THE EMPIRE

The Empire is the greatest of mankind's realms in the Old World. Founded by the man-god Sigmar, it has endured for two and a half millennia, surviving countless invasions by the many dread forces that threaten its borders. Protected by faith and steel, defended by tireless citizen soldiers and valiant heroes, the Empire stands firm against all its foes.

IRON COMPANY
Chris Wraight

When retired engineer Magnus Ironblood is tempted into one more campaign, he finds himself working alongside some unlikely allies. Sent as part of an Imperial force to bring to heel the secessionist forces of Countess von Kleister, this rag-tag army finds themselves outgunned. Digging deep into their reserves of courage and ingenuity they must fight the enemy forces with everything they have.

GRIMBLADES
Nick Kyme

When orcs and goblins invade the Empire, the Emperor Dieter IV does nothing. While the other elector counts bicker, Prince Wilhelm is left to defend the Reikland alone. The Grimblades are among his brave army that opposes the greenskins. Amidst desperate war across the Empire and a plot to kill the prince, the Grimblades must survive this orc invasion and claim victory.

WARRIOR PRIEST
Darius Hinks

Jakob Wolff, warrior priest of Sigmar, sets out on a holy crusade to track down his brother, whose soul has been tainted by the Ruinous Powers. Family must be put to one side as Wolff battles to prevent the Empire from sinking into Chaos, with only his strength of arms and the purity of his beliefs to call upon.

By the same authors

· ORION ·
Darius Hinks
Book 1: THE VAULTS OF WINTER
Book 2: TEARS OF ISHA
Book 3: THE COUNCIL OF BEASTS (2014)

· TIME OF LEGENDS: THE WAR OF VENGEANCE ·
Nick Kyme and Chris Wraight
Book 1: THE GREAT BETRAYAL
Book 2: MASTER OF DRAGONS
Book 3: ELFDOOM (2014)

· STORM OF MAGIC ·
Darius Hinks, Chris Wraight and C L Werner
Book 1: RAZUMOV'S TOMB
Book 2: DRAGONMAGE
Book 3: THE HOUR OF SHADOWS

· DWARFS ·
Nick Kyme and Gav Thorpe
(Contains the novels *Grudge Bearer*, *Oathbreaker* and
Honourkeeper)

· SCHWARZHELM & HELBORG:
SWORDS OF THE EMPEROR ·
Chris Wraight
(Contains the novels *Sword of Justice* and *Sword of
Vengeance*)

· LUTHOR HUSS ·
Chris Wraight

· SIGVALD ·
Darius Hinks

· MASTERS OF MAGIC ·
Chris Wraight

A WARHAMMER OMNIBUS

THE EMPIRE

CHRIS WRAIGHT • NICK KYME • DARIUS HINKS

BLACK LIBRARY

A Black Library Publication

Iron Company copyright © 2009, Games Workshop Ltd.
Grimblades copyright © 2010, Games Workshop Ltd.
Warrior Priest copyright © 2010, Games Workshop Ltd.
'As Dead as Flesh' first published in *Inferno!* magazine,
copyright © 2004, Games Workshop Ltd.
'Dead Man's Hand' first published in *Tales of the Old World*,
copyright © 2007, Games Workshop Ltd.
'Sanctity' first published in *Invasion*, copyright © 2007, Games Workshop Ltd.
'The Judgement of Crows' and 'The Miracle at Berlau' first published in
Death and Dishonour, copyright © 2010, Games Workshop Ltd.
'The March of Doom' first published in *Black Library Games Day Anthology 2011/12*,
copyright © 2011, Games Workshop Ltd.

This omnibus edition published in Great Britain in 2014 by
Black Library,
Games Workshop Ltd.,
Willow Road,
Nottingham, NG7 2WS, UK.

10 9 8 7 6 5 4 3 2 1

Cover illustration by Daren Horley
Map by Nuala Kinrade

A CIP record for this book is available from the British Library.

UK ISBN 13: 978 1 84970 586 8
US ISBN 13: 978 1 84970 587 5

See Black Library on the internet at

www.blacklibrary.com

Find out more about Games Workshop
and the world of Warhammer at

www.games-workshop.com

Printed and bound by CPI Group (UK) Ltd, Croydon, CR0 4YY

This is a dark age, a bloody age, an age of daemons
and of sorcery. It is an age of battle and death, and of the
world's ending. Amidst all of the fire, flame and fury
it is a time, too, of mighty heroes, of bold deeds
and great courage.

At the heart of the Old World sprawls the Empire, the
largest and most powerful of the human realms. Known for
its engineers, sorcerers, traders and soldiers, it is
a land of great mountains, mighty rivers, dark forests
and vast cities. And from his throne in Altdorf reigns
the Emperor Karl Franz, sacred descendant of the
founder of these lands, Sigmar, and wielder
of his magical warhammer.

But these are far from civilised times. Across the length
and breadth of the Old World, from the knightly palaces
of Bretonnia to ice-bound Kislev in the far north, come
rumblings of war. In the towering Worlds Edge Mountains,
the orc tribes are gathering for another assault. Bandits and
renegades harry the wild southern lands of
the Border Princes. There are rumours of rat-things, the
skaven, emerging from the sewers and swamps across the
land. And from the northern wildernesses there is the
ever-present threat of Chaos, of daemons and beastmen
corrupted by the foul powers of the Dark Gods.
As the time of battle draws ever near,
the Empire needs heroes
like never before.

North of Here Lie The
Dreaded Chaos Wastes.

f Claus

Erengrad.

"Here Be Trolls..."

Praag.

middle mountains.

lenheim.

Kislev

Kislev.

Wolfenburg.

Talabheim.

The Empire

Altdorf.

Karak Kad

Nuln.

The
Moot.

Sylvania.
Dracken
-hof.

Zhufbar.

Averheim.

Black
Water.

Black fire Pass.

Karak
Norn.

CONTENTS

IRON COMPANY
Chris Wraight

CHAPTER ONE

'There are many who pour scorn on the engineers. They call us mad-men, fools, or worse. We have no honour in the Empire, nor in the lands beyond. And yet I foresee a great change coming. When the sword fails and where the spell miscasts, iron and blackpowder will still retain their merit. Our time has not yet come. But as the days grow darker, it surely will. Only when all the Emperor's companies are Iron Companies will the future of our race be secured. Then we shall no longer be scorned, but lauded and justly appraised as the mightiest and most learned of men.'

The Notebooks of Leonardo da Miragliano

It was the end of winter, and the worst of the ice had retreated north at last. The ground still lay as hard as bone, and the trees were bare. Their black trunks rose starkly into the grey air. Men wrapped themselves heavily against the chill. The countryside was silent but for the echoing croak of ravens. When the sun rose, it was weak, its light watery. When it set, the cold came creeping back from the mountains, and families huddled around meagre fires, watchful of the flickering shadows.

The streets of Hergig were almost empty. In the faint light of dusk, the narrow houses clustered together tightly, rising from the filth of the streets in uneven, jagged rows. The most elaborate of the buildings were roofed with slate and had frames of oak. The poorest looked tired and stained with age.

Hochland was not a wealthy place, and there were more poor places than rich. The elector count and his court preferred to dwell for most of the year in their private estates near the southern borders. Only in the deep winter did they trail back to Hergig, sheltering in the massive Kristalhof in the centre of the city. The vast keep ensured they were isolated from the worst squalor of their subjects. Those who could afford it constructed their town houses around the prestigious Hofbahn district, as close as they could get to the keep. Those who couldn't took their chances in the lower town, where the squalid dwellings were rammed up against one another and the militia patrolled in teams.

Magnus Ironblood took a look around him. He felt tired and grimy. Of all the houses before him, only one was lit. A hand-painted sign hung on battered hinges: *The Boar.* There were a thousand inns with that name in the northlands. This one looked no different to the rest. The light coming from the doorway was dim. There was no sound of carousing from inside, just a low, surly murmuring.

Still, the place served beer, and that was the important thing. Magnus walked towards it, his long leather overcoat swirling as he went. The expensive garment marked him out in such places. He no longer cared. Fitting in had never been his principal strength.

He pushed the door open. The inn was little more than the lower room of a private house. Old straw lay on the floor, reeking. Tallow candles burned in alcoves, leaving black streaks against the daub walls. There was no bar, just a long table on which dusty bottles and kegs of beer had been piled. A shrewish woman sat behind it, counting copper coins into a jar. There were a few more wooden tables in the centre of the room, and long benches against the walls. As Magnus entered, some of the drinkers turned their heads towards the door. There weren't many of them. They were all men, all old, all clothed in heavy cloaks and jerkins against the cold.

Just like me, thought Magnus, dryly. This is what I've become.

The drinkers went back to nursing their flagons. One man looked at Magnus for a little longer. He had a sparse grey beard and glittering eyes, and hunched over his drink protectively. He kept up his gaze for a few moments, before turning back to his beer.

Magnus ignored him, and walked over to what passed for the bar. The old fool probably lusted after his coat. He could try and get it if he wanted. Better men had failed.

'Beer,' Magnus said to the woman, curtly.

She gave him an irritated look, as if serving customers was something to be avoided, and put her coins down.

'Keg, or bottle?' she asked.

To have beer from a glass bottle was a rarity. Magnus looked at the ones on show carefully. The glass was deep green and thick, with long corks protruding from the neck. They had foreign characters on the labels, angular and unreadable. Plundered stock, then. Anything could be in them.

'Keg,' he said, throwing a single coin onto the table.

The woman got up and filled an iron tankard with a dark brown liquid. There was virtually no head on it. It smelled almost like beer. There was more than a hint of the drain about it too.

Magnus took it up and wandered over to one of the benches. He sat heavily. As he did so, he noticed that the man with the beard had left. None of the other patrons paid him any attention. He took a sip of his drink. It had a sour finish, but he'd had much worse. It was wet, it would take the edge off his mood, and nothing much else mattered.

He pushed himself back against the wall, letting his legs stretch out against the floor, watching the furrows his heels made in the dirt. His boots had once been something to be proud of. Expensive leather, expertly sewn. Now they were just like him, faded and battered. He looked down at his legs. Though it was hard to remember, Magnus had once been considered tall. Handsome, even. Now he just looked big. The muscles that had pounded hammers on anvils were still there, but lay under an unwelcome covering of fat. His features had become lined and hard from the elements. His dark hair, jet-black when he'd been in Nuln, was now ragged and flecked with grey. At least they matched his eyes now. Just like his father's, pale grey irises like the flank of a Middenheim wolf.

The beer went down well. Before he knew it, the flagon was nearly empty. Magnus left the dregs where they were. You never really wanted to know what was in them. He gestured to the woman for another. She brought one over, grumbling as she came.

'And?' she said, holding out a grimy palm.

Magnus paused. His payment should have been good for more. His were rare coins, minted in Nuln, almost the last remaining from his final cache. He thought about protesting, but the beer had sunk deep into his body, making him lethargic. Who cared if he was being cheated? The money would be gone soon enough anyway.

He pressed a second coin into her hand, and the woman skulked off. Magnus took a thoughtful sip. For what he was paying, he might as well try and enjoy it.

As he lowered the rim of the tankard, the door opened again. A gust of frigid air sighed into the room. A man entered. He looked nothing like the others. His flesh was smooth and clean, his robes expensive. Aside from the thin layer of mud lining his soft boots, little of the street clung to him. As his fingers moved, the weak light caught on metal. He was wearing rings on his pale, effeminate fingers. Walking around Hergig like that was dangerous. He was either very stupid, or very powerful.

The man pushed his long cloak back, revealing a sleek, rounded stomach. Everything about him was self-satisfied, from his grooming to his pink, fleshy face. The woman hurried up to him, her earlier irascibility swept away.

'Herr Grotius,' she said, handing him a bottle of beer. 'You do us honour.'

The man looked at her distastefully, and reached for some payment.

'Not necessary, not necessary,' the woman said. 'Will you have anything else?'

The man Grotius looked around him. His expression seemed to imply that nothing, absolutely nothing in this miserable place could possibly be of the slightest interest to him.

'No,' he said. His voice was syrupy, and conveyed a casual disdain with a minimum of effort. 'I won't be here long.'

The woman withdrew, looking back at the newcomer nervously as she did so. A few eyes around the room were raised in his direction, but flicked down again as soon as he looked around. Magnus suddenly felt a chill run through him. Grotius was walking towards him.

'Herr Magnus Albrecht Ironblood?' he said.

Magnus nodded warily. The man pulled a chair from a nearby table, wiped its surface with the corner of his cloak, and sat down carefully.

'May I join you?'

Magnus looked at the man with suspicion. The rest of the drinkers seemed to know who the newcomer was, and went back to their low-voiced conversations.

'Do I have a choice?' asked Magnus.

Grotius smiled thinly.

'Of course you do. But I'd recommend spending a few moments in my company. We have something of significant mutual interest to discuss.'

Magnus took a deliberate swig of his drink, weighing up the situation. The man had the air of an official, a court flunky. If that were true, it boded badly for him. He had never had a good experience with officials. They were parasites, paid gold to administer the affairs of their benefactors while the masses starved.

'Is that so?' said Magnus. 'Then you won't mind telling me who you are, who sent you and how you knew I was here.'

The man raised an eyebrow.

'You really don't know who I am?' he said, musingly. 'They told me you were new to Hergig, but still.'

The man took a sip from his bottle, and winced. He put it down as if it was full of wasps. As he did so, the doors of the tavern burst open. They slammed against the walls heavily, and a group of men burst in. Three or four of them, plus a slovenly woman with a painted face. They called out for beer. Their red cheeks and bleary eyes indicated they'd already had a lot.

The woman frantically tried to calm them down, but one of them broke into a song. Magnus sat back, smiling. The lyrics were enlightening, something about a miller's daughter and an oversized grindstone. Grotius, however, didn't see the funny side. He stood up, and fixed the ringleader with a cold stare.

For a moment, the man kept going. But his friends saw the danger. He was dragged into the shadows and hastily quietened. As realisation dawned, Magnus saw the man's face turn ashen. He slumped into the corner and was given a dirty flagon to cool his spirits. They clearly knew who Grotius was. It was only him, it seemed, who was at a disadvantage.

Grotius's gaze swept the rest of the room. All eyes were lowered. The hum of conversation returned. The man sighed irritably, and looked back at Magnus.

'My name is Valerian von Grotius. I'm an agent of Count Ludenhof. My duties are many. You should know from the outset that I'm in the complete trust of the elector. That may inform our discussion, since you're clearly new to Hochland.'

Magnus maintained his sceptical expression. This was getting worse.

'As for how I found you,' said Grotius, 'it was a simple matter. The name Ironblood still carries some weight in the Empire, no matter how much you've tried to extinguish it. Even now, despite your lamentable fall from prestige, you don't much resemble the scum from around here. When news reached me that you'd ended up in Hergig, I was able to draw on a few outstanding debts. In that, as ever, I was ably served.'

Magnus inclined his head sardonically.

'Glad to hear it,' he said. 'Your sort never seem short of willing helpers.'

Grotius ignored Magnus's tone.

'A happy consequence of office,' he said, looking down at his rings absently. 'I've been waiting to meet you for several days. I'm glad to finally have the honour.'

Magnus belched loudly.

'So now we're all happy,' he said. 'Suppose you tell me what you want, and then leave?'

A flicker of annoyance crossed Grotius's features for the first time.

'I'll be pleased to leave you to your many pressing affairs,' he said, looking at Magnus's stained jerkin with faintly veiled disgust. 'Do you think I enjoy coming to such places?'

He collected himself.

'You're unfamiliar with the politics of Hochland,' Grotius said, settling against the creaking back of his chair. 'Let me illuminate you. Much as we might wish it otherwise, the benign rule of Count Ludenhof is not as universally appreciated as it might be. As with all the states of the Empire, there is discontent, there is envy, and there are rivals to the sovereign office. Through the enlightened policies of his advisers, the count has maintained the security of his position with considerable efficiency. But there are always issues, always the threat of strife.'

As he spoke, Grotius looked genuinely pained by the spectre of disloyalty to the count. Magnus sighed, took a deep swig of his drink and slumped further against the bench.

'There is a woman of noble birth, the Margravine Anna-Louisa Margarete Emeludt von Kleister,' continued Grotius. 'She's the mistress of several familial estates to the north of the province, bordering on the Hochland Mittebergen, the Middle Mountains. The source of her wealth has never been entirely clear, but she has deep pockets. Among her possessions are several mines. It's possible she's discovered a hidden source of precious metal, maybe even gold. If so, that gives her substantial independent means. She could mint coinage, even hire mercenaries. It is a situation which has proved increasingly intolerable.'

'Sounds like some woman,' said Magnus. 'Maybe we should meet.'

'I'd like nothing better,' said Grotius. 'But you might find it difficult. For over a year, she has rebuffed any attempt to draw her back within the fold of legitimate government. Reasonable requests for a tithe of her wealth have met with no reply. Repeated embassies have returned with no response. She has, in effect, become a rebel.'

Magnus sighed deeply. Grotius looked in the mood to spin out his tale. Magnus was tired, and the potent ale was beginning to generate a low throb behind his eyes. The murky business of Hochland's internal politics was no concern of his.

'So bring her to heel,' he said. 'Ludenhof will have to learn to control his women.'

Grotius looked awkwardly at him.

'The thought had occurred to us. Sedition is not tolerated here any more than it would be in Nuln or Altdorf. When it was clear the margravine had ceased to fall within the writ of the state, an armed delegation was sent to her estate with orders to arrest her. She was not there. According to reports, she had raised her own troops with gold and promises, and set up court in a remote citadel in the mountains. The implication of this is clear. She intends to resist arrest, and build up her strength over the winter. In the spring, she may have gathered enough men to move against the elector. Obviously, this situation could not be tolerated. One of our agents reported that she had amassed a considerable store of arms which could only grow. On my advice, an army was mustered and sent to bring the rebels to heel.'

Grotius's sense of awkwardness seemed to increase. Some of his easy self-assurance had dissolved.

'That was over a month ago,' he said, quietly. 'They have not been heard of since. We have no idea of their fate. There are many, myself included, who believe them destroyed.'

Magnus let out a low whistle. Despite himself, he was beginning to become intrigued.

'You lost an army?' he said. 'Careless. If you ask me, heads should roll. Right at the top.'

Grotius gave him a withering look.

'And so we come to the present situation,' he said. 'There is a rogue margravine hidden in the Mittebergen, gathering fresh troops to her side with every passing week. No attempt to contact her has been successful. The integrity of the state is compromised. The count is greatly troubled, and has sworn to bring the affair to a speedy conclusion. Funds have been transferred from his personal account in Altdorf for the raising of a second army. He is determined to crush the rebellion before it can blossom further. Hochland will not be divided.'

Magnus drained his tankard, and looked at Grotius.

'Fascinating,' he said, licking his lips. 'But I'd listen a lot better if...'

Grotius snapped his fingers irritably, and the woman at the table instantly began to pour a fresh flagon of ale. The drunkards in the corner were getting steadily louder again. One man was gnawing at a chicken bone in the shadows, the pink juices running down his chin. Another had brought out a scrawny fighting cockerel and was showing it to the woman proudly. All across the Empire, in every squalid hole and cranny, similar scenes were being played out. It was a dreary thought.

'So now we come to it,' said Grotius, watching as the beer was delivered. 'The army is gathered and is nearly ready to march. All is in place, save for one element. Our master engineer, Marcus Frölich, was on the first campaign. His machinery, his crews, all are lost. We have guns in Hergig, but no one to operate them. We could send for a replacement from the college in Nuln, but our request would take days to arrive, and weeks to respond to. So when I discovered that an Ironblood was in Hergig, you can imagine my satisfaction. You are here, and, despite everything, your name still means something. Or at least it does to those who know about such things. There is money in this, Herr Ironblood. Money, and a chance to recover yourself.'

At that, Magnus let slip a long, bitter laugh. He looked at Grotius, a wolfish smile playing on his lips.

'Ah, my friend,' he said. 'You've been badly advised. If you need a master engineer, look elsewhere. There are good reasons for my leaving the service. Yours was a nice story, and I feel for your loss, but you'll need to find someone else to be your gunnery captain.'

Grotius maintained his equable expression, and placed his hands comfortably across his broad stomach.

'You would do well to consider the proposal,' he said, weighing his words carefully. 'The count himself has been told of your presence here. Matters have been set in motion. Decisions have been ratified. I trust you know what that means?'

Magnus felt his anger rising. He placed his tankard down roughly on the bench beside him. This would have to be cut off before it could go any further.

'Sigmar damn you!' he hissed. 'You have some guts to come here and talk to me like I was some boy of your master's. I've served in armies larger than you've ever seen. I've commanded batteries of a hundred guns and answered to Marshal Helborg himself. If I had a weapon…'

Grotius's eyes went flat.

'But you don't, do you?' he said, acidly. 'Even I've heard of the Ironblood pistol. Where is it now? In the hands of some strumpet witch hunter? You've squandered everything, Ironblood. Whoever you used to be, whatever you used to command, now you're just another feckless wanderer, ripe for nothing but the press or the poorhouse.'

Magnus's eyes blazed, but the words died in his throat. Despite it all, the accusations hit home. Grotius had done his work well, and knew where his vulnerable points were. The agent's lip curled slightly in a sneer.

'I began reasonably, in the hope that you might be persuaded to see the gracious opportunity the count has extended you,' Grotius said. 'He's a man who's used to having his wishes granted. I suspect he would be extremely disappointed to learn that his offer has been turned down.'

Magnus felt his anger sink into a kind of dark resignation. He was new in Hergig, and the few friends he had here would be no protection if he made enemies of the authorities. He knew just enough of the ways of the Imperial hierarchy to appreciate the position he was in.

'Now that you put it like that,' said Magnus, not bothering to hide the scorn in his voice, 'I'm inclined to listen further. Tell on.'

Grotius let his vicious expression slide, and the benign air of satisfaction returned. The man had all the deceit and silky manners of a career diplomat.

'The resources at your disposal would be considerable,' he said, matter of factly. 'There are several big guns, many smaller pieces, and the crew to man them. There are also companies of handgunners, some equipped with the famous Hochland long guns. They'll all need close supervision. The commander of the army, General Scharnhorst, is not a believer in the new sciences. That is to be regretted, and is also why we need you. Since you're so proud of your prior experiences, I cannot believe a man such as yourself would have much of a problem with our requirements.'

Magnus found himself only half-listening. The evening had gone from merely bad to terrible.

'I suppose you have the plans all prepared?' he said, looking at the thin foam on his beer grimly.

'The place the margravine has chosen is called Morgramgar,' he said. 'I will arrange for our charts to be sent to you. It is a citadel, high up in the mountains, reputedly built on a single spur of rock. She has not chosen the location idly. Morgramgar was built to withstand a siege. It will be hard to reach, and even harder to storm. I won't lie to you, Ironblood. The task will be arduous. There is much about the rebellion we don't know. And if tales of Kleister's riches are to be believed, we cannot be sure how many men she has bought. We need commanders of calibre, not hired swords.'

Magnus drank again, feeling the sour liquid slip down his throat easily.

'You paint an attractive picture,' he said. 'No wonder you're having trouble recruiting. What of this Scharnhorst? Is he good?'

Grotius couldn't conceal a slight flicker of discomfort before his face resumed its habitual smoothness.

'He's one of Hochland's most decorated soldiers,' he said, lowering his eyes. 'He has commanded many of the elector's armies.'

Magnus leaned forward, and placed his tankard on the table roughly.

'Look,' he said, his eyes glinting. 'I don't care what you think of him. This whole province is a backward hive of peasantry. Commanding a Hochland battalion is about as impressive as organising a village fayre. You may have a few decent handgunners up here, but that's it. I'm going to need more than that. Sending an army into the mountains with a provincial hick at the helm will be suicide, for all of us. You'll have to do better than that.'

Grotius's eyes went flat.

'If we're so backward here,' he said, slowly and deliberately, 'then it was a poor choice you made to live amongst us. You may not have appreciated it yet, being so new, but we are a proud people. You would do well to remember that. Not all Hochlanders are as tolerant as I am.'

Magnus snorted with derision.

'You need me,' he said. 'If you didn't, you'd have dragged me to the gaol already. I know where we stand here, Grotius. If I refuse, I'll suddenly find my every doing a matter of interest to the local sergeant. I'm too old and weary to play that game.'

He fixed the agent with a dark look.

'I can do your work for you,' he said. 'You know that. But I want payment up front, and I want the money to do it properly. My own team, and funds to hire whatever I think I need. And I want full command of the engineer companies. This Scharnhorst can do what he wants with the halberdiers and the archers, but I don't want any interference with the guns.'

Grotius returned the glare coolly.

'You'll get money,' he said. 'For yourself and for your company. The gunnery crews will answer to you. But don't attempt to cross Scharnhorst. He's the general, and he's in command. I warn you, he won't tolerate any attempt to undermine that. You've served before. You know how it is.'

Magnus drained the last of his tankard. Three flagons' worth already. How had he become so accustomed to it, so quickly?

'And I command the heavy iron,' he said. 'I won't tolerate any attempt to undermine that, either.'

He placed the empty tankard on the bench beside him.

'I'll have to meet this Scharnhorst,' Magnus said, wearily. 'Perhaps we can come to some arrangement.'

Grotius shrugged, pulled his cloak about him and looked over to the door. As he moved, all eyes around the tavern turned to him. The conversations ebbed again. The desperation to see him leave was palpable.

'That's your business,' he said. 'Now I must go. There's much to arrange. Where are your lodgings? I'll have the documents sent to you.'

'Above the blacksmiths on Karlfranzstrasse,' said Magnus. 'There's a coaching inn on the corner of the street. Get your man to ask for directions there.'

Grotius nodded, and rose. As he did so, he threw a couple of coins onto the bench.

'I'm glad you saw the opportunity here, Ironblood,' he said, failing to keep the edge of disdain from his voice. 'That concludes our business. I'll be in touch. In the meantime, enjoy a drink, courtesy of the count.'

Magnus bowed ironically, leaving the coins where they were.

'I'll be sure to thank him when we next meet.'

Grotius turned and walked back towards the doorway. A few of the drinkers raised their heads slightly, but kept their eyes low. The cockerel squawked, and was silenced. The door opened, and the chill of the night rushed in once more. It slammed shut with his passing, and the flimsy wood shivered.

The room relaxed. Conversations became more animated, and furtive glances were shot in Magnus's direction. The slovenly woman began to cackle. Magnus ignored her and looked at the coins before him. They shone dully in the dirty light. The sum was derisory. He'd been suborned so cheaply, with so little struggle. Even a year ago he might have laughed off a man like Grotius. The coins would have been hurled back at his preening, prancing face. He could have resisted the commission, taken his chances with the militia, broken free of Hergig and laughed in the faces of his pursuers.

Not now. When the spirit had been broken, the carrion crows began to circle. With a heavy sense of futility, he picked up the coins. Magnus looked up at the serving woman, who was glaring at him with suspicion and hostility.

'Another,' he said in a thick voice.

CHAPTER TWO

'Is there anything which embodies the might of the Empire of man more than the cannonry it can bring to bear? What other nation of the world has mastered such dread science? What other race can deploy the lines of death-dealing iron as we can? With every passing year, our metallurgists discover more, and our alchemists distil purer and more potent strains of the blackpowder. Though the lost souls of Chaos may sweep down from the Northern Wastes, and the savage greenskins assail us from their foul holes in the mountains, we have nothing to fear as long as we remain true to the sacred lore of the machine. In it lies our salvation, our redemption, and our one true hope.'

Address given by Solomon Grusswalder
Master of the College of Engineers, Nuln

Thorgad Grimgarsson waited silently in the shadows under the trees. Glamrist felt light in his gnarled hands. It always did, when the time came. A thin reflection of moonlight gleamed along the blade. The edge was as sharp as the High King's own. He'd ground it himself. The only way to get it done properly.

Ahead, the faint light pooled in the narrow clearing. There was movement. Thorgad narrowed his eyes. Years of living in the lamplit halls of his ancestors had made them almost as good in the dark as they were under the sun.

'Grobi,' he mouthed, letting his lips curl with disgust.

He ran a finger lightly along the axe blade. Even in the weak light, the runes were visible. They gave him comfort. Soon they would be drenched in black blood. It had been too long since Glamrist had drunk deep. The spirit of the weapon was taut with readiness.

There was a low chattering. The grobi were careless. Too rarely were they disturbed in the heart of the forest. This was their realm, a world of throttlings and chokings, a miserable life of preying on the unwary and the foolish. Even if he had not been schooled to hate the race from birth, Thorgad would still have despised them. There was nothing in the world more deserving of death than a goblin.

One of them shuffled into full view. It was wearing a dark cloak. A hooked nose poked out from under it, and there was a quick flash of curved yellow teeth. Others scuttled into the clearing. They were excited. One of them had picked up a trail of something. They clutched their weapons in scrawny hands. Gouges, sickles, nets, twisted scimitars. The chattering grew louder. They were moving off.

The time had come. Thorgad made a final assessment of their numbers, then hefted Glamrist expertly.

'Khazuk!' he bellowed, and burst from the undergrowth.

In a second he was amongst them. The axe whirled in the air. A slick of blood splattered across Thorgad's beard and breastplate. The stench of it clogged his nostrils.

The goblins broke like animals, squealing and squawking. Some leapt up into the trees, scrabbling at the bark. Others darted into the foliage. Thorgad went after them like a hunter after rabbits, swinging the heavy blade with abandon. The muscles in his powerful arms responded instantly. It had been too long since they had done anything but hammer iron. The change felt good.

The slowest of the grobi were soon cut down. Their twitching bodies lay amid the bracken. Tattered cloaks hung from briars. The sound of their screams echoed from the tree trunks.

But then it changed. One of them must have noticed Thorgad was alone. A series of barked orders ran through the forest. The dwarf stood in the centre of the clearing, panting. Silvery light limned the open space. Beyond, the shadows clustered, as dark as nightshade. The squawking stopped. The rustling branches fell still.

Then, one by one, points of yellow light appeared. Dozens of them.

'Grungni's beard,' muttered Thorgad. 'More than I thought.'

He spat on the ground, turning slowly, watching the sets of eyes multiply in the gloom. He was surrounded. Still they waited. He let his breathing return to normal. His eyes narrowed. They would have to rush him to have any chance. Who would be the first to try it? He found himself grinning.

'Come on then!' he roared, breaking the eerie silence.

They came. A wave of chattering, snickering hate. In the half-light they looked like rats, swarming across the ground. The first of them reached him. One leapt up, its thin face distorted with fear and malice. A second later it fell to the ground, nearly sliced in two.

More came at him. Thorgad felt something grasp his ankle. A scimitar whistled past his neck. Fingers as hard as iron rods scrabbled at his cloak. He kept moving. Glamrist was working quickly now. He hurled it in wide arcs, smashing apart any grobi that got too near. The shining blade was soon as black as pitch, stained with a thick layer of gore. He could feel his own blood trickle across his right arm. One of the grobi knives had hit home. In his activity, he'd hardly noticed it. The axe sang. The squawking rose in volume.

Still they came. More were arriving from the deeps of the forest. Thorgad swung round, looking for an escape route. There was none. Much as he hated to admit it, he might have been a little ambitious. A vicious-looking grobi leapt up towards his face, teeth snapping. Thorgad felt the spittle on his skin, smelt the putrid stink. With a snarl of disgust, he brought his left fist up. Bone crunched, and the cloaked horror crumpled. Thorgad spun around again.

Too late. He felt the sharp pain of the gouge as it bored into his thigh. Glamrist flashed, and the grobi staggered backwards. Its entrails spilled, gleaming in the starlight.

Thorgad grunted as the pain radiated up his leg. This was getting difficult. More grobi fell. His arms were streaked with blood, his face spattered with it. Still they jumped towards him. He felt something grab hold of his cloak again. The grip held. Two more sprang towards him, flails spinning. In their hateful eyes, there was the glint of victory.

Thorgad roared with frustration. He jabbed and hacked the axe head into the attackers. He wrenched his arms around, trying to dislodge the clutching hands. He could feel himself losing balance. The axe was ripped from his fingers. From somewhere, he heard a high cackle of glee. Even as he was dragged down into the undergrowth, he managed to take two more with him, smashing their brittle heads together until their eyes popped and the skulls fractured. As he felt them clamber over him for the killing blow, he had time for one last curse.

'Grimnir take you all!' he spat, watching the scimitar blade rise above him.

It never fell. Something spun across the narrow clearing, flashing in the starlight. There was the whine of crossbows. Bolts thudded into their marks. The blade fell uselessly from the goblin's hands. It tumbled back to the ground. The squealing broke out again. More shafts found their targets.

Then the dwarfs came, charging across the clearing, axes swinging. The grobi broke and ran. These odds were less to their liking. They were pursued, driven back into the endless shadows of the forest. From the depths, the sound of killing began again.

Thorgad pushed the limp body of the dead grobi from him. He shook his head to clear it. That had been too close. Painfully, feeling the deep wound in his thigh, he hauled himself back onto his feet.

'What are you doing here?' came a gruff voice.

Thorgad looked up. The dwarf before him was almost entirely encased in ornate armour. His helmet was engraved with the likeness of Grimnir, and he carried a heavily decorated warhammer, already running with goblin blood.

Thorgad grimaced as he leaned on his wounded leg.

'Heading east,' he said, retrieving Glamrist from where it had been dropped.

'You almost lost your blade,' the armoured dwarf said, disapprovingly. 'That would have been a great shame on your family.'

'My family already bears shame,' said Thorgad. 'It's why I'm here. But you have my thanks.'

The armoured dwarf took off his helmet and extended a gauntlet. His hair was ivory-white and his beard was long and pleated. A venerable warrior, then.

'Snorri Valramnik,' he said. 'And you owe me nothing. Killing these vermin is its own reward.'

Thorgad grasped the dwarf's hand.

'Thorgad Grimgarsson,' he said.

Valramnik raised a bushy eyebrow.

'Grimgarsson?' he said. 'That explains why you're here. You should be more careful.'

Thorgad didn't reply. He tore a strip from a dead goblin's cloak, and begun to wind it around his wound. The bleeding was already slowing. It would heal soon. The dawi were made of strong stuff.

Valramnik looked over his shoulder. His warriors were returning to the clearing. The last of the grobi were either dead or driven far off.

'We can't stay long,' the old dwarf said. 'A debt of honour takes us south. But this meeting may be more than chance.'

He leaned towards Thorgad, and his voice lowered.

'I know what you seek,' he said. 'Your time may be at hand. The umgi are fighting over the Morgramgariven. War will come soon. A good dawi knows how to take his chance.'

Thorgad looked at Valramnik steadily. He gave nothing away.

'How do you know this?'

Valramnik laughed, and his barrel chest shook.

'Never you mind how I know,' he said. 'I speak to many folk, dawi and umgi. You can listen and profit, or ignore me and your grudge will never be erased. The Empire is no place for you, Grimgarsson. You should listen to advice when it finds you.'

Thorgad grunted, trying not to show his interest too much. He began to clean the gore from Glamrist. Inwardly, however, his heart had begun to race.

'If this is true,' he said carefully, 'I will be in debt to you twice over. A chest of gold would be too little reward.'

Valramnik laughed again. His warriors had all returned, and he put his helmet back on.

'Don't incur debts you can't pay!' he said. 'But if you wish to clear them, look for me in Karak Hirn. Until then, Grimnir be with you.'

With that, he turned back into the shadows and stalked off. His entourage went with him, and soon they were lost in the darkling trees.

Thorgad stood silently for a while, pondering the strange ways of fate. After some time, he collected himself, and slung Glamrist across his back. His face gave little away. Despite the grobi, despite the unexpected reprieve, despite the tantalising news, his expression remained stony. With a halting limp, he turned west, and began to plough through the forest once more. The coming days would determine the truth of Valramnik's news. But it was worth following the lead. At least it gave him some purpose. After weeks in the wilderness, now Hergig awaited him.

Magnus came round. The world gradually made its presence felt. It was cold, pale and unpleasant.

He half-sat up in bed, and took a look about him. He was in his garret above the blacksmith's. It was filthy. Dirty linen was strewn across the bare wooden floor. Harsh light fought its way through the narrow, grimy window ahead of him. In the corner of the room, a pile of heavy, huge chests sat, covered in rumpled sheets. They were the only items of any worth in the chamber. The wood was oak, dark with age. All were banded with iron, and there was a strange rune on the lock. Dwarfish make. Despite hundreds of years of artistry in the Empire, still nothing could compare to them when it came to making things to last.

Magnus pushed the sheets from him, and carefully rubbed his chin. It was thick with stubble. A line of drool ran across one cheek. His breath was foul. The room stank. His temples began to hammer.

Shakily, mindful of his eggshell-weak head, Magnus staggered to his feet and headed for the chamber pot. A wave of nausea lurched across him. When done, he shuffled to the window, shoved the rotten frame outwards and hurled the contents into the street below. There was an outraged curse, followed by raucous laughter.

Magnus smiled grimly. He still felt sick. Most of his clothes from the night before had been thrown across a rickety chair. He pulled them back on. Their stale aroma blended artfully with the other malodorous smells in the room. The icy morning air, now rushing into the bedchamber through the open window, did little to dent the seamy atmosphere.

There was a metal bowl on a shelf next to the chair, and a chipped pitcher of water. The surface was lined with scum. Magnus poured it into the bowl, dipped his head towards it and splashed his face. The chill water brought a rush of blood to his face, and his head thumped more strongly. He shook it, and his unruly hair whipped across his cheeks.

Magnus took a deep breath, feeling himself gradually come back together. He looked out of the open window. The sun was still low in the sky, but it must have been at least mid-morning. His room was on the second floor of the blacksmith's rambling house, and he could see a landscape of sloping roofs in every direction. Mud-coloured smoke rose lazily into the pale sky. The chatter of the street filtered up towards him. It was lively, vital, obscene, good-natured. Everything that Magnus wasn't.

He opened the draughty door to his humble chamber, and stomped down the creaking stairs. Two storeys below, the forge was clearly at work. With each clang of the blacksmith's hammer, the veins in his forehead gave a sympathetic spasm of pain. Wincing against the hammering, Magnus entered the wife's private domain in the floor above the forge.

As he stumbled in, Frau Ettieg turned to greet him. She had been cooking, and her cheeks were crimson from the heat of the oven. She wiped her hands on her grease-stained apron, and frowned.

'Drunk again?' she asked.

The blacksmith's wife was a solid, heavy-boned woman with a face like a man's. She rarely lost her frown, which made her look even more masculine. Magnus felt sorry for her. Her husband, the swarthy, violent Herr Ettieg, had been enjoying the favours of the maid Brigitta for some time. It was common knowledge in the neighbourhood, especially since the plump, bright-eyed Brigitta was pretty indiscreet about the whole thing. In Frau Ettieg's situation, Magnus wouldn't have looked his best either.

He ignored her comment, and sat heavily at the table. The smell of oily pancakes wafted from the oven.

'Anything to wet a man's lips?' Magnus said. Even he was surprised at how gravelly his voice sounded.

Frau Ettieg shook her head disgustedly, but got him a cup of small beer from one of the cupboards. She put it down in front of him, still shaking her head.

'It's not good for a man to drink all day and all night,' she said. 'You'll end up in the gutter. And you owe Pieter a month's rent. He won't wait forever.'

Magnus took a swig of the weak, foamy beer. It tasted more like dirty water than ale, but he felt his body respond almost instantly nonetheless.

'I'll be fine soon,' he said, without much conviction. 'I'm waiting for something to come in. Trust me.'

As he spoke, Magnus dimly remembered something about last night. Some promise of money. He frowned, and pushed his hand through his oily hair. What was it?

Frau Ettieg sighed, and went back to the oven.

'A man came for you this morning,' she said, absently. 'He left you a message. It's on the table.'

Magnus winced. People calling for him was never a welcome sign. He looked across the table. There was a roll of parchment lying on it, bound by a leather cord. There was a seal. Count Aldebrand Ludenhof's seal.

His stomach gave a sudden lurch, and the small beer rose uncomfortably in his gorge. It all came rushing back. Grotius. The assignment. That was why he'd got so drunk.

Magnus reached for the parchment and unrolled it. There were letters of commission from the count's private office, all signed in sweeping flourishes of black ink and stamped with the official marks. Grotius had written him instructions. The Hochland Grand Army's store yards in Hergig had been alerted to the situation. He was expected to pay them a visit at noon. General Scharnhorst was also down to meet him in the afternoon.

Magnus rolled his eyes. Grotius had been nothing if not efficient. The little worm.

'What time is it?' he asked Frau Ettieg, leafing through the dense roll of orders and instructions.

'Late,' she replied, keeping her attention on her cooking. 'You've been snoring like a pig for hours. Do you want a pancake?'

Magnus shook his head, and rose from the table.

'I've got to go,' he said. 'You should have told me about this earlier.'

Frau Ettieg turned, placing her hands on her barrel-like hips crossly.

'And go up to that pile of filth you call your room?' she asked. 'Not likely. If you're going out, I'll get that little slut to clean it.'

Magnus swallowed the last of the beer, spat into the corner of the room and brushed his clothes down casually.

'Tell her to keep away from the chests,' he said. 'I'll be back at the end of the day.'

Frau Ettieg came up to him. She frowned, and flicked some of the detritus of the night from his leather overcoat. She could be strangely maternal at times.

'Take this,' she said, pressing a steaming pancake into his hands. 'You're a disgrace. Your father would weep to see you.'

Magnus shrugged. Once so many people told you the same thing, it lost its power to shock.

'Thanks,' he said, munching on the cake. It tasted of fat and curdled milk. 'I'll enjoy it on the way.'

The vast mass of the Kristalhof loomed into the pale grey sky. Its enormous walls sloped slightly inwards as it rose from the chaos of the streets around it. Its dark flanks were brutal in their simplicity. There was no adornment, no decoration. It had been built for war. The towers at each corner were broad and squat, banded with lines of granite. If the count and his court were inside, there was no visible external sign. A few crows flapped lazily above the keep. They were mere specks against its bulk.

Magnus looked up at it grimly. In an ugly town, it was the ugliest building. It might have even been the ugliest building in the entire Empire, although there were plenty of contenders for that crown. He was glad he was not going inside. The store yards of the Hochland Grand Army were in a compound under the shadow of the Kristalhof.

The 'Grand' Army was nothing of the sort. Unlike the drilled perfection of the Reiksguard or the massed ferocity of the Middenheim regiments, the Hochlanders were slipshod and slovenly. The store yards were a case in point. Piles of halberds and pikes lay across the muddy yards, their tips gently rusting in the damp. Blackpowder kegs were left next to bales of dry straw. Rows of cannons had been left exposed to the elements with not so much as a sheet across them. As he toured the yards, Magnus's temper worsened. By the time he came across the quartermaster, his mood had become black.

'Who're you?' said the quartermaster, a thick-set man with weasely eyes and a broken nose. He looked hostile and dishonest, much like quartermasters across the whole Old World.

Magnus handed him his letters of warrant from Grotius.

'This place is a disgrace,' he said, looking sourly at the chaos around him.

The quartermaster looked back at him stupidly. Despite the letters of warrant, he looked deeply suspicious of Magnus.

'You're an Ironblood?' he asked, leering with his tiny eyes.

Magnus glared at him.

'I am,' he growled. 'If you knew anything of your trade, you'd know that. Look at those guns! You're a damned fool.'

Magnus walked up to one of the great cannons. It had a long iron barrel, about six feet. It was functional rather than decorative, but well made. He ran his finger across the pitted outer surface. A Gottekruger, a minor marque from Nuln. Solid, dependable, accurate. It deserved better treatment. The rim of the gun had corroded, and the axle had rotted almost entirely away. It would need a week's work before it would fire again.

Looking insulted, the quartermaster limped after him.

'Begging your pardon, sir,' he said, disingenuously. 'We don't get the funds we need. What are you after?'

Magnus gave him a withering look.

'Everything that works,' he said. 'Which I'd say is about half of what you have. We need as many heavy cannons as you've got. The bigger the better. They're for breaching walls. I was told you have rocket batteries and volley guns too, though Sigmar only knows what condition they're in. Is this true?'

The quartermaster looked evasive.

'You mean the Helblasters?' he said. 'We might have two left. I'd have to look in the sheds. It'll take time. Of course, I'd go a lot quicker if you could see your way…'

The man squinted at Magnus, and didn't finish his sentence. Magnus felt his heart sink even further. The quartermaster was as corrupt as a Tilean. On another day, Magnus might have paid him something, just to oil the wheels of business. But the quartermaster had picked the wrong time to angle for payment. Magnus's headache had settled into an acute, stabbing pain behind the eyes. He needed another drink.

His temper snapped. Magnus suddenly swept down on the quartermaster and grabbed him by his collar. He pushed his grizzled face into his, knowing that his breath would still be as foul as a gnoblar's crotch, and bared his teeth.

'I don't know what kind of peasants you've been used to dealing with,' Magnus hissed, keeping his gaze locked on to the other man's irises, 'but fool around with me and I'll tear your eyes out for shot. My papers are from Valerian von Grotius. Give me any trouble, and I'll be straight on to him. He'll be glad to deal with any parts of you still remaining alive after me and my lads have given you a proper going over. Is that understood?'

The quartermaster's eyes were now filled with fear.

'Yes, sir,' he squeaked, and his body went limp.

Magnus let him go, and brushed his coat lapels down.

'I'll leave the list with you,' he said, coolly. 'You have until sundown to prepare an inventory. I want everything specified on the list to be ready for when the army leaves. If you have to get help in, that'll come out of your own fat pocket. You'll get your fee when I'm happy, and not before.'

The quartermaster looked at him with an expression of pure loathing.

'Yes, sir,' he said once again, bowing unsteadily.

Magnus turned away from him imperiously, and walked back past the lines of decaying ordnance. The quartermaster looked spiteful enough to do something to the guns in revenge, but hopefully his fear of Grotius would put some speed into the man's work. For the first time that day, Magnus felt something approaching pleasure. His blood was pumping, and his head was clear. He still had it, despite everything.

'Herr Ironblood!' came a gruff voice from close behind him.

Magnus froze. The pleasure evaporated immediately. Whoever that was, it didn't sound good. He turned to see a tall, raven-haired man in a long dark green cloak looking at him coldly. The top of the man's head was bare, and his bald pate glinted dully in the pale sunlight. He was wearing a fine jerkin and cloak. A broadsword rested against one thigh. An exquisite blade. An iron star hung from his breast, bearing the crest of Ludenhof.

So. This was the general.

'Herr Scharnhorst,' said Magnus, and bowed. 'I was on my way to see you.'

Scharnhorst raised an eyebrow.

'Our appointment was an hour ago,' he said. His voice sounded like iron scraping across ice. His face was lean and angular. A long, old scar bisected one cheek. 'I saw you having a discussion with my quartermaster. Is anything amiss?'

Magnus paused. This was their first meeting. Diplomacy was normally a good plan. But the man clearly knew nothing about gunnery. There was no point in hiding the truth.

'This yard is not up to scratch, general,' said Magnus bluntly. 'The ordnance is rotting away. We have a long trek to the Mittebergen. If I'm to deliver you guns capable of breaching the walls of Morgramgar, your man will have to do his job better. And not for a fee.'

Scharnhorst didn't respond at once, but his thin lips pursed. A crow cawed in the far distance, and for a moment Magnus could imagine the general's head transposed with it. They were remarkably similar.

'I see,' said Scharnhorst. 'You're to be commended on your diligence. I'll have a word with Gruber.'

Magnus bowed.

'That would be appreciated, general.'

Scharnhorst remained stony.

'Walk with me, Ironblood,' he said, and began to amble towards the yard entrance. Magnus fell in beside him.

'You've chosen to be blunt with me, Ironblood,' said Scharnhorst. 'I admire that in a man. I'll be similarly blunt with you.'

He turned to look directly at Magnus. The scar made his face look almost like a death mask.

'There is a great schism at the heart of the Empire,' he said. 'There are those who place their faith in the tools of Sigmar. The sword, the axe, the warhammer. You know the sort. But there are also those who have departed from his teaching. They look to the ways of the sorcerer, the scholar and the—'

'The engineer,' said Magnus, finishing his sentence for him. A deep weariness had settled within him. He'd heard this speech a thousand times, and from a hundred different soldiers.

Scharnhorst let slip a wintry smile.

'Quite so. And, in the name of honesty, you must know that I am in the former camp. You people kill as many of our own kind as the enemy. On every campaign I have conducted, some disaster has befallen our engineers. If it were not for the urging of Herr Grotius, I would not have taken a master engineer at all. The cannons would have been under my command. That you should know.'

Magnus bit his lip. That was idiocy. There was probably no one left in Hergig besides him who knew how to transport and deploy the heavy guns properly. Leaving it to a man with ice in his veins and lead in his head would be a disaster.

'Grotius made the better choice, I'd say,' said Magnus, keeping his voice just on the right side of insolence. 'With respect, these things aren't toys. They can win you a war, but only in the right hands.'

Scharnhorst looked at Magnus doubtfully. His eyes crawled across his mud-streaked coat, and seemed to linger on every patch of grease, every tattered hole.

'And you have the right pair of hands?'

Magnus could well imagine how he looked, with his ragged clothes and unkempt hair. Scharnhorst couldn't be blamed for underestimating the command of his art. Only the night before, Magnus had been little better than a vagrant. A commission didn't change that. It would take time to get back into his old role.

'I'm an Ironblood, general,' he said. 'Ask anyone. Grotius had to search for me by name.'

Scharnhorst looked doubtful.

'They told me Ironblood was a famous name in your trade,' he said. 'They also told me you were washed up. I don't know about the first of those, but I can see the second is true. You should get yourself cleaned up. You're a mess.'

Magnus absorbed the insult without flinching. He was getting used to it. Being labelled a disgrace had become almost second nature.

'This has all happened quickly, general,' said Magnus. 'Until last night, I didn't know I'd be travelling with you at all. You have to make some allowances.'

Scharnhorst gave him an icy look.

'Don't tell me when I may or may not make allowances,' he said. 'I'll be the judge of that. And I don't care about your problems, Ironblood. You can drink yourself to death in as many inns as you like, just as long as you're not under my command when you do it. You are now, so you'd better get yourself together. Next time I see you, you'll have shaved, and at least tried to look like an officer worthy of respect from the men. And do something about your stench. Even the flagellants don't smell as bad.'

Magnus tried to look as deferential as he could.

'Very good, general,' he said. 'I'll get right on it.'

Scharnhorst nodded.

'You do that,' he said. 'We don't have much time.'

With that, he turned on his heel and left as abruptly as he'd arrived. Magnus watched him walk up towards the Kristalhof. No doubt he had some banquet to attend or audience to conduct. The life of a member of the noble classes would always be different.

He left the store yard and began to head back towards the blacksmith's house. He'd have to tell Frau Ettieg that he'd be away for a while. She'd miss the rent money, but little else. As he walked through the streets, Magnus caught sight of a promising-looking sign. *The White Hart*. It even looked pretty clean. He stuffed his hand in a pocket, and was pleasantly surprised to find a few coins. That improved his mood. Scharnhorst was right: if he was going to try and pull an Iron Company together he would have to pull himself together first. But that could wait. Right now, he needed a drink.

Silvio Messina regarded the man before him coolly. The drunkard was a vast, hulking brute. Ill-shaven, stinking, poorly clad. Like all the inhabitants of the Empire, he didn't know how to look after himself. It was pitiful.

Silvio ran a finger through his own elegant jet-black mane of perfectly glossy hair, and sighed. Hergig was a tiresome place, and this episode was more tiresome still. He certainly knew how to pick the wrong tavern. It just wasn't his night.

Lukas edged towards him, looking anxious.

'Do you want me to call for the militia?' he hissed in a worried whisper.

Silvio irritably gestured for him to withdraw. It was bad enough getting into bar fights in such a hole. Having a wide-eyed youngster to look after too was almost too tedious for words.

'So keep out of this, *ragazzo*,' Silvio said. 'It'll be over in a moment.'

As he spoke, the brute came at him, arms flailing wildly. There was an appreciative roar from the rest of the drinkers in the tavern. The animal was clearly well known here, and fancied himself as the cock of the walk. The fact that this knuckle-headed ass was the best on offer was another damning indictment of the provincials and their backwardness.

Silvio waited until the last moment before slipping to one side. He evaded the cartwheeling fists of the drunkard easily. As the thick-set man reeled at him again, Silvio stuck out an impeccably crafted leather boot, and watched his assailant career into the beer-soaked floor of the inn. A roar of laughter broke out around the room, and tankards were thumped against tables.

The man thumped his fists on the ground with frustration. Slowly, cumbersomely, he got up, and turned to face Silvio once more. As he did so, his eyes went wide. The rage left his face, and his hands fell to his sides. He stood, stupidly.

Silvio allowed himself a dry smile of victory. His pistol, an exquisitely crafted gun from the studios of Salvator Boccherino of Luccini, was pressed lightly against the fat man's forehead. Even in the dull light of the candles around them, its silver shaft glistened. The intricate engravings of the famously beautiful courtesans of Luccini graced the chamber, while the handle was inlaid with a flawless panel of mother-of-pearl. It was a beautiful thing. An elegant thing. No doubt the beasts of Hergig had never seen such finery. It was worth more than their pox-ridden inn and all its contents.

But that wasn't the best part of it. Most importantly for his current purposes, the pistol was utterly deadly. The barrel had been ground by Boccherino himself, and dispatched shot as straight and true as a virgin's promise. Not that Silvio was worried about missing his target on this occasion. The brute was trapped like a pig in its pen, blinking and wondering desperately what to do.

'Now then,' said Silvio, calmly, relishing his control. 'I expect you're reconsidering your position. What was it you were going to do to me? Now I recall it. Drown my head into your... what you call it? That *firkin*. And hold me down while I died in the muck you people call *ale*. Doesn't look so likely now, does it?'

A line of sweat ran down the man's temple. From the corner of his eye, Silvio could see that the rest of the tavern's occupants were staying in their seats. Some looked transfixed. Others were merely enjoying the show. He let his finger run up and down the length of the solid silver trigger mechanism, savouring the power.

'As I see it, you have no idea what kind of gun this is,' said Silvio, sadistically. 'If you were forty feet away and running into the dark, still she couldn't miss. You're out of your depth, fat man. Count yourself fortunate I was only after your wife. If I wanted your hovel and your stash of coins, I could take them too. Any time.'

The brute was becoming enraged again, but held his position with difficulty. He knew that a single move would finish him. Silvio enjoyed watching the tortured expression on his face.

'So I tell you the truth,' said Silvio, toying with his prey like a cat. 'It's probably not so bad a thing that you found us when you did. I hate to tell it to you, but she's really not that good. I mean it, have you people ever heard of a *bath*?'

That was possibly taking things a bit too far. There was a low murmur of anger from the seated drinkers around them. They didn't mind one of their number being humiliated, but casting aspersions on all of them was dangerous. This thing had better be wrapped up.

'You're lucky I'm in such good mood,' he said, pressing the muzzle of the pistol more firmly against the man's flabby flesh. 'Another day, I'd leave a hole in your skull. Now, back away, slowly. You let my companion and me leave this place in peace. Come after us, I'll not be so forgivable. Do not forget, my aim is true, in shooting as it is with all things.'

His hands shaking, either from rage or fear, the drunkard slowly took a few steps backward. His tiny, piggish eyes blazed with an impotent fury. Silvio checked to see that Lukas was by his side before retreating towards the doorway. He kept the pistol raised, his eyes sweeping the tavern for threats. The natives seemed cowed by his display for the time being.

As he reached the door, Silvio allowed some of his customary swagger to take over. He bowed to the assembled gathering in mock salute.

'Thank you, fine sirs, for your most exquisite entertainment,' he said, his voice silky. 'I am overjoyed to learn that men of Hergig are as hospitable and accommodating as their wives and their daughters. When this silly business is over, we may think of coming to visit again.'

That final insult lit the fuse. Chairs were kicked over and tables rammed to the walls as the tavern rose up in a wall of rage. Silvio turned to Lukas, a wicked smile on his lips.

'Run!' he shouted.

The two of them turned and fled into the night, curses and bellows of spluttered anger following them as they went. Thankfully, the pursuit did not last long. The denizens of the tavern were mostly too drunk to stand, and those with some sense were wary of the pistol. After a show of chasing them from the inn, they gave up the hunt, grumbling and muttering as they returned to their lukewarm drinks.

Once they were sure the last of them had stumbled off, Silvio and Lukas stood panting under the eaves of a half-derelict town house. Silvio felt a thrill run through his refined body. This was why he loved being a mercenary. There was nothing quite like the rush from taking advantage of the stupidity of the locals. And if things ever went wrong, his most loyal companion, the esteemed Boccherino pistol, was always there to ensure a hasty exit.

He turned to Lukas, and grinned.

'This is life, eh?' he said, his teeth flashing white in the dark.

The sandy-haired youth from Averland didn't look too sure. He was still too timid, too green. Like all the men of the Empire, he didn't have enough imagination.

'You're a madman,' said Lukas between breaths. 'We could've been killed.'

Silvio laughed.

'By that rabble?' he said, disgustedly. 'By Luccina, I'd have been ashamed to have been *scratched* by one of them.'

'You're right,' came a voice. It wasn't Lukas's. 'That would have been sloppy.'

Silvio whirled around, raising his pistol quickly.

'Declare yourself!' he hissed.

A man's shape emerged from the shadows. He was as dishevelled and grimy as the wretches they had left behind in the tavern. He was heavy-boned, and wore a long leather overcoat. His greying hair hung in lank curls to his shoulders, and the stench of drink hung around him. Only his bearing gave him away. He might have looked like a vagrant, but Silvio could see he was nothing of the sort.

'Put your gun down, lad,' the man said, walking towards them casually. 'It's a nice piece. A Calvasario?'

Silvio kept the pistol raised, watching the newcomer with suspicion.

'Close,' he said. 'You know your marques. How does man of Hergig acquire such knowledge?'

The man laughed, a strange, bitter sound.

'I'm no man of Hergig,' he said. 'So it's a Boccherino. Very nice. Though

I dislike Tilean pieces. Flashy, but temperamental.'

Silvio kept his aim steady.

'I told you declare yourself,' he said in a low voice.

The man shrugged.

'You don't scare me, lad,' he said. 'You put on quite a show back there, but you were never going to shoot. I'll give you a name, though, for what it's worth. Ironblood. No doubt you've heard of it.'

Silvio frowned. It was familiar. Where had he heard it? Somewhere back in Tilea, perhaps. He had an image of a pistol. An outrageous, three-barrelled monster. A work of genius. Surely, it could have nothing to do with the man before him. The man looked little better than a wandering savage.

'It means nothing to me,' he said. 'What do you want?'

Ironblood shrugged.

'Have it your way,' he said. 'As for what I want, that should be obvious. You're here to fight. I'm here to hire. You've worked in an engineer's company before?'

Silvio nodded cautiously.

'Many times. In the Border Princes, Ostland. I had given up on work here. The Hochlanders don't seem to know what any one of them is doing.'

Ironblood smiled grimly.

'Then we're agreed on that, at least,' he said. 'They have guns, though. Heavy cannons, mortars, some lighter pieces. And they have handgunners. Some of them are very good. Huntsmen, mostly, drafted in by Ludenhof from the countryside. They just need someone to lead them. Someone who does know what they're doing.'

Silvio let his finger relax on the trigger. Beside him, Lukas stayed mute. This was interesting.

'Can you afford me?' said Silvio, letting his habitual confidence bleed into his speech. 'You'll not find a better master of handgunners. I can shoot golden tassel from Karl Franz's nightcap at hundred paces. What's more, I can teach the others to do the same. If these Hochland guns are all they're told of, of course.'

Ironblood shrugged.

'Some of the older ones are,' he said. 'What can your friend do?'

Silvio started to reply, but Lukas spoke over him, the words spilling out in his enthusiasm.

'I've studied at Nuln, sir,' he said in his young, high voice. 'Under Captain Horgrimm. I can handle a long riflegun, and man a standard mortar battery too. I know the theory of the volley guns, and have been second in command of a rank of cannons. Big siege cannons, they were. I even took over once, when one of the recoils caught the captain.'

Ironblood looked at Lukas with a mix of scepticism and amusement.

'Can you command men, boy?' he asked.

Lukas looked downcast.

'I'm learning,' he said, weakly.

'The boy's new,' said Silvio. 'I teach him what he needs to know. His family is Herschel. He comes with me. But I'll say again, how much are you offering? We are not some flea-infested dogs of war. I'm not so sure you can pay our price.'

Ironblood laughed at that, and his heavy body shook with mirth.

'Don't try to bargain with me, lad,' he said, grinning. 'If you weren't for sale you wouldn't be here. And you'll get no better offer. Unless you fancy joining the flagellants or the halberdiers. I can't quite see that, looking at your fine clothes.'

His expression became more serious.

'Listen, the money's good,' he continued. 'I'm under commission from the count's agent, and you won't want for payment. We'll be a small company. Half a dozen men, at most. There'll be little glory in this messy campaign, but there will be gold. So what will you say?'

Silvio thought for a moment. The man Ironblood spoke the truth. It was probably going to be the best offer they'd get. Slogging along in the mud with the regular state troops was not something he was prepared to do, even for a generous share of the bounty. As he looked into Ironblood's eyes, Silvio could see that the man was used to command. If he and Lukas weren't going to leave Hergig and look for some other fight to take up, this was the obvious thing to do. And once on the road, there were bound to be possibilities. There always were.

'How long do we have?' he said, retaining his sceptical expression for the sake of form.

'The army leaves in four days,' said Ironblood. 'You'll need to give me your answer in the morning. You'll find me at the Grand Army store yards. Ask for me by name.'

'Very well,' said Silvio, keeping his voice neutral. 'So we'll think about it.'

Ironblood nodded.

'You do that,' he said. 'But don't take too long. And for the sake of Sigmar, stop pointing that pistol in my face. You look like a fool.'

Silvio bristled a little, but lowered the weapon. As he did so, Ironblood bowed to take his leave, and retreated back into the night. Silvio watched him walk off, consumed by his thoughts. This looked like a good bet, but it never paid to be hasty.

'What are you doing?' said Lukas urgently, once Ironblood was out of earshot. 'We should be jumping at this! It's why we're here, after all.'

Silvio looked at him wearily. He liked Lukas, and the boy was a good engineer. But he would have to learn some guile, or his career would be short and painful.

'We'll do it, don't worry,' said Silvio, casually extinguishing the taper on his pistol and sheathing it in its holster. 'But I don't want him to think we are too keen. That is fatal.'

He took a deep breath, and looked around him. The dark streets were nearly empty. Lukas waited expectantly.

'Come on,' said Silvio at last. 'There will be another inn open somewhere. If we're going to join this strange thing, we'd better make most of what's on offer.'

He looked down at Lukas. The boy was as eager as a puppy.

'Just don't embarrass me,' Silvio said, stalking off with Lukas in tow. 'I still haven't given up on finding wench. You make them nervous.'

CHAPTER THREE

'These are nice drawings. They are by your children, yes?'

Reputed remarks of High King Thorgrim Grudgebearer, on being presented with
a copy of the Notebooks of Leonardo da Miragliano by the Emperor Karl Franz

Hergig was poor, and it showed. The thoroughfares were narrow, the buildings old and shabby. Most were made of wood. Aside from the imposing Kristalhof, there were few stone constructions. Even the city walls seemed in poor repair, despite the fact they had been necessary for the city's defence many times in living memory. The skulls of slaughtered beastmen still hung over the main gates, presumably intended as a warning to their kin not to come back. Magnus didn't blame them for staying in the forests.

The morning had dawned cold again. He had a hangover again. It was thirsty work, recruiting. His mood was dark. Why had he come to such a place? What had possibly drawn him to this Sigmar-bereft wasteland? The people were stupid and superstitious. There were more temples to Shallya and Taal than to the divine protector of the Empire. Perhaps it had been the reputation of the gunners. The Hochland long gun was undoubtedly a piece of engineering mastery. Even the gunsmiths of Nuln admired the best examples. But when Magnus had arrived in the city, he had been disappointed. There were few smiths left. Many had fled south to escape the endless wars. More had been poached by richer employers in the lands to the south, their secrets scattered across the

Empire and feverishly copied by less-skilled hands. A genuine Hergig piece was now a rare and precious thing. Magnus wondered if there was anybody left in the city who really knew how to make one.

Even if there had been, there was still more talent in his own blood-stream than in the whole province. The Ironblood pistol was whispered about reverentially in the corridors of the College of Engineers. True flintlock, a rarity in the Empire. Three barrels. Exquisitely bored. The cleanest workings you could imagine. Nearly impossible to fire without igniting truly. And the deadliest aim of any gun he had ever used. The very fact that his name was associated with such a masterpiece occasionally filled him with a terrified awe. Only three had ever been made. Now two were lost, and the third was in a crystal casket deep within the college vaults. He had heard rumours that a second was still in use somewhere in the Empire. A witch hunter. A woman. From time to time, he pondered trying to track her down.

The same thing stopped him every time. Shame. He had not made the guns. His father had, the great Augustus Ironblood. The old White Wolf of Nuln, so-called because of his mane of ivory hair, sweeping down from his severe, lined face. At one time Magnus had wanted nothing but to follow in the old man's footsteps. And he had started well. Too well, perhaps. And then...

Magnus looked down at his filth-spattered coat. He held his hands up. They were dark with long-ingrained grime. His nails, once worn to the quick by honest work, had grown effeminately long. Frau Ettieg was right. Augustus would have wept.

He took a deep breath. Such thoughts depressed him. There was no use dwelling on them. Nothing could change what he'd become. He was the product of fate, like everyone else.

Magnus stepped around a pool of something foetid and unidentifiable. On the far side of the street, it looked like a fight was breaking out. A man in ragged robes broke from a crowd and tore off towards the poor quarter. He was followed by a scrum of angry townsfolk. Some were newly-arrived mercenaries, by their look. No doubt they'd been trying to buy luck charms or some other nonsense. Paying for a bundle of crow-bones from a street wizard was stupid and dangerous. Trying to cheat your customers was even more stupid. From behind a row of houses, the man's voice rose in panic. It looked like they'd got him. He wouldn't last long.

Magnus sighed, and pressed on. Soon he had reached his destination, a low-beamed house on the fringes of the Hofbahn. The door was open and light streamed from the room within. There was the noise of a man's laughter, and children squealing, and a woman's high voice chiding them all mockingly. Magnus smiled in spite of himself. There were some things in life he couldn't be cynical about. He smoothed his hair down again and brushed some of the muck from his coat. Knocking on the door frame to announce himself, he ducked under the lintel and entered.

The doorway led straight into a kitchen, warm with the smells of cooking. A vast man sat at a long wooden table. His beard was a fiery red, just like that of a Bright wizard. His girth was enormous, and he seemed to fill half the narrow chamber by himself. When he saw Magnus enter, his smile froze for a second on his lips. Then he recovered himself, and let out a bellow of delight.

'Ironblood!' he roared, and rose from his seat.

Magnus smiled, and stood patiently to embrace the bear hug.

'How are you, Tobias?' Magnus said, feeling his ribs groan under the pressure.

Tobias Hildebrandt stepped back, still grinning.

'As well as ever,' he said. 'Life is good. And you?'

Magnus ducked the question, and turned to the woman.

'Anna-Liese,' he said, bowing his head politely.

Hildebrandt's wife looked back at him guardedly. She was a pretty, brown-haired woman in the prime of life. If she looked a little tired and distracted, then she had every right to be. There were four children clustered around her, staring at Magnus with alarm. They knew who he was, but they had never seen him looking quite so shabby. He suddenly felt self-conscious. He should have made some effort to scrub the worst off. Perhaps the smell of beer was still on his breath.

Magnus looked at Hildebrandt, not enjoying the awkward silence.

'Could I speak with you?' he asked.

Hildebrandt shot his wife a glance. She understood at once.

'Children, come,' she said in her gentle, remonstrating tone. 'Your father has business to discuss.'

Quietly, efficiently, they slipped out of the room. Anna-Liese closed the door behind her. With a pang, Magnus realised he'd broken up a precious family moment. He envied Hildebrandt. The man had achieved everything that Magnus had been unable to. In a dark and brutal world, there was still space for the simple pleasure of hearth and home. That, Magnus thought dryly, was what they were all fighting for, after all.

'So,' Hildebrandt said, in his rumbling voice. 'What's all this?'

Magnus sat down at the table, and Hildebrandt resumed his seat.

'A commission,' said Magnus. 'I've had a look at the documents. It's worth a lot. It could wipe out our losses. Interested?'

Hildebrandt looked at him warily. Magnus could see the indecision. He understood the man's doubts. About everything.

'What kind of commission?' asked Hildebrandt.

Magnus explained the story of the margravine.

'We'll have several companies of gunners,' he said. 'There are some big pieces too. Cannons, some mortars. Ludenhof's been something of a collector. There's a Helblaster or two, maybe some rocket batteries.

They're serious. They have the ironwork. They just need crew to man them.'

Hildebrandt took a deep breath. As he did so, his massive lungs slowly filled, and took just as long to slowly empty. His face was marked with doubt.

'I thought you weren't–' he began.

'I don't have a choice,' said Magnus, cutting him off. 'Ludenhof found out I was here. They're short-handed. And anyway, I need the money. I'm going to do it. Are you with me?'

Hildebrandt sighed again. He was beginning to resemble a bellows, sucking in air and expelling it again.

'It's not easy,' he said, grudgingly. 'There's Anna-Liese. She'd hate for me to leave again. We've not been in Hochland long. And the children. I don't know, Magnus.'

Magnus knew his old friend better than that. Anna-Liese would miss him, to be sure. But he would miss her more. Hildebrandt had always been a family man. For him, the fighting had always been about the money. Money to secure their future, to pay for an education at the temple, to lift them out of the gutter. Unlike Magnus, he hadn't drunk it all away. He could afford a modest house, to keep his children in clothes, to put meat on the board and ale in the cellar. What reason could he have to go back to it all?

'You don't have to decide now,' said Magnus, trying to keep the disappointment out of his voice. 'I can come back later.'

Hildebrandt looked torn.

'We're getting older, Magnus,' he said. 'There comes a time in a man's life when he's no good on the field any more. We've done our bit for the Emperor. Do you have to take this commission?'

Magnus felt a sour taste form in his mouth. It was all very well for Hildebrandt to talk of picking and choosing commissions. He didn't have Grotius on his shoulder, nor a pile of debt on his back. The man had become comfortable. Soft. Perhaps this had been a bad idea.

Magnus rose.

'Think about it,' he said. 'I've got things to see to. You know where I am.'

Hildebrandt stayed seated. His face creased with concern.

'How much are you drinking, Magnus?' he said. 'You don't look well. Why not come and stay with us for a few days? Just until you get things back in order. I have connections. We could keep it quiet.'

Magnus stopped in his tracks. For a moment, for just a moment, he had a vision of what that might be like. Laundered sheets. Hot water in the copper. A warm hearth. Evenings surrounded by a proper family, rather than the transient scum he associated with. The vision was uncomfortable. Painful, even. He shook it off.

'I'm expected in the Kristalhof,' he said, gruffly.

Without waiting for Hildebrandt to reply, he turned and left. From within the house, there came a sound of a long, final sigh.

The weather lifted slightly, but not enough to drive the chill from the air and the damp from the walls. A steady drizzle had been falling for two days, turning the normally muddy streets into teeming rivulets. The inhabitants of the city went about their business with hoods drawn tightly over their heads. The heavy swell of the Talabec glinted dully under the grey sky, and the ravens stayed gloomily on their branches.

Gradually, painfully, Ludenhof's army had taken shape. Money had changed hands, and more mercenaries had arrived. The inns and brothels of Hergig found their takings rising sharply, as did the cutpurses. Honest residents of the town stayed behind locked doors after dark, nervously watching the columns of staggering soldiers reel through the streets, carousing as they went. The songs were a weird mix. Reikspiel was blended with Tilean, Estalian, Bretonnian, even the harsh tongue of Kislev. Wherever there was fighting to be had, the jackals would cluster from all over the Old World. They were never short of work.

Not all the recent arrivals were dogs of war. Outside the city walls, a ramshackle camp had been erected. The sound of tolling bells could be heard emanating from it at all hours of the day and night. A crude representation of the twin-tailed comet, hewn from old, rotten wood, stood lopsidedly in the centre of the settlement. The inhabitants had grown quickly from a few dozen to over a hundred, and still they came. The folk of Hergig shunned these newcomers even more than the mercenaries. They could hear the crack of whipcord and the shrieks of pain. Flagellants were seldom welcomed by the ordinary folk of the Empire. The wretches had come to Hergig to do the only thing they still knew how to do. Labour, fight and die.

Magnus lifted his head from the pitcher of water, feeling its cold touch revive him. From his garret room vantage point, Magnus could just about see the edge of the camp beyond the city perimeter. It had been positioned on a marshy curve by the riverbank. No doubt the mud and mosquitoes would be seen as more blessed penitence from Sigmar. He felt nothing but disdain. However far he fell, he would never be as bad as those foam-mouthed fanatics. Magnus shook his head.

Behind him, the door suddenly slammed open. Magnus's heart sprang up into his throat, and he whirled around. He clutched for a sword at his side, but it wasn't there. He was barely dressed.

In front of him, there was a bearded man. No, too short for a man. A dwarf. He stood with his legs apart, arms by his sides. A huge axe was clenched in his right hand. Magnus's eyes flicked over to the nearest chest. Too far. He'd be dead before he could get halfway.

He looked back at the stranger. With effort, he forced his heart to stop hammering. If the intruder had wanted him dead, he would be so already. He calmed himself down, and waited for what was coming.

'Very wise,' came a low, rumbling voice, seemingly aware of his thoughts.

'Who are you?' said Magnus, struggling to keep his voice steady. His mind was working quickly. He had no weapon to hand, but he was a big man and knew how to use his fists. But a dwarf was something else. They were like a ball of solid granite, bound with iron and crested with something sharp. He'd never seen a man take one on by choice.

'Thorgad Grimgarsson,' came the answer. The voice was harsh, scraped raw by a life spent fighting in the deeps of the earth. 'You, I know. At least by reputation.'

Magnus took a better look at the intruder, feeling his thumping heart begin to return to normal. Thorgad looked like all the other dwarfs he'd known. There was the unnatural stockiness, the exposed arms of pure bunched muscle, the heavily decorated beard with its elaborate plaits and rings of iron. Thorgad's hair was a dark, deep brown, almost black at the lips and eyebrows. His squat nose and cheeks were heavily tanned, and the ink-blue shapes of old tattoos ran across every inch of exposed skin. He wore a heavy leather jerkin and a round iron helmet. His boots had iron tips, and were covered with old, dry mud. He had a bandage around his thigh, and there were other fresh wounds. Like all of his kind, his expression was hard to read, and his origins hard to guess. To the extent he could tell, Magnus thought he looked old. His hands were laced with scars, and his eyes bore the confident glint of a seasoned warrior.

Magnus leaned back against the wall. The dwarf didn't look like he'd come to fight. In his heavily indebted situation, though, you could never be too careful. Bounty hunters were not unknown in Hergig. He kept his fists bunched, and his eyes open.

'Well then, Master Grimgarsson,' said Magnus. 'You've come into my room and given me a scare. Well done. There was a time when that would have been an achievement. Now you're here, you'd better tell me what you want.'

Thorgad fixed his steel-trap gaze on Magnus. He didn't smile.

'You're mixed up in this new army,' he said in his growling voice. 'That's what I heard, at any rate. Ludenhof has got this damn-fool idea into his head, and he's trapped you in it.'

'It's a commission,' said Magnus, guardedly. 'I'm a master engineer. I choose the ones I take and the ones I don't.'

Thorgad raised an eyebrow.

'So you say,' he said. 'Or it might be that you've run out of money and luck, and this is all that's left.'

Magnus felt his temper begin to rise.

'Watch your stunted tongue,' he said, conjuring as much menace as he could, given the situation. 'State your business, or get out.'

Thorgad ran a thick finger along the edge of his axe.

'Get me out?' he said. 'And how would you do that? If you fancy your chances against a dawi, then bring it on. I won't stop you.'

Magnus scowled impotently. The dwarf might have been shorter than him, but Magnus knew from long experience that an experienced warrior like Thorgad was a match for all but the toughest of human fighters. It was not for nothing that the dwarfs looked down on men, despite the height difference. For a moment, Magnus pondered rushing him, trying to knock him off balance before he could get hold of the axe properly. It was futile, and they both knew it.

Thorgad scowled.

'Enough of this stupidness,' he said, hefting the heavy bronze-inlaid axe head as if it were made of straw. 'I'm not here to kill you. Or even to make your life more difficult than it already is. You haven't worked it out yet? I want to join you.'

For a moment, Magnus couldn't believe what he was hearing. A dwarf joining an engineering company wasn't unprecedented, but it was rare. The stunted folk believed themselves the most accomplished engineers in the Old World. Magnus had known many of them from his long years studying at Nuln and fighting in the Emperor's armies. If a human created a faster-loading gun, a dwarf would look down the barrel and sniff at its inaccuracy. If a human made a cannon capable of smashing ten-foot-thick walls apart, a dwarf would ask why it couldn't demolish mountains. For all he respected their achievements, Magnus mostly found dwarfs insufferable. They were arrogant, prickly and far too easily angered. Having one along with him on the campaign, all things being equal, would not be a good idea.

'You've a strange way of asking for a favour,' Magnus said.

Thorgad frowned. Or, at least it looked like frowning.

'A favour?' he said. 'If you think going on this journey will be a favour, you can't know the land around Morgramgar.'

He leaned forward. Under his bushy eyebrows, his deep-set eyes glinted brightly.

'I guess you haven't been told much about this campaign yet,' Thorgad said. 'That's no surprise. The count doesn't know what he's doing. No one here does. I've seen cack-handed umgi campaigns before, but even by your standards this is bad. You've already had one army destroyed. Sending another one into the mountains before finding out what happened is stupid. Really stupid.'

Magnus tried to interrupt, but was halted by Thorgad's stare.

'Let me tell you about Morgramgar,' said the dwarf. 'It is old. Very old. The battlements may be the creation of your Empire, but the foundations are not. It has been built to survive, carved from the living rock by folk who knew what they were doing. It stands on a spur of solid stone, and its dark walls rise a hundred feet from the plains below. Water bubbles from the deeps beneath, shielded by solid stone, impervious to spoiling. There are storehouses hewn from the earth within capable of holding months' worth of food. An unprepared army would break against those walls like the tide while the defenders drank and ate their fill within.'

Magnus looked doubtful.

'I've seen some drawings,' he said. 'It doesn't look that big. I've run sieges before.'

Thorgad shook his head.

'Size is not the issue, manling,' he said, scornfully. 'You're twice my height, but I could stand you on your head before you could reach for your sword. The point is this. Morgramgar is nigh-on impregnable. You won't break it without help. You need me. I can deliver the citadel to you.'

Magnus saw that the dwarfish sense of modesty was still much as it had ever been.

'Oh yes?' he said, unconvinced. 'And you're prepared to prove it, I suppose. Talk is common, particularly from your kind.'

Thorgad's eyes darkened at the insult, and Magnus saw his hand grip the axe more tightly.

'Don't mock me, manling,' he growled. 'I travelled far to find you. You should listen to wisdom when you have the chance. Don't become more of a fool than you already are.'

Magnus sighed inwardly. This was why dwarfs were so wearisome. They handed out insults like cheap coins, but could never take one back. He'd never met a stunted one who didn't have a rampaging sense of personal pride. Perhaps it was a height thing.

'I've worked in the mines under the Worlds Edge Mountains since before your esteemed father was alive. I've marched in more armies in the dark places of the world than your race will ever know. I have hewn stone apart like flesh, tunnelled under sheer mountainsides, brought down centuries of labour with a single blow of an axe. It's in my blood. If you want to take this citadel, then I'll say it again. You need me. Take me with you. You need not pay me a florin. I scorn your gold. I just need to be there.'

Magnus raised an eyebrow.

'You scorn my gold?' he said, genuinely amazed.

Thorgad shook his head disgustedly, and said no more. Magnus looked at him intently. This was an unexpected development, albeit one with possibilities.

'Suppose you tell me why you're so keen to come along?' he said. 'I can believe you know what you are doing. I've never met a dwarf yet who didn't know the right way to point a cannon. But you're not in it for the money? That I find hard to believe.'

Thorgad still didn't reply at once.

'My reasons needn't concern you,' he said at last, the words dragged from his lips. 'My task in Morgramgar is my own. But I will swear loyalty to you and your company. If you know anything of the dawi, then you'll know what that means. My oath will bind me until the task is accomplished and the citadel is broken. Then I will go my own way. All debts paid. That's the offer. You would do well to accept it.'

Magnus silently weighed up the options. Although the dwarf wasn't to know it, the company at present still consisted solely of himself and the Tilean. Hildebrandt might waver, but Magnus hadn't found any other engineers of adequate quality. To turn down a concrete offer would be difficult. The fact that Thorgad would work for free was incredible, if troubling. But he knew the value of a dwarf oath. Whatever reason Thorgad had for wanting to get inside Morgramgar, it was clearly powerful.

Magnus ran a weary hand through his unkempt hair. Thorgad waited patiently.

'Very well,' said Magnus at length. 'I'll take you on. But if you're going to do this, then be aware that I command this company. I don't care how things are done in Karaz-a-Kazoo, or wherever you're from, but we do it my way in my command. That goes for you as much as the other lads. Can you do that?'

Thorgad looked sourly back at Magnus, clearly not relishing that prospect.

'You have my oath, manling,' he said, grudgingly.

Magnus spat on his hand, and held it out.

'Then we'll seal it,' he said.

Thorgad spat a thick gobbet of phlegm onto his own palm, and walked towards Magnus. The two clasped hands tightly. Magnus felt the iron-hard grip of the dwarf fingers, and spasms shot through his arm. Taking on the dwarf in combat would have been madness. It was lucky Thorgad had intended him no harm.

'When do we leave?' said Thorgad, releasing Magnus's hand and wiping his own on his jerkin.

'There are a few things still to do,' said Magnus, truthfully enough. 'Scharnhorst aims to leave tomorrow. The muster will be at dawn, in the shadow of the Kristalhof.'

'I will see you then,' said Thorgad, and started to walk from the room.

'Wait!' said Magnus. 'There is work for us to do. I know nothing of what your skills are.'

Thorgad shrugged, and kept walking.

'That can wait,' he said, flatly. 'I have business elsewhere. I'll see you at dawn. Look for me at the castle.'

With that, he was gone, clumping down the stairs in his heavy iron-shod boots. Magnus stood for a moment, unsure of what to do with himself. From downstairs, he heard Frau Ettieg's squeal of alarm, followed by a door slamming.

Eventually, Magnus walked over to the bed and sat down heavily. That had been unusual. The disturbance had upset his rhythm. Normally, he might have had a drink to calm his nerves. But he was trying to cut down. Scharnhorst's words had hurt him more than he liked to admit. He needed to clean himself up. Perhaps this was a chance to turn things around. Or get killed. One of the two, certainly.

Magnus sighed. He'd rather have had Tobias beside him. But Hildebrandt would have to make up his own mind.

CHAPTER FOUR

'Forget all you have been told about the heroic legends of the Empire. Forget tales of bravery and sacrifice. Forget the legends of the runefangs and Ghal Maraz. Do you really think that we would remain the mightiest realm on the earth if we relied on those magical trinkets in battle? I will tell you the truth. Every battle is won or lost before a sword is even picked up. The real glory of the Emperor's armies lies in one simple, mundane thing. Planning. If you have no stores of blackpowder, no ledgers for payment, no lines of supply, no schedule for armaments, you are doomed. I will also tell you the most potent weapon in all the armies of men. Though you may not believe me now, you will when the time of testing comes. Curb your laughter, and listen to me. It is the baggage train.'

From an address given by General Erasmus Jasper von Mickelberg,
Chief Instructor at the Imperial College of Arms, Altdorf

The new day dawned, cold and wreathed in rain. Heavy clouds were being driven south-east by winds from the far steppes of Kislev and the gloomy plains of Ostermark. The rain-bearing palls were piled up on the northern horizon, discharging their load in heavy, lightning-laced storms against the flanks of the distant mountains. The bleak forests of Hochland were damp and sodden. The worst of the winter chill was leaving the lowlands, but the spring rains had been quick to take their place.

Ludenhof's army had been assembled on a wide area to the north of the city. Normally the space was flat and dry, kept free of farms and woodland for the purpose of mustering soldiers for the endless wars of the north. Now it had been turned into a vast pool of slick mud, churned up by the ceaseless movement of men. Horses laboured and whinnied as they were whipped to their stations. The infantry hauled their wargear through the mire, cursing as the grime clutched at their boots. Dampened by the incessant drizzle, drained by the filth underfoot, the army presented a dismal aspect.

The count himself was nowhere to be seen. Members of the nobility had ridden out at first light to inspect the progress of the campaign. Otherwise, it had been left to Grotius and Scharnhorst to ensure that the men were put in order. The Imperial agent sat on his horse atop a low rise, impassively looking over the mass of striving figures beneath him. All across the open plain, the shouts of sergeants and the groans of their charges filled the air.

Despite the short time given for preparation, Grotius had performed his task well. There were nearly four thousand troops assembled, organised in rows of companies according to their function. The bulk of the men were state troopers and drafted militia, arrayed in the Hochland colours of red and forest-green. Some attempt had been made to impose a modicum of uniformity on them, but for every smartly arrayed soldier in well-kept hauberk and helmet, there were a dozen wearing hastily dyed rags and clutching pitchforks rather than halberds. Alongside the regular troops were the mass of mercenaries, some decked out in a close approximation of Hochland livery, most wearing whatever they had come to Hergig in. They were under the command of their own captains, grim-faced men bearing the scars of battle. Most had better weaponry than the state troops, and knew how to use it too. The dogs of war sharpened their blades with expert relish, no doubt eager to spill the blood that earned their keep.

Set aside from the great bulk of troops were the more accomplished elements of the army. There was a small company of knights, clad in dark armour and mounted on heavy chargers. They were not enough to form a proper cavalry charge, but looked well-equipped and practiced in the arts of combat nonetheless. There were no pistoliers or outriders alongside them, but several companies of handgunners had been assembled. These were composed of hunters and trappers from the highlands, drawn into the army with the promise of gold and the threat of the gaol. They were tall, bearded men, uncomfortable in the squalor of the city but deadly in the harsh wilderness. They spoke little, and cleaned their prized guns with quiet dedication. Of all the native soldiery, they looked the most efficient.

And then there were the artillery brigades. Several dozen large items had been prized from Gruber's store yards. In pride of place were the iron-belchers, the huge siege cannons. They were drawn by teams of two carthorses each on great metal-framed wagons. Each was massive, forged in the furnaces of Nuln or Middenheim and decorated with the devices of those cities. Benedictions to Sigmar and Karl Franz had been draped across them by the superstitious crews, which now hung limply in the rain, the ink running down the parchment in rivulets. Other, lighter cannons were drawn in their wake, their slender barrels raised into the air like the snouts of beasts. Behind them all were more canvas-covered carts, each hauled by fresh teams of horses. Within them was stored the shot, the balls of iron grape, the kegs of blackpowder, the rams, the tinder, the spikes, the hammers and all the other equipment needed to keep the mighty machines of war firing true.

But the conventional cannons were not all. Despite Gruber's slovenliness, there were also carts laden with other artillery pieces of arcane design. Most were covered in waxed sheets to keep them from the rain, but here and there outlandish muzzles poked from their shielding. A practiced eye would have seen the telltale outlines of mortars, squat and wide-bellied in shape. They would also have spotted two large machines, tightly bound with rope to their platforms and weighed down with lead balls. The Helblaster guns, as volatile as a Marienburg fishwife and almost as deadly. Non-engineers steered well clear of such contraptions. Even before battle had been joined, their fearsome reputation went before them. Just as dangerous, and as unpredictable, were the Helstorm rockets, of which there were also a couple of examples amidst the artillery column.

As in the case of the cannons, these engines of war were attended by horse-drawn carts laden with ammunition, parts and supplies. Getting them all to the battlefield in one piece was a minor miracle in itself. Together, the massed ironwork had the potential to devastate an opposing force, whatever its origin. Cannons feared no monster of Chaos, and were indifferent to the horror inspired by the rampaging greenskins. Their deadly cargo was as effective against the sorcerer and the heretic as it was against mortal soldiers. And yet in the wrong hands, such mighty engines could wreak havoc amidst the ranks of the faithful too. Not for nothing did the ordinary infantryman look on them with a mix of respect and revulsion. Only the wizards inspired greater feelings of ambivalence amongst the ordinary folk of the Empire.

On the edge of the massed ranks of soldiers, the final contingent of troops lay. The flagellants had grown in number considerably, and now formed perhaps a tenth of the entire complement of infantry. They had made no attempt at all to don the colours of Hochland, and were arrayed in their usual batch of rags and tattered cloaks. Some were naked to the waist, their chests laced with self-inflicted wounds, daubed slogans and tattoos. They seemed impervious to the biting wind and driving rain, no doubt sustained by their endless chanting to Sigmar. Cowled priests went among them, sprinkling holy water from great brass censers and leading the liturgy. They were a breed apart, the flagellants, looked on with uncomprehending eyes by the bulk of the troops. Hochland was no centre for the cult of Sigmar, and the zealots were often seen as little better than madmen.

From his vantage point close to the army commanders, Magnus gazed over the ragged host. He was surprised that so much had been accomplished in such a short time. No doubt it was mostly down to Grotius. The man may have been a slimy toad, but he was clearly an astute one. As he pondered how such a creature had risen to his current position of power, the man himself came riding over.

'You're still with us, then,' he said from atop his horse, giving Ironblood a supercilious smile.

'It was too good an offer to turn down,' said Magnus, dryly.

'Very wise,' said Grotius, bringing his steed to a standstill. 'And I hope you're impressed with what's been accomplished. The count's army would not disgrace any battlefield in the Empire.'

Magnus wasn't sure about that. A massed charge of Reiksguard would make short work of the little cavalry they possessed, and he'd seen much tougher-looking ranks of state troopers from other provinces. But he did have to admit that the number of halberdiers was impressive, as was the artillery train.

'Shame the count's not here to see it himself,' said Magnus.

Grotius's face registered a faint flicker of disapproval.

'The count is detained with many matters of state,' he said. 'I'm sure he would be here if he could.'

'The elector's place is with his men,' came a new voice from behind them. It was harsh and grating, as if scarred by a lifetime of barked orders.

Magnus turned, and saw a warrior priest standing before him. The man was tall and powerfully built. Like most of his order, his head was bare. His torso was encased in thick plate armour, and dark red robes hung to his ankles. He carried an iron warhammer in his right hand, crowned with spikes and engraved with passages from the holy books. His eyebrows were low and dark, causing shadows to bleed across his eyes.

'Ah, Kossof,' said Grotius. 'This is Herr Magnus Ironblood, our master engineer. I assume you've not had the pleasure of each other's acquaintance.'

The two men looked at each other darkly.

'Why we tolerate the blasphemy of the new science in the Emperor's armies I will never understand,' said Kossof in a low voice. 'If Holy Sigmar had sanctioned the use of such infernal machines, he would have written of it.'

Magnus snorted derisively.

'I don't think there were many great cannons around when Sigmar was on earth,' he said, keeping the contempt in his voice to the fore.

Kossof scowled, and looked as if he had discovered a new and disgusting kind of beetle on the underside of his iron-tipped boots.

'I have come to expect such disrespectful blasphemy from those of your twisted persuasion, Ironblood,' he said. 'One day you will realise the folly of your pursuit of knowledge. If we did not live in such craven times, I would be empowered to show you the error of your ways.'

Ironblood took a step forward, reaching for the short sword at his belt.

'Oh, really?' he said. 'And how would you do that?'

'Gentlemen!' said Grotius, in a weary-sounding voice. 'As entertaining as your little disagreements are, this is hardly the place for them. You should continue your theological discussions some other time. Preferably after your task is accomplished and your orders have been carried out.'

Magnus looked between Grotius and Kossof, unsure which of them he found the most objectionable. In their own very different ways, they embodied everything he hated about the Empire.

'I'll leave you to it,' he growled, turning on his heel without giving Kossof a second look.

Behind him, he could hear the two men start to confer. He ignored them. Grotius was not coming on the campaign, so if they had some petty conspiracy between them, it mattered not.

As Magnus walked somewhat aimlessly in the direction of the artillery train, he saw a familiar shape come up the hill to meet him. At once, his mood lifted, and Kossof was forgotten.

'Tobias!' he cried, and ran over to the huge man. 'It was good of you to come. Anna-Liese has given you the afternoon off, then?'

Magnus found himself grinning as he spoke, but he meant no disrespect. Hildebrandt's well-ordered family life was what made the big man so admirable.

'Something like that,' said Hildebrandt, looking sheepish. 'Magnus, I'm coming with you. I've thought it over, and we could do with the money. Anna-Liese has come round. She doesn't like it, but a man has to be master in his house.'

For a moment, Magnus stood stunned. He had resigned himself to a long, dreary journey with the inscrutable Thorgad and the untried duo of Messina and Herschel. Hildebrandt coming with him was a completely unexpected boon.

He clasped his old friend's hand, speechless for a moment.

'That's... *good*,' was all he could muster. 'Really, that's good. I thought you'd decided against it.'

Hildebrandt looked pleased, but there was something else behind his expression. Worry, perhaps. Or maybe regret.

'I couldn't let you go on your own,' said the big man, not entirely convincingly. 'You'd blow yourself up. Or someone else. And it's been too long since I did some real work. Got my hands dirty. You know what I mean.'

Magnus looked at him closely. There was something the man wasn't telling him. But he was in no mood to inquire too deeply. The fact that he had an ally, someone he could rely on to get things done properly, was more than enough. He smiled again, uncaring of the rainwater running down his lank hair.

'There'll be five of us,' he said. 'Two men I've hired, and a dwarf who's coming for his own reasons.'

'A dwarf?' said Hildebrandt, eyebrows raised. 'I thought you hated dwarfs.'

Magnus shrugged.

'I'm not paying him,' he said. 'And there's been little enough time to arrange anything else. Come, I'll take you to meet the others. We'll have to divide up the workload differently now, but another pair of hands will help.'

Hildebrandt looked across the plain, his expert eyes picking out the heavy guns and already making an assessment of their best deployment.

'Let's go then,' he said. 'I don't like the way those volley guns have been stowed, for a start.'

The two men walked down the hill briskly, over to the staging area for the gunnery crews. As they went, they were soon lost in a technical discussion of firing rates and powder delivery.

All around them, men marched with growing purpose, their faces set grimly against the drizzle. Horsemen rode between the milling companies, delivering messages and carrying orders. Everyone could sense that matters were nearly set in place. Whispers had gone round that Scharnhorst was on his way. The signal to break camp, a series of braying notes from the horns, would soon sound. The preparation had been done, the gold had changed hands, the men had been found.

The wait was over. Hochland was going to war.

Once the orders to move out had been given, the army roused itself like a massive, sluggish animal. The knights had ridden out first, along with the commander's retinue. Scharnhorst rode at the head of the line on a giant black stallion. It was a fine-looking beast, stamping and shaking its head as it walked, and it wouldn't have looked out of place in the stables of the Knights Panther. His retinue was composed of the usual senior officials, clad in the finest armour and draped in the red and green of Hochland. Despite their impressive appearance, most were there to oversee the distribution of food, the maintenance of discipline in the ranks, and the protection of the army's chests of coins and other things worth stealing. Scharnhorst's most useful captains marched with their men.

All in all, Magnus thought Scharnhorst's commanders looked pretty competent. They shared their commander's savage demeanour, and spoke little as they rode. That was good. Having been commanded in the past by effete sons of the urban nobility, Magnus could appreciate when the conduct of the campaign was in the hands of proper soldiers.

After the captains came the small company of knights, followed by rows and rows of marching infantry. The state troopers went reasonably quickly, cheered by the prospect of getting under way at last. Though few of them relished battle, standing around in the rain waiting for their orders had blighted their spirits. It was better to be moving, whatever that entailed in the future.

Despite their size, the formations moved from the staging area and on to the main road north with little fuss. Magnus watched the outriders move up and down the columns of men, barking orders and dragging the serried ranks into a close approximation of good order. Things had started well enough. The army looked like it could fight. He'd been in many that had never looked like that.

Finally, behind the last of the swaggering lines of mercenaries, the artillery train was given leave to pull off. Magnus shouted out a series of orders to the drivers of the carts. Ropes shivering, the horses leaned into the task. Gradually, with much swearing and beating, the heavy wagons broke into movement. Gouts of mud were thrown up from hooves and wheels, but the big guns were under way. Magnus walked over to his horse, a lumpen, dull-eyed creature with a shaggy mane and matted coat, and mounted expertly. He cast his eyes across the slowly moving column of wagons, and felt a glow of satisfaction. He had the tools with which to work.

A sudden craving for a drink came over him. Magnus swallowed, feeling the rise of the nausea within him that always accompanied periods of sobriety. Not now. Things were just getting going. He had to stay clean.

He kicked his steed into a steady walk, and rode over to where the rest of his company were mounted, waiting expectantly for him.

'So here we are,' Magnus said, putting a brave face on his craving. 'Back in the saddle. Anything to report?'

'Food's lousy,' said Silvio. 'Hochland troops smell worse than greenskins, and those guns won't fire without much of my work.'

Lukas grinned.

'At least we'll be kept busy,' he said, brightly.

Thorgad looked up at Silvio. Unlike the others, he went on foot. He'd been offered a mountain pony, but that had met with nothing but scorn. So the dwarf laboured in the mud, his cloak already stained with the filth of the road. Magnus knew from experience that dwarfs could march a long way before they became weary. But still, Morgramgar was many miles distant. A strange race.

'If you keep complaining,' Thorgad said to Silvio darkly, 'I might come up there and give you something to complain about.'

Hildebrandt looked at the wagon train with concern, ignoring the bickering between the Tilean and the dwarf.

'Messina's right, sir,' he said to Ironblood. 'I've not been here long, but we've pieces here that'll shatter when we put the fire to them. This won't be easy.'

Magnus sighed, and let a tolerant smile spread across his face. The guns he had were faulty, the rain was incessant, he felt terrible, and his men were already arguing amongst themselves. In Scharnhorst and Kossof he was surrounded by officers who would rather he wasn't there at all. All things considered, that wasn't bad. At least no one had tried to kill him yet.

'All right, lads,' he said, raising a hand to silence the squabbling from Messina and Thorgad. 'We'll take another look at the cannons when we reach camp. For now, I don't want to lose our place in the column. There's plenty here who'll rejoice to see us fall behind, so I don't want them to have the satisfaction. Keep an eye on the ironwork. Don't let any of those damned zealots near the blackpowder. Otherwise, relax and enjoy the journey. We'll be busy soon enough.'

He kicked his horse again, and shoved his way to the front of the artillery column. Hildebrandt followed him, while the others spread out along the lines, watching the swaying wagons carefully.

Magnus felt the pleasure of command dilute his lingering nausea. No one had called him 'sir' for a long time. Not since…

But it was better not to think about that. He drew in a long draught of cold, rain-laced air, and looked up at the distant northern horizon. Even so soon into the campaign, his heart had begin to beat a little faster, and some of the sickly pallor had left his cheeks. They were under way, and battle would not be long in coming.

The ascent from the plains around Hergig to the highlands was tortuous. As a province, Hochland was covered in mile upon mile of dark, twisted forest. Some called it the Eastern Drakwald, an offshoot of the mighty woods that cloaked Middenheim in fear and mystery. Others called it the southern edge of the Forest of Shadows, the Hochland Deeps, or simply the Dark Country. Even more so than the rest of the sparsely populated Empire, the depths of the Hochland forest were unexplored and untouched by the hand of man. Mighty ravines scored their way across the tumbled landscape, draped in grasping ranks of sleek-barked trees and tangled undergrowth. At the base of those ever-shadowed gorges, barely lit by the shrouded rays of the sun, all manner of primordial beasts dwelt in a perpetual twilight realm. Only the foolish or the mad sought them out. Every child in Hochland knew the dangers of the deep forest.

The beastmen were the most feared and hated. Some said they were the changeling children of impious parents, left to fend for themselves amongst the crushing briars. Others said they were the true soul of the forest, remnants of a time before Sigmar when men lived in scattered bands and feared every fleeting shadow. Yet more said that they were a portent of the future, a grim warning of the End Times when the final hosts of Chaos would rise up again and mankind would fall before the limitless legions of the damned.

Whatever the truth, it seemed that the numbers of beastmen rose every winter. At night, their bellows and whinnies could be heard in outlying villages and towns, causing grown men to pull their bedclothes over their ears and women to weep into their nightdresses. And all sensible folk knew that there were worse monsters lurking in the forgotten places. Tales were told of the creeping dead, limping through the marsh gas when the fog rolled down from the high peaks. Whispers ran through Hergig of skeletal witches, summoning all manner of foul sorcery over their bubbling cauldrons of maidens' blood. There were legends of fey elven spirits flitting between the boughs, spiteful tree-sprites conversing in forgotten tongues under the sickle moon, and scuttling giant spiders ridden by their cackling goblin masters in the endless, cloying gloom.

In the past, when the Empire had been stronger, perhaps not all those stories had been believed. Now, as the enemies of man multiplied once more and the undergrowth was alive with scurrying horrors, there were few who did not place credence on the old tales. The most outlandish myth of all, that the very cities themselves were riddled with the warrens of warp-spawned rat-men, sounded less crazy than it once had. They were truly dark times when such madness was believed even by learned men.

Every so often, the terror would be banished for a time. A crusade would be launched, and pious men of the Empire would sweep into the dark places with cleansing flame. Priests of Sigmar would banish the horrors, and the blood of the beastmen would stain the earth. The famed Boris Todbringer was still worshipped by the far-flung folk of the northern Empire. Whenever there was a break in the endless warfare on his northern borders, he would muster companies of his grim-faced Knights of the White Wolf, and the creatures of darkness would cower in their forsaken hollows. And yet, once the slaughter was over and the proud warriors of Ulric had returned to their homesteads, the shadows would lengthen once more. No living man had penetrated the heart of the forest, and none would ever do so. The Empire could limit the spread of the ancient woods, but it could never hem them in entirely.

Magnus reflected on that as the army wound its way north from Hergig and began to climb up into the highlands. They went by the ancient forest roads, the highways of the Empire in the north. The trees had been felled far from the trail, and the surviving trunks lurked sullenly in the distance on either side. All knew that such ways had not been made by men. Older hands had carved them from the living forest, and strange spells had been placed on them in time immemorial to ward off the throttling branches. Men were only the latest to make use of them, ignorant of their origins.

As the ranks of men passed through the trees they sang bawdy songs of waylaid virgins and genial foresters, swinging their packs with abandon. The humour was forced, however. All stayed wary. The army was large, but not powerful enough to scare off all denizens of the woods. They all knew the beastmen were there, watching, waiting.

As they passed through a particularly deep gorge, its sides rising high and jagged into the pale air, Lukas came alongside Magnus. His face was still cheerful, though the edge had been taken off it by the bleak country around them.

'This place is like nothing I've seen before,' he said, looking at the dark eaves of the trees doubtfully.

'No place for men,' agreed Magnus, avoiding peering too closely at the shadows. 'You're from Averland, yes?'

'Right,' he said, unable to keep his eyes off the forest. 'We keep the land tilled there. I never thought I'd wish to see another farmstead again in my life. But after this...'

'Don't look too closely, lad,' said Magnus. 'We'll be out of it in time. The mountains have their own dangers, but at least the air is pure and the stone is clean. This is cursed country.'

The army went quickly, perhaps part-driven by some vague sense of fear, but mostly by Scharnhorst's iron will. They set up camp infrequently, and only when the trees pulled back and the air was free of the rustle of hostile branches. Even then, at night there were howls from the tree edge. Some of the scouts, foraging far ahead to pick out the best route north, never came back. None asked after them. The men pressed on, hands on pommels, eyes flickering back and forth watchfully.

Despite the clipped pace, it took them several days of marching for them to clear the bulk of the forest. Whenever they camped for the night, they piled the fires high. Tired limbs made for heavy sleep, but only the bravest slumbered completely through the strange calls and shrieks from the darkness. Just once did they come into the open, bellowing and whinnying. The first engagement of the campaign was short and vicious. The beastmen were routed quickly, driven back by a hail of arrows and shot. After that there were no more raids. But the songs ceased. The soldiers kept their eyes on the northern horizon, desperate to leave the oppressive, endless ranks of trees.

When the breakthrough came, it was surprisingly sudden. The columns of men had been toiling for hours up a sharp defile, choked with roots, boulders and brambles. The horses were skittish, and the wheels of the carts fouled and needed to be freed often. For the first time since leaving Hergig, the pristine ranks of marching men broke into confusion, and the shouted orders from the sergeants and captains were abrasive and replete with curses. But then, just as the ascent seemed destined to go on forever, the vanguard broke into easier ground. The rest of the army coiled up after them. Rank by rank, company by company, they left the forest and marched into the open.

At the rear, behind the long trail of infantry, the engineer companies were last to climb the steep ascent. Magnus had remained at the very back, marshalling the route of the heavy guns as they crawled up the treacherous ground. By the time they had reached the final ridge, the flanks of the horses were shiny with sweat, and the axles of the carts groaned under their load.

When the last of them had crested the rise, Magnus looked up and surveyed the scene. The land yawned away in gentle curves of steadily rising wilderness. The peaks of the hills were bare of trees and covered in a dense carpet of gorse and heather. A mournful wind scraped across the open country, rustling the grass and sedge. After the close air of the forest, the highland seemed both severe and fresh. The army spread across it, grateful for sight of the horizon once more.

And then, far in the distance, Magnus saw their destination for the first time. On the northern edge of his vision, the mountains rose, grey and purple against the haze. They looked impossibly far. The margravine had chosen her bolthole well. Climbing through the passes to Morgramgar would be a trial for the best of commanders. Magnus could see that others in the army thought the same thing, and low murmurs of discontent rippled through the infantry companies.

But Scharnhorst was in no mood to indulge petty gossip. Within moments of the last carts breaking into the highlands, the horns were sounded. Whips cracked, and the steady beat of hide drums started once more. Like a sullen beast of burden, the army started to march again. There would be no rest until the walls of the citadel stood before them. And then the real work would begin.

CHAPTER FIVE

'After the slaughter at Skaalgrad, General Horstmann was taken before the Grand Council of Enquiry in Talabheim. He was unrepentant, despite losing the field and over half of his men to the foul Norscans. When asked what had precipitated his downfall, his answer was simple. Division in the ranks. He seemed to think that no further explanation was required.'

Record of the trial and execution of Alberich Horstmann
Talabecland State Archives

For a few days, the rain had held off, and the worst of the stink over the soldiery ebbed. Clothes dried out, and rust was cleaned from the blades of weapons. Morale was high. But then the clouds closed once more, and the weather turned. Rain fell in steady streams without break or let. It got everywhere, into the kegs of dried food, into the crates packed with straw and iron shot, even through layers of wood and waxed cloth into the powder stores. It was relentless, an endless torrent of grey, cold misery, hammering on the downcast heads of the army as it toiled across the highlands. The ground became boggy and treacherous, and the horses stumbled as they went. In every direction, the sky was low and dour, mirroring the spirits of the men.

Hildebrandt wiped his brow clear again, watching as the water slewed from his shoulders onto the ground below. He was relatively lucky, with a stiff leather jerkin and heavy hood. The ordinary infantrymen trod sullenly in their inferior gear, moving onwards only to keep the chill from their breasts, soaked to their hides.

The big man looked back over the row of lurching carts. The going was tough in the mire. Axles creaked, and lashings came loose. Trying to keep such temperamental machinery on the road was worse than keeping a woman happy. At least women gave you some reward for your pains. The guns were fickle mistresses indeed.

Not for the first time, he wondered whether he'd done the right thing in taking up Ironblood's commission. Hildebrandt was old enough to escape the Imperial draft, and could have been expected to live the remainder of his days out in relative peace. It was not so much that he was too old to serve, but more that he'd done his time. There were only so many dead bodies a man could see before his mind began to turn. He'd witnessed old soldiers in the gutters of Nuln and Hergig, wedded to the bottle, dousing their self-pity in strong ale before the cutpurses finished them off. That was no way for a man to go. Not when he had a brace of children waiting for him by the hearth and an honest woman to warm his bed.

Despite all of that, the decision had not been hard to make. He owed it to Ironblood. The man had saved his life in the past, and they had fought like brothers when they were young. Hildebrandt had watched the man's descent into squalor with alarm. Now that Magnus seemed to have rediscovered a spark of self-command again, Tobias had a duty to see him through the campaign. One more failure would finish Ironblood. That could not be allowed to happen. Once this campaign was over, they could both think again. For the moment, cracking Morgramgar open was the only thing they could look forward to, the sole object of their attention. The alternative was to repeat the past. Hildebrandt knew some of what had happened back then, but not all. What he did know was enough to make him want to ensure that it never took place again.

He raised his eyes from the slow-hauling carts and squinted up the trail ahead. The land was rising rapidly. They were passing into a narrow gorge at the foot of the peaks. On his left, the earth was gradually falling away as the trail rose. On his right, the cliffs were soaring into sheer walls of striated stone, as sharp as teeth at the summit and flecked with sparse vegetation. The road wound between the extremes. Soon it would be little more than a ledge between the mountain's shoulder and the chasm to the left.

Hildebrandt pushed his horse into a canter, and joined Magnus further up the column. He looked grey and tired. An empty gourd flapped at his side. Hildebrandt could smell ale on his breath.

'This is dangerous,' he said, grimly. 'Wide enough for the guns?'

Magnus nodded. He seemed alert enough.

'I was thinking the same,' he said. 'We'll have to go in single file.

Carefully. Is everything lashed securely?'

Hildebrandt looked back at the ramshackle caravan.

'Aye,' he said. 'But the rain plays havoc with the bearings. Some of these carts would come apart at a sneeze.'

'Get Messina, Herschel and the dwarf to spread out down the train,' said Magnus. 'First sign of trouble, shout. I don't want to see Gruber's precious machines at the bottom of the gorge, and neither will Scharnhorst.'

Hildebrandt pulled his horse round, and trotted back down the line of heavy-laden carts. The drivers looked nervous, and kept tight under the shadow of the cliff on their right hand. The horses knew the danger, and their eyes rolled as they strained. The creatures were tired, and their spirits looked fragile. After several days in the wilds, Hildebrandt knew how they felt.

The column crawled on, climbing ever more steadily into the heart of the mountains. The rain fell remorselessly, scything through the gusting wind as if it wasn't there. Streams formed along the rock-strewn passage, gurgling and bubbling down the trail, making footing treacherous. Men swore under their breaths as they hauled their gear. No songs were sung, and the only speech was the hoarse yelling of the captains, urging one more push before they laid camp for the night.

Hildebrandt rode ceaselessly up and down the train, watching the progress of the wagons intently. Messina and the boy did the same. As the path narrowed and the drop to their left became more sheer, the tension mounted. It would only take one wheel to go.

After another hour of solid, nervous progress, at last the landscape seemed to relent. Ahead of them the path widened as the gorge closed, and they reached the head of the pass. Hildebrandt felt his fingers loose their clamped grip on his reins, and he let a low sigh of relief escape his lips.

An axle snapped. It sounded like a tree falling. With a heave and snap of splitting wood, the wagon in front of him lurched drunkenly to its left. The horses reared in their tethers, and the wheels ground down into the soft earth. Shouts of panic came from up ahead. The wagon veered near the cliff edge, only pulled back by frantic hauling on the reins from the driver.

'Cut the harness!' came a desperate cry.

The horses had got trapped, and were going mad. One of them reared again, fighting to get loose of the cart. The waterlogged earth seemed to dissolve under it. It was carrying one of the siege guns. Tobias heard the snap of leather stays going, and the cart slid further towards the abyss.

'Cut the damn harness!' came the cry again.

The horses were scrabbling in the mud, unwittingly pulling the cart nearer to disaster. Tobias saw men leap from the wagon. The driver was still fighting to keep it on the path. He was going down.

Hildebrandt knew what he had to do. His heart beating powerfully, he leapt from his horse and ran up to the stricken cart. The ground beneath his feet was liquid. It felt like the entire hillside was sliding. If the cannon took the whole ledge down with it, there would be no hope of getting the other wagons past the breach.

Tobias sped past the reeling wagon and under the flailing hooves of the terrified horses. He was a big man, but under their flanks he felt little more than a child. He pulled his sword from his belt and slashed at the leather harness. Two swipes, and the straps sprung free, whipping at his face as they did so. One of the horses bolted up the path, neighing frantically, rearing afresh as its path was blocked by the men ahead.

Everything seemed to be in motion. The earth was slick and wet, the cart was churning its way closer to the edge, the second horse was prancing jerkily in its harness. Tobias felt his nerve nearly go. In an instant, he saw a vision of himself being dragged over the edge. The cannon was huge. Getting caught up in the cart's demise would be fatal.

Hildebrandt cursed, and plunged towards the tethered horse.

'Jump, man!' he yelled at the driver. The man was still trying desperately to right the wagon. 'Get away!'

Tobias had a vague impression of a white-faced, terrified figure pulling at the reins, and then it was lost in a whirl of movement. He felt the rock give way under his feet. With a lunge, he managed to cut the final cords of the harness, and the foam-flecked horse bolted. Its legs buckled on the edge of the precipice, and it went over. The animal screamed, an unearthly sound, before being dashed against the rocks below.

The horses had been cut free, but it was too late to save the wagon. The momentum of the cart was carrying it past the edge. Even as he tried to scramble out of the way, Tobias could see the heavy iron muzzle of the cannon leaning over the brink. The driver of the cart, still trapped on the swaying wreck of twisted wood, was shrieking like a woman. He was lost. There was no way back.

'Leap!' cried Hildebrandt one more time, though he knew it was hopeless. He was in danger himself. His boot caught in a rope trailing from the broken cart. He felt the sudden tug on his thighs. For a second, pure panic gripped him. He could feel himself being pulled over. Frantically, Tobias hacked at the rope. He was dragged along, hauled from his feet. His free arm hit the ground heavily. His fingers scraped across the loose earth, tearing through the mud.

His sword bit home. The rope snapped, and with a sigh the entire cart seemed to collapse in on itself. The lip of the path crumbled, and the broken structure swung over the edge, trailing rope and twisted planks of wood. The driver, still caught in the mechanism, let out a strangled scream as he was borne over into the gorge. His voice trailed horribly for a moment, echoing up from the chasm, until it was obscured by the crash of iron against rock. Then nothing.

The danger wasn't over. Hildebrandt was still on the edge, and the earth continued to slide. He was on his stomach, trying to pull himself free of the landslip. It wasn't enough. He was falling. It was like trying to swim up a waterfall. For a moment, he saw Elena's face, staring at him with reproach. Then the last rock disappeared from beneath his boots. He was over the void.

A hand grasped his wrist. The grip was firm and unyielding.

'Help me, damn you!' came a gruff voice, full of fear. 'He's heavy as a bear!'

More hands pulled at him, dragging him from the brink. Tobias looked up, his heart still pumping. He was surrounded by men. Ironblood was there, as was Thorgad. Shakily, he pulled himself to his knees. The ledge had held.

'Mother of Sigmar,' said Magnus, looking pale. 'I thought we'd lost you.'

Hildebrandt took a look over his shoulder. The cart had caused ruin on its descent, and a jagged gouge had been cut into the edge of the path. Stones still clattered down the slope. All along the surviving portions of the ledge, men stood, mouths agape, looking with horror at the broken cannon in the chasm below.

Tobias felt his arms begin to shake uncontrollably. With shivering hands, he made the sign of the comet across his breast.

'Thank you,' was all he could say to Ironblood, his voice thin and weak. 'By all that's holy, thank you.'

Scharnhorst looked coldly at the engineers. They presented a sorry aspect. Ironblood's appearance had improved slightly since Hergig, but the man still looked slovenly and grime-covered. His company were little better. The big one, Hildebrandt, seemed to have lost his nerve entirely, and stood silently to one side. The others, a Tilean and a young lad from Averland, were withdrawn and mute. Worst of all, there was the dwarf. It was embarrassing to have one of them witness this shambles. Though many commanders considered it an honour to have dwarfs marching alongside them, Scharnhorst was a Hochlander. He had little dealing with the dwarfs in the province, and he distrusted anything unusual.

Scharnhorst sighed.

'So you got the rest of the guns up the hillside?' he said.

'Yes, sir,' said Ironblood, looking almost belligerent. His eyes were rimmed with red. 'Despite the landslide, we drew the remaining pieces through. It was hard work. We had to shore up the left hand of the ledge. That's why it took so long.'

The men were all in Scharnhorst's canvas tent. The day was waning, and candles flickered in the half-light. All around the camp, fires were being kindled. The troops were exhausted after the climb. Aside from Ironblood and his motley company, Scharnhorst had his senior captains with him, including the leader of the flagellants. They all sat in the shadows, regarding the engineers darkly.

Scharnhorst sighed.

'Herr Ironblood,' he said, wearily. 'You seem to think that losing one cannon is little cause for concern. And yet, if I understand it correctly, the one we let slip was one of our largest pieces. If we lose many more of them, getting to Morgramgar will be a waste of time. What do you expect me to do? Go up to the doors and knock?'

Ironblood remained impassive. The man looked tired. That wasn't surprising. They were all tired.

'It's a matter of regret,' said the engineer, keeping his voice steady. 'But we couldn't account for the ledge giving way. We did all we could. Without Hildebrandt here, it would have been much worse.'

Scharnhorst sniffed. He was unimpressed.

'From what I was told, the spark that set this off was a broken axle,' he said. 'On a baggage cart in your care.'

Ironblood visibly bristled at that.

'I can only work with the material I'm given,' he said, and the insolence in his voice was evident then. 'If I could have chariots of iron to carry our guns up the mountainside, then I would use them. I remind you, sir, that everything we're using comes from your store yards.'

The warrior priest Kossof hissed from the shadows. In the flickering candlelight, his face looked like a mask.

'Perhaps it is a shame that the whole train didn't fall into the abyss,' he said, his voice a sibilant rasp. 'Then there would be nothing to blast apart our brave troops from behind our own lines.'

There was a murmur of assent from some of the other captains. Thorgad took a step forward, his face glowering with scorn. Scharnhorst fixed Kossof with a withering look.

'Enough,' he said. 'Don't be a fool. We need as many gunnery pieces as we can get.'

He turned back to Ironblood.

'When Grotius told me we needed a master engineer to oversee our artillery, I was hardly persuaded,' he said. 'He assured me that one of your sort was necessary. To ensure that there were no mishaps with the great guns. Needless to say, I am hardly reassured by your progress so far.'

Ironblood looked like he wanted to interject, but Scharnhorst talked over him. The little man would have to wait for permission to respond.

'According to the plan, we should be coming to the approaches to Morgramgar soon. We're now far behind, held back by your antics in the passes. It's not good enough, Ironblood. I won't tolerate another delay at your hands. Is that clear?'

Ironblood had by now gone red with rage. Scharnhorst could see the man clenching his fists, trying to suppress the protests that were undoubtedly building within him. The general didn't care to hear excuses. It was results that mattered.

Eventually, Ironblood controlled himself.

'I understand, general,' he said. He looked like the words were being dragged from his mouth. 'I'll speak to the men. We'll look at the carts again. We'll make any repairs necessary tonight.'

Scharnhorst nodded.

'Good. See that you do. Now go. I have matters to discuss with the others.'

Ironblood baulked at that also. No doubt he thought of himself as a senior commander. The man would have to learn his place. He was a technician, nothing more. If he couldn't look after his own little realm, then he could hardly be expected to take his place at the high table of command.

The engineer bowed stiffly, then turned on his heel and left the tent. Awkwardly, the others followed him without a word. The flaps fell back into place, and the candle flames guttered.

Scharnhorst looked around at his advisers. They looked half-drowned. The rain continued to fall, drumming on the tent roof, and their spirits had sunk.

'Anything to say?' he snapped, trying to rouse some response from them.

Johann Kruger, the captain of the Knights of the Iron Sceptre, looked up. His lean, aristocratic face looked less lined with fatigue than some of the others.

'The engineer Ironblood spoke the truth,' he said, calmly. 'The artillery train is in bad shape. Your man Gruber gave them little of quality to work with.'

Scharnhorst sneered.

'You're defending him, Kruger?'

Kruger shrugged.

'We'll need those guns when we reach Morgramgar,' he said. 'Don't make an enemy you don't need.'

Only one of the noble blood would dare speak so freely to a general, Scharnhorst thought. Kruger was bound by allegiance to himself and Sigmar only. Scharnhorst despised the attitude, but needed the man's expertise. One of the wearying aspects of command.

'The same advice goes for you, master knight,' said Scharnhorst, adopting a warning tone. 'I'll heed your advice, but remember who's in command.'

Kruger looked unperturbed by the admonishment, and sank back into contemplation. In his place, Kossof spoke again.

'Is this not a sign, general?' he said, making an effort to knock the rough edges from his normal harsh speech. 'We can bring this heretic to heel without the use of the new science. Why else would Sigmar send the rain? Why else would our prized gun be the first to fall?'

Scharnhorst didn't like the look of smug triumph in the man's eyes. Something about Kossof turned his stomach.

'I won't tell you again, Kossof,' said Scharnhorst. 'The plan of campaign calls for artillery, and as long as we arrive with any pieces intact, we'll use them.'

He leaned forward, and pointed a lean finger at the priest in the half-light.

'And I warn you,' he said, 'don't pursue your superstitious vendetta against Ironblood behind my back. If he rectifies his error and proves himself on the field, I'll bear the man no ill will. You should do the same. There'll be no dissension in the ranks of this army.'

Kossof glared back at Scharnhorst for a moment, clearly taken aback. No doubt the man had thought he was reinforcing the general's own views. The priest would have to learn otherwise. Scharnhorst was a fair man. Hard, perhaps, but fair. The only thing he didn't tolerate was failure. Beyond that, there were no favourites.

'I understand,' said Kossof, bowing slightly. 'Herr Ironblood needn't fear interference from me.'

'I hope not,' said Scharnhorst, putting feeling into the words.

He reached for the charts and ledgers. There was much business to get through before he would let the officers back to their beds. The start of the campaign had been bad enough. If they were going to get to Morgramgar without some serious infighting breaking out, things had better improve soon.

The dawn broke. The rain had stopped falling at last, and a frigid wind tore across the highlands, freezing the sodden troops as they huddled together in the mud. Only the officers and knights had tents to shelter them from the elements. The ordinary soldiers slept in thin blankets, wrapped tightly around them to ward against the worst of the chill. Many of them had stacked their wargear on top of them as they slept, partly to keep it out of the mire, partly to add a little more protection from the knife-sharp wind.

Magnus woke suddenly, his body somehow remembering the routine of battle from all those years ago. His head was sore, buffeted both by the cold and the iron-hard ground. Every muscle ached from shivering, and his joints were as stiff as an elector's starched collar. He opened his eyes and looked around. The fire had long gone out, and there was just a meagre patch of damp, charred earth where it had been. The other engineers lay huddled around it, still asleep.

Hildebrandt snored loudly. The man had hardly spoken since his encounter with the cliff edge, and had drifted into a deep slumber as soon as he'd hit the ground. Magnus had never seen him so scared. There was a time when both of them would have laughed at a brush with death. Maintaining a front was all-important. It would not do for the men to think you were weak. But Tobias seemed to have forgotten that. He'd been shaken, and badly. Perhaps he now had more to lose. Whatever the truth, he hadn't spoken to Magnus about it, and Magnus hadn't asked.

Messina and Herschel slept also. The two of them had worked hard the previous night, checking the gun-hauling wagons and making minor repairs. Ironblood had been impressed by the Tilean. Despite his raffish appearance and superior bearing, he knew what he was doing. He was strong, too. The boy Herschel had been keen, and worked hard under Messina's direction. Any misgivings Magnus had about bringing him along looked like they'd been misplaced.

Groaning slightly from the effort, Magnus hauled himself from his tangled cloak, and stood up. The wagon nearest him was piled high with crates and tarpaulin-covered chests. Just to be safe, Magnus went up to one of them and pulled the material back. His own collection of ancient chests were still there, all still locked, all still safe. He gazed at the ornate metalwork of the nearest, and let his finger run down the side of it absently. Had he been foolish to bring all the gear along? Probably not. In his absence, Herr Ettieg would no doubt have tried to break into the stash. Safest to keep it by his side, however expensive and difficult it was.

'There's something special in there, no?' came a familiar voice from a few yards away.

Thorgad was sat on a pile of sacking, puffing on a long clay pipe. He was looking at Ironblood steadily.

'None of your damn business,' said Magnus, irritably. He pulled the tarpaulin back hurriedly, and walked away from the cart. 'How long have you been up?'

'A few hours,' said the dwarf. 'I'm amazed at the sleep you umgi need. I can remember campaigns under the earth where we went without sleep for days at a time. None of us suffered from it.'

Magnus ignored the boast, and came over to sit by the dwarf. His bones felt like their marrow had been replaced with rods of ice.

'Got any food?'

Thorgad handed him some strips of dried meat. The donating animal was unidentifiable, and they were almost black with age. Magnus took one, and ripped a corner with his teeth. It was like biting into cured leather, and he felt his jaw ache with the effort.

'Traggot,' said Thorgad. 'Broiled wolf hide. Dried over peat. Not many umgi get to try it.'

Magnus grimaced.

'They're missing out,' he said, still chewing.

'We're nearly there,' said Thorgad, letting gouts of smoke drift up into the grey air. 'Whatever your general says, we haven't lost much time. The loss of one cannon will mean little when we get to Morgramgar.'

Ironblood gave the dwarf a sidelong look. Was Thorgad trying to make him feel better? That was out of character, and something to worry about. When a dwarf turned his hand to sympathy, then things were truly bad.

'Let's hope so,' said Magnus, attacking the chunk of meat. It remained solid and unmoving in his mouth.

'Tell me,' said Thorgad. 'Your name is a famous one among your people. I've asked around. Ironblood brings respect. And yet, when I met you, you looked like you were ready for the dung heap. What went wrong?'

Ironblood looked at him sourly, swallowing the meat at last with some difficulty. It had been hours since he'd allowed himself even a sniff of ale, and his mood had soured.

'Are you always this direct?' he said.

Thorgad smiled bleakly.

'Aye, manling,' he said. 'No point in beating about the grobi nest.'

Ironblood felt the lump of wolf gristle slide down his gullet slowly. He'd be digesting it for the rest of the morning. Dwarf stomachs were strange and terrible things.

'I'll say it again, then,' said Ironblood. 'Mind your own damn business.'

He pulled his cloak tight around him, feeling the blood beginning to pump back into his feet and fingers.

'We'll be on our way soon,' Magnus said, changing the subject to something more immediate. 'And I'm glad it's not far. This whole campaign can't end soon enough for me.'

Thorgad spat on the ground, and looked disdainful.

'You really don't understand, do you?' he said, his voice growling with displeasure. 'You and that idiot general think you'll arrive at the citadel, lob a few pounds of iron at the walls and then come merrily home again when they fall down. Believe me, it's not going to be that way.'

Ironblood felt sure he didn't want to hear what was coming next, but kept listening. The dwarf seemed to know what he was talking about. You could never tell when one was just boasting for the sake of it, but Thorgad had an air of casual knowledge that held his attention.

'You've forgotten a whole army's been lost up here already,' said the dwarf. 'That doesn't happen by accident. Even an umgi general couldn't massacre the men under his command single-handedly.'

The dwarf's eyes shone. He seemed to be taking a kind of sadistic pleasure in recounting the tale of human weakness.

'This country will get very hard. Very hard, very soon,' he said. 'We'll be passing through the perfect terrain for an ambush. Do you think this von Kleister will let you walk up to her gates without a fight? No. She's not stupid, that woman. I'll wager she's got more sense than your man Scharnhorst, at any rate. Expect an attack, and soon. Her troops know the country. They'll strike by night, or when we're breaking camp. When we're weak.'

Ironblood looked sceptical.

'There are four thousand men in this command,' he said. 'It'd be brave to attack us in the open. We have archers and handgunners to guard the flanks. Some of them know this country too.'

Thorgad shrugged.

'So you say,' he said. 'We'll see what happens.'

Then he leaned over to Ironblood, and fixed him with a level stare.

'But just remember,' he said, and his voice was low. 'I'll say it again, so the importance of it isn't lost on you. There was a whole army sent up here ahead of you. None of them came back. None of them. Does that sound like something to take lightly? You should be more afraid, master engineer, and not just for the axles on your precious carts.'

Thorgad sat back, looking grimly satisfied. Magnus wanted to say something to puncture the dwarf's insufferable pride, but nothing came to mind. If he was honest, Thorgad's words had unsettled him. The mountains were a cold, unforgiving place. He looked up at the peaks around them, pale in the morning air. Mist rolled lazily down their flanks, wreathing the valleys in shadow. They were silent, cold, inscrutable.

Then, just as he began to feel the full effect of the dwarf's portentous warning, the horns sounded to rouse the sleeping army. All around them, men groaned, and rolled over in their cloaks. In an instant, the sergeants were on their feet, wiping their eyes and barking out orders. Irritably, blearily, the camp began to rise. Magnus's thoughts were broken, and the harsh reality of the present rushed in to take their place.

He took a deep breath, and looked down at Thorgad.

'So be it,' he said. 'One more march, and we'll be right under Anna-Louisa's petticoats. And then we'll really see what's been going on up here.'

With that, Magnus got up and stomped off to wake the others. As he left, Thorgad stayed seated, gently smoking his pipe. His expression was hard to read, but his eyes glittered like flints.

CHAPTER SIX

'The engineer can create machines to counter all foes. From the precision fire of the master-crafted pistol, to the massed volleys of the handgunners, there is little that can stand against the effective deployment of blackpowder weapons. But there is one thing he cannot counter, no matter how skilled he is with iron, steam and steel. That is fear, the devourer of men. Let terror enter the hearts of your troops, and all the guns in the Old World will not be enough to ensure victory.'

Master Engineer Lukas Grendel
Address given at the College
of Engineers, Nuln

As the army climbed ever higher, the weather became steadily colder. While the lowlands around Hergig were enjoying the first few days of spring, the mountains remained as hard and cold as marble. The snowline was still far above them, but the biting wind made the air frigid. Men, shivering in their damp clothes, bent their heads low and gritted their teeth as they marched. Several had fallen sick in the grinding conditions. There was little to be done for them. Those that could still walk were given such crude potions as existed and propped up by their fellow soldiers. A few poor souls, lost in fevers or defeated by the high airs, had been left behind. They would either have to find their way back to Hergig somehow or die out in the wilds.

For those that had made it up into the Middle Mountains, the white summits now rose around them on all sides. The army had reached the heart of the high country, and the road rose and fell constantly, winding and diving around great outcrops of grey-banded rock. The few trees that grew in such places were dark pines, grasping on to the edges of the mighty cliffs with gnarled roots. Thin grey grasses rustled endlessly in the wind, a constant susurration that set even the most experienced soldiers' nerves on edge.

As he rode, Magnus found himself drawn to the high peaks, now ringing the horizon. The mountains gazed down at the massed columns of men as they toiled up towards their goal. They looked pitiless and bleak, crested with glittering crowns of rock-broken ice. There was an air of menace emanating from them. Every so often, as the wind moaned and eddied against the raw, jagged rocks, Magnus thought he caught the echo of fell voices, whispering malicious words just beyond mortal hearing.

There were tales about the mountains, just as there were tales about the forest. Strange things gnawed their way under the rock, it was told. All knew that high up in the snow-covered heights, far beyond the reach of mortal men, ancient creatures lived. Armoured dragons, crouching over their hoards of ice-crusted gold. Fur-covered monsters in the shapes of men, howling their loneliness to the glittering stars. Magnus had never really believed such stories. But now, looking up at the sheer flanks of the great mountains, he felt his nerve begin to fail him. He had been dry for almost two days, and it played havoc with his nerves. There were surely secrets hidden in those terrible heights, secrets that mortal men were never destined to discover. This was not their place, no more than the deep forest was.

Suddenly, his thoughts were interrupted by shouts from the men in front of him. Something was going on further up ahead. Magnus rose in his stirrups, trying to make out what was happening. Bugles had been sounded, and captains of the handgunners were riding up towards the vanguard of the army.

Magnus turned in his saddle, and called over to the others.

'Hildebrandt, Thorgad, you come with me,' he said. 'Messina and Herschel, stay with the guns. We'll be back soon.'

He kicked the flanks of his horse, and broke into a canter. Hildebrandt was soon at his side, lumbering along on his giant carthorse. Thorgad broke into a run, cursing as he tried to keep up with the horses. A low stream of obscene Khazalid pursued them as they rode up through the ranks.

Magnus was soon joined by other company captains, summoned by the call of the horns, each with the same look of consternation on their faces. The signal for battle had not been given, so the massed ranks of footsoldiers stood down, grateful for the rest. For some reason, Scharnhorst wanted his commanders to come together at the head of the army. That was unusual, and whatever was unusual was a cause for concern.

Passing four thousand men took some time, even on a fast horse. Eventually, Magnus and the others reached the vanguard. Thorgad arrived some time later, his cheeks blood-red. No one dared so much as smile at him.

The army had halted at the entrance of a sheer-edged valley running roughly north-west. Its flanks rose like the inside of a clay bowl, smooth and free of vegetation. The road at its base ran swiftly into shadow, for the sun failed to penetrate far down into the deep gorge. It was hard to make out much beyond the first few hundred yards, but it seemed from the curve of the rock as if the valley continued for at least a couple of miles.

Magnus looked at it with distrust. A natural place for an ambush. The enveloping cliffs could hide a whole regiment of archers. Once within the welcoming embrace of the slopes there would be little an army could do to defend itself. Within the bowl-shaped depression, the wind moaned and echoed mockingly, as if daring them to enter.

'What is this?' asked Magnus, bringing his horse alongside Kruger, the captain of the Iron Sceptre knights.

'The scouts have returned,' said the knight, peering into the valley beyond with a grim look. 'The enemy is nowhere to be seen. But there's… something else.'

Magnus didn't like the expression on the man's face. He was about to quiz him further when Scharnhorst came riding up with his retinue. He looked even more sour than usual. The cold air and dry wind suited his personality perfectly.

'Kruger, Kossof, Ironblood, Meckled-Raus, Harrowgrim, Halsbad,' Scharnhorst said perfunctorily. 'Come with me. There's something you should see.'

Without waiting for them to reply, he pulled his horse round and rode up towards the maw of the valley. The named captains broke into a canter and followed him. Many of their retainers did too.

'You should come,' said Ironblood to Hildebrandt and the dwarf. 'I don't like the look of this, but we should all see it.'

They rode swiftly from the head of the pass and into the long shadow. Once out of the light of the sun, the temperature plummeted even further. The sheer sides of the chasm soared into the pale air like battlements, cutting off the sunlight and amplifying the scraping sigh of the wind. Within those terrible walls, everything became bleak and colourless. The few trees clinging to the rock were small and stunted, their bare branches groping up into the air like crone's fingers. Aside from clatter of the horses' hooves, there was almost no sound at all. It felt as if they were riding into the mouth of the underworld.

Magnus looked up at the rock around them warily. He could see no sign of movement up above. It was the scouts' task to make sure that such places would be free of snipers or longbowmen, but you could never be sure. He half-expected a hail of arrows to come spinning down from the bleak heights at any moment.

They kept riding. They had gone nearly a mile when Thorgad noticed the stench.

'Grimnir's beard,' he spat, shaking his head with disgust. 'That's as foul as a slayer's gruntaz.'

Soon afterwards, Magnus realised what he meant. A familiar aroma wafted up from the valley before them. For an old soldier, it was as commonplace as the smell of sour beer and sweat. Death. The reek of death. It was everywhere. His heart began to beat more heavily. There could be only one explanation.

The company rode on, eventually cresting a narrow ridge across the valley floor. Only then did Scharnhorst give the signal to halt. The captains formed a line on the rise, looking ahead with grey faces. None of them spoke. None of them needed to. They had found the army that had gone before them.

Strewn from one side of the valley to the other, corpses lay in twisted formations on the ice-hard ground. Old blood, brown and cracked into flakes, was streaked across the stones. Swords lay where they had been dropped, wedged between rocks or half-buried in loose gravel. One of Hochland's battle-standards still stood, its tattered flag fluttering in the wind. The insignia of Count Ludenhof had been replaced by a crudely daubed death's head. Obscene insults had been scrawled across the rocks around it.

Many of the bodies had been stripped of their armour, their boots and even their clothes. Some were headless. A few had been cruelly hacked apart, their limbs lying like discarded toys amongst the carnage. The icy air had preserved the corpses from decomposing entirely, but the steady onset of putrescence had turned the scene into a stinking, rotting charnel house. Magnus saw Hildebrandt pull a piece of cloth to his mouth, trying not to gag. Thorgad looked on impassively, his snub nose wrinkled against the foul odour.

So this was what had become of them. Killed to a man. No survivors.

'I don't want the men to see this,' said Scharnhorst. His voice was thin and unforgiving. A kernel of anger underpinned it. It was the first time Magnus had heard emotion in his speech. 'We'll find another route to the citadel. But we cannot pass without finding out what happened here.'

Kruger raised an eyebrow coolly.

'We can see what happened,' he said. 'What good will it do us to linger over it?'

Scharnhorst continued gazing over the scene of desolation before them, as if by boring his eyes into the rocks he could bring the silent corpses back to life.

'Look again, master knight,' he said, coldly. 'How many battlefields have you ridden across? When did you ever see one like this? Do not look for what is there before you. Look for what is not.'

Mutely, Magnus turned back to the ranks of broken cadavers along with Kruger and the others. To look on the scene for more than a moment was hard. It seemed somehow disrespectful. Though they were now grey-skinned and hollow-eyed, the victims had once been men like him, full of blood and clothed in flesh. For a moment, Magnus couldn't see what Scharnhorst was going on about. He resented having to peer at the dead for longer than was necessary. Then, gradually, he began to understand.

All of the stricken men were wearing the colours of Hochland. The first army had clearly been more organised than the second. There were no mercenaries among them, and no livery from other states of the Empire. As Magnus's eyes swept across the benighted scene, his suspicion was confirmed. There were no enemy troops there at all. All the corpses were clad in the remains of Ludenhof's colours. It was as if an invisible enemy had come down from the heights and struck them as they marched.

Though some distance away, Magnus could still make out the look of terror and amazement on the dead men's faces. He'd never witnessed a battlefield like it. Even in the most heinous one-sided slaughter, a few troops from both forces ended up lying in the blood-soaked mire. Here, it looked as if the wind itself had borne death on its wings. The steady thump of his heartbeat began to quicken again. This was a silent horror beyond anything he had encountered. He reached for his gourd. It was empty. If the mountains themselves had risen up and destroyed a whole army of men, what hope did they have? They would be dead before a single shot was fired on the walls of Morgramgar. There was some bestial presence in the peaks, something they could never hope to resist. They were dead men, just like the ones lying in the dirt before them.

Magnus could sense that others were thinking the same thing. A shiver of unease passed along the line of commanders. One of them, a lieutenant of Kruger's, started to retch dryly into a rag.

'Do not forget yourselves, men,' said Scharnhorst, sternly. His voice still had an edge of anger in it, and trembled as he spoke. 'These were good folk of Hochland once. They deserved better than this, a cold grave in the mountains with no blessing or hope of burial.'

He looked at his men on either side of him, and a frown of disgust passed across his features.

'For anyone thinking that this is the work of some unnatural spirit or vengeful shade, forget that now. These men have been killed with steel and shot, just like any other troops. The battlefield has been cleared. They've done it to unnerve us. Do not let them have this victory. You are men of the Empire. Find your courage.'

As Scharnhorst spoke, Magnus recovered himself. Of course, that was what had happened. The awful smell, the moaning wind, it was beginning to get to him. He shook his head, trying to shrug off the persistent feeling of doom and hopelessness.

'It's not a pleasant task,' continued the general, looking back over the corpses with distaste, 'but we have to do it. There will be clues. Things we can use. I'll give you an hour. Move amongst the dead. Find out what happened. Then we'll ride on by another path. Whatever happens, we must not repeat their mistakes.'

Magnus exchanged glances with Hildebrandt. The huge man clearly wanted nothing to do with the fields of slowly rotting cadavers. Magnus wasn't too keen on the idea himself. The captains hesitated, regarding the mangled limbs with revulsion.

'Damned weaklings,' muttered Thorgad, and unbuckled his axe from its leather ties. He stomped down the ridge towards the battlefield. That was enough to shame the others into action. With a sigh, Magnus and Hildebrandt did likewise, following the dwarf down into the stinking pit, their faces pale.

'I saw a tapestry like this once,' said Hildebrandt, clasping a scarf to his face as he walked. 'In the Temple of Morr in Wurtbad. A vision of the afterlife.'

'Something to look forward to, then,' said Magnus. Everywhere he looked, the glassy eyes of the dead stared back at him. Those which still had eyes, that was. The crows had been busy at the sockets, and every exposed flap of dead flesh was scored with peck-marks. The smell was overpowering.

'What does he expect us to find?' grumbled Hildebrandt, picking his way through the decaying ranks. 'These bodies are weeks old. The battlefield has been cleared.'

Magnus shrugged, and looked up again at the steep defiles on either side of them.

'They were ambushed,' he said, grimly. 'Volleys of fire from up there would cause havoc. Block the valley at either end, and you have a massacre on your hands.'

'Why don't they try it on us?' he said, following Magnus's gaze into the heavens.

Magnus shook his head, trying to avoid breathing deeply of the noxious air around him. He remembered Thorgad's words. They'll come at night, or when breaking camp. When we're weak.

'Maybe they lost more men than they'd hoped for,' he said, knowing his words sounded hollow. 'But I don't trust our scouts. This place feels wrong. There are eyes on us, or I'm a greenskin.'

Hildebrandt didn't reply, and started kicking away some of the discarded blades that littered the ground. The two men were in the thick of the ruined army, and the piles of bodies lay almost on top of one another.

'There's nothing to see here but death,' he murmured, bitterly. His great face was heavy with grief.

Magnus lifted his eyes from the ranks of bodies and looked at Hildebrandt with concern. The man was in a bad way. The fall had knocked some of the spirit from him. This field of decay was doing the rest. Perhaps it hadn't been right to bring him along. The man's courage was not what it had been.

Magnus was about to tell him to return to the ridge when a hoarse shout came from Thorgad. The two men hurried over. Unlike the others, who had trodden lightly and with distaste through the sickening scene, Thorgad had rummaged vigorously amongst the bodies. Any remaining gear had been rifled through. The enemy had looted most of the objects of value, but such had been the scale of their victory that the defenders' weapons lay where they had fallen. Clearly, the rebels had had no great need for more swords or spears.

'I've found something,' the dwarf said, gruffly.

Thorgad had a sliver of metal in his palm. It was about five inches long, curved like an elongated *S*, and artfully carved. He gave it to Magnus.

'A serpentine,' Ironblood said, turning the object over in his hands. It was the device used to lower the burning match into the pan, employed in long guns to detonate the blackpowder charge.

Thorgad nodded.

'Aye,' he said. 'The only piece of gunnery I've found. Whoever stripped this place has done good work. They might have had a dwarf's eyes. There's nothing left of them. Nothing at all. It's as if they were never here.'

'Apart from this,' said Magnus, thoughtfully. He pulled a monocle lens from his jerkin, and fixed it to his right eye. He drew the sliver closer, and peered intently at it. The mechanism was familiar, and yet unfamiliar. He could clearly see how it fitted with the rest of the gun, but the shape was more angular than was common in Imperial weaponry. It was not from the north of the Empire, that was for sure. Hochland guns had their own unique workings of which their gunsmiths were fiercely proud. It might have come from Nuln, though there were also subtle differences from the products of that city's great schools. The serpentine wouldn't have fitted any of the guns in his handgunner companies. It was too big, and too bizarrely shaped.

Magnus paused, unsure of himself.

'This is new to me,' he said at last, putting the eyeglass away and holding the metal up to the meagre light. 'There was a time when I could have told you where every bearing from every working in the Old World came from. Now I'm no longer so confident. But I'd say this is new. From a new mechanism, too. I've never seen its like.'

Hildebrandt took the serpentine and examined it intently. Thorgad nodded his squat head in agreement.

'You should ask yourself something, Ironblood,' the dwarf said. 'Those peaks on either side of us are high. Very high. Could your gunners hit a target from there? If the ambush was raised from those cliffs, their guns can shoot a long way. I don't think any umgi weapons are that good.'

Magnus squinted as he gauged the distances. The dwarf might have been right. If they had fired from so far, the range of their weapons must have been good. Worryingly good.

'There's something else,' said Thorgad, taking the piece back from Hildebrandt. 'This design has something of the dwarfs about it, or I'll shave my beard off. Your race would never carve something this way. You don't have the tools for it. See the angle here, where the pin is fixed? That's dawi design. I'd stake my hold on it.'

Magnus took another look. He was no expert on dwarfish manufacture, but Thorgad had a point. It had the mark of the stunted folk. The quality, too. He frowned, thinking hard.

'Are there dwarfs in these mountains?' he asked.

'There are dwarfs all over the Empire,' said Thorgad, dismissively. 'But in numbers? Not here. There's nothing of value to us in these hills. In any case, my people wouldn't be getting involved with your fights. Why would they risk their necks for Anna-Louisa when there are grudges to avenge in the east?'

Thorgad stowed the serpentine safely in a pouch at his belt.

'No,' he said. 'If dwarfs are involved, then there are few of them. Perhaps some smiths, working for hire.'

Thorgad didn't look at Magnus as he spoke, and Ironblood thought the dwarf wasn't telling all he knew. He pondered pressing him for more, but decided against it. If Thorgad had his secrets, no amount of cajoling would prise them from him. They would come out in the end, one way or another.

'So we know this,' said Magnus, resignedly. 'They have good guns. Of their own design, by the look of it. I don't like that. You're right about their range. We have nothing to match it. I should tell Scharnhorst.'

'He won't be happy,' said Hildebrandt.

'Have you ever seen him happy?' asked Magnus. 'I'll tell him myself. The scouts must be forewarned.'

Magnus looked out over the scene of desolation. Whatever guns the enemy possessed, they had wreaked terrible destruction. The thought of it sent a tremor down his spine.

'They're not perfect,' he murmured, thinking of the serpentine. 'They didn't erase all the evidence. That's something.'

As he spoke, Magnus found that he didn't believe his own words. The more they discovered about the unseen enemy, the more Magnus found himself full of misgiving. Why hadn't they shown themselves? Were they tormenting them? Letting the army exhaust itself in the ascent before letting their full force loose on them? He felt his stomach begin to rebel. The noxious odour of death was intensifying. There was little more they could do in such a place.

'Come,' Magnus said to Thorgad and Hildebrandt. 'We should go back. This battlefield sickens me. We'll think more on it once we're marching. Messina might know more – it could be a Tilean design.'

Thorgad nodded curtly, and the three of them began to pick their way over to the ridge, stepping around the forests of warped and mangled limbs as they went. Far above them, the cold wind whined. The stone itself seemed grim and hostile. This was a cursed place. The sooner they were out of the valley of the dead, the better.

With the valley route denied them, the army had to take a circuitous path to their eventual destination. They had been barely a day's march from Morgramgar on discovery of the site of the massacre, but Magnus guessed that the detour would take them at least twice that. With no sign of their goal, the men had become fractious and restive. The endless cold, poor diet and lack of decisive action were all playing their part. Fights broke out for the smallest of reasons. The harsh regimen of the sergeants was redoubled, and it became common to see soldiers dragged from their companies to face the lash for insubordination. As with all the campaigns Magnus had ever been on, the longer it lasted without combat, the more the cohesion of the army was put under strain.

If Scharnhorst realised the scale of the unrest, he gave no sign of it. The pace remained punishing. Kruger and his Knights of the Iron Sceptre rode ceaselessly along the flanks of the marching companies, urging greater efforts for the glory of the Emperor. The captain and his men became hated by the common infantrymen, who had little in common with the noble riders on their powerful steeds. At the rear of the entire host, the trail of carts and wagons crawled onwards painfully slowly. No matter how hard the drivers whipped and goaded the straining horses, there was only so much progress the beasts could make. Several of them had collapsed from the strain. When resuscitation proved impossible, their necks were cut, and they were left for the wolves. There were now no spare horses to pull the great guns. If any others failed to make it, the engineers would have to commandeer replacement steeds from the cavalry units. That would be neither easy nor popular.

The day waned to dusk. In the far north, strange shapes could be seen flying low on the jagged horizon. Birds, perhaps. But they were big ones, and their wings were like those of a bat. As the light died, they passed from view.

Scharnhorst's men cleared a series of rubble-choked gullies and emerged onto a wide plain several hundred feet above their starting position. The land was flat, stony and scored with great cracks. Little grew on it but lichen, clinging to the underside of great boulders. With nothing to break its path, the wind tore across the bleak landscape, whipping at the clothes of the soldiers and making the standards snap and ruffle. When the order to cease marching and form camp was given, men fell to their knees with exhaustion, heedless of rank, deployment or the need to organise sentries. As the heavy wains were hauled up the last few hundred yards, campfires were lit on the bare stone, and thin gruel slopped into tin pails. The dark was coming quickly, and the shadows were long.

Magnus and the engineers were, as ever, busy with the rearguard. Corps of handgunners had been called back to assist the safe mooring of the gunnery train. Messina and Herschel rode amongst them, threatening and encouraging as necessary. There was work to be done before night fell, but few of them could think of anything but their bellies and a snatched night's sleep. The gruel was little better than water, but at least it was hot.

As the sun sunk towards the serrated west, Magnus looked at the scene before him wearily, feeling a heavy tiredness eke away at his bones. It had now been days since he'd had a proper drink. Up in the barren wilderness, even the sparse comforts of Frau Ettieg's homestead suddenly took on a strangely wholesome aspect. He found himself salivating at the prospect of a tankard full of frothy, well-drawn beer. Once, it had been such a common pleasure. Now it had become the stuff of dreams. For a moment, just a moment, he forgot about the burden of command, the endless complaints of the wain drivers, the worry over the state of the big guns, and imagined sipping a warm, thick, foamy draught of properly bitter, malt-soaked home-brewed ale. Magnus half-closed his eyes, and let the reins of his horse fall slack. His fingers crept towards the gourd.

The first shot rang out.

'Cover!' came a panicked voice, and immediately the camp burst into action. Men scrabbled for their guns. Fires were doused. Pails of gruel were knocked over. Some men lay on the floor and didn't move. The shots had been well-aimed.

Magnus slid from his horse. He looked around quickly, trying to see where the others were. There was no sign of them. This was bad. The troops were exposed, and the light was almost gone. Picking out the enemy snipers was going to be difficult.

Keeping his body low, Magnus ran over to the nearest company of handgunners. Several of them had been felled. The rest were frantically pulling their long guns from leather holsters and striking flints to light the matchcord.

'Keep calm!' cried Magnus. 'Remember your training. They can't fire again for a moment. Load your guns and wait for my signal.'

As the words left his lips, the dusk was lit with a barrage of light. The sound of blackpowder cracked in the air. On Magnus's left hand, a man crumpled heavily, clutching his eyes and screaming. He rolled away, blood pumping from the wound. Magnus looked down in horror, transfixed.

'That's impossible,' he breathed. 'No one could reload that quickly. How many ranks have they got?'

His mind was racing. This was dangerous. He turned to the handgunners.

'Form a line!' he shouted, seizing the stricken gunner's weapon from where he'd dropped it. 'Wait for my mark!'

The men around him hurriedly finished loading their guns, blowing powder from the sealed pans and replacing the scouring sticks. They crouched down in a long, ragged line facing away from the lines of carts. Elsewhere in the camp, the sound of gunfire echoed. Shouted orders and screams of pain rose up from the length of the column. It sounded disorderly. This was a shambles.

Magnus rammed the shot home, checked the burn of his matchcord and hoisted the gun to his shoulder. He was lucky. It was a genuine Hochland long gun. It would fire true.

'Raise your weapons!' he shouted. On either side of him, muzzles fell into line. It was slow, though. Far too slow.

There was nothing to aim at. Nothing to see. The shots had come from the murk beyond the camp perimeter. They would have to shoot blind. It would be a miracle if they hit a thing.

'Fire!' cried Magnus.

The guns recoiled as the serpentines snapped back and blackpowder burst into flame. With a ragged snap, a volley of shot was sent sailing into the gloom. Smoke from the ignited powder floated across the camp. There were similar jarring cracks from elsewhere in the camp. The defenders were slowly responding. Magnus wondered if any of them could see more than he could.

'Reload!' he yelled, knowing that time was of the essence.

He crouched down low. The matchcord was taken off and pan exposed. He spilled a leather pouch of iron balls into his palm, drew out the scouring stick and rammed one into the barrel expertly, keeping a close eye on the spare powder. This was complicated, dangerous work. If something hit the stores, they would all be immolated. Best not to think about it.

Magnus raised himself to one knee.

'Quicker, damn you!' he growled. The handgunners were taking too long, fumbling as the light failed. This was going to be a massacre. He remembered the grey faces in the valley. They never stood a chance. 'Sigmar flay you, load the damn guns!'

There was a flash of light from far off. Magnus ducked. A fresh volley of shot slammed into the camp. Men were hurled from their feet. Shot ripped through leather and ricocheted off iron. Fresh cries of sudden agony rose up. The lines were wavering. To their left, the defence was broken, and men were fleeing from the danger. Magnus pushed himself back into a crouch. How in the name of Morr were the attackers loading so fast? They'd released three heavy, disciplined volleys so far, and the defenders had barely got one away.

'Raise your guns!' he shouted. 'Aim for where the powder flashes!'

It was almost useless advice. They were firing blind, hoping against hope that their shot would somehow hit the right target. The enemy had no such worries. They knew where to aim, and their target was huge. Every volley would hit something or other. The dark was their ally.

Slowly, clumsily, the handgunners assumed the firing position. There were fewer of them. Some of the gunners' matchcord had extinguished, some had shattered scourers, others lay face down against the rock, blood pooling.

'Fire!' bellowed Magnus.

The guns cracked once again, sending the iron balls screaming into the dusk. It wasn't clear that they'd hit anything at all. The position was hopeless. Where was the cavalry? Why hadn't the scouts secured the area?

'Reload!' croaked Magnus, his voice breaking and going hoarse. With trembling fingers, he reached for more shot. The barrel of his gun was hot, and the stench of blackpowder was close in his nostrils. He kept low, heart beating hard. At the rate the bastards were firing, it couldn't be long before…

The muzzle flashes came again, and more shot whined over his head. With terrible repetition, more men cried out in pain as the shot found its targets. The rate of fire was unbelievable. How many attackers were there? Were they advancing? How far away were they? It was impossible to tell. It was a fiasco. They were being picked off like grouse.

At last, Magnus heard the bugles ring out. Someone had taken charge. The order to advance was given. There was no option but to take the fight to the enemy. Torches had been hurriedly lit, and Magnus heard the thunder of hooves as the knights charged in the direction of the incoming fire. Kruger was there, his voice raised in dreadful anger. It was horribly dangerous in the low light, but it was the right tactic. The only tactic.

'Take up your guns!' cried Magnus, lifting his own to his chest and cradling the all-important cord. 'Follow me!'

At last, the men had some direction, something to get their teeth into. With a roar of aggression and rage, they rose up as one and charged across the broken stone. Magnus was at the forefront, eyes wide, sweat starting from his skin, expecting to hear the blast and whine of gunfire at any moment. He muttered a quick prayer to Sigmar. All there was now was luck, or grace. The light had almost gone entirely, and every black shape against the earth looked like an enemy soldier. His heart banged in his chest, his lungs laboured. Battle had come at last.

They kept running. No shots echoed. The bugles rang out again. Some of the knights had overshot, and were cantering back. The air was filled with the shouts and war cries of the defenders, but no guns fired. It was as if the enemy had never existed.

A cold shiver passed through Magnus's stomach. They should have been hard upon them by now. They were being drawn out. The snipers had withdrawn. It was a trap.

'Hold fast!' he screamed, juddering to a halt and holding his hand up. All around him, men ran heedlessly onward, consumed with the desire to spill blood.

Finally, the guns rang out again. The noise came from further away. Magnus flung himself to the ground. Hot blood splattered across him. The handgunner on his right side slumped to the rock, scrabbling at his torn stomach, squealing like a stuck pig.

Magnus rolled away, sick with rage and impotent fury. They were being played for fools. It was the oldest tactic in the sniper's manual. Hit hard, withdraw. Hit hard, withdraw. The defenders were being strung out in an attempt to engage an unseen foe. Soon the light would fail entirely, and shooting would become impossible for both sides. Their only hope was to keep together, keep their volleys disciplined.

'To me!' Magnus roared, standing up. He cared nothing for the danger now. Their only chance was to stop running after shadows and stay in formation. 'Form a line! To me, men of Hochland!'

The survivors heeded his call. Soon he was surrounded by a dozen men. In the low light, their faces looked bewildered and angry.

'Raise your guns and aim for the flashes!' bellowed Magnus, trying to instil some sense of purpose. 'Fire on my mark, then withdraw. Damn you all, this is a bloodbath!'

The men crouched down, and long guns were prepared. On Magnus's mark, the entire line let off a rippling wave of fire. Once again, the shot whined into the dark. Whether it hit anything, no one could tell.

'Withdraw!' cried Magnus, pulling at the handgunners nearest him as he fell back. 'Don't go chasing phantoms! We must keep our shape!'

Gradually, the rest of the army seemed to be adopting the same strategy. The ranks of gunners were holding now, retreating step by step. Every so often, the crack of detonation would echo into the darkening air from the lines of defenders. There were no more volleys from the hidden snipers. They had gone. Like shades of death, they had retreated back into the shadows. As the night fell, even their guns would be no use. Somewhere in the night, the knights were riding hard, trying to find them.

'Mother of Sigmar,' breathed Magnus, feeling disgusted and dejected. He and his men retreated back to the camp perimeter. There were bodies everywhere. Some moved weakly, crying in pain. Others were as still and cold as the rock around them. The toll had been dreadful.

Gradually, the sounds of battle ebbed. Once Scharnhorst's commanders realised the attackers had fled, they reined in their men to conserve ammunition. Chasing after them in the dark would be suicidal. In any case, it was clear that the attackers had planned to strike and then retreat. The defenders had been out-thought, out-manoeuvred and out-shot. It was a disgrace.

Magnus reloaded, just in case, and sat heavily on a wooden crate. There were no more shots from the dark. Around him, handgunners stood stupidly, wondering whether to fire blindly or just hold their position. Magnus ignored them. They would have to absorb this lesson in tactics, and learn from it. There was nothing they could do now until the morning.

From the gathering darkness, a man walked towards Magnus. It was Messina. He had his flintlock pistol by his side, and the muzzle still smoked. A smouldering fury was in his eyes.

'Where were damned scouts?' he spat. 'It was like trying to shoot *fantasmi*.'

Magnus looked up wearily. The man was right to be angry.

'The knights might catch some of them,' he said, though he knew it was unlikely. 'We can't chase after them in this light.'

He looked at the handgunners. They were still waiting for orders. Now that the short, vicious firefight was over, many looked shocked.

'Make sure you're loaded and ready to fire again,' said Magnus to them, testily. 'We'll organise patrols, and get proper sentries for the camp edge.'

The gesture would give them something to do, but Magnus knew it was futile. The enemy wouldn't be back tonight. They relied on surprise to offset their lack of numbers. It had been a devastating tactic. He spat on the ground, got up and started to walk off towards the centre of the camp. All around him, torches were being lit and men were running to their stations. Too late. All much too late.

'Where you going?' asked Messina, looking exasperated.

Magnus turned to face him, his lined face lit up by the dancing flames.

'To Scharnhorst,' he said, his voice flat. 'We've got some talking to do. If he still doesn't think he needs a proper strategy for the guns, then he's a bigger fool than I thought he was.'

With that, Magnus turned and stalked towards the general's tent. His mood was black. All around him, the night was filled with the cries of the dead and the dying. The first encounter had come and gone. And they had lost.

CHAPTER SEVEN

'Never forget that behind the sights of the gun there lies a man. He must be trained to use his weapon, just as he would a pike, a broadsword or a loom. The tools of war are dangerous and fragile things, and blackpowder makes them more so. The mastery must be taught slowly. Repeat the lessons, and repeat them again. Once on the battlefield, it will be too late for further schooling. If they enter battle not knowing how to kill, all they will learn is how to be killed.'

Heinz-Karl Fromann,
Chief Instructor, Stirland
State Gunnery School

Messina was fuming. The campaign was turning into a dangerous and exhausting farrago. A half-competent general would have laid in precautions for a raid against their position, especially as they were now closing in on Morgramgar. The scouts and outriders had been dispatched far too easily. Even now, far into the mid-morning, several were still missing. Scores of soldiers had been killed before they'd even had a chance to pick up their weapons. For an army the size of Scharnhorst's, the casualties were bearable. But the blow to morale was real. The men were already teetering on the edge of fatigue and disrespect. Now that the incompetence of their masters had been fully exposed, they were even more so.

What made it worse was that the attackers had all used long guns. There was not an arrow in sight amongst the bodies of the slain. The ordinary halberdiers now looked askance at the engineers. Messina knew exactly what they were thinking. That the enemy was being better led, and was better equipped. And that their own commanders were arrogant fools.

'Again,' snapped Messina, looking down the line of handgunners. 'We'll do it again until you get it all right.'

Under Ironblood's orders, he had taken several dozen of the best troops in the gunnery companies, and was now drilling them mercilessly. Their performance had been sloppy. Damned sloppy. Whatever training they must have had in the past was clearly poor. While the bulk of the army was busy putting the camp into some kind of order, Messina and Herschel had been trying to instil discipline into the Hochlanders' firing. If they were attacked again with such rates of fire, they would lose as many men again. Speed of reloading was everything.

In front of his unforgiving gaze, the state gunners filled the pan, charged the barrel, loaded the shot, rammed it down, replaced the rods, fixed the cord, raised their rifles and fired into the distance. Their movements were getting better. The shame of the debacle the night before had driven them to improve. Some of the Hochland hunters were good shots. But they were slow, terribly slow.

After releasing their flurry of shot, they stooped quickly and reloaded their guns. A second volley cracked out across the echoing plain. That was better. Not as good as the enemy had been, but better.

Messina felt a presence at his shoulder, and turned. Herschel was observing quietly. The boy looked like he hadn't slept much. For all the Tilean knew, it might have been his first taste of real combat, and Messina could imagine that it hadn't been what he'd imagined.

'Keep it up, *ragazzi*!' he shouted to the handgunners. 'I want twelve more before you return to camp.'

He turned away from them, and walked slowly back to the wagons. Herschel came with him.

'How's it going?' said the young man.

'They are not bad soldiers, I think,' said Messina. 'But their training has been poor. I don't have the time to turn things upwards. We must accept they are the better shots.'

Herschel nodded. He looked worried.

'Herr Ironblood took some men out this morning,' he said. 'To see where the attackers had come from. We found footprints. They'd been taking aim from an incredible distance. There's no way we can compete with that.'

Messina stroked his elegant chin thoughtfully. Despite everything, he still took care over his looks. He was clean-shaven, and his clothes looked almost clean. That marked him out from the bulk of the officers, let alone the average infantryman.

'So they can fire further as well as faster,' he said. 'That is unfortunate.

I'd put my money on these Hochlanders to hit their targets, but they have to get into their position first.'

Herschel took a deep breath, and the worry remained heavy on his face. The lad was inexperienced, but was still nobody's fool. In the short time Messina had known him, he'd been impressed by the boy's knowledge of ballistics. When he spoke, the men listened to him. That was no easy feat.

'Can I ask you something, Silvio?' Lukas said, cautiously.

Here it came.

'Of course.'

'You've been on many campaigns,' said Herschel. 'You've served under many master engineers. What do you make of Magnus Ironblood?'

Messina drew in a breath of cold air. This was delicate. Unity was a virtue. But the truth was even more valuable.

'I have heard the name, of course,' he said. 'I am sure you have too. But names don't command armies. You remember how he looked when he found us? Something made him into that state. He has fallen. Perhaps he can't get it back. I don't know.'

Herschel looked pensive.

'I don't mean any disrespect,' he said, keeping his voice low. 'But we were badly beaten last night. There should have been plans in place. Any rabble could have attacked the camp. There was nothing arranged. Frankly, I could have done…'

He trailed off, and gave Messina a worried look.

'Don't worry, lad,' said Silvio. 'You can speak freely with me.'

Herschel shook his head, clearly full of doubt.

'I know how to fire a long gun,' he said. 'I know all the technical matters. But commanding an army… Perhaps I should keep my mouth shut.'

Silvio smiled at him.

'Perhaps you should,' he said. 'But not with me. I think that you are right. We've got to get things up together, and soon. We're nearly at the place, but there's time for more of those attacks. Ironblood thinks we'll just have to put them up, hold formation and suffer the losses.'

Silvio glanced over his shoulder at the practising handgunners. The volleys were still erratic. They were up against a foe they couldn't hope to match.

'Luccina only knows why we're so outgunned,' he murmured. 'These places should be home to nothing more than bandits and sheep. There is something strange going on. If we're going to think it through, we'll have to be creative.'

He clapped his hand on Herschel's shoulder and drew his face close to the boy's.

'I have some ideas myself,' he said, in little more than a whisper. 'Ironblood won't like it, but he'll never have to know. Are you in the mind for some danger? If we carry it off, there might be money in it.'

Herschel looked uncertain.

'What do you mean?' he asked. 'Ironblood ought to know about anything we're doing.'

Silvio smiled tolerantly. The lad was young. He'd have to grow up quickly.

'You may have noticed that our captain is not as respected as he would like,' he said, keeping his voice to a confidential murmur. 'Now, I do not suggest that we do anything disloyal. He is paying us, after all of it. But reputation is everything. If we were to do something by ourselves, something that might turn things just a little in our favour, it would do no great harm. To catch a general's eye is never a bad thing. We have to think of our own position.'

Lukas still looked unconvinced.

'What do you have in mind?' he said eventually, his mind clearly working through the possibilities.

Messina grinned.

'I thought you might never ask me,' he said. 'Come with me. But keep it to yourself. We've a lot to gain, and a lot to lose. And that's just how I like it.'

Hildebrandt watched Magnus walk heavily back into the camp and collapse onto a pile of old sacking. The man looked spent. He'd been busy most of the night organising watches to prevent a repeat attack, and most of the morning leading search parties to track down the snipers. Both efforts had been unfruitful. The attackers weren't fools. They would choose their moments, sweeping down when they weren't expected, and retreating as soon as the army could respond. It was a dirty kind of fighting, but effective nonetheless.

'Did you find much?' asked Hildebrandt, warily.

Magnus snorted.

'More of the same,' he said. His voice was thick with tiredness. Magnus looked almost as bad as he had done in Hergig. His hair was lank, and there were hollows of grey under his eyes. 'They'd slit the throats of the outriders. Crept up as the night fell. Nothing left behind. Just some powder-burns on the rocks, the odd piece of shot. Like ghosts. Damned ghosts.'

Ironblood sighed, and let his powerful shoulders relax. Hildebrandt looked on with concern. The big man was feeling the effects of his brush with tragedy still. The entire army was strung out on its feet. There were whispers amongst the soldiers. Most of them didn't bear repeating.

'Their guns are better,' said Hildebrandt, simply.

Magnus rolled his eyes.

'You think I don't know that? What are we supposed to do about it?'

Hildebrandt paused.

'You brought the chests with you,' he said. 'The machine from Nuln. I saw it. Do you plan to use it?'

Magnus sat up sharply, his eyes flat with suspicion.

'Have you been spying on me, Tobias?' he said.

Hildebrandt sighed with irritation.

'Of course not,' he said. 'It's there for all to see. But I know what's in them. The others don't.'

Magnus scowled. When he was tired, he became belligerent.

'You have no idea what's in them,' he said, scornfully, hauling himself to his feet.

Hildebrandt felt his own anger rising. After being persuaded to come on this terrible campaign, the least he deserved was some respect.

'It's the Blutschreiben, isn't it?'

There was a smug note of victory in his voice. He was closer to Ironblood than anyone. Despite all that had happened, Hildebrandt knew he wouldn't have left the past entirely behind.

Magnus didn't reply at once. He had a dark look in his eyes.

'It's locked away,' he said finally. 'That's how it'll stay.'

There it was. That old defiance. That old pig-headedness. It would be the death of both of them.

'Morr rot your bones!' spat Hildebrandt. 'How long are you going to let it hold you back? It's brilliant! Your father never got it right. You were almost there, Magnus. Almost there!'

Magnus took an angry step forward, his hands trembling.

'Almost!' he cried. 'How good is almost? It wasn't good enough for us last night. It won't be good enough if the siege guns crack when we roll them up to Morgramgar. And it wasn't good enough back then either.'

His voice wavered. Old memories were rising to the surface like oil in water.

'It wasn't good enough for him,' he said, softly, withdrawing, his eyes losing their focus. 'There's been enough death. It's not ready.'

From the shadows, Thorgad emerged. He was carrying a huge pile of cannon shot, half his own height. The dwarf had been working flat out since the attack. His axe had been little use in the fracas, and he seemed ashamed not to have contributed more. When he saw Hildebrandt and Ironblood in conference, he put down his burden and came over to them.

'A damn mess this has been,' he growled, rubbing his beard.

At the sight of the dwarf, Hildebrandt felt his own anger ebb. The strain was getting to all of them.

'I'm sorry, Magnus,' he said, bringing the debate to an end. 'I shouldn't have spoken. But it's frustrating, knowing…'

'I know,' said Magnus, quietly. 'They're out shooting us. But we can weather the storm. They're only coming at us now because they fear the siege. Once we have the heavy iron lined up, then they'll be in trouble. We have to hold our nerve.'

Ironblood looked at Hildebrandt directly. Amidst all the sullen weariness, there was a spark of defiance left. Not much of one, but it was there nonetheless. The old man was hard to grind down.

Thorgad spat on the ground.

'So what's next?' he said.

'We'll keep drilling the men,' Magnus said. 'They've got to get their rates of fire up. As for the rest, the knights and the lunatics, that's not our task. Scharnhorst can look after them.'

Hildebrandt nodded. The knowledge that the Blutschreiben still existed, albeit packed away and dismantled, was tantalising. But now was not the right time. He could return to the subject later.

'Very well,' he said. 'Messina and the boy have been busy with them all morning. I'll lend them a hand. We'll be at Morgramgar soon enough anyway.'

Thorgad looked doubtful, but said nothing. Magnus let out a deep, shuddering sigh, and sat back down again.

'By Sigmar, I hope so,' he said. 'When those cannons are delivered and we're sending death at them from a safe distance, then I'll relax. Until then, we've got a contest.'

At noon, the army moved onwards once more. The dead were disposed of quickly and with little ceremony. There was no time for burial, and the bodies were merely piled together and thrown into a crack in the granite plain. Lime was thrown over them, and Kossof gave a blessing. As he spoke to the assembled ranks, hostile eyes were directed at the engineers. Whispers had spread throughout the troops that Ironblood was still drinking, that he had spiked the defenders' guns to make them fire more slowly, that he was somehow in league with the enemy. It was wild talk, and baseless, but fatigue and fear did strange things to the men's minds.

When they returned to the march, they made slow progress. The land wound inexorably upward. The path passed between two mighty shoulders of hard, tumbled rock. It was dark and scoured of all but the hardiest grasses by the wind. The wains struggled, the men laboured, and the chill air bled the last of the energy from tired legs.

The very landscape seemed set against them. But there was more than cold stone to contend with. In the constant moan of the wind, there were fragments of fell voices. It might have been imagination, might not. High up in the crags, there were definitely things moving. Stones would skitter down slopes, clattering into tired ranks of infantry. Echoing roars sounded from far off in the peaks, and were answered by distant hammer-blows. These were not portents of Anna-Louisa's men. They were the noises of the unknown mountain reaches, far above the tolerances of mortal men. Whatever dread sentience dwelt in those terrible extremes, it did not descend to trouble them. But all were aware of its presence, and the knowledge added to the febrile atmosphere in the army itself.

Throughout all of this, Ironblood rode ahead of the gunnery companies, keeping himself to himself. He spoke rarely, and solely to Hildebrandt. Tobias was similarly quiet, locked in thought. Thorgad seemed utterly content in his own company, and strode tirelessly alongside the straining horses. Only Messina and Herschel still kept up something approaching banter with the men. They had been the most heavily involved with the punishing rounds of firing practice, and were looked on by many of the troops as their real mentors.

The warrior priest Kossof made the most of the situation. He and his acolytes had become the most animated of the army's many ranks. Every fresh adversity seemed to swell their sense of righteous fury.

'Trust not in the new science, brothers!' Kossof cried cheerfully, as the snap of whips and shrieks of the faithful rang out into the air. 'Keep faith in Holy Sigmar! The sword and the spear are the blessed weapons! The time when we will use them is coming! Keep faith!'

The gunners looked darkly on him as he passed them, but the words found resonance with the halberdiers and pikemen. They had been largely redundant on the journey so far, unable to respond quick enough to the night-time raid. Their skills would only come into play when they arrived at the citadel, and until then they looked restive and surly.

The other component of the army which retained its vigour was the Knights of the Iron Sceptre. They had the luxury of superior rations and the best equipment. While the bulk of the men shivered in the biting wind, they still rode up and down the lines, secure within heavy suits of armour. Though they were resented, they were also admired. The knights had done more than any others to chase down the night-time attackers, and they were trusted far more than the flighty bunch of engineers and their drunkard commander.

Despite the harshness of the terrain, they made steady progress. Scharnhorst had sent many men ahead as scouts on the few remaining horses. They patrolled in groups of six, mindful of the possibility of ambush. The rest of the army kept as bunched together as they could, all eyes on the shadows in the rocks.

After another day of heavy toil, the men crested the last of the great ridges before the valley in which, so the charts said, Morgramgar lay. The citadel itself was some miles distant, and the depression was wreathed in a heavy fog. Mindful of the mistakes of the past, Scharnhorst called a halt as the sun began to wane. They were in a shallow, wide valley surrounded by broken country. It was the only location wide enough to accommodate the whole army, but it was hardly ideal. There were vantage points in the hills around. All knew what that meant, and the men's eyes flickered nervously up at the jagged rocks enclosing them.

With an hour to go before nightfall, the camp was rigged properly, and sentries were posted on the high ground beyond. Fires were lit all around the perimeter, and gunners placed on every vantage point. They knew the enemy would come again. This was the rebels' last chance to strike before the siege was laid. At least they would be prepared this time.

As the final glow of the sunset ebbed behind the mountains to the west, Magnus sat on his horse, staring moodily at the dying of the light. Thorgad stood alongside him, scouring the mountains ahead.

'Tough country,' he muttered, seemingly to himself.

Magnus paid no attention. He knew his mood was weakening his authority with the men. They were looking for a decisive sign, and he was giving them none. His whole body ached for a drink. The scale of his dependence had begun to frighten him. Had he really sunk so low? How close had he been to losing himself entirely? It was a frightening prospect. And yet, despite knowing how ruinous it had been, how close to the edge it had taken him, every fibre in Magnus's body yearned for one more swig.

His sombre gaze swept across the ranks of gunners. They were primed and ready, muzzles arranged in long rows, ready for the assault. Their faces were grim in the failing light. They knew that they presented a big target. The enemy would not have to be accurate. Somehow, the defenders would have to pick their opposite numbers in the murk. What was worse, their guns were inferior. Magnus wanted to offer some words of comfort and encouragement. He couldn't think of any. His mind was sluggish and morbid. They would just have to cope as best they could.

Just as before, the attack came without warning. Scharnhorst's extra scouts had clearly not done their job. The night was suddenly lit from all around with muzzle flashes. An instant later, and the harsh sound of the blackpowder igniting echoed from the mountain flanks. Shot spat into the close-packed ranks of men. The sickeningly familiar cries of agony rose into the night.

'Keep your formations!' cried Magnus, suddenly galvanised into action. 'Remember your training! Return fire! Aim for the flashes!'

The response was less chaotic than it had been. Despite their losses, the lines of handgunners held their shape, and a disciplined volley whined off back into the night. Some of them might have even found their mark. It was hard to tell. Seeing anything in the gloom was nigh on impossible. As long as they retained their positions, though, they would get through it. The temptation to go charging off into the foothills was strong, but it must be resisted. The enemy would just draw them on, picking them off as they stumbled up the slope.

A second wave of incoming shot slammed into the defenders' lines. So quick. Most of the handgunners were still reloading when it impacted. Magnus saw one man take a musket-ball in the face as he stooped to pick up fresh shot. He spun round from the force of the blow, his skull caved in. The gunner fell without making a sound, and lay immobile. On either side of him, his comrades worked grimly to prepare a second volley.

'Keep your shape!' yelled Magnus again, knowing they would be itching to run. It was hard to fight the instinct. 'Fire in rounds! Hold your positions!'

Then, without warning, something new happened. From the far side of the camp, there were three mighty crashes. There was a high whine that slowly disappeared into the night. Something had been launched. There was a trail of smoke just visible against the darkening sky. Magnus followed the curve of the projectiles, his mouth hanging open in surprise. They were rockets. But he hadn't ordered any fired. They were for the siege. How had they been found?

'What in Sigmar's...' he began.

Then they detonated. The explosions were massive, and the earth seemed to vibrate under his feet. Three huge blooms of red cascaded over their heads, fizzing and drifting to earth slowly. These were not his rockets. The entire space was lit up with a lurid illumination. The outlines of men were suddenly visible on the ridges around them. The light didn't die away, but kept burning in the air. Spinning sparks flew from the floating shards, picking out every detail of the rocky hills above them in stark detail.

There was a roar of excitement from the men in the encampment. This was what they needed. From somewhere amongst the press of troops, orders were barked. Infantry began to swarm up towards the rocks. Kruger was at the forefront, his armour still glinting in the poor light, his charger labouring up the slope.

'Keep your formation!' shouted Magnus again to the gunners, but his words were ignored. More rockets screamed into the sky, bathing the land around them in fresh layers of harsh colour. The attackers were exposed. With all the energy born of days of pent-up frustration, the defenders broke out. Murderous oaths were sworn, and a savage light was in their eyes.

Powerless to prevent it, Magnus spat a curse and joined the surge up the shallow slope. He kicked his horse viciously. He must have presented a tempting target so high above the shoulders of his men, but he didn't care. Someone had usurped his authority and fired rockets. He didn't know whether to feel angrier with himself for not thinking of it, or his subordinates for going behind his back.

'Messina,' he hissed to himself. 'Those are Tilean flares. No one makes them like that.'

Then he was amongst the fighting. The snipers on the ridges had been surprised. The enemy. Face-to-face at last. They hastily tried to withdraw. With their positions exposed, retreat was impossible. The knights had been primed, and were heavily engaged, hacking and slashing from their steeds. The halberdiers, desperate for a fight, had joined the fray. In the blood-red light, the combat was murderous. Men grappled against each other like daemonic creatures, their eyes staring with hatred. The chance for revenge had come, and they were seizing it with both hands.

Magnus drew his sword, and rode into the morass of grappling bodies. A man leapt up at him, using his long riflegun as a club. Magnus swung the blade, feeling its keen edge snag on flesh and bite deep. Blood spat up, smearing across both him and his steed. It was hot and thick. The smell was overpowering. It took him back instantly to the battles he'd fought as a young man, back when he'd still eagerly rushed into combat, the thrill of it running through his veins. Before he'd lost his nerve.

Magnus ploughed onwards, swiping with his sword like a harvester in the fields. The snipers were pitifully unprepared. They'd expected to release a few rounds of shot into a supine enemy, then shrink back into the darkness. Many of them didn't even have swords with them. Just guns. And they were next to useless in a close press.

More rockets screamed into the sky above them. Fresh explosions detonated, showering the scene with more light. It looked as if blood was raining down from the heavens. Magnus pulled his horse round, facing a terrified enemy gunner. The man dropped his weapon and raised his hands. He was unarmed. Scared. Alone. For a moment, Magnus met his gaze. The gunner was a Hochlander, just like the ones running amok amongst his comrades. For this evening at least, he'd picked the wrong side.

Magnus rode him down, blocking the screams from his ears as the horse's hooves trampled the man into the ground. Another sniper emerged, and he cut him down too. There was no honour or glory in it. The tables had been turned, and the hunters had become the prey. As Magnus hacked and stabbed with a vicious fury, there was one nagging thought at the back of his mind. The victory hadn't been his doing. When this was over, there would have to be a reckoning.

The fires still burned. Some of the knights had yet to come back, and were pursuing their prey as far as the rockets would allow them. In the rest of the camp, raucous songs rose bawdily into the night. Ale had been released from the supply wagons, and the officers let their men indulge in it. After so many days of hardship, a victory, even a minor one, was worth celebrating.

Scharnhorst sat on a low stool by his tent, feeling a cold satisfaction within. They were nearing the end of the long trek north. After so many days in the wilderness, Morgramgar was now in range. Their losses had been serious, but not out of the ordinary for a major campaign. Perhaps two hundred had been slain in the raids, mostly gunners or poorly armoured flagellants. More had died on the ascent, and there had been some desertion. They could absorb that. More importantly, they had struck back at last. The price in dead was immaterial. It was the effect on morale that was important. When the morning came, they would march to the citadel walls, knowing that the enemy was vulnerable.

His captains stood around him, sharing in the satisfaction. They had all been involved in the rout. Many had flagons of ale in their hand, and blood on their tunics. Now they looked like real soldiers. The Tilean engineer, Messina, held pride of place amongst them. He had drunk deep, and had a ruddy glow in his lean cheeks.

'You did well,' said Scharnhorst, allowing a thin smile to crack across his stern face. 'If I'd known your rockets were so potent, I'd have ordered them used before.'

Messina grinned back, his eyes shining with pride and ale.

'They're of my own design,' he said. 'Brought specially in private stores. You won't see flares like that just anywhere. The recipe is a secret.'

'How many are left?' asked the general.

Messina shrugged.

'Not many,' he said. 'They will be less good when we lay siege. But they did the job I asked of them.'

Scharnhorst nodded.

'That they did. You are to be commended. I take it that your superior officer approved these plans?'

'He did not.'

The voice was Ironblood's. Magnus pushed his way to the front of the charmed circle of men. His leather coat was streaked with mud and gore. In the flickering light, his face was terrible. His sword was still naked in his hands, and it dripped steadily. He had been drinking. He looked worse than he'd been in Gruber's yards.

'Put your weapon away, man,' hissed a voice. It might have been Kruger's. Ironblood ignored him.

'I authorised no use of rockets,' he said, staring at Messina with fury.

Scharnhorst rose from his seat. His satisfaction turned instantly to irritation. The man was a liability.

'You have some nerve, approaching me like this,' he said, his voice low. 'You would do well to remember your place, Ironblood.'

Magnus looked up at him. His eyes were wild.

'Yes, it *is* important to respect rank, it is not, general?' he said. 'If your subordinates start to act without your explicit orders, then there'll be no discipline left. Isn't that right?'

Messina said nothing, but his face was disdainful. At his shoulder, the young Herschel stood, hovering uncertainly.

Scharnhorst took a deep breath.

'If you'd run your company with more competence, I'd have some sympathy,' he said. 'Your men have had to do your job for you. Your comrade has dipped into his personal stores for the cause. As a result of his actions, we have had a victory. Perhaps you should learn from his example.'

Magnus's eyes circled around the gathering of captains. He looked like a trapped beast, surrounded by hounds. Messina met his stare with a blank insolence. Herschel lowered his gaze. Ironblood looked like he was about to speak again, but then his colleague, Hildebrandt, came bursting out from the circle of men.

'I apologise, sir,' he said to Scharnhorst, bowing quickly. He grabbed Ironblood's arm, and began to pull him away. 'The battle has been hard. He doesn't know what he's saying. He needs rest.'

Magnus briefly resisted, sullenly snatching his arm back. But then the fire left his eyes. He looked defeated. With one last poisonous glare at Messina, he let Hildebrandt draw him away. The two of them stalked into the darkness, and were gone.

For a moment, no one spoke. Even Kossof seemed embarrassed, and stared intently at the ground. The fire crackled. The sound of singing rose into the air from elsewhere in the camp.

At length, Scharnhorst sat down again.

'A volatile man, that Ironblood,' he said. 'Perhaps we will have to look at the division of responsibilities again. Maybe Grotius was wrong about him.'

Scharnhorst looked up at Messina, who hadn't moved.

'You seem like an enterprising young man,' he said. 'We're nearly at the point where our engineers will be most useful. Do you have any more ideas for taking the fight to the enemy?'

Messina smiled, and his eyes glittered darkly.

'Indeed I do, sir,' he said, his voice glossy with satisfaction. 'Indeed I do.'

CHAPTER EIGHT

'Do not trust the seeker after knowledge! The boastful mind is the most dangerous enemy of man. Our proper task is to till the earth and guard the hearth. Those who seek truths amongst the stars or dabble in the new sciences are at the root of our downfall. Whenever a man of learning turns to the dark powers, then the Ruinous Gods laugh at our folly. Each time a child opens a book and is taught to read the signs within, the day of destruction looms nearer. Forget what you have been told by the foolish and the worldly! Ignorance of forbidden knowledge is power. Shun the wizard, the seer and the engineer. Only in faith and labour shall we be preserved!'

Luthor Huss
The sermon at Erengrad

In the heart of the mountains, a wide valley had been carved from the sheer rock by millennia of scraping ice. Like the rest of the highlands, it was bleak and barren. The rock was grey-banded granite, abrasive to the touch and tough as the bones of dragons. On all sides of the valley, the cliffs rose up tall and sheer. Their summits were jagged and impassable. Snow still clung to the uttermost peaks. The wind tore through the narrow gaps and skirled across the valley floor, tousling the few plants that grew and scraping the rock ever drier.

At the southern end of the valley there was a break in the otherwise perfect wall of cliffs. From this gap, the trail to Morgramgar wound steadily, picking its way across the desolate valley floor and looping around the many piles of boulders and mighty stone formations. The outcrops of rock were massive, and stood like the statues of some long-forgotten race of giants amidst the emptiness. An observant traveller, if any had existed so far into the wilds, might have picked out strange shapes on their flanks, almost like carvings. No doubt he would have put them down to the wind. In such a barren place, what else could they be?

The path ran for three miles before it reached the head of the valley. There, the mighty cliffs rose up once more, sealing the enclosed space in a circus of stone. Beyond those vast ramparts, there was no more travelling. The peaks piled up on top of one another, rising ever higher, until the land and sky seemed to meet in a haze of distant whiteness. The road ended.

At the point where the trail gave out, a mighty spur of black rock jutted out from the base of the towering cliffs. Unlike the dove-grey stone around it, the spur glistened darkly from many chiselled facets. It didn't belong. It looked like it had been hurled down from the heavens in some ancient war among the gods. It was shaped like the prow of a ship, sloping upwards and into the air of the valley. The wind broke across it, and no snow marred its surface. It was cold, hard and as slick as glass.

On top of the spur, a hundred feet above the valley floor, rose the isolated citadel of Morgramgar. The point where its dark walls met the stone below was indistinct. It seemed to loom from the cliffs around it, like some spell-induced growth from the roots of the mountains themselves.

Its base was solid and angular. The walls were arranged in a star shape with five points facing outwards. The blocks of stone were massive, each one the size of a peasant's hovel. They were rectangular and smooth, fitted together so perfectly that the joins were barely visible. The windows in that sheer surface were few. Every so often, a narrow shaft could be seen, set back far into the heavy stone and lined with iron. Pale illumination shone from some. In others, a deep red glow bled out into the cold air. Near the base of the citadel, the noise of a low throbbing could be made out, as if some vast machine was turning in the stone beneath. The rocks reverberated with it, sending a faint hum out into the valley beyond.

Further up the flanks of the citadel, the walls became taller and thinner. A cluster of towers burst from the foundations. They were slender and angular, clad in the same dark stone and topped with razor-sharp turrets. Flying bridges and twisting balustrades ran between them, fragile and perilous-looking in the high airs. Where there were windows, they glowed an eerie pale green. The narrow slots had glass panes in them, and strange shapes were carved around the frames. The stone was scored and pitted with age. Drab banners hung from the highest balconies. Once, the emblem of Hochland had been displayed proudly by loyal margraves. Now new insignias had taken their place. A long sable standard hung from the highest tower. It was unmarked, save for a grotesque death's head etched in crude lines of white. The hollow eyes gazed back down the empty gorge, daring any intruders to approach it.

At the top of the central tower, a soaring pinnacle which reached several hundred feet above the plain below, a large chamber had been constructed. It was too big for its base, and sat awkwardly atop the dark and forbidding citadel. More pale green light leaked from its many windows. More so than the death's head below, the chamber gave off the aspect of a terrible, sentient awareness. It was as if the windows were eyes and the jagged roof above it the horns of some ossified daemonic entity. Chains hung in great loops from beneath its overhanging eaves, clanking and swaying in the ever-present wind.

Within that chamber, Anna-Louisa had set her seat, and peered south across the valley. Her mighty armies were housed below, stationed in the vast halls that ran beneath the walls. The real glory of Morgramgar was not in its jagged pinnacles and towers. Deep within the foundations, ancient workings scored their way into the shadows beneath. There were massive chambers in the stone. Over the centuries, they had been allowed to fall into disrepair. That had changed. Now they were full of provisions, armaments, billeted men and, so rumour had it, deadly machines of war. Morgramgar had been restored, turned into a place of death, a citadel against which armies would break themselves like stones under the hammer.

On a narrow balcony overlooking the plain, set halfway up the sheer walls of the central tower, two men stood. They were both clothed in black, and their hair rustled in the chill air.

'They will be here soon,' said one of them.

He was a high-browed man with receding dark hair. His skin was pale and his eyes had deep bags under them. He looked like the kind of man who spent his days in the dark, by the forge, or in long-forgotten subterranean chambers. He wore a heavy amulet of silver around his neck. His cloak was of fine quality, and a collar of ermine trimmed his neck. He would have passed for a noble-born in many cities of the Empire, but some features of low birth gave him away. His gnarled hands spoke of manual labour, and he stooped as he stood, almost as if he expected some blow to rain down on him from a superior. Despite this, his gaze was proud. His lips curled around the words as he spoke.

'Indeed so, Rathmor,' said the second. 'But they've been blooded. We could have hoped for little more.'

Rathmor's companion was cut from different cloth. Though he wore the same dark robes, his frame was heavy. He had a neatly clipped silver beard and a mane of white hair to his shoulders. His features were blunt, and his skin was tanned and weather-beaten. Like Rathmor, his hands were scored by years of labour, but from wielding swords and shields rather than the machines of the forge. He bore himself proudly, leaning into the wind, his wide shoulders set back. He had the look of a man who feared little and ran from nothing. A warrior, then. Unlike his companion.

'I do not like your complacence, Esselman,' said Rathmor, pursing his thin lips distastefully. 'We don't have unlimited resources, despite her largesse. We lost too many of our men when you persuaded her to march against the first of these armies. I still think that was a mistake.'

Esselman sneered at the smaller man, not bothering to hide his contempt.

'What would you have done?' he asked. 'Stayed here, crouching behind your walls as they came to get you? You're a coward, Rathmor. I can't fathom what the lady sees in you.'

Rathmor took the insult in his stride, as if he was quite used to it.

'What she sees in me is my incomparable genius,' he said, unself-consciously. 'If I weren't here, you'd be nothing more than a rabble, squatting in the mountains waiting for your mistress to drag you out to your deaths. Admit it, Esselman. Without the modifications to your guns, you'd never have crushed Ludenhof's men.'

Esselman shrugged.

'We had the advantage of surprise,' he said. 'But I admit you've improved our range. Which is why we should have ridden to engage them again. This hiding and fleeing is hateful.'

Rathmor let a superior smile creep across his features.

'You're a warrior,' he said. 'All you think of is standing up and fighting. If the Empire were run by the likes of you, we'd be little better off than the beastmen.'

He leaned over the edge of the balcony, peering down towards the outer walls, far below. The sound of the muffled workings wafted upwards. A faint tremor could be sensed in the stone itself. It was as if all Morgramgar was a giant machine, and they were merely passengers on it.

'You're backward-looking,' said Rathmor, looking at the iron and stone around him. 'You belong to the past, when men hid from monsters in the shadows like children. The new science is everything. Blackpowder machines. With such tools, we could banish the scourge of Chaos for-ever. Even the elves would sit at our feet as slaves, and man would be master of the world.'

There was a strange light in the man's eyes as he spoke. Esselman looked weary. He had heard the speech a dozen times.

'Your toys are useful,' he said, grudgingly. 'The lady likes them. That's why we tolerate you. But they'll never replace a good man with a sword. Don't get carried away.'

Rathmor's expression wasn't dented. He was lost in a reverie of his own.

'A man with a sword?' he repeated, mockingly. 'Can a man with a sword fell a marauder at a hundred paces? Can he tunnel down to the deep ores and extract gold from the roots of the world? Can he throw fire into the air and immolate whole companies of our enemies?'

He laughed scornfully.

'Your age is passing, old warrior,' said Rathmor, gleefully. 'A new time is coming. The time of steel and steam. All it takes is vision. The Emperor will never allow it. There are too many in Altdorf with closed eyes and slow minds. But they'll see. When the spring comes and we sweep down from the mountains, then they'll see. The Empire needs shaking to its rotten core.'

Esselman's face remained impassive.

'So you keep saying,' he said. 'You've convinced von Kleister. How you did it, I'll never know. But you have, and so here we are. Stuck in a hold in the mountains. We've turned Ludenhof against us, and if we ever escape Hochland we'll have the armies of three more states hard on our heels. Your strategy's worked a charm so far.'

Rathmor's laugh was replaced by a scowl. His expressions changed quickly, like a child's. On the fringes of his wizened, clever face there was an air of petulance.

'Things are just as they should be,' he said. 'Our strength is still growing. The machines aren't complete. We just need time. Morgramgar is impregnable. We'll wait out the siege, hold for our moment. This army will be destroyed, just as the first was. The rumour of our success, and the gold beneath our feet, will spread. When the time is right, we will march south. But only then. Not before.'

Esselman gave the man a warning look.

'Remember your place, Rathmor,' he said. 'The lady tolerates you, but I'm the master of her armies. I need your machines, but I won't be dictated to. We'll march when I say so.'

Rathmor gave a mock bow, his sardonic smile returning.

'Of course, my lord,' he said, silkily. 'Yours will be the word of command for the men. But we still need more time. The forges are busy, but we cannot rush the work. There is still much to learn, much to discover.'

Esselman turned back towards the empty valley stretching before them. There was still no sign of the approaching army. No living creature stirred against the bleak backdrop of granite.

'Is the infernal engine ready?' he asked. 'That's the one thing I'm interested in. That's something I could use.'

Rathmor gave Esselman a knowing look, almost a leer, and shook his head.

'Patience, my good general,' he said. 'It needs more work. I would not send it out against such a rabble. Its time will come when we are fully revealed at last. Then the whole Empire will see the greatness of my work. Just as they should have done, all that time ago. They were fools then, and they're fools now. We have nothing to fear from any of them.'

Esselman didn't share Rathmor's look of confidence. He squinted his eyes against the pale southern horizon, scanning carefully for any sign of movement.

'You can keep it under wraps for now,' he said, gruffly. 'The lady agrees with you. But if it's needed to break this siege, I'll call on you again. I won't stay cooped up in here forever. A man should take the fight to the enemy when he can.'

Rathmor didn't like the sound of that, and said nothing. He flexed his crooked fingers against the stone balustrade and rocked back on his heels. He seemed ill at ease standing still. His whole body itched for some kind of activity. He cut a nervous, strained figure next to his more assured companion.

'Your impatience will ruin everything,' he muttered. 'We have all we need. Gold, men, the citadel and the support of the lady. I'll say it again. All we need is time. Time to perfect the machines. Hochland has no engineers capable of breaching these walls. They're a race of goatherds and drunkards. Wait a little longer. When all is ready, I will give you your war.'

Rathmor's speech became more excited. He was drifting into a reverie again.

'You will ride into Hergig at the head of an army the likes of which the world has never seen. If you think the weapons I've given you so far are good, wait till you see what's coming from the forges. If I could somehow do without the necessity of flesh to man my creations, I would. That's the only weak link. Otherwise my machines are perfect.'

Esselman recoiled slightly from Rathmor. The two men clearly had different philosophies.

'I sometimes wonder,' he said, slowly, 'why you didn't stay at Nuln. If your genius was so evident, they would surely have made some use of you.'

A look of aversion filled Rathmor's eyes, and he rocked back away from the balcony's edge.

'Everything has its price!' he said, his voice rising in pitch. 'What does it matter that a few men died? That's the price of progress!'

A sneer crept across his womanish lips again.

'They couldn't pay it,' he said. 'We had to leave. Me, and the other one. We both had to leave. All the visionaries did. They're as blind as their masters in Altdorf.'

Esselman looked at Rathmor with distaste. The little man was consumed by a sudden vitriol. His hands shook, and spittle flew as he spoke.

'That, my friend, will be the sweetest moment,' Rathmor said. 'Only when the walls of Nuln are besieged with ranks of the infernal machines. Only when the college is wreathed in fire, flames they cannot put out, will I return. Only when they're on their knees, begging for forgiveness and to recognise my genius, will I deign to speak to them again. The dogs. The damned, blighted dogs! Only then will I go back.'

Rathmor's speech had become shrill and repetitious. He shook slightly, and the strange rocking motion started up again. Esselman stepped away from him, looking revolted.

He was about to speak, when a chime sounded deep within the tower behind them. Both men froze. Rathmor's face was already pale. It seemed to lose even more blood in an instant.

'What does she want?' he hissed, looking at the skull-like chamber suspended above them. The light from the stained-glass windows was green and sinister.

'Who knows?' said Esselman, taking a final look down the valley. It remained empty. 'But I'm not going to keep her waiting. You'd better come too.'

The echoing chime sounded again. It was strangely redolent of a child's toy. A glockenspiel, or a clockwork model. And yet its effect on the men was immediate. With a look of extreme reluctance, Rathmor smoothed his dark clothes over his chest, and steadied his shaking fingers.

'Damn her,' he whispered, looking extremely perturbed.

'Don't let her hear you say that,' replied Esselman. 'Genius or not, you'd better keep that tongue under control.'

Slowly, with reluctant steps, the two men withdrew from the balcony and retreated into the tower behind them. Unseen hands slammed the doors shut. The chill breeze wafted across the vacant platform.

With their passing, no other movement was visible on the spiked battlements. No watchmen patrolled, no scouts rode from the gates, no defenders paced across the bleak courtyards. But from deep below, Rathmor's engines continued their ceaseless grinding. The chains below the high chamber swung in the wind, and the hidden forges burned. Like some nightmare creation suddenly bereft of human controllers, Morgramgar waited for the coming battle, its mysteries hidden for the moment, its depths uncovered, its terrors veiled.

CHAPTER NINE

'What limits their powers, these engineering geniuses? I am not sure that anything does, apart from the moral law given us by Sigmar and Verena. If the engineer was allowed to indulge his every speculation without constraint, then the race of man would soon descend into barbarism. There are sketches of machines in the vaults of the college that defy belief. I have been shown them. Unholy amalgamations of human flesh and iron workings. Mixtures of steam technology and the art of the wizard. These things must never be allowed to see the light of day. You have my word that I am a supporter of the new science, but perversion is perversion, wherever it is found, and a matter for the witch hunters.'

Elector Emmanuelle von Leibwitz
XVth Report of the Imperial Commission
on the College of Engineers

At last, Morgramgar had come into view. The vanguard climbed the final few yards up a slope of loose scree, and the valley unfolded before them. The citadel was a mere speck of darkness against the distant cliffs. Only as the army marched down the bare valley floor did its true scale become apparent. The fortress was small only in comparison with the gigantic cliffs behind it. An observer on the ground could see its titanic scale well enough.

Scharnhorst maintained his habitual pace, and the road was traversed quickly. The victory against the snipers had restored the spirits of both men and commanders. Half a mile from the enemy ramparts, the general called a halt. The various companies spread out across the plain. All eyes were fixed on the dark, strange edifice before them. Morgramgar was a twisted construction. In the harsh mountain light, it looked almost as if it had been forged from iron rather than built up from stone. There was no sign of movement anywhere near it. The road leading to the gates was silent. The massive entrance was shut. Doors of age-stained wood were enclosed in a frame of black metal. The portal was carved into the shape of a gaping wolf's mouth. Two eyes burned above the lintel with some strange fire. Even in the harsh daylight, the effect was unsettling.

Bugles sounded across the army, signalling the deployment pattern for the siege. State troopers fanned out, led by their captains. The halberdiers, pikemen, swordsmen and mercenaries, by far the largest component of the army, arranged themselves in a long line facing the enemy walls. The knights were deployed in the reserve, far out on the right flank. Their cavalry charges would be little use unless a sortie emerged. Scharnhorst and his retinue took up position on a broken rise, well behind the bulk of the army. The flagellants were deployed in a ragged group on the left flank. They were kept well away from the main soldiery by Scharnhorst, a situation which pleased everyone. As soon as the deployment was complete, the fanatics started their imploring benedictions to Sigmar, and their thin, warbling voices drifted over the empty plain.

Once the last of the carts had been hauled up, Magnus, Hildebrandt and Thorgad began to oversee the unloading of the heavy guns. Most had survived the journey in more or less one piece, but several had suffered damage and needed running repairs. The dwarf seemed to take this personally, and spent his time tutting with disapproval. Herschel and Messina were nowhere to be seen. They had become increasingly a law unto themselves since the last attack.

If anything, Scharnhorst seemed to be encouraging the split in the corps of engineers. Magnus had seen the Tilean ride closely alongside the general's staff on the ascent. It put his teeth on edge, but there was little he could do. In the cold light of day, he was ashamed of his performance. The outburst had been an aberration, even for someone in his weakened state. For so long, he had held out against the lure of drink. His one slip had carried a heavy penalty. The only response was to make amends on the field. He found some comfort in the heavy, repetitive work of deploying the guns and organising the crews. There was much to do before all would be ready, and it was in such situations that the art of the master engineer came into its own.

He was marshalling the unloading of one of the huge iron-belchers, a massive piece with the fanciful name 'Brunhilde' engraved on its iron barrel, when Hildebrandt rode up towards him.

'Why are you here?' the big man said, looking exasperated. 'Scharnhorst's called a council of war.'

Magnus's heart sank. He hadn't even been informed. Messina had replaced him in the general's estimation. Magnus carried on with what he was doing, tightening a series of thick leather straps around the unwieldy machinery to allow it to be lifted down.

'I guess I wasn't required,' he said nonchalantly, concentrating on his work.

Hildebrandt dismounted heavily, and strode up to him.

'Listen to me,' he said, pulling Magnus around to face him. 'This is pathetic. You've given up. Messina's a pushy bastard, but he's half your age. He hasn't served as long as either of us. If you let him walk over you, you'll become a laughing stock.'

Magnus smiled wryly.

'Am I not already?' he said, looking around at the busy gunnery crews. 'The men are whispering behind my back. They think I can't hear them. Perhaps it's best to let the young blood take over.'

Hildebrandt looked disgusted.

'When I knew you of old, you'd never have let things come to this,' he said. 'Mother of Sigmar, Magnus. You've changed. It's humiliating, watching you like this.'

Magnus failed to respond to that. He felt as if all the fight had been beaten out of him. He had returned to the shell of a man he'd been in Hergig. Whatever Grotius had roused in him, it hadn't taken long to die.

'What does it matter?' he said. 'We'll be paid in any case. I'll clear my debts. You can put your children into a trade. Everyone's happy.'

Hildebrandt shook his head.

'Not if that preening fool gets us all killed. He's no idea what he's doing. Scharnhorst is impressed with his rocket trick, but Messina has no idea how to deploy the heavy guns. And if you think the boy Herschel will do any better, you're madder than he is. You need to put a stop to this, Magnus. Morr's blood, man. You're being turned into a fool by your own crew. I never thought I'd live to see it.'

Finally, Magnus felt the sting of shame. Hildebrandt stood before him, his face torn between accusation and pity. That was hard to bear. He could take anything from Tobias, even contempt. But not pity. They had come too far together. Even after his fall from grace, the bond of friendship and respect had never completely severed. It would break his heart to see it snap now.

'Where are they placing the wall-breakers?' asked Magnus. He was too weary for another battle with Messina and Scharnhorst, though he knew it had to come.

'Messina wants them over on that ridge,' said Hildebrandt, pointing to a shallow hillock directly in front of the first ranks of handgunners. 'They'll be close enough to send shot over the lower battlements. He's got some Tilean contraptions. He says they'll kindle fire once they land.'

Magnus frowned.

'That's too close,' he said. 'For all we know, they've got guns on those walls with a greater range than ours. I wouldn't put anything past them.'

Hildebrandt let out another infuriated breath.

'Exactly!' he cried. 'You need to tell Scharnhorst that. Messina's all over him. If the defenders get their own shot amongst our cannons, we'll have hauled them up here for nothing. You're still in command. Put an end to this madness.'

Magnus looked back towards the distant walls of Morgramgar. There wasn't any sign of gunnery on the walls. But that meant nothing. It was already evident that the enemy's artillery commander was highly skilled. It wouldn't be hard to conceal barrels behind those massive walls. The more he looked, the more sure he was that there was something hidden behind the blank, dark facade. Some of the openings below the battlements looked very strange indeed.

'I'll have a word with the general,' said Magnus at last. 'He's got to have forgiven me by now, hasn't he?'

Hildebrandt clapped him on the shoulder.

'I'll oversee the rest of this,' he said. 'Just make sure these pieces get put in the right place.'

Scharnhorst gazed at Magnus with his familiar expression of wary disregard. The general was standing amidst the command retinue in his full ceremonial dress, a brass spyglass clutched in his hand. Kruger, Kossof and the other commanders were with him as always. Towards the rear of the group, Messina lurked, keeping his head down. Magnus had no doubt that he'd been active in talking to Scharnhorst behind his back. For the moment, Ironblood chose to keep his thoughts to himself. After his outburst the previous night, his position was precarious to say the least.

'And what, may I ask, is the point of bringing our big guns all this way, if we can't place them within range of the castle walls?' said Scharnhorst, his tone sarcastic.

Magnus worked hard to keep his voice respectful.

'I'm not sure who advised you to do that, sir,' he said. 'Of course we need to place our artillery pieces in range of the walls. But sending shot high over the battlements will require them to be moved too close. We need to proceed with caution. We've already seen that the enemy possesses handguns far superior to ours. It is reasonable to assume they've prepared heavy artillery too. If we rush into this, we'll lose our advantage.'

Scharnhorst pursed his lips.

'What would you suggest?' he asked.

'Deploy our guns immediately in front of the ranks, with companies of halberdiers on hand to defend them against raids. They won't be able to lob shot right over the battlements from there, but they'll be close enough to blast at the foundations. That's all we need to do. One crack in the walls, and we've got our entrance.'

Kruger turned his aristocratic head towards the citadel.

'I don't know, Ironblood,' the knight said. 'Those walls have been designed to withstand punishment. I think we should be aiming higher. I've seen the effect of fire within a closed space. We'll cause panic. We should aim to make this siege as short as possible. I don't want to be here longer than I have to.'

Magnus stifled some smart remark about needing to head back to the estate to oppress the serfs. No one here knew anything about ballistics. Apart from Messina, that was.

'I could be wrong,' Magnus said, speaking slowly and carefully, trying to stay humble. 'I'm aware we haven't exactly covered ourselves with glory. But I've got a strong feeling about this. We've been drawn up here by them. They wanted us to come to them. If they were worried about us deploying our cannons so close, they'd have tried to frustrate us. But they're waiting. They want to make it look as if we can just walk up and start firing at them. I don't believe it for a second.'

Scharnhorst was listening carefully. Magnus had to give the man his due. He was sceptical, but he was paying attention.

'You asked me to run your gunnery for you, sir,' Magnus said, completing his case. 'That's my advice. Deploy as far back as you can. It'll take time to find our range in any case.'

Scharnhorst rubbed his chin thoughtfully, looking back and forth between the ranks of his own men and the silent walls of the citadel in the distance.

'Messina,' he said, sharply. 'What do you think?'

Silvio came forward. He at least had the decency to look abashed, and didn't meet Magnus's eyes.

'Herr Ironblood is master engineer,' he said, disingenuously. 'His view carries the most weight. With all respect, though, I disagree.'

His shifty eyes flickered around the assembled men nervously. Magnus could guess his predicament. The man's stock had risen after the deployment of the flares. But those around him were officers, to whom the chain of command was near-sacred. Kruger looked at him suspiciously. The Tilean would have to play his hand carefully. Magnus kept silent, waiting to see how things would unfold.

'Those walls are thick. They are designed to take our heavy shot,' said Messina. 'You can see that from here. I've seen stone like that before. The shape of the star makes it strong. If our shot is just hitting the base of walls, we'll be here for weeks. We don't have unlimited cannonballs, and our lines of supply are long.'

For a moment, Silvio's gaze alighted on Magnus. Ironblood stared back at him implacably. Messina's eyes quickly moved back to Scharnhorst.

'We have explosive charges,' he said, quickly. 'Like mortar rounds, but lighter. They're an invention of mine, and I've used them before with success. They're caskets, tied with steel wire and capable of surviving a detonation in the barrel, but full of quick-fire which explodes on hitting. *Fuoco del muerto*. An apt name. Once it is lit, it's hard to douse quickly. If we keep up a volley, we can clear the walls. Maybe even in hours. They'll be so busy running after those fires, you will be able to attack the gates in safety.'

Scharnhorst remained silent, pondering the options. Kossof, standing at the rear of the captains, muttered to himself.

'What does it matter which of these heretics we listen to?' he said under his breath. 'They're both as bad as each other. We should be storming the gates!'

Scharnhorst ignored him. The general looked supremely irritated. Magnus felt an acute sense of shame begin to creep across him. This situation should never have arisen. If he'd been a proper master of his company, Messina would never have been able to undermine him so completely. Now that it had happened, he would just have to wait on the general's decision.

'We'll deploy on the forward ridge, as planned,' said Scharnhorst. His voice had a tone of finality about it that brooked no disagreement. He turned to Magnus. 'This is nothing personal, Ironblood. But I can't see any ordnance on those walls, and the scouts report nothing either. You've been too cautious all through this campaign. If we can get those lower levels on fire, our task will be made that much easier. And if we end up spending weeks up here waiting for the walls to crack, we'll start running low on supplies.'

Magnus felt his heart sink. The final humiliation. His command of his men had been undermined again. He pondered protesting, but then saw the implacable expression on the general's face. The man wasn't going to change his mind.

'I want you to oversee the deployment as soon as those guns are unloaded and prepared,' said Scharnhorst. 'You're the master engineer. Make sure that they can clear the battlements.'

The general turned to Messina.

'Take your orders from Ironblood,' he said, though his voice didn't quite carry the conviction it had earlier. 'He's the superior officer. Remember that.'

The two men bowed, and left the group of commanders together. As they walked down from the retinue, the remaining captains fell into discussion about other aspects of the siege. There was much to organise, and the day was waning fast.

Magnus gave Messina a hard stare. The Tilean said nothing, and had trouble meeting the older man's gaze. It was the first time they'd spoken since Magnus's performance in front of Scharnhorst. As they walked on, there was an uneasy silence.

'Why are you doing this, Messina?' said Magnus at last. His voice was neither accusatory nor whining. He just wanted to know. 'We'd be better working together. You can't hide behind the general forever.'

Messina kept his eyes on the floor.

'I do not know what you're talking about, sir,' he said. 'General Scharnhorst asked for my advice.'

Magnus laughed, a bitter sound with no mirth in it.

'So you're playing that game,' he said. His pained smile left his face. 'Listen, lad. You're young. You know how to fire a pistol, and you're good with the machinery. That's why I hired you. But don't play politics. You may think you can run with Scharnhorst and come away with something extra from this, but you'll burn your fingers. I've served with his sort before. He doesn't think much of me, and that's given you your chance. But overplay your hand, and you'll regret it.'

Messina remained stony-faced.

'Where do you want me starting on these guns?' he said.

Magnus sighed. There were fights he enjoyed, and fights he didn't. This was one he didn't.

'The iron-belchers are ready,' he said, motioning towards Hildebrandt and a gang of gunners. 'I'll look to the lighter ordnance. If I'm right, and I hope I'm not, it's all we'll have left in a few hours anyway.'

By mid-afternoon, the guns had been hauled into position. Crews milled around them, piling shot in neat pyramids behind the heavy iron cannons and laying out the rest of their equipment on sheets of leather. The artillery pieces were the largest in the army's arsenal, designed to break down castle walls or send heavy shot hurtling into massed enemy formations. Magnus had seen similar guns in action on many battlefields in the past. Used rightly, they were devastating. Used wrongly, they were expensive, dangerous follies. It all depended on who was in charge.

Each cannon had a crew of up to half a dozen men attached to it. The most important member was the master gunner, responsible for sighting the gun. This was an inexact science, mostly involving ramming wooden wedges under the great wheels to raise the barrel to the required angle. The master gunners had travelled with the same weapon for years, though, and knew all its idiosyncrasies and kinks.

The master was accompanied by a gunnery crew who had responsibility for loading, sponging and firing the mechanism. One man carried the heavy ramrod used to thrust the shot and cartridge of blackpowder deep into the barrel, while another had a stave-mounted sponge of rags covered in wool used to clean the interior after a detonation. There were pails of dirty water next to every piece, needed for when the iron barrel reached dangerous temperatures. During a heated exchange, this could happen with unnerving speed.

When the shot was loaded and rammed, the gun aimed in the right direction and at the right elevation, the gunnery master would step forwards with a lighted wick. The flaming kindling would be dropped into the pan, filled with blackpowder. All being well, the detonation would be immediate. The blackpowder would cause the cartridge within the iron shaft to explode. The cannon would rock back on its wheels, slamming against the back of the chassis and jumping like an animal. With any luck, the crew would have got out of the way in time, cowering behind whatever shelter they had to hand. Gunnery hands soon learned to move quickly.

With a well-bored piece, the shot would be sent high and true, and the cannon would come back to rest on its chassis, ready for reloading. But such was the way of things that the cartridge was perfectly capable of rupturing the shell of iron around it, or blasting the breech out backwards, or shattering the wooden framework beneath, or a dozen other calamitous things. Not for nothing were prayers whispered to Morr every time a great cannon was deployed. They were ferocious devices, but also capricious. If the barrel exploded, the worst of all the things that could happen, then there was little hope for the crew.

To his credit, Messina worked hard on the deployment. Magnus watched him closely. In another situation, he would have agreed with the Tilean's strategy. But this was different. Having been stung once by the range of the handguns, he had a deep-seated feeling that their deployment was ruinously close. Something about the enemy's equipment scared him. The serpentine was part of it. For all Thorgad's words about dwarfish design, there was something familiar about it. Nothing he could put his finger on, just a vague recollection of something from the far past. He took the shard of metal out of his pocket and looked at it again. It winked in the sunlight, looking as innocent as a lady's necklace. Only an engineer would know it for what it was, the trigger that ignited the destructive power of the weapon. It was a piece of exquisite, and dangerous, machinery.

Magnus sighed, and put it away. Messina and Herschel were coming towards him. The Tilean had recovered most of his habitual self-assurance, but the lad from Averland looked uncertain whom to defer to. Ironblood almost felt sorry for him.

'We are in place, sir,' said Messina. 'Will you give the order to fire?'

Magnus looked along the line of cannons. The crews gazed back at him expectantly. The fuses had been lit, and the first volley of Silvio's strange shot had been loaded and rammed. Thorgad and Hildebrandt stood some distance away, looking unconvinced. Neither spoke.

'Very good,' said Magnus, and glanced up at the silent walls of Morgramgar. There was still no movement visible on the high walls. The dark citadel remained entirely silent, entirely still. Only the slight movement of the death's-head standard and the swaying of the strange chains broke the impression of implacable hostility. It was an unnerving construction.

The walls looked as smooth and unbroken as ever. If he didn't know that the citadel was swarming with troops deep inside, Magnus might have presumed it had been abandoned.

From several yards away, Scharnhorst stood peering at the ramparts through his spyglass. All other eyes were on the artillery rank.

Magnus pushed that out of his mind, and raised his hand.

'On my mark!' he cried.

The master gunners shuffled to their positions. Magnus could feel his breathing begin to speed up. There was an air of stifled expectation across the whole army. This was what they had come for.

He muttered a brief benediction to Sigmar, then raised his eyes to the walls once more.

'Fire!' he cried.

The wicks fell. Almost immediately, the cartridges in the cannon exploded. In a ragged line, the great guns leapt back on their chassis, and the air was filled with the noxious stench of blackpowder. Messina's ingenious shells were blasted high into the air.

Magnus followed their progress intently, shading his eyes against the white of the sky. The master gunners had done their job well. Only one shell spun off target, smashing into the rock in front of the gates. It exploded messily, spreading an orange carpet of flames across the stony ground. The rest sailed over the tops of the ramparts. They ignited against the dark walls, spreading their deadly cargo across the battlements.

There was a roar of appreciation from the men of the army. Fists were raised. Lines of ink-black smoke began to coil from the citadel's lower levels. Still there was no sign of movement from within.

'Reload!' cried Magnus.

Messina was standing close to him, watching the progress of his inventions with concern. Thorgad and Hildebrandt came closer, each staring intently at the walls.

The gunnery crews worked quickly. Sponges were loaded with cold water and rammed into the smoking barrels of the guns. Men slopped more water over the ironwork, watching anxiously for any signs of over-heating. Fresh cartridges of compressed blackpowder were delivered, and hastily thrust back against the breeches. Then more shot was delivered. The men carried Silvio's bundles of death warily, walking slowly across the uneven ground and taking care where they trod. The loads were placed in the cannons, and the crew pressed them against the cartridges gingerly.

Magnus stole a last look at the walls of the citadel. The fires did not seem to be catching. There was some smouldering somewhere behind the towering walls, but not the inferno Messina had promised. He didn't know whether to be pleased by that or not.

He turned his attention back to the row of artillery. They were ready to fire again. One by one, the gunners finished their preparations and looked up at Magnus, waiting for the word.

'Fire!'

Again, only one misfire. One of the cannons recoiled too heavily, spinning on its axle and slewing to the left. A young lad was caught by the rebounding iron. His scream was drowned by the heavy detonation along the line. Fresh shells soared into the air. They were well aimed. All cleared the first line of battlements, and the sound of their explosions cracked across the valley. The men cheered again. More smoke rose.

'Reload!' cried Magnus. 'Get that man out of there!'

Something was wrong. The fire wasn't kindling. Morgramgar remained defiantly unharmed. The fires were being put out as soon as they started. There was still no visible movement on the walls.

The crews worked hard. The man who had taken the brunt of the misfire was dragged back from the ranks. His leg was a mangled mess of blood and tendons. His screams continued, only ebbing as he was pulled away from the vanguard and towards the makeshift apothecary's tent.

Messina was looking worried.

'The lower levels should be now on fire...' he muttered, looking at the walls with suspicion. 'Why isn't it catching?'

Magnus ignored him, and prepared a fresh volley.

'Fire!'

The shells rose up once more. No misfires. All found their target. Briefly, flames licked the flanks of the citadel. Smoke rose. Then it died, extinguished by the ever-present wind. The cheers lost some of their vigour. The troops could see that the volleys were having little effect. Still Morgramgar remained implacable. The standard still hung. The chains still revolved. The silence was unnerving.

Magnus looked over at Scharnhorst. The general gave no sign.

'How many of these things do you have?' Magnus hissed to Messina.

'As many as we have need of,' said Silvio, looking distractedly at the fortress. 'Keep it going! It only takes one to catch.'

Magnus doubted that. It wasn't working. He considered ordering a halt, drawing the cannons back to a safe range. He dismissed the idea. One more round. Scharnhorst would expect him to give the strategy a fair shot.

'Reload!' he shouted, feeling his voice begin to hoarsen.

As he did so, something began to change on the walls of Morgramgar. A sick feeling took hold of him. He knew it. There was machinery there, embedded in the stone. Plumes of steam escaped from the ramparts, billowing into the air and drifting across the battlefield. The red fires in the wolf's eyes burst into a full blaze. The unnatural light in the citadel windows glowed more fiercely. Massive clangs echoed from deep within the fortress. Signals, perhaps. Or maybe the operation of giant machinery.

'Hurry it up!' bellowed Magnus, not liking the look of what was happening at all. The crews rushed to comply. The rest of the army, lined up some distance behind them, had ceased making any noise. They were looking at the walls.

There were resounding booms from the citadel. High up in the outer ramparts, stones suddenly seemed to withdraw and slide to one side. The scrape of wheels against iron was clearly audible. From the gaps in the wall, round muzzles were thrust forward. There were over a dozen of them. They were huge. Sculpted wolf's heads and skulls had been placed over the cannon shafts. From the holes behind them, smoke boiled and ran down the walls, collecting at the base of the citadel. With more grinding, the guns were run out. The largest extended at least six feet over the plain below, hanging precipitously.

Magnus knew at once that they were within the range of such monsters. The guns were a third bigger than his own largest iron-belchers. Not only were their own guns within range, but the rest of the army was as well.

'Get back!' he cried, hoping Scharnhorst would hear him. 'The troops must withdraw!'

The crews around him kept working. They had little choice. There were more ominous rumbles from Morgramgar. There was still no sign of any human activity. The terrible row of wall-mounted cannons seemed to operate as if possessed of a morbid will of its own. Smoke continued to pour from the gaps around the barrels, draping the walls in a curtain of foul-smelling gloom. Echoing booms sounded from within the structure. Whatever had been unleashed was coming to fruition.

'Fire when ready!' yelled Magnus, desperate to get the shot away.

From behind him, he could hear men scrabbling to retreat. The troops weren't stupid. They knew they were in too close. Messina's strategy was unravelling fast.

In a ragged, undisciplined sequence, Ironblood's cannons fired again. Just as before, their deadly cargo hit the target. The flames recoiled from the dark stone as if it were glass, cascading back to earth in rapidly cooling gouts. The plan had failed.

'That's enough!' cried Ironblood. 'Pull back! Get those guns moving!'

It was an impossible task. The cannons took time to move. Even working flat out, there was no hope of getting them all away. The crews complied as best they could, dousing the steaming barrels, kicking the wedges from the wheels, dragging horses over to haul the guns from danger.

Messina's eyes were staring. The man was losing his composure.

'What are you doing?' he hissed. 'We can still make it all work!'

Ironblood gave him a weary look.

'Forget it, Silvio,' he said, curtly. 'I counselled against this from the start. We're exposed. Help me withdraw, or get out of the way.'

Messina hesitated for a moment, clearly torn. But the crews needed no urging. They were working hurriedly, shouting orders to one another, desperately trying to pull back before they were covered in shot.

Magnus stole a look towards Scharnhorst's position. Even the general was pulling back, surrounded by his escort of knights. Only the flagellants were staying put. Their leaders were hurling invective at the citadel, utterly undaunted by the bizarre mechanisms being unveiled before them.

Then, it happened. The entire valley was rocked by a huge row of explosions. Men fell to the ground, covering their ears. The blasts echoed from the rock around them, booming and amplifying. The air was filled with the screaming sound of iron tearing through the air. Magnus fell to the ground immediately.

The shot impacted. It was grape, bags of leather stuffed with twisted fragments of iron and bursting gobbets of blackpowder. When it hit, storms of metal flew through the air, tearing apart anything it passed through. Men screamed, clutching faces and torsos. Blood stained the rocks.

The retreat instantly became a rout. There was no standing up against such a withering volley. The front ranks of the army were sliced apart, their ordered ranks dissolving into ruin instantly.

Magnus got to his feet shakily. If the enemy cannons were as quick-loading as their guns, a second round would be imminent. His palms were sweaty with fear. He should have withdrawn sooner. The signs had been there.

He took a hurried look around him. Some of the cannons had been hitched to their steeds, and were being dragged back. Others had been abandoned. There was no hope of retrieving them. They would be isolated, free for the enemy to pound into scrap at their convenience. Even as he ran from the scene, Magnus's fists balled in frustration. After so much effort, so much time, to lose guns in such a manner was a bitter blow.

The booms rang out from Morgramgar again. The grape fell shorter. They were going for the artillery lines. There were fresh explosions as the shells of the cannons, still hot and steaming from their bombardment, were blasted apart. The acrid stench of burned metal and blackpowder wafted from the ridge, mixed with the sickening aroma of roasted flesh. Not all the crew had got away.

The army continued to withdraw. All across the plain, the bodies of the slow and the unlucky were strewn, twitching weakly or torn apart. Gradually, the range of the defenders' guns was exceeded. Even the flagellants were forced to flee from the scourging grapeshot, screaming curses incoherently as they staggered from danger.

More booms rang out from Morgramgar. The echoing blasts were like nothing Magnus had come across before. Even seasoned warriors cowered under the resounding report. The waves of noise rebounded staggeringly from the valley walls around them.

Magnus stopped running. Like the bulk of the men around him, he knew he was now clear of the enemy guns. He turned, watching the grim evidence of the botched deployment. The abandoned artillery pieces were being turned into worthless shards. As the defenders' cannons found their range, every last item was pounded into the hard ground. The approach to the citadel was turned into a pitted morass of blood and churned earth.

It seemed to go on forever. Even once the army had been driven away, the bombardment continued, ramming home the message of their inadequacy and futility. The surviving troops looked on, horror-struck. Any satisfaction in their minor successes had been entirely erased. The scale of the task now became horribly apparent.

Magnus limped across the ranks of disheartened men to Scharnhorst's retinue. The expressions of the captains were grim. Kossof had been silenced by the thunder of Morgramgar's arsenal. Kruger's face was pale.

Scharnhorst saw Ironblood approach, but said nothing in greeting. He looked shaken by what he had seen. Magnus waited for him to speak. He felt little emotion. Vindication had arrived, but at a terrible price.

'How many pieces did we lose?' Scharnhorst said at last. His voice shook, and this time not from anger.

Magnus took a deep breath.

'By my reckoning, half the big guns,' he said. 'Those we salvaged don't have enough range to hit the walls without being blasted apart. If you want to break this citadel, general, we're going to have to think of something else.'

Scharnhorst pursed his lips, and his gaze passed back to Morgramgar. The guns had fallen silent at last. The fortress returned to its air of horrifying stillness. Smoke idly drifted across the pockmarked battlefield. The moans of the wounded and dying rose weakly into the air. None ventured forth to try and retrieve them. For the time being, the battle was over.

CHAPTER TEN

'Gah! The umgi have never understood warfare. They think the whole world is flat. Their minds work in two dimensions. If they had ever defended holds from grobi and thaggoraki, they would know that battle may be joined from above and below. I do not ever expect them to master mechanical flight, for their minds are weak and limited. But I cannot understand their aversion to tunnelling. Perhaps they are afraid. Yes, that must be the explanation.'

Hadrin Yellowbeard
Ironbreaker Champion,
Karak Azgal

The sun set. Scharnhorst withdrew the army back down the valley, and a guard was set on the approaches to Morgramgar. Sealing the citadel was easy. There was only one way in and one way out. For as long as the besiegers stayed out of range of the monstrous guns, they were masters of the land around the fortress. Mindful of the possibility of a sortie, Scharnhorst trained his remaining cannons on the land immediately before the gates. Companies of halberdiers and handgunners were rotated regularly, keeping a close watch on the eerily quiet walls.

Quiet they were, but not silent. As the evening darkened into night, men became aware of the low hum emanating from the dark towers. Some even felt the earth drumming under their feet. The series of throbbing vibrations was not always audible. It ebbed and flowed. But when the muffled rhythm made itself known, a sense of dread filtered across the entire army. The noise was unnatural, like massive wheels turning endlessly down in the roots of the mountains. Combined with the strange, glowing lights high in the topmost pinnacle, it was enough to make the hardest hearts quaver. Some openly questioned whether Morgramgar was inhabited by humans at all, or whether some other nightmarish force had taken roost in its angular towers. Few of the soldiers planned to sleep much during the night, whatever their superiors instructed them to do.

Once the wreckage of the initial bombardment had been cleared away, Scharnhorst called a fresh council of war. By the light of huge bonfires, the captains of the army gathered together. The mood was grim. They had been given a lesson in the power of the cannon. Hundreds had been killed by the whirling grapeshot. Several battalions had lost nearly all their men. The flagellants had been decimated. The largest guns had been destroyed. What was left was clearly incapable of breaching the walls.

All sat around the fire outside Scharnhorst's tent with slumped shoulders, speaking little. Tensions between the various factions within the army had subsided. Now that the scale of the task before them had been made clear, the mood for infighting had dissolved.

Eventually, Scharnhorst himself arrived. He had been touring the defences on the perimeter of the camp. Despite the long, grim day, he looked as vigorous as ever. Unlike some of his commanders, his bearing remained proud and upright. He still wore his ceremonial dress, and the iron symbol of the Grand Army was displayed prominently on his breast. All could see that he was angry, though the rage was buried deep. When he spoke, his voice was as controlled as ever.

'So,' he said at last. 'We have come through peril and extremity to this. The enemy is content to remain in the citadel. We do not have the guns to trouble him. Is there any way around this?'

Kruger spoke first, as always.

'We don't have the means to break the walls,' he said, simply. 'Our only option is to starve them out. We do have the numbers to ensure than none within can escape.'

Scharnhorst shook his head.

'Did you not listen to Grotius's assessment?' he said. 'Morgramgar has its own sources of water which we cannot interfere with. They have stores for months. How will we keep ourselves supplied? It would be ruinously expensive.'

Kruger looked a little stung.

'We have to show them we're committed to the long haul,' he said. 'A siege will be drawn-out and difficult. But the count has resources. He must raise more money, send more supplies.'

Scharnhorst let slip a thin smile.

'You do not know the count as I do,' he said, 'nor the state of the

Hochland gold reserves. We're on our own, at least for now. If all else fails, I will send to Hergig for aid. But don't expect to hear anything more than expressions of regret.'

Kruger stood down, unsatisfied. The warrior priest Kossof spoke next.

'Can we not assault the walls directly?' he said. 'There would be losses, of course. Those unholy guns have already slain many of my men. But the bulk of our infantry is still intact. A sustained charge against the gates would surely force them in. And once we're inside, we can bring our superior numbers to bear at last.'

One of the captains of the halberdiers, a tall, blond man named Dieter Halsbad, shook his head scornfully.

'Haven't you seen those gates?' he said. 'We'd need a heavy ram to break them down. All the time, we'd be under attack from those cannons.'

Kossof snarled at him.

'Of course I've seen them!' he snapped. 'But those cannons are high on the walls. Once we're under their range, we'll have a free hand.'

Kruger shook his head.

'I don't think so,' he said. 'We don't have siege engines. Those walls are too high for grapnels, and they look stronger than many I've seen. If the order's given, then I'll ride with you all the way. But it would be a bloodbath. We aren't equipped to storm that place without a breach from the guns.'

Kossof scowled, thought for a minute, then withdrew, glaring at Iron-blood and the engineers. Magnus, who was tired after another long day restoring the surviving guns back to working order, felt his temper rise.

'Don't blame the engineers,' he said, hotly. 'We work with the materials we're given. There are no cannons in all of Hochland capable of matching theirs. Sigmar alone knows how they've come by such machines. If you want more siege engines, then look for them yourself. I'll wager there's nothing between here and Talabheim to match their defences.'

Scharnhorst raised his hand impatiently.

'Enough,' he snapped. 'Arguing will get us nowhere. We have what we have. And I do not intend to go back to Hergig while Morgramgar remains intact. If any of you have any better ideas, now is the time to speak.'

Halsbad spoke up again.

'If we can't assault them directly, nor bring down the walls with cannonfire, can we not get at them from below? What are our engineers for, if they can't undermine the foundations? There are more ways than one to topple a rampart.'

All eyes turned to Magnus.

'You're asking more than you know,' he said. 'That place is built on solid stone. There's not a patch of honest earth in this whole valley. It's all damned granite. But if a weak point could be found, then maybe we could do something. I don't have answers for you now, but I can study the possibilities with my men.'

Scharnhorst looked at him slightly less coldly than usual. Though he would be the last to admit it, the general was no doubt aware that his judgement over the placing of the great cannons had been faulty. Magnus's stock had not exactly risen, but that of his main rival had fallen, leaving them more or less where they had been at the beginning of all this.

'Very well,' said Scharnhorst, curtly. 'We'll adjourn to let the engineers do some work. We'll convene again at dawn. Whatever answers we have then, we'll need to make a decision. I'll not waste my men away on this Sigmar-bereft plain while the margravine mocks us from the comfort of her perfumed boudoir.'

He turned on his heel, and stalked back to his tent. Slowly, and without speaking, the commanders rose and returned to their companies. For once, Kossof had little to say. He seemed to have been taken aback by the slaughter of his followers. The flagellants had been the slowest to pull back, and had suffered terrible losses. The crack of the whip had been savage in penitence since.

As Magnus walked back to the gunnery companies, Hildebrandt came alongside him. His hands were black from working on the guns.

'What did Scharnhorst have to say?' asked the big man, bristling with curiosity.

Magnus shrugged.

'Not much,' he said. 'The man has no ideas. Those Morgramgar guns have surprised everyone. Including me. They're monsters.'

Hildebrandt looked like he was angling for something.

'And have you come up with anything yourself?'

Magnus shook his head.

'Not yet,' he said. 'I played for time. There are some tricks I can remember from the old days. We might be able to do something with the Helstorms. Or a tunnel. I need to think about it.'

Hildebrandt lost his patience.

'You know what I mean, Magnus,' he said. 'The Blutschreiben. You can't keep it hidden any longer. It was designed for a situation like this.'

Magnus looked at Tobias in frank amazement.

'I told you it wasn't to be used,' he said. 'Do you know nothing of me at all? I haven't kept it hidden out of spite. It doesn't work! Let that be an end to it!'

Hildebrandt let out a frustrated breath.

'Then why have you still kept the components, stashed away in those crates of yours? It could be reconstructed in a day. With the barrels of the guns we have left, we have something that would make those great cannons look like ladies' pistols.'

Magnus turned on Hildebrandt, his gaze low and threatening.

'Enough,' he said, his voice flat. 'It will not be used. I won't debate with you. We'll have to find some other way to solve this puzzle.'

Magnus didn't wait for a reply, and stalked off into the darkness. After letting a long, weary sigh escape his lips, Hildebrandt did likewise. His huge shoulders were slumped in resignation.

Only after they were gone did two more figures creep from the shadows.

'Sounds interesting, wouldn't you say?' said Messina coolly.

Herschel gave him a warning look.

'I think we've done enough,' he said, his voice full of worry. 'We're just making things worse.'

Messina glared at him.

'You're in this already, Lukas,' he said, his voice harsh. 'Come with me. I've an idea what they're talking about.'

The Tilean strode confidently off towards the baggage train. Only later, and reluctantly, did Herschel follow him, looking over his shoulder as he went.

When Magnus returned to his place in the camp, a fire had already been lit. Sitting next to it was Thorgad. He was smoking again, and rings of vapour were floating gently into the night air.

'Where've you been?' growled Magnus. The dwarf had been missing for some time. His help would have been invaluable when reconstructing the damaged artillery pieces.

'You haven't done well, Ironblood,' said Thorgad bluntly. 'I've not seen a campaign run this badly since my youth. And that was many lives of men ago.'

Magnus scowled. He was in no mood to indulge the dwarf's insufferable arrogance. Despite Thorgad's eagerness to join the company, he had done little enough to justify his place. He was becoming a liability, just like that snake Messina and his lapdog.

'Watch your tongue,' Magnus said sullenly. 'This is not a good time.'

Thorgad snorted. It might have been a laugh. Or perhaps just an expression of contempt.

'There hasn't been a good time since we left Hergig,' he said, his eyes twinkling with malice. He hefted his axe lightly in his left hand. In the firelight, the keen edge sparkled. 'This is Glamrist. As old as that citadel over there. I brought her with me to cleave heads. She's thirsty, but there's no blood to drink. I'm beginning to wonder why I bothered.'

Magnus knew he was being goaded. He was almost too tired to care.

'Then go back,' he muttered. 'You seem to know your way around here.'

'Maybe I will,' Thorgad said. 'But that would be a shame. Because then you'd never find your way into Morgramgar. Which is what I'm here to show you.'

For a moment, Magnus felt his heart leap. So the dwarf knew the way in. But then scepticism rushed back in. If this was some kind of sick joke, then the stunted bastard would feel the force of his bunched fist, and damn the consequences.

'All right,' he said, warily. 'You've got my attention. Now I suppose you're going to tell me the solution's obvious, and only a thick-headed umgi could have missed it.'

Thorgad placed Glamrist down beside him, and beckoned Magnus to come closer.

'You remember that I told you Morgramgar was old,' he said. 'I doubt the humans in there have any idea how old. These mountains have seen many inhabitants come and go, and few remember them all. There are strange places under the earth here. Rock halls, glittering with amethyst. Mighty caves worn by the ever-grinding of unseen rivers. All of them overlooked by your folk. You've never been much interested in what's beneath your noses, always chasing after the next flashy thing on the surface. Just like the elgi, curse them.'

Magnus had to work to conceal his impatience. Like most dwarfs, once Thorgad got going with a story he was hard to rein in.

'The point of this, as you'll have grasped if you had any wit about you, is that if you can't get into a place by going over ground, then you'll have to consider going under it. It's that simple.'

Magnus felt his earlier excitement ebb. The dwarf was proposing nothing he didn't know about. But delving into the solid rock around Morgramgar would take a legion of men, and equipment they didn't have. He felt sarcastic and disappointed.

'So what do you suggest?' he said. 'Start digging from here? We should emerge under the citadel in, say, a few months. Perfect. I can already see the look on Scharnhorst's face when I tell him this.'

Thorgad didn't reply for a few moments. He looked like he was weighing up whether it was worth going on. His face was openly scornful.

'There are times when I can't guess what other men see in you, Ironblood,' he said at last, his voice dripping with irritation. 'Your men have made you look a fool, and you're no closer to finding a way to break the citadel open. If I were you, I'd listen to good advice. I'd say you need as much of it as you can get.'

Magnus felt his temper bubble up within him. Days of setbacks and humiliation had taken their toll. He was near the end of his strength. He could see himself reaching out to knock the smug stunted one from his complacent perch. He hadn't been in a fight since Hergig. Perhaps it would do him some good.

Thorgad must have noticed the murderous look in his eyes. Maybe for the first time in his life, he backed down. Clearly, there were more important things at stake than pride. And, for a dwarf, that said a lot.

'Enough of this,' Thorgad said, shaking his head. 'While we bicker here, time is being wasted.'

He leaned forward, his face now deadly serious.

'You took me on this campaign with nothing but my word,' Thorgad said. 'Never let it be said that a dwarf doesn't know how to repay his debts. Come with me. I'll show you a way to the heart of the citadel.'

Magnus was about to pull back, but something in the dwarf's eyes held his attention. Thorgad was in deadly earnest.

'How do you know this?' said Magnus warily.

'You don't need to know,' replied Thorgad. 'But you're in need of something. I'll take up less than an hour of your time. Can you afford to pass the chance by?'

Magnus thought for a few moments. His body ached. His mind was sluggish with fatigue. A large part of him wanted nothing more than to roll himself up in a blanket and fall into a deep sleep. Thorgad could have been talking rubbish. But, once again, the dwarf's eyes held him. They were deep, set under protruding eyebrows, and caught the glint from the firelight. Thorgad's gaze didn't waver.

'Very well,' said Magnus, half-cursing himself. 'Show me what you're talking about. But it had better be worth seeing.'

Thorgad nodded, and got up laboriously.

'You'll need to come with me now. There's some walking to do. Take a weapon.'

The two of them walked across the camp swiftly. Around them, men were settling down for the night as best they could. It was still bitterly cold, and the harsh terrain offered no respite from the chill. The bonfires burned all across the plain. Above them, in the distance, the unearthly illumination from Morgramgar stained the crisp night air. The towers were black against the black of the night, punctuated only by the shining windows. At the very summit of the central tower, the glowing lime-green glass leered out across the plain like a collection of deathly eyes.

'You're not taking us anywhere close to that, are you?' said Magnus. He was no coward, but the citadel had an unclean, unnatural aspect. Under his feet, he could still detect the constant hum of something working.

Thorgad smiled grimly.

'Close,' he said. 'But not so close that we'll be seen. You asked me where I'd been. Scouting. I need to show you what I've found.'

They crept towards the edge of the camp. When they reached the perimeter, the watch challenged them. Ironblood's face was recognised, as was the dwarf's. They were waved through, though they were watched long after they had passed from the glow of the massed fires and into the dark of the night.

It took Magnus's eyes a moment to adjust to the darkness around them. The stars were out, but the sickle moon threw little light across the barren landscape. Thorgad went surely and swiftly, but Magnus found himself tripping over every rock on his path.

'Slow down!' he hissed, as the dwarf threatened to leave him far behind.

Thorgad waited for him to catch up, drumming his fingers against Glamrist with impatience.

'How long do you want to be out here?' he said, irritably. 'You've longer legs than me. Use them!'

They carried on walking, Thorgad leading, Ironblood traipsing along behind. From the camp edge, they struck out east towards the nearest valley wall. When they reached it, they turned left and followed the sheer rising cliff for some distance. Morgramgar was ahead of them and to their left, its lights shimmering in the deep dark of the cliff base. They were edging closer, creeping along the extreme right hand of the valley floor. In the dark, the going was slow, but soon the far end of the valley was nearing, and the citadel loomed massively to their left.

'Won't they have watchers on the walls?' said Magnus, looking up in fear. The fortress ramparts were altogether too close.

'They'll struggle to see anything down here,' said Thorgad, looking unconcerned. 'We're just two black specks against the black rock. They'd have to have the eyes of a daemon to see us.'

Magnus found himself wishing Thorgad hadn't used that word. There was something strangely daemonic about Morgramgar. He looked over his shoulder. In the distance, the lights of the camp twinkled. With any luck, any watchers in the citadel would have trained their eyes on that.

'Where are you taking me?' he whispered, feeling altogether too exposed. The unnatural throbbing was stronger the nearer they came to Morgramgar. The mountains themselves seemed to be alive with a faint, repetitive movement.

'We're almost there,' said Thorgad, curtly. 'Stop asking questions, and hurry up.'

They crawled on, heads low, hugging the shadows of the steep rise to their right. The further they went, the closer they came to the mighty cliffs at the very end of the gorge. The spires of Morgramgar were now visible in some detail, their edges sharp against the starlit sky. The citadel gave off an aura of palpable dread. Magnus found his eyes repeatedly drawn to it. He was both repelled and strangely attracted to the cluster of green windows at the summit. In his weariness, it was easy to imagine that the structure was some massive, primordial beast, hunched up against the mountain and staring balefully out at the valley beyond.

Magnus blinked, trying to retain his concentration. He was losing his grip.

Finally, thankfully, Thorgad halted. They were several hundred yards from the right-hand flank of the citadel, wreathed in darkness and hard under the lee of the valley wall.

'Here it is,' said Thorgad.

He was pointing to a deep cleft in the stone to their right. It was hidden on either side by massive outcrops of granite. Perhaps only a dwarf would have noticed it. To the casual eye, it looked just like a thin shadow against the endless screen of stone. But, as he came closer, Magnus could see that the cleft headed swiftly downwards. Just beyond the lip of the entrance, the space rapidly expanded.

Thorgad crept up to the narrow chasm, and stepped inside. There was a spark, and the dwarf held a small lantern above his head.

'You'll need this,' he said, beckoning to Magnus.

Ironblood followed Thorgad into the opening, squeezing through the tight gap and grazing his shoulders against the rough edges. The light of Thorgad's lantern bounced and reflected off a dazzling wall of smooth, dark chinks. The chamber was little higher than a man, and not much wider either, but it ran off into the distance ahead. As far as Magnus could make out, it went steeply down, before veering suddenly left. Beyond that, Thorgad's light didn't penetrate.

'I followed the fissure for some distance,' said Thorgad. 'It runs deep into the mountain root. Further along, there is a vaulted cave. You could house a dozen men there in comfort. The air is pure, and the earth solid. It can't be more than five hundred Imperial yards from there to the foundations of the citadel.'

Magnus looked around him, suddenly seeing the possibilities.

'This rock is like iron,' he said, doubtfully. 'We don't have a team of miners with us. As for me, it's been years since I oversaw anything like this.'

Thorgad snorted derisively.

'What do you need umgi miners for?' he scoffed. 'You have me. And if you have blackpowder for blasting, and axes and hammers for gouging, then you'd be able to delve this stuff. It's not as hard as the bedrock under a karak, not even close. We would set our young ones on such stone to test their arms.'

For the first time that evening, Magnus's mood had improved sufficiently to appreciate the dwarf's boast. A team of men, working in shifts, could carve a tunnel under the foundations of the citadel. It would be hard work, but he'd seen such things done in sieges before. The fact that the cleft existed made it possible. They could work in secret, and far underground. If done right, the defenders would know nothing of it.

'I take back my earlier words, dwarf,' said Magnus. 'Once a tunnel runs beneath the foundations, everything changes. We have charges for detonation. Or perhaps a way could be made for a raid. In either case, we'll be safe from those guns.'

Thorgad frowned.

'Don't get carried away,' he said. 'This is difficult and dangerous work, particularly for you. You won't seize the citadel this way.'

Magnus nodded, his spirits undiminished.

'I know,' he said. 'But it's a start.'

He turned to face the dwarf, the first genuine smile on his face since the discovery of the stricken army in the vale below. At last, there was something for him to begin proper work on. Messina would be kept away from this. He would need a few dozen men, no more. And Scharnhorst would have to hold it secret from the others. It could be done. It just needed planning.

'That's all I need,' said Magnus, his voice quickening with excitement, considering the possibilities. 'A start. My friend, I believe our luck has changed at last.'

CHAPTER ELEVEN

The earth was riven by torment. Deep under the mountain, mighty machines toiled. The rock chamber was lit by dozens of braziers, and blood-red light swam across the stone. The space was vast, supported by massive columns. Flames burned in sunken channels scored across the floor. Booming, repetitive drum-rolls echoed through the cavernous emptiness. The voices of men rose in labour. There were hundreds of them, black shapes against the firelight, hammering at anvils, or tending the huge mechanical devices around them.

Every so often, plumes of steam would spurt from some hidden pipe or valve. Pistons revolved slowly in brass sheaths. Metal was beaten against metal. Sparks skittered across the smooth floor. Furnaces roared insatiably, fed by lines of labourers bent double under their loads of wood. The heat was intense, the stench of burning heavy.

Far under the surface of the earth, down in the very bowels of Morgramgar, Anna-Louisa's forces were being armed. Wickedly curved spear-tips cascaded into waiting baskets and were dragged off into the armouries. Swords were drawn from the forges, still shimmering with heat, and plunged into water before being taken to the grinding stones. Iron crossbow bolts were sharpened and hardened, then added to the forest of shafts already fashioned. Deeper within the windowless chamber, more esoteric creations were being crafted. Strange pieces of metalwork were lovingly chipped and polished, then sent down along the lines of workers to be assembled into machines of war. Men pored over gun barrels, trigger mechanisms, blackpowder assemblies and all the other paraphernalia of the gunsmith's art. Master gunners walked up and down the rows of craftsmen, picking up components and staring at them through round eyeglasses. The slightest flaw was noticed, and the piece rejected. Under their exacting tyranny, the surviving pieces were flawless.

Further down into the mountain heart, right down in the very base of the castle's foundations, the armouries were full to overflowing. Anna-Louisa had more arms than she had men to bear them. Such was her policy. When the spring came, and the promise of endless gold spread across the impoverished Empire, then they would come. Mercenaries, state troopers, princes. All would flock to her banner, eager to use the tools of death her funds had created. Secure within the cold walls of her impregnable citadel, with every passing hour her store of deadly artistry grew. Soon there wouldn't be room for all of them, even in her near-boundless storerooms.

Rathmor looked over the scene with satisfaction. He stood on a narrow platform high up in the wall of the chamber. The balcony jutted less than four feet into the smoke-stained air, and an angular rail of iron ran around it. From the vantage point, he could see the rows of men work, the hammers rising and falling in rhythm. The sight enthralled him. At last, after so many years, he had a workshop worthy of his talents. Even Nuln, the centre of the Empire's industrial might, had nothing to compare to this. Nowhere in the lands of men were such weapons created. It was the start of a bright new dawn.

Perhaps this is how it had been in the glory days of the dwarfs, he thought. Maybe the old karaks had echoed to the synchronised pounding of metal and the roar of fire once. No longer. They were half-empty now, and the oldest forges were cold. Only Rathmor, possessed of long-forgotten knowledge and a mind capable of using it, had grasped what needed to happen. The long years of ridicule were drawing to a close.

'Magnificent,' he breathed, his eyes sweeping across the nightmarish vista. 'Perfection. Excellence. Unmatchable.'

His thoughts were interrupted. From behind him, Rathmor heard the clatter of armoured feet. There was a narrow corridor leading up to the balcony, carved into the raw stone. It was filled with figures. One shadow was intimately familiar to him. Rathmor's heart sank. Esselman had come to monitor progress.

The warrior strode onto the balcony. He looked over the scene with distaste. His retinue stayed back respectfully. Rathmor nodded briefly in greeting. Esselman barely acknowledged his presence.

'You have turned this whole level into a smithy,' he said, coldly. His ivory hair was tinged with red from the fire.

Rathmor sneered.

'I was told to build you an army,' he said. 'You need tools. I merely provide.'

Esselman didn't look convinced. Something about the mighty contraptions of bronze and iron clearly appalled him. In the perpetual gloom, they hissed and pounded like unbound creatures from a nightmare.

'Where are the infernal engines?' he said, peering into the fiery murk below.

'Only one is ready,' said Rathmor. 'It will be many weeks before another can be completed. This is delicate work. We are on the frontiers of knowledge. I can't rush it.'

Esselman snorted.

'We may need them sooner than you think,' he said. 'Have you seen the size of Ludenhof's army? They're biding their time. We should have attacked them in the passes. Now they're encamped before us. We're hemmed in. I don't like it.'

Rathmor laughed, a scraping sound that was swiftly lost amid the pounding below.

'Why so scared?' he said, mockingly. 'It's not like you. There's nothing they can do to us in here. Their pathetic Tilean fire has been doused. It would never have kindled on this stone. Half their cannons have been smashed. The rest are barely capable of denting these walls, let alone break them. Let them starve in the open! After a few weeks of this, the machines will be ready. If they thought our earlier show was pretty, they'll love the encore.'

Esselman's severe face remained impassive.

'Perhaps you're right,' he said, in a tone that gave away his doubt. 'But it's a craven strategy. I'd rather strike now than later. It's been too long since I had a sword in my hand and some natural air in my lungs. Your filth poisons me.'

Rathmor smirked.

'Then petition the lady to let you go outside. I'd love to hear what she'd have to say.'

Esselman couldn't suppress a momentary shudder.

'Your case has been made now,' he said, turning away from the furnaces. 'We'll stay cooped up in here until our leashes have been removed. I'll not try to convince her again.'

Rathmor smiled.

'I'm glad you've seen reason,' he said.

Esselman gave him a dark look.

'I hope you're right about this, Rathmor. This is a fearful risk. Your contraptions are powerful, I'll give you that. But what we're doing hasn't been attempted for a generation. When the rebellion spreads from Hochland, there are mightier powers than Ludenhof to worry about.'

'So there are,' said Rathmor. 'But it can be done. Remember Marienburg. Where is your faith?'

As he spoke, the hammers rained down, the sparks flew. The flames leapt high against the chiselled rock face, and the giant cog wheels turned slowly in the darkness.

'If I had any faith, I wouldn't be doing this,' muttered Esselman. 'And that's what worries me.'

As he turned to face Rathmor again, Esselman towered over the hunched engineer.

'But, to give you your due, you've created all manner of toys down here,' he said. 'I know how deadly they are. And that's why I've come down. I want you to use them to make this place safe. Forget churning out more spikes for the lady. We need to make sure the citadel is secure.'

Rathmor's petulant expression returned.

'What do you mean?' he said. 'What more protection do you want? The walls are twelve feet thick.'

'I've conducted a siege before,' Esselman said. 'A castle is never as strong as your pride makes it. There are always weak links. You've boasted that your weapons are like nothing used before. Prove it to me. Lace this place with them. String your damned firecrackers from every archway in the citadel.'

He leaned over towards Rathmor, and the light of the fires below caught in his eyes.

'If they get in here, I don't want any of them to get out,' he hissed. 'Make this place into the father of all deathtraps. If those walls are breached, I want to hear them burn as they enter.'

A slow smile grew across Rathmor's lips.

'Traps?' he said, and his tongue briefly flickered with relish. 'I see what you mean. Well, a little extra security wouldn't hurt. And it would be a pleasant intellectual diversion.'

Esselman made to withdraw. It looked like he was keen to leave the foundry.

'Diversion or not, you'll do it,' he said. 'Just don't take too long about it. They'll come at us soon. I can feel it in my blood. I've seen the way you use fire. Start on the main tower, and work out. Everything needs to be covered. It may not come to it, but if it does, their flesh will be the fuel. We can't allow them to get this far in. There are secrets in the tower that would damn us all.'

Rathmor bowed his head. When his face rose again, it had a hungry look.

'I'll get right to it, general,' he said. 'It will be a pleasure. A genuine pleasure.'

Magnus squeezed himself down into the tunnel once more. He didn't like working underground. The spaces were too confined. Whenever he descended into Thorgad's workings, he couldn't forget the layers of stone pressing heavily down on the roof above. It wasn't natural. Not for a man.

Ironblood had never been one for earthworks. Many of his colleagues in Nuln had loved them. Those who had completed their training without being crushed or suffocated had found long and profitable service with the armies of electors, for siegecraft was highly valued. But for Magnus, the joy of his profession was the blackpowder lore. That was where the childish excitement of the engineer really lay. He could still remember seeing the first demonstration given to him by his father, more than thirty years ago. Back then he could only watch, wide-eyed, his child's face lit with the sparking of the unnatural candles Augustus Ironblood had placed all around the floor of the forge. Only later had he been allowed to take the work on himself, to experiment with fuses, explosive charges and burn-times. That was where the magic was, in the unpredictable, capricious nature of the augmented fire, the plaything and the servant of the gunnery schools. And the danger too, of course.

Magnus pushed forward, past the narrow entrance and into the wider tunnel carved by Thorgad and his team of sappers. The work had been done brilliantly. Under cover of night, men had sneaked materials into the narrow cleft hard against the shadow of the valley wall. They had moved in small groups, taking as little with them as they could each time. All the tools, the gouges, axes and hammers, were kept underground. No wooden frame supported the fragile ceiling of the tunnel. Thorgad had insisted on this. It would be too easy for the enemy to spot large groups of men carrying heavy planks and beams into the rock opening, even at night. Instead, the dwarf had used his race's long knowledge of the bones of the mountains to direct the delving. The tunnel snaked through veins of solid, hard-wearing rock. The process made excavation dangerous and exhausting, but reduced the risk of collapse. Pillars were left standing at regular intervals, shaped into cunning forms by Thorgad himself. These columns carried the weight of the whole earth above. Every time Magnus brushed past them, he made the sign of the comet against his breast.

From the natural opening in the valley's side, the carved corridor ran steadily down into the heart of the mountain root. It didn't take a straight path, but ran unevenly through the most suitable rock. The gaps were just tall enough for a man to walk along, his body bent double. Thorgad stomped up and down the tunnel unhindered, but Magnus had to stoop low, his fingers inches above the floor.

After several days of unforgiving labour, the underground path now reached far under the valley floor, and drew near to the foundations of the citadel at its head. The men worked long through the night, relying on the ever-present hum of the fell machines in the bowels of Morgramgar to drown the noise of their hacking and chipping. Even in the face of solid rock, they used little blasting powder. On the few occasions when the only option was to crack open the rock ahead with a charge, Magnus had arranged for Scharnhorst to launch a volley of fire from the remaining iron-belchers. It was a crude tactic, for the cannons they had left were barely capable of hitting the walls at their current range. For the time being at least, though, it seemed to have worked. There was no sign that any of the defenders knew anything of the tunnelling going on beneath their feet. In fact, there was still no sign of any defenders at all. The citadel remained as chill and impassive as ever.

Magnus pushed himself into an even smaller gap, and felt his breathing grow more rapid. There were torches fixed to the walls of the tunnel. By some art of Thorgad's they burned brightly and with little smoke. But there was no escaping the cloying, deadening impression of being buried far beneath the earth. The air was hot and close. As Magnus neared the head of the workings, he could hear the men cursing. The smell of sweat was heavy. Iron clanged against rock, and the gloom was lit by sparks as well as fire.

'How goes it?' said Magnus, panting heavily and pressing his hands against his thighs. His palms were moist, and his linen shirt clung to him under the leather of his coat.

The dwarf turned from the rock face, and smiled. Thorgad was happiest underground. His mood was rarely as good in the sunlight.

'It goes well!' he growled, his eyes glittering with satisfaction. 'We're nearly through. Now all you have to do is work out what to do when we're in.'

Magnus sank back against the wall, letting his breathing ebb to normal. The tunnel was a hateful place.

'I showed your drawings to Scharnhorst,' he said. 'He's pleased. I think he might be starting to trust us again. That's good.'

Thorgad stomped over and leaned on Glamrist. The dwarf never used the axe to hew stone, but kept it by his side at all times. The ornate blade seemed to be some kind of talisman for him.

'So what did he say?' asked the dwarf.

'He wants the guns taken out,' said Magnus. 'The ones on the ramparts.

With them out of the way, he thinks he can unleash Kruger, Kossof and the others on the gates. I told him I thought we could do it. What do you think?'

Thorgad blew out loudly, his scarred cheeks puffing out.

'Grungni's beard, human,' he said, shaking his head. 'How do you propose we do that? I can get into the lower levels, but what are you going to do after that? Storm the place yourself?'

Magnus smiled grimly.

'Not on my own,' he said, dryly. 'We have some tricks up our sleeve. Messina's not the only one with gadgets.'

He reached into his clothes, and withdrew a small metal sphere, studded with rivets and wrapped in a leather strip.

'Know what this is?'

Thorgad eyed the device warily.

'I've seen similar,' he said, distrustfully. 'Some kind of blackpowder weapon?'

Magnus nodded.

'These are charges,' he said. 'My own design. Small enough to fit a dozen on a belt, but nasty enough to clear a room of men. Pull the strap clear, and the wick ignites with a flint. Take care to get far enough away before it goes off, though. They're devastating.'

Magnus grinned, and tossed the ball lightly in his palm.

'These are from my own stash,' he said. 'The last I salvaged. They have a few extra tweaks.'

Thorgad frowned.

'Then stop throwing it around like a fool,' he growled. 'What's your plan?'

Magnus put the sphere away carefully.

'Two dozen men. Six armed with these, the rest with pistols and knives. Any more than that, and we'll need a bigger breach. Come out into the level immediately under the main walls, and we'll fight our way to the guns. We'll lace the lot of them with these bombs, shoving them into the breeches, and then withdraw. By the time they know what's going on, they'll have a brace of exploding barrels to contend with. Then we'll be out of the tunnel and away.'

Magnus sat back, satisfied.

'Scharnhorst liked the idea,' he said. 'He's asked me to pick the men.'

Thorgad glowered.

'That's a damn fool plan, if ever I heard one,' he muttered. 'You've no idea what that place is like inside. For all you know, we'll break into a guardroom stuffed with soldiers. Then your precious bomb-toys will be little use.'

Magnus looked at the dwarf tolerantly. He hadn't expected effusive praise from Thorgad. That wasn't really his way.

'We have old plans of the fortress,' he said. 'Scharnhorst and I looked over them. And you claim to know this citadel too, though Sigmar only knows how. If you can bring us up under the left-hand side of the main gates, we'll come through into one of the store chambers. There won't be guards there. Who'd expect an attack from beneath them? The soldiers will be up on the walls, and in the tower garrisons, and manning the forges. If we move fast, we can hit them hard and get out again. From the store levels, a spiral stair takes us up to the main ramparts. We'll need a bit of luck from there, but those gun platforms are big. We should be able to see them as soon as we're in range.'

Thorgad gave Magnus a sidelong glance.

'Your optimism commends you,' he said. 'But that's if all goes well. You're just as likely to be killed as you emerge, like rabbits from a warren.'

Magnus wasn't in the mood to be deterred. With war, there was always risk.

'They won't know a thing about it,' he said, confidently. 'We'll go in and then get out. Just as they did to us in the mountains. But they've got nowhere to go. Once those guns are out of action, we'll see how cocky they are.'

Thorgad frowned.

'I'll keep digging,' he said. 'If that's really what you want, then I can get you under the gates by dawn tomorrow. I don't like your plan enough to let you go in there alone, though. When the rock's breached, I'll come in with you. Glamrist is aching to cut flesh, and I won't dull its edge on this rock.'

Magnus grinned.

'That's good to hear,' he said, his eyes glinting in the darkness. 'They'll not expect to hear Khazalid, and an extra pair of hands will be useful.'

He turned around clumsily, and made to shuffle back down the tunnel towards the cold night outside.

'Send word when you're nearing completion,' Magnus said. 'I'm heading back to the camp to train up the attack party. Those bombs need some experience to handle.'

Thorgad nodded.

'I'll let you know,' he said, casting a critical eye over the men hammering away at the rock face.

When Magnus had moved back up along the narrow way and was beyond earshot, the dwarf shook his shaggy head.

'Damned fool umgi planning,' he muttered, walking back over to the head of the mine. 'This grudge had better be worth it.'

And then he was at the raw edge of the rock again, directing the work, striding back and forth like a general. Slowly, achingly slowly, hidden in darkness and sheathed in solid granite, the tunnel snaked on towards its destination.

* * *

Messina placed the papers down on the table with a flourish. There were several sheets. Scharnhorst took his time to leaf through them. Silvio could sense Lukas's agitation from next to him, but paid it no attention. The boy was a sack of nerves.

They were alone with the general in his tent. From outside, Messina could hear the routine noise of the camp. Fires were being laid, weapons sharpened. Raucous cries and insults ran back and forth amongst the men. There was even the sound of an obscene song drifting across from the other side of the sprawling settlement. Messina, though he normally enjoyed such things, was glad that the words were impossible to make out. He doubted that Scharnhorst appreciated the finer points of the tavern singer's art.

Under the thick canvas sheets, the general's tent was as austere as his character. There was a thin roll of fabric laid on the ground against one edge, no doubt for sleeping on. A simple table next to it held a wooden bowl and a pitcher of water. There was a heavy ironbound chest in one corner, and a simple desk and chair. Messina had seen generals' accommodation before, and most often it was like being in a temporary palace, stuffed with flagons of claret and barrels of fine meats. Scharnhorst, whatever his faults may have been, wasn't one of those gluttons. He slept on the stony floor like the rest of his men. Messina wondered if he even took off his sword belt.

The general sat at the desk, while Messina and Lukas stood before it. Herschel's head scraped the fabric ceiling. Like so many Averlanders, he was too tall for his own good. Scharnhorst took his time, turning the fragile sheets of parchment carefully. Some of them were very old, and flaked away in his hands as he did so.

'I won't pretend I can read all of these plans,' he said, lifting his severe face from the drawings. 'It looks to me like some kind of many-barrelled cannon. With wheels. No doubt you're here to tell me more about it.'

Messina nodded.

'It is a weapon, sir,' he said, 'but not like the ones you've seen deployed. You have heard of the steam tank of da Miragliano? This is a lesser device, though it operates on similar principles. But, if constructed right, has properties all of its own. It has two barrels, linked together and capable of being swivelled and targeted with great accuracy. It needs crew of only one to operate, although there is room for more. The gunner sits in this chair – here – and directs the firing mechanism. Loading of charges is automatic, performed by this hydraulic mechanism. I will not go into all the details, but the system is quite ingenious. The ammunition is fed in here, and the circulatory system channels it straight to the breech. Jams are prevented by means of the steel…'

Scharnhorst held his hand up impatiently.

'I don't need to know how it works, man,' he snapped. 'Just tell me what it can do.'

Messina felt his cheeks go hot. He had to remember than not everyone found the details of gunnery as interesting as he did. Even a first-year engineering student could have grasped how revolutionary the machine on the drawings was. Scharnhorst, however, like most men, had little patience for such things.

'It is battlefield piece,' said Messina, checking his enthusiasm. 'It cannot bring those walls down by itself, but it can bring havoc against enemy troops. The Blutschreiben, as I call it, can fire into massed infantry once every minute. The rate of fire is only matched by its power. The barrels are capable of tearing plate armour as if it were matchwood. With its unique targeting quadrants, it will hit even distant objects square on. Once the proper battle is joined, this machine is the one piece of artillery capable of turning the sea in our favour. Trust me, general. Whatever weapons they have hidden away inside that fortress, it is as nothing compared to this.'

Scharnhorst rubbed his chin absently, looking at the plans with care.

'And you say you can have this assembled soon?' he said.

Messina nodded.

'Very soon,' he said. 'Many of the components are prepared. They just need putting together, basic assembly and linking to the barrels of our cannons. Herschel and I have already identified two of our iron-belchers which we can use to construct the Blutschreiben. It will mean losing them, of course. But when you see the difference this machine will make, I tell you, you will never regret it.'

Scharnhorst looked up from the desk. His piercing eyes fixed on Messina firmly.

'What does your officer, Ironblood, make of this?'

Messina felt his palms quicken with sweat. This was where the deception lay.

'He is in agreement with me,' Messina said, working hard to keep his voice nonchalant. 'He is now fully occupied with the dwarf Thorgad on plans for the siege, and so delegated this task to me. Herschel and myself are quite capable of constructing the device. Once you give order to advance, it will be ready.'

Scharnhorst maintained his steady gaze, and Messina felt a trickle of sweat run down the base of his spine. Lukas's face was white. It had been a mistake to bring him along. The boy would ruin everything.

Eventually, Scharnhorst sighed.

'Listen, I don't care what politics are still brewing between you,' he said. 'If you think I've any interest in trying to sort out feuds within the gunnery companies then you underestimate how busy I am.'

The general rolled the parchment up and handed it back to Messina.

'You have my leave to construct this,' he said. 'If what Ironblood tells me is true, you have at most two days before the citadel is stormed. Make the most of it. If you haven't finished by then, I'll need you to marshal the artillery with the others. Can you do that?'

Messina swallowed. That was hardly any time. There were still aspects of the mechanism he didn't understand. But it was still possible. Everything was possible.

'Of course, sir,' he said, taking the roll of parchment from Scharnhorst's hand. 'So I'll deliver you a weapon the likes of which even your Marshal Helborg wouldn't dream of.'

Scharnhorst didn't look pleased by that. As ever, his expression remained thunderous.

'Get on and do it, then,' he snapped. 'When the time comes, report to my aide-de-camp. You'd better be right about this. You've already failed once. Don't let me down again.'

Messina bowed, and withdrew from the tent. Like a scared child, Herschel followed him, tripping over his feet as he stepped through the canvas opening. They hurried away from the general's quarters.

'I still don't think this is wise!' the boy hissed as they walked. 'You've no idea how to make that thing work.'

Messina rounded on him, jabbing a finger against Lukas's chest.

'Stop your whining!' he growled, his eyes savage. 'You did agree to work with me on this thing. If we get it right, we will walk away from here heroes. The mortars will be forgotten. We will have made our titles. What are you so worried about?'

Lukas looked daunted, but he held his ground. The men lounging around them on the rocks took little notice of the discussion. Arguments broke out all the time across the camp, and were hardly worth remarking on.

'There must have been a reason Ironblood didn't want it used,' Lukas insisted. 'You heard what he said to Hildebrandt. If Scharnhorst tells him…'

Messina laughed scornfully.

'Why would he do that?' he said. 'You heard the man. The sick blood between me and that *ubriacone* is none of his business.'

Messina felt his temper boil, and had to work to quell it. He stopped, took a deep breath, and some of the irritation left his face. There was no use getting angry with Herschel. The lad was just naïve, and he'd be needed to help build the weapon.

'Scharnhorst's no one's fool,' said Messina, more calmly. 'He will be happy to see rivalry between his engineers as long as it doesn't harm his own position. He will not tell Ironblood. And as for the danger, you must learn to live with it. Ours is a dangerous trade, ragazzo. Always it has been. If you can't live with that, you would be better off doing something less arduous.'

Lukas looked only half-convinced. There was still indignation in his features.

'Come on, lad,' said Messina, adopting a more fatherly tone. 'This will be good exercise for you. We will together see if we can make sense of Ironblood's plans. If we can't, then we must stop work. What do you say?'

Lukas hesitated, his open face clearly torn. For a moment, his eyes flickered over towards the edge of the valley, where Ironblood toiled under the earth with Thorgad. Then they flicked back to the rolls of parchment. His mind was being made up.

'We'll give it a go,' he said at last, though with no great conviction. 'But if we can't make it safe, we should stop. This is my first battle. I don't want it to be my last.'

Messina felt a wave of relief pass through him. Most likely the Blutschreiben would be mortally dangerous. But from the drawings he could see it would also be murderously powerful. Some gambles were worth taking.

'Of course,' Silvio said, comfortingly, putting an arm around Lukas's shoulder and steering him back towards the artillery lines. 'We'll take it slowly, checking every stage as we go. But remember – we have to keep secret from the others. Ironblood and Thorgad will not be a problem for us, but we'll have to stop that big man Hildebrandt from nosing around. He's too loyal to be brought along. Can you do that?'

Lukas nodded.

'I guess so,' he said.

Together, the two men headed across the camp, through the rows of idle men and towards the artillery pieces clustered at the rear of the army lines. There, Ironblood's stock of chests lay hidden. Once they had contained the plans and parts for the Blutschreiben. Now they held only straw and stones, the locks having been expertly picked and resealed. The prior contents were now in Messina's possession, carefully unpacked and ready for assembly.

With a sudden lurch in his stomach, Messina felt his earlier anxiety transform into excitement. The tools were all there. They just had to be put together correctly. And then the stage would be set for the entrance of the most devastating machinery of death ever to grace the battlefields of the Old World. It would be his name, Silvio Pietro de Taglia Messina, not Ironblood's, etched in the roll of honour in Nuln.

Messina smiled inwardly at the prospect, and felt a glow of pleasure. War could be a dirty business. But at times, just now and then, it was a thing of exquisite beauty.

CHAPTER TWELVE

'It grieves my heart that the Church of Sigmar distrusts us so. While we remain divided, our enemies muster beyond the mountains, an everlasting tide of darkness that lusts for nothing more than our destruction. What more could we accomplish together! Perhaps the day will come. If the art of the engineer could be allied to the fervour of the noble warrior priesthood, I fervently believe that no force in all the Old World, not even the hordes of Chaos themselves, would be sufficient to stand against us.'

The Notebooks of Leonardo da Miragliano

The torches burned low. The atmosphere was close and stifling. Magnus, Thorgad and Hildebrandt stood with the other men of the raiding party just inside the entrance to the tunnel. There was barely room for all of them. Each could feel the breathing of the others. With the expectation of battle, all hearts beat a little faster.

Night had fallen once more, and Morgramgar was lit by its sinister green light. After driving the men hard for two further days, Thorgad had completed his excavation. Only a thin wall of rock now lay between the hidden workings and the foundations of the citadel beyond. Scharnhorst had given the order to conduct the raid, and now the infiltrators waited nervously, just inside the protective lip of the rock cleft, unwilling to go further. Down the tunnel, the lattice of charges lay.

'How long were those damned fuses?' hissed Magnus to Thorgad.

The dwarf scowled in the darkness.

'Long enough,' he snapped. 'Don't tell me my business.'

Down in the depths, at the rock face, kegs of blackpowder had been laid against the remaining rock, and metal spikes had been driven artfully into the stone. Once the kegs went off, the wall of the chamber would collapse. Sigmar willing, it would also blow a hole in the adjacent citadel foundations large enough for them to enter by. If not, then all their work would be undone and the surprise would be lost. As he waited, Magnus couldn't help letting his nerves get the better of him. He knew that once the fighting began he would be fine. It was the hanging around that did for him.

He clutched his torch tightly in his left hand, took a deep breath and tried to calm himself. For some reason, he found himself remembering standing outside the college in Nuln, nearly a lifetime ago. The day before his entrance examination. Was that the last time he'd been as scared? Of course not. He'd been in many battles since. Every one scared him. He was no Helborg. Perhaps that was why he'd been attracted to engineering. You didn't need to be a hero, although there was a kind of bravery to it. The kind that let a man stand next to a lit iron-belcher and hold his ground. Or ram the shot into a long gun when the wind was blowing the powder across the matchcord. Many a knight would have refused such odds. It was a unique profession, and not without honour. So his father had always told him, anyway. Before he'd died.

Wincing, Magnus brought his thoughts back into the present. At his belt, the rows of little blackpowder charges clustered. In his right hand, his naked sword blade glinted from the flames. All the other men were arrayed in a similar way. The plan was simple. Once a way had been blasted in, they would burst into the fortress, find their way as quickly as possible from the deeps up to the gun levels, lay the charges and withdraw. If they did it quickly enough, they might escape with no need for fighting at all. Magnus knew that was unlikely. Morgramgar may have seemed silent and empty from the outside, but the place was stuffed with Anna-Louisa's soldiers. They were bound to run into some of them, even if they were quick. It was a fearful risk. Better than freezing to death out in the open, but still a risk.

From far ahead, deep down in the tunnel, the noise of fizzing suddenly echoed back up. Something was happening.

'Hold your positions,' he said in a low voice, bracing himself against the rock wall.

Around him, men gripped their swords more tightly, or adjusted their torches, or checked the leather straps on their charges for the final time.

When it came, the explosions were strangely muffled. There was a great boom, and the ground shook underneath them. The rock seemed to buckle, and some of the men briefly staggered. Lines of rock particles cascaded from the roof, making the torches flicker and gutter. But

Thorgad's mining skills had been superb. The tunnel held.

From ahead of them, a wall of hot air and blackpowder-laced dust rushed upwards. More crashes could be heard rumbling deep within the earth. The dwarf's network of charges was going off, tearing down the remaining stone, blasting its way through the mountain like an animal. Only after several more detonations did the last of the crushing explosions die away. That was it. Now they had to trust to fate.

Magnus looked around his men one last time. In the flickering torchlight, their faces were tight with fear. But there was something else. Eagerness. The wait had been long. Now they needed to release their aggression.

'Remember your orders,' he said simply. He'd never been one for battlefield oration. 'Keep together. Sigmar be with you. Let's go.'

Magnus set off down the tunnel at a loping run, keeping his torch low against the ground and watching out for rubble in his way. The route was tight, and he had to stoop as he went. Behind him, he could hear Hildebrandt's heavy tread and the clatter of Thorgad's iron-shod feet.

They went down the winding corridor quickly, stopping only to squeeze past obstacles where necessary. The air was thick with dust and the stench of blackpowder. Magnus stifled a coughing fit as he went. There was no time to stop and cleanse his lungs. Everything depended on speed.

They arrived at the rock face. The air was hot. The final few yards of standing stone had been utterly destroyed. Thorgad's last chamber, lovingly hewn from the mountain bones, lay in ruins. Part of the ceiling had collapsed, blocking off a large area to their right. The torches had been blown out by the blasts, and the only light was from their own flaming brands. The air was thick with floating dust. It was hard to make anything out. For a terrible moment, Magnus thought that the blast had done nothing but close the end of the tunnel off for good.

Then, he saw it. High up on the left-hand side, there was a gash in the rock. A jagged slope of tortured and broken stone led upwards steeply. At its summit, the uneven surface of the mountain's innards gave way to the regular outline of walls. Thorgad had been right. The explosion had shattered the foundations of a storeroom right at the base of the citadel. The gap was narrow, but just wide enough for a man to slip through. They had their way in. The dwarf had been as good as his word.

'Follow me,' said Magnus, keeping his voice low. The enemy was sure to have been roused by the explosions, but there was no harm in keeping their presence hidden for as long as possible.

Magnus scrambled up the loose pile of rock. It was awkward work. He slipped several times, sending scree down behind him onto the heads of those following. Curses, and the sounds of men losing their footing, followed him up. Some of the rocks were still hot from the blasts, and Magnus felt the savage aftermath of Thorgad's fireworks even through the soles of his boots.

He crested the summit. The hole was dark, and there were no sounds from beyond. There was little time for caution. Magnus thrust his torch through the gap, and took a quick look. He'd emerged into a narrow room, walled with bare stone and piled high with crates of salted provisions. Some had burst open from the force of the blast, and there was a jagged crack in the wall on the far side of the chamber. Flagstones had been pushed upwards, and the footing looked treacherous. There was no sign of any resistance. The plans had been reliable. Either that, or they'd been very lucky.

Magnus pushed his way through the gap, and turned to haul Hildebrandt up. In a few moments, the raiding party had all squeezed into the chamber. From above, Magnus could hear footfalls. A bell was ringing far away, and its chimes resounded through the stone. The alarm had been raised. They only had moments.

'Come,' he said, and ran towards a doorway on the far side of the room. The door had been blown from its hinges and hung to one side. Magnus kicked it away, and burst into the corridor beyond.

There were torches still lit against the walls, and it became easier to see what was happening. The stone inside Morgramgar was dark and smooth, just like the exterior. Despite the noises from above, there was still no sign of any guards. For a moment, Magnus felt his nerve fail. This was too easy. Why weren't there any soldiers?

He pushed such thoughts to the back of his mind. The corridor led away in both directions. At the far end of the left branch, a narrow doorway led to a spiral stair. Just as the map had said it would. Magnus ran towards it, keeping his torch low and his sword raised. Once inside Morgramgar, the noise of the machinery was everywhere, making the walls vibrate with its constant presence. It was oppressive, and jarred his senses. No normal fortress should house such monsters.

The men came on behind him, keeping tightly together. Magnus reached the doorway, and plunged into the dark stairwell beyond. It was narrow and tight. He ran up the steps two at a time, hoping against hope he wouldn't meet a defender on the stairs.

A forlorn hope. He turned a corner, and ran straight into a soldier coming the other way. The endless grinding of the machines had hidden the sounds of his approach. For an instant, Magnus could see the staring eyes of the soldier, white in the darkness. The man fumbled for his sword. With a savage swipe, Magnus slashed across his neck, more by luck than judgement, spraying blood across the stairway. With a gurgled scream, the soldier collapsed, tumbling down at Magnus's feet, clutching at his pumping wound.

Magnus kicked him away with disgust. In the narrow space, he had to clamber over the still-hot body to keep going. Beyond him, the stair opened out into a larger room. He climbed up. Behind him, he could hear the rest of the men shoving the body of the guard unceremoniously down the spiral.

The room at the top of the stairs was large and better lit. The stone was black and as smooth as glass. It had a strange sheen to it. No wonder Messina's baubles had failed to kindle. There was nothing for them to latch on to.

Doorways led off in three directions. There was no sign of any more guards. Despite the rapid ascent, they were still down in the depths of the citadel.

'That one,' said Thorgad, pointing to one of the doors.

Magnus didn't wait to ask him how he knew. With the dwarf at his side, he ran towards the empty doorway. Hildebrandt and the others were hard on his heels. As they reached it, finally more guards emerged. One charged at Thorgad.

'Khazuk!' cried the dwarf, and hurled himself forward. Glamrist glittered as it was swung. Before he'd time to react, the soldier had his legs hewn from under him. He screamed horribly before Thorgad's second swing ended his agony. Magnus thrust his torch into the face of the other, briefly blinding him and sending him staggering back. The engineer stabbed his sword into the man's stomach. When he withdrew it, the blade was slick with blood. The guard slumped, his lips a red froth.

'There'll be more!' cried Magnus. 'Keep going!'

He and Thorgad raced through the doorway and up a second wide flight of stairs. These led to more corridors and more ascents. As they went, there was more sporadic resistance, but it was clear they'd surprised the enemy. The soldiers were disorganised, and came at them in twos and threes. They were all Hochland regular troops, just like the ones who'd attacked them in the mountains, and just as poorly prepared for a close fight.

After helping dispatch a scared-looking patrol of three more startled defenders, Magnus ran around a final corner and found himself in a long, wide gallery. They were making good progress. The company had climbed quickly, and was now well above ground level. There were windows high above them now, carved deep into the walls. From their narrow panes, starlight filtered down into the interior. Deep below, the machines continued to growl ominously.

'There,' said Thorgad, gesturing towards a narrow door. 'That's the way to the gunnery level.'

Magnus rushed over to the door. It was bolted. A heavy iron padlock hung from the latch. He shook the door on its hinges, but it remained fast.

'Stand back,' said Thorgad. Behind them, the rest of the raiding party clustered, looking over their shoulders nervously.

The dwarf swung Glamrist easily round his shoulders, building up momentum. He swung it hard against the bolt. With a flash of sparks, the metal severed cleanly. The door shivered, and swung open.

'Come on!' said Magnus, and plunged into the gap. He could feel his brand begin to flicker. They would not have light forever.

The band of men followed close behind. The door guarded another narrow winding stair, and soon their serried boots were thudding against the stone steps. As he sprinted up them at the head of the party, Magnus turned briefly to Thorgad.

'That's some blade,' he said, breathing heavily. 'Magic?'

Thorgad snorted a laugh.

'Not as you reckon it,' he said. 'Just sharp.'

The stair led out into a long, low chamber. It stretched off into the darkness, its far end hidden in shadow. More starlight filtered in from narrow windows. Magnus suddenly realised they were high on the south-facing walls, the ones that dominated the valley beyond. They'd come further up than he'd thought. They must be just below the level of those terrifying guns. There were no guards around, though the noise of commotion throughout the citadel was growing. They'd be discovered soon.

'Now where?' he said to Thorgad.

The dwarf grinned, and pointed upwards. Magnus followed the gesture, lifting his torch high. About six feet above their heads, massive gantries had been constructed. Mighty beams of steel-bound wood thrust themselves forward. Dimly, Magnus could see the dark barrels of guns laid over them. There were what looked like iron rails, wheels and chains looping below the huge mouths of the guns. Beyond the silent maws of cannons, there were hatches in the walls.

They were standing directly under the gunnery-level platforms.

'Majestic,' breathed Magnus, despite himself. The construction was awesome. To balance cannons that large over such a fragile-seeming mechanism was a truly marvellous feat. No doubt, when some signal was given, the doors in the walls would be opened and the huge weapons slid along the rails. Then the carnage would begin, just as it had done before.

'We don't need to climb up there,' said Hildebrandt, coming up alongside Thorgad. 'Destroy those rails, and the guns will come down sure enough. We can turn this chamber into a firestorm.'

Magnus drew a charge from his belt, and fingered the leather strap. A sudden, strange feeling had come over him. The artistry was too good. He could see the dull glint of hydraulic workings in the tangle of beams and ironwork above. It was a crime to demolish such finery. There were secrets here, secrets worth the lives of many men.

He hesitated. The bell continued to chime from far above. At the base of the stairs, he could hear the clatter of steel against stone. They were coming.

'Spread out!' he barked at the men. 'A charge under each gun, unprimed. Leave the rest in the chamber. Then get out! We'll have some fighting before we're done.'

The men ran down the chamber, torches held aloft, spreading out down the long, eerily silent space. As they went, their tread echoed strangely from the heavy iron frames above. It was an odd sensation, to have so many tons of metalwork hanging over their heads. Soon, if Sigmar so willed, it would be lying in a pile of twisted rubble and wood on the stone floor.

Thorgad, Hildebrandt and Magnus stayed at the near end of the chamber, guarding the entrance. No men came up the stairs. The dark was still their friend, and the soldiers were hunting in the wrong places. But it could only be moments before someone saw the broken doorway.

After just a few moments, the men came back. The charges had been laid, hurled up into the gantries and lodged against the bearings and hauling cables. Now they lay like eggs, nestled in the ironwork.

'Down the stairs!' yelled Magnus. 'Back the way we came! It's time to go.'

As he shouted the orders, he could hear the door being slammed open below. The guards had come at last. Without pausing, Thorgad charged down the steps ahead of the others, Glamrist whirling over his head, shouting curses in Khazalid. Hildebrandt followed close behind, his sword glimmering menacingly.

Magnus hung back, a blackpowder charge cupped in his palm. He unbuckled the remainder of the bombs from his belt, and sent them skittering across the stone floor. With one last regretful look up at the engineering above him, he tore the leather strip from the charge in his hand. The flint caught, and the wick sparked into life. This was the one, the flame that would ignite the rest in a frenzy of immolation.

'Burn well, little destroyer,' he whispered, and hurled it into the darkness above.

Then he turned and fled. From behind, Magnus heard the charge clang off the barrel of a cannon and come to rest somewhere in the gantry. He tore down the steps at the end of the chamber, knowing he had only moments. Before he hit the bottom, the bomb went off. There was a deafening crack, and the stairway behind him filled with flame and light.

That was just the beginning. One by one, the rest of the charges were kindled. Crushing booms blossomed, shaking the stone around them. There was the sound of tortured iron and snapping wood. The guns were falling. There were more explosions, and the acrid stench of blackpowder caught in Magnus's nostrils. Masonry fell down the stairwell after him. He was nearly caught by a heavy piece of stone tumbling down the steps. The blasts continued.

Magnus reached the bottom of the stairs, his breathing heavy and thick with dust. In the confusion, he'd lost his brand. He had his sword, and that proved well. The corridor at the base of the stairs was heaving with men. The citadel's defenders had found them, and now the raiding party was locked in a furious fight to escape.

'Sigmar!' bellowed Magnus. He launched himself into the press of men. His charge knocked a soldier from his feet. Magnus stamped on his neck and plunged his sword into his midriff, ignoring the strangled cry of agony.

Around him, the fighting was vicious. The raiders and citadel guards were locked together, grappling furiously at close quarters. Some had fallen already, though it was hard to make out from which side. Hildebrandt was in the thick of it, wading through the tangled mass like a giant, hammering at the hapless figures around him. Thorgad's voice echoed from the stone walls. The dwarf was clearly busy.

Magnus smashed his pommel into an attacker's face. He followed up quickly, ramming the man against the wall. The soldier had lost his helmet in the fray. His face was full of fear. In the flickering light of the torches, he looked young. Just a boy, like Herschel. Probably his first fight.

Magnus head-butted him savagely, and watched him slide down the wall, blood trickling from his ears. He didn't finish him off. There was little room for sentiment, but he was not quite lost in savagery yet.

He whirled round quickly, sword held high. Hildebrandt and Thorgad had turned the tide, and the fight was ebbing. The few remaining defenders were being driven off. Some of them were being pursued.

'Come back, you dogs!' yelled Magnus. 'Let them go! There'll be more. We need to get out!'

He set off at once, retracing the way the company had come just moments before. From above, the last few remaining charges were going off. A series of thuds shook the ceiling of the corridor, and a long crack snaked across it. The whole section of the citadel was being shaken. It could go down at any moment.

Aware of their plight, the company ran back hard through the network of corridors and stairways. Any resistance they met was swept away like chaff. A feral mood had kindled in Magnus's soul. His breeches were caked in blood. He could almost taste it. As he ran, he could feel his old heart pump powerfully within his breast. There were so few guards. They were going to do it. They were going to get out.

He ran down the last of the spiral stairways before the exit. The storeroom was just ahead, around the corner. Magnus made to cry out, rallying his men for one last dash, but the shout died in his throat. The corridor ahead was blocked with men. Enemy soldiers, standing in ranks of three deep. From behind them, there was the sound of more coming. At the last, they had been caught in a trap. The defenders had found the breach. It had been too good to be true.

Thorgad looked up at Magnus darkly as he loped along, not missing a stride.

'We nearly made it,' he said, dryly.

Magnus didn't stop running. He cast his flaming brand to one side.

There was enough light from the wall-torches. He drew a long dagger from his side.

'We'll take some of them with us,' he replied, grimly.

Magnus and Thorgad ran headlong into the waiting rows of guards. The clash of steel echoed from the narrow walls. Hildebrandt was close behind, and he mowed his way into the combat like a harvester. One soldier was lifted from his feet and slammed into the wall. Magnus squared up to his opponent, blocking a hesitant sword thrust with his blade and stabbing back with his dagger. Thorgad was soon at his side, spinning and hacking away with Glamrist.

They were hemmed in. The corridor allowed no more than four men to stand shoulder to shoulder. The guards pressed against them, a wall of steel between them and the way out. When one fell, another took his place. Agonisingly close to the tunnel entrance, Magnus and his men were pushed back. There were too many of them.

With a cry of frustration and rage, Magnus smashed aside the man before him. Too slowly he saw the blade flicker at him from the side. It pierced his flesh, digging deep just below his outstretched arm. Pain flooded across him, and he staggered, his vision cloudy. He had a dim impression of Thorgad at his side, and the blade was withdrawn suddenly. There were shouts and screams all around. In the half-light, it was hard to make out what was going on.

A man leapt over him. It was Hildebrandt. The big man had gone mad with rage. He was swiping wildly in every direction. For a moment, the soldiers were driven back. Magnus looked up, blearily. He could feel the hot blood, his own this time, slick against his side. Thorgad leaned down, his face lined with concern.

'All right?' he said, sharply.

Magnus nodded weakly. He was far from all right. He could feel his blood pumping strongly from the wound.

'I...' he began, but his voice failed him. He slumped further against the cold stone floor.

Even Hildebrandt was now in trouble. Many of the raiding party had now been cut down, and he was isolated. Thorgad sprung up from Magnus's side and raced to join him. Magnus could feel his vision darkening further.

So this was it. For some reason, amid all the carnage, he saw an image of his father loom up before him. It was as if his leonine head was leaning over him, looking at him sternly. That was too much to bear. The old man had always been disappointed in him. Magnus felt a strange kernel of determination harden within. If he was going to die, then it would at least be with a sword in his hand. He fumbled for the blade. Shakily, his head hammering and his hands cold, Magnus hauled himself upright.

The fight was almost over. Hildebrandt was trying desperately to hold three soldiers off at once. Thorgad had been backed into a corner, though it had taken a dozen guards to keep him there. Most of the other raiders were dead, and the few that remained were being butchered.

A guard, rushing to join the attack on the dwarf, suddenly caught sight of Magnus. He looked amazed, and then laughed.

'Not dead yet?' he asked, and walked casually up to him.

Magnus gritted his teeth, and held his sword in front of him as firmly as he could. In what seemed like the distance, there was the sound of fresh cries and shouts of anger. The fight was not quite over.

'Come and get me,' he said weakly.

The soldier laughed. He swung his blade at Magnus with a contemptuous ease. Magnus parried, and his sword was knocked from his numb fingers. It flashed as it bounced across the flagstones. There was a rapid movement, too fast for him to catch. His vision darkened, then cleared again. Everything was spinning.

Fighting the confusion, Magnus looked up. The soldier loomed over him. The engineer worked to keep his eyes open. He clenched his fists, determined not to flinch. But there was no killing blow. The soldier's face suddenly seemed familiar. There was a tattoo, and a bald head, and wild, staring eyes. And there was no sword, but a warhammer. In the flickering torchlight, it took him a few moments to work out who it was.

'Kossof!' he hissed, sliding back down against the wall.

Rough hands grabbed at him, pulling him back up. Magnus had the vague impression of more men running into the narrow corridor. There was a stench of incense, and ritual cries to Holy Sigmar. The flagellants. The place was full of them.

Kossof dragged Magnus from the front line of the fighting, away from the soldier, who lay on the floor, his neck broken. Kossof's own cloak was streaked with blood, and his eyes had a savage light in them. Magnus had to work to keep consciousness. He knew he'd lost a lot of blood. He was losing his grip on his surroundings.

'A bold plan,' said Kossof, pulling the engineer towards the storeroom door. 'But guns are no substitute for steel.'

Gradually, Magnus pieced together what was going on. The flagellants had come up through the tunnel. They had fought their way to his position. He looked over his shoulder. The remains of the raiding party and the flagellants were fighting a rearguard action, gradually withdrawing towards the breach in the foundations. He could still hear Thorgad in the thick of it. There was no sign of Hildebrandt.

'What...' he began, but his mouth was dry and his throat constricted.

Two of Kossof's men came up out of the darkness. The warrior priest handed Magnus to them, and he felt their rough hands prop him up. Kossof turned to head back into the fighting, hefting his warhammer with intent. Before he left, he fixed Magnus with a strange look.

'Perhaps I was wrong about you, Ironblood,' Kossof said. 'You started this. We will finish it. In all events, Sigmar will be honoured.'

Then he was gone, tearing back towards the press of fighting men, wielding his hammer like a scythe.

Magnus could barely see a thing. His vision was cloudy, and his whole side felt numb. He had the vague impression of being dragged into the darkness. The sounds of fighting died away. Around him, he could feel the swish of rough woollen cloaks. There were torches, and the noise of men rushing to and fro. Someone brushed past him, and the wound in his side sent out fresh spears of pain.

Then he was out. The night air was chill. Suddenly, his senses revived. Magnus shook off his helpers, and shivered weakly. He was back at the cleft in the rock, at the head of the tunnel. There were men milling all around. Kruger was there.

He looked up. The vast bulk of Morgramgar loomed up into the night. Its battlements were aflame. Great gouts of crimson fire soared up from the ramparts. Cracks had appeared in the walls. The green lights at the summit burned fiercely. The hum of machines still throbbed against the earth, but they sounded strained and labouring.

'What's happening?' Magnus asked, his voice cracking.

Kruger rushed over to him.

'You've been wounded, Ironblood,' he said, grabbing his arm to shepherd him away from the scene.

Magnus shook him off impatiently.

'Why's Kossof here?' he snapped, feeling the cold air restore his awareness. The pain in his side was crippling.

'He saw your handiwork from the camp,' said Kruger. 'Scharnhorst thought you might need some help getting out.'

All around them, men were being pulled from the tunnel entrance. Deep within the earth, the sounds of fighting continued, resounding outwards from the narrow cleft.

'Come with me,' said Kruger, taking Magnus's good arm again and dragging him from the tunnel.

'Wait!' cried Magnus, struggling weakly against the knight's iron grip. 'Hildebrandt's still in…'

Before he could finish speaking, there was a huge, thudding explosion. A mighty plume of smoke burst from the tunnel entrance, showering the men around with debris. Kruger was knocked from his feet. He dragged Magnus down with him, who fell painfully on his side. The shards of agony returned, and he almost passed out.

Desperately, filled with a terrible fear, Magnus pulled himself onto his hands and knees. The men around him were regaining their feet. The smoke from the tunnel continued to rise. There were further distant booms, and the sound of cascading stone. Magnus looked at the ruined cleft in horror. Whoever had been in the tunnel was surely dead. He felt sudden, fearful tears spike at his eyes.

'So you made it too,' came a familiar voice.

Magnus looked up. Hildebrandt was at his side, cradling a bleeding forearm and looking pale. Beside him, Thorgad was limping, as were several of the survivors from the raiding party.

A combination of relief and surprise washed over Magnus. He staggered to his feet. The pooled tears ran down his cheek. He felt himself becoming faint again. His left side was drenched in blood. Every time he moved he could feel it sticking against his flesh.

'What happened?'

'Kossof,' said Hildebrandt, his voice hollow. 'His men filled the breach. They pushed the guards back. That got us out. I saw him. He was like a man possessed. Then...'

He stopped speaking, and looked at the tunnel.

'They blew it up behind them, Ironblood,' said Thorgad. Even his stoic dwarfish face looked shaken. 'They sealed the breach with their own men, then set off more charges.'

Magnus followed Hildebrandt's horrified gaze. The last of the smoke curled lazily into the night air. The tunnel had become their rescuers' tomb. And they had done it deliberately.

Kruger came over to join them.

'We need to leave,' he said more urgently. 'It's not safe, so close to the citadel.'

Magnus ignored him.

'Of all the unexpected...' he started. 'Kossof.'

He shook his head. The pain was getting worse. He could feel the bleeding start up again. Somehow, it didn't seem to matter.

'Ironblood,' said Kruger again, his voice commanding. 'We need to leave.'

Magnus turned at last to face him. The knight was beginning to annoy him. He was tired, and good men had died. Even men he hadn't thought of as good had died.

But then the last waves of fatigue and pain came crashing down. When the end came, it was sudden. Magnus fell back to his knees, barely feeling the sharp stone as it dug into his flesh. The whole world seemed to tilt on its axis, and his vision went dark. For a moment, he had the impression of falling, falling wildly, deep into a pit that went on forever. He thought he caught a last glimpse of Kossof's face, set grim against the light of torches, and then it was gone.

Magnus slumped to the ground, and knew no more.

CHAPTER THIRTEEN

'What are the origins of the Engineers? None know for sure. It is true that the great Leonardo came from Tilea, as have many of the finest minds in our field. There are numerous others who could lay reasonable claim to founding the new science. But my judgement is that all of these are wide of the mark. There is little under the sun that men have truly created. We have learned our arts of magic from the elves. We have learned our ways of battle from our ancient enemies, the greenskins and the beastmen. If you ask me where the roots of our engineering lie, you must look under the mountains themselves. For the fathers of our art, there can be little doubt, are the dwarfs.'

*Some Principles of Battlefield Gunnery, as
Observed by a Practitioner, Ludwig von Meinkopt*

With the coming of the dawn, the fires on the ramparts had died out. The sun brought a cold, grey light to the dry valley before Morgramgar. The wind, the never-ceasing scourer of the land, continued to blast away at the thin grass and dry rock. The south walls of the citadel were dark and charred. Huge rents had been opened in the parapet. Thick black smoke continued to churn from some of the blasted holes. It drifted heavily from the damaged walls, before dissipating slowly into the pure, high airs of the mountains.

Magnus looked at the scene dispassionately. His side ached horribly. He shifted slightly to one side, and spasms of pain ran through him. He winced, and clutched at the bandages swaddling his ribcage.

'You've been lucky,' said Thorgad, munching on a cold chicken leg. Juice ran down his chin and into his voluminous beard. 'I thought you'd been stuck good.'

Magnus knew the truth of it. When he'd awoken with nothing more than a bad headache and a painful torso, the extent of his luck had become apparent. The apothecaries had done well, for once. He'd lost a lot of blood, but nothing vital had been pierced. If the blade had been just a few inches higher, then things might have been very different.

The engineer was sitting with Hildebrandt and the dwarf on the ground in front of the artillery train, enjoying an improvised breakfast of cold meat and stale bread. Before them, the whole of Scharnhorst's army was aimlessly preparing for the labours of the day ahead. There was little urgency about their movements. One of the great misconceptions about life in the armies of the Empire was that it was filled with constant action. In reality, most of the time was spent in either back-breaking labour or mind-numbing boredom. The moments of extreme danger or glory were rare. None of which made them less overwhelming when they came. And, as danger went, the raid into Morgramgar had been pretty extreme.

Magnus sighed, and chewed gingerly on the last of his bread. Every movement of his jaw seemed to create an echo of dull pain in his ribs.

'If it's luck,' he said, 'it doesn't feel much like it.'

He squinted into the distance. Beyond the ranks of slowly moving men and the half-mile of bleak, windswept valley floor, Morgramgar still lurked. If anything, the pall of smoke hanging over it seemed to amplify the sense of quiet dread that infused the place. After everything, all the bloodshed and explosions, still the citadel made no external sign of life. The battlements were empty. The chamber at the summit of the highest tower continued to glow a lurid green. The fires in the wolf's head over the gate burned. And beneath them, low and at the edge of hearing, the wheels still turned. It was impossible to escape that noise. The machines hidden deep within the vaults still ground and hummed. Their brief foray inside now seemed like a strange and unreal daydream. Even now, Magnus had trouble reconstructing what had happened.

Thorgad followed his gaze for a few moments, then lost interest.

'Gah,' he said, wiping his mouth. 'You're lucky you have me, for a start. You'd never have got in otherwise.'

Hildebrandt looked at Thorgad with disapproval.

'You should watch your mouth,' he said, spitting a knob of gristle onto the ground beside him. 'We did what we set out to do. The guns are silent. And some men didn't come back.'

Thorgad raised a bushy eyebrow, but didn't seem perturbed.

'I didn't say it wasn't a success,' he said. 'It damn well ought to have been, as well. That was a lot of digging, even for me.'

Magnus didn't join in the banter. He felt a conflict of emotions within him. It had been a long time since he'd been as close to death. He could still see the face of the arrogant soldier, his expected executioner. If Kossof had been a few moments later, then the result would have been different. He let a long, slow sigh escape his lungs, and tried to sit back on his hands. With difficulty, he managed it. Perhaps his ribs were knitting back together after all.

Of all the strange things about the assault, the role of the flagellants had been the most perplexing. Like all good folk of the Empire, Magnus had always looked down on them. Crazies, they were called. Morrslieb-touched, Sigmar's idiots, lash-lovers and worse. Kossof had seemed to Magnus just another in a long list of fanatics. To a man of science, the Sigmarites were the ultimate expression of the Empire's barbarism and backwardness. In every college of learning in the Old World, from Nuln to Wulfgard, they were regarded as little better than madmen and criminals.

Perhaps that view would have to change. In all his years as a soldier and engineer, Magnus couldn't remember anything braver. Now many of them lay dead, their bodies buried under the mountain. If any had been taken alive, their fate was probably much worse. Those that had not been part of the desperate rescue, the bulk of the many hundreds in the army, had taken the losses in their stride. They had appointed a new leader, Kossof's deputy, a man with bloodshot eyes called Johann-Mark Leibkopf. The sounds of whipcord and frenzy rose into the cold air of the camp just as they had done the day before. The regular soldiers still looked at the religious contingent with suspicious eyes, but there was less open scorn in their expressions now.

'We should have planned better,' said Magnus, a bitter tone creeping into his voice. 'It was foolish to think we'd get out on our own.'

Hildebrandt looked at Magnus carefully. The big man carried his arm in a sling. Just like Ironblood, he'd been lucky. The wound wasn't deep.

'Don't blame yourself,' Tobias said, his voice rumbling warningly in his barrel chest. 'Scharnhorst made the right decision to send them after us. And you delivered what you promised. The guns are silent.'

'Yes, so you keep saying,' said Magnus.

He found he couldn't stay bitter for long. The taste of fresh air and the knowledge that he'd cheated death once more was as effective a tonic as anything else. He reached down to pick up the iron tankard by his side. There was still a slop or two of small beer in there. He raised it in the direction of the tunnel, and saluted.

'I never thought I'd say it,' Magnus said. 'But thank Sigmar for Kossof and his fanatics. Who knows? Perhaps they're on the right track with all that holiness. In any case, I'm glad they came along.'

Hildebrandt raised his tankard too, though with less conviction. Thorgad gave them both a contemptuous look, and shook his head. When he saw the dwarf's sour face, Magnus laughed.

The mirth didn't last long. His sides were too painful.

'So, what's next for this glorious campaign?' he said, changing the subject. 'We've bloodied them twice, but we're still no nearer taking the walls. Any news from our esteemed general?'

Hildebrandt tore off a fresh hunk of bread.

'From what I hear, the assault will be soon. Scharnhorst wants another council before letting the army loose. He's worried about how few guns we have. And the experience of being too hasty with the iron-belchers has taught him to take his time. You've got a day or two for your bruises to go down, I reckon.'

Magnus winced. He could already feel his stitches begin to itch.

'Well, if he wants someone to sort out the rocket launchers, he'll have to wait a few hours at least. After last night, I'm not moving, general or not. He'll have to come to me.'

Hildebrandt grinned. Thorgad squinted at him while eating.

'Not very wise, I should think,' the dwarf said. 'You've forgotten about your problem with Messina. He's been hanging around the general for a while now like a penniless harlot. I think Scharnhorst likes the idea of an engineer he can manipulate. You'd better watch your back.'

Magnus snorted bitterly, forgetting again how much it tortured his wounded flank.

'That womanish bastard?' he said. 'I'd forgotten all about him. Frankly, with all that's gone on, I don't really give a damn what he's up to. We've shown General Ironguts what we're made of, and he'll have to pay attention to rank from now on. As for that Tilean pretty-boy, he can hang himself up by his glossy locks and swing in the wind for all I care.'

Hildebrandt looked at Magnus, startled. Then his big face creased into a laugh, and it rolled out into the chill morning air. Even Thorgad was tickled, and his strange, gravelly chuckle joined Tobias's. It proved infectious. In the middle of the camp of war, surrounded by the weapons of death and the cries of the wounded, the three engineers gave up their habitual reserve, and laughed. For a moment, just a fleeting moment, the cares of battle lifted from them.

Magnus joined in, heedless of the pain in his ribs. It was good to feel the layers of care fall from his shoulders for a moment. Soon they would be back again. The assault couldn't be far away. And then all smiles would be banished, perhaps forever.

Messina cursed floridly. A stream of Tilean expletives, most involving the parentage of the Empire's ruling class, emerged from the wooden framework around him. Lukas looked at him anxiously. This was not going well. The Averlander scratched the back of his neck, and stood away from the carcass of the Blutschreiben. It was still far from complete, and time was running out.

The two men were hidden under one of the larger canvas coverings at the back of the artillery encampment. Messina had hired several of the gunnery crews who had lost their great weapons to act as guards. A few pieces of exotic 'silver' pieces from Luccini had been enough to buy their loyalty. They would only discover the coins were a worthless tin alloy when the campaign was long over.

Under cover, and with a constant guard stationed outside to prevent casual spies, Ironblood's plans, long in the devising, were finally coming to fruition. The design was fiendishly complex. In essence, the Blutschreiben was a massively powerful mobile repeating cannon. It used two standard iron barrels, mounted on an elaborate wooden chassis. The genius of it, though, lay in three particular things.

First, the gunner was mounted on a seat on top of the structure and could direct the firing of the mechanism with consummate ease. A series of ropes, pulleys, brass dials and levers controlled every aspect of the gun's movement and detonations. The complicated and finely wrought gear mechanisms for this had been made by Ironblood himself. Like all the detailed sections of the machine, they had been taken from the great chests and bolted on to the crude wooden frame.

Second, there was an ingenious system for loading ammunition. Unlike the laborious process of sponging, ramming, firing and cleaning required for an ordinary cannon, in the case of the Blutschreiben everything was automatic. The complexity here was quite astounding, and the barrels of the cannons were surrounded with a lattice of greased ropes and linked chains, each with a specific function. Should any part of the system not work as expected, then the whole was liable to collapse. Given the amount of blackpowder contained within the machine's innards, a malfunction was not something the gunner would welcome.

Third, the barrels could be swivelled around on a great brass-lined turret. When the chassis had chugged its way into position, the gunner could dispense with any further movement, and spin his position around in a ninety-degree arc by using the steam-powered controls. A mighty furnace, perilously close to the blackpowder caches, provided the locomotive power for the pistons which drove the targeting. As ever, Ironblood's machinery for delivering such power was monstrously involved. A maze of copper piping sprouted from the rear of the gun platform. Only half of this had been connected thus far, and it already looked like a nest of baby snakes. The rest lay on the floor of the tent, jumbled in a heap where a frustrated Messina had dumped them.

Lukas looked over their handiwork so far, and sighed a weary sigh. He hadn't slept much since Messina had convinced Scharnhorst to let them build the damned thing. While Ironblood had been busy with the tunnelling, it had been relatively easy to keep the construction under wraps. Now that the engineers had returned, it was only a matter of time before they discovered what Messina and he were up to.

Though Lukas didn't know why Ironblood was quite so set against the use of his master weapon, he could take an educated guess. Like all experimental projects, the thing looked horribly dangerous. A standard cannon, with its relatively simple firing mechanism, was liable to blow up at any moment, scarring or killing its crew and showering debris across the battlefield. This monster, which could in theory hurl round after round of heavy ammunition through the air with barely a pause, using only the power of steam and mechanics, was liable to be an absolute nightmare to keep under control. And that was assuming they could put it together remotely correctly. As Messina's frequent cursing testified, that couldn't be relied upon either.

The Tilean emerged from under the chassis looking harassed. His normally glossy locks were matted and tangled. His olive skin was marked by blotches of grease and powder-burns. His fine clothes were ruined.

'How's it going?' asked Lukas, tentatively.

Messina gave him a dark look which spoke volumes.

'Have you deciphered secondary lubricant system yet?' he said by way of reply. His voice was tired and clipped.

Lukas pulled one of the many sheets of parchment from the jumbled pile on the floor. It was scored with notes and hastily scrawled diagrams. Deciphering it was like trying to read elvish. Not impossible for a human, but close to being a lifetime's work.

'I think so,' he said, cautiously. 'When you're finished working on the turret traction, I could attempt to fix it in place. We might be able to get shot-loading working then.'

Messina took a deep breath, and looked back at the half-finished machine. There was hatred in his eyes.

'By Luccina,' he spat, wiping his hands on his expensive clothes. 'If I'd known how complicated the damned thing would be…'

He didn't finish his sentence, but walked over to a low bench by the entrance to the tent. There was a flagon of watered-down wine. He picked it up and took a hefty swig.

'What time is it?' he asked, slumping onto the bench and looking exhausted.

Lukas shrugged.

'Mid-morning, I'd say. We've not got long before Scharnhorst'll want to know if it's ready.'

Messina shot him a poisonous look.

'Really?' he said, sarcastically. 'So that is news to me.'

He took another long swig. When he wiped his mouth, a long trail of some dark, oily substance was left against his cheek. Lukas kept a diplomatic silence.

'Do you think we'll make it?' the boy said, frowning as he looked over the semi-complete structure.

Lukas's moment of doubt seemed to galvanise Messina. He let out a derisive snort, and got up from the bench.

'By all the lawful gods, yes,' he said, putting down the flagon firmly. 'This is our chance, boy. He's had a success, that drunk man, with his tunnelling. We need one of our own. This will be it. When we advance, I will be sitting in that chair, sending death into the ranks of the enemy. There'll be no standing against us. That is all that matters.'

There was a familiar dark fire in his eyes as he spoke. Lukas knew better than to contradict him.

'Then we'd better get back to work,' he said, picking up his tools wearily. They had already been at it for hours. With a dreadful certainty, Lukas knew that the night ahead would be a long one.

Rathmor was consumed by a cold, malevolent rage. He stalked down the long corridors of the citadel, his black robes fluttering behind him as he went. His guns, his beloved guns, had been destroyed. There was no humiliation greater for an engineer. They should have been safe. They were within the walls. Someone would suffer for it. They would all suffer.

He pushed the door to Esselman's chambers open roughly. A startled guard standing in the antechamber raised his sword briefly in challenge before recognising who it was.

'Sir,' he said, nodding his head in acknowledgement.

Rathmor ignored him and ploughed on into the inner sanctum. There was a pair of metal-lined doors ahead of him. He pushed them both open, and they slammed back against the walls on either side.

Beyond was a large torchlit room. From far above, daylight weakly filtered down from windows high up on the eastern walls. Esselman's room was near the summit of the soaring citadel.

Only two men were in the room. One was Esselman himself. The other was one of the insurgents. A warrior priest. He was tied tightly to a wooden chair with leather straps. His robes were torn and singed. His severe face was bruised and lacerated. Either he'd picked up those wounds in the fighting, or Esselman had not been kind to him.

The captive priest barely seemed to notice Rathmor's entrance. His eyes flickered weakly towards him, then went back to blankly staring into space. He had a strange, resigned expression on his face.

Esselman slammed a fist against the wall in frustration.

'These damned priests!' he spat, and turned away from the captive. He walked over to a side table, and poured a tankard of dark ale. He drank deeply before lifting his head to acknowledge Rathmor.

'What do you want?' he asked.

Rathmor controlled his anger with some difficulty. After all that had happened, to be forced to treat with such insolent fools was almost beyond toleration.

'The lady is furious,' he snapped back. 'She's been tearing her chamber to pieces. Her staff don't dare enter.'

Esselman gave a hollow laugh.

'You think I don't know that?' he said, and a faint sliver of fear entered his words. 'By Sigmar, this is a damned mess.'

'Dare not take his name in vain, heretic,' hissed the priest, defiantly.

Esselman strode over to the bound man and struck him hard in the face. Unable to protect himself, the priest's head cracked sickeningly against the frame of the chair. For a moment, the man's eyes went glassy, and a trickle of blood ran down from the corner of his mouth. He recovered his poise with effort, and fixed a gaze of controlled hatred at Esselman. Even in his current predicament, the priest seemed unbowed.

Esselman cradled his fist in his other hand gingerly, and looked at Rathmor sourly.

'These damned priests,' he said again. 'I hate them. Ask any question you like, and all you get back are platitudes about the coming wrath of the comet. They disgust me.'

Rathmor looked at the priest with renewed interest, and a greedy look passed across his face.

'What do you want to know?' he asked, his mouth twisted into a leer. 'I have special instruments down in the forges. They would soon loosen a reluctant tongue, blessed by Sigmar or not.'

The priest gazed back at him fearlessly, as if daring him to bring on the tools of torture. Esselman regarded Rathmor coldly.

'What do you think I am?' he said, disdainfully. 'I'm a warrior, not a bastard witch hunter. There'll be none of your perversions while I'm in charge of the citadel.'

He rubbed his hands wearily across his face and took another long swig of ale.

'We'd learn nothing much in any case,' Esselman said. 'What's there to find out? That the army is intent on driving us out of here? That we know. There are no secrets in this war. They'll attack the gates soon. We have no guns to repel them. You'll have to trust to force of arms sooner than you would wish, Rathmor.'

The engineer shook his head reluctantly.

'It's still too soon,' he whined, looking at the priest with hatred. He would have loved to have spent some time alone with the wretched man, if for no other reason than to work out his frustration on some unwilling flesh. Esselman's warrior code could be inconvenient and frustrating.

Esselman spat on the ground contemptuously.

'You've run out of time, my friend,' he said. The word 'friend' was intoned coldly. 'She won't stand for it any longer. You've had months to get this army ready. Now we'll see how good it really is.'

Rathmor had to stop himself from bursting into an incoherent rage. It wasn't fair. Things were conspiring against him. Just as always, the ignorant were rushing his work. When it failed, as it always might, he would get the blame.

'You have no idea what's at stake here!' he cried, and spittle flew from his pale lips. 'There are still things I don't understand! The book...'

Then he stopped, as if an invisible hand had clamped itself over his mouth. Esselman looked at him warily.

'What book?' he said.

'Forget about it,' snapped Rathmor. 'That's not important. What is important is getting rid of this army of fools and fanatics.'

He shot an acidic look at the priest as he spoke.

'You know as well as I that the charade of gold will only last so long. We must move on. Von Kleister can keep the men fooled for a month or two, but it won't last. Everything depends on getting the machines together, and taking the fight to Ludenhof. Everything!'

Esselman gazed down at the hunched body of Rathmor with disgust.

'Don't try to tell me my duties,' he said irritably. 'If your precious guns had been less fragile, we wouldn't be in this situation.'

That was almost the final straw. Guarding the gunnery was Esselman's province. It was bad enough that the man's negligence had let a raiding party in to blow them up. To be blamed for their fragility was an insult too far. Rathmor's eyes bulged, and his thin fists clenched. He could feel his rage boiling to a climax. He tried to find the right words, but it was as if his jaw had been clamped shut. The veins on his temples bulged, and sweat broke out across his forehead.

Esselman must have seen the signs. He shook his head in resignation, took a final draught of beer, and some of the belligerence left him.

'Oh, don't get worked up, Rathmor,' he said disgustedly, walking over to the table and replacing the tankard. 'That'll do no one any good.'

Esselman leaned against the stone wall, and looked uninterestedly over towards the bound priest. Slowly, painfully, Rathmor suppressed his anger. One day, when he was at the head of a reformed New College of Engineers, his wrath would be feared across the entire Old World. He would be able to lash out, unrestrained, whenever the mood fell on him. For now, though, he needed men like Esselman. For now.

'We have things to do,' Esselman said, curtly. 'I don't care what the dangers are, we need your infernal machine. Now. And I want your traps laid, just as we agreed. If they'd been in place earlier, that little raiding party wouldn't have got far. You promised to turn the lower levels into a firestorm.'

Rathmor shivered with anger, but kept control of himself. Just.

'The machine will be ready,' he said, his voice shaking slightly. 'When they attack the gates, I'll let it loose. And fear not for the traps. If they breach the walls a second time, none of them will get out alive.'

Esselman seemed satisfied with Rathmor's vehemence.

'Good,' he said. He turned back to the warrior priest, who had been listening in silence, his eyes alert and his expression intent.

'Did you hear that, you damned zealot?' Esselman asked, a grim smile on his lips. 'I should have you killed. But I might just let you stay alive long enough to see your comrades burn. It'll be a fitting end to your doomed campaign.'

Esselman loomed over the warrior priest, his fists bunched. It looked like he might strike the man again, either out of spite or from simple frustration.

But then, a chime sounded. Just as before, the childlike noise echoed down the corridors. Both men froze instantly. Rathmor forgot his bubbling anger, and looked at Esselman, wide-eyed.

'What do you think she wants now?' he hissed.

Esselman swallowed, and looked suddenly uncomfortable.

'No idea,' he said, his voice quavering slightly. 'But we'd better not keep her waiting.'

The chime sounded again, quiet but insistent. Esselman looked at the priest sourly.

'We'll continue this conversation another time,' he said, and turned on his heel. He left the chamber, and Rathmor scuttled along at his heels. They were like curs summoned by their mistress. The door opened and closed with a slam. Their footfalls echoed through the antechamber and out into the corridor beyond. Then they were gone. With their absence, the room fell into silence.

Seemingly forgotten, the warrior priest Kossof sat as immobile as a graven image. Despite his ordeal, his body remained upright and his eyes glittered with a keen light. In the dark and the quiet, his lips began to move soundlessly.

'Vengeance,' he breathed, lips curling into a smile. 'Vengeance.'

The sun sank towards the western horizon. The peaks began to cast their long, jagged shadows over the valley floor. Despite being wrapped in layers of clothing and encased in his long leather coat, Magnus was cold. His wound ached dully. The thirst had returned and every movement provoked a fresh spike of pain. It made him irritable and easy to anger. After the euphoria of the attack, the campaign, the lull before the storm. Though he could see the benefit of planning properly, he was itching to get back into the thick of things. The men were tired, driven into a sullen sluggishness by the endless cold, the moaning of the wind and that terrible, maddening throbbing that seemed to shake the very earth under their feet.

He wrapped his arms about himself, and stamped to try and generate some circulation. Perhaps he was still short on blood. He stalked off to find some more meat and drink. As he walked towards one of the provision wagons, he met Hildebrandt coming the other way.

'How are you feeling?' asked the big man.

'Not too bad,' Magnus replied. 'I've had worse.'

Hildebrandt looked preoccupied.

'Do you have some time to spare?' he asked, looking around him.

'Bags of it,' he replied. 'We're not doing anything until dawn.'

'Then come with me.'

Magnus followed Hildebrandt to the shadow of a row of artillery wagons, each still covered with canvas and kept under tight wraps. When they were out of sight of most of the soldiers, Hildebrandt took a bundle of rags from under his cloak and unwrapped it. Inside there were pieces of metal. They glinted weakly in the failing light.

'Recognise these?' said Hildebrandt, turning the fabric over and letting the pieces clink against one another.

Magnus took one and held it up, peering at the shard of steel intently.

'They're gunnery pieces,' he said, looking at it with expert eyes. 'Where did you get them?'

'One of the guards in the citadel had a pistol,' said Hildebrandt. 'I had time to take it with me when we left. I've been taking it apart.'

Magnus drew his eyeglass out, and studied the component carefully.

'Just like before,' he said, thoughtfully. 'This is good quality. Better than I've seen in a long while.'

Hildebrandt handed him some more. They were all of the same standard.

'What else do you see?' he asked.

Magnus pursed his lips. He handed the pieces back.

'They're dwarfish,' he said.

Hildebrandt nodded.

'Just like the one we found in the passes. They're all the same. We've got to face the truth, Magnus. These men are being armed by dwarfs.'

Magnus frowned, and took another look.

'I'm not sure,' he said. 'Thorgad thought they were dwarfish too, but only in origin. We don't know where these were made.'

Hildebrandt lowered his voice.

'Why's the dwarf here, Magnus?' he said. 'Something's going on in that fortress that he knows about. If his kind are arming our enemies, how do we know we can trust him?'

Magnus let slip a cold smile.

'If you fancy trying to prise the truth from him, you're welcome to try,' he said. 'I'll leave you to it, though. Thorgad's got no explaining to do to me. He's just one of the crew. And without him, we'd never have got inside the citadel.'

Hildebrandt looked unconvinced.

'He's got his own plans here, and you know it. It's no good. There's some secret about the weaponry in there, and he knows things he's not telling. We could be better prepared. I don't want to lead men into a bloodbath like we had in the passes. You should press him for what he knows.'

Magnus felt the smile leave his lips. He was loath to look into a man's secrets. He had plenty of his own. Sometimes he wondered if they were all that he did have.

'He'll tell me nothing. You know that. If I anger him, he'll leave. And then we'll never find out what reason he has for being here.'

Hildebrandt collected the pieces together, and wrapped them carefully up once more.

'So be it,' he said, looking disappointed. 'I can't force you. But I'm keeping my eyes open around him. Messina may be a rat, but at least he's a stupid one. There's something about Thorgad, though. I hope you don't live to regret not finding out what it is.'

Magnus placed a hand on his old friend's shoulder.

'We're nearly there, Tobias,' he said. 'They don't have the men to withstand a full assault. It won't be long before we're picking up our bag of gold and heading back to Hergig.'

Hildebrandt didn't smile. An unfamiliar look played out on his large, open face.

'Don't try to reassure me, Magnus,' he said. 'I've been in too many campaigns for that. There's something wrong with that place. Their equipment's too good. They have machines. Even the troopers can hear them working. I fear for you if you enter there. I fear for all of us.'

Magnus let his hand drop. Hildebrandt stowed the metalwork back under his cloak. Without saying anything more, he walked off into the gathering dusk.

Magnus watched him go. Then his eyes flicked up to the mighty citadel, still silent, still lit by the series of unearthly lights. The clouds of smoke had dissipated, and now it lurked like a shadow at the base of the distant cliffs. Hildebrandt was right. There was something unnatural about it. They would assault it soon. More men would die, just to satisfy the ambition of a distant count who barely left his summer palace. Such was the way of the Empire.

He sighed, and turned away.

CHAPTER FOURTEEN

'Why are men so afraid of the power of artillery? Because every state trooper knows that one day all warfare will be conducted behind the barrel of a gun. In the future, the sword and the spear will disappear from our battlefields, and the ranks of gunners will take their place. It matters not how many nobles complain of this, nor how many witch hunters confiscate our untried machines and devices. Our day will come. History demands it.'

Attributed to Frau Meikle of Waldenhof

The day dawned chill and grey, like all days in the high peaks. During the night, high clouds had been driven south, and now the sky was as clear and white as a pearl. There was an ominous cracking from the far heights, as if mighty sheets of ice were grinding past one another. Down in the valley where the army still camped, the stones were as hard and pale as bone. It was a harsh place.

Though the sun brought little warmth, it did give light. As the first rays crept over the eastern line of mountain edges, trumpets were sounded by Scharnhorst's heralds. The time had come. Sergeants and captains sprung from their hard beds on the stone, and rushed to don their equipment. Soldiers were kicked from sleep. Cold fires were stoked into life, and pails of icy water were rushed from the stores. Reveille had arrived, and food was delivered swiftly to hungry mouths. The slop and meat stew had been made marginally thicker than usual. The men would need their energy for the fight, and even the flint-eyed, penny-pinching cooks knew it.

Magnus roused himself with difficulty. His wound had been plaguing him through the night, and his sleep had been fitful. For some reason, he had dreamed of his father again. The White Wolf of Nuln. For so many years that name had been both a blessing and a curse. A blessing, as it had got him into the college and secured his future in the trade. A curse, as he could never hope to live up to the mighty reputation. Even in death, the magisterial figure of Augustus haunted him. There was no escape, either at the bottom of a keg of beer, nor back on the hard road to war.

Magnus shook his head to clear it, and ran his fingers over his heavily stubbled chin. No time to shave. Things were moving. He pulled himself from the ground, wincing as his ribs creaked and the cold morning air flooded under the blanket. He reached for his overcoat with trembling hands, and wrapped himself in it. The mountains were hateful, and no place for honest men.

All around him, machinery of war was being pulled forward. The time for the great cannons had passed. Now the instruments of choice were the rocket launchers, the volley guns and the other deadly tools of the battlefield engineer. Stomping to restore his circulation, Magnus walked over to the first wave of guns. The crews were pulling the covers from their pieces and dusting the fragile firing mechanisms down. When they saw him coming, they stood to attention and saluted. Magnus grinned wryly. Since the successful demolition of Morgramgar's heavy guns, his stock had clearly risen with the men.

'What do you call her?' he said, stopping by a Helblaster and its crew.

'Murderous Margrita,' came the reply, without a trace of irony. Crews often gave their artillery pieces names, and always those of women. For the men who knew they could lose a limb to the whims of their devices, it seemed appropriate.

'Very good,' said Magnus, casting his eye quickly over the machine. Helblasters were equipped with nine ironbound barrels. The top three fired in unison. Once the shot was clear, the whole edifice could be rotated on a central axis, bringing a fully loaded trio of barrels to play in an instant. In all, nine shots could be released before the contraption had to be reloaded. Magnus had seen them used many times in many campaigns. They were devastating, capable of cutting down entire ranks of oncoming enemy troops. When they worked, that was. Like all complex pieces, the mechanism had its flaws. Even the slightest misalignment could ignite the blackpowder charges too early. An exploding Helblaster was one of the most spectacular sights on the battlefield. Anyone within twelve yards of it would be lucky to escape with just his legs missing.

'Murderous Margrita' looked in good condition. Several days in the mountains had not obviously done anything to dent her martial prowess. The bindings looked secure, the breeches were clean and well-oiled and the wooden chassis was neatly painted. The wheels and axle were solid, and the ornate triggers gleamed proudly in the weak light.

'You should be proud of her,' said Magnus, with approval. 'Keep with the others, though. A massed rank of firing does more damage than a dozen individual volleys.'

The crew nodded respectfully, even the old master gunner. He looked like a veteran of the capricious ways of gunnery, with several fingers missing and a wooden pole in place of his right leg. When he smiled, Magnus noted that there were only two teeth left in his head and his nose had been badly broken. He shouldn't have peered into the breech, then.

Magnus kept walking, observing with some pleasure the efficiency with which the guns were being broken out and rolled into position. Things had come a long way since the store yards of Hergig. The men had been drilled hard, and they'd learned much on the job. There was no greater tutor than the fear of death and dishonour. Every element of his command, from the ranks of the handgunners to the thunderous power of the heavy iron, was in better shape than when he'd found it. From what he'd seen of the enemy's capabilities, that was no bad thing.

Next in line was a slightly off-kilter looking Helstorm battery. These things were Magnus's pet hates. All knew that the design was an inferior copy of a template from the far-off East. Unlike the Helblaster, which was dangerous enough, the Helstorm had almost nothing to protect the crew should something go wrong. Like most examples of its kind, the Helstorm in front of him had a complement of nine rockets arranged on a fragile-looking frame. In theory, each could be fired independently. In practice, the fuses were so close together that several would often be unleashed at once. Given that the rockets were placed in different positions, this resulted in unpredictable behaviour. Magnus had seen volleys of rockets plough into the rear of lines of allied troops, causing huge bloodshed and confusion. He had also seen Helstorms literally launch themselves into the air when a rocket got jammed, taking their crew with them and hurling them across the battlefield. When Magnus saw a Helstorm, he had some sympathy for the ordinary soldier's dislike of war machines. They were devastating, in every sense.

Magnus looked at the example in front of him warily.

'Name?' he said, but without much enthusiasm.

'We haven't got one yet, sir,' replied a cheery-looking youth. The other members of the crew hung back. The master gunner wore an eye-patch. Never a good thing to see from the man responsible for aiming the thing. 'She's a new-build. Just out of the smithy in Hergig. We'll see how it goes, and name her when we learn her character.'

Magnus raised an eyebrow.

'This hasn't been fired?'

The crew looked sheepish, and said nothing. Magnus sighed, and looked at the mechanism. It all looked in order, but you could never be sure.

'Keep to the right flank,' said Magnus, sharply. 'Take double care over everything you do. If I see one of these rockets go into our own troops, I'll have you strapped to her yourself and fired into the ground.'

Without waiting for a reply, he stalked off further along the line. From behind him, there was a nervous muttering. There were a dozen or so more pieces all told, plus some mortars and the lines of handgunners. It was a good complement for an army of their size. More than enough to trouble whatever was in the citadel, certainly.

The light was growing rapidly, and around them the army was moving into position for attack. His inspection complete, Magnus called out down the line.

'All right, men!' he cried, standing on a shallow ledge overlooking the land in front of the fortress gates. 'You had your training. You know the plans. Keep disciplined, and keep together. We know the enemy has some tricks, but we've shown they can be beaten. Cover the infantry when they advance, and for the sake of Sigmar don't fire on our own people. Only advance when you get your orders. Good luck, and Sigmar be with you.'

It wasn't a very inspiring speech. There were a few half-hearted cheers from some of the younger crews. Most of the rest just got on with things, harnessing the horses and pulling their war machines into position.

'They're shaky-looking machines,' came a familiar voice next to Magnus. Thorgad stood next to him, looking disapprovingly at the devices.

'Glad you could join us,' said Magnus, dryly. 'This isn't really your sort of work.'

Thorgad shook his head.

'Agreed. I'll be happier when I've got flesh to cleave. But there's a place for blackpowder. I reckon you'll need it.'

Magnus looked up over the battlefield. Morgramgar stood on the far side of the wide open space, as dark and inscrutable as ever. The death's-head standard moved slightly in the breeze. The humming was still there, but it seemed reduced in volume. Whatever dark purpose the machines had been put to was clearly achieved. They knew battle was coming. On the tall ramparts, there was a telltale glint of steel. At last, there were sentries visible. Things were coming to a head.

'Have you seen Hildebrandt?' asked Magnus. 'We'll need him.'

Thorgad shook his head.

'He'll be along. But you should be more worried about your rival, Messina.'

A sudden feeling of uneasiness made Magnus pause. He'd almost forgotten about the wayward Tilean. The tunnelling had taken up so much time and energy that Messina's actions had seemed almost inconsequential.

'What do you mean?'

Thorgad shook his head dismissively.

'Too late to do anything about it now,' he said, looking over towards Scharnhorst's command retinue. 'Human business is none of my concern anyway. I think the signal's about to be given.'

As the dwarf finished talking, there was a loud blare of trumpets from the heralds. Riders broke from the cover of high ground, and began delivering sealed orders to the various captains arranged across the open ground.

From his vantage point at the rear of the entire deployment, Magnus had a good view of the preparation. Men were hurriedly taking their positions, rushing to form lines and complete detachments. Slowly, with some confusion and much yelling of orders from harassed sergeants, the familiar patchwork of an Imperial army began to take shape. Scharnhorst's forces were strung out in a long line facing Morgramgar's south-facing walls. On the left flank, the flagellants clustered. Heedless of orders, they feverishly banged drums and blew horns, chanting the name of Sigmar over and over. They had passed into their strange battlefield trance. Magnus had seen it before. They would be almost impervious to wounds once they were unleashed.

On the right of the flagellants were the first companies of halberdiers and pikemen. They were mostly composed of mercenary companies, and wore a variety of colours. Aside from the flagellants, they were the least orderly of the army's detachments, and Magnus could make out officers moving between them, trying to knock them into shape.

Beyond them, at the centre of the assault, were the Knights of the Iron Sceptre. Kruger was visible at their head, mounted on his giant sable charger. In their spotless armour and perfect formation, they were a formidable company, the iron heart of the entire army. On their right, the Hochland companies of halberdiers and handgunners had been arranged. They were kitted out in the red and green of their state, and stood silently in neat regiments. Unlike the flagellants, they made little noise. Most of them knew they would soon be fighting their countrymen, and there was little stomach for the forthcoming slaughter. Their commanders marched among them, trying to drum up some aggression. Magnus watched the spectacle grimly. When the blood started flowing, then they would remember how to kill.

On the extreme right flank of the army were the shorter-range artillery pieces, the Helstorms and the Helblasters. They were protected by a sullen-looking company of state troopers. Standing in front of a row of those monsters couldn't have been a popular assignment. Behind them on slightly higher ground were placed the long-range guns, the mortars and the surviving cannons. Their crews were still busy with the final adjustments to their range. All were pointed at the gates. With the removal of covering fire from the walls, they were now perfectly capable of hitting them. Once they were down, the charge would be ordered. For now, all eyes were on the guns.

Magnus looked back towards the centre of the deployment. As before, Scharnhorst stood on a low mound just behind the main companies of Hochland troops. He was peering through a spyglass, looking intently at the enemy fortifications before giving the orders to commence battle. Around him, his commanders shouted orders, which were quickly relayed down the lines. There were only three reserve companies held back. When the time came, the general clearly wanted a swift kill.

'Here he comes,' said Thorgad, motioning down the slope.

Hildebrandt was walking up to meet them, red in the face.

'Where have you been?' asked Magnus. 'This is about to begin.'

The big man looked worried.

'Your chests,' he said. 'They've been tampered with. The Blutschreiben components. They've been taken.'

Magnus felt as if the earth had been knocked from under his feet. He stared back at Hildebrandt stupidly for a moment, taking in the news slowly.

'How do you–' he began.

'I went to the wagon to retrieve the last of the ammunition for the big guns. We were unloading crates when a chest of yours was knocked from its place. The lock broke. There's nothing but straw in there.'

Magnus's incredulity turned quickly into rage.

'So that's what he's been doing!' he cried, his fists balling in impotent fury. 'The little bastard! He has no idea what he's doing. It doesn't work! If he tries to use it–'

His tirade was broken by a fresh blast of trumpets. Scharnhorst had given the signal. The barrage was to begin.

'Where is he?' hissed Magnus, his cheeks red with anger.

'You've got no time,' said Thorgad. 'The order's been given.'

Magnus looked around him. The gunnery captains looked back at him. For a moment, he considered leaving them in Hildebrandt's hands. He needed to track down Messina before he did anything stupid. But it was impossible. Scharnhorst's eyes were on him. His duty was clear.

'Damn it all,' he muttered. 'Messina can wait. He can't have done much with the pieces yet.'

He rose to his full height, and turned to face the waiting gunners.

'On my mark!' he cried, his harsh voice echoing down the lines of artillery.

The crews sprang forward, flaming brands at the ready. The spongers and master gunners stood back. Their work was done.

Magnus took a last look at their trim and angle of the guns, and the position of the barrels. There was nothing out of place. He looked up at the walls. They were as blank as ever, dark and sheer. Only the blast marks near the parapet gave away the effects of their raid.

'Fire!' he cried, and his voice bellowed out down the lines.

As one, the crews ignited the fuses. There was a short gap as the cord burned down. But then, one by one, the mighty engines let loose their deadly cargo. Mortars sent their charges looping high into the clear air. They rained down on the battlements heavily. There was no Tilean fire in them this time, but honest explosive charge and searing grape. Stone cracked and buckled under the onslaught.

With a screaming *whoosh*, the Helstorm rockets streaked towards their targets. Most hit the target, spinning into the gatehouse and exploding in a messy plume of fire. Only a few careered off course, slamming into the ground before the walls, or spinning wildly off into the skies before fizzling out and falling to earth in the far distance. The Helblasters joined in, sending ranks of piercing heavy iron shot against the distant gates, slamming into the stone and metalwork with a series of heavy, echoing blasts.

The ridge was engulfed with drifting smoke. Crews battled to reload their weapons amid the eye-watering clouds. Those soldiers closest to the artillery lines shifted away nervously, holding their ears against the splitting cracks and booms.

'Maintain your fire!' cried Magnus, though his voice was hardly audible in the cacophony. 'All guns to be aimed at the gates!'

Finally, as if held in reserve to remind all of their peerless power, the last of the great cannons were unleashed. Massive, ground-shaking booms rang out as the fearsome machines of war detonated, sending their iron shot spinning across the open ground. The noise of impact resounded heavily between the valley walls. Round after round slammed into the gates. Huge metal shot alternated with explosive rockets and dispersed grape. The citadel was being battered into submission.

Along the ranks of waiting soldiers, a low murmur began to pick up volume. There was no response from the fortress. It was as grim and unmoving as ever. But damage was being done. The rounds of stone-tearing ammunition kept hitting. The master gunners had done their targeting work well. Cracks began to appear in the masonry. The wolf's head lost its flame.

'Keep firing!' bellowed Magnus.

As he spoke, there was a shuddering crash to his right. He whirled around to see one of the Helblasters listing to one side, its barrels split open and steaming. A man was trapped under the wreckage, squealing in agony. Others rushed to pour water on the red-hot metal and haul the man free. Hildebrandt left his station to oversee the withdrawal of the piece. Magnus turned his attention back to the firing.

'Keep at it!' he cried again. 'No respite!'

The heat of the guns was now almost tangible, even in the ice-cold air. Another round slammed into the distant walls. All along the ranks of the army, men strained to see the results of the battery. Still there was no answer from the citadel. Their teeth had been drawn. The gate was defenceless against ranged fire. Magnus felt a grim sense of satisfaction. It was almost too easy.

Then, at last, it came. One cannonball, hurled far into the air and sent hurtling towards the gates, found its mark perfectly. The edifice, weakened by the ferocious waves of shot, crumbled. A huge cheer went up from the assembled ranks. Despite the drifting layers of smoke, they could see what was happening. The lintel had fallen. The arch was going down. The gates were broken.

More projectiles were hurled. Rockets spun into the ruin. Mortars sent their deadly contents into the breach. Flames sprang up as the entire gatehouse slid into rubble. On either side of its mighty frame, the walls began to splinter. All of a sudden, Morgramgar looked vulnerable. The way was open. The wolf had been thrown down.

Trumpets sounded once more from the command group.

'Cease firing!' cried Magnus.

It took a while for his order to be heeded. Some of the more enthusiastic crews managed to get another round away before they were dragged back by their counterparts. The smoke rolled across the vista. Morgramgar was revealed again. Its walls were still smooth and unbroken. But where the gates had stood, there was now a gaping hole. The doors had been utterly destroyed, and the pillars on either side of them were bent and sagging.

Magnus smiled thinly. He had done what was asked of him. Now the army could be unleashed at last. He looked over at Scharnhorst, and nodded.

More trumpets rang out, and a series of signals passed along the ranks. With a roar, of relief as much as anything else, the long held-back ranks of footsoldiers were loosed. Like a herd of wild beasts, they rushed forward, brandishing their weapons in the harsh morning sun, yelling and shouting with abandon. At their side were the flagellants, outdoing all others in ferocity, scourging themselves into a frenzy even as they charged headlong towards the breach. The handgunners advanced too, keeping further back, held from the vanguard by their stony-faced commanders. Slowly, cautiously, Magnus gave the order for the artillery to be hauled to closer quarters. There was still work for them to do, but they would need to be nearer.

At the very centre of the huge mass of bodies, the Knights of the Iron Sceptre were the foremost. Their long black pennants streamed outwards as their steeds tore up the stone from under them. The noise of their massed hooves rivalled the blasts of the smaller guns. Magnus could see Kruger at the forefront, his standard held high, his black helm catching the sun and glinting like polished onyx. Despite himself, Magnus felt his heart surge. The sight was glorious. After so long trudging through the passes, hauling the machinery, putting up with one slight after another, the moment of release had finally come.

But just then, even as the vanguard thundered towards the gates and the hordes of men followed eagerly in their wake, there was a gigantic, resonating boom from the citadel. Silent for so long, it suddenly burst into life. Fires were kindled, and flames shot up from the battlements. Rows of archers appeared along the lower walls. From the gate there came the sound of brazen trumpets. Drums started up, beating wildly and echoing from the valley walls. As if waiting for Scharnhorst's men to commit themselves, Morgramgar finally stirred. The army it had been cradling within its deep vaults, so long rumoured, was finally disgorged from the broken gates.

With a blood-freezing shout, ranks of black-clad infantry poured from the breach to meet the onslaught. They kept coming. Rank after rank. There were gunners amongst them. The crack of their shots was audible even over the tumult. And there were mounted soldiers, armoured in plate and wearing black death's-head emblems. They looked as well armed as the Iron Sceptre knights, and charged towards the invaders with as much ferocity.

Still they kept coming. There were marching ranks of halberdiers, pouring from the shattered gates like ants spilling from a disturbed nest. The gap between the two armies narrowed. There was no let up. Each hurled themselves towards the other as if the End Times were upon them. Magnus narrowed his eyes. The vanguards would clash while still a long way from the gates. Had the enemy intended this? Why had his forces been kept in reserve for so long?

He turned back to the guns.

'Haul them faster, damn your eyes!' he bellowed, urging the men on. It took time to drag a whole artillery line into a new position. The guns needed careful handling. The barrels were red-hot still, and the horses were nervous and skittish from the explosions. The longer the crews took, however, the longer the footsoldiers were without heavy artillery cover.

Magnus looked back. Thorgad had scrambled on top of a pile of ammunition kegs to get a better view. He looked anxious to join the fray. The knights had reached the front lines of the advancing enemy. Behind them, footsoldiers piled in. Horses slammed into the front ranks, tearing a swathe through the oncoming infantry. Steel clashed against steel. The crack of long guns opened up from the right flank, and more men stumbled into the dust of the field. The pungent aroma of blood was mingled with the bitter stench of the blackpowder. The drums rolled. The fires burned. The war machines roared.

Battle was joined.

CHAPTER FIFTEEN

'Guns! Explosions! The smell of fire and fear! Gentlemen, there is nothing better, nothing on earth. What sport would war be without it? They say that the age of Sigmar was the age of heroism. Don't believe a word of it! These are the days of glory, my friends! The time of blackpowder and steel! May it last forever!'

Reported last words of Master Gunner Augerich von Mettelblicken

Messina and Herschel were still working. The thunder of battle was all around, only slightly muffled by the thick canvas about them. The whine of rockets and the thud of the mortars broke the uniform clamour of arms. Below it all, the distant machines under Morgramgar still turned, and the heavy drums still rolled.

'Nearly there…' said Messina, clambering over the huge frame of the Blutschreiben. He had two different gauges of spanner in each hand, and was tightening the last of the bolts on the exterior of the wooden skeleton. Against all the odds, it looked like they would make it. The chassis was complete. The furnace was stoked, and thick black smoke was pouring from the rear stacks. It billowed out of the open tent doors. There was now no hope of secrecy, but the need had passed. The machine was functional. Its time had come at last.

'Is the locomotive bearing connected correctly?' asked Lukas, his voice sounding thin and scared. 'I don't think we're ready for this, Silvio.'

Messina laughed. His spirits had not been as high for days. Ironblood may have been a tyrant and a drunkard, but he knew how to build a war machine. The Blutschreiben stood nearly ten feet high at its tallest point. Its four massive wheels, adapted from the largest of their wagons and studded with iron spikes, turned effortlessly at the press of a lever. The enormous power of the furnace made the whole structure vibrate, like an animal eager to be released. Atop it all, the confusion of piping, bracings, gun housings, armoured plates, pulley mechanisms and gear chains, was the glory of the thing. A rotating chair, set on a ring of brass and festooned with controls of every sort. Though it was mostly constructed from wood taken from common wagons and iron stripped from existing artillery pieces, it was finer to his eyes than all the golden thrones of Araby.

Messina clambered into it, dropped the spanners and took control of the main set of levers. With a judder and a gout of soot, the machine rolled jerkily forward.

'She moves!' cried Messina, wild with triumph. He felt the same way he always did at the prospect of a fresh new conquest, of whatever sort. He could sense the enormous latent power of the machine beneath him. 'A work of genius! Why did the old fool not build it?'

Lukas hung back still.

'Are you really taking it out there?'

Messina looked down at him scornfully. He felt like some obscenely powerful potentate of the lands of legend, housed in his own steam-powered device of ruin.

'So what do you think?' he said, witheringly. 'Why would I build it, if not to use in battle? We aren't too late! This is our time!'

'There's been no testing!' cried Lukas, suddenly looking angry with his mentor. 'Ironblood knew there was something wrong with–'

Before he could finish, one of the gaskets within the maze of piping blew. A column of scalding steam shot backwards. The chains driving the wheels shuddered, then went limp. The smoke coming out of the main furnace began to splutter and spit out dark gobbets of oil.

'Shut it down!' cried Lukas. 'It'll blow!'

Messina, flustered, pulled a couple of levers in front of him and depressed a great brass-tipped column. The engine heaved and coughed, then went dead. Slowly, with a last parting shudder for good measure, the contraption came to a halt.

The air was thick with smoke. Soot had caked the entire rear end of the machinery. Steaming water leaked from the pipes under the chassis and pooled against the rock. The thing seemed to sink back a little into the earth.

Messina peered over the edge of the turret, his spirits still high. It was a setback, nothing more.

'It moves!' he said again, his face still filled with a childish delight. 'Help me get it working again!'

Lukas looked out of the tent entrance, clearly torn between making the machine safe and rushing to help with the fighting. For a moment, he hesitated, a sword in one hand, a wrench in the other.

'Come on,' said Messina, smoothly, knowing the lad was suggestible. 'We've spent days making this thing. All the problems have been solved. With this, we can turn tide of the battle. If we make a name for ourselves, what is the harm? We're so close!'

Lukas looked up at him, and his gaze was accusatory.

'This is all about the gold, isn't it?' he said, and he dropped the wrench. 'Enough. You've kept me tied up with this folly long enough. No more.'

He brandished his sword, and shot one last, dark look up at Messina. 'You've taught me a lot, Silvio,' he said. 'Perhaps in more ways than you know.'

And then he was gone, his blond head ducking under the tent flap and out into the camp beyond.

'Come back!' cried Messina, struggling to extricate himself from the narrow turret. 'Damn you, Herschel! It's not about the gold! It's about–'

His foot slipped. His hands scrabbled onto the brass lip of the chair, but missed their aim. For a sickening moment, he felt nothing beneath him. Then he was on the hard floor with a heavy thump, his head cracking against the near wheel of the Blutschreiben. His vision went black, and waves of blood-red pain started behind his eyes.

'Mother of Luccina!' he hissed, getting up with difficulty.

Messina staggered to the tent entrance. To their credit, the hired guards were still at their stations. They peered at Silvio as if he were some bestial creature from the wilds. The Tilean clasped a hand to his aching head, and scowled at them.

'Do not stand there stupid like Bretonnian pigs,' he snapped. 'There is three more silver pieces for each of you if you will come inside and help me get this thing working. Keep your mouth shut and don't ask questions, and I will make you all rich men.'

The venality of soldiers was always worth a punt. The three men looked at each other for a moment, then the most senior of them nodded.

'Very well. What needs to be done?'

Messina smiled through his rapidly developing headache. Who needed Lukas?

'Come inside, my good men,' he said. 'Steady yourselves when entering, and I will show you one of the wonders of the Old World.'

Rathmor stood on the balcony, high up on the leading wall of the citadel. He gazed over the battle, raging far below on the plain. The wind tore at his cloak, pulling it over his shoulder.

His expression was sour. There was no art in such warfare. The brutish clash of arms did nothing to stir his sensibilities. Only in the subtle arts of slow pain, or the mighty contest between machines, was there any glory. Above all, he valued the duel between masters of the single-shot gun. That was where the majesty of combat lay. To wield a true-firing pistol against one's opponent was the highest form of civilised conflict. Almost everything else was tedious barbarism. It was a pity that he'd almost certainly not have the opportunity to indulge his passion in this messy engagement.

He was shaken from his introspection by a familiar sound. Once more, like a recurring bad dream, Esselman had come to bother him. The man was irritating beyond words. His soldier's mind was pathetically limited, and his endless interference had become wearing. It seemed to Rathmor as if he'd never be left alone with his high, lofty thoughts. When all of this was over, he would really have to see whether the lady could do any better for her generals.

Esselman arrived on the balcony, stood beside him and looked over the same scene. His face was grim. There was a lurid weal on one cheek. The results of his last meeting with the lady, no doubt.

'You've set the traps, as we discussed?' he said, his voice clipped.

Rathmor nodded.

'All the inner levels have been rigged,' he said. 'If the need comes, we can turn this place into a pyre. But only if the need comes. The treasures in the forges are beyond price, even for the lady. We'll never see their like again.'

Esselman grunted in reply.

'Good,' he said. 'My place is on the field. I'll leave you to play with your toys.'

Rathmor bristled at the insult, but said nothing in reply. It was his 'toys' that powered the whole enterprise. Without them, Esselman would be nothing more than a provincial commander.

'There's one last thing,' said the general, curtly.

Rathmor waited. He knew what was coming, but Esselman would at least have to ask him outright.

'The infernal machine.'

Still Rathmor didn't reply.

'I know it's ready,' continued Esselman, his voice failing to hide a note of urgency. 'You told me yourself. Tell me where it is. I'll have a gunner assigned to it. They'll break against it like rain on the hills.'

Rathmor stayed unresponsive for a moment longer, but then his resolve failed. It was only a matter of time. He couldn't keep it safely stowed forever. This wasn't the proper moment for it, but the situation was difficult. He could hardly deny the man his tools now.

'Very well,' he said, turning to face Esselman and fixing him with as stern a look as he could generate. 'You can take it out. There are men in my retinue who know how to power it. If you truly need it to guarantee victory, that is. But I'd planned to unleash them all together. Alone, the infernal machine can cause havoc. In formation, they will be unstoppable.'

Esselman nodded. That was as close to thanks as he was ever going to get.

'It must be deployed now. They have the advantage of numbers. We need to break it.'

Rathmor looked back over the sea of men below. It looked like a tide of darkness, ready to wash against the foundations of the citadel. Much as he hated to see his beloved creations sent out prematurely, he couldn't help but suppress a smile at the thought of the carnage they would wreak.

'I'll come down with you. You will have your precious machine on the field in moments. Who knows? I may even join you out there. It's been too long since I tasted the aroma of blood on the air.'

The two men turned and walked back from the balcony. They disappeared into the tower behind, and the great doors were slammed shut. Far above them, the death's-head standard fluttered once, caught by the wind, and then hung still.

Thorgad had gone. The dwarf could not be restrained, and had charged down the slope into the thick of the fighting. Even over so many other sounds, Magnus could just about hear him. His strange battle cries were like no other shout from the field. The engineer couldn't suppress a faint smile. Dwarfs were irritating and irritable in roughly equal measure, but they were peerless fighters.

He looked over his shoulder. The artillery pieces had been dragged forwards into their new firing positions. Hildebrandt had taken control of the longer-range pieces, and was already goading the crews to reload. Magnus turned away. That was no longer his job. He was with the handgunners. In a close melee, they were the ones to turn the battle.

'Form up!' he cried. The two detachments of Hochland handgunners under his direct command responded quickly. They were getting better.

The regiments were a few dozen yards from the press of the fighting. The battle was evenly poised. The enemy sortie had prevented the attackers from reaching the gates, but they had been unable to break through Scharnhorst's lines. Now the Hochland army had pinned the defenders back, and the hand-to-hand combat stretched in a long line before the citadel walls. For the moment, it was a stalemate. The conflict was ferocious, but it had yet to resolve one way or the other.

Some of the handgunners had already charged into the fray, dragged into it by their enthusiasm and foolish captains. That was not the way to conduct ranged battle. The guns were only effective at a distance, and could only bring their power to bear in coordinated volleys. The key was discipline.

'Keep together men!' bellowed Magnus, and looked down the lines of gunners severely. 'Fire, advance, then fire again. Any man who gets out of line will have me to answer to! And pick your targets. It's a mess out there.'

He raised his hand, and the gunners lifted their weapons to their shoulders. At the edge of their range, the boiling mass of fighting men struggled. It was hard to make out who was who. Then there was a break, and a contingent of Anna-Louisa's troops charged towards them. They were dressed in the black livery of the citadel, and were armed with swords and axes.

Magnus smiled. Fodder for his guns.

'Fire!' he cried, and there was a instant rolling crack along the lines.

Shot spun into the advancing attackers, felling a dozen instantly. The charge broke, and some even turned back.

'Reload!' shouted Magnus. 'Hold your positions! Quicker, you dogs!'

The men struggled to replace their shot. They were faster at it than they had been in the mountains, but still far off perfection. Anna-Louisa's men rallied, and the braver attackers started to advance again.

'Fire when ready!' said Magnus, seeing the danger. The gap was closing fast, and he drew his sword in readiness.

With a rippling series of detonations, the guns fired again. Their aim was good. The entire front rank of the oncoming troops collapsed in on itself. Men fell to the ground, legs cut from under them or torsos punctured. That was enough to break their spirit. The unit splintered, and began to stumble backwards.

'Do not run!' yelled Magnus, seeing some of the younger gunners eager to pursue. 'March forward, then fire on my mark!'

In a single, unbroken line of green and red, the Hochland men advanced, their guns held high. The enemy was melting away. There was no answer to the volley of concentrated fire. Nothing, not even the raving hordes of Chaos, could stand up to a properly commanded gun-line.

'Cease marching!' cried Magnus. 'Reload, and fire at will!'

The men applied more shot, and once more their deadly iron was unleashed. The solid core of handgunners became an island of order within the sea of confusion around them. Allied troops latched on quickly, and protective detachments were formed on their two flanks. The enemy attempted to charge again, but once more the withering fire cut them down yards before their goal. They advanced again. Once more, the defenders fell back.

Magnus stepped back from the lines of gunners, satisfied with his handiwork. They continued to advance without him. He ran back up a shallow incline over to his left to get a better view of the battle around him. Some of the halberdiers from Halsbad's company had withdrawn from the heaviest fighting, and were doing the same.

'Going well, eh?' said Magnus, almost beginning to enjoy himself.

One of Halsbad's troops looked at him coldly. He had a jagged cut on his left arm, and his face and neck were splattered with blood. The close-combat troops were seldom friendly with those who delivered death at a distance.

'There's going to be another push,' the man said. 'Scharnhorst's throwing the reserves in.'

Magnus shaded his eyes, and looked out over the plain. The enemy was being pushed back on all fronts. The Knights of the Iron Sceptre could be seen in the very thick of it. None were standing against them. Anna-Louisa's men were better armed and equipped, but they were outnumbered. Far over on the left flank, Scharnhorst's reserves were indeed mustering behind the disorganised ranks of flagellants. Magnus could see what was happening. When the signal was given, they would charge through their own men, their movements shielded by the shrieking fanatics in front of them. If it worked, it would break the enemy's far flank altogether. Magnus looked over to Scharnhorst's command group, safely removed from the fighting and standing clustered on a ridge behind the reserve companies. The trumpets were being raised. A thrill of anticipation passed through him.

The signal never came. As if to pre-empt Scharnhorst's manoeuvre, a tremendous roll of drums suddenly burst from the citadel. Fresh troops poured from the shattered gates. These looked like nothing Magnus had ever seen. They were clad in armour like knights, but the plates were dark and ornate. The helmets were carved in the likeness of the death's head, bone-white and gruesome. They carried huge double-bladed halberds, which they swung around them as they advanced. Unlike the ordinary troops, they didn't charge into battle, but advanced steadily and in formation. Magnus squinted to try and get a better look. They looked formidable.

But they were only the honour guard of what was to come. From behind them, a monster emerged. Huge plumes of ink-black smoke wreathed its passage. Six iron wheels churned the ground beneath it. Three tall ironbound chimneys belched vapours. The death's head was inscribed on its forward armour, etched in ivory against a black background. In front of its tall, curved fore-armour, massive iron spikes rose up cruelly. On every side, heavy plates had been riveted, inuring it to harm. As it rolled forward, a few arrows and shot clattered harmlessly from its flanks. More smoke billowed upwards as it laboured. Troops on both sides gaped at it open-mouthed. The momentum in Scharnhorst's men suddenly flagged. A ragged cheer rose from Anna-Louisa's.

Its progress was slow, like an insect steadily crawling towards its target. But Magnus immediately saw the danger. There was nothing on the battlefield to hurt it. It was smaller than the famed steam tanks of da Miragliano, but not that much. He had seen the devastation caused by one of those things many years ago. What was worse, there was something horribly familiar about the design of the war machine.

'Rathmor,' Magnus breathed, hardly daring to utter the words. 'Could it be?'

The machine ground its way forwards. No horse would come near it. Men fell back before it, unsure how to attack it. In their confusion, the dark-armoured halberdiers advanced unfought. A wedge was being driven between the attackers' forces. Heartened by the new arrival, Anna-Louisa's men renewed their attack. Scharnhorst's men, by contrast, were suddenly consumed with doubt. The charge of the reserves was halted. The knights rode back, rallying men around them as they did so.

Magnus suddenly realised he was standing transfixed, like so many others. He shook himself free of stupor, and ran down the rise, over to where Hildebrandt was frantically trying to aim his guns at the approaching behemoth.

'Have you seen that thing before?' Magnus said, urgently.

Hildebrandt, busy with fuses and quadrants, looked back irritably.

'Now isn't the time, Magnus,' he muttered. 'We need to take it out.'

'It's Heinz-Willem Rathmor's,' said Magnus with certainty, looking back at the machine grimly. 'We worked on it together. It's his Blutschrei-ben. He finished it. By Morr, he finished it.'

Hildebrandt brushed past him, a heavy round cannonball in his hands.

'I don't care,' he said, loading it into one of the iron-belchers. 'I don't care what you two worked on at Nuln, and I don't care what that thing is. We need to stop it.'

Magnus felt the blood draining from his face. It was getting closer.

'You can't,' he murmured. 'I know how it's built. We've got nothing to touch it.'

'Then get out of the way!' cried Hildebrandt. 'We've got to try.'

Magnus stepped back. Hildebrandt lit the fuse on the cannon.

'Fire at will!' the big man cried. 'Target the machine!'

His cannon, the largest they still had in operation, detonated. The iron shaft slammed back against its braces, and the chassis quivered. The shot was sent high and fast. Hildebrandt was a good aim. But cannons were not designed to hit precision targets. The ball thudded into a cluster of men advancing to the right of the infernal machine. They were scattered in all direction, stone and gore flying high from the impact and tearing a hole in the enemy formation. A good result. Not good enough.

More guns blazed. Rockets spiralled in on the creeping tank, mortars peppered its road, Helblasters launched volley after volley at its iron flanks. Some rounds hit. The monster shrugged them off, rocking slightly on its massive axles from the impact, but unhindered. Shrouded in smoke, it crawled on. Even the craters placed in its path by the cannons were no obstacle. Agonisingly, going at a slower pace than a man's walk, it kept coming, driving inexorably into the heart of the battle, striking the attackers down with fear and instilling new resolve into Anna-Louisa's hordes.

'Here it comes,' said Magnus, feeling hollow. 'It's moving into range.'

As it did so, two of the heavy iron panels at the front of the machine were drawn back. Just as had happened on the citadel walls, two gun barrels were thrust from the gaps. They were heavy and ringed with bronze. Wolf's heads had been carved over their mouths. From the gaps behind the muzzles, fresh smoke poured out, running down the sides of the tank and staining the ground as it came.

All could see what was happening. Those in the path of the machine scrabbled to race backwards. Formations were broken, and counter-charges were halted. The war machine halted. From its rear, bracing rods were extended. There was the sound of something being ignited.

Magnus threw himself to the ground. With a roar of fire, Rathmor's infernal engine let loose. Volleys of grape seared through the air. The twisted metal spun and bounced along the ground, slicing through limbs, armour and mounts. It fired again. A great channel opened up before it, cleared of men by the scourging power of its two cannons.

The retreat became a rout. Hildebrandt trained more guns on it. None were capable of breaking the heavy armour. The knights attempted to outflank it, perilously extending themselves by charging into the implac-able armoured bodyguard on either side. They were repelled with losses.

Hildebrandt had joined Magnus on the ground. He looked shaken.

'Any suggestions?' he said.

Magnus poked his head up above the dirt. The machine was advancing again. On either side of it, Anna-Louisa's men were swarming around, preventing attack from close quarters.

'It's only a matter of time before it heads this way,' Magnus said, grimly. 'Let's use these guns while we've got them. Who knows? We might get a lucky shot.'

The two men sprung up and raced back to the line of artillery. Some of the machines had been abandoned. An air of panic had settled over the whole army.

'Get back to your positions, you fools!' cried Magnus, feeling a dark sense of resolve return. The shock of seeing the design he was so familiar with emerge from nowhere was wearing off. There were many questions to be answered. Right now, they would have to wait. Survival was the first priority.

The crews worked frantically to turn the heavy pieces around. The progress of the war machine was slow, but it still needed constant adjust-ment to keep up with. Gradually, the cannon barrels were trained on it once more. Wedges were driven under the wheels of the great guns, and master gunners took their last measurements. Time was running out. The infernal machine was closing. Even now its guns were turning in their direction.

'Fire!' cried Magnus. Despite himself, an echo of panic entered his voice. He could see the muzzles of the enemy guns train in on his position.

The cannons roared. The remaining rockets were dispatched in a flurry of smoke and blackpowder. Dozens of Anna-Louisa's men, advancing blithely in the lee of the war machine, were hurled to the ground, cut down by the hail of fire. The device itself was rocked, knocked back a yard by the ferocity of the rounds that hit. Some of the iron panels were knocked in, and one of the wheels shattered. Like a boxer reeling from a blow, the tank sagged in the ground.

'Mother of Sigmar!' exclaimed Hildebrandt. 'We got it!'

'No, we didn't,' said Magnus, his brow furrowed in confusion. 'We can't hit anything that hard.'

He looked back over the ranks of Scharnhorst's army. On the ridge behind the general's position, a new shape had emerged. It looked just like Rathmor's infernal engine, but without most of the armour cladding and decoration. It could have been designed from the same drawings, so similar was it in dimensions. There were only four wheels to the machine's six, and much of the chassis looked jury-rigged and liable to fall apart at any time. The guns were hastily bolted-together shells of cannons, held in place by an artful scaffold of iron bars and braces. Even more than Rathmor's machine, the newcomer was shrouded in thick black smoke. Naked flames coursed from the rear, licking the copper piping and sending plumes of steam far into the air. As it came forward, it wheezed and rolled, drunkenly heading directly into the path of the armour-clad monster.

'Messina!' cried Magnus, at last realising what he'd been doing. His stomach lurched with horror. All at once, nightmares from the past and present were converging. 'The madman! He'll kill us all!'

The flamboyant Tilean, exposed to the elements in his bare-bones contraption, took off his hat and waved it wildly over his head. Scharnhorst's men stopped in their tracks. Some of them stood stupidly, as if startled by the end of the world. Others roared with relief and raced towards it. For a moment, the broadsides from the first tank halted. Messina brought the Blutschreiben forward. As it came, the whole structure groaned and shifted. It looked liable to collapse at any moment.

'How did he–' started Hildebrandt.

'There's no time for that,' snapped Magnus, reaching into his jacket for the last of the blackpowder charges. 'He's doomed himself. But it'll give us the diversion we need. Gather the handgunners. We'll need to finish that monster off ourselves.'

Rathmor's war machine was turning, away from the ineffective lines of artillery and towards its new challenger. Like two great bulls, they squared up to one another.

Somehow, Messina was able to fire first. His two mighty gun barrels blazed. The whole shell of the tank rocked back, and several minor components spun into the air, knocked loose by the discharge. The volley hit home. Rathmor's tank was blasted sideways again. More of the iron panels were gouged inward, and several were ripped free altogether.

The men around the tank were driven from it by the remorseless power of the impact. They scattered like children. The entire battle became focussed on the duel between the iron machines.

Magnus and Hildebrandt pulled together all the gunners who remained close to hand. The melee before them had become confused as companies from both armies scrabbled to get out of the way. Most of the enemy troops close to Rathmor's tank had been driven off, and the way through to the infernal engine was no longer barred.

'We're going closer!' cried Magnus to the handgunners Hildebrandt had gathered. 'We just need to get near enough!'

Some of the soldiers looked back at him as if he were mad. Others, inured to grim fatalism by long experience, picked up their guns and started to prime them for the attack.

'What are you going to do?' asked Hildebrandt, pulling his sword from his sheath and grabbing hold of two of the blackpowder charges.

'I know that machine,' said Magnus, taking up his own blade. 'The Blutschreiben's already blasted half its armour off. If it gets a shot of its own away, then Messina's a corpse. But he might have given us a way in.'

The gunners were ready.

'To me!' cried Magnus, and charged down the slope to meet the lumbering machine. The men followed him, fanning out on either side. Hildebrandt brought up the rear, as slow as an ox and already breathing heavily.

They descended into the heart of the battle. All pretence at ordered regiments and lines had been shattered by the arrival of Rathmor's war machine. Soldiers, heedless of orders, were grappling with each other, running from the scene, or merely trying to make sense of what was going on. Like so many battles, it had descended into a confused mess.

Magnus and the gunners kept together. Enemy troops in their way were knocked back with a volley of shots. The guns blazed, and swords flickered. Resistance was sporadic. All eyes were on the two war machines.

Messina had brought his machine into dangerously close quarters. Magnus risked a quick look over at it. It was trundling ever closer towards Rathmor's model, leaking oil, water, steam and smoke as it came. The first device was still crippled. Something had jarred with the drive mechanism, and three of its wheels spun uselessly. It lay heavily over to one side, and the choked wheeze of its steam engine was clearly audible.

Then, something seemed to click. The infernal engine righted itself, swaying on its wheels heavily, before turning to face the onslaught of Messina. The Tilean was less than twenty yards distant. He looked feral, his face fixed in an exhilarated mask of triumph as he worked the controls. His machine was still reloading. The infernal engine took aim.

'Merciful Verena…' breathed Magnus, hardly daring to look.

The guns fired. Rathmor's damaged machine shuddered as its payload was discharged. One of its other wheels shattered. Iron panels were shed from its side like scales. The machine had been badly damaged, and it showed. The wooden interior of the device was exposed, as was its lone crewman.

It mattered not. One shot was enough. The twin shells hammered into Messina's lumbering contraption. Already frail, the structure simply exploded. With an echoing smash, the entire frame blasted apart, throwing beams, wheels, barrels and chains high into the air. The furnace ignited with a thunderous boom, immolating the surviving shell in a ball of flame. Men too close to the impact fell to the ground, clutching at their faces or frantically trying to douse the fires kindling on their clothes. A second resounding blast swept across the battlefield. The Blutschreiben was gone, almost as soon as it had arrived. A spiked wheel came rolling crazily from the carcass, bouncing over the uneven ground, before clattering over. Then nothing. There was no sign of Messina.

Magnus turned his face away grimly. He had warned Hildebrandt it wasn't safe. Now Messina had paid the price.

'Keep going!' he yelled, urging the gunners on. Despite the jostling press of men around them, they had carved a route into the heart of the enemy ranks. Soldiers on both sides were still sheltering from the falling debris. Rathmor's monster was tantalisingly close.

This was the chance. Heedless of the danger, Magnus flung himself forward. One of the death's-head guards, turning slowly from the spectacle of the Blutschreiben's demise, spotted him. He swung a halberd. Magnus ducked under it, still running, not stopping to engage him. A gun fired from behind him, and the halberdier fell to the ground, a neat hole scored in his helmet. The handgunners were still close, then.

Only a few yards. The battered sides of the steam tank loomed up. Magnus could see the face of the man inside, white with fear, trying to bring it round. It was too late. The Blutschreiben had done its work. The armour hung from its flanks loosely, exposing the unprotected innards of the machine.

'For those who died in the passes,' muttered Magnus, bitterly, tearing the leather from the blackpowder bomb in his hand.

With all his remaining strength, he hurled the charge hard into the crippled tank. It lodged somewhere in the piping at the rear, deep within the remaining armoured shell and behind the pilot's head. The man inside stared at it, unsure what to make of the innocuous-looking egg.

Magnus turned away, only to see the gunners he'd brought with him either fleeing or slain. There were enemy soldiers all around. Hildebrandt had been tied up in combat some distance away and was bellowing with rage. The battle was closing back in around him. Magnus was alone, isolated and in the heart of the enemy ranks. Another of the machine's strange bodyguards loomed up before him, halberd raised. The blade flashed in the morning light, ready for the downward blow.

The charge went off. Magnus was hurled forward, his head slamming against the rock. His side exploded with pain where his stitches dragged along the harsh stone floor. He had a vague impression of men being thrown around like dolls, and heavy objects whistling over his prone body. A scorching wind rushed past him, hot as a furnace.

His heart still hammering, Magnus looked up. The machine was gone, replaced by a crater of steaming, twisted metal. It shimmered with heat. Debris continued to fall, some of it heavy chunks of iron. Anyone within yards of the explosion had been knocked from their feet. Slowly, painfully, soldiers were hauling themselves up. Some lay still, blood seeping from their prone bodies. The explosion had caused carnage.

Magnus shook his head, trying to clear the black, spinning shapes from his vision. Dimly, he was aware of the still form of the enemy halberdier by his side. The man had fallen on his weapon, and a long trail of blood ran like a stream over the stones.

A shadow fell across him. Hildebrandt. The big man extended a hand. He was breathing heavily.

'We have to get back,' he gasped. 'They're regrouping.'

Magnus nodded weakly, feeling himself being pulled upwards roughly. His side felt as if it was on fire, and a line of hot blood dripped into his eyes.

Painfully, haltingly, barely aware of what was going on, he was dragged from the scene. Behind them, soldiers staggered back to take up their positions. Smoke drifted across the field from the source of the devastation. Trumpets blared from far away, a desperate attempt by the army commanders to marshal the troops again. They sounded thin and ineffectual after the echoing blasts from the tanks. The shock of the machines' arrival had knocked all shape out of the formations, both attacker and defender. Only slowly was the gap filled by fresh troops. The newcomers tore into one another once more, cutting the dazed victims of the blasts down where they stood. Amid them all, the two wrecks smouldered, surrounded by dozens of the slain.

As he was pulled away to safety, a dark thought entered Magnus's head. He had been responsible for both dreadful war machines. They were his designs. Now two other men had taken them and used them for their own ends. One was Messina, who had died for his ambition. The other was Heinz-Willem Rathmor, a name from the distant past. Suddenly, Magnus understood. The guns, the cannons, the cunning artistry of the weapons. There had never been a better mind than Rathmor. Even his father had said so.

'Tobias,' gasped Magnus, feeling the pain in his side begin to ebb. 'He's here.'

Hildebrandt finally halted, and set Magnus down against the charred ruin of a cannon housing. They had withdrawn behind their own lines. The battle still raged, but some way off.

'So you said,' replied the big man, collapsing heavily on the stones beside him. 'I thought he'd died.'

'So did I,' said Magnus, and a shadow passed across his features. 'If I'd known he were here, I might have told Grotius to stuff his commission.'

He felt faint. He'd been hit on the head by something, and his vision was still blurred at the edges. Every bone throbbed.

'Now that I know he's here, though,' Magnus said, his voice low, 'there's only one thing to do. I'm going to have to kill him.'

Hildebrandt looked at him. His face was drained of blood, and he seemed exhausted.

'Let it go, Magnus,' he said, his eyes almost pleading. 'There's enough for us to worry about here without making this personal.'

Magnus spat on the ground contemptuously. The spittle was laced with blood.

'You know me better than that,' he said, and his voice had a kernel of steel. 'Whatever else happens here, I'm going back in there. And when I do, I'll track him down. He'll know soon enough there's an Ironblood in Scharnhorst's army. I want him to know it. I want him to be afraid. He ought to be. I'm coming for him.'

CHAPTER SIXTEEN

'So turns the path of war. The foolish commander is the one who trusts too deeply in his tools. Your wizards may falter, your artillery may misfire. Only one thing remains trustworthy, even when all else fails. The spirit of vengeance in men. When all other things desert you, rely on the capacity for hatred. That quality alone is what a wise commander cultivates in his soldiers, and no great battle has been won without it.'

Grand Marshal of the Reiksguard Kurt Helborg
Memoirs, Vol. XII

Rathmor stormed down the corridor. History was repeating itself. Once again, he felt the kind of anger and frustration that comes from a sudden bereavement. He had never really cared for the loss of men he had known in life, nor even that of members of his own family. Esselman's entire army could be slain, and he would feel little emotion. But his machines, they were something else. Rathmor had an emotional attachment to each of them, from the lowliest barrel to the mightiest steam-powered monster of destruction.

The infernal machine had gone, laid low by the unlikeliest of chances. There should have been nothing in the enemy arsenal capable of piercing its armour. Even the luckiest of shots from a standard artillery piece should have been repelled with ease. But then the Blutschreiben had arrived. Against all hope, like a nightmare out of the past, a mere skeleton of what it could have been, the machine had appeared. Iron-blood's machine.

Rathmor spat on the ground as he walked, heedless of the running men around him and the gongs echoing deep within the vaults of the fortress. Magnus Ironblood had come back. This put a whole new complexion to the campaign, and one that Rathmor didn't like.

They had been together in Nuln, the two brightest students of their generation. Ironblood had always been too cautious, but his mind was brilliant. Rathmor had taken up the mantle of creation for both of them. He had no illustrious father to dog his every move. He could indulge the wilder flights of his imagination with freedom. The pair of them, with Ironblood's rigour and Rathmor's powers of creation, had been an unbeatable team. Everything came easily, everything was enjoyable. After only a year at the colleges, poring over manuals of battlefield gunnery and the principles of the new sciences, their instructors were running out of things to teach them. The whisper had gone round that one of them would become Master of the College one day. The only question was which. Would the Ironblood name rise to even higher positions of honour and esteem? Or would the outsider, the hunched genius from Ostland, take the ultimate prize?

Rathmor felt his stomach clench inside him. Even to think of those days brought bile rising in his gorge. They were a long way off, those years of toil and humiliation, but the memory was still raw. The wounds had not healed.

The irony was that it had been Ironblood, usually so plodding and careful, who had created the Blutschreiben. Working alone and in secret, he had studied the forbidden drawings of the steam tank of da Miragliano. The secret of the massive war machines had long been lost, and even the most basic aspects of their maintenance had become a dark art in the fraternity. Only the sketches remained, recondite and incomplete.

That wasn't good enough for Magnus. Back then, he had believed engineering was the salvation of the Empire, that all problems were soluble. So he had spent long candle-lit hours in the deeps of the ancient library, squirrelling out facts from barely legible tomes. His reputation had granted his access to vaults normally hidden from students, and he'd amassed a huge stash of wondrous material. Rathmor could still remember the feelings of excitement when he'd seen them. A mobile gunnery platform, virtually invulnerable, powered by steam and hydraulics, capable of destroying almost any target with ease. The Blutschreiben was a marvel. Almost on a par with the steam tank itself. It promised to revolutionise the art of war and turn the Empire into the most powerful force in the entire world.

He carried on walking, oblivious to the commotion around him. He knew it wouldn't be long now before the enemy was in the citadel. He didn't care. With the destruction of the infernal machines, the way was now open. His plans lay in tatters. Another month, maybe two, and Anna-Louisa would have had her invincible army. Now it was wrecked, and by a man whom Rathmor thought had drifted into drunkenness and squalor. What was worse, the origin of his art was now at risk. Above all, even if von Kleister and her idiot general were slain, the secret in the depths of Morgramgar could not be discovered. There was too much at stake. He had to reach it before the invaders did.

Rathmor descended stairwells quickly, heading down level after level, leaving the inhabited parts of the citadel behind him. It got darker. The corridors got narrower. Soon the noise of the great wheels in the forges was ringing in his ears. They carried on churning out weapons blithely, oblivious to the coming storm. The air became hotter as the furnaces neared. The anvils were empty. The channels of fire were untended. All hands had been rushed to the defence of the walls. He was alone in his underground kingdom.

He looked up. Far away, high above the dark vaulted ceilings, the sounds of fighting filtered down. The invaders were inside. It would not be long now.

Rathmor turned, and slipped down the secret ways only he knew. He could still salvage something from this mess. The book was still there, and his drawings were with it. If he was careful, he could emerge unscathed, ready to try his designs somewhere else. He was still young enough, and the Empire was full of disaffected nobles with money to spend. He just had to retrieve the important things, and evade the hunters for long enough.

Deep down, though, he knew that there was only one man he needed to evade. Ironblood must surely know he was in Morgramgar by now. The design of his machines was unmistakeable, as good as a signature on a piece of parchment. And if Ironblood knew that Rathmor was here, then he'd be coming. Some crimes were too heinous to forget, and Rathmor knew that the passing years would have done nothing to heal the wounds.

With trembling hands, he withdrew his pistol from his jacket, and began to nervously clean the mechanism. Before the battle was over, he knew he'd be called on to use it.

Lukas looked up, feeling the blood trickle down from his forehead and mingle with sweat. For a moment, he could barely remember where he was or what he'd been doing. Then it all came flooding back. The blasted crater before him was still smoking heavily. It was hard to make out anything within its rim. There were a few iron struts, bent out of all shape and blackened from the fire. Most of the wooden shell of the machine had been completely destroyed. Here and there, strewn all over the battlefield, a few pieces of the larger beams smouldered. It had taken days to build, hours of work both day and night working from plans neither he nor Messina fully understood. To have got it working at all had been a miracle. All for nothing. It had barely lasted minutes on the field.

Lukas pulled himself upwards, feeling his battered body protest. Though his memory of it was hazy, he could recall running towards Messina, desperate to stop him advancing. Then the opposing war machine had fired, and the Tilean had gone. All his flamboyance, his artistry, his arrogance and charm, lost to the world forever with a single blast of the device's guns. Messina had been exasperating at times. But he'd taken Lukas under his wing and given him a trade. Many fathers did less for their sons.

Lukas felt his senses returning. There was no time to mourn. All across the field, soldiers were recovering from the twin blasts, shaking their heads and gingerly getting back to their feet. Those who had been further away were closing in fast, advancing across the pitted earth, intent on closing the temporary gap in the fighting.

He clambered back up, legs shaky, and brushed himself down. He'd been hit on the head by something, and his left ankle was twisted and swollen. He'd been lucky, though. There were bodies on either side of him that still hadn't moved. The death of the steam tanks had taken many dozens of troops with them, from both sides.

Lukas looked around, and began to hobble back to the relative safety of his own lines. As he did so, he felt some strength return to his leg, and he picked up pace. The smoke was clearing, and the shouts of battle were rushing back in.

As he stumbled onwards, he was overtaken by a ragged-looking group of men. Their uniforms were torn, and they carried a mix of halberds and shortswords. Lukas suddenly realised he was unarmed. His sword must have been knocked clear when the Blutschreiben had exploded. He raised his fists desperately, aware even through his panic how futile and stupid the gesture was.

Then he saw the livery of Hochland, and a wave of relief washed over him.

'What are you doing here, soldier?' came a harsh voice from among them.

A burly man, the captain, grabbed him roughly by the shoulder and brandished a blade in his face. Lukas's vision swam. He was still shaken from the blast, and his grip on his surroundings was weak.

'You'll get yourself killed out on your own,' snapped the captain, taking a spare sword and pressing it into his hands. 'Stick with us. We're going back in.'

As the man spoke, Scharnhorst's trumpets blared out once more. From all along the lines of attackers, answering blasts rang. On either side of the halberdiers, ranks of soldiers began to advance. In the distance, on Lukas's left, disorganised bands of flagellants tore towards the citadel, shrieking and howling with incoherent rage. In their wake, rows of foot-soldiers came onwards more cautiously. Some order had been restored to their detachments. Men who had been cut off from their companies like Lukas were absorbed into the oncoming formations and carried along with the advance.

There were none left behind. Scharnhorst had finally committed the reserves, and the entire army pressed forward, rank after rank of soldiers moving in concert.

Lukas grasped the handle of his sword, and gripped it tight. The feel of the blade in his hands was comforting. It was an honest weapon, not like the crazed constructions of his fellow engineers. For the first time in a long while, Lukas felt like he was among equals. The men on either side of him were from similar stock. There were no handguns, spyglasses or mortars here. Just faith and steel, the bedrocks of the Empire.

Across the pitted battlefield, the enemy had formed up too. With a yell, Anna-Louisa's men rushed forward, their blades flashing in the sun. Lukas's company didn't hesitate. To a man, they let rip a ragged answering shout, and charged towards the approaching enemy.

Lukas was carried along. As he ran, a kind of exhilaration took hold of him. He joined in with the chorus of war cries, feeling his hot blood pound through his body. His blade felt light in his hands. His injuries were forgotten.

The lines closed in on each other. As the fighting broke out once more, the last thing Lukas thought was how simple the way of a non-engineer was. How much better it was to be amid a company of proper soldiers, shoulder to shoulder, wielding the weapons of Holy Sigmar, with only a natural and honourable death to fear. It was the life of an Imperial soldier. It was the life of a man.

Then the detachments crashed together. All was forgotten save the desperate struggle of arms. Lukas was lost in the melee, his blond head just one in a crowd of dozens, hundreds of others. Steel rang out against steel, flesh against flesh. The final push had begun.

Scharnhorst smiled. Slowly, bitterly, the defenders were pushed back to the citadel walls. Bereft of the imposing presence of Rathmor's war engine, they were beaten back by the Hochlanders' superior numbers. The close fighting gave no opportunity for them to bring their superior long guns to bear. Men grappled with men, fighting with swords, pikes, halberds, clubs, fists and teeth. There was little glory in it. Apart from the knights, who launched glorious charges into the heart of the boiling mass, the rest of the combat was brutal and ugly. Soldiers were dragged down to the ground by weight of numbers alone, throttled in the press and suffocated in the shadows. Eyes were gouged, fingers broken, scalps ripped, any mean or vicious trick to gain an extra yard of ground.

The greatest losses had been among the flagellants. They had flung themselves at the defending lines with utter abandon. Many had been mown down remorselessly with gunfire. Once they came too close for the enemy guns to be effective, they were sliced apart by the disciplined ranks of the defending halberdiers, working in concert like a team of harvesters before their crop. But it mattered not. Though the flagellants were slain in droves, they punched holes in the regiments of defenders through the sheer force of their charge. These were then exploited by the ranks of state troopers behind. Time and again the zealots would be hurled forward, only to be followed by orderly lines of soldiers ready to pile in and finish the task.

Across the rest of the field, the story was the same. Anna-Louisa's men, well drilled and superbly equipped, were borne down by the volume of bodies coming at them. The deathmask bodyguard of the war machine, the best close-combat troops in the defending army, cut down three men for every one of their number they lost. But it was still not enough. Inexorably, they were harried back towards the shattered gates of their citadel.

Watching all of this unfold with an expression of impassive flint, Scharnhorst stood with his retinue on the low mound that served as his outpost. Every few minutes, reports were brought to him by red-faced functionaries, detailing the progress of the assault. The news was mostly good. Where changes needed to be made, trumpets sounded in a series of signals, and the captains reassigned regiments and redeployed companies. Though every step was paid for in blood, the noose was closing in.

The Knights of the Iron Sceptre were continually in the thick of the fighting. On a rare lull between charges, Kruger rode up from the field and dismounted beside the general. His cheeks were heavily flushed from his exertions, and he wore a bloodied bandage on his left arm. Otherwise, he looked the same as ever. Haughty, aristocratic, implacable, deadly.

'We near the gatehouse, sir,' he said, pulling his helmet off and walking up to the command retinue. 'Your orders?'

Scharnhorst put his spyglass down. Though it was now almost imperceptible, the faint smile still played across his lips.

'They've been playing us for fools for days,' he said, a vicious edge in his voice. 'We've lost too many good men to their cowardly guns. Now they'll pay for every drop of blood spilled. Let us finish this. Take your knights and marshal the final charge. We'll assault the gates and push on within the citadel. Slay them all. We will make an example of this little rebellion, and the fear of it will resonate to the Talabec and beyond.'

Kruger looked over his shoulder at the battlefield. For a moment, he seemed hesitant.

'Are you sure?' he said in his unconsciously arrogant way. No other member of the army would have dared to question Scharnhorst. 'Ironblood thought there would be hidden dangers inside.'

Scharnhorst turned and made a signal to one of his aides. A horse was led up the hill, a huge chestnut stallion with an armoured faceplate and the colours of Hochland emblazoned on its tabards.

'The order has been given, master knight,' the general replied, reaching for the reins of his steed. 'I have been ordering the siege from the rear for too long. I myself will lead this charge. Muster your company. You will be my escort.'

Kruger bowed, and rushed back to his mount. In moments, the heavily armoured Iron Sceptre knights were assembled for another charge, their horses stamping at the ground and whinnying impatiently. Scharnhorst and his personal guard mounted. The finest armour Hochland could produce was on display. The general himself donned a heavy steel helm, emblazoned with Ludenhof's family emblem, the boar's head, and crowned with green and red plumes. He drew his broadsword, and its blade glinted in the sun. The day was waxing fast, and noon was now long past. The battle would be decided before it rose again.

'Men of Hochland!' the general bellowed, bringing his huge steed around to face the citadel. Before him, his entire army was laid out, locked in a pitiless battle with the beleaguered defenders at the walls. 'This is the turning point! Show no mercy! Death to the traitors! Forward! For Ludenhof, Karl Franz and the Empire!'

The men closest to the general cheered wildly, and surged forward. The knights kicked their horses. With a noise greater than the machines still churning in the bowels of the earth, the charge began. They swept down towards the gates, swords shining, hooves drumming. Behind them, trumpets gave the signal for the final assault, and fresh cheers rose from the furthest reaches of Ludenhof's army. The tide of men pressed towards the fortress. Notched blades rose and fell, throwing blood high into the air. The final push had begun.

Magnus and Hildebrandt fought together, their shoulders touching, their weapons working in unison. The time for gunnery was long over. Artillery still fired sporadically from the ridge far behind them, but the combat was now so close that there were few clear targets for them. The handgunners had put down their long guns and picked up swords. The final hundred yards of ground before the gates were contested in hand-to-hand combat, close, visceral and brutal.

After the reserves had been mustered and all men had been thrown into the fray, the two engineers had ended up in the forefront of the attack on the right-hand flank. Around them were ranks of state troopers, most armed with halberds, swords and spears. The going was hard. The close press of men meant that swinging a blade properly was difficult. The fighting was a cramped, stabbing affair with little skill and plenty of trust to luck. Amid the grasping, thrusting morass, Hildebrandt towered like a giant. Men rallied to him, and he stood at the centre of a remorselessly advancing knot of soldiers.

Magnus was happy to fight in his shadow. The knowledge that Rathmor was in the citadel had thrown all thought of fatigue from him, and he hacked and stabbed at the men before him as if he were in the prime of his youth. His wits hadn't entirely left him, though. He knew he was wounded, and that he needed to conserve his strength. If Rathmor was the same man he had been so many years ago, he would have made precautions for an assault on the citadel. There would be devices in place to frustrate the attack. Even though the defenders of Morgramgar were reeling, there was still danger.

Hildebrandt roared like a bull, and ploughed on, bringing down two men in front of him with the sheer mass of his body. Magnus rushed to support him, thrusting expertly with his sword and parrying the return blows. The years of indolence and drunkenness were falling from him, and his muscles were remembering how to wield a blade once more. Though his arms ached, he carried on pounding and hammering at the defenders. It was as if they were pieces of metal on the anvil, ready to be smashed into shards. If Frau Ettieg could see him now, his eyes shining with a grim ferocity, she wouldn't have dared to call him a disgrace.

The gate was nearing. Over to the left, the knights had almost fought their way to the shattered pillars. Scharnhorst was with them. Magnus caught a glimpse of the general's cloak rippling in the wind, surrounded by the glittering armour of his bodyguard. Kruger was wielding his mighty longsword with a roaring, concentrated fury. Few could stand against him. The end would not be long now.

'We have to be at the front of that assault,' hissed Magnus, pushing his hapless opponent backwards and head-butting him viciously.

Hildebrandt brought his blade down with a crunch on the shoulder of the soldier before him. He smashed another in the face with his free fist. He was splattered in gore, and his face was crimson.

'Morr's teeth, Magnus,' he muttered, his lungs labouring. 'We don't belong here. Leave the hacking to the knights.'

A defender crept beneath Magnus's guard and flashed his sword upwards. The man was felled by the spearman on Ironblood's left, skewered from neck to stomach, leaking intestines and gibbering horribly. Magnus nodded quickly in thanks, wiped the gore from his face and pushed on.

'He'll be down below. Down where those machines are. We have to find him.'

Hildebrandt grunted something inaudible in reply, and strode powerfully ahead. His mere presence seemed to daunt the defenders, and the lines wavered. Anna-Louisa's men were being pounded hard on every front, and now held only a small patch of land in front of the gatehouse. They were being driven in.

When the break came, it was sudden. The defenders' rearguard seemed to crack all at once, turning and bolting through the crushed gates. The ranks in front of them buckled. Scharnhorst saw the change, and the knights wheeled their horses around and hurled themselves directly at the breach. A fresh cheer rippled through the attacking forces, and the pressure built.

For a moment, Anna-Louisa's remaining men held the line, the heavily armoured bodyguards bellowing defiance. But it couldn't last. The ranks broke, and attackers poured into the breaches. Caught in the stampede, the defending troops were trampled underfoot or cut down where they cowered. Many of those fleeing were hacked apart by the knights. Kruger made the gates, and rode under them with a great roar of triumph. His fellow knights surged after him, Scharnhorst among them. The last defenders were swept aside, and the citadel was breached. With shouts of both scorn and triumph, Ludenhof's men piled into the gap.

'This is it,' said Magnus. 'Keep with them.'

Faced with nothing but fleeing defenders, Hildebrandt did his best to slow down, but the pressure of men moving all round them kept him and Magnus heading for the breach. It would have been near impossible to turn round, even if they'd wanted to.

'Back inside again,' he said, resignedly, wiping his sword blade as he pressed forward. 'This time by the front door.'

As they approached the gates, the ground became choked and pitted. The evidence of the earlier artillery fire was everywhere. The craters at the base of the ruined gatehouse were full of corpses, most of them still warm. Blasted remains of shot and cartridge casings were everywhere. It was hard to keep a secure footing, and Magnus felt himself stumble often as the baying crowds around him carried him onward.

The gate itself was the width of two carriages. Its span had been reduced by the piles of debris, and Scharnhorst's men had to squeeze themselves through at no more than four men abreast. From the far side of the walls, inside the citadel, the sounds of fighting could already be heard. The defenders may have been driven in, but there was clearly resistance still.

Eventually, after much shoving and cursing, Magnus and Hildebrandt reached the gates. On the far side, the first of Morgramgar's many courtyards opened up. It was hewn from the same dark stone that the walls were. Even full of clatter and noise, it was a mournful space. Dreary black walls enclosed the far three sides, each studded with narrow windows.

Beyond the opposing wall, the bulk of the citadel rose up imposingly. From ground level, the place looked like a vast cluster of broad-trunked towers, each connected to the others by a series of spiralling stairs and twisting buttresses. Everything was tall, narrow and tortured. The architects of the citadel, having had little space on which to build, had packed as much as they could into the few natural platforms. As a result, the whole place looked like a thicket of trees in a dark primeval forest, jumbled on top of one another and grasping upwards for light. Above them all, towering two hundred feet from the courtyard, the mighty central shaft rose. The summit of that tower was still crowned by the strange bulbous chamber, illuminated from within by the lurid green light.

The first courtyard was secured quickly. Scharnhorst and the rest of the knights dismounted. The winding stairs and narrow corridors would be impossible to negotiate on horseback. All of them knew that the rest of the fighting would be on foot, locked tight in the close halls of stone.

The few of Anna-Louisa's soldiers that had made it through the gates were now being beaten back into the interior of the citadel. A couple of narrow doorways were still held, and arrows had begun to spin down into the courtyard from windows high up in the towers beyond. It was a barely token effort. The retreat had been disorderly, and Scharnhorst was clearly keen to keep up the momentum.

'Spread out!' he yelled, brandishing his broadsword and looking murderous. 'Hunt them down! The traitors are up in the towers! A gold crown for the man who brings me the head of Anna-Louisa von Kleister!'

That ratcheted the frenzy up another notch. Soldiers, their faces distorted by bloodlust, tore across the courtyard, hammering down doors and crashing their way up the narrow stairs beyond and into the towers. There were more behind them, pushing from the rear for the chance of getting involved with the slaughter. Like the sea bursting through the breach in a tide-wall, Morgramgar was filling up with men.

'Are you with me?' cried Hildebrandt, carried along with the throng despite his vast bulk.

Magnus held back.

'Rathmor won't be up there!' he cried. Hildebrandt was already several yards away. Magnus kept his position with difficulty, ducking and shoving past the rows of rushing, eager bodies. Like some street urchin of Altdorf, he crouched down and scampered out of the main press. With much elbowing and jostling, he was soon at the right-hand edge of the horde, away from the main current of men surging ever upwards.

'I'll find you!' came Hildebrandt's roar, now some distance ahead. Magnus looked over to where he struggled. The big man had been pushed into the forefront of the assault. Fighting had broken out once more at the far end of the courtyard. A brief counter-attack from the tower beyond had been launched. The defenders weren't finished yet.

Magnus looked down to his right. There was a little door sunk far back into the wall. It led downwards, towards the lower levels of the citadel. The forges. If Rathmor was in the fortress, he would be there, down amongst his machines, cornered like a badger before the dogs.

Magnus looked back up for the last time. Hildebrandt was gone, caught up in the thick of the fighting. He knew he should go after him, stand beside him. Just as the big man had done for him, so many times. It was his duty.

But there was a stronger urge within him than duty. A cold flame had been kindled. He had long thought it extinguished, doused in ale and bitterness, but the sight of the war machines had brought it back.

Rathmor was here. His old colleague. The one who had stolen the Blutschreiben designs. The one who had built the experimental war machine in the foundries of Nuln, and paraded it as if the drawings were his. The one who had convinced that old man of engineering, the peerless White Wolf of Nuln, to pilot the first prototype. Rathmor had somehow convinced the magisterial figure that it was safe, that the flaws had been worked out of it. And he had then watched from safety as the magazine had exploded, cascading the watching professors with burning shards of iron and burying the dream in ignominy.

The memory was etched into Magnus's mind. He could remember his frantic last effort to halt it. On the day itself, he had come tearing into the parade ground after discovering the truth, too late to prevent it, but in time to witness the final explosion. His father, Augustus Iron-blood, slain by a weapon of his own designing. From that day, from that moment, he had been doomed to live with the guilt. That was what had driven him away. The brilliance had gone forever. Never again did he innovate. He had lost his nerve. The drinking began. And there was never enough of it. Never enough to forget.

But guilt could be overcome. Revenge was the antidote. The man who had taken everything from him was near. Magnus took out the pistol from within his shirt, and began to prepare it. The time had come. He slipped from the ranks of the invading army, still heading up and into the heights of the citadel, and passed through the narrow door. The forges awaited, and vengeance.

CHAPTER SEVENTEEN

'The engineers pride themselves on their scientific minds. But scratch under the skin, and you'll find them as passionate and irrational as the rest of us. They may claim to find pleasure in the mechanical workings of their machines, but put a pistol in their hand, and their blood will run as hot as any man's. Indeed, it has often been my supposition that the hearts of our famous mechanical scholars may be particularly prone to excitement in the heat of battle. Their imaginations are fertile, and their capacity for rage strong. If it were otherwise, how could they come up with such dreadful devices?'

The Emperor Karl Franz

Lukas didn't look back. He had been swept along through the gates like the rest of them, caught up in a tide of moving bodies. He still clutched his sword tightly, and the blade ran with blood. The spirit of exhilaration had ebbed slightly. He felt as if he had succumbed to a kind of madness during the assault. He had grieved for Messina with every blow struck. In a strange way, the fighting had been cathartic. No one noticed tears in the heat of battle.

The troopers around him pressed forward. The gates were coming closer. As Lukas passed under them, he marvelled at the destruction. The stone had been cracked and shattered. Metal bindings lay shredded and hanging. The ground had been turned into a morass of debris and churned earth. The blood had seeped into the meagre soil, and had been ground into a dirty slurry of deep red.

Beyond the gates, the courtyard was full of men. The knights had pushed far ahead, up into the towers. The last of the enemy soldiers had been driven up before them. Now the real fighting had moved upwards. But Morgramgar was a warren of passageways and corridors. There was plenty of opportunity to get your hands bloody if you knew where to look.

'Over here, lads!' cried the captain of the halberdiers. Lukas realised suddenly that he didn't even know the man's name. There was little enough time for introductions in the heart of the fighting.

He followed the captain's pointing finger. A door over on their left was still barred and locked. The main mass of the army had swept past it. The halberdiers broke from the ranks and raced over to it. One of the men, a brute with a swathe of tattoos on his exposed arms and a dark forked beard, slammed his shoulder into the wood. It shivered, and the hinges buckled. More men joined him. After several more heavy blows, the iron severed and the door fell open. A wide corridor stretched away on the far side. Noises of men running could be heard in the distance.

'That's our prey!' cried the captain, and tore down the passageway. His men were quick to join him. Like hounds after the fox, the halberdiers ran down the stone corridor, hollering and baying for more blood. Lukas went along with them, but remained quiet. He was no veteran of such assaults, but it seemed to him that things were a little too easy. Why were the enemy falling back so quickly? They had superior gunners. They knew the citadel better than the invaders. Doubt began to gnaw at him.

The corridor led up and round in a long curve. It was steadily climbing, heading from the cramped cluster of buildings at the base of the citadel to the higher levels. There were windows carved into the stone on their left. As they climbed, the west flanks of the citadel were exposed. Lukas gradually began to make sense of the place. It was built on a number of clear stages. Each one got narrower as they climbed. All ways led to the upper pinnacle, the strange emerald chamber.

They kept running. There was no sign of the defenders. Lukas felt his foreboding grow. They were being drawn onwards and upwards. He turned to catch a glimpse from the nearest window. As he did so, his foot caught on the edge of something, and he tumbled to the ground. He hit the stone hard, and was winded. The rest of his company ploughed on upwards. There was the sound of coarse laughter.

'Catch up, youngster!' cried one of them.

Then they were gone, lost around the corner up ahead, the sounds of their footfalls and battle cries echoing into the distance.

Lukas shook his head and took a series of deep breaths. He looked down at his feet. He had tripped over a length of twine. He hadn't noticed it earlier. It ran the whole length of the passageway, shoved tight against the outer wall. It looked familiar. For a moment, he didn't know why. Then he recognised it. It was a long fuse. The twine was dry and quick to kindle. If lit, it would burn furiously. Its flame would travel up the corridor far more quickly than a man could.

Lukas's foreboding turned into a cold dread. They were being lured into a trap. The citadel had been prepared for them. He had to warn the others.

Still groggy from his fall, he pulled himself upright and broke into a halting run once more. The others were now far ahead of him. Lukas reached the end of the passageway, and entered a narrow chamber. From the sound of running and clattering, he could tell that the halberdiers had pressed on upwards. But there were other doors leading from the room. One was small and ordinary-looking. The length of twine ran directly under it. The fuse had been placed in the shadows between the stone flags. It was hardly visible even when he was looking for it.

Lukas stopped. He let his sword fall to his side. The sounds of pursuit died away, and the room became almost silent. His heart beating quickly, Lukas went over to the door. It was unlocked. He pushed at it, and it swung open easily. For a moment, he couldn't make out what was inside. It was growing darker outside as the day failed, and the light from the windows was weak.

Then his eyes adjusted to the gloom. It was a cache of some kind. There were objects piled up in the narrow space. To an ordinary soldier they might have seemed innocuous enough. But there were signs Lukas could read. Some of the objects had metal casings, studded with rivets. Some looked more like Messina's incendiary mortars. There were powder kegs amongst them. And more twine extended from the pile of explosive devices, some of it looping up to holes in the ceiling of the room, more leading off through narrow gaps back down towards the lower levels.

Lukas knew exactly what he was seeing. Just one node in a network. The citadel had been laced with such caches. There could be a dozen of them, or a hundred. It didn't matter. If the army continued to advance recklessly, they were heading for disaster.

Lukas left the chamber, and headed back down the corridor, his mind working furiously. He began to run back down, picking up speed as he went. He let the halberdiers carry on without him. There were more important men to warn. He had to find Hildebrandt. Or Kruger. Or even Scharnhorst. Someone had to be informed. Lukas fought to control the panic rising within him. As if blinded by their bloodlust, the army was rushing headlong into an inferno.

The air was becoming hot. The torches had burned low, and many had gone out altogether. Deep in the vaults beneath the courtyard, the shadows hung from the stone. An eerie quiet had descended over the dark corridors. Every so often a rumour of the fighting above would filter down, echoing from wall to wall. The sound was distorted, twisted by its long journey from the far pinnacles of the towers. In the deep ways, the stone absorbed everything. Light and sound sunk into the black, smooth surface like water draining into a sponge.

Magnus went slowly, waiting for his eyes to adjust to the dim environment. His pistol was loaded and ready to fire. It felt heavy and reliable in his hand. An old make, a Gruningweld, one his father had recommended, years ago. One of the very first flintlocks. An exquisite piece. Magnus let his finger run along the trigger. One shot would be enough.

The floor of the corridor sloped steeply downwards. The blank rock walls were familiar enough from his last excursion into the citadel. Just as before, the throbbing of the engines in the foundations hummed through the whole structure. Magnus placed his fingers lightly against the wall. Faintly, very faintly, they were drumming with the vibration. Despite everything, the wheels still turned. Rathmor's forges had not yet fallen silent.

He crept on. The deserted passages were eerie and unnerving, much more so than they had been when enemy soldiers had run down them, hunting the infiltrators. Now all the guards were in the upper levels, grappling for control of the spires. All except one. With a dreadful certainty, Magnus knew that Rathmor was somewhere down below.

The corridor terminated in a small octagonal chamber. In the centre of it, a wide shaft had been delved and a spiral staircase wound downwards. The glow of flames emanated from the lip of the stairwell. There were noises too. Churning noises, like a vast beast bellowing in the far, deep forest. Magnus shook his head, and placed such thoughts from his mind. His senses were liable to play tricks on him. He felt alone, surrounded by the dark and the phantoms of the imagination. He gripped the holster of his pistol more tightly, and stepped down into the stairwell.

As he descended, the noises of battle died out completely. The black, steadily glinting stone was everywhere. It was just as it had been back in the tunnel. Close, cloying, heavy, oppressive. The walls lost the appearance of human construction. They looked like channels carved into the living rock by some awesome natural process. Magnus was no longer in the citadel. He was descending into the mines and tunnels below, the realm Rathmor had created for himself. As Magnus went ever downwards, the heat and noise increased. He was coming to the heart of it.

The stairway finally ended. Another long, winding corridor stretched away. There were a few torches still smouldering, but they weren't needed. At the far end of the underground passage, the stone was limned with crimson. There was an opening, and beyond it the play of flame was obvious. Firelight glimmered from the many facets of the stones. Magnus felt as if he had entered some replica of the underworld. He looked over his shoulder, back to the stairway he had come down. It curled off into the darkness. He looked back at the fires ahead. There was only one way.

He went on, feeling his heart thump in his chest like the machines below him. A thin layer of sweat collected on his brow, though his flesh was clammy and cold. Despite the heat, a chill had entered his limbs. The further he went, the more oppressed he felt.

The corridor came to an end. It opened out into another wide chamber. Just like the one on the level above, it was octagonal. That was strange. Imperial architects mostly disliked anything other than a crude rectangle. By the firelight, he could just make out markings on the walls. They were squat, angular shapes. Not human writing. These were the arcane symbols of the dwarfs. Runes. It was hard to see the detail in them, but they looked old. Very old. The edges were worn smooth. Only at the corners of the eight walls did enough depth remain in the scored characters to make out anything of their nature.

Magnus didn't stay to try and decipher their message. He knew no Khazalid. The dwarfs taught it to none but their own kind. At the thought of dwarfs, Magnus suddenly remembered Thorgad. Where was he? Most likely in the heart of the fighting, whirling Glamrist around his head and spitting obscenities. Then again, perhaps not. There was some strange connection with the dwarfs here. There had been connections with the dwarfs all along. Thorgad had said that men hadn't built the foundations of Morgramgar. Having seen them for himself, Magnus could see what he had meant. There were older delvings in the roots of the hills, perhaps even older than the kingdoms of men themselves.

He returned to the task at hand. There were two doorways in the chamber, the one he had entered through and another set in the opposite wall. As before, a well lay in the centre, though there were no stairs leading further down. A bright red light burned from the edge of the octagonal stone lip. Magnus edged closer, and peered over the edge. Hot air surged up to meet him, singeing the tips of his straggling hair. The vivid light was blinding after the gloom of the descent, and his eyes watered. He stumbled onwards, over towards the far door. The noise of the machines was stronger. It came from beyond the narrow gap. Even before passing through it, Magnus could see that it opened into some kind of hall. The noises echoed and overlapped with one another, like ritual chants in a cathedral of Sigmar. The leaping light of great furnaces was visible, sending long shadows curling up the rock walls and flickering over the floor of the chamber.

Magnus pressed himself hard against the near wall of the chamber and edged towards the door. Slowly, carefully, knowing he'd make a tempting target for any sniper lurking in the wide space beyond, he gingerly pushed his head around the stone doorframe. As he did so, he brought his pistol up gently to his breast, keeping his finger resting lightly on the trigger. The blood in his temples beat thickly, and a thin line of sweat ran down the small of his back. His eyes peered around the rough rock edge.

The vista beyond took his breath away, and for a moment Magnus forgot his danger entirely. The hall was vast. Vast beyond his imagination. He had come down to floor level, and a wide, paved surface stretched off into the distance. It looked like polished obsidian, and was marked by huge, intricate geometric patterns. In the flickering light, Magnus thought he could make out more runes, but their shape was indistinct and strange.

Fire was everywhere. It ran in long stone channels across the floor, hung in great braziers suspended on chains, was trapped in massive ironbound lanterns, rotating gently under the influence of some unseen force. The air was hot and thick, and the stench of tar and blackpowder was pungent. The noise was now ever-present. It filled every corner of the mighty arena, and the rock itself seemed to vibrate to the noise of the devices caged within it.

And what devices they were. The chamber rose to the height of a castle wall, disappearing into darkness before the roof came into view. Massive, vaulted pillars carried its weight, inscribed with great, jagged runes. Between them, huge wheels turned with a glacial slowness. They were fashioned of jet-black metal, hammered into a smooth surface and studded with iron rivets. They churned the channels of fire endlessly, and dripped with the liquid heat. From the wheels, heavy shafts turned. The flames glinted from their bronze flanks. At the end of the shafts, all manner of engines laboured, sending columns of thick black smoke, black even against the everlasting gloom of the high vaults, coiling upwards into oblivion.

Each of the machines was made differently. Some were for the smelting of metals, and the raw heat within their innards glowed brightly, ready to receive the next batch of unworked metal. Some were made for the forging of weapons, and their steam-powered hammers rose over anvils, poised to crash down and beat blades into shape. Others contained gigantic coppers in which strange liquids boiled furiously. Magnus recognised the process of blackpowder creation, but on a scale he'd never witnessed before.

The vast machines were far larger than their counterparts in Nuln. In forgotten Morgramgar, right on the edge of the Empire, deep within the frigid roots of the mountains, a factory of awesome power had been constructed. Despite his danger, despite the sense of latent fury which had been roused within him by Rathmor's presence, Magnus couldn't help but let a sigh of admiration escape his parched lips. It was a magnificent creation, the work of a masterful engineering mind.

Gradually, he forced himself to return to the reason for his being there. He was exposed, vulnerable. Magnus screwed his eyes up against the shadowy, shifting air. There was no sign of movement in the hall, besides the endless turning of the wheels and the flickering of the flames. The machines themselves lay idle, waiting for their crews to tend to them once more. There was no sign of any men among them. All had left, called away to defend their mistress high up in the towers.

Drawing a shallow breath and whispering a quick prayer to Verena, the protector of the settlers of debts, Magnus slipped out from the chamber and shuffled over to the nearest of the mighty pillars. As he went, he thought he heard an echoing movement from far down the hall. His eyes snapped round, but there was no sign of anything. Just flames and smoke. Magnus reached the shelter of the pillar, and pressed himself against the hot stone. The girth of the columns at the base was easily the width of six men standing shoulder to shoulder. Safe for the moment in its shadow, Magnus checked his pistol over quickly. When the time came, it would have to fire truly.

Rathmor had to be somewhere in the vast forge. This was his place. Though not a superstitious man, Magnus knew with a dreadful certainty that he'd be waiting. There was a certain order to things. They had both been summoned to Morgramgar for a reason. Now all their affairs would be settled.

'Greetings.'

Magnus felt his heart leap in terror. He pressed himself hard against the hot stone. It was a voice from the past, rebounding from the iron and stone around and fracturing into echoes. He couldn't tell where it was coming from. It might have been above him. It might have been far away, past the rows of gently rotating shafts. He gripped his pistol tight.

'I saw your machine on the battlefield,' came the voice again. It had a strange, wheedling edge to it. 'So you finished it, the Blutschreiben. I'm glad. It was a worthy match for my own creations. They were all from the same drawings. As you should know.'

Magnus made no reply. After so many years, to hear Rathmor's voice again was a torment. In the shifting light, just as he had before, he saw a sudden vision of his father's face. He screwed his eyes closed.

'We needn't be enemies, Magnus,' came the voice. It sounded like it was coming from somewhere different, but it was unclear where. It was as fleeting and insubstantial as the leaping flames themselves. 'What happened was years ago, and much blood and water has flowed since. You needn't hunt me like I was some kind of fugitive. We're the same, you and I. Cut from the same cloth. Will you listen to reason?'

For a moment, Magnus felt himself harking to the seductive words. They had been close, back then, the two of them. United against the ignorance and suspicion of the colleges. So long ago. It had seemed then that the new science would usher in an age of hope and progress. They had been at the forefront, the bright hope of the colleges, of the Empire itself.

But that was then. Too much had happened since. And some betrayals were too profound for forgiveness. He would not listen to reason.

Not now. It was the application of reason that had led him to create the Blutschreiben. He didn't know who he hated more, Rathmor for building it, or himself for coming up with the plans.

Magnus took another deep breath, and felt the ash-flecked air fill his lungs.

'I'll not listen to your arguments, Heinz-Willem,' he said out loud. His voice echoed from pillar to pillar, and spun into the reverberating darkness. He knew he was taking a risk, and made his preparation to move. 'What would either of us gain? You've kept building them, kept working on the plans. You know I can't let you carry on. It's a monster. When would you give up on it? How many have to die first?'

He'd given away his position. Magnus looked over to his left. One of the huge machines loomed only a few yards distant. It rose, tall and dark, high up into the firelit vaults.

A thin laugh echoed down from the shadows. It seemed to come from everywhere and nowhere.

'That is the price!' cried Rathmor. His voice sounded on the edge of hysteria. 'You know that. Think what could be achieved, if we could perfect the designs. We'd surpass the art of da Miragliano. Princes would come and beg at our door, just for a glimpse at the power we could give them. That's what you're throwing away, Magnus.'

Ironblood tried to gauge the distance between the pillar and the shelter of the machine. Just a few strides in the open, then back into cover. He crouched low, tensing his muscles.

'Are these the words you used to convince my father?' Magnus said, letting the long years of anguish poison the words. 'Do you really think you'll make me follow him? If you'd had any shame, you'd have done what I did. Tried to forget. Instead, you persist in your delusions. It has to end, Heinz-Willem. It may as well be me that does it.'

Once again, the laugh echoed down from wherever Rathmor crouched.

'That's your final offer? There's nothing I can do to dissuade you from your pointless quest for revenge?'

Magnus tensed. This was it. Surely now the man had an aim. This was Rathmor's domain, after all. He knew all its ways.

'You know the answer!' Magnus cried. 'Never!'

As the words left his mouth, he pitched forward. He felt the shot as it whistled past his shoulder and cracked into the pillar. He kept going, legs pumping, until he was in the shadow of the nearest machine. He placed his hand on the metal housing, and snatched it back. It was fiery hot. Shaking, he crouched down, looking all around him, trying to see some clue in the smoky gloom. There was nothing.

Then there was the sound of running, far down in the vast hall, echoing into the void. Rathmor had withdrawn. To reload, no doubt. For a moment, Magnus's nerve failed him. He could still withdraw. He could run back up the winding stairs, up towards the light where his allies were fighting. He looked back over to the doorway into the octagonal chamber. It was still close. Tantalisingly close.

Magnus turned back to face the hall. He would only leave the forges when his task was done. Either that, or die here, the second Ironblood to be murdered by Rathmor.

Grimly, Magnus took up his pistol once more. Hugging the shadows, lurking like some creature of darkness against the heels of the churning machines, he crept forward. Step by step, he headed deeper into the heart of the mountain.

Scharnhorst pressed forward, a savage light in his features. Though few of his men would have guessed it, he hated standing safe from harm at the rear of his armies with his officers, ordering their movements through messengers and bugle-signals. For the most part, it had to be done that way. No commander could order his troops from the thick of battle. He had to have an overview of the whole, and a clear sense of which way the winds of fate and circumstance were blowing.

Not now. Thank Sigmar. The time for cold-blooded strategising was long gone. His men were running amok through Morgramgar, and the defences had crumbled. At last, he could take his proper place at the tip of the spear, sword in hand.

Scharnhorst swung his broadsword in a wide arc, and the defenders fell back again. On either side of him the heavily armoured knights rampaged, slicing their way through any resistance. Their armour was scratched and dented, their breastplates streaked with blood, their plumes ripped and tattered. They looked like death incarnate, tearing their way through the corridors and stairways of the upper citadel. None could stand against them.

They had fought hard up the many stairways and hidden chambers. Every bridge, every archway, every postern had been held against them. Each redoubt had been stormed, cleansed of the traitors who still clung to them. Anna-Louisa's men knew better than to expect mercy. The Imperial electors were not merciful men. Scharnhorst had his orders, and they all knew it. So they fought like ferrets in a trap, desperately clinging on to every slight defensive position, only ejected after all had been slain. It was dirty, tiring work. But it felt good. Scharnhorst was a patriotic Hochlander. The rebels were vermin. They had forgotten their allegiance, and in a world of war, that was all that mattered. Removing them from the realm of the living would make the remainder purer. Even in their deaths, they were doing Sigmar's work, after a fashion.

Scharnhorst looked over his shoulder. The vanguard was still at his heels. The knights clattered up the stone passageways to join him. Behind them, the state troopers clustered, baying for blood. He could dimly make out the vast shape of that engineer, Ironblood's deputy. The man looked good in a fight.

The general turned back to the task ahead. They had fought their way to the base of the central tower. The bulk of the citadel now lay beneath them. The valley floor was several hundred feet distant, and wreathed in the shadows of the gathering dusk. Fires had been started in the lower levels behind the walls, and their flickering light bled up the steep slopes of the inner walls. The first level of the fortress had been taken, and the last of the guards were being remorselessly hunted in the shadows. The second level was now contested. Knowing the value of striking at the heart of the contagion, Scharnhorst had not tarried, but had carried on upwards, fighting all the way, clearing the stairwells of Anna-Louisa's traitorous minions, pressing on to the central tower.

Now it loomed before them, stark and tall against the gloaming. There was a great courtyard set at its base, wide and paved with stone. At the edge of it there was an ornate parapet. The rest of the citadel was below that edge, and the stench of its burning rose above it.

In the centre of the courtyard, a wide stair rose. It ascended for many dozens of steps, and could have accommodated a whole company of knights. At the summit of the stairs, the huge tower soared into the air. Though only a single tower, it was larger than many small fortresses. The base was over forty feet wide, and the vast bole rose sheer and smooth from it. Studded into the courtyard-facing aspect were narrow windows, glowing with a lurid light.

Right at the top, leaning out over them, far above, was the final chamber. After everything, despite the ruins of the rest of the fortress, the windows of that bulbous pinnacle still shone with a bizarre green illumination. Far out into the gathering night they shone, staining the smooth stone with a sickly sheen.

Scharnhorst watched with satisfaction as his men cleared the courtyard of the final few defenders. His victory was almost complete. Only the tower remained. Its massive doors were barred, but that was of little consequence.

'Knights, to me!' he ordered.

Kruger and his company were immediately by his side.

'This is the final element,' said Scharnhorst coldly, gazing up at the tower. 'I will make the final kill. You will come with me.'

Kruger pulled his helmet off, leaned on his longsword for a moment, and wiped his brow. His face was flushed and ran with sweat, but his eyes were as piercing as ever. He looked at the doors doubtfully.

'We'll need a ram for those,' he said. 'Men won't bring them down quickly.'

Scharnhorst smiled grimly.

'I disagree,' he said, and turned around, back towards the press of men at his back. 'Where is the engineer?' he bellowed, his voice rising above the tumult. 'The man who was in Ironblood's company? I saw him.'

There was a brief commotion as the state troopers tried to find the man the general wished to see. After a few moments, Hildebrandt was located, and pushed to the front of the crowd. He emerged looking more weary than surprised, and bowed clumsily.

'What's your name, man?' asked Scharnhorst.

'Hildebrandt, sir,' replied the engineer, giving no hint of resentment at not being recognised. Both he and Scharnhorst knew that they had met and spoken many times on the long journey into the mountains, but it was not a general's responsibility to remember such things.

'Where's Ironblood?' asked Scharnhorst.

'Fighting in the lower levels,' replied Hildebrandt without hesitating.

Scharnhorst smiled. The man was loyal at least.

'Then you'll have to do,' he said. 'I know of the blackpowder bombs. The ones you used to destroy the guns. There's one last task for them. Can you break down those doors?'

Hildebrandt looked over them, and nodded curtly.

'I can.'

He reached to his belt, and pulled two of the round charges from it. There were leather straps around them. In Hildebrandt's hands they looked little more than hens' eggs.

'Then do it,' ordered Scharnhorst. 'Blow them down on the first attempt, and I'll forget any harsh words I've said concerning engineers. And you shall have the honour of being in the vanguard for the final assault.'

Hildebrandt didn't need to wait for further instructions. He strode forward. Behind him, the ranks of men in the courtyard shuffled back. There was soon a wide gap between the doors and the first ranks of Scharnhorst's army. Hildebrandt ascended the stairs, looking up as he went at the strange, silent bulk of the tower. There was no movement from above. As the evening waned towards night, it remained implacable.

Hildebrandt reached the top. He placed both of the charges where the massive ironbound doors met. The man retreated down the stairs far more quickly than he'd ascended them, and came running back to the protective ranks of soldiers. As he reached the safety of the general's retinue, the charges went off. Two sharp cracks resounded across the courtyard, and twin orbs of fire rushed outwards. The doors rocked. One was blasted clean from its massive hinges. The flames and smoke cleared, and the damaged door swung open on one iron bracket. A dark green light leaked out from the interior.

For a moment, the men in the courtyard hung back. There was something unwholesome about the green glow coming from the shattered doorway. Scharnhorst himself felt an unusual pang of foreboding. What had been unleashed? Would a brace of daemons spill from the gap? Though the sounds of combat and looting still rose into the air from down below, the high courtyard was seized with a sudden hush. There was no movement from the tower. It stood darkly, looming over them like a noiseless portent of death.

Scharnhorst took up his sword, and was comforted by the weight of the steel in his hands. His doubts began to ebb away.

'Come,' he said, quietly but firmly. Around him, the knights raised their weapons as one. 'The bitch von Kleister is there. The one who has brought this bloodshed on our land. Follow me. The time has come to end this.'

As the last natural light bled from the west, the vanguard strode up the stairs, towards the ruined gates and into the last tower.

CHAPTER EIGHTEEN

'I have learned, over long years of study, not to judge the exterior of any object without knowing the full details of its interior. The grandest building may conceal a rotten core, and the meanest-looking pistol may hide the finest rifling workmanship within it. That seems to me a good maxim for any engineer. We have often discovered that the way a device looks is no guarantee of its quality. In fact, though I hesitate to make the comparison directly, the same may too be said of men. Some of us who seem most fearful by reputation may turn out, on closer examination, to be nothing but weaklings and cowards. Conversely, even those who have sunk low, almost to the point of becoming nothing, may carry within them the smouldering spark of greatness, ready at any moment to leap once more into flame.'

The Notebooks of Leonardo da Miragliano

The machines toiled. Even after being abandoned by their makers, the valves and pistons still turned in the darkness. The channels of fire still burned, and the vaults still echoed. It was as if the place had a vital spirit all of its own, an animal awareness that filled its iron sinews and copper muscles.

Magnus steeled himself. The sound of Rathmor's footsteps had died away, and the cathedral-like forge was free once more of human sounds. Clutching his pistol carefully, poised to fire at the slightest movement, he crept free of the lee of the vast machine that sheltered him. Far ahead, the light of the fires seemed to ebb. Magnus went towards the end of the hall warily, keeping close to the cover of the mighty devices and hugging the shadows of the columns. Every so often he would jump as a sudden spurt of steam or belch of liquid fire caught him off guard. Then he would spin around, or flatten himself against the hot stone, his heart beating. But Rathmor had gone, fled into the lower levels, further into the dark heart of his kingdom. For the moment, Magnus was alone.

He took a deep breath. He could still taste the ash on his lips. He went on. The columns passed by in stately succession. As he padded silently, each fresh machine emerged from the fiery murk, and passed back into it behind him. He lost count of how many there were. Each one was more elaborate and heavily ornamented than the last.

Eventually, Magnus reached the end of the long rows of foundries. The final mechanical device in the hall had a great wolf's head carved from metal on its summit. Just like the gates. Thick brown smoke rose in a steady, boiling pillar from its central chimney. It smelled foul, and a brackish ooze lapped at its base. Magnus stepped around it carefully, knowing enough of Rathmor's ways not to get any of the strange liquid on his clothes. The pool looked poisonous in the gloom.

The light of the fires was losing its vibrancy. Most of the great channels of magma were now far behind him. Magnus began to descend again. He screwed his eyes against the perpetual murk. There were more chambers ahead, soaked in shadow, lit by measly, smoky torches. Their filth clogged the already acrid air. He had to stop himself coughing. Grimly, he pressed a rag to his mouth, and carried on.

It got darker, and lower. Magnus passed huge storerooms. Some of the contents of them could only be guessed at. They looked like they'd been bored directly into the rock. It was hard to gauge their size. In the gloom inside them, row upon row of weapons waited. Spears were piled in huge bales next to sheaves of swords. And there were guns, placed in racks and hanging side by side. They were long guns, the kind that had been used against the army in the passes. Even in the thick murk, Magnus could see the distinctive serpentines adorning their barrels. So they had been forged here, wrought using Rathmor's diabolical machinery. There were none quite like them in all the Old World. Dwarfish, and yet not dwarfish. There were still riddles to unravel.

The atmosphere started to cool. The fires were left behind. Magnus pulled his leather coat closer round his shoulders. The fine cloud of dust and soot lifted, and the air became sharper. It smelled dank. As the last of the fire-pits diminished into the distance, the light once more became dim. The few torches bracketed against the walls were scant compensation, and threw a thin orange light across the uneven floor. The elaborate paving of the hall was forgotten. The roof of the chamber had sunk to little more than a few dozen feet high. The magnificence of the forges was replaced by a cold, forgotten procession of dreary tunnels and store-chambers.

In one of them, great dark shapes loomed in the shadows. They were covered in some kind of fabric. There were no torches flickering above them, but their outline was unmistakeable. Infernal machines. Rathmor's devices. A dozen more. It was hard to tell if they were finished, waiting for deployment at a moment's notice, or still in construction. All had the basic outline of the Blutschreiben. They were copies. Shams. But still deadly, for all that. Magnus shook his head in disgust. They were abominations. If Rathmor was allowed to complete his plan, it would spell destruction on a terrible scale for the Empire. Magnus felt the smooth weight of his pistol in his palm, and it reassured him. There was still time to halt it all.

He walked on further in the gathering gloom. He had begun to lose track of distance. The storerooms came to an end, and the darkness grew. Magnus stopped, and listened carefully. It was hard to make out much ahead. He felt as if he'd descended to the very root of the mountain. The shadows were as cold and ancient as any in the world. Going any further would be hard without a torch. But carrying a flame would make him an easy target. He decided to do without. It made his progress even slower. At any moment, Magnus expected to hear the report of a pistol. Even as he walked, his every muscle seemed to tense.

But there was nothing. Rathmor seemed to have shrunk back into the very rock itself. The more that Magnus crept onward, the more silent and ominous his surroundings became. The ceiling carried on descending. Soon he was walking down corridors not much taller than he was. The rock had been carved roughly around him, and there were faint track marks in the jagged floor. Every so often, he would pass some abandoned cart, knocked onto its side and left to decay in the eternal shadow. There were still torches, even so far down. They flickered and guttered. Some had gone out for lack of fuel. The others would follow them soon enough. Then the night would close over him, and he would be totally blind.

That thought was strangely terror-inducing, and Magnus pushed it out of his mind. He kept going, his feet treading silently on the unseen floor, his fingers running along the walls, tracing the serrated pattern of the stone under them. The churn of the machines was a distant whisper now. There were no other noises. It was as if he was lost at the centre of earth. The memory of light and wind felt distant.

There was a noise. Magnus pushed himself hard against the near wall, his pistol raised. His breathing quickened, and he strained to see ahead. There was no repeat of the sound. He couldn't even tell what it had been. But where there was noise, there was movement. And where there was movement…

Magnus waited for his breathing to calm, and set off again. It felt like he'd been walking for hours. Gauging time was near impossible. And then, he got the impression of space once more. The gloom around

him was almost complete, but there was something in the air that told
him the tunnel had opened out into a hall once more. Magnus slipped
over to the near wall again, wary of the wide space. He paused, listening
hard for any sound. There was nothing, except for maybe the slightest of
moans as the air from above shifted down the miles of tunnel and chamber. No water dripped, no torch sparked. Something within Magnus told
him that he'd reached the end. There were no chambers below this one,
no more machines. Whatever had been done here, it was still a secret.

He looked down at the pistol in his hands. He could just make out its
outline in the gloom. The last torch, some yards back, still lent a dim
glimmer to things.

Then it went out. Caught by some freak gust of chill air, or doused by
a malevolent hand, the light died. Magnus was plunged into complete
darkness. He might have been swimming in the void before the creation
of the world. Panic rose in his throat. He had been a fool. There was
nothing he could do in such a place. He was blind, and alone. He had
to get back, find a way towards the light.

Magnus whirled around, back in the direction he thought the tunnel
lay. For a moment, he felt the urge to cry out loud, to scream, to do
something to break the endless, terrible silent darkness.

Then he felt the cool metal press against his temple.

The invaders climbed the steps swiftly. Kruger and his knights were in the
lead, powering up the twisting stairs even in their heavy plate armour.
Hildebrandt struggled to keep up with them. Night had fallen, and he
felt his fatigue latch on to him like a heavy cloak. The long, cold days in
the mountains had taken their toll. His arms ached from wielding his
weapon for so long, his legs ached from the endless climbing. It felt like
they'd ascended halfway up the side of the peak itself. Only now were
they nearing the uttermost pinnacle, the final chamber of the citadel.

Moonlight shone weakly through the windows of the tower, but there
was little other light. The shadows clung to the walls like ink. Men's faces
distorted in the murk, and Hildebrandt felt his mood become more
febrile. The green tinge on the edges of the stone was growing. As they
clattered up the narrow, twisted ways, it became steadily more intense.
The nearer the summit they went, the more it looked as though the walls
had been doused in some unholy alchemical substance.

There was no resistance on the stairs. The promised army of defenders looked to have melted away. Hildebrandt wondered if the strength
of Anna-Louisa's forces had been overestimated. Certainly, since their
initial setbacks in the passes, the battle had swung decisively their way.

The stairs went on, winding tighter and tighter as the tower drew
towards its peak. Hildebrandt could feel his lungs labour. His breathing
began to come in shuddering heaves. He was too old and too fat for
this. His hands shook from tiredness. With a dogged growl, he pressed

on, determined not to be outdone by the armoured men around him. Even after hours of fighting and pursuit, they still fought and climbed as keenly as ever.

Just as Hildebrandt began to think that they'd be plodding up the stairway forever, it came to a sudden end. There was a narrow antechamber ahead. Three iron lanterns hung from the ceiling. The glass in the panes was lime-green. They threw a sickly light across the stone. The walls were almost bare. Here and there, a few gold trinkets had been hung. It was an incongruous sight. In the eerie light, they looked strangely sinister.

Scharnhorst was waiting in the antechamber, as was Kruger and many of the other knights. There was space for several dozen men, no more. At the far end of the chamber, a large pair of doors was bolted against them. There was still no sign of any guards. The room was quiet. From down the stairs, the noise of men clattering to a halt on the stone echoed upwards. Hildebrandt came to a standstill amid the knights, his chest heaving. It didn't look like Scharnhorst was in any hurry to break the doors down.

'What's going on?' Hildebrandt asked a soldier next to him.

The knight had taken his helmet off, and his jet-black hair cascaded in curls almost to his shoulder. He looked young. No more than twenty summers. The battle hardly seemed to have touched him.

'Can't you hear it?' he replied in an aristocratic accent, inclining his head towards the doors. 'It's unsettled him.'

Hildebrandt paused, and listened carefully. For a moment, there was nothing. Just the ragged breathing of the men around him and the muffled sounds of soldiers coming up the stairs behind them.

But then he caught it. A high, wandering voice. Like a little girl's. It was some kind of whimsical tune. Hildebrandt thought he recognised it, but he couldn't quite place the name. Then it came to him. It was a lullaby. He'd sung it to his own daughter Hannelore. Beyond the mighty oak doors, right at the bitter summit of the dark citadel, in the heart of the pitiless mountains and surrounded by the dead and dying of two armies, someone was singing a lullaby.

Hildebrandt couldn't believe it. He looked over at Scharnhorst. For the first time Hildebrandt could remember, the general looked nonplussed. He stood by the doors, unmoving, his naked sword still in his hand. Around him, the knights waited for their orders. The assault had come to a grinding halt. Men waited on the stairs below, their vigour transformed into uncertainty. The singing continued, reedy and insubstantial. In the lurid green glow, the effect was more than strange. It was otherwordly.

At length, Scharnhorst turned from the doors. He had a strange expression on his face.

'There's some devilry here,' he muttered, before turning to Kruger. 'These doors are unlocked. We must enter and see this thing through. Come with me.'

Scharnhorst's eyes swept the assembled throng, and settled on Hildebrandt.

'You too,' he said. 'And bring one of those charges. Just in case.'

Without waiting for a reply, he turned and placed his hand on the doors. Kruger and Hildebrandt pushed their way through the crowd of soldiers to stand at his shoulder. The general hesitated a final time, and then pushed. With a long, sighing creak, the doors swung inwards. From inside, green light flooded the antechamber. The three men walked forward. This was the final room. There was nowhere else to go. They were at the pinnacle of Morgramgar. They entered the chamber.

Magnus froze, his own weapon by his side. He could feel the heat of another body close to his. A man's breath grazed against his cheek.

'Brave,' came a voice, close by. 'Very brave. But useless.'

The voice sounded sad, like a child who has had to put away his toys at the end of the day. Magnus stayed perfectly still. The gun's muzzle rested against his flesh. If he moved, he was dead. His mind raced, his heart thumped, but he resisted the urge to flail or plead. He would never plead.

There was a sigh from the darkness beside him.

'I really don't want to do this,' said Rathmor, resignedly. 'Do you think I desire the fate of two Ironbloods on my name? It's hard enough having responsibility for one. Though I don't feel I should share all the blame for that.'

Magnus kept his position with difficulty. His only chance lay in Rathmor making a mistake. If the man wanted to talk, so much the better. These moments were precious. He was painfully aware they could be his last.

'Why didn't you finish the Blutschreiben yourself?' the traitor engineer asked, and his voice became wheedling again. 'If you'd been open to persuasion, we could have completed it together. Then I wouldn't have had to go behind your back. You've seen that I've nearly perfected it. There are a dozen more down here, almost finished. Imagine them on the battlefield at once! Nothing could stop them. Even here at Morgramgar, the only thing that could break its armour was a half-finished machine of your own design. And I've improved it since Nuln. It's almost there, Ironblood.'

The voice broke a little. It sounded as if Rathmor was trying to convince himself.

'Almost there,' he said again, bitterly. 'I just needed a little more time.'

The pressure of the muzzle lessened. Rathmor was drifting into some kind of reverie. This was the moment.

Magnus spun round, wheeling in the dark, and knocked Rathmor back. There was a cry, and a dull thud. Magnus sprinted forward, blind and terrified, waiting for the blast to finish him. In the dark he ran straight into a wall, and fell heavily. Blood streamed from his nose. Frantically, he scrambled along the stone, certain to feel the explosion of pain at any moment.

It didn't come. Trembling, Magnus turned back. He could see nothing, just the endless black of the tunnel. Rathmor didn't speak. He didn't fire his gun. It was as if he'd never existed at all.

Suddenly, a spark lit. A flame burst into being nearby. The mouth of the tunnel was illuminated, and Magnus could see how narrow it was. The walls of the subterranean cavern soared upwards into the preternatural gloom. The far end was lost in shadow.

His eyes adjusted slowly. Rathmor lay a few yards away, his limbs twisted awkwardly. His neck was severed nearly straight through. Dark blood still pumped down his jerkin and over the stone. His eyes were unfocussed, but his face was set into a mask of surprise. His pistol lay on the floor, forgotten.

The fire had come from a flint-strike onto a flaming brand. As the flame grew, the red light blossomed. The torch was held low to the ground. For a moment, it was hard to see who the bearer was. Then the dark shape of Thorgad emerged. The blade of Glamrist was red from the flame and from Rathmor's blood. The dwarf had a strange look in his eyes, at once full of triumph and emptiness.

'I told you,' he said gruffly, and his eyes glinted like jewels in the darkness. 'You'll be glad to have me along, I said. And I was right, was I not, Ironblood?'

Hildebrandt looked around him with amazement. In all his years of service, he had seen nothing like it. The room was circular, and huge. Great stained glass windows had been constructed on all sides. The moonlight streamed through them. Just as it had been outside, the glass was green. The panes were irregularly shaped, and threw odd patterns of emerald light across the floor. Everything was bathed in the lurid glow. More lanterns hung from the distant ceiling, also throwing a green light across the space. Hildebrandt felt a tremor of nausea just looking at it all. There was no escape. The effect was sickening. He fingered the last of his blackpowder charges nervously.

The walls of the chamber were covered in paintings. They looked like the daubings of a child. In fact, crude representations of children were everywhere. There was a portrait of what might have been the goddess Shallya too, and another of some kind of Sigmarite betrothal ceremony. The brushstrokes were heavy and artless. Some images had been scored out with thick black ink. Others had been savaged, slashed apart, and from these the canvas hung down in tatters. Those that were left were bizarre and malformed.

Across the floor, wooden toys were scattered. Most of them lay forlorn in the sickly shadows, forgotten or broken. There were ceramic dolls with no eyes. Wooden soldiers were everywhere. All were mutilated in some way. Many had no heads. There was a wooden rocking cradle near the far side of the room. The sheets had been ripped from it, and several of the legs were broken. A music box lay next to it. It looked exquisitely made, with silver bindings on the rosewood case. But it too was broken. Shards of metal were scattered around it, and the lid was cracked. It would never play again.

Hildebrandt felt a horror well up within him as he gazed around. The men beside him said nothing. It seemed almost indecent to be there, as if they had intruded into some profoundly personal nightmare. Reluctantly, the big man let his eyes follow the sound of singing. Part of him didn't want to look. But it was impossible to avoid. In the very centre of the chamber, the margravine was sitting, staring at them.

She was in bed. Her huge four-poster bedframe dominated the room. It was lined with silk sheets and linen hangings. Once they must have been fine things, fit for a lady of noble birth. Now they were stained and tattered, and fluttered limply. The bedclothes were strewn with more dolls. One hung from the frame over the centre, a little noose around its diminutive neck. Others had been warped or disfigured.

Propped up by enormous bolsters, Anna-Louisa Margarete Emeludt von Kleister, commander of the rebel armies and mistress of Morgramgar, looked at them with glassy eyes. She kept singing, mumbling the words over and again. As she did so, she tugged weakly at her straggling dark hair. Strands of it lay all over the sheets in clumps. Her flesh was pallid. Dark lines had been scored under her eyes. What little she had left of her looks had been pasted over with heavy layers of rouge. Her lips were haphazardly painted. She looked a little like one of her own dolls. The stench of perfume was everywhere, powerful and pungent. It was a scene of madness and degradation.

She kept staring, but said nothing. Her singing petered out. The chamber fell silent. Eventually, Scharnhorst took a deep breath.

'Madam,' he said, falteringly. 'By the warrant of Count Ludenhof of Hochland, Elector of the Empire, I have come to end your treachery.'

Anna-Louisa didn't reply at once. It looked as if her mind, or what was left of it, was wondering. Then her eyes seemed to gather some focus. She gazed dreamily at the general.

'Have you come to marry me?' she said. 'It's about time. I've been waiting so long.'

A stray tear ran down her cheek, blurring the heavy make-up. Scharnhorst looked at Kruger, and his brow furrowed in confusion. The knight raised an eyebrow, but said nothing. Then Anna-Louisa shook her head, and laughed. It was a strained, gurgling sound.

'Of course you're not here to marry me!' she said, brushing her tear away. 'You're soldiers. They told me you would come. To take away my gold.'

She picked up one of her dolls, looked at it dispassionately for a moment and in a casual gesture twisted its head off. As she did so, a faint growl passed her cracked lips.

'My gold,' she said again. 'That's what they want me for. That clever man Rathmor. And my soldier man, Esselman. They told me they could buy men with it. And then we could break down the Emperor's palace, and he would have to marry me. And then I would have an heir. A little child. To play with. It's been so lonely here without one. So I gave them my gold. That's how it happened.'

A strange eagerness seemed to strike up in her eyes, and she leaned forward. As she did so, the blankets fell from around her. Hildebrandt could see that she was emaciated under her flimsy nightdress. Her movements were like that of a spider, stilted and creeping. Scharnhorst remained silent. He looked horrified.

'Do you know how much gold there is under these mountains, soldier man?' asked Anna-Louisa, looking suddenly delighted. 'Endless gold! The little men mine it for me, and then I buy more of them. Every day, more men come to serve me. Soon we will have enough, and Esselman will take them to break open the Emperor's palace. It won't be long now!'

Scharnhorst took a deep breath. Now that the shock of the sight was wearing off, he looked like he was tiring of the woman's babbling.

'My lady,' he said, choosing his words carefully. 'I fear you have been deluded. Your mind is deranged. Whatever plans you had have ended. Your armies are destroyed. Your citadel is taken. Any gold you have will be confiscated and withdrawn to the treasury of Count Ludenhof.'

As he spoke, Anna-Louisa's eyes seemed to lose their focus again. She started playing with one of her toys.

'My orders were to destroy your citadel and execute you for high treason,' said Scharnhorst, his expression full of doubt and his speech slow. 'Now that I see the truth, I must surmise that you have been misled. The real traitors are those who have told you such lies. I cannot judge this matter. I will take you to Hergig. Wiser heads shall determine what shall be done with you. You are ill, my lady. Very ill. Will you relinquish yourself to my stewardship? You will not be harmed. It may do your cause some favour, were you to come of your own free will.'

Anna-Louisa looked up vaguely.

'Give myself up?' she said, in her childlike, wandering voice. 'They told me you would say that. Let me think. My soldier man told me you would say that. And there was something I had to say. What was it?'

Scharnhorst looked sourly at the scene before him. Anna-Louisa was clearly too far gone in madness to debate with.

'Enough,' he said. 'Whatever your commander told you is not important now. The citadel is ours. At first light, you will come with me to Hergig.'

At that, Anna-Louisa suddenly leapt up from the bolsters. Her hair flew wildly, and settled in straggling lumps about her face.

'That's it!' she cried. 'I remember now!'

She giggled maniacally.

'There was something I had to tell you when you got here,' she said, in a girlish whisper, looking inordinately pleased with herself. 'That man said that you would come up the tower. Then I had to say that he is still on the second level, hiding. When you're all up here, he will come out. And there are special fireworks all over the second level. They were made by that clever man Rathmor. And he's going to set them off! We are all going to burn! Isn't that very funny? We're all going to burn!'

Scharnhorst looked at her intently, a sudden sharp concern in his eyes.

'What do you mean?' he snapped.

Before Anna-Louisa could reply, there was a commotion behind them. Hildebrandt turned round to see Lukas pushing his way through the crowded antechamber and into the room. The lad was dishevelled and panting heavily. He must have shoved and jostled his way up through the whole company of men lining the spiral stairs.

'Sir!' he cried, his voice desperate. 'You must withdraw! It's a trap! There are explosives lining the citadel! We've been drawn up here!'

For a second, panic rippled across Scharnhorst's features. He turned back to Anna-Louisa, then to Lukas again. He didn't know what to do. Despite the general's rank, Lukas looked exasperated. He was at the end of his strength, and a dreadful certainty was in his expression.

'Sir, we have to withdraw!' he cried again. 'There are enemy troops hidden on the second level. They will detonate the charges!'

Still Scharnhorst hesitated. The men looked to him desperately. Some began to shuffle back towards the stairway nervously.

'I–' he began, but he was cut off.

Deep below, a familiar booming had started. There was a distant crack of blackpowder. The green windows were tinged with the red of fire. Screams filtered up from the lower levels. Rathmor's final trap had been sprung. Down in the courtyards and armouries, the corridors and mess halls, the storerooms and cellars, the bombs were going off.

Magnus sank back against the hard stone walls. His heart was still racing. His head was hammering from the impact of his fall. He felt as if his stitches had opened again. There was a sharp pain in his side, and a hot, sticky feeling of blood against his ribs.

Thorgad blew softly on his brand, and fed it some powdery substance. The flame flared up, throwing long shadows up the rock walls. The dwarf placed the torch against the wall, where it continued to burn.

The two of them were standing in a wide, tall cavern. Behind Magnus, the tunnel led back to the forge level. On the far side of the chamber, more tunnels led off into the endless night beyond. They were roughly hewn from the bare rock, and showed signs of recent wear and tear. The stone floor was littered with rubbish. Old leather gourds, discarded rags, animal bones and broken tools cluttered the dark recesses of the cavern.

Thorgad looked at Rathmor's corpse dispassionately. Magnus felt his equanimity gradually returning. His heartbeat slowed to nearly normal.

'So, what are you doing down here?' he said at last, looking at Thorgad with a mixture of relief, fatigue and confusion.

Thorgad turned from Rathmor, and rested his gnarled hands on Glamrist. In the half-light, he looked like a graven image of one of the dwarf lords of old. He could have been made of stone himself.

'I might ask you the same thing, umgi,' he said. There was a resentful edge in his voice. 'Your people don't belong here. These are our delvings. The fortress above is a mockery of what was once here.'

Magnus leaned back against the rock, weighing the dwarf's words carefully. He had a feeling some truths were about to be revealed.

'You intimated as much when we met,' he said. 'So you wanted to revisit the place. I can understand that. A dangerous way to go sightseeing, though.'

Thorgad scowled. He looked in no mood to humour Magnus.

'Don't mock me,' he said, and his voice had a low, warning tone. 'These mines are older than your Empire. Older than your race itself, maybe. Do you think I would come here lightly? It has been many hundreds of years since the dawi dwelt here. Only in song do we remember this place. And many have forgotten even that. Shame on them.'

Magnus looked at Thorgad afresh. The dwarf spoke with a voice of reverence. The engineer said nothing in reply, but sat and listened.

'Perhaps you know something of grudges,' continued Thorgad, leaning heavily on his axe. 'They are debts of our race, to be paid in respect of some great wrong. They can stretch back for a thousand years, longer even than the long lives of my people. They are recorded with care, set down on tablets of stone and in the ironbound books of the karak archives. Though years may pass before they may be returned to, they are never forgotten. Such is the way of my race. We cannot let the debt go. Though the whole world may fall into fire and the karaks sink into shadow forever, while there is still a single dwarf alive the list of grudges shall be in his mind, driving him to rectify the wrongs done to us through all the long bitter years.'

Magnus could feel his side spasm with pain. He stayed stock still and kept his mouth shut. Thorgad was eager to talk. That was rare for a dwarf. The opportunity might never come again.

'You asked me why I wished to join you,' Thorgad said. 'This is why. To fulfil a grudge held against my clan. In the past, long before the towers of Altdorf had been thought of or the foundries of Nuln first lit, one of my ancestors lost a thing of great value. A book. It is old beyond measure, and even my folk do not remember its origins. In the long years of war and strife, it was almost forgotten. But not quite. The record of grudges sets down that it was one of my blood who let the book slip through his fingers. Its whereabouts remained unknown, but it was enough that the deed had been done by one of my own kin. The shame has hung around my neck since I was a beardling.'

Magnus watched the dwarf intently as he spoke. Thorgad's eyes were not fixed on anything in particular. They seemed locked on something far away.

'Then, against all hope, there came word of an uprising in Hochland. A rebellion from the mountains. And it came to my ears that the traitors were using weapons of great quality. So good, in fact, that they surpassed the best that men could create. They were so good, I was told, that they even rivalled the guns of the dwarfs. And then a thought entered my mind, and it began to wear at me. These men were holed up in Morgramgar. I knew that the place had long ago been one of the halls of my people. It was called Karak Grimaz then, and its mines were famous. The name you give it is a corruption of its other title. The Morgrammgariven. The Halls of Silent Stone. Though the citadel above us was built by men, there were always the workings underneath, quiet and undisturbed. Umgi have never penetrated far into the deep places. Not unless driven there by some great need. But what if the book had been discovered there? I asked myself. And what if one of you man-creatures had the wit to use it? That fear wore at me, and I had no rest from that day onwards.'

'This book,' said Magnus. 'It had some secret techniques in it, then? It was a manual of some kind?'

Thorgad didn't reply, but unstrapped a large object from his back. It was nearly as big as he was. Carefully, his hands working with surprising gentleness, he unwrapped layers of sacking and soft fabric. Soon, in the gently burning light of the torch, a thick tome lay. The leather covers were black and cracked with age, and the spine and corners were studded with a tarnished bronze-like metal. A single rune had been engraved into the cover. The pages were bound closed with many straps, but the buckles on them had been broken.

'The Book of Khazgred,' said Thorgad, solemnly. 'In here are secrets no man has the wit to understand, even were he to spend a lifetime studying it. There are marvels inside beyond any of your short-lived kind. This Rathmor had barely scratched the surface of it. But what he learned was enough to make the long guns we found, as well as the cannons. He was clever. It was his cleverness that gave him away. How long had he had this thing? I do not know, but it must have taken him years to decipher the few passages which he did. He only gleaned a little, but even that was sufficient to make a leap into the unknown. The forges you see here, the machines, they are all but copies of the designs of Khazgred. In the days of our glory, we would have laughed at such follies. Even now, the great anvils of Karaz-a-Karak make them look like the work of children.'

Magnus leaned forward, ignoring the pain in his flank. His fingers crept gingerly towards the book, almost unbidden. So that was how Rathmor had managed to create such monsters. One of the fabled dwarfen manuals of arcane science. Just to peer inside for a moment would be the dream of a lifetime. He looked up at Thorgad, and an eager hope lit in his eyes.

Thorgad smiled grimly, and replaced the coverings over the book.

'This is not knowledge for you,' he said. 'Rathmor has paid for his insolence. I would not have Glamrist employed to keep your mouth shut as well.'

Magnus looked over at Rathmor's corpse, and shuddered. His spirits sank. Thorgad had spoken, and there was no point in arguing over it. The blade of the axe was too sharp, and he was too exhausted. He sighed. So he had just been a tool in Thorgad's long plan of vengeance.

'So you needed us to get you inside,' said Magnus, a little resentment creeping into his voice. 'That was your only purpose here.'

Thorgad nodded, and swung the tome onto his back once more.

'I never lied to you, Ironblood,' he said. 'Your war was your own business. It was merely my opportunity. You have my thanks, and that is not lightly given. But do not forget your debt to me, too. You'd have found it hard to scale these walls while the cannons were still blazing.'

Magnus hung his head. After all the anguish, all the labour, it seemed a bitter ending. An obscure book of the dwarfs. A human engineer with dreams of worldly domination. Both lost. Poor reasons to go to war.

'What'll you do now?' he said, his eyes still lowered.

Thorgad pulled his cloak about him, and hefted Glamrist in one hand.

'Go back to the east,' he said. 'The book will be returned to its rightful place in the archives. The grudge will be scored from the record. The honour of my clan will be restored.'

Magnus nodded resignedly.

'So be it,' he said. 'Then there's nothing more to do here.'

He felt battered, bruised and weary of the world. Slowly, awkwardly, he hauled himself to his feet.

'It must be night by now,' he said, wincing against the pain. 'As a last favour, can you help me find the way back up to the forge level? Your eyes are better down here than mine. I need to find Hildebrandt. The fighting in the citadel should be over by now. He'll want to know what happened to Rathmor. He knew him too, once.'

Thorgad gave him a strange look then, and his eyes glittered brightly.

'Don't be so sure the fighting is over, Ironblood,' he said cryptically. 'But I'll come with you, at least to the forges. Then you'll need to make your own way. Before we move, however, there's one last thing.'

He shuffled over to a small pile of rocks in the corner of the chamber. He filled both hands with small nuggets, and walked back to Magnus.

'These mines were the source of this von Kleister's wealth,' he said, disdainfully. 'It was with the promise of gold that she drew her mercenaries here. But that story had always seemed hollow to me. If there was still gold in these tunnels, there would still be dawi here. I've been exploring a little. This is what the woman has been building her army with.'

He emptied a pile of nuggets onto the floor at Magnus's feet. The last handful he gave to the engineer. Magnus took them. In the gloom, they glinted and twinkled. He frowned.

'Gold,' he said.

Thorgad snorted with disdain.

'Grungni's axe!' he spluttered. 'Even now, you amaze me. Do you know nothing at all? This is kruckgol. Fool's gold, man. If this is what she's planning to pay her men with, they're in for a shock.'

The dwarf stood back, and let Glamrist swing in a gentle arc towards the ground. As it hit the pile of nuggets, they shattered, skittering off into the shadows. The ingots were as brittle as rusted iron. Magnus stared at the ones he held in his hand. They were worthless. Rocks, just like any other. The rebellion was built on sand. The final irony.

'We should go,' said Thorgad, sharply. 'This torch won't last forever, and even my eyes can't guide us quickly with nothing to see by. Come. But bring some of those nuggets with you. As much as you can carry. They may come in useful.'

Magnus did as he was asked. Then he and Thorgad set off, as quickly as the poor light would allow. Behind them, the cavern sank back into darkness once more. The shadows over Rathmor's body lengthened, then deepened, then closed over him for good.

CHAPTER NINETEEN

*'This is at the heart of all we do. The power of fire. Consider the irony
of it. We rely on it for the most mundane tasks of the hearth and
the kitchen. Without it, we could neither survive the winter nor feed
ourselves in the summer. And yet, in the hands of a skilled craftsman,
it turns into the direst of all our many weapons. Let that be the legacy
of the engineer, if you wish to find one. That he turns the means by
which we sustain ourselves into the great destroyer of men.'*

Ludovik von Rassingen
Professor of Engineering,
Imperial College, Nuln

Morgramgar was aflame. The level behind the outer walls was a sea of
fire. As the contagion spread, more blackpowder kegs ignited, blasting
stone and tearing down walls. Some of the more slender towers collapsed entirely, falling in on themselves with an agonising slowness and
showering the men beneath with charred masonry.

The roars of triumph and vengeance were replaced with screams
of agony. Caught between the stone and the fire, Scharnhorst's army
panicked. Men pushed past one another, trampling the weaker ones
underfoot, pushing the slowest against the walls, desperate to find a way
out. The flames leapt high into the night sky, bathing the mountainside
beyond with a sheen of blood-red.

Scharnhorst finally reacted. Anna-Louisa was laughing uncontrollably,
hugging her skinny sides and rocking back and forth on the bed. The

general looked at her with disgust, then turned to Kruger.

'Rally the men at the courtyard below. Bombs or no, we'll have to cut our way down.'

The knight captain nodded curtly, and replaced his helmet on his head. His company began to head down the stairway. From below, the noise of men shouting and running could be heard.

Scharnhorst looked at Lukas darkly.

'How did you find out?' he asked.

Lukas was still out of breath.

'I found a cache,' he said. 'They've been well placed, and well hidden.'

Scharnhorst walked over to the nearest window, and gazed down on the levels below. The red glow of the fires mixed with the green sheen of the panes to create a strange muddy mixture of the two. The bedchamber looked more unnatural than ever.

'There are unharmed areas,' he muttered, looking over a trio of dark columns to the west of the central tower. 'They'll be there. Waiting for us to lose our nerve.'

He spun round on his heel, and his cloak swirled around him.

'Come,' he snapped, looking at Hildebrandt. 'This isn't over yet. The men must be rallied.'

Hildebrandt bowed, and the three of them went back through the antechamber and down the stairs. From behind them, Anna-Louisa's fey laughter degenerated into a series of sobs. Then she was forgotten. Scharnhorst's mind was working quickly. The situation was dangerous. But he still had the bulk of his army intact. The enemy commander had not been found, but even if he'd managed to hide some of his forces from the assault, they would still be outnumbered. It was all about holding the core of the army together. Once panic set in, the advantage would be gone.

Scharnhorst emerged from the tower at the summit of the wide leading stairway. Before him, a scene of devastation lay. The courtyard was high up on the southern face of the citadel, and it looked down over the valley and all the levels below. From beyond its wide parapet, huge flames danced like snakes. Smoke rose into the night air, blotting out the stars and polluting the light of the moon. Below, the rest of the fortress burned.

Lit by the firelight, his men milled around without direction across the wide expanse. For a moment, Scharnhorst couldn't see why they lingered. If they'd had any sense, they would have begun to descend into the lower levels and tried to find a way out. But the exits were blocked. From hidden passageways, Anna-Louisa's guards had at last emerged in numbers. They were all around the edge of the courtyard, and pinned Scharnhorst's men in and back towards the foot of the tower. There were many of them. They had gunners. The snap of blackpowder fire rang out in the night air. In their wake, Anna-Louisa's footsoldiers charged into the fray, bearing the look of men who had nothing to lose. To the east and west of the courtyard, where lesser towers reared their curved, spiked roofs into the air, arrows began to whine down. Scharnhorst's army was trapped, hemmed in on all sides. Any reinforcements must have been trapped further down. Scharnhorst shuddered. He didn't want to contemplate their fate.

'Men of Hochland!' he roared, swinging his sword around his head. He was heedless of the threat from the archers. The army needed leadership, or all would be lost. 'To me, men of Hochland!'

At his side, one of the Knights of the Iron Sceptre unfurled Ludenhof's standard. It rippled out in the fire-flecked wind, dark against the black of the stone behind it. A trumpet sounded. Slowly, with much confusion and labour, his men began to respond. Kruger strode down into the fray, barking orders and pushing troopers into position. Defensive lines began to form. The stream of arrows from above was met by a return volley from below. There were few archers in Scharnhorst's army, but at least it was a start.

The general remained at the top of the stairs leading to the tower, gazing at the battle intently. His soldiers had formed a wide defensive semicircle in the centre of the courtyard, their backs to the stairway. From the many steps leading up to the parapet from lower down, fresh troops poured in. They wore the black armour of all of Anna-Louisa's men. There were more than Scharnhorst had counted on. Where had they been hiding? It mattered little now. They were here, and a way had to be found to resist them.

His eyes swept across the scene. It was hard to make out any detail in the low light. The fires down below threw a red aura high into the sky, but against it the men were little more than grappling shadows.

Then, far off, he saw his adversary. A man, standing much as he was at the rear of his forces on the other side of the courtyard. He was on the edge of the parapet. His mane of silver hair was swept back and rippled in the wind. He stood with the confidence of a leader of men. Having seen the pitiful state of Anna-Louisa, Scharnhorst now knew who his real enemy was. He narrowed his eyes towards the unnamed opponent, and whispered a curse on him. Then he hefted his sword lightly in his right hand, and strode down the steps towards the front line. His bodyguard, a quartet of knights in the colours of the Iron Sceptre, fell in alongside him.

'Sir, is this wise?' asked one of them, his expression hidden behind his helmet.

Scharnhorst fixed him with a look of disdain.

'My place is with my men,' he said, curtly.

And then he pressed on, pushing his troops aside to get to the thick of the fighting. As he went, a shout went up from the knights.

'Scharnhorst!' they cried in unison. 'Scharnhorst for Hochland!'

The standard followed him into battle. When his men saw it, they seemed to garner fresh resolve. Scharnhorst took some comfort from that. The front neared. He whispered a prayer to Sigmar, and then hurled himself into the combat.

Hildebrandt and Lukas were together, fighting almost back to back. It was hard to make out what was going on in the dark, but they could tell things were going badly. The series of explosions below had turned everything on its head. The lower levels were lost, cut off by flames and the resurgent enemy. The tables had turned once again.

Still, Hildebrandt found that he preferred being in the thick of battle than being in that dreadful chamber up above. For all its horror, there was an honesty to combat with a sword. His opponents were men, just like him. They had the same aspirations as him, the same weaknesses and capabilities. But that horror in the upper room was like nothing he'd ever seen. Even as he swung his heavy sword against a row of desperate-looking attackers, he found himself chilled by it. There was something uniquely terrifying about the descent into madness of one who must have once been so privileged. Amid his revulsion, there was also a spark of sympathy. The carnage had been caused by other men. Anna-Louisa had just been a tool, a means for them to raise the money they needed.

Driven by outrage, Hildebrandt roared his defiance and lunged forwards at the advancing ranks of black-clad men. Lukas was at his side, fighting with considerable skill for a lad of his years. Just as before, Scharnhorst's men clustered around Hildebrandt's imposing presence. He became a focal point in the struggle for survival. On either side, a hundred similar little battles took place. No ground was given, no backwards step was taken. Though knocked off-balance by the lines of bombs, the men had recovered. For the last time, the forces clashed. This would count for all.

As he worked, swinging his blade with heavy strokes, Hildebrandt suddenly found himself wondering where Magnus had gone. A pang of worry hit him. He had been heading for the mines. Had he got back up before the bombs detonated? Even if he had, he might have walked right into the middle of the enemy. There was no telling where he'd ended up, or if he was even alive. The prospect of his old friend's death galvanised him even further, and he let slip a frustrated bellow of rage. Enemy troops scattered before him, and he waded forward, his sword sweeping in mighty heaves. The men beside him joined in, shouting with scorn and mockery as they pressed forward.

Then, something changed. A ripple of confusion seemed to pass through the soldiers on both sides. Orders continued to be spat out by the captains, but there was a distraction. The fighting became sporadic. Some detachments even disengaged entirely. The attackers in front of

Hildebrandt seemed to lose heart, and hurried to withdraw. In the brief lull, Tobias looked around him. Lukas had turned from the fighting too. Others had done the same. Despite the urgings of their commanders, soldiers from the two armies were pulling free from the combat and looking up at the tower.

Twisting around awkwardly, unwilling to let his guard down entirely, Hildebrandt did the same. The smooth stone soared high into the air above them. Its flanks gleamed in the firelight. The pinnacle glowed brightly. Hildebrandt found the effect no less oppressive for knowing its cause. Now more than ever it reminded him of a cluster of eyes.

For a moment, he couldn't make out what the great distraction was. But others had seen it. Though some fighting continued, many men stood idly, looking up at the tower, mouths gaping. Hildebrandt screwed his eyes up against the night sky.

Then he saw it. She had emerged. One of the windows had been opened. Far up the tower there was a narrow balcony. Anna-Louisa stood against it, her skirts fluttering in the smoky air. She was too far away for Hildebrandt to make out much of her expression, but it seemed she was smiling. The effect was mesmerising. Soldiers of Scharnhorst's army who had been fed the story of Margravine von Kleister's power and majesty now stared at the frail woman standing over them. Her own troops were similarly transfixed. Many looked horrified, discovering for the first time the true nature of their dread mistress.

'O men of Hochland!' she cried. Her voice was high and fragile, but it carried down to the courtyard well enough. A crazed edge was still apparent in it. 'Why do you fight in my castle? Do you not know that soon we shall all march to Altdorf together? Put away your toys! It is time for bed!'

Her words had an instant impact. Soldiers of the citadel stood staring, or shook their heads in disbelief. From parts of Scharnhorst's regiments, a raucous laughter broke out. Commanders bellowed in anger, urging their men back to the fighting, but it was no good. Anna-Louisa had stolen their thunder. Like some grotesque ghost of childhood, she loomed over them. As her fortress burned down below, she let slip a giddy laugh.

'You look so funny down there!' she giggled. 'Stop your nonsense now. Where is my soldier man? He should have come to see me.'

More laughter broke out amongst the soldiers. Anna-Louisa's troops fell back, some openly disputing between themselves. The unveiling of their commander had broken their vengeful spirit. Hildebrandt could see the look of horror on the faces nearest him. He could understand it well enough. Many of them had died. They had been promised much. It would be a hard lesson, to learn how far they had been deceived. Some of the troops even put down their weapons, throwing their hands up in disgust. Their commanders began moving through the ranks, cursing them and ordering them to take up arms again.

They responded only slowly. The momentum of the battle had been broken, and it was slow to recover. The long days of fighting, the endless cold and privation, had broken the martial spirit of many of the men. It was not as if they were struggling for survival against one of the dread foes of mankind. They were all Hochlanders, all simple men of the Empire, locked in combat due to the whims and obsessions of their distant superiors. Like beaten animals, they were herded back into combat. The commanders barked orders, cajoled with promises of plunder, threatened with the prospect of punishment.

Slowly, unwillingly, the men took up their swords. Anna-Louisa continued to laugh and rave. The knights charged, and the spell was broken. Scharnhorst's troops reformed their defensive positions, and Esselman's contingents renewed the press towards the tower. Steel clashed against steel, and the cries of anger and agony drowned out the crackle and spit of the flames. The distant roar of the fires in the keep had grown louder, and the columns of smoke curling into the night were thick and dark. Anna-Louisa was forgotten, a pathetic figure railing from the balcony unheeded.

Then the assault stumbled again. A single shot rang out across the courtyard, echoing from the walls around it. Another voice was raised in a great, resounding shout. It came from one of the lesser towers on the east side of the courtyard. There was a balcony set high up. A man stood at it. He had long, grey hair and wore a leather coat. He leaned over the masses below, pressing against the iron railing just as Anna-Louisa had done. In one hand he held a laden sack. In the other he held a pistol.

'Men of Hochland!' he cried, and his voice echoed around the strangely quiet scene. 'You have been lied to! You were told there was gold for you at the end of your glorious campaign. You were told that your patron was a woman of power and wealth. All of these are lies. You can see with your own eyes that the margravine is mad. She has been used by evil men. Forget their stories! One of them is dead. The other still leads you. Reject him! He has nothing to offer you but this!'

At that, he swung the sack over his head several times, before launching it out over the heads of the two armies. It spun in the air, spraying its cargo in every direction. At first, it seemed as if the bag contained a collection of blood-red jewels. The nuggets rained down, bouncing from the stone and clattering across the flags. As they landed, the soldiers cowered, expecting some new engineering terror. But no fire exploded over their heads, and no strange blast kindled on the hot stone. The pebble-like projectiles lay against the flags, glinting in the firelight. Seized with a sudden realisation, men scrabbled after them.

'Gold!' came the cry. The scuffle became a frenzy. Fights broke out instantly. All discipline had been broken. The courtyard descended into confusion once more.

'My gold!' came a wail from the tower. Anna-Louisa had climbed onto the balcony edge, her face creased with distress. 'Do not take my gold!'

The man in the leather coat laughed, and the sound of it echoed even above the growing commotion below.

'Fear not, lady!' he shouted. 'It is worthless! Like your promises!'

The truth of it was gradually emerging. As men fought over the nuggets, they shattered and broke between their fingers. Greed turned to anger. A low murmur began to build across Anna-Louisa's forces. Hildebrandt, standing amid the ranks of Scharnhorst's troops, looked over towards the rear of the courtyard. The enemy command group was besieged by their own men, and had drawn arms.

'My gold!' shrieked Anna-Louisa, and stood, precariously, on the rim of the railing. She seemed to be stretched out into the void, desperately clawing at the air. Hildebrandt looked up. With a sudden feeling of nausea, he could see what would happen.

'Get out of the way!' he shouted. It was hopeless. There were dozens of men directly beneath her. They were squabbling over the fool's gold, all thought of the conflict lost.

There was a desperate, last flail before her balance was lost completely. Anna-Louisa grasped the railing, her eyes wide and staring. For a brief second, her gaze seemed to clarify. She looked out over the ruins of her fortress. The flames burned, licking even up the parapet of the courtyard. A wan smile crossed her ruined features. The madness in her eyes dimmed. Her features relaxed. For a moment, she seemed as she must have done, years ago. She lingered for a heartbeat longer. Then her fingers unclasped. Without a sound, she dropped from the balcony. Her nightdress flapping, she plummeted. Hildebrandt averted his eyes. There was a heavy crack, and then nothing.

The fires were growing. The armies were seized by a dark and mutinous mood. The grip of the commanders was loosened, and murderous fighting broke out again. Madness swept across the regiments, as the utter futility and desperation of their situation became apparent. They would get no money. There would be no plunder. All that remained was a blind rage, the fury of the mob. At the base of the tower, the storm of anger swirled. Hochlanders put down their long guns and picked up blades. Morgramgar had become a pyre, a gruesome monument to the folly of Anna-Louisa and the ruthless response of Ludenhof.

It seemed as if both armies would be consumed with the same primal rage. Once the lust for blood was kindled, it was hard to douse. But Scharnhorst was still at the heart of the fighting, and his knights were clustered around. The kernel of his army remained true, a fixed point around which the madness revolved. Slowly, his iron will began to exert itself. Regiments of Ludenhof's Grand Army were beaten into shape by their captains, and formed up to charge into the demoralised, shapeless ranks of Anna-Louisa's men. The Knights of the Iron Sceptre, noble warriors who had little need for more gold, kept their heads. Scharnhorst's army gradually recovered its poise, and began to push out from the steps around the tower. Slowly, and with each step contested, they pressed against the noose around them, driving the encircling ranks of soldiers back towards the parapet.

There was no disciplined response. Anna-Louisa's army had turned in on itself. It was an army of mercenaries, hired by the promise of riches. Seeing the ruin of their hopes, many of them tried to flee. Others went berserk in their frustration and bitterness, attacking anyone who came near them, friend or foe. Knots of desperate men dragged their own commanders down. Throats were cut in the dark, and scores settled.

The rot of mutiny spread fast. The most bitter of the fighters, professional murderers and brawlers, the dogs of war, needed a culprit for their loss. Too late did the command group see the danger. The rear ranks of Anna-Louisa's forces turned tail and surged towards Esselman. There was a murderous sheen in their eyes. Their swords dripped with gore as they came.

There was nowhere for the general to go. He was pinned at the back of the courtyard with only the sheer drop down to the next level behind him. One by one, Esselman and his commanders were set upon and pulled into the maw of the mob. Far from help, swords rose and fell quickly, and the cries of Anna-Louisa's captains were brief before being silenced. The orgy of rage was ratcheted higher. Soldiers trampled over their comrades, just for the chance to desecrate the corpses of the men who had betrayed them. Fists hammered down, feet stamped, fingers gouged. The stones were covered in a thick carpet of blood. With a roar of empty triumph, the mutineers dragged the corpses to the edge of the parapet. With little ceremony, the bloodied bodies were stripped of their armour and valuables, then hurled over the edge and into the inferno below. Esselman was the last. As his blackened, mutilated body sailed into the void, a huge cheer broke from the armies. Both of them.

Lukas looked at Hildebrandt, a mix of amazement and uncertainty in his expression.

'What is this, Tobias?' he said.

Hildebrandt leaned on his sword. He could see Scharnhorst and his commanders surging forward, slicing through the broken ranks of the enemy. The standard of Hochland was being carried into the heart of Anna-Louisa's forces. Their formations were broken, their hopes ended. All that was left was the final bout of killing, the final snuffing of the candle.

'This is the end, Lukas,' said Hildebrandt, wearily preparing to join the assault for the last time.

There was no triumph in his voice. All around them, Morgramgar burned. And in the firelight, crushed underfoot, the nuggets of fool's gold twinkled, a final mockery to heap insult onto the memory of all those who had died.

CHAPTER TWENTY

'The fact that I have become, by dint of my skill and labour, one of the pre-eminent engineers in the Empire, is a matter of considerable pride to me. Not a day goes by without me giving thanks to Sigmar for his grace in granting me my gifts of invention and the moral character to use them wisely. And yet all these things pale into nothingness beside the greatest creation of my life, the one that fills me with joy beyond compare, and in earnest of which I would gladly give up all else. My son, Magnus, the priceless jewel for the sake of which all else has been done. I am proud of him, though he doesn't know it as he should. I am old now, and I write these words for posterity. One day he shall rise up and shake the Empire with his deeds. He has the skill. And, in time, if the fates are kind, he will discover the will.'

Augustus Ironblood
*Private diary. Recovered and preserved
in the Imperial College, Nuln*

The smoke drifted down the valley, staining the clear mountain air. Dawn had broken several hours since, and still the lower levels of Morgramgar burned. Scharnhorst had long abandoned the attempt to save the citadel. The survivors of the assault had been withdrawn. Those who had fought for Anna-Louisa were disarmed and interned. Their trials, or what passed for them, would take place in Hergig. After a day of being near abandoned, the camp was inhabited again, and the men wearily went about gathering their supplies for the long march back to the lowlands. All were exhausted. There was no mood of victory. Morgramgar had held neither riches nor glory. It had been cursed, a monument to the madness and greed of the noble classes and nothing more.

Magnus sat on one of the artillery wagons back in the encampment, gazing over the ruins before him. They smouldered darkly under the shoulder of the mighty crag beyond. Every so often a muffled boom would announce that some hidden cache had gone off. The proud aspect of the fortress had been mauled beyond recognition. Many of the towers had fallen. Those that were left were charred and cracked. The forges, deep in the heart of Rathmor's conflagration, were lost forever.

Magnus thought of the rows of infernal machines hidden in those dark storerooms. And the ranks of forges, now silenced. Perhaps it was for the best that they were destroyed. There was some knowledge that the world was better off without.

His thoughts were interrupted by a massive, rolling blast in the distance. He lifted his eyes in time to see the central tower, the emerald-encrusted pinnacle, slowly crumble. With a muffled roar, it toppled over, throwing a cloud of dust high into the air. With it gone, the citadel lost its residual terror. It was now nothing more than a collection of ruins, high in the wastes of the Middle Mountains. They had done what they came for. Kleister's fortress had been razed.

There was a movement at Magnus's shoulder. Hildebrandt came and sat down by him. He watched the same spectacle grimly for a while.

'What do you think will become of it?' he said in his deep, rolling voice.

Magnus shrugged, not really caring.

'Who knows?' he said. 'Maybe Ludenhof will have it rebuilt.'

Hildebrandt turned away from the citadel, and looked at Magnus.

'You were in the vaults,' he said. 'How did you get out of there? The whole place was on fire.'

Magnus smiled weakly.

'It helped having a dwarf at my side,' he said. 'As ever, he knew all the hidden ways.'

Magnus sighed, and looked away from the wreck of Morgramgar.

'He's gone now,' he said. 'It turned out that this was more about him than any of us. He's happy, at least.'

Hildebrandt didn't ask what that comment was about. For a moment, the two of them sat in silence. Two old friends, perched on a ramshackle cart on the edge of the civilised world. All around was wasteland, desolation and destruction.

'So was it worth it, this commission?' asked Hildebrandt, finally.

Magnus didn't reply immediately.

'Not for the money we'll get,' he said at last. 'And Messina's dead. I regret that, despite everything. I should have worked harder with him.

He had no idea of the danger he was in. And the Blutschreiben has gone forever. I now know what Rathmor did after leaving Nuln. We've stopped him spreading his madness further. That's something, I suppose.'

Hildebrandt nodded, but without much enthusiasm.

'I suppose so,' he said.

Ahead of them, amongst the toiling ranks of men dismantling the camp ready for the journey home, Magnus suddenly caught sight of Lukas. The boy was laughing and joking with a band of halberdiers. In the sun, his flaxen hair looked bright and unsullied.

'The lad,' Magnus said. 'He was with you at the end, yes?'

Hildebrandt nodded.

'Will he make it, do you think? Will he become an engineer?'

Hildebrandt thought for a moment, before fixing Magnus with a level gaze.

'Maybe,' he said. 'But he's seen what can be done with the machines. He saw what it did to Messina. If that's the future, I'd wager he wants no part of it.'

'You sound like I did,' said Magnus. 'Back in Hergig. You don't regret what we've done, do you?'

Hildebrandt looked back over the smoking ruins of Morgramgar, and his expression was bleak.

'You persuaded me to come with you, Magnus,' he said. 'Truth be told, I came to protect you from yourself. Maybe this will be the saving of you. I hope it is. But there's nothing for me here now. A man grows sick of the killing. When we're back, that's it for me. No more campaigns. You'd do well to do the same. Find an honest trade. Leave the fighting to younger men. Our time has passed.'

Magnus said nothing, but followed his friend's gaze out towards the broken fortress. The smoke still poured out.

'The Empire will always need Iron Companies,' he said, though his heart was not quite in it.

'So you say,' said Hildebrandt, and neither was his.

In the distance, a series of trumpets were blown to mark the lifting of the camp. Horses were whipped into action, and the loaded wagons and carts began to move. Men shouldered their weapons and pulled their packs onto their backs. In the midst of them were the handgunners. Their numbers were sorely reduced. There were few cannons left too. Hochland's arsenal would take months to recover its strength. The entire state had been weakened, its strength sapped by the feuds between powerful men. Even as its armies were drained of their potency, the foes of mankind multiplied in the wastelands beyond. The whole affair had been dirty, vicious, demoralising and dangerous. If this was victory, it was a sour taste to savour.

Hildebrandt said nothing more. After a few moments, he got down from his seat and walked over to the remnants of the artillery train. His voice was soon raised in the distance, shouting orders to the men, getting the caravan into order.

Magnus watched him for a moment, before turning his gaze one final time back to Morgramgar. The thought that Rathmor, the architect of the disaster which killed his father, lay buried under the mountain was some consolation for all that had happened. And despite everything, there was a flicker of pride deep within his breast.

He reached down for his gourd. For the last few days, he had barely thought of having a drink. Now, with all the excitement over, he surely deserved a swig. As he drew the leather to his lips, he paused. For some reason, the smell of the ale repelled him. Perhaps it had finally turned. Of perhaps finally he had.

He let the gourd fall down at his feet. The beer ran from the neck, foaming brown. It seeped into the rock. There suddenly seemed so little point to it. He had drowned in drink to forget the past. Now the past had returned, and its horrors had been more fragile than he'd remembered.

Magnus took a deep breath, feeling the pure, cold air enter his battered frame. The craving had left him. Perhaps not forever, but for the moment. And as he had once said to Thorgad, a start was all he needed. For the first time he could remember since the accident at Nuln, Magnus reflected on the legacy of Augustus and felt no shame. He was complete. He was healed. All men had ghosts, but his were no longer vengeful. As the high clouds drifted past the ruined towers, he thought he caught the phantasm of his father's face one last time. The craggy features, the mane of hair. But no disapproval. Not any more.

Magnus sighed, and the daydream rippled out of existence. The wind was getting up again. He could feel his wounded side ache from the chill. He had to go. There would be plenty of time to decide whether he wanted to take on another assignment when he got back to Hergig. Perhaps Hildebrandt was right. Perhaps he should look to retire. And yet a part of him wondered if he would ever do it. The Empire would always need engineers. There would always be madmen like Rathmor to counter, always walls that needed to be breached. For all their dangers and temptations, the new sciences were still the future for mankind. For better or worse Magnus had always been a part of that. Maybe he always would be.

He turned his back on the smoking ruins, and headed back down towards the baggage trains. As he went, the cold air moaned across the stone of the valley. He passed the ruined iron of the cannons and joined the mass of men marching back the way they had come. For a moment his long leather coat was visible. Then Magnus vanished among them, just another face in the numberless armies of the Empire.

The campaign was over. They were going home.

GRIMBLADES
Nick Kyme

PROLOGUE

Iron Gate, dwarf-held bastion of Black Fire Pass,
690 miles from Altdorf

They came from the east. The green tide that swept across the Worlds Edge Mountains went through its southern causeways with the pounding of drums and the call of beasts. They burned and sacked as they went. The sky blackened with the smoke of their charnel fires. Horns and bestial roars announced them. Tribes upon tribes heard the call to arms: the Waaagh! One by one the orcs and goblins emerged from their caves, bringing cleavers and spears and a brute desire to kill. This was the greenskin way, and with each fresh warband the horde swelled and its belligerence grew.

Black Fire Pass – the name was legendary. Orcs had come here before, and would again. Over two thousand years ago, they fought the nascent Man-God and were defeated. Now, a goblin led them. An apparent lesser cousin of the orc was the goblin, but not this beast. This beast was different. It was driven. It was ruthless. It was deadly. And neither dwarf nor man who guarded the gates of this ancestral battleground would oppose it.

'Name the dead!' King Bragarik boomed above the battle. He could barely think, such was the thunder coming from the orc drums. His skull throbbed with it, and their debased chanting.

'Thord Helhand, slain by an urk's blade; Norgan Stonefinger, crushed under a grobi chariot; Baldin Grittooth, bard of the halls, eaten by a troll…' The dwarf king's grudgemaster reeled off the names of the fallen as if he were inventorying weapons from the hold's armouries.

There was no time for remorse, or for grief. Dwarfs were pragmatic, especially about death. Retribution was all that mattered, and a levelling of the scales made in blood.

Life was balance. A death for a death. Blood for blood. The grudge-keeper's way.

Grudgemaster Drengk scribed perfunctorily, in the same manner as his declarations. There might be no time later. If he died, who then would remember the fallen? Who then would scribe his name in the book? The 'book' was a massive, hide-bound tome which hung around his neck as heavy as a millstone. But dwarfs were stout and strong: they worked and lived underground, digging, mining, hauling rock and ore. Drengk wore his discomfort, as all dwarfs did, with a stoic scowl.

In front of king and grudgemaster were Iron Gate's hearthguard, its hammerers. These redoubtable warriors were the king's own and they stood in file with shields locked. Hammers rose and fell like pistons and oaths were hurled like spears into the greenskin hordes trying to punch through them. King Bragarik was at their centre, his grudgemaster just behind him.

The hammerers' gromril armour was dented and stained from hard fighting. Each suit was an heirloom, worth as much as a human town. More than one hammerer had lost his battle helm. Dark, hateful eyes were revealed underneath, where before they'd been occluded by a mass of beard and metal. The elite of the dwarf hold brought low by cleavers and clubs.

King Bragarik hadn't escaped without injury. His mail gorget was split and the links spilled down his armoured chest. A cut just above his brow drooled blood, gumming his left eye and making it dark and rheumy. Bragarik had discarded his own shield. A troll's mace had shattered it. The beast was destroyed – the dwarf king had burned it with his rune axe – but so too was his shield.

Even Loki and Kazûm, his bearers, laboured underneath him with injuries. A long hard fight. One the dwarfs were losing.

For a moment, the line bowed as a renewed thrust came from the rear of the orcs and rippled forward to the fighting ranks. A hammerer screamed and fell with a black haft protruding from his neck, only to be lost from view in a red haze.

'Close ranks,' bellowed the king. A blaring warhorn answered above the rumble of drums. Blood laced his gilded gromril armour, painting its runes black as he severed an orc's neck. He crushed the skull of another with his gauntleted fist. Below him, his shieldbearers hacked furiously with their axes.

When the killing abated for a moment and the line was strong once more, King Bragarik scowled back at Drengk.

'Godrin Stoutbellow,' the grudgemaster concluded, 'killed by an urk spear.'

'Let it be known,' proclaimed the king, 'that on this day they did fall and were revenged.' His eye traced the line of battle, too long and too thin for his liking, strung out across the width of Black Fire Pass, its valley sides teeming with greenskins. Bragarik saw his hammerers, a cliff of gromril breakers against a green and turbulent tide. To their right were the Venerable, silver-haired long-beards that had lived for centuries but whose place by the eternal hearth was calling. Most were older than the king, and twice as cantankerous. Every one of their dead was not only the loss of a dwarf, but an end to a piece of living history. The warrior clans followed them: metalsmiths, fletchers, candlemakers and rockshapers all – the craftsdwarfs of the hold arrayed in battle and fighting alongside their brothers.

Quarrellers regimented upon a shallow mound filled the air with shafts from their crossbows, exacting a heavy toll. Thunderers boomed just below, between their volleys, spewing smoke and fire. More greenskins fell to their fusillades too, but it wasn't enough; not nearly enough.

Rodi Coalthumb's miners were overrun. Bragarik saw the thane laying his oathstone as he prepared a final stand.

Drongi's rangers had long been lost to the greenskin swell, swept up like sticks before a rushing river.

The king's own son, Orig, lay on a bier of shields in a cold room, silently reposed. It had been a bitter blow.

Yes, only retribution was left to the dwarfs now as Black Fire Pass filled with orcs and goblins, just as it had done in recent years when man and dwarf first stood together.

'Is there sign of–'

A blast of cannons behind him smothered even Bragarik's imposing voice.

'Their chieftain,' he tried again. 'Is there sign of him?'

Skane, the hold's banner bearer, was standing on top of a small hillock and gazed across the field beyond the rolling gun smoke.

'I see him, thane-king.' He pointed to the east, his grubby finger encrusted with rings.

Bragarik's eyes narrowed when he saw the Paunch.

The bloated goblin king spewed curses with every breath as he hacked and hewed with a double-bladed axe.

Bragarik hawked and spat, before despatching another orc with his rune axe. He'd dearly love to vent his wrath on the fat goblin swine.

A shadow crept across a lightning cracked sky. Fell voices churned the air, deep and animalistic – the Paunch's shaman was abroad.

The voice of Hungni, runesmith of the hold, rose up to challenge it. Orcish sorcery met dwarf tenacity and the heavens burned with green fire.

Emboldened by their shaman's magic, the greenskins pushed and the dwarfs gave. Just one step, but Bragarik felt it all the way down the line as his shieldbearers retreated.

'At this rate, the walls of Iron Gate will be at our backs,' snapped the king, to no one in particular.

And then there would be no more ground to give.

He turned again to Skane.

'To the north, does he come?'

The hammerer line rippled with another greenskin assault, bringing shouts, death cries and more naming of the dead from Drengk.

Rodi Coalthumb was gone. Laments from slayers weighted the air, doleful and fatalistic.

Skane shielded his eyes against a pellucid light above that was far from natural. Hungni was losing to the shaman. The beat of a wyvern's wings was drawing nearer...

Unmoving as a rock, Skane did not waver. He looked northward. A speck was growing there, like a piece of grit at first. It became larger as a grim wind began to build. The edges of Skane's cloth banner shivered.

The dwarf line withdrew another step.

'Skane!'

The banner bearer let his hand fall. 'He comes, my king! He comes!'

Cresting the mountain crags around Iron Gate, a figure ran slowly but steadily towards the king. The dwarf's cheeks were puffed, his armour split. A cudgel blow dented his helm.

Six messengers the king had sent and only one returned. He had a scroll tucked in his belt. Bragarik's eyes were keen and he saw a wax seal upon it, wearing the Imperial crest of Emperor Dieter IV.

'Let him through!' he bellowed. More horns conveyed the order, and the dwarf rearguards parted like a metal sea to admit the messenger.

As the dwarf approached, he was still catching his breath. Bragarik's attention was half elsewhere, looking askance at the eastern flank crumbling as a force of orc boar riders rolled over it.

Drengk's voice was hoarse by now. It vied with the heavy report of drums and the shouts of thanes as they fought to shore up the broken flank.

Heavily-armoured Ironbreakers were already moving in to intercede against the boar's riders and they planted their banner firmly.

'Speak quickly,' snapped the king.

The messenger proffered the scroll to him.

Leaning down to snatch it from the messenger's grip, Bragarik split the seal, unfurled it and read swiftly. Hope faded as vitriol clouded the king's granite features. He crushed the scroll in his fist and let it fall.

The king looked at Skane. 'Signal the retreat.'

'Thane-king?'

Bragarik's beard quivered with rage, setting the torcs and ingots bound there jangling.

'Do as you're bidden!'

He turned back towards the line and looked over the wall of hammerer shields defending him.

'The day is lost…' he growled to himself, and then in a smaller, hate-filled voice. 'Old oaths are sundered.'

Skane raised the hold banner and gave the signal to retreat. All across the killing field, horns sounded and drums crashed. The line narrowed, its long haft becoming a hammer's head as the stoutest dwarf armour put itself between its retreating brothers and the greenskins. They withdrew by steps, slow and reluctant. King Bragarik was amongst the last to leave.

Bodies of dead dwarfs were revealed in their wake amidst a mire of broken blades and shattered hafts. Snapped shields stuck out of red-rimed earth like partly excised teeth. Fallen battle helms served as paltry grave-markers. Greenskins littered the field, too, together with the carcasses of slain beasts. Already, they had begun to stink and a pall of decay hung over the air.

Bragarik's nose rankled as he surveyed the dead.

Drengk had lost his voice and scribed silently in his tome of remembering, the hold's book of grudges, its *dammaz kron*, where all the ills done to its many clans were recorded.

Bragarik wagered that several dark chapters would be writ by the grudgemaster's hand before the day was out.

Bitterly, the dwarfs left the field of battle. Their hammerers and iron-breakers guarded the retreat, but the greenskins did not pursue. The Paunch had not come here to taste dwarf flesh, nor did he want to fight a siege against an intractable foe. As the dwarfs fell back, so too did the way into the lands beyond the pass open. Here was the Empire, the heartlands of the greatest realm of men.

Iron Gate shut its hold tight with a forbidding clang and as the last of King Bragarik's warriors came to stand with their brothers, darkness reigned in the outer hall.

'Keep 'em doused,' the dwarf king snapped at his lamplighters. They could see well enough without light.

'Think of brothers lost,' he said, his voice sounding louder in the gloom. 'Remember the dead. And remember aid asked for but not given. Men have no honour this day. They break old pacts sworn by High King Kurgan. They bring dishonour to his name too.' King Bragarik was breathing hard and fast, his anger only just contained. 'Let the grobi go, and the urk and the troll. No rangers will oppose them, no watchtowers will warn of their approach. *Umgi*-men are alone in this,' he swore in a voice that held enough canker to scour iron. 'Let them look to themselves against the greenskins. For the dawi will not come. We will not come.'

CHAPTER ONE

Rousting in Reikwald Forest

Reikland border, domain of Prince Wilhelm III,
185 miles from Altdorf

Crouched in the lee of a gnarled oak, Eber adjusted his sallet helm for the fifth time. Unlike the rest of his Reikland uniform, it was too big. It kept slipping over his eyes and obscuring his view of the shadowed boughs of the Reikwald. His grey-white tunic and red-slitted hose stretched to contain his bulk, but the buttonholes still gaped with the tension from his muscles.

Eber was his family name. His first name was Brutan, given to him by his father. A cruel joke as it turned out. Even as a boy, it summed up his intimidating physique. 'Dumb ox', 'clumsy oaf' and 'fat brute' were some of the less flattering appellations his father had also chosen when the mood took him or when he had no more coin to stay in the tavern.

Those nights were the worst for Brutan and his waif-like mother. Violent, drunken, red nights; they were filled with accusation, ridicule and resentment. Brutan was tough, like a slab of butcher's meat, and his father had turned to his frailer wife when he'd been frustrated at the tenderiser's block. Brutan still remembered her pleas, her screams. Sometimes they went on into the night even now, years later. Brutan had clenched his thick, ham-like fists, but had done nothing. By the time he grew out of adolescence he was twice his father's size, but years of indoctrinated fear had left him scared of the man. Not a father; more a monster, like those he hunted in the forest at this very moment.

No, Brutan had lacked the courage to act then. Instead he had simply balled his fists impotently by his sides and stared at his feet, his large, ungainly feet, and done nothing.

'*Hsst!*'

The sound came from Eber's left and broke his unhappy reverie.

'Eber, advance!'

It was old Varveiter, glaring at Eber out of his good eye, giving him his parchment-cracked voice. The other eye was misted over with cataracts, but old Varveiter often claimed that he'd lost the sight in it fighting orcs in the Middle Mountains.

The veteran soldier had seen greener years. His beard was wiry and thin, with more grey in it than brown. The leather hauberk he wore under his plate cuirass was a similar texture to his skin, only not as cured, and black instead of tan. But he was strong and held his halberd haft with a soldier's purpose.

Varveiter nodded ahead as the line began to move: Eber, Rechts, Lenkmann and Varveiter with Sergeant Karlich at the centre keeping them spread out and steady. Masbrecht and Keller ranged on the extreme left and right, each guarding a flank.

About fifty feet ahead were the scouts, Volker and Brand, their advance low and silent. Heinrich Volker had a hunter's gait, a trapper's poise. He went without a helmet and his short, black hair was bound with a band of crimson cloth. He led the way towards the beastman encampment. Whilst scouting, Volker eschewed his halberd for a long dirk. Markus Brand was no poacher, but he moved with silent menace. He wore a tan leather cap with a short, protruding feather over his helmet. A long vambrace up his left arm supported three small knives. Brand was a killer, a quiet man but with violent urges that he sated on the battlefield. He too carried a long dagger, but its blade was serrated and the metal dark from use.

Together, they were the front rankers of the Reikland 16th Halberdiers, also known as the Grimblades. The rest of the forty-strong regiment waited several hundred feet back in a partial clearing. Surprise, according to Sergeant Karlich, was best effected in smaller numbers.

The foul stench that had polluted the shallow breeze wafting through the forest for the last hour abruptly intensified and Volker raised a hand for the halberdiers to stop.

Karlich didn't need to relay the order to his men. A low clanking of metal breastplates and tassets sounded in response to Volker's warning. It lasted just a few seconds as each man in the rank became still and watchful.

Hunched silhouettes cavorted in the gloom ahead. Karlich saw the suggestion of horned heads and shaggy-hided bodies in those shapes that parodied men. Hooting and braying carried on the charged silence around the Grimblades. Wood smoke and something else... burning meat, supplemented the rank odour of the beastmen. Somewhere in the Reikwald depths a fire cracked. There were no animals here, no deer, no birds. Beastmen were unnatural creatures, their very presence was repellent to the native denizens of the forest.

Volker was moving again. Karlich could only just make out his route through the undergrowth by the faintest tremble of bracken or a carefully parted branch. Brand matched the scout's step exactly. Karlich saw him pull a knife from his vambrace before he too was lost from sight. He ordered the rest of the front rankers forward.

Masbrecht and Keller closed in on the flanks. Rechts and Lenkmann kept close to their sergeant. Varveiter just about kept pace, sweating profusely under the weight of his armour and his years. Eber stayed close to the old soldier. They were only fifty feet or so away, close enough to taste the corruption emanating from the beasts, when Eber set off a poacher's trap with the haft of his halberd. The trap sprang shut with a loud clang, disturbing a flock of ragged carrion crows. Kindred of the beastmen, the wretched birds cawed loudly as they pierced the forest canopy overhead.

The cavorting stopped abruptly, and the beastmen snarled and brayed at the men in their camp. Once Volker had established the likely spot of the beasts, Karlich had chosen to approach downwind of them. Like most animals, natural or otherwise, beastmen had a strong sense of smell and Karlich wisely didn't want to alert the creatures to the halberdiers' presence by their scent. That mattered little now. The beasts had seen them and bayed for the taste of man-flesh. Snatching up crude spears and bone clubs, the beasts charged straight at the Grimblades.

Volker and Brand were the first to be discovered. The Reikland hunter rose from the foliage to stab a beast in the arm. The creature howled and made to strike back when Volker cut it again, this time across the belly, spilling its rancid guts. They were ungor, the smallest of the beastmen broods, but no less vicious or bloodthirsty. Brand took one in the throat, ramming his dagger in all the way to the hilt before yanking it free and releasing a long spurt of blood. The ungor crumpled with a burbled rasp. He killed a second with a throwing knife, the beast's head snapping back with a jerk as the blade filled its left eye socket.

The element of surprise lasted seconds. After their initial kills, Volker and Brand were on the defensive, ungors chasing them as they ran.

Karlich swore. Abandoning his initial plan, he turned to Rechts and Lenkmann.

'Sound the attack, signal the rest of the regiment!' He drew his sword. 'Grimblades! Forward!'

Rechts beat out a battle rhythm on the small drum lashed over his shoulder for his brother soldiers to follow. Lenkmann found a clear spot and unfurled the banner that had been on his back. Swinging it back and forth, he signalled their position to the other Grimblades.

Cursing his own stupidity, Eber snapped the end of his halberd haft with his foot to free the weapon from the trap, and stormed at the beastmen.

From either flank came the growling of hounds, the ungors' whelp creatures, too muscled and hairy to be mere dogs. Out the corner of his eye, Eber saw Masbrecht and Keller move to intercept the hounds. A tract of heavy scrub and bracken stood between him and his fellow halberdiers.

Volker had given up the fight now. He was simply running for his life. Brand lingered, stopping occasionally to gut an ungor. One that had got ahead of the fleeing halberdiers raised its club to stave in Volker's skull before Brand used the last of his throwing knives to kill it. The hunter flinched as the blade whipped past his face, but nodded a hasty thanks to Brand.

'Move, Grimblades, move!' Karlich raged. He held the line with Lenkmann but could have overtaken Varveiter who was finding the pace hard to match. Eber outstripped the old soldier by many yards, spurred on by guilt.

Rather than negotiate the foliage, Eber just barrelled through it. He met Volker first and kept on going, smacking straight into a chasing ungor with all the force of a bull. Eber used his shoulder like a battering ram. He felt the crunch of bone as he met the beast, the impact throwing it off its feet. Another came at him from the shadows, shrieking like some mutant swine. Eber swept his halberd in a high arc and cut off the ungor's head. He impaled a third with a thrust. He cried as a club smashed against his shoulder guard and dented the metal. Numbness spread up his arm like ice, and he nearly dropped his weapon. To be disarmed was to die, so Eber held on.

A slew of blood arced from the ungor's neck and it fell, Varveiter's halberd following it.

'Eager for the killing, eh, Eber?' Varveiter said between breaths.

Eber nodded as a deeper cry tore from the forest depths. Ungor corpses littered the floor, but more were coming and something else, something larger.

A muscled gor, a much bigger beastman kindred, emerged out of the gloom. A coiled goat's horn hung from a ragged belt attached around its thick waist, and it clutched a rusty cleaver in its massive hand.

Tilting its head back, the gor released a ululating bellow that resonated around the Reikwald, setting a tremor off in Karlich's spine. The remaining ungor gathered to the stronger beast, acknowledging its superiority. More whelp hounds stalked at the periphery of the group.

'Hold, lad,' gasped Varveiter. 'We need to wait for the others and form rank.'

But Eber was already plunging forward to meet the gor's challenge.

'Wait!'

Eber wasn't listening. He was determined to make up for his earlier mistake and if that meant fighting the gor, then so be it.

With the gor easily a foot taller, even the mighty Reiklander appeared puny next to the brawny beastman. The lesser creatures seemed to sense the challenge unfolding between their herd-leader and the man-skin and didn't interfere. Instead, they sped forward on reverse-jointed limbs to fight the others.

'Eber!' Varveiter cried out as the gor loomed over his Reikland brother. But his attention was quickly forced elsewhere as the ungor came at him. He blocked a knife slash with his haft then punched the creature in its snout to daze it. Ignoring the pain in his fist, Varveiter swept his halberd around to cut the goat-like legs from under another creature whilst the first ungor staggered. A thrust to the belly did for that one too.

'Eber!' he cried again, only able to take a few steps before another ungor blocked his path. Its spear thrust was deflected by Varveiter's tasset, but it deadened his leg and he half-collapsed. Seizing its advantage, the beastman dropped its weapon and tried to rip Varveiter's throat out instead. The old soldier turned just in time, putting his armoured forearm into the creature's mouth. He roared when the ungor bit into the leather of his vambrace. Though small, the beast had a jaw like a blacksmith's vice and kept on pressing.

Its foul breath assailed Varveiter, redolent of rotten meat and dung. Just when he thought he'd pass out from the pain, the ungor's eyes widened and it let go.

Brand was revealed behind it, wiping the flat of his dagger on his tunic. His cold, dead eyes regarded Varveiter for a moment before he offered the old soldier a hand up.

'Thank you, son,' he said as he was being hauled to his feet.

Brand gave a curt nod.

'Are you hurt, Siegen?' It was a voice like a blade being drawn from a scabbard, but it held a note of familial concern. Brand was not Varveiter's son but the killer regarded him like a father figure nonetheless, and was the only Grimblade left who used his first name.

'I'm fine. Go help Eber.'

The brutish Reiklander was holding his own against the gor. Trained to use polearms in the Grünburg barracks, Eber made the most of those lessons now and kept the beastman at bay with sharp thrusts from his halberd. But the tactic also served another purpose. The gor was getting more and more frustrated, and increasingly reckless. It stomped and snorted, aiming savage swipes that sliced only air or clanged against Eber's blade. One attack overstretched it, bringing its head forward. Seeing his chance, Eber lashed out and cut off one of its ram-like horns. Howling, the gor backed off a step and the Empire soldier came forwards. Eber jabbed his halberd into the beast's thigh and drew blood. But it wasn't enough to slow the creature, let alone kill it, and the gor came on with renewed fury.

Varveiter looked on as Brand ploughed into the forest after Eber. He could barely move, the pain in his leg was so bad. The bruised flesh pressed against his tasset as it swelled and drove hot pins of agony in the old soldier's thigh. Despite the danger, he bent down to loosen the buckle and strap. A shadow passed across him as Varveiter came back up and was face to face with a snarling ungor. He scrabbled for his halberd, ramming the tip of its haft into the ground like a defensive stake. The charging ungor impaled itself, spit through like a boar, but left Varveiter defenceless as a pair of whelp hounds scrambled through the brush to savage him.

The old soldier licked his lips before balling his fists.

'Come on then, you ugly bastards.'

One of the hounds leapt at him, as the second rounded on Varveiter's blind side to come at his unprotected flank.

He grimaced, but the expected impact didn't come. There was a loud *thunk* of flesh on metal as Sergeant Karlich put his shield between Varveiter and the leaping hound. A yelp came from the second as Keller stuck it with his halberd's point. Masbrecht, also returning from the flanks, staved in the creature's skull with a hammer.

'Sigmar's breath, they do stink!' he spat.

'No worse than Eber,' laughed Keller, a cruel smile splitting his hawkish features.

'Aye, and he'll be worse still dead,' said Karlich. 'Now shut your mouths and follow me.'

The sergeant led them the rest of the way to Eber, forcing back the ungors and what was left of the hounds. More were coming though, summoned by the death cries of their herd and the reek of blood.

'Form rank!' shouted Karlich when Rechts and Lenkmann had joined them.

'The rest of the regiment is just behind us,' Lenkmann reported, planting the banner and drawing his sword.

Rechts beat out the order to form up with his drum. The others fell in dutifully.

When it saw the gathering of men the gor backed away, recognising a threat. Eber was content to let it go. His muscles burned from the effort of fighting it, but he still took up his post in the fighting rank.

'They're regrouping for another charge,' said Varveiter. He'd freed his halberd and levelled it forward at the same angle as the others. Volker too had his familiar polearm, as did Brand, both collected from Rechts who'd strapped the weapons to his back before the engagement.

'Hold this line!' hollered Sergeant Karlich. The beasts outnumbered them, but they were a rabble. The front rankers only needed to keep them back until the rest of the regiment arrived. Already, he could hear soldiers crashing through the undergrowth behind them.

The gor herd-leader roared, snarling and lashing at the ungor trammelling the foliage to close with the man-skins.

'Brace and meet them!' bellowed Karlich. In response, the angle of the halberds lowered again by just a fraction. Each man put his foot behind the base of the haft. Maddened by bloodlust, the ungors and whelp hounds struck the thicket of steel and were scattered. Some were shredded, others impaled. Any that got through were cut down by Karlich's sword or brained by Masbrecht's hammer.

'Thrust!' came the sergeant's next order and each man drove his halberd forward to strike a second wave of ungor. Rechts cried out when a rusty blade pierced his shoulder. Karlich battered the creature senseless with a blow from his shield before it could follow up, then Lenkmann stabbed it in the throat whilst it was prone.

'Stay together.'

At least a dozen more dead and injured ungor littered the ground, but with the gor at their backs the rest dare not falter.

'Taal's mercy, how many more of these swine are there?' asked Volker.

'Come on, come on…' Karlich muttered under his breath. The sound of reinforcements was close, but was it close enough?

The battle was fierce, and Karlich dare not avert his attention from it for even a second. In the end, it was the ungors that gave him his answer. The vigour drained out of them like air from a pig's bladder and they retreated. Even the brutish gor lost its nerve. The scent of so much man-flesh and Empire-forged steel spooked rather than emboldened it. Bringing the coiled horn to its bovine mouth, it blew a long discordant note.

Like cattle fearing the drover's whip, the beasts took flight. Some reverted to all fours, galloping awkwardly alongside the hounds; others jerked with two-legged strides.

Karlich felt the rest of his regiment at his back and found his confidence renewed.

'All Grimblades,' he rallied, 'advance!'

Rechts drummed the pace as Lenkmann raised the banner. The forest was thinning and the beastmen headed to a clearing.

Forty men drove nigh-on seventy beasts, broken by their good order and stolid defence.

About twenty feet from the forest's edge, Karlich called a halt. He could see through the trees and scrub to the broad clearing beyond. Caught up in a fleeing frenzy, the beasts didn't stop until they burst through to the other side.

Captain Leorich Stahler waited for them there with a block of fifty Bögenhafen spear and two lines of twenty handguns from Grünburg.

An explosion erupted in the previously peaceful clearing as all forty handgunners discharged musket and shot. Smoke billowed in a vast cloud, swathing the field and drenching it with the acrid stench of blackpowder. Those beasts that survived the fusillade wandered from the grey smoke pall dazed and confused. A clipped command from Stahler sent the spearmen forward to mop them up. Some of the ungor at the rear of the herd had the sense to turn and flee but were swept up by Karlich's Grimblades in short order.

It was all over in a few bloody minutes and by the end all seventy-six beastman corpses were accounted for. Stahler killed the gor himself, when the two balls of shot embedded in its chest didn't stop it. His sword flashed once with military efficiency and the herd-leader's head was parted from its shoulders.

'No trophies,' warned the captain calmly, as Karlich's halberdiers emerged from the tree line. 'Burn them all, every one.'

Stahler was a tall, stocky man with a thick moustache and a dark beard. His lacquered armour was black and etched with Imperial motifs, amongst them the blazing comet and the rampant griffon. His longsword carried a laurel emblem just above the hilt and the pommel flashed as its embedded ruby caught the sun. A hat and helm sat snug in the crook of his arm, and his black hair was lathered in sweat from where he'd taken the headgear off.

'Well met, Feder,' he said warmly, using Karlich's first name and seizing his hand in an iron grip. 'Any casualties?'

'Mercifully none, though it was close.'

Stahler raised an eyebrow, but the sergeant shook his head.

'Nothing that troubled us unduly, sir.'

'Good. We're making camp in the next clearing. This one will stink to high heaven by the time we're done with the pyres.' Stahler's nose wrinkled as if he could already smell them. 'The Reikwald is our pitch for the night. Come the morrow, we cross the Reikland border into Averland.'

Karlich nodded.

'Shall I have my men help with the building of the pyres, sir?'

Stahler clapped him on the shoulder and leaned in. 'You've done enough for one day, Feder. Head for the clearing and break camp. Your men have earned a rest.'

'Thank you, sir.'

'Rousting's over, Feder,' Stahler continued, staring into the middle distance. 'Prince Wilhelm is on the march and all musterings are to meet up with him on the Steinig Road, four days' march from Averheim.'

Several days ago, word had reached the western provinces of an incursion from the east through Black Fire Pass. Though it was impossible to substantiate any of the reports, the news from road wardens and outriders that had made it across the Averland and Stirland borders was that a huge greenskin army was on the move, sacking towns and burning villages. The Emperor's response to the threat was, as of yet, unknown, at least to the likes of Stahler and Karlich. By contrast, Prince Wilhelm III of Reikland had raised what regiments he possessed, as well as a good number of citizen militias from his provincial villages and hamlets, and ordered them to march forth in defence of their eastern brothers.

'Any news from the other provinces?' Karlich asked. 'Are we to ally with their forces on the border or at some other strongpoint?'

Stahler laughed. It was a hollow sound, without mirth, and did nothing for Karlich's confidence.

'You know as much as I do. Though you'd think an orc and goblin invasion through Black Fire Pass would get some attention, wouldn't you?'

'Aye. But I'm surprised we're not marching for the pass itself in that case. Couldn't the dwarfs hold them?'

Stahler's gaze narrowed and he turned to Karlich again.

'By all accounts, the dwarfs stepped aside.'

'Why?'

'I don't know,' Stahler admitted darkly. 'We follow orders, Feder, you and I both. As soldiers that's all we can really do. Prince Wilhelm marches, so do we.' He allowed a long pause as if deciding whether or not that made sense to him too, then added, 'Faith in Sigmar.'

'Faith in Sigmar, sir.'

Eber watched from a short distance as Captain Stahler departed. He was overseeing the other regiments in the muster, making sure every single beast was hauled onto the pyres erected by the village militias and then set on fire.

Sergeant Karlich walked past him, but didn't meet Eber's gaze at first.

'You've earned a reprieve from pyre duty,' he said without smiling. 'Volker, we're setting up in the next clearing. Go on ahead and lead us through.'

The Reikland hunter nodded and peeled off into the forest. Nearer to the Reikwald's edge, the dangers within lessened. The Grimblades had driven the beasts some distance in the end, and the next clearing took them even farther from the forest's arboreal depths. A stream could be heard, babbling through the trees. There was a village nearby too, Hobsklein it was called. Some of the militia had come from here. They, like the rest of the village's inhabitants, were grateful to the Empire soldiers for rousting out and destroying the beastmen, and were only too happy for them to share a patch within sight of their stockade walls.

'The rest of you, stay in formation until you're on the other side,' the sergeant continued. 'Then you can break ranks.'

Karlich let them go on alone, turning his back and pulling a stubby pipe from his tunic pocket. One of the village militia came past with a torch and Karlich stopped him so he could stir some embers to life in the cup and light his pipeweed.

When the militiaman was gone, he took a long draw to steady his nerves. It was closer than he'd let on to Stahler. A bloody miracle, in fact, that no man had died in the forest. The bones scattered around the beasts' squalid encampment could quite easily have been theirs.

'You have your orders,' he said to thin air.

Eber shuffled into his sergeant's eye-line.

'Sir...'

Karlich's face was hard at first. They'd been lucky and no thanks to Eber's lack of concentration, but the halberdier had fought well in the end.

'It's all right, Eber. Any of us could have sprung that trap.'

The big Reiklander's expression suggested he thought differently.

Karlich sighed and his face softened. 'Go on, join the others.'

Eber nodded, hurrying to catch the rest and take his place in the front rank.

'Saw the way you faced off against that gor, Eber,' said Rechts from down the line, smiling through his ruddy beard.

'He cut off its bloody horn!' added Volker, alongside him.

Varveiter chuckled but was robbed of his humour by the pain in his leg and grimaced.

Eber felt a little lighter, but he still knew he could have cost them all their lives.

They emerged through to the next clearing – there was only a relatively short tract of sparse forest between it and the last one – and Rechts drummed for them to break ranks. Baggage train camp followers were already pitching tents and lighting fires before night crawled in. The watchtower torches of Hobsklein were visible a few hundred feet distant. Some of the Grimblades shook hands, patted one another's backs or expressed other gestures of camaraderie as they wandered off into smaller groups.

The clearing was a broad expanse, mainly flat ground of soft grass and loamy soil. Had the villagers dared to, so close to the forest, they might have planted seeds in the patch of ground and a very different group of rank and file could've held sway in it.

The Grimblade front rankers stayed together and made for the nearest pitch. Other regimental troops were slowly making their way through in dribs and drabs. Volker would return soon, hopefully with game, but the others were content to wait.

Eber was about to follow when Keller crept up alongside him and leant near his ear.

'Fat oaf,' he snarled. 'Get yourself killed next time and spare us all your idiocy.'

Like a shadow passing over the sun, Keller drifted away, calling and joking out loud to the others.

Eber stopped. An ache was building inside him. He hated Keller, hated him for saying what he'd just said; hated him for making Eber hate himself. He wanted to lash out, to strike Keller and wipe away his cocky smirk. Instead he merely clenched his fists and looked down at his feet.

CHAPTER TWO

Campfires

Village of Hobsklein, on the Reikland border,
190 miles from Altdorf

Evening had drawn in, but the sky above was dark and clear. Stars shimmered in the firmament and the moon was full and bright.

By now, the campfire was burning well and gave off the succulent aroma of cooking guinea fowl. Volker had caught the birds an hour earlier, plucked the feathers and spitted them over the hot flames. Fatty juices dripped from the birds' carcasses, six in all, and made the fire below spit and crackle.

'Smells good,' said Keller, licking his lips.

'Better than trail rations at any rate,' added Rechts, taking another pull on the bottle of Middenland hooch. The drummer was a resourceful alcoholic and had procured the liquor from a peddler he'd met on the road to the Reikland border.

'Nothing wrong with salt-pork and grits,' said Varveiter, stretching out his injured leg and hissing through his teeth as he eased it into position.

'Aye, if you've got a stomach like a warhorse or your tongue is so old and leathery that you're past caring about taste.' Keller laughed, and the others laughed with him. All except for Brand, who kept a yard or two away from the rest. He stayed to the shadows, sharpening his blades on a whetstone. Occasionally, the light caught in his eyes and they flashed with captured fire.

Varveiter grumbled something derogatory about Keller's mother under his breath and went back to massaging the stiffness from his leg.

There were several separate campfires set around the clearing. The sounds of good-natured jostling, tawdry songs and the clatter of knives on plates emanated from them. Smoke from slowly-burning kindling and pipeweed scented the cloudy air. Tents stood in ranks or half circles, blades and polearms racked outside or leaning against trees. With the destruction of the beastmen, the mood was relaxed. Even the sentries stationed at all the cardinal points of the encampment looked undisturbed. It was a good time, and those came very rarely on campaign.

'By Taal, you're a good hunter, Volker,' said Rechts when he was given his first strip of guinea fowl. He devoured it whole, wiping the juices from his bearded chin and sucking at the heat baking his tongue. 'Why did you end up joining the army as a halberdier and not a huntsman?'

'State troopers' pay is better,' Volker answered simply. 'Even if the company's not,' he added with a wry smile.

Now it was Rechts's turn to laugh out loud, so hard that he jarred the shoulder wound from the ungor's blade. He winced and clutched at the bloodstained bandage.

'I could see to that for you, brother,' offered Masbrecht. As well as something of a Sigmarite puritan, Masbrecht also had some skill as a chirurgeon. His father had done it as his profession, and passed some of his skills onto his son before he died of pox nearly ten years ago. The death of the man he had idolised had hit Masbrecht hard and the youth fell into bad ways for a time until he found religion and the cult of Sigmar.

'It's fine,' snapped Rechts, as the mood abruptly soured, 'and I'm no brother of yours.'

'We're all brothers of Sigmar, Torsten.'

Rechts stood, leaving the rest of his guinea fowl but taking his half-empty bottle. 'Piss off, Masbrecht, and leave your sermonising for someone else. Don't call me that, either. My friends call me Torsten. You're just another soldier I happen to serve with.' He turned, stumbling a little with the grog, and stalked off.

Silence descended for a while before Keller let out a long, high-pitched whistle.

'What crawled up his arse and died?'

Masbrecht paled and kept his mouth shut.

'I heard he was victimised by zealous preachers when he was young,' said Brand, so grim the air seemed to get colder with his voice. 'Executed his family, left him for dead.'

More silence. Brand had as much of a knack for killing the mood as he did for killing in general.

'Ah, don't worry about that miserable whoreson,' said Keller, trying to lighten the atmosphere. 'Come and bless me instead, Masbrecht. Sigmar knows, I need it!'

He laughed again and drew some humour back out of the night.

Volker chuckled, though it felt forced.

'What about you, Eber?' Lenkmann piped up, his opening a little awkward. He was better accustomed to polishing his tunic's buttons or pressing the creases from his hose than conversing with his comrades. 'Why did you join up?'

The big Reiklander had been quiet until then, content to fade into the background. His guilt still felt heavy, like a lead ball in his gut, and he was hoping the night would pass without any further attention. The others were of the same mind, only poor old Lenkmann was about as intuitive as a rock.

'I, er… used to be with a band of travelling carnival folk–'

'A bumbling klown, no doubt,' quipped Keller, keeping his malice hidden from everyone except Eber and, unbeknownst to him, Brand too.

'Strongman,' Eber corrected.

To Keller's annoyance, the others appeared interested in Eber's secret life.

'What did you lift?' asked Volker.

'Ale barrels, anvils, that kind of thing,' said Eber. 'Once, I lifted a cart mule.'

Lenkmann was impressed. 'What, over your head?' He mimed the feat as he imagined it.

'Aye, just so.'

'Sounds likely…' Keller's sarcasm was biting.

'It's true,' said Eber, quietly. Evidently, the carnival was not a place of happy memories for him either.

'I believe him,' said Volker.

Keller sniffed impatiently, shaking his head. 'Aw, why are you even talking to the lout? He almost got us all killed today,' he said, adding under his breath. 'Dumb ox.'

Eber heard him, and it made him angry. 'Don't call me that.'

'What? Dumb or ox?'

'Leave him alone, Krieger,' Volker pleaded. He had been looking forward to a quiet evening of simple pleasures, of good food and reasonable company, when they could leave the horrors of the Reikwald behind them, if just for a night. Everyone else on the patch was getting on, why not them?

Keller turned on the huntsman.

'Why? But for Karlich's quick thinking, the oaf's stupidity could have seen us all dead.'

'Everyone makes mistakes, Keller,' offered Lenkmann, distinctly uncomfortable at the sudden turn.

'Mistakes that'll get us all killed, one day,' Keller replied, focusing back on Eber. 'Should've stayed at the circus, klown.'

Socially awkward as he was, the banner bearer could think of no way to defuse the rising tension. Volker had said his bit. Masbrecht was content to stay out of it, after Rechts's earlier outburst. He looked to Brand for support, but all he got was cold, hollow eyes, narrowed like knife slashes in the campfire gloom. In the end, it was old Varveiter that had the answer.

'He showed more bravery than some.' The old man was staring into the dark, picking at his guinea fowl idly.

Keller bared his teeth.

'What's that supposed to mean?'

'It means that I saw you, more than once, skulking in the shadows on the flank, keeping your head down and your blade unsullied.'

'I'm no coward, Varveiter.' Keller was on his feet. Brand made to move, too, his hand disappearing into the dark folds of his tunic before the old soldier warned him off with a look.

Varveiter fixed the other halberdier with a stony glare.

'Well, let's just say all of your enemies usually have their wounds in the back.'

'I *outmanoeuvre*, you bast–'

Varveiter cut him off.

'No need to sour the evening. And in my day,' he added, 'that kind of… *outmanoeuvring* was called cowardice.'

Keller snorted, backing down a little when he realised the old soldier was actually spoiling for a fight.

Lenkmann caught onto the ploy late: Varveiter was baiting Keller, just like Keller had been baiting Eber. It took the attention off the big Reiklander who didn't have the wit to match him and was already torn up with guilt so as not to be thinking that straight.

'In your day, our troops wore loin cloths and tattoos.'

'That so? I must be ancient, then. Well you should have no trouble besting me, should you?' Varveiter got up with a grunt and a grimace. Unbuckling his breastplate, he let it fall to the ground.

'Now, come on…' Lenkmann began, half an eye on the nearest campfires, but was far, far too late. The wheels had been long in motion by the time the danger presented itself to him.

Varveiter raised a hand. 'It's all right, Lenkmann. Keller wants to show us his skill. I'm happy to let him. Don't tell me you've never brawled with comrades before? Good for camaraderie, or so we *old* campaigners say…' He glanced at Keller, who suddenly looked less sure of himself.

'What are you doing, old man?'

'Readying for a fight,' he answered, rolling up his sleeves and rotating his shoulders. 'Come on, son, don't disappoint me.'

Keller caught another twinge as Varveiter moved. The old soldier betrayed the weakness in his bruised leg and stood awkwardly.

Fair enough, he'd dump the geriatric on his arse and then see what he had to say about 'cowardice'.

'You should've hung up your blade a long time ago, Varveiter. And now I'm going to show you wh–'

Varveiter lunged forward and punched Keller hard in the gut. The mouthy halberdier doubled over and heaved up his guinea fowl.

Backing up, he raised a hand.

'Bastard!' he managed through hard breaths. 'I wasn't ready.'

'I was,' replied Varveiter, and swung again. This time the move was slow, and Keller saw it coming. Dropping his shoulder, he took the punch on his back, most of the force lost through the extra distance the blow had to travel. Varveiter wasn't done, though, and threw in a left hook that Keller had to step back from to avoid.

The old man was breathing in short, sharp gasps. That last combination had taken something out of him. Keller smiled thinly, like a snake sizing up a mouse, and leant in with a quick jab. He struck Varveiter on his upper torso then he rained in another blow that clipped the side of the old man's head. It was like striking iron.

Much to Keller's delight, Varveiter was backing up. A space had cleared around the campfire, Masbrecht, Volker and Lenkmann moving from the 'arena' to avoid getting hit by a stray blow or a falling body. Eber was on the other side of the flames and well out of it. Brand just kept his seat and watched. If Karlich had been there, he'd have put a stop to it. Lenkmann, however, had lost the reins of the situation long ago, before he'd even realised it was brewing.

'Not so bullish, now, eh?' Keller goaded.

Krieger Keller was a small man. Not physically, but mentally and morally. And he *was* a coward, just like Varveiter had said. It was the truth of his remarks that set Keller off in the first place. He didn't like feeling small, and any chance to vent his wrath, his sense of inadequacy on something smaller, frailer, he took it. Eber was an easy target. A big man but a dumb man, without the resolve to fight back. Keller had heard his wailings in the night, about his mother and his abusive father. Eber was easy meat. And now he'd prove his superiority over Varveiter, too.

The old man didn't reply, just kept his guard up and spat out a gobbet of blood from where Keller had caught him in the mouth. He beckoned the younger man on scornfully.

Filled with over-confidence, Keller came forward again. He feinted with a punch to Varveiter's strong side then aimed a kick at his bad leg when the old soldier's guard was down.

Varveiter cried out, and the pain was there on his face for all to see. Lenkmann went to intercede but something in the old soldier's eyes told him not to. It had gone beyond a brawl. This was personal. Even Brand kept his seat, but his gaze never left the two pugilists.

'Aiming for a weak spot...' gasped Varveiter. 'Good tactic...'

'With you, your whole body is a weakness,' Keller snarled and threw an overhand meant to finish the old man off.

Varveiter was ready for it. He ducked beneath the punch, sending an uppercut into Keller's stomach at the end of the move.

'Yours is your pride, lad,' he hissed.

He followed the uppercut with a heavy jab to the man's ribs, not so hard as to break one, but hard enough to bruise and hurt like hell. The air was blasted from Keller's lungs as if he'd been hit with a hammer. The hammer came next.

As Keller bent over again, spewing up his empty guts, Varveiter smashed his elbow against the younger man's back, flooring him. By the end, it was Keller that was gasping for breath, puking bile and crumpled in a heap. Varveiter stood over him, all of his feigned fatigue abruptly gone.

When he leant down to pick up his breastplate, he whispered in Keller's ear.

'Don't let's you and me have this talk again, you little shit, or I will break something next time. Permanently.'

Keller scowled through his agony, having finished dry heaving, and nodded meekly.

'See?' said Varveiter out loud as he yanked Keller to his feet. 'Good for camaraderie.' He slapped the other halberdier hard on his back, a little harder than he really needed to.

Keller smiled thinly. His eyes conveyed all of his shame and impotent rage. They said something else too, a message just for Varveiter.

This isn't over between us.

Varveiter stared back, as stoic as stone. He'd had more than one run in with a fellow soldier in his career, men much tougher than the one before him now. Keller was just a jumped up little snot who needed taking down a peg. He wasn't even slightly worried. Other concerns were on his mind right now.

'I reckon that's enough excitement for me for one night,' the old man said. 'I'll bid you all a fair evening. You too, Krieger,' he added with a final glance in the seething halberdier's direction. Varveiter walked away in the night, heading for one of the tents.

After Volker had bid the old man good night, and Masbrecht had muttered a benediction to Sigmar for him, the familiar silence returned.

Keller decided he couldn't take it and, clutching his stomach and snarling, stomped away in the opposite direction to Varveiter.

'An eventful evening,' Lenkmann began after a minute or so, trying ineptly to leaven the heavy silence.

Volker chewed on his guinea fowl, but set the strip down after a few bites. He'd suddenly lost his appetite. Eber looked as sullen as ever, his brawny arms and legs tucked tight into his body despite the fact it wasn't a cold night. Masbrecht nodded to Lenkmann, just as awkward as the banner bearer, before his eyes dropped and he fumbled at the Sigmarite talisman hung around his neck.

Another silent minute passed before Brand got to his feet and went off without a word. Before he left the fireside, he leant down to put a dagger in Volker's guinea fowl, pausing to look at the hunter with the blade barely an inch away.

'Eat up,' invited Volker. 'No sense in it going to waste.'

Brand took the meat, devoured a strip off the blade, and walked on.

'Just we four then,' Lenkmann said optimistically after a few more seconds.

No one answered him.

The small stream babbled along with the placid night sounds of the forest. With the taint of the beastmen scoured from its boughs, at least the small tract of trees within sight of Hobsklein, the sinister pall that had lingered there had gone. In its place was life; good, wholesome, natural creation.

Varveiter liked listening to the nocturnal movements of the Reikland. It brought a small measure of peace, especially in a land that saw so little. If the coming war was as bad as he suspected it would be, he would likely not experience peace for some time after. He made the most of it and drank in the atmosphere of the night.

He'd come to the stream deliberately, picking out a secluded spot safe from prying eyes. After the fight with Keller, he'd only loosely strapped his breastplate back up. Now, by the water's edge, he shrugged it off his body. Fresh spikes of agony, worse than those he'd felt at the fireside, clawed at him. The injury he'd feigned in front of Keller hadn't been feigned at all, it was the outward strength he'd been lying about.

Next came the leg, and here Varveiter was afraid to even look. Easing himself into the stream, feet first once he'd struggled off his boots, he allowed the cool water to numb his thigh before he rolled up his hose. Varveiter hissed with pain as he did, forced to keep his tongue behind a cage of his own teeth lest he cry out. An ugly, black bruise showed itself as he peeled the garment back. There was some crimson too, where the blood vessels had burst painfully below the surface of his skin. Feeling daggers of fire with every step, Varveiter shuffled a little deeper and bent down as far as he could to splash the bruised leg. It was scant relief, but it was something.

When he was done, he clawed his way back out of the stream – he couldn't remember how – redressed and collapsed on the bank next to his discarded armour.

'Siegen?'

Varveiter was only semi-conscious. He'd slipped into a sort of fugue state, his body's reaction to the pain. Shadowed images of green trees and golden fields of corn filled his mind. Wood smoke carried on the breeze and somewhere a woman was singing.

'Siegen?'

Her voice was like warm fires on a cold day and cooling wind in the summer heat. She lifted him with her siren-like song. The sun was streaming through her auburn hair, and in his vision it blazed with the flames of her passion and spirit.

'Siegen?'

A hand was shaking him, it felt firm but tender. Varveiter opened his eyes and saw Brand looking down on him.

'Sigmar's arse!' he swore, and would have flinched had he been able.

'I brought some meat,' said Brand, offering the last strip of guinea fowl he'd taken from Volker's plate.

'Thank you, lad,' Varveiter said, pushing himself up into a seated position.

'Are you all right, Siegen?' Brand asked when he saw the discomfort in the old soldier's face.

'Fine, lad. You just disturbed a pleasant dream, that's all.'

'I don't dream,' said Brand flatly. The coldness returned to his eyes like hard steel. 'As long as you're all right,' he added, before heading off deeper into the night.

Varveiter watched him go and thought again of the enigma that was Brand. Whenever encamped, he would often wander out into the dark and only return again come morning. No one ever asked him about it. Karlich didn't care enough to bother, and Varveiter thought a man's business was a man's business and the others were too scared.

Still, it did perplex him.

As rested as he could be, Varveiter was pulling on his boots when he got his second visitor of the evening. When he heard the crunch of grass nearby, he thought of Keller at first and went to grab his dirk.

'As bad as that, was it?'

Varveiter realised it was Karlich and he moved his hand away again.

'Sir?'

'Don't play coy with me, you sly goat,' said Karlich, as he stepped into view. 'And don't call me "sir". You'll make me feel as old as you are.'

The burn scar on the left side of the sergeant's face looked livid in the moonlight, and he'd taken off his hat and helm to reveal the shaven scalp beneath it. Karlich still wore his breastplate, though, and had a long dagger strapped to his left leg.

'A lesson was needed, is all,' Varveiter explained, getting to his feet and stretching out the fresh aches.

'Long as that's all it was.' Karlich cracked his knuckles. He wore leather gloves. In all the years under his command, Varveiter could never remember seeing the sergeant without them. 'Keller's a whoreson bastard,' he went on, 'but he's our bastard and I like to keep him on a tight leash. Last thing I need is you stirring the hornet's nest.'

'It won't happen again, si– *Karlich*.'

'Good, now share some of that meat with me. I'm bloody starving.'

'Volker left a place for you by the fire,' Varveiter returned, passing a piece of now cold guinea fowl to his sergeant.

'Needed some time by myself,' said Karlich. His gaze was on the distant village of Hobsklein. The stream ran right up to its stockade walls. As they'd been talking, a Taalite priest had emerged from behind the gates, ushering out a small group of villagers bringing barrels of ale, sacks of grain for the horses and raw vegetables. One youth even dragged a sow by a rope, such was the Hobskleiner's gratitude at ridding their patch of forest of beastmen. They'd obviously waited until all the tents were pitched, the men settled and sentries posted before coming out. They probably wanted to be sure all of the beastmen were dead, too.

'I *feel* old,' Varveiter confessed out of nowhere.

'Eh? What are you talking about? You're a warhorse, Siegen, proud and strong.' Karlich clapped him on the back.

'Am I? I don't feel it. It's like my muscles are ropes that have been stretched too tautly and left to sag. And the bruises linger, and the blood. I can't remember the last time I didn't go through a day without tasting blood in my mouth.'

'You're just tired,' Karlich replied. 'We all are. It was a hard fight in the forest. In any case, I need you to help me keep the rest in line,' he laughed, though it failed to convey much mirth.

Varveiter faced him, a terrible sadness coming over his face.

'If I could no longer soldier, Karlich, I don't know what else I would do.' His voice cracked a little with emotion.

'You've many good years left in you, yet, warhorse,' Karlich said, doing well to hide the lie in his words. 'Go back to camp and get some sleep,' he ordered. 'I'll be along in a while. We march at first light.'

Varveiter nodded, before saluting his sergeant and heading back to camp.

When he was alone, Karlich looked back at the procession of villagers. He'd seen another figure abroad in the night, but moving away from him and towards the village itself. He rode an armoured steed and wore a black, wide-brimmed hat. As he stooped to address the village priest, the figure's coal-dark cloak drooped downwards, revealing a studded hauberk the colour of burnt umber and a brace of pistols cinched at his belt. An icon hung from his neck, too. It was of a silver hammer, the sigil of Sigmar and the holy seal of his templars, the witch hunters.

Karlich's eyes shadowed as he saw him. Rubbing his gloved hands reflexively, he shivered at first, before a hot line of anger came to quash his fear.

CHAPTER THREE

The Emperor's New Court

Along the River Reik, near the Bögenhafen road,
7 miles from Altdorf

They stuck to the banks of the Reik, keeping the river in sight at all times and watching the boats, skiffs and trawlers as they plied the waterways in packs. It was a light evening, but the mood was heavy. The prince wore a severe expression, as impenetrable as a mask, and rode his steed intently. The other riders with him, plate-armoured Griffonkorps whose own faces were hidden behind shining war helms, were as cold and impassive as statues. It was not their lot to question or to challenge; they obeyed, protected without pause. It was the job of others to probe the prince's mind.

'We could have taken a river barge, you know,' said Ledner. He rasped when he spoke, an old neck wound covered by a Reikland-red scarf affecting his voice. Riding at the front of the retinue with the prince, Ledner was able to turn and look at his patron directly.

Prince Wilhelm, the third Wilhelm after his father and grandfather, glanced askance at his captain.

'And be caught behind Dieter's gilded barges from Nuln? I think not.'

The captain looked again at the mighty river. Even this late, the Reik was thronged with waterborne traffic, bearing the many trappings and fineries of their glorious Emperor Dieter IV. The 'Golden Emperor' some called him, on account of his gilded palace in the capital at Nuln. Perhaps 'Yellow Emperor' would have have been more apt given the current state of affairs.

'War brews in the east and Black Fire is broken through, and what does he do?' continued Wilhelm. 'He moves his court farther west to Altdorf.' The prince knew he spoke out of turn to discuss his lord Emperor so disparagingly and in open company, but he was exasperated at Dieter's reaction. Lines of barely restrained anger marred his handsome features, a noble bearing born of pure Reikland stock. He wore his gilded breastplate with its lion rampant proudly. The colours of his state, the red and white of the Reikmark, were entwined in his elegant riding tunic and leggings. Even his black, leather boots carried an eagle icon. It represented Myrmidia, patron deity of the art of war and one Reiklanders held in great reverence, second only to their progenitor, Sigmar.

As he rode with greater impatience, his crimson cloak billowed behind him. Ledner found it hard to keep up.

'Altdorf will still be there if we tarry a little, my prince.'

Ledner wore a breastplate, too, but it was unlike those worn by the rest of Wilhelm's charges. He was no Griffonkorps, no warrior-knight. Ostensibly, Ledner's rank was that of captain, but his influence and importance to the prince went much deeper than that.

'It's not Altdorf that concerns me,' returned the prince, casting a weary eye on the vessels ferrying chests, barrels and even servants down the wide, black ribbon of the Reik. 'It's what my cousin is doing to the rest of the Empire.'

Prince Wilhelm spurred his horse to a gallop. Over the next rise, the great city of Altdorf loomed. It had been some time since he'd last entered the capital. At least that's how it felt to him. When news had drifted west that a huge army of greenskins had broken through Black Fire Pass and were invading the Empire, bound for its heartlands, two things happened almost simultaneously: Emperor Dieter moved his court west, away from the battles; and Wilhelm relocated his princely lodgings east to the town of Kemperbad, where he could keep a better eye on Reikland's border. Given all of his letters and petitions had fallen on deaf ears, and his messengers had been ousted back to Kemperbad, Wilhelm had had little choice but to return. It was hardly a chore. Altdorf was a city he loved dearly, warts and all. The only thing that might mar his homecoming was the man who sat upon its palatial throne.

Late into the evening, the smoke from tavern fires and smiths still plumed into the night air, settling over the city in a grubby pall. Towers reached up like clawing fingers, trying to scratch out the moon. Tenements and warehouses, revealed on the higher contoured islands above the wall, squatted on top of one another. In the distance, the shadow of one of the Colleges of Magic could be seen. Eldritch lightning crackled in the clouds around its borders, evidence of the wizards and magisters at work within its clandestine halls. Rising proudly above the squalor of the lower, lesser districts was the University of Altdorf, a seat of learning and enlightenment like no other in the entire Old World. There were other landmarks, too: the recently commissioned Imperial Zoo, the austere and forbidding Temple of Sigmar and the many marvellous bridges fashioned by the School of Engineers at Nuln, spanning the numerous waterways flowing through Altdorf from a confluence of the Talabec and the Reik upon which the city sat. Wilhelm felt its presence as surely as his own thumb or finger.

'First city of the Empire...' he breathed reverently as the shadow cast by a white wall passed over them, 'with a Stirlander sullying your glorious throne.' Reikland was in his blood in more ways than one.

The walls were high, watch lanterns lit, crossbowmen patrolled Altdorf's ramparts and a great gate bearing the icon of a griffon barred passage into the aspect of the city that Wilhelm and his entourage now approached.

'Welcome home, my prince,' uttered Ledner as the gates parted with a cry from one of the watchmen. The Prince of Reikland's banner was upraised for all to see, his knights a formidable talisman of his heritage and identity.

'Aye, let us see what kind of a welcome Dieter has for us.'

Galloping under the great triumphal arch, Wilhelm led the way up the Reikland road, north to the palace where the Emperor had made his court. He didn't slow, not for the peddlers, or the ranks of soldiers marching three abreast – for Dieter had moved troops as well as trappings to the city – not even for the nobles as they entered the Rich Quarter and closed on the palace. Griffonkorps bellowed for the way to be cleared, a preceptor lifting his face mask to shout through his long, curled moustaches. There was no time to waste, no time at all.

The audience chamber was filled with tension. Wilhelm felt it emanating between the Lord Protector of Stirland and the Count of Talabecland in particular. The antipathy of these two closely bordered states was well known. Their enmity stretched back to the Time of Three Emperors, before Magnus the Pious had united the land and the Empire was engaged in a bitter power struggle that led to bloody civil war. Some wounds went deeper than a blade cut or an arrow gouge; they lingered through time and hereditary, passing on to scions and then their sons in a destructive, feuding circle. Neder von Krieglitz of Stirland and Hans Feuerbach of Talabecland epitomised this.

Strange that the Emperor Dieter, also a son of Stirland, did not regard Feuerbach sourly. Perhaps this was the reason why Krieglitz, Dieter's cousin, was similarly disaffected towards his provincial lord and Emperor, though he would never voice it in open company. Such were the vagaries and conundrums of Imperial politics.

By contrast, Markus Todbringer, Count of Middenland, remained stoically silent as he stood in the ostentatiously appointed room. It had once been Wilhelm's audience chamber, but the prince didn't remember the gilding and ornamentation lavished on it. Portraits of the Emperor bedecked the walls of the long hall, and there were additional tapestries, statues and other artistic luxuries on show. He suspected that Dieter was making himself at home. There were chairs, finely upholstered and opulently decorated, but no one sat. Stately ritual demanded that they wait for their potentate and sit only after he was first seated. The Emperor, though, had kept them standing for longer than was reasonable.

Tempers were beginning to fray.

'Wissenland hides behind his towers and fortifications. What other explanation is there for his absence?' said the Lord Protector of Stirland. Though not an elected official, in the same way as the counts, he watched over Stirland in the Emperor's stead, whose business kept him in the capital and now Altdorf. 'No surprise, really,' he continued. 'It would be just like Pfeifraucher to shut the gate to his province. He has the mountains at his back after all, and need only defend one open border. Not like us at Stirland. We face foes in every direction.'

'You whine like a maiden, Krieglitz,' sneered Feuerbach, the Count of Talabecland. 'Show some stomach like your ancestors.'

Feuerbach referred to Martin von Krieglitz, Neder's grandfather, who had famously slain the undead fiend Mannfred von Carstein and ended the so-called Vampire Wars that had plagued Stirland in particular for generations.

'You speak of stomach, yet it was your antecedents that declared Ottilia Empress despite our own claimant's Imperially sanctioned ascension to the throne. That is the calibre of Talabecland.'

Feuerbach laughed derisorily.

'Over a thousand years passes and still the backward-looking folk of the Stir cannot let old grievances go. No wonder you're all mentally-stunted peasants.'

'We have long memories,' growled Krieglitz. 'And I'll see you on the duelling field for insulting my people.'

'With what? Your pitchfork and hoe?'

Krieglitz went for his runefang, one of the twelve dwarf-forged blades given unto Sigmar and his barbarian chieftains.

'Nobles,' Wilhelm's voice broke in, 'hold your anger for the foe banging on our gates. Old rivalries mean nothing compared to the greenskin horde from the east.' He scowled at both men. 'And act like your station, not like tavern brawlers drunk on ale and bravado.'

Chastened, Krieglitz let it go. He muttered something in Feuerbach's direction but the count either ignored it or didn't hear.

Feuerbach looked about to send a final parting shot to end the debate on when the huge double doors at the back of the audience hall opened and Emperor Dieter stepped through.

The doors were thick oak, inlaid with silver filigree that depicted a griffon rampant on either smoothly carved face. They were lacquered black and reflected the refulgent gleam of the Emperor's own finery. Dieter wore a long velvet gown, traced with gold and studded with amber. A thick cloak sat upon the already voluminous gown, again velvet but of a darker, less verdant green. Upon his brow, he carried a crown. This too was encrusted with jewels. The rings on his fingers *clacked* as he drummed them idly against the hilt of an ornamental dagger at his waist. His boots were deerskin, pale and pristine in the glow of the lamps ensconced on the walls. Dieter walked between the pools of light they cast in a processional fashion, his lackeys and fawners in tow like a clutch of parasitic birds, flapping this way and that, eager for a crumb of the Emperor's attention.

Salted pork and grain had been all Wilhelm needed to sustain him on the long journey from Kemperbad. It was at risk of being shown again to all present, such was his disgust at Dieter's brazen opulence. The toadies were artisans and craftsmen; a tailor examined the fit of his latest creation upon his Imperial master. In relation to its provincial brothers, Stirland was a poor state but one of solid men with strong characters and hardy hearts. Dieter, as its elector count and now Emperor, had risen high and yet, at the same time, fallen far.

The four nobles acknowledged the Emperor immediately as he approached, bowing as one.

'My lord–' Wilhelm began, stepping forward, before Dieter gestured for him to be silent. He held up his finger, glaring through small, widely spaced eyes that glittered with some private amusement. An inane smile rippled across a face fattened by decadence and largesse. His aquiline nose appeared to point upwards as if he was always sneering down at those beneath him. Clean-shaven to the point of pre-adolescent smoothness and with blond curls spilling down from his head to rest upon his shoulders, Dieter had the look of an overweight child about him. In many ways, he was exactly that.

Dieter shushed his obsequious entourage with an angry hiss, and then sent them scurrying away into numerous anterooms flanking the audience hall with a flick of his other wrist. His finger was still upraised as if he were remonstrating a naughty child, and Wilhelm reddened with anger.

As soon as the doors to the anterooms closed and the toadies were all gone, fresh footsteps filled the brief silence that followed their departure. Looking over Dieter's shoulder, Wilhelm saw four burly men, strapped in arms and armour bearing the red and blue state colours of Altdorf. Between them they hefted a large, ornate throne, carved from Hochland cedar, lacquered and furnished with gold. It could not have been an easy burden, and the men sweated and heaved as they carried it across the length of the hall. Dieter never even glanced at his retainers as they set the throne down. They merely bowed and left again as the Emperor took his seat.

After a bout of shuffling to get his corpulent behind in just the right position, Dieter let his hand fall and looked up.

'Be seated,' he beckoned with a mirthless smile.

All four of the nobles sat down.

'My lord,' Wilhelm began again, unable to conceal his frustration. 'War comes from the east and yet our combined armies remain listless and profligate behind city walls, in barrack houses and bastions. We must act against this threat,' he implored.

'I know of no threat, cousin,' said Dieter. His mood was idle as he rubbed the rings on his fingers with his thumb. 'I hear... *talk*. Rumours of a rabble come through Black Fire. A pass, I'd like to note, that is supposedly guarded by the dwarfs, our sworn allies since the time of Sigmar.'

All except Todbringer muttered a small prayer at the mention of the Man-God's name.

'It is worse than that, Emperor,' Wilhelm persisted. Despite the fact they were related, the Prince of Reikland observed due deference. 'I've sent numerous letters and petitions to your court here in Altdorf, and all were either ignored or rebutted. You've forced me to ride over three hundred miles from Kemperbad–'

'Well you needn't have come so far, dear Wilhelm,' Dieter interjected, his tone innocent and benevolent. 'I told you a place was set for you here. Simply because I have moved west, does not mean you need move east. Altdorf is large enough to accommodate both its Emperor and its prince.'

'I moved to Kemperbad to better watch the border, but that isn't the point. Why did you ignore my petitions?'

'We are constantly at war, cousin. If the Emperor were to leap up and rally his armies at every drawn sword, every razed village, his armies would be quickly exhausted and his elector counts as dependent as a newborn calf. I saw no need to reply.'

Exasperated, Wilhelm got to his feet. As he did, he noticed one of the statues shift at the side of the room. It was then he realised that the penumbral shadows between the lamps held more than carved effigies. Armoured knights were poised in the half dark too. And was that movement he heard from the balconied gallery above them, and the suggestion of a crossbow cradled by a marksmen's silhouette? Dieter was as paranoid as he was decadent it seemed.

'If you won't acknowledge the severity of the threat facing us, then at least commit some troops,' he said, easing down again. 'The few state levies and Griffonkorps at my disposal aren't enough. Altdorf and Nuln have the largest and best-trained standing armies in the Empire – they must march east to the aid of their beleaguered brothers.'

Dieter looked unimpressed. 'Have you seen this greenskin horde for yourself? Do you know first hand what threat they truly possess, Wilhelm?'

The prince had to bite his tongue for a moment before he replied. 'No, I have not. But there are reports–'

'Not worth the tongues that gabbled them or the muddy parchment on which they are writ.' Dieter flapped his hand in a lazy, dismissive gesture. 'The orcs and goblins will turn to squabbling soon enough and this whole crisis will blow itself out.'

'When? At the point where our villages and towns are ash and ruins? The Empire is burning, my lord! If you don't believe me, then listen to the testimony of your other nobles.' He gestured to Krieglitz, who cleared his throat before speaking.

'It's true, my liege. The river patrols have seen orc and goblin war-bands marching uncontested. Averland is under almost perpetual siege, Wissenland cannot be reached and has shut all lines of communication behind border walls and watchtowers, and more greenskins pass through my borders daily. Only Sylvania is untouched, but then no sane creature would ever wander there without good reason,' he added gravely.

'Refugees dog the edges of Talabecland,' Feuerbach said. 'I have no wish to see Stir folk flooding my hinterlands, poaching and begging. I have enough peasants.' He glanced daggers in Krieglitz's direction. The Lord Protector of Stirland clenched his fists and looked about to draw his weapon again. Were it not for the crossbowmen above, he might have.

Instead he stood.

'My lord,' he said to the Emperor. 'I apologise, but there is urgent business that requires my attention in Stirland. It cannot wait and I beg your leave.' A hot vein of fury laced Krieglitz's forehead, directed at the slightly smirking Feuerbach.

Dieter waved a hand impassively, acceding to the lord protector's request.

'I'm sorry, Wilhelm,' said Krieglitz in an angry whisper as he turned to leave the chamber, 'but there can be no alliance with Talabecland. None at all.'

Krieglitz left and Wilhelm sighed in his wake. His case was growing thinner with each passing moment. Even if he could convince Dieter to act, there was nothing to say his provincial brothers would take up arms together. Right now it seemed just as likely they would kill one another before marching under the same standard. In spite of it, he went on.

'So far, the greenskins are at large in most of the east and north-east provinces,' he said. 'If we unite our armies now and march to the orcs, they will get no further westward. They cannot simply go unchallenged. I beseech you, Emperor, unleash your armies and ally this nation under a banner of war.'

Dieter appeared not to notice the prince's urgency and instead gazed around the room. 'Do you like what I've done with your audience chamber, cousin? I thought it too stark and utilitarian before, not fit for royal habitation.'

Wilhelm shook his head incredulously. Even Todbringer exchanged a curious glance with Feuerbach.

'What possible bearing does my opinion of your decorations have on the war that will soon be at our borders?'

The mood changed abruptly. Dieter exchanged languor for anger. 'It will endure,' he said darkly. 'When the war is done and all the dead are accounted for, all of this,' he spread his arms to encompass the room, 'will still be here. *I* will still be here. There are deeper matters of state for me to consider. This greenskin rabble does not warrant Imperial attention. What's more, I tire of this conversation.' He glared at Wilhelm intently. 'Your request for troops is denied. The provinces must look to their own borders. I cannot rescue them at every calamity.' He turned and showed his cheek. 'Now go.'

Exhaling his anger, Wilhelm rose without another word. His jaw was gritted so hard he thought he might snap a tooth. Feuerbach was the next to leave, bowing swiftly and getting on his way. Perhaps he hoped to catch Krieglitz and continue their feud on the duelling field after all. Todbringer followed, utterly unmoved and unconcerned.

As Wilhelm turned to go, he was stopped by a final few words from his Emperor.

'This matter is concluded,' he said. 'Don't return to Altdorf, *Prince* Wilhelm. Her gates will be barred to you.'

'As you wish,' Wilhelm said through clenched teeth. Just as he was passing back through the entrance way, he heard the double doors at the back of the audience hall open again. Out of the corner of his eye he saw three men enter, nobles by the look of their lavish attire. There were enough gemstones and gilding upon their vestments alone to buy a small town, lock, stock and barrel.

'My lords...' He heard Dieter declare with false bonhomie, before the door was closed and the rest of the meeting left a mystery.

He met Todbringer on the other side, talking quietly with one of his aides.

'Markus...'

The Count of Middenland turned at the sound of Wilhelm's voice. They shook hands, favouring the warrior's grip.

'I had hoped for more support from you,' said Wilhelm honestly.

Todbringer released his grasp.

'I've already committed all the troops I can afford to your army, Wilhelm,' he answered. His voice was cold and gravelly, as if it had been hewn from the rocky steppes of the Fauschlag itself. 'Averland and those other peasant provinces are far from Middenland. When the City of the White Wolf is in danger, then I'll act and bring the fury of Ulric down on the greenskins' heads.'

'You sound no better than Feuerbach, full of provincial rivalry and bad blood,' Wilhelm accused.

'Had the Emperor agreed to go to war, I would have backed you brother, but the fact is we *are* divided and noble as your spirit is, you cannot bring us together. If the greenskins rampage through the east and north-west, so be it. By the time they reach Middenland, my army will be ready and they will be worn down from fighting the other states.'

'So you'll wait in Middenheim until the enemy is at your gates and crush them after they've spent their wrath killing your Imperial kin.' Wilhelm shook his head in disappointment. 'I had thought better of you, Markus.'

'I'm a pragmatist, just like you, Wilhelm,' said Todbringer, starting to turn away. 'You do what you feel you must to protect the Reikland, it is no different for me and Middenland.'

'I assume your troops will be feeding your generals regular reports of the greenskins' martial strength and advance.'

'You know they will.'

With that, Markus Todbringer showed his back and walked away with his aide in tow. 'Good luck, Wilhelm,' he called.

Wilhelm sagged, feeling the weight of his armour and his runefang as never before. He couldn't let the Empire burn, nor his brothers struggle. The campaign would go ahead as planned.

His thoughts were interrupted by Ledner, the captain approaching silently despite his armour and other trappings.

'We must join our forces, Ledner. Victory can come no other way,' said Wilhelm without looking at him. 'But it cannot work like this.'

'Then what must be done?' asked Ledner in his rasping voice.

Wilhelm looked around. There were Altdorf soldiers and Dieter's lackeys everywhere.

'Walk with me.'

After passing through a number of corridors that led them back out of the palace and into the wide esplanade of a courtyard, Wilhelm spoke again.

'Dieter was meeting with more nobles after we left,' he said. 'Marienburgers, I think. He's up to something. The rest of the Empire is slowly being crippled by the greenskins, yet funds are coming into Altdorf from somewhere to gild his rooms and furnishings.'

'I saw no less than five mercenary companies pass through the palace gate whilst you were gone,' offered Ledner in a shadowy tone. 'High price too, by the looks of them. No rabble or criminal sell-swords, they were professional soldiers. Some from Tilea, and with Marienburgers in their ranks to boot.'

'What is he planning?' Wilhelm asked as they reached the stable yard and their horses. Word had reached the Griffonkorps that their prince was ready to depart and they were already mounted and vigilant.

'I don't yet know, my lord,' admitted Ledner, helping Wilhelm into his saddle.

'Find out for me. Do whatever is necessary.'

Ledner nodded slowly. 'As you wish, my prince.'

CHAPTER FOUR

First blooding

Captain Stahler's encampment, Reikland border,
190 miles from Altdorf

Rechts woke to a murderous hangover. After leaving the campfire, he'd found two more bottles of Middenland hooch in his belongings and drunk them both. Masbrecht's presence, his predilection towards religion, had stirred up some uncomfortable memories for him. Crackling thatch, plaintive screams and the stench of burning flesh had come to him in his drunken dreams. His tunic and hose were sodden, and not just from alcohol sweats.

'Walk it off, Rechts,' growled a deep voice.

The Grimblades' drummer looked up. Through bleared vision he saw Karlich, sitting on the hewn stump of a tree, pipe in hand. The sergeant looked as grey and ragged as he felt.

'Yes, sir,' Rechts replied, surprised to find his voice so hoarse, adding, 'Karlich?'

Blowing a long plume of smoke, the sergeant regarded him.

'Have you even slept, sir?'

'Worry about yourself, soldier. Walk it off. Go on.'

Rechts did as ordered, aiming himself in the vague direction of cooking smells emanating from the camp. He suspected Volker was up already and preparing breakfast before they marched. Dawn was still a couple of hours off, or just a little less. Rechts would eat and sober up as much as he could.

Karlich watched him go, taking a long draw from his pipe to still his nerves. He'd watched the witch hunter until he'd finished talking with the priest and entered the village through its stockade wall. After that, he'd found the tree stump, taken a seat and waited the night out. He'd seen daemons in the darkness, heard them whispering to him on the breeze as the boughs of the Reikwald shifted. They were not real, of course, just apparitions from his past, coming back to taunt him, as they always did, when the world was still and peace within his grasp.

No peace for you, Feder. Peace must be earned and you have yet to pay its price.

He waited there for another hour, until the camp followers came to pack up tents and clear the pitch for the baggage trains. Stiff from staying in one place for too long, Karlich stretched his unyielding bones and rubbed his legs to get the circulation going again. Wiping the tiredness from his eyes and running a hand through his mousy hair, he started walking to the Grimblades' pitch.

On the way, he saw the encampment was busier than before. Several regiments had joined them in the night from the north. Their banners could be seen hanging low, stirred by the faint pre-dawn breeze. Karlich recognised the red and black of Carroburg, their famed greatswords no less, and the deep blue of Middenland. He heard the latter northerners before he saw them, boasting and pushing their weight around.

'Swordsmen...' he said beneath his breath, noticing their swagger and arrogant nonchalance as they barracked a group of militia huntsmen for some cooked pheasant.

'You'd be doing a service for the Empire, lad,' a brawny-looking Middenlander was saying to a huntsman with downy hair instead of thick stubble around his chin. The boy must have been all of sixteen and was obviously terrified of the bearded northerner. To the youth's credit, he was steadfast.

'Get your own meat,' said another boy brave enough to speak up. 'This is ours, we caught it.'

'Ask yourself one question,' invited a different Middenlander, a grey-haired veteran with a bare chin and long moustaches. He was the regiment's sergeant. 'When we meet the orc on the road to Averheim, who will be doing most of the fighting?'

The youth shook his head and pulled the meat close to his chest as a third Middenlander, blond-bearded with a shaven scalp, spoke up.

'Hand it over, boy,' he warned in a deep voice. When the youth protested still, blond-beard cuffed him hard around the ear and took the meat anyway.

'Now we'll take all of it,' declared the grey-haired sergeant in a low voice.

'Stay seated,' ordered the brawny Middenlander as one of the huntsmen made to stand. Four more northerners stomped over their camp, taking the cooked pheasant, together with what the huntsmen had flensed onto their clay plates, with them. One raised his voice in anger, pulling a dirk halfway from its sheath only to stop when he felt the touch of cold, Middenland steel at his neck.

'Don't make me blood you, peasant,' said blond-beard.

Karlich was almost to the camp and about to intervene when someone else beat him to the punch.

'Give it back,' said Volker. He had Rechts and Eber with him.

'It's only vittels for the Empire's *fighting* men,' explained grey-hair coolly. Karlich saw the Middenlander's hand had strayed to his pommel. 'What need have scouts and peasants for food?' he added. 'Let them eat when battle's begun.'

'Don't make me ask you again.' Volker patted the dirk at his belt.

Grey-hair laughed. 'What are you going to do with that? Cut my thumb?'

'No, your throat,' hissed a voice in his ear.

'Oh sh-' Karlich began, hurrying over. Brand had crept up on the Middenland sergeant. His serrated dagger was pressed against the northerner's neck.

'Grimblades!' yelled Karlich. 'Men of the Reik, stand down.'

The Middenlanders had drawn swords as soon as they'd seen the blade at their sergeant's throat. Some were shouting. Blond-beard merely glared at Brand, his eyes conveying murderous intent. More were coming, too: Grimblades and Middenlanders. A few more minutes and a regiment against regiment brawl would be in prospect. Stahler would hang those responsible if he found out.

Only the Carroburgers looked unmoved by the whole affair, sitting just a few feet away in their own private encampment, supping pipes and talking quietly over cups of steaming broth. They could have interceded at any time, and likely broken up the impending brawl before it had escalated – none with any sense would challenge a soldier of the greatswords – but they chose to keep to their own.

'Brand!' Karlich bawled. 'Put up your blade or face charges.' The threat of charges was moot. Karlich knew that Brand cared little about facing military discipline, but the sergeant hoped he respected him enough to do as he'd told him.

Reluctantly, Brand edged his blade away from grey-hair's throat and backed off a step with hands raised.

'And the rest of you,' Karlich added. 'Back to your pitch. Get your arses ready to march. I want you all armoured with halberds by the time I get there.'

Volker looked reluctant to go. Brand merely waited impassively for the rest, watching blond-beard. He'd do whatever his brother halberdiers did.

'Do it!'

Volker acceded, and they sloped off, casting dark looks at the Middenlanders as they went.

Freed from Brand's blade, the grey-haired northerner walked up to Karlich, still rubbing his throat at an imagined wound.

'If he'd meant to cut you, he would have,' the Reiklander told him.

The Middenlander smiled, and left it alone. 'Well met,' he said, offering his hand. 'Vankar Sturnbled.'

Karlich declined his handshake.

'Feder Karlich,' he answered curtly. 'Do you mind telling me what you and your men were doing, sergeant?'

Sturnbled let his hand fall. His comradely mood went with it.

'Just sport, sergeant, is all it was. Surely, as a fellow warrior, you can appreciate that. Or do they not have sport in Reikland?'

'Aye, we have sport, and we have bastards like you and your men too, so I shan't judge your entire state on the example you've set,' Karlich replied. 'Give the huntsmen back their meat. Take a strip each to save face, but leave the rest.'

Sturnbled's face darkened and he lowered his voice so only Karlich could hear him.

'We've never met before, Reiklander, and I'm a forgiving man, so I'll consider this a mistake,' he said. 'But address me or my men like this again and you'll see just how inhospitable the north can be to soft southerners like yourself.'

Karlich kept his silence and looked Sturnbled in the eye. With his men gone, he was surrounded by Middenlanders.

Sturnbled held his gaze for a few moments more, and when it became obvious that Karlich wasn't about to look away, turned to his men.

'Steel Swords! One strip each and back to camp,' he snarled. 'Give 'em back the rest.'

Blond-beard's face was sour enough to scorch steel, as the other swordsmen sheathed blades and went back towards their camp amidst disgruntled mutterings.

'You too, Torveld.'

The stern-faced Middenlander put away his sword and stalked off.

'He doesn't like backing down,' explained Sturnbled as he turned to Karlich again. 'None of us do.'

Karlich was still deciding if it was meant as a promise or a threat, when Sturnbled took his leave.

One of the huntsmen nodded curt thanks in the Reikland sergeant's direction, which he reciprocated.

Bad enough that there were orcs abroad, now the Grimblades faced an enemy within as well. As he went on his way, Karlich wondered if Rechts had any more hooch. He needed a strong drink right about now.

As he passed the greatswords on his way to the encampment, Karlich caught the eye of their leader.

'Why didn't you stop it?' he asked. 'None of them would dare challenge a greatsworder. You could've ended it before it had begun. Blood could have been shed and men lost their lives to a fellow soldier's blade or the noose.'

The greatsworder straightened. In his black plate-mail he looked massive and imposing. His shaven head was grey with stubble and his silver moustaches immaculate. A leather eye patch gave him a grizzled appearance that suggested he was a campaign veteran. 'Not our fight,' he answered simply.

Karlich scowled, continuing on his way.

'Bloody Carroburgers...' he muttered.

Smoke marred the Averland horizon, too thick and black to be cook fires. Somewhere up ahead, over the grassy rise, a village was burning.

Stahler's army had crossed the border into Averland at dawn, just as the captain had predicted. The camp had broken up, all tents and trappings secured on the modest baggage train and the troops, except the militia levies, organised into marching order by their sergeants.

A small stone bridge over a stream had conveyed them into the province, a wide and open plain known for its horses. Much of Averland was flat with little undulation. It made for perfect equine breeding terrain. So far, they had seen no horses save for a forlorn pair of dead horses, rotting and alive with flies, across the width of the Aver. The mighty river, almost as thick as the Reik and just as impressive, barred the way into Averland proper. Most of the byways and ferry crossings were burned or abandoned. Some supposed the Averlanders had done it after fleeing their borders to prevent pursuit or to stop enemies from crossing the river on the Stirland side. For Stahler and his men, it made life difficult. The few fords and crossings they had encountered were unsuitable for the baggage train, so the order had gone down the line to follow the river until a more substantial bridge could be found.

It wasn't only dead horses that they'd passed on the other side. Trains of refugees spilling from undefended villages trudged vacantly along the river's course, heading for the border, clutching their meagre possessions. One little girl, her face blackened by smoke, clung to a wooden toy. It was hard to tell what it was supposed to be, so bad was the fire damage. The Middenlanders had ignored them, treating the miserable wretches with the same disdain as the grass under their feet or the hot sun on the backs of their necks.

Masbrecht and Lenkmann had wanted to go and help the Averlanders, but Karlich had forbidden it. He did allow Rechts to break ranks and holler directions to the border at them. The drummer had an excellent singing voice and could project loudly. Even still, the refugees looked not to notice his words and trudged on indifferently.

The soldiers saw other Averlanders huddled around roadside shrines.

A priestess of Shallya tended to one ragged mob, leading them in a prayer for succour from her goddess. So far, it appeared that Shallya's mercy was absent from these lands. The devastation was a shock to all. No one in the army, even Stahler, had suspected the greenskins had advanced this far into the Empire, and so quickly. It showed a determination and purpose the beasts were not known for. It was reasoned to be a vanguard, for they would have seen the greenskins had they been it a full army.

A short while after this the Reikwald huntsmen had spotted the smoke. Another mile and they could all see it, heavy and dark like a storm cloud but promising death instead of rain.

'So, I heard you had a run in with the northerners,' Varveiter said quietly to Brand. The old soldier had been sleeping when the ruckus had broken out, but Lenkmann had told him everything that happened. 'That you put a blade to one of their necks.'

'Sergeant,' Brand replied without emotion. 'I put a blade to their sergeant's neck.'

'Ah yes, their sergeant...'

Brand gave Varveiter a side glance, expecting to be chastised.

'Sorry I missed it,' the old soldier admitted with a chuckle.

Brand allowed himself a mouth twitch that for him approximated a smile, before his sergeant's voice interrupted.

'Can you smell that?' Karlich asked Lenkmann.

The banner bearer marched doggedly at the head of the group, he and Rechts on either side of their sergeant in a rank of three. He sniffed loudly.

'Whatever it is, it reeks like old boots left out in the sun,' offered Rechts as he too detected the stench. Lenkmann nodded as he wrinkled his nose. It was coming from up ahead, from the same direction as the smoke. As far as the Grimblades knew, it *was* the smoke.

'Are you saying it's worse than Eber's feet?' chimed Volker, from two ranks behind.

Karlich cast a look over his shoulder. 'Or your breath.'

The smile vanished off Volker's face and he was silent. Eber jabbed him playfully in the ribs as he marched alongside him, which drew harsh mutterings from the scout. Unusually for him, Keller stayed quiet. He was in the second rank with Varveiter and Brand. That left Masbrecht in the third rank next to Volker, and the other Grimblades behind them, marching in time to Rechts's drumming.

The halberdiers were third in the line of march. Ahead of them were the handgunners from Grünburg. The Middenlanders – the Steel Swords – took the lead with Captain Stahler. Behind the Grimblades marched fifty Bögenhafen spearmen, their spear tips pointed towards the smoke-stained sky. The greatsworders kept the rearguard, arguably the most dangerous part of the column. Karlich had learned their champion's name was Reiter von Rauken and his men the so-called 'Carroburg Few'. It was an apt way to describe them; aside from the militia levies that ranged either side of the column or with the dawdling baggage train as bodyguards, the Carroburgers were the smallest regiment in the army at only eighteen heads. It didn't make them any less fearsome, or Karlich like them any more or less than he already did. Rauken and his men could have stopped the fight that was brewing between his men and the other northerners, but they didn't. That was a black mark in the Reiklander's book, and he didn't strike them out easily.

'It doesn't smell like any meat I've ever tasted,' said Eber. The stench was really noisome now, and infected the breeze like a miasma. The Grimblades were just cresting the grassy rise after the handgunners. Karlich noticed that some of the Grünburg men had stopped to gag. He heard another retch up his trail rations shortly afterwards.

'That's because it's not any meat a man would ever feed himself with…' Varveiter's expression was grave as he came over the hill and saw what had upset the Grünburgers.

Eight wooden stakes lined the road ahead, fashioned from charred timbers. At first it was hard to tell just what was fastened to each because it moved in the sunlight.

'Carrion,' uttered Brand, as if that explained everything. The marching column had ground to a halt and several of the rear rankers, including the Bögenhafen spearmen, had started to complain about the hold up.

'Quiet your men!' Karlich snapped to the Bögenhafen sergeant, calling down the line. Something in the other Reiklander's eyes told the leader of the spearmen that he should do as asked.

Feathers. It was feathers that were moving on the wooden stakes, crows mainly and the odd raven. Carrion birds, just as Brand had said.

When Lenkmann realised what they concealed, he retched too and only just held on to his breakfast. In the valley below the rise, Captain Stahler stepped out from the Middenlanders and fired his pistol into the air. The birds scattered, a living carpet of darkness sent fleeing by the report of blackpowder, to reveal the corpses of eight road wardens. The men were obviously dead and horrifically picked at by the carrion crows. Every one had red-rimmed sockets where their eyes should be. The eyes were always the first to go: easy meat, full of nourishment and quick to reach for snapping beaks. The dark cavities that remained seemed to go on forever as if the manner of such a death had condemned these poor men to eternal torture in limbo. A wooden crossbar bisected the upright stake, and the road wardens' arms had been hung over them to look like gruesome scarecrows. The irony of their appearance was not lost on Karlich. If anything, the corpses had enticed the hungry birds.

Thick, crude iron spikes had been hammered into the men's torsos, some even in the groin; the wrists and ankles too. Their skin was flayed in places, their bodies opened up by a ragged blade just below the stomach so that their entrails spilled out like so much offal. Karlich hoped that this last torture had been done after death, and heard Masbrecht mutter a prayer to Sigmar at the sight of such degradation.

'Bring axes!' A weary-looking Captain Stahler called from the base of the valley. 'Cut them down... cut them all down.'

Militiamen came with axes, and together with volunteers from both the Reikland and Middenland regiments, the dead road wardens were cut down. Baggage train trenchers and sappers dug shallow graves alongside the Aver, just deep enough to keep casual predators away, and the men were laid to rest. Masbrecht said a few words over the corpses, as the army possessed no priest. Rechts was absent from the short ceremony.

After that, the Empire army carried on their way. On the flat Averland plain the village was still visible, despite the smoke wreathing it like a funeral veil. The same stench that had emanated off the poor road wardens was coming from there too.

The village's name was Blösstadt. At least that's what the fire-blackened sign lying before the broken gate and shattered stockade wall said. Furriers, smiths, farmers and muleskinners had all lived here once, venturing out to ply their trades and wares on market days in the nearby towns. No anvil sound rang upon a breeze, foetid and rank with decay; no horses whinnied, nor did their hooves clack against the cobbled village square as they were led to market; no voices came at all as the Grimblades passed through the gate and into a scene of utter destruction.

It was as quiet as his father's mortuary, or so Masbrecht thought, levelling his halberd warily at every shadow. The quietude was unsettling, almost unnatural, and he was glad he wasn't alone. Eber and Volker had joined him as he walked towards the village square, a gravel road to guide them. A strange drone pricked at his left ear and he waggled a finger in it experimentally to see if he could shift it. Then he saw the first of the bodies and realised the drone came from the flies buzzing around it, feeding off death.

'Parasites!' he raged, rushing over to the bloodied body of a farmhand and trying to shoo the flies away.

Volker gripped Masbrecht's arm firmly before he got too far.

'Keep it quiet,' he hissed. 'No telling what we'll find here and I'd rather find it before it finds me. Understand?'

Masbrecht nodded, and Volker let him go. The scout patted his arm where he'd seized it. 'Sorry, Pruder,' he said, calling the other soldier by the name his mother had given him. 'Just be mindful.'

After that they continued their slow advance into the village, the flies returned to their putrid feast.

On the other side of the village, losing sight of Volker's group each time they passed one of the large stable yards that Blösstadt had used for its horses, Varveiter led Brand and Rechts along the inner side of the stockade wall. They too found bodies, human and mutilated cattle. So far, they had also seen no sign of life.

'Quiet, but not peaceful,' muttered Rechts. He had his drum slung to one side and a drawn short sword in his fist.

'Aye,' hissed Varveiter in reply. The old soldier had seen villages ravaged before, by bandits, beastmen and orcs as well, but this looked different somehow. 'It's the stillness of the dead, a feeling the living, at least the right-minded of them, can't abide.'

He let Brand move ahead. The other halberdier was silent too. He knew the feeling Varveiter was talking about, he'd known it many times, and here in Blösstadt it put him on edge.

Karlich was approaching the lookout post, a small hill near the middle of the village. There were the remains of a watchtower at the crest of the rise. The corpse of a milkmaid hung slackly over its damaged palisades, doubtless seeking refuge when the greenskins came or trying to bring a warning to her kith and kin. She'd probably known it was a lost cause, but she'd done it anyway. Karlich wondered if she was pretty under all that blood and matted hair.

The watchtower was unsafe to climb, but the hill itself offered a reasonable vantage point from which to view the rest of Blösstadt. The huntsmen Captain Stahler had sent in ahead, while he remained outside the village with the rest of the army, had reached the inn and hovels at the village's southern end. They moved through the narrow lanes with their bows held low but nocked and ready. Nearby there were several hay barns, locked and shuttered. Farther still, Karlich made out a small mill, a waterwheel just dipping into a shallow stream that bisected Blösstadt into two uneven portions. The Grimblades took the larger east section, whilst the smaller regiment of Middenlander Steel Swords took the west.

Karlich caught Sturnbled's eye as he led one patrol. The northerner returned his gaze without expression and then looked away. The Reiklander was glad that the stream kept the two regiments apart. The bad feeling between them had surfaced quickly but would be slow to submerge again, if at all. Where the stream broke the village in two, the Reikland and Middenland patrols did overlap, however.

Somewhere in the distance a dog was yelping. In the abject silence, its presence startled Volker before he realised what it was. He followed the noise to an outdoor privy, the handle tied shut to the doorframe with a length of fraying rope. The poor mutt's wailing awoke something in Volker and he made for the privy at once, crossing the stream and wetting his boots to do so.

'Volker, where are you going?' asked Masbrecht. 'What happened to keeping quiet?'

'A creature is in distress, maybe hurt,' Volker replied, not looking back but forging on instead, 'and I intend to rescue it *quietly*.'

Masbrecht turned to Eber for support, but the big Reiklander merely shrugged and went after Volker.

A few feet from the privy and the blond-bearded Torveld came into view, together with another Middenlander called Wode and Sergeant Sturnbled just behind them.

'What have we here…' said Torveld, slashing open the privy with his dagger. The door flew open almost at once as the burly Middenlander was pitched off his feet by a sudden rush of fur and fangs. The dog was a brutish and well-muscled mastiff. It had black fur and a tan leather eye patch over its right eye with a single stud in lieu of an iris. The beast growled and took a nip at Torveld but did very little damage, before bounding off the Middenlander and growling a warning at the strange-smelling men in its village.

'Little bastard…' snarled Torveld, his pride more wounded than his skin. He bundled to his feet, retrieving the dagger he'd dropped when the mastiff had sprung out at him. 'I'll gut you!'

'Leave the dog alone,' warned Volker calmly. 'It's just scared.' He approached the mastiff, which was now shivering with anger and fear, and when he was only a few feet away, crouched down to his knees.

The crack of a pistol's flintlock arrested his attention from the dog. Sturnbled had drawn and was levelling the weapon at the mastiff.

'It's rabid,' declared the Middenlander sergeant, his arm arrow-straight as he aimed down a small, round sighter at the end of his pistol's barrel. Froth was spilling from the mastiff's jaws, and ran off its chin to pool on the ground.

'The poor beast has dry-mouth, it's not rabid, you idiot,' replied Volker. Ignoring Sturnbled, he cupped his hands to draw water from the stream and offered it to the mastiff. Wary at first with the rest of the soldiers looking on, the beast padded up to Volker, sniffed at the air around him and then started lapping at the stream water. It was thirsty and went back several more times as Volker fetched more. By the third time, the Reikland hunter was patting the mastiff's forehead and stroking its muzzle. After he'd smoothed down its flanks and given it a strip of salted pork from his trail rations, Volker stood up.

'See. Not rabid, just hungry and thirsty. As you would be if you'd been locked up in there for days.'

'More like hours,' snarled Torveld, gesturing towards the nearby corpse of a blacksmith. Volker wondered briefly if it had been the man's dog. 'The blood here is still fresh.'

'How fresh?' asked Masbrecht, a note of concern in his voice.

Torveld rounded on him. 'Like I said, Reikland sop, a few hours.'

Masbrecht still pressed. 'How fresh *exactly*?'

A foul stink pervaded the air suddenly like corpse gas escaping from the recently dead.

'Draw your swords…' Sturnbled told his men, then looked directly at

Wode. 'Find Hallar, have him signal the others.'

'What's happening?' asked Eber, scanning the middle distance.

'We didn't meet the greenskins on the road...' answered Volker, the mastiff at heel beside him but growling.

'And? So what? I thought that was a good thing.'

'We didn't meet them on the road because they are still here. Look!'

Now Eber saw them, two orcs attempting to creep up on them, using a narrow tethering pole to hide behind despite their obvious bulk. It was ludicrous, but then they *were* greenskins. They weren't alone.

A garbled scream came from up ahead. It was one of the huntsmen.

Varveiter had lost Brand when he'd disappeared into the ruined shack. A few minutes earlier, they'd heard something coming from the ramshackle abode a few feet ahead of them, one of a small clutch of three arranged in a half circle. The laconic Reiklander had glanced at Varveiter, signalling his intent to investigate, before jogging ahead and then into the shack.

Rechts had wanted to go after him, but Varveiter had made him stall.

'Let him check it first,' the old soldier had told him.

Rechts looked nonplussed.

'He's quieter than you or me,' Varveiter explained. 'If there's danger he'll find it, and if he can't kill it he'll come running.'

They were both standing at the threshold to the shack. The door was off its hinges with more than one axe hole in the wood. Less a door and more a shattered window now.

'Easy...' whispered Varveiter, using his polearm to ease the door remnants open a fraction. Cold, harsh light spilled in from the outside reluctantly as if afraid to enter. Bare wood and bloodstains were revealed. Varveiter looked back at Rechts. The drummer's eyes were wide and his knuckles white where he gripped his short sword too tightly. His attention back on the door, Varveiter blew out a calming breath and took a step inside.

Slowly scanning the shadows, he found Brand crouched motionless in the corner of the shack's single room. A small pottery cauldron was upturned in the centre; spilled broth washed the floor like vomit, mingling with the blood. There were two beds, the thin sheets and sacking mattress dark with vital stains. Bodies lay unmoving in both. Varveiter counted five in total but couldn't tell if they were male or female because of the darkness and the blood. Another body was strewn on the floor, a cleaver blade still wedged in its back. From the build, it looked like a man. A woodcutting axe lay a few inches from his grasping fingers. He too was dead. The woman mewling quietly before Brand was not.

Varveiter went to his fellow Grimblade whilst Rechts watched the door nervously. His hands were shaking a little, and not just from delirium tremens.

'Merciful Sigmar…' Varveiter breathed as he took a knee beside Brand. He grimaced from the pain in his thigh but took care not to let it show.

Brand was holding the woman's hand. It looked limp and pale like a dying fish. She appeared incoherent, on the verge of death. Doubtless, she'd seen her family butchered by the greenskins and it had deranged her.

'They stood no chance,' uttered Brand without emotion.

'Poor bastards.'

The woman opened her eyes, a jerk of nervous energy impelling her. Whether she'd snapped into lucidity briefly or Varveiter's words had brought her around, it was impossible to tell. Her mouth started moving, but she could form no words because she had no tongue. Blood trickled down the edges of her mouth and Brand dabbed it carefully with his tunic sleeve. The dying woman's eyes widened and she appeared desperate to speak. A waft of something unpleasant drifted through the doorway, like spoiled meat and dung.

'Shit…' hissed Varveiter, recognising the signs and getting to his feet. 'Out of the house,' he said, then louder. 'Get out of the house!'

Placing his hands almost lovingly upon the woman's cheeks, her slowly nodding as he did it, Brand broke her neck with a savage twist to end her suffering. Varveiter was limping for the door, calling to Rechts. Brand followed them out into the gloomy day and saw the greenskins that he already knew were there.

It all happened terrifyingly fast. One moment they were scouting through the village, picking past corpses and the ruins of burnt buildings, the next the greenskins were upon them. Karlich saw the ambush unfold from the summit of the lookout point. In truth, it was poorly executed. Several orcs sought to hide by lying down under paltry scraps of hay. Others merely stood still, buckets over their heads. The goblins showed more cunning. They at least stayed out of sight, closing off escape routes when bands of scouts spotted the orcs easily. The poor huntsmen were the first to die. Three made it from the area around the inn but didn't get far. As they emerged into the street, goblin archers put several arrows in each Reiklander's back. The charging orcs that followed, trussed in chainmail and wielding cleavers, cut down the injured. Karlich saw one man, the brave youth who'd spoken out against the Middenlanders at the camp, crawling for some cover before a blade struck him in the back and he was still. His murderer snarled and roared in exultation of its kill before barrelling on after its rampant kin.

Throughout the entire village, orcs and goblins were emerging from concealed positions, out of hovels, from hay bales, even underneath piles of corpses. The stench of the dead had masked their scent, but now it drenched the air like a contagion. The Empire troops had sprung the ambush early, thanks mainly to the stupidity of the orcs. It gave the soldiers precious minutes to prepare.

Brutish and wild, their porcine faces studded with rings and nuggets of iron, the orcs were a fearsome sight. Karlich had fought the beasts before. Easily the equal of a man, he knew orcs to have tough skin like leather and almost unbreakable skulls. He had even seen one studded with arrows, its left arm severed at the shoulder, still fight on and kill two more men before it was brought down. Orcs lived to fight and as a consequence were very good at it.

Goblins followed in their wake. Smaller and weaker, goblins possessed a low cunning and if anything were more malicious than orcs. It was not unknown for goblins to torture the victims of their raids, exacting the cruelty they suffered at the hands of their orcish brethren upon the poor humans at their mercy. Essentially, they were cowardly creatures, but revelled in hurting anything smaller or weaker than themselves.

'Lenkmann, raise the banner and rally the rest of the men to this point,' said Karlich, heading for the watchtower.

'Some of the others on the east side of the village may not see it,' offered Keller quickly. 'Should I go and warn them, sergeant?'

Karlich paused to think: Brand, Varveiter and Rechts were on the eastern side. 'Do it,' he said quickly, 'but be careful. The greenskins are everywhere.'

Keller nodded and sped off.

Lenkmann looked to his sergeant as he threw open the door to the watchtower. 'And what will you be doing, sir?'

'Signalling reinforcements. If Stahler doesn't get in here quick, we are all dead men,' Karlich said and raced inside, the door banging shut behind him.

Karlich had his shield strapped on his back and was able to take the watchtower steps two at a time with his sword drawn. He reasoned the villagers had made them close together so children or women could also 'garrison' the tower as required. There was no blood on the steps and they were largely intact despite the damage.

The wood creaked ominously with his every footfall though, magnified by the silence inside the tower. By the time Karlich neared the top, the tremors of battle sounded on the breeze: the clash of steel, the shouts of men and the roar of beasts. He knew he had to gather the regiment quickly. His men were spread too thin around Blösstadt. Without regimental coherency, the greenskins would pick them off without a fight, but he needed Stahler and the rest of the army even more.

His mind was racing as he burst through the trapdoor that led to the tower's parapet, so much so that he didn't see the goblin lurking in the shadows waiting for him. Hot agony seared Karlich as a ragged blade stabbed into his breastplate, glanced off and scraped rib bone at his side. The wound quickly became wet with blood, but the armour had saved his life. Not expecting its prey to survive, the goblin was on the back foot when Karlich stabbed it in the throat. The greenskin died, gurgling blood. Kicking it from his path, Karlich moved further onto the parapet. He spared a glance for the slain milkmaid hanging over the palisade like a red, rag doll and was tempted to pull her down for the sake of her dignity but knew there wasn't time. Instead, he went straight for the watchtower's warning bell. Sheathing his sword, Karlich yanked on the clapper so hard he almost pulled the bell from its yoke. A warning ring pealed over Blösstadt, carrying to every part of the village and beyond.

CHAPTER FIVE

Ambushed

Blösstadt village, Averland,
319 miles from Altdorf

The report of Sturnbled's pistol was smothered by a series of loud clangs as Blösstadt's watchtower bell pealed its warning. Powder smoke discharged silently into the air like a gust of grey breath. The Middenlander's shot was true and struck the charging orc in the forehead. Blood, brain and bone fragments blew from the back of the greenskin's skull in a ruddy plume. The beast staggered a few more steps, slumped down and was still.

Another trampled over it as if it was just another obstacle to be trammelled in the pursuit of violence. A further two orcs followed: one carried a long spear with a barbed tip, the other a rusty sword and a shield. Goblins had joined the greenskin vanguard too, and rushed ahead of the burly orcs. One came at Sturnbled. With no time to reload, the Middenlander twisted his pistol around so he could use its weighted butt like a club. In his other hand, he'd drawn his sword. Parrying the wild slash of the goblin's blade, Sturnbled brained it with the pistol. A second died to Torveld's expert sword thrust, before the orcs caught up and the fight was on.

Despite bracing himself, Volker was barrelled off his feet by a charging orc. It was the beast bearing the shield. The orc had used it like a battering ram and now had the Reiklander at its mercy, until the mastiff pounced, wrapping its frothing jaws around the greenskin's forearm and biting down hard. Shaking its sword arm fervently, the orc took several seconds to shrug the hound off. The mastiff went scrambling off into the dirt but had clung on long enough for Masbrecht and Eber to end the greenskin with their halberds. Undeterred, the mastiff bounced to its paws and launched itself at another goblin. The greenskin squealed in pain and shock as the vicious dog tore its throat out. Volker was back on his feet by then.

'Good dog!' he praised, weighing in against another orc fighting Masbrecht. The sounds of battle had drawn more Reiklanders and Middenlanders from the surrounding streets and they came with weapons bared. It was hectic and blurred, filled with blood, grunting and metal clashing against metal. Sweat stung Eber's eyes and orc stink rankled in his nose, but he kept on swinging until there was nothing left to kill.

Sturnbled reloaded his pistol, the greenskins kept at bay by Torveld and his other men, and another blast filled the air, this time without the ringing of the warning bell to silence it. Two goblins took flight at the noise and the smell. One was dragged to heel by Volker's mastiff, the dog's master finishing what it had begun with the point of his halberd; the other Torveld killed with a flung dagger.

It was over in minutes, but each man was heaving for breath and red-faced with effort. A soldier wearing a Reikland uniform was lying face down on the ground, blood seeping from a wound to his head. Masbrecht knelt by his side and whispered a few words of prayer, but didn't turn the poor wretch over.

'It's Gethin,' announced the other Grimblade that had come with him to join the fight. 'Fourth ranker.'

Volker knew the speaker to be a man called Lodde, and laid a reassuring hand on his shoulder. Eber looked on grimly at the morbid scene. He hoped he would not die face down in the dirt like that.

The Middenlanders weren't spared from grief, either. One had been decapitated by an orc's blade, so Torveld took the deceased's cloak and shawled it over the body. In lieu of a funeral, it was the best he could do.

'Ulric will keep them to his breast,' said Sturnbled solemnly, casting a glance in Masbrecht's direction as he performed the benediction. 'Aye, and Sigmar too,' the Middenlander concluded.

By the end of it, four orcs and six goblins were dead, compared to the one each of the Reiklanders and Middenlanders. But it wasn't over, not nearly done. More greenskins were coming, many more. Another horde erupted from the opposite direction in a running battle with some more of Sturnbled's men.

'Get them to the hill,' the sergeant told Torveld, recognising the sense in Karlich's plan to rally there. It was painfully clear the Empire men were outnumbered and the only way they'd survive long enough for reinforcements was to stage a dogged defence. For that they needed a strongpoint, and in a village like Blösstadt the lookout hill with its watchtower was as good a place as any.

Torveld started bellowing at the retreating men, seeing Wode amongst them and pointing him to the hill where the Reiklanders were already gathering. He tried not to balk at the sheer number of greenskins in pursuit, nor the horde that had now emerged from the same direction as the initial vanguard they'd just despatched.

Varveiter heard the tolling bell as he came out of the shack. Another three Grimblades had been drawn to the woman's soft pleas and were outside in the small square of dirt before the hovels. One was already dead, his helmet split in two by an orc's cleaver. It could have been Mensk. Varveiter had seen death on the battlefield many times, he was no stranger to it, but even so he tried not to look at the slain Reiklander. The other two, Prünst and Otto, were fighting hard against a pair of orcs. Brand went into the fray, just as another orc and a pair of goblins rushed into the lane facing the hovels, bellowing war cries.

Gutting the first orc, but not quick enough to save Prünst, Brand then moved on to the second with Rechts in support. The three halberdiers overwhelmed the beast with sheer weight of numbers. As it died, Otto went to give Brand his thanks but the words died on his lips with a gurgle of blood. His legs twisted beneath him and he crumpled, a black-feathered shaft protruding from his neck. The goblins were carrying short bows.

'Shields!' cried Varveiter, bringing up his own shield to protect him. While the others had been fighting, he'd moved ahead to waylay the second group of greenskins. The arrow hitting his shield made him slow a little, enough for Brand to catch up. Rechts was on his heels. Together, Brand and Varveiter presented a wall of halberd points for the orc to career into, which it did with bloodthirsty abandon.

Though impaled, the beast still swung wildly at them with a rusty axe. It caught Rechts on his shoulder as he tried to stab the greenskin with his short sword. The tunic ripped and blood welled in a narrow gash, making the drummer cry out with pain as the old spear wound from the ungor opened up again.

'Die you dirty, green swine,' spat Varveiter, shoving the halberd deeper into the orc's gut. Arrows *thunked* into the creature's broad back as the Grimblades put the orc between them and the goblin archers. Brand twisted his blade then secured the haft in the dirt with his foot as the orc squirmed. Rechts had backed off, pressing at the gash in his shoulder and trying to staunch the blood flow. It left only two of them to hold off the beast.

Pinioned to both halberds, the orc had little movement save to slash madly with its axe. Ducking one swing that tainted the air with the reek of old blood, Brand went around the creature's blindside. He idly killed one of the goblins with a throwing knife – the other had run out of arrows – before pulling out his dirk and ramming it straight into the back of the orc's skull. He needed to use both hands to make it penetrate. Varveiter grimaced in disgust as the blade point punched through the greenskin's eye on the other side, rupturing it like a red grape. At last, he yanked out his halberd but the dead orc stayed upright affixed to Brand's weapon. Together, all three men rolled the creature over and onto the ground.

When Brand had retrieved his weapons, he turned to Varveiter who was leaning on a horse trough and breathing heavily.

'You all right, Siegen?'

'Fine, lad. Go get that little bastard, before it fetches more of its kin.'

After loosing all of its shafts and seeing its fellows slain, the last goblin had fled further north into Blösstadt. The way ahead looked clear for now, most of the fighting sounded like it was happening across the stream on the other side of the village.

Brand nodded and started to jog in that direction. He was of the killing mind now; Varveiter saw the feral spark in his cold eyes. Rechts was about to go after him, when he decided to lag behind for the old soldier, who was gasping for breath.

Varveiter waved him on.

'Go! Make sure he doesn't get himself killed.'

Rechts looked at Varveiter then around the hovels at the bodies of man and greenskin. There were no enemies nearby.

'Be right behind us, old man.'

Varveiter scowled as only the curmudgeonly can but caught the note of concern. 'Get gone!'

And he did, short sword in hand, after Brand.

As soon as the drummer was out of sight, Varveiter staggered and nearly fell. The pain in his leg was bad. Much worse than he'd let on to Rechts or Brand.

Just wait a while, and I'll be fine, he told himself. Can't let them see me like this. I need to fight, I need to be a soldier, I–

A dizzy spell came and went. Varveiter sorely wanted to take off his helmet and breastplate, the tasset that felt as if it was cutting off the blood to his leg, but knew that was foolish. So he gritted his teeth and bore it.

To be duped into an ambush was one thing, but for it to be perpetrated by orcs was just galling. Even as badly executed as it was, even with the corpses masking their stench as well as concealing the greenskins physically, it should not have got to this. It was rare cunning, and Varveiter suspected a goblin's nous. Orcs had no aptitude for anything except violence. A man will recoil from an effigy representing his own mortality. He will not look too closely at the dead. They are repugnant, tragic; a cautionary tale that there but for the grace of Sigmar goes he. Yes, the goblins were wise and now with their larger brethren they were upon them.

Gauging their position by concentration of stench, and the likely sites for an ambush, Varveiter reckoned on the bulk of the greenskin horde being across the stream in amongst the more densely-packed buildings. It would be too risky for the creatures to try and stay concealed any closer. No orc could pull it off, for sure. They wouldn't stray too close to the lookout post, either. Maybe just the odd lurking sentry, looking for a quick and dirty kill. It was largely open ground and with few places to hide, save the watchtower. Put too many greenskins in there and they'd be dead within minutes as the Empire men burned it to the ground. The situation was grim. Orcs would be flooding the village and Karlich would no doubt send a warning to Captain Stahler, hence the tower bell, and rally the rest to the lookout.

Varveiter only hoped he had the strength and will to join them.

Agony flared up his side again, the focus of which started at his thigh where the beastman had stabbed him. Vomit regurgitated into his mouth, and he tasted the acrid sting of bile at the back of his throat. The dizziness came back with a vengeance as Varveiter took a tentative step from the horse trough he was using as a crutch. He stood upright in spite of it. Blood pulsed in his ears, louder than Rechts's drum at full marching beat, and black fog billowed threateningly at the edge of his vision. He was close to passing out, so bit his lip hard. He drew blood, the copper taste of it filling his mouth, but the fresh pain kept him from falling. Then he heard him.

'Warhorse...'

A shadow clouded over Varveiter, smothering the old soldier in shade. When he realised it wasn't his failing eyesight, he turned and saw Keller.

'What'd you want?' he snapped with more conviction than he truly felt.

Perplexity turned to horror when Varveiter discovered he'd been stabbed in the side through a gap in his armour. Funny, he couldn't remember Keller getting so close to him. Maybe he'd blacked out for a second. Survival instinct took over now. Keller was close, but that also meant he was in reach of the old soldier's hands. He'd killed men with those bare hands before; men he'd had no grudge against. This was different. Varveiter seized the wiry Keller around the neck and squeezed. The younger man's weasel face contorted as he struggled to breathe, but Varveiter kept up the pressure. Something warm was running down his side, dampening his leg and collecting in his boot. It sloshed as he adjusted his footing to get a better grip and take the weight off his ailing thigh.

Panicked, Keller dropped the knife now slick with Varveiter's blood and pawed at the old man's leathery fingers. They were like petrified oak: unyielding and rigid. Desperation crept into his movements now, as the life was slowly being choked out of him by a vengeful veteran with an aptitude for pugilism: an aptitude that had seen him humiliated and stoked an ember of resentment and bitterness into flaming rage within Keller's core. He lashed out, striking the old soldier's wounded thigh.

Varveiter screamed as lightning tore through his lower body, shocking him with tiny forks of pain. His leg crumpled and he lost his grip. Keller heaved in a relieved breath. The world was fading around Varveiter. Keller was saying something to him but it was as if his voice was too far away to make out the words, as if he was at the top of a long well and Varveiter was at its bottom. He fell, a cynical punch to his jaw putting the old soldier on his rump. Keller kicked and the lightning flared again, building to a thunderhead of agony. He couldn't feel his leg at all now, and looked dumbfounded at his red palm and fingers as he brought them up to his face. He'd lost a lot of blood. It was pooling under him in a sticky morass.

Suddenly, Keller was gone. A strange silence descended, an eerie peace. Shadows were moving in the narrow lanes of Blösstadt. It took a while for Varveiter to realise they weren't phantoms at the fringes of his clouding sight. The goblins had returned, or perhaps they were different creatures – Varveiter could no longer tell. He reached for his halberd. He didn't remember dropping it, but there it sat in the dirt. Even as his fingers closed on the haft, he knew he couldn't grasp it. He was too weak from blood loss.

You bastard, Keller, he thought, his mind the only faculty left to him he could rely on in his final moments. Didn't even have the guts to do it yourself...

Blood pulsing from his side, slumped in the dirt without his weapon in his hand, it wasn't the way Varveiter had wanted to die. The last thing he saw as his vision faded was the goblins stowing their cudgels as they approached him. Instead, they drew daggers and Siegen Varveiter realised then his death would not be quick...

Karlich emerged from the watchtower pale and out of breath. The wound in his side was still bloody, despite the rag of tunic he'd tied off to stymie it.

'Found more than a dead milkmaid up there, eh, Reiklander?'

The Grimblade sergeant gave Sturnbled a dirty look as he reached the summit of the hill and approached him.

'How many men do you have left?' asked Karlich, ignoring the jibe.

'Just over twenty. What's your plan?'

Karlich trudged a few feet down the hill to where his men were gathering. In the distance, he saw the greenskins hustling towards them in a mass, coming from all four compass directions. The last few halberdiers were just ahead of them, emerging from Blösstadt's eastern side. They slogged the final steps across the partially forded river, one man losing his footing and then his head to a flung axe as he went to rise. The stream ran red with his blood.

'Form ranks!' bellowed Karlich, half in answer to Sturnbled's question. He regarded the Middenlander over his shoulder, who was priming his duelling pistol. 'We need to cover every aspect of this hill,' Karlich told him. 'Make two half-circles – my men to the north and east, yours to the south and west. We make our stand as low as we can, while maintaining the advantage of height and retreat by steps as necessary.'

'You want to hold out for Stahler to save us, then,' Sturnbled replied, as if unaccustomed to the concept of being saved and not being the one doing the saving.

'Yes.'

Sturnbled didn't like it, but knew enough to realise they were out of options. He hastily organised his men and ordered them to lock shields. Just over twenty Middenland Steel Swords and maybe thirty-five Reikland Grimblades opposed the greenskin hordes swarming Blösstadt – less than sixty men against twice that number or more in orcs and goblins.

Keller returned to the ranks and hurriedly found his position alongside Rechts. They were strung out in a long file of twelve men, just three ranks deep with some stragglers. It meant Keller was pushed up to the front.

'Where's Varveiter?' asked Lenkmann, starting to raise the banner.

Keller's face darkened. He couldn't help but glance in Brand's direction, who was also in the front rank but on the opposite side of the command section.

'He's dead then,' said Karlich bitterly, not feeling patient enough to wait for Keller to find the courage to spit out his words.

'I was looking for Rechts and Brand when I found him,' Keller said. His gaze went involuntarily to Brand again.

The other Reiklander gave away nothing – the whitening in his knuckles could just be tension before battle. Brand's expression was cold, but he saw what the others did not. He saw the finger marks around Keller's throat where someone had tried to throttle him; too large for goblins, too thin for orcs. He knew the truth and if they survived this, knew what he was going to do to Keller.

'The old man was bound to get himself killed someday,' muttered Volker, wiping away a tear. Behind him, Masbrecht intoned a quiet litany that made Rechts stiffen in anger despite its intent. Eber was dumbstruck and hung his head a little, as a dog might when it loses its master.

'Did he die with a weapon in his hand, Keller?' asked Karlich, fighting hard not to show emotion. Varveiter had been a father to them all of sorts by the end.

Keller nodded meekly, afraid his voice would give away the lie.

'Then it's as he'd have wanted.'

'Likely we'll all die in this Sigmar-forsaken place anyway,' said Volker, grabbing the mastiff by its scruff and dragging it close. The beast had bonded with the Reikland hunter and snarled at the approaching orc horde.

'Shut up, Volker,' snapped Karlich. 'Speak like that again and you'll be lashed when this is over. Stahler will come,' he said. 'We just have to hold out long enough for it to matter when he does.'

There was no more time for talk or grief, only time for fighting. The greenskins had arrived.

CHAPTER SIX

A captain's duty

Blösstadt village, Averland,
319 miles from Altdorf

The warning bell pealed long and loud beyond the stockade wall of Blösstadt and fed all the way to Stahler's position a few hundred feet from the gate. The captain recognised its urgency and shouted the order to march. Von Rauken's Carroburg Few took the lead, the greatsworders keen to face danger but still highly disciplined as they advanced. A block of handgunners followed them, then the spearmen and finally the second regiment of gunners. Stahler joined the spearmen to better view the entire line and not be too far from any one element of it. Besides, he knew that Von Rauken was a capable leader and didn't need the morale-boosting presence of a captain. The militia units, a few scattered free companies and archers, ran alongside and to the rear of the column. Most stayed with the baggage train and camp followers a few yards behind the professional soldiers.

They were only fifty feet or so from the looming stockade wall when the air was split with the sound of battle cries. The harsh and ululating timbre of those cries told Stahler that the greenskins had planned more than one ambush. Shading his eyes from the sun that was beginning to dip behind some cloud, Stahler made out a patch of dust billowing on the horizon. From a shallow valley, large enough to hide a cavalry force, a horde of orc boar riders barrelled forth. The greenskins hooted and brayed, banging shields with their crude weapons, whilst their shaggy mounts snorted through ringed snouts. Another cry echoed across the flat land – a hidden dip on the opposite side of the column concealed further riders. As the orcs crested a small, grassy rise, Stahler raised his sword aloft.

'All troops to the village! Run for the stockade wall!'

Out in the open, surrounded by the greenskins' shock cavalry, the Empire troops were severely outmatched. At least in Blösstadt there were buildings and lanes to defend, walls to impede an otherwise devastating boar charge.

Armour plates clanked and scabbards slapped, regimental sergeants bellowed frantic orders and the column began to move. For a time the Empire force lost its coherency in the mad dash for the walls. The gaping gatehouse offered salvation, a promise of possible survival within the confines of the stockade that surrounded Blösstadt. That promise was shattered abruptly when a fully laden lumber cart rolled into the gap, blocking off the gate, and burst into flames.

Arrows whickered through the fire, the silhouettes of goblins just visible through the haze and smoke. One of the greatsworders was struck in the armpit and cried out; others took the crudely-feathered shafts against their full plate armour and marched into the arrows stoically.

They were trapped with the orc boar riders bearing down on them, and had only a few minutes to do something about it. As Stahler marshalled his thoughts and tried to devise a plan that wouldn't end with them all dead on a bloody plain outside Blösstadt, a discordant war horn reverberated in his ears. He winced at the noise, a whining and tuneless clamour, and saw more riders. This time they were goblins, clinging maniacally to giant, slavering wolves. One of the diminutive greenskins was so fervid that it fell, and several wolves broke from their loose formation to feed on it. The act of wanton savagery barely slowed them. They were heading for the baggage train.

'Signal the militia to surround the carts, archers behind free company men,' he snapped to the spearmen's standard bearer, a soldier named Heiflig. The banner went up and in concordance with the regimental horn blower conveyed the message. Stahler didn't wait to see if they'd respond. He couldn't do any more for them. If they failed, they were dead – it was that simple. Instead he yelled loudly.

'Break column and form square!'

The spearman musician blew again, this time accompanied by the beating of drums from the Grünburg gunner regiments. Cavalry were deadly to long lines or unguarded flanks. They could reap right through them, cutting men asunder with no reply, come about and then charge all over again. Blocks of infantry facing every aspect were a much tougher prospect, where weight of numbers and the reassuring presence of rear ranks would count for something. Stahler knew it, as did every Empire captain worth his salt, and watched with grim satisfaction as the units in his command reformed.

Only the greatswords differed in their formation, making a tight circle of blades, every man three feet apart. The gaps in the line were risky, but necessary as they provided clearance for the swings of the Carroburg Few's mighty double-handed blades. It also made the most of the greatsworders' prodigious fighting strength – every one of von Rauken's men would face an enemy.

With the appearance of the greenskin riders, the greatswords had allowed the handgunners to pass them and close on the gate. It meant von Rauken was close enough to Stahler to be heard as he shouted.

'We need to get inside. We'll be slaughtered out here, in squares or not!'

Stahler knew he was right, and was about to shout back when a percussive bark erupted from the handgunners closest the gate. The goblin archers disappeared from view. No more arrows whickered from the flaming cart.

Deciding he didn't wish to debate strategy across their regiments, Stahler broke off from the Bögenhafen spearmen and jogged quickly over to the greatsworders. He kept low and behind the regiments. Some of the wolf riders carried short bows and he couldn't risk being killed by a lucky arrow. He needed to make it fast. The greenskins had started far off, using distance as well as terrain to hide their ambush, but now they were closing.

'I agree,' said Stahler, a little breathlessly. He had one eye on the advancing greenskins and one on von Rauken who glowered at him like an armour-plated juggernaut. The greatsworder was easily a head taller than Stahler and his eye-patch and thick moustaches made him look imperious. But Stahler wasn't intimidated; he'd faced off against lords and counts before now. 'Hit and run tactics will decimate us,' he added. 'But we aren't getting into the village until that obstruction is out of the way.'

Von Rauken nodded and gestured to a pair of handgunners who had joined them whilst Stahler was talking.

'Sergeant Isaak and his best marksman, Utz,' said von Rauken by way of introduction. The two Grünburgers nodded curtly. 'Tell the captain what you told me,' he invited, fixing them with his iron-hard glare.

To his credit, Sergeant Isaak didn't wilt, but his marksman looked a little peaked.

'My lord,' Isaak began, thumbs tucked into a thick weapons belt off which hung two large pistols, 'Utz here,' – he nodded towards the marksman, who had his harquebus slung over his shoulder and was wringing a leather cap in his hands – 'believes he has a way we can breach the gate.'

Stahler regarded the man at once, as did they all.

'Then speak, Utz, the enemy will be upon us in short order.'

'Grenades, m-milord,' Utz stammered in a thick accent, reminiscent of the Grünburg boatyards.

Stahler raised a questioning eyebrow at Isaak.

'His father is an engineer,' the sergeant explained. 'Lad's picked up a thing or two. There's nothing he doesn't know about blackpowder, sir.'

The hooting cries of the orcs and the bray of their boars was coming closer. Peeling off from the main horde, the wolf riders had already engaged the militia, circling the baggage train like predators circling their prey. Out of the corner of his eye, Stahler saw three men were dead with black-shafted arrows sticking out of their bodies.

'How quickly can you do it?' he put to Utz.

'We'll need socks and caps for the powder, more than just the bags we carry,' Utz replied. 'Then twine. It shouldn't take more than a few minutes, my lord.'

'Get to it then.'

Utz and Isaak hurried off to the regiment, the sergeant already calling for every man to relinquish his socks or cap if he had them.

Left with the burly greatsworder, Stahler had one thing left to say before he ran back to the Grünburg spearmen, who were looking anxious in his absence.

'Keep them safe, von Rauken. If we don't break though that barricade–'

'Then you and I will be dining in Sigmar's longhouse before the day is out,' the greatsworder replied.

As Stahler nodded and then went to his men, von Rauken rejoined his own.

'Carroburg Few…' he called, taking his place between standard and drum, 'we bloody few. Steep your blades this day. Steep them in the red of your tunics. Steep them in greenskin blood. Let all remember the Siege of Carroburg and how our courage was measured and made.'

A clash of blades, the slip of steel on leather greeted von Rauken's proclamation as the Carroburg Few drew swords and prepared to meet the enemy.

Thick, black smoke was visible from his vantage point on the hill. Karlich was familiar enough with Blösstadt's layout to realise it was coming from the gate. He'd also heard the faint echo of horns – not the trumpets and clarions of the Empire, but the throaty, strident blaring of greenskin pipes – and knew that Stahler was cut off. It changed nothing, only his resolve to dig in harder and make the orcs pay for every inch they took.

'Hold together!' Karlich shouted, blocking the swipe of a rusty cleaver before stunning the orc he faced with a stiff punch to the nose. It was like striking granite but the beast felt it too and backed off just enough for Karlich to finish it with his sword. Respite was brief, more of the porcine brutes were clamouring to the battle.

The sheer swell of it was incredible, like the pitch and yaw of a ship in a stormy sea. With the initial charge, the halberdiers' line bent, but then reasserted itself like steel flexing back after being tested. They braced hafts into the hill soil and levelled blades outwards in a dull, grey metal palisade. Orcs were skewered, goblins kicked and split by swords but still the greenskins came. Gazing through the gaps in the fighting, Karlich dared not make a headcount – beyond the Grimblades' front rank, there appeared to be no end to the orcs.

Backing up the slope with the massive press of the horde, Keller slipped. Brand was beside him immediately and kept the soldier on his feet. Keller only had time to flash a brief glance in his direction. It was met with icy cold and if it wasn't for the greenskins to his front, he'd have been reluctant to turn away.

'It won't be in your back,' he heard Brand whisper, before he was lost from view in the melee.

Lenkmann and Rechts fought doggedly by Karlich's side, protecting his flanks and hacking furiously with their blades. The drummer closed his ears to the sound of Masbrecht's vocal devotions, concentrating on the scrape of metal, the grunts of the embattled and the cries of the dying.

Volker felt the line thinning. The front rank was dug in hard, a core of strong men, he knew, that had fought many battles together and lived to tell of it. No doubt they missed Varveiter, the old soldier was the source of much inspiration, but they were holding. Volker's keen eyes picked out goblins creeping through the orcish wall of muscle and fury. He'd slain two already, the corpses had rolled down the hill to be crushed underfoot. Another pair had dragged a Grimblade, Jorgs, to his death by first stabbing him in the legs when his attention was on the orcs. Once Jorgs was down the malicious creatures had gone to work with their knives. Volker had seen the man collapse and heard him screaming as the goblins took him. Keeping his eyes low and high at the same time was impossible, but the mastiff guarded his master's legs, tearing out goblin throats and keeping them at bay with its frothing bark and bite.

The edges of the line were being hit hard. Eber felt it like a physical blow. Several men had lost their lives on the flanks as the greenskins levelled most of their strength at the 'hinges' between the regiments. Though Eber couldn't really see that well, he realised the Middenlanders were struggling to hold off the beasts just as they were. Cutting down another orc, splitting its skull with a roar, he vowed to make the greenskins fight for every step. Eber was strong and his harsh upbringing, first at his father's hand and then as part of the circus troupe, had made him tough but the orcs were testing his limits. He buried his halberd into the face of one, imagining it was his abusive father and the killing came easier.

'Retreat two steps,' hollered Karlich. 'In good order, Grimblades.'

Eber moved with the rest of the line. He could feel the summit of the hill getting closer.

* * *

A raking discharge from the Grünburg guns filled the air with a flurry of smoke. Another crack of flintlocks immediately followed it as the second of the handgunner regiments fired its weapons. This was a much lesser discharge, as a quarter of its number was preparing grenades under the tutelage of marksman Utz. Sergeant Isaak stayed with the greater regiment, unleashing his pistols one at a time to maintain a steady rate of fire.

The orcs bore the brunt of the fusillades on their shields. Powder and shot left wood chips and dented plate in its wake. Despite the heavy barrage – a fact made possible by firing in ranks, whereby rear rankers replaced front rankers with fuses primed in a constant cycle of powder, shot, ram, fire – the greenskins had lost few riders and fewer boars. They circled the Empire infantry squares like carrion choosing the tastiest morsels to descend upon. Several of the handgunners were dead already, slumped in the dirt with axe and spear wounds. Every death meant one less ball of shot to unleash at the orcs.

'Stay together!' shouted Stahler, as an orc bounced off his shield and nearly felled him as it careened past. 'Maintain square,' he urged, once he'd righted himself.

Boar stink and foetid orc spore had turned the air around them into a febrile soup. Several spearmen gagged, but kept their polearms steady under the gaze of the captain.

Stahler wiped away the sweat streaking his face, sparing a glance towards the Carroburgers and Utz's forlorn hope. The greatswordes were fighting hard and had yet to lose a man. Through the melee, the Empire captain couldn't tell if the grenades were ready yet or not. He hoped it would be soon. They were holding right enough – even the militia were doing a satisfactory job of protecting the wagons – but holding was not enough. His instincts told him the orcs were merely toying with them and that a concerted push was coming.

It arrived sooner than Stahler thought.

From out of the boar riders' ranks, which until then had been a blur of snorting, dark-furred hide and metal, emerged a massive creature too large and imposing to ever be called a mere boar. It was more like a hairy bull, thickly muscled and armoured like the caparisoned steed of a knight, albeit with crude plates and belts of chainmail. Its tiny eyes shimmered red and it snorted a long drizzle of mucus. It might have been a challenge, Stahler was unsure. The deep bellow from the dark-skinned orc upon the boar-beast's back could be nothing other.

Digging its spiked heels into the boar's flank, the greenskin chieftain drove at the greatswordes and Stahler saw the orc in its full terrifying aspect. Curled rams' horns extended from a black iron helmet; chainmail draped its obscenely muscular body like a second skin; fists the size of circus dumbbells gripped a pair of axes, notched from the kills it had made and dark with old blood. It was a monster, a thing of nightmares and it was coming for von Rauken.

Stahler knew the strength and courage of the greatswordsers, and Carroburgers were tough men. But their thin line could not stand against this beast and his entourage. They would stand but shatter soon after, driven under hooves or before rusty blades and then there would be nothing between Utz's men and certain death. The death of Utz meant the death of them all, and the orcish chieftain was cunning enough to realise this.

There was little time to act, and Stahler knew if he thought too hard about what he was going to do he might falter and it would be too late. So instead, he roared.

'Charge!'

Galvanised by the presence of their captain, the Bögenhafeners went from a steady jog to a run. They barrelled into the path of the boar riders, bellowing war cries to stump up their courage.

'Forward in the name of Prince Wilhelm,' shouted Stahler, 'and for the glory of the Reik!'

In the path of the charging boars, there was little time to set themselves and level spears. The men of Bögenhafen did what they could before a thundering wall of fur, fangs and tusks exploded into them. It was like being struck by a battering ram full in the chest, the earth trembling underfoot.

Stahler lost his helmet and very nearly his shield. He clung to it, this lifeline on a thread of leather, by sheer will alone. Spearmen were tossed into the air like dolls, limbs flailing. Others were ground under hoof or gored by tusks and blades. One man had his neck cleaved in twain, and the decapitated head bounced amongst his brethren like a grisly ball. Blood and screaming, the hoot of beasts and the desperate reek of combat filled the air around them. The standard almost fell, poor Heiflig gutted by an orc's cleaver, before one of the rear rankers came forward to seize it. The war horn was forgotten, in favour of the grunts and cries of desperate battle. In the initial boar charge, the Bögenhafen spears had lost almost their entire front rank – only Stahler and the musician remained. And yet they held.

'Spears!' shouted Stahler, though he hardly needed to as the second rank thrust their polearms over the first who went down on bent knee to let the steel tips pass over their shoulders. Several orcs and boars were pinioned, two even fell to mortal wounds but the greenskins were not done.

After hacking off an orc's hand at the wrist then ramming his shield into its boar's snout, Stahler saw the chieftain a few paces down the line. Its axe blades were a crimson blur, reaping heads and limbs like a farmer reaps corn during harvest. Except this was a visceral, bloody yield.

'Fight me, pig-face!' shouted Stahler. He didn't relish taking on the beast. It was almost twice his height without the mount; with it, the orc was utterly monstrous. Yet he couldn't let it attack the spearmen. They would simply be butchered, and any hopes of survival with them.

'Come on, you stinking scum!' he roared, stabbing a boar rider in the gut as it leaned to strike at him and very nearly losing his head as it swung back.

A line of blood laced Stahler's face, still warm on the orc's blade, and he fought not to gag. A spear to the beast's throat ended its life, but he couldn't see who'd done it. It was impossible to discern anything in the madness. Stahler's focus was just on the orc chieftain.

'To me, you spineless bastard!'

At last the orc took notice, this squealing piece of manflesh rattling his puny shield with his tiny knife. Though man and orc did not speak the same language, understanding between them was absolute. Throwing back his head, the greenskin chieftain emitted an ululating cry that drove the warriors from its path.

Challenge accepted.

Stahler fought to quell his fear. The battle around him appeared to lull. The world slowed, but it was as if the orc chieftain were moving outside of time as it came on inexorably and at speed. The captain's longsword was no ordinary weapon. Myrmidian priests had blessed it and a single rune was forged into the blade. Despite the keenness of its edge, the magical sharpness parted mail links like they were parchment, Stahler balked at the thickness of the orc's armour, its flesh and brawn.

'Sigmar protect me...' he whispered, making the sign of the hammer with his shield arm then bringing it up to meet the charge of the beast.

'Last step!' cried Karlich as they reached the summit of the hill. Through the fog of battle, the Grimblade sergeant vaguely made out Sturnbled issuing a similar warning to his men. The Middenlander had given up on his pistol and fought with sword and buckler instead. Torveld fought beside him and, despite his disliking of the northerners, Karlich had to admit they were ferocious fighters.

Twenty minutes is a long time on the battlefield where seconds can stretch to lifetimes and every swing of your sword or sweep of your halberd feels like lifting a tree. Proud of them as he was, Karlich knew his men were flagging. Another of the Grimblades – Helmut? – was struck down, and the line thinned again. It had been some time since they'd had two full rear ranks and the gaps were telling. Three times Karlich had narrowed the formation already, the small circle of soldiers around the hill tightening as they ascended its rise, as if pulling their own noose. Occasional peals of Rechts's drum relayed the command to close ranks, whilst Lenkmann hollered and cajoled them to maintain good order when they did.

Smoke was still rising from the gatehouse. If Stahler didn't make it through soon, this would be one of the shortest Imperial campaigns in history.

* * *

The world was drenched red before Stahler's eyes as the blow against his shield forced him back. He staggered with the sheer strength behind the attack. Putting his weight on his back foot, he lashed out wildly with his blade. Laughing – a deep, throaty noise full of malice – the orc chieftain merely swatted the sword aside with the flat of its axe. It sported long cuts, the odd gouge in its skin and armour, but these small blows Stahler had inflicted only enraged and empowered the beast.

Blood was leaking into Stahler's eyes from a cut on his forehead that he couldn't see or feel. A deep throbbing in his head dulled the battle noise, but he thought he heard the final pulses of his heart in this world as the orc came again.

Stahler lunged in an effort to maybe put the orc off balance, salvage a little more time for Utz, but the beast swatted the weapon away again. Leaning down from its mount, the chieftain seized Stahler by his tunic. Snarling stinking spittle into the man's face, the orc butted him hard.

The red world turned black. It was like being hit by granite. Stahler felt his nose break. He became vaguely aware of being spun around, his shield fleeing from his grasp, sword slipping from his nerveless fingers.

'Wilhelm...'

The words brushed past his lips like a death rattle as the long well came for him. It was cool in its shadowy depths and the water was dank. Old things lingered in it: old unquiet things that he would soon be joining. Earth came up to meet him, the bloody mire embracing Stahler's body like he was a babe in arms. For he was a child of war and she, the battlefield, was his dark mother.

Thunder boomed above, and with the last of his fading sight Stahler saw dead, bloody faces staring back at him, welcoming him.

Join us...

An almighty crack announced the destruction of the gates. Karlich saw it happen as surely as he felt the greenskins falter. Flaming debris and smoke plumed fifty feet high in an orange, grey bloom that expanded into the orcs around the gates. The greenskins were engulfed, riddled by wood splinters the size of swords, burned to death in the booming conflagration.

Some of the orcs and goblins fighting the Grimblades were looking over their shoulders. Confidence that had been so abundant moments ago ebbed like water in a punctured skin.

Something else was happening too. There was thunder, only not from the heavens. This thunder shook the earth and sent it trembling all the way up to the summit of the hill.

'Wilhelm...' breathed Karlich, in revered thanks for their deliverance. Having planned to join his armies on the road to Averheim, the Prince of Reikland had come. He had come and they were saved, but only if they were still willing to save themselves.

Karlich saw his chance.

'Grimblades! Push them back!'

As one the halberdiers thrust forward, leading with spikes and cleaving with blades as they surged down the hill, scattering the greenskins before them. There came the sound of powder cracks from a fusillade as beautiful and welcome as an orchestral chorus. Smoke plumed the air like grey pennants billowing on the breeze, announcing the arrival of salvation.

No longer pressed from all sides, greatsworders, handgunners and spearmen spilling into Blösstadt to leaven the intense pressure, Grimblades and Steel Swords reforming their ranks in a thick, narrow fighting block. Shields and blades went deep, as deep as they could. The greenskins were broken, all sense of purpose and coherency lost in a moment. The men of the Empire were merciless as they routed them.

Outside it was a similar glorious story. Karlich and the others would not get to see the magnificent charge of Prince Wilhelm and his knights, nor would they witness the efforts of the regiments from Kemperbad, Auerswald and Ubersreik. There were scores of militia soldiers too, drawn from the surrounding Reikland villages, all impassioned by a prince's cause and a desire to protect their borders and the borders of their neighbours. If they did not look to the defence of their Empire, then who would? It was a rare moment of solidarity in a land rife with internal strife and politicking, but then Wilhelm was an inspirational man and ruler. He spoke to men's hearts, not their heads or their coffers.

The goblin wolf riders broke first. The sight of such enemy numbers bearing down on them from the west – the serried ranks of pikes, halberds and swords all eager for blood – was enough to put them to flight. The militia regiments protecting the wagons cheered and jeered at the fleeing greenskins but knew, deep down, how close they had come to being food for the worms.

Prince Wilhelm was at the tip of a gleaming lance head, driving his knights forward from the back of a barded steed. Captain Ledner was at his right hand, Preceptor Kogswald at his left. With their banner unfurled and a blazing clarion call bursting from a silver bugle, the Griffonkorps rode onto the bloodied field like avenging warrior angels laying waste to the foul and the wicked.

Trapped between the doughty spearmen of Bögenhafen and the irresistible charge of Wilhelm and his knights, the orc boar riders were split apart like rotten kindling and scattered to the wind. Only the chieftain and his loyal bodyguard cadre stayed, recognising the prospect of a good fight and unafraid of death.

Griffonkorps lances skewered the first, splintering shields, piercing armour and flesh. Orcs were flung from their mounts as if punched by a cannon ball and those boars not kicked to death by the knights' armoured horses, were stabbed with longswords.

Even after penetrating the first greenskin line, the impetus of Wilhelm's charge was not spent. It rolled on, gathering momentum like a tidal wave. As its apex, the Prince of Reikland met the orc chieftain in single combat. Storm clouds were billowing across the heavens, as if the elements heralded the battle about to unfold, and dry lightning raked the sky in jagged forks.

'In the name of the Empire and Reikland!' shouted Wilhelm, his gleaming runefang held aloft as the thunder answered.

He struck just as the lightning cracked, a close heat drenching the field in a feverish sweat. Haze flickered in the distance and the air thickened. The ancient runefang descended like a comet and cut the chieftain down. Axe hafts splintered, armour parted, flesh and bone were cleaved – nothing could stop it. The chieftain died, split in two, both halves of his body spilling gore and viscera onto the earth.

It proved the end for the greenskins. Fear ran through them. In that moment, the heat broke and the clouds, as if they had been holding their breath, let go and the rains came. Wilhelm rode into Blösstadt like a warrior-king of old. Orc blood ran down off his armour, washed away and purified by the rain.

'Victory to the Empire!' he cried, as the fires around him died and the last death throes of the battle with the greenskins played out. 'For the Reik!'

'For Prince Wilhelm!' the men of the Empire replied, and Wilhelm knew then that his people loved him. Perhaps they could win this war and send the Paunch back over the mountains to the east.

Little could Wilhelm have known the futility of that dream and the dark days that lay ahead.

CHAPTER SEVEN

Good counsel

Prince Wilhelm's encampment, Averland,
324 miles from Altdorf

It was claustrophobic in the war tent, and the air was thick with pipe smoke. Sergeant Karlich didn't mind the latter, but he found the presence of the great and good a little hard to bear. He was not a politic man; he was a soldier, plain and simple. He knew how to fight, how to command men and get the best from them. He understood tactics and he feared death – any man that didn't was not to be trusted – but here, in this war tent, before his lords and masters, he felt profoundly out of his depth.

'You are all known to me, so I'll speak plainly,' Wilhelm began. The Prince of Reikland was still wearing his golden breastplate but had removed his greaves and tassets. The vambraces on his wrists carried the symbol of a rampant griffon. His blond hair, slightly damp and unkempt from wearing his helmet, shone like fresh straw in the lamp-light, and his blue eyes flashed like sapphires. Noble blood was obvious in his features and bearing.

'No aid comes from Altdorf.' The prince's conclusion landed like a hammer blow.

Preceptor Kogswald bore this statement with knightly stoicism and gave nothing away, but the others present, Captains Vogen of Kemperbad and Hornstchaft of Auerswald, Engineer Meinstadt and Father Untervash of the Holy Order of Sigmar, balked at this news. All had thought Altdorf would respond to the threat, that its vast armies would march in support of the prince. If Altdorf had closed its gates, then Nuln had too and that meant the Emperor was content to hole up behind the walls of Prince Wilhelm's former domain.

'What of the other states? What of Talabecland and Stirland? Does Wissenland answer the call to arms? Its borders are under threat too,' asked Vogen, a portly man with thick plate armour, and a feathered helmet sat in the crook on his arm. He sported a dark brown beard to hide his jowls and double chin.

'None are coming. Middenland, too, has sent what troops it is willing to commit,' said Wilhelm before his expression darkened. 'We are alone in this.'

'Ha!' scoffed Hornstchaft. 'So Middenland waits for the storm to vent its wrath against our bulwarks, only to then see it dashed upon its own when it rolls over the eastern Empire and the Reik. I'm surprised the northerners sent men at all.'

Where Vogen was all bulk and flab, Hornstchaft was hawkish and slim. Slightly taller than his counterpart, he held himself straight like a rod, and wore light chain armour. A small breastplate, emblazoned with a laurel and skull, finished the ensemble. He preferred a wide-brimmed hat over a helm. His had three griffon feathers sticking out of it.

'If our brothers do not come, then why are we marching out to Averheim? Why aren't we looking to our own borders? Tell me that,' said Meinstadt. The engineer was a fastidious man, his buttons and buckles polished and pristine. His face was pale and narrow from too much time spent in his workshops, and his hands bore powder stains like faded lesions. He wore a monocle with what appeared to be a targeting reticule placed over it in thin strips of brass. Leather, part smock, part armour, covered his upper body and carried an icon of the College of Engineers, a sideways image of a cannon. Evidently, Meinstadt was a gunnery captain. Karlich had seen no artillery in the camp, though.

'By marching to Averheim, we *are* defending our borders,' countered Wilhelm. The frustration of the prince was obvious, but he had encouraged his officers to speak plainly. He reminded himself of the fact that he already knew this news and that he had asked the very same questions himself during the long ride from Altdorf.

Another figure stepped forward from the shadows. This man, Karlich knew, was Adolphus Ledner. He held the nominal rank of captain, but most who knew him were aware of other *services* he provided for the prince and the Empire. Ledner was a scary bastard. Thin-faced like a blade, with hooded eyes that could pierce a man's soul and an aura of inscrutable intensity that made his mood impossible to gauge. Whenever Karlich had seen him, Ledner had always been wearing a red scarf around his neck. Some in the army suggested it was to cover a neck wound from where one of his many enemies had tried to slit his throat. Karlich could believe that. Exploitation, assassination and intimidation were Ledner's forte. He was as secretive as a witch hunter, and twice as resourceful. He traded in information, lies and half-truths and Wilhelm, for the good of the Reik, was content to turn a blind eye to most of it.

'Uncontested, it will not be long before the orcs drive westward,' he said. Ledner's voice reminded Karlich of a snake. It was harsh and rasping, but when he spoke all in the tent listened. 'And as they rampage, burning villages and murdering as they go, other tribes will gather to their banner.' He leaned forward on the table in the middle of the tent that was covered in maps and hastily written reports, and shadows pooled in his face from the lamps, making him appear ghoulish. 'This "Grom the Paunch" is like no other greenskin we have fought in recent times. It has an army large enough to sack Altdorf and if we do not meet it now and stop it, then that is exactly what it will do. Irrespective of whether the Emperor can see the danger or not, we must preserve our greatest cities. Nuln too, is under threat and we cannot allow the capital to fall without a fight. This goblin king must not cross the Averland border. It must not reach the Reikmark.'

Meinstadt's jaw clamped shut like a trap. Ledner, and therefore Prince Wilhelm, had spoken – it would not be wise to contest further.

Karlich cleared his throat, breaking the sudden silence. 'So what must we do?'

All eyes turned to him, and he felt suddenly very small and insignificant.

Wilhelm's was the first face to soften. 'I am glad there are some soldiers in our midst,' said the prince. 'How is your captain, Sergeant Karlich?'

Taken aback that Wilhelm even knew his name, Karlich faltered before replying.

'Fighting for his life in the chirurgeon's tent, your majesty,' he said at last, unsure if he should bow and instead producing a sort of half nod.

Stahler had been dragged off the battlefield by what was left of the Bögenhafen spearmen. His bravura had saved many of their lives, but left the captain badly wounded. Most of the blood that soaked his clothes had been his.

'Then we should all pray to Sigmar that he recovers to fight again.' Wilhelm half glanced at Father Untervash as he said it. The bald-headed warrior priest, who was even thicker set than Eber, gave a barely perceptible nod and touched the hammer icon hanging by a chain over his breast.

'Sigmar does not abandon his fighting sons,' he intoned, his voice full of sepulchral import. 'Your captain will take up his blade again. It is the will of the Hammer.'

Somewhere in the shadows, Karlich thought he heard someone cough, though he couldn't see who made the sound and realised there was another present whom he had yet to meet.

Wilhelm made the sign of the hammer before addressing the room. 'Averheim is under siege and we go to lift it if we can.' He gestured to some of the reports written by his scribes from the findings of the army's scouts. 'Greenskins push north, south and west. Stirland's borders are breached in a dozen or more places, entire tribes move on Wissenland despite its watchtowers and walls. None are untouched. But Averland is overrun and needs the aid of its brother states. We march on to the state capital and will meet with whatever provincial forces remain outside the city.'

At this remark, Preceptor Kogswald stepped forward.

'A local baron has marshalled a small army and moves westward,' said the knight commander, his tone as hard and haughty as his bearing. 'There are other temple knights with him and a small portion of state troops. We will intercept them, gather what information we can of Averheim's plight and march to the capital.' He brushed aside a clutch of scattered reports to get to the provincial map underneath. Kogswald's gauntleted finger pressed down on a dark blue band running along Averland's north-east border. 'The river Aver,' he said. 'We are currently on its north-east side. If we are to enter Averheim, we must find a large enough crossing to get us to the south-east side. That is our first obstacle, for the greenskins will be guarding the bridges, most likely destroying all but the few they require to move up from Averland and into Stirland.'

'Do we know how our military assets compare to that of the orcs?' asked Vogen, striking up his pipe.

'We are fewer by at least ten to one,' Ledner answered flatly, causing Vogen to almost choke.

'Breath of Myrmidia...' uttered Hornschaft. He failed to notice the raised eyebrow from Father Untervash at the invoking of a lesser deity's name. 'How can we prevail against that?'

'With faith in *Sigmar*, captain,' said Untervash.

Hornschaft turned on the man. 'We will need more than that, priest. I hear the Paunch's forces are not merely restricted to greenskins,' he added. 'That there are trolls and other beasts amongst the horde. I even hear tell of a shaman, one that rides a flying lizard!'

'A wyvern,' said a deep voice. It rumbled low and steady like an undercurrent of thunder. Karlich looked again to the shadows from where the voice had come and saw a cerulean flash light up the darkness, which came from a man's eyes. He was hooded and wore dark robes, but Karlich sensed they merely hid some grander attire underneath. Though the mysterious man was illuminated only briefly, Karlich saw he carried a jagged silver staff with a comet symbol at its tip. He had a forked beard that jutted impossibly from his chin, and there was the suggestion of a skullcap beneath his voluminous cowl. When he spoke again, Karlich felt a charge in the air and was put in mind of tempestuous storms and raging winds.

'The goblin's pet sorcerer rides a wyvern,' he confirmed. 'Do not fear it, though...' he added, opening his palm flat. Within, a tiny ball of lightning coruscated and forked, 'we are not without magic of our own.'

Karlich swallowed audibly. Truly, he was rubbing shoulders with gods and giants. When the council of war was finally over, he couldn't wait to get back to his men.

Eber shovelled the last of the earth onto the grave and wiped his brow with the back of his forearm. His back was sore from all the digging, but he had insisted on doing it alone. Varveiter's final rest was upon a grassy hill, radiated by shafts of sunlight. Eber had made it deep and buried the old soldier face down. He'd wept as he'd dug, the other Grimblades who knew Varveiter best looking on silently.

Rechts had left before Masbrecht could utter a benediction, walking away from the site with a bottle in hand and a scowl on his face. Keller had followed soon after, a dark mood over him that veiled his ordinary good humour. The other mourners thought it was grief. Only Brand, as still and lifeless as stone, knew it was actually guilt. When it was done and the others had started to walk away, Brand remained. None questioned it, or intervened in any way. They knew better.

Lenkmann did look back though and saw the man kneel and mouth a silent vow to the dead. Before he turned away, he watched Brand pull out his knife and cut his palm. He didn't know the ritual. To him it looked barbaric, but each of them would have to deal with Siegen Varveiter's death in a different way.

The old soldier was not alone, of course. Others joined him in death. A way outside Blösstadt tiny mounds littered the grassy knolls and plains. They were marked by blade hilts, broken helms or shields. Father Untervash blessed every single one to ward away necromantic interference. The village itself was no more. Greenskin spore blighted it. Fire had ravaged many of its buildings and destroyed large sections of the gate and stockade wall. Blood soaked its lanes and violence tainted its memory and spirit. Its people were dead. All of them. Wilhelm had ordered it burned down and razed from existence. Nothing good could come of its lingering ruins. Dark creatures, carrion and bandits would be drawn to its rotting shell as parasites are to a corpse. There were enough shadowed places in the Empire already without adding to them.

'Looks like the war council is over,' said Masbrecht, nodding towards the distant figures emerging from Wilhelm's tent. The encampment had been erected hastily, a few miles from Blösstadt and upwind so the smell of burning flesh from the pyres didn't infect it. The village was just an orange smudge on the horizon that no one cared to look at for the dark memories it held.

'So, does this mean Karlich will be leading the footsloggers in Captain

Stahler's absence?' asked Volker. He'd knelt down to pet the mastiff, his newfound companion that he had named 'Dog'. The creature licked his face eagerly.

Lenkmann opened his mouth to answer when another spoke in his stead.

'The beast likely has pox or worms.' It was Torveld, passing by the Grimblades' pitch with two other Middenlanders. 'You'd do well not to let it lap at you, southerner. Better still, let me slit its throat so it can't spread disease.'

Volker stood and drew his dirk. 'Try it,' he warned. Dog knew its enemies, and growled.

Torveld had stopped to level his threat and laughed out loud at the Reiklander. 'Still have the stomach to fight, eh?'

Eber stepped forward, balling his fists.

'Move on,' he said in a low voice. Varveiter was dead. His comrades in arms were dead. But *they* had fought and lived. That meant something. He would be cowed by bullies no longer. His strength was not just in his arm, it was in his heart too. Varveiter had taught him that. To do anything less than stand up would besmirch his memory. Eber took another step forward but kept his weapons sheathed. For the honour of his regiment and the memory of the dead, he would crush the Middenlander's skull with his bare hands if he had to.

'Hold your bear back, southerner,' Torveld warned Volker, all the sarcasm and cruel mirth disappearing from his face.

'Please, we are all allies here,' said Lenkmann, hands raised plaintively. 'We fought alongside one another. There is no need for this. We are all at war together, on the same side.'

Torveld snarled. 'It is not *our* war, though, is it Reiklander?'

Lenkmann was slightly dumbfounded. 'It will come to us all if we do not act now and together. We are all sons of Sig–'

'We are not,' Torveld cut him off. '*We* are winter wolves and our borders are far from here to the north. Don't forget that.' The Middenlander looked like he wanted more, that he wanted to vent his wrath against the southerners. His fists clenched. There were only a few feet between the two groups and now more swordsmen had joined Torveld and his companions.

'Bury your dead,' came Brand's voice from Torveld's left. The swordsmen turned to see him walking slowly towards them. 'Before they start to rot,' the Reiklander added.

Torveld paused. He could sense the danger, the potential violence of this man. It made even his northern blood run a little colder.

'Torveld,' said the gruff voice of Sturnbled from behind him. The grey-haired sergeant looked as grim as ever. He needn't say anything further. Muttering beneath his breath, Torveld turned and walked away taking the other Steel Swords with him.

'They are belligerent bastards,' said Lenkmann when they were gone. The others looked around at him. The standard bearer rarely swore, but he was clearly shaken and angry at what he saw as a breach of the soldier's code. Men who had fought side-by-side, shed blood together for the same cause, should have respect for one another. It offended his sense of honour and propriety that the Middenlanders did not.

'What did you expect,' said Karlich, stepping in amongst his men. 'They are northerners.'

Lenkmann saluted crisply at the sudden return of his sergeant. The others mainly nodded. Brand just looked him in the eye. Rechts lazily waved a hand.

'So what now, sergeant,' asked Volker, 'or should we call you "captain"?'

The corner of Karlich's mouth twitched in what could have been a grin. 'You sorry lot aren't shut of me yet,' he replied. 'I'm still a Grimblade, thank Sigmar.'

'When will Altdorf and Nuln join us?' asked Lenkmann.

'They won't,' Karlich answered flatly, not waiting for questions or protests. 'We march on to Averheim to death or glory, by the grace of Sigmar.'

CHAPTER EIGHT

On the road to Averheim

*Near the town of Streissen, Averland,
378 miles from Altdorf*

The way to Averheim was paved with misery and hopelessness. The closer they got to the capital, the more frequently they came across bedraggled regiments in Averland black and yellow. In truth, they were scraps of soldiers. Most were deserters or utterly routed troops. Encountered at a distance on the opposite side of the Aver, the broken merely trudged onwards, aimless and despairing. Those on the same side of the river fled like scared rabbits when they saw the column of Reikland troops. They wanted neither succour nor aid, instead fearing to be pressed into service by another lord. Many were wounded. Some carried dead and injured comrades over their shoulders, ignoring the stench of gangrene and decomposition.

There were human refugees too, alone and alongside the broken Averland troops, much like the ones the foot regiments had met earlier when Stahler was still in command. Dour priests of Morr walked with them, ministering to the dead and dying, flocks of ravens shadowing their every step.

Amongst a copse of trees, the army's scouts found a trio of hanged soldiers. From the scattered rocks beneath their dangling, bootless feet, it appeared they had committed suicide. Two more Averlanders were found slumped against the bole of the hanging tree. Their wrists were slit and bloodied daggers lay in their dead hands. Evidently, the desperate men had run out of rope for all five of them and didn't want to cut down the others to reuse what they had.

Mercifully the army did not meet any more orcs, nor did it stop at any other villages, empty or not. Deserters, refugees and suicides were not their only encounters, however. Late into the evening, just before the captains announced they would break camp, a single rider and a ragged band of followers on foot joined them, having come from the west.

Karlich shuddered inwardly when he recognised the same witch hunter from Hobsklein. The man had almost forty degenerates in tow. Around half were armoured to the hilt and carried an assortment of weapons. An eclectic mix, including a pair of dwarfs and several dark-skinned men foreign to the Empire, they could be nothing other than mercenaries. The rest were made up of flagellants and seekers, the latter being the homeless, pitiless wretches who had lost everything to the dark creatures that predated on the innocent and weak, and who longed only for vengeance or death. Dangerous men all, but nothing compared to their mounted leader.

'In search of gold and retribution,' remarked Volker from the second rank when he noticed Karlich looking at them. The Grimblades marched in column, three files wide, like the rest of the foot regiments. They were midway down the order of march, unfortunately, right behind the Steel Swords.

'Aye,' Karlich replied, keeping his feelings hidden from his men. 'Not a good combination.'

'Parasites and degenerates,' muttered Rechts to the sergeant's right, spitting out a gobbet of phlegm.

'Undesirable allies, indeed,' noted Lenkmann.

'All faithful men are soldiers of Sigmar,' said Masbrecht. 'We should not judge them harshly for that.'

Rechts glared over his shoulder at the man. 'Shut up, Masbrecht! No one cares what you think.'

'Both of you be quiet,' snapped Karlich, quickly nipping the situation in the bud before it could develop. 'Silence until we break camp,' he added afterwards.

The witch hunter and his 'soldiers of faith' joined the rear of the column, happiest with the militia companies and baggage train. Runners informed the prince of their presence. Encouraged by Father Untervash, Wilhelm tolerated them. He needed every man he could get if he was to lift the siege over Averheim.

Once they were out of sight, the rest of the army almost forgot about them. All except Karlich that is. The image of the witch hunter, attired in black and carrying his silver talisman like a death warrant, was burned into his mind. He could no more forget the man's presence than he could his own name. Was it just war and suffering that had drawn him to them, or did the Templar of Sigmar ride the plains of Averland for another reason? Was he, in fact, looking for someone?

Karlich did not consider himself to be a paranoid man. He met fate head on and didn't look over his shoulder for shadows in the night. The appearance of the witch hunter from Hobsklein had changed all that though.

Baron Ernst Blaselocker lolled in his saddle like an overweight klown. His steed, a stubby-legged mare, was as bulky as her master. Its bright yellow caparison hurt the eyes if looked at too long. Rings filled the baron's fat fingers and a great golden amulet rested on his breastplate which stuck out on account of his girth. A peppering of stubble swathed his triple chins but made him look neither swarthy nor rugged. All it actually did was to reinforce the baron's gluttonous image. His yellow and black tunic, echoed by the tiny pennant banner affixed to the back of his cuirass, affirmed his allegiance to Averland. A helmet, its visor raised, sat upon his head and failed to hide his thinning ginger hair. A broadsword sat in a scabbard at his waist which slapped against the man's bulging thigh in time with his wobbling jowls.

'Prince Wilhelm!' exclaimed the baron, throwing out an arm in over-enthusiastic greeting. 'It does my heart good to see that Reikland has not abandoned its brothers.'

The prince rode ahead of the army with Ledner, Preceptor Kogswald and a small contingent of Griffonkorps.

'Ernst,' the prince replied. The man was known to Wilhelm. They had attended Imperial functions together at the Emperor's Palace in Nuln. Baron Blaselocker was a toady, a lower ranked noble who sought to improve his station by association. More than once he had tried to court the prince's favour with offers of banquets or rides through his lands around the town of Streissen. Wilhelm had refused every one. Politely, of course. Emperor Dieter's functions were a trial he had no choice but to bear; Blaselocker's company was not.

Had he been able to choose his allies, Wilhelm would have placed the baron near the bottom of a long list. But such luxuries were not available to him. Every sword was welcomed to the cause, even Blaselocker's. To his credit, the baron had brought a decent-sized force with him. True to Preceptor Kogswald's word, there were a number of temple knights alongside the footslogging state troops. Wilhelm didn't recognise the order but judged them to be Sigmarite given the blazing comet device on their shields and banner. The rest of the army comprised spearmen and crossbows, with a few free companies. It was about a third the size of Wilhelm's force.

'A large army to escort a noble of my mere stature,' said the baron when he saw the marching column of men behind the prince's small entourage.

Wilhelm's brow furrowed. 'You misunderstand, Ernst. We aren't here to escort you anywhere. We march to Averheim to try and lift the siege.'

The baron's ruddy face paled at once.

'W-what? I thought...' The good humour vanished and his hands started to tremble a little.

'We march to Averheim, and so do you,' asserted Wilhelm. 'Now tell me, how bad are things at the capital? What forces do we face?'

The baron swallowed deeply and started to shake his head. 'N-no, no, no,' he blathered. 'You don't want to go there. We should head west to Reikland. I'm sure the Emperor will grant us protection in Nuln.'

'The Emperor has moved west himself already and resides at Altdorf,' snapped Ledner, 'you'll find no protection there. Now, do as your prince bids before I smack you off that horse, you fat oaf!'

As quickly as it came, Ledner's anger subsided, leaving Blaselocker dumbstruck.

'Speak to me, Ernst,' said the prince. 'Tell me what you know, and do it now.'

Keller shook the dirt and stones from his boot, sitting by the side of the road and trying not to lift his gaze from the ground. He'd been seeing things in the shadows, in the lee of trees, at the crest of hills, in the cool quiet of valleys. During the march from Blösstadt, he'd noticed a shape flitting occasionally at the edge of his vision. But when he went to catch it the shape had gone, evaporated like mist before the hot sun. He knew what it was and begged for it to stop, before telling himself to get a grip on his senses. The shadow didn't listen. It dogged him every step he took. It haunted his every waking thought and came again, as a much more grisly apparition, not merely a shadow at all, in his nightmares. Even now, basking in the glory of the midday sun, whilst the regiments from Averland were integrated into the order of march, he felt it. There at his shoulder, he perched like a harbinger of Keller's own inexorable fate. His penance. Thankfully, none of the other Grimblades had noticed. At least not yet.

They rested briefly in a grassy plain with a few dotted trees and near a shallow stream. It was a minor tributary of the mighty Aver, which was visible as a glittering silver-blue band in the distance.

Almost as long and wide as the Reik, the river was an impressive sight. Ordinarily, skiffs and boats would ply its depths for trade and passage across. The Aver was strangely empty this day, and had been for several days before it. Even the river birds, the fishermen and waterborne creatures were few and far between. It was as if life had ceased to be along its banks, as if the river were abandoned in the face of the greenskin invasion, its own refugee columns passing unheeded in the night.

Rechts stretched his legs, and rubbed at the fading wound in his shoulder. He winced, but the pain was not nearly as bad as it had been. It had been a long march from Reikland and now, closing on Averheim and the enemy, the soldiers of the Empire were starting to feel it. Even Volker, a seasoned ranger and hunter used to trekking the wilds, rubbed at his back and grimaced.

'How much farther to Averheim?' said Rechts.

Though he'd asked no one in particular, Lenkmann took it upon himself to answer.

'Another thirty miles or so, just over that next rise,' – he pointed to the distant horizon – 'and we should see it. From there, I'd guess a day's march, maybe two.'

'Are you keen for a fight or something, Torsten?' asked Volker of the drummer.

'Not especially, but anything is preferable to this.'

'Maybe Eber could carry you,' laughed the Reikland hunter, one eye on Dog who was scurrying around the long grasses chasing imagined prey.

'Strap a cart onto his back and we could all travel in relative comfort,' scoffed Rechts, before leaping onto Eber's broad back. 'To Averheim, beast of burden!' he cried.

The big halberdier laughed loudly, seizing Rechts's ankles and then dumping him to the ground. 'This beast is not for riding,' said Eber, helping the drummer back to his feet, who was rubbing his sore rump.

By now, most of the Grimblades were laughing. Even Lenkmann managed to snigger. It was a welcome relief after the sombreness of Varveiter's death. Brand was nowhere to be seen, having wandered off. Likely he was sharpening his blades by the edge of the stream where a good number of soldiers were dunking their heads and washing their filthy pits, or refilling skins. The latter seemingly unbothered by what the former were doing in their future drinking water.

'Keller…' Masbrecht began, noticing the down-turned face of his comrade, 'are you all right? Not in the mood for banter? If you wish, I can bless you with–'

'*Go away!*' hissed Keller, risking a glance at a lonely tree a little way in the distance. Its limbs were swaying as if beckoning and a leaf cascaded forlornly from one of its branches. '*Leave me alone… please.*'

'Sorry, brother. I didn't mean to cause offence,' said Masbrecht and walked away to join the rest.

When he was gone, Keller looked up.

'What?' he asked of Masbrecht's departing back, only just realising he hadn't been alone.

Karlich had a sour look on his face as he returned to the regiment and his men. He'd been listening to one of Prince Wilhelm's messengers, who related some change in orders directly from a scroll. The sergeant had neglected to even look at the parchment, let alone keep it, and instead nodded curtly to the runner before showing him his back and walking away.

'News doesn't look good,' whispered Rechts.

Even from behind him, Masbrecht could smell the alcohol on the drummer's breath but chose to hold his tongue. It awakened something in him, an old dependency and desire he thought was long buried. Clenching his jaw, Masbrecht pushed it back down into the deep places of his soul where it belonged. Lenkmann, standing rod-straight along-side the Grimblade drummer, failed to notice Rechts's booze breath. His gaze was fixed on Karlich.

'It will be what it will be,' he replied. 'We'll perform our duty all the same.'

'Definitely not good,' hissed Volker.

They were back in formation and arrayed in column with the Averland regiments. A few of the officers had received messages from the prince and the army was awaiting their return to the ranks before marching on to Averheim.

'Who is that overstuffed peacock riding behind him?' asked Keller. His voice was a little hoarse; he'd barely spoken at all in days.

They all saw the corpulent noble atop his stubby-legged steed swaying behind Karlich. Even mounted, the man was slower than the Grimblade sergeant by a good two strides. Karlich reached the men first as the noble slowed and then came to a stop a few regiments ahead of them, next to von Rauken's Carroburg Few. The stern greatsworder champion looked about as pleased as Karlich to be in the mounted noble's presence, but then his mood was perpetually dour.

'Sergeant,' said Lenkmann, addressing Karlich with a clipped salute.

'You're probably wondering who that is,' began Karlich, not deigning to wait for questions. 'It's Baron Ernst Blaselocker of Streissen. His Averland regiments are the reason for our swelled forces.'

'Why is he riding with us?' asked Volker.

'He has replaced Captain Stahler,' Brand replied, prompting a glance over the shoulder from Karlich.

'Is he leading us now then?' asked Rechts, failing to keep the disappointment out of his voice.

Karlich was stoic in response. 'The baron has command of the Reik and Averland foot, until such time as Captain Stahler is fit to retake the field.'

'And how long will that be?' asked Masbrecht.

'How am I to know!' snapped Karlich. 'I have yet to visit the chirurgeon's tent and enquire after the captain. His screams suggest it will not be before we reach Averheim, if at all.'

'Let's hope it's soon…' mumbled Volker.

'I heard that!'

Volker bowed his head contritely at the sergeant's reprimand.

'Tender mercies of Shallya, can he even fight?' hissed Lenkmann, as surprised as anyone at his own impropriety.

Karlich knew something of the noble who now led them. He'd heard talk in the Averland camp and knew that some called him the 'Yellow Baron' and not on account of his allegiance to the province either. Together with the appearance of the witch hunter, Stahler's injury and now this, it was turning into an arduous campaign.

Karlich sighed. It was a question to which he suspected he knew the answer already but, for the sake of morale, chose not to voice. Instead he replied with as much tact as he could muster.

'We'll find out soon enough.'

CHAPTER NINE

Rivers of blood

Brigund Bridge, Averland,
409 miles from Altdorf

Though not as long or wide as the Reik, the River Aver was still a formidable waterway. Its silvery expanse hugged the northern border of Averland and was as much a defensive barrier as it was a route for trade and commerce coming out of the east. Beyond the capital Averheim and along the edges of the Moot, the land of the halflings, it divided into two large tributaries, the Aver Reach and Blue Reach. Crossing it was a simple matter of securing passage upon a barge or finding a bridge or a ford near one of its narrower junctions. For a large force of men, together with baggage and beasts of burden, it was a more difficult prospect. The fact of the greenskin invasion made that prospect doubly problematic.

Out of tactical acuity or simple wanton destruction, the orcs and goblins in the Paunch's horde had destroyed most of the major crossing points over the Aver. Bridges were left fire-blackened ruins, ferrymen and their barges slain and burned, fords clogged with rotting corpses and the wreckage of the greenskins' violent rampages.

The search for a suitable crossing, large enough to accommodate his army, drove Wilhelm north-east. They shadowed the mighty river all the way. Every step closer to Averheim brought increased atrocities visited upon its people by the orcs. Isolated greenskin warbands were spotted across the far side of the Aver. Many of the men, particularly the Averlanders, wanted to engage them but Wilhelm forbade it – they had to reach the capital. Every moment wasted was time for another nail to be driven into Averheim's coffin. If the city was nought but a smoking ruin when they arrived then everything they'd endured so far would have been for nothing. The greenskins hooted and jeered at the passing army, loosing arrows ineffectually to land in the river's midst or break on the rocks of its bank. Angered, but maintaining discipline, the army of the Empire ignored them and marched on.

'Our fight will come soon enough,' Wilhelm had told them. 'Save your blades and your fury for that.'

It was to come soon, upon the Brigund Bridge, and the river below would run red with the blood of both man and orc.

A chunk of Averland stone barrelled through the air, twisting slowly like a leaf caught in the wind. Empire men watched it as it turned. They looked with morbid fascination, wondering bleakly if they would be struck or spared. Reaching the end of its parabola, the rock crashed into the ground with a shower of earth, chalk dust and grit. A regiment of Averland pike was crumpled by it, their shields and their screams doing nothing to prevent the rock trammelling their ranks. Men were crushed to paste. Some became tangled around the rock as it rolled onwards, using its momentum to furrow the earth and churn up soldiers like they were dolls.

'Drive on, Grimblades!' bellowed Karlich, ducking instinctively as another chunk of masonry spiralled into the sky. Beyond the waves of orcs and goblins holding the bridge, he made out distant batteries of catapults. The launching arm of one snapped, sending three of its goblin crew into the air instead of its stone cargo, which was dumped onto its orc overseer instead. He smiled grimly at the greenskins' misfortune, but knew it meant little. The Paunch had not only burned and ravaged on his bloody way through the Empire, he had constructed and fortified too. Much of the material, including its ammunition used to build the catapults, had been taken from barns, homesteads and watchtowers. Crude, certainly, but effective and deadly too, and in abundance. Through glimpses between the ducking and rallying, Karlich counted at least ten onager and mangonel-like war machines. The barrage was almost unceasing. It was making a real mess of the foot troops.

Blaselocker had no answer, even though his objective was a simple one: take and hold the bridge, and do not yield it until Wilhelm and his knights arrive. Karlich had seen the tactic used by the Empire many times. The foot regiments drive the army's centre, claiming a strategic position by sheer weight of numbers. Once taken, they must then keep it until a smaller, but more powerful, force attacked from the flank. The idea was to frustrate an enemy into throwing everything at the defenders to try and break them. Whilst he vented his strength and his wrath to his front, he would be vulnerable to his flank and rear. The flanking force would tear into that weakness and rip out the enemy's heart. A determined push from the hitherto static foot soldiers would press the enemy to his front aspect and thusly surrounded would result in the enemy being broken and routed.

Military theory was one thing. Textbooks and scrolls relayed the tactic in impersonal terms, with the added benefit of strategic maps. They did not tell would-be generals of the reek of blood, the stench of men as they piss and shit themselves before the first push, the deafening clamour of steel or the wailing of the dead. They did not reveal how your heart beat louder than a drum in your chest, so violent it felt like it would burst right out of your ribcage. Nor did it make reference to the enemy launching chunks of rock the size of cattle at you, or of air so thick with arrows and powder smoke it was as if the sun had been permanently eclipsed. It told of none of these things, because to do so would stop any young officer from taking to the field and likely have them seek out a softer profession as a merchant or craftsman.

So it was that Karlich and the Grimblades, together with the rest of the foot regiments, were to be the rock around which Wilhelm's plan depended, holding long enough for the prince to launch his crippling counter punch at the head of an armoured wedge of charging steel. Only before they could hold the bridge, they had to first take it. In the way of that were the orc war machines. Two waves comprised the assault: the Grimblades were in the first. Smash a hole through the greenskin ranks, drive on to the machineries and destroy them. A simple enough plan with one subtle flaw, how can you fight back against a chunk of hurtling stone?

Yet another rock thudded into the ground just to the Grimblades' right. It sank down into the earth and didn't roll, but still spread a clutch of charging militia across the ground like crimson butter. Chips of broken stone spat out from the impact like pistol shots. One hit Gruber in the shoulder, making the Grimblade from the back ranks cry out and fall; another scythed Brand across the cheek, but he merely grunted and took the pain without slowing down.

A slow jog built to a flat out run from the Empire foot troops as the greenskins came within charging distance. The soldiers roared until their lungs burned, dredging courage from within. The war machines had to be destroyed. Wilhelm and his knights could not flank attack until they were gone, for even the formidable armour of the Griffonkorps and the Order of the Fiery Comet was as linen against several tons of falling masonry.

To his right, Karlich saw the shadow of a great flying beast passing across the smothered light of the sun. The air around it crackled, promoting the gathering of storm clouds tinged an ugly dark-green. Fell voices filled the air. Their bestial words were indiscernible to the sergeant but their meaning was clear.

Bring war and death to men.

As quickly as he had seen it, the shadow of the beast was gone, lost beyond Karlich's peripheral vision, taking its master with it towards where he knew Wilhelm and his knights were riding. Karlich mouthed a silent prayer to Sigmar for the prince's triumph and forged on.

Regiments closed on either side of the Grimblades, the anchors to their flanks. On the immediate left, Averland swordsmen began to raise shields; on the right the remnants of the Bögenhafen spearmen, who had overrun the broken militia unit formerly attached to them, now levelled their polearms. On the extremes of the formation were the Steel Swords and Carroburg Few, to the left and right respectively. Blaselocker led from the rear, urging his men to charge behind a solid wall of shields and blades.

Overhead, arrows and crossbow bolts soared like flocks of barbed-beaked birds. Powder cracks came and went like thunder, accompanied by smoke and the reek of fire and soot. Karlich saw a distant line of greenskins fall to the wave of missiles. Goblins span on their heels, choking with arrows in their throats or clutching stomachs where iron shot had torn them away. Several fell with bolts to the brain, transfixed through the eye as if sprouting a black-fletched whisker.

The orcs were more resilient. Their armour was thicker, they wore helmets and carried shields – many tore out the shafts sticking from their bodies or barrelled on with them still embedded in their flesh like spines. Goblin short-bows were loosed sporadically in reply, but failed to have much of an impact. It didn't really matter. The horde was huge. Hand-to-hand was where it excelled, where the strength and brutality of orcs found domination.

The greenskins were coming up fast. A wall of rampant orcs and goblins was held together in ragged formations, clutching crude spears, clubs and axes. The beasts were daubed in blood and war paint, their round wooden shields smeared with orcish icons and tribal symbols. Their banners were fashioned from flesh and hide, baked black in the sun, and carried further sigils. They reminded Karlich of totems; skulls and other trophies rammed on their spiked tips in grisly stacks. Horns blared and drums beat, vying against the Empire's own, order meeting discord in a cacophony.

'In the name of Prince Wilhelm!' shouted Karlich, and his cry was echoed by the other sergeants down the line. The clash was just seconds away. The edge of the bridge was so close, just a few feet, but swamped with greenskins. He felt his heart beating, so loud it deafened the noise around him. Gripping his sword, the earth pounding by beneath his feet, the pull of the wind and the stench of greenskins swirling, he raised his shield and met the foe.

Several died in the initial rush, impaled on blades and spears, smothered in the crush, battered senseless against shields and unyielding bodies. It was over in moments. Then came the drive and the real killing began.

Karlich cut to his right, severing an orc's jugular. A fine spray of dark blood painted his breastplate. Turning towards a flash of green to his left, he impaled another orc through the neck, nearly ripping off its head as he withdrew the blade in a welter of gore. Something smashed against his shield and he would have fallen if not for the man behind him pushing him upright.

'In Sigmar's name, sergeant!' shouted Masbrecht from the second rank, thrusting his halberd over Karlich's shoulder to pierce an orc's torso. When the halberd spike was ripped free it released a gushet of blood and greenskin innards, spilling them like offal onto the ground.

'Aye, for Sigmar,' breathed Karlich, thrusting his shield forward to smash a goblin's nose and committing back to the fight.

At the end of the front rank, Eber grunted and blew, his halberd rising and falling like a pendulum in his thick-fingered grasp. He cut off a goblin's head, the wretched creature was still snarling even after it was decapitated, then lunged into another orc's body. Eber held the beast as it flailed at him, before Brand finished it with a downward cut that split its skull.

'Push forward!' the voice of Karlich was muted by the sheer madness of the battle around them. They saw Lenkmann raise the banner and heard the beat of Rechts's drum, conveying the order to press.

A tangible swell came from behind them as the rear rankers heaved. On either side, the flanking regiments of swords and spearmen did the same. The entire Empire battle line was making a concerted push against the greenskins. The orcs and goblins on the near side of the Brigund Bridge were only a vanguard, the bulk of the greenskins were on the other side. Still, all the Grimblades needed to do was punch a hole through the centre, surge through to the other side and assault the war machines.

Volker was breathing hard. The greenskins were everywhere, but he tried to keep focused on those in front of him, trying to kill him. Like they had at Blösstadt, goblins sneaked through the orcish ranks, aiming for legs and ankles with their knives as they emerged amongst the enemy. The tactic was less effective this time. The Empire men had learned to look below as well as in front. Dog patrolled his master's legs, savaging any goblins that came close, ripping out their throats and keeping pace with the push.

The orc vanguard was breaking. Keller felt it from the second rank as surely as the wood of the Brigund Bridge beneath his boots. Blaselocker's determined push up the centre was actually working. Panicked, huge swathes of orcs and goblins fled backwards through their own ranks. Too slow to turn and join the flood, some were crushed underfoot. Others tumbled over the sides of the bridge to a watery doom in the Aver below. Suddenly an ever-widening streak of daylight began to emerge between the Empire forces and the retreating greenskins.

'Tighten formation!' The order reverberated down the line to the tune of trumpets and drums. As they gained the bridge, running past its midpoint in pursuit of the greenskins, Keller felt the files narrow and the ranks thicken. To his right and left, men withdrew to make additional ranks and deepen the Grimblades' formation. The spears and swords on either side did the same. Von Rauken's Carroburg Few and the Middenland Steel Swords closed in and the entire Empire battle line became a giant stopper, plugging up the bridge along its width.

'Advance!' shouted Karlich, screaming to be heard above the din of the battle. The greenskin vanguard was in full retreat. Other regiments on the far side of the Brigund Bridge were closing fast to seal the gap but were slow and unruly to respond. Bickering had broken out amongst several mobs, so all that stood between the Grimblades and the greenskin catapults was a thin line of goblins wielding short bows.

'Forward now! Charge you whoresons, charge!'

It was like breaking the surface of the sea having been submerged below its watery depths as the Grimblades burst from the battle line and headed straight for the goblin archers. Arrows whickered into them from the goblins' vantage point on the lowest step of a shallow hill. At the summit, the war machine crews looked on helplessly, the Empire men too close to target with the catapults. The Grimblades' momentum had carried them a long way across the short tract of plains that led up to the hill. Behind them, the other regiments had closed the gap, effectively 'shutting the gate' back onto the bridge for the other greenskins.

Eber felt an arrow glance his arm. He grimaced as it tore his tunic and opened a wet, red line in his skin. Another Grimblade fell somewhere behind him, gurgling blood from a neck wound, trampled to death in the maddened dash for the hill, but this was the only casualty. Seeing their arrows were ineffective, the goblin archers balked and some even started to run as the Grimblades charged them.

Ascending the hill in long strides, the Empire soldiers fell upon the hapless goblins in a hacking, lunging wave. The entire front rank of the greenskin archers was butchered in seconds. The few that remained squealed and ran. Some were swept up by the triumphant halberdiers as they drove on to attack the catapults; others were sent sprawling down the hillsides, breaking their necks and limbs. Fewer still just kept on running, abandoning the field and Averland for good.

The war machines were no greater challenge. Mainly crewed by goblins with the occasional orc overseer, the ones that didn't flee on sight of the massacred archers soon fell beneath the halberdiers' blades. The fight had lasted only minutes, but the catapults were silenced and as they took stock of the carnage around them, the Grimblades realised just how far from the battle at the bridge they had come.

Marshalling some order at last, huge mobs of orcs and goblins had started to converge on the bridge, determined to take it back. Massive brutes wielding double-bladed axes and feral beasts with bones through their noses, wearing furs and carrying stone clubs, roamed amongst the throng. Trolls lolled between the mobs, goblin overseers prodding them enthusiastically with long, barbed tridents. One of the witless creatures took offence at being goaded and ate one of its tormentors in a single bite. An armoured orc with a spiked whip took the dead goblin's place and the troll was driven forward again. Other, smaller beasts scurried between the unruly ranks. Reddish-orange, bulbous and festooned with warts, Karlich recognised them as squigs. Little more than fangs on legs, squigs were vicious creatures, the absurdity of their appearance belying their ferocity.

Von Rauken and the others faced a stern challenge to hold the bridge, but at least the war machines had been silenced. At least Prince Wilhelm and the knights were not far off, now the way was open.

Karlich looked to the east. A storm raged there, cerulean lighting clashing with green fire in the heavens. Clouds boiled up in anger, summoned by their masters as an unseen magical duel took place. Wilhelm and his entourage would be in its eye.

'They've met them…' said Lenkmann, proudly holding the banner aloft.

All eyes went to the Brigund Bridge where the greenskin mobs had finally clashed with the Empire defenders attempting to hold it.

'Madness,' breathed Masbrecht upon witnessing the carnage. 'Sigmar protect them.' He made the sign of the hammer.

'We fought in something similar,' Rechts shot back, but realised von Rauken and the others were in a fight for their lives.

'Where is Prince Wilhelm?' asked Volker, looking to where the magical storm cracked and thundered.

Karlich had his eyes on the battle for the bridge. 'Waylaid,' he muttered. He looked around him. The orcs and goblins were leaving them alone for now, a wide gulf of open ground churned by booted feet but empty of foes, encircled them.

'We should hold the hill, sergeant,' said Lenkmann, guessing what Karlich was thinking. 'Those are our orders.'

Karlich grit his teeth. 'I know.' His gaze went eastward again. There were no trumpets, no calls to arms, only sorcerous thunder. All the while, more and more greenskins poured into the forces at the Brigund Bridge. It was impossible to see anything in the chaos. Did the orc mobs advance a step? Karlich couldn't be sure.

'What shall we do?' asked Brand. Several other Grimblades around him looked eager to hear the sergeant's answer.

Again, Karlich looked to the east.

'What if he doesn't come?' asked Eber, frowning at the thought of what might happen if Wilhelm didn't arrive.

'Something's happening!' said Lenkmann, pointing his sword towards the bridge.

Karlich went a few steps down the hill. 'What's he doing?' His eyes narrowed as he tried to see.

Masbrecht saw it before the rest. His voice was cold and distant.

'He's ordering a retreat…'

Scowling, Karlich turned to face him. 'What?' He looked back. Masbrecht was right. The troops in the rear ranks were pulling back. Blaselocker had taken his fill of bloodshed and death and decided he didn't like it.

'Von Rauken won't give up the bridge,' said Keller, blinking hard as if trying to shake off the sight. 'Have you ever known a Carroburger to relinquish anything?'

'Then he'll die,' said Rechts. 'They're fatalists, as well as stubborn bastards.'

'Aye, and for nothing!' snapped Karlich, then muttered, 'Blaselocker you spineless cur…' He strode back up the hill to address his men.

'We're going down there, aren't we?' said Lenkmann, his tone resigned.

'We are,' said Karlich. 'Into formation!' he cried to the regiment.

Rechts beat out the order on his drum.

'Tight ranks, narrow frontage,' hollered Karlich. 'We'll punch through like a lance.'

'Not wishing to speak out of turn,' muttered Rechts, 'but this is suicidal, sergeant.'

'Have some *faith*,' Karlich replied, deliberately bitter. 'Prince Wilhelm will come. Succour isn't only found at the bottom of a bottle, Torsten.'

The drummer shut his mouth and waited for the order.

Karlich gave it swiftly.

'Forward, in the name of the Reik and Prince Wilhelm!'

Unimpeded by the open terrain, the Grimblades marched quickly to the battle site. Karlich steered them on an oblique route that would see them hit the weakest flank of the greenskin line, using the river itself as a natural anchor to their own flank.

A ragged band of goblins were the first enemies to oppose them. Karlich and his men fell upon the smaller greenskins with fury. The Grimblades cut the goblins down ruthlessly, the greenskins' bloodied-eye banner soon crushed underfoot by the rampant halberdiers. Karlich finished the goblins' champion himself, severing the creature's neck and head. It proved too much for the greenskins, who turned and fled into the packed ranks before they'd barely struck a blow in reply. The large mob of orcs behind them, swathed in metal scale and carrying broad wooden shields and spears, were a different foe altogether. They killed their cowardly goblin cousins as they ran into the unmoveable line of their shields. It only set off the orcs' bloodlust. They whooped and hollered at the prospect of a real fight presented by the overrunning Grimblades.

'Into them!' Karlich was hoarse from battle, but made his voice heard above the clash of steel and the grunt of beasts.

Hitting the orcs was like driving at a stone wall; hard and unyielding. They had the greenskins in the flank, robbing them of much of their fighting strength and stopping their chieftain from bringing his axe to bear, but still they fought ferociously. So intent were the greenskins on getting to the bridge that their ranks were utterly rammed, like forcing an apple through the eye of a needle. The smaller beasts were crushed by the bigger ones. Karlich saw trolls, slime-skinned monsters with manes of lank seaweed-like hair and scales like fish, looming head and shoulders above the brawling mobs. Occasionally one would reach down and pluck a greenskin from the mob, biting off its head or swallowing it whole before it was brought to heel again by spears and whips. Patches of animosity broke out amidst the clamouring horde, so in the end it was hard to tell who was fighting who.

Through the carnage, Karlich could see von Rauken and his men fighting like heroes to hold the bridge. He saw too that the greatsworders noticed the allies in their midst and redoubled their efforts. The Carroburgers were not alone, either, and it sent a shiver of fear down Karlich's spine when he recognised the mercenary rabble of the witch hunter. Whether to hold the bridge or simply to bring death to the enemies of Sigmar, or even for the templar's promised coin, the sellswords, flagellants and seekers stuck doggedly to the task when everyone but the greatsworders had already fled.

Madmen… thought Karlich, but perhaps the templar would be slain?

He dared to hope, then felt a heavy blow against his shield. Karlich was battered back but stuck out his sword and was rewarded with a porcine squeal of pain. He then righted himself, parrying a cut that would have cleaved his own head, and jabbed again. Steel met flesh and the orc assailing him, seen only in flashes from behind Karlich's shield, before it crumpled to the ground with its throat slashed open. After that, Karlich forgot about the witch hunter and put his mind wholly on staying alive.

With their brutish kin around them, the orcs were not giving an inch. The Grimblades had killed several and, fighting the beasts to their unprepared flank, had taken few casualties in reply, but the orcs were digging in and more were coming.

Rear rankers, impatient to get into battle, had now seen the flank attack by the Empire soldiers. Horns brayed and hooted and drums pounded out the order to reform and manoeuvre around the flank. Locked in combat, Karlich realised with rising horror that the Grimblades were exposed.

'Push them back, break through!' he urged, but it was like telling the wind not to blow or the mountains to part ways – the orcs were implacable.

Glory was not something that had ever concerned Karlich. He was a soldier, content with a soldier's lot. But throwing away the lives of his men because of a rash decision did not sit well with him. Suddenly, he wished they had stayed on the hill and the bridge be damned.

Blaselocker, you bastard, he thought. You've doomed us all with your cowardice.

Eber anchored the end of the line with Brand behind him, then Leffe and Gans in the rear ranks. His halberd was slick with greenskin blood and his muscles burned from the killing. Corpses littered the ground at his feet but for a moment there was respite as the orc back ranks had been despatched and others were still struggling over the dead to fill the gaps. Out of the corner of his eye he noticed another mob approaching. They were the biggest greenskins he had ever seen, as broad as oak trees with skin twice as thick as bark but just as gnarled. Huge black metal plates covered their bodies, dripping with swathes of chainmail. Horned helmets rose up in exultation to their heinous gods, a challenge and an invocation in one. Gauntleted fists, as large as a horse's head and studded with spikes, wrapped around thick-hafted glaives that glinted dully in the half-light. Graven totems, tiny skulls and rings of brass and copper, jangled against the metal like cruel laughter.

'Monsters...' Eber breathed, and for the first time in his life found something that frightened him more than his father. 'Brand!' he cried.

'I see them,' said Brand, levelling his halberd at the onrushing greenskins. They were like charging bulls, and lowered their horned helms as they closed.

'Do you believe in the power of Sigmar, Brand?' asked Eber. The other two Grimblades, Leffe and Gans, had swung around too but kept quiet.

The bull-like orcs were just twenty feet away.

'I believe a man must save himself if he wants to live. Sigmar protects the strong.'

Eber muttered, 'I wish Masbrecht were here beside me...'

The Empire men roared, prepared to meet their enemy defiantly, when a blinding flash lit up the gloom. Thunder, loud and percussive as cannon fire, erupted a split-second afterwards. Eber blinked back the after flare of lightning, the reek of ozone heavy in his nostrils, and saw a row of charred corpses where the monstrous orcs had been.

Brand noticed the hairs on his hands were standing up. His teeth ached.

'Maybe I was wro–'

Another flash... this time they saw it come from the heavens, splitting the darkness like sun pierces cloud. Brand managed to keep his eyes open long enough to see the orcs struck, to see the lightning arc race through all that metal, burning and shocking as it went.

The storm came again, several bolts coursing from above like spears of righteous anger. They weaved and raked, splitting and coruscating through the greenskin mobs like hot, angry fingers. Wherever they touched, death followed. The stink of smouldering orc flesh was soon heavy on the breeze.

Eber was laughing, loud and booming in concert with the thunder.

Brand laughed too. It was a wicked sound, full of malice and sadistic joy.

'Burn you bastards, burn!'

Some of the greenskins were running. Karlich felt the rout before he saw it, a sudden shifting of weight to their embattled front. He'd lost sight of the flank by then, so buried was he in blood and bodies. Something lit up the battle, too stark and short-lived to be sunlight.

Did I just hear laughter?

The tide had swung again and he didn't need to see the banner of Altdorf snapping on the breeze to know the self-same saviour had delivered them again.

Thunder came from the east. It wracked the heavens above and shook the earth below. Hooves pounded the dirt, clarions announced a glorious charge. A sudden rush of movement came upon the greenskins as if an unseen wind was propelling them west, away from the storm of steeds and lances. They panicked as one, some flailing into the Aver to be drowned in its unforgiving depths. Others were crushed in the relentless press from the Brigund Bridge now that Blaselocker, with victory in sight, had re-committed the troops. Despite the fact they'd been fighting longer than any other regiment, the Carroburg Few led the rampant pursuers.

For his part, Karlich ordered his Grimblades to hold. The bridge was won and they would keep it that way. He contented himself with watching the enemy flee, safe in the knowledge that no more of his men would die, for the moment at least. A blur of silver, gold and red sped past them, so long that he had time to strike up his pipe and stand in awe of it.

Karlich could only glance at Wilhelm riding at the head of the Griffonkorps, the horses were moving too swiftly for a longer look. The gold-armoured Order of the Fiery Comet drove alongside them, their flanged maces spitting arcs of greenskin blood when they rose and fell. The prince was majestic, his runefang like a streak of captured fire in his hand. On his left, Preceptor Kogswald, his own blade etched in enchanted sigils; on his right, the wizard Karlich had seen in the command tent, no longer wearing a dowdy cloak and cowl. Stars and comets decorated his robes of deep, cerulean blue. Silver edged the cuffs and trims. Constellations stitched into the fabric appeared to shimmer and shift. Lightning bolts and other heavenly symbols hung from chains on his belt and around his neck. Even the skullcap the wizard wore carried the image of celestial phenomena.

Hope sparked within the sergeant, kindled by the lightning that had raged from above and so decimated the greenskins. Perhaps victory at Averheim was possible after all.

'Quite a sight, isn't it?' Von Rauken's voice brought Karlich around.

The greatsworder champion was walking towards him with some of his men. The lacquered black plate of his cuirass was dented and smeared with blood. He'd removed his helmet, revealing a few strands of hair covering an otherwise bald head.

'Comes from living in Carroburg,' he said. Von Rauken grinned, showing a missing tooth. Evidently, the greatsworders had hung back after all and had merely moved aside to allow the fresher regiments to pass.

'Aye, I hear you're a serious people. A little levity and you might have some hair to warm that pate of yours.'

Von Rauken smiled and held out a gauntleted hand. It looked massive and the leather palm was well worn from sword wielding.

'Your service to Carroburg, and to the Few, will not be forgotten, Sergeant Karlich.'

Karlich gripped the greatsworder's hand firmly and nodded.

'Call me Feder.'

Von Rauken clapped him on the shoulder. 'Very well, Feder. I am still von Rauken.'

At that the two men laughed loudly. There was palpable relief in it, of a battle over and won, of having survived to tell of it and endure the nightmares later. It passed to the men around them and soon Grimblade and Carroburg Few were exchanging names and stories in the way that Lenkmann had expected of the Steel Swords.

For their part, the Middenlanders were livid. Glory had been denied them, supplanted by ignominy at being part of Blaselocker's retreating force. They strode across the bridge wearing scowls like masks, not meeting any other soldier in the eye. Sturnbled looked ashamed, but used his pride to conceal it. Torveld was looking for someone to blame for this smear on their honour. His gaze fell upon the Grimblades and was then lost again to the middle distance.

The battle was done, the greenskin army in full rout. Most of the Empire regiments had given up pursuit and were consolidating at the bridge. Even as they spoke, Karlich and von Rauken were being joined by troops from the north side of the river. The wagons, too, were now starting to move across. Priests of Morr went with them, leather-bound 'death-books' clutched in their bony fingers, ledgers for the prince's quartermasters when they had to reorganise the army in the face of casualties.

Blaselocker trotted over last of all, his bodyguards surrounding him, glad their faces were obscured by battle-helms. The baron would have to answer to Prince Wilhelm now.

'A pity he did not die in the battle,' spat von Rauken, his mood souring at the sight of the pompous Averland noble.

Karlich was a little taken aback by the blatant outburst, even though he felt the same. He supped on his pipe to cover his surprise, but found himself liking the outspoken greatsworder more and more.

'He'll wish he did if Ledner is allowed at him,' he replied.
Von Rauken smiled again, but this time humourlessly.
'Then let us hope for that.'

CHAPTER TEN

Licking wounds

The town of Mannsgard, Averland,
383 miles from Altdorf

Ledner closed the tavern door and turned to face an almost empty room. An iron tub sat in the middle of it where Prince Wilhelm was taking a hot bath.

'How is it?' asked the prince, whilst a local priestess of Shallya rubbed healing salts into his heavily-bruised shoulder. The charge by the prince and his knights might have been glorious, but the battle to fend off Grom's shaman and his 'flying lizard' was not. The beast had raked Wilhelm's pauldron before he'd nicked its snout with his runefang and sent it fleeing for the sky.

'Quiet,' said Ledner. His gaze went to the armour and clothing slumped on a chair near the tub. Wilhelm's runefang rested on top of it, inside its scabbard. The captain noticed his liege kept the blade within reach. A sensible move. Perhaps the young prince was learning to be cautious after all. 'Mannsgard might as well be a tomb,' he went on. 'The townsfolk that haven't fled or been killed cower behind locked doors carrying picks and cudgels. The few people we have encountered offer limited services and don't indulge in much talk.'

Wilhelm frowned at the annoyance in Ledner's voice.

'And this bothers you?' he asked.

'Yes, it bothers me. Where are the peddlers and the whores, the illicit traders and profiteers? War brings death, my liege, but it also brings opportunity for those who have a will and a way to make coin.'

Wincing with the pain in his back and shoulder, Wilhelm sat up in the bath.

'They're mostly dead, Ledner. That or they've run westward with the refugees,' he explained needlessly. 'We are less than ten miles from Averheim. I can almost hear the greenskin chanting on the breeze and smell their spore tainting it. Is it really any wonder that the land, this town, is abandoned, even by its human carrion?'

Ledner's face darkened.

'No, my liege.'

'So, how do we fare?' asked the prince, glancing at the death-books piled in one corner of the room.

They were in the tavern's taproom. The floors were timber, the wood stained but worn. A simple bar sat to the left at the back. Most of the alcohol was gone. A stairway curled up to an upper floor. The iron tub had been moved from one of the upper rooms – 'guest quarters' a placard read – and brought down to the prince. It looked almost ludicrous in the expansive room, the many tables and chairs that might once have stood there having been either looted or used as barricades.

Though the day's march from the Brigund Bridge to the town had proven uneventful, Mannsgard had suffered many attacks since the invasion. The town's walls were thick, hewn from rough stone taken from the mountains, and overlooked by watchtowers. Its militia regiments had been many, several bands of soldiers seeking refuge had also added to its garrison, but still they had suffered. The cemeteries and mortuaries were full. Even the temples of Shallya, Sigmar and Verena could hold no more bodies. So much corpse traffic had been foisted upon the gardens of Morr that the old prefect had died himself, of a heart attack. Ledner heard talk of a town watchmen finding the poor old bastard, his withering body food for the crows.

Morr giveth, Morr taketh away...

A black mood pervaded here, the final rest before the march on Averheim. It was like a funeral veil, only no one had said when they could stop mourning. At least, the presence of the army meant that greenskin raiders would think twice before attacking again. Not that there'd been any sign for several days, not according to Mannsgard's gate sentries anyway. Ledner supposed the orcs and goblins had been drawn to the Brigund Bridge instead and the army of 'humies', as they called men in their crude speech, gathering there. A black stain was upon this place. It was no different to Blösstadt, only unlike the village they'd been forced to put to the torch, Mannsgard didn't realise it was already dead. Old men and withered women mainly populated the town now, its youth having been cut down in its prime, an end to its legacy and future.

'Adolphus?' Wilhelm pressed.

Ledner blinked, recognising his first name, and realising he hadn't answered the prince's question. Sometimes the dark moods came when he least expected it. Usually he could master them, the baggage of too many years of war and blood. Occasionally they got the better of him.

'We lost a lot of men at Brigund Bridge. More than we could comfortably spare.'

'Any loss like that is uncomfortable to me, Ledner,' chided the prince, standing and accepting a towel from the Shallyan priestess.

'I meant no offence, but it's simple numbers my lord. We can't hope to prevail at Averheim with the forces we have left. At best our chances are slim and bloody.'

Stepping from the tub, Wilhelm's brow furrowed. He looked heavy, as if he still wore his armour. Ledner continued.

'Of course, our dear ally the baron was somewhat instrumental in that debacle.'

'I heard Karlich's men helped hold the bridge with the Carroburgers.'

'Stubborn bastards,' muttered Ledner, before a stern look from Wilhelm forced an apology. 'They are certainly resourceful, and brave, these halberdiers. True sons of the Reik,' he added, cracking his knuckles, just another of his idiosyncratic traits. 'Vanhans and his rabble earned their keep, too.'

'The witch hunter?'

'Yes, my lord. They are camped outside the town walls. The templar claims there is only "debauchery and unholy art" to be found within.'

'I'm surprised he hasn't come in to burn and stake it all then. Watch him,' said Wilhelm, finishing up drying off. He handed the towel back to the priestess, who bowed and took her leave.

'Like a hawk, my lord.'

A pregnant pause invited Ledner's next question. He waited to ask it until they were alone. 'Would you like me to remonstrate with Blaselocker?'

Wilhelm pulled on his undergarments and hose. 'If I wanted to find him hanging by his medallion from the rafters or drowned in his own drink, then yes. I'll deal with him,' the prince asserted. 'The Averlanders need a figurehead, even one as craven as he. What of Sirrius?'

'Weak from his exertions. It doesn't take an augur to know he won't be fighting again for a few days. Even if we wanted to move on Averheim tomorrow, I wouldn't advise it, not without the wizard.'

Wilhelm considered that for a moment before his mind went elsewhere. 'Any word from the other provinces?'

'Messengers were sent as requested, but none, as of yet, have returned. The scouting parties have come back though, some of them. They report Stirland is under almost perpetual siege and that greenskin armies are as far north as Talabecland.'

'So we are alone in this, after all, just as the Emperor predicted.' Wilhelm couldn't hide his bitterness. After buttoning his tunic, he sat down heavily in the chair, his sword and armour now resting against the leg. 'I love the Empire, Ledner...'

'As do we all, my liege.'

'But I love the Reik more. What are we doing here, old friend? Is this really our war? Was Markus right? Should I be back at Kemperbad, strengthening our border for the inevitable tide?'

'Someone must stand for the Empire when its emperor does not,' Ledner answered plainly. 'I am not a righteous man. I have killed and bribed, extorted and committed larceny to keep my province safe. I do it knowing I must live a life of compromise, because that is who I am and my lot. You, my lord, *are* a righteous man.' Ledner paused to look outside, an old habit, to make sure no one was within earshot. He looked back at Wilhelm. 'Dieter is a fatuous emperor. His time is ending. Whatever business he is brokering with Marienburg will undo him, and when he falls the Empire will have need of a decent man, a strong lineage to guide it.'

'I don't make war five hundred miles from home as part of a bid for succession, Ledner,' said the prince, slightly perturbed.

'I know, my liege,' the captain replied, 'and that is what makes you just.'

Wilhelm tugged on his boots and strapped on his breastplate. He cinched his runefang to his belt with care. What the sword stood for had faded in the current time, yet the prince still believed. 'Perhaps, but it'll all be for nothing if I cannot bring allies to my banner, Ledner. The only Empire left to govern might be a tattered ruin by the end.'

'So you still plan to ride to Wissenland. It's several days' journey from Mannsgard. Are you sure that's wise?' said Ledner. 'Send me in your stead.'

'I must go. If Pfeifraucher can be convinced to fight, then it will only be done by my intervention. I'll have the Griffonkorps to protect me.' Wilhelm smiled, hooking his cloak to his pauldrons and picking up his helmet. 'In any event, I need you here to be my eyes and maintain order in the ranks.'

Ledner bowed. 'As I knew you would, my liege. As I also knew you would not rest at Mannsgard, either.'

'The soak has eased my bones. How can I rest when my land is in danger? If I am the just and noble heir apparent you say I am, then I must act.'

'Send the count my greetings,' said Ledner as Wilhelm was making for the door.

Outside the tavern, a small band of Griffonkorps were already gathering. The prince's empty steed was with them.

'I want Pfeifraucher to join us, Ledner,' Wilhelm replied as he was leaving, 'not lock his gates even tighter.'

Both men laughed, but their humour was fleeting. A dark road lay ahead for Wilhelm, darker than he realised.

When the prince had gone, Ledner's face fell. If they could not unite their provincial brothers beneath one banner, this war would very likely be the death of them both.

All of the regiments in Prince Wilhelm's army, together with their officers, were billeted in Mannsgard. Foreign soldiers outnumbered Averland citizens now. They would need to make the most of their respite. Word had already reached the masses that the prince rode with all haste to Wissenland, at least a three-day journey there and back. After that, irrespective of Count Pfeifraucher's decision, they would march on Averheim and try to lift the siege. Some of the soldiers went carousing in the towns in what many had started to call 'the last days'. Though most of Mannsgard was empty or simply waiting for death, there were still pleasures to be found, booze to be drunk if you knew where to look. Others sought out notaries and scribes, eager to make their last will and testament before the march. Many went to the temples, to pray for their loved ones or make peace with Sigmar or Morr.

Keller was not a praying man, though he had given some thought to it recently. Instead, he had found a different vice to assuage his guilt. The One-Eyed Dwarf was one of the few taverns left in Mannsgard that still carried alcohol. Most of the others had already been drunk dry by the nervous townsfolk or their stock carried away in the refugee wagons. It wasn't a wise move. Orcs and goblins ranked ale and spirits a close second to brawling and rampaging.

Rechts was asleep in one corner of the small establishment. He'd kicked off his boots and propped up his bare feet with a stool. The drummer's drunken snoring echoed around the almost empty bar. Across the room was the tavern's only other patron, a dwarf with an eye patch, a tramp by the look of his festering clothes. Keller wondered if it was coincidence or whether the dwarf had been there since the tavern existed, hence the name above the door outside. The dwarf held a dead fish in one gnarled hand and piped up when he saw Keller looking.

'Dead fish!' he raved, in thickly-accented Reikspiel. Obviously he was an expatriate, an exile from the Vaults or Black Mountains. 'Keeps ogling me,' he added. With a shout he slammed the fish against the table where he was sitting. Judging by the stains and fish scales in the wood, it wasn't the first time he'd done it. 'Not natural when it's dead.'

Keller moved on, ignoring the dwarf. There was no barkeep, so he poured himself a drink. The liquor was hot and abrasive when it hit his throat. Coughing, he poured another and then a third. He kept the bottle next to him like an old friend and had drained half of it when someone whispered in his ear.

'Drowning your sorrows or trying to take the edge off?'

Keller swallowed hard but could no longer taste the alcohol.

'Thought you said you wouldn't do it in the back,' he said. His voice came out in a rasp.

'That's why you're going to turn around.'

So he did, and came face-to-face with Brand. Keller gave a half glance at Rechts.

'He won't help you,' said Brand, his icy stare chilling Keller to the bone. 'Shout out and I'll do it here, now. It'll be messy, painful.'

Keller nodded. Tears welled in his eyes.

'Drinking with a friend?' asked Brand, when he saw the two glasses on the bar. One of them looked untouched and had two shots of grain whisky in it.

'S-something like that…'

'He wouldn't have drunk with you anyway.'

'Probably not.'

Silence fell in the tavern as Brand stared. His gaze was more piercing than steel.

'Are you sorry for what you've done?' he asked. 'I am,' he added, without waiting for an answer. It was the most and the longest Keller had ever heard Brand speak, but he still wasn't done. 'I've killed men, lots of them. Innocent and guilty. It's why I joined the army. I could tell you my upbringing was violent or some trauma made me this way, but it isn't true. I've always *needed* to kill. I'm trying to make up for it, now,' Brand said, looking over at the empty glass and the empty seat before it. 'Their faces come in the night, the ones I've killed.' He looked back at Keller. 'Like you're seeing a face right now, aren't you, Krieger?'

Keller nodded meekly. Warm piss trickled down his leg, staining his hose.

'I scream for them. In the night, I find a quiet place and inside I scream,' Brand said. 'War is one thing, but it takes a lot to kill a man in cold blood. A part of it clings to you, like their phantom unwilling to let go. It'll drag you down, Krieger, if you don't master it. You're not like me…'

Krieger was shaking his head. He was crying. When he realised, he wiped at his face.

'You can't keep the guilt,' Brand continued. 'Bloody hands lead to retribution in the end. Mine will come one day. Yours has already found you.'

Keller pointed feebly at Brand. The other Reiklander nodded slowly.

'I won't do it when your back is turned, you're right. You'll die with a weapon in your hand, but you will die. Varveiter's honour demands it. Now,' said Brand finally, 'take your dagger and come with me.'

Keller was already standing up, legs shaking, when Eber and Volker came in. The huntsman knew something was up at once.

'Too late for a drink, or are you moving on?' he asked.

Eber's forehead wrinkled, as if he knew something wasn't quite right but couldn't put his finger on it.

Keller sat back down gratefully, trying to obscure the wet patch in his hose.

'I'll take another.' He sounded a little breathless.

'Some other time,' said Brand, though it wasn't clear if he was talking to Keller or Volker. He was heading for the door, about to leave, when more would-be patrons joined them.

Torveld, Wode and three other Steel Swords stood in Brand's path.

'Popular place,' said Torveld, smiling thinly.

Brand backed up. So did the other Reiklanders. They moved farther into the room, pushing aside the few chairs and tables as they went.

The Middenlanders stepped after them slowly, Torveld taking the lead. A few feet of open floor stood between them.

'A good day for you at the Brigund Bridge,' said Torveld. He was armed. So were his compatriots. The Grimblades just carried dirks. Their halberds were stocked at an armoury in the town. Sturnbled must have dished out the blades to his men.

'What do you want, northerner?' Volker got straight to the point. Dog was with him and growled at the Middenlanders.

'*Him*,' Torveld snarled, pointing at Rechts.

Eber gave his slumbering comrade a shove. Unfortunately, the big Reiklander didn't always know his own strength and Rechts was dumped off the chair and onto the ground.

'Whoreson! Wha–' he began, scrambling to his feet and reaching for his dagger before he saw Eber. Then he noticed the others, and Torveld glaring at him. Indignation became mockery on the drummer's face. 'Ah, the Yellow Baron's lackeys have come to schlow their courage, have they?'

Wode balled his fists, prompting Eber to step forward, but Torveld kept the Middenlander back.

Rechts was steaming drunk. He slurred his words and belched loudly. Three empty bottles of hooch rolled around his feet as he stumbled a little before standing straight.

'What have you been saying, Rechts?' hissed Volker, one eye on the belligerent Middenlanders.

The drummer looked offended. 'Jusht the truth,' he said, licking his lips. 'They schwagger about, arrogant bashtards,' – he imitated the movement by swaying his shoulders and putting on a disdainful sneer – 'but when push comes to shove, they run like milkmaids.'

'Shut up, Rechts,' Volker warned him.

Torveld was shaking his head. He and his countrymen had heard enough.

Eber made fists. Keller looked relieved that the attention was no longer on him. He wrapped his hand around the half empty whisky bottle. Brand just stood with his hands by his sides, taking it all in, planning to kill Torveld first.

'I'm going to gut you like a pig, southerner.' Torveld was looking at Rechts.

'Shure, you are…' he replied, before promptly passing out and crashing to the floor.

The Middenlanders had half drawn their blades when the tavern door opened again. Everyone turned to see who it was. Captain Stahler stood in the doorway, ashen-faced and looking far from pleased. Von Rauken and several of his greatswordres accompanied him.

'Put up your blades,' he said calmly to the Middenlanders.

'This is a matter of honour, they've–' Torveld began.

'Put 'em up! Do it now!'

The Middenlanders obeyed, stepping aside as Stahler stalked into the room appraising all present with a filthy look.

'Get to your billet,' he said to the Steel Swords, 'and tell Sergeant Sturnbled I want words. Go on, get out!'

Torveld was livid, but he held on to his temper. He nodded with a last look in the Grimblades' direction before storming out with his men.

'Now you lot…' said Stahler, once the Middenlanders were gone. The captain wore his breastplate, but had yet to don his helmet. He walked with a limp and the effort clearly pained him, but he was still formidable. The greatswordres stood behind him like plate-clad sentinels. Von Rauken was doing his best to keep the smirk off his face. Concealed behind his beard, no one could see it anyway.

The Grimblades were downcast, suddenly ambivalent about their captain's return. Volker was about to speak when Stahler cut him off.

'Not a damn word!' He looked over his shoulder. 'Karlich, get in here.'

A stern-faced Sergeant Karlich entered the tavern, Lenkmann and Masbrecht in tow. He was shaking his head and scowling. He looked more annoyed than Stahler. 'It appears my return was timely,' said Stahler. 'Blaselocker is gone,' he added flatly. 'I'm back and this kind of behaviour in my regiments won't be tolerated. If we weren't so short of bodies you'd be flogged. Some of you would swing. Do your killing on the battlefield. Don't worry, you'll get your chance, we all bloody will.' He glared for a few moments, regarding each man in turn before facing Karlich.

'I'll leave this rabble to you.'

Karlich saluted, waiting for Stahler and the greatswordres to leave, before turning his attention on the Grimblades.

'Captain Stahler has recovered well enough to fight, praise Sigmar,' he recounted deadpan. 'We are heading out. On patrol. Now.' Karlich punctuated the last word firmly.

'Those northern scum–'

Karlich cut Volker off.

'Are out for blood, I know. But it'll be Stahler who has it if you carry on like this. All of you, with me, right now,' he said. As Karlich was leaving, he added, 'Eber, get him up and make sure he's sober by the time we reach the gate.'

Eber nodded and hauled Rechts onto his back, carrying him like a sack of grain. The big Reiklander remembered seeing a horse trough a little way from Mannsgard's gate. Rechts would either be sober or drowned by the time he was done.

CHAPTER ELEVEN

A dark discovery

*Outside Mannsgard, Averland,
386 miles from Altdorf*

Several miles outside Mannsgard, the land grew wilder. Though still largely flat and open, the Averland forests were thicker here. Men had not come with fire and axes to clear them. There were no other towns. Even villages were sparse, just smoking shadows on a distant horizon.

Volker noticed an isolated farm up ahead, not reported by the other patrols. The eight Reiklanders had met the last party on the way out, a tired-looking band of Averland pike. They had nodded and exchanged muted greetings as they'd passed one another, but that was all. The Averlanders had been south-east but found nothing. Volker had brought them westward and to the farm. He stopped a few hundred feet from it, waiting for the others.

'Looks deserted,' said Masbrecht as he joined the huntsmen.

The farm was ramshackle, comprising a small stone house, a barn and some stables. There were wooden fences and several fields could also have been part of the farmer's land, but no animals grazed in them and there weren't any crops either. A stream ran through the land, its banks coloured by blood. Volker had followed the watercourse all the way to the farm.

'Best be sure,' said Karlich. The sergeant's mood hadn't improved. He had other things on his mind, too. Like the witch hunter's encampment they'd passed when leaving Mannsgard. Of the templar, there'd been no sign. Small mercies. He looked at Rechts. 'You first, soldier.'

Hung-over and red-eyed, but sober thanks to the liberal dunkings in the horse trough by Eber, Rechts nodded and headed up to the farm. The regimental drum and banner were back in Mannsgard, so at least he didn't have anything to weigh him down. As Rechts came within the farm's boundary line, he drew his short sword.

Volker looked nervously at his sergeant.

Karlich sighed. 'Try and make sure he doesn't get himself killed.'

The huntsman saluted and jogged after Rechts.

'The rest of you, come on,' added Karlich, and continued tramping through the high grass after the scouts.

Up close, the farm and its buildings looked even more wrecked than at a distance. Much of the wood from the barn was rotten. Several of the stones that made up the house had slipped or were cracked. After Rechts and Volker had scouted out the land around the buildings to check for ambushers, Karlich had divided them into three groups to take the house, barn and stables respectively. A shallow wind howled across the plains. As it passed through the open buildings, it took on an unnatural sound. It disturbed Lenkmann greatly, who paused as he was about to enter the stables.

'Do we really need to go in?' he asked.

Brand shook his head and walked right past him.

'Orcs or goblins, more likely, could be hiding inside,' said Masbrecht. 'Part of a vanguard or a splinter from the horde besieging Averheim. Either way, we have to know. How would Prince Wilhelm react if his troops allowed the greenskins to sneak up on us, waking up to find the walls of Mannsgard surrounded, as well as those of Averheim?'

'The prince is in Wissenland, or on his way at least.'

As they'd left the town behind, they'd seen Prince Wilhelm and his Griffonkorps riding hard for the provincial border. They needed to move swiftly. Not only were greenskins abroad, but with every day that went by Averheim was squeezed further by Grom the Paunch. If Wilhelm's army didn't march soon, the goblin king might have crushed the Averland capital to rubble by the time they arrived.

'Come on,' Brand called from inside. He lingered just beyond the stable threshold, not willing to commit himself in case he found a goblin dagger in his back.

Lenkmann gave the skeletal structure a sour look. The wasted timbers reminded him of bones. Shadows loomed within the stable's creaking confines and he could hear the buzzing of flies against the wind. Lenkmann was not a cowardly man. He'd do his duty to the Empire, fighting greenskins or beastmen. Even marauders from the north held no true terror for him. But the unquiet, the revenant scratching at its coffin lid, digging through its earthy grave, that did unsettle him.

'Masbrecht...' he said.

The other Reiklander smiled and made the sign of the hammer.

'I always feel better when you do it,' Lenkmann admitted.

'There's nothing to fear, brother. Sigmar is always with us.'

'I'm not afraid,' snapped the banner bearer. 'Just being careful,' he added, striding into the stables with unnecessary gusto.

The farmhouse was quiet except for the creaking of its only door on broken hinges. Karlich was the first inside, pushing the door with his sword tip so it was wide enough to enter.

The stench in the room had faded, but Eber still wrinkled his nose.

'That's a foul reek,' he said, peering over Karlich's shoulder to get a better look.

'Don't blame me,' snapped Keller. He held his arm low instinctively, trying to conceal the stain on his hose. The tang of it still lingered in his nostrils, even though it had long since gone. Like Karlich, his mind was also on other things. He kept his gaze ahead, not wanting to look at the lonely cart dumped next to the house with no mule to pull it. Something else was standing by it. Keller had glimpsed its presence in his peripheral vision before looking away. He didn't want to see it directly. It had… *changed* in the last few days. To look upon it now… Keller feared he'd cry out in spite of himself.

Though he'd secured the door, Karlich still heard creaking. It got louder as he went inside. The house had one room. There was a simple bed, table and chair. A wool rug, dirty from use, covered a small patch on the stone floor. A thatch roof overhead filtered the sun in thin, grainy beams. Though gloomy, there was enough light to see the farmer hanging two feet from the ground.

'Sacred Morr,' breathed Eber when he noticed the corpse.

Keller made the sign of the hammer, determined to make the penitent streak stick.

'How long?' he asked.

'A while,' said Karlich, approaching the body. Its sunken flesh was grey and ghoulish. Empty sockets remained where the eyes had been. Rigor mortis curled the farmer's toes and fingers into claws. Rough clothes hung off the body like flaying skin.

There was no sign of greenskins, none at all. Karlich supposed the farmer had heard of the invasion while in town for market day, returned to his farm and decided it was better to take his own life than face possible torture and certain death by the orcs. How could he have known the greenskins would miss him? At least the house was clear. It was bitter compensation.

'Shallya's mercy,' Karlich muttered. He sounded weary. 'Cut him down.'

Rechts was still dizzy. The open air was doing nothing for him. About to enter the barn, he staggered and would have fallen if not for Volker catching his arm.

'Easy does it,' said the huntsman in a low voice. 'Let me go first.'

Rechts gladly moved aside and followed Volker in through the half-open barn door.

Despite the shafts of sunlight lancing the cracks in its roof, it was dark inside the barn. The air was stale and smelled of hay and dung. Bales were bound up with string in the two far corners. Stacked on top of one another, they stretched halfway to the door. Vertical beams supported the roof, hung with chains, sickles and scythes. It didn't look like they'd been used for a long time. A loft loomed above. It was the perfect place for an ambush, so Volker kept his eyes on it.

'Something's off,' he said to Rechts, who had just sidled through the door.

'Hot in here.' The drummer looked nauseous.

'Quiet!' hissed Volker. The huntsman had moved under the trapdoor that led up to the hayloft. A length of rope dangled to the ground from it. Volker wrapped the rope around his fist and pulled. The trapdoor doubled up as a ramp, and an entire section of the loft floor came down to rest on the ground. Standing near the foot of the ramp, Volker secured the rope on a hook attached to a wooden beam and waited.

Now Rechts could smell it too. Something was definitely off in the barn, and it was coming from the hayloft. Hangover forgotten, he edged closer to Volker. They needed to be careful. Karlich had split them up to search all three structures at the same time. Help, if they needed it, would be a little way off.

Volker whistled sharply. A few seconds later, Dog trotted into the barn from where it had been told to wait outside. After a gesture from its master, the mutt ran up the ramp and into the hayloft.

'Now we wait,' said Volker, the sound of snuffling and rooting coming from above them. Then Dog barked, low at first but building in pitch with each successive sound.

Volker moved up the ramp, keeping low.

Rechts followed, amazed at his comrade's stealth. Volker barely made a sound.

The hayloft was almost full. A pitchfork stuck out of the loose stacks like a marker, but Dog wasn't interested in this. It was scratting at the far end of the loft, pushing its muzzle eagerly into the piled hay. It was a gloomy spot. The loft's open window was on the opposite side. Glancing at it only seemed to make the patch where Dog stood even darker.

'Come!' said Volker, and the mastiff stopped rooting to rejoin its master.

Crossing the loft to the site of Dog's interest felt farther than it actually was. Volker kept his eyes on the stack the entire time, his dirk held low and close to his body. A faint crunch of hay assured the huntsman that Rechts was right behind him.

'Grab that,' he said, indicating the pitchfork.

Rechts went over and took the implement. He then passed it to Volker, who hadn't moved and was waiting for him. Stalking the last few feet to the haystack, Volker prodded carefully with the fork. The first attempt went straight through, the second hit something. He lunged harder and the pitchfork came back with blood on it. Using the pitchfork in a scraping motion, Volker dragged away some of the hay. There was a body lying beneath, dead a few days but no more. The seal on its tunic was familiar. It was the griffon rampant of the Emperor.

'Go find Sergeant Karlich,' Volker said, stepping away. His hands were shaking, but he couldn't explain why. 'Right now!' he snapped, when Rechts didn't move straight away.

Stumbling a little at first, and not from the hangover, Rechts ran out of the hayloft and across the barn. Only when he reached Karlich at the house, did he stop to puke. An already long day was about to get much longer.

The dead messenger lay on the floor of the hayloft in full view. After Rechts had gone to get the others, Volker had carefully cleared away the hay concealing the body.

'Altdorf colours,' said Karlich, under his breath. Under a long tan cloak, the dead messenger's tunic was red and blue. His garments looked fine and unroughed. His boots were expensive and polished. One of them lay on the floor alongside the body. Even the man's stockings were clean and white. He looked lean and healthy, except for the dagger sticking out of his chest.

'From the royal house,' said Masbrecht. He noted the dead messenger's hands: they were clean, his nails manicured. 'An aide, perhaps?'

'This is how you found him?' asked Karlich, weighing up Masbrecht's theory with some of his own.

Volker was crouching next to the body, examining the wound, and nodded.

Except for Brand, who knew something about dagger wounds himself, the rest of the Grimblades were down in the barn. Rechts was sitting on a hay bale, nursing his head and stomach. Keller kept to himself, his eyes on the ground, whilst Lenkmann and Eber watched the door.

'That's no orc blade; it's Empire,' said Karlich, stooping to get a better look at the dagger.

'Greenskins didn't kill him,' said Brand, lurking in the shadows. 'The cut is too precise, one thrust right into the heart.'

Karlich turned, suddenly feeling a little colder. 'And?'

'It's assassination work.'

And you would know, I suppose, thought Karlich. Sometimes he wondered how they all slept at night with Brand around, then he remembered the man was on their side and that was how. Since Varveiter's death, Brand had retreated further into himself. They all missed the old warhorse, Karlich especially. But for Brand, Varveiter had been the one stable element in his life. Now he was gone, bloodily, and that bothered Karlich, more than he wanted to admit.

'You search him?' he asked Volker.

'Found this.' The huntsman gave Karlich a scroll of parchment. 'Hidden in his boot.'

'What's on it?' Karlich asked, noting the broken seal as he unfurled it. The scroll was actually a map that showed Averland and Wissenland. Several landmarks were detailed, including Mannsgard and Pfeildorf, the capital of Wissenland and Prince Wilhelm's destination. A route was marked out between the two locations with a line that ended in an arrow leading back to Mannsgard. A small red 'X' fell about halfway along it where some hills were also sketched.

'What does it mean?' asked Volker.

Karlich looked back down at the body, then at the Reikland dagger plunged into its dead heart. Brand was already heading down again. He knew they were going back.

'I don't know,' Karlich lied. He had some ideas. 'We should return to Mannsgard and report it. We go now.'

CHAPTER TWELVE

To save a prince

Outside Mannsgard, Averland,
386 miles from Altdorf

The Grimblades ran the five miles back to camp. The high grass made hard work of it and all except for Brand were gasping for breath by the time they reached Mannsgard's gates.

Old Varveiter would have been complaining, the last to come in. Eber missed it. They all did. Or at least, that's how it appeared. Keller had said nothing since the barn. He was finding it increasingly difficult to lift his eyes off the ground lately. Masbrecht had asked him about it, but Keller just mumbled something and walked away. Masbrecht dropped it after that.

Karlich had said nothing to those who were down in the barn when the body was being examined. Rechts knew of it, of course, and they knew what he knew, but only Volker, Brand and Masbrecht were privy to the map and the dagger. Karlich had worried at it all the way to Mannsgard, trying not to jump to conclusions. Captain Stahler would know what to do. He was billeted in an old counting house close to the gate. At least they wouldn't have to slog through the streets to reach him.

'You three, come with me,' said Karlich, upon entering the town. 'The rest of you will wait at The One-Eyed Dwarf until I come and get you. Understood?'

Brand, Masbrecht and Volker stayed with the sergeant. As the others were moving off, Karlich added, 'And stay out of trouble.'

Lenkmann saluted, and assured the sergeant that wouldn't be a problem.

When they were out of earshot, Masbrecht asked in a low voice, 'Why meet so close to Mannsgard? The messenger and his would-be killer, I mean.'

'Closeness to his mark,' said Brand. 'He can observe and predict, gather information first hand if he needs to. The messenger obviously came from the prince's camp. He served his purpose and was silenced.'

'Perhaps Templar Vanhans or one of his faithful saw something,' offered Masbrecht.

Karlich stiffened at the mention of the witch hunter's name. He tried not to react and focused on getting to the counting house.

'Scouts and patrols are leaving the town all the time,' said Brand. 'A lone rider would be lost with the rest.'

'Shut up, both of you.' Disturbed also by Brand's knowledge of contract killing, Karlich had finally listened to all he could take. Bad enough that they'd found the dead messenger at all, they didn't need someone overhearing them on the street. Things were complicated as it was. When they reached Stahler's billet, the matter became tangled even further.

The counting house was a dusty place with grey walls, full of wooden furniture. It had two floors, the upper one had an archive and vault but was boarded over; the lower had a hallway leading to a small office with a writing desk and was full of old ledgers. A side room contained a bed and chair. It was close to the Temple of Shallya, so Stahler was in reach of ministration if he needed it.

The shutters were drawn and the counting house was dark when the four Grimblades entered. Smoke hung in the air, obscuring the view further.

Karlich went in first, his men a few paces behind. Their steps sounded loud and echoing as they walked down the hallway. Upon reaching the office, Karlich saw a silhouette sitting at the writing desk. Stahler was smoking a pipe, though it didn't smell like his usual tobacco. Perhaps the priestesses had provided a curative leaf. Karlich had heard of such things, though didn't place much stock in them.

'Sir,' he ventured. 'We've made a disturbing discovery.' Stahler was little more than a black outline against a dark-grey canvas, but he sat up when Karlich spoke. The sergeant took it as an invitation to speak further.

'There's an old farmstead about five miles west of Mannsgard. The farmer was dead. There was also another body,' Karlich paused, choosing his next words carefully. 'It was hidden in a hay loft and wore the trappings of an Altdorf messenger, one from Prince Wilhelm's camp.'

As his sight adjusted, Karlich began to see Stahler's eyes in the gloom. They narrowed at the mention of the prince and suddenly the sergeant felt that something was wrong.

'You're not Captain Stahler,' he said flatly, straightening his back to show his annoyance. Karlich didn't like being fooled. He liked liars and charlatans even less. 'Who are you?'

The silhouette struck a match, lighting up a nearby lamp. Ledner was revealed in its wan glow. Shadows pooled the crevices of his thin face, making him appear gaunter than he actually was. Ledner kept the light behind him, blinding his visitors but enabling him to see them clearly.

'You were saying, sergeant?'

'I thought I was speaking to my captain. I'm sorry, sir. There's been a mistake.' Karlich went to go, not sure what Ledner would make of what he had heard so far, when the voice of the prince's spymaster stopped him.

'The only mistake would be to leave this room,' Ledner said calmly. 'Please go on. Captain Stahler is with the sisters of mercy having his wounds redressed.'

Karlich wished he had had the temerity to ask what then Ledner was doing in his captain's billet with his aide obviously elsewhere. In the circumstances, he didn't think it wise. He took the map scroll from where he'd secured it in his belt and unfurled it on the desk.

'And what is this?' Ledner asked.

'A map of Averland and Wissenland,' said Volker, nonplussed. Karlich glared at him and the huntsman shut his mouth like a trap.

Ledner smiled thinly. His eyes were predatory as he regarded Volker.

'What is its meaning?'

'The messenger was carrying it when he died,' said Karlich.

Ledner began to study the map. He traced a thin finger down the line describing Wilhelm's route.

'How was he killed?'

Karlich cleared his throat, making Ledner look up.

'We think he was assassinated. An Empire dagger had pierced his heart.'

Ledner sighed, rolling up the parchment. 'Well, that would do it I suppose.'

When the spymaster permitted a long silence to descend, Karlich told him, 'Something must be done.'

Ledner fixed the sergeant with a cold stare that bled all heat from the lamp. Karlich felt a shiver but suppressed it.

'About what? What is it you think is happening here, sergeant?' Ledner was enjoying the inquisition and suddenly Karlich could imagine many men who had fallen under the spymaster's scrutiny. He thought those 'conversations' would be markedly less pleasant than this one. That they would end with hot steel and fire, maybe the noose or rack. Ledner was famed for his strong stomach and his sociopathic nature. A keen combination in a torturer and confessor.

Karlich drew off his courage, speaking aloud what he had believed since finding the body and seeing the map.

'Prince Wilhelm is in danger, my lord. I think someone's planning to kill him.'

Ledner smiled again. There was no warmth in it. It was a gesture as far from humour as it was possible to get.

'You were wise to come to me, sergeant. Even if it was by accident,' said Ledner. 'You are certain this messenger was slain by an assassin, the same man you think is after the prince?'

'It may already be too late,' said Karlich. 'If the prince's would-be killer attacked him on the way to Pfeildorf... My lord, I must speak to my captain at once. Something must be done.'

'No you won't,' Ledner replied, standing.

'I beg your par–'

'You won't, because the fewer people who know about this the better.' Ledner opened up the lamp's shutter, exposing the flame within. 'Who else was with you?' he asked. 'Just these three?'

'No. There were four others, all men of my regiment.'

'Where are these men now?'

Karlich's brow furrowed. 'At a tavern in the town. What does it matter?'

Ledner opened the oil valve on the lamp so the flame burned at its fiercest. He took the map and poked one corner in through the shutter.

'What are you doing?' Karlich reached out for the parchment, which was already burning, but Ledner seized his wrist in a grip as strong as a serpent's jaws.

'You remember the location on the map, the low hills, the mid-point between Prince Wilhelm's route?' He sniffed scornfully. 'Of course you do. A man like you, sergeant, would have seared it into his mind. Am I right?'

Karlich backed down. He nodded slowly and Ledner released him so he could continue burning the map. The flames seemed to fill his eyes, revealing a dark glint in the pupils. When he was done reducing the parchment to charred fragments, he turned his gaze back on Karlich.

'A plot against the prince that comes from within his very camp,' said Ledner. 'No one is to be trusted, sergeant. You shouldn't even have trusted me but then you had little choice in the matter since you had to do *something*. No one else can know of this – *no one*. If word slipped out of an assassination plot against the prince, by his own court no less, two things would certainly happen. Our killer would realise his plan was compromised and change it, thus denying us the opportunity to stop him. Furthermore, this campaign, the Empire itself, would be thrown into even greater turmoil. We are divided enough as it is without talk of assassination within our own ranks.

'What do you think would happen next? Electors, barons, earls, they'd be even more paranoid than they are now. Instead of one assassin, you would have hundreds.' Ledner breathed deeply, as if making up his mind. 'Stahler cannot know,' he said. 'But here is what you'll do. Fetch your men, the other four who saw the body, and bring them here to me.'

'Why? What do you plan to do?' asked Karlich, forgetting his place for a moment.

'Other than finding out who ordered the contract on the prince, *I* am not going to do anything. *You* however will be responsible for stopping this assassin.'

Karlich was already shaking his head when Ledner interrupted him.

'This must not get out. Be very clear on this. So far, the only ones who know of it are you, your men and I. Keep it that way or risk far more than the death of a beloved prince.' Ledner waved a finger at him. The glint in his eye returned. 'Civil war, sergeant, just like in the old days.'

Karlich still wasn't convinced.

'There must be those better equipped than us to deal with this matter.'

'Yes, of course there are,' said Ledner, 'but we've been over this. The fewer people who know, remember?'

'Sigmar be damned,' muttered Karlich, and knew they had no choice. A trained killer against him and seven of his men. Were it not for Brand, he wouldn't have liked the odds.

'Halberds are hardly made for stealth,' Karlich added.

'Get your men, bring them here. I will have weapons waiting,' Ledner told him. 'You can use a pistol?' he asked.

Karlich nodded.

'Anyone else?'

Volker raised a hand, as Masbrecht shook his head.

Ledner's eyes went to Brand, who had watched the whole affair intently from the darkness.

'Oh, I bet you can use one. I bet you're no stranger to having blood on your hands, are you?' The spymaster's smile was almost venomous.

Brand never moved.

Ledner looked as if he was about to say something else to him, but he turned his attention back on Karlich.

'The prince will make his return in just over a day. You need to be in those hills and root out the killer before the prince reaches them.' He doused the lantern, plunging the room back into darkness. 'Go,' he added, sitting down again. 'Weapons will be waiting for you.'

Karlich didn't know what else to say. He turned on his heel, glad to be leaving the counting house and Ledner behind.

Eight Grimblades left the town of Mannsgard just before dusk, armed with short swords and bucklers. Three men also carried pistols. Ledner had met them at the counting house and told them to wait until night was approaching to make their way out. Patrols were not that uncommon at the end of the day and their presence would barely raise an eyebrow amongst the watchmen and gate guards. By way of a parting gift, Ledner provided fur-lined cloaks for them all. Without the sun to warm them and few trees and valleys to shield against the wind, the plains would be bitterly cold after dark.

They were to travel on foot, a journey that would take the entire night and most of the next morning. Ledner reasoned that the prince and his Griffonkorps would likely ride from Pfeildorf at dawn, bringing them to the assassination site – the hilly valley denoted at the map – no earlier than late morning. The Grimblades had to find the assassin and kill him before then. They'd be cutting it fine.

Without the crackle of a fire for company, it felt eerie on the grassy heath. Some of the Grimblades huddled together against a harsh wind, as it tossed their cloaks about, trying to work them free with its chill fingers. The fur lining might as well be soaked through for all the protection it offered; blowing from the east, the wind was like daggers shearing through their clothes. It brought the smell of burning meat with it from the huge ritual pyres erected by the orcs. It wasn't animal in origin; the stench was human.

'If I imagine a fire, will that warm me?' said Rechts. He was shivering more than the others, a grey pallor affecting his face.

'Aye, and draw fewer greenskins and other beasts to our camp than a real fire,' Karlich replied with a scowl. He nursed a pipe in his hands, taking care to shelter the small flame.

'Wish I was still drunk,' Rechts muttered.

'Perhaps if you'd stayed sober you wouldn't feel the cold so much,' snapped the sergeant. He was starting to lose his patience. They all were.

Since leaving Mannsgard that evening, the men had said little to one another. Each had his mind on his thoughts and the awful truth that someone within the Empire, within their camp, was plotting to kill Prince Wilhelm. Worse still, they were the ones supposed to prevent it. Karlich, for one, didn't appreciate the burden. He'd noticed something cruel in Ledner's eyes when he'd sent them off. The spymaster didn't expect them all to return.

What are men like us to men like him, he thought bitterly? *Just fodder for his schemes and lies.*

A low howl from the distant hills to the south startled them. Volker turned quickly, soothing Dog who had been lying beside him but was now on his feet and growling. He made out a silhouette on the far away hills, of a beast prowling the moors near the Wissenland border. All men of the Aver had heard tales of the balewolf. It was a legend spun by housewives and bored soldiers. The Grimblades had listened to a veteran piker tell it in Mannsgard. Now it came back to haunt them with the shadows, real or imagined, on the wind-tossed grasslands of the wild.

'Easy boy,' he murmured, using the tone of his voice to quieten the mastiff. Volker blinked and the silhouette was gone, like a wisp of smoke carried off by the breeze.

'Good dog...' said Lenkmann, reaching over to pat the mutt's head. He snatched his hand away when Dog snapped at him, fangs bared.

'Not really,' Volker replied with a smile. The moon was high overhead, revealed through scudding cloud, and it cast his face in a sinister light. 'It means no offence. Just knows its master.'

Lenkmann mumbled something before planting his hands firmly back inside his cloak.

Volker tickled Dog under the chin and the savage beast growled appreciatively before licking the salt off his fingers.

'It scents evil,' said Brand. He was sitting a little way back from the circle of men, who turned suddenly at the sound of his voice. 'Can't you smell it, too?'

Masbrecht made the sign of Sigmar and watched the darkness where the beast had been with fearful eyes.

'Smell what?' asked Eber. Of all the Grimblades, the big Reiklander appeared least troubled by the cold. The layers of muscle obviously made for good insulation.

'Orc spore. It's thick.'

Now they all smelled it, coming from the east on the same breeze that brought the reek of burning meat. Orange smudges blighted that part of the horizon from the villages and towns still ablaze. Men and women would be burning. Some might have fled if they were lucky. Perhaps the fell beasts of the wild had easier prey that night than the Grimblades.

Overhead, there came the flapping of wings and a shadow passed over them like a curse. Every man, even Brand, flattened to the ground and didn't look up again until the shadow was gone.

'We all saw that, right?' asked Volker, wanting to be convinced he wasn't just hallucinating.

Keller nodded meekly. Like in the barn, he'd kept his eyes on the ground for most of the journey, using whoever was in front of him as a guide. No one questioned him about it. They all knew something had happened to him since Blösstadt. Only he and Brand knew the truth.

'It was the shaman and his wyvern,' said Karlich, trying to slow his racing heartbeat.

Keller's teeth were chattering, and not from the cold. Masbrecht was muttering a prayer of warding under his breath. The others just huddled, trying to look as small as possible. Even Brand was shaken. If this was the effect that the creature caused hundreds of feet away, up in the air, then how could men face it on the battlefield? It only made Wilhelm's victory at the Brigund Bridge, when he had driven the beast and its master off, all the more impressive. It also convinced Karlich that they had to save this man, that without him they would surely fail. He'd been right in the tent all those days ago: men like Wilhelm were greater than he, capable of doing great things.

Several minutes passed before they felt comfortable enough to return to the circle. No one spoke of the wyvern again, nor did they look in the direction of its heading if they could help it. In the end, it was Rechts who broke the fearful silence.

'What are we doing out here, sergeant?'

It was a valid question, one Karlich had asked himself several times already. But it wasn't what Rechts really meant. What he really meant was: why us? Karlich's answer, as he'd already told himself, was simple.

'Our duty to prince and province,' he said.

'To Ledner, you mean. That bastard doesn't care if we live or die. He probably hopes we don't survive.' Rechts was emboldened by his anger, grateful to it for smothering his fear. 'And if we succeed? What then? What recompense will we get?'

Karlich was tiring of the drummer's belligerence. He knew he was only scared, just like the rest of them. But this wasn't helping.

'Nothing! We get nothing, save the knowledge that we prevented the murder of our liege-lord and prince,' he snapped. 'Is that not enough? It should be enough.'

Rechts bowed his head, shamed.

'Aye, I thought so,' muttered Karlich and instantly regretted it.

After that the rest of the night without incident, but it was long and uncomfortable, filled with the shadows of monsters and the howl of wolves.

CHAPTER THIRTEEN

Ghosts

Averland plains,
411 miles from Altdorf

The dawn brought little comfort for the Grimblades, despite the rising sun. It had yet to warm the plains or their aching bones. Breath still ghosted the air. It came out in white gusts as Karlich had coughed and wheezed. They'd slept sitting up, and there was nothing to pack, though Lenkmann had leaned over onto Eber's shoulder and was profoundly embarrassed when he woke.

'Didn't even buy him a drink!' Rechts had chortled with uncommon good humour. He'd obviously slept off the booze at last.

Brand had stayed awake all night. Volker, who'd been the first up, would later say how he rose to find the cold eyes of the man regarding him through the twilit mist. Volker didn't stay to chat. In minutes he was gone, scouting off into the distance with Dog.

Few words were exchanged when the others stirred and began to move. No one felt like talking after a harrowing night. It was a while trudging through the long grasses before the grim silence was lifted.

'Who would want to kill the prince?' asked Eber, unaware of the sour mood and more out of exasperation than any desire to actually know. 'I can't understand it.'

'All political figures have enemies, Brutan,' Lenkmann replied. 'Wilhelm is no different. It could be one of a hundred or more men.'

'It's poor timing,' muttered Keller, his displeasure at the mission currently outweighing his other 'concerns'.

'So there's a good time to try and kill a prince of Altdorf?' asked Karlich. He looked towards the sun, gauging its position and therefore the time. By his reckoning, they had maybe three hours before the prince could arrive at the valley. The pace suddenly didn't feel fast enough. 'Hurry it up,' he said, eyes front, hoping to see Volker. The huntsman was still ranging ahead with the mutt, keeping them away from any greenskins that might be roaming nearby, and leading them to the hills. His last report had been some time ago.

'When his back is turned and his guard is down,' said Brand to the sergeant's first comment.

Karlich scowled at the dry humour, finding it inappropriate.

'I wish Varveiter were here,' said Lenkmann, to Karlich's right. 'We could use his wisdom now.'

'Aye, he might've been canny enough for us to get us out of this shitheap we currently find ourselves in,' said Rechts, his humour fleeting.

Masbrecht looked affronted. 'Saving a prince is an *honour*, brother. It is Sigmar's work we go to do this day.'

Rechts was livid. 'He calls me "brother" one more time and it won't be Wilhelm's assassin you'll be stopping.'

'Shut up, Rechts,' snapped Karlich. 'Whatever it is between the two of you, deal with it. This is the most important deed you'll ever do in your entire life, don't wreck it,' he warned, before turning his anger on Masbrecht. 'And you. Save the sermons. You know he doesn't like it. Not all of us are willing converts.' He wanted to say more, but saw Volker running back towards them.

'Just beyond the next rise,' he said. 'The land slopes downward and lifts again to a set of hills. That must be the place.'

'You sure?' asked Karlich.

'As I can be. The map was quite well detailed and there are few hills in Averland, especially so close to the road.'

'Makes you wonder why the prince came this way at all,' said Lenkmann. 'A valley is a good place for an ambush.'

'The road is the most direct route, I suppose,' said Karlich, 'but who's to say the prince even chose it.'

None of it really mattered. The morning sun was high and its rays were creeping steadily across the plains. Time was running out.

Cresting the rise, the Grimblades had the sloping plain laid out below them. A short distance and the flat land rose up again, the road bending with it, and there were the hills. Strewn with rocks, hollows and wild bracken, it was a rugged place full of shadows.

'Lots of places to hide,' observed Volker.

They came at the hills from an oblique angle, ever watchful for movement, keeping the sun behind them all the way.

'He'll be up high,' added Brand, 'probably with a bow or harquebus. He'll want to kill the prince from a distance, so he doesn't have to fight his Griffonkorps.'

'So we're looking for a marksman, then,' said Karlich. 'Perhaps we'll be able to stop him, after all.'

'A marksman, yes,' said Brand. 'And a swordsman and a knife-wielder, and a pugilist. Assassins are killers. They're trained well in the art. Don't make the mistake of thinking just because he wants to shoot the prince that he can't execute him, or us, in ten or more other ways.'

Yet again, Karlich felt a cold shiver but couldn't deny the sense in what Brand was saying. He decided to change tack.

'He could be anywhere, behind any rock, hunkered down in any hollow, hidden in the long grasses or crouched upon any ridge, as still as the earth,' said Karlich. 'We root him out before the prince gets here. He cannot know of it. To do so would mean this whole dirty business gets out and, alive or dead, the prince and his cohorts can't ignore it. You heard Ledner – the Empire would fracture under the strain. We'd have civil war.'

Karlich eyed his men and felt a surge of pride, even for Keller who he considered a bastard of the highest order.

'We're not assassins or spies; we're just men, soldiers of the Empire who face a difficult duty. This is an enemy like any other. At Blösstadt you gave me your resolve, at the Brigund Bridge your courage. Now I ask for cunning. Find this whoreson, stop him and stay alive into the bargain.'

He allowed a short pause to think, how in Sigmar's name did we ever get here? and then deferred to Volker, who knew the ways of hunting better than any of them.

'We split into pairs, four groups, one compass direction each. Start wide and move in slowly. Stay low and keep your eyes open. Chances are, he's already in there, waiting.'

'Sobering thought,' muttered Rechts.

'Just as well, where you're concerned,' said Karlich, before addressing his men. 'No heroics,' he said, looking at Brand in particular. 'Find him, signal your comrades and we'll silence this cur together without our blood being spilled to do it. Faith in Sigmar,' he added.

The Grimblades echoed him, all except for Rechts.

'And Morr be damned,' said Karlich to himself, trudging down towards the road where the hills loomed with quiet menace.

Eight against one. So, why did it feel like they were the prey?

Up close the hills were vast, easily sprawling a half mile either side and along the road. They dipped, rose and undulated as if in a pact with the assassin to frustrate the Grimblades' search. Patches of scree and loose rocks made the ground treacherous. There were small ravines and caves.

Crags and sheltered gullies were everywhere. Each and every nook had to be searched. Other creatures might lurk along the hillsides. It wasn't unknown for trolls or even larger beasts to make their lairs in such places. Keller, for one, hoped that wouldn't be the case.

Maintaining his concentration was hard, what with the *other* looking on and dogging his every step.

'*Leave me be,*' he hissed. A side glance revealed his plea had gone unheeded. '*Plague me no more!*' he said louder, prompting an angry look from Volker who he was paired with. Even Dog looked annoyed, but then that little bastard always did.

Keller allowed himself a smirk, the first for some time – Volker loved that mutt more than he did his own family. Back in Mannsgard, he'd seen the beast lick the huntsman's feet. Volker slept in his boots. He was not one to take them off regularly. Keller assumed the affection between mutt and man was probably mutual.

The sliver of his old self passed, like a flash of sun on metal, as the *other* reasserted its presence again. Still no sign of the assassin. The two men carried on.

Lenkmann stumbled and cursed through his teeth. He'd jarred his ankle. It was painful as he felt down at it, but he could still move well enough. The sun was high now, and he had to squint when he looked up. Morning was nearly done. Brand was leaving him behind, hurrying through the hills like a wolf hunting deer, or maybe another wolf.

There was something of the bloodhound in the man, so driven to find the assassin was he. Lenkmann noticed he'd left his pistol unloaded. Brand wanted to face his adversary up close, push steel into his flesh, so the assassin knew who had killed him, who was his better. It was as if *need* compelled him. Lenkmann had seen Brand in battle before, the man was frightening, but this was different. This was a whole other side to him. And as he struggled to catch Brand, so intent on his prey, so utterly possessed with scarcely restrained violence, Lenkmann thought this was the truest side of the man. Brand had been a mystery until then. Now Lenkmann saw him for what he really was and it scared him more than the wyvern.

A green ocean stretched before them and the hills were its waves, and the rocks its shore. Here they trawled for a single fish, one with hollow eyes, black and lifeless as a doll's. Karlich felt those eyes upon him. Ever since entering the hills, he'd not been able to shake the feeling of being watched. Paranoia was becoming an unwelcome bedfellow for the sergeant.

The sun was rising and though it warmed his face, it also sent the shadows fleeing into the deeper crevices of the land, filling them with darkness. Karlich began to imagine enemies lurking there: a masked assassin, wraith-like and undefeatable; Vanhans the witch hunter, armed with murderer's noose and a traitor's brand.

Karlich gasped when he felt Rechts's hand on his arm.

'Sergeant, you all right?'

He found his composure quickly, hiding his surprise behind annoyance.

'Fine! Never mind me, Rechts. Keep your eyes on the hills. He's here, I can feel it.'

They forged off together in silence.

Karlich was annoyed at himself for allowing his mind to wander. If the assassin had been watching then he would have loosed an arrow or shot in the sergeant's back and ended him then and there.

Idiot!

He didn't mean to take his anger out on Rechts, either. At least the drummer was sober and alert. It was more than could be said for him. Rechts needed watching closely. If nothing else, he needed keeping apart from Masbrecht. He'd developed a passive loathing for the man, taking umbrage at his piety. Karlich had no desire to see that become more than angry words. Honestly, he wasn't sure what Rechts was capable of. He knew something of the man's past. He'd spoken of it once after their first battle together. Rechts wasn't a drummer back then and Karlich only just a sergeant. The Reikland border was under attack by beastmen out of the Reikwald. It had been a tough fight and many good men had not seen the sunrise. Perhaps being faced with mortality, so close and immediate it could be felt as a shiver in the bones, Rechts had decided to talk of his troubles. It had just been the two of them, huddled over mugs of strong spirits in a booth in some tavern, the name of which Karlich could no longer remember.

Through slurred whispers, Rechts had told of the day a mutant was discovered in his village. A boy back then, he'd been fishing in a stream nearby his village when a girl had cried out. A sullen child, who kept to himself, was being bullied by the edge of the stream. He scuffled with his attackers: a blacksmith's son, his head full of soot, and a farrier's lad who'd been hit on the head with too many horseshoes. There was low cunning in these boys, who pulled at the sullen child's clothes, intent on first stripping him then dumping him naked into the stream. They'd succeeded in removing his boots and leggings when the girl, skimming stones on the bank, had noticed something terrible. The sullen child had fleshy webs between his toes and a small tail of bone protruded from the base of his spine.

Cries of '*Mutant! Unclean!*' echoed across the stream and down to the village. Men with hooks and staves came running with the local priest in tow.

The sullen boy was crying, tugging on his leggings and reaching for his boots when the village men seized him at the priest's orders. So disturbed was he by what he'd seen, the old cleric sent messengers to the nearest town and the chapter house of the Order of Sigmar there.

Everything changed when the witch hunters arrived. Their leader was a brutal man on a crusade that was anything but righteous. Rechts never saw the sullen boy again, but he knew what happened to him. The 'purging' didn't end there. In a fit of pious rage, the witch hunter declared the entire village spoiled by Chaos. He found signs of taint where there were none and condemned innocents to the pyre and noose. When some of the villagers resisted, it only enflamed him further. Rechts's mother could see to the end of what was happening. She took her son away from the village square where a mob was baying for blood, little realising that soon their own flesh would crispen on the pyre.

For the witch hunters brought men with them, hard men who served the order in a grim, unspoken role. At the points of their swords, they herded the villagers one-by-one into the flames. Only the priest was spared, baying for blood and retribution, transformed by fear into a madman. From his hiding place under the floorboards of his house, Rechts could hear their screams. He covered his ears against the terrible noise and screwed his eyes shut. By the time he opened them again, the village was quiet. Smoke and the smell of cooked meat lingered on the air. The stench aroused no hunger in him; he retched and fetched up an empty stomach in the street. Rechts emerged to find his village was gone, just a burnt out skeleton of wood and scorched stone. Piles of ash and charred bones were all that remained of his kith and kin. Though he searched on his knees, tears streaking his soot-stained face, he never found his mother amongst the remains. A part of him hoped she had escaped, but knew deep down that his fingers might have brushed the ash of what she had become in the pyre's flame.

Desolated and alone, Rechts had wandered down the road leading from his village wishing for death. Against the odds, he reached Grünburg and lived on the streets until he was old enough to take a piece of silver and join the Emperor's armies.

Even as a boy, Rechts had been a survivor. It was no different when he became a soldier but he bore the mark of that day in the village deeper than any physical scar. He never trusted priests again and hated witch hunters with a passion. In that, he and Karlich had an accord. Karlich had listened to the tale quietly and consoled him at the end. It was like talking to stone for all the emotion Rechts had shown him. Neither man could have known that Karlich would meet that self same witch hunter many years later, and that the zealot would not live to torture another innocent. The man was gone, but his legacy remained, and like a shadow creeping over the face of a setting sun, it was getting closer to Karlich.

A flash of light caught Karlich's attention. Something glinted in the morning sun.

Metal?

He followed a second flash south-east and what he saw turned his blood cold.

Prince Wilhelm and his knights were on the road and heading towards them. Still several miles distant, there could be no mistaking the Griffonkorps banner and the troop of armoured men on horseback. Karlich surveyed the hills quickly out of instinct, as if the murderer would present himself now the moment drew near, but he saw nothing. Just rocks and rugged earth, patches of gorse and bracken, a hundred places where the shadows could hide Wilhelm's would-be slayer.

The flash of light came again. Soon it would be a flash of blackpowder and a prince's blood would be sullied on the ground.

Eber squinted and scowled. He rubbed at his eyes as he was momentarily blinded by something shining into them. Shielding the sun overhead with one meaty hand, he tried to blink away the after flare but it came again. He tried to follow its origin. Too late he saw the mirror being used to blind him. Too late he realised the blurry shadow figure was coming for him. Eber heard Masbrecht cry out a warning. The burly Reiklander wasn't fast enough as he brought his shortsword up to guard.

'Fat pig, you're so slow!' said his father's voice, echoing in his head from beyond the grave.

Then he felt the knife enter his body. The first few stabs were hot and sharp, but the ones that followed grew cold and numb. Even Eber with all his strength couldn't stop the blood flowing from his body. As when his father used to beat him, his arms fell to his sides, his head went down to his boots and he could do nothing.

CHAPTER FOURTEEN

An unexpected murderer

Averland plains,
413 miles from Altdorf

The first moment Karlich knew something was wrong, Masbrecht was shouting.

'Eber's dead! He killed him! He's here!'

That couldn't be right. He'd seen Eber but a half hour ago, he was fine. A strong ox of a man was Eber. No, he couldn't be dead. There must be a mistake.

Then came the running, Karlich and Rechts together, Karlich's legs working in advance of his mind, his fingers tugging the pistol from his belt before his brain had told them to.

Eber *was* dead. The assassin had killed him.

A sound like thunder echoed throughout the hills, the natural depression within the valley rebounding and intensifying it so it was loud and difficult to pinpoint. A rock just above Karlich's head exploded a half-second later.

Karlich cried out as stony shrapnel embedded in his cheek like hot needles. He went down behind some scattered boulders lodged in the hillside – so did Rechts – and not from the injury. The next shot could be his skull instead of a rock.

'Grimblades!' he roared, trying to staunch the blood flooding down his face and neck, spilling through his fingers and soaking his shoulder. Karlich searched the hills. His head was down but he saw his men moving through the gaps in the rocks. The sun was in his eye-line, partially blinding him.

The bastard had been waiting all along, waiting for the perfect moment.

Grimacing with the pain in his cheek, Karlich cursed and stepped out from behind the boulders. He had to join the hunt. He just hoped the assassin had switched aim or the next iron ball would indeed be in his head.

Brand kept his anger like a caged thing, deep inside him. Now it was threatening to spill over, so annoyed was he about being on the wrong side of the hills. He bolted like a maniac across the road, leaving Lenkmann behind. Intent to the point of recklessness, he powered up the opposite hillside in long, rangy strides. He met Eber a short distance up, ashen-faced and lying on his side in a pool of his own blood. The red rivulets coming from his body were like thick veins threading the grass. Brand barely glanced down as he raced past him.

Masbrecht was knelt beside him. 'I didn't see, I didn't see...'

Brand wasn't listening.

Not far now.

He ran harder.

Volker drew his pistol when he saw Eber go down. It was so quick. A snatch of movement, the fading memory of a lithe figure in dark-brown and green felling an oak in the time it should take to cut down a sapling. Then the assassin was gone and Volker lowered his pistol with a curse.

'He's here. Come on!' he urged Keller, who looked like his wits had deserted him.

'*Get away! Get out of my head!*' he murmured, staggering after Volker and Dog. The mutt was barking loudly, drawing the others to the fight.

'Good boy, good boy,' said Volker, bounding across the hillside, his words coming out in a breathless rush. He ducked through tight ravines, hooked around boulders, leapt over mounds of earth. Just the flicker of his enemy, the waft of something incongruous on the breeze, kept him on the assassin's tail.

As a huntsman on his native lands, during all the years he'd been in the Reikland army, Volker had never tracked a prey so elusive. The assassin left foils and false signs everywhere he went. He had just seconds to do it, and Volker had even less time to decipher them. He went on a winding path, first down and then up again, across the length and breadth of the hillside.

Volker lost concentration for a split-second when he saw Brand barrelling up to meet him. In the corner of his eye, he noticed Karlich and Rechts too. In that moment, he lost his prey. Volker paused, annoyed at himself and felt a slight shift in the air nearby. Ducking out of instinct, he heard something whip over his head that ended in a dissonant *clang* against the rocks beside him. Volker was swinging the pistol around when he saw the assassin. Lithe and tall, he wore a tight leather bodice tied off down the middle. Their leggings and boots were of a dark animal hide. No skin was visible, hidden as it was behind long sleeves, gloves and a mask to cover the face. Something flashed between the eye-slits. It looked like enjoyment. The assassin had blades up his arms, daggers at his belt, a short sword down one leg and some kind of rifle, like no harquebus Volker had ever seen, on a strap slung over his shoulder.

The huntsman's skill at observation had always been keen, and all this he discerned in the moment it took for the assassin to loose another throwing dagger and end Volker's life.

Fate intervened in the huntsman's favour, a burly mass of fur and fangs smashing into the assassin and spoiling his aim. The dagger clattered harmlessly to one side and Volker was on his feet a moment later. Dog was fastened to the assassin's arm, biting down and growling. It elicited a screech of pain from the masked killer, a lot higher in pitch than Volker was expecting. Before he could get there, the assassin threw Dog off. The mastiff rolled and leapt again, but faltered in mid-flight. Volker thought he'd seen the killer raise a hand in warding, a natural reaction to a savage beast coming at him, but as Dog yelped and crumpled to the ground, he suspected something else. Horror built in Volker's gut, all thought of stopping the assassin momentarily forgotten in his concern for Dog. The mastiff wasn't moving. Something bubbled from its maw amidst the foaming saliva.

Frantic, Volker searched Dog's cooling body for sign of injury. Under its chin, he found a tiny dart. So innocuous-looking, yet so deadly. He went to tear it out before realising the barb was poisoned. Dog was dead. There was nothing Volker could do.

Brand got the assassin's attention simply by running towards her at speed. He redoubled his efforts when he saw the mastiff fall to the dart. Unless the assassin's attention was elsewhere, she'd gut Volker next while his grief made him defenceless. No such weakness from Brand. He knew her, this killer, because he knew himself.

Karlich and Rechts were coming from below. Even Keller was catching up to where Volker cradled his beast's lifeless head. The others were not far, either. They were herding her. She knew it. But Brand knew that an animal was deadliest when cornered. He followed her as she raced up the hillside. She was trying to reach higher ground and find an escape route. Perhaps, with Wilhelm closing by the moment, she merely wished to stall her attackers and execute her mission and the prince with a kill shot from the summit of the hill. The rifle she wore on her back looked like it was up to the task.

With Volker incapacitated, Brand easily outstripped the others for pace. Powering up the rugged slope, he had the assassin exactly where he wanted her – to himself.

Weaving around a rocky outcrop, Brand saw the flash of steel just in time. He parried with his blade, sparks and metal slivers shearing off in the air like falling stars. The second thrust came just as swiftly and he was forced to deflect low to avoid having a knife in his abdomen. The assassin, surprised her victim had lasted this long, drew a second dagger. Brand stepped back, pulling a throwing knife from his vambrace and using it like a foil. Her attack exploded against him in a rain of blows. High and low thrusts, wide slashes and overhand cuts prodded and probed the Reiklander's defences, seeking an opening.

She was good, faster than him. Brand knew he couldn't beat her while she had the upper hand. But all he had to do was hold her off and wait for the others. He'd wanted the assassin for himself, but was pragmatic enough to accept help when he needed it. A flurry of blade strokes pushed Brand back. A hot line of pain seared his arm as she opened up a bloody gash in his wrist. A well-aimed kick punched the air from Brand's lungs and sent him sprawling down the slope. Winded, but with anger fuelling his body in lieu of air, Brand scrambled back after her.

'Bitch…' he muttered in a rare moment of pique.

Then he saw the rifle levelled almost point blank at his chest and knew he'd made a mistake. Closing his eyes, Brand accepted the inevitable. He heard horses in the distance and men shouting from the valley below. But when the shot rang out, he felt no pain. He didn't fall with an iron bullet in his heart.

Brand opened his eyes.

She was dead, the left eye-slit of her mask exploded outwards in a bloom of bloodstained leather. Volker was revealed behind her, an empty look on his face, a smoking pistol in his hand.

Eber felt cold and clammy to the touch as Karlich stooped beside him. Masbrecht was crouched next to the sergeant, tearing strips from his cloak and jerkin, and pressing them against Eber's flowing wounds.

'I was wrong. He's alive,' said Masbrecht.

Below, the prince's entourage could be heard charging past. It was likely they'd heard the shot, but impossible to know what they made of it. Bandits and rogues of all stripes were common in the wild and often attacked travellers on the road. In truth, it seemed most of these reprobates had abandoned ambushing the Imperial byways in the wake of Grom's invasion, but Wilhelm and his Griffonkorps couldn't be certain of that. At least it was easier to countenance than an assassin hired to slay him from the shadows.

Karlich had seen the assassin fall to Volker's bullet. At least they'd managed that. It would all be for nothing if the prince discovered the truth, though. The Grimblades kept down, staying out of sight to add weight to the lie that errant bandits were lurking on the hillside. Rechts threatened to shatter the deceit with what he said next.

'We should hail them. Eber's alive and he needs help,' he pleaded to Karlich. 'A horse will get him back to Mannsgard faster than we can.'

Masbrecht replied before Karlich could answer. 'I can help him.' He felt Eber's trunk-like neck. 'His pulse is weak, but he's a strong one. I can help him,' he repeated.

Rechts balled his fists as his jaw set in a firm, unyielding line. 'If you say you'll pray for him…'

Masbrecht turned to him, stony-faced. 'My father was a physician. I learned some of his trade.'

Rechts wasn't convinced. The horses were almost gone. He went to Karlich for a second opinion.

The sergeant considered hard.

'We can't risk it,' he decided in the end.

'Eber will probably die!' said Rechts.

'We can't risk it!' Karlich hissed, his eyes urging the drummer to be quiet and stay down like the rest of them. 'One life for the fate of the Empire. I won't do it, Rechts. Stay down.'

The clacking of hooves against the road slowly receded into the distance. Morning had passed, the prince and his knights were gone.

The leather mask was almost black. It had two angular eye slits and bent outwards along the middle to accommodate the nose. It came off easily when Karlich pulled at it, sticking only slightly to the bloodied mess underneath.

Lenkmann had joined them and gave a sharp intake of breath as the assassin's identity was revealed.

Prince Wilhelm's would-be killer was a woman, a pretty one if not for the bullet hole ruining one side of her face. Only Brand had known it beforehand.

'Doesn't look Imperial,' said Rechts.

The dead assassin had olive skin with big, dark eyes and hair like sable to match.

'She's a hireling, a sell-sword,' said Brand. 'A dog of war.'

Karlich felt that same tremor of unease whenever Brand spoke of things that hinted at his old life. It had been a short while since Wilhelm had passed through the valley, alive and well. Together with his Griffonkorps, the prince was just a dust cloud on the horizon now, riding hard for Mannsgard. Karlich wondered idly if their entreaties to Wissenland had been successful. He suspected not. He winced when a bitter smile pulled at his injured cheek. Masbrecht had removed most of the stone shards but it was still painful. Dried blood covered one half of the sergeant's face like a mask. The shoulder of his jerkin was caked in it.

Four men surrounded the corpse. Volker was off somewhere, burying

Dog. He'd not spoken a word since the mastiff's death. He didn't appear to be distraught or even angry, just null of feeling, as if he were made of marble. Masbrecht was still tending to Eber, fulfilling his promise to help the burly Reiklander if he could. With Eber's wounds bandaged, there was little more Masbrecht could do. Eber remained unconscious, his breathing laboured. The paleness of his skin suggested he'd lost a lot of blood. Some of it stained Masbrecht's sleeves and stuck between his fingers and under his nails. It wasn't a pleasant sensation.

Keller sat off to the side of the group of four around the assassin. He was downcast, lost in his thoughts.

'Looks like a tattoo,' remarked Rechts, noting the mark on the side of the assassin's neck. Brand had brushed aside her hair and revealed it.

'Do you know what it means?' asked Karlich.

'No,' said Brand. 'I don't recognise this one.'

This one... thought Karlich.

'But I know what this is,' Brand added. From a small pouch tied to the assassin's belt he produced a gold coin.

Karlich took it to examine it.

'Stamped with the burgers' seal,' he muttered. 'This is Marienburg gold. Freshly minted too, if the sheen is anything to go by.'

'I don't understand,' said Lenkmann.

Karlich's face darkened as the possibilities ran through his mind. This business was growing murkier by the minute.

'Neither do I,' he said.

'She was expensive,' Brand told them. 'Those blades, that rifle... Doesn't come cheap. And she was good. Really good.'

Karlich thought he heard a note of reluctant admiration in the other Reiklander's voice.

'Have you ever seen anything like that?' asked Lenkmann.

He was pointing at the rifle next to her. The lacquered wood stock was finely carved and it had a metal barrel and trigger. It was much longer than an ordinary harquebus with a deeper, narrower barrel. It was una- dorned, though a gunsmith's mark was engraved in the wood of the butt. A small circlet of iron with a cross through it was hinged to the end of the barrel. A sighter of some description.

'It's Tilean, like her,' said Brand.

Karlich knew little of Tilea, save it was a country far south of the Empire renowned for thieves, sell-swords and adventurers. She certainly had a foreign cast to her features and Tilea had a prominent and pow- erful assassins' guild whose reach stretched through much of the Old World. He couldn't be sure, though. He wanted to know how Brand could be.

'How do you know?' Karlich asked.

'I've been there.'

Karlich was incredulous. He didn't know of any soldiers that had travelled beyond the Empire. 'When?'

'I was sixteen.'

Karlich waited but when it was obvious no further explanation was coming, he dropped the subject. Brand's past was as cloudy as the Reik during fog. Instead, he focused back on the rifle and the question of what to do with it.

'We have to destroy it,' he said.

Lenkmann made to protest. 'Such a masterpiece weapon, couldn't we–'

'How would you explain it when we return to Mannsgard? We can't just say we found it in the wild. Questions would be asked. The truth would come out.'

Lenkmann had no answer.

'Every trace of her must disappear,' Karlich concluded.

Rechts pulled off his cloak and rolled up his sleeves.

'Then we'd best get started.'

CHAPTER FIFTEEN
Old wounds

The road warden's rest, Averland woods,
408 miles from Altdorf

They buried the assassin on the hillside in a shallow grave. There was no time to dig a deeper one and Karlich hoped that scavengers might unearth and then devour her. It was a gruesome thought, and no one voiced it out loud, but they'd been forced to compromise ever since discovering the Altdorf messenger's corpse and becoming Ledner's thugs. Brand dismantled the rifle, smashing its mechanical parts beyond repair with the butt of his pistol and setting fire to the wooden components.

Eber lived, for the moment. His breathing was still shallow and he hadn't regained consciousness yet. By the time they were able to move him – lifting his body with a pair of cloaks like a hammock and carried between two – evening was already drawing in.

It was Volker who found the road warden's rest, a small shack well hidden in the woods with a second outbuilding that served as a watchtower nearby. It was bare wood, but sturdy and well kept. Judging by the dust and the smell, it hadn't been occupied in weeks. As they entered the hut where the road warden would sleep and eat his meals, Karlich was reminded of the crucifixes they'd found on the way to Blösstadt. The fluttering of dark wings, the frenzied pecking and the excited caws of crows came back to him, unwelcome as bad eggs.

The hut was sparse with a small iron stove in one corner, an empty skillet perched on top. There was a bed. It had mildewed blankets and was stuffed with straw for comfort. This was where they laid Eber, his bearers grateful for not having to haul him around for a while. A stool sat by the bed – Karlich imagined the road warden tugging on his boots or sharpening his blade. A hook on the wall contained the empty echo of a crossbow, a darker patch in the wood where the light hadn't touched it. A small cupboard revealed salted meats and a barrel of warm ale. The Grimblades tucked in without thought, not realising how hungry they actually were until presented with food.

Small windows revealed a dingy view. The shack had a flat roof but angled at one end. It had started to rain, thunder in the east announcing a heavy downpour, and it teemed over the window in thick streaks. Through it there was the watchtower, a hundred feet or so from the hut and a small tethering pole where the road warden would have secured his horse. They'd found rope and spare iron horseshoes in the shack, but there was no animal in sight. The entire place was desolate and forlorn, as if missing the presence of its occupants.

'This is a cold house,' moaned Rechts, huddled in his cloak. His gaze went longingly to the empty iron hearth and the weeks-old soot coating it.

On Karlich's orders they'd kept the fire doused. Like much of the shack, it was well tended. Apart from the recent soot, the stones were swept and the iron grate that kept the logs in place was brushed. A small chimney poked from the canted roof. Smoke would be a certain signal that the shack was occupied. The road warden had picked his spot well. It was untouched because no one, save an expert tracker, would know it was there. Even Averland, with its abundance of plains, had its forests. Like all the places of the Empire, darkness lurked there too, out of sight in the shadows. With greenskins and other beasts abroad, Karlich had reason to be cautious.

As an added precaution, the sergeant had posted a watch. The small outhouse was a perfect location for sentry duty.

'These are cold times,' added Lenkmann, 'as bleak as winter.'

With the bed occupied by Eber, most of the Grimblades squatted on the floor. It *was* cold but warmer than the outdoors, and at least they had a roof over their heads. Masbrecht sat on the stool, keeping an eye on his patient. He'd redressed the bandages and cleaned the wounds with water from a well around the back of the hut, but there was little more he could do for poor Eber. While he lived, there was hope. He was a strong man. Masbrecht prayed silently for him to pull through.

'What do you make of the gold?' asked Rechts, trying to occupy his mind with something other than how chill his bones were. It was the first time anyone had said anything of it or the assassination plot since they'd left the hillside. With the few words he'd spoken, Volker reckoned they were well over halfway to Mannsgard, possibly another day's journey encumbered by Eber.

Prince Wilhelm would have returned already and by the time the Grimblades got back to town, preparations would be underway for the march to Averheim. Karlich hoped they wouldn't be missed. Ledner probably hoped they were all dead.

'Marienburg seal, clearly fresh,' said Karlich, bringing the coin to his mind's eye. Like her trappings, the coin had been buried with the dead assassin. 'I'm not sure what to think. Honestly, I don't really want to.'

'I cannot countenance a prince of Reikland would be the victim of a blade in his own camp,' added Masbrecht. 'We are not savages. Sigmar-fearing men are godly and honourable, they–'

'Stop your preaching,' snapped Rechts with the weary ire of a frustrated drunk.

Karlich intervened before it went further. 'First time was a warning, Rechts. Don't make me come over to you.'

Rechts scowled behind his cloak, but backed down.

'I only meant it is hard for me as a devout…' Masbrecht paused when he saw Rechts glaring at him '…for me to believe a Reiklander could wish harm upon his own prince. Have we fallen so far?'

'We are not on the Warrior's Hill, if that's what you mean,' said Karlich.

Warrior's Hill was where in ages past that Sigmar gathered his chieftains and had them swear allegiance to an ideal, to the birth of an Empire. It was an act of fealty, not just to an emperor, the first emperor in fact, but to each other and the realm of man as a whole.

'Dreams fade with the dawn, Masbrecht,' Karlich continued. 'Like a wisp of cloud, they are at once beautiful and lofty, but also unreachable, transient. At best, they're a memory. At worst, they're entirely forgotten.'

'Gods, but that's bleak,' said Lenkmann, shaking his head.

Karlich was impassive. 'I'm a realist, that's all. I've seen the dark things men do.' His eyes met with Rechts's out of reflex rather than design. He went on. 'What remains after idealism is gone is life.' Karlich was almost sanguine. 'It is the pledges we make to one another, on the field of battle, in this very room.' He spread his hands and looked at Masbrecht again. 'Not all men are as pure-hearted as you, Masbrecht. Even I have… *regrets*.'

For a moment, Karlich went to a place inside him, where he kept his own dark truths. Whenever he opened that door, he smelled smoke and felt again his hands burning in the pyre, tearing at the ropes that held *her*… then pushing *his* face into the mud when he knew it was too late and *they* were gone…

Masbrecht wasn't done. His voice brought Karlich back. 'We're expected to keep all knowledge of this to ourselves, of what we did,' he said. 'I'm not sure I can do that.'

Karlich looked serious now. 'Well you must. We all know what's at stake.'

'If we don't, yes I know. But what's at stake if we do keep our mouths shut?' He put it to all of them. 'One killer has failed, but who's to say others won't be sent for the prince. He must be told his life is in danger.'

'We've been through this already, *brother*.' Rechts's upper lip curled into a snarl.

Karlich sighed deeply. 'Yes, there may be others. Perhaps this is also an end to it, we can but hope. But I doubt they'll strike now Wilhelm is back in Mannsgard with the army. Assassination will be the least of his concerns. Greenskins await us at Averheim, a horde the likes of which we've never seen if the scouts are to be believed.

'There is much we don't know here, Masbrecht. Don't act before being certain of the facts at hand.'

Masbrecht wasn't happy about it, his moral code was a strict one, but he nodded his agreement all the same.

'Ledner knows more than he's saying,' said Volker, sticking to the shadows, a few feet from the rest of the group. Lenkmann offered him a strip of salted beef but he declined.

'You could hang princes on that man's secrets,' Karlich replied in a bitter voice. The irony of the statement was not lost on him. By using Wilhelm as bait to draw out the assassin, Ledner had almost done just that.

There were rumours that Marienburg desired independence from the Empire. Karlich had heard traders in Altdorf and on the Reik claiming as much. It was so far fetched an idea that it had become something of a joke, an idiosyncratic quirk of a people joined by land but divorced in ideology. A rich state wanting to get richer. Even the underclass were well heeled.

There are no peasants in Marienburg, so the popular myth went, *because they can't tend fields with all those rings on their fingers.*

'And what if he hangs *us*?' added Volker.

Lenkmann raised an eyebrow. 'A dour thought, Volker.'

'I have plenty to be dour about.'

Lenkmann was closest to him and reached over to pat his shoulder. The gesture was a little awkward, but his expression conveyed sadness. 'It was a brave animal.'

Something dark flashed across the huntsman's eyes as he looked back. 'It was a mean bastard.'

Karlich was looking around. 'Speaking of which, where is Brand?'

All eyes went to one corner of the room. Brand had been sitting there, almost invisibly in the deepest shadows. Now he was not.

'I could've sworn…' Lenkmann began.

Karlich was on his feet. His anxious mood passed to the others, a sudden sense of urgency charging the air. He asked a question to which he already knew the answer.

'Who is on watch?'

Masbrecht was the first to answer. 'Keller.'

Karlich left the door banging loudly in the wind as he bolted from the shack.

* * *

Slipping out was easy. It was gloomy in the shack and filled with shadows. A few candles had been scavenged from a drawer but they were stubby and weak. Karlich was wise to light only a few. Any more and the fiery glow would have attracted more than just moths. Just like smoke from a chimney, larger nocturnal predators would be drawn to a flame, drawn to the warmth it promised and that of the humans crowded round it.

A back door led out into a small yard where they'd found the well. Without a handle or any discerning marks, it was hard to see. Brand had found it easily enough, though. Easier still was disappearing when the debate about Wilhelm's would-be killers was going on.

No one noticed the slightest flutter of the candle flames or the faint draft of cold air, so fleeting it could have been imagined.

Brand was out in the rain. To some it would be a cleansing experience, but no amount of rain could purify the taint Brand felt on his body like a second skin. Rain reminded him of drowning, only by degrees, one drop at a time. He'd led a violent life, and associated everything with death. Brand circled around the back of the hut, staying low and moving steadily but calmly. Sudden movements, even out in the rain-drenched darkness, might attract the attention of his comrades, and they had no part in what he was about to do.

Brand knew his chance would come again. Keller was a slave to his guilt now. He couldn't stand to be in the presence of others for fear that the sickening lump behind his ribs would make him speak out and confess his sin. Blood, Brand knew, especially old blood, was heavier than it first appeared.

The outhouse was ahead, little more than a silhouette, like a piece of driftwood sticking up from a clinging sandbank. The earth around it, despite being sheltered by the canopy of the forest, was sodden like a quagmire. Brand trod lightly and swiftly once away from the shack and in the open.

He barely noticed the rain anymore as he approached the door. Somewhere behind him another door was banging. It was hard to hear, muffled by the weather. The door to the watchtower was unlatched. Easing it open with his foot, Brand drew his dagger. Inside, Keller was waiting.

Nearly slipping several times on the mud, Karlich reached the watchtower a little out of breath. He drew his sword, vaguely aware of the others behind him. Throwing open the door, he rushed inside expecting to see Brand murdering Keller. It had taken him a few days, but he'd realised there was something between the two men. He didn't know what precisely, but suspected it had something to do with Varveiter's death. He'd watched Brand ever since, but had let him slip from his sight when his guard was down.

Keller *was* dead, but not from Brand's dagger. He swung by a rope tied around his neck. A stool lay on its side nearby. The tips of Keller's boots barely scraped the floor. By the pallor of his skin, he'd been dead for some time.

Brand was sitting on the floor, sobbing into his hands. For a moment Karlich was taken aback. He'd never seen the man cry. Ever.

The others were coming in from the outside.

Karlich slammed the door in their faces, locking it shut.

'Get out! Go back to the hut,' he said, shouting so they wouldn't question him. Someone tried the door. He heard Lenkmann's voice but the meaning of his words was lost in the rain. 'Do it now. That's an order.'

When he was sure the others had gone, Karlich turned back to Brand. His gaze drifted upwards to Keller's swinging body. The rope groaned with the weight. In that gruesome moment he realised what must have happened at Blösstadt.

Keller had murdered Varveiter in retribution for humiliating him at the camp, and the guilt of it had driven him to hang himself. Brand had known it too, much sooner than Karlich, and had planned revenge of his own. Only Keller had robbed him of it, too afraid to face the consequences of his actions.

'I would've done it,' sobbed Brand, as all of his grief flooded out. 'I wanted to do it.'

Karlich sheathed his sword and knelt down beside him.

'I know, brother.' He made to touch Brand's arm but stopped short, letting his hand fall to his side. *When soothing a wounded wolf, it's wise to keep your hands to yourself.* Karlich had heard that spoken in Middenheim once. 'It's all right.'

They sat like that in the silence and the dark for a while, until Brand stopped crying and Karlich decided to cut Keller down.

No one would ever know the truth, nor would they ask for it. The Grimblades had been through much together and knew when to leave things alone.

Keller was dead. Karlich had told them he thought the man simply couldn't take the pressures of the war and the burden placed upon them by Ledner, and it was left at that. All had noticed how withdrawn he'd become since their first engagement at the slaughtered village. It wasn't so beyond reason – men had taken their own lives for less.

An unmarked grave was Keller's only legacy. Volker had found a suitable spot in the forest that was shaded and the soil less like the sucking bog surrounding the watchtower. Masbrecht had delivered a short sermon, a soldier's prayer. Rechts had stayed, but made his discomfort obvious. It wasn't that the drummer didn't believe in Sigmar, far from it. His faith had been shaken, yes, but it was priests and dogma he had issue with. Karlich knew that, and recognised himself in that conviction.

It was why he tolerated the outbursts and the drunkenness.

Even Brand had attended in the end. Karlich assumed he had his reasons.

When it was done, when Keller's bones were laid to rest, Rechts had sung a solemn lament. It was a marching song of Reikland, *My brother in our Land*, one that commemorated the fallen and asked their comrades to remember them. The rain had persisted until morning and framed a sullen scene around the grave.

There was no time to tarry. As soon as Rechts was done they left the road warden's rest and headed back to Mannsgard. The mood was grim, but Eber, at least, had shown some signs of life. Masbrecht had performed his task well. The burly Reiklander would live.

CHAPTER SIXTEEN

Marshalling for war

The town of Mannsgard, Averland,
383 miles from Altdorf

An army was growing outside the town by the time the Grimblades returned. Imperial banners caught on the wind, snapping against their poles as if fighting to be free. Soldiers in the colours of Averland, Middenland, Reikland and Carroburg gathered. There was a hubbub of voices and the dull *clang* of metal from breastplates and tassets as the soldiers slowly formed into regiments. The lines of men filing from the gates seemed endless. An entire town emptied, leaving only its graven citizens behind. Karlich would later remark that he couldn't tell if they were pleased or distraught to no longer be harbouring soldiers.

Pikemen, spear, swordsmen and halberdiers stood shoulder to shoulder with archers, crossbowmen and handgunners. Militiamen roved in loose bands until their sergeants bellowed for order. To their credit, the free companies made rank and file quickly. Mules dragged baggage caravans or hauled cannons and mortars, gunnery crews shadowing them like dutiful hounds. Engineers rode in the wagons themselves, together with their best journeymen. Karlich saw one muttering to his war machine and smoothing the barrel in the same way he'd stroke a beloved pet.

Madmen, he thought. Blackpowder was as dangerous as sorcery. Only the insanely brave or the bravely insane dallied with it. Exploding shrapnel could kill a man as easy as a blade or bow and before an enemy had even deigned to launch its first attack. He remembered an incident a few years back when a gunner had lost his head to a spinning axle flung from his machine when it misfired. The irony of it was the battle was already won, and the guns were being fired to salute their victory. Since that day, Karlich had vowed to give war engines and their like a wide berth.

Mad they may be, but compared to the footsloggers the gunners looked positively sanguine. Most of the infantry were drawn and pale, moving with the uncertain purpose of condemned men. It wasn't so far from the truth.

Karlich had yet to see the cavalry as he and the others walked past the processional exodus from Mannsgard. He assumed they'd be last, after the foot soldiers were readied to march.

It was mid-morning, the sun was rising quickly and the last of the night patrols were returning. Karlich had blended his own troops in with them, so as not to arouse suspicion. Passing the last of the thronging soldiers on their way through the gate, he noticed von Rauken and his Carroburg Few. The hoary old veteran nodded with the slow certainty of iron. Karlich returned the gesture and tried to hide his nerves. Though he was the last man he wanted to see, he had to find Ledner and tell him what had happened.

Karlich found the spymaster at the counting house where they'd met in secret two nights ago, gathering up maps and charts from the desk.

It was still gloomy, though the window slats were open and allowed a little light in. Dust whirled about the air in thick, grey clumps. Karlich coughed, giving away his presence.

Ledner did well to mask his surprise when he looked up at him.

'It's done.' Karlich was in no mood for niceties. He wanted to get away from this man and this place as soon as possible. He was alone, having left the others to find the rest of the regiment. If Captain Stahler asked, Karlich was giving his report to one of Wilhelm's scriveners for the prince's perusal later.

'Fine work,' said Ledner. Something flashed behind his eyes. Karlich thought it was amusement, but the kind of emotion shown by a snake as it circled a plucky mouse.

'Not without cost.'

'Yes, I heard you lost a man. And the one who was injured?'

'He's with the chirurgeon. He'll live, but won't fight at Averheim.'

'You'll miss his blade.'

Karlich was downcast. 'Aye, I will.'

Ledner went into a drawer in the desk and tossed a heavy-looking bag in front of Karlich.

'What's this?' he asked, not bothering to keep the angry tone from his voice.

A few coins spilled out onto the desk, the weight of the pile inside the bag pulling it over.

'Your payment.' Ledner didn't look up as he sorted the last of the charts and scrolls. 'There's five crowns each in there. Two more for you as sergeant.'

Karlich dumped a large bundle on the desk. It struck the bag of coins and scattered them over the scarred wood.

'Your guns and blades,' he said.

Ledner barely glanced at the leather skin binding the weapons together.

'And the cloaks?' he asked, rolling up the last of his scrolls.

'We'll keep 'em, if it's all the same to you. Nights on the Averland plain can be cold. You can keep the blood money.'

If Ledner felt the barb, or even cared, he didn't show it. He ignored the scattered coins, too.

It would be just like the man to leave them out of spite or to demonstrate just how much higher in the Imperial hierarchy he was, thought Karlich. We are little more than insects to men like him. He suppressed the urge to punch Ledner in the face. Karlich fancied his dagger-like nose would break fairly easily.

'There's more?' asked the spymaster, when Karlich didn't leave.

'Don't you want to know about the assassin?'

The sergeant was genuinely nonplussed.

'You stopped him, that's all that really concerns me.'

'The assassin was female, a Tilean by her cast and features.'

Ledner kept silent, inviting more.

'She was a sell-sword hired with freshly-minted Marienburg gold but then I suppose that doesn't really surprise you, does it?' Karlich couldn't keep the sneer from his tone or his face.

Now Ledner looked up at him. 'And what makes you say that, sergeant?'

'Only that you know more than you're telling me.'

The spymaster laughed wryly. 'You knew what was needed,' said Ledner. 'A little information can be a dangerous thing, especially if it is heard out of context. I'm sure you're aware of that, sergeant.'

Karlich felt a sudden chill enter his spine. He swallowed hard. Did Ledner just allude to something in his past?

Does he know about Vanhans?

The look of playful humour vanished off Ledner's face, as if deciding he'd pushed far enough for now.

'You should get back to your regiment,' he said, returning to the scrolls. 'If you're late for mustering, questions might be asked.'

Recovering his composure, Karlich said, 'Well then, let me ask you one more thing.'

Ledner peered up at him from the table. 'Go on.'

'What was Count Pfeifraucher's answer?'

'You'd like to know your sacrifice wasn't in vain, that the prince's journey wasn't a needless waste of time and effort?'

'Just tell me.'

Ledner snorted at some private amusement. 'Have you looked around the town or at the army gathering outside? What do you see, sergeant?'

Answering questions with questions, how like a spymaster.

'I see nothing different, except perhaps a few more unhappy faces.'

Ledner collected the scrolls and charts under his arm. As he walked past Karlich on his way out, he said, 'Well then, there's your answer.'

Karlich *really* wanted to hit him now. He clenched his fists and it took all of his considerable willpower not to do it. He realised Ledner was trying to goad him. Execution was the punishment for striking a senior officer and Ledner knew it. So instead, Karlich kept his back to him and let the spymaster go.

'I'll send someone back for those pistols, unless you want to take them?' Ledner didn't wait for an answer, the sound of the door closing echoed in the man's wake.

'I have somewhere you can put them...' Karlich snarled at the gloom. He waited until he was sure Ledner was gone then left the counting house to go and find his regiment. Any longer away from the gathering army and Stahler might begin to miss him.

Captain Stahler couldn't believe what he was hearing. Judging by the reaction of Prince Wilhelm's other officers, neither could they.

'So we'll return to Reikland then, fortify our borders,' said Captain Hornschaft, 'and consolidate our forces with the Averlanders,' he added when he caught a petrified look from Baron Blaselocker. The Yellow Baron, as he was now known around the camp, was really just an officer in name only. He had no troops to command, save his own retinue, and his position on the field would be at the rear, near the war machines where he could cause the least amount of trouble.

Prince Wilhelm had pointed it out on one of the maps before him only a few moments ago. It was a few moments after that when he idly let slip that Wissenland had refused all overtures of alliance with Reikland and Averland. Just as before, they were alone in the liberation of Averheim.

'Why do you think we are going over strategic plans of attack, Hornschaft?' asked Preceptor Kogswald. The Griffonkorps captain had a way of making even the simplest question sound like an impatient challenge. His mood was sour, and he flushed angrily behind his oiled moustaches – Kogswald had vehemently opposed the prince's diplomatic mission to Wissenland.

The captain from Auerswald balked a little before the knight's ire. He removed his wide-brimmed hat to mop his brow. 'Without Count Pfeifraucher, we are badly outnumbered.' He appealed to Wilhelm who was watching his officers keenly. A general could tell a lot about the men of his command when they were under pressure. Who would fight, who would rather flee to die another day. He was still undecided about Hornschaft.

'And yet, here we are,' said Vogen. The captain from Kemperbad stabbed a gauntleted finger down onto the map, which showed the lay of the land near the outskirts of Averheim, as if to suggest that battle was now a formality in his eyes.

Wilhelm smiled privately.

A fighter, that one.

'So, what's to be done?' asked Stahler, displaying the earthy pragmatism he was known for. Truth was, though, he agreed with Hornschaft. Marching on Averheim with an under-strength force was near enough suicide. The difference was, Stahler's pragmatic streak also manifested as a stoic adherence to duty.

At that moment Ledner entered, throwing a shaft of light into the darkened confines of the tavern. Wilhelm had hastily summoned all of his military officers to his temporary lodgings in Mannsgard. He'd hoped against hope that Wissenland would answer the call to arms and fight beside its brothers. But instead of solidarity in the face of a common enemy, all Pfeifraucher had offered was a provincial mindset that saw him shutting his borders for good. Well, at least until the orcs moved farther south-east and tore them down.

All of the captains were present, including Engineer Meinstadt who'd remained in pensive silence since the council began. Preceptor Kogswald of the Griffonkorps was seldom far from his prince's side if he could help it, and represented all of the templar knights in the army. Vanhans and his 'soldiers of faith' were, obviously, excluded.

Of the others, Father Untervash was outside the town leading his fellow priests and novitiates from regiment to regiment, offering blessings and instilling the courage of Sigmar where it was needed. The wizard had removed himself, meditating in solitude to consolidate his magical strength. Apparently, his powers were all but returned since the exhausting battle near the Brigund Bridge.

The light died quickly as Ledner shut the tavern door, as did the warmth in the room. Fear mongering and disinformation were the man's stock-in-trade, and rolled off him like a mist wherever he went.

'Apologies, my liege,' he said to Wilhelm in his familiar rasp, the other officers parting to allow him a place at the strategy table. 'A matter arose that required my attention. Also, I needed to gather the additional charts and scrolls for our quartermasters.'

The prince nodded once, in a gesture that all was well, before Kogswald outlined the plan of battle.

'There is an army within Averheim. Trapped behind its gates, there is little it can do but defend the walls,' he said, taking a nub of charcoal from a clay pot on the table. 'Our force is not insignificant,' he added, starting to draw. 'We bring the greenskins on to us with artillery fire, archers and shot...' Crosses represented the missile troops. Three arrows, arcing from where Averheim was depicted on the map to the crosses he had just drawn, represented the enemy's movements. 'Thus leavened, the wall guard can be thinned, its surplus used to form a large sortie in the courtyard.' Kogswald looked up and smiled. The expression was a grim rictus, framed by his moustache. Steel coloured the emotion in his eyes.

'No less than five knightly orders are holed up within Averheim. By pulling the greenskins towards us and using our cavalry to cut a path through to the gate, we can unleash them. Caught between a massed force of knights and the infantry, the greenskins will soon become disorganised. Rout, after that, is inevitable.'

Kogswald stood straight after leaning over the table for so long. He looked pleased with himself.

Prince Wilhelm waited patiently for the reaction.

The other captains were nodding. Vogen folded his arms to suggest it met with his approval. Even Hornschaft looked mollified by what he'd heard. Stahler had to admit it sounded like a winning strategy, but he also saw the burden it would place on the infantry. When the orcs came at them, goaded by the guns, it would fall to the foot soldiers to hold them off and prevent the line from being overrun. Despite his ardent loyalty to the cause, he was starting to find the role of punching bag a little wearisome.

'And what if the greenskins will not be baited or if they maintain their order?'

Kogswald swung his gaze over to Ledner. He shook his head. 'They are orcs,' he said, confused at what his fellow captain was implying. 'Ignorant beasts that are easily distracted and dissuaded. It is their nature. They can no more fight it than you or I could renounce our duty to the prince. It is what they are.'

Ledner's eyes never wavered. He met Kogswald's indignant steel with silken guile. 'And yet, the question remains...'

Kogswald laughed again, not bothering to hide his scorn and incredulity. He looked about to reply when he went to the prince, instead.

'My lord–' he said, half as a question, half exasperation. Kogswald opened his palms as if to say, *Are you going to listen to this snake's drivel?*

Wilhelm breathed deeply, his eyes blind with thought. Wrong-footing them all, he turned to Meinstadt.

'Master of the Guns, how much artillery do we have?'

The engineer adjusted his monocle, by way of nervous affectation. He loudly cleared his throat.

'Six great cannon, one volley gun, three mortar and ninety-six harquebus, my lord.'

Stahler was taken aback at Meinstadt's rapid inventory. He'd heard little and seen less of the war engines in the army's arsenal. True, there were wagons driving out of Mannsgard with machineries aboard but he had not known of the volley gun, nor had he appreciated the sheer numbers. Engineers were secretive bastards, and evidently Meinstadt believed in that clandestine code, but they were also notoriously eager for 'trialling' their weapons of mass destruction. Stahler assumed Prince Wilhelm had instructed most of the artillery be held back and saved for breaking the siege at Averheim.

'Keep a portion of the guns in reserve,' said the prince. 'I'll leave it up to you, Meinstadt, to decide what is appropriate.' Now he addressed the entire council. 'If our attack falters, or the orcs surprise us all and hold their ground, we'll cover our retreat with artillery. Nature or not, no mortal creature would gladly walk into a fusillade of shot if there are easier pickings elsewhere.'

The engineer was nodding at this wisdom when Wilhelm glanced at him. 'Do it now. Make your preparations.'

Meinstadt was already leaving when the prince spoke again.

'We are done, my captains. We march to Averheim, to glory or death.' He nodded with a knowing sort of fatalism. 'To blood, certainly. Fight for me,' he added. 'Fight for the Reikland and the Empire. Turn the tide.'

The gathered captains stood a little straighter, a little taller and saluted together. Hornschaft was nodding again. With all the feathers on his hat, it put Stahler in mind of a bird pecking at its feed. Vogen puffed up his chest with war-like pride. Kogswald was imperious as ever. Ledner gave away nothing.

These were the men that would deliver Averheim or see it fall, of this Stahler felt sure. The air felt cold. It was the touch of death closing, of Morr's heavy sword above all their heads. It only made Stahler more determined.

'Faith in Sigmar,' said the prince.

His captains answered as one.

'Faith in Sigmar!'

It would need to account for much in the hours to come.

As the officers departed to their regiments, Stahler made an excuse to linger behind. Ledner and the prince were still inside. With the others gone, he went around the side of the tavern. When Stahler was sure no one was watching he bent double, hands on his knees to hold himself up. Sweat cascaded off his forehead as he removed his hat and helm. It felt as if an anvil were lying on his chest.

'*Gods...*' Stahler was surprised at the breathless rasp that came out of him. At Blösstadt the orc's wound had gone deep – deeper than he'd realised. He clutched at his breastplate, it was like a vice seizing his body. When he drew away his hand it was dappled with blood.

* * *

When Karlich returned to the regiment, a surprise awaited him.

'Refugees from Averland,' Lenkmann explained after a crisp salute. Karlich eyed the new recruit in his ranks wearily.

'Just one? Doesn't seem worth it,' he chuntered to himself.

'Welcome back, sergeant,' Lenkmann added facilely. He stood forward of his comrades, as if distancing himself in the relative pecking order.

'I've hardly been away,' Karlich muttered and approached the fresh blood. He was young, that much was obvious, with the slight tan of a life lived on the Averland plains. The uniform was mismatched with yellow, black hose and a red tunic. The leather jerkin he wore over it had a crimson and white ribbon tied to one of its straps. He had one around his arm too. A metal gorget protected his neck and he had a peaked helmet.

Karlich beckoned the lad forwards. He came to stand beside Lenkmann.

'You a halberdier, son?'

'As sure as Siggurd!' the lad answered forcefully.

The perplexed look on Karlich's face made him go further.

'I mean, yes sir, I am. Gerrant Greiss, formerly of the Grenzstadt Fifth,' he added.

Karlich sized him up. He scowled as if unimpressed. Behind them, Rechts and Volker were trying to keep a straight face.

'You've fought "the Paunch" many men are speaking of?'

'Not face-to-face, but our lord general did. At the Averland border, our army watched the western end of Black Fire Pass. We were amongst the first to resist the greenskins.'

'Your lord, where is he now?'

'His head is mounted on the goblin king's banner, sir.'

Averlanders were a straightforward, earthy people. Perhaps it was why they enjoyed such good relations with the dwarfs. Even still, Greiss's forthrightness caught Karlich unawares.

'I see,' he said, recovering. 'Rejoin your comrades. Welcome to the Grimblades, Greiss.'

Karlich looked around at the growing army. Blocks of troops were discernible now. An order of march, come through from the returning officers, was slowly being established. The Grimblades had yet to learn of their position in it. Stahler, much to Karlich's relief, still hadn't shown up.

He did see that other regiments, besides his own, had been swelled by refugee recruits too. Some, like Greiss, wore spare uniforms or elements thereof. Many looked incongruous amongst their new postings, however, wearing only a regimental ribbon on their arms to identify them.

'Reappropriated after Captain Ledner's instructions to the quartermasters,' Lenkmann said when he saw his sergeant surveying the army.

Karlich remembered the charts and scrolls in the counting house. He vaguely recalled a number of the so-called 'death-books' amongst them.

As his gaze continued uninterrupted, Karlich noticed further additions.

He saw a large regiment of dwarfs, probably expatriates from the Grey Mountains given their obvious penchant for Imperial trappings such as feathered helms and slitted tunics. Karlich had met Worlds Edge Mountain dwarfs before, and they did not dress like that. He also saw halflings, likely travelled from the Moot. More diminutive than dwarfs, but not as stocky and without beards, halflings were regarded as something of a nuisance in the Empire. Still, they were braver than they looked and fairly stout on account of their well-fed bellies.

These halflings were an odd band, well-armed despite the shortness of their weapons and stature. They carried short bows and a variety of small daggers and dirks. One wore a kettle for a helmet, another a pot with a ladle tucked in his belt. Karlich spotted forks and spoons too, even a frying pan. Satchels slung over the halflings' backs were stuffed with vittels. A chicken's foot poked from one, the stopper from a jug of mead from another.

'At least they've brought their own food,' said a familiar voice. Von Rauken blew a plume of smoke as he chewed on his pipe. He smiled when Karlich saw him.

'Are you jesting, greatsworder? That's just a morsel to those gluttons!'

Von Rauken laughed with a sound like grinding iron and the two men shook hands warmly. 'Aye, you're probably right,' he said.

'Once done with the supply wagons, they'll be on to the horses,' Karlich replied.

Von Rauken laughed louder. His humour was infectious and as far removed from the grim champion as Karlich had ever seen.

'Levity is good before battle,' he said, the dourness returning. Something unspoken passed between the two men, a shared desire that both should survive what was to come at Averheim.

Von Rauken clapped Karlich on the shoulder and nodded.

'We'll drink to it after.' With that, he turned away and went back to where his greatswords were waiting.

Karlich replied in a quiet voice, 'Aye, after.'

'The army grows, but why does it feel like the end of times, like our last battle?' Lenkmann asked after a moment of silence.

Around them the infantry was almost ready. Heavy horse could be heard above the muttered voices of the throng. The cavalry was leaving Mannsgard. They were about to begin marching to Averheim.

'Because it is, Lenkmann,' Karlich told him. His tone was slightly wistful. 'It probably is.'

Thunder trembled in the heavens. Lightning drew jagged arcs across a steel-grey sky a moment later. Karlich's eye was drawn to a desolate heath, a mile or so from the town. There he made out the wizard he had met in the war tent. He was channelling the storm in and out of his body, like a lightning rod. His hair stood on end, ablaze with celestial fury. A tempest was growing to the east. The faintest echoes of it whirled around the army and tore one of the banners free from its pole. Karlich watched some men reach for it, but it got caught up in the wind and gusted away. Ragged and forlorn, it sped back towards the Reikland.

The thunder came again with renewed vigour, filling Karlich's world with noise.

CHAPTER SEVENTEEN

Besieged

Outside Averheim, capital city of Averland,
483 miles from Altdorf

The earth trembled under the hooves of Wilhelm's horse. Loud and deafening, the guns reminded him of thunder.

The great cannons fired one after the other, each fresh report adding to the resonance of the ones before it. Smoke spewed from their iron barrels, the ends fashioned into the mouths of mythical beasts, and thronged the air with the stench of blackpowder. A second percussive blast provided a deeper chorus, just beneath the sound of the cannon. These were the mortars, their fat shells whining overhead to land in the packed greenskin ranks.

Wilhelm tried to follow the destructive course of the war machines but was too far away. Together with the cavalry, amounting to six lances of templars and a roving band of pistoliers, Prince Wilhelm occupied the far right flank of the battleline. He was nearly a hundred feet from what could be considered the war front. The *refused flank* was a well-known military theorem in the Empire. Here, on the killing fields before Averheim, it would be tested in practice.

Averland's capital looked like a broken silhouette in the distance. Like most large cities, it was surrounded by a wall. It had suffered badly under the attentions of the greenskins. Their crude catapults were too far advanced to be hit by the Imperial cannonade. Mangonels and onagers loosed relentlessly. Walls and towers, even sections of the heavily fortified gatehouse, resembled the nubs of broken teeth. Even at a distance, Wilhelm could tell that men hung dead in some of the ruins. The clouds of flies made it gruesomely obvious.

At other parts of the wall, the orcs launched continuous assaults with ladders, ropes and log rams. Through a spyglass, the prince made out an orc slavemaster urging a band of trolls to heave a battering ram against Averheim's main gate. The ornate carving that had once adorned it had been bludgeoned into oblivion. Dust and grit from the neighbouring gatehouse walls shook loose with every fresh blow. Wilhelm could already imagine it splintering. It was making the wait worse, so he lowered the spyglass.

To his left, he knew, was the rest of the army.

The rear was anchored by Meinstadt and his war machines. Two brace of cannon and a pair of mortars comprised the battery. The remaining engines were primed but left unfired.

Five regiments of handgunners stood sentinel before the larger guns above and behind them. Little did Wilhelm know, but Utz and his sergeant, Isaak, were amongst them as part of the Grünburg contingent. Due to their longer range, four regiments of Averland crossbowmen were stationed a step above them.

In order to accommodate the blackpowder troops and the gunnery crews, Imperial sappers had been forced to raise earth embankments. They did this by digging trenches and then heaping up the mud. It had to be packed hard so the weighty machineries didn't sink. It also needed shoring with timber along its sides. Palisades were erected at the base by way of a makeshift rampart to protect the handgunners. The trenches were filled with abatis as a final deterrent. It was backbreaking work and the labour gangs earned their bread and coin that day, but it was also necessary. The land around Averheim was very flat and Meinstadt needed elevation for his guns if the plan was to succeed.

Militia were interspersed between the blackpowder troops. Their ranks were much deeper, their frontage narrow by comparison. They were to act as foils should the greenskins break through to the guns.

In front of them came the infantry.

A huge wedge of Empire soldiery dominated one half of the plain beyond the ersatz embankment. Three lines, ten regiments each, made up the infantry throng. Swordsmen and halberdiers took the back line. The dwarfs from the Grey Mountains were deployed here too, together with large groups of militia. No regiment was less than six ranks deep.

A second line of halberdiers and swordsmen stood in front of the first. Here the Grimblades were stationed. Von Rauken's greatswordors were nearby, occupying a central position. His smaller regiment was in addition to the main body of troops but no less imposing for its smaller size.

The front line had the pike and spears. Vanhans's mercenaries and desperadoes pitched their banner here too. It would fall to all of these brave souls to bear the brunt of the greenskin attack and weather it if they could. Once battle was joined, they'd narrow their formations and allow the rear line to engage.

Roaming just in front of the formal infantry wedge were free companies, huntsmen and archers. The halflings were amongst them. It was the job of this skirmish line to frustrate and disorganise the orcs as much as possible before they charged. By pulling and dividing them, it was hoped the greenskins wouldn't attack as a cohesive mass, thusly making it easier to resist them.

Across the line, drums beat and horns blared. They were challenges, designed to goad the greenskins and bolster the Empire's fighting men.

They will need it, Wilhelm thought grimly, donning his helmet as the orcs began to turn.

The greenskin army was like a tide.

'Have you ever seen such a horde?' Lenkmann uttered from the front rank. Even the banner he carried sagged in assumed defeat.

'I can feel Morr's breath on my neck,' said Volker, one rank behind him. His mood had turned maudlin ever since the death of Dog.

'Enough of that!' snapped Karlich. 'It doesn't matter if there is one orc or a hundred thousand. You can still only kill them one at a time.'

But even he had to admit the enemy was vast. Unlike the precise and militaristic order of the Empire army, the greenskins were a densely packed rabble.

Through gaps in the Empire's own ranks Karlich made out tribal banners that appeared to unify certain mobs. To his dismay, several carried the desiccated remains of Imperial soldiers. Other greenskins could be identified by markings and tattoos. Brawling was mandatory. Smaller goblins bickered continuously, whilst their larger cousins engaged in more violent acts against their own kind. Rival clans fought tooth and nail in the rear masses.

Even as the cannon balls bounded through their ranks, chewing up bodies and ripping off limbs, they still brawled. Only when explosive mortar rounds blasted them apart, separating combatants, did the orcs stop fighting one another and turn to the 'humies on the hill'.

It was slow at first, like a boulder rolling down a lightly canted slope. It took time to build and spread like an angry flame through the greenskin ranks. But gradually, and with fearsome momentum, the orcs began to charge.

Bellows and war cries accompanied the shuffling gait of greenskin feet. The dark sea surrounding Averheim rippled. They thumped their chests and smashed cleavers against chipped wooden shields. Standard bearers rattled totems, cursing the weakling men who had chosen to pick a fight with them. Huge flesh-skinned drums beat. Raucous pipes screeched. The ocean of green was moving.

Amongst the bestial mob were larger beasts, creatures that shared the greenskins' desire for carnage and cruelty. Lumbering trolls, pugnacious ogres and gangling giants roamed alongside orcs and goblins of every tribe.

Hooded in black cowls and cloaks, festooned with bone charms, armoured with thick dark plate – the one known as 'the Paunch' had allied a massive and diverse horde together. With guile, intimidation, sheer strength or perhaps all three, this warlord, this 'Grom', had overcome the single greatest weakness of the greenskin race, the one thing that had, until now, prevented their wanton destruction of the Empire – animosity. Gathered in warbands, orcs were fearsome and tough enemies. Amassed in their tens of thousands, they were nigh on unstoppable.

The end of times, indeed, thought Karlich with a morbid smirk.

As the greenskins came on, surging full pelt at the waiting Empire infantry, riding beasts broke out from the ranks. Wolves and boars scurried and snorted in packs, but Karlich also caught flashes of other things bearing greenskins to battle. Hulking cave spiders carrying tattooed goblins scuttled hideously. Ovoid squigs, all fangs and rough, red hide bounded on two legs, their hooded riders hanging on by their claws. Karlich hadn't realised the monsters grew to be that big.

The roar of the guns intensified, as desperate as their firers. Cannons boomed, loud and dissonant behind the infantry. The sharp cracks of harquebus accompanied them in a ballistic symphony. Though they were far from the front, overlooking the battlefield on the embankment, the artillery batteries and their ranks of gunners could still hear the rage.

'*WAAAAGHHH!*'

It was like a primal invocation, bursting from greenskin mouths in a tumult of sound. Men fell, as if struck by a physical thing. A soldier in a sword regiment from Streissen dropped dead from fright. Several others soiled themselves, unable to control their bowels. Behind the Grimblades, a militia band broke and fled.

Several others turned, thinking about desertion too. Karlich saw them out the corner of his eye. They held, for now.

'Merciful Sigmar, even the sky is turning…' Masbrecht pointed to the heavens where dark, myrtle-tinged clouds had begun to boil. Fell voices wreathed the air, now thick with unnatural heat. The sun was smothered, snuffed out like a candle and a gloom sullied the field of war, tainting everything green.

Shadows lingered in the firmament. Karlich saw the suggestion of a sloped brow, a jutting chin. Eyes like malevolent red stars burned in those clouds. There were two of them, two hulking figures so massive and terrible that he knew if he looked upon them any longer his mind would shatter.

Suddenly, Karlich felt a tremendous weight upon him. His arms and armour seemed heavier than before. He realised it was despair, sapping at his strength and resolve. The others felt it too. Volker had shut his eyes. Masbrecht was praying under his breath. Rechts licked his lips, in need of a drink. He'd never felt so dry. Even Brand twitched as he experienced the oppressive presence of the entities in the storm above.

'*Faith in Sigmar…*'

Karlich heard it distantly.

'*Faith in Sigmar…*'

Louder now, he recognised the voice of Father Untervash.

'Faith in Sigmar!' On the third time, Karlich shouted too. 'Give me your courage, men of the Reik!'

The shadows above chuckled at his defiance. It sounded like malicious thunder. A spit of green lightning threaded the clouds. Karlich bit his lip, drawing blood, and used the pain to shut it out.

'Grimblades!' He roared it like a call to arms.

Across the line, other regiments were refinding their purpose too. Empire men gripped their hafts a little tighter, brought their shoulders closer to one another. Together they were strong. Sigmar had taught them that. Banners that had dipped rose again. Drums and pipes struck up against the orcish din crashing into them like a disharmonious wave.

Above, the clouds began to recede. The shadows there grew fainter.

'*He* is with us…' Masbrecht was weeping. He clutched a talisman of a hammer in his left fist.

Even Rechts was moved.

A clarion sounded from somewhere near the army's centre. Other horns took up the call that spread slowly down the line. More than two dozen banners thrust into the darkling sky. Wilhelm's banner was proudest. It rose like a rallying cry. Eldritch wind buffeted it but it snapped and thrashed defiantly.

We shall not be bowed. We are Empire. Sigmar is with us.

Though the prince himself was not riding alongside the army banner, all who saw it recognised its authority and the order to march.

'We are to meet them then,' Volker hardly sounded pleased.

'You hoped to cower behind pikes and spears?' said Karlich.

'Stay together, brothers,' said Greiss. 'They can't break us if we keep to our bonds of soldiery.'

Nodding, Volker looked girded by the newcomer's words.

Karlich peered over his shoulder at Greiss, who was part of the second rank next to Volker. 'Well spoken,' he said. 'You sure you're not a Reiklander?'

They all laughed, even some of the rear rankers who were in earshot.

Levity was good before battle.

Captain Stahler bellowed above the throng. The din of over two thousand tassets and breastplates rattled into movement. The Empire began to march.

CHAPTER EIGHTEEN

Battle is joined

Outside Averheim, capital city of Averland,
483 miles from Altdorf

Wilhelm's warhorse had caught the scent of battle and strained at the bit before the prince reined it in.

'Easy now…' he soothed, patting the beast's armoured flank.

They were all eager, not just the steeds, but the men too. The orcs had been goaded by Meinstadt's cannon and though mauled by guns and bows, they had engaged the infantry. The skirmishers were either fled or consumed. Only the plucky halflings and a few isolated groups of huntsmen remained. Even now, they were being harried by goblin scouts. Sensibly, the Mootlanders had found a rocky outcrop on which to stage a desperate defence. The huntsmen were in the open though. A large band of Wolf Riders swept over them. When they'd passed, the Empire men were dead.

At the battle line, the bloodshed was even worse.

Within seconds, ranks of spear and pike just disappeared, swallowed by the green tide. So furious was the melee between the Empire's front and the greenskin rear mobs, it was tough to discern anything of meaning. Already, the corpses had begun to pile up. Those orcs and goblins slain by the artillery barrage were lost from view, crushed underfoot by their own kin. The bodies of men, butchered and bloodied, joined them on the killing field. Heaps of them rose up like fleshy bulwarks on the churned earth.

Though at first Grom's green horde had appeared endless, gaps were emerging between the warbands. Prince Wilhelm had been cunning in his deployment of the army. They occupied an area of the battlefield at an oblique angle to the orcs. It meant when the beasts engaged them they would have to charge *away* from Averheim and the gathered knights. As the seconds passed and the greenskins pressed more and more tribes into the fray, the aspect facing the Empire cavalry thinned and presented its flank.

'We should ride now,' advised Kogswald, impatient to bloody his lance.

Wilhelm lowered his spyglass for the second time.

'Hold,' he warned. 'We wait until the way is almost open.'

'It may shut again if we don't act,' Kogswald replied.

'Just wait,' said the prince, about to look through the spyglass again but stopping himself.

He'd hoped to see some sign of Grom, but had failed to find the goblin king in the masses. Likely, the beast was closer to the gate. It would show itself soon enough.

'I've heard talk that the greenskin warlord cannot be killed,' uttered Ledner, as if reading his liege's thoughts. 'That it ate the flesh of a troll and has a girth to match. No less than three lords, a knight templar amongst them,' he added with a wry smile at Kogswald, 'have alleged inflicting a mortal blow and yet here we are before Averheim's ragged gates.'

'What do we do with trolls, preceptor?' Wilhelm asked.

Kogswald's indignation turned to spite. His moustache curled up in a feral grin. 'Burn them, my liege.'

'Just so…' He tapped the pommel of his runefang. *Dragon Tooth* it was called. Its inner fire raged with all the fury of its namesake. He slammed down the visor on his helmet. The green waves had parted. Wilhelm drew his sword and raised it high.

'We ride!'

The sky was boiling. Clouds tinged green billowed and twisted, occluding the sun. The presence of the orcish deities in the gloom had lessened but not abated. Like a looming threat they feasted on the greenskin rage swamping Averheim and the land around it. Their chanting voices bubbled on the air like a feverish sweat.

They were not alone.

Another accompanied them. Not a deity but a totem of its fell gods' power. Its shadow soared through the clouds on leathery wings, a dreaded silhouette once witnessed on a desolate plain at night.

'Wyvern!' yelled Rechts, gesturing to the sky as the Grimblades were driving forward. 'The greenskin shaman is abroad.'

'Eyes ahead,' said Karlich. The pikes in front were barely holding. Just a few feet separated the two regimental lines. The Grimblades and the second front could enter the fray at any moment. Their booted feet marched in unison, matching the pace of the halberdiers from Auerswald to their right and the Middenland swordsmen to their left. Mercifully, there'd been little time to mingle with the belligerent northerners, though they'd scowled and muttered amongst themselves upon seeing their neighbours in the line of deployment.

Nearby, Karlich heard von Rauken urging on the Imperial soldiers nearby. He sounded impatient for blood. The warrior priest in his ranks was adding fervour to his steel.

'Sigmar is my shield, the hammer in my hand. I shall not fear darkness,' cried Father Untervash, hurling dogma as if it were a spear.

Beyond a mass of cluttered pikes, Karlich made out the greenskins. Shouts of men merged with the brays of orcs into a cacophony. Though only glimpsed through a press of bodies, he could tell the fighting was fierce.

It was but a piece of a much larger struggle.

From his vantage point mounted on a warhorse, Stahler watched the pikemen crumple and give. They'd held off the orcs as long as they could. Their defensive formations had done a lot to staunch the initial rush, but now they were shedding men like autumn leaves. Tattooed orcs, their shoulders like fat slabs of meat, hacked into them as they fled. Their snarling white faces were painted to resemble skulls and they wore no armour, save their beast-hide jerkins. The Imperial spear regiments were losing a similar war of attrition. In the end, they had to break and fall back or risk being annihilated beneath the greenskin tide.

Stahler held his sword aloft. Its single rune glowed defiantly, throwing light across the blade. He winced but tried not to let it show. His wound still ached like hot pins in his gut. It was why he rode a horse rather than went on foot. Stahler had always warred on foot. He preferred to be near his men, in the dirt and the mire. Soldiers respected a captain who was willing to bleed and stand with them. But he feared if he did, he might not stand at all. Perception was everything. He had to inspire and embolden. Stahler couldn't do that doubled up in pain or flagging in a fighting rank.

The left flank was buckling. Spears from Kemperbad and Bögenhafen, and four blocks of Averland pike, were in danger of being overrun. Three regiments of halberdiers including Karlich's Grimblades, of whom Stahler was fond but would never show it, and a pair of sword regiments out of Streissen and Middenland was ready to fill the gap soon to be created by the fleeing polearms. Thankfully, the infantry centre and its front line right flank were holding. Despite his loathing of the fanatics, Stahler had to admit that Vanhans's soldiers of faith were proving resilient. They'd moved to the centre and girded it with their reckless passion. It struck him as ironic that the witch hunter fought like a man possessed.

To the right of the Grimblades von Rauken's greatswordsers moved up, eager for carnage.

'Second line...' Stahler roared, '...forward, in the name of Prince Wilhelm!'

Most of the pikes and spears retreated in good order, though they were still bloodied before the halberdiers and swordsmen could relieve them. There was the swift beat of drums to signal the charge then came the clash of steel and the grunting of men.

On the left flank, battle was joined with the second line.

Stahler rode up just behind them. His face was an ugly grimace. He prayed he could stay the course.

Screaming pike and spearmen barrelled through the Grimblades and the halberdiers from Auerswald.

Karlich ordered his men to let them through and come together again once they'd passed. Panic must not spread. The broken could be allowed to flee but must not get swept up in their fear.

'Hold true,' he cried. 'Maintain rank and file!'

It was hard to think, let alone speak. The clatter of arms and armour was everywhere, growing louder by the second. Blood scent reeked on the air. Steel and leather, too.

They were beyond the fleeing spearmen, a frantic blur of yellow and black disappearing in the Grimblades' peripheral vision. A slab of orcs with bloody cleavers and studded-leather hauberks confronted them, eager for more.

Karlich roared without words. His heart pounded like a blacksmith's hammer. Then there was the rush and the carnage that followed. He took a blow on his shield, hard enough to jar his shoulder. Karlich ignored the pain and stabbed the snorting greenskin in the face. Dark blood gushed from the wound, threading from his withdrawn blade in an arc. A line of halberds slammed down in unison, splitting two orcs apart. Someone screamed. Karlich didn't recognise who. A rear ranker moved up to fill the gap.

Stabbing and thrusting now, the halberdiers fought hard to keep the greenskins at bay where their strength and brutality would count for less.

Karlich cut again, slashing an orc's thigh. He barely saw the beast. His enemies were a haze of snarling slab-browed faces and jutting jaws. Taking a punch to the side of the face, Karlich nearly fell. He almost lost his shield. Strong hands behind him held him up, while a halberd blade thrust overhead into the orc's neck. It died choking blood.

'As one we stand,' he heard the voice of Greiss saying. No one other than Brand could have applied the deathblow.

Back on his feet and fighting, Karlich felt the weight of his warrior brothers at his back and knew that Greiss was right.

The Grimblades held. The Auerswalders and the Steel Swords held. With

Father Untervash, von Rauken's greatsworders were reaping a heavy toll of greenskins. But the orcs refused to yield. Even the goblins were undaunted.

The bloody day was far from over.

Kicking its flanks, Stahler rode his warhorse in a loop around the back of his command. The second line was holding. In the gap between it and the third, a decent amount of pike and spear had rallied and were already reforming. Their drums and horns carried orders on the air, though some had lost their banners in the panicked rush to flee.

Captain Hornschaft was supposed to be leading the front line. Stahler had lost sight of him ever since the greenskins' initial charge. He hoped, a little forlornly, that he was still alive.

A cry echoed loudly from the far right, accompanied by the shrilling of silver trumpets. Stahler's pride soared when he saw Prince Wilhelm and his knights ride onto the field of war. Over a hundred templars and half as many pistoliers again charged with glorious voices. Break through the greenskin horde, reach the gate and free the army of Averheim. Stahler willed them on, his voice escaping as a breath.

'For Sigmar, noble prince…'

He averted his gaze when another, much less inspiring, sight seized his attention.

Trolls were lumbering through the greenskin rear ranks, swinging tree trunks and the bodies of dead Averheimers like clubs. Orcs and goblins were left bludgeoned in their wake. Others, battered aside in the beasts' eagerness to feed, flew like broken dolls over the heads of rival mobs much to their cackled amusement. Plucked from amongst its kin, a goblin squealed before being devoured, a quick morsel before the feast to come. An orc flayed by acidic bile collapsed into a pile of sticky bone. The troll responsible wiped its drooling maw with a meaty hand. Vomit hissed and burned against its craggy skin before evaporating. The beasts lived only to eat and to kill. Food was neither friend nor foe. Goaded by orc slavemasters, the trolls would reach the second line soon.

Stahler was about to spur his horse – he'd need to reach his men before the trolls – when he hesitated.

A black shadow drew over him and the Grimblades, eclipsing what little light shone on the battlefield. Evil lurked within that shadow.

Blacktooth…

The name was uttered like a curse into his mind, and the minds of those who saw it, in a guttural cadence. The breath snagged in Stahler's throat, as if too afraid to escape. Whinnying in terror, his steed caught the scent of the monster before seeing it.

A wyvern, an old beast from deep within the mountains, loomed over them. Mounted on its back in a crude saddle was the orc shaman. Blacktooth wanted a fight.

* * *

Huge, beating wings funnelled the scent of the wyvern's rage and hate towards the puny men who could only cower. Akin to a giant winged lizard, the monster's hide was thickly scaled and shone with a gelid lustre. It put Karlich in mind of dank places, of ancient slime-skinned caves where men should never venture. A ribbed belly, thicker than a cannon's barrel, heaved and sucked with the effort of keeping it aloft and steady. Its barbed tail quivered, seeping poison. Fangs as long as swords, and broad as axe heads, were stained crimson. Trying to muster his courage, Karlich imagined the wyvern's appetite for flesh was not yet sated.

Men howled before the beast wrenched straight from the depths of their darkest nightmares. Scenting fear, the wyvern roared. An ululating, unnatural din resounded over the battlefield. Those who heard it felt their blood freeze and their bodies stiffen in fear.

A band of militia, a detachment of a much larger regiment of halberdiers from Streissen, panicked and fled. Blacktooth snarled his displeasure. As the shaman sat up in rusted-iron stirrups, Karlich got a better look at him.

Blacktooth was festooned with skull charms and totems. He clutched a strange wand in his right fist, some bizarre daemon-head charm hammered onto a stave of dark iron. A dirty, furred jerkin of many colours swathed his body. Blacktooth was barefoot. A horned hat, crested with a halfling's skull, covered his head. He held a notched cleaver in his other hand. One of the large fangs protruding over his upper lip was blighted with decay.

The fleeing men didn't get far. Blacktooth unleashed a blast of green lightning from his eyes. The militia never even had time to scream before they blackened and died.

'Sigmar preserve us!' someone shouted from down the line.

'Morr's shadow is upon us!' said another.

Masbrecht was praying in the front rank. His eyes were closed and he clasped the hammer icon around his neck as if it could make him invisible.

Karlich wanted to speak, to galvanise his men, but found his mouth was dry and his tongue leaden. The urge to run, to save himself, was strong. Burning meat was redolent on the breeze. He did not want that fate.

Blacktooth and his beast aimed their malign gaze at the Grimblades. There was a form of low intelligence there, capable of much cruelty.

'T-tur…' Karlich could barely speak.

Run, run! his mind pleaded.

Try as he might, he was fixated on the terrible wyvern and its master. Something else was moving behind the orc hordes too. A caustic stench came with it. Karlich thought he could smell sulphur.

Were all the creatures of the dark beneath the world coming for them?

A bright light surged into being to Karlich's right. He blinked, fighting the after flare. Dimly, he was aware of the greenskins squealing in pain.

It took a supreme effort of will to tear his eyes off the wyvern and look past it but, with his vision returning, Karlich saw the greenskins in front of them were blinded. They scratched at their eyes, thumped their kin with clubs or hacked with cleavers. Enraged and afraid, the orcs were cutting themselves to pieces.

The cold dread he had felt was scoured away by a sensation of heat. Suddenly emboldened, Karlich followed the source of the light.

Father Untervash glowed with an inner glory. His every pore exuded stark and blazing fury. It filled his eyes and made them burn. The warrior priest's voice resonated with power as he stepped forward from the front rank of the greatswordsers.

'Denizen of the deep, foul spawn, with the wrath of Sigmar I will smite thee!'

Holy fire coursed over the priest's warhammer, flickering along the haft and up Father Untervash's arms. He swung it three times in a wide arc then planted the head into the ground where a pulse of fire erupted. Orcs within its path were seared. Blacktooth and his wyvern were assailed by the backwash but didn't yield to it.

A horrible, bestial grunting came from the orc shaman when it was over. The sound was deep and abyssal, drunk with unfettered power. Blacktooth shucked up and down. It took Karlich a moment to realise the orc was laughing.

'In Sigmar's name, I denounce thee wret–'

With a serpent's reflexes, the wyvern snapped at Father Untervash and seized him in its jaws. Blood spewed from the warrior priest's lips, preventing him from finishing the holy diatribe. Gasps of shock echoed through the Imperial soldiery as their keeper of the faith slowly drowned in his own blood when his chest was crushed.

Defiant to the end, Father Untervash spat through red-rimed teeth and tried to lift his hammer. His pain and anger ended when the beast snapped its jaws and him in two.

'Morr protect my soul!' One soldier from Auerswald fell to his knees, awaiting the end. Several more from the same regiment ran, discarding their banner as all hope faded.

The light, in many ways, died with Untervash.

Ragged halves of his torso fell out either side of the wyvern's mouth, trailing ribbons of red meat and crumpling to the ground like scraps. Somewhere farther down the line another regiment fled. The gruesome display and the presence of the monster had unmanned them. Karlich felt the shift all the way to the front rank. Part of the second front was overrun, the pressure telling at their flank. They at least had to hold.

Without the priest to repel them, the orcs returned. Mercifully, Blacktooth took to the sky but Karlich sensed he was far from done with them. Guttural chanting infested the breeze as the shaman channelled a more powerful spell.

Remembered terror still numbing his bones, despite Untervash's holy aura, Karlich was fighting for his life again. The orcs were badly burned by the priest's holy fire, and they were angry. In the madness, it felt as if there was no end to them.

They'd barely begun to swing their halberds again when darkness loomed above the Grimblades. At first Karlich thought it was the wyvern returned to devour them but then he saw the giant orc foot manifesting in the clouds. One of the hulking orc deities laughed and snorted as it prepared to flatten them.

Even as he cut and hewed at the enemy to his front, wary of the devilry above, a feverish sweat overcame him. Karlich's hackles rose. His armour became hot to the touch. Glancing skyward between thrusts, he saw tendrils of green cloud spool off the giant foot as it plummeted with inexorable finality.

Ahead, the stench of sulphur got stronger as the trolls reached them. 'Helena, forgive me...' He used his dead wife's name like a blessing.

But the orcish foot did not fall. Winds billowed from the west, carrying a figure of silver and azure. Borne aloft on a wisp of cumulonimbus, Sirrius Cloudcaller stalled the wrath of gods with sorcerous will.

One hand halted the foot's descent, a gulf of turbulent air between them. The other hand spilled lightning from its fingertips. Forks of it lanced down and burned the trolls to charred meat. Even their incredible regenerative powers were unable to mend them.

Blacktooth bared his fangs, sweeping down to confront the Celestial wizard up close. The shaman growled and clenched his fist. The orcish foot descended again but crashed against a shimmering, azure shield. Sparks cascaded like dying comets as Sirrius Cloudcaller put all of his effort into resisting Blacktooth.

The magical shield glittered like a false firmament of stars. It cracked with the immense pressure, but held. Taking a deep breath, the Celestial wizard exhaled a blast of wind that forced the shaman back. Even his wyvern could not keep them from spiralling.

Sirrius soared into the storm-wracked heavens after him. Soon he was nothing more than a shadow chasing another, climbing, ever climbing into the sky above.

A patch of fiery amber began to glow in his wake. It tinted the clouds where the Celestial wizard had pierced it to pursue Blacktooth. The edges of the ragged hole slowly blackened and there rose a sound like the world cracking along its seams. Incredible, intense heat turned the clouds to steam as a flaming meteorite tore through the gloom with a blazing tail.

The fire-wreathed rock struck somewhere far behind the orcs. Hundreds died in the crater, their bodies reduced to cinder. A wave of fiery debris claimed hundreds more. The din of its impact was felt all the way to the Imperial line and brought the Grimblades and the rest of the soldiery to their knees. Mobs of orcs and goblins were destroyed utterly. Others were left decimated.

The tribe fighting Karlich's men lost three rear ranks in a single blow. The rest were seared by heat and left dazed and dying when the Grimblades charged. Karlich hadn't wanted to grant them mercy, but their deaths were swift.

A few hundred greenskin dead counted for little in the overall scheme of the battle, but it meant the way lay open for the infantry to advance.

The entire left flank butchered their way through the orc and goblin remnants at the edge of the meteor blast and marched onto the still smoking ground, slightly awestruck by what they'd just witnessed. Already, though, orcs and goblins were moving through the heat haze. Earth turned to glass crunched beneath their feet.

Wiping off his blade, Karlich cursed when he saw the Steel Swords advancing. Eager to chase down and slay a mob of shattered goblins, they had gone too far and left the Grimblades' flank exposed. The Middenlanders were heedless to the risk, ploughing on. A disingenuous part of Karlich believed the other regiment had endangered them deliberately.

'Sturnbled and that rabid dog Torveld would see us dead,' griped Rechts, beating the order to march on his drum.

'They may not have long to wait,' said Greiss, pointing from the second rank. A band of Wolf Riders was loping through the carnage. A manic goblin in the lead was cackling and pointing back. Its warriors did so too, sharing some unheard joke.

Karlich knew what it was. In moments they would be engaged by the vast goblin mob to their front, only to be charged a second later by the Wolf Riders. They'd be fighting towards two aspects at once.

'Wheel formation!' he shouted, causing Lenkmann to signal with the banner and Rechts to alter the tune of his drum. They'd try to face both enemies to the front. The Grimblades slowly pivoted on their right flank, the left shuffling forward using it like a fulcrum and angling their frontage.

A low explosion suddenly erupted behind them. It sounded distant, as if it came from the embankment. Leiter, who'd replaced Keller in the front rank, turned to look but a goblin arrow from the Wolf Riders pierced his neck. Gushing blood, he fell and Ensk took his place.

They braced halberds when the goblin mob struck but, to Karlich's dismay, the Wolf Riders arrested their charge at the last moment and skittered around them. The slight delay was hardly costly. They engaged the Grimblades' flank.

Pressured from two sides, the rear rankers found it hard to lend their support. Karlich felt the goblins pushing incessantly, even as he cut at them with his sword. It only got worse when the sergeant glanced to his left and saw Vanhans and his soldiers of faith. The witch hunter met his gaze and glared briefly before Karlich lost him in the ebb and flow of the melee.

Fatigue gnawed at him now, like an unwelcome guest who wouldn't leave. Karlich felt like giving in. They'd endured almost a half hour of unbroken fighting. Across the line, it was beginning to hurt. Troops that had regrouped from the original front were moving in support, plugging inevitable gaps, but they could only do so much. Every man was tiring. Karlich had hoped the enemy would be too. But they showed no sign of doing so; the greenskins' stamina seemed limitless.

CHAPTER NINETEEN

The death of honour

Outside Averheim, capital city of Averland,
483 miles from Altdorf

Stahler knew wizards had power, but until he'd seen Sirrius Cloudcaller summon the chunk of flaming rock, he'd not realised just how much. Deep down, it frightened him that some men could wield such a thing like he would wield a sword. He wondered at the price of it, at the sacrifice it must require.

His awe had banished his fear at least, and with the wyvern gone he could concentrate on the battle. It stuck in his craw that he couldn't commit to the fight. He had to lead, to guide tactically, so as many men as possible survived the next dawn, if there was one.

The left flank was beginning to push the orcs and goblins back. Though, to Stahler's chagrin, both the centre and right flank were making better progress. Buoyed by victory, the regiments commanded by Vogen were forging ahead. It meant the line angled awkwardly and Stahler wished he could haul them back, but he was too far away.

Behind him, smoke and fire billowed across the embankment. It was hard to make out but it looked like one of the great cannons had misfired and exploded, killing its crew. Meinstadt was still alive, labouring to free an iron ball stuck in the mouth of one of the mortars. Through the fog, Stahler discerned another of the cannons had slipped down the hill, part of the makeshift embankment crumbling beneath it. Gunnery crews pushed and heaved on ropes to bring it level again but were making little inroads.

The war machines had done their part. Meinstadt's reserves remained, but only in extremis. That left one cannon. It was up to the infantry now. They were fighting hard, gaining ground, but it was a ripple against an ocean.

Stahler had no illusions. Prince Wilhelm needed to break through and release the army inside Averheim very soon.

Wilhelm and his knights punched through a trailing warband of orcs, burst right through their flank and scattered them. Kogswald sang ancient war ballads as he slew, whereas Ledner was deathly silent and killed with brutal efficiency. Both such fine warriors, such contrasts in light and shade.

Dragon Tooth was well bloodied by now. The orc filth slipped off its blade like water, leaving it bright and unsullied as if newly forged. The Griffonkorps and the Order of the Fiery Comet hadn't lost a single rider. There was still some way to go, a field of orcs and goblins stretched ahead of them, but the Averheim gates were in sight.

Wilhelm's eyes narrowed, akin to when a hunter in the Reikwald spots prey. Free of the orcs, now either dead or fleeing, he was able to focus his attention on a figure standing out amidst the thronging battle for Averheim ahead.

It was distant, glimpsed through a clutch of swaying beasts and banners, horns and totems. Wilhelm could not believe the creature's size. The rumours, all he had heard and largely discounted, did not prepare him.

Grom the Goblin King was immense.

At first, the Prince of Reikland mistook him for an orc. No goblin had any right to be that big. Grom's girth was incredible, the paunch for which he was so famed. It spilled out from under dirty chainmail in a solid mass of flesh and muscle, pockmarked with warts. A helmet fashioned from a horned skull sat on his ugly, leering head. A necklace of claws and finger bones looped around his neck. The furry hide that served as a cloak was spattered with dried blood. Grom was in the killing mood, and Wilhelm need rely on rumour no more as he could now see the goblin's strength and prowess for himself.

A sortie of templar knights who'd possibly seen Wilhelm's gambit was trying to fight a route through to him and open up the way to Averheim. They had stalled upon hitting a vast swathe of miniscule greenskins. Though weak and diminutive, the creatures known in the Empire as snotlings were in such numbers that the brave knights were dragged down and engulfed. Vaguely, Wilhelm made out a mass of tiny jaws with teeth like pins gnawing at the stricken templars. The snotlings inveigled their way into armour plate, under chainmail, hungering for soft, yielding flesh they could feast upon.

Though they struggled, once off their horses the knights were as good as dead. Other, larger goblins armed with nets and barbed tridents hurried in stabbing and prodding at gaps in their armour.

Bravely, some had broken through and Grom was cutting them down. They barely made it twenty feet from the gate when the goblin king was amongst them, his double-headed axe cleaving limbs and reaping a bloody toll.

The knights didn't last long. None returned to Averheim.

Wilhelm was horrified. This menace had to be stopped. His determination to meet Grom in single combat and end the war grew.

The small tract of open ground they'd found upon smashing through the orc mob was coming to an end. A band of night goblins – hooded creatures that usually dwelt in caves and seldom fought in the day – scurried into the path of Wilhelm's knights. Ranting on behind the Paunch was his standard bearer. The nasty little creature spat and stuck his tongue out as he raved at the other goblins, urging them to charge.

Several mobs had allied together under a single banner, a jagged, bleeding eye. There were maybe eighty to a hundred of them. Wilhelm gauged they'd last less than half that number in seconds against his knights.

Just as he leaned in, lowering his body closer to his steed for the initial impact, he caught a final glimpse of Grom, looking at him over his shoulder, before he sidled away.

Was the goblin warlord grinning?

Seeing another opportunity to bloody his lance, easy pickings at that, Kogswald spurred his knights.

'Allow me, my lord,' he said, slamming down his visor and kicking his steed. '*H'yar!*'

He'd scythe the goblins down like chaff.

Moments from impact, the other lanceheads just a few seconds behind him, Kogswald's eyes widened and he tried to rein in his horse. The other knights followed suit but some were too slow and piled up behind those in front. A stray lance raked a horse's flank, tearing into its barding and eliciting a whinny of pain. Others crumpled against the armoured backs of the lead animals. Necks and limbs broke with an audible crack of bone. Men fell from their saddles and were crushed underhoof. But the carnage had only just begun.

Bursting out of the night goblin ranks came six greenskins each wielding a massive ball and chain. They swung the ridiculously huge weapons in an arc, slowly at first and then gradually gaining momentum until the displaced air from them whirling around created a low *whomp* with each successful circle. Frothing at the mouth like rabid dogs, the goblin fanatics were clearly insane. Their maddened voices were oddly distorted as they spun, like a reverberant howl growing and diminishing at rapidly increasing intervals.

One of the horses strayed into the whirlwind of iron and was instantly bludgeoned. Its rider raised his shield ineffectually. The desperate knight was battered into a greasy paste before he had time to scream. Unperturbed, the goblin fanatic carried on trammelling through the warriors behind. The other five inflicted similar devastation, their course unpredictable but deadly. One of the Griffonkorps tried to stab down at a greenskin with his longsword but succeeded in only snapping his blade and then losing his arm as it was dragged in to the goblin's killing arc and crushed.

In just a few seconds, Wilhelm's proud lancehead was in tatters. Almost half of his knights were dead or dying. The attack on the Averheim gate ground to a terrible halt.

Brand stabbed a goblin wolfrider in the neck, releasing a plume of gore just as the rain began to fall. It was light at first, a low *plink, plink* against their armour, but then it grew to a downpour. Tunics and hose were quickly sodden, leather stained dark like blood. It was so heavy it became hard to see much farther than a foot or so in front of their faces. Brand didn't mind. He only needed to see what he had to kill and that usually fell into those parameters. Disembowelling a giant wolf, he decided the rain had done nothing to cool the battlefield. In fact, the heat was more oppressive than ever. If anything, it made it more clammy and humid. As it died, the wolf upended the goblin on its back into a worsening swamp. Brand put his boot on the creature's head, holding it down while he fought another. A line of sweat was rekindled down his back and made him itch. He would have scratched were it not for all the greenskins on the flank trying to gut him.

Brand was at the 'hinge', where the front and rear ranks met. He protected Masbrecht's back, who was in the front rank fighting the horde of goblins on foot. Alongside him was Greiss, the recruit from Averland. The man was skilled and held his own. He had an aptitude for killing. His tally rivalled Brand's own.

At the front, Brand was dimly aware of Karlich shouting curses at the greenskins and encouragement to the men. Brand generally hated officers, but he respected Karlich. Not as much as Varveiter, but he held the sergeant in high regard. It was the only reason he hadn't killed him after he'd seen him break down in the watchtower at the road warden's rest. That was a distant memory now, only Keller's face remained and the sense of his retribution being denied that Brand felt at the other soldier taking the coward's way out.

It was hard fighting, some of the toughest Brand had faced. The noise was intense and blended together into a hellish sort of din. Some men, if they survived, would not get over it. It would likely drive them mad. Brand had known soldiers, harder men than those around him, who had taken their own lives because of it.

Pressure could be felt on both sides, ever pressing. It was a task just to keep the goblins back, let alone defeat them. As he killed another wolfrider, Brand heard a man farther down the flank gurgle a death cry as one of the mounts ripped his throat out. Greiss still refused to yield. For Brand, it was like looking into a mirror, a cracked and slightly dirty mirror.

Karlich disliked the Middenlanders almost as much as he hated the goblin hordes trying to kill them. After hacking apart a goblin's skull with his sword, he spared a glance at Vanhans's men. They were true butchers. The ruthless mercenaries and insane flagellants laid into a band of orcs with bloody abandon. Like madmen, they died in droves but fought without fear. The paid mercenaries were more careful but equally brutal. A promise of further coin was all that kept them in the fight, though. Karlich only glimpsed the witch hunter, a sliver of black, a flash of silver, but his voice was wholly apparent. Every cut came with a curse, a hateful catechism spat with phlegmy vitriol. If animus was a weapon then Vanhans's blade was sharper than the keenest diamond.

Ahead was no better. After plunging forward heedlessly, the Steel Swords had now stalled, forming a shieldwall against a mob of heavily-armoured orcs. Trying to stay alive and kill his enemies at the same time, meant Karlich couldn't see how they were faring. He cursed the Middenlanders all the same for having left his own regiment vulnerable, goaded by the promise of glory denied them at the Brigund Bridge. He only regretted he wouldn't get to pay them back for their dissension.

Just as Karlich was preparing to make a last stand, to be reunited with his wife and daughter in Morr's afterlife, the pressure on the flank lifted. Looking out the corner of his eye for as long as he dared, he saw the telltale black and red of Carroburg.

Sigmar bless his blade, von Rauken had come to their aid.

With greatsworders cleaving into them mercilessly from behind and the halberdiers giving them hell from the front, the goblin Wolf Riders scattered and fled. The few that weren't slain in the retreat barrelled southward for the Black Mountains. Karlich fancied even Grom could not get them to turn, so badly had the Carroburg Few mauled them.

The goblin horde fighting to the Grimblades' front capitulated soon after. Worn down by Vanhans on one side, and the greatsworders on the other, Karlich and his men were at last able to overwhelm them and put the creatures to flight.

Several still lived, eighty or more goblins from the same tribe, but their will was broken. Their retreat left a short spurt of open ground before them. Karlich used the time marching into it to catch a breath and share a word with von Rauken.

'A good time to repay a debt of honour,' he said.

The greatsworder champion merely grinned, showing a lost tooth.

'There's more blood to be shed still. Don't thank us yet,' growled the Carroburger.

Karlich's reply was arrested by the storm cracking above. He looked up and saw the Celestial wizard and the shaman duelling inside a massive thunderhead. Lit from behind by lightning, they appeared as frozen silhouettes. Every flash revealed a new vista, as if held in transparent amber, only for it to fade and reappear a moment later in a different duelling pose. Wizard and shaman were just ephemeral shadows painted on the underside of clouds, so high, so far away. It was impossible to tell who was winning.

Respite was brief. More orcs and goblins were coming.

Karlich cast a glance over his shoulder. Smoke was wreathing the embankment, spilling down onto the battlefield in a creeping, grey veil. Something was happening up there but he couldn't tell what. From the sound of the explosion he heard earlier, it couldn't be good. Peering through the smog he noticed that the back line had moved up and a good hundred feet or so now separated them. In the tight confines of the battlefield ahead, it felt like a gulf.

Gaps were forming in the battle. Whereas before it was clogged without room to manoeuvre, fleeing regiments and mobs had pulled at both armies. Formations and battle lines were breaking down. Together with the natural ebb and flow of combat, discrete masses were slowly emerging. A regiment from Grünburg and another from Streissen fought a savage orc mob and a horde of forest goblins. A stolid wedge of halberdiers struggled against a smaller band of trolls, their numbers dwindling. A force of pike and swordsmen clashed with a grunting tribe of orc boar riders, keeping the beasts at bay with a wall of shields and polearms. Each fought their own personal battle. Suddenly the wider war had become less important and immediate than merely living out the next minute.

Stahler knew how to read an engagement as easily as he discerned the palm of his own hand. The struggle for Averheim was reaching a crucial stage.

Between the fighting, patches of open ground strangled with the dead and dying were revealed. Like pulling back a dirty curtain, broken blades and shields, bloodied leather and mail was found cluttering the earth like scrap. From every struggle, fresh horrors emerged from underfoot as man and orc jostled for superiority.

The Imperial infantry was pressing ahead. Stahler knew it was important to maintain momentum, especially with such a large army arrayed against them, but he was weary about leaving the rear line and their support so far behind. Soon the men would tire too. Nothing could be worse than being stranded beyond help, surrounded by foes and with a heavy sword arm. They had to press on, though. If they could hold, even break through to Averheim, then the two armies would surely crush the greenskins. Perhaps the war could be won here after all.

Don't get ahead of yourself, old man. Damn fine way to get killed.

A wry smile turned to a grimace on Stahler's face when a jab of pain shot up his arm and side. Clutching his chest, he gasped. It was like breathing piping hot cinders. A clatter of metal announced he'd dropped his sword. Stahler watched it hit the ground. Sagging in the saddle, he almost followed it. Seizing the reins with his other hand, he tried to hold on.

Can't... see me... like this; even the voice in his head sounded agonised. He needed to get up. He thought about reaching for his blade.

Forget it, there's no way.

Stahler realised if he dismounted or leaned down to retrieve it, he might never get back up again.

'Merciful Shallya,' he rasped. The sound was wet and ragged. Stahler tasted copper in his mouth.

Darkness blinded him for a split second before he blinked it away. Tremors of mild panic went with it. The soldiers' backs were still hazy. It might have been because of the smoke. He wasn't sure.

Blackpowder smoke was creeping down the embankment. It swept the field in a dark grey fog from the constant discharge of harquebus, mortar and cannon. The rear echelons of the army were smothered and it was slowly layering the entire plain. Still groggy but mastering the pain, Stahler saw a scattered band of goblins approaching him through the murk. Some of the greenskin mobs had overshot or been left behind in the massive push by the Imperial infantry. Crossbowmen and handgunners were picking them off with isolated *clacks* of their weapons, but some were still getting through. Most of the greenskin remnants fled but some were prowling the dead and dying, stealing and murdering as they went. They wouldn't tackle a regiment, but a lone rider would be fair game.

Stahler realised abruptly that he was separated from the line, in a sort of grey no-man's-land. Mist and gunsmoke coalesced into a dark fug that made it hard to see. The goblins were coming for him. He sneered, annoyed with himself.

Easy meat.

Stahler drew a pistol from his belt. He had already dropped his shield when he went for the reins. With both hands free, he wrenched a short sword from its scabbard on his steed's barded flank.

Something told him he was dying, that the wound he'd received at Blösstadt was mortal, only he hadn't known it. Until now.

By the gods, he'd take some more of the bastards with him before he fell.

Six against one.

The first of the goblins emerged from the smoke and mist, its pointy nose cutting through it like a knife.

Stahler levelled his pistol and fired.

Make that five.

Kogswald was dead. Bludgeoned by a huge iron ball, the spikes upon it had ripped his armour apart. The preceptor was lying on his slain horse with a chain wrapped around his crushed neck and torso. He hadn't even lifted his sword. It was an ignoble end for a noble warrior.

Several other knights, both Griffonkorps and Order of the Fiery Comet, joined him in grim repose. Their limbs were twisted, tangled together with one another and their horses, mashed beyond recognition by the deadly goblin weapons.

Cavalry killers. Wilhelm had heard of goblin fanatics before. Intoxicated on cave fungus, they were insane and utterly immune to fear and doubt. He had never fought against them, though.

'Ride through!' urged the prince. What was left of the knights charged on. Babbled hooting from the whirling goblins assailed them through their battle-helms as they thundered past.

In the frantic dash to escape, Wilhelm noticed one of the demented greenskins spin off wildly and into a patch of rock. It left a messy stain against the grey stone as it died. Another collided with one of its comrades and the two wrapped around each other in a fatal embrace. A fourth ran out of fervour and collapsed, its overworked heart giving out convulsively.

That left only two. The gauntlet was at least now runnable. Hot air whipped past the prince's face, displaced by a heavy ball and chain. Shards of debris carried along in its wake stung at his skin. He resisted the temptation to lash out. If he did, he'd lose his arm to one swing of the deadly weapon.

Despite the damage inflicted by the fanatics, Wilhelm and his charges cut through the night goblins that had harboured the fanatics with relative ease. Ploughing through the greenskin ranks was akin to butchery, not battle. By the time they'd reached the other side, the knights were less than half their original strength. Around fifty remained and even they were bruised and battered. Cracking flintlocks erupted from the few surviving pistoliers. Tiny plumes of blackpowder smoke erupted from their firearms before the last of the fanatics were shot and killed.

Relieved, Wilhelm turned to look at Kogswald. Lifting his visor, he gasped for breath. He'd known the man all of his life. He'd been his retainer and protector for almost thirty years. The sight of him so cruelly slain, bereft of glory, was almost too much.

'He's gone,' Ledner's snake-rasp banished the prince's nostalgia. Nothing could be done for the preceptor. Ledner's pragmatism outweighed sentiment every time. There was no love lost between the two men. Neither, to their credit, had pretended otherwise. But Ledner recognised the great shame in what had happened to his sparring partner.

Ledner was wounded too. He held his reins gingerly with one hand, the other clutching his sword. His arm was either twisted or broken, possibly at the shoulder. Ledner didn't let it show, despite his bloodied face. A cut above his right eye drooled gorily, but he was defiant as ever.

When the prince didn't reply, Ledner rode up alongside him and leaned in close so he could whisper. 'Marshal your knights!' he hissed between clenched teeth.

They'd stalled a little, the impetus of their charge faltering once free and clear of the night goblins. 'They need you to lead them. Do it!'

As if waking from a dream, Wilhelm came around. The knights were milling around, lacking in purpose. The prince reined his horse about, facing the enemy ahead. The briefest of nods in Ledner's direction acknowledged the service he'd just performed for his master.

'Onward,' cried Wilhelm, raising his sword. 'The gates of Averheim are close. We're nearly there. For Kogswald and our slain brothers!'

The knights cheered, though it was a dark and vengeful cry. Even in the face of death, their spirit was indomitable. It was what made them better than ordinary men.

Under fifty knights, just two and a half lances, to take the gate and release the Averheim army – Wilhelm had Sigmar's name upon his lips as they charged again.

His steed had saved his life, or at least prolonged it for another, perhaps more peaceful death. Unlike most soldiers, Stahler had no wish to die on the battlefield. It was a lonesome, depressing place. Death and death alone belonged there, not glory. He wanted to meet his end in the arms of a beautiful woman; or in a tavern, surrounded by friends and comrades; or old aged before a slow burning hearth, a smouldering pipe in his hand and a contented smile on his face that said: I'm ready now, I've lived.

Even as his warhorse had staved in the skull of the last goblin, the other four dispatched between them, Stahler knew that was not his fate. He'd die here in the mire, alone yet surrounded by his men. As if to punish him for his killing efforts, the pain in Stahler's arm and side returned. He stifled a cry. The tears in his eyes were from agony, not anguish.

Stay alive, he kept repeating to himself. Stay alive and make it count for something.

The rain brought him around. It *tinkled* against his armour. Rivulets inveigled their way down his back, chilling him. The effect was mildly reviving. It wasn't to last.

Only shortly after it had begun, the rainstorm stopped abruptly. The clouds persisted but they no longer shed their tears. Mist followed in its wake, rising swiftly like an ethereal tide, smothering the battlefield. The smoke from the hillside rolled into it, turning it into dense smog.

He'd experienced foggy nights in Altdorf, the mist creeping off the Reik, when you could only just see the hand before your face, where visibility had been better than this. The battle had just become many times more treacherous.

It was as the grey smog clawed its way across the plain that everything began to go wrong.

An almighty flash ignited the heavens just as the Grimblades were about to engage yet another greenskin mob. Something plummeted from the sky, blazing like a falling comet.

Whether it was denial or the simple fact of distance, it took Karlich a few seconds to realise it was Sirrius Cloudcaller.

Blacktooth had won. The Celestial wizard was dead.

A bizarre after-flare was frozen against Karlich's eye. As he blinked he again saw Sirrius etched upon the clouds in agonised silhouette.

'Fight on, fight on for the Empire!' Von Rauken had seen it too and was doing his best to rally them.

Without the wizard… Karlich dare not contemplate further. The crash of blades was coming fast, so he bellowed as hard as his lungs would allow and lost himself to the madness.

Wilhelm's knights were riding at the orcs' backs now. Charging along the rear of the greenskins engaged with the Empire troops, it was tempting to wheel off and gut a mob from behind. Wilhelm felt sure even the hardest orcs would crumple beneath their lances and their righteous anger. Part of him wanted to, needed to, vent his frustration at the death of noble Kogswald. It would be an outpouring of grief. Averheim demanded his attention, though. He would be its saviour. He would save the Empire and take Dieter to account for his lassitude, feathering his nest as he brokered deals with greedy Marienburgers and the rest of the Empire burned. It made the prince's blood hot that an Emperor could abandon his lands to despoliation. If he survived this, there would a reckoning. All the mercenaries and sell-swords in Tilea couldn't prevent it.

With thoughts of vengeance plaguing his mind, the prince failed to notice the shadow in the clouds growing above them. It wasn't until Ledner cried out, an oddly strangled shriek due to his old neck wound, that Wilhelm knew of the danger in their midst.

'My lord, get down!' Ledner threw himself at the prince, leaping off his own steed to do it. The two men slammed into the earth and rolled as something large and scaly raked overhead, a pair of screaming knights gripped in its clutches. It was a miracle they weren't killed or seriously injured in the fall. Several more knights were scattered across the ground, their bodies and their horses broken. Trying to heave the air back into his chest, the ache of sudden bruises from the fall muddying his senses, Wilhelm looked into the sky and saw the wyvern turn. It tossed a dangling figure from its mouth as it dove for them.

The prince rose unsteadily before Ledner tackled him again, grunting as he jarred his injured arm. Warm air and the foetid stink of the beast washed over them. Ledner yelped in pain as a talon clipped him, tearing a bloody gash in his wounded shoulder.

'It wants you,' he snarled from the agony. 'Get your wits first then face it.'

He rolled off from where he'd pinned the prince. Wilhelm nodded curtly, found his breath at last and got to his feet.

The wyvern was circling around for another pass. The shaman on its back cackled wildly, enjoying the spectacle.

Dragon Tooth was in the prince's hand as he took up a swordfighting stance. Since he'd been a boy, Kogswald had taught him how to fight. As the wyvern knifed through the clouds at him, Wilhelm recalled a lesson where the preceptor had tutored him in the art of engaging a horseman on foot. It required balance and timing. The prince adopted those sage tactics now.

'See this blade,' he muttered to the beast as it grew in his eye line, 'do you remember it?' They were just moments away from impact. 'It remembers you...'

Dragon Tooth caught an errant shaft of sunlight and flashed in agreement.

The sunlight died when the wyvern eclipsed it, hurtling at Wilhelm like a thrown spear but with all the force of a battering ram. Its eyes glinted like malevolent rubies, its claws and fangs promised gruesome death. Saliva drizzled from its open mouth as the beast savoured the scent of royal flesh.

Purge your mind of all doubt. You and your blade are as one. Kogswald was with him again, only fifteen years ago.

The rising mist swept up in front of the beast, masking it from sight. Wilhelm closed his eyes until the beat of its wings nearly deafened him, then he pivoted his body aside in a wide arc and lashed out with *Dragon Tooth*.

He was buffeted hard by the wyvern's bulk as it arrowed past him. A ribbon of heat opened up in his thigh and he realised it had cut him. Almost simultaneously he felt the enchanted blade dragging through hide and flesh, eliciting a bestial screech of agony.

Dragon Tooth hissed and spat as the wyvern's blood touched the blade as if whispering a curse. The wound went deep. Wilhelm knew it by instinct. Dizzy, one hand clutching his injured leg, he turned in time to see the wyvern careening off into the distance. The membrane from its right wing hung like a ragged sail. It made the beast flail in the air like a stricken ship on invisible waves. Blood threaded the earth like a red, throbbing vein from where Wilhelm had cut the wyvern to a furrow in the ground where it eventually pitched. It wasn't dead, a terrible mewling sound reverberated from its nose, but it was down and so was the shaman.

'Nicely done, my lord,' said Ledner running up beside him. Even he couldn't hide his awe at what the prince had just done.

Wilhelm was breathless with effort. 'It's a little different with horses.'

Ledner didn't know what he meant, so ignored the comment. 'Can you walk?'

The prince nodded.

'Then you can ride.' Ledner turned and hailed two of the knights.

Wilhelm paled. They numbered less than twenty. Some were injured and would never fight again. Many were dead. The wyvern's monstrous strength was awesome to behold.

Across the plain towards Averheim, whose hopes were fading like a candle at the end of its wick, several bulky shadows were plunging through the mist. The grey veil was thinnest near the city, without the powder smoke to pollute it, and Wilhelm made out a squadron of chariots heading towards them.

When the two knights reached Ledner they dismounted.

'Here, my lord,' Ledner invited.

Wilhelm frowned. 'Where is my steed?'

'Dead. Now take the saddle.'

Ledner helped the prince up and then mounted the other horse.

'Come, my lord,' he said, reining his borrowed horse towards the Imperial line. 'There's little time.'

'What are you doing?' Wilhelm didn't bother to hide his anger. 'Averheim–'

'Is lost,' snapped Ledner, 'and so will we be if we delay further. This way, my lord. The knights will cover our retreat.'

'Sacrifice their lives you mean.'

'If that makes you follow me now, then yes, they will. Don't let it be in vain.'

The proud remnants of the Griffonkorps and the Order of the Fiery Comet aligned their steeds in a long fighting line. Many had lost their lances. A lone survivor of the pistoliers mixed in with their ranks, a templar in all but name for his bravery. Those on foot stood either side of the horses. Some men were praying. More than one kissed the blade of his sword and showed it to the heavens. The shaft of sunlight that had lit up *Dragon Tooth* returned to bathe them briefly in its lustre but then was gone.

Wilhelm made to ride up alongside them, but Ledner snatched his reins and stopped him.

The chariots were closing all the while. They'd been held in reserve for this very purpose. Grom was as wily as he was obese.

'You are the prince of Reikland. You must not fall!'

Ledner's anger shook Wilhelm into understanding. His defiance crumpled into an expression of profound sadness.

'Sigmar be with you…' he murmured to the knights. He nodded slowly, almost imperceptibly, before he and Ledner rode for the Imperial line as if all the hounds of Chaos were at their heels.

It was over. Wilhelm had failed.

CHAPTER TWENTY

The better part of valour

Outside Averheim, capital city of Averland,
483 miles from Altdorf

The sight of Wilhelm quitting the field sent shockwaves through the rest of the army. They couldn't reach Averheim and free the elector count's army. A full retreat was ordered almost immediately. The orcs fighting the Grimblades seemed to sense the sudden weakness. It intensified their strength and with the burly greenskins pressing hard against them the halberdiers gave and broke.

Somewhere between running and shouting orders, Karlich fell. The damned smog was everywhere, choking the plain in a charcoal shroud. It was a curse and a blessing. For some, it meant they could retreat without fear of pursuit; for others, it meant getting lost in the darkness and stumbling into the enemy, or worse, the blades of their own panicked kinsmen.

Panic was the only way to describe it. Monsters lived in the mist and smog, some real, some imagined. Their grunting bootsteps thudded behind… or was it in front? Their snorting rage was omnipresent.

Karlich didn't know how far they'd already run. He went to get up when he was kicked in the stomach and fell down again. It wasn't a greenskin. The immediate view was hazy, but he thought he saw an Imperial uniform disappearing eerily away from him. He was suddenly disorientated. Perspective and direction lost all meaning in the smog.

He tried to rise again, this time managing to get to his feet and realised he was alone. Something came at him swiftly from the murk. He gutted it on his blade, belatedly glad it was a goblin. The greenskins too were running scared. Though entirely natural, the smog had taken on an eldritch quality. Snaps of harquebuses were muffled by it. Karlich thought he saw the vague blossom of their flaring flintlocks as the hand-gunners fired, and headed for them.

His sword wouldn't move. Karlich wrenched at it but it wouldn't give. It was stuck fast in the dead goblin's body. With no time to pull it free, he left it. He didn't know what had happened to the other Grimblades but, with only his dirk to protect him, hoped they were close. One moment they had been running together, trying to maintain some form of good order, the next he was tumbling into the hard earth and all was grey and dark around him.

He thought about shouting out for his comrades, but decided against it. There might be more greenskins, bigger ones, lurking in the smog and he didn't want to risk attracting them.

Warily, he trudged towards the flare of guns. He remembered it was only about a hundred feet to the rear line and safety.

It might as well have been a hundred miles.

The going was slow. Littered with fallen blades and the dead and dying, the ground was treacherous. Karlich saw the shadow of an Empire soldier rushing blindly through the smog and impaling himself on a discarded spear jutting from the earth. The poor sod gurgled once and then died. It was only when Karlich saw the hulking silhouettes drifting ahead of him, too large and broad-backed to be men, that he realised he was really in trouble.

In their eagerness to chase down their defeated enemy, some of the orcs had got in front of him. Briefly fixated on the orcs, he heard the light thud of charging feet too late.

Karlich turned, just as a black-swathed figure rammed into him. He gasped as the air was smashed from his lungs. The sergeant kicked out and was greeted with a satisfying grunt of pain. Despite the fact he was gagging for breath, he tried to shove the body off him but his arm was pinned beneath what felt like his attacker's knee. The scuffle came in flashes – a whipping cloak, black but dirty with caked mud; a silver talisman, gleaming and forbidding; the snarling face of a man he feared but barely knew. Vanhans straddled Karlich, locking his arms with his knees, and seized the sergeant's neck in both hands.

'Murdering heretic,' he snarled, his venting spittle wetting Karlich's cheek.

Karlich jarred a knee into Vanhans's back and he relented enough for the Reiklander to take a breath.

'What are you talking about, maniac?' he hissed through clenched teeth before the witch hunter reasserted his position but this time pushed the flat of his hand under Karlich's chin.

'Lothar Henniker,' he said. 'You know.'

And he *did* know. Vanhans had just used Karlich's real name.

He couldn't have known. There was no way, despite the fact they had later fought together, that Karlich could have realised the crazed butcher who had burned down Rechts's village and condemned its inhabitants to death would visit Karlich years later. The madman's name was Grelle the Confessor, a self-proclaimed title, and he was the worst of the Order of Sigmar's chaff. Death warrants were issued without cause, businesses and homes were put to the torch, innocents dangled from the noose. All of it served Grelle's paranoid fixation with purity and what he believed was a Sigmar-given duty to rid the world of the wretched and the unclean.

Grelle was the worst kind of charlatan: one who didn't know it. Karlich, then Lothar, had turned a blind eye at first, hoping that the witch hunter and his retinue would soon leave. He resented him for the burnings and the deaths, but so long as it didn't touch him or his family, he would keep his peace. Who knows, perhaps the victims of Grelle's purgings were not victims at all? Perhaps they really were heretics? That was the mentality of fear talking, the desire to avoid persecution through acceptance, no matter how abhorrent. Lothar only realised this later and to his cost.

It all changed when his wife, Helena... *my beautiful Helena*... cured an old man's sickness with a herbal panacea. It was nothing more than alleviating the symptoms of a cough but Grelle saw only witchery in her selfless deeds. When Lothar was out gathering wood for the fire, the witch hunter and his cronies took his wife and daughter... *oh, Sigmar, not Isobel*... from their home and burned them both as witches.

Lothar had seen smoke issuing from the village square and wondered why they'd lit a bonfire. A moment later he was running, the gathered firewood scattered in his wake. To that very day, Karlich couldn't explain where the sense of urgency that filled him came from but he had never run harder in his life, nor since.

Entering through the village gates, he inhaled the stench of burning meat. The fat sizzled and crackled in his ears like cruel laughter. It was too late for Helena, too late for his daughter. Battering his way through the jeering crowds, Lothar ripped at the fire-wreathed pyre, burning himself badly in the process. Rough hands seized him by the shoulders and he was hoisted off his knees where he wept and scrabbled at the smoking wood.

Two of Grelle's henchmen held him before their master.

'Conspirator!' Grelle denounced. 'Warlock!' he accused. The witch hunter's face was partially hidden behind a cage-like helmet, his skin a patchwork of self-inflicted scars. He wore little more than leather and rags. His calloused feet and hands were bare. The stink of urine and stale sweat emanated off Grelle in a pall. His breath was redolent of dung. *This* was the wretched creature that had executed his beloved family.

Lothar snapped. He cried out with such anguish and apoplexy it was as if his heart were breaking.

Throwing off the minions, Lothar threw himself at the witch hunter. A charred log had rolled off the pyre and into the village square. He seized it and battered Grelle until his cage-helm was staved in and split his ugly visage. The henchmen, nothing more than bullies motivated by persecuting the weak and credulous, stood back in shock as Lothar brutalised their master. Even the rabid onlookers had lost their fervour. Stunned into abject silence, they could only watch.

Grelle mewled in pain and self pity but Lothar pounded relentlessly through the man's pleading. Red rimmed his vision. When the log finally broke, he cast it aside and shoved Grelle's face into the wet mud. It had been raining since dawn, though not enough to quench the fires that had so cruelly robbed Lothar of his family. The witch hunter suffocated in the mud. His thrashing protests didn't last.

Only when it was over did Lothar realise what he had done. His hands were bloody. His wife and child were nought but blackened corpses. Lothar fled, there and then, out into the forest. He'd killed a Templar of Sigmar. Others would come looking for him. Stay and he condemned everyone around him. More would die needlessly. That day Lothar Henniker died too. Feder Karlich was born in his stead.

But now his old life had returned, like an exhumed corpse. The buzzing of its flies, the stink of putrefaction gave him away. He'd been careful, leaving only a shadow of his former existence, but even shadows can be caught if they spend too long near the light.

The present rushed back to the sound of heavy guns. Meinstadt was firing the cannons held in reserve. The artillery was meant to pave the Empire army's retreat, but it was more treacherous than being surrounded by orcs. A gout of earth exploded nearby, showering the struggling men with dirt. Karlich and Vanhans were in no-man's-land, where the dead would soon linger.

'You'll kill us both,' Karlich snarled, finding it difficult to speak with the witch hunter's iron-hard palm pressing against his chin.

Either Vanhans wasn't listening or he didn't care.

'Lothar Henniker,' he declared, 'I accuse you of heretical murder and consorting with witches most foul.' He reached for something with his free hand and pushed it against Karlich's cheek.

The sergeant screamed as red-hot iron seared his face.

'See how the non-believer burns!'

Vanhans was drunk with his ravings. He'd heated his talisman in one of the many fires around the battlefield, using it to convince himself of his own deluded mania.

The thunderous retort of great cannon was getting louder.

Vanhans tore the icon away, wrenching melted skin from Karlich's face with it.

'I name you daemon, skulking in the guise of man. The order will have vengeance, Sigmar demand–'

Something hot and wet rained on Karlich's face. At the same time he smelled warm iron and felt the passage of a large object soar overhead. The pressure at his chin lessened abruptly, enabling him to look down.

Vanhans was dead. He'd been beheaded by a stray cannon ball. The bounce had taken off his skull at the chin. Lolling macabrely for a few seconds, his corpse collapsed, the Sigmarite icon still clenched in his fist. Rigor mortis would make it hard to reclaim later.

Overcoming the shock, acutely aware that Meinstadt's cannonade went on unabated, Karlich shoved off the witch hunter's body and staggered to his feet. A cannon ball whined past him nearby and he cowered for a moment before ploughing towards the flash of harquebuses again.

Shadows loomed in the smog, the orcs he had noticed earlier. Now they noticed him too, drawn by Vanhans's ravings. They had his scent and grunted in anticipation of the kill.

There were only two of them.

Unarmed, it was one more than needed to kill Karlich. He'd lost his dirk in the scuffle.

Fleeing was suicide. The greenskins were behind him and now they were in front of him, too. Something glinted nearby in the smog, catching what little light penetrated the gloom. Karlich reached for it, even as the pair of orcs closed, and his fingers gripped the hilt of a sword. It was Stahler's. He recognised the rune on the blade. Without time to wonder what had happened to his captain, Karlich took up a fighting stance.

A fight it was then.

He'd need to make it quick. Despite the smog, the rest of the greenskin army couldn't be far behind. Even deterred by the cannonade, some would still get through.

The first lunged through the grey gloom, its silhouette resolving into an ugly visage of tusks and raw aggression. Karlich let it come, ducking its clumsy swipe and slicing it along the belly. Armour and flesh parted easily and the beast was disembowelled in a single cut. The second went to cleave off Karlich's head but stopped mid-swing when it found a blade transfixed through its beady, red eye. Drooling blood, the orc collapsed a moment later.

Karlich marvelled briefly at whatever craft had wrought the runeblade. Truly, there was power in the world of which he had no comprehension.

Another explosion tinged the grey smog a fiery orange, spitting hot earth and shrapnel in a deadly cloud. Marvel or not, the runeblade wouldn't stop him from being slain by a cannon ball. Karlich needed to get out of no-man's-land, but he was like a ship without a compass. His bearings, despite the muffled din and flare of harquebus, were off. Salvation came from an unlikely quarter.

'Sergeant Karlich! Sergeant Karlich!'

He heard Lenkmann's voice before he saw him and the Grimblades' banner. It fluttered like a beacon in the smog. Hazy and indistinct, yes, but imposing enough to be visible from a longer distance. Karlich made for it at once.

Lenkmann wasn't alone. He had Volker with him.

'Though you were dead,' the Reikland huntsman hugged his sergeant warmly, who looked awkward at the gesture. 'Sorry, sir,' he added afterwards.

Karlich smiled. 'Forgotten,' he replied. 'Where's the battleline?'

Lenkmann looked to Volker, who frowned and looked around in the smog.

'Volker?' asked the banner bearer.

'We're close,' he said. 'Hard to get a strong trail in all this smoke.'

Cannon balls and the dense impacts of mortar shells resonated around them with growing regularity.

'Can't we just go back?' asked Karlich. 'How did you find me?'

Lenkmann shrugged. 'Blind luck. I heard someone speaking through the mist and then I heard what sounded like your voice, too, sir. I followed it. Volker came with me.' He glared at the huntsman who stayed close but was becoming indistinct in the mist with every foot that he trailed a route back. 'The idea was for him to guide us back.'

'Stop moaning, Lenkmann,' Volker replied. 'Must've got turned around. If Dog was alive...' he muttered the last part.

Nearby, they could hear more greenskins closing.

'Whisper!' Karlich hissed. 'We don't want that filth finding us in all this bloody smog. If only there were–' the sergeant stopped abruptly when he saw another shadow heading for them in the gloom.

'Captain Stahler?'

It was hard to see for sure, but the figure wore Imperial trappings synonymous with Karlich's captain and nodded. Keeping his distance, he beckoned them to follow him.

'This way,' Karlich said to the others. He made off after Stahler. 'Captain,' he added, brandishing the runeblade before him. 'I found your sword.'

Stahler's response was to plough on through the fog and smoke, always a few feet again, just barely discernible.

It wasn't long before the grey veil receded and the rugged shape of the embankment began to form. Sporadic explosions illuminated it in grainy white light, banishing the darkness briefly before it reigned again.

The heavy report of the volley gun was intense and devastating. Karlich had never seen one used in battle before. It fired with a *crank-choom, crank-choom* cadence, spitting out tongues of flame with every shot.

As they were emerging from the smog, Karlich realised he'd lost sight of Captain Stahler. His attention had lapsed for only a few seconds, drawn by the spectacle of the guns.

'Where is he?'

'Where's who?' asked Volker.

Karlich fixed him with an angry glare. 'Now isn't the time. Stahler, where is the captain? I just saw him a moment ago. He led us out of the killing field.'

Lenkmann was shaking his head. 'It was just the three of us. I thought you had found a route through the smog...' The banner bearer paled a little and looked as if he were about to vomit.

The sight of Masbrecht, Brand and Greiss running towards them prevented Karlich's immediate reply.

'Sigmar's blood, it's good to see you, sergeant.' Masbrecht clapped Karlich on the shoulder and nodded to the others.

'We very nearly didn't make it back at all,' said Volker.

They walked and talked. The rest of the Grimblades were just beyond the embankment with the rest of the Empire army. They were pulling back the entire force.

'Wilhelm's retreating,' said Brand flatly. 'The greenskins have won. So how did you get back?'

Lenkmann's eyes were hooded and he looked down.

'The sergeant found a way,' said Volker.

'And I thought you were the scout,' offered Greiss with a grin.

Volker gave him a stern look but in mild jest.

Much of the urgency surrounding the withdrawal had subsided. The spiked palisades were lowered over the abatis-filled trench, spanning them for the retreating regiments to cross. At least Wilhelm's escape plan was proving successful. The cannonade combined with the confusion of the smog had dissuaded all but the dumbest or most bloodthirsty greenskins from pursuit. The few that did make it through were soon cut down and those numbers dwindled by the minute.

Over the hill, past the slowly reforming lines of handgunners and crossbowmen, there was a scene of mass upheaval. Captains and sergeants bellowed for order, shifting banners hither and thither in an effort to achieve some kind of cohesion in the ranks. Many soldiers had been separated in the rout, those who lived were only just returning to their regiments. Horns and drums were beating in a cacophony. Runners ferried messages back and forth with frantic gusto. Waggoneers and drovers laid carts with remaining supplies. Some of the baggage train carried the dead and wounded. Hundreds would have to be left in the smog for the greenskins to eat and butcher. No one spoke of it.

Slowly, laboriously, a line of march began to form. Wilhelm was seen near the front, at a distance, marshalling his officers. The cadre had thinned distinctly since the battle. Ledner was alive, much to Karlich's disappointment. He was exchanging words with Captain Vogen, about halfway up the line. Instructions from the prince, no doubt.

Journeymen in teams of five and six hurried past Karlich and the others, bound for the war machines. The last of the army was packing up and readying to move to Sigmar only knew where. Defeat at Averheim was not fully countenanced, it seemed to the sergeant. What happened next was anyone's guess.

Karlich surveyed the milling crowds as Lenkmann led them back to the rest of the Grimblades.

'Where is Captain Stahler?' asked the sergeant. 'I want to return his sword.'

Brand looked over his shoulder. His face was cold like an iron mask.

'It's yours now, sir,' he said in all seriousness.

Karlich frowned.

As they neared the regiment he noticed a sullen-looking wagon with a bodyguard of six silent Griffonkorps, last survivors of the goblin fanatics. Three bodies were lying on it, partially covered by red blankets with gilded trim. They looked like the dead warriors' cloaks. One face was visible, the other two were shrouded.

It was Masbrecht who spoke. His tone was sombre and sepulchral. 'Captain Stahler is dead. Someone found him on his horse. His body had no fresh injuries. It was like he'd just died.'

Karlich tore his eyes off the corpse as a priest of Morr driving the wagon covered its face.

Somewhere behind the sergeant, Lenkmann threw up.

CHAPTER TWENTY-ONE

The long retreat

*Beyond the Stirland border, Stirland,
433 miles from Altdorf*

Averland was no longer deemed safe. Harried all the way by warbands from Grom's army, Wilhelm led his troops north across the border and into Stirland. Here in peasant country, the lay of the land was no better. As in Averland, villages and towns were burning. Some of the smaller hamlets were little more than ashen husks; Grom had made bonfires out of them. Doomsayers and refugees littered the province like disconsolate sheep.

Whereas Averland was largely flat and wealthy, Stirland was rugged and poor. To the east was Sylvania, a shadow of a land that lingered like a dirty secret everyone already knew. The von Carsteins had once ruled over it, a house of aristocratic fiends whose last scion had fallen to Count Martin's runefang. Strangely, in the vampires' absence, it was even more a haunted place of which few Stirlanders spoke and fewer still ventured. As for Stirland itself, it was hilly and the last tranches of the Great Forest crept over its northernmost reaches as if to colonise it with its forbidding arbours. Rural, down to earth, Stirland's people were slow to change and quick to cast suspicion, especially on outsiders. It made for a bleak and unwelcoming vista as the army crossed the border, most of its watchtowers already smoking ruins.

On the third day of the march, armed outriders approached the column. They rode black mares that matched the colour of their hair, and carried harquebus and bows. Most of the riders wore dark caps of Stirland green. Their leather hauberks, hose and tassets were grimy. A quick parley with the leader of the fifty-strong group, a dirty-faced sergeant with an eye-patch and a dark beard, went down the line in short order. Wurtbad was the nearest, possibly the only, safe city in the province.

Despite the obvious provincial differences, Wilhelm was still a prince of the Empire and as such the Stirland outriders insisted on escorting him to their capital. Faster riders, without armour and carrying dirks, were sent ahead to bring advance word to Lord Protector Krieglitz.

All being well, the Reiklanders and their guides would reach Wurtbad in two days.

Wurtbad was not like Altdorf. Nor did it resemble Averheim. To the rest of the Empire, these were magnificent cities, shining testimonies to the achievements of man. Wurtbad, despite its bustling trade, its markets and its white walls, was a grim place. The mood was hardly helped by the greenskin hordes rampaging not so far from its border. They'd sent flocks of refugees before them, like cattle chased by the drover's whip. Rustic, backward and generally unwashed, they lent an air of bigotry and superstition that the count would rather leave in his hinterlands, not confront on his doorstep.

Karlich scowled back at a native Stirlander who was passing by in the near-deserted street. Though Lord Protector Krieglitz had allowed the Reiklanders entry to his capital, the army was to be billeted outside in tents. Only Wilhelm and his entourage were permitted to lodge within its walls. Forays into town by small bands of the soldiery were allowed, however, in order to drink and forget their troubles, if only for a short time. Such 'excursions' went by rote, a few regiments at a time. Karlich and the Grimblades were currently enjoying their rotation in what was regarded 'the wine capital of the Empire'.

Good news for Rechts, he thought bitterly, and wondered if a drunken stupor would ease his pain.

The sheer scale of the defeat at Averheim was barely just setting in. Fighting for your life, even trudging down the Old Dwarf Road, ever fearful of greenskin attack, tended to occupy the mind. Now, in the quiet and the solitude, the dust had begun to settle. It smelled of the grave and itched with despair. Suicides had already been reported by several sergeants. Mercifully, desertion was scarce. It was mainly Averlanders, sneaking back across the border, wanting to meet the end in their own lands. Karlich couldn't blame them. He felt a long way from home.

In the aftermath, Wilhelm's quartermasters had taken a tally. The death-books were growing into quite a compendium. He'd lost a large body of troops at Averheim, together with nearly all the knights. Middenland had almost none of its original contingent.

It gave Karlich no pleasure that the Steel Swords had not returned from the plains. Even though they had left his Grimblades vulnerable to a flank attack and were, in no uncertain terms, the biggest whoresons he had ever met, Karlich could not bear a fallen soldier ill will. For all their faults, Sturnbled had led his men bravely, fighting in a war they didn't understand or believe in. They deserved to die in the land of Ulric with their forefathers, not in some foreign field.

True survivors that they were, the greatswords and von Rauken still lived, though 'Carroburg Fewer' might be a more appropriate name now. At his last count, Karlich gauged there were no more than ten of the greatswords left. They bore it all stoically, of course.

That left mainly citizen levies and those infantry regiments raised in Reikland townships and trained as professional soldiers. Then there were the few remaining Averlanders, dwindling by the day. It wasn't much.

Most of the war machines and engineers made the journey. Meinstadt was one of the few officers Karlich had met that was still breathing. Stahler was gone – it left a hole in his stomach and a chill down his back to think of it. Karlich pushed the memory of what he'd seen – *or had he?* – on the plains outside Averheim to the back of his mind. No good could come of digging there. Lenkmann had refused flat out to acknowledge it. To him, it never happened. The banner bearer was right at home with the superstitious Stirlanders. Of the rest, Hornstchaft was assumed slain in the initial charge, though his body remained unrecovered, and Preceptor Kogswald had met his end protecting the life of the prince, or so the propaganda went. Ironically, Blaselocker of Averland had died when the cannon misfired on the embankment. By seeking refuge behind the massive iron gun he had actually doomed himself. The demise of Father Untervash, Karlich had witnessed himself. The sight of the warrior priest being bitten in two still haunted his nightmares.

Thankfully no one had questioned the death of Vanhans. With the witch hunter gone, the funds from the temple dried up. Without coin, the mercenaries left the following morning. Most of Vanhans's faithful horde disbanded too with no shepherd to guide the fervent flock.

Karlich had the blood of two templars on his hands. Both were madmen to his mind. After the campaign, assuming he survived, he might have to move on again, lest the spectre of Lothar Henniker catch up with him.

Bleak. Yes, it was the only word Karlich could think of to describe their situation as he sat outside an inn with too few customers and sipped at hot ale.

'Apparently, it's the custom,' said a familiar voice behind him.

'Eh?'

Masbrecht came into view and gestured to the clay tankard Karlich was cradling.

'I've heard they use a poker from the fire to warm it.'

Karlich smacked his lips and scowled. He'd been holding the tankard so long, the heat had long since stopped emanating off it. 'Tastes like soot.'

There was a long pause. Masbrecht looked uneasy and rubbed his chin.

'Spit it out then,' said Karlich.

'Sir?'

'Whatever it is you've come to speak to me about, say it.' Karlich set his tankard down on the stumpy table beside him. The two men were alone.

'It's not right,' Masbrecht uttered simply.

'What isn't? The ale, the war, our defeat? There's much in the world that isn't right, Masbrecht. You'll need to narrow it down.'

Masbrecht barely moved. 'You know what I'm talking about.'

'Ah,' said Karlich, stretching his legs and pulling his pipe from his tunic pocket. '*That*.' The cup was already packed with tobacco. It was late, night was drawing in. Karlich leaned over to a candle stuck to the table with its own wax and coaxed his pipeweed to life.

'Are you really surprised we lost at Averheim?' Masbrecht continued. 'Even the greenskins can form an alliance. We are at each others' throats!'

'Hardly,' Karlich said through piping smoke. 'We've been left to our own protection, Masbrecht. There's a difference.'

'Someone within Wilhelm's camp, someone who could be *here*, now, wants our prince dead. How can you stand idly by and let it happen?' Masbrecht sat down next to Karlich. 'At Averheim, it was different. Surrounded by the army, the prince was safe. But here, now–'

'Ledner said he'd take care of it. We've done our part for prince and province.'

'You trust *him*?'

'Not as much as a goblin, but what other choice is there?'

Masbrecht's body language was beseeching. 'Let's tell the prince, warn him of the danger he's in.'

'We don't know he's in danger. The assassin's dead, remember.'

Masbrecht's expression darkened. 'Eber's blood was all over my hands and he's still not fit to fight. I remember well enough.'

'Look, I'm sorry. Morals are all fine and good but they're not always practical. If word got out...' Karlich sucked a breath in through his teeth. 'Well, let's just say the consequences could be ugly.'

'Or the culprits could be found and brought to justice,' said Masbrecht. 'The prince's reputation is reinforced and would-be betrayers will think twice before plotting against him. Moreover, we'd be rid of the traitors in our midst!' He was agitated, breathing hard. Karlich had seldom seen him so passionate about something other than religion. He saw it for what it really was though. Refutation. Disbelief.

That men could turn on their own, on someone as pure and noble as Prince Wilhelm, dented Masbrecht's faith. Belief in Sigmar was really all he had. Without it, he was a shadow. Karlich saw that now, just as he saw the look that flashed across Masbrecht's face when he'd regarded the cup of ale. It was *need*. The absence of one thing meant its replacement by another. Small wonder he was so puritanical about Rechts's drinking.

Karlich leaned forward and hissed: 'We stopped an assassination. I wouldn't say we rested on our laurels, Masbrecht. What more would you have us–'

The inn door slamming open interrupted him.

'What's he doing here?' a surly voice asked. It was Rechts, nursing his own hot ale, one of several he'd already imbibed by the look of him. 'I said I didn't want to drink alone, but I'd rather that than share ale with this naysayer. The mood is grim enough.'

'Drunkenness will do that to a man,' Masbrecht replied. Anger underpinned his voice. He was already in a pugnacious mood.

'Voice of experience, *brother*?' Now Rechts was goading him.

Karlich went to intercede but Masbrecht cut him off.

'Are you a heretic, Torsten, is that it?'

Karlich quickly got to his feet. 'That's enough!'

Rechts had just sat down and was about to get up again when Karlich pushed him back onto his stool. There was silence as the drummer gritted his teeth and rode out his anger.

'They were burned,' he said eventually. '*All* of them, my entire village.'

Masbrecht found he was wrong-footed. 'Wha–'

'A templar came to us, a servant of Sigmar, or so he claimed. A boy was found with a webbed toe. Fearful of mutation, the villagers took him before the witch hunter.' As darkness crept across the sky, the shadows pooling in Rechts's face made him look cadaverous. Too much drink and lack of proper sleep had worn the man down. As he spoke, it didn't appear to lessen his burden. 'I never saw the boy after that. Trials followed, then executions. Soon the trials were abandoned altogether and it was just about the burning. Our village preacher let him do it. His voice was loudest in the mob. I only survived because my mother hid me. When I came out, they were all dead. My mother, my whole family were ash. The witch hunter and his cronies had moved on. So, forgive me if I do not trust those that preach the word of Sigmar as readily as you do.'

Rechts stood up. Karlich let him, showing his palms in a gesture for the drummer to stay calm. He did. Until Masbrecht opened his mouth again.

'That boy could not have burned for no reason, he must–'

Rechts exploded. Spittle was flying from his mouth, 'Whim, brother. That was all. Whim and the will of a raving mad man, clad in Sigmar's cloth. Preaching fear and doubt, an entire village turned on itself. The hammer is not a death warrant, yet there are those who brandish it like one.' Rechts was clenching and unclenching his fists. The old pugnacity had returned. Karlich edged around the table so he could get between them if he needed to.

'*Reason!*' Rechts went on. 'Reason doesn't come into it. An innocent boy burned, an untainted village destroyed, all at the hand of our self-proclaimed protectors. Show me the reason in that.' In a much smaller voice, he added, 'I can still smell my mother's ash on my hands…'

Masbrecht was indignant. 'I still don't–' he began, Karlich already frowning and about to tell him to close his trap before Rechts interceded.

'Speak further and I'll cut out your tongue.' He'd ripped a dirk from its scabbard and held it levelly, especially considering he was well inebriated.

'Put it away, Torsten,' said Karlich in a firm voice. 'Trooper Rechts!' he added a moment later.

Rechts obeyed, looked at Masbrecht once more, who was paling a little by then, and left.

Karlich watched him wander off down the street. Come the morning, he'd send Volker to look for him. He turned to say something to Masbrecht but he was leaving too, heading in the opposite direction. That was something, at least. Karlich sat down, his bones never more weary. As he sipped at his tepid ale, he scowled.

'Definitely tastes like soot.'

CHAPTER TWENTY-TWO

Festering wounds

Wurtbad, capital of Stirland,
398 miles from Altdorf

Two concessions were made concerning the admittance of foreign troops into Wurtbad. The first allowed a few regiments at a time, no more than two hundred men, to spend a night in town away from the pitched encampment outside the border walls. The second instructed that all injured men in need of care beyond the skill of army chirurgeons would be housed under the auspices of the Temple of Shallya until such time as they could return to their regiment.

These hospitium were not merely found in the temple itself. The badly wounded and the dying were in such numbers that it would not have coped. Inns, stately abodes, barracks and even barns were given over to the ministration of the sick and ailing. Locals avoided such places; they were grim and unpleasant to look upon. The stench of necrosis and old rot made the air inside them rank and noisome. Wailing and moaning was a common, morale-eating chorus. Few soldiers emerged alive, let alone whole. Several of the town's sawbones had already earned tidy profits from the Prince of Reikland's coffers for their diligent labours over the gangrenous and diseased. Shallyan priestesses moved between sweaty cots with a tireless grace and brought blankets from the recently deceased for the newly admitted. Steamed over the hot springs which Wurtbad was famous for, the blankets were damp and reeked of latent death. Dingy, so as to hide the horror of it from their inmates and nurses, the hospitium maintained an air of the desolate and gladly forgotten.

Eber was one of the fortunate. He would live and escape with all his limbs. Strong as an ox, determined as an Ostland bull, his natural stamina and phlegmatic humour had seen him through the worst. Masbrecht had applied bandages expertly on the heath and likely saved the burly Reiklander a lot of blood, possibly even his life. The battlefield was still beyond him, but a few more days of healing and rest would see Eber take up his halberd again. He longed to be back amongst his brothers.

Sitting up in his cot, Eber bowed his head as a grey-faced priest of Morr drifted by. Cadaverous and silent within his black robes, he was more wraith than man. A quiet prayer of warding and the sign of the raven would have to keep the God of Death and Dreams at bay. At least, Eber hoped it would.

Once the priest was gone, off to perform the final rites of soul binding for some poor wretch, Eber looked around. It was almost smoky in the dim lantern light but his heart spiked painfully in his wounded chest when he saw someone he recognised just a few cots away from his.

Torveld was sitting over the edge of his cot wearing a blank expression. He was being attended by a Shallyan matriarch. Her robes were grimy and stained with blood but she still managed to look pure. She carried a candle, perfectly poised, in one hand. She was discussing Torveld's condition with one of the army's quartermasters, a slightly corpulent man who dabbed his forehead with a rag every few seconds and whose leather hauberk strained at the gut. Eber wondered how long before he was being ministered by the sisters of mercy. They spoke in low voices, but Eber still overheard them.

According to the matriarch, Torveld had lost his memory. Leastways, he had no recollection of the past few months. His head wound was well healed, though. Physically fine, he could return to his regiment and the campaign.

At this brief summary, the quartermaster nodded and went to a large book of parchments he had in his hand. Torveld was still wearing his bloodstained uniform and the quartermaster leafed through the broad pages laboriously. It was hard to see, but Eber made out heraldries, regimental markings and banner icons as the pages were turned. Having found what he sought, the quartermaster frowned.

His voice was a low murmur. Even though he couldn't hear it, Eber knew what was said: Torveld's regiment, the Middenland Steel Swords, were dead. He was the only survivor. The northerner appeared not to understand the import of the quartermaster's words. Eber imagined a mental shrug in the man's neutral demeanour.

'Well, he can't stay here in the temple,' said the matriarch. Her voice was soft but her message unyielding.

'It's a return to the army then, my lad,' the quartermaster addressed Torveld directly. 'There'll be a use for you there.'

Torveld was then led away by the quartermaster, a walking husk awaiting a soul to fill it. Confident whatever choleric intent the Middenlander
harboured was lost to amnesia, Eber eased back onto his cot. The pain
in his chest flared. His wounds were still raw. A gentle touch soothed
his shoulder. A priestess of Shallya calmly requested that he should lie
down. Eber was sweating. Blood darkened his bandages in faint blossoms of vermillion. He did as asked, turning his head to watch Torveld
leave the temple and his sight.

Nothing to worry about there, he told himself, nothing at all.

The sun hurt his eyes as Evik Torveld left the temple. He was only half
listening as the quartermaster gave him directions to the town gate.
Once at the encampment, he was to report to Sergeant Hauker for
duties. A moment later, the quartermaster had returned inside to assess
some of the other wounded and Torveld was left alone.

He was still finding his bearings when he noticed another soldier
walking through Wurtbad's streets. The uniform triggered something
buried in Torveld's damaged mind. His hand went to the head wound
out of reflex. Anger burned through the fog clouding Torveld's memory,
a line of heat that left a core of rage and vengeance behind.

Sturnbled, Wode... all his brothers of Ulric, all dead.

'Grimblades...' he muttered like a curse.

Torveld clenched his fists until the knuckles whitened, then headed
after the soldier.

For the first time in years, Masbrecht needed a drink. He felt the familiar
gravel taste in his mouth, the cotton tongue behind itching teeth. Sweat
soaked the back of his tunic. Just a tiny patch in the small of his back,
but it told him the craving was upon him. He'd fought hard to deny it,
burying the little voice inside him under the weight of faith and religion. Foolishly, he thought he'd beaten it but it was there, waiting for a
moment of weakness.

The streets were quiet. Most Wurtbad residents stayed indoors after
dark, fearing attack from the greenskins. Others never left the taverns,
satisfied to drink themselves into oblivion until the dawn. Being insen-
sible made it easy to forget, if just for a while. Masbrecht didn't want to
go to a tavern. He wanted to drink alone, to indulge and be damned.
The brewhouses were shut and bolted. He wandered down a side alley.
It was cluttered with refuse and other scraps. Urine ringed the air in an
invisible pall. Drunken shapes lolled in its darkest recesses.

Masbrecht walked over to one. The man was filthy and wore the remnants of a docker's garb. He was snoring loudly, clutching a grimy bottle.
His pepper-stubble cheeks blew in and out with every laboured breath.

Without thinking, Masbrecht snatched the bottle. He took a quick
pull. The liquor was fiery hot. It burned the back of his throat and he

coughed hard, bringing up phlegm. Wiping his mouth, he took another, wincing as the liquid went down.

All the deaths, all the lies and compromises of the last few days and weeks would disappear in a fog of drunkenness. Masbrecht embraced it, tears welling in his eyes. Cold, grey faces came to him as he closed his eyes to the pain.

Varveiter, lost at Blösstadt…

Eber, brutally stabbed and fighting for his life…

Keller, hung by the neck with his own rope…

Captain Stahler, cold and lifeless on a death priest's cart…

It didn't feel right. It wasn't right. None of it was. As Masbrecht supped, filling his body with the poison he had renounced for over five years, the old docker slowly stirred. Like a child without its blanket, he missed the presence of the bottle. He awoke with a grunt, then was screaming unintelligibly at the man who had stolen his grog.

Surprised, Masbrecht pulled his dagger and brandished it at him.

'Stay there, you old dog,' he cried. 'Stay there or I'll cut you!'

The old docker recoiled, holding up his hands and pleading clemency.

'Give mercy, milord. Don't tar your blade with an old sot like me, I beg ya.'

Reality hit Masbrecht like a flood. The bottle shattered on the ground before he even knew he'd dropped it, waking up the other drunks.

'In Sigmar's name…' He fled back out into the accusing night.

'Bastard…' he heard from down the alley. 'My grog…'

Masbrecht got as far as a tinker's before he had to stop and be sick. The liquor came back just as hot and unpleasant. Putting his fingers down his throat he puked again, just to be sure he was rid of it.

Kneeling in his own vomit, Masbrecht clasped his hands together in a desperate prayer. They were shaking.

'*Merciful Sigmar, guide me in my time of need. I am lost without your hand upon my shoulder.*'

Somewhere in the distance, bells were tolling. Masbrecht had heard them before. They belonged to the Temple of Sigmar near the town square. Salvation was close. He made for the bells at once, unaware that someone was following him.

CHAPTER TWENTY-THREE

Hard truths

Wurtbad, capital of Stirland,
398 miles from Altdorf

Krieglitz's hall was empty and echoing. The blazing hearth crackled, rudely invading the quietude and casting flickering grey slashes against the walls. A portrait hung above the fire, hinted at through the passing shadows. A noble bearing suggested itself and Wilhelm, pondering over his goblet of mulled spice-wine, thought it was probably Martin, one of Neder's most famous ancestors.

The lambent light gave the room a warm impression. Thick, woollen rugs swathed the floor, a patch of flagstone visible here and there between them. Bare wooden beams stood in ranks along the walls and arched overhead like dark, embracing arms. A pair of crossed swords, a halberd and spear hung between the vertical beams. Tapestries were lost in shadow.

Wilhelm found the rustic aesthetic pleasing. It was a blessed rural tonic compared to Dieter's lavishly appointed chambers. He eased into the furs draped across the back of his chair, still leafing through a series of missives and reports.

'Averheim holds at least,' he said with a hint of bitter irony.

'The beast is moving, Wilhelm,' said Krieglitz. 'It has sated its lust for carnage in our hinterlands and seeks fresh enemies.'

Wilhelm looked up at Krieglitz, wearisome at the bleakness in the reports and returned petitions.

The two men faced each other across a table of rough-hewn oak. They had stripped out of their battle gear, in favour of light clothes and short cloaks. A change of attire was most welcome in Wilhelm's opinion, though that and a bath had done nothing to cleanse the taint of defeat and loss. Six days in Wurtbad so far for the army to regroup and for Wilhelm to decide what to do next. Several officers had requested an immediate return to Reikland. The Lord Protector of Stirland was right, Grom and his horde *were* moving, likely westward to the heartlands of the Empire. The fact remained though that Wilhelm's army, especially depleted as it was, could not match the greenskins. He needed allies. Petitions for aid had been sent to all states and provinces upon his arrival in the Stirland capital. The first replies to those missives had arrived that evening.

'No word from Wissenland?'

'Pfeifraucher hasn't changed his position, nor will he,' Krieglitz returned.

'And what about you, Neder? What's your position?'

The mounted head of a great boar, the cured and stuffed carcass of an elk caught Wilhelm's eye. The shadows and the fire gave them a strange sense of verisimilitude. The prince suddenly imagined them roaming the wild, straying into the hunter's sights... He felt an uncomfortable empathy with the beasts' plight.

'Orcs and goblins still rove my lands,' replied Krieglitz. 'Even if I wanted to, I can't join your crusade, especially not with victory so uncertain. As Dieter's regent, I can hardly go against him either.' His face darkened as he drew back into shadow. Wilhelm thought it might be shame that made him do it.

'And I cannot leave the Reikmark to be ravaged, either,' he said. 'Is there nothing you can do?'

'I don't think a prince has ever pleaded with me before.'

Wilhelm's reply was curt.

'Not pleading – *asking*.'

'Sorry, brother.' Krieglitz looked downcast. He was only a lord protector and had no right to address a royal son of Reikland like that. 'I can provide an escort to the border but that's all. Don't forget, as well as greenskins, I have Sylvania stirring in the east.'

There was no better news in the returned missives. Wilhelm stood up abruptly.

'Then there's nothing further to discuss. Thank you for the wine, but I've lost my taste for it.'

'Wilhelm...'

The prince was turning to leave and glanced back sharply.

'Save your contrition, Neder. It counts for nothing on the battlefield.'

Wilhelm was walking away, disappearing into shadow, when Krieglitz spoke up.

'What will you do?'

Wilhelm stopped.

'Try to find more troops at Nuln, rally the townships and citizen militias, whatever I can. Perhaps Dieter will deploy his armies when the goblins are at his gates, but I doubt it.'

Krieglitz left an awkward pause before replying.

'I am sorry, brother.'

'The army will be gone by morning,' said Wilhelm, then carried on walking.

Rechts and Masbrecht were missing. Outside Wurtbad in the pre-dawn light, a muster was forming. The Grimblades were supposed to be a part of it. Except Karlich and a small group were still in the town square, two bodies short. It was finally time to return to Reikland.

'Find them both,' he said to Volker, his annoyance obvious. 'Bring them back here to me. We might have an hour before Vogen starts asking questions.'

With the tragic death of Captain Stahler, Vogen had taken over command of all the remaining infantry regiments. A tall order, but most of the soldiers that comprised it were veterans and could look to their sergeants for guidance. Vogen was enough of a pragmatist to let this happen and oversee where needed.

Volker nodded and jogged off into town.

'And us, sergeant,' asked Lenkmann, 'what should we do?'

Brand stood silently alongside him, together with Greiss. The rest of the Grimblades were already outside Wurtbad's gates on the mustering field, which now closely resembled a cesspool after several thousand men had been camped there. Small wonder that the Stirlanders were glad for the foreign exodus.

Karlich looked sour and he glared at the banner bearer.

'We wait.'

Volker found Masbrecht in a pool of his own blood. The Temple of Sigmar was the first place he thought to look, but he was unhappy at the discovery he made there. Fortunately, there was no one else present save for the old priest who ministered it. From him, Volker learned that several Wurtbad folk had already seen the body. That in itself wouldn't be such a problem were it not for the fact of what was written in the blood.

Masbrecht was on his knees, as if in penitent genuflection. In death, he slumped against a statue of Sigmar, just below a set of stone steps leading up to the temple's main altar. Dried blood streaked his neck where it looked like he'd slit his own throat. The wound gaped like a red smile that was anything but humorous. The tips of Masbrecht's fingers were red too. His confession was written in blood alongside him. It told of the assassination attempt on Wilhelm, of a 'traitor in the Reikland' and his guilt in what he saw as complicity in keeping the threat of it secret.

'Incredible that he wrote so much when his lifeblood was ebbing like that,' said Lenkmann.

As soon as he'd found the body, Volker had instructed the old priest to seal the temple until his return, which he did along with Karlich and the others. They'd all been staring for almost a minute before Lenkmann had broken the silence.

'I've seen men do more than that,' offered Brand.

All except Karlich turned to regard the unsettling Reiklander.

'What's he holding in his left hand?' asked the sergeant.

'Must've missed that...' muttered Volker and crouched beside the body. It was hard to see in the murky confines of the temple. Masbrecht's left hand was also crushed up against the statue where he'd slumped.

Volker prised a scroll loose. The dead man's body had yet to rigor.

It was a map Masbrecht was clutching in his bloodied fingers.

'Where in Morr's name did he get *that*?' asked Volker.

Karlich recognised the self-same piece of parchment Ledner had showed him before they'd been charged with the prince's preservation on the heath. Except, it couldn't be. Ledner had burned it.

'Who else has seen this?' asked the sergeant.

'Several of the townsfolk. News will be spreading,' said Volker.

'Like fire...' muttered Brand, kneeling down next to Masbrecht. 'It's no suicide.'

Karlich glared at the Reiklander, demanding more.

'Too clean, too obvious,' Brand replied without even catching his sergeant's look. 'If you wanted to confess, why stab yourself in the neck and then use your own blood to write it?'

'Guilt can do strange things to a man,' suggested Lenkmann. His hollow voice reminded them all of poor Keller.

Brand shook his head. 'Doesn't feel like something Masbrecht would do. He'd go to Vogen, the prince even, confess and then await judgement. He wouldn't kill himself.'

'How can you be sure?' asked Greiss.

Brand turned and held the recruit's gaze. 'I just *know*.'

'So he was murdered,' said Greiss, 'and in his dying moments, unburdened his soul to Sigmar. Sounds like the actions of a devout man.'

No one spoke for a few moments as reality sank in.

Masbrecht was dead. Someone had murdered him.

'We can do nothing about the confession,' said Karlich at last. 'That horse has bolted. Ledner may have us all hanged on account of it. We'll tackle that in turn.' He turned to Volker. 'Any sign of Rechts?'

It was the first time anyone had mentioned the drummer's name, but long after they'd all been thinking it.

'Would he...'

'I don't know.'

'How deep did their enmity go?' asked Greiss.

'Shut up!' Karlich snapped. The two men had almost come to blows before. The argument outside the tavern had been one of the worst. What if this time they'd met again and no one had been there to stop them? Premeditated murder was not *in* Rechts, but a fight that got out of hand... and if he was still drunk?

'Lenkmann,' said Karlich, 'wait here for the watch. Vogen or even Ledner may follow.' Karlich glared at the banner bearer intently to emphasise the import of his next words. 'Say nothing,' he said, turning briefly and taking in the other Grimblades in a glance, 'that goes for all of you. We keep quiet, try and fathom what happened. Lenkmann, you found Masbrecht here and have no idea why he did it or what his bloodied confession refers to. If anyone asks, I'm gathering the last of the regiment for the muster. Understand?'

Lenkmann nodded.

'The rest of you,' added Karlich, already walking out of the temple. 'Every alehouse, every tavern in Wurtbad. Find him.'

No drunkard in all of Wurtbad would have visited as many alehouses as they had in such short order. Rechts was at none of them, and now Karlich was beginning to despair they'd ever find him. A niggle at the back of his head mooted that the drummer *had* killed Masbrecht and fled town for fear of repercussions. Karlich crushed that voice mentally underfoot and trusted in his instincts that Rechts was a good man in a bad way.

He was alone. By splitting up, the Grimblades had a better chance of finding Rechts quickly and quietly. As Karlich gazed around, something caught his eye. Like a lot of Stirland towns, Wurtbad's rugged landscape encroached within its walls. It had several hills and narrow winding lanes that led to their summits. One such grassy knoll caught his attention. A thin smoke trail emanated from it.

Karlich turned abruptly, half expecting to see someone behind him, but the townsfolk had moved on and scowled less. Putting it down to tension, he made for the hill in long, determined strides.

The knoll was at the outskirts of town and overlooked much of its rural market. Even early as it was, traders were setting up stalls and wares for the coming morning. There were many gaps. Much of the usual bustle had been dented by the invasion. People still needed to eat, though. Trade offered a sense of order and normality fearful and superstitious folk needed. Count Krieglitz was a wise ruler, not a mere peasant lord as some of his contemporaries snidely branded him.

Rechts was smoking a thin bone pipe when Karlich found him. In the other hand, he cradled a bottle of Middenland hooch. It was empty, barring the dregs.

'Come to drag me to muster?' he asked without looking back.

Karlich didn't answer but walked closer and kept his dirk within reach.

'Just needed a little peace,' Rechts continued. 'Old memories sting when they're poked at.' Now he faced Karlich. He looked crapulous and melancholic. 'I wouldn't have cut out his tongue, you know. Thumped him, yes,' he added, nodding at the idea, 'but not cut him.'

And then, as he experienced the ambivalence of feeling relief that Rechts hadn't murdered Masbrecht but then concern that his killer was still unknown to him, Karlich noticed a shadow fall upon them both. Rechts's eyes widened and he tried to stand when he saw who loomed behind his sergeant.

Karlich moved just in time, ripping out his dirk and parrying Torveld's thrust out of instinct. Another slash came at him, opening up the sergeant's shoulder. Karlich yelped aloud, dropping his dagger as a hot dark line spoiled his tunic.

'Southern dog,' spat Torveld, drunk with anger. 'They're all dead.' He lunged, and Karlich dodged aside.

Comprehending that Torveld was alive and not slain with the other Steel Swords as he originally thought, it all made sudden, terrible sense to Karlich. The Middenlander had killed Masbrecht out of a misguided fit of revenge. Blood for blood – that was the Ulrican way. Torveld blamed the Grimblades for the death of his comrades and was here to exact the price he saw was owed.

Rechts bull-charged him, even as Karlich was backing off to try and find some even footing, but Torveld barged the drunken Reiklander aside. The drummer's momentum took him careening halfway down the hill, where he landed with a grunt.

'Your brothers died in battle. It wasn't down to us,' Karlich told him, glancing around for a weapon, anything. 'This is murder, Middenlander. Vogen will see you swing for this.' It was an empty threat considering he'd killed already. As Torveld came on, Karlich decided to change approach. 'I thought Ulricans were proud, honour-bound warriors–'

Torveld thumped his chest. 'Winter wolves are the fiercest and most honourable.'

It was the most heartfelt and tragic affirmation Karlich had ever heard.

'Then why slit a man's throat? Why kill my brother in arms and try to hide it with deception?'

Torveld's face went blank for just a second. He had no notion of what Karlich was talking about.

'I lost the other and followed you he–' was all he could manage before Greiss knocked him unconscious from behind.

'Masbrecht is dead?' Rechts was scrambling up the hill, sometimes on four limbs, sometimes two but was dumbstruck when he realised what had happened.

'Yes,' said Greiss, his iron-hard gaze fixed on Karlich. Even unarmed, the sergeant was at least sober and presented the greatest threat to his mission.

'He killed him, Torsten,' said Karlich. 'I'm sorry I ever doubted you.'

Rechts's confusion only grew. He struggled upright, still wavering. 'What's going on?'

Karlich wasn't really listening. His eyes were on Greiss.

'Who do you serve? Ledner?'

Greiss nodded, seeing no harm in the admission now. The assassin had clubbed Torveld over the head with a *main gauche*, parrying dagger. He also had a duelling pistol snug in his belt.

Karlich gestured to the weapons. 'Gifts from your master?'

'These are mine,' said Greiss with a voice so cold it practically chilled the air. Ice flowed in his veins now. 'Commendable,' he added. 'Stalling for time, devising my true nature. Your time is almost up, yours and your men's. If you don't struggle, I'll make it quick.'

'So Ledner didn't trust us to keep quiet after all,' said Karlich.

'No more words,' Greiss told them. 'Face away from me, kneel down and prepare to meet Sigmar.'

Rechts roared and drove at Greiss. Maybe it was the grog, maybe he was just slower, but Greiss was able to turn and plant his dagger into Rechts's neck before the drummer even got his hands up to try and choke him. Rechts burbled blood-flecked curses.

Karlich saw a slim chance and went for the assassin himself, but the pistol was in Greiss's hand as if it had always been there. A shot boomed across the knoll and Karlich spun with the impact of it in his shoulder. He staggered and fell. The bone was shattered and he cried out, clutching at it through his oozing blood.

Greiss withdrew the main gauche. Rechts was already dead when he slumped to the ground. Torveld was stirring too. Greiss lunged and pierced the Middenlander's eye. He died instantly.

Then Greiss turned to Karlich.

'You and me left,' he said with the hint of a smile. 'I offered you quick, you chose slow...'

'How about a third choice?'

The voice behind him made Greiss flinch.

Brand stepped from the shadows creeping back down the knoll in the face of the rising sun. 'Me.' He glanced at Rechts and his jaw clenched.

Too late to save one...

'Was hoping I'd kill you last,' Greiss replied. Karlich was in no shape to face a trained assassin but he kept half an eye on the sergeant anyway. 'Thought I'd lost *you* in the market,' he muttered.

'You're not the only one who can follow a lamb.' Brand drew his dirk.

There was the slightest of nods and then Greiss attacked.

Steel flashed in a grey blur, thrusting, lunging slashing for any of several death-wounds. Brand parried or dodged them all.

'Knew you were too good for a common soldier,' he snarled, raking his blade against the edge of Greiss's. Metal shards and sparks cascaded like flickering rain.

Greiss growled at him though his gritted teeth. 'So are you.'

They broke off, circling before leaping in again, their dagger strokes ringing like a blacksmith's anvil.

'Campaigning's made you rusty,' said Greiss, a second blade flashing into his hand from a concealed spring-mounted bracer. He plunged it into Brand's shoulder, drawing a cry of pain from the Reiklander. With the other hand Greiss pressed for Brand's throat. He dropped his dirk and held on to the assassin's wrist. 'One by one, you're all dead men. I'll gut y– *urrghh*!'

Greiss spat a gob of blood that ruined his tunic with a long, viscous streak. He looked down at the gory length of steel rammed up into his back that punched out through his chest. Karlich whispered in his ear behind him before Greiss died.

'*Grimblades fight as one.*'

Brand pushed the main gauche away from his throat and pulled the dagger out of his shoulder with a wince. Both Reiklanders backed away. Karlich left the sword embedded and watched Greiss buckle and fall. He knew he had lost a fair amount of blood but he'd be damned if he was going to lie down yet. His breath rasped a little as he spoke.

'Ledner really didn't want us to talk, did he?'

Brand had already strapped up his shoulder with a piece of cloth and knelt down by Greiss's body.

'Small wonder given he knew about the prince's killer and used our liege-lord as bait to draw the assassin out,' the sergeant added. 'Civil war be damned, Vogen is hearing of this.'

'It is worse than that,' said Brand, turning Greiss's head. There was a tattoo on the dead man's neck which exactly matched the one they had found on the Tilean assassin. 'No Marienburg gold this time.'

'That bastard…' uttered Karlich.

The killers were both Ledner's. With that truth came a chilling revelation. Not only did he know of Prince Wilhelm's assassination, he had orchestrated it. Ledner was the traitor.

CHAPTER TWENTY-FOUR

Patriotism

*Outside the walls of Wurtbad, capital of Stirland,
398 miles from Altdorf*

By now, all of Wurtbad and the mustering army beyond its walls knew of the foiled attempt on Prince Wilhelm's life. Most of the common soldiery were shocked and angered, others simply assumed it was the price of being Reikland royalty. Officers expressed outrage. Privately, they harboured suspicions that the prince's cousin, Emperor Dieter himself, was somehow responsible. This last rumour was perpetuated by cohorts of Adolphus Ledner. Like any good spymaster, he had many lackeys in his employ. But Ledner, usually ubiquitous in the presence of his lord, was not present when Wilhelm gave his reaction to the news.

'It changes nothing,' he said, fastening his scabbarded sword and tightening the straps on his breastplate. He was in one of Krieglitz's armouries, with the Lord Protector of Stirland looking on.

'Defy the will of the Emperor and expect consequences, is that the way of it?' he said. 'I heard the assassin's bribe was Marienburg gold. What do you think that means?'

Wilhelm glared at him as he was adjusting his leg greaves. 'You should not speak ill of your liege-lord and Emperor. As for the burgomeisters,' he added, 'who knows what those greedy merchants are up to. I had hoped Ledner would have discovered something by now.'

'Nuln's Golden Palace wasn't gilded by taxes alone, I'd say.'

Wilhelm paused in his battle preparation. 'Be careful who you say that to, Neder.' It wasn't a threat, more an expression of concern.

Krieglitz smiled thinly. He changed tack. 'Word will have reached most of the other provinces by next morning,' he said. 'You'll be a legend, Wilhelm – the noble Prince of Reikland who rode out to defend his Empire and crushed the vipers in his nest trying to stop him.'

'Am I so glorious? What have I achieved? Averland is ruined, much of Stirland is also devastated,' – Krieglitz's face darkened at this remark – 'and now I've failed to dismantle the greenskin horde and left the Reikmark open to invasion. Assassin or no, it's a bitter draught to swallow. *Legendary* is not how I would describe it.'

'Even still, you've made friends of the other electors and nobles. Backbone and courage, that's what the Empire needs most.'

'Just not friendly enough, eh, Neder?' The bitterness in Wilhelm's voice was obvious.

Captain Vogen appeared at the armoury door before Krieglitz could reply.

'Beg your pardon, lords,' he said, 'we are all but ready to march.'

Wilhelm nodded to the officer. 'Get them into order, captain. The orcs move west, so will we, and get ahead of them if we can.'

'Are we still bound for Nuln?' Vogen asked.

Wilhelm sheathed a dagger at his hip, the last of his war trappings. 'The beast will want to sack the capital and with it all but empty, there's nothing to stop the greenskins doing it.'

Vogen saluted and left to perform his duties. Just as he was going, Wilhelm stopped him.

'Have you seen Captain Ledner?'

'Not recently, my liege. But I could easily have missed him during the muster.'

Wilhelm gestured that he could leave.

'A concern?' asked Krieglitz when Vogen was gone.

'No,' Wilhelm decided. 'He'll turn up when he's needed, probably when I least expect it. Adolphus Ledner always does.'

Karlich was hurrying through the Wurtbad streets, taking side alleys and backways to avoid the commotion outside the Temple of Sigmar near the town square, when he heard a sharp *click* from the shadows behind him. He stopped sharply and found a pistol trained on his torso as he turned.

'Couldn't let you run off to Vogen or the prince before we'd had a chance to talk,' said Ledner. His sibilant voice creaked like an old coffin.

'Slay me here and you'll bring the Watch running, quartermasters too and who knows who else,' countered Karlich, hiding his nerves.

'There are a hundred ways I could explain the gunshot and your corpse,' Ledner told him, stepping closer so the errant shafts of sunlight bathing the backstreet hit his face. The contrast of light and shade only made it more forbidding.

'For a man who claims to be a patriot, plotting to kill your own liege-lord seems like the deeds of a traitor,' said Karlich.

'Where are the rest of your men?' asked Ledner. 'The ones that still live,' he added without malice.

Karlich imagined wrapping his hands around the spymaster's throat and squeezing until all vitality had left him. 'Returned to the regiment, but you already knew that.'

Ledner allowed himself a small grunt of amusement. 'Yes, I did. Though, they are actually with my sergeants-at-arms, awaiting interrogation. Witnesses to murder,' – Ledner counted on his fingers – '*four* times over? Yes, the Middenlander makes four. Questions must be asked.'

'As we're about to march to Nuln? How did you explain that to the prince?'

'Wilhelm trusts my counsel, *sergeant*. You should know that.'

'Then he trusts a serpent!' Karlich spat, making fists. 'You're a snake in more than just your voice, *captain*.'

'Barbs are only painful if they're real,' Ledner told him. There were only a few feet between them. 'You're much too clever for a mere soldier–' A hacking cough stopped the spymaster. Karlich went to grab for him before the pistol came back up and Ledner regained his composure. 'Don't make me revise my opinion of you!' he snapped, still spluttering.

'Choking on your own lies?' Karlich framed a bitter smile.

'Amusing. You are quite a resourceful man. I never expected you or your footsloggers to best my Tilean, let alone kill Greiss,' said Ledner, more hoarsely than usual. 'He was from the Border Princes, not Averland, by the way.'

'Can't say I care. Dead is dead. Is this where you ask me to join your brood?'

'No,' Ledner said flatly. 'You have the wit for it, but not the moral ambiguity or ruthless pragmatism I require in my agents.' He paused to size Karlich up, gauging whether to kill him or let him live. 'I organised the assassination, the one I tasked you to foil,' he admitted at last. 'You already know this. Wilhelm was either supposed to die or be badly injured in the attempt. Either way, sympathy for our cause and that of the Empire would soar. Martyrs are potent rallying symbols.'

Karlich's anger was almost palpable. 'You said we could speak nothing of it, for fear of civil war.'

'Don't be naïve. You're better than that. Your success on the road back to Mannsgard was as unexpected as your discovery of my messenger. The Marienburg coin you found–'

Karlich interrupted, 'Was left for others to find in order to discredit the Emperor. Even my thick, *soldier's* ears have discerned some of dealings with the burgomeisters. Every sane son of Sigmar in the land knows of it.'

'By finding that wretch in the barn, you became a thorn. When my

counter plan also failed, I decided to bring about the same result by killing you and letting slip that Wilhelm was attacked in the same breath.
The prince's reputation will soon be enhanced. I confess, I had not
thought of it originally but this is a better outcome. This way Wilhelm
lives.'

'And us, my men and I, what is our fate?'

'I *am* a patriot of the Empire, but the Reikland above all else. Emperor
Dieter's efficacy as ruler of our lands is questionable at best. I would
also scrutinise his loyalty, for his Marienburg allies are no friends of
the Empire.' Ledner dabbed a trickle of blood that had seeped from the
corner of his lip. He'd coughed it up and Karlich wondered what else
the man was hiding beneath his crimson scarf. 'Understand me, Karlich.
Know that when I say I would do anything to protect the Empire and
the Reik, I mean *anything*. Wilhelm is a brave leader but he could not
challenge or overthrow the Emperor. Only as a martyr and the catalyst
for revolution could he do that... until now.'

'How do you sleep with such plans twisting inside your head?'

Ledner smiled, as if the man before him had seen a measure of his
soul.

'I don't want to kill you, Karlich,' he said.

'What's a little more blood? We'll all be drowning in it soon enough.'

'I hadn't thought of you as a fatalist. You're not like that shackled wolf
in your regiment – the killer of killers.' Ledner raised his eyebrows, as if
considering. 'Now, *he* would suit my purposes greatly, if I believed he
could be controlled. No, you're a different animal altogether I think,
much more savage.' He showed his teeth. '*They* don't see it, your precious
Grimblades but *I* do, Lothar. I know it all too well, Lothar Henniker of
Ohslecht. That was the name of your village, wasn't it? The place where
you killed a Templar of Sigmar?'

Karlich's blood ran cold. He thought that part of his old life had ended
with the headless witch hunter on the killing fields outside Averheim.

Ledner went on. 'I'm sure he and that brutal bastard Vanhans deserved
it. Unfortunately for you, though, Templars of Sigmar are a persistent,
vengeful breed. They'd likely torture you first if they found you. *If* they
found you. Do we have an understanding?'

Karlich was breathing hard through his nose, something between rage
and fear. Compromise or death, why did it always come to those two
choices with men like Ledner? After a few moments, he spoke.

'Release my men. Never approach or threaten me again.'

Ledner lowered his pistol. 'I knew you were wise, much too good to
be a sergeant. I don't need to tell you what would happen if you broke
our agreement. If any of you did...' He backed away until the shadows
of the alley swallowed him.

Karlich waited until he was sure Ledner was gone then staggered
up against the wall, hands bracing him as he retched. By the time he

reached the army outside Wurtbad, what was left of his regiment would be waiting for him released from the sergeants-at-arms' custody. They'd survived Ledner's machinations, at least for a time. Now they just had to survive the green horde.

One way or another, it would end at Reikland.

CHAPTER TWENTY-FIVE

A return to the ranks

*Stirland border, north-east of Averland,
394 miles from Altdorf*

Ledner rejoined the army several miles on the road out of Wurtbad. A long trail of soldiers, ranked in order of march and followed by baggage trains, streamed from the encampment site at the edge of town. A virulent scar was left in their wake, the remains of latrines, cookfires and earth churned by many booted feet. It would be weeks, assuming a cessation to the greenskin invasion, before the land could be restored.

Though the orcs and goblins were moving, bands of raiders still lingered in the province. Hunkering down in the hills and scratches of forest, it might be years before the recalcitrant greenskins were rooted out and expunged.

Krieglitz's huntsmen took the army south-east, down the Old Dwarf Road at first. They could make good time and try to forge ahead of Grom's horde pushing westward towards Reikland. Swift riders had already been sent to the province to warn the garrisons still manning Blood Keep, Helmgart and the barracks at Grünburg. Wilhelm doubted his cousin would admit, let alone heed his urgent missives. The Emperor's concerns were elsewhere, wrapped up in Marienburg gold and the charms of some courtly maidens, no doubt. Such languor while the Empire suffered made the prince sick with anger.

Barring its beleaguered capital, Averland was overrun so the southern border of Stirland was to be avoided. Nor did they wish to be slowed by the larger tributaries of the River Aver that bled into the province. In all likelihood, the crossings would be watched or even impassable. It was only a short way south-east before the army left the Old Dwarf Road and went west with the hills to the south instead. They would hug the northern border, close to Talabecland, make first for Kemperbad and any troops the prince still had there and then on to Nuln, hopefully ahead of the horde. The journey would take several days, possibly longer.

'Am I on a fool's errand, Ledner?' asked the prince as the spymaster rode up alongside him.

'Even if you were, I would keep such truths to yourself, lord. Our army is ragged enough.'

They were mainly an infantry force now with a predominance of citizen soldiers. Meinstadt's war machines were few and largely inconsequential. The knights were almost vanquished to a man. Those that remained stayed by the prince's side always, especially since the news of the assassination attempt had broken. From behind their visored helms they regarded every man who came into their liege-lord's presence as sternly as an enemy to be slain on the battlefield.

Some more Mootlanders had joined them, so too did the dwarf exiles march to Nuln, but half-breeds would hardly swing the balance of the war for Wilhelm or the Empire.

Krieglitz relented to an extent, impassioned by Wilhelm's stalwartness in the face of what he believed was Dieter's treachery. He made a cohort of his household guard available to the prince. The Hornhelms wore battered plate armour and their steeds could hardly be considered magnificent, but the knights-at-arms would accompany Wilhelm all the way to Nuln and fight for him as if he were their own lord. The huntsmen too, their guides along the northern border, would stay and fight. They were all Krieglitz's representatives while he and his army ventured forth to tackle the larger greenskin bands shed by Grom's immense horde still in his province. To the goblin king, they were just dregs. His army was formidable without them. To Krieglitz they were a pest threatening his subjects.

'Where have you been, Ledner?' Wilhelm asked after he'd allowed a brief silence to fall between them.

'With the quartermasters, dragging the walking wounded into the line of march. We'll need every spear and blade we have. Arrangements also had to be made for the dead and dying. Several of Morr's own raven-keepers had remained behind at Wurtbad.'

Wilhelm rode ahead but instructed his lead infantry officer to maintain the same pace. He also urged Ledner to follow. The Griffonkorps remnants came too, Wilhelm's armoured shadow. They would fight and die only. Ears and eyes closed to the prince's private dealings, the knights were as disciplined as statues in this conviction.

'Did you know?' he asked when they were out of earshot.

Ledner pursed his lips.

'Of course you did,' said the prince, 'you know everything concerning my business, even when I do not.' The remonstration in his tone bordered on outright anger.

'Had I acted sooner, the perpetrator would have escaped, slipped its noose,' Ledner replied. Utterly calm, it was hard to tell he'd incurred the ire of an Imperial prince, one that could have him executed with but a command to his knights. 'You'd be supping poison in your evening tonic or finding a viper in your bathwater, my lord. Perhaps a keg of blackpowder, fused and lit, rolled into your tent or a dagger in the back as you consulted your officers. Murder needn't be subtle or clean. But this I know: if you have an assassin within your grasp, you let him come...' Ledner made a fist, '...and crush him when he's close enough to touch.'

'You've made your point, Adolphus,' Wilhelm conceded, 'but if I find out you've used me as bait again, we will have words, you and I. Don't think me one of your tools to be manipulated.'

Ledner nodded contritely. 'Understood, my prince.'

'Good.' Wilhelm slowed his steed to allow the line of march to catch up. 'Now, tell me what faces us at Nuln.'

Ledner looked westward, his gaze unwavering. 'Blood, my prince. Rivers of blood are what await us there.'

Eber was saddened to learn of the death of his comrades. He rejoined the regiment outside Wurtbad, one of the many 'walking wounded' pressed back into service for what was being called the 'Preservation of Reikland'. He had liked Rechts most of all, despite his bad temper, and Masbrecht had always struck him as a gentle soul. These men were more than his comrades; they were his family, in lieu of the one that had cast him out so cruelly when he was a boy.

He ached when he moved. His gait felt awkward and his breath came laboured after walking long distances. After the horrific knife attack, Eber was not the man he once was, the ox no longer. That saddened him too, but he vowed to stand and fight anyway, to ensure no more of his brothers in the Grimblades died if he could help it.

Something was going on. Two days of silence with Nuln growing closer all the while told him that. It was more than just grief affecting the other halberdiers. Eber had wondered if Ledner was the cause, that there was more to the deaths of his fellows than first appeared. Allegedly, the Middenlander Torveld had killed them. He'd also learned from Karlich that it was now a matter of military record that the soldier had done it out of revenge for what he saw as the Grimblades' culpability in the destruction of his regiment. A head wound supposedly afflicted the poor man, 'affected his humours' so the scrivened words of the physician went.

'Madness took him and it ended in blood,' Karlich had said, though it was clear he did not believe this fully, and that to utter the half lie rankled with the sergeant. Later, when he was sure prying eyes weren't watching, he'd spoken differently. 'Torveld was a bastard,' he'd said, whispering, 'but not a murderer, not like that.'

Eber had then learned of some of Ledner's role, at least that he was involved somehow, but nothing more. It was another reason for Karlich to hate the spymaster. Rumours abound that witnesses had been paid off or silenced in order to foster Ledner's lie. The soldiers in the Grimblades' regiment were painted as victims of circumstance, which they were, only not in the way the spymaster had portrayed.

Eber was not gifted with the quickest wit; he knew that and accepted his limitations. Some people regarded him as credulous and gullible, but even he knew the story was a falsehood before Karlich had confided in him. He didn't dig for further answers, assuming they were best left unearthed, but it laid an uncomfortable pall over his brothers in arms that he didn't like.

He decided to do something about it and broke into bellowing song.

'The Burgher of Bögen had such girth, 'tis a wonder his mother did give birth…'

He'd learned the ditty years ago. Though his voice was not as strong as Rechts's had been, Eber gave it his all.

'…to a brute of a son without much grace, feet from the Moot and a round, red face!'

At the end of the front rank, he glanced sideways at Karlich who joined him in the second verse that added further scorn on to the Burgher of Bögen's 'legend'. Pretty soon, all of the Grimblades were singing. Volker, who became drummer in Rechts's absence, beat out the marching rhythm. It spread down the column. The Averlanders and Stirlanders in the army took up the song, too. They didn't know the words but it was unimportant. The halflings brought out pipes and spoons by way of instrumental accompaniment. Even the dwarfs *hrummed* and *hroomed* to the tune. It was a strange, discordant sound, likened to the filling and exhaling of bellows or the slow movement of earth. No man could repeat it.

Eber came to the end of the song, a rousing crescendo supplied by the enthusiastic Mootlanders and the mood lightened.

Volker laughed loudly, there was relief in the gesture, and slapped Eber on the back. It drew a wince from the burly Reiklander that he hid well behind a broad smile.

'It's been many years since I heard that marching song.' It was Vogen, touring the line on his steed, seeing to the courage and morale of the men. His task was almost done for him and he smiled, twisting his large moustaches upwards. He trotted over to Karlich, maintaining pace with that part of the column.

'Captain,' said the sergeant, and the others in the front ranks followed suit.

'Your voice would benefit from some melody, though,' Vogen said to Eber with a subtle wink at Karlich.

Eber nodded then flushed a little.

'No need to stand on ceremony,' the portly captain from Kemperbad told them, whilst adjusting the belt at his waist. 'I am not Stahler, but he told me much of the men in his command,' he added, smoothing his beard with a gauntleted hand. Vogen was so bulky and broad he had more in common with the dwarf exiles than his own kith and kin.

'Then he would've said the Grimblades respect their officers,' answered Karlich. It was the first time he'd really spoken to Captain Vogen. With Nuln looming like a black cloud on the horizon, he wondered if it would be the last.

Further down the line another marching song began.

'We'll need our spirits up for what's to come,' said Vogen. It was like he'd reached in and grasped at Karlich's thoughts. He found he liked the man at once. The captain looked down at the sergeant's hip.

'That was his sword, wasn't it?' There was sorrow in his voice.

Karlich nodded humbly.

'It's good that you keep it,' Vogen told him. 'Stahler would've wanted that, to fight with us at the end.'

'And is it "the end"?' asked Karlich, the old scars on his face starting to itch.

Vogen looked to the west, as if trying to scry their destinies. 'Of the campaign? Yes, I believe it will end in the Reik. We'll give our blood for that land, more than any other. No son of Reikland will abandon it. Our bodies would litter the fields before that ever happened.' The grim mood returned for a spell. Sensing it, Vogen changed the subject.

'We'll be joining up with reinforcements from inside the province,' he said. 'Garrisons from Blood Keep and Grünburg are assembling to the north of the city. It's mainly a citizen militia force but these are Reikland men with Reikland blood – I'd take that over hirelings any day of Mitterfruhl. The barrack houses will arm them and we must be ready to meet them near the border. Together, we'll turn back the green tide.

'We need only bloody their nose. Survival of the Reik, and by extension the Empire, is all that matters now.'

'Sir...' Volker interrupted.

Karlich shot him a stern glance before following the scout's pointing finger towards the horizon. They'd just crested a rise and the lay of the Reikland had unfolded before them in the distance. It was not all they saw.

A thin haze of smoke drifted languidly above another range of hills.

The spate of singing stopped as the other regiments saw it too.

Lenkmann narrowed his eyes. 'What is that?'

A solitary horn rang out. Captain Vogen was needed at the head of the column. He rode off without a word.

'It's Nuln,' said Brand, voicing aloud what everyone was thinking. The capital of the Empire was already burning.

CHAPTER TWENTY-SIX

Burning in black

Outside Nuln, capital of the Empire,
289 miles from Altdorf

A day later they reached Nuln. There was little of the city left. A flickering shell of a city danced with shadows created by the fires within. Nuln's once proud walls were ransacked and gaping, like a festering wound. A killing field littered the land outside it. Men in the black tunics of the capital lay dead in their droves, broken remains of war machines were scattered around like chaff and fat flies droned about the carcasses of steeds in noisome clouds.

Before coming to the capital, Wilhelm had almost emptied Kemperbad on the way. There was just a skeleton garrison left behind. The reinforcements were mainly citizen levies again, the prince's legend having spread to all men of the Reik, who pledged to his cause as their worthy and noble saviour. The army's stay was brief but as Wilhelm and his warriors rode through the square, children placed garlands around their necks, women gave prayers and men their strength of arms. Young and old, strong and infirm, all swore to fight for Wilhelm and the Reikland.

At Nuln, they barely reached the city's outer milestone. At Kemperbad, Wilhelm not only gained troops and goodwill, he also discovered that Nuln's army had been defeated, the city sacked. The forces due to meet them from Grünburg and Blood Keep had apparently joined up with the defenders. How many now survived was unknown. It might be none.

Grom had moved on but some of his warbands remained. They'd come to a nervous halt and the Empire column broke ranks as the men, unable to comprehend the horror of their glorious capital as a blackened ruin, wandered loose and suddenly bereft of hope.

A ragged-looking scout approached Prince Wilhelm, who rode a little way out to meet him with three of his Griffonkorps in close attendance. The boy was almost battered to the ground by a knight's armoured steed before the prince ordered them to stand back and let the poor wretch through.

'Nothing left, my liege,' he said, breathlessly. A runner from the baggage train brought him water and he drank deeply before continuing. 'The army was defeated. All except Lord Grundel, who holds the west quarter of the city…' At that the distant echo of cannon fire rang out.

'Albrecht Grundel,' muttered Ledner, close by. 'He was… *vocal* in court at the lassitude of the Nuln army. Likely, he kept his household troops well drilled, unlike the city-state forces.' He looked down at the messenger from atop his steed and gestured to the fallen soldiers in the distance. Wilhelm had ordered the column be brought up short of the city after hearing the news out of Kemperbad. 'Where are the rest, boy? This can't be it.'

'Altdorf, my lord. The rest fled to Altdorf.' The scout ferreted around inside his jerkin, pulling out a scrap of parchment. 'I was given this by Captain Dedricht.'

'Do we know him?' Wilhelm asked Ledner in a low voice.

'Commander of the Grünburg force,' he said, as one of the Griffonkorps dismounted and stalked up to the boy. Snatching the parchment, the knight delivered it to the prince a moment later before getting back on his steed.

Wilhelm frowned as he read.

> *Retreated across the hills. Nuln is defeated. Blood Keep and Grünburg are still at fighting strength. More regiments are arriving from Helmgart and Ubersreik. Will meet on the Axe Bite Road between Bögenhafen and Altdorf. Faith in Sigmar.*
> *Capn. Elias Dedricht*

'Faith in Sigmar,' Wilhelm muttered and clenched the parchment in his fist. The prince's face was grim. He lifted the spyglass to his eye. Nuln's gatehouse was badly breached and offered an unobstructed view into the heart of the city. His expression hardened further.

'Ranald's teeth, the Paunch will pay in blood! I see chariots roaming Nuln's streets and orcs run amok.' He put down the spyglass before he broke it in a fit of rage. The scout balked beneath the prince's glare.

'What's become of the Golden Palace?'

'S-stripped b-bare, my liege. It's nothing but a pen for the greenskins' beasts.'

The poor lad was on the verge of collapse. They'd get nothing further from him. Ledner was about to press for more when Wilhelm raised a hand to stop him.

'Enough. Go to the baggage train,' he said to the scout. The lad blinked back tears from inside a soot-blackened face. Dried blood caked his dirty hair. 'Tell them to give you food and water. You're to ride in one of the carts until we reach Altdorf. Tell them it's the prince's order. Now go.'

The lad bowed profusely and scurried off towards the distant baggage trains.

'What now?' asked Ledner. 'What of the capital?'

'Men grew fat and rested on the laurels of old glories, Ledner,' he said, 'sure in the knowledge that no foe would ever venture as far west as Nuln. Now look at it.'

The city was a wraith, looming across a sea of dead. It was a charnel house and although Wilhelm railed at leaving Albrecht Grundel unreinforced, he had no choice but to press on and try and save the city that was still intact – *his* city.

'Nuln is lost,' was the prince's dire proclamation. 'We go to Altdorf. The dead here are barely cold. There might be time enough to overtake the goblin warlord before he reaches the city.' Wilhelm considered it before he continued. 'There are passes through the hills that the greenskins won't know about. It's rugged land but fit enough for marching. We'll use one to get ahead of the horde.'

'We'll join with Dedricht's force?'

'Even our combined army can't match the greenskins,' said Wilhelm. 'I have another idea. Get three of our fastest messengers and meet me at the front. Do it quickly.'

Wilhelm reined his steed around and rode back to the head of the army. The column was reforming as Ledner went the opposite way to gather the messengers the prince requested.

As they marched on with despair in their hearts, the desolate boom of cannons raked the blood-scented breeze.

CHAPTER TWENTY-SEVEN

The valley of death

*Reikland hills, on the Bögenhafen road,
34 miles from Altdorf*

Grom's green horde swept down the Reikland hills like a contagion, defiling everything it touched. To the naked eye it appeared as if the land undulated with an obscene tempo. Orc and goblin heads bobbed in the tide, jeering and bellowing. It was hard to define tribes – the beasts massed in a stinking ruck, the larger battering the lesser and so on to the smallest creature. Like their enemies, the earth was beaten and brutalised beneath the greenskins' chariots and hobnailed boots. Their dung choked the very life from it, the once verdant Imperial fields reduced to a cesspit of filthy mud. Such was the price of open war.

A paltry force of defenders defied the orcs at the bottom of a small valley. It rose sharply behind them and would make any retreat difficult. Beyond that rise was the road to Altdorf. Grom had marched the most direct route. There would be no further delays. The Empire was within his meaty goblin fist. Altdorf represented its last defiant bastion. Every man amongst the defenders knew it couldn't get that far. They might have no choice. They were ragged and despairing in their serried ranks, so bedraggled that they looked incapable of flight even if they had to. This would be a last stand.

The valley sides were just as sheer as its mouth and the orcs funnelled into it in a screaming flood. Grom wanted Altdorf. He wanted to sack this proud city of men, the ancestral capital of Sigmar, as he had already sacked Nuln. And he didn't want to wait.

Prince Wilhelm's jaw was set as hard as stone as the greenskins came for them. He waited in the centre of a long battleline of roughly a thousand men, mounted on his warhorse. Captain Dedricht was to the east side of the valley, grim-faced and on foot, gripping his halberd like it was life itself. Aside from the Griffonkorps bodyguards, the rest of the force was also on foot. They looked worn and tired. They were – the passage across the hills had been hard. Their uniforms were ripped and scuffed, and they stank of sweaty fear. Banners dipped as the thin breeze wafting down through the valley ebbed to nothing. Even dug in behind make-shift barricades and several upturned carts, the Empire army couldn't hope to hold for long.

The noise of charging greenskin feet and rumbling chariots built to a crescendo. It was deafening, made louder by the dense, hard rock of the enclosed valley walls.

For a moment, the chariots pulled ahead but then foundered when they hit a patch of rough stones strung out in a line that extended the full width of the valley. Here was the first of Wilhelm's deterrents. The greenskin mobs behind the previously faster machineries overtook them. Picking their way through the rubble, some of the larger orcs upturned several of the lighter chariots, so eager were they to bloody their blades.

The natural funnel of the valley pressed the orcs and goblins tighter. Grom was somewhere amongst them, snarling commands and keeping order. It was hard, even for the Paunch. The greenskins recognised the Empire army in front of them was bloodied, like a wounded animal. They wanted to put it down. No greenskin could resist bullying the weak and these men were laid low. Even the goblin king could not deny his own nature. He too bayed for manflesh, held so tantalisingly before his tongue.

Deep into the valley bottom, well below the ridges on either side and with the greenskins barely a hundred feet away, a banner rose up in the Empire ranks. A chorus of muted trumpets rang out, signalling to all.

Far from holding the line and giving up their blood for the Empire, Wilhelm and his army fled.

They had seen the sheer strength of Waaagh! Grom and quailed.

It only goaded the Paunch all the more. His prize was running up the valley ridge, directly away from his horde. Urging his mobs to greater efforts, he was determined to catch the 'humies' before they reached the summit.

Wilhelm, cantering in order to keep pace with the foot troops, did not get to the valley peak, nor did he intend to. Instead, he came up about twenty feet short. Another banner went up, more clarion calls echoed on the dead air. The Empire line reformed, became much tighter, much denser than before, its ranks packed and deep. Shield walls were raised and locked, spears levelled. A ragged band of defenders became a tough and determined rectangle of soldiers. The second part of Wilhelm's plan happened a moment later.

Imperial war cries spilled down over the east and west ridges, thousands of men followed them, two flanking forces comprised of state regiments and citizen militia. The western force contained the Hornhelms, the flower of Stirland's cavalry. Several stern-faced state regiments accompanied them. The slowly-dipping lances of the knights sent a shiver of fear through the greenskins they barrelled towards. The eastern force was on foot, led by Captain Vogen. Stolid dwarfs joined the Empire ranks of swords, pikes and militia. Mootlanders ranged their flanks.

Behind the prince, who had resumed his position in the centre of the battleline, a fourth force appeared. The remnants of Meinstadt's war machines and all of the harquebuses were suddenly levelled at the onrushing green horde. The goblin frontrunners faltered in places and there was a collision of bodies. The larger orcs remained uncowed and hacked through their more timid brethren if they held them up.

Like a piece of meat, Wilhelm had dangled the prospect of a quick and bloody win before the Paunch. He was greedy, this Grom, and he had taken the bait readily. Though still outnumbered, the Empire had trapped the greenskins in the narrow defile and could attack on three aspects at once. Victory was far from assured, but at least now they had a fighting chance.

Karlich's shoulders ached from heaving the carriage of the great cannon up to the ridgeline. Several regiments were positioned with the war engines, partly to defend them, partly to get them where they needed to be. The first task was done – blackpowder smoke already laced the air from the opening salvoes, and set ears ringing with *thudding* reports – the second, keeping the machines from harm, would not be as easy.

The Grimblades made ranks quickly, stationed just below one of the two great cannon. Meinstadt still had the volley gun and one of the mortars left too. The latter was aimed at the rear of the greenskin lines, where its explosive shells would cause maximum damage but pose minimum risk to friendly troops. A deadly barrage landed deep in the valley, throwing greenskins and dirt plumes into the air with brutal ease.

Lenkmann pumped his fist, thrilled at the ingenuity of the Empire taking such a toll on the beasts, but the hole in the mobs was quickly filled and his optimism disappeared with it.

'It's as if it never happened, just like at Averheim,' he said, holding onto his banner with both hands as if it supported him. 'They're endless.'

'You expected any different,' grumbled Volker, sticks held fast against his pigskin drum. The instrument still felt awkward, as if he were wearing a dead man's coat that didn't fit. Rechts had been the Grimblades' beating heart. To carry his drum felt like a transgression, not an honour. Volker wondered if it was time to leave the army.

Karlich intruded on his thoughts. 'We don't need to beat them,' he said, rotating his shoulder blade where it was still sore, 'just bloody them enough to force the greenskins out of Reikland.'

'I thought orcs liked to fight?' queried Eber. The big man was a welcome presence in the ranks, though the bindings around his chest suggested he might not have much fight left in him. 'Won't that just make them want to fight more?'

'Anything that lives doesn't want to die,' Brand told him. 'Greenskins are no different.'

'There'll be much dying this day, before it's out,' said Volker.

Karlich adjusted his shield straps, looking down at the throng below. 'Be thankful you're up here and not amongst that.'

Farther down the valley from the Grimblades' position, Wilhelm's baiting force made a slow advance. With higher ground and Imperial discipline to gird them, the ragged soldiery could effectively 'bung' the valley. They were so closely packed, they'd be hard to rout. Wilhelm's presence, shining in his gilded armour plate, would galvanise them further. Even still, it was a meat grinder.

Hope, what there was of it, seemed very far away.

'Should we make our farewells now?' asked Lenkmann with genuine regret.

Volker went to reply, when Karlich stopped him.

'Leave it unsaid. It's a bad omen to honour the dead before they're in the ground,' he added. 'Tends to end up putting them there.'

Another blast of powder smoke obscured the footsloggers before they met with the first of Grom's orcs. Karlich was still wiping soot from his eyes when the clash of arms resolved itself on the low breeze.

At the valley sides, on the east and west slopes, similar struggles played out. The high ridge and the backline afforded a strong vantage point from which to see the entire battle. Maybe that's why Wilhelm appointed Ledner to marshal the rearguard force. Karlich had seen the spymaster only once after deployment. Even as he surveyed the carnage below, as the Hornhelms split off from combat and reformed for another charge, as pike and sword met with cleaver and club, as skulls were split and bodies sundered, Karlich knew Ledner was close by. It felt like a blade against his back, poised to thrust.

Smoke rolled down into the valley like fog. It was not so different to Averheim, but here it gathered in the valley's low trough. Wilhelm's horse fought the reins a little as the grey-white mist engulfed them. With the weak breeze unable to shift it, the smoke lingered at the valley bottom in a thick pall. It smothered the greenskins, making them appear numberless as they emerged from it in droves.

The element of surprise was spent. The fighting was fast and dirty now. Wilhelm's runefang was well bloodied as the giant black orc loomed into view. It appeared as a shadow at first, like a beast of the deep oceans slowly surfacing. He felt the Griffonkorps close protectively around him. The axe, too large and heavy for a man to wield, cut through the mist first. One of the Griffonkorps fell away with hardly a sound but minus his head. The carpet of fog swallowed him like he was just a memory.

A second knight managed to angle a sword thrust before the black orc's claw snapped out and seized him by the helmet. The Griffonkorps elicited a sort of squeak as his skull was crushed.

In the intervening seconds, Wilhelm pushed forward ahead of his protectors. The black orc emerged fully from the pooling smoke. It was huge. Eye-to-eye with the prince, despite the fact he was mounted, it snarled and bit off the horse's head. Part of the poor creature's skull remained as it collapsed to the ground, gushing blood, taking Wilhelm with it. The horse's demise was slow enough for the prince to leap free and still keep his feet, after a fashion. All around him, the desperate fighting went on. Parts of the shield wall nearby crumpled against the enemy's savagery. Spears were snapped like twigs but the Empire line held.

The shadow of the axe swept over Wilhelm, hard to discern in the press of bodies and the tumult of battle. Another Griffonkorps gave his life so the prince might live, horse and knight cleaved almost in two. Wilhelm used these seconds to get a solid footing. The black orc beast was not alone. Its slightly smaller, but no less brutal, brethren crowded out the other Empire soldiers near the prince's side. He would face the beast alone. Somewhere, probably during the fall, he'd lost his shield, so he held *Dragon Tooth* two-handed. Wilhelm knew he'd only get one chance at the monstrous black orc and he'd need all of his strength to kill it, even with the magical dwarf blade.

Obviously a warlord and one of Grom's chieftains, the orc's skin was like dark leather only more rugged. Thick mail armour swathed a heavily-muscled body that heaved with barely fettered rage. The axe was the size of a cart wheel, notched with use and stained crimson. Spiked boots added unnecessary height, while the black orc's skull was stitched with scars. Around its neck it wore a ring of desiccated halfling corpses as a man might wear a charm of wolf's teeth. The beast bellowed, showering the prince with foul spittle. Its rancid breath stank of rotten meat.

The clash of arms surrounded Wilhelm. He was in the eye of a massive storm but the war had narrowed into this one fight, this moment of kill or be killed. The prince tried to step back, telling himself it was for a better fighting stance and not because he balked at the ferocious creature, but found there was no room. It didn't matter anyway. The black orc had issued its challenge. Now it advanced, axe swinging like a deadly pendulum.

'Strength of Sigmar,' Wilhelm muttered, kissing his blade in the manner of the old ways, and went to meet the beast.

* * *

Staring into nothing was getting maddening. For the last few minutes Karlich had watched the belt of thickening smoke, alert for the first sign of a greenskin breakthrough. He blinked away several imagined horrors in the mist, before realising all was well. Sweat sheened his forehead, though he wasn't hot. With the pale cloud wreathing the field, tendrils of it reaching up to them on the ridge, a nervous tension gripped the valley. There was little to see now, even from on high, just half-shadows moving in the false fog and the sounds of battle.

It was eldritch, unsettling. Lenkmann clamped a hand over his mouth to still his chattering teeth. The grey-white smoke played on his fears, reminding the banner bearer of something unnatural. Lenkmann saw ghosts in that growing cloud. In some respects, it wasn't so far from the truth. Some of the shadows were soon just echoes where once they'd been lives. The smoke deadened, evoking a sense of the strange and disquieting. It was made worse by the presence of the great cannon so nearby.

The fate of Blaselocker was put into Karlich's mind as the war machine boomed only feet above them. The baron's shredded remains had to be portioned away in separate sacks when the cannon had exploded alongside him. The raven-keepers were still removing iron shards from his flesh when poor Blaselocker was half assembled on a slab in the Temple of Morr.

The cannon thundered again, rocking on wedged wheels. Karlich winced, dipping his head against the noise. When he opened his eyes, he noticed the pommel of his inherited blade glinting. It brought back the memory of Stahler. He'd be laughing at him, no doubt. Karlich drew comfort from the imagined presence of his old captain embodied by the sword. Some of the smoke had cleared a little when he looked up again and saw Stahler's replacement, Vogen, fighting hard on the east flank.

Fortunately the greenskins had yet to right themselves. The smoke added to their disorder and confusion, and they fought at a disadvantage. Without more manpower, though, the Empire couldn't press it. Attrition governed the battle at that moment. With the greenskins' superior numbers, it meant the balance would soon shift as the casualties mounted on both sides. They needed to find a way to break the orcs, and soon.

Ledner's choke-rasp shouting above brought Karlich from the throng below and back up to the ridge. He was directing some of the cannon fire for Engineer Meinstadt, picking out targets in the fog. Somewhere in the distance, a goblin chariot exploded in a shower of wooden splinters. They'd navigated the rocks intended to foul them and were roaming the flanks. There was little room, but the narrow machines snuck through.

Shifting his gaze, Karlich found the centre of the battlefield to be almost occluded but the smoke was slowly beginning to dissipate. He recognised the Carroburg Few and wished they were side-by-side. Von Rauken's men slowly resolved in the fog, fighting hard against a mob of massive, dark-skinned orcs. Something even bigger bellowed and hollered in their ranks before a belt of fog veiled them again.

Karlich said a quiet prayer that it wasn't the last time he'd see them alive.

The irony wasn't lost on Ledner. Despite his stern words to the spymaster on the road to Altdorf, Wilhelm had offered himself up as bait to draw the Paunch out. He suppressed a wry smile at that thought, allowing only a moment of reflection, before turning his attention back to the cannon. The goblin king, his death or serious injury, was key to victory. As it so often did, greenskin supremacy depended on the strength and willpower of its warlord. Without Grom, the disparate tribes would quickly fragment, lesser chieftains would vie for the leadership of the army and the Waaagh would slowly dissipate.

Bloody their nose… It was a phrase Ledner had heard much of in the intervening hours since leaving Kemperbad and before the battle.

The Paunch was shrewd, far shrewder than any goblin had a right to be, he would not be goaded easily. Wilhelm had to offer up a trophy for his rack the greenskin could truly savour. The only bargaining piece that the prince had, though, was himself. It was a risk Ledner didn't like. Using Wilhelm to reveal an assassin, with potential benefits resulting from either outcome, was one thing; the prince's death on this fog-choked field would mean the sack of Altdorf. The spymaster could see much at stake, and much that could go wrong. It wasn't a game he liked playing, when the odds were evenly stacked.

These machinations had been flooding through Ledner's mind like irritated moths bouncing off the glass of a lantern. Worse still, Wilhelm had ordered him to the ridge. War machines were dangerous, the province of madmen, but it was the fact that he couldn't be by the prince's side that bothered him the most. Ledner suspected their earlier 'words' had something to do with that. Or perhaps it was a less emotionally-driven decision than it first appeared, and Wilhelm was merely being practical. If he fell in battle, then it would be up to Ledner to rally the troops or marshal the retreat. Either way, leadership would be needed.

It didn't matter. Fate was not yet done with the Prince of Reikland, nor was it done with Adolphus Ledner.

He waited for a short subsidence in the cannonade before turning in his saddle to address Meinstadt.

'Engineer, how long can we keep this up?'

The cannons bellowed again, their iron cargo buoyed on fat streams of powder smoke spat from fire-blackened mouths.

Meinstadt hollered at one of the gunnery crew with the volley gun to rotate its barrel array – Ledner eyed the so-called 'wonder weapon' suspiciously, glad he was well away from it – before replying.

'We're low on ball and powder,' the engineer said, leaving an oil smear across his forehead after mopping his brow. Most of the gunnery crew had shed their tunics and let the sweat sheathe their brawny, smoke-stained bodies. They were as black as coal miners, and twice as grim. 'When that's done, we'll go to grapeshot. Hope you've a few coins in that expensive-looking attire you're wearing, captain,' he added wryly. 'We might need them.'

Ledner's retort was lost in the gunfire, and he gave up repeating it. Before he returned his attention to the field, he bemoaned the lack of ammunition to which Meinstadt gave the equivalent of a vocal shrug then went back to his labours.

One saving grace was that at least the prince had arrayed some decent troops around him. Though now he looked more intently, through the spyglass Wilhelm had given him to observe the field, Ledner saw the Griffonkorps had thinned to almost nothing and the greatsworders were struggling against a mob of hulking black orcs. Their banner dipped and swayed frantically as they tried to reach the prince. They had good reason – Wilhelm was facing an absolute monster. Ledner had only seen ogres as big. Had the beast not been green, he would've assumed it *was* an ogre.

Something caught Ledner's eye, just at the periphery of his vision. He angled the spyglass eastward and caught sight of the prince's prey. It was Grom, ranging along the flank, content to let the battle unfold and develop, so he could better read it.

Ledner shook his head, disbelieving.

Truly, this fat brute was unique – he could think! He plotted and planned like a man! Mercy of Shallya, not all greenskins are created thusly or the Empire would drown in its own blood. It might yet!

Fascinated, Ledner watched the Paunch catch and commandeer a chariot that was slow to build momentum after stalling on the rocks. He hauled the crew off and took their place. As he climbed aboard, the carriage of the chariot dug into the earth like a wooden plough, dragged down by Grom's heavy body. The wolves pulling it strained at their crude tresses, struggling to ferry the obese goblin king. Under his fierce goading, they picked up speed. Fear lent them vigour.

Greenskins in the Paunch's path either stepped aside or were crushed under the chariot's ironbound wheels.

Ledner guessed at Grom's direction. He followed the path suggested by his erratic journey on the chariot and found Wilhelm at the end of it. The prince was engaged with the giant black orc and hadn't seen the goblin king approaching.

A pang of something resembling anxiety twisted Ledner's gut. It was a fleeting emotion, hard to discern. He seldom felt anything but calm detachment.

'This is why I never leave your side, my lord,' he muttered bitterly. Ledner urged his steed forwards, heading for the slope and Prince Wilhelm.

CHAPTER TWENTY-EIGHT
The value of sacrifice

*Reikland hills, on the Bögenhafen road,
34 miles from Altdorf*

Feint. Evade. Strike. The words of Kogswald entered Wilhelm's mind from the past: *remember these three rules when fighting a foe bigger and stronger than you. Move quickly and attack when your opponent tires, victory by a thousand cuts is still victory.*

But the giant black orc showed no sign of tiring, nor would it die by a thousand cuts. One chance, one cut, was all that Wilhelm would get, if that.

A small arena of dirt had grown around the two combatants, despite the efforts of the Empire troops to reach their lord. Wilhelm was glad of it; at least he didn't feel like a drowning man anymore. When the black orc attacked, it charged like a bull. When it passed for a third time, Wilhelm heard deep grunting before its bulk was reduced to a shadow in the fog. It struck a glancing blow to the prince's pauldron. Only the virtue of the armour's forging kept his shoulder from shattering. The monster came again, turning quickly on its heel and resolving through the gloom. Something hot struck Wilhelm's face. Belatedly he realised it was freshly shed blood from the black orc's axe.

This time the prince stood his ground. *Dragon Tooth* had taken on a strange, dull glow in the fog. An overhead swipe drove towards his head. He only just parried it, jarring both arms, but deflecting the blow downwards. The axe was buried deep in the ground. Pounding greenskin feet had loosened the soil at the valley bottom and the earth received the blade gratefully.

Wilhelm took his chance. The effort of parrying sent his runefang away from the black orc, but he used the momentum of the attack to carry on the swing. It went full circle in the time it took for the black orc to realise his axe was snared, and impaled the monster's skull.

The black orc shuddered, the pathetic halfling corpses around his neck quivering as if they were dancing. Wilhelm pushed hard against bone until his runefang pierced the greenskin's tiny brain. The black orc let go of its axe, still refusing to yield and acknowledge it was dead. Wilhelm wrenched *Dragon Tooth* free. The enchanted blade tore through the monster's head, decapitating it from the chin upwards. The slab of stinking skull and meat sloped off the ruddy stump like a cut from a butcher's block. Its claws stopped grasping, inches from the prince's throat and the giant black orc slumped into a heap.

A spike of dissolution shot through the other black orcs, stunned at the chieftain's death. Sensing a turn in the fight, the Carroburg Few drove even harder at the greenskins. Together with a large regiment of Auerswald spearmen, they broke the black orcs and sent them reeling. Several goblin mobs which had previously been eager to join the winning side lost heart and fled too. Wilhelm ordered the line to hold and reform.

'Draw out the warlord,' he shouted. The prince was still stranded in the open, unaware that he already had.

He was marshalling his strength when a spectacular explosion lit the ridge behind him, sending burning shrapnel into the ranks below. Men standing several feet away were struck and killed. Wilhelm turned, along with others in the army, to witness a massive fireball ignite the ridge.

Karlich tasted earth as he was thrown down and scattered with the other halberdiers by a tremendous blast wave. Heat pricked the hairs on the back of his neck and despite the grubby tang of soil in his mouth, he embraced the instinct to sink his face down further.

It had come from the vicinity of the volley gun, he guessed, though it was hard to tell with his senses momentarily shredded. He still couldn't see or hear properly. Soot stained the air black, making it hard to breathe. Somewhere amidst the deafening explosion of blackpowder a horse shrieked.

'Come together, come–' Karlich's voice was choked by coughing. Smoke filled his lungs and he brought up thick black phlegm. Wiping his mouth, he looked around. Shapes emerged as the black clouds slowly cleared. He was still dazed, only vaguely aware he was alone, when he noticed dead men strewn upon the ridgeline. War machine crew and harquebus gunners were the main casualties. Meinstadt's voice rose above the panicked clamour, attempting to restore order. Karlich thought the engineer had been with the volley gun and wondered briefly how he'd managed to survive the blast before he saw the dead horse.

Though peppered with hot metal from the sundered cannon, its insides now its outsides, Karlich recognised the steed as Ledner's. Following the unfortunate beast's path, he found its master not far away, rolling on his back, dazed. He was quite far from the summit of the ridge. Ledner had been moving away when the volley gun misfired. If not, he'd surely be amongst the dead.

The world had dimmed into a narrow half-blur, as if he was seeing it through an underwater tunnel. Karlich's hearing was still affected too, but he didn't let it stop him stumbling towards the spymaster.

'On your feet,' he snarled, feeling his hate for the man anew. Karlich seized Ledner's hand, almost got him level, then slipped, sending the two of them back down again.

A bestial cry echoed from farther down the valley, tinny with the explosion still reverberating in Karlich's skull. Orcs had broken through the first line, part of the east flank crumpling when one of the militia regiments had made for the edge of the valley in utter terror. They were big, not the size of black orcs, but burly and thickly armoured.

'Get up!' said Karlich with more urgency than bile this time. His hearing came back in a crash of sound. He staggered at first, but quickly composed himself. 'I said up, you bastard.'

Ledner smiled, drooling blood from where he'd lost a couple of teeth. He had a cut across his forehead, too, and held his wounded arm gingerly as he rose.

'Here's your chance, *Lothar*,' he said. 'I'm at your mercy. I can see it in your eyes!'

Karlich had his dirk and Ledner was injured and unarmed. A swift glance behind revealed they were separated from the rest of the men, a belt of thick smoke clouding the view.

No one would ever know.

All the things Ledner had done, the way he'd manipulated them. He'd cost Karlich friends and comrades, forced them to compromise their own morals to serve his shady ones. This was a man willing to sacrifice his prince and liege-lord. However noble the cause, nothing could excuse that. Karlich had him by the scruff of the neck.

It would be easy.

All this flashed through the sergeant's mind before he made his decision.

'No.' He pulled Ledner up, helped him onto his shoulder. 'I killed in cold blood before,' he said, walking him back up the ridge. 'I did it for love. I won't do it for hate, not for you. And in any case,' he added, whispering into Ledner's ear, 'your death will come soon enough. I saw the blood on your lip in the alley. Lung rot is a painful way to go.'

The mask slipped for a moment before Karlich looked away again, all of Ledner's insecurities and fears revealed to him. Let him die in agony; Karlich's conscience would be clear.

Ahead of the two men, the Grimblades were reforming. Mercifully, it looked like no casualties had been sustained in the blast, just pounding heads and grazed knees. Karlich was already shouting up to the great cannon, warning them about the approaching orcs when Ledner found his wits and pointed to the opposite side of the valley.

'No, there!'

Meinstadt never saw Ledner. His eyes were on the orc mob advancing on the war machines. Fearing they'd be overrun, he ordered up pails of coins, nails, spoons and anything else they could find to stuff the cannon with and fire grapeshot. It would render the weapon useless for the rest of the battle but at least they'd survive a little longer. The beasts were bearing down on them. By the time the cannon was turned and primed, they'd be too close for an iron ball.

Karlich followed Ledner's outstretched hand. He saw Grom, riding a lop-sided chariot, heading for the prince who'd just despatched a monstrous black orc and hadn't seen the goblin king.

He looked back down the ridge. The armoured orcs were clanking up the slope, gathering momentum. They looked tough. The Grimblades were still shaken from the explosion. Across the valley, Prince Wilhelm stood in the path of the goblin king's chariot. The cannon couldn't pepper the orcs with grapeshot *and* fire on the chariot. The latter was a risk, but without intervention the prince would be run down.

Grom was getting close...

Karlich made up his mind. He had to shout to be heard.

'Save the prince, we'll hold off the orcs.'

Meinstadt, a dishevelled, slightly blackened figure, nodded and ordered the great cannon turned about. He was already giving out miniscule adjustments to elevation and amounts of blackpowder when Karlich resumed his position in the Grimblades' front rank.

Ledner was alongside him.

'This is my captain's sword,' he told the spymaster. He drew the blade and it shone star-like in the light. 'I don't plan on dishonouring it today, nor should you.'

Ledner had picked up his own sword when they'd staggered back up the ridge. He held it in one hand, shakily due to his injuries.

'I knew you had balls, sergeant,' he rasped. 'That's why I've always liked you. That's why I haven't had you killed.'

'Sigmar be praised, then,' Karlich replied. The orcs were close enough to taste their foetid aroma on the breeze.

Ledner gave him a quizzical look, to which Karlich answered, 'That you spared me long enough for this bloody end.'

Behind them, the great cannon boomed.

* * *

Wilhelm was alone when the chariot burst out from the greenskin ranks. Grom had weaved around the back of his mobs, waiting until the last moment to charge. Bearing down on Wilhelm now as it did, there was no time to mount a defence against the deadly machine. Its spinning scythed wheels were mesmerising... The cries of Wilhelm's men rushing to try and save him were moot, their desperate actions fated to always be too late.

In the wake of the fleeing black orcs, a mob of tattooed greenskins with bones through their noses, wearing animal hide and wielding crude stone axes charged into the open ground, wailing.

Caught between a goblin king and a sea of frenzied green, thought the prince.

Wilhelm saluted his forefathers and then his enemy. He levelled his runefang at Grom and prepared to meet him.

'*Deus Sigmar...*' he murmured, and closed his eyes.

At the sound of splintered wood and half-heard goblin curses, he opened them again.

Grom's chariot was wrecked. The Paunch was flattened underneath its carriage in a heap. One of the scythed wheels was still spinning, but pointed harmlessly in the air. The other had broken off and rolled away somewhere out of sight. The wolves were dead, crushed or impaled. A cannonball was lodged in the ground nearby, exuding smoke. It had upended the machine, flipping it dramatically to land just short of the prince.

When Grom didn't move at first, Wilhelm dared to hope the goblin king was dead. But then a piece of debris trembled atop the wreckage and fell off. Other larger pieces followed until the Paunch was back on his feet. He wrenched a stake of wood from his chest. Wilhelm's eyes widened as the wound closed behind it, and he saw all of Grom's cuts and bruises heal as if they had never been there. He recalled Ledner's words about the rumour the warlord could not be killed. Despite the evidence of his own eyes, he forced himself not to believe it.

Abruptly, Wilhelm became aware of Empire troops rushing to his side.

Grom's minions did the same. The savage orcs subsumed him into their ranks, while the Paunch's standard-bearer laughed and capered beside him. A brutal cuff from Grom to the little wretch's head curbed his enthusiasm.

Seeing the prince, Grom snarled and spat a gob of blood on the ground. He brandished his axe meaningfully before ordering the charge.

Up close, Grom looked even bigger. Eating troll flesh had done this to him, so it was reckoned. It accounted for the creature's massive belly, swollen with carnage, glutted on war.

Wilhelm allowed himself a murderous grin that narrowed his eyes. 'What do we do with trolls...' he said, before muttering a word of power that ignited a bright red flame along *Dragon Tooth*'s blade.

Kogswald's reply in the war tent returned to him in a whisper as the Empire men charged.

We burn them.

Several of the armoured orcs rushing up the slope towards the war machines jerked and fell but the desultory harquebus salvo didn't slow them.

'For Reikland and Prince Wilhelm!' cried Karlich, before storming down the slope with his men to meet them.

Even Ledner roared, a hoarse unsettling noise, as a fatalistic abandon gripped the Grimblades.

Despite the fact they occupied the higher ground, the impact of the armoured orcs was brutal. Heifer and Innker, two recent stand-ins for the front rank, died at once. Heifer lost his nose and most of his face when a spiked club staved it in; Innker slipped on his own innards before realising he'd been opened up by an axe and died spewing blood down his tunic. Others, who Karlich failed to recognise in the maddened scrum of the fight, moved up from the back ranks to replace the fallen.

Eber took a blow to the stomach, more haft than blade, and grunted in pain. He stuck the orc on the end of his halberd and kept pushing until it was dead. Gore streaked the haft when he jerked it loose.

Brand abandoned his polearm completely, having dragged a hammer from the carnage and used that to bludgeon the greenskins. Bone chips and brain matter flicked off every strike he made. Stooping in the melee, he picked up a fallen sword and wielded it in his free hand. Stabbing and swiping, he was more frenzied than the savage beasts escorting the goblin king down in the valley. There was no finesse in this, no killing art. It was raw and primal with men reduced to beasts, desperate for survival.

For a fleeting moment, Karlich thought they could win. He felt determination in his troops and an overwhelming desire to live. Even injured, Ledner was devastating, a true swordsman compared to his own clumsy efforts. Stahler's sword was the leveller, though, shearing armour like parchment and cleaving off limbs like they were dead twigs.

But it wasn't enough. Karlich's misplaced optimism crumpled when Volker's lifeless body spun away from the orc chieftain leading the mob, impelled by the cleaver blow that had ruined his face and ended his life. The Reikland hunter disappeared in the mass as he fell and was trampled underfoot. Karlich wanted to reach for him and save Volker the indignity of being ground into the dirt but it was impossible.

Someone cried out. It sounded like Eber. Pain or anguish, it was hard to tell for sure.

They were losing. Karlich felt it in the surge of hopelessness that threatened to end him. A back step became three. Lenkmann looked to him for a sign. His left eye was gummed with blood. Karlich couldn't actually see it for sure. It didn't appear to concern him. Lenkmann's banner, his charge and solemn responsibility, was flecked with a comrade's blood.

Volker's dead.

'Hold! Hold!' rasped Ledner, shoving Karlich's shoulder in a gesture of defiance.

If they fled now they would not escape. The greenskins would catch them and they'd be slain to a man. Do or die – Karlich knew it was this he'd agreed to when telling Meinstadt to save the prince. No sacrifice comes without cost.

Behind them, men were running. Karlich heard the distant bootfalls getting closer and realised they weren't running away.

A burst of staccato *cracks* sounded near to his left, or was it his right? He wondered if he'd got turned around in the battle. Several orcs fell dead with smoke oozing from holes in their armour. The *cracks* came again, to much the same effect. Then a band of brawny gunnery crew led by Meinstadt slammed into the side of the orcs and laid about them with hatchets, hammers and other tools. With their machinery's ammunition exhausted, the engineer had pressganged the mortar crew into combat.

Meinstadt discharged his pistol at close range. The repeating mechanism fired three shots that sank an orc to its knees where he finished it with his sword.

Renewed hope filled Karlich, and the sergeant used it as a vessel for his anger. Armoured orcs died beneath Stahler's blade. It was the like the old captain lived on through it.

The greenskins thought they'd broken the Empire men. When they held on, rallying to Lenkmann's soiled standard, the orcs' pugnacity faded. The Grimblades had fought back the ground they'd lost, grinding the greenskins back down the slope, when a cry came from the ridgeline.

'Down!'

To a man, the halberdiers and gunnery crew dropped. Above them, a burst of grapeshot shredded what was left of the armoured orcs and broke them, but finished the last of the war machines.

None of the halberdiers gave chase. They'd hung on long enough for the great cannon to reload. Several of the Grimblades were dead, Volker with them. Karlich and Brand dragged his battered body from amongst the fallen.

They tried not to look at the dead man's face. They wouldn't have recognised it anyway. Brand shawled the poor sod with his cloak and dragged him farther up the ridge. Karlich ordered them all up there. With the cannons spent, it made no more sense to stay below them, they might as well occupy the highest vantage point where they were not so far from the ranks of harquebus. Grief was a luxury to feel later.

Karlich noticed Eber had not moved. He was on his knees, half sunk in the blood-soaked earth. His halberd rested limply in the crook of his arm like a fallen flag. The sergeant winced as he went down to him. A cut in his leg gave him discomfort, but he neither cared nor had time to staunch it.

'Higher ground, Eber,' he said, aware of the battle raging below them and that another greenskin breakthrough could be imminent. 'Come on, I'll help you up.'

He reached under Eber's thick arm but it was like heaving dead weight. Then he saw the burly Reiklander holding on to his sides. He was whispering something.

'Sergeant!' Lenkmann cried. The banner bearer's tone was urgent but Karlich waved away his concern without looking. Instead, he leaned in and listened.

'Like thread, like thread...' Eber muttered, and Karlich noticed the big man's fingers were ruby red and slick with his own blood. 'Feels like... sides splitting... I'm coming undone...'

'Lenkmann! Brand!' Karlich cried when he saw the wounds reopened in Eber's ox-like chest.

So much blood, so much blood, was all he kept thinking.

Eber was staring at him when he turned back. An incongruous look of serenity softened his face.

'I always thought of you...' he said with the last of his breath, '...like a father.'

When Brand and Lenkmann arrived, Karlich was crouched down shaking his head. His eyes were rimed with tears. It would be easy to give in then, but the battle wasn't done. A prince fought for his life, fought for all their lives in the valley below.

'Help me carry him,' said Karlich in a distant voice. Gazing down into the cauldron below, he hoped the sacrifice they'd made would be worth it.

For a fat brute, Grom was quick. And he fought with the fury of a caged boar. A savage punch sent hot spikes of agony rushing through Wilhelm's jaw where the goblin king had connected. His eyes filled with white needles that threatened to turn to black. The prince shook off the nausea and disorientation that tried to overwhelm him. He bit his lip, finding clarity in pain, before fending off Grom's bearded axe with *Dragon Tooth*'s blade.

Around him, the prince's charges fought so their lord might get his chance, his one chance to defeat the Paunch and end the war – at least for Reikland. Greatswordsmen from the Carroburg Few, led by their grizzled champion, fought side by side with spearmen from Auerswald and citizen militias from countless villages and small towns. The Reikland had rallied for their province and their prince. Wilhelm was determined not be found wanting, but reward their faith in him.

Grom came again, the low *thwump* of his axe like a death knell when it swept overhead. It met Wilhelm's runefang with a dissonant *clang* and forced the prince back a step. Another swing, overhead and hard.

Wilhelm parried high, pushing the axe blade out and wide, before driving into the beast with his armoured shoulder.

It was like hitting a wall of lead. Grom's flesh was as unyielding as it was obese. Though he'd jarred his shoulder, Wilhelm was close enough to yank the dagger from the belt at his hip and stab the greenskin king in the neck. He drove it deep, one-handed – the other gripped *Dragon Tooth* – until the fat brute squealed.

Grom used his bulk to drive Wilhelm off, the dagger wrenched from the prince's grasp but still embedded in the goblin's neck. Grom yanked it free with a spit of dark blood. In moments the wound closed and the Paunch smiled through spine-like teeth the colour of rust.

Wilhelm rolled *Dragon Tooth* around in a circle, tracing arcs of flame in the air that vanished in seconds.

'Just a taste,' promised the prince, but inwardly he despaired at the goblin's apparent invulnerability.

Grom snorted, belched and came at him again. One solid hit from his axe, which was no ordinary blade, and Wilhelm was sure he'd be maimed or dead. Anger made the goblin king reckless. His first strike cut thin air. Wilhelm went to counter, but Grom's wrath also lent him strength. Another punch crumpled the prince's fauld and sent lances of agony into his abdomen. This time he embraced the pain and fashioned a lunge into Grom's exposed thigh.

Dragon Tooth went deep and the rancid stink of burning meat clouded the air. Wilhelm ignored it, goring with his blade, dragging a deep and painful cleft in the greenskin's seemingly regenerative flesh.

Grom squealed, porcine and high in pitch. So close, their bodies touching, he leaned over to bite the prince's shoulder. Wilhelm's pain escaped in an agonised yelp, but he kept the pressure up and drove his runefang deeper. Grom stopped the biting when he threw his head back to squeal again. Wilhelm was reminded of hunting swine in the Reikwald Forest. Stuck boar made a similar noise. This was no prize to mount on the mantle, no hog roast to enjoy by a roaring hearth; it was a dire foe that had brought the Empire to its knees.

'I'll cut you dow–'

Grom butted the prince hard, stalling his vow. Wilhelm's sword didn't leave his grip as he fell back, and the blade pulled out from the goblin king's leg with the tearing of flesh. The axe blow that followed would have finished the prince were it not for the last Griffonkorps selling his life to save his liege-lord. Plate parted before Grom's crimson-edged blade, cutting the gallant knight in two and spilling him all over the field like offal.

Wilhelm feared the goblin king was restored again and back for more, but when the dizziness abated he saw the wound *Dragon Tooth* had scored was not closing. That last axe strike was the lashing of a desperate beast in terrible pain. The skin on Grom's leg was burned black, seared by a captured flame.

Kogswald had been right about the trolls, and the goblin king's miraculous healing was due to the physiology of those beasts. Fire was anathema to them, and so it was to Grom. The Paunch was in agony. Two large savage orcs held him upright as he cursed and frothed. With their overlord's wounding, the fight was ebbing from the deranged greenskins. Their berserker's fervour was almost tapped. A rank of the beasts went down to spears and greatswords as the Empire men fought to hold the advantage.

Grom looked about to rally, digging deep of his pain to find the molten anger at its core. When Wilhelm showed him *Dragon Tooth* and flared the blade into fiery life, the goblin king faltered. He shied away from the ancestral sword, fearful of its burning edge, afraid for his precious flesh and acutely aware of his own mortality.

Goblins were craven creatures, even brutes as large and cunning as Grom. He knew this was a fight he was unwilling to pay the cost to win. Snorting in the crude language of the greenskins, Grom ordered the savage orcs to withdraw and bear him away from the fire-blade into the bargain.

Across the valley, the Empire and their allies sensed the balance shift in their favour. At either flank they pressed the greenskins even harder, a final effort to send them from the field. Wilhelm led the centre, his victorious warriors butchering the orcs and goblins too belligerent to buckle with their warlord.

From the ridgeline harquebuses cracked, harrying the greenskins at every step, until their shot and powder were exhausted. As the smoke settled and the noise of battle died to be replaced by the sullen moans of dying, the Empire was left on the field.

They had bloodied Grom's nose. The Paunch was far from defeated, but they had repelled him from Reikland and kept Altdorf safe.

Wilhelm would learn later that Grom had turned northwards, across the border and into Middenland. Todbringer would have to face the greenskin horde now and see if his armoured bulwarks could weather the vented storm as he had hoped.

For Reikland's part, they let the goblins go. The battle was won but there were precious few troops left alive in the valley to savour it. Certainly, there was not army enough to follow the Paunch north all the way to Middenheim.

Instead, Wilhelm raised the army's banner. It was soiled and bloody from where it had fallen in the earth as the last Griffonkorps had died. Still, it fluttered proudly in the prince's grasp. He lifted *Dragon Tooth* to the heavens and a great cheer went up, hounding the greenskins all the way past the border.

Victory was Reikland's.

And upon the ridge, a sergeant and his men praised almighty Sigmar for that.

EPILOGUE

Reikland prairie, on the outskirts of Altdorf,
Eight miles from the new capital of the Empire

The grey day matched Karlich's mood as he surveyed a steel sky from a rocky outcrop. It was a day of reunion and remembrance. Four years had passed since Waaagh! Grom had blighted the Empire and brought his country to its very knees.

Karlich was proud to have been there at the end, at least for Reikland. Tales still drifted down to southern provinces of the razing of Middenland and the destruction of a temple of the White Wolves at Middenheim. Grom's anger hadn't been sated at Nuln, that much was obvious. After that, the beast had carried on northwards to the ocean and lands far beyond the Empire's and even the Old World's shores.

It was a day of great change, too. Altdorf, in all its magnificent glory, lay below. Wagons entered the city in their droves. For three days and nights it had been thus, as the Golden Palace of Nuln was stripped of its ostentation and Dieter's ill-gotten wealth redistributed. Even years later, there was much that needed to be rebuilt. Grom's invasion had left a lasting and destructive legacy behind it. The poorer villages and hamlets felt its bite more than most. Here was where the money was needed. Wilhelm, Saviour of the Reik, would see it was spent wisely.

It turned out the assassins and the dealings with Marienburg were but scraps of a larger treachery, some of which was, admittedly, perpetuated by Ledner. Karlich didn't know many details, save what he had heard down the years. It seemed Dieter's Golden Palace, all of his accumulated wealth, had been garnered from bribes. Marienburg had recently seceded from the Empire, its independence bought through Imperial corruption. At his prince's behest, Adolphus Ledner had uncovered documents and witnesses that would attest to Dieter's role in it. Many were sick of his indolent rule and like sharks scenting blood, descended upon the Emperor. It had taken time to expose these dealings, especially in the aftermath of the war, but in the end an emergency council at Volkshalle in Altdorf had seen the then Emperor deposed. He'd fled to Marienburg, in fear for his life. Rumours abounded that an army from Reikland was headed to the Wasteland to bring him back. Wilhelm was his worthy successor. With a new Emperor came a new capital, and for the first time in many years that honour was Altdorf's again.

'Grim day for a coronation,' remarked a voice Karlich knew from behind him.

'Lenkmann!' He shook hands with his old banner bearer in the manner of a firm friend.

Since the war, the Grimblades had been disbanded. There were so few of them left that there seemed little point in going on. Even with recruits, it wouldn't have been the same regiment – not anymore.

Lenkmann wore a sergeant's silver laurels on his lapel now. Karlich had heard the lad got his own command. It was well deserved.

'Pristine as ever, I see,' he said, clapping Lenkmann warmly on the shoulders and looking him up and down. Not a buckle out of place. He was immaculate in his dress attire.

'Some things don't change,' Lenkmann replied, with a note of sadness he couldn't hide.

'And this?' asked Karlich, pointing to his eye.

He'd lost it during the battle in the valley, which the poets had dubbed 'Glory at Bloody Gorge'. Well, the bards were right about one thing.

'I think the patch gives me an air of danger.' Lenkmann laughed, not deigning to touch it. Several years without his left eye, but he still hadn't fully adjusted. Perhaps he never would. 'We all lost something that day, though.'

Karlich smiled but his face still matched the brooding sky.

'I heard you're no longer serving in the army,' Lenkmann ventured after a moment's silence.

Karlich looked to the city. Several regiments were already trooping through Altdorf's gates to observe the pomp and ceremony. He recognised the banner of von Rauken's Carroburg Few and hoped the veteran champion was still amongst them. Their ranks, so badly battered during the campaign of four years ago, had been swelled by fresh blood.

'Not sure it's in me anymore. I only joined to escape the past. This'll be the last time I don armour and uniform,' he said.

Unlike Lenkmann, Karlich felt ill at ease in the dress attire he'd been given. The coronation not only celebrated the crowning of the new Emperor, it also commemorated and honoured those who had fallen to secure Reikland's sovereignty almost five years ago. Karlich was amongst the esteemed guests, one of few that no longer served but had survived the battle.

'Ledner's dead you know. You've nothing to fear from him or his lackeys anymore.'

He'd told them all, those who still lived amongst his closest companions, about Vanhans and even Grelle the Confessor. Not a man amongst them raised so much as an accusing eyebrow, not even Von Rauken. It was past, another life.

'Lung rot, I heard.'

'Painful way to go,' said Lenkmann.

'He'd earned it.'

'Yes he had.'

Karlich took out his pipe. Smoke drifted on the breeze after he'd fired it up, carried down to the city below them.

'Did you bring it?'

When Karlich faced him again, he saw Lenkmann was cradling a dusky-looking bottle in his arm.

'Wasn't easy to procure.' Lenkmann held it up to his eye. 'But this is it. Middenland hooch. Rechts must've had a stomach like a horse.'

'And a face to match,' added Karlich.

They laughed at that, but not for long.

Karlich surveyed the sloping outcrop behind them. It was studded with rocks and wild grass, but nothing else.

'Doesn't look like he's coming. Shame that,' he said genuinely.

'Let's get to it, then. Captain Vogen will flay me if I'm late for the Emperor-elect.'

Lenkmann offered the bottle to Karlich, who declined. 'First honours are yours, Bader.'

Lenkmann gave his old sergeant a reproachful glance, before uncorking the hooch and taking a swig.

Coughing and spluttering, he handed it over to Karlich. The ex-sergeant was more of a hardened drinker and took the pull without complaint.

'Not to your taste,' he smiled, wiping a trickle of brown liquid from his lip.

'I prefer something with *taste* other than that of neat alcohol, if that's what you mean.'

Karlich grinned, before assuming a solemn expression. He turned to the horizon and slowly upended the bottle. The dark liquid trickled out over the grass, a last drink to old friends.

'To the fallen,' he said, drawing Stahler's sword and planting it in the alcohol-soaked ground.

'Aye, to Varveiter and Eber, to Keller and Rechts…'

'To Volker and Masbrecht,' said Karlich, 'to all the Grimblades. And to Stahler,' he added.

'May Morr take them to his breast and Sigmar welcome them in the halls of heroes.'

Karlich let the bottle fall after Lenkmann had finished.

'It's done then.'

'It's done.'

Lenkmann faced him, saluted once and outstretched his hand. 'It's been an honour, sir.'

Karlich ignored the hand and hugged him warmly like a brother.

Lenkmann was taken aback at first but reciprocated the gesture.

'Come on,' said Karlich as they parted. 'Mustn't keep Emperor Wilhelm waiting.'

They left the outcrop together just as a shaft of sunlight poked through the clouds.

When they were gone, another figure came out of hiding to stand upon the rocky ridge overlooking the city, a mean looking mastiff following at his heel.

Remembrances were best observed alone, Brand always thought. Besides, a reunion would only raise awkward questions. He had no intention of returning to Altdorf or the army. An old profession had come calling again and Brand meant to heed it. This would be his last act as a Grimblade.

He regarded the spilled alcohol and the gleaming sword. He was tempted to take it, such was its craftsmanship, but that would dishonour the captain and he couldn't have that. Instead, he saluted once, a final acknowledgement to old friends and an old life.

Brand didn't linger. He was bound for the port of Marienburg where a ship would take him to Tilea. He hadn't been there since he was sixteen but had heard of openings in various guilds for men of his calibre.

The small parcel in his hands contained his old uniform. Beneath the paper, it was still stained with blood. Brand laid it down and walked away.

'Come, Volker!' he snapped, and the mastiff dutifully followed.

WARRIOR PRIEST

Darius Hinks

CHAPTER ONE

Tannhauser's Gift

Captain Kurdt Tannhauser was dead. His heart was still hammering fiercely beneath his breastplate, but he knew that each powerful thud only took him closer to the grave. As his charger tore onwards through a blur of steel and fire, the screams of his dying men trailed after him. There would be no triumphant homecoming tonight.

Most of the soldiers who had struck out from Mercy's End had fallen far behind; or just fallen. Bergolt and Gelfrat were still alive, but they were mired in a forest of axes and swords. The panthers emblazoned on their banners were scorched and torn and their sword strikes grew weaker with each desperate blow. Within minutes, they would be dead. The artillery had fallen silent and even the roguish Ditmarus and his pistoliers had vanished from view. Tannhauser could only assume they had finally achieved the glorious end they had always joked about.

Turning away from the bloodbath that surrounded him, he steered his mount towards a single glittering point. Perched on a nearby hilltop, surveying the carnage was a dazzling figure: a sliver of light in the darkness, sat calmly amidst the shadowy hordes with six shimmering wings arching upwards from its back.

Freed from the twin constraints of fear and hope, Captain Tannhauser charged up the hill towards this beautiful horror. Axes and spears hurtled towards him, but his speed confounded even the most practised aim. He rose up in his saddle and held his sword aloft, so that the light of the moons ran along its battered edge. With his other hand he removed his helmet and cast it down onto the mud, revelling in the wind, rain and blood that lashed into his face. 'Join me, Mormius,' he whispered, as he raced towards the gleaming figure. 'Join me in death.'

At the brow of the hill, a wall of tusks and muscle barred his way. Towering men in greasy animal furs and crude iron armour charged to meet him as he neared their champion. The pounding rain blurred their forms, making iridescent ghosts of them, but even the terrible weather could not shield Tannhauser from the extent of their deformity. Elongated arms reached out towards him through the downpour; arms contorted beyond all recognition, ending in cruel, serrated beaks. As he bore down on them, Tannhauser struggled to distinguish one shape from another: arachnid limbs, twisted muscles and gnarled tusks all merged into a nightmarish whole.

The marauders held fast as the captain's mount slammed into them, ripping through the horse's chest with their strange claws and cutting its legs from beneath it. As the animal toppled, screaming to the ground, Tannhauser flew from the saddle, tumbling through the air over the marauders' heads and slamming into the muddy hillside.

Behind him, the grotesque figures struggled up from beneath the dying horse, but they were too slow. Despite his burning lungs, Tannhauser climbed awkwardly to his feet and ran towards Mormius, grunting with pain and exertion as he stumbled through the rain and filth.

As the captain approached his foe, he saw the reason for the pale light playing across his armour. Mormius was clad entirely in faceted crystals that shifted and whirred mechanically as he raised his sword to defend himself. He towered over Tannhauser, at nearly seven feet tall, and as his wings spread out behind him in the moonlight, the captain felt as though he were facing a god. Hatred carried him through his doubt though. He grinned with triumph as he finally swung his sword at the monster that had robbed him of life.

Mormius parried and with the dull *clang* of steel on steel, the fight began.

The captain knew he had precious seconds before the champion's guards pulled him apart, so he attacked with breathtaking speed, landing a flurry of blows on his opponent and leaving him reeling in the face of the onslaught. As Mormius staggered backwards, the captain called out the names of his fallen comrades in a furious roll call for the dead.

Mormius's huge wings began to beat frantically as he slipped through the mud and corpses. Finally, the captain smashed the champion's blade aside and Mormius stumbled back over a broken cannon, his chest exposed. Tannhauser raised his sword for the deathblow.

Then he froze.

He found himself face to face with a proud knight of the Empire. The man's skin was drawn and pale with passion; blood and filth covered his armour and his dark, rain-sodden hair was plastered across his ivory brow. It was the knight's eyes that most arrested him, knifing into

Tannhauser with a terrible look of despair.

With dawning horror, the captain realised that this lost soul was his own reflection, trapped like a caged animal in the glimmering plates of Mormius's armour. He was so shocked by his appearance that his sword slipped from his fingers. The war had made a ghoul of him. He was a monster. For a few seconds he forgot all about the battle as he studied the tortured lines of his own face; then, a hot bolt of pain snapped him out of his reverie. As the searing heat grew he looked down to see Mormius's sword, embedded deep in his belly.

The champion began to laugh as Tannhauser dropped silently into the mud.

Mormius's huge command tent was sewn from the hides of fallen soldiers, and as he lit a brazier in its centre, a dozen eyeless faces leered down at him, reanimated in the flickering green light. The champion sat down, cross-legged at the captain's feet and removed his helmet, allowing a shock of lustrous ginger ringlets to roll down over his shoulders. Tannhauser struggled against the tiredness that threatened to overcome him, but a great weight seemed to be pressing him into his chair. He struggled to rise, but found his limbs paralysed, all traces of strength gone from them. He stared curiously into Mormius's face. 'You're a child,' he said, through a mouthful of blood.

It was true. The face before him was that of a youth barely out of his teens. Mormius looked like a pampered aristocrat, or maybe the son of a wealthy merchant. His soft white skin was flawless and his languid blue eyes gazed out from beneath long, feminine lashes. His plump lips were so glossy and pink, that the captain wondered if he were wearing make-up.

'It would appear so to you, I suppose,' replied Mormius with a voice like velvet. He moistened his lips and revealed his perfect ivory teeth in a warm smile. 'I was born in the time of your forefathers, Kurdt, way back when Sigmar's progeny were still little more than beasts, crawling around in their own filth.'

Tannhauser grimaced. 'I would take a quick death over a life such as yours.' He managed to raise a hand and wipe away the blood that was muffling his words. 'What use is an eternity of life, if it's spent in the service of such wretched masters?'

'A commendable sentiment, Kurdt,' replied Mormius as his smile turned into a giggle. 'In fact, now I hear it put like that, I might be forced to reconsider my position.' His laughter grew until his whole body was rocking back and forth and his eyes filled with tears. He lurched to his feet and whirled around the tent, carelessly knocking over furniture of incredible antiquity. Gilt-edged mirrors and crystal bowls smashed across the ground as Mormius's mirth grew, becoming a succession of hiccupping yelps. Then the laughter shifted seamlessly into a scream of rage and the champion flew at Tannhauser, his face contorted with fury. 'What would you know of eternity?' he screamed, slapping the knight with such force that the chair toppled beneath him and he sprawled on the floor. 'You're nothing but an unwitting slave. Since the day you were born you've been ensnared, a plaything of the Great Conspirator.' He crouched down, grabbed Tannhauser's head and howled into his face. 'You're the child! Don't you see? All of you strutting soldiers, celebrating your petty, ridiculous victories. You're just pawns. Not even that. You're a punchline to a joke you couldn't even understand.' He screamed again, but his rage was now so intense it strangled his words into a garbled whine.

As Mormius's anger increased, his features began to change, shifting and sliding in and out of view. Tannhauser saw a bewildering series of faces flash before him: old men, children and crones, all wailing with fury. Then, as suddenly as it began, the screaming ceased.

Mormius covered his mouth and flushed with embarrassment. 'Forgive me, Kurdt,' he whispered, loosing his grip on Tannhauser's head. His voice was gentle again and his face was his own once more. He helped the captain back up onto the chair and dusted him down with his soft white hands. He smiled apologetically. 'I've spent so long with these creatures,' – he gestured to the walls of the tent and the shadows of marauders passing by outside – 'I sometimes forget my manners.' The cheerful smile returned and he stepped over to a table laden with food. 'I haven't even offered you a drink,' he said, filling a silver goblet with wine and bringing it to the captain. 'You must think me quite the heathen.'

Tannhauser simply stared at him in mute horror, so Mormius placed the drink on the floor next to him and returned to the brazier in the centre of the room. 'It's a good vintage,' he muttered, as he measured out an assortment of coloured powders and dropped them into the green flames, filling the tent with thick, heady smoke. 'It would ease your suffering,' he added, with a note of apology in his voice.

As the clouds of smoke grew, the captain strained to follow Mormius's movements. His willowy shape slipped back and forth through the cloying fumes, dropping tinctures and leaves into the brazier like a master chef, humming merrily to himself as he worked. The walls of the tent gradually slipped away behind a haze of coloured smoke. Tannhauser felt himself falling into a realm of shadows. He wondered if his tired heart had finally released him.

A shape caught his eye, to the left of the brazier. It was a large net of some kind and at first he thought it was full of animal carcasses. He saw ribs, gristle and strands of wet meat. To his horror, he noticed the mass of flesh was moving slightly, as though breathing. He looked closer and saw that the organs and limbs were melded together into one grotesque being, layered with glistening viscera and dark, pulsing tumours. As he watched, the pile of meat shifted and several eyes suddenly peered out at him. The sack's thick cords strained as it started to slide across the ground in his direction. Tannhauser gasped as a grey, elongated face looked from beneath the folds of flesh. Then he noticed rows of hands, all reaching towards him from the mass of body parts.

Mormius heard Tannhauser's gasp and rolled his eyes in irritation. He strode across the tent and gave the meat a series of fierce kicks, until the struggling shape crawled back into the shadows. 'Family,' he said, shaking his head despairingly. 'What's to be done with them?' He stooped to wipe some blood from his boot. 'Still, I suppose they have sacrificed much on my behalf.'

Mormius gently fanned the smoke with his broad, silver wings, and Tannhauser sensed another presence, watching him intently. He peered through the fug, trying to spot the new arrival but, to his dismay, he realised that it was not in the tent, but in his mind, a strange sentience, spreading at the back of his thoughts like a shadow, tentatively probing the recesses of his consciousness. Images arrived unbidden in his head: glimpses of places and people he could never have seen. A range of mountains reared up before him, with peaks so sheer that they defied all logic. Then came vast armies of creatures so warped and grotesque he wanted to shield his eyes from the awfulness of them, but the visions were deep within him and however he squirmed, he could not escape them.

Tannhauser realised Mormius was crouched before him again, watching eagerly. The knight looked down at his hands and saw that they were rippling and swelling as the presence exerted its influence over his body. The bones in his back cracked as they stretched and elongated, arching up in a long curve. His head jolted back and with a shocking flash of pain he felt his head rearrange itself into a long beak-like curve.

Tannhauser opened his mouth to cry out, but another sound entirely emerged; a hoarse scraping that ripped through his throat. He was vaguely aware of Mormius, giggling with delight. The alien screech began to form words from Tannhauser's protesting vocal chords. At first it was no more than a jumble of screeched vowels, but then a distinct word filled the tent: 'Mormius.'

'Yes, master,' cried the champion, his voice wavering with emotion. 'You're so kind to spare me your–'

'Failure,' shrieked the hideous voice, forcing Tannhauser's head back even further.

Mormius's smile faltered. 'Failure, master?' He gestured to the door of the tent. 'We're in the very heart of Ostland. I've killed so many in your name, they're already writing songs about me. The province is on its knees.'

A furious chorus of screeches greeted Mormius's words. 'What of the capital? What of Wolfenburg? What of von Raukov? Why are you here? Your idleness is treachery.' As the words grew more enraged, the flames in the brazier began to gut and flicker, plunging the tent in and out of darkness. 'Do you wish to serve me, or make a fool of me?' cried the voice. 'Have you forsaken me? Are you enamoured of another master?'

Fear twisted Mormius's chubby face into a grimace. 'Master,' he gasped. 'Please understand – I've marched ceaselessly for weeks, but I need to gather my strength before I move on. The Ostlanders have refortified an old castle, called Mercy's End. It has already been ruined once by Archaon and we'll easily sweep it away, as surely as everything else, but I must wait for the rest of my army before heading south.'

'No!' screamed the voice, with such force that Tannhauser's throat burst. His whole body began to spasm and twist, like a broken marionette, and blood started rushing quickly from his exposed vocal cords. 'Strike now, or betray me.'

Mormius pawed pathetically at Tannhauser's jerking limbs and began to whine. 'Don't say such things, master. Of course I haven't betrayed you. Strendel, Wurdorf and Steinfeld are already in ruins. The north of the province is overrun with my men and they're all marching to meet me here. The surviving Ostlanders are massing in that crumbling old wreck, but they've picked a poor place to make their stand. We'll be there within days and we'll smash through those old walls like firewood. Then the whole province will be ours.' There was no reply, so he grabbed his sword from the ground and lifted it up over his head. 'As you wish then. We'll leave now. The stragglers will just have to catch up with us as best they can. I won't betray you, master.' There was still no reply and Mormius dashed to the captain's side, falling on his knees and grabbing Tannhauser's bloody hands in his own. 'Master?'

The captain lay slumped in the chair and however much Mormius pleaded and shook him, no more words came. 'Of course,' muttered the champion, rising to his feet and looking anxiously around the room. 'Of course, I must strike now. You're right.' He dashed from the tent and left Tannhauser to bleed alone.

The flames in the brazier flickered and finally died, plunging the tent into darkness. The captain's body was twisted beyond all recognition, but as the afterimage of the fire played over his retina, a faint smile spread across his torn lips. His heart finally accepted the truth of his death and gratefully ceased to drum. As his last breath slipped from his lungs, Tannhauser looked down at a sharpened ring on his finger, glistening with a jewel of Mormius's blood. He wondered how long it would be before the champion discovered the gift he had left him.

The keep reared up from the hillside like a broken tooth. Firelight flickered from its narrow windows and above its crumbling battlements a banner was flying in the moonlight: a single bull, glowering defiantly from a black and white field.

All around the building, a great army was massing, swelling like waves beneath the quickly moving clouds. Mormius mounted a white, barded warhorse and rode to the brow of a hill to look down at the ranks flooding the valley. A grotesque figure shambled out of the darkness and stood at his side. Mormius looked down at his captain with distaste. The thing's serpentine limbs dragged behind him through the mud and silvery mites rushed over his scaled, eyeless face as he grinned up at his general. 'Your army is almost ready, lord,' he said, in a retching, gurgling voice. He lifted one of his writhing arms and gestured at the scene below. 'I've never seen such a gathering. No one could stop it. By tomorrow night we will have a force like nothing they've ever seen.'

'We must leave now,' said Mormius. 'We've rested long enough.'

The creature's smile faltered and a strange hissing noise came from deep in his throat. 'Now, my lord?'

'Yes, now. For every day we spend waiting, Mercy's End grows a little stronger. I have no desire to spend a week tussling over that backwater. I should be within sight of the capital by now, not wasting my time on these parochial skirmishes.'

'Well, master,' the marauder said, shrugging helplessly. 'I'm not sure that will be possible. Many of the troops are still fighting their way through Kislev. Ivarr Kolbeinn has gathered a great number of ogres and they're just a few days north of here. And Ingvarr the Changed has hundreds of men marching with him.' He grimaced with all four of his mouths. 'We should at least wait for Freyviòr Sturl and his horsemen.'

'Didn't you hear me?' said Mormius. 'We attack in the morning.' He grinned. 'Or do you think my skills as a strategist are insufficient?' His shoulders began to shake with amusement. 'Maybe it would be better if you made the tactical decisions from now on?'

At the sound of Mormius's laughter, the colour drained from the marauder's face. He backed away, shaking his head. 'No, of course not, you're absolutely right.' He waved at the keep. 'These fools won't see the dawn. I'll see to it.' He lurched awkwardly away through the rain. 'We'll be marching south within the hour.'

With some difficulty, Mormius managed to stifle his laughter. Once he was calm, he smiled with satisfaction at the great army arrayed before him. The standard bearers had unfurled their crude colours to the wind: the eight pointed star of Chaos, daubed in the blood of their enemies. It was a terrifying sight and his heart swelled with pride.

As he watched the endless stream of troops swarming out of the darkness, Mormius noticed a small hole on his left gauntlet. As he watched, a spidery, black patina began to spread over the crystals that surrounded it. He peered at the dark stain for a moment, then promptly forgot all about it as he turned his attention to the battle ahead.

CHAPTER TWO

Merciful Justice

'Envy never dies,' said the old man, leaning in towards the assembled crowd. His voice was low, but his whole body was twisted with hate. Spittle was hanging from his cracked lips and his gaunt face was flushed with emotion. 'The old gods are always there, waiting for revenge; waiting to rise again.' His frenzied, bony arms snaked back and forth across his chest as he spoke and a sheen of sweat glistened over his ribs. A blistered symbol was scorched across his belly: a single flaming hammer.

Anna was torn between fascination and disgust. From her vantage point, up on top of the pyre, she could see how easily he manipulated the mob. Some of these people had recently trusted her with their lives; only the night before, most of them had still doubted her guilt. Now, they could smell blood on the morning air and they would not rest until more of it was spilled. As the old man continued his tirade, she saw life slipping from her grasp. Scarlet tears began to roll down over her bruised, swollen cheeks and she prepared herself for death.

'Their obscure plots always surround us,' continued the old man. 'A tide of unholy filth hides behind the most innocent of faces. Even the most vigilant of Sigmar's servants can struggle to spot the signs.' The crowd murmured their assent, beginning to warm to his theme. 'Look at her,' he hissed, stretching his frail body to its full height and pointing theatrically at Anna. 'See how this "priestess" whimpers for forgiveness. See the cold tears that run from her pitiless eyes. Even now, with judgement at hand, she is unrepentant. If you hesitate, if you falter even for a moment, she will worm her way out of justice. Trust me, my friends, that pretty young face hides an old, terrible evil; there's murder in her heart.' The crowd's murmurs grew louder and many of them cast nervous, furtive glances up at the priestess.

Anna shivered. Dawn light was spreading quickly over the village, but the witch hunter's henchman had torn her white robes as he fastened her to the pyre. Her exposed flesh was wet with dew and the autumn breeze knifed into her. She prayed that one way or another, her ordeal would soon be over. As the crowd began to chant along with the old man's liturgy, she looked out across their heads to the fields beyond the village; out towards the distant forest. Crows were hopping across the ploughed fields and heading towards her. She took a strange comfort in the sight. As mankind acted out its bloody rituals, nature continued unabated. The world marched on, blind to her fate. Even as the crows picked at her charred remains, she would become part of a timeless cycle of rebirth. There was solace in such things, she decided.

'Riders,' she muttered, surprised by the hoarse croak that came from her throat. The blood in her eyes had painted the horizon as a crimson blur, and for a while she doubted herself, but as the shapes grew nearer she was sure: it wasn't crows, but men who were moving towards her. Two horsemen had emerged from the distant trees and were slowly crossing the fields towards the village. She looked down to see if anyone else had noticed, but the old man had the mob in the palm of his sweaty hand. As he lurched back and forth, singing and cursing ecstatically, they cheered him on, waving knives and pitchforks in approval and edging towards the pyre.

'Look around,' he continued, gesturing towards the ruined houses. 'These truly are the end times. Judgement is finally at hand. Only the most pious will survive. Corruption and decay is crawling across our blessed homeland and only those with the faith to stare it down can escape damnation.' The villagers nodded eagerly at each other, unable to dispute the logic of his words. Life had always been hard, out here on the very edge of the Empire, but in recent months even the most hardened Ostlanders had begun to know doubt. Streams of blank-eyed refugees passed through almost daily now, bringing news of terrible defeats in the north. There wasn't a young man left in the village who wasn't fighting for his life in the war, or already cold in the ground.

The old man scampered, spider-like onto the remains of a barn wall and slapped the crumbling stone. 'Bricks and mortar can no longer keep you safe, my friends. The creatures that watch from the trees do not care about walls or doors. They're filled with mindless, animal hate. No mortal protection can stop them. They'll soon be back to finish the job. Yes! And burn down the rest of your homes.' He scratched frantically at his thin beard. 'And if you don't show the strength of your faith, you'll burn along with them.' He levelled a trembling finger at Anna. 'And *she* has brought this upon you!'

The crowd erupted into raucous cheers. 'She must die,' screamed an old woman, grabbing a lit firebrand and holding it aloft.

'It's true,' cried a blacksmith, nervously twisting his leather apron as he rushed to the old woman's side. 'Before the priestess came, we were safe, but now the creatures come almost nightly. I've heard her singing songs in a foreign language.' He looked around at the other villagers. 'I think she's calling to them.'

The old man nodded encouragement as the crowd began hurling a stream of evidence at Anna.

'She cured old Mandred with nothing more than a garland of flowers.'

'She goes into the forest alone, unafraid of the creatures.'

Anna was barely conscious of the accusations. A steady stream of blood was flowing from her head and reality kept slipping in and out of grasp. Visions of her childhood blurred into view and she whispered the name of her abbess, begging her to forgive her for the miserable end she had come to. She still could not be sure if the two horsemen were even real. Certainly none of the villagers seemed to have noticed them. The men's silhouettes were now quite clear as they trotted through the morning mist, but the mob was fixated on the old man. She blinked away her tears. Yes, she was sure now, it was two men, both mounted on powerful warhorses. Admittedly, the first was little more than a boy. His wiry body barely filled the saddle and his limbs flapped around clumsily as he steered the horse over the furrows; but even at this distance she could see the determined frown on his face as he strained to control his mount.

The second rider was another matter altogether. He was a little further back and still partly shrouded in mist, but from his posture Anna could tell this was no travelling merchant or itinerant farmer. He handled his horse with the calm surety of a veteran soldier, his chin raised disdainfully as he surveyed the scene before him. He was a shaven-headed giant, with a broad chest clad in thick, iron armour that glinted dully in the morning light. A great warhammer was slung nonchalantly over his wide shoulders. Anna felt a thrill of hope. Was this her saviour? Her pulse quickened and for the first time she tested the strength of the bonds that held her. She was strapped to a stout post with her hands above her head. The witch hunter's henchman had done his job well, but maybe if she just twisted a little…

'You are wise people,' said the old man, hopping back down from the barn wall. 'I can see it in your eyes.' He hugged and patted those nearest to him, blind to the grimaces his sour odour induced. As he moved amongst the crowd, he handed out small wooden hammers, muttering a blessing to each recipient in turn. The villagers grasped the icons with joy, pressing them to their chests and muttering prayers of thanks. The old man stroked the hammer emblazoned across his puckered belly. 'This symbol is no gaudy badge of honour. No shallow boast. The hammer is a mark of our heavy burden. It's no easy thing to hand out unerring judgement.' He gave the old woman a toothy, yellow grin as he took the flaming brand from her hand. 'Believe me,' he said, as he approached the pyre and looked up at the desperately struggling Anna, 'mercy would often seem the easier path.'

The crowd fell silent as he raised the brand and closed his eyes, as though in prayer. For a few minutes, the crackling of the flames was the only sound, and then, when he spoke again, it was in a dull monotone. 'It is to the merciful justice of Sigmar that I commit you, servant of the Ruinous Powers. May your soul find peace at last in the cleansing flame of his forgiveness.' Then the old man opened his eyes and Anna saw again how unusual they were; the irises were of such a pale grey that his pupils seemed to be floating in a pair of clear, white pools. He gave Anna a kind smile as he thrust the fire into the kindling at her feet.

The crowd gasped and backed away from the pyre, as though suddenly realising the magnitude of their treachery. The kindling was still damp with morning dew and for a while nothing happened; but then, to Anna's horror, thin trails of smoke began to snake around her feet.

'Don't be afraid,' said the old man, signalling for the mob to approach. 'The punishment of Sigmar only falls on his most errant children. You've all done well to reveal this woman's heresy. Now be stout of heart, and see the task through to its end.' He plucked a scroll from his robes and, as Anna began to moan in fear, he started to pray. He left the pyre and scampered back up onto the barn wall, proudly lifting his chin and addressing his words to the indifferent sky. One by one, the villagers stepped nervously back towards the growing fire, murmuring along with his prayers. Soon, the old man's passion started to infect them. Their doubt passed as quickly as it had come and they pressed closer, eager to see the witch burn.

Anna strained at her bonds, but they simply bit into her slender wrists all the more, until fresh blood began to flow down her arms. The smoke was quickly growing thicker and she felt the first glow of warmth under her feet. She strained, trying to stretch herself away from the fire, but it was useless. She wondered desperately whether she should try to inhale the smoke and escape into unconsciousness, but the thought appalled her; she was not ready to give up on life yet. She looked out through the cinders and heat haze and felt a rush of excitement. The two riders had almost reached the square and they were heading straight for her.

Now that she saw the larger of the two men at close hand, he looked even more impressive. The lower part of his face was hidden behind an iron gorget, but the battered metal could not hide the fierce intensity in his dark, brooding eyes. He was obviously a priest of some importance. Crimson robes hung down from beneath his thick, plate armour and the cloth was decorated with beautiful gold embroidery. Religious texts were chained to his cuirass and around his regal, shaven head he wore a studded metal band, engraved with images of a flaming hammer. Anna's heart swelled as he steered his horse towards the baying mob and looked her straight in the eye.

The crowd stumbled over their words and fell silent as they finally noticed the two horsemen. As the priest and his young acolyte approached, the villagers looked nervously towards the old witch hunter for reassurance. He was lost in prayer, swaying back and forth on the wall and muttering garbled words to the heavens. 'Banish, O Sigmar, this Servant of Change. Dispel her unholy form. I invoke Your name. Let me end this Heresy. Let *me* be the instrument of Your wrath!'

The warrior priest dismounted and lifted his warhammer from over his shoulders. He surveyed the scene, taking in the wide-eyed villagers and the quickly growing fire. As his metal-clad fingers drummed on the haft of his weapon, a scowl crossed his face. Then he spotted the babbling old man, crouched on the barn wall. With a nod of satisfaction he marched straight past the priestess, pausing only to pick up a long wooden stake from the pyre. As the gangly youth tumbled awkwardly from his horse, he gave Anna an apologetic frown, before rushing after his master.

Anna gasped. They had no intention of saving her. They were bloodthirsty Sigmarites, just like the old man; blind to anything but their own hunger for war. She groaned with the horror of it. 'Have you no compassion?' she tried to say, but her lips were thick with dried blood and the words came out as a mumbled croak. She spat into the growing flames, cursing the hammer god and all his witless minions. Let the fire take her. There was no hope for a world ruled by such monsters. She would rather take her chances with the creatures of the forest than face another holy man.

The old man finally noticed the priest striding purposefully towards him. He tugged excitedly at his straggly hair as he saw the holy texts and hammer icons. A broad grin spread across his face. 'Brother,' he cried, skipping down from the wall, 'you've joined us at a crucial moment.' He spread his arms in a greeting and rushed towards him.

The priest remained silent as he approached. Upon reaching the old man he lifted him from the ground, as easily as if he were a small child and carried him back to the wall. Before the witch hunter could mutter a word of protest, the priest raised his great hammer and with one powerful blow pounded the wooden stake through the old man's chest, pinning him to the wall and leaving him dangling, puppet-like a few feet from the ground. Cries of dismay exploded from the crowd as a bright torrent of blood rushed from the old man and began drumming across the dusty earth. For a few seconds he was mute with shock, staring at the priest in confusion, then, he too began to scream, clutching desperately at the splintered wood and trying to stem the flow of blood.

The priest seemed oblivious to the pandemonium he had triggered. He calmly wiped the old man's warm blood from his armour and stepped back to survey his handiwork.

'What have you done?' screamed the old man in disbelief, thrashing his scrawny limbs like an overturned beetle. 'You've killed me!' He looked over at the crowd. 'Somebody stop him. He's a murderer.'

The crowd backed away, suddenly afraid, as the warrior priest turned to face them. His black eyes flashed dangerously from beneath thick grey eyebrows and when he spoke it was with the quiet surety of a man used to being obeyed. 'Leave us,' he growled.

The villagers looked around for support, but only met the same fear in each other's faces. With a last disappointed look at Anna, they shuffled back towards their homes, muttering bitterly at being deprived of their sport.

The priest turned back towards his prey, who was still howling with pain and fury. 'Adelman,' cried the old man, scouring the upturned carts and ruined houses, 'where are you, you dog? I'm injured.' But however much he called, no one came to the witch hunter's aid.

The priest and the boy watched in silence as the old man continued his frenzied attempts to remove the stake. After a few minutes, he realised that each movement simply quickened the blood flow. At last, as his face began to drain of colour, he realised death was at hand and fell silent, looking over at the priest in wide-eyed terror. 'Who are you?' he said, shaking his head in dismay. 'Why've you done this to me?'

The priest nodded. 'Greetings, Otto Sürman. My name is Jakob Wolff.' He stepped closer to the old man. 'You may remember murdering my parents.'

Sürman's face twisted into a grimace of horror. 'What? I've never met you before, I…' His voice trailed off into a confused silence. 'Wait,' he said, peering at the priest, 'did you say Wolff? I *do* know that–' A fit of choking gripped him and a fresh torrent blood ran from between his crooked teeth. When the fit had passed, he sneered dismissively and spat a thick red gobbet onto the floor. 'Oh, yes, it all comes back to me now. I remember your wretched family, Jakob.' He shook his head at the towering warrior before him. 'And I don't regret a thing. Corruption runs in your people like the rot. I'm only sad I let you live.'

The acolyte flinched at Sürman's words and looked up at his master to see his response. The priest remained calm. The only outward sign of his anger was a slight tightening of his jaw.

'You're a liar,' he replied. 'It has taken me thirty years of false penitence to realise my mistake, but finally I understand. My parents weren't guilty, any more than I was guilty for accusing them.' Colour rushed to his cheeks and he suddenly gripped the stake. The wood was embedded just below the old man's shoulder and with a grunt the priest shoved it even deeper. The noise that came from Sürman's throat sounded barely human. 'You murdered them, knowing my accusations were wrong. I was an innocent child. You knew they weren't occultists.' His voice rose to a roar. 'Admit it, you worm!'

'Save me,' whimpered Sürman reaching out to the young acolyte. 'Don't let him do this to me, I beg–'

'Admit it!' cried Wolff again, ramming the wood even deeper into the ragged wound.

'Yes,' wailed Sürman, arching his back in agony and beginning to weep. 'Yes, yes, yes, you're right, I knew it wasn't them.' He grabbed the priest's arm and gave out a strange keening noise that echoed around the village streets. 'But *you* summoned me. You made the accusation, and someone had to pay the price.' He gave the priest a look of desperation. 'Once the wheels have begun to turn, it's hard to stop these things. I can't...' His words disintegrated into incoherent sobs.

Wolff stepped back and looked up at the sky, considering the old man's words. 'I understand your methods, Sürman.' He shook his head. 'It's to my eternal shame that I did not then. It still haunts me to think that I betrayed my own parents to a villain such as you. Even after a lifetime of penance I can't come to terms with it.'

The witch hunter looked down at the blood that was pooling beneath him, and groaned with fear. 'What do you want with me?' he pleaded, reaching out to the priest. 'It's been thirty years, Jakob, what can I do now? I'm an old man, for Sigmar's sake!'

The priest lowered his gaze and looked back at him. 'We both know my parents were innocent of the crimes they died for; but there's another lie here; one that can't be left to fester.'

The witch hunter's eyes bulged and he shook his head frantically. 'What? What lie? What could you want to know after all these years?'

'Who was the true guilty party, Sürman? Who was the real occultist?'

Sürman gave a strangulated choke of laughter. 'What?' he said, sneering in disbelief. 'You don't even know?' He began to jerk back and forth with deep shuddering laughter, baring his bloody teeth in a feral grin. 'He doesn't know who it was.' Tears continued to flow over his cheeks as he giggled hysterically and pointed at the priest. 'It's almost worth dying, just to see what an ass you've grown into. And to think your parents thought so highly of you. How could you not spot corruption in the face of your own brother?'

Wolff moved to strike the old man, but then the strength seemed to go out of him. He stumbled and leant heavily on the wall next to Sürman.

The old man's face was now just inches from the priest's and he whispered gleefully in his ear. 'Yes, you pompous oaf, you know it's the truth. Fabian was the only occultist in the Wolff household, and he's let you carry his guilt around all these years while he spreads his poison over the Empire; praying to the same unspeakable horrors you've spent your life trying to destroy.'

'Fabian?' whispered Wolff, as he slumped against the wall. 'My own brother?'

'Your life's a joke, Wolff,' spat Sürman. 'You've wasted thirty years in penance for another man's crime.'

Jakob finally gave into his fury and grabbed Sürman by the throat, raising his hammer to dash the old man's brains out. 'It can't be true,' he snarled. 'If Fabian was worshipping the Dark Powers, why would you let him go free? You may be a filthy, deluded monster, but you imagine yourself to be some kind of witch hunter. You even fooled me into believing you were a priest. Even by your own twisted logic you should have wanted Fabian dead. If he were a cultist, why would you let him go free?'

Sürman shook his head and grinned slyly at the priest. 'You're no wiser now than you were at fifteen, Jakob.' He gestured wildly to the pyre. Anna had finally slipped into unconsciousness as the flames rose around her. 'I burned your parents, you fool,' he said in a thin, agonised whisper. 'Do you think I'd be such an idiot as to admit my mistake?' He slapped the hammer on his belly and looked up at the sky. 'I still had important work to do, Jakob. I couldn't risk execution for the sake of one deluded conjurer. Just a few days after you left Berlau, Fabian signed up with the Ostland Black Guard. Sigmar knows what mischief he was planning to wreak there, but three decades have passed since then. I imagine he's long dead.' He shook his head imploringly. 'What can I do about it now, after all this time?'

'The Black Guard?' said Wolff, tightening his grip on Sürman's throat. 'What else do you know of him? Speak quickly, if you–'

An explosion echoed around the village, drowning out the priest's words. Wolff whirled around to see his young acolyte perched awkwardly on top of the flaming pyre, reaching desperately for Anna as the burning wood collapsed beneath his feet. 'Master,' he cried, pathetically, as he lurched through the smoke and attempted to grab onto the lifeless priestess.

Jakob grimaced, looking from the bleeding old man to the pyre and back again. 'I'm not finished,' he said, freeing Sürman's throat and dashing towards the fire.

While the priest had been interrogating Sürman, villagers had gradually been creeping back out of doorways and alleyways to witness the spectacle. Wolff had to barge his way through the growing crowd to reach the pyre. Once there he paused. The flames had now fully taken hold and the heat needled into his eyes. The acolyte cried out again, stranded next to Anna as sparks and embers whirled around him.

Wolff shook his head at the boy's foolishness. Then, clutching his warhammer tightly in both hands, he strode into the fire. Charred wood and cinders erupted all around him as he scrambled through the blaze. At first he made good progress, moving quickly towards the stranded couple. Then, his foot dropped through a hole and he found himself waist deep in flaming wood. Wolff howled with impotent fury at his predicament. Try as he might he could not climb any further. Smoke engulfed him and he felt the stubble on his head begin to shrivel as fire washed over him. He realised the horror of his situation. History was on the verge of repeating itself: another Wolff, burned alive on Sürman's pyre. Hot fury burst from his lungs in an incoherent roar. He lifted his warhammer and, swinging it in a great arc, slammed it into the pyre's central pillar.

The acolyte's eyes widened with fear. 'Master,' he shouted, struggling to keep his footing as the pyre shifted beneath him. 'You'll kill us.'

Wolff was deaf to his cries and swung the hammer again. The pyre belched great gouts of flame but he kept swinging, striking it repeatedly and enveloping himself in an inferno of heat and smoke. Finally, with a sharp *crack*, the priest smashed through the post. The whole structure teetered for a second, swaying drunkenly, then it collapsed in on itself, hurling blazing wood spinning across the village square.

Finally free, Wolff patted himself down, extinguishing the fires that covered his robes. Then, slinging his hammer back over his shoulder he strode through the scattered flames. He lifted the dazed acolyte from beneath the wreckage and with his other hand he grabbed Anna. Then, as the astonished villagers backed away from him, he emerged from the fire, dragging the two bodies behind him like sacks of corn. He dropped Anna and the boy to the ground and collapsed to his knees, gulping clean air into his scorched lungs.

'She's a witch,' cried a fat old militiaman, rushing forward and kicking Anna's prone shape. 'The witch hunter found her guilty.' He grabbed Anna's blistered body and lifted her head from the ground. 'It's all her fault. Everything that's happened to the village these last months.' His voice grew thin with hysteria. 'She *has* to die.'

The other villagers stepped back from the man, nervously eyeing the priest's warhammer. Most were not as keen to pit themselves against someone who had just walked so calmly through fire.

As the militiaman's vengeful screams continued, Wolff stayed on his knees, with his hands pressed into the earth and his eyes closed as he struggled for breath.

With a retching cough, the young acolyte sat up. His hair was twisted and black and his face was flushed with heat. He had the look of a wild-eyed prophet. He saw the villager grappling with Anna and leapt towards him. 'Leave her alone, you brute,' he cried, landing a punch on the man's face and sending him sprawling across the ground. He followed after him, windmilling his arms and landing blow after blow on the militiaman's head. 'You don't know anything. You're listening to the words of a murderer. Sürman's no priest. He's not even a witch hunter; he's just insane.'

The militiaman recovered his composure and rose to his feet. He took a cudgel from his belt and slammed it into the boy's stomach. As the acolyte fell to the ground, doubled up in pain, the militiaman kicked him viciously in the side and looked up at the other villagers. 'The boy's in league with the witch,' he announced, calmly.

The other villagers shuffled towards him, still looking nervously at the choking priest.

'Stop,' gasped Wolff, glaring at the militiaman. 'You're making a mistake. Sürman isn't to be trusted. Let the boy go.'

The militiaman's jowly face grew red with anger and he grabbed the boy by his blackened hair. 'What right do you people have to stop us defending ourselves?' He gestured to the pitiful ruins that surrounded them. 'Look at us. We're barely surviving. Year after year we've fought back monsters you can't even imagine. What do you know of our lives? And now, when we have a minion of Chaos in our very midst, you would free her.' He threw the acolyte back to the floor and levelled a finger at the gasping priest. 'In fact, how do we know you're not in league with her? How is it that you arrived, just as we were about to rid ourselves of this evil?'

Angry mutterings came from the crowd and a few of them nervously fingered their clubs and sticks as they stepped up behind the militiaman.

Wolff took a deep, rasping breath and rose from the ground. He dusted the soot from his armour, lifted his hammer from his back and turned to face the villagers. 'Let the boy go,' he repeated quietly.

'She must burn,' cried the militiaman, pointing at the unconscious priestess. 'And the boy with her. He was clearly trying to save her. I won't let you bring a curse on what's left of this village.'

Jakob gave a rattling cough and stepped forward, straightening up to his full height and lifting his hammer to strike.

The militiaman fled with a yell, leaping over the smouldering remains of the pyre and disappearing from view. The other villagers quickly backed away from the priest and hid their weapons as Wolff helped the acolyte back to his feet.

'Are you hurt?' asked the priest gruffly, dusting the boy down.

'No,' replied the acolyte, with an embarrassed smile. 'I'll think twice about leaping into another fire though.'

The priest nodded and gave a disapproving grunt, before turning to the crumpled priestess.

The boy rushed to the woman's side and lifted her head from the ground. Her long hair had shrivelled to a blackened frizz and her tattered robes crumbled to ash in his fingers, but her chest was still rising and falling as she took a series of quick, shallow breaths. 'She's alive,' he whispered and took a flask of water from his belt, pouring a little into her mouth. At first the liquid just ran over her chin unheeded, but then she gave a hoarse splutter and opened her eyes, pushing the boy away in fear. 'She's alive,' he repeated, helping her to sit up.

'Stay back,' gasped the priestess, shoving the boy away and attempting to stand. Her legs immediately gave way and she toppled to the floor, but she was now fully awake and looked around in confusion. 'The pyre,' she said, looking at the smouldering ruin. 'Did you save me?' she asked, grabbing the boy's arm.

'Well, not exactly,' he replied, blushing. 'It was more–'

'Yes,' snapped Wolff, striding forward and lifting her to her feet. 'If it wasn't for this foolish child, you'd be dead.'

Anna flinched from the priest's grasp, looking nervously of his brutal demeanour and Sigmarite garb. 'Who are you?' she asked, staggering away from him. Then her hand shot to her mouth and she looked around in a panic. 'Where's the witch hunter?'

Wolff spun around to find that barn wall was empty, apart from a dark crimson stain where he had left Sürman. He cursed under his breath and ran across the village square to investigate. 'Sürman,' he cried, dashing in and out of the houses. 'Come back, you wretch.' His face grew purple with rage. 'Where's my brother?'

Wolff tore through the village, turning over carts and barrels, but a fit of coughing overtook him and after a few minutes he dropped to his knees again. With a strangled bark of despair he slammed his hammer into the ground and spat sooty phlegm into the earth. 'Where's my brother, you murdering dog?'

CHAPTER THREE

Sigmar's Heirs

'Ratboy?' asked Anna, laughing as she dragged a knife over her scalp. 'What kind of a name is that?'

'I've grown used to it,' replied the acolyte, with a shrug. He looked around. They were sat on the bank of a small stream and Ratboy couldn't help but smile at the unexpected beauty of the scene. As the morning sun cleared the distant blue hills of Kislev, it gilded the shallow waters, transforming the blasted valley into a memory of happier times. They were in a small clearing, and the scorched trees and shrubs that surrounded them took on a kind of grandeur as they bathed in the dawn glow. Even the rain seemed reluctant to mar the idyllic scene, coming down in a fine, warm drizzle that hissed gently across the stream's surface.

'I can barely remember my childhood,' he said. 'I'm not even sure if this was originally my homeland. Truth is, I can't remember much at all before Master Wolff took me in. He found me scavenging for food and rescued me from a bunch of meat-headed halberdiers from Nordland.' His eyes glazed over for a moment as he sank into his memories, then he shook his head with a laugh and ran his fingers through the water. 'They weren't quite as sympathetic as my master. I think they might have been the ones who named me. I'm quite happy to be a Ratboy though.' His smile grew and he briefly met the priestess's eye. 'Rats are survivors.'

Anna dipped the knife in the water and continued shaving her head, frowning with concentration as she followed her undulating reflection. The crisp remnants of her flaxen hair fell away easily in little clumps that drifted off in the current. As Ratboy watched her discreetly from the corner of his eye, he couldn't help noticing that even without hair she had an ethereal beauty.

The events of the previous day had left her bruised and weak; so weak, in fact, that he had practically carried her down to the water's edge. But despite her terrible ordeal, there was something noble in Anna's piercing, grey-green eyes. They had been chatting for a few hours now, and Ratboy had never met anyone quite like her. There was such intensity in her gaze that he found it hard to meet her eye. He guessed she was only a few years older than he was – early twenties at most – but he felt childlike in her presence. He wondered how he must look to her. A ridiculous figure, probably, with his gangly limbs and tatty clothes. Not the kind of man to turn her head, certainly. He suddenly felt ashamed of himself for thinking such thoughts about a priestess and looked down into the palms of his hands, trying not to think about how full and red her lips were. Anna continued shaving her head, oblivious to his admiring glances. 'So, tell me about Wolff,' she said.

'Jakob Wolff,' sighed Ratboy. 'He's a bit of mystery to me, I'm afraid. He's not what you might call a great talker, so even after three years in his service, I don't know too much about him.' As the topic of conversation shifted onto another person, Ratboy's confidence grew, and he met Anna's eye with a little more surety. 'Although, that said, I've seen him turn the tide of a whole battle with nothing more than words.' His face lit up with enthusiasm as he warmed to his subject. 'I've seen dying men claw their way up from beneath mounds of the dead, just to fight by his side.' He shook his head in wonder. 'Despite his hatred of sorcery, there's a kind of magic in Brother Wolff.'

'Really?' asked Anna, wiping the knife on her tattered robes and looking at Ratboy with a bitter expression. 'I've met many of these Sigmarites. In my experience their faith seems little more than glorified bloodlust.' She shuddered. 'Is he really so different from the man who tried to burn me yesterday?'

'Sürman? He's no priest. He's just a cheap fraud, exploiting people's fear to pursue his own tawdry ends.' Ratboy shuddered at the thought of the man. 'He calls himself a witch hunter, but the title's just a mask he hides behind. And he's certainly no templar. I think he may once have been a catechist – a lay brother that is – but Wolff told me Sürman has no connection with the church at all now. He's just a very dangerous man.' He paused and looked around the valley, to make sure they were alone. 'He killed Wolff's parents,' he whispered.

Anna's eyes widened and she handed Ratboy's knife back to him. 'Killed them?' She shook her head. 'That would explain things, I suppose. I thought at first he'd come to spare me from the flames, but I quickly realised that he had other priorities.'

'He did save you, eventually.'

'Really? It was you I saw fighting through the flames. After that I can't really remember too much.' She placed a hand on Ratboy's arm and smiled. 'You risked your life for me. I won't forget it. Maybe Wolff played his part, but I'm not sure I'd still be here if I had relied on the compassion of a warrior priest.'

Ratboy blushed and withdrew his arm. 'My master's a devout man. He would've saved you, I'm sure. You must understand though, his thoughts haven't been clear of late. He became a wondering mendicant when he was very young, as a kind of penance. But he was tricked. It's only very recently that he's learned the truth. He'd always believed he had blood on his hands.' Ratboy paused, unsure whether to continue. 'Everyone looks to the priesthood for guidance. When things seem this hopeless, they're the only ones we can really trust. We all rely on them so heavily to revive our faith when it flags, but what if...' his voice trailed off and he looked awkwardly at Anna.

She continued his thought for him. 'What if a priest begins to know doubt?'

Ratboy nodded and leaned towards her, speaking in a low voice. 'Nothing made sense to me until I met Wolff. Everyone else is so twisted and broken. Everyone I ever met seemed damaged, one way or another, but not Wolff. His faith was always so unshakable. So bottomless. All I've ever wanted was to become more like him.' He frowned and looked at Anna with fear in his eyes. 'But recently, he seems unsure of himself. Maybe after witnessing so many horrors, even he could lose his faith?'

Anna smiled and shook her head. 'Anyone can feel afraid, Ratboy, but with such a devoted friend as you by his side, I think he will find his way.' Ratboy's eyes widened. 'Friend? I'm not sure he'd—'

'Ratboy,' called a voice from further down the valley.

They looked around and saw the towering figure of Wolff, shielding his eyes from the light as he walked out from beneath the blackened trees.

'Yes, master,' replied Ratboy, leaping to his feet and stepping nervously away from Anna. 'I'm just here with the priestess. She needed to use my knife.'

'I'm sure she has little use for your weapons, my boy.'

Anna rose to her feet and made a futile effort to dust down her robes. She barely reached Wolff's chest, but sounded undaunted as she addressed him. 'Apparently, I'm in your debt, Brother Wolff,' she said brusquely. 'Sürman was quite determined to make charcoal of me.'

Wolff massaged his scarred jaw as he studied her. 'Sürman's a clever man, sister, but I doubt he could've turned a whole village against you. Not without some cause.' He peered intently into her eyes. 'What might that cause have been I wonder?'

Colour rushed into Anna's face and she laughed incredulously as she turned to Ratboy. 'What did I tell you? These hammer hurlers are all alike: sanctimonious killers, the lot of them.'

'I merely asked you a question, sister.'

Anna shook her head. 'Questions lead to bonfires, Brother Wolff. At least where you and your brethren are concerned.' She turned to leave. 'I'd be better taking my chances with the damned.'

Wolff placed one hand on her shoulder and the other on the haft of his warhammer. 'An answer please, sister.'

There was an awkward silence as Anna looked from Wolff to Ratboy. Then her shoulders dropped and she nodded. 'My crime was a simple one, Brother Wolff. I've been working my way around this province for months now, trying to salvage a little hope from the chaos.' She sat down heavily on the grass and sighed.

'It's been a losing battle. The woods are crawling with...' she shook her head in despair, *'unspeakable* things. I was travelling with a regiment of halberdiers from Wendorf, but even they weren't safe: with all their armour and weapons they were powerless to stop the awful things we saw. They were heading to the capital, but I decided to stay here and see if I could help these poor people. I suppose I'm deluding myself though. What could I really do? The whole of Ostland seems on the verge of collapse.'

'Believe me, sister, we're well acquainted with the situation,' replied Wolff.

'Really? Do you know how scared these people are? Those villagers were so glad to see me when I arrived. They were terrified of their own shadows. They begged me for help, so I gave it to them. Healing those I could and praying for those I couldn't. The Weeping Maiden doesn't make petty distinctions though. I found a man, dressed in mockery of the creatures that haunted his nightmares. He was covered in his own filth and praying to his livestock, so I attempted to help him.'

'Was the man corrupted?' asked Wolff, crouching next to her.

Anna's eyes filled with tears as she gestured at the smouldering ruins that surrounded them. 'Look around, Brother Wolff. *Everything* is corrupted. This province has been ripped apart. Such terms have lost their meaning. Living or dead. Sane or mad. They're the only distinctions worth making nowadays.' She took a slow breath to calm herself.

'I don't think he was worshipping the Ruinous Powers, if that's what you mean. I think he'd lost his reason in the face of all this madness, but who could blame him for that? The villagers didn't agree though. They found me trying to help him and added me to their long list of suspicions. The witch hunter arrived the following day and happily took matters out of their hands.' She looked up at Wolff with a sneer of disdain. 'I imagine you'd have done much the same.'

The priest shook his head. 'Maybe not, sister. I've seen a good many things I'd rather forget, but I don't think my mind has become quite as twisted as Sürman's. Not yet, at least.' He stood up and looked out across the glittering water. 'You're not the first Sister of Shallya to fall foul of an overzealous witch hunter and I'm sure you won't be the last. Sürman's no brother of mine. Monsters like him are a stain on the good name of my order.' Wolff removed one of his gloves and held out a hand. 'If there's anything I can do that would give you a better opinion of us, I'd be glad to help.'

Anna looked at Wolff's open hand with suspicion. His broad fingers were misshapen with calluses and scars and there was dried blood beneath his splintered fingernails. Finally, she placed a hesitant hand in his and gave a reluctant nod. 'I think I should return to my temple. I imagine they're quite overwhelmed by now, but I think I may need a little healing myself. It's just a few miles north of Lubrecht. If you're heading that way, maybe we could travel together?' She gave a hollow laugh, and looked down at her scorched, battered limbs. 'I'm not sure I'd make it very far on my own.'

'Gladly,' replied Wolff, and helped her to her feet.

Ostland was a land long accustomed to war. From as far back as Ratboy could remember, the province had been fighting for its life, but recently the stout hearts of its people had begun to falter. As the trio rode north he looked out over its gloomy forests and meadows. To the west reared the ragged outline of the Middle Mountains. He had never ventured any closer than the heavily-wooded foothills, but even Ratboy knew the legends associated with those towering peaks. The myriad caves and crevices all sheltered some terrifying abomination: ogres, beastmen, every kind of monstrosity that could keep an honest man awake at night. Then he looked east, to the distant realm of Kislev, realm of the Ice Queen, with her fierce fur-clad hordes; and then, covering everything in between, the Forest of Shadows. The woods of Ostland had always been a fearsome place, but until now the villages and homesteads had stood firm: staking their claims with axes, muscle and sheer bloody-mindedness. Over the last few months, however, Ratboy had seen his countrymen driven from their homes by a foe so numerous, and terrifying, that even the province's cities were now in ruins. Only the capital, Wolfenburg, was still fully intact. Every face he saw, from infantryman to farmer, was filled with the same terrible questions: how much longer can we hold out against this onslaught? How long before I am trampled under the cloven hooves of the enemy?

'This must be the village you were looking for,' called Anna, from further up the trail. The ancient trees leant wearily over the path, making it hard to see through the arboreal gloom, but Ratboy could clearly hear the concern in Anna's voice.

He turned to Wolff, who was riding beside him, and grimaced. 'That sounds like bad news to me.' The warrior priest's only reply was a stern nod, as he spurred his horse onwards.

The village of Gotburg sat in a small clearing, not far from the road to Bosenfels. Wolff had insisted they make a slight detour so that he could visit the place, but Ratboy struggled to see why. It was a pitiful sight. Like every other village they had encountered, its stockade was breached and burned, and several of the houses had been levelled. Unlike some of the others, however, it still boasted a few signs of life. As the trio arrived at the ruined gate, they saw a crowd gathered in the village square.

Ratboy gasped in dismay as he saw what they were doing.

Several dozen villagers were on their knees, thrashing their naked torsos with barbed strips and chanting frantically as blood poured from their scarred flesh. As the rest of the crowd looked on, the penitents were gradually whipping themselves to death. It was not just this that made Ratboy gasp; it was also the man who was the focus of their prayers. They seemed to be worshipping a corpse. A skeletal body was strapped to a broken gatepost with a sign hung around its neck. Its pale, naked flesh was lacerated all over with countless knife wounds, many of which were in the shape of a hammer. Scrawled on the sign, in dark, bloody letters, was a single word: REPENT.

Ratboy realised that slurred, feeble words were coming from the body's cracked mouth. He looked up at Wolff in horror. 'Is that some kind of revenant?'

Wolff scowled back at him as he dismounted. 'Don't mention such things, boy. These are Sigmar's children.'

Anna had already tied her horse to a fence and rushed over to one of the spectators. It was a ruddy-faced old woodcutter with a chinstrap beard. As she approached him, the man waved her away furiously. 'Stay back, healer. We don't need your meddling hands here. The flagellants will save us from further attacks.' He gestured to the emaciated figure that was leading the prayers. 'Raphael has foretold it. But only if they sacrifice themselves in our place.' He grabbed her by the arm and pulled her close. 'It's what Sigmar demands! There's nothing you can do for them now.'

Ratboy noticed several of the villagers blanched at the woodcutter's words. They looked anxiously at Anna as their friends and family spilled themselves across the dusty ground; but none of them seemed brave enough to contradict him. As the priestess looked to them for support, they turned away, blushing with shame at the horror being perpetrated on their behalf.

'"He that cleaves his flesh in my name, abideth in me,"' quoted the man strapped to the post, raising his voice to regain the crowd's attention and rolling his bloodshot eyes at the heavens.

Ratboy stepped a little closer to the gruesome display and realised the man was repeating the same words over and over again: 'He that cleaves his flesh in my name, abideth in me.' He couldn't understand how such a skeletal wretch could still breathe, never mind drive dozens of normal people to such a sickening death.

'Wait,' cried a deep powerful voice, and Ratboy saw that Wolff had strode up to the front of the group.

The skeletal man faltered, stumbling over his words as he tried to focus on Wolff's thick claret robes and ornate, burnished armour. As the man's words slowed, so did the frantic, jerking movements of the crowd. They lowered their whips and looked up expectantly at Wolff from beneath sweaty, matted hair.

The priest unclasped a small leather-bound book from a strap on his forearm. A confused silence descended over the square, as Wolff began to leaf through the text, frowning as he searched for the right passage. Finally, he paused, and smiled to himself, before looking out over the panting, bleeding congregation and addressing them in a voice that boomed around the square. 'The quote is from the *Book of Eberlinus*,' he cried. It reads thus: "He that cleaves flesh and blood in my name, abideth in me, and I in him."'

The crowd looked at him open mouthed, uncomprehending.

Wolff nodded, willing them to understand. 'Your faith is a glorious gesture. A gesture of defiance. I heard tales of your devotion as far away as Haundorf. It's a wonder to behold such belief in the face of the countless evils that assail us.' He gestured towards the surrounding forest. 'Your very survival hinges on it. So many have fallen by the wayside, but you, my pious children of Sigmar have survived everything, simply by the virtue of your faith.' He closed the little book with a *snap* and when he spoke again, his voice trembled with emotion. 'If I had an army of men with hearts like yours, the war would over by nightfall.'

The flagellants began to nod and smile at each other, revelling in the priest's praise. A few of them climbed unsteadily to their feet, wiping the blood from their eyes, and trying to calm their breathing enough to speak. 'Priest,' gasped a middle-aged woman, with tears welling in her eyes. 'I don't understand. What you said about the quote – are we doing wrong?'

Wolff shook his head. 'You're not doing wrong, child, far from it. This man...' He turned to the skeletal figure slumped behind him.

The man's eyes bulged in their sunken sockets and he trembled in awe as Wolff addressed him. 'Raphael,' he whispered.

'Raphael,' repeated Wolff, 'has filled you with the light of Sigmar, and none of you will ever be the same again.'

The congregation gasped and moaned with delight. Several of them crawled forwards and pawed at the hem of Wolff's robes, sobbing in ecstasy and pressing their faces into the embroidered cloth.

Ratboy and Anna watched in amazement at how quickly Wolff had entranced the crowd. Even the spectators began to fall to their knees, muttering prayers of thanks and crossing their chests with the sign of the hammer.

'No,' continued Wolff, 'you're very far from doing wrong, my children.'

Wolff paused and strapped the book back onto his arm. 'However…' he allowed the word to echo around the square, 'if you have the strength for the task, I would ask a favour of you.'

Raphael strained to free himself from the post. 'Anything, father,' he gasped, pulling at his bonds until fresh streams of blood erupted from his wounds. 'Let us serve you, I beg.'

'Aye,' cried the middle-aged woman, rushing over to Wolff and falling at his feet. 'Let us serve you, lord. What would you ask?' She waved a trembling, bleeding arm at the assembled crowd. 'We've tried to be penitent.' She grabbed a knife from her belt and held it to her own throat. 'Should we try harder?'

Wolff placed a hand on her arm and lowered the blade. 'Wait, daughter of Sigmar. Eberlinus's words were not "He that cleaves *his* flesh in my name," they were "He that cleaves flesh in my name". The difference is subtle, but important.'

The woman frowned. 'Then whose flesh should we cleave?'

'The enemy's,' gasped Raphael, finally freeing himself and tumbling to the ground at Wolff's feet. 'You wish us to march with you.'

Wolff gave Raphael a paternal smile.

CHAPTER FOUR

Blood Sports

Music was drifting across the ruined landscape. As a merciful dusk fell over the crumbling farms and villages, chords echoed through the smoking wreckage and as the three riders steered their mounts north, ghostly harmonies drifted out of the dark to meet them.

Wolff rode up the side of a hill to find the source of the strange noise. 'Hired swords,' he said, beckoning to Anna and Ratboy to come and see. They rode up beside him and saw a merry trail of lights snaking through the hills towards them. Several regiments of soldiers were travelling north. Proud, armoured knights on barded mounts. Over their heads fluttered banners bearing a symbol Ratboy didn't recognise: a pair of bright yellow swords, emblazoned on a black background. The men wore the most incredible uniforms Ratboy had ever seen. Huge, plumed hats and elaborately frilled collars, all dyed with a yellow pigment so bright that even the chill gloom of an Ostland evening failed to dampen its cheeriness.

'Who are they?' he asked, turning to his master.

Wolff wrinkled his nose with distaste. 'Southerners,' he muttered.

'Southerners?' asked Ratboy. 'From Reikland?'

Wolff shook his head. 'No. They're a long way from home, by the looks of them. Averland, maybe, although half of them look like Tilean freelancers. Sigmar knows what would drag them so far north, but I'm glad to see them here – whatever the reason.' He leant forward in his saddle and peered through the darkness. 'Although, I fear their general may have already been injured. See how he rolls in his saddle?'

Ratboy and Anna followed Wolff's gaze. Near to the front of the regiment, surrounded by standard bearers and musicians rode a knight whose armour was even more ornate than the others. His winged helmet was trimmed with gold, and as he lolled back and forth on his horse, the metal flashed in the moonlight, drawing attention to his lurching movements.

'Strange music for times such as these,' said Anna.

The drummers and pipers that surrounded the general were skipping merrily through the long grass, oblivious to the gentle Ostland rain that was banking over the hills. They were playing a jig and the snatches of song that reached Wolff and the others sounded oddly raucous. In the face of the shattered homes and towers that covered the landscape, it seemed almost disrespectful.

Wolff nodded. 'Indeed.' He turned his horse around to face the shambling figures that were staggering up the hillside behind them. Raphael was too weak to walk, so the rest of the flagellants had fashioned a makeshift litter to drag him along on. As they climbed slowly towards the priest, the sound of their whips could be clearly heard, along with their frantic prayers. 'Just a little further,' he called out to them. 'There's an army ahead. I must speak with the general. Wait here and I'll send word if it's safe to approach.'

Raphael waved weakly in reply.

Anna watched as the penitents stumbled towards them. She shook her head in dismay at the awful violence they were inflicting on their own flesh. 'At a word from you they would drop those whips,' she said, glaring at Wolff. 'Have you no pity?'

Ratboy flinched at the venom in her voice, but Wolff simply ignored her.

As the three of them rode down the hill towards the troops, they saw the injured general summon an officer to his side, who then rode out to meet them. As he approached, they saw he was rake-thin with a long aristocratic face that sneered disdainfully at them as he approached. He carried a brightly polished shield, engraved with the same yellow swords as the banners, and as he reached the top of the hill Ratboy marvelled at the fine, gold embroidery that covered his clothes. He'd never seen such a flamboyantly dressed man. He wore a wide drooping hat, topped with ostrich feathers and studded with pearls, and his slashed leather jerkin was stretched tightly over a bright yellow silk doublet that shimmered as he moved. His short cloak was edged with lace and even his elaborate codpiece was stitched with gold thread. With his fine attire and twirled, waxed moustaches, Ratboy imagined he would be more at home on an elegant, sunlit boulevard than a muddy Ostland battlefield.

'Good evening, father,' he said, with a curt nod to Wolff. 'I'm Obermarshall Hugo von Gryphius's adjutant. He sends you his regards and offers you his hospitality.' The valet looked less than hospitable however, and his thickly accented voice was cool as he continued. 'We'll be making camp soon and Obermarshall von Gryphius would be interested to hear news of the war, especially from a senior priest such as yourself.'

'We'd be glad of the general's protection,' replied Wolff, 'but I'm afraid we're only just heading north ourselves. I doubt we know much more than your lord.'

The valet pursed his lips in irritation, but gave a stiff bow all the same. 'Very well, I'm sure my lord would still be keen to speak to you.' He looked briefly at Anna and then waved his frilled sleeve down the hill, signalling for them to lead the way. 'He generally takes pleasure in good company.'

'I have a group of followers with me-' began Wolff.

'I'll see to them,' snapped the valet, and gestured towards the army again.

As they followed the soldier down the hill, Ratboy felt as though he were entering a strange dream. The musicians were dancing in and out of the horses, dressed in elaborate animal costumes and banging tambourines as they whirled back and forth through the rain. The swarthy soldiers eyed the new arrivals suspiciously from beneath their sallet helmets, but they seemed too exhausted to give them much attention and soon looked back down at their mud-splattered horses, riding onwards through the valley with a slow determination that hinted at months of travel.

The obermarshall was as unlike his adjutant as he could possibly be: a short, pot-bellied lump, with a soft, ebullient face that seemed quite out place in his finely wrought helmet. His small, ebony eyes sparkled with pleasure as he saw Anna, and his olive skin fractured into a network of wrinkles. 'What a joy to encounter friendly faces in such grim surroundings,' he said in a thin, piping voice.

Ratboy frowned. The general seemed barely able to stay in his saddle, but bore no obvious signs of injury and he wondered what ailed the man. As they reached his side, however, he had his answer: rather than wielding weapons, the general had a bottle of sherry in one hand and a large glass in the other. As he enthusiastically hugged each of his guests in turn, they winced at the thick stench of garlic and alcohol that surrounded him.

'You poor things – what's happened to you?' he asked, noticing their scorched, bloody clothes.

Wolff studied the wine and food stains that covered the general's armour, before replying. 'We're at war, obermarshall, like the rest of this forsaken province.'

The general seemed oblivious to the disapproving tone in Wolff's voice. His eyes lit up with excitement and he leant forward in his saddle. 'Ah, yes, the war. That's exactly why we're here.' He took a swig of sherry, spilling most of it down his tunic. 'In fact, once we've made camp, I'd like to pick your brains. I believe it's all happening north of here some-where? Is that right?' He chuckled and slapped Wolff's armour. 'These things usually happen somewhere in the north, don't they?'

Wolff's nostrils flared and he drew a breath to answer, but then he seemed to think better of it and simply nodded.

'Christoff,' cried the general. 'Pitch my tent over there, near that willow tree. I think it would make a pleasant subject for a sketch or two.'

The old valet gave a little bow and backed away, snapping orders to the surrounding guards and stewards as he went.

The general tumbled awkwardly from his warhorse, and gestured for Wolff and the others to sit next to him on the grass. 'So,' he continued, once they had dismounted, 'tell me about yourselves. What are your names?'

'I'm Brother Jakob Wolff, and this is my acolyte, Anselm, although he goes by the name of Ratboy.'

Gryphius took in Ratboy's scrawny frame and tattered tunic and burst into laughter. 'Ratboy! Of course he is! That's wonderful.' He grabbed Ratboy's shoulder and gave it a firm squeeze. 'Ratboy,' he repeated, 'that's why I love you country folk. Always so quick to laugh at yourselves.'

Wolff raised his eyebrows and remained silent until the general man-aged to stifle his mirth.

'And this is Anna...' he looked over at her enquiringly.

'Fleck,' she snapped, glaring at the priest. 'I'm a Sister of Shallya, lord,' she continued, softening her voice and turning to the general, 'and I'm trained in the healing arts, so if any of your men have injuries, I'd be happy to assist them.'

'Of course,' replied the general, taking another swig of his sherry. 'There'll be plenty of time for that kind of thing later though. You all look quite ravenous.' He lurched to his feet and looked out over a teetering mass of tent poles, flaming torches and ascending banners. 'Christoff,' he cried. 'People are starving over here. Bring food for my guests, man. Where are you?'

'On my way, lord,' came a reply from out of the darkness.

'You look as though you may need medical assistance yourself,' said Gryphius, sitting down again and looking at Anna's scorched, shaven head. 'And I'm sure we could find you some more feminine clothes.'

'These will be fine,' she replied, clutching her tatty white robes protec-tively. 'Although a needle and thread would be appreciated.'

'Christoff,' bawled the general, 'bring the seamstress too.'

'I don't recognise your heraldry, obermarshall,' said Wolff, gesturing to the swords on Gryphius's ornate chest armour. 'Where have you travelled from? Averland?'

'Averhiem,' replied the general.

Wolff nodded, but Ratboy gave the general a look of helpless confusion.

Gryphius frowned. 'It's the home of the artists Tilmann and Donatus, and the composer, Ortlieb. You must have heard of the playwright Eustacius at least?'

Ratboy shook his head.

Colour flushed into the general's round cheeks and he gave an embarrassed cough. 'Well, I can assure you, he's quite a talent. Prince Eustacius enjoys the patronage of the Emperor himself.'

'But what brings you so far from home?' asked Wolff, keen to change the subject. 'Of all the provinces in the Empire, Ostland's not the safest place to be at the moment. These are dangerous times to be abroad, obermarshall. You're lucky to have got this far without encountering the enemy.'

The general grinned, revealing a row of small, uneven teeth. 'But that's exactly why I'm here.' He patted the rapier on his lap. 'I wish to test my mettle against the minions of the Dark Gods.' He puffed out his chest and attempted to suck in his paunch. 'In Averheim, the name von Gryphius is a byword for fearless heroism. There are few foes I have yet to pit myself against: greenskins, dragons, necromancers; all have learned to fear my name.' He leant forward and spoke in a conspiratorial tone. 'I've heard there's a great champion leading this new incursion into your Empire – even greater than the one called Archaon who preceded him.' He drew his sword, narrowly missing Ratboy's face as he waved it at the sky. 'Imagine the glory of slaying such a monster! The name von Gryphius would echo down the centuries.'

'But my lord,' replied Anna, 'the whole province is overrun with marauders and bandits. Even the capital's half ruined. Those who can have fled south, to Reikland. Is it wise for you to risk your men in such a campaign?'

The smile slipped from von Gryphius's face. 'I can assure you, Anna, I'm not one to avoid danger. Your elector count needs brave men at his side in times such as these, and mine are amongst the bravest. If there's anything we can do to help von Raukov repel these fiends, then we'll do it.' He sheathed his sword and smiled again, picturing his glorious, impending victory. Then, remembering his guests, he patted Ratboy's leg. 'But enough about me, what drags you three so far north?'

'We're looking for a regiment named the Ostland Black Guard,' Wolff replied. 'I believe they're engaged in the same conflict you're heading towards. And, of course, I wish to lend my support to the army. They will need great spiritual fortitude in the face of such foes. "By Sigmar's light may we know what is to be done; and only through his strength may we avoid the abyss."'

'Indeed,' replied Gryphius, winking at Anna and taking another swig of sherry. 'My thoughts exactly.' He offered the bottle to his guests and when they declined, he shrugged and drank a little more. 'I can see that you would wish to join the army as quickly as possible, but what is the importance of this Black Guard? Is that a regiment you have connections with?'

Wolff paused before replying. 'Of a sort,' he said, making it clear he did not wish to discuss the matter further.

'I see.' Gryphius slapped his thigh and lurched to his feet. 'Well, I believe that's my tent ready,' he said, offering Anna his hand. 'Let's go and make ourselves a little more comfortable. I'll see if Christoff has found you some food yet.'

A grand pavilion had appeared behind them, and as Gryphius staggered towards its black and yellow domes, he regaled them with tales of his chef's wonderful creations.

'I feel it's important to maintain one's standards, even during times of hardship,' he explained. 'At all times I include in my entourage a chef of the very best quality,' – he waved at the musicians dancing around the growing campsite – 'as well as entertainers and artists of renown.' He paused and looked earnestly at Anna. 'I'm something of a patron of the arts,' he said. 'In fact, I'm more than just a patron.' As a bowing Christoff opened the door of the tent, Gryphius strode inside and gestured to an array of canvases that were scattered across the silk cushions within. 'Many of these are my own work.'

'Really?' replied Anna, feigning interest. They all paused to look at a large canvas that Gryphius held up to them. It was a seemingly random collection of black brushstrokes.

'As you can see, it's after Vridel,' he explained, looking at them eagerly. 'Are you admirers of the Heinczel school?'

Anna turned to Wolff and Ratboy for support.

'Generally, Ostlanders don't have a lot of time to study paintings,' answered Wolff.

'Is that so?' replied the general, shaking his head sadly. He dropped the canvas to the floor and waved at the cushions that filled the tent. 'Well, make yourselves comfortable, please.'

'Did you mention food,' asked Ratboy, eyeing up a heavily laden table at the back of the tent.

'Of course,' exclaimed the general, 'tuck in, my boy, tuck in!'

Ratboy and the others hesitated for a moment, daunted by the exotic array of strange dishes. Brightly coloured fruits with thick rubbery skins and unfamiliar cuts of meat were arrayed in a fantastically gaudy display. None of them had ever seen anything like it before; but Ratboy's hunger soon overcame all other concerns and he began to wolf down the strange food, murmuring with pleasure as he devoured the rich morsels on offer.

'Please, I insist,' said von Gryphius, nodding encouragingly to the two hesitant priests.

'Well, maybe a little bread,' replied Wolff and began to eat.

Anna followed suit and all conversation ceased for a few minutes as the grinning general watched them eating.

A little while later, sprawled sleepily on silk cushions and surrounded by the soft glow of a dozen candles, the three travellers finally began to relax. They stretched out their aching, bruised limbs and massaged their stiff joints as von Gryphius's servants flitted discreetly back and forth.

The general was slumped on an ornate throne and the sherry was finally starting to take effect; every few minutes he would make himself jump with a little snore, and then gradually nod off to sleep again. At the far end of the tent, a harpist played a gentle lament while a dancer twirled back and forth, dressed as a signet.

'Obermarshall,' said Wolff, causing the general to snort in surprise and sit bolt upright.

'Yes?' he replied, giving the priest a bleary eyed grin. 'Make yourself at home,' he muttered. 'Christoff has seen to your men. You can sleep here in my tent tonight. We'll sort out your own accommodation tomorrow.'

'I just wondered, lord. If we might make a slight detour tomorrow.' He looked at Anna, struggling to stay awake at his side. 'Sister Fleck's hospital is not far from here. Could we escort her home? I'm sure she has little desire to travel any further in my company.'

'Of course,' replied the general with a dismissive wave of his hand. He looked at Anna with heavy, half-lidded eyes. 'I should be glad to assist her in any way possible. We can leave most of the troops to rest for the morning and head out by ourselves.' He grinned toothily at Anna. 'In a more intimate group.'

'I was a foundling – like many of the sisters,' explained Anna as her horse picked its way through a grey smudge of clinging mist and drooping, dew-laden boughs. 'The matriarch is a wonderful, inspirational woman – an abbess, called Sister Gundram – and she made me a ward of temple. It's a very isolated existence, as you can imagine. For the first ten years of my life I never so much as laid eyes on a man.'

At this, Gryphius looked up from the churned muddy path they were following and gave her a sly smile, but Anna was lost in her reverie and carried on oblivious.

'I couldn't have wished for a more caring family – the sisters even taught me to read and write.' She nodded at Wolff, who was riding a few feet ahead, talking to some of Gryphius's guards. 'And, unlike other priesthoods, the Shallyan faith is not above explaining the beliefs of the other churches, so I gained an understanding of the less,' she paused, searching for the right word, 'open-minded faiths.'

'It sounds like an idyllic childhood,' said Gryphius, nodding his head and adopting a more serious expression.

Anna nodded. 'Having seen the conditions of other children in the province, I think I was probably very lucky.' She looked Gryphius in the eye. 'You must understand though, the abbey is a working hospital, so from as soon as I was able to hold a pail of water, I've been helping the sick and the injured. It wasn't always the easiest place to grow up. My childhood prayers were often drowned out by the screams of the dying.'

Gryphius leant a little closer and placed a comforting hand on Anna's arm.

'Obermarshall,' called one of the soldiers and Anna and Gryphius followed the man's finger to see an even darker smudge up ahead.

'I think that's the abbey,' muttered Anna, peering through the morning mist and frowning, 'but I'm not sure. There's something not right. Why does it look so dark?'

Wolff's heavy brow knotted in a frown as he led his warhorse towards the building.

As they moved closer, the explanation for the darkness was clear: the Temple of the Bleeding Heart had been put to the torch.

Ratboy felt Anna's pain, as he saw that the simple, white-washed building was now little more than a blackened ruin.

'What kind of monsters could do this?' Anna groaned, pawing desperately at her pale scalp as she rode closer. 'What of my sisters? What of the children?'

Wolff shook his head in anger, before steering his horse up the hill at a quick canter. Ratboy rode quickly after him, along with von Gryphius and his guardsmen.

'We must find Sister Gundram. She's the abbess,' gasped Anna, looking around desperately as they rode closer. The fear in her voice made Ratboy wince. 'I beg you, help me find her.'

The temple must once have been an impressive complex, thought Ratboy as they approached it: infirmaries, chapels and a domed chapterhouse in the centre, all surrounded by a low wall in the shape of a teardrop, but almost all of it had been razed to the ground. The violence went beyond mere vandalism, though. As they reached the top of the hill, they began to notice charred human remains littered throughout the ruins.

The colour drained from von Gryphius's face and he turned to Anna. 'Wait here,' he snapped, signalling for his men to guard her. 'Let us scout ahead first.'

Anna's eyes were wide with shock and she seemed too dazed to disagree. She gave a mute nod as Gryphius rode ahead.

As they entered the central courtyard, Wolff dismounted and approached one of the corpses. The blackened bodies were barely recognisable as human, but as the priest crouched next to them, he gave a little sigh of relief. 'These aren't children,' he breathed through gritted teeth. 'State troops by the looks of them.' He gestured to a broken sword lying on the ground. 'There was some kind of defence here at least. The priestesses didn't meet their fate alone.'

'Maybe the children were evacuated then?' said Ratboy, dismounting and rushing to his master's side.

Wolff nodded. 'It's possible. We must look inside.' He looked up at the general in surprise as he realised he was unaccompanied. 'We might need at least a few of your men, obermarshall.'

Von Gryphius gave a loud, slightly forced laugh. 'What, and share all the fun? Is that wise, priest?' he asked. He gestured to the swords and pistols that hung from his belt. 'I'm sure we can handle a few cowardly temple thieves.'

'Obermarshall, the minions of the Dark Gods may not be the easy prey you're expecting. These creatures are unlike anything you will have faced before.'

The general grinned. 'Of course, Brother Wolff – that's why I'm here.' He looked at the shattered buildings. 'I can't imagine there's anyone alive in there anyway.' He toppled from his charger and drew his rapier, swaying slightly as he squinted into the smoke-filled ruins. 'Lead the way, priest.'

More bodies were scattered around the cloistered pathways within. Ratboy tried to avert his gaze, but couldn't help noticing that some of the shapes were clad in white robes and were clearly not soldiers. He pictured Anna, waiting on the hillside below, and felt his eyes prickle with tears. Who could do such a thing, he wondered?

'It looks like we've found your prey, obermarshall,' snapped Wolff, kicking one of the corpses.

They rushed to his side and saw a large, smouldering body lying at his feet. It was as scorched and broken as everything else, but even the ravages of the fire couldn't hide the thing's monstrous shape. Ratboy grimaced at the stink emanating from it, but stepped closer nonetheless, curious to study the monster. It was vaguely man-shaped, but its shoulders and limbs were grotesquely swollen and muscled, and covered with a thick, greasy hide. Wolff used his iron-clad boot to roll the thing over onto its back, revealing a head that was bloated and distorted into a roughly bovine shape, with great gnarled horns sprouting from its face.

'What is it?' whispered von Gryphius, his eyes wide with shock.

Wolff looked up at him in surprise. 'This is the evil that plagues us, obermarshall; *this* is the great prize you've been seeking.' He ground his boot into the thing's hide and grimaced. 'This is the embodiment of corruption. "By the simple undividedness of Sigmar's being, the faithful will find truth; as surely as the deceiver's form will reveal that which his words would hide."'

He shrugged and led the way towards the chapterhouse, which was the only building not to have been completely destroyed by the flames. As they approached it, the number of bodies increased, as did the awful stench that came from the fallen beastmen.

'The fighting seems to have been fiercest here,' commented Wolff as he stepped up to the shattered door that led into the building. As the others gathered behind him, weapons at the ready, Wolff used his warhammer to shove the door open. The splinted wood screeched noisily as it swung inwards, but the darkness inside was complete. The pale grey sun seemed afraid to cross the threshold and illuminate the bloodshed within.

Wolff gripped his hammer tightly in both hands, and then disappeared into the blackness.

After a second's hesitation, Ratboy followed.

At first the gloom seemed impenetrable, but as his eyes grew accustomed to the dark, vague shapes began to emerge and he saw that the floor was littered with overturned tables and chairs. It looked like the scene of some final defence, with the priestesses and soldiers barricaded inside the chapterhouse. From the shattered state of the door and the broken furniture, Ratboy guessed that some kind of battering ram must have been used to smash the barricades aside. He looked around but could find no sign of such a weapon.

Movement caught his eye, and he saw a towering shape rush towards him out of the darkness. He lifted his knife, and then lowered it again as he recognised Wolff's chiselled features glowering down at him.

'They're all dead,' muttered the priest, shaking his head and gesturing to the white shapes slumped on the floor around them. 'I believe I just found the abbess.' He held up a ring. It was hard to make out in the darkness, but as the metal rolled between the priest's fingers, Ratboy realised it was decorated with a white dove carrying a golden key. There was an unusual note of emotion in Wolff's voice as he continued. 'These women desired only to help. They bore no allegiance to any army or lord. They didn't deserve to meet their end in this way.' He closed his fist around the ring and secreted it within his robes. 'Come,' he said, stepping back towards the door.

The light vanished before either of them could reach the doorway, plunging them into a darkness even more profound than before. A colossal shape had blocked their way, towering over even Wolff. Ratboy heard the deep, rattling breath of a large animal.

Wolff shoved the acolyte violently across the room and as he tumbled over the broken furniture, Ratboy heard a great weapon slam into the ground where he had just been standing. He gasped in pain, winded by a chair leg that jabbed him in the stomach as he landed. As he rolled onto his back, groaning, shapes whirled around him in the darkness, crashing into walls and tables and grunting with exertion.

Sparks flew as weapons collided and in the brief flashes of light, Ratboy saw Wolff fighting desperately against a creature so big it had to stoop beneath the chapterhouse's vaulted ceiling. The light was gone too fast for him to be sure of the monster's shape, but he was left with a vague impression of massive, coiled muscle and long, curved horns.

Ratboy tried to draw breath, but retched instead, powerless to call for help. As he felt around in the dark for his knife, he heard Wolff muttering something nearby. Then, as the priest uttered a final, fierce syllable, glittering light flooded the chamber and the creature looming over them was revealed in all its monstrous glory. It was obviously the same species as the bodies outside, but even more grotesquely oversized. As holy light poured from Wolff's hammer, shimmering and flashing off the whitewashed walls, the creature bellowed and swung an axe at the priest's head. The weapon was almost as big as the priest himself, and as he leapt out of the way it smashed into the wall, cutting into the stone with such force that the whole building shook, sending masonry tumbling from the ceiling. The priest's warhammer slipped from his grip as he landed, clattering across the flagstones and disappearing from view.

The room plunged into darkness once more.

The grunting and smashing sounds continued until Ratboy heard Wolff cry out with pain. As the monster moved back and forth, brief bursts of light crept in from the outside, and in one such flash he suddenly saw the beast lifting Wolff from the ground, about to smash him against the wall, swinging him as easily as a straw doll.

Ratboy tried desperately to rise, but he was still unable to breathe and fell to his knees again, whimpering pathetically as he crawled towards the two combatants.

There was a final, deafening *bang* and then silence filled the chapterhouse.

As Ratboy crawled painfully towards the doorway, the acrid stink of saltpetre filled his nose and he saw another figure stood just inside the doorway, with a thin trail of smoke drifting from its raised hand.

'I told you we didn't need more men,' said von Gryphius, lowering his flintlock pistol with a high-pitched laugh. The colour had drained from his face and his eyes were rolling with fear. As he helped Ratboy to his feet his thin voice sounded slightly hysterical. 'What exactly was that?' he asked, gesturing to the huge mound that lay at his feet.

'Good work, obermarshall,' came Wolff's voice from the darkness. He stepped into the shaft of light coming through the doorway and looked down at the monster's body in confusion. 'I'm amazed your shot could pierce such a thick skull.'

Von Gryphius nodded slowly, still staring at the huge corpse in amazement. 'I'm a regular at the Giselbrecht hunt,' he muttered. 'And that fellow's left eye was conveniently large.'

The ghost of a smile played around Wolff's lips as he studied the general, then he took Ratboy's arm. Once outside, they both fell to the ground, exhausted. When he had caught his breath, Wolff took the ring from his robes and looked at it thoughtfully as it glittered in the sunlight. The dove was stained with the blood of its previous owner.

'I must talk with Anna,' he said.

CHAPTER FIVE

The Restless Dead

Recently, Erasmus had begun to speak to the bodies as he worked. He knew it was a little odd, but with each passing day, he found the mortal world harder to understand and had come to think of these waxy, shrouded shapes as his friends. Their stillness comforted him and sometimes he would give them voices; replying to himself as though the dead were answering. His talk was endless and anodyne: the changing of the seasons and the consistency of his porridge were the most regular topics. He doubted the corpses minded though. After all, his were the last mortal thoughts that would ever be directed at these poor, lost souls.

The garden of Morr at Elghast was a humble temple, but its crypt was a bewildering maze of tunnels and chambers. The priest's flickering lamps had only ever illuminated a small fraction of it. Four generations of his family had tended the dead in this place, but as far as he knew, no one had ever attempted to map out the full extent of the catacombs. The limestone arches had once been ornately carved in the likeness of skulls and black rose petals, but over the centuries the pillars and cornices had shrugged off their sculpted edges, reasserting their natural, ragged shapes.

A more inquisitive mind might have wished to explore the distant, ancient chambers, but not Erasmus. As he performed the funerary rites, he sometimes heard movements from deeper inside the network of tunnels, and felt obliged to investigate, but it usually turned out to be nothing more than rats, feasting on the dead. The rest of the time, he left the rows of crumbling mausoleums alone.

The clapping of large wings announced the arrival of Udo, fluttering in through the half open door that led back up to the temple. As the raven settled on her perch, she cawed repeatedly at the black-robed priest, tilting her head to watch him as he shuffled from corpse to corpse.

'Really?' replied Erasmus, pausing in the act of cleaning a knife to look up at the bird. 'That's most unfortunate, old girl, but owls have as much right to eat mice as you do. All creatures have a right to live.' He carefully lifted a shroud and plunged the knife into something soft and yielding, causing a thin arc of fluid to patter gently across the stone floor. 'At least, for a while they do.'

He chopped and sliced in silence for a few minutes, frowning in concentration. Then he paused. 'Now then friend, what's this?' he muttered, tugging an arrowhead from his subject's chest with a moist popping sound. He held the bent piece of metal closer to his lamp and peered at it. 'I don't think you'll need this in the afterlife.' He dabbed at the wound with a cloth and muttered a quick, sonorous prayer, before dropping the arrowhead in a little copper bowl with a *clang*. 'Was it really worth it, I wonder,' he said, taking a jug of oil from a nearby table and tipping a little onto the corpse's chest. As the chamber filled with the scent of rosewater, he shook his head. 'What cause was worth losing everything for, at your age? How old were you exactly?'

'*Early thirties,*' he replied to himself in a deep voice. '*Thirty-five at most.*'

'I see. Old enough to have a family then, maybe, and people who loved you, but that wasn't enough – you had to look for something more. Something exciting.'

'*There's no love out there anymore, father: covetousness, maybe; the desire for other men's land; bloodlust perhaps, but no love.*'

Erasmus sighed as he continued to anoint the body. 'Yes, I suppose you might be right.' He paused, frowning at something. Then, with another wet *pop*, he removed a second arrowhead. 'There certainly doesn't seem to have been much love for you.'

He wiped down the second wound and finished applying the scented oil. Then, placing the knife back in a leather roll, he shuffled across the chamber to a small recess in the damp rock, filled with a collection of bottles, jugs and mildewed books. He selected one of the texts and returned to the body, where he began to pray. He wished the deceased a quick journey to the afterlife and begged Morr to grant him safe passage.

Natural light hardly reached down into the crypt, but after a few more hours' work, Erasmus's stomach announced quite clearly that it was midday. He stroked his tonsured head and gave a little yawn. 'Oh, Udo, I think it might be time for some lunch.'

The raven gave no reply.

He extinguished all the lamps apart from the one in his hand and fully opened the door that led back up to the temple, allowing a little more distant, grey sunlight to penetrate the immemorial gloom. He extinguished his final lamp and began to climb the rounded steps, holding out his arm for Udo to perch on. 'Bless me!' he exclaimed, slapping his head with his hand and turning around. 'I'm such a doddering old fool. I forgot all about our new guest.' He climbed back down, relit his small, iron lantern and closed the door again, shuffling back towards the furthest recesses of the chamber. The single flickering light picked out a corpse that was such a recent arrival the priest had yet to find a shroud for it. 'I can't leave you like this all afternoon, now can I?'

'*No,*' he replied to himself. '*You should at least show a little respect for a fellow priest.*'

'I know. I know. I'm sorry, brother,' he muttered, lifting some muslin from a shelf as he approached the body. 'Are you actually a priest though?' he wondered aloud, holding the lantern over the remains. The body was that of a wiry old man, with thin, greasy hair and puckered, weather-beaten skin. 'This certainly seems to suggest you were a man of faith,' he said, holding the light over a symbol on the old man's stomach. The sagging folds of skin below his ribs were branded with the shape of a flaming hammer. 'But there's something about your expression that makes me wonder.' He stooped until his clouded, myopic eyes were just an inch or two from the corpse's face. 'There's something a little wild about you.'

'*I'm a mendicant,*' Erasmus said to himself in the same sonorous voice he gave all the dead. '*That's why I look so emaciated.*'

'Well, yes, that would explain the sunburned skin too, I suppose, but what about this injury? It looks to me more like the wound of a soldier, or a fanatic even. You certainly didn't get this in a temple.' He moved the lantern across the body, illuminating a large, ragged hole, just beneath the man's left shoulder. 'And I suppose this must have been the work of your servant,' he said, fingering the crude attempts at bandaging.

'*You're a naïve old fool,*' Erasmus replied to himself in a deep voice. '*Hiding away in the dark for all these years, as the world turns on its head. You think that priests don't get murdered? No one's safe anymore. Violence is the only currency people understand in these dark times. You remember what Ernko said, when he delivered his brother's remains. The whole of Gumprecht is consumed with madness – they've turned on each other, hunting down their own families like dogs. They've burned their own houses to the ground. All because they think there's a heretic somewhere in their midst – someone who might draw the gaze of the Ruinous Powers in their direction. And remember that ferryman from Hürdell? He said the people from his village had begun dressing as goats and eating grass, in the hope it would appease the creatures of the forest and spare them from attacks. And if that merchant from Ferlangen was correct, half the cities in the province have fallen to the enemy.*'

Erasmus shook his head in surprise as he peeled back the dark, damp rags that covered the wound. 'What kind of weapon did this to you?' he muttered. In truth though, after the horrors of the last few years, there was little that could shock the priest anymore, and he began to hum a little ditty to himself as he worked. He reopened his roll of tools and fetched another bottle of ointment. Then, he paused. 'Looks like you've still got something in there, friend,' he said, peering into the bloody hole. 'Is that a splinter of wood?' He took a small scythe-shaped tool from his roll and slid it into the wound.

The corpse gave out a deafening, tremulous scream.

Its eyes opened wide in terror and one of its sinewy hands shot up, grabbing Erasmus's shoulder in a tight grip.

Erasmus dropped the knife to the floor with a clatter and stared back at the animated corpse in confusion; then he began to scream too. He tried to pull back from its grasp, but the corpse's second hand shot up, grabbing him firmly by the other shoulder.

The corpse's face was twisted in horror and confusion as it looked from Erasmus to the surrounding darkness. The vague shapes of the other bodies were just visible, and the corpse shook its head wildly, before turning back to the priest. 'I'm not dead,' it breathed in a croaky whisper. 'For Sigmar's sake, I'm alive!'

'I work here mostly on my own,' said Erasmus, shuffling cheerfully in and out of his bedchamber. 'My brother, Bertram, visits occasionally.' His lips twisted into a grimace. 'He only comes to help when he has to, thankfully – only when there's too much embalming for me to handle alone. Mind you, that seems to be more often than not lately.' He lifted Sürman up into a sitting position and handed him a cup of water. 'Lately it seems like the dead outnumber the living.' He chuckled as he pulled open the shutters, filling the small room with flat grey light. 'Another cheerful Ostland day,' he said, watching the autumn rain slanting across the forest below.

Sürman watched him carefully over the top of the cup as he took a gulp of the water. He immediately spat the liquid out and burst into a series of hacking coughs, spraying flecks of blood all over the bed's woollen sheets.

'Be careful,' said Erasmus, dashing to his side and snatching the cup from him. 'You need to drink it slowly.' He shook his head and gently patted Sürman's bony, hunched back. 'It's a miracle you're alive. That wound must have missed your heart by an inch.' Once the coughing fit had passed, he handed the cup back and sat on a stool next to the window. 'Your man brought you to me certain that you were dead.' Erasmus looked at the floor to hide his embarrassment. 'There are various tests I would have performed before beginning the embalming, of course. I was just going to remove a couple of the splinters.'

Sürman sipped the water again, carefully this time, and he managed to hold it down. His hollow, stubbly cheeks were still as grey as the rain clouds rushing past the window, but his breath was coming a little easier now, and he was beginning to think he might even survive. 'Who brought me here?' he asked in a strained whisper.

Erasmus's long, pale face lit up with a smile. 'You sound so much better!' He clasped his tapered fingers together and muttered a prayer. 'My skills as a healer are rarely called upon. It's been a long time since I practiced herb lore. I wasn't sure if that poultice would be powerful enough to draw out the illness.' He shook his head in amazement. 'You're made of sterner stuff than you look, old man.'

No hint of emotion crossed Sürman's face. He took a slow breath and then repeated his words a little louder. 'Who brought me here?'

The eager smile remained on Erasmus's face as he replied. 'As I said, it was your man.' He looked up at the ceiling and drummed his fingers on his knees. 'I think he said his name was Albrecht or Adolphus, or–'

'Adelman,' interrupted Sürman, with a note of impatience in his voice.

'Yes! That's the one. He'd travelled with you for days, trying to find help, but he'd finally given up hope of reviving you.' Erasmus narrowed his eyes and looked back at Sürman. 'He seemed eager to leave. As though he were worried I would ask him the reasons for your condition.' He shrugged. 'But the truth is, my friend, the actions of the living are rarely Morr's concern. Whatever we do in life, we all reach the same destination.'

'There are many different routes to that destination,' muttered Sürman, looking down at his ruined body.

'Aye,' replied Erasmus, finally letting the smile slip from his face. 'That there are.' He gestured to the hammer on Sürman's stomach. 'Are you some kind of priest then, friend?'

'My name's Otto Sürman, and yes, I'm a High Priest of Sigmar.'

Erasmus raised his eyebrows and smiled. 'A *High* Priest, you say? I'd have expected a little more finery.'

'Adelman has robbed me, you idiot,' snapped Sürman, rising up from the bed and twisting the sheets in his bony fists. He looked up at the ceiling of the priest's cell and groaned with frustration. 'That witch did this to me. She must have summoned Wolff somehow – knowing he would save her. And now she goes free and Adelman has taken everything.' He flopped back onto the bed and glared at Erasmus.

Erasmus looked appalled. 'Your servant hasn't robbed you. At least, I don't think so.'

'Idiot. Do you think I travel the province naked and penniless? Adelman's taken my robes and my books too.' His eyes bulged as a terrible thought hit him. 'And all of my relics – my priceless relics.' Sürman drew a breath to hurl more insults at the priest, but before he could speak, the bed dropped away from beneath him and his stomach lurched horribly. He groaned with nausea and clamped his eyes shut in fear. When he opened them again, he was still lying in the priest's bed and Erasmus was watching over him with a concerned expression on his face.

'You should calm yourself,' urged the priest. 'You're not through the worst of it yet. The wound was full of illness and spores of corruption. I was forced to use a more powerful mixture than I would've liked.'

Sürman's vision blurred and his temples began to throb. He tried to focus on the priest, but as he peered at him, Erasmus's long, patrician features began to stretch and elongate: sliding from his face to reveal vivid pits of red flesh beneath his eyes that gradually drooped down towards his mouth. Sürman tried to reach out and push the flesh back into place, but his limbs refused to obey and he groaned in fear. 'Your face…' he murmured, as the walls closed in around him.

'What is it?' asked Erasmus, leaning forward, so that the remaining flesh peeled back from his head and revealed the glistening skull beneath. 'You should rest,' he said, splashing thick blood all over the bed, but Sürman's eyes were already closing as sleep washed over him.

Anna had sprouted great, black, oily wings and as she stepped towards Sürman she croaked in a harsh, inhuman voice. She drew a knife from beneath her feathers and brandished it playfully at him. Catching the candlelight on the edge of its curved, serrated blade.

Sürman was sprawled on a mortuary slab and all his strength had gone from him. As the witch approached he was powerless to move and he felt impotent fury rising from deep within him. 'You'll die, Anna,' he said, glaring into her black, lidless eyes. 'Your wound is full of the spores of corruption.'

The witch spread her wings and laughed, before flying up onto the slab and crouching low over him, so that her mouth was almost touching his. She twisted her screeching voice into words he could understand. 'What are you talking about Otto?' she said, holding the knife up to his face. 'How could you ever find me without your eyes?'

'I have eyes!' cried Sürman, straining to twist his head out of her reach.

'You did have,' replied the witch, smiling as she brought the knife down towards him.

Sürman cried out in fear and clamped his eyes shut. 'I'll still find you, witch!' he cried.

Anna's only reply was harsh, bird-like squawks of laughter.

The expected pain never arrived and after a few moments Sürman opened his eyes to find he was back in the priest's cell. It was still morning, but the sky outside was clear and bright, and he guessed this was not the same day. He reached up to feel his eyes, and sighed with relief.

A loud cawing filled the room and Sürman screamed with terror.

He looked around and saw a large raven, sat on an old chest at the foot of the bed, eyeing him warily.

Erasmus burst into the room with a bloody, curved knife in his hand and a look of dismay on his face. 'What's happened?' he cried, placing the knife on the chair and clutching Sürman's hand. 'Are you alright?'

'There's a bird in here!' exclaimed Sürman, crawling fearfully beneath the sheets. 'She tried to steal my eyes.'

The priest laughed gently and patted Sürman's arm. 'That's just Udo. She won't hurt you.' He held out his arm, and the bird flew across the room and perched on its master. 'Come on, old girl. You're scaring our guest.' With another smile at Sürman, he left the room, taking his bird with him.

Sürman shivered. His body was covered with cold sweat. 'He's poisoned me,' he muttered to himself, pulling the sheets up to his chin, and looking warily around the room. 'Another witch. Just like Anna Fleck.' He heard a distant door slam and the sound of voices talking somewhere on the floor below. 'They're all trying to kill me,' he moaned. 'In league with the witch.' He noticed Erasmus's knife on the chair and smiled. He pulled himself to the edge of the bed. His limbs trembled with the effort, but he wasn't sure how long he had and his fear gave him strength. With one hand on the cold stone floor, he reached out to the chair. 'Got it,' he gasped, clutching the knife in his hand. With a grunt, he pushed himself back onto the bed and hid the blade beneath the blankets. With a smile of relief, he lowered his head onto the pillow, and quickly slipped back into his strange dreams.

'Otto,' said Erasmus, gently shaking him awake. 'I have news.'

Sürman lurched into a sitting position and groaned, looking around at the room in confusion. 'What's that?' he said, rubbing the sleep from his eyes.

Erasmus laughed at his sudden movements. 'You seem stronger,' he exclaimed, handing him a bowl of stew. 'Try and eat some more of this. You threw up most of the last bowl.'

Sürman took the food from the priest and began to eat, surprised by his own hunger. 'The last bowl?' he asked, eying the priest suspiciously. 'What last bowl?'

Erasmus chuckled. 'Don't you remember?'

Sürman shook his head, spilling a little of the broth down his stubbly chin.

'You've been here for nearly a week now, my friend,' said Erasmus. 'I thought I'd lost you a while back, but you seem to be a lot better today.' He gestured to the quickly emptying bowl. 'I'd take that a bit slower though.'

Sürman flinched as the raven flew into the room and perched at the end of the bed.

'Don't worry, Udo won't hurt you,' laughed the priest. He adopted a serious expression. 'Anyway, as I was saying, I have news.'

Sürman grunted, without lifting his face up from the bowl.

'I've been talking to my brother, Bertram, and he tells me that your servant, Adelman, is still in the village.'

Sürman paused with the spoon halfway to his mouth, and a piece of unchewed meat hanging from between his teeth.

'Bertram is a constable of the watch, you see.' Erasmus frowned. 'I wonder sometimes if he's really the right man for the job. Some of his decisions seem a little harsh to me.' He leant forward and lowered his voice a little. 'He's not really the brightest–'

'Adelman!' snarled Sürman, sending the piece of meat flying from his mouth. 'Where is he? Where are my belongings?'

Erasmus looked blankly at him, confused for a moment. 'Oh, yes, your servant.' He frowned. 'Well, it's a sad tale, really. Thinking that you were dead, he took a room at the Bull's Head, and has been there for days, drowning his sorrows.'

'What about my things?'

'Well, according to Bertram, he arrived with two heavily laden saddlebags, and as far as anyone can tell, they've never left his room. I told Bertram not to ask too widely though, for fear of stirring up interest in the value of your possessions.'

Sürman sank back into the bed, trying to still the fevered visions that kept seizing hold of him. Erasmus had no intention of letting him live, he saw that quite clearly. The old priest would simply keep poisoning him until he passed away in his sleep. Then he would send his brother to murder Adelman and claim the relics and books for himself. He hugged his frail body and his powerlessness tormented him. A vision of Anna filled his thoughts, mocking him as she strode away from the pyre. The thought that he would die and she would live was too much. His eyes rolled back into their sockets and his muscles began to spasm as a kind of fit came over him. Suddenly, he remembered something and slipped a hand down beneath the blankets. He smiled as his hand closed around the cold metal of the knife.

'Are you alright?' asked Erasmus.

Sürman gave him a strained smile. 'Tell me,' he gasped, trying to hide his growing excitement. 'How did you heal me?'

Erasmus leant back in his chair and shrugged modestly. 'Oh, it was simple herb lore really, nothing mysterious. Long ago, before I was even an initiate, I used to dabble in such things. I just applied a poultice: a little brooklime, mandrake and figwort, and then an infusion of Queen of the Meadow. Then nothing more than rest and a light broth to keep your strength up until the fever passed.'

Sürman nodded. 'And how did you learn this "herb lore"?'

'Ah, well, my mother was,' he laughed, 'well, I suppose you'd call her a kind of wise woman. She knew all sorts of things: weird folk legends, and strange rites; you know the kind of thing.' He shook his head and looked wistfully out of the window. 'Sometimes I wonder if we've lost something, by neglecting all the teachings of the Old Faith.'

'Old Faith?' asked Sürman, continuing to smile. 'Old gods do you mean?'

'Well yes, I suppose so.' Erasmus shrugged. 'There's often a lot of wisdom in those more ancient forms of worship.'

'Sorry,' muttered Sürman, tightening his grip on the knife handle. 'Could you come a little closer, I can't quite hear you.'

Erasmus frowned. 'Are your ears infected too?' he asked, leaning towards Sürman.

Sürman's smile spread into a wolfish grin as the priest drew nearer. He slowly slid the knife up from beneath the blankets.

A terrible screeching noise filled the room and Erasmus jumped up from his chair.

Sürman cursed under his breath and slid the knife back down the bed.

'What's the matter, old girl?' cried Erasmus, dashing across the room to the raven. The bird was hopping back and forth in a frenzy and cawing repeatedly at Sürman.

Heavy footsteps pounded up the stairs and a large man blundered into the room. He was a towering, lantern-jawed brute, wearing a filthy buckskin coat that could barely restrain the proud swell of his stomach. His freckled, hairy forearms were about as wide as Sürman's waist, and the witch hunter groaned with frustration as his chance for escape slipped away from him.

'What're you playing at, brother?' the man barked at the priest. Erasmus was still trying to placate the raven, however, and not waiting for a reply, the newcomer strode past him and approached the bed. He grinned down at Sürman and enveloped his frail hand in his own meaty paw. 'Pleased to make your acquaintance, milord. Erasmus tells me you're a priest of some kind.'

Sürman's stomach knotted with anger and he remained silent, glowering up at the man from the bed.

'Don't say much, does he?' said the man, continuing to grip Sürman's hand. 'Is he a bit deaf?' He moved his broad, florid face a little closer and bellowed into Sürman's ear. 'I'm Bertram. The village constable.' He patted a short wooden club attached to his belt. 'You might say I'm the Emperor's legal representative around here.' He loosed his grip and smiled proudly. 'I'm the one who's been investigating the whereabouts of your missing servant, Adelman.'

'Get me out of here,' gasped Sürman suddenly, sitting up in the bed and casting a fearful look at the priest. 'Your brother's trying to kill me.'

The constable paused, and frowned at his brother. 'Is he still wrong in the head?'

Erasmus gave Sürman an embarrassed smile as he stepped to his brother's side. 'I mentioned that the poultice I applied might have confused you a little. It's not that you're–'

'Take me to Adelman,' cried Sürman, grabbing Bertram's arm. 'I must speak with him as a matter of urgency.' He gave a groan of exertion and climbed out of the bed, hanging on to Bertram for support as he stood before them, trembling and naked. 'I'm surrounded by witches!' he cried, spraying spit into the constable's face. 'You must get me out of here.'

'Calm yourself, Otto,' said Erasmus, trying to usher him back into the bed.

Sürman batted him aside with surprising strength and looked at Bertram with desperation in his rolling eyes. 'I demand you take me to the Bull's Head. There's a powerful enchantress at large in this region.' He slapped the hammer on his hollow stomach. 'Anyone who fails to assist me shall be considered an accomplice.' He let go of the constable and managed to stand unaided as he levelled a finger at him. 'Are you going to help me, or should I consider you an occultist too?'

Doubt flickered across Bertram's simple face. He looked at his brother, but Erasmus looked as anxious as he did. 'Well, father,' he shrugged, 'if you really wish to leave, of course I'll help. It's just…' He looked at the bandages around Sürman's shoulder. 'Are you sure you're strong enough?'

Sürman swayed a little on his spindly legs as he turned towards Erasmus, who was hovering nervously by the doorway. 'I have my suspicions, priest,' he snapped, 'but fortunately for you, I have more important concerns at present. Fetch me some clothes and let me leave immediately, and I will try and forget your talk of "old gods" for a little while.'

Erasmus's face drained of colour, as he finally realised the nature of the man he had been treating. 'Y-Yes, of course' he stammered, rushing from the room.

Sürman's feverish mind was still lurching in and out of reality as he staggered into the Bull's Head. He peered uncertainly into the lounge of the tavern and flinched at the sight of the jostling figures moving through the smoky candlelight. Most of the villagers were crowded around a huge inglenook fireplace, warming themselves against the cold, drizzly evening that was tapping against the mullioned windows. They were simple farmers and woodsmen mostly, but to Sürman, the raging fire seemed to be melting the flesh from their faces, dripping rubbery strings of skin into their tankards. His stomach turned at the sight and he felt his legs starting to give way. He spotted a chair in a dark corner and collapsed into it, his head spinning. He closed his eyes for a few moments and tried to calm his breathing.

'Is everything alright, sir?' someone asked.

Sürman opened his eyes to see a barrel-chested man, clearly built from the same mould as Bertram. He had a long, greying beard though, and from his apron and the empty tankards in his hands, Sürman guessed he was the innkeeper.

'No,' muttered Sürman, pulling himself up in his seat and sneering at the man. 'No, it is not. My wretched servant is staying at your fleapit of an inn and every penny he's spending is pilfered from my purse.'

The innkeeper's face flushed with anger, but he refrained from acknowledging Sürman's insult. 'What name's he travelling under?'

Sürman grimaced as he noticed the man's skin growing translucent, revealing the pulsing organs and arteries beneath. He shook his head and looked again, to find the hallucination had passed. 'The useless dog is called Adelman.'

The innkeeper gave a brusque nod and stormed away.

Adelman had once been a stevedore, working on the docks in Altdorf. His neck was as thick as a tree trunk and his arms were like knotted steel, but Sürman had often wondered if he might have taken a blow to the head in his youth. As he rushed through the busy inn towards Sürman's table, his mouth was hung open with the same perpetual look of slack-jawed confusion he always wore. 'Master,' he exclaimed, dropping to his knees at Sürman's feet and hugging his legs. As he did this, his broad shoulders connected with the next table and sent it toppling over, scattering empty jugs and plates across the dusty floor.

'Watch yourself, you oaf,' hissed Sürman, batting his servant around the head until he loosed his legs and looked up at him. It always seemed to Sürman that Adelman's features had fallen into the middle of his face somehow. His eyes were nestled too close together, on either side of a small snub nose, surrounded by a vast expanse of cheekbone. And as he smiled, Adelman revealed a row of gleaming, tombstone teeth.

'You're not dead,' he said in a bass rumble.

'Quick witted as ever, I see,' muttered Sürman. 'Are my things safe?'

Adelman nodded eagerly. 'They're locked in my room. Shall I fetch them?'

Sürman shook his head. 'If you've not spent all of my money on these luxurious lodgings, would you be so good as to fetch me some food first?'

As Adelman rushed enthusiastically off to the bar, Sürman tried again to take in his surroundings. Seeing a familiar face, even one as ridiculous as Adelman's, had reassured him a little, and he felt his grasp on reality tightening. Maybe the priest's poison was finally wearing off? The woodsmen and labourers gathered round the fire were little more than shifting silhouettes, but from the raucous sound of their laughter, he could tell they had been drinking for hours. Harvest time was long past, and the woodsmen probably spent as little time in the forest as possible these days. Around the edges of the long, rectangular lounge, various other groups were huddled in the shadows, telling tales of the war and attempting to lift each other's spirits for a while.

The only group he could see clearly was sat at a table directly opposite. Several young farmhands were crowded eagerly around an older woman, who was obviously delighted with all the attention. She was dressed in a gaudy array of flowery silks and cheap trinkets, and every now and then she would lift her heavily made-up face to the beamed ceiling and burst into trilling song. She was obviously some kind of entertainer and by her odd, lilting accent, Sürman guessed that she was not from the province.

As he waited for his food, Sürman found himself listening along with the spellbound youths as she spoke.

'Obermarshall Hugo von Gryphius is the kind of man who appreciates the charms of an older woman,' she said, batting her lashes and pursing her scarlet lips, as her audience erupted into a chorus of laughter and lewd comments. 'But not only that,' she continued, adopting a more serious expression. 'He appreciates the arts in all their forms. He employs actors and musicians from every corner of the Old World.' She leant across the table, distracting the boys with a brief display of her cleavage. 'In fact, he wrote to the academy at Kleinberg, personally requesting my presence in his entourage.'

'But what's this "obermarshall" doing in Ostland?' asked one of the farmhands.

'He sees warfare as just another one of the great arts,' she explained. 'He heard that your province was battling against a terrible foe, and he was eager to join the performance.'

The farmhands' laughter stalled as they recalled the war. 'I'm not sure it will be as much fun as he imagines,' muttered one, taking a deep swig of his ale.

Adelman reappeared with a plate of nondescript meat and some grey bread. Sürman grimaced at it, before starting to shovel down the hot food. Adelman began to speak, but Sürman signalled for him to be silent and continued listening to the singer.

'So why are you no longer travelling with his army, then?' asked another youth.

The singer curled her lip with distaste. 'He found another distraction.' She cried with disbelief. 'A priestess of Shallya no less.'

Sürman paused, with a fork of steaming offal hovering near his mouth.

'A priestess?' exclaimed one of the farmhands. 'What kind of entertainment is he expecting from her?'

The boys all burst into hysterical laughter, and the singer had to raise her voice to be heard. 'He's obsessed with her, for some reason.' She shook her head. 'And she hasn't even got any hair!'

This last comment was greeted with such howls of laughter that even the innkeeper looked over to see what was so funny.

'What happened to her hair?' asked one of the farmhands.

'Well, apparently, she fell foul of some kind of witch hunter and he tried to burn her to death.'

The farmhands' laughter tailed off again at the mention of a witch hunter. Their guffaws became quiet chuckles as they wiped the tears from their eyes.

Sürman was already struggling to his feet as the woman continued.

'Some warrior priest rescued her, but not before her golden locks had been burned clean off. She was called Anna something.'

'Fleck,' snapped Sürman, staggering up to the table and slamming his hands down on the gnarled wood.

'Eh, what's your game, mister?' cried the woman in surprise.

'Watch it,' growled the largest of the farmhands, as they all rose to their feet and stepped between Sürman and the woman. 'Just who might you be?'

Sürman managed to stand erect and jabbed a bony finger into the lad's chest. 'I'm the witch hunter you were just discussing.' He pulled open the black robes Erasmus had loaned him, to reveal the hammer burnt across his flesh.

The youths fell silent and backed away from him, suddenly feeling very sober. 'There's no reason to get yourself all worked up, mister.'

'I've done nothing wrong,' cried the woman, with a note of panic rising in her voice, as her audience all dissolved into the shadows.

Sürman gave her what he imagined was a reassuring smile and gestured to her chair. 'Please, don't be alarmed,' he said, sitting down next to her. 'I just wanted to ask you a couple of questions.'

The woman's face was pale with fear as she looked around the inn for help. The drunken farmers had started singing, however, and no one had noticed her predicament.

'Adelman,' snapped Sürman, 'fetch the lady another glass of wine.'

Once they were both seated, Sürman took the woman's hand. 'Am I right,' he asked, 'was the priestess called Anna Fleck?'

The woman was wide-eyed with terror as she replied. 'Yes, I think so.' She shook her head urgently. 'I had little to do with her though. I was simply employed as a dancer for von Gryphius. The priestess has been travelling with him for the last week or so, and I just asked her how she lost her hair.'

Sürman nodded, and squeezed her hand a little tighter. 'Is she still riding with von Gryphius?' he asked, looking hungrily into the woman's eyes.

'She was, as of this morning. I think they had planned to leave her at some kind of temple, before they encounter the enemy, but when they got there, the temple was already destroyed. When I last saw her, she seemed to have lost all reason. There's an important priest of some kind with her – a warrior priest, by the look of his armour – and she rides on the back of his horse now. She doesn't even speak, or eat, or anything. She just clings on to the priest in silence as the army heads north.' The woman eased her hand from Sürman's and frowned. 'I'm not sure she's long for this world, to be honest.'

Sürman allowed himself a little chuckle. 'You're right about that, if nothing else.' He slicked his long, lank hair into a side parting and looked at the woman thoughtfully. 'There's just one more thing,' he said, 'do you have any idea where they're headed?'

'Von Gryphius?' The woman shook her head. 'Well, north, looking for the enemy, but that could mean anywhere.'

'Think,' urged Sürman, with a hint of menace in his voice. 'It's very important. I must find this woman.'

The singer looked up at the ceiling, desperately trying to think of a place name. 'Oh, wait!' she exclaimed, grabbing Sürman's hand. 'I heard von Gryphius mention a friend. An old countryman of his. He wanted to visit his castle as they marched north. They were headed that way when I left them. It's somewhere north of Lubrecht.' Her face lit up in a triumphant smile. 'His name was Casper von Lüneberg. That's where they were headed – to Castle Lüneberg!'

Sürman leant back in his chair with a satisfied nod. Then, after a few minutes, he gave the singer a questioning look. 'Did you say you spoke with Anna?' he asked, signalling for Adelman to approach the table. 'What exactly would a dancer have to discuss with a sorceress?' He gave her a wolfish grin, as he lifted a long knife from his servant's belt. 'Unless, of course, the two of you had something in common.'

CHAPTER SIX

Fair-weather Friends

Von Gryphius's soldiers grimaced and pulled their thin, silk cloaks a little tighter as they rode into the bitter north. For the last week, the only change in the monotonous weather had been from cold, miserable rain to cold, miserable sleet. A grey mist lay over the tree-lined hills and the sun was no more than a silver ghost, hovering nervously behind mountainous clouds.

At the head of the long column of grumbling men, the general raised a gauntleted hand to shield his eyes against the fierce downpour and squinted down at the figure running beside him. His adjutant was jogging by the side of his warhorse, slipping through the mud and trying not to drop a silver tray piled high with small pastries. Gryphius puffed out his flabby cheeks in disgust, straining to be heard over the sound of the rain as it pinged off his winged helmet. 'I *am* making allowances, Christoff, but it's not even fit for the dogs.' He spat a mouthful into the mud. 'Is there even any sugar on there?'

There was no hint of emotion in Christoff's reply. 'I believe the pastry chef thought the raspberry jam would add sufficient sweetness, milord. Would you like to try one of the custard tartlets?'

'What's the point?' cried Gryphius in despair. He waved at the sodden musicians to his left. The ears of their animal costumes had drooped in the downpour and they made a pathetic sight as they tooted tunelessly on their waterlogged instruments. 'No one seems to be prepared to make any effort today.'

'I'll ask Chef to try again,' said Christoff, turning to leave.

'Wait,' cried Gryphius, shaking his head and grabbing a few pastries. 'I need to eat *something* this morning.'

As the general chomped unhappily on his mushy breakfast, a horse broke ranks and trotted up alongside his. Its thin, hooded rider leant over to speak to him. 'Will we reach Castle Lüneberg today, obermarshall?'

For a few seconds the general did not reply, pouting instead at the pastry disintegrating in his hand. 'This has never been near a raspberry,' he muttered to himself, before realising he was being addressed. 'Ah, Ratboy,' he replied finally. 'Your province gives quite a welcome to its would-be rescuers,' he laughed, waving at the rain. 'It's enough to make one feel quite unwanted.'

Ratboy shrugged. 'I'm afraid this is quite normal for this far north, obermarshall. It's only going to get worse as we approach the Sea of Claws.'

The general gave him a pastry and a smile. 'You should come with me to Averheim some time, my boy, and get a bit of southern sun on those pallid cheeks of yours.' He washed his tart down with some sherry and waved the bottle vaguely at the waterlogged landscape. 'Casper's letter said he was just a few miles north of here. Next to a small town, called Ruckendorf. It should be somewhere around here.' He looked up at the rolling clouds. 'If it hasn't sunk, that is.' His eyes misted over as he remembered his old friend. 'In his youth, Casper was a very promising poet, you know. Back in Averheim, the name of von Lüneberg was often heard in the highest echelons of polite society.' An unusual note of regret entered his voice. 'It's strange the way things sometimes work out.'

He noticed Ratboy's downcast expression and shook his head, adopting his usual cheerful grin. 'Anna will recover, lad, don't you worry. She's an Ostlander.' His eyes widened with surprise as a long, rattling belch erupted from his mouth. Then he patted his prodigious belly and looked up the clouds. 'I hope Casper still keeps a well stocked larder.'

Ratboy gave a weak smile and twisted in his saddle to look back through the forest of spears and banners. Wolff and his ragtag band of followers were trailing a little way behind them, and he could just about see the figure of Anna, slumped on the back of Wolff's horse, with her head nodding listlessly in the rain. 'I'm sure you're right. She probably just needs a little time to grieve,' he said.

A shimmering figure loomed out of the rain, riding along the grass verge at the side of the road. As it came closer it gradually assumed the form of a scout. 'Ruckendorf, sir' he cried, pointing down the road, 'around the next bend.' He paused, and shook his head. 'The enemy's already been there. The buildings are ruined.'

'Really?' snapped Gryphius in a shrill voice, clutching at the hilt of his sword. Then, remembering Ratboy was at his side, he adopted a stern expression and raised his chins proudly. 'We may not get the friendly welcome we were expecting.' He turned to one of his captains. 'Tell the men to ready their weapons. We're finally going to fight through something other than mud.'

They entered the small town through the west gate and found most of the locals waiting for them. A huge mound of bodies was piled in the market square: soldiers, woodsmen, merchants and farmers, all jumbled together in a bloody mound of twisted limbs and broken weapons. The gabled townhouses and inns were blackened and smashed and the blood of the townsfolk had been daubed across their own ruined homes.

'Sigmar,' whispered Ratboy, grimacing at the smell of rotting meat as he steered his horse slowly through the ruins. 'Is anyone in Ostland still alive?'

Von Gryphius eyed the bodies warily as he rode towards them and lifted a perfumed handkerchief to his nose. Then he nodded towards a large building on the far side of the square. Its proud pillars and wide steps must have once been the dominating feature of Ruckendorf. 'Looks like the town hall is still occupied.'

Ratboy followed his gaze and saw a few sodden figures, cowering pitifully behind a decapitated statue of the Emperor.

Gryphius led his army towards them. The horses' hooves clattered across the square as they skirted around the morbid display at its centre. For once, though, the men rode in silence, with swords and halberds at the ready as they eyed the wreckage for signs of the enemy.

'What happened here?' cried the general, as they neared the statue.

The cowering figures hesitated for a few moments, before one of them, a grizzled old infantryman, stepped out of the shadows. His jerkin was stained and torn and one of his arms was strapped across his chest in a bloody sling. His eyes were wide and unblinking as he addressed them. 'Ostland is doomed, stranger. I'd start running now if I were you. It's probably already too late, but maybe a few of you might still survive.'

'I'm an old friend of your lord,' answered Gryphius, ignoring the man's gloomy tone. 'Is Castle Lüneberg near here?'

The infantryman's face twisted into a snarl. 'An old friend, you say?' He took in Gryphius's yellow, silk breeches and high, lacy collar with a sneer of disdain. 'That would make sense.' He pointed his broken sword at the pile of corpses. 'That's what happens to old friends of Casper von Lüneberg.'

Wolff steered his horse across the square and halted next to Gryphius. 'That's no way to speak of your lord, soldier.'

The soldier glared back at the warrior priest with a mixture of fear and pride. 'I have no lord anymore, priest,' he cried, sending his sword clanging down the steps of the town hall. 'Save perhaps Morr, and I've already made my peace with him.' As he turned to leave, he waved dismissively around the side of the building. 'Keep going as you are. Meet your end with that old fool, if that's what you wish.'

Gryphius turned to Wolff with a confused expression. 'It's odd that he should be so rude. Casper always used to have such a way with people.'

Castle Lüneberg was perched high up on a rocky promontory, overlooking the town: a picturesque mass of twisting spires and gracefully arching buttresses, looming watchfully over Ruckendorf. The duke's black and white banner was still flapping bravely against the driving rain, but as Gryphius's men trudged up the steep, twisting road to its gates, their hopes gradually sank. As they approached the castle, they saw that many of the doors had been smashed from their hinges and ragged holes had been blasted through the outer wall, leaving several of the chambers exposed to the elements.

A horse and trap was hurtling down the road towards them. Its canvas sides bulged with servants and their belongings and as the driver steered the cart in their direction, a long trail of buckets and pans clattered in its wake.

At the sight of Gryphius's army, the driver pulled over to the side of the road and stared in amazement. As the troops in the vanguard marched past the cart, a row of shocked, pale faces gawped out from beneath the tarpaulin, whispering to each other and pointing at the soldiers' outlandish uniforms.

'I would have expected more of Ostlanders,' called von Gryphius, lifting his chin haughtily as his horse trotted past them, 'than to abandon their master in his hour of need.'

Most of the servants were too terrified to reply to such an august personage, but after a few seconds a buck-toothed girl popped her head out of the back of the cart. She yelled defiantly at the receding general. 'We didn't want to go nowhere, milord. The master's banished us, on pain of death. We hung on longer than most. He's swore to kill us on sight if we return. We ain't abandoning no one.'

'A likely story,' called back Gryphius. 'Why would Casper wish to be without his servants, even if the wolves *are* at his door?'

'He ain't got no need of anyone anymore,' answered the girl. 'You'll see. 'Cept perhaps some pallbearers – I guess he'll be needing them soon enough.'

Gryphius rolled his eyes at Ratboy, and led the way through the castle gates and into the courtyard. He opened his mouth to hurl another insult back at the woman, but the scene that met him stopped the words short. There were more bodies, scattered all around the central keep: sprawled across the flagstones and slumped against broken doorframes. From their bloodstained black and white armour, it was obvious that most of the dead were state troops. There were other corpses too, though: fur-clad marauders from the north, clutching brutal-looking axes and scarred with the grotesque sigils of the Dark Gods. The whole place was stained with drying blood. As the rest of the troops filed in behind Gryphius, the eerie silence snatched the words from their lips. Even the general seemed reluctant to break it, shaking his head at the carnage as his servants rushed to help him dismount.

With a horrendous scraping sound, the flagellants dragged Raphael's litter into the castle. They were still muttering prayers to him and lashing their naked, emaciated bodies with straps as they stumbled, barefoot over the broken masonry. As Ratboy looked back at them, he winced at the sight of their prophet. Raphael's skeletal frame was arched in pain, and his anguished face was raised up to the brooding clouds in supplication, but as the litter bounced across the flagstones, his body remained frozen in a motionless spasm. His pale, scarred flesh was as rigid as the statues that lined the courtyard.

'Master,' said Ratboy, turning to Wolff, 'is that man–?'

'Hush, boy,' said Wolff, giving him a stern look as he climbed down from his horse. 'Raphael is their inspiration. He fills them with hope.' He placed a hand on Ratboy's shoulder. 'And hope is a rare thing.'

Ratboy nodded mutely as he helped Wolff lift Anna down from the saddle. She was as limp as a doll as they placed her on the ground and there was no hint of life in her eyes as Wolff gently took her arm and led her over to the general.

'Obermarshall,' said Wolff, gesturing to the destruction that surrounded them. 'This battle has already been lost. There's nothing to be done here now. I suggest we just–'

Gryphius rounded angrily on the priest. 'Lüneberg was my friend,' he cried, in a voice that cracked with emotion. 'I *must* see him again.'

An awkward silence followed his words. Gryphius saw how shocked his men were by his outburst and colour rushed to his cheeks. When he spoke again, his voice was softer. 'There are things we need to discuss. It's important that I find out what's happened to him.'

Wolff shrugged and waved at the bodies. 'Very well, obermarshall, but I'm not sure you'll like what you find.'

A rolling, musical cry echoed around the courtyard: 'Oh, sweet, tender voice! Slicing through time's torpid veil.' Hands reached out into the rain from a vine-covered balcony above them. 'What bliss is this? Can it be that when everything seems darkest, I hear the beloved voice of Hugo von Gryphius?'

'Casper!' cried the general and his face lit up with pleasure. He stepped backwards into the centre of the courtyard to get a better view of the balcony. 'Is that really you?' He slapped a hand against his breastplate and fell to his knees. 'Old friend, I never thought I'd see you again.'

Gryphius's servants had quickly filled the dying castle with the illusion of life. Candlelight, song and the comforting smell of roasting meat filled the great hall for one last time. As the torches burst into flame, they gave the slashed tapestries and bloodstained walls a homely warmth, despite the broken windows that lined one side of the room.

As Ratboy stepped awkwardly to his master's side to serve him, the flickering light from the candelabras revealed his blushes. He had insisted that this duty was his alone, but as he carried the steaming food towards Wolff, he suddenly felt ashamed of his dusty travelling clothes and his simple, country manners. His stomach knotted as he looked at the grand nobles arrayed before him. Casper Gregorius von Lüneberg, Duke of Ruckendorf, was seated directly opposite Wolff, wearing a beautifully embroidered black tabard and a thick gold chain around his neck, from which dangled his badge of office: a proud, brass bull. Next to him sat his old friend, Obermarshall von Gryphius. The general had insisted on changing before dinner and was now squeezed into a plush, ruby red doublet that stretched snugly over his potbelly and tapered down towards his oversized codpiece. Gryphius had also replaced his collar with an even higher one, and as he leant hungrily over his venison, the starched lace tinkled and shimmered with tiny jewels.

As Ratboy placed the food down before his master and stood discretely behind him, he noted the priest's lack of pretension with pride. Wolff's only concession to vanity had been to let Ratboy remove his plate armour and wipe a little of the mud from his vestments, but even in such simple attire, he carried himself with a quiet dignity that, to Ratboy's mind, set him above all the other guests.

Sat silently next to Wolff was the forlorn, mute figure of Anna, and the rest of the seats were filled with Gryphius's officers, heedlessly splashing wine over their canary yellow doublets as they lunged playfully after the serving girls.

At the far end of the hall, next to a raging fire, the general's musicians launched into another frenzied jig, giving the room the feel of a joyous, rowdy tavern, rather than a doomed citadel at the edge of the world.

Casper Lüneberg was as short as Gryphius, with the same olive skin and dark, oily hair, but he carried none of the obermarshall's extra weight. He was a slender, ethereal figure, who waved his arms like a conjuror as he spoke and let his unruly, black locks trail down to his goatee beard as he addressed them. 'Foes and maladies unnumbered; murmuring terrors and the mindless multitudes; none could touch me, in such crystal company as this!'

Gryphius grinned proudly at Wolff over the jellies and guinea fowl that sat between them. 'See? I told you he had a way with people! Such beautiful words!' He wrapped an arm around their host's shoulders, giving him a fierce hug and planting a loud kiss on his cheek. 'By Sigmar, Casper, it's good to see you!'

Lüneberg smiled wistfully. 'Your voice is like an old, beloved song, Hugo. It would rekindle my soul to see your blessed face one last time.'

The smile fell from Gryphius's lips as he looked at the bandage over Lüneberg's eyes. 'What caused this blindness, Casper? Was it old age?'

Lüneberg chuckled. 'Remember, I'm two months younger than you, old man. No, for once time was not the enemy; this veil was lowered by another hand.' The smile dropped from his face and he took Gryphius's hand, speaking so softly that Ratboy could only just catch his words over the music. 'How did we come to end our days so far from home, Hugo?

What a lachrymose end to our ridiculous tragedy.'

The mood at the table changed noticeably. Gryphius's shoulders sagged and his mouth twisted into a grimace. 'Old friend,' he muttered, before lowering his gaze to the table and falling silent.

There was obviously some unresolved tension between the two men and Wolff left them to their thoughts for a while. He turned to the other diners and grimaced with distaste, as they grew loud and clumsy with drink. Eventually, he sipped from a glass of water, cleared his throat and addressed von Lüneberg. 'Tell me, duke, when did the attacks begin?'

Lüneberg did not seem to hear the priest at first; then he shook his head. 'Sorry, Brother Wolff, what was that?'

'When did the attacks begin?' he repeated. 'You've obviously fought bravely in defence of your dukedom, and presumably with such a great castle as this came a force of some size. How it was that things started to turn against you?'

Lüneberg flicked his hair to one side, revealing a set of thick, gold hoops that dangled from his ear. 'Things were ever against me, Brother Wolff. When I came to this province I had nothing to live for.' Gryphius looked up at these words, but the duke continued, oblivious to his friend's pained expression. 'So I pitted myself against these unending hordes that plague the Ostlanders. I had some skill with a sword and plenty of money to buy and equip an army. And, most of all, I was look-ing for something to distract me from my past.' His words trembled with growing anger. 'And yes, you're right, I *have* fought bravely, and not just in the defence of this wretched backwater. I've marched alongside the elector count in countless hopeless engagements, but to what end? What was my glittering prize?' He waved at the broken windows and the pitch dark outside. 'A dukedom on the edge of sanity and the unruly damned on my doorstep. They've drunk my southern soul like an exotic wine.' He waved his hand in a theatrical flourish and his gold rings flashed in the candlelight. 'I have already passed beyond.'

Wolff leant across the table. 'Are *all* your men dead then?'

Lüneberg shook his head. 'Vanity would have finished them though, every one, if I'd let it. Even blind, I thought I could lead them to victory. Even after a thousand mindless, mournful endings I thought I could deliver them. I thought I could loose the cord around their throats, but I only pulled it tighter.'

The duke turned his head vaguely in Wolff's direction and spoke with a sudden urgency. 'But what are you doing out here, father? I know Hugo's story – it's a sad one, and his wounds run even deeper than mine. I know the bitter discontent that haunts him, but *you* still have strength left. I can hear it in your voice. Why would you squander it here? Why did you not head south, while you could? Von Raukov has assembled a great army in Wolfenberg to fight this latest abomination. A man of your faith could have been of use to him.'

Wolff was a little taken aback by the duke's words, 'I do intend to find the main force. I mean to aid the elector count in any way I can,' he hesitated, 'and also, I'm seeking my brother, Fabian Wolff, who I believe is fighting in a regiment called the Ostland Black Guard.'

'But you're too far north,' cried the duke, with surprising vehemence. The rowdy officers at the other end of the table fell silent, looking over at him in surprise. 'The enemy has already swept though this whole region,' continued the duke, shaking his head in confusion. 'You must have passed them in the night somehow. Don't you realise? You're already *behind* the invasion. They marched through here two days past, slaughtering everything in their path. While my servants cowered in the cellars I threw myself at the monsters and begged them for death; but they saw that it would be crueller to let me live. My grief is a torment worse than anything they could have inflicted.' He shivered. 'There's a gentle-tongued devil leading them, a giggling grotesque that introduced himself as Mormius. The fiend charged through here so fast he didn't even wait to see his army destroy me. He did, however, pause long enough to do this.' The duke lifted his bandage briefly, to reveal two swollen lines of stitches where his eyes should have been.

Wolff grimaced at the sight of the thick, red scars. 'Why would he blind you but let you live?'

'He's utterly insane. Even by the standards of his own kind. He'd somehow heard of my love for literature, and as his soldiers tore down the walls and butchered my friends, he attempted to discuss poetry with me. I told him it was impossible that such a drooling animal could ever understand anything of beauty or the arts.' The duke shook his head. 'Something about my words seemed to amuse him – he became quite hysterical in fact. Then he threw me against the wall and gouged out my eyes with his thumbs. A day later, unable to even see my own sword, I tried to lead these poor wretches against his army as they rushed south.' His voice hitched with emotion. 'It was a shameful farce. They turned their full force against us and I ordered a retreat, but it was far too late. Half of the townsfolk had already been ripped to pieces by those dogs. What madness made me lead them into battle I'll never know.' He shook his head. 'So much death...' He lifted one of his ring-laden hands to his mouth, as though he could not bear to hear any more of his own words.

'You did what you thought best,' said a soft voice.

To his shock, Ratboy realised the words were Anna's. Tears were flowing freely from her eyes as she looked up at the blind duke. It was the first time she had spoken to anyone since Wolff had told her that the abbess was dead.

Lüneberg flinched at her words, as though she were insulting him, but he drew a deep breath and lowered his hand from his mouth, seeming to regain control of himself. He took a sip of wine and turned towards Wolff. 'I wouldn't hold out much hope of a reunion with your brother.

If he's spent any amount of time in von Raukov's army, he's probably dead by now, but even if he isn't, there's no way you could reach him. You've come too far to the north-east. We're completely surrounded out here. The only way you could rejoin von Raukov's men now would be to fight back through Mormius's entire army from behind. It's impossible.'

The rest of the officers were now following the duke's words in attentive silence. At the word 'impossible' they looked towards their general for his response. Conscious of all eyes being on him, Gryphius puffed out his small chest and placed his hands firmly on the table. 'Impossible? I don't think so, old friend.' He shrugged off the gloom that had settled over him and grinned at his captains, raising his glass aloft. 'Finally, it sounds like we have a fight on our hands!'

The officers exploded into raucous cheers and whistles, banging their fists on the table and filling each other's glasses.

Lüneberg frowned. 'I understand your reasons Hugo, but there are others here who might not be so eager for the cold embrace of the grave.' He gave a grim laugh. 'Well, I suppose you would have the element of surprise though. They won't expect anything to come from this direction, other than more of their own kind.'

'Where was this Mormius headed?' asked Wolff.

'Wolfenberg,' replied Lüneberg. 'His only strategy is to race to the capital as fast as possible. But they have one last hurdle to cross before they can head south unimpeded. There's a young captain named Andreas Felhamer whose banner has become something of a rallying point. He's gathered the last of the northern garrisons together into a single force. He's quite the firebrand and his passion does him credit, but I'm not sure his judgment is sound. He's gathered all this flotsam and jetsam into an old ruined keep, named Mühlberg. The locals call it Mercy's End, in memory of its former glories, but these days the old place barely has the strength to support Felhamer's banners.'

'What of von Raukov?' asked Wolff. 'You mentioned that he's gathered a great force. Where does he intend to strike? Maybe we could join him in the counterattack?'

'He's racing north as we speak. He's heard of Felhamer's heroics and ordered him to hold Mercy's End, until the main force arrives to relieve him.' Lüneberg shook his head. 'The poor, brave child. They'll all be dead a long time before that. Mormius drives his army with a fierce determination. I've never seen anything like it. He's careless of anything but the race south. Felhamer's military career will be a short one, I'm afraid. I imagine von Raukov knows that though.' Lüneberg patted the table till he found a fork, and shovelled some food into his mouth. 'I fear that the elector count is simply using the captain as a sponge, to soak up some of the enemy's fury for a while, and buy him a little marching time. No one expects him to leave Mercy's End alive.'

Gryphius leant forward, so that his eyes glinted mischievously in the candlelight. 'Well, Captain Felhamer might find he has a little Averland steel to keep him company in his final watch.' He lurched unsteadily to his feet and clambered onto the table, raising his sword to his men and sending food and wine clattering across the floor. 'Tomorrow, we march to war, my friends.' The officers lurched unsteadily to their feet and drew their own swords in a solemn reply. The general took a swig of wine and grinned at them. 'But tonight, I think we need a little dancing.' He jumped down from the table and marched towards the musicians, grabbing a serving girl's hand as he went. The officers scrambled after him, laughing and shouting as they barged past Ratboy and left Wolff, Lüneberg and Anna alone at the table.

The music swelled in volume and the room filled with whirling, dancing shapes. The officers began spinning drunkenly in and out of the shifting shadows, as vague and insubstantial as the ghosts they might soon become.

Lüneberg smiled indulgently. 'He makes a good show of it, doesn't he? You'd think him quite the hero. It wasn't always so. He's not the man he pretends to be.' He winced suddenly and placed a hand over his bandage.

Anna rose from her chair and rushed to his side. She placed her hands over his and lowered her head, whispering a few soft words in his ear as she did so.

At first the duke looked irritated at being manhandled in such a way, but then a relieved smile spread across his face. 'Who is this worker of miracles?' he asked, squeezing her hands gratefully.

A faint smile played around Anna's mouth as she replied. 'No miracle worker, my lord, just someone with a little compassion for a tired old soldier.'

Lüneberg held onto her hands for a while longer. 'A Sister of Shallya, then?'

Anna frowned. 'I think so, my lord. In truth, I've been quite lost these last few days, even from myself; but hearing the pain in your voice reminded me who I am.' She freed her hand from his and placed it on his shoulder. 'You can't carry the fate of a whole nation on your shoulders, my lord. If you hadn't led these people to war, someone else would simply have had to do it in your stead.'

Lüneberg nodded slowly and chuckled. 'It's been decades since I last saw Hugo, but he obviously hasn't lost the knack of surrounding himself with powerful women.'

Anna blushed and returned to her seat. As she stepped past Ratboy she gave him a shy nod, as though seeing him for the first time in days.

He smiled awkwardly in reply, relieved to see a little of the old determination back in her steely eyes.

'So, tell me, duke,' said Wolff, a little while later, 'how did you find yourself so far from Averland? Did you and von Gryphius set out together?'

'Ah, therein lies a tale, Brother Wolff,' replied Lüneberg with a wry smile. 'And not a happy one I'm afraid. Hugo was not always the valiant hero you see now. As a youth, his only interest was in the arts, and the idea of dirtying his hands in combat repulsed him.' He waved over to where Gryphius and his men were dancing drunkenly around the ruined hall. 'There comes a time however, when all men must fight for what they love.

'Averland is a land of rich pastures and even richer palaces. The sun smiles down on Sigmar's southern heirs with the kind of indulgence his hardy northern offspring can hardly imagine. But even in such a paradise, there are wars to be won, and enemies to repel. Hugo knew this, but his head has always been full of music and poetry.' The duke paused and tilted his head to one side, trying to reassure himself Gryphius was still out of earshot. 'He has a big heart, that one, but it is the heart of a child – easily distracted by new passions, and new ideas; sometimes he's neglectful of the things that really matter.' Lüneberg fanned out his tanned, bejeweled fingers across the table. 'These are not the hands of a natural fighter, but it was these hands that Gryphius entrusted with the safety of his young wife. Not once in his short life had he heeded the call of battle, and as bandits struck closer and closer to his ancestral home, he found an excuse to be elsewhere. The artist, Schüzzelwanst had opened a new exhibition in Altdorf and, despite the danger looming over his home, he decided he had to meet the great man, leaving me in charge of his garrison.

'Even if Gryphius had been fighting by my side, he couldn't have saved his wife, but in his heart he knows he should have been there.' Lüneberg shook his head. 'If only so he could have died by her side.'

Ratboy was so caught up in the duke's tale he forgot himself and leant across the table to speak. 'But how was it that you survived?'

Lüneberg shrugged. 'It seems to be my destiny to fail those I'm responsible for and live to tell the tale.' He lifted his clothes to reveal a thick old scar, snaking down through the grey hairs on his chest, all the way to his groin. 'They gutted me like a fish, and the pain was unimaginable,' he gave a grim laugh; 'but I couldn't bear to die until I'd seen Gryphius, and confronted him over his cowardice. To see a man's wife destroyed in such a way, when he should have been there to defend his home, gave me a bitter vitality. When he finally did return though, he blamed me for her death and we–' He paused and took a sip of wine. 'Well, let's just say, her death changed things. Our friendship was over, and neither of us could bear our pampered, pointless existence for a minute longer. We exiled ourselves from our homeland. My shame drove me north to war and Gryphius, well, he adopted the role of a rootless hedonist. He has to avoid his own thoughts at all costs, and any distraction will do: wine, food, bloodshed, fear or even death, it's all the same to him now. He just wants to be dazzled by experience, feeling everything to the full, with no concern for the consequences. He won't rest until he's ruined himself in some glorious endeavour. It's ironic, really, that we are surrounded by so much death and the one man who would welcome it has survived.'

Ratboy looked over at the general, stumbling and leaping gaily around the room. Maybe it was his imagination, but as he studied Gryphius's round, grinning face, he thought he could pinpoint a subtle hardness behind his eyes; and perhaps even a glimmer of fear.

Wolff talked to Lüneberg for a little longer, probing him for descriptions of the surrounding countryside and the nature of Mormius's army, but the life seemed to have left the duke, and eventually he rose from the table and gave them a small bow. 'Wake me in the morning, before you leave, and I'll set you on the right road,' he yawned.

'But won't you join us?' asked Anna, her voice full of dismay.

The duke shook his head sadly, as one of Gryphius's servants took his arm and began to lead him away. 'No, child, it sounds like you have a hard road ahead of you and my fighting days are long over.' He waved at the ruined hall as he shuffled away from them. 'This seems as good a place as any to meet my end. Good evening, my friends.'

Wolff and Anna retired to their rooms shortly after, but the tale of Lüneberg and Gryphius haunted Ratboy, and even after a long day's marching, he felt oddly restless. Once he was sure his master had no further need for him, he sat on a stool to watch the duke and his men dancing. The entertainment was short-lived, though. Tiredness and alcohol gradually overcame the company and one by one they slumped to the floor. Finally, there was just a single fiddle player, dressed as a goose and playing a series of discordant notes as he skipped around the room, leading the duke in a ragged, lurching jig around the hall.

The duke was still drinking heavily as he danced and something about his desire for oblivion repulsed Ratboy. He wandered out onto the battlements, to clear his head. As he stepped out into the moonlight he turned his collar up against the cold and looked down on the sleeping army. Gaudy yellow and black tents were pitched all over the courtyard and the lights of torches moved back and forth between them, as the quartermaster and his men prepared for the next day's march. The rain had eased to a fine, billowing drizzle, but it quickly seeped through Ratboy's clothes, chilling his slender limbs. After a few minutes he headed back inside to find a corner to curl up in.

As he approached the door, a strange noise caught his attention and he looked out over the other side of the tower. The scene below chilled him even more than the rain and the memory of it stayed with him for a long time afterwards. The penitent villagers from Gotburg were still awake and had crowded around Raphael's litter in prayer. They had propped up his twisted, broken corpse with a stick and as his glassy eyes stared lifelessly out over the courtyard, they called out to him for guidance and lashed themselves repeatedly with sticks, mingling their blood with the soft Ostland rain.

CHAPTER SEVEN

Righteous Fury

They headed west, with the sun at their backs, looking for the war.

Ratboy gazed back over his shoulder at Castle Lüneberg, silhouetted against the dawn glow. He thought he could still just make out the lonely figure of the duke, with his hand raised in a silent farewell. 'What will become of him?' he muttered, turning to his master.

The priest replied with a hint of irritation in his voice. 'What concern is that of yours? He's made his choice and we must respect it.' He shrugged his hammer into a more comfortable position on his back and kept his gaze on the road ahead. 'Such hedonism rarely ends well.'

Gryphius's army marched behind them, carving a noisy path through the dewy forest glades, like a fast flowing river of yellow cloth and burnished metal.

Wolff, Anna and Ratboy rode at the head of the column, alongside the general and his officers. Trailing behind the main force came the flagellants, still carrying Raphael's corpse on the slowly disintegrating litter. Ratboy looked back at them in confusion. 'Master,' he said, 'the villagers from Gotburg – there seems to be more of them than before.'

Wolff nodded, without turning to face his acolyte. 'Such fervour is infectious. In times such as these, people are forever on the look out for salvation. Raphael's new followers are mostly Lüneberg's former servants, plus some of the injured soldiers who were still hiding out in the castle. I imagine their numbers will continue to swell as we approach Mercy's End.'

Ratboy shook his head in amazement, looking at the broken body on the litter. 'But don't they realise that Raphael has died?'

Wolff looked around with a dangerous glint in his eyes. 'Watch your words, boy. Who knows what they think. Some of them may believe he's in a trance, and that he is communicating directly with Sigmar himself. And it may even be that they see things more clearly than you. The edifying effects of hunger, and constant pain can have unforeseen results. Who are you to be so mocking of their faith?' He slowed his horse, until he was riding beside Ratboy. 'Such scepticism does not become you. If you truly wish to enter the priesthood you must understand how important such fierce belief can be. It's all too easy to let physical comfort come between you and religious truth.'

'So you think they might be right?' replied Ratboy, incredulously. 'That he hasn't thrashed himself to death, he's just in some kind of holy sleep?'

Wolff shrugged. 'My thoughts on the matter are irrelevant. I've seen many things that defy explanation, and have learned enough humility to bite my tongue rather than make rash judgements. The only thing I'm sure of is the limits of my own knowledge. My understanding of the spiritual realm is like a single candle, flickering in the dark. There is much that I cannot see.'

Ratboy blushed and looked away from his master, feeling that he had made a fool of himself.

Wolff noticed his embarrassment and softened his voice. 'There are other considerations, too. The role of a warrior priest is to ensure the survival of Sigmar's heirs and also the survival of His doctrine. Sometimes that relies as much on tactical thought as it does on revelation. Soon, we'll need to fight our way through an army of immense size. From what the duke told me last night, Mormius's army numbers in the thousands. And somehow we must slice through that foul canker to reach von Raukov's men.'

He looked Ratboy in the eye, lowering his voice even more. 'You know that I've had doubts of my own recently. Even I began to question my purpose, Anselm. After all these years of fruitless, endless war, I had begun to doubt that I could have any effect.' He pounded his fist against the dull metal of his breastplate with a hollow *clang*. 'But now I *know* I have a duty to fulfil. My own brother is ahead of us, marching with von Raukov's army. And I know now he's filled with corruption of the worst kind. Who can say what he intends to do, but I have to find him.' He patted the broad knife wedged in his belt. 'And stop him, somehow.'

He waved his gauntleted hand at the lurching, bloody figures trailing behind the litter. 'I have a suspicion that such fanatical faith will be invaluable. I can guarantee you that even if every man in Gryphius's army lay dead around them those villagers would still be defending their prophet. With their hands and teeth if they had to.'

After that Ratboy rode in silence, mulling over his master's words. Was

Wolff saying that Raphael's followers were inspired, or merely useful? Surely they were indulging in a kind of idolatry? The litter was strewn with a strange mixture of objects, all placed there by the flagellants. Mounds of herbs and berries were draped over the corpse, and sheets of parchment were nailed to the wood, covered in manically scrawled prayers and poems. Someone had even fastened a wooden hammer to Raphael's rigid right hand, which bounced from side to side as the litter gouged its way along the forest path. Ratboy shivered. He couldn't be sure whether he was imagining it or not, but he thought there was a sickly sweet smell of rotting meat on the breeze, coming from Raphael's discoloured flesh.

The morning wore on and Ratboy's thoughts wandered onto less gruesome matters. Anna was riding a few horses ahead of him and each time she turned to give him an encouraging smile, he felt his stomach flip. Since talking to the duke she had regained a little of her straight-backed dignity and even seemed eager for the challenge ahead. Ratboy sensed that despite the horror of losing her matriarch and fellow sisters, there was still a mysterious strength in her. She fascinated him. Even riding alongside such strutting, feathered popinjays as Gryphius's captains, Ratboy found her simple white robe utterly hypnotic. He followed the cloth as it shifted up and down her pale, slender arms.

With a rush of shame, he noticed that Wolff was studying him intently. He smiled awkwardly at his master and returned his gaze to the road ahead.

There was a clatter of boots and hooves as the army crossed an old wooden bridge and left the shelter of the trees for a while, marching out across an expanse of wide, open grassland that stretched ahead of them for several miles. The musicians struck up a jaunty tune and danced around the marching troops, leaping up and down in the tall grass and trailing brightly coloured streamers behind them as they sang. As the hours wore on, Ratboy grew to hate their piping whistles and clanging bells. He glared at their painted, bestial masks, willing them to be silent, but their energy seemed boundless.

Gradually, the sun overtook the army and began to descend ahead of them, causing the soldiers to pull their helmets down a little lower over their faces and squint as they rode.

'What's this?' slurred Gryphius as a rider headed back towards him out of the sunset. The general's face was flushed from the previous night's drinking and as he leant forward in his saddle to see who was approaching, he clutched protectively at his bloated stomach.

The slender figure of Christoff made his way down the line of men with his chin lifted haughtily. It looked to Ratboy as though he imagined himself to be the Emperor himself, inspecting a trooping of the colour. He bowed almost imperceptibly to the general. 'Obermarshall,' he said, 'the scouts have spotted an abandoned farmhouse and they suggest it would make an ideal place to camp tonight. The owners have all been slaughtered, but not before they dug several trenches and fortified the outbuildings, so it will be easily defended.'

'Much good it did the previous occupants,' said Gryphius, trying to smile through his nausea. 'Very well, let's head for the farm.' He grabbed Christoff's puffed sleeve. 'Just make sure there's a reasonable meal waiting for me when I get there. No more of this northern rubbish. I want something with a little flavour, not another bucket of grey mud.'

Christoff tipped his plumed hat. 'Of course, obermarshall.'

The army pitched its tents with the quick efficiency of men eager to get their heads down. As twilight fell over the old farm, Ratboy hunkered down next to a fire with the other servants, while Wolff and the general's captains pored over maps and discussed the impending battle. He stretched his aching limbs out across the grass with a groan of relief, and as he drifted off to sleep a strange jumble of images filled his head: Anna's delicate features morphed and decayed into Raphael's greying flesh, before being replaced by his master's flashing eyes, scowling down at him from a pulpit.

'Sigmar's blood,' exclaimed Gryphius, as he reined in his horse and looked down over the valley below. 'Is that an army or a nation?'

A silver thread of sunlight was just beginning to glimmer on the horizon and as the dawn light grew, it picked out tens of thousands of men, sprawled across the landscape, carpeting the fields as far as the eye could see in either direction. Pitched in the centre of the valley were a couple of command tents, but mostly the soldiers had just fallen where they stopped, sleeping in ditches and the hollows of trees.

Ratboy grimaced at the sight of the army. It marred the landscape like a dark, ugly scar. Severed heads dangled from their bloodstained banners and brutal, iron weapons lay scattered across the grass. A few of the soldiers were already beginning to rise; pouring filthy water over their greasy manes and flexing their fur-clad muscles as they looked across the fields towards the growing dawn.

'Down,' hissed Wolff, steering his horse back away from the brow of the hill and dismounting. 'A few more minutes and we'll be visible.'

The others followed suit, leading their horses back down the hill and then crawling back up to the hilltop to peer out through the tall grass at the marauders.

'That's it,' said Gryphius, grinning at his captains and pointing past Mormius's army to a tall, slender shape on the horizon. It was hard to see clearly in the half-light, but the general had no doubt as to the building's name. 'Mercy's End,' he hissed, drumming his fists against the ground like an excited child. 'It's the ruined castle that Lüneberg told us about. *That's* Ostland's final hope. And we're just in time to join arms with our northern brothers, before they make their last stand.' He turned to Wolff. 'We must strike now while the enemy are still rising. We could slaughter half of them in their sleep. It's all they deserve, the filthy blasphemers.'

Wolff shook his head. 'There are so many of them,' he muttered, clenching and unclenching his gauntleted hands as he looked down on the monstrous shapes. 'We'd never make it through them all.' He signalled for the others to crawl back down the hill. Once they were sure it was safe they climbed to their feet. Gryphius's captains all looked to Wolff for his guidance, a little unnerved by the brittle grin on their general's face.

'We've been very lucky, it's true,' said the priest. 'From what the duke said, this Mormius has been driving his men mercilessly for weeks without rest, but we've managed to arrive at the end of the one night they've been allowed to sleep.'

Gryphius drew his sword and held it aloft. 'I hear you, Brother Wolff. This is a unique chance. We'll take them all on. The people of Mercy's End will wake up to see a pile of corpses at their gates.'

Wolff grasped the general's arm and snarled at him. 'They outnumber us ten to one, obermarshall, if not more. We'd never reach the citadel.'

'So what are you suggesting,' snapped Gryphius, freeing his arm and replying in a tone of haughty disdain. 'That we return to Castle Lüneberg and wait there to be slaughtered in our beds?'

'No,' replied Wolff. 'Mercy's End must endure, at least for a while, if Raukov's army is to stand any chance of halting this incursion.' He waved at the captains who were hanging on his every word. 'And an army such as yours could make all the difference, obermarshall. But only if they aren't slaughtered before they reach the citadel.' He frowned. 'We need some kind of diversion.' He looked down the hillside at Gryphius's army, and beyond, to the ragged lines of flagellants, prostrating themselves before Raphael's corpse. 'I have an idea,' he said, and strode down the hill.

As the sun cleared the horizon, the flagellants descended on Mormius's army, pouring down from the hills like the end of the world.

Ratboy shook his head in wonder. The fury of their charge was breathtaking. He finally understood his master's respect for them. Raphael's cult had swelled beyond all recognition into a terrifying horde of willing martyrs. Their eyes burned with holy wrath as they ripped into the side of the sleeping army. Their screeched prayers echoed around the hills and their wiry, scarred limbs flailed up and down, hacking furiously at the confused marauders.

'Holy Sigmar,' muttered Ratboy, as he watched the carnage from the other end of the valley. 'They're going to slaughter the whole army.'

For a while it seemed he might be right. As the drowsy marauders lurched to their feet, scrabbling around for their discarded weapons and blowing their horns to raise the alarm, the flagellants tore through their ranks in a frenzy of righteous bloodlust. They wore no armour, but seemed mindless of the vicious weapons that lashed out at their naked flesh. Even from the safety of the hilltop, Ratboy found it hard to see such bloody passion heading towards him.

'What did you say to them?' asked Anna, with a note of disgust in her voice. She grimaced as the flagellants threw their naked selves into the melee, ripping at the marauders' faces with flails, clubs and broken, bloody fingernails. 'You've sent them to their deaths,' she muttered.

'We prayed together for a while,' said Wolff, ignoring the disapproval in her voice. 'And then I explained the truth of the situation.' He gestured to the litter behind them. Raphael's rotting corpse was lashed securely to the planks, which in turn were strapped to a pair of horses, in readiness for the charge ahead. 'There's only one chance that their prophet could reach the safety of Mercy's End, and it will require a great sacrifice on their part.' He rubbed his powerful jaw as he watched the shocking violence below. 'And sacrifice is the one thing they have no fear of.'

With a scrape of metal, the priest slid his great warhammer from his back and pointed it down at the battle. 'Feast your eyes on this scene, my friends. Fix it deep in your hearts for all eternity. You will never again see such a beautiful display of pure, unshackled faith.' As Raphael's followers bathed in the blood of their foes, Wolff crossed himself with the sign of the hammer and muttered a prayer for them. 'You're witnessing Sigmar's legacy in all its unstoppable glory. These people have His blood in their veins and His strength in their hearts. While such devotion still exists, this blessed Empire will never fail.'

He turned towards Gryphius. 'Are your men ready, my lord? Our time is short. Their passion will only carry them so far. A few more minutes and the enemy will start to realise what a small force they're facing. Then things will be over very quickly.'

The general's eyes glistened with excitement as he fastened his winged helmet onto his head. He turned to his waiting army, arrayed on the hill-side below. The yellow and black of their banners whipped gaily in the dawn light, and a thousand expectant faces looked back at him. 'Sons of Averland,' he cried, lifting his sword and turning his face to the sky. 'Ride for your life! Ride for the Empire! Ride for Sigmar!' With that he turned his horse and charged down the hill towards the enemy, screaming with fear and delight.

With a great thunder of hooves and armour, his troops charged after him.

'Stay close,' barked Wolff to Ratboy, as he snapped his reins and disappeared over the brow of the hill.

It was all Ratboy could do to cling desperately onto the reins of his horse as it careered wildly after the others. The general's quartermaster had buried him in armour way too big for his wiry frame: an oversized hauberk, a billowing yellow tabard and a helmet that immediately fell down over his eyes, leaving him blind and helpless as he plummeted towards the enemy.

He dared to loose a hand from the reins and lift his visor. The eyes of the surrounding horses were rolling with terror as the army plunged into the valley at incredible speed. The world rushed by in such a sickening blur that Ratboy thought he might lose his breakfast. Wolff was directly ahead, leading the charge with Gryphius, holding his hammer before him like a lance and bellowing commands as he went.

Where's Anna? wondered Ratboy suddenly, remembering that she had refused the offer of armour. He tried to look back, but it was too late. With a deafening crash, Gryphius's men slammed into the enemy troops.

Shreds of steel, teeth and bone exploded around them as they collided with the stunned marauders.

Ratboy clamped his legs tightly around his steed and ducked low in his saddle as violence erupted all around him. Horses fell and pieces of armour whistled past his face. A chorus of screams filled his ears, but in the chaos it was impossible to tell if they were war cries, or the howls of the dying.

As his horse's hooves drummed furiously beneath him, Ratboy tried to take in his surroundings. It was hard to be sure what was happening, but things seemed to be going to plan. The formation of the troops was still vaguely intact: pistoliers in the vanguard, followed by ranks of flamboyantly dressed knights and then, at the rear, the dark-skinned freelancers from Tilea. As Wolff intended, Mormius's soldiers had all been rushing towards the screaming fanatics, so this new attack had caught them unawares for a second time.

The Averlanders did not pause to press their advantage, however. They ploughed onwards at a furious pace. The plan was simple: race for the citadel; keep their heads down; pray for deliverance.

A succession of snarling faces flashed before Ratboy. They howled curses as they rushed by, barking at him in the thick, guttural language of the northern wastes. Their savage weapons clattered uselessly across his borrowed armour, but he felt far from heroic. A broadsword hung at his belt – another gift from Gryphius's armoury, but he couldn't bring himself to remove his hands from the horse's reins. Terror locked them to the leather straps. The noise and fury of the battle was like nothing he'd ever experienced. Fortunately, his steed was more experienced than its rider, pounding across the valley floor in an unwavering line and smashing straight through everything in its path.

He heard Wolff calling out from somewhere ahead. 'Raise the corpse,' he was crying, his voice already hoarse from shouting. 'Raise him up so his followers can see.'

Ratboy risked a glance up from his horse's neck and saw his master.

Wolff was still at the head of the charge, smashing through the thick press of bodies like a vision of Sigmar Himself. He was stood high in the stirrups, swinging his warhammer from left to right in great sweeping arcs, leaving a trail of splintered limbs and shattered armour in his wake. 'Sigmar absolves you,' he cried repeatedly, slamming his hammer into faces and shields with such force that his broad shoulders jolted back with the impact of each blow. Hastily fired arrows whirred towards him, clanging against his breastplate, but he rode on oblivious, dealing out Sigmar's judgement with ten pounds of bloody, tempered steel. The priest vanished briefly behind a flash of claret, and Ratboy thought he had fallen; but then he reappeared, swinging again and again as his war-horse galloped towards the citadel.

Gryphius was next to him, laughing hysterically as he fired his flintlock pistol blindly into the rolling clouds of dust and gore that surrounded him. His wavering tenor rang out through the screams. 'For Averland! For the Emperor!'

Ratboy looked back over his shoulder and saw that they were already half way across the valley. We're going to make it, he thought with a rush of excitement. The ragged line of charging horses was unbroken. The vivid black and yellow banners had already cut a swathe right through the heart of the reeling marauders. The speed of the charge was so great that hardly a single knight had fallen. Most of the marauders were still busy with the frenzied figures at the other end of the valley. To Ratboy's amazement, he saw that dozens of the penitents were still hacking their way across the field. The fury of their attack had carried them almost to the command tents in the centre of the valley, but it looked as though their luck might soon run out. Mormius's army was finally on its feet, swirling like an ocean around the villagers; hungry for vengeance.

Hot, blood-slick hands snapped Ratboy's head back and his horse suddenly staggered under the weight of a second rider. Ratboy clasped desperately at his throat just in time to stop the blade that was shoved towards it. His hand split open like a ripe fruit and a thick torrent of blood pumped up over his face. He felt rancid breath on his ear and a steel-hard grip tightening around his neck. His attacker tried to draw the knife back for another attempt, but the blade locked between Ratboy's splintered finger bones. However furiously the knife's wielder wrenched at it, it would not come free.

The pain seemed remote and unreal. Ratboy knew he was seconds from death and clutched at his sword with his one good hand, swaying wildly in the saddle as he loosed the reins. He grasped the hilt of the weapon and began to slide it from his belt, but before he could use it, his assailant hurled him from the saddle and he slammed onto the rock-hard ground.

Agony stabbed into Ratboy's face as it crunched into the dry earth. He felt something click in his neck as the whole weight of his armoured body piled down on it. Instinct forced him to roll to one side, just in time to avoid the marauder's axe as it slammed into the ground beside him.

He lurched unsteadily to his feet, feeling as though his head was the size of a cart. His eyes were full of blood and the world swam wildly in and out focus, but he couldn't miss the figure striding towards him. It was the marauder who had destroyed his hand: a beetle-browed goliath, with a neck as thick as a tree and a great two-handed axe clutched in his meaty fingers. His scarred flesh was naked apart from a ragged loincloth and a battered iron helm topped with a long, curved tusk. 'Wolff,' gasped Ratboy, as he drew his sword to defend himself, 'help me.'

The marauder grinned down at his prey, revealing a mouthful of blackened stumps as he leant back and swung the axe at Ratboy's head.

Ratboy tried to block the blow, straining to lift his sword one-handed, but the marauder's taut, knotted muscles were the result of a lifetime devoted to war. The axe slammed the sword aside with such force that the impact made Ratboy howl. His forearms jangled with pain as the sword buckled and bounced from his grip. He staggered backwards and tumbled to the ground.

The grinning marauder advanced on him, drawing back his axe for another blow. Horses and soldiers screamed past, heedless of Ratboy's fate and he raised his hands feebly at the approaching warrior, horrified that no-one would even witness his death.

The marauder's head collapsed with a wet *crunch* as Wolff's hammer pounded into his face.

'Sigmar,' gasped the priest, dealing him another hammer-blow to the head, 'absolves you.'

The marauder swayed back on his heels and gave a bovine rumble of pain. Then he righted himself and grinned up at Wolf, snapping his nose back into place and laughing as he spat his few remaining teeth from his ruined mouth.

Wolff dropped from his horse and the two men circled each other, panting and looking for a chance to strike. There was little between them in bulk, but Ratboy could see that his master was exhausted. His breath was coming in short, hitching gasps and the joints of his armour were clogged with mud and gore.

The marauder saw a chance and swung for Wolff's legs.

The priest dodged the blow with surprising agility for such a large man, leaping high in the air and bringing his hammer down with a grunt. It thudded into the marauder's thigh and the warrior's femur disintegrated beneath the weight of the blow.

The marauder howled and fell to his knees, with vivid shards of bone erupting from beneath his leathery skin. His cry became a death croak, as a second hammer-blow knocked his head back, snapping his neck like kindling and killing him instantly. He thudded to the ground with a whistling sound, as a final breath slipped from his severed windpipe.

The momentum of Wolff's strike sent him staggering forwards into the fray and for a second, Ratboy lost sight of him. Then he lurched back towards him with a look of wild fury on his face. 'I told you to stay close,' he snapped, grabbing the whimpering acolyte's arm and wrenching him to his feet. 'You could've been hurt.'

More marauders were sprinting towards them as Wolff climbed back onto his horse and hauled Ratboy up behind him. He floored the nearest with a fierce blow to the side of his head, then charged after the Averlanders.

The pain in Ratboy's hand was growing quickly. He held it protectively to his chest, not daring to look at the damage.

'Obermarshall,' cried Wolff, banking his horse from left to right as they pursued the receding line of Empire troops. 'No!'

Ratboy strained to see around his master's bulky plate armour. He saw immediately that the situation had worsened. The Averlanders were still ploughing through the enemy at a fantastic pace, but the marauders were now massing around them in much greater numbers. Within the space of a few seconds he saw several of Gryphius's men torn from their saddles and dragged down into a fury of hacking, tearing blades. The obermarshall's adjutant, Christoff was riding alongside Wolff when he suddenly jolted back in his saddle, clutching at his throat. He tumbled from view before Ratboy had chance to see what had killed him.

Then he saw Gryphius and understood Wolff's alarmed cry. The general had broken away from the main column and was veering off to the centre of the valley. Along with thirty or so of his men he was attempting to make a dash for Mormius's command tents. 'What's he doing?' he gasped into Wolff's ear.

'Risking everything,' grunted the priest, racing after the general. 'He's forgotten that Raphael's followers are just a decoy.' He pointed his hammer north towards a small bedraggled group, still tearing their way towards Mormius's tents. 'Gryphius thinks he can join them in beheading this invasion.' He drove his horse even harder. 'He's a damned fool, and he's going to lead his whole army to its death.'

Ratboy looked back and saw the truth of his master's words. The main column was already faltering and splitting in confusion. The soldiers didn't know whether to do as they were ordered – keep making for the citadel, or rally around their valiant general instead. As the Averlanders floundered, the marauders tore into them with renewed vigour. Howling obscenities as they dived into the confused rout.

'Obermarshall,' cried Wolff again, as they closed on the general. 'We *must* make for Mercy's End!'

The general looked back, his eyes bulging with passion and fear. 'We can take them, Wolff,' he called, blasting his flintlock into the face of another marauder. 'I know it! We can reach Mormius!'

The command tents were still several minutes' ride away, however, when the sheer volume of howling, spitting marauders slowed Gryphius and his captains to a canter. The general's battle cries took on a more desperate tone as the grotesque shapes pressed around him. The marauders here seemed even more corrupted and deformed than the others. Ratboy saw men with drooling mouths gaping in their chests, and gnarled, eyeless beaks where faces should have been. It was like descending into a nightmarish bestiary.

They had nearly reached Gryphius when the general flopped back in his saddle, clutching his side with a high-pitched yelp of pain. His horse spun in confusion and Ratboy saw the thick shaft of a spear embedded in Gryphius's side.

'Thank Sigmar,' muttered Wolff under his breath.

Gryphius's officers rallied round him, slashing frantically at the sea of blades surrounding their wounded general.

'Lead him back to the others,' bellowed Wolff, still racing towards them. As they neared the crowd around Gryphius, Ratboy saw the terror on the men's faces. They were completely encircled. However fiercely they swung their weapons, there was no way they could hack their way back to the main force. One by one the knights tumbled into the bristling mass of swords, as the marauders cut away the legs of their horses and pulled them down into the slaughter.

'Master,' cried Ratboy, as he saw that they too were completely hemmed in. Countless rows of marauders were swarming around them. 'We're trapped!'

Wolff planted his boot in the face of nearest marauder, grabbing a broadsword from his flailing hands as he toppled to the floor. 'I know,' he grunted, handing the weapon to Ratboy. 'Do something useful.'

As the misshapen figures reached out towards him, Ratboy lashed out with the crude weapon. Fear gave him strength and his blade was soon slick with blood as he hewed limbs and parried sword strikes. His mind grew blank as he fought. He was aware of nothing but the screaming pain in his muscles and his desperate desire for life. The odds were impossible though. Gradually the wall of vicious, barbed blades pressed in on them. For every marauder that fell, ten more leapt to take his place, each more fierce than the last.

Finally with an awful, braying scream, the horse's legs collapsed beneath it and Wolf and Ratboy crashed to the ground.

A tremendous roar of victory erupted from the marauders as they saw the priest drop from view.

Ratboy's sword flew from his grip as he rolled clear of the thrashing horse. He wrapped his trembling arms around his head and clamped his eyes shut, waiting to feel the cool bite of metal, slicing into his flesh.

Heat washed over him instead.

As Ratboy curled into a ball, gibbering incoherent nonsense to himself, he felt fire rush over him, shrivelling the hairs on his forearms and scorching his broken fingers. He looked up in confusion to see Wolff kneeling beside him, with his head lowered in prayer and his gauntleted hands resting calmly on the head of his warhammer. The light pouring from his flesh was so bright that Ratboy's eyes immediately filled with tears. He squinted into the incandescent halo and laughed in wonder. It was like looking into the sun, but he couldn't tear his eyes away. It was more beautiful than anything he had ever seen. Slowly, the nimbus of light expanded, washing over the confused marauders. As it touched their flesh they lit up like candles, blossoming in thick white flames that leapt from their skin and engulfed their flailing limbs. Their cheers of victory became wails of despair as their eyes exploded, bursting in their sockets with a series of audible pops.

Ratboy looked down at himself in dismay, expecting to see the flames covering his own body, but there was just a pleasant heat; no more painful than a fierce midday sun. Unlike daylight, though, this heat seemed to seep in through his pores, rushing through his veins and flooding his heart with passion. He leapt to his feet and flew at the stumbling, burning shapes; tearing into them with his broken fingers and howling in a voice he could barely recognise. As he kicked and thumped at the screaming marauders, a phrase came unbidden to his lips. The words were unfamiliar, but he howled them with such vehemence that his voice cracked. 'Every man hath heard of Sigmar,' he cried, grabbing a knife from the ground and thrusting it into bellies and faces. 'Every man hath learned to fear His blessed wrath.'

Ratboy gave himself completely to the animal rage and later, he found it difficult to say how long he had fought, or how many marauders he had butchered. It always chilled him to consider what might have happened if he had not been interrupted.

Wolff's calm voice brought him back. 'I think they've learned enough, for now,' said his master, placing a hand on his shoulder.

Ratboy lurched to a halt, looking down at his gore-splattered limbs in confusion. Then he turned to face the priest. Traces of the holy light were still streaming from his eyes and, as he smiled, it poured from between his teeth. All around them the ground was flattened and scorched, as though Sigmar had sent a comet to smite his foes. Ratboy tried to speak, but his voice was ruined and he could only emit a pitiful squeak.

Wolff nodded, as though he understood, then gestured to Gryphius's officers who were still circling around them. They were leading a riderless horse and as Wolff jogged towards it, he dragged Ratboy behind him. 'We don't have long,' he said, mounting the horse and lifting Ratboy up behind him.

Gryphius was slumped over the back of another knight's horse and as they raced back towards the main column of troops, Ratboy couldn't tell whether the general was alive or dead. Many of his men were clutching wounds of their own and swaying in their saddles, but as the marauders reeled from Wolff's holy fire, the Averlanders saw their one chance for escape and took it. Driving their exhausted horses forwards, through the charred remains, in a last, desperate charge.

The righteous fury that had washed over Ratboy gradually receded to reveal an impressive selection of pains. As he bounced weakly on the back of Wolff's horse, he realised that he was covered with dozens of cuts and grazes, but it was his left hand that worried him most of all: it was little more than a torn rag of glistening muscle and splintered bone. He gripped his master a little tighter as they left the radius of Wolff's blast and crashed back into a wall of living foes. The knights made no pretence of fighting, heading straight for the citadel in a desperate rout. Many of them dropped armour and swords as they charged, hoping to gain a little more speed over the final approach.

The ruin rose up ahead, so close Ratboy felt he could almost touch the figures watching eagerly from the battlements.

'Ride for your lives,' cried Wolff, raising his hammer and trying to drag a last burst of effort from the men. 'We're almost through.'

Ratboy looked back to see hundreds upon hundreds of marauders crossing the valley towards them. There was no sign of the flagellants, and he guessed Raphael's followers must have finally achieved the ultimate sacrifice in the name of their prophet. Raphael's corpse was gone too: dragged down to the killing floor along with the riders who carried it.

As he looked back over the desperate faces of the charging Averlanders, something caught Ratboy's eye. Far across the valley, near the command tents, a flashing light glimmered though the early morning gloom; lifting slowly above the heads of the marauders and heading towards them. 'Master,' Ratboy croaked, but his ruined voice was lost beneath the thundering of the horses' hooves.

As the flickering shape moved towards them it picked up speed and after a few minutes Ratboy realised it was a man of some kind, covered in reflective, glassy armour and hurtling towards them with the powerful thrust of six colossal wings. Despite his fear, and the awful pain in his broken hand, Ratboy felt anger well up in him. This creature was responsible for everything; this was the reason for the slaughter at Ruckendorf and Gotburg and Castle Lüneberg; this was the fiend behind the deaths of Anna's sisters.

At the thought of Anna, Ratboy gasped. Where was she? He looked around at the riders on either side of him. She was nowhere to be seen and Ratboy's anger grew all the more as he looked back at the winged figure racing towards them.

Ragged cheers broke out ahead, as they neared the crumbling walls of Mercy's End. He turned away from the flashing figure and saw the marauders on both sides falling to their knees, pierced with dozens of black and white tipped arrows. Archers had lined the walls of the keep in their hundreds, firing great banks of arrows over the heads of the Averlanders as the towering castle gates began to slowly open.

The pain of Ratboy's countless wounds finally began to overcome him. The last vestiges of Wolff's light slipped from his throat in a tired groan as his head lolled forward against the priest's back. He was vaguely aware that up ahead hooves were clattering against cobbles, rather than blood-soaked earth, but before Wolff's horse had reached the gate, Ratboy's strength left him. He loosed his grip on Wolff's back, slid down towards the rushing ground and knew no more.

CHAPTER EIGHT

Unwelcome Guests

The sound of approaching horses dragged Casper von Lüneberg from the relative warmth of his bed. He cursed as he shuffled across the bitterly cold bedchamber. 'I told them to leave me be,' he muttered, draping blankets over his royal robes as he descended the winding stairs to the great hall. 'I can't help you now,' he called out, assuming that some of his servants must have returned. Several days' worth of stubble had softened his angular features and his unwashed hair sprouted from his woolly cocoon like a collection of strange antennae. As he entered the hall, it was only the flashes of gold on his fingers that distinguished him from any other deranged refugee.

He paused on the threshold and tilted his head to one side, listening to the sound of the hooves crossing his courtyard. 'Two horses,' he said. 'Warhorses.' He stepped up to one of the broken windows and grimaced into the icy blast. 'Who's there?' he called out. 'Lüneberg is dead. There's no one here but us ghosts.'

There was no reply, but the duke heard the men dismount, drop to the ground and tether their horses. There was a clatter of metal falling to the cobbles and a furious voice rang out. 'Adelman, you oaf, be careful with that.'

A vague premonition of danger tingled in the duke's mind. There was something in the sharp, stentorian voice that worried him. 'What does it matter,' he said, with a shrug, but his words didn't quite ring true. Despite himself, Lüneberg felt a sudden lust for life. He stumbled back into the hall, grasping at chairs and walls for support.

He heard the sound of the strangers' boots as they entered the inner keep and pounded up the stairs towards him. Hearing the approach of his executioners was altogether different from picturing his death as something remote and abstract. The duke began muttering under his breath. 'Where did I leave my sword,' he said, patting the surface of the long table that divided the room. 'There must be something in here.' His fingers touched upon a variety of useless objects: cups, bowls, spoons but nothing he could use as a weapon. 'It's next to my bed,' he said, heading for the door, but as he rushed across the hall, he stumbled on a broken fiddle and fell heavily to the floor. He tried to lift himself, but couldn't seem to catch his breath.

The door flew open with a loud bang and footsteps rushed towards him. 'My lord,' cried the voice he had heard outside, 'are you injured? Adelman, help him up.'

A pair of enormous, rough hands grasped the duke, lifted him to his feet and placed him on a chair.

'Who are you?' he gasped, still struggling for breath.

'Otto Sürman, Templar of Sigmar,' replied the voice, twisting itself into a gentle croon. 'Do I have the honour of meeting Duke Casper von Lüneberg?'

The duke gripped his knees and hitched his shoulders up and down as he grabbed a few short breaths. 'Yes,' he managed to exclaim after a few minutes, 'I'm Casper von Lüneberg.' He gave a grim laugh. 'But as far as the dukedom is concerned, I fear I may be in dereliction of my duties.'

There was a pause, and the duke assumed his guests were looking around at the ruined tapestries and broken furniture.

'We saw bodies in the village, duke. Was this the work of the same Chaos force that laid waste to Strendel and Wurdorf? The marauders heading for Wolfenberg?'

Lüneberg shrugged. 'There is some kind of *thing* leading them, named Mormius. He didn't have much time to discuss tactics with me, but yes, I believe he was headed for the capital. Mercy's End still blocks their way, but I doubt it will be much of an obstacle. I've never seen such an army.'

'Mercy's End?'

The duke thrust his head towards his interrogator, as though willing his severed optical nerves back into life. 'What are you doing here? There's nothing here for you, or your god. Whichever one you profess to serve. I'm through with creeds and wars and stratagems. You can expect no help from me.' He sneered. 'I gave everything for this Empire and it spat me out like a rotten fruit.'

The duke felt a gentle hand on his, as the crooning voice replied. 'My lord, we require no help. Far from it – I simply wished to enquire after a friend of mine.'

'Which friend?'

'A priestess of Shallya, who goes by the name of Anna Fleck. I believe she's travelling in the company of one of my brethren – a warrior priest named Jakob Wolff.'

The duke blushed and shook his head, embarrassed by the harshness of his words. 'You must forgive my rudeness, Brother Sürman, I didn't realise. Any friend of that woman is a friend of mine.'

'No forgiveness needed, duke. We live in dangerous times. It's wise to be wary of strangers.'

Lüneberg heard the scraping sound of a chair being pulled alongside his, and when the soft voice spoke again, it was so close he could feel the priest's breath on his ear. 'Are you a good friend of Anna then, duke?'

The duke smiled as he remembered his encounter with the priestess. 'It seems strange to say it, after such a brief acquaintance, but yes, I feel as though I know her very well.' He leant back in his chair. 'She's of a kind though, I suppose. There are those who destroy and those who create, and I fear Anna's breed are in the minority.'

'I think I understand you, duke.' There was a slight urgency in Sürman's voice as he asked his next question. 'Is she here?'

'Oh, no, I'm afraid not, Brother Sürman. She left with Gryphius's army, two days past. She has no intention of fighting, though. They couldn't even get her to wear armour.' The duke's smile slipped from his face. 'She hopes to bring a little love to this wounded land, but I fear she might be too late for that.'

'I see. And where did Gryphius plan to go from here? South?'

The duke gave a hollow laugh. 'South? You don't know Hugo von Gryphius. He's heard that the whole weight of the Chaos realm is pressing down on Mercy's End, so he wants to be there when the hammer falls. He intends to throw in his lot with those poor, doomed souls.'

'And Anna went with him?'

'Yes, along with the warrior priest and his acolyte.'

Sürman fell silent as he considered Lüneberg's words and for a few minutes the only sound was the duke's laboured breathing.

'Tell me, duke,' said Sürman eventually, 'what happened to your eyes?'

The duke placed a protective hand over the stained bandage. 'The thing called Mormius didn't approve of my reading habits.' He shrugged. 'I'm not sure what he is, exactly, but he's indulged in the worst kind of occultism and I think it's sent him mad. His whole body has been transformed by depravity, so I suppose it makes sense that it would have warped his mind too. He has six, huge wings sprouting from his back and eyes that could flay the skin from your bones.' He shuddered at the memory. 'He treated me quite politely at first, but when I commented on his obvious heresy, he became completely unhinged.'

'So, not only did this daemonic entity enter your castle,' asked Sürman, with a slight tremor in his voice. 'You spoke with it, too?'

The duke nodded and hugged himself, suddenly remembering the cold. He waited for Sürman to continue speaking, but no words came.

Instead, he felt the priest rise from the chair and step away. There was a low muttering sound as Sürman spoke to his companion, then a brief click of metal against metal.

'Tell me, duke,' said Sürman, from somewhere behind him, 'why did this child of the Old Night allow you to live?' The gentle croon had vanished, to be replaced with a contemptuous sneer. 'What perverted bargain did you make to buy your freedom?'

'Bargain? What are you talking–' The duke cut himself short with a wry laugh. 'Oh. Of course. I see.' He laughed a little harder and shook his head in disbelief. 'So this is how it finishes. What a pitiful end to a farcical life.'

'It is to the merciful justice of Sigmar that I commit you, servant of the Ruinous Powers,' replied Sürman. 'May your soul–'

'Don't waste any more of my time, you pathetic dupe,' snapped Lüneberg. 'Do whatever you imagine you must, but please don't make me listen to that puerile dogma.'

The duke barely noticed the pistol as it was pressed to the back of his head. He was already far away, in a country of golden, rolling fields and unstained friendship. 'Hugo, old friend,' he breathed, 'forgive me.'

By the time the gunshot had echoed once around the empty hall, Lüneberg was dead.

CHAPTER NINE
Men of Ostland

The darkness was all encompassing. It cradled Ratboy, caressing his damaged flesh like swaddling and easing him towards oblivion. Brutal memories tried to pierce the gloom and it was his own brutality that haunted him most of all. But for every glimpse of frenzied hands and pulsing viscera, another wave of blackness came, dragging him further and further down.

A voice interrupted his descent. 'Ratboy,' it called. The sound of his own name reminded him again of his bloody deeds and jolted him back up from the abyss. 'Stay with us.'

The soft, familiar tones gave Ratboy another memory: a brief glimpse of sunlight beside a quick, winding stream and a woman's eyes, looking into his with unashamed affection. Suddenly the darkness seemed a little less enticing.

'Try and drink this,' said the voice and he felt a cup pressed gently against his mouth, moistening his lips with warm, aromatic liquid.

He swallowed a little of the drink and opened his eyes.

For a while he only registered Anna's face, leaning over his and lit up with a broad grin. Her ivory skin was bruised and scratched, and he could see faint worry lines at the corners of her eyes that he suspected had not been there just a few short weeks ago. Her hair had grown back as a halo of glinting stubble and she had tears of relief in her eyes.

'You're alive,' he muttered.

Anna burst into laughter and leant away from him. '*I'm* alive? You're the one who vanished just as we reached our destination.' She gestured to his tightly bandaged hand. 'And you're the one who decided to grab the wrong end of a knife.'

Ratboy's nose wrinkled as he noticed a strong smell of manure. He looked around at his surroundings. He was lying on a bed of straw in the corner of a stable, surrounded by a forest of horses' legs and piles of dung.

'It was the warmest place we could find,' laughed Anna, noticing his look of disgust. 'Most of this place fell down centuries ago, but the horses do quite nicely for themselves.'

'Where's Brother Wolff?'

'Recovering, I imagine. After he rescued you, he seemed quite overcome with exhaustion. He'd barely dragged you through the gates when he collapsed. I'm not sure what he did out there – that awful light that came down on him seemed to melt flesh from men's bones.' Her eyes widened with horror at the memory of it. 'He suffered horribly for it afterwards though. His face was greyer than Raphael's corpse. I didn't think he would survive.' She gave Ratboy another sip of the tea and smiled at him as he gulped it down.

Ratboy struggled up into a sitting position with a look of concern on his face. 'So, is he asleep still? Has he recovered from his exhaustion?'

Anna pressed him gently back onto the straw. 'Don't alarm yourself. He's awake and talking to Captain Felhamer – the officer in charge of this place.' She grimaced. 'Well, I say "in charge", but the captain has quite a few egos to contend with. Everyone in here seems to have some ridiculous, vainglorious title: Kompmeister or Kriegswarden or something else that justifies their pompousness. And they all think they should be making the big tactical decisions.'

'But what of the enemy?' Ratboy's eyes grew wide with fear. 'I saw a shape pursuing us. A creature, that flew at the head of the marauders.'

Anna nodded. 'Yes, you saw the thing the duke referred to as Mormius. He said it's some kind of daemon spawn.' Her cool, grey eyes clouded over. 'It's Mormius who murdered Sister Gundram, my matriarch. And he massacred Lüneberg's men. He's the one leading the enemy against us.'

'Then are we under attack?'

'Not yet.' Anna looked at Ratboy's bandaged hand. 'It seems that our ill-advised charge may have bought Captain Felhamer and his men a little time. They were expecting the assault to begin this morning, but between us and the penitents, we left the enemy quite disconcerted.' She sighed. 'It's the briefest of respites though. Wolff and Felhamer both expect them to strike at nightfall.'

Ratboy frowned, still trying to piece together his memories of the morning's events. 'Why did you call the charge "ill-advised"? We made it to Mercy's End, didn't we?'

Anna hesitated before replying. 'Well, yes, or at least *some* of us did.'

She smoothed down her white robes and looked at her long, delicate fingers. 'The obermarshall confused things greatly by attempting to reach the flagellants. Barely half of his men reached the citadel and few of them are without injuries.' She frowned. 'And of course, every single one of the villagers from Gotburg was butchered. Just as your master knew they would be when he sent them into battle.'

Ratboy blushed at her angry tone. 'They had chosen their path before they even met Master Wolff.'

Anna shook her head, but seemed unwilling to argue the point.

'And what of the obermarshall himself?'

Anna shook her head again. 'I've done as much as I can for him, but I couldn't remove the weapon from his side without risking more damage.' As her eyes met Ratboy's, they were full of regret. 'The most I could do was remove some of the spear and bandage the rest up. I don't expect him to see the morning.'

Ratboy nodded and fell silent. He recalled the frenzy that took hold of him during the battle and shuddered. He looked down at his chest and saw that his borrowed yellow tabard was torn and dark with blood.

Anna followed his gaze and gave him an odd, forced smile. 'Your master was pleased with your bravery. He feels that your determination did you credit.'

Ratboy closed his eyes, trying to rid himself of the awful images that plagued him. 'I'm not sure it was determination as such,' he said. 'The light that came from Brother Wolff seemed to change me. And there was so much blood everywhere, I lost track of things.' He grimaced. 'I wasn't myself.'

Anna raised her eyebrows. 'If you wish to follow in Wolff's footsteps, you'll need to accept such violence.' She shook her head. 'It's not the path I would've chosen, but the life of a warrior priest is full of such horrors. It's a path of pain, as well as prayer.'

'Of course,' replied Ratboy, a little indignantly. 'I'm not quite as naïve as you imagine, sister. My master has trained me in the martial arts as carefully as the holy texts. It's just that...' his voice trailed away and he looked down at his blood-caked hands in confusion. 'I didn't expect to find it so enjoyable.'

He looked up in time to catch the horrified expression on Anna's face. 'My motives were pure,' he said, grabbing her hand and willing her to understand. 'For a while, I felt as though I could tear down all the evil in this world. Pull it apart with my bare hands. I wanted to rip the corruption from the heart of the Empire. And as my master's light surrounded me, it seemed as though I finally could. Finally make a difference.' He shrugged, embarrassed by the passion in his voice. 'That's all I meant by enjoyable.'

She gave a stiff nod and withdrew her hand. 'Yes. I understand. I've heard such sentiments before.' She looked down at him with a smile that did not reach her eyes. 'Your master has trained you perfectly. You're already beginning to sound like him. I've no doubt that you'll make a fierce defender of the Sigmarite faith.' She rose to her feet. 'I must inform Wolff that his brave protégé is awake.'

Ratboy watched Anna's slender form as it slipped away between the restless horses. Her tone had sounded more accusatory than praising and he felt a sinking feeling in his stomach. 'Sigmar,' he muttered, looking down at the bloody lump that had once been his left hand. 'What a mess.'

Despite its crumbling masonry and broken rafters, the central hall at Mercy's End was a beautiful sight. A high, vaulted ceiling reached up over a broad, circular chamber that managed to be imposing, yet light and airy at the same time, thanks to a series of tall, stained glass windows that flooded the room with coloured light. As Ratboy entered, he kept his eyes focussed respectfully on the floor, noticing that every polished flagstone was inlaid with glittering images of twin-tailed comets and the Ghal Maraz.

At the centre of the chamber was a round stone table and as he approached it Wolff rose to greet him, gesturing to the one empty chair.

'Tell us what you saw,' said the priest, placing his hand on Ratboy's shoulder, 'as we were approaching the gates.'

Ratboy looked up from the table and felt his tongue freeze in his mouth. A circle of regal, patrician faces surrounded him, and from the elaborately waxed beards and furrowed brows, he took them to be generals and captains of the highest rank. Their clothes were uniformly bloodstained and torn, but it was obvious from their thick, velvet doublets and intricately worked hauberks that they were great leaders. All of them had seen better days though. Their faces were lined with exhaustion and several of them carried fresh scars.

With a shock of recognition, Ratboy realised that one of the men was Gryphius. The obermarshall's olive skin had drained to a sickly greenish hue and his face was contorted with pain. He nodded vaguely at Ratboy, but there was no trace of his habitual grin.

'Well, um,' Ratboy stammered, unnerved by the dramatic change in the general, 'I can't recall exactly, but–'

'What's that he says?' bellowed a silver-haired old brute, with a fierce, bristling beard and red, rheumy eyes. 'Tell him to speak up, priest.'

'I said, I can't remember too clearly,' said Ratboy, raising his voice a little. 'But I know I saw a winged creature of some kind, flying after us.'

'Winged, did he say?' barked the old soldier, looking around furiously for confirmation.

'Yes, Oswald,' snapped the man to his right – a handsome youth with short-cropped blond hair and piercing blue eyes. 'And maybe if you bite your fat old tongue for a second, he might be able to say a little more.'

The small patches of Oswald's skin that weren't covered by beard flushed red and he leapt to his feet, thrusting forward a barrel chest as broad as a shire horse. 'You're not the elector count just yet, Captain Felhamer,' he yelled, glowering down at the younger man. 'And it wouldn't harm you to show a little respect to your elders.'

Wolff raised a hand and all eyes immediately turned towards him. 'Gentlemen,' he said quietly, 'we don't have much time.'

Oswald continued to scowl at Captain Felhamer.

'Apologies, marshall,' said the captain with a shrug, 'I meant no offence. Please, take your seat and let's hear what the boy has to say.'

The old soldier gave a snort of disgust and dropped heavily back into his chair.

'Please,' said the young captain, gesturing for Ratboy to continue.

'Well, that was it really. I saw a winged figure and he seemed to be made of silver, or glass, or something shiny at least. I believe it was the thing that Duke Lüneberg called Mormius.'

A babble of voices erupted around the table, as the officers turned to each other and began talking urgently.

'Gentlemen,' said Wolff, raising his hand again, and silence descended over the chamber once more. The priest turned to Ratboy. 'Did you see anything else?'

Ratboy looked down at the table's scratched stone and frowned. 'Well, I passed out soon after I saw him. But I recall that he was surrounded by soldiers who seemed larger than the others, and some that weren't even human.' Ratboy looked up at his master with fear in his eyes. 'They had so many limbs and mouths, and they scrabbled along the ground like spiders. I...' his voice trailed off as he recalled the full horror of what he saw. 'And there were other shapes following him, that were even more monstrous.' He shook his head. 'They were the size of trees.' His voice became shrill at the memory. 'They were twice the size of the marauders and they carried great clubs and axes.' He grabbed Wolff's sleeve and looked desperately at him. 'They were eating corpses as they marched.'

The man sat next to Ratboy whistled through his teeth. 'Ogres of some kind then,' he said, looking around the table. 'This is going to be some night.'

'The whole thing is madness,' cried another officer. 'We're all going to be butchered. Why aren't we pulling back to Wolfenberg, while there's still time?'

'Diterich is right,' cried a sharp-featured, beak-nosed man, wearing a monocle. He slammed his gauntleted hand down on the stone table. 'Why make a useless sacrifice of ourselves here? There's no way we can make an adequate defence of this ruin.'

'There was something else,' said Ratboy, closing his eyes in concentration.

The soldiers fell silent and waited for him to continue.

'Just before I passed out I noticed something strange about Mormius.' He opened his eyes and looked up at Wolff with excitement. 'He was injured. His right arm was all shrivelled. It looked as though there was a kind of black acid eating through his armour – stretching out like veins from his hand.' Ratboy looked down at his own bloody fingers. 'Like there was some kind of disease, or poison eating him up.'

'Tannhauser!' cried Captain Felhamer, leaping to his feet and clenching his fists with excitement. 'Maybe he reached him after all? The boy might have seen the effects of his poison. Sigmar's Blood, this could be our chance!' There was a cobalt fire burning in his eyes as he looked round the table. 'If we leave Mercy's End now they'll hunt us like rats – ripping us apart before we've gotten a mile from this valley. Our only chance is to make a stand here. If the boy's right, Mormius could be on the verge of death. Tannhauser could have reached him somehow.'

Wolff shook his head. 'Tannhauser?'

'One of my bravest captains,' replied Felhamer, his eyes bulging with passion. 'The marauders butchered his regiment as they slept, and it sent him half mad with grief. Several days ago he set out to avenge them. I tried to stop him, but he wouldn't listen.' Felhamer gave a short laugh. 'To be honest, I cursed his name at the time. Some of my best knights left with him. There was no hope of success, but he was inconsolable. He wanted to join the fight for the northern garrisons so he could try to get close to Mormius. He said he had a ring filled with some kind of poison. I thought he was raving, but from what your acolyte has described, I think he may have achieved his goal.' Felhamer laughed again. 'He was a very unusual man, Captain Tannhauser. I think I may have underestimated him.'

'But what does it matter?' cried Oswald. 'We've gathered every last vestige of our strength into one convenient slaughterhouse. Even if you're right about this lunatic, Tannhauser, which I doubt very much, the marauders have ten times our numbers. Mormius or not, we can't win here. We should be splitting our forces and choosing battlegrounds more suited to our strengths. That's the only way we can save Ostland from destruction.'

'The marauders annihilated the northern regions in a matter of days,' replied Felhamer, levelling a trembling finger at the northern wall of the chamber. 'If they're left to march any further south, there'll be nothing left to save.' He dropped back into his chair, with a despondent sigh. 'We have to hold them here for as long as we can and give the elector count time to bring the battle away from Wolfenberg. I have orders from von Raukov himself, requesting me to do just that.'

'So we're a sacrifice, is that it?' cried Oswald, looking at the other soldiers with an incredulous expression on his face. 'Is that all von Raukov thinks we're worth? A minor distraction, to give him time to polish his armour and rehearse his victory speech?' He drew his sword and slammed it down on the table with a clatter that echoed around the vaulted ceiling. 'I came to fight, not play games. If we stay here, we're as good as dead.'

There was murmur of disgruntled voices around the table, and most of them seemed in agreement with Oswald. Ratboy looked at his master apologetically, feeling that he was responsible for the discord.

Wolff rose from his chair with a slow majesty that silenced the debate. The light from the stained glass windows played across the iron band on his shaven head as he nodded slowly in agreement. 'It's true,' he said, 'that if you stay here and fight, it's likely you will die; if you flee, however, it's certain.' He tapped his ironclad finger against the brass hammer on his gorget. 'But, more than that, if you flee, you will have betrayed your faith, your families and your emperor.' His eyes flashed dangerously beneath his heavy brow as he looked around the table. He strode across the chamber and when he reached the nearest pillar he slammed his fist into it. The officers jumped in surprise as a cloud of dust exploded around Wolff's gauntlet. 'This is good Ostland stone,' he said. 'A little old maybe, like the rest of us, but good nonetheless. Don't let those horrors soil one blessed inch of it.' He looked directly at Oswald. 'Those afraid to give their lives in the name of Sigmar are free to leave, but I have a suspicion Ostland ran out of cowards a long time ago.'

There was a ripple of nervous laughter and even Oswald smiled, nodding in agreement as he sheathed his sword. 'It's true,' he said, 'Ostland *isn't* the easiest place to grow a few ears of corn.'

Shoulders visibly relaxed and hands were loosed from sword hilts as the tension around the room dissipated.

Wolff looked up at the crumbling masonry. 'Life is fleeting. We inhabit a tiny sliver of existence, surrounded on all sides by an endless void. We only have one chance to make a difference. One chance before we return to the endless night. Death today, or death tomorrow, what does it matter if we don't lead a life worth living?' He lifted his warhammer up into one of the shafts of light and slowly rotated it, scattering jewels of colour across the walls of the chamber and into the faces of the assembled officers. 'You're Sigmar's heirs. No one in this room was ever destined to eke out their days in a sick bed. We are the elect few, chosen for hardship and greatness. Whether it's today, or next year, your end will be glorious and godlike. And if this is your day to die, then by Sigmar make it a good day!'

Ratboy's heart swelled at his master's words and he noticed several of the officers nodding eagerly in agreement.

'I hear you, priest,' replied the beak-nosed officer, 'but your words might carry a little more weight if your friend Gryphius hadn't told me that you yourself are planning to flee south at the first opportunity.'

Captain Felhamer looked at Wolff in dismay. 'Is that true?' he asked.

Wolff nodded and returned to his seat. There was no trace of shame or embarrassment on his face as he replied. 'Yes,' he said. 'It's true. I must leave tonight.'

'Why?' cried the beak-nosed man, glaring incredulously through his monocle. 'We have need of you here. How can you advise us to hold this pile of rubble, when you yourself will not even stay to help?'

Wolff returned the officer's glare with a calm nod. 'I understand your concern, Marshall Meinrich, but I assure you, I would rather meet my end here, covered in glory, than pursue the miserable errand that waits me.'

Captain Felhamer rose to his feet, his pale cheeks flushed with colour. 'But Brother Wolff, after what you've just said, what could be more important than helping us defend Mercy's End?'

'I'll help all I can,' replied Wolff. 'There are things I can do before I leave.' He ran a hand over his shaven head and closed his eyes. 'I have a little strength left. I'll pray with your men and bless them. And I'll join you in the initial defence.' He opened his eyes and looked Felhamer in the eye. 'But I cannot neglect my duty.'

'At least tell us *why* you won't stay and fight,' said the old, bearded man, named Oswald.

'There's a traitor marching with von Raukov's army,' Wolff explained. 'He's a worshipper of the Dark Gods, named Fabian. He's a murderer and a heretic and a threat to the whole war effort. He must be stopped before he can achieve whatever perverted end he has in mind. And I'm the one person in all Ostland who could recognise him.' The priest gave a long sigh. 'He's my brother.'

Silence greeted Wolff's admission as the officers considered how exactly Wolff might stop his brother.

'If I stay here and fight,' the priest continued, 'I may be of some use to you. But in the meantime, Fabian will be free to wreak havoc on von Raukov's army. I haven't seen my brother for decades. I don't even know what name he will be using now. Who knows how high he has risen through the ranks. He may even be close to the elector count himself. Close enough to assassinate him maybe.' Wolff looked around the table. 'We could give our lives holding Mercy's End, only to find that von Raukov's army has been devoured from the inside.'

Felhamer shook his head and looked down at the table in despair. 'Then you must abandon us to our fate.'

'No one here is abandoned!' Wolff cried, slamming his fist against his breastplate. 'Sigmar is here, in our hearts and our swords. A priest is just a touchstone. A conduit. You don't need me to lead you. There will be a warrior god marching by your side.'

A small voice piped up from next to the Wolff. 'It's true,' said Ratboy, looking up at his master and nodding. 'This morning, during the battle, I was sure everything was lost: my hand was ruined; the enemy were all around us; but something carried me through it. I felt Sigmar, guiding me.' He laughed and looked around at the officers. 'I had no weapon and the marauders towered over me, but I still took them.' He gave a fierce grin. 'I tore them apart.'

Von Gryphius rocked back in his chair and gave a weak snort of laughter. For a brief moment his old, playful smile returned. 'If a one handed, unarmed child can fight these pigs, then I don't see what you're all so afraid of.' He climbed slowly to his feet, wincing with pain, and lifted his rapier over the table. 'Priest or not, I make my stand here. Are you all with me?'

For a few seconds there was no response. Ratboy noticed the monocled officer was studying him closely; taking in his scrawny frame and tattered, stained clothes. Finally, the man climbed to his feet, drew his broadsword and held it out over the table, so that the tip clattered against von Gryphius's sword. 'Forgive me, captain,' he said, turning to Felhamer. 'I forgot myself. It shouldn't have taken the bravery of a child to remind me of my duty, but if you'll still have me, I'd be honoured to die by your side.'

One by one the other soldiers stood and drew their weapons, creating a canopy of battered steel over the old table.

Captain Felhamer's handsome face cracked into a broad grin and his blue eyes sparkled victoriously. 'Let this Mormius make his move,' he said, rising to his feet and clanging his sword on top of the others. 'There's life in these old stones yet.'

CHAPTER TEN

Mercy's End

As Wolff climbed up onto the ramparts, all eyes were on him. Felhamer had gathered over two thousand men beneath his banner; only a fraction of the numbers arrayed against them, but a glorious sight nonetheless. Archers, spearmen, handgunners, greatswords and engineers stood side by side with battle-hardened militiamen and stony-faced villagers, who gripped their clubs and spears firmly, despite the fear written across their faces. From high above their plumed helmets the stubborn bull of Ostland glowered down expectantly, emblazoned across a dozen rippling flags.

As Wolff reached the top step, the soldiers nearest to him dropped on one knee and lowered their heads in genuflection. The priest placed his right hand on their shoulders, muttered a quick prayer from the book held in his left hand and then strode on. As he walked along the castle wall the scene was repeated again and again, and as each of the soldiers climbed back to their feet, the fear vanished from their eyes; replaced with the fierce light of hope. As Ratboy followed behind his master, carrying his hammer for him as he blessed the troops, he recognised the light as the same force that had earlier driven him to such frenzy. He both envied and pitied the men as they crowded around his master, desperate for the touch of his hand. Many held out their swords and spears and Wolff placed a hand on every weapon that was passed his way.

As they made their way around the castle wall, Ratboy looked out over the battlements, down into the valley below. It was now mid afternoon and there was no hiding the size of the army moving towards them.

The attack had already begun, he realised with a jolt. Countless rows of bare-chested northmen, were running towards the castle with shields over their heads and ladders under their arms. As Wolff continued, the captains on the wall signalled for the archers to take their positions, but Ratboy could not help wondering if they had enough arrows to take down so many men. It looked like there was a whole ocean of jagged metal and scorched wood rushing towards them. Why don't they shoot? he wondered, as the marauders raced closer and closer. They must be in range by now.

Captain Felhamer was perched at the top of a bell tower that looked down over the wall, and as the charging marauders approached, the sergeants all watched for his signal. His hand was raised above his head, ready to launch the defence, but as the marauders sprinted across the bloody ground towards the castle, he kept his hand aloft, as though waiting for some invisible sign. Finally, as the enemy were almost at the castle gates, he brought his hand down in a cutting motion.

Ratboy immediately saw the reason for his delay.

The earth around the castle collapsed with an immense explosion of mud; disappearing from beneath the feet of the charging marauders with a booming groan of collapsing boards. They toppled in their hundreds down into a broad trench, letting go of their shields as they crashed helplessly onto a bed of thick, wooden stakes. As the marauders screamed and howled with rage and panic, the archers finally launched their first volley from the castle walls.

'It's the old moat,' cried Ratboy. 'They'd hidden it!'

Wolff took a break from his prayers, to give his acolyte a short nod. 'Captain Felhamer has been preparing this wreck for weeks. I believe he has quite a few such tricks up his sleeve.'

Banks of arrows arced down into the writhing mass of stranded, thrashing figures. The dazed marauders tried to crawl back out of the moat, but the archers fired with incredible speed and accuracy, loosing arrow after arrow into the river of flailing limbs. The moat quickly became clogged with the dying and the dead.

The enemy were charging forward in such massive numbers, that the men further back had no idea what had happened at the foot of the castle wall. Waves of them rushed unwittingly towards the trench. As the first group tried to clamber back to safety, their comrades crashed into them from the other direction and the crush of bodies, spears and ladders all tumbled down into the moat, to the cheers of Felhamer's archers.

Ratboy looked down on the confusion in amazement. The scene quickly took on the appearance of a slaughterhouse as the moat filled up with broken weapons and bodies. Despite their aching arms the archers kept up the furious pace and it seemed as though the whole army was going to pour into Felhamer's trap.

Finally, Mormius saw what was happening and horns began to sound along the enemy lines, calling a retreat. The warriors nearest the castle were so enraged by the waves of arrows, that they continued trying to reach the walls, clambering over the mounds of skewered corpses and slamming their ladders against the old stone. A few of them even managed to start scrambling up towards the archers, but before they had climbed even a few feet, Felhamer brought down his hand a second time and barrels of hot oil poured down from the embrasures, sending the marauders screaming and gambolling to their deaths.

The horns continued to blow, but the northmen were now so consumed by rage and bloodlust that many of them broke ranks and continued ploughing forwards through the mayhem. The charge quickly became a directionless rout and still the endless clouds of arrows rained down on them.

Finally, Wolff blessed the last soldier in the line and turned to stand beside Ratboy. They both looked down on the massacre below. 'Barbarians,' the priest muttered, shaking his head in disgust. 'If only all our enemies were so undisciplined.' He held his hand up to shield his eyes against the light and then cried out in alarm. 'Down!' he yelled, throwing Ratboy to the ground as a cloud of arrows whirred angrily over their heads.

All along the wall, soldiers howled in pain as the enemy's arrows found their mark. Dozens of men tumbled back from the wall, spinning down towards the courtyard below, or dropping to their knees and clutching at pierced throats and chests.

Ratboy looked up at the crumbling bell tower. Felhamer and the other officers had vanished from view and he prayed they had ducked in time. His fears were quickly allayed. As the clouds of enemy arrows dropped away, Felhamer rose up and held his two-handed sword aloft, signalling for his archers to return fire.

Ratboy peered out through a loophole and saw that the marauders were finally backing away from the trench and staggering towards their own lines. Before they had got very far, the Empire archers loosed another volley down on them, dropping dozens more of the northmen in their tracks. Ratboy counted no more than fifty or so survivors who reached the safety of the main army.

A roar of victory erupted all along the walls of Mercy's End. Almost a thousand marauders lay dead or dying in the ditch below them, and only a handful of Ostlanders had fallen.

Ratboy noticed that his master did not join in with the celebrations. The priest was peering out over the battlements and frowning. 'Something else is coming,' he muttered.

Ratboy followed his gaze and saw a vague shape break away from the bulk of the enemy army and start rushing across the valley floor towards them. 'What *is* that?' he asked. The shape was charging towards them so fast and with such strange, spasmodic movements that he could not be sure what he was looking at. Strangely, as it neared the castle, the shape became harder rather than easier to define. Ratboy had an impression of limbs and maybe even faces, but rather than troops, it seemed more like a mass of pink and blue energy, rippling across the ground. Ratboy turned to his master for an explanation, but Wolff had opened one of his holy books and was leafing through the pages with such a grim look of concentration on his face that Ratboy didn't dare interrupt him.

The cheers along the wall faltered as the soldiers noticed the strange sight rushing towards them. As the pink and blue shape reached the trench, the ground seemed to warp and bulge, as though reflected in a curved mirror and even the corpses appeared to writhe and shift like smoke.

Felhamer signalled for the archers to open fire, but it was too late. The pink shape washed over the moat like quicksilver and flooded up against the castle.

'Sigmar help us,' gasped Ratboy as he finally saw what was heading towards them. The pink mass was made up of hundreds of twisted, writhing limbs and wide gaping mouths that oozed and coagulated with a peculiar elasticity. The figures giggled and snarled as they billowed upwards in a torrent of rippling flesh. Faces appeared in bellies and contorted into long arachnid limbs before bursting and reforming into other shapes. It looked like a sea of pure Chaos was rushing up towards the ramparts.

Screams of horror erupted from the Empire soldiers as the shapes flooded over the battlements and washed down onto them.

'Hold your line!' cried Felhamer, as he sliced one of the creatures in two with his greatsword. The thing immediately became two smaller shapes and leapt up at him again. He staggered backwards, wrestling frantically as the writhing mass enveloped his chest. Then he disappeared from view.

'Master,' screamed Ratboy, as one the shapes flew at him. It cackled as it latched onto his neck with dozens of slippery, grasping tentacles. Pink energy hissed around its torso and a wide mouth burst from its flesh, baring rows of serrated teeth as it struggled to press its twitching body against him.

Wolff gave no reply, but as Ratboy stumbled past him, fighting for his life, the priest rose to his feet and smashed his hammer down onto the ancient stonework. White fire erupted along the entire length of the wall, enveloping the pink creatures in a dazzling inferno of energy. As the flames touched their jerking, snapping bodies, the creatures screeched in pain and dropped to the ground, contorting as they floundered, trying to escape from the blinding light.

The soldiers needed no order from the tower. They fell on the stunned shapes with knives, spears and swords, hacking the monsters limb from limb until nothing remained but a mess of purple viscera.

The creatures' organs continued to writhe and crawl across the ground and for a few moments the only sound was the squelch of boots, grinding the remains into the stone, as the soldiers ran about, stamping on rows of snapping teeth and pulling grasping fingers from their armour.

Once the shapes had finally become still, the soldiers looked around at each other with ashen faces. They were hardened veterans of countless wars, but none of them had ever encountered anything quite so sickening as this.

Howls began to echo along the wall once more and Ratboy looked to see if there was another wave of creatures coming up the walls. It was worse than that. Some of the men who had been attacked by the monsters had begun to change. Where the creatures had gripped them for several minutes, or sunk teeth though their armour, the men's flesh had become oddly deformed: sprouting serpentine growths that quickly grew in strength and size as the soldiers looked on in horror.

One of the mutated men was standing near Wolff. The soldier groaned in disgust as the skin on his neck and face rolled and bubbled, struggling to contain the frantic changes occurring beneath. His groan turned into a muffled wail, as glistening pink tendrils rushed from behind his eyes and enveloped his face, sliding back into his head through his mouth and beginning to suffocate him.

Wolff stepped calmly forwards and slammed his hammer into the man's head. The soldier was dead before he hit the floor. Writhing shapes squirmed from his shattered skull, reaching out for something to latch onto, but Wolff stamped down on them with his iron-clad boot until they were still. Then he looked up at the horrified circle of onlookers. 'Kill the corrupted,' he said, loud enough for his words to carry all along the crowds of shocked soldiers. 'They're beyond saving.'

The soldiers whose flesh had been changed raised their hands protectively as the other men surrounded them, raising their swords but still unsure whether to strike.

Wolff leapt up onto the wall and cried out in furious, commanding tones. 'Do it now, or we all die!'

For a second, the soldiers still hesitated to kill their former friends, but then one of them screamed out in dismay as a forest of pink tendrils burst from the man nearest to him and latched onto his head, dragging him towards a gaping mouth that had suddenly opened in the mutant's neck. The soldiers attacked the men with axes and swords, slicing desperately at them before they themselves became corrupted. This was the only signal the others needed. All along the wall the Ostlanders attacked anyone who showed the merest hint of mutation, eager to save themselves from the same fate.

Ratboy reeled in horror as he watched the Ostlanders hacking at their own countrymen. To see former comrades turn on each other in this way was more than he could bear and he covered his eyes.

Wolff grabbed his hand and pulled it firmly away from his face. 'This is Sigmar's work, boy,' he gasped, glaring at his acolyte with such fury that Ratboy struggled to meet his gaze. 'Don't you dare avert your eyes.'

Ratboy nodded, and dutifully took in the full horror of the scene. The soldiers were eyeing each other warily as they backed away from the dying mutants. In just a few short minutes, they had gone from being a unified fighting force, to a collection of rabid individuals, terrified that some subtle transformation of their flesh might mark them out for execution. Rather than looking out towards the massing ranks of the enemy, they circled each other, clutching their blood-drenched swords in fear.

We're lost, thought Ratboy, watching as old friends become wary strangers and rows of drilled soldiers splintered into a paranoid mob. He looked to his master for guidance, but Wolff had slumped weakly against the wall, gasping for breath, his face drawn and grey with exhaustion. Accusations began to fly back and forth between the terrified men as they rounded on anyone who displayed even so much as a limp.

'Wait,' cried Ratboy, but his voice was lost in the general tumult. He leapt up onto the stonework and called out again. 'Wait,' he cried with more determination. 'The enemy is out there, don't do their work for them! Remember who you are, men of Ostland!'

A few faces turned to see who had spoken, and Ratboy noticed that one of them was the sharp-featured officer named Meinrich who had earlier accused Wolff of cowardice. His black and white tabard was torn and scorched, but his monocle was still firmly in place and he nodded grimly back at Ratboy.

Meinrich stretched up to his full height and his willowy frame towered over most of the men that surrounded him. 'The boy's right,' he yelled, clanging his sword on his breastplate. 'Hold your swords. Resume your positions. Man the wall!' The soldiers looked shamefully from Meinrich to Ratboy and lowered their weapons. They picked the crackling remains from their armour with distaste and stepped back into line, readying themselves for the next assault.

Ratboy dropped back down from the wall and saw Wolff, still stooped and straining for breath, but looking up at him with a grim smile. The priest nodded and gripped his arm in silent approbation, before standing up and looking out towards the enemy.

'Sigmar's blood,' he muttered, opening his prayer book once more. 'This is going to be a long night.'

Ratboy looked out over the battlements and saw another pink mass of swirling shapes rushing across the valley towards them. He gasped in horror and backed away.

Wolff was still holding his arm and pulled him close. 'I have the measure of you now, boy,' he said, squeezing his arm so hard that his metal-clad fingers bit into the boy's flesh. 'You were born for this. I thought it before and I know it now.' The priest looked deep into the aco-lyte's eyes. 'Keep close by my side, Anselm. Sigmar's grace is written all over you. I can see His holy wrath in your eyes.' He tightened the straps of his armour and looked up at the darkening sky. 'These fiends are no match for *two* blessed sons of the Heldenhammer.'

For the next three hours they fought wave after wave of the hideous, shifting shapes. As the crimson sun dropped slowly towards the horizon, Wolff, Ratboy and Meinrich dashed along the wall, rallying the men each time they faltered and hacking their way through the tormented shapes that poured over the walls.

The soldiers' initial terror gave way to a grim determination not to be corrupted. As the prayers of Wolff and Ratboy rang constantly in their ears, they butchered the monsters with a mute, machine-like efficiency; fighting through their exhaustion and pain until the stones were slick with the blood of their enemies.

Wolff's praise affected Ratboy even more powerfully than the holy light had done. As he strode along the battlements, his gangly frame seemed to grow in stature, and his hoarse cries rang out over the cacophony, galvanising the soldiers as they sliced furiously through the torrent of limbs and teeth.

Despite the orders yelled down from the bell tower, it was Wolff and Ratboy who became the focus of the Ostlanders' defence. Every time the line faltered, the priest and his acolyte rallied the men and fought alongside them: Wolff with his pounding hammer and Ratboy with a borrowed sword clutched tightly in his one good hand.

As the hours rolled by, the tide of corruption slowed and then finally ceased. A sanguine dusk flooded the valley as the castle's defenders lowered their weapons. They leant weakly against each other and looked down at their handiwork. Mounds of warped, broken shapes lay all along the wall and across the courtyard, but after the initial assault, only a handful more of the Ostlanders had fallen. Lamplighters picked their way through the corpses, setting torches and beacons alight in every corner of the castle. Captain Felhamer and the other officers descended from the tower, embracing the soldiers in fierce hugs and praising them for their bravery, while Wolff followed behind, anointing the battered swords and shields that were lifted up to him.

Ratboy noticed a white-robed shape flitting across the wall towards them. It was Anna, and as she moved through the ranks of tired soldiers, she held a small bottle to their lips: a restorative of some kind, he guessed, from the colour it brought to their pale cheeks.

Joining Ratboy and Wolff, Anna shook her head at the grotesque shapes that surrounded them. On Wolff's orders, the bodies were being shovelled down into the courtyard to be burned, and as a nest of twitching limbs was hurled past her, Anna recoiled. 'What are they?' she asked.

Wolff looked up from his work, and shrugged. 'Daemons of a kind,' he replied. 'Lesser minions of the Ruinous Powers.' He shook his head. 'Such things have no right to exist in our world: they're torn from somewhere beyond the corporeal realm. Only the most powerful, unspeakable magic can wrench such horrors into the mortal world. This Mormius, or someone in his service, is a practitioner of the very darkest arts.' The priest looked out across the valley at the thousands of torches that had begun to punctuate the shadows. 'He must have expended great energy summoning such unholy regiments. No doubt he will be furious that they fared so badly against the simple faith of Felhamer's garrison.'

'So you think Felhamer still has a hope?' asked Anna, incredulously.

'Of course he has hope,' snapped Wolff. 'But hope is not always enough. This is just the beginning. I doubt Mormius will have expected such fierce resistance.' He waved at the crumbling walls. 'Not from such a wreck as this. He probably thought this would be the briefest of struggles – a mere prelude to the main act – but Felhamer's men have forced him to reconsider. Mormius has wasted huge numbers by throwing his force against them so carelessly. He'll plan his next move more carefully.'

'And what of us, master?' asked Ratboy. 'Are we to stay and fight after all? What of your brother?'

The priest frowned and looked away. 'Felhamer and his men are brave beyond anything I could have expected. They're sacrificing themselves, with no expectation of survival, in the hope that others might live. They're prepared to die for the good of an Empire that will never even know their names. These soldiers are everything that's strong and pure about this land.' He sighed. 'To abandon them is a betrayal of the worst kind – a betrayal of my own vows.' He turned to face Ratboy and Anna with doubt in his eyes. For a brief moment, his fierce mask slipped to reveal the face of a tired, confused old man. 'Everything has become so clouded this last year,' he said, rolling his head back across his broad shoulders and stretching the bones in his neck with a series of audible cracks. 'Sometimes it seems that there's no clear path any more.' He looked down at his friends' concerned faces. 'Can you understand? If I leave, these men will die, but if I stay, the whole campaign will be at risk – the whole province even.'

Ratboy shook his head. 'But in the meeting earlier you said–'

'I said what they needed to hear,' snapped the priest. He took a long, weary breath to steady his voice. 'I've struck a deal of sorts with Felhamer. If I fight with his men, until nightfall, he'll show us a passage up through the hills. There's an ancient network of tunnels beneath the citadel. No one knows who built them, but they predate even the tribes of Sigmar's day. It's a maze of dead ends and impassable doors, but Felhamer has a map. With his help, we can flee Mormius's hordes and abandon these poor souls to their fate.' He looked out at the quickly sinking sun. 'Soon, I'll have fulfilled my part of the bargain and we can go.'

Ratboy felt anger and confusion well up in him as he watched Anna sneering at his master. It enraged him to see the disgust in her eyes, but he could not help sympathising with her. When his master had addressed Felhamer and the others, his words had struck a powerful chord within him. He had accepted the truth of Wolff's speech as completely as the scriptures of the *Deus Sigmar*; but now he saw the words from another perspective entirely. He realised that Wolff knew all along that the men had no chance of victory. His words were calculated, cynical even, intended only to shame the men who had suggested a retreat. Ratboy opened his mouth to accuse his master, but the words dried up in his throat as he saw the anguish in Wolff's eyes. He nodded in silent agreement instead.

'I must do what I can for the captain,' said Wolff, taking his hammer from Ratboy and pointing it back at the castle's central keep. 'Prepare your things and meet me by the postern gate in ten minutes.' With that, he strode off through the milling crowds of soldiers, in the direction of Felhamer and the other officers.

'As old as it is, Mercy's End wasn't the first bastion to be built on this site,' explained Captain Felhamer as he led them through the deserted streets. 'When my ancestors laid the foundations, many centuries ago, they discovered the remains of an even older fortress.'

Ratboy looked away from the captain and noticed that Anna was listening to his words with a rapt expression on her face. He felt an odd rush of nausea as he saw the blushes that coloured her usually pale skin. What's so special about him, he wondered, looking at Felhamer's strong jaw, perfect teeth and tall, powerful physique. If you removed all those plates of armour and gaudy feathers he would probably look much like me, he decided.

'The architecture was like nothing they'd ever seen, or even read of,' continued Felhamer. 'The ruins were full of delicate, serpentine columns and tall arching windows – all crafted with incredible skill. Despite the obvious age of the stonework, almost all of the rooms were still intact.' The captain placed a hand on Anna's arm and gave her an excited grin. 'Imagine it,' he said, 'the handiwork of a forgotten race.'

Anna's blushes deepened and she smiled back at him, before lowering her gaze to the floor.

'People weren't so enlightened in those days, though,' he said, loosing her arm and turning to Ratboy. 'They were afraid of the strange sigils that adorned the walls, and imagined they had stumbled across some shrine to the Dark Gods.' He shook his head sadly. 'So they smashed the beautiful statues and filled the elegant rooms with rubble. Then they built Mercy's End right over the top of the old castle and forbade anyone to ever speak of it again.'

He led them into a tumbledown outbuilding and paused by a large set of trapdoors, half hidden beneath mounds of straw and dung. A group of bored-looking sentries leapt to attention as he approached, clanking their iron-clad boots and straightening their wide, felt hats.

Felhamer nodded brusquely at them, before clearing the straw away from the doors with his boot and turning to face Wolff and the others. 'For centuries the old ruins lay forgotten, until my great, great grandfather, Ernestus, ordered the building of a new well to cope with the demands of an expanding populace, and discovered this.' He reached beneath the slashed leather of his doublet and withdrew a slender knife, holding it out so that it glinted in the torchlight.

Anna gasped and stepped closer to Felhamer.

'Beautiful, isn't it?' asked the captain.

Ratboy shrugged and scowled at his feet, but Wolff answered. 'I've never seen anything quite like it,' he said, peering at the delicately engraved silver. 'Unless...' He looked closer, but then shook his head and said no more.

'Most of the relics have been lost over the years, but a few of the rooms have been unearthed.' The captain gave a proud smile. 'Many of them during my own tenure, actually. Most of the site was destroyed during the building of Mercy's End, but we've managed to clear several of the larger chambers, and we reopened a long passageway that emerges almost half a mile south of here, on the other side of the valley.' He gestured to one of the doors and a guard rushed to unlock it. 'I had a suspicion that it might come in useful some day,' he said, bending down and wrenching open one of the doors.

Wolff pulled open the other door and they all peered down into the oily blackness. The torchlight only reached the first few steps, but they were obviously made by master craftsmen, and still sound, even after centuries of neglect.

Felhamer took three torches from the walls of the outbuilding and handed them to Wolff, Anna and Ratboy. 'These should see you through to the other side,' he said, 'if you don't dawdle.' Then he took a scrap of parchment and handed it to the warrior priest. 'It's a simple map. There are only a few rooms still passable, and once you're into the main passageway, you just follow it till you reach the steps at the far end.' The captain stepped back and looked out at the encroaching darkness. His smile faltered as he remembered the task that awaited him. He shook his head at Wolff. 'Are you sure about this?' he asked, with a slight tremor in his voice. 'Is there no way you could stay? Even for a few days?' He gripped the priest's shoulder and his eyes filled with passion. 'With you to lead us, I believe we could hold back anything.'

Wolff looked away with a pained expression on his face. 'I can't,' he muttered. He handed his torch to Ratboy and placed a hand on the young captain's arm. 'Join me in prayer, for a moment,' he said. He led Felhamer to the far corner of the old barn and they knelt together on the straw. Ratboy could not hear their words, but as the priest led Felhamer in a series of muttered catechisms, the air began to hum with a tangible energy that tingled deep in his bones and raised the hairs on his arms. The torches spat and flickered oddly, and a sense of foreboding filled the room, as though a great storm were brewing. Ratboy saw that Anna and the guards had noticed it too; they were looking around nervously at the lurching shadows and had placed their hands on the hilts of their weapons, as though expecting an attack.

After a few minutes, Wolff and Felhamer rose to their feet and returned to the top of the steps. The captain's face was transformed. The fear had vanished from his eyes and there was a stern, determined line to his jaw. As he gripped Wolff's arm, his hand was trembling with emotion. 'Good luck, Brother Wolff,' he said. 'I shall not forget what you did for us here today. Whatever unholy powers your brother has allied himself to, I doubt they'll be a match for such unshakable faith as yours.'

Wolff nodded but his eyes were full of doubt. He gave no reply as he stepped down into the darkness.

CHAPTER ELEVEN

The Warrener

'Stay close,' muttered the priest as he trotted quickly down the steps. As his boots clattered across the ancient stone, the sound was swallowed by the thick gloom. The light from their torches only reached a few feet either side of them, but every now and then Ratboy glimpsed pale, delicate columns, rearing up into the blackness.

'Who could have built these rooms?' he whispered, afraid to disturb the centuries-old silence.

'Who can say?' replied Wolff, without breaking his stride. 'The world is old beyond reckoning. Man was certainly not the first race to inhabit these northern regions. Older, stranger folk came here long before we did.' As he turned to face Ratboy and Anna, the flickering light threw deep shadows across his brutal features. 'Some say that it was the dabbling of those ancient peoples that unleashed the winds of magic on the world; that they unshackled the Ruinous Powers and gave them access to our realm.' He shrugged and turned away. 'But if such a people ever did inhabit this place, they fled long ago, leaving us to deal with the consequences of their hubris.'

Wolff paused as they reached the bottom step, and held his torch over the map Felhamer had given him.

As the priest frowned at the scrap of parchment, Ratboy held his own torch aloft, peering into the gaping void that surrounded them. His light revealed nothing but rat bones and a few pale spiders that scuttled quickly back into the shadows. The air seemed different this far down though, and his throat grew tight at the thought of all the earth above their heads. A thousand childhood tales nagged at the edge of his memory: tales of creatures that lived below the earth. Were these chambers really uninhabited, he wondered?

'This way,' barked Wolff as he strode off to the left.

Ratboy and Anna had to move quickly to keep pace with the priest's broad strides, but they were keen not to lose sight of his torch. Without a map, it would be all too easy to get lost in the maze of archways and tunnels. They rushed through a succession of ornately carved doorways and Ratboy sensed from the echoes of their footfalls that each room they entered was slightly smaller than the last. As they crossed the third room, a flash of light caught his eye. Something was reflecting the glare of their torches. He guessed it was only a few feet away and veered off from Wolff's light for a minute to get a closer look.

'Ratboy,' snapped Anna, from behind, 'what are you doing?'

Her voice echoed strangely through the darkness and Wolff stopped immediately to see what was happening.

'There's something over here,' replied Ratboy, lowering his torch towards the glittering object. As the light washed over the dusty stone, a pale face grinned up at him and Ratboy yelped with shock.

'What's that?' cried Wolff, dashing over to his side and thrusting his torch towards the object. A skeleton lay sprawled across the flagstones. It was fractured, ancient, and obviously not human. The limbs were unnaturally slender and the skull was elongated in a way that none of them had ever seen before. Clutched in its hand was a slender, curved sword. Most of the blade was hidden beneath centuries of dust and cobwebs, but a tiny section of the hilt flashed merrily in the shifting firelight.

Anna staggered back from the bones with a look of horror on her face. 'Don't touch it,' she gasped, 'it's some kind of daemon.'

Ratboy didn't hear her. The glittering metal entranced him and before Wolff could stop him, he reached down and grabbed the sword.

'Let me see that,' growled the priest, snatching it away from him. He wiped away the dust and muck and held the sword up to his face. The blade flashed in the torchlight, scattering lances of brilliance around the chamber and revealing tantalising glimpses of the crumbling architecture. The sword itself was a thing of incredible beauty, and of a similar design to the knife Felhamer had showed them earlier. Delicate scrollwork ran along its entire length, depicting astrological symbols, and a series of long, sculpted characters were entwined around single red stone embedded in the hilt. Wolff peered at the sword for a few minutes, turning it slowly in his hands. Then he shrugged, and handed it back. 'This is no ordinary weapon,' he said, looking closely at Ratboy, 'but I can't see anything *unnatural* about its manufacture.' He watched as Ratboy cradled the sword in his trembling hands. 'It seems strange that it's lain here for all these centuries, hidden from everyone and yet the second you entered the room, you noticed it.'

Ratboy boy's eyes were wide with excitement as he ran a finger along the edge of the blade. He snatched his hand away with a gasp and placed his finger in his mouth. 'Still sharp,' he muttered, 'after all this time.'

Wolff nodded. 'It's a good sword.' He placed a hand on Ratboy's shoulder. 'Just be sure to tell me if you notice anything strange about it.' He looked at the twitching shadows that surrounded them. 'Well made is one thing, but an aspirant priest should always be on the look out for any signs of sorcery or occultism.'

Ratboy's face flushed with pride at the suggestion he could even aspire to being a priest. As they marched out of the chamber, he felt as though he had discovered two prizes in the dark beneath Mercy's End.

They passed into another chamber that smelled strongly of damp and rotting vegetation. Ratboy frowned at the overpowering stench and, after slotting the sword securely in his belt, he held his hand over his mouth to try to block out some of the stink. He looked back at Anna and she twisted her face into an exaggerated grimace.

They reached a doorway so wide that even when Ratboy stretched his arms out to their full extent, he couldn't touch the sides. It led into a broad, empty passageway that continued onwards, arrow straight for as far as they could see. 'This is the central route that leads up into the hills,' said Wolff, pausing for a moment so that they could catch their breath. He removed one of his vambraces and massaged the bruised muscles of his forearm. 'The next attack will have already begun,' he said in a voice tinged with regret. 'And I fear we hadn't seen the half of what Mormius had in store for Felhamer.'

Anna shrugged. 'I don't think we saw all that Felhamer had in store for the enemy either. There's a strength in him that won't be easily broken.'

Wolff nodded as he pulled his armour back on and strode forwards. 'You're right, sister,' he said, as they rushed after him. 'But I can't help feeling I've sent a good man to his grave. Many good men, in fact.'

Anna gave a hollow laugh that echoed strangely around the passageway. 'Isn't that your job, Brother Wolff?'

They walked in an awkward silence for a while, each lost in their own thoughts. After a while, the passageway began to slope upwards and the atmosphere grew a little less oppressive.

'This must be it,' said Wolff after nearly an hour had passed. Their torches lit up a pair of massive stone doors at the end of the passageway. 'If Felhamer was right, they should open out onto the far side of the valley.' As he reached the doors, he pressed his shoulder against them and shoved. The hinges groaned and the doors moved, but only an inch or so, and Wolff gave a bitter laugh. 'They're locked,' he said, peering through the gap. 'There's a chain on the other side.' He stepped back and lifted his warhammer from his back. 'Stand clear,' he said, as he prepared to smash it against the stone.

'Wait,' cried Anna, grabbing his arm. 'You must be joking. Those doors are a foot thick. You'll break your arm.'

'Master,' said Ratboy, rushing up to the door and drawing his new sword. 'Let me try.'

Wolff drew breath to speak, then shrugged and stepped back.

Ratboy peered through the gap and then slid the slender blade carefully through it. After a moment's pause, he lifted the sword and then brought it down with a grunt of exertion. It sliced downwards with a flash of sparks and clattered on the flagstones. Ratboy turned to give Wolff a mischievous grin before gently pushing the doors open to reveal the star-laden heavens beyond. The chain dangled at the edge of the door, sliced neatly through the middle. 'Well made indeed,' he said, proudly twirling his sword as he strode out into the cool night air.

As Felhamer had promised, they emerged nearly a mile away from Mercy's End. The door was cut into the far side of a small hollow, and the Forest of Shadows was spread out below them, for as far as the eye could see. They closed the doors carefully behind them and replaced the nettles and branches that grew over them. As they stepped out onto the hillside, Ratboy noticed with surprise that the doors had completely disappeared from view. He remembered his master's instruction to be vigilant for signs of sorcery, but bit his tongue. If the doors had remained hidden for all these centuries, he did not think he should be the one to ask why.

They clambered up to the top of the hill, savouring the cool night air and the open sky above their heads. Once they had reached the summit, they looked back towards the castle. It was adrift amongst an ocean of flickering lights and even from this distance there was something sinister about the fires. Greens and blues mingled with the more natural yellows and every now and then great gouts of flame would erupt from one of the lumbering, indistinct shapes that towered over the crush of smaller figures.

'They're still holding on,' said Wolff, with a note of awe.

Ratboy peered at the castle and saw that his master was right. Fire had spread all along the battlements, but Felhamer's banners were still flying. The black and white designs were tinged a sickly green by the daemonic fires raging beneath them, but they were a clear sign that the citadel had not fallen.

'What happened to Gryphius?' exclaimed Anna suddenly. 'Is he still down there?'

Wolff nodded. 'I think I may have underestimated him. I took him for a mere dilettante, but he has proved himself to be much more than that.' He turned to Anna and noticed the tears that suddenly glistened in her eyes. 'There's nothing to be done for a man such as that, sister. His wounds are old and deep. But I assured him that he will find peace at last in this battle – whatever the outcome.'

'Peace in death, you mean?' she snapped. 'Do you really think the only way to ease a broken heart is to stop it?'

Wolff shrugged. 'We should keep moving,' he said, ignoring her question and turning away from the besieged ruin. 'We aren't safe travelling in such a small group. The sooner we can find von Raukov's army the better.'

With that he jogged down the hill towards the trees, leaving his acolyte to bear the brunt of Anna's fury.

'Pig-headed hammer hurler,' she muttered, scowling at the priest's back. She turned on Ratboy. 'Why do you people always believe bloodshed is such a cure-all?'

Ratboy shrugged, in unconscious imitation of his master and moved to follow him.

'Wait,' said Anna, grabbing his arm. 'How's your hand?'

Ratboy paused as she removed the bandages.

'Improving a bit, I think,' she said, in the same angry tones. She unclasped a small bag that was slung over her shoulder, and removed a large dried leaf. As she pressed it onto the wound, Ratboy's eyes widened with pain. 'Don't be such a child,' she said as she replaced the bandages and rushed after the quickly disappearing Wolff. 'It will do you good.'

As they reached the edge of the trees, Wolff paused and looked up at the shadow moon, Morrslieb. It was hanging unusually low in the sky and seemed to be almost resting on the black, shifting peaks of the forest. As Ratboy and Anna approached, gasping for breath, he turned to them with an odd smile. 'What a choice,' he said, gesturing to the trees. 'Take our chances beneath these malign boughs, or risk the open country.'

'I've spent my entire life crossing this forest,' replied Anna. 'The trees themselves are no more dangerous than a field of corn.' She shrugged. 'And wise travellers know how to move without calling too much attention to themselves.' She waved at the hills that surrounded them. 'Mormius will doubtless have many more recruits heading this way. I think it would be safest to use the cover of the trees.'

Wolff nodded. 'You're right, of course.' He glanced up at Morrslieb again and frowned. 'Let's tread carefully, though.'

Their feet sank deep into the loamy, grey soil as they crept beneath the sombre boughs of the forest. Countless tiny creatures scampered away at their approach. Aspens and pines reached up over them, fracturing the lurid moonlight and scattering it across the ivy, bracken and brambles that carpeted the ground.

They moved forward in a watchful silence, slipping lightly through the shadows and over the fallen leaves and branches. Ratboy shivered and pulled his cloak a little tighter. Ostland was rarely warm, but as they moved onwards through the dewy groves the trees seemed to amplify the autumnal chill.

Anna seemed quite at home in the forest and scouted ahead, creeping quickly through the thicket and pausing every now and then to unearth toadstools and seeds and drop them in her bag. As she reached the edge of a small clearing, she paused and crouched low to the ground, pressing her hands down onto the springy turf. She turned back to Wolff and Ratboy and raised a finger to her mouth as they approached.

They stooped down beside her to see what she had found. At first Ratboy could see nothing in the pale moonlight, but Anna traced her finger around a series of shapes embedded in the grass. It looked like the tracks of a large, hoofed animal, but as Anna glanced nervously around the clearing, Ratboy guessed these were no natural tracks.

Anna's eyes were wide with fear as she rose to her feet and pressed her finger to her mouth again, before skirting around the edge of the clearing. They re-entered the trees and continued on their way, but Anna was now moving much slower and with even more care than before. After ten minutes or so, she crouched behind a tree trunk and signalled for them to approach quietly.

Wolff and Ratboy crept up beside the priestess and followed the direction of her gaze. Down below them was a small gulley, cutting through the trees, and a column of figures was hurrying silently along it. Ratboy felt a rush of fear as he watched the shadowy procession. There was something dreamlike about the scene. It was hard to see clearly in the dark of the forest, but they were clearly not human. Their broad, naked chests were covered with a thick hide of fur and their bestial heads were crowned with gnarled, vicious horns. Talismans and fetishes dangled from their massive, tattooed arms and cruel, ugly weapons hung from their belts. An acrid, animal stink came from them that was so powerful the three travellers instinctively covered their noses. Beastmen, thought Ratboy, clutching his sword with fear. He had encountered such creatures of Chaos before, but had never become accustomed to them. He looked up at his master, wondering what they would do.

Wolff's face was filled with disgust as he watched the creatures rushing by, but as he caught Ratboy's questioning look he shook his head and gestured for them to back away.

They crept with painstaking slowness away from the gulley, and only after several minutes, did anyone dare to speak.

'We're safe for the moment,' whispered Anna. 'We're downwind from them,' she explained, with a grimace at the awful smell that had followed them from the gulley. 'And they seemed to be in quite a hurry.' She frowned. 'In fact, they were oddly disciplined for beastmen. From what I know of their nature, they rarely behave like that.'

'They were probably headed for Mercy's End,' replied Wolff. 'Mormius must have great power at his command to bring order to such rabble.'

'Is there nothing we can do to stop them?' asked Ratboy. 'Felhamer has so many men pitted against him already. Maybe we could set up some kind of ambush?'

Wolff shook his head. 'There are far too many of them. We can't risk it. And anyway, even if we could stop this one small group, what difference would it make? Remember why we left Mercy's End. I have to find out what part my brother has to play in all this.'

Anna nodded eagerly, keen to stay as far away from the beastmen as possible. 'If we keep to the higher ground, they won't even know we were here,' she whispered, and started clambering up a steep escarpment that led away from the gulley.

After five minutes or so they reached a wide, moonlit plateau that reared up above the treetops and gave them a clear view over the surrounding forest. Far behind them, they could make out the silhouette of Mercy's End. The ruin was still bejewelled with the strange lights, but it was impossible from this distance to see how the battle was progressing. Ratboy took comfort from the fact that there was clearly some kind of movement along the castle walls.

At least it hasn't been burned to the ground, he thought.

'What's that?' asked Anna, pointing in the opposite direction.

West of the plateau, was another collection of lights, nestling in the northern foothills of the Middle Mountains. 'Is that Ferlangen?' she asked, peering through darkness.

Wolff shook his head. 'We're still too far east.' He frowned as he studied the lights. 'There are no cities in that direction. It must be an encampment. And a large one at that.'

'Von Raukov?' asked Ratboy, hopefully.

The priest nodded. 'Let's pray that it is.' He looked down at the forest that lay between them and the distant lights. 'If we make good speed, we could reach them by tomorrow night.'

Ratboy looked around with disappointment at the soft turf that covered the hilltop. 'I suppose that doesn't leave any time for a quick rest?'

Anna shook her head in disbelief. 'Have you forgotten what we just saw? These trees are probably crawling with those creatures. Would you really be able to shut your eyes with such horrors for bedfellows?'

'Quite,' said Wolff, answering for him. 'We keep moving.' He waved back towards Mercy's End. 'Felhamer's garrison could be defeated at any time, and this whole region will be overrun with Mormius's horde.'

They spent the rest of the night rushing through the trees in complete silence. After the sight of the beastmen, none of them wanted to risk drawing any attention to themselves and Ratboy had to bite his tongue on several occasions, as his imagination painted horned shapes on the sombre shadows. The threat was not always in Ratboy's mind, however. On one occasion they were forced to clamber into a ditch as a band of mounted marauders broke from the trees, heading north to join the battle. It was only Anna's keen sense of smell that saved them. Noticing an odd scent on the wind, she herded Ratboy and Wolff into the ditch, just seconds before the horsemen charged by. The priest was forced to give her a grudging nod of respect as they dragged themselves back up from the bed of damp, rotten leaves.

Gradually, as dawn approached, the trees began to thin out, interspersed with large areas of scrub and bracken. The sky behind them shifted from black to a deep azure, and a chorus of birdsong erupted from the branches. Wrens and nuthatches scattered at their approach, trilling petulantly as the heavy-footed interlopers hurried past.

As the first rays of sunlight began to warm the backs of their necks, the scattered trees were replaced by featureless moorland, and Wolff began to pick up the pace, urging his already exhausted companions into a brisk jog.

'Look,' hissed Anna, as they approached a long, winding hawthorn hedge. 'It's one of the creatures.'

Wolff and Ratboy stumbled to a halt as they saw what she was referring to. Something was curled up beneath the hedge. It was mostly hidden from view by the thick mass of leaves, but the grubby fur on its twisted, hunched back was clearly visible and as they slowly approached, a croaking snore rang out.

Wolff and Ratboy cautiously drew their weapons as they approached the hedge.

They were within a few feet of the sleeping figure, when it sensed their presence and lurched up out of the hedge, staggering towards them with its arms raised.

Wolff raised his hammer to strike, but Anna grabbed his arm and cried out in alarm.

'Wait,' she cried. 'He's human.'

'Sigmar, you're right,' gasped Wolff, lowering his weapon and looking down at the creature with amazement.

But as the man shuffled towards the three travellers, rubbing the sleep from his eyes, Ratboy wondered if Anna might be mistaken. His spine was so hunched and twisted that his face barely came up to Ratboy's chest, and he had to wrench his head awkwardly onto one side to look up at them. His whole misshapen body was wrapped in a stinking mass of old, mangy rabbit skins and strange contraptions of metal and wire that clattered as he moved. Ratboy guessed that some of the metal objects were traps, but there were many other things he couldn't identify: clumps of feather, tied together with thick cords of grass, little idols made of shell and animal bones that rattled as he reached his crooked arms out towards them. His loose, wet lips sagged down in a duck-like pout, but as he looked up at Wolff, they spread into a grin of recognition, revealing a single, large tooth. 'Priest,' he said in a thick, phlegmy voice.

Ratboy flinched at the sight of the man's face. Dozens of warts and growths had warped his pale, pockmarked flesh so that he almost resembled the mutated creatures they had fought on the walls of Mercy's End.

Anna noticed Ratboy's disgust and gave him a quick scowl of disapproval before stooping to speak to the strange man. 'Who are you?' she asked gently, taking his gnarled hand fearlessly into her own.

'Helwyg,' grunted the man, gripping her hand tightly and licking his wide, drooping lips in excitement. 'The warrener.' As he spoke to Anna, his large, watery eyes kept flicking to Wolff and he seemed eager to speak to him.

'Your names?' he asked, struggling a little to force the words from his deformed mouth.

'Anselm, Anna and I'm Brother Jakob Wolff,' replied the priest, stepping closer. 'What are you doing out here alone? These forests are crawling with the enemy. It's not safe to walk alone.'

'Soldiers need food,' said the little man with a grin, licking his lips again. 'They sent the warrener for coneys.' He shrugged. 'But Helwyg is no hunter.' He gestured to the hedge. 'Got tired. Sat down.' He chuckled. 'Fell asleep.'

'Soldiers, you say?' asked Wolff. 'Whose army are you travelling with?'

'Iron Duke,' replied Helwyg with a moist lisp. He shuffled towards Wolff and pawed at his scarlet robes. 'The saviour,' he explained, spreading his arms with a rattle of springs and bones, 'of the Empire.'

'The elector count, you mean,' asked Wolff, frowning. 'Are you talking about von Raukov?'

Helwyg shook his head.

'Is it Ostlanders you're marching with?'

Helwyg gave a vague nod, but his attention seemed to have wandered. He was fingering the thick chains that fixed Wolff's holy texts to his cuirass and eyeing the gold filigree that decorated the edges of his gorget. 'Mighty priest,' he muttered. 'Jakob Wolff.'

Wolff nodded impatiently and backed away from the strange, hunched figure. 'Can you lead us to the army?' he asked, trying to hide his disgust as the man's grasping fingers followed him.

The warrener grinned, and began to stroke the objects that were strapped across his furs, eying Wolff's armour the whole time. 'Yes,' he said. As he turned and began lurching slowly away, he clapped his hands with excitement. 'Priests are better than coneys.'

After the race through the tunnels, Helwyg's awkward, shuffling gait seemed painfully slow, but from what little they could see of him, beneath the layers of grubby fur, his legs were as ruined as the rest of him. Ratboy, for one, was glad of the slower pace, and took the opportunity to examine his new sword a little more closely, tracing the strange runes on its hilt with his finger and wondering what they might mean.

After a couple of hours, Anna grew impatient with Helwyg's tortuous slowness. She began scouting ahead and peering into the growing light to see if she could spot the army. Finally, as the sun reached its zenith and a light rain began to waft across the fields towards them, she called back from the top of a small incline. 'They're here,' she cried, pointing in the direction of some low, quick-moving rain clouds. 'We've found them.'

The others rushed to her side and looked down over a wide plateau. A huge army was spread out before them, camped under a dazzling panoply of banners bearing not just the bull of Ostland, but the emblems of several other provinces too. The rain was coming down harder with every minute, and it was hard to see the encampment clearly, but Ratboy guessed there must be thousands of men down there, cleaning their weapons and preparing for battle.

'Thank Sigmar,' said Wolff, turning to the others. 'These must be von Raukov's men. And they're not much more than a day's march from Mercy's End.' He lifted one of the books that hung at his side and kissed it. 'My brother must be down there somewhere.'

'Brother?' asked Helwyg, shuffling towards him.

Wolff gave a brusque nod, but said no more on the subject as he strode off down the hill.

Close up, the scale of the army became utterly bewildering. As they entered the encampment a crush of figures barged blindly past them: soldiers, swineherds, blacksmiths, ostlers, merchants and messengers, all dashing through streets of gaudy canvas as the army prepared to decamp. Ratboy had never seen such a gathering of humanity and without Wolff to lead him, he would have cowered beneath the first available cart. The mouth-watering aroma of frying sausage meat mingled with the tang of unwashed bodies and the sweet stink of infected wounds. His master strode purposefully onwards through the pandemonium. He picked out a black banner, emblazoned with a golden griffon and headed straight towards it.

Helwyg strained his neck to look at the distant banner and grinned. 'Priest has priestly friends?' he asked, hobbling after Wolff and clutching at his burnished armour.

Wolff gave a brusque nod. 'It's unusual to see Knights Griffon so far from Altdorf,' he said.

'Knights Griffon?' asked Ratboy.

Wolff gave a sigh of annoyance at being asked so many questions. 'Yes, Knights Griffon. They're closely linked to my own order,' he snapped. 'As you should well know.' At the sight of Ratboy's blushes, he softened his voice a little and gestured to the crowds of soldiers that surrounded them. 'A familiar face might be useful if we want to find out what's happening here.'

As they neared the banner, Ratboy saw flashes of polished steel glinting between the tents; then, as they turned a final corner, he saw the Knights Griffon revealed in all their glory. Seemingly blind to the chaos that surrounded them, the knights were lined up in calm, orderly ranks as their captain rode slowly between them, carefully inspecting their gleaming armour and their impressive array of weaponry. Ratboy had never seen such an obvious display of wealth and power. Everything about the knights, from their polished, plumed helmets, to the scalloped barding on their destriers, was intricately worked and lovingly polished. Even the dour Ostland rain only added to the effect, as it washed over the oiled steel of their visors.

The captain was a grizzled old veteran, whose short, silver beard seemed as hard and glinting as his fluted helmet. At the sight of Wolff, his leathery face split into a broad smile and he threw his arms open in greeting. 'Brother Jakob Wolff, as I live and breathe,' he said, with a voice like the rumble of thunder. 'What an unexpected blessing.'

The captain dismounted and the two towering figures embraced with a clatter of armour. Then they stood back and peered into each other's faces.

'I seem to remember a little black amongst the grey,' said Wolff, nodding to the knight's fringe of silver hair.

'Well, yes, some of us *were* young once, Jakob. Unlike your good self of course – I'm reliably informed that you left the womb with a shaven head and the Holy Scriptures in your fist.'

A strange growling noise came from Wolff's throat and after a few seconds Ratboy realised it was laughter. It was a sound he'd never heard before and he turned to Anna with a bemused look on his face.

The priestess rolled her eyes.

'Maximilian von Düring,' sighed Wolff, visibly relaxing at the sight of his old friend. 'It's good to see you, baron. I have much to ask.'

Maximilian dismissed his knights with a wave of his hand and gestured for Wolff to follow him to his tent. 'If your squires speak to my quartermaster, he'll find them some food,' he said.

Anna's eyes flashed with indignation and Wolff shook his head. 'Ah, no, Maximilian, let me introduce–'

He paused as he noticed the expectant face of Helwyg looking up at him. 'Thank you for your help,' he said, nodding to the warrener. 'You may return to your work.'

Helwyg looked a little disappointed at being dismissed, but nodded all the same. 'Always glad,' he slurred, before shuffling away into the jostling crowds of lackeys and liegemen.

'As I was saying,' continued Wolff, 'this is my noviciate Anselm, who goes under the name of Ratboy, and our travelling companion is Sister Anna Fleck, of the Order of the Bleeding Heart.'

Maximilian frowned and gave a deep bow. 'Apologies,' he said. 'I should have noticed your clerical robes. This miserable Ostland weather paints everything a muddy brown.'

Anna gave a brisk nod, but Ratboy mirrored the baron's deep bow and his face lit up at being greeted so graciously by a knight of such high rank.

'Let's get out of this rain for a minute,' said the baron and gestured to his tent. 'Mobilising a force of this size takes a while. We still have an hour or two at our disposal, I should think.'

The baron's tent had the austere look of a monk's cell. Beyond a few sheets rolled up in the corner there was just a small table and a couple of books. The four of them sat on the ground, just inside the door, as the rain drummed on the canvas stretched above their heads.

'Something has changed in you since we last met,' decided Maximilian, once they had finished exchanging the usual pleasantries. He peered closely into Wolff's eyes. 'And I don't just mean a few extra grey hairs.'

Wolff looked a little awkward under his friend's intense stare and seemed unsure how to reply to so direct a statement. He glanced at Ratboy, as though ordering him to bite his tongue. Then he shrugged. 'The last year or so has been difficult for everyone. I imagine we're all a little changed.'

The baron nodded, slowly. 'That's true, Jakob, but you of all people know how to find comfort in the sacred texts and scriptures. Your belief has been a constant inspiration to me whenever I felt afraid. I know the strength of your faith: it is as immovable as the earth beneath our feet; but I see some kind of doubt in your eyes that wasn't there before.' He leant forward. 'Tell me, old friend, what's brought you here, at this precise moment?'

Wolff examined the back of his gloves, spreading his fingers thoughtfully and then clenching his fists, before meeting the baron's gaze. 'I entered the church at a very young age,' he said quietly, 'as you know. But I only intended to become a sacristan or an archivist of some kind. My interest was chiefly in the study of holy tracts and sacred artefacts, rather than in the martial aspects of our faith.'

A look of surprise crossed Anna's face and she moved to speak, but Wolff continued.

'I only decided to devote myself to the life of a mendicant warrior priest as penance for what I believed was a terrible betrayal,' he lowered his voice even more, 'of my own parents.'

Wolff paused, seemingly overcome with emotion at the memory.

His three listeners waited patiently for him to continue.

'However,' he continued, looking up at Ratboy, 'penance can only carry one so far. I've failed and abandoned so many stout-hearted friends that I began to feel a fraud. I felt as though my faith was built on foundations of sand.' The baron shook his head urgently, but Wolff continued. 'And then, to top it all, I recently discovered that the crime was never mine to pay penance for. It was another man entirely who betrayed my parents.' He shrugged. 'But, in a way, that discovery gave me a new resolve. The man I speak of is a cultist of the worst sort.' He looked desperately at Maximilian. 'And I believe he's right here, marching in von Raukov's army.'

The baron shook his head. 'This army is von Raukov's in name only.

The elector count was seriously injured during the recent defence of Wolfenberg. He'll be bedridden for weeks, if not months.'

'Then who's leading you?'

The baron smiled. 'A great general indeed,' he answered. 'They call him the Iron Duke. He shares your surname, actually,' he said with wry smile. 'His name is Kriegsmarshall Fabian Wolff.'

Helwyg shuffled slowly though the crowds as pavilions toppled all around him, crumbling to the ground in great billowing piles of muddy canvas. Even the thick hides that enveloped him could not hide the odd, jerking nature of his movements. The soldiers were too busy checking their weapons and readying the horses to pay him much attention, so he was able to snake undisturbed through the encampment. After nearly an hour, he reached the command tents: towering, bunting-clad behemoths that loomed over everything else. As he lurched towards the largest tent, the Iron Duke's honour guard eyed him with distaste from beneath their lupine, sculpted helmets, but made no move to prevent him entering.

Once inside, Helwyg fastened the doors behind him and looked around the tent to make sure it was empty. Then he approached an ornate throne, silhouetted against a row of torches at the back of the tent. He fell awkwardly to one knee and lowered his head respectfully, then climbed to his feet again and began to remove his grubby furs. They dropped to his feet in a stinking pool of sweat and mud and he stepped to one side, completely naked. Deprived of its protective covering, the extent of his body's deformity was revealed. His limbs were crooked and twisted almost beyond recognition and the serpentine curves of his spine were clearly visible beneath his filthy skin.

He began to scratch at the greasy strands of hair that crowned his head, digging his fingers deep into his scalp with such force that streams of dark blood began to flow quickly over his face. He showed no sign of pain though, and as his dirty fingernails sliced under the skin, he pulled it away from the bone. A thick flap of scalp came free with a soft tearing sound. He pulled it forwards, down over his face, to reveal a mass of blood-slick feathers beneath. The streams of blood became rivers as he wrenched open his chest cavity, spilling his organs across the ground in a steaming mass, revealing his true form: a small, willowy man, covered in blue iridescent feathers that shimmered as he moved. He stretched to his full height and sighed with relief. 'I've found him,' he said, with a proud smile spreading across his thin, avian features.

'Are you sure?' came a low voice from the throne.

'Yes, my lord,' piped the creature. He stepped closer, wiping the blood and sinew from his feathers. 'It was your brother. I heard his name quite clearly: Jakob Wolff.'

A tall, slender knight rose from the throne and stepped slowly into the torchlight. His face was long and aristocratic. The flames were reflected in his coat of burnished mail, and in the jewels that adorned a leather patch over his left eye. He stepped towards the feathered man and took his head in his hands, stooping to plant a passionate kiss on his bloody forehead. 'Then your soul is assured its place alongside mine in eternity, Helwyg.' He twirled his elegant, waxed moustache between his fingers and turned away from his servant. 'How did you discover him? Is his presence widely known?'

Helwyg skipped lightly after him. 'In all truth, lord, he found me. I'd given up the search. I was planning to return this very morning and inform you that you must be mistaken. Then, as I took a brief nap, just outside camp, he stumbled across me, looking for a guide.'

Fabian's shoulders shook with laughter. 'How delicious are the devices of our master?' He looked down at Helwyg. 'And who knows of his presence?'

'As you predicted, kriegsmarshall, he made straight for the Knights Griffon and has approached no one else.' He shrugged, 'Wolff is a common enough surname, and in a gathering of this size, no one will guess at any connection. He wouldn't be foolish enough to openly accuse you. Apart from maybe to his pious friend, Maximilian; but what could they do alone? Who would believe them? After all your glorious victories, these men would slit the throat of anyone who spoke against you. And how could Jakob prove you're his brother?' Helwyg looked up at his master. 'You don't even look alike.'

Fabian nodded and a smile lit up his hawk-like features. 'It's true, I always did take after mother.' He returned to his throne and sat down. 'You've done well, Helwyg. I now have my brother exactly where I wanted him. Whatever he has planned, it's safest that I keep him close to me. Watch him closely. At *all* times.' He looked up at his servant. 'You can't leave like that though, Helwyg,' he said, nodding to the shimmering feathers.

Helwyg's narrow shoulders slumped dejectedly and he pouted. 'I've been limping around in that warrener's body for weeks,' he said, wrinkling his nose. 'And he stank even before I killed him.'

Fabian narrowed his eyes.

'Very well,' muttered Helwyg, peevishly. He scoured the shadows of the tent and after a few moments he pounced, flying across the room in a blur of talons and feathers. There was a muffled squeak and then a rat scampered out of the darkness. It nodded its head once at Fabian and slipped away, through a small gap at the bottom of the tent doors.

Fabian leant back in his throne with a sigh of satisfaction. Then, he lifted his patch to reveal a running black sore where his eye should have been. The scab glistened with moisture and it swelled and bulged as a shape began to move beneath it. After a few seconds, the scab parted like a small mouth, dangling strands of white pus over a black, featureless orb. 'O Great Schemer,' said the general, 'guide me.' The orb began to roll in its socket, as it perceived a torrent of shapes and colours. For a while the general could not discern anything beyond the vaguest outlines and textures, but soon he began to make out specific images: tall, crooked trees, looming over a gloomy forest path; an ancient grove, throbbing with eldritch light; a narrow defile, clogged with weeping, dying men and finally, a glittering, winged knight bearing down on him with a long sword in his hand. A breeze slipped beneath the canvas walls and became a whisper, calling to Fabian from the shadows. 'Deliver me from Mormius,' it said. 'Send him to the abyss. I will raise you up in his place.'

'But master,' replied Fabian, gripping the arms of his throne. 'What of my brother?'

There was no reply, and as suddenly as they had come, the visions ceased. Fabian replaced the patch and sat back in his throne with a frustrated sigh. 'Oh, Jakob,' he breathed. 'A promise is a promise, no matter how many years have passed. How can you dare to approach me, even now?' He closed his uncorrupted right eye, and cast his mind back through the decades, to a distant summer's day and a room in his father's house.

CHAPTER TWELVE

Blood Ties

'Fabian,' called a thin, musical voice. 'Come and say hello to your brother.'

Fabian stared morosely through a wide bay window onto the secluded valley outside. He was only fourteen, but already felt as though life had betrayed him. He pressed his face to the warm, leaded glass and as he looked out at the sunlit idyll of his parents' estate, he wept. A glorious jumble of orchards and wildflower meadows lay sleepily across the hillside, surrounding the long drive that led down to the gatehouse, where the servants were unloading his father's coach. He lolled back into a mountain of damask cushions and wiped away hot, angry tears. 'I'm busy,' he replied, picking up a book of folk tales that lay forgotten on the table next to him.

An azure cloud of embroidered silk bustled into the drawing room. 'Fabian,' scolded his mother, frowning at him through her pince nez. 'Don't pout. We haven't seen Jakob for months. Brother Braun said in his letter that he's done exceptionally well in his studies.'

'Really,' replied Fabian, nonchalantly turning a page and refusing to look up from the book. 'You *do* surprise me.'

'Fabian…' repeated his mother in a stern voice, gesturing to the open door.

'Very well,' he replied, accepting defeat and snapping the book shut. 'Although I really don't see why everything must stop at merest mention of the word "Jakob".'

He followed his mother out through the carpeted reception rooms and into the garden. The verges and borders were ablaze with colour and he immediately felt his nose tingle at the scent of the honeysuckle that trailed over the house's pink-grey stone. He held a handkerchief to his face, in the hope it would give him some protection.

The façade of Berlau house was covered with dozens of tall windows, and as the new arrivals approached, they had to shield their eyes against the inferno of light reflected in the glass.

'Jakob,' cried his mother, unable to contain her excitement at seeing her firstborn. She dashed across the small courtyard and threw her arms around the youth, smothering him with kisses. 'I swear you look even taller,' she exclaimed, hugging him tightly.

'Margarethe,' said the elegant, elderly gentleman next to Jakob. 'Really – you'll suffocate the poor boy.' Even dressed in his mud-splattered travelling clothes, Fabian's father looked every inch the nobleman. The nostrils of his long, aquiline nose flared at such a gaudy display of emotion and he ground his heel angrily into the cobbles. Despite his annoyance, though, he could not hide the proud gleam in his eye as he placed a hand on Jakob's shoulder. 'Let him change, at least, before you drown him in syrup.'

Margarethe stepped back, and allowed the boy to head inside. 'You are cruel to me, Hieronymus,' she said, giving her husband a coy smile. Then, she nodded to the old priest waiting patiently next to her husband. 'Brother Braun,' she trilled. 'It's good to see you.'

The man nodded his tonsured head. 'Frau Wolff,' he said, kissing the fingers she dangled before him. 'The pleasure is all mine, I assure you.'

'Come inside,' she said, taking his hand. 'You must be tired out in this heat. I'll order us some drinks and you can tell me your news.'

As the priest entered the house, he bowed to Fabian, who was slouched just inside the entrance hall.

Fabian nodded slightly in reply but did not return the priest's smile.

'Busy as ever, I see, Fabian,' said Hieronymus, as he approached his son.

Fabian gave his father an ironic grin, before sauntering back into the house and following his brother upstairs.

He found Jakob in the library, replacing a few books he had taken at the start of the summer. Unlike the rest of the house, the library was swathed in a cool gloom, and as Fabian approached his brother he squinted, purblind, at the texts. 'The Relations of Matter and Faith,' he read. 'Sounds gripping.'

'Hello, Fabian,' replied Jakob, continuing to slide the books back into the dusty spaces on the shelves.

Fabian studied him. Since his revelation a few years earlier, Jakob's passion for all things ecclesiastical had transformed him. Not just spiritually, either. His burgeoning faith seemed to have fed his adolescent body too. He now towered over his slender young brother, and there was a wholesome robustness about him that nauseated Fabian. He was a vision of perfect Ostland youth: even, white teeth; thick, black hair; broad, muscled shoulders and clear, intelligent eyes. Everything about him seemed designed to show the slight, bookish Fabian in an unfavourable light.

'What's dragged you back amongst us weak sinners?' he asked, dropping into a chair. 'I thought you'd end your days in that draughty ruin.'

'Brother Braun's temple *is* a little ramshackle,' replied Wolff, coming to sit next to Fabian and starting to unlace his muddy jerkin. 'But too many home comforts can be a distraction from contemplation.'

'I'm quite fond of my home comforts,' said Fabian, before breaking off into a series of hacking coughs. 'Wretched flowers,' he wheezed asthmatically, sitting bolt upright as he tried to calm his breathing.

Jakob eyed his brother with concern. 'Can I help?'

Fabian shook his head and took a few more whistling breaths before replying. 'You could pray, maybe,' he gasped. Once he had wiped his streaming eyes, Fabian looked at his brother. 'Tell me,' he said. 'While you're contemplating, do your thoughts ever include the shameful state of your own family?'

'Shameful? The name Wolff is a well-respected one,' replied Jakob, frowning in confusion. 'It has been for centuries.'

Fabian gave a hollow laugh. 'You've been away a long time, brother. Things have changed.'

'I'm not sure I understand you,' replied Jakob, rising to his feet and eyeing his brother suspiciously. 'But I can see at least one thing that hasn't changed. You're as angry and ungrateful as ever. Look at you – born into the lap of luxury and as bitter as a starving orphan. What have you got to complain about?'

'Our father's become a laughing stock, Jakob,' said Fabian, flushing with anger. 'Even a dullard like you, with your head full of prophets and miracles, must be aware of it. He thinks of nothing but the Sigmarite Church. While the stewards rob us blind, marauders are running unchallenged across our estates. The whole of Ostland is almost overrun and the elector count needs every sword he can get, but our father spends all his time praying.' He clenched his fists. 'And signing away our inheritance to charitable causes.' He levelled a finger at his brother. 'And all because of the sycophantic drivel Braun pours in his ear. He can't think about anything useful since that senile old fool convinced him you're some kind of holy protégé.'

Jakob's lip curled in a sneer of disgust. 'Maybe if you didn't spend your whole time reading ridiculous novels, *you* could achieve something with your life. Then you might not be so consumed with jealousy.'

Fabian leapt to his feet and squared up to his brother; undeterred by the fact that his face barely reached Jakob's broad chest. 'The bailiffs all laugh at him behind his back, Jakob. They take wages for soldiers they sacked months ago, and leave the gatehouses unmanned. They pocket the profits from the harvest and tell him the crops all failed. But the old fool won't believe me when I tell him what a bunch of crooks they are. Berlau is barely defended at all these days. But father just tells me about the new chapterhouse he's funding or shows me a sketch of some new chancel in Wolfenberg that Braun has convinced him to pay for. He's pissing all over our family name, Jakob. He's forgotten his heritage. Another few years of this neglect and Berlau House will be as ruined as Braun's temple.'

'I'm not in the mood for this rubbish, Fabian,' said Jakob, turning to leave. He paused at the door and glared back at his brother. 'You're not a child anymore. You should learn to be a bit more respectful when talking about our father. He's a good man.'

'Really?' replied Fabian, striding after him and jabbing a finger into his chest. 'You think you can come back here, after spending months peering into your navel, and tell me what kind of man our father is?'

Jakob grabbed his brother's shoulders and slammed him back into the bookshelves. 'Watch yourself,' he whispered as leather-bound volumes thudded to the floor around them. 'Sigmarite doctrine doesn't tend to preach forgiveness.' He pushed Fabian back against the shelves, so that the boy grimaced with pain. 'Don't take me for a pious sop. I'm still a Wolff.'

For a few seconds the boys stood there, glaring at each other with complete hatred. Then Fabian flared his nostrils and twisted his face into an exaggerated frown. 'The blood of a Wolff runs true,' he said, in note-perfect imitation of their father's low, booming voice.

Jakob held his brother for a few more seconds, scowling furiously, then the tension suddenly exploded from his lungs in a bark of laughter. He stepped back, shaking his head and started to giggle 'The blood of a Wolff,' he gasped, in the same ridiculous low voice Fabian had used, 'does indeed run true.'

'Boys,' came their mother's voice. 'Stop playing and come down for a drink. We're in the Long Gallery.'

The two brothers were still chuckling as they marched obediently down the stairs.

'There's only so much I can teach him,' Braun was saying as they entered the room. He was stood in front of a window that looked out onto a sun-dappled orchard and as he spoke he dabbed repeatedly at his face with a damp handkerchief. 'He's already surpassed me in several areas,' he explained, waving at Jakob. 'Your son can recite *The Life of Sigmar* in its entirety as easily as I can recall a simple prayer.' He shook his head in wonder. 'I've never seen anything quite like it, to be honest. I've already allowed him to perform some important ordinances and observations, and he executed them with startling success. For instance, only last Wellentag he recited the most beautiful threnody for a recently deceased goat.' He paused, and closed his eyes, seemingly holding back tears. 'Old Man Göbel loved that animal more dearly than his own children and your son's eloquence was a great comfort to him.'

'Then what are you suggesting?' asked Hieronymus. There was no trace of emotion on his stern face, but a slight tremor in his voice betrayed his excitement. 'Is the boy ready to be fully ordained into the church?'

Braun shrugged. 'It's always hard to gauge such things. One must be wary of subjecting a noviciate to the trials prematurely, but he certainly shows unusual promise. I've been corresponding with an old friend of mine in Altdorf, Arch Lector Lauterbach, regarding the matter, and he has requested that I bring your son to the capital, so that he may test him more thoroughly in the Cathedral of Sigmar.'

Hieronymus could control his features no longer. His eyes bulged as he looked from Jakob to Braun. 'An Arch Lector? I had no idea you had been discussing the matter with such senior figures.' He placed a hand on Jakob's shoulder and allowed himself a slight smile. 'Of course you can take him to Altdorf, Brother Braun. It would be a great honour for us.' He puffed out his chest and dusted an imaginary piece of fluff from his jacket. 'In fact, it is a long time since I visited the capital myself. If it would be of use, my wife and I should be glad to accompany you.'

Braun raised his eyebrows in surprise. 'Well, no offence to your lordship, but I had really imagined it would just be Jakob and myself.'

Hieronymus's face remained impassive, but Fabian noticed the slight tightening of his jaw that usually preceded an explosion of anger. 'I imagine the priests would be keen to meet such a generous benefactor as myself, Brother Braun,' he said in carefully controlled tones.

Braun opened his mouth to speak, but then seemed to reconsider. He gave a wide smile and bent his frail old body into a low bow. 'Of course, that's absolutely right your lordship. And it would be a perfect opportunity for you to see some of the work you've contributed to. I would be delighted if you and Frau Wolff could accompany us.'

'Excellent,' said Hieronymus, clapping his hands down on his thighs. 'Then we'll leave as soon as possible.'

Fabian backed cautiously towards the door.

Hieronymus grabbed him by the shoulder. 'You too, boy. It will do you good to see a little of the real world, instead of wasting your time on all those infantile myths you seem so obsessed with.'

'But father,' whined Fabian, 'the priests have no interest in meeting me.'

Hieronymus gave a short bark of laughter. 'You think I'd take you to the cathedral? And let you ruin your brother's future with some petulant remark?' He loosed Fabian's shoulder and shook his head in disbelief. 'I think not. But I won't leave you here to wreak havoc in our absence. I dread to think what we'd return to. And you may even be able to make yourself useful in Altdorf. You'll stay with my cousin Jonas, and if you value your hide, you'll do as he asks. Spending time with an educated gentleman such as Jonas might give you a little of the intellectual ballast you seem so sorely lacking in.'

'Altdorf,' murmured Margarethe, looking nervously up at the religious plasterwork that decorated the ceiling. She took her husband's arm. 'Is it wise to travel at the moment, Hieronymus? Altdorf is such a long way from here and the roads are so dangerous.'

Hieronymus nodded his head firmly. 'A journey to the very heart of the Empire is just what these boys need.' He noticed Margarethe's concerned expression and took her hand. 'Don't worry yourself unduly. We'll take guards. There won't be a problem.'

Servants bustled into the room and handed out slender glasses of wine. Brother Braun took a tiny sip and placed the glass carefully on a table. 'There's actually another small matter I wished to discuss with your lordship,' he said, taking the seat that was offered him. Once he was settled, and the others had taken their seats too, he continued. 'There has been some concern over the last couple of weeks that...' he paused, unsure how to continue. He was suddenly unable to meet Hieronymus's eye and as he continued, he fixed his gaze carefully on the elaborate wallpaper behind the noble's head. 'Well, some of the villagers feel that they've been somewhat abandoned.'

Braun noticed the expression on Hieronymus's face and hurried to finish before he was interrupted. 'It's not that they mean to criticise your lordship's management of the estate in any way, it's just that at this particular time they would be grateful–'

'What *exactly* is the problem?' interrupted Hieronymus.

Braun took a deep breath and frowned. 'It's one of my own brethren, I'm afraid,' he said. 'Well, at least I believe he's a lay brother of some kind. I'd been turning a blind eye to his eccentricities, but now he's taken it on himself to pass a very harsh judgement on one of your villagers.'

Hieronymus shrugged and sat back in his chair. 'Surely I have men to deal with this kind of thing, Braun. Do you really need to bother me with such matters?'

'There are no men, father,' snapped Fabian, his voice squeaking with excitement. 'I've already told you: your stewards have been lying to you for months. The militia's almost non-existent. We're left open to every fraud and charlatan who wants to fleece the good people of Berlau. In fact just last–'

Hieronymus silenced his son with a raised hand and a glare. 'Who is this lay brother, Braun, and what exactly is he trying to punish?'

'His name's Otto Sürman,' answered Braun. 'I know very little about him. When he arrived last summer, I took him for a devout man of learning. He attended a few of my services and asked if he could make use of my library. To be honest, I had suspicions from the first, but I could see no reason to be rude to the man, and I let him stay. Recently, though, it seems he's assumed the role of judge, jury and executioner.

I'd heard several rumours from my congregation and dismissed them as idle fancy, but now I've seen an example of his cruelty with my own eyes.'

Hieronymus nodded for him to continue.

'There's a boy in the village who goes by the name of Lukas. He's a little simple maybe, but nothing more than that as far as I can see and Sürman has accused the poor lad of the most terrible crimes. He claims he has been communing with the gods of the Old Night.'

'And has he?' asked Margarethe, her face filled with concern.

Braun shook his head. 'The boy's a bit of a loner that's all, but I hear that Sürman's had his eye on him for a while. Lukas is not so bright and maybe a little odd, so the other villagers tend to steer clear of him. His only real friends are a bunch of carrier pigeons he keeps in a small cage. They're a mangy bunch, and useless as messenger birds, but he dotes on them.'

'Where's the crime in that?' asked Hieronymus.

'There's no crime that I can see, but this Sürman character noticed the boy talking to the birds and claims they were responding to his commands – as though he was talking to them in their own language. He decided that such behaviour – along with Lukas's other eccentricities – marks him out as a witch of some kind.'

'How ridiculous,' exclaimed Hieronymus. 'I believe I even know the boy. There isn't an ounce of evil in him. What has this lay brother done to the poor soul?'

Braun grimaced. 'He told the villagers that Lukas is possessed by some kind of bird spirit. They're a superstitious lot, but even they found that a bit hard to swallow, so Sürman offered to prove the boy's guilt with a trial. He got the carpenter to construct a huge birdcage, then he locked the boy inside it and had him hoisted up thirty feet from the ground.'

Margarethe gasped. 'What on earth does he intend to prove by doing that?'

'The cage is open-topped but there is no way the boy could reach the pole to climb down. He'd break his neck if he even tried. Sürman has convinced the villagers that if they leave him up there long enough, the daemon will be driven mad by thirst and hunger and break free from Lukas's flesh. He claims it will fly to freedom – thus freeing the boy from possession.'

'And the villagers have allowed this to happen?' asked Hieronymus, shaking his head in disbelief.

Braun nodded. 'You must understand, lord, they're all terrified of Sürman. He's told them he works for the church as a witch hunter, so they're desperate not to anger him in any way.'

At the words 'witch hunter', Margarethe raised a hand nervously to her throat and looked at her husband. 'Perhaps we shouldn't become involved in a dispute like this. If he believes this boy is possessed, maybe he is. Who are we to deny the will of Sigmar?'

'The man is nothing to do with Sigmar,' replied Braun, shaking his head. 'I've made enquiries, and there's no record of him ever being ordained.' He placed a hand on Margarethe's knee. 'The countryside is overrun with such charlatans, my lady. In dark times such as these, simple rural folk are easily swayed. Their paranoia robs them of good sense.'

'Still,' replied Hieronymus, frowning, 'if he has the will of the people behind him, it might be dangerous to stir up trouble. Maybe my wife is right.'

'Father,' cried Fabian, leaping to his feet. 'Remember who we are! We are Wolffs. Are we to hand over control of our estates to any witless vagabond who wanders across our borders?'

'Watch your manners, boy,' snapped Hieronymus and Fabian sat down again with a sigh.

'Very well,' said Hieronymus. 'Let us make a compromise. I have no desire to delay our journey and get caught up in some petty legal dispute, but for once I think my son may have a point. This kind of bullying will lead to trouble if left unchecked.' He rang a little bell that was hung on the wall near to his head.

After a few minutes, an ancient hunchback shuffled into the room. Conrad Strobel had been the Wolffs' retainer since the time of Hieronymus's grandfather. Despite the heat, and his advanced years, Strobel was dressed for war. A thick leather jerkin enveloped his frail torso and his pinched, shrew-like features were almost completely hidden beneath a battered old helmet. 'M'lord?' he asked.

'How many of my personal guard are on duty today?' asked Hieronymus.

The old man's rheumy eyes grew even more clouded and he began to mutter under his breath.

'What was that?' asked Hieronymus.

'Three,' Strobel replied, raising his tremulous voice.

Colour rushed into Hieronymus's face, but he refused to acknowledge the smug expression directed at him by Fabian. 'Three units, do you mean?'

Strobel slowly shook his head. 'Three men,' he replied. There was a hint of accusation in his voice as he continued. 'I did inform His Lordship when I was forced to lose Ditwin and Eberhard.'

Hieronymus's eyes widened and his cheeks darkened to a deep purple, but he replied calmly. 'Of course. Have the three of them ride into the village would you, Strobel? There's a man by the name of Sürman who's causing a bit of trouble.'

'Should they arrest him?' asked the retainer.

Hieronymus stroked his long chin and thought for a moment. 'No, just have them free the boy he's imprisoned and then banish Sürman from my estate. Tell him that if he ever returns, I'll have him up before the magistrate.'

'Very good,' replied Strobel and left with the same chorus of sighs and wheezes that accompanied his arrival.

'Is it wise to antagonise these people, my dear?' asked Margarethe, obviously uncomfortable at the thought of banishing a witch hunter.

'I'm not antagonising him, I'm removing him,' replied Hieronymus sharply. 'Now, I'd rather not spend the whole afternoon discussing such tedious matters. Brother Braun – let's retire to my study and plan the route to Altdorf.' As he rose to his feet his eyes were gleaming with excitement. 'Imagine it, a personal invite from an Arch Lector.' He looked down at his sons. 'And your first visit to the capital. Believe me boys, you'll barely recognise yourselves by the time you return to Berlau. Altdorf is a city like no other. Nobody who passes through those hallowed gates is ever the same again.'

CHAPTER THIRTEEN
The Unknown House

'Is that the drains or the locals?' asked Fabian, wrinkling his nose in disgust as they drove into the Königplatz. His impression of the city had so far been less than favourable. Their coach had approached the great north gates at a painful crawl, as the driver steered carefully through the flea-ridden lake of slums and refuges that had besieged Altdorf. Pock-marked fingers had reached up to them as they passed, begging for alms or passage into the city, and the driver had been forced to fend off hordes of naked, filthy orphans who clambered onto the roof and pleaded for food. It had been a miserable end to a miserable journey.

Once through the gates, things hadn't got much better. Fabian baulked at the confusing maze of crowded, narrow streets and tall, teetering townhouses. The filthy, cramped buildings of the city grew more bloated with each wonky storey, so that by the third or fourth floor their half-timbered facades were almost touching the houses opposite: arching over the bustling streets like bridges and plunging the flagstones below into a constant gloom.

There was a brief glimpse of blue sky overhead as they entered the Königplatz, but the broad square was no less crowded than the streets that led onto it. As Fabian tried to climb down from the coach, grinning, shouting hawkers clutched at his clothes, thrusting their wares into his face and vying aggressively for his attention.

'Fabian!' cried his father. 'Back in the coach, now! They'll have the shirt off your back if you give them half a chance.'

Fabian climbed back inside and looked in amazement at his parents.

'What a hellish place,' he muttered. 'And what *is* that smell?'

To his annoyance no one seemed to hear him. They were all peering through the windows, engrossed by the mayhem outside. Despite his loud sighs, they continued to ignore him, so he followed their example, squeezing his face next to Jakob's and looking out through the coach window.

Every form of life was parading through the square. The coach rocked constantly as the crush of bodies barged past it and the hawkers outside pressed dolls and clothes to the glass. A few feet away a man was driving a train of cages through the crowd and each one was filled with a menagerie of incredible creatures, half of which Fabian couldn't even name. Birds with dazzling, rainbow-coloured feathers dozed on their perches and giant cats with ragged, white manes gazed idly out from their prisons. Further into the square, rows of striped awnings shaded produce from every corner of the Old World: fruit, livestock, fish and leather passed over the heads of the jostling figures as they haggled and joked with each other. Further still, in the heart of the square, ranks of crumbling statues towered over everything; made faceless and nameless by the elements, they watched the turmoil at their feet with a regal, patrician disdain, marred only by the thick layer of bird muck that coated their faces.

Fabian fastened a handkerchief over his nose and settled back in his seat. The thick odour seeped through the cotton. It seemed to be a powerful mixture of horse piss and rotting fish, with a persistent, acrid bass note that he guessed was coming from the open sewers.

'There's our man,' cried Braun, pointing out a young priest fighting his way through the crowds towards them. 'I'd never forget that face.'

Fabian raised his eyebrows as the slender youth neared the coach. The boy's appearance certainly *was* memorable. His head was shaven, as with any other novitiate, and his vestments were simple and unadorned, but his face seemed to have slipped to the sides of his head. His broad, watery eyes were closer to his ears than his wide crooked nose, and his broad mouth was so big it seemed to hinge his whole head as it broke into a broad smile.

'Brother Potzlinger,' cried Braun, shoving the door open and fighting his way down to embrace the youth. 'It's *so* good to see you.'

Potzlinger gave a hyena laugh and patted Braun's back enthusiastically. 'And you too, brother.' He turned his head to one side with an odd, bird-like movement and looked up at the Wolffs with one bulging eye. 'Welcome to Altdorf,' he cried, struggling to make himself heard over the cacophony.

Hieronymus climbed down and took his hand. 'It's good to meet you, Brother Potzlinger,' he said waving his hand back at the coach. 'This is my wife Margarethe, and our sons Fabian,' he paused for dramatic effect, 'and Jakob.'

'Ah, yes, Jakob,' said Potzlinger, reaching up to take the boy's hand. 'We've learned so much about you from Brother Braun's letters. I feel as though I already know you.' He looked around at the square and grimaced. 'We should find somewhere better to speak though. Königplatz is like this every Aubentag. I'm not sure what the river wardens do with their time, I'm really not – it seems like we let any old riffraff into the city these days.' He shrugged. 'Well, we may as well make straight for the cathedral. We can have a little peace there. I believe the Arch Lector has arranged some accommodation for you.' He held a hand up to Margarethe. 'It's probably easier if we walk. Your boys will see more of the city that way anyway.'

'Oh no, Fabian isn't accompanying us,' explained Hieronymus hurriedly. 'He'll be staying with his Uncle Jonas. The driver knows the way to the house.' He narrowed his eyes as he put his head back inside the coach. 'Just sit tight until you get there, Fabian. We'll only be gone for a few days I should think, so try keep your head down and not cause your uncle any trouble.' With that he slammed the door shut, cutting out at least a little of the racket from outside.

Fabian watched his family struggling across the square, as Brother Potzlinger pointed out the various landmarks to his wide-eyed brother. Then, as the coach began to edge cautiously back towards the narrow streets, he sat down and hissed through his teeth. 'What a place,' he said, pressing the handkerchief to his face and shaking his head in disgust.

He soon lost track of their route as the coach bounced and clattered through the labyrinthine maze of streets. The houses pressed closer and closer overhead and just as there seemed barely enough room for the coach to squeeze any further, they reached their destination. They had left the noise of the market place far behind, and as Fabian climbed down onto the grimy cobbles, he felt oddly nervous. The townhouses that surrounded him were all four or five storeys tall and as they leant out over his head, leaving just a narrow slit of sky, their small, deep-set windows peered down hungrily at him.

'It's that one,' muttered the driver, nodding towards the last house on the street. It was even taller and more asymmetrical than the others. A mixture of architectural styles had been piled on top of each other to create a haphazard column of crumbling render and gnarled timbers. It looked to Fabian like a stiff breeze would send all five of its crooked, gabled storeys tumbling to the ground. There was a sign over the gate, beautifully painted in gothic script that announced enigmatically: The Unknown House.

'Are you sure this is the right place?' asked Fabian, turning back to the coach, but the driver just gave him an odd smile as he dropped the luggage at the gate and climbed back onto the coach.

Fabian sighed, hefted his bag onto his back and climbed up the flagged path to the front door. There was a large iron knocker in the shape of a snarling wolf, and he clanged it three times, before stepping back to wait for a response.

No one came, and after a few minutes he pressed his ear to the door and listened for footsteps. He heard another sound instead: a mournful, unearthly moaning that throbbed gently through the wood. Fabian felt a tingle of fear. No mortal being could make such a noise. He stepped back again and turned to speak to the coachman, but he was gone. The coach was already turning a corner and disappearing from view. I wonder if I could find the cathedral, he thought, looking back down the winding street.

With a screech of rusted hinges, the door opened.

The eerie droning sound flooded out onto the street and Fabian turned to face a towering, fur-clad giant of a man, who had to stoop to fit his broad shoulders out through the doorframe. 'What do you want?' he growled, through a long, shaggy beard. He spoke in such a thick Kislev accent, though, that it sounded more like: 'Vwaht do you vwant?'

'Uncle Jonas?' asked Fabian, doubtfully.

The giant's eyes narrowed beneath his thick brow. 'I'm no one's uncle, child,' he said. 'I'm no one's anything, thank the gods.' He eased his massive bulk back in through the doorframe and stepped to one side, signalling for Fabian to step into the gloomy interior. 'Jonas probably won't return until tonight. You'd best speak to his wife, Isolde. Come inside.'

Fabian hesitated, looking wistfully back over his shoulder at the street, before stepping into the house. He found himself in a muddle of narrow corridors, cramped staircases and sombre, dark panelling. The Kislevite had to remain stooped as he led the way beneath the low, beamed ceilings. Strange objects pressed in on them, crowding the shelves and cupboards that lined the walls: china dolls and stuffed birds crowded every available space and crooked pictures shook on the walls as the man stomped across the uneven floors. The whole place was filled with the odd, whirring buzzing sound and as they approached a door at the far end of the hallway, it grew louder. The only light came from a single, filthy window, and it was hard to see clearly, but Fabian thought he could make out two large sentries flanking the door. As they reached it, however, he realised he was mistaken. The bulky figures were actually the stuffed carcasses of two massive bears. They were an imposing presence, despite their dusty, moth-eaten fur and Fabian found it hard to look at their snarling faces as he hurried though the doorway.

They had entered another narrow hallway that ended in a rickety spiral staircase. The Kislevite waved one of his meaty fur-clad paws at it. 'She'll be in the Tapestry Room. Second on the left.'

Fabian nodded, and squeezed past the man towards the stairs. 'Thank you…' he said, waiting for the man to supply his name.

The giant gave a low chuckle and nodded back. 'Kobach,' he said, in an amused rumble, before stomping away.

'Kobach,' repeated Fabian quietly to himself; not sure if it was a name or an insult. The stairs shifted unnervingly beneath his feet as he climbed up to the next floor. There was another door at the top, and as he pushed it open and stepped onto the landing, the droning chorus grew even louder. As Fabian looked down the long, twisting hallway, he thought he could discern some kind of melody in the noise, as though the house were humming a lullaby to itself.

As he passed the first door, he noticed that it was open and squinted through the gloom to see if the room was empty. It wasn't. His pulse quickened as he realised at least two of the shadows in there were alive: a couple of hooded monks were sat close together, whispering to each other in hurried, urgent tones. They looked up angrily at Fabian's approach and one of them leapt to his feet and slammed the door shut. Fabian only caught the briefest glimpse of his face, but it was enough to unnerve him even more. The man's pale, narrow features were beaded with sweat and his bloodshot eyes were running with tears.

He hurried onwards, towards the awful sound. Finally he reached the next door. There was something strange about the frame. At first he struggled to see what exactly it was in the half-light, but after a few seconds he realised the entire structure was carved from the jaw of some monstrous leviathan. With a grimace of disgust, he saw that its bleached teeth were still in place, surrounding the door with rows of jagged canines.

This close, the sound was really quite terrifying and Fabian looked back down the corridor, wondering if even now it might be possible to escape. He could imagine how amusing his brother would find it though, if he arrived at the cathedral, having been too scared to wait in his own uncle's house. I'd never hear the end of it, he decided and after taking a long, hitching breath he tapped gently on the door.

The noise stopped immediately, as though the house were holding its breath.

The door opened slowly, flooding the hallway with smoke and warm, yellow light. A beautiful woman looked out at him with sleepy, half-lidded eyes. Her pale skin was flushed with warmth, or alcohol and her thick black tresses were tousled and unkempt, as though he had woken her from a deep sleep. She gave him a languid smile and stooped to place a long, moist kiss on his forehead, as though they were old, intimate acquaintances. As she leant back again, Fabian's eyes rested briefly on the expanse of ivory cleavage straining at the emerald-green velvet of her dress. He blushed as he realised she had noticed the direction of his gaze and the woman's smile broadened as she stepped back into the room and signalled for him to follow.

It was a large room, but every inch of it was crowded with crates, chests and piles of books. The walls were lined with thick, faded tapestries depicting a gaudy multitude of creatures, both mythical and real. There was a large, canopied bed in one corner and next to it an oil lamp was quietly hissing, filling the room with soft, shifting shadows. The light also picked out a haze of scented smoke that was hovering at about the level of Fabian's face. He couldn't place the aroma, but as he inhaled the fumes he felt a pleasant heaviness in his limbs and suddenly realised how tired he was.

'Take a seat,' said the woman in a soft voice, waving vaguely at the jumble of furniture that cluttered the room. Then she yawned, reaching up in a slow, feline stretch, obviously conscious of how flattering the light was as it played across her curves. As the light shimmered over her hair, Fabian noticed it was bejewelled with dozens of tiny, yellow flowers. Once she had finished stretching, the woman curled up in a large, leather chair and rested her chin on her hands, gazing through the smoke at Fabian's discomfort with obvious amusement.

He finally found a chair and perched awkwardly on the edge of it, looking everywhere but at the woman. 'Your servant told me it was best to wait here,' he muttered, 'until my uncle returns.'

'Of course,' she replied, nodding sagely. 'And who is your uncle?'

Fabian frowned and finally met her eye, wondering why on earth she had kissed him so fervently if she had know idea who he was. 'My... my uncle is Captain Jonas Wolff,' he stammered, wondering if he had come to the wrong room.

The woman flicked her ebony hair back from her face and looked up at the ceiling as though trying to recall something. 'Jonas Wolff is my husband's name too,' she said, seeming a little confused. 'How odd.'

Fabian waited for her to continue, but she just frowned up at the ceiling in silence. He took the opportunity to admire the long, pale curve of her neck and as he did so, he noticed a silver chain that pointed enticingly to the neckline of her dress. The chain ended in a small, ivory figurine of some kind, but Fabian could not quite make it out through the heady fug. After a few minutes, the silence began to seem a little odd. 'Then, are you Isolde?' he asked.

The warm smile returned to her face and she looked back at him. 'Of course I am, silly boy.' She rummaged down by the side of her chair and lifted a strange contraption up onto her lap. It looked like an oversized violin, but it had a cranked wheel attached to it and the soundboard was covered with a row of small teeth-like keys. 'Are you a fan of the wheel fiddle?' she asked. Before he could reply, she began to turn the handle, filling the room with the awful whining buzz he had heard earlier. As she played, the woman closed her eyes and mouthed a stream of silent words. She seemed to quickly forget all about her guest.

As the droning notes washed over him, Fabian felt his head growing lighter and his eyelids growing heavier. He tried to keep himself awake by studying the animals depicted on the tapestries, and to his delight he realised they were moving, dancing across the walls of the room in time to the music and fluttering gaily across the ceiling. Scale seemed to have no meaning for the crewelwork creatures. Rats pounced viciously on horses, wrestling them to the ground with their teeth, and monkeys rode on the back of goldfinches, waving little flags above their heads as they circled the light fittings and skipped around the doorframe. Fabian laughed to himself, thrilled to think that Jakob had missed out on this incredible carnival, just so that he could be lectured by a bunch of sour-faced old priests. The music eddied and swelled, enveloping his thoughts with its odd, serpentine phrases. After a while, he slipped gratefully into unconsciousness, dragging the creatures down with him into his dreams.

'Isolde, what have you done?' cried an angry voice and Fabian woke with a start. For a moment he could not place his surroundings. The oil lamp had burned itself out and the only illumination was a few shards of moonlight knifing through the gaps in the wooden shutters. He saw the dark-haired woman curled up on her chair, fast asleep, but still clutching the strange instrument to her chest. With an inexplicable feeling of guilt, Fabian remembered what had happened and lurched up from his chair. His head spun sickeningly and he felt as though the floor was giving way beneath him. He turned towards the door, to see the owner of the voice.

An elderly gentleman was stood in the doorway, and Fabian immediately realised it must be his uncle. He had the same regal bearing and aquiline features as his father, but if anything, they were even more refined. He was obviously much older than Hieronymus: in his late seventies possibly, and he had to support himself on a long, delicate cane; but his clothes were perfectly tailored. His doublet, jerkin, and hose were all jet black and embellished with delicate silver needlework, and he wore a high, ermine-lined collar, ribbed with sparkling leaves of silver. His long, grey moustache was waxed in a flamboyant curl and as he took in Fabian's slender form, he dipped his head in a graceful bow. 'Fabian, I presume?' he said, annunciating each syllable with the soft, precise tones of a poet.

'Yes, my lord,' gasped Fabian stumbling through the chaos and taking the man's hand. 'I was instructed to wait here by your servant, but I was tired after the journey and–'

'I can imagine what happened, child,' interrupted the old man, giving Fabian a kind smile. He eyed the sleeping woman with concern. 'My wife has been a little unwell of late.' He placed a hand on Fabian's shoulder and looked deep into his eyes. 'Don't give any credence to anything she might have told you. The poor thing has become slightly confused. She inhabits a strange fantasy land half the time.' He gestured to the wheel fiddle. 'She finds it helpful to indulge her passion for music.' He chuckled. 'But it's not always so helpful for everyone else.'

He steered Fabian out of the room and quietly closed the door behind him. 'As you have no doubt guessed, I'm your Uncle Jonas,' he said, leaning on Fabian's shoulder for support as they headed off down the corridor. 'I had hoped to be here to meet you, but I got caught up in a dispute with some rather disreputable foreigners.' They entered a smoky, book-lined study. A small, cast iron fireplace filled the room with light from its merry, crackling blaze and Fabian helped the old man into a seat beside it.

'Did you mention a servant?' asked Jonas, signalling for Fabian to sit next to him and handing him a small glass of thick, ruby liquid.

Fabian eyed the glass suspiciously, still feeling unsteady from his unexpected nap. 'Er, yes,' he replied. 'Your butler, I think. A large Kislevite man. He showed me to your wife's chambers. I think he was called Kobach.'

Jonas leant back in his chair with a snort of amusement. 'So, Kobach Ivanov has returned to Altdorf!' He shook his head. 'That man is bound for either greatness or the executioner's block, but I wouldn't like to bet which.' He noticed Fabian's look of confusion and patted his knee reassuringly. 'I'm sorry, lad – I'm not laughing at you. You should learn not to make such quick assumptions though. If Kobach had realised that you mistook him for a servant, I wouldn't like to imagine where you'd be now. This house is a refuge for some of the city's more interesting visitors; many of them are very powerful men in their own countries, but they're all a little dangerous in their own way.' He drained his glass and waved at the drink in Fabian's hand. 'Drink up, son. We have a whole city to explore and you'll need little fire in your belly to survive your first night in Altdorf.'

Fabian looked out through a small leaded window at the darkness outside. 'We're going out now?' he asked.

Jonas shrugged. 'Well, you can retire to your bed if you wish. There's one all made up for you if you'd like an early night.' He leant forward, so that the flames flashed mischievously in his eyes. 'I just have a feeling you're a little more adventurous than that.'

No adult had ever spoken to Fabian in such conspiratorial tones before and he was unsure how to respond. He realised that despite the physical similarities, this man was nothing like his father. There was a hint of danger in the old man's voice that both troubled and excited him. It did not take him long to make up his mind. He emptied the glass with one hungry gulp and as the potent drink filled him with warmth he grinned. 'I'm not really *that* tired,' he replied.

'They call this the Street of a Hundred Taverns,' explained Jonas as they fought their way through the jostling crowds of revellers. He was leaning heavily on Fabian for support, but his eyes sparkled with excitement as he waved his cane at the array of inns and clubs that surrounded them. Despite the late hour, the street was ablaze with light and crammed with people: lame beggars grasped at their legs as they passed; drunken dock-hands hurled red-faced abuse at each other; nobles barged past in gaudy, flamboyant palanquins and sinister, hooded figures watched attentively from the ill-lit side streets. Despite his fear, Fabian felt more alive than he could ever remember feeling before.

'This is the vital, pounding heart of the city,' continued Jonas, tapping his cane on the filthy cobbles. 'The whole Empire even.' He pointed out an incredible array of characters to Fabian, from infamous crime lords and legendary war heroes, to distinguished plutocrats and revered musicians, all crushed together in a whirling mass of drunken faces and raucous song. 'Anything worth knowing is being discussed right here, right now. There are deals being struck in these taverns that will influence military strategy in every corner of the Empire. Kingdoms have been toppled as a result of a chance remark uttered in the back alleys and cellars that surround us.'

He shouldered his way towards a narrow, anonymous-looking door, tucked away beside a rundown theatre. He tapped firmly with the knocker and after a few minutes a shutter snapped to one side and a pair of suspicious eyes glared out at them. 'Ah, Captain Wolff,' came a voice. 'Back so soon?' There was a *click clack* of locks being turned and the door opened inwards onto a surprisingly plush interior. Candles lined the walls of a wood-panelled hallway and a liveried butler bowed graciously at them, waving for them to enter.

'Thank you, Vogel,' said Jonas, handing the man his hat and cape as he entered.

The butler was a flame-haired youth, whose pale, freckled face split into a grin at the sight of Jonas. 'Always a pleasure, captain,' he replied. After hanging the hat and cloak in a side room, he leant close to Jonas and whispered conspiratorially in his ear.

Jonas laughed and clapped him on the back. 'Ah, yes – I thought as much. I'm not afraid of a few half-soaked Tileans though, Vogel,' he said. 'Anyway,' he continued, nodding at Fabian, 'I have some muscle with me tonight.'

The butler laughed and waved them down the hall.

At the far end was another door, much grander than the first. It was a broad, venerable thing, made of polished oak and elaborate brass hinges. There was a large letter R engraved in the central panel, framed within a cartouche of writhing serpents. Jonas gave Fabian a sly wink and shoved the door open to reveal a wide, carpeted drawing room, lined with tapestries and curtained booths. Deep, high-backed chairs were scattered around the room and several distinguished-looking gentlemen were sat reading books or talking. There was a haze of pipe smoke that made it hard to discern the club's patrons very clearly, but as Fabian caught glimpses of their exotic clothes and heard snatches of their foreign accents, he deduced that many of them were not from the Empire. The place throbbed with an undercurrent of danger and he looked nervously at his uncle, but Jonas placed a reassuring hand on his shoulder and grinned. 'Welcome to the Recalcitrant Club,' he said proudly.

'Jonas,' said an unfeasibly obese gentleman, as he waddled slowly towards them. He wore his dark hair slicked back from his jowly face in a greasy bob, and his small, porcine eyes nestled behind a pair of round, wire-rimmed glasses. Blue robes billowed around him as he embraced Jonas and placed a kiss on his cheek. He studied the noble's slender physique. 'The years have been kind to you,' he said, in a creamy, effeminate voice. 'I doubted I would ever see your dear face again. What a delightful surprise.'

Jonas smiled and squeezed the man's shoulder. 'I only saw you this morning, Puchelperger,' he replied, 'so I'd hope I've not worn too badly.' He looked down at the man's vast, trembling paunch. 'I see times haven't been too hard for you, either.'

Puchelperger raised his eyebrows. 'I endeavoured to keep myself hale and hearty in the hope of your eventual return.' He gestured to an empty booth. 'Let me buy you a drink and you can introduce me to your new friend.'

They settled back into plush, leather couches and a waiter discretely deposited three tall glasses on their table.

'This is my cousin's son, Fabian,' said Jonas, smiling paternally, and patting the boy on the shoulder. 'It's his first time in Altdorf.'

'Ah, an innocent,' said Puchelperger with a glint in his beady, black eyes. 'Well, my boy, you couldn't have wished for a better guide.' He gestured to the tall glass in front of Fabian. 'Please, I insist,' he said.

Fabian's thoughts were already a little muddled from his previous drink and he looked at his uncle with a worried expression.

Jonas laughed. 'It won't harm you, boy,' he said, taking a swig from his own glass. 'I'm not sure how they do things in the country, but I think you're old enough to sample a few of life's more cosmopolitan pleasures.'

Afraid of appearing a fool in front of his urbane new friends, Fabian emptied the entire glass in one swallow. He felt a sudden rush of euphoria followed by an equally sudden rush of gas. He grinned at his uncle, as an explosive belch ripped through his throat.

The two men burst into raucous laughter.

'Ah, yes,' cried Puchelperger, clapping his chubby hands, and causing the table to rock as his belly jiggled up and down. 'He's a Wolff alright!' He leant as far forward as his stomach would allow. 'Tell me though, boy – what brings you to this noble city?'

The smile dropped from Fabian's face. 'My brother,' he muttered. 'He's some kind of *wonderful* student. The priests wanted to interview him at the Cathedral of Sigmar.'

Jonas noted Fabian's sullen tone with interest. 'And you? Have you studied the holy texts?'

Fabian gave a harsh laugh. 'No, uncle, to be honest, I find all that stuff as dull as ditchwater.' The rush of euphoria was still growing in his head and he felt his shyness slipping away. He raised his eyebrows disdainfully and his voice rang with a new-found confidence. 'I find it a facile ideology at best. I've read many of the older, epic poems and they seem to me far more interesting.'

Jonas and Puchelperger both fell silent at these words and Jonas continued to study Fabian intently.

'Interesting,' said Puchelperger, giving Jonas a knowing look as he emptied his own glass. 'Well, I'm sure you won't find it dull spending an evening in the company of your uncle.'

Jonas smiled. 'I have a few interesting diversions in mind.'

'Jonas Wolff,' barked a harsh voice and Fabian turned to see a leathery, olive-skinned rake, wearing a colourful gypsy bandana and scowling at Jonas with evident rage. 'I was hoping to see you in here,' he said in a strange, lilting accent. The man was slender, but with the taut, sinewy physique of a dancer or an acrobat, and as he leant over the table, Fabian noticed he was clutching a long, needle-thin knife. A group of similarly flamboyant men were stood behind him, all holding knives of their own.

'Calderino,' replied Jonas, with an amiable smile. 'What charmingly rustic manners you have. And it's always such a delight to hear your interpretation of our language.'

The man's teeth flashed, bright white against his tanned skin as he snarled his reply. 'We had a deal, Jonas. I secured the books for you.' He grabbed Jonas by his tall collar and pulled him across the table. 'Where's my money?'

Jonas slapped the man's face with such force that he loosed his grip and stepped back, holding his hand to his cheek in shock. 'Not in the club, Calderino,' Jonas hissed, gesturing to the red-haired butler, Vogel, who was watching them from the doorway with an anxious expression on his face.

Calderino looked around to notice that the room had fallen silent and all the other club members were watching him over their papers, scowling with disapproval. He took a deep breath and removed his hand from his face. 'Well, whatever happens Wolff, I *will* have my payment,' he whispered, levelling his slender knife at Jonas. Then, with a flamboyant flourish of his short, silk cape he stormed out of the room, leaving his friends to hastily finish their drinks and rush after him.

Jonas smiled apologetically at the butler and settled back in his seat. 'The books were all forgeries,' he explained to Puchelperger, loud enough for the rest of the club to hear. 'And not even good ones.'

Puchelperger shook his head and sighed despairingly at Fabian. 'See what I mean?' he said. 'Whatever else he might be accused of, your uncle is rarely boring.'

For the next hour or so, Fabian listened respectfully as the two men exchanged anecdotes and discussed the state of the Empire. Another drink appeared mysteriously before him, but he drank this one a little slower, already feeling as though he might need to borrow his uncle's cane when it was time to leave. As the conversation turned to politics, his mind wondered to Jonas's strange young wife. She could not have been more than thirty, and she was strikingly beautiful, yet she was attracted to a man of Jonas's advanced years. He wondered if he could ever learn to be as witty and assured as his uncle. How different he was from his pious, bumbling father. Fabian shook his head as he considered how much more there was to life than the simple, god-fearing dogma his brother had adopted.

'I sense we're boring you, Fabian,' said Jonas, finishing his drink and rising from his chair. 'I find it all too easy to while away the hours in this genial haven, but there's so much more I'd like to show you tonight.'

Puchelperger bade them an enthusiastic farewell and as they headed for the door, several of the other club members gave Jonas their regards and commented on the poor manners of the foreigner who had accosted him.

As they left the warmth of the club, the cold night air left Fabian reeling. He felt his uncle's steadying hand on his arm though, and quickly recovered his composure.

'Are you alright, son?' asked Jonas, with an amused smile.

'Yes, uncle,' said Fabian with a manly cough, but as they re-entered the crowded street he found it difficult to focus on the multitude of shapes and colours rushing by.

As they made their way south down the Street of a Hundred Taverns, the constant stink of the city became more focussed. The smell of the sewers and livestock was eclipsed by the overwhelming stench of fish and brine. And beneath the calls of beggars and drunks, Fabian thought he could make out a vague sloshing sound.

They reached the end of the road and Fabian gasped. A broad expanse of moonlit water lay stretched out before him, carving right through the heart of the city, and dotted with small islands, all linked by a myriad of crowded bridges.

Dozens of galleons and barges were moored up at the quayside and even at this late hour, crowds of sailors and stevedores were rushing to-and-fro along the gangplanks, laden with exotic goods and yelling commands to each other in a wonderful variety of accents and languages. Fabian looked up at the nearest ship in awe. Its mountainous, barnacle-encrusted hull reared up over him, and he felt a cool spray landing on his upturned face as the sails snapped and boomed over his head. On the far side of the river lay the rest of the city: a teeming mass of spires, roofs, domes and bridges. The combination of the alcohol rushing through his veins and the incredible panoply arrayed before him left Fabian's heart racing. He suddenly felt as though he might burst into tears at the sheer spectacle of it all.

'Quite a sight, isn't it?' said Jonas, looking out over the water. 'It's best to keep moving though,' he said, steering Fabian back into the flow of people. 'The docks aren't the safest place to be at night.'

Fabian did not really need his uncle's warning. Most of the figures rushing by looked as though they would slit his throat as easily as asking him to step aside. He saw hostile eyes watching from every alleyway and violence filled the air as palpably as the stink of fish. He shuddered and stepped a little closer to his uncle.

'Watch yourself,' laughed Jonas, as a pile of brawling drunks scattered across the cobbles in front of them. With surprising agility, he dragged Fabian around the mass of flailing limbs and turned up a quiet back street. It was so steep and narrow that they had to walk in single file as they clambered up past the shuttered warehouses and dingy archways. As they reached the summit, Fabian noticed a light was flickering through the window of one of the buildings. A small, battered sign was hanging above the door, in the shape of an open book.

'Those dusty old fools in the university district will tell you they're the keepers of Altdorf's entire reserves of knowledge,' said Jonas, pausing outside the shop. 'But there's much more to be learned in this city, for those willing to look.' He tapped on the door and stepped back into the street to wait for a response.

After a few minutes the door squeaked open and an elderly woman peered myopically out at them through the thick, scratched lenses of her spectacles. Her skin was as shrivelled as a dried fig and her back was so hunched by age that she was barely four feet tall.

'Frau Gangolffin,' exclaimed Jonas, giving the old lady a gracious bow. 'I hope I didn't wake you.'

'Don't be cruel, Jonas,' she replied with a voice like sandpaper on gravel. 'You know perfectly well how little sleep I get.' She peered up at Fabian and shook her head. 'At my age I'm lucky if I can close my eyes for so much as an hour.' Without another word, she shuffled back into the shop, leaving the door swinging open behind her.

Jonas smiled mischievously at Fabian and ushered him inside.

Every inch of the shop was crammed with crooked, heaving book-shelves and teetering piles of dusty, leather-bound folios. The comforting smell of old paper was almost enough to mask the stink of the river and Fabian took a deep, grateful breath. There was an oil lamp sat on a desk at the foot of a narrow staircase and the glow of the shifting flame danced across the rows of foiled spines. Fabian sighed as he took in the wealth of obscure bestiaries and ancient poetry anthologies. He reeled from shelf to shelf, unsure where to look first, dazzled by the wealth of esoteric learning on display.

He noticed that Jonas was chuckling softly. 'It's quite something, isn't it?' he said. 'Choose any book you want and consider it a gift.' He nodded to the old woman, who seemed to have already forgotten them. She was hunched eagerly over a parchment on her desk, peering at it through a large magnifying glass. 'I have an account with the old dear,' he said.

'Frau Gangolffin,' said Jonas, waving to the narrow stairs. 'Do you have the books I ordered?'

The old woman still had the magnifying glass in front of her face as she looked up, giving her the appearance of a confused, whiskery cyclops. 'Ah, yes,' she croaked, with a look of recognition. She placed the lens back on the cluttered desk and started climbing very slowly up the stairs. 'They did arrive, I think, with the last Estalian shipment. They should be up here somewhere.'

'Take your time, my boy,' said Jonas, waving at the bookshelves. 'Who knows when you'll be here again.' With that he followed the woman upstairs.

Fabian immersed himself in the books, comforted by the creak of the floorboards overhead and the muffled sound of his uncle's voice as he chatted to the old woman. Finally, after nearly an hour had passed, Jonas climbed back down the stairs with a pile of books under his arm. 'Find anything of interest?' he asked.

Fabian held up a handsome volume, bound in white leather, with a gold knife foiled on the front. 'Is this too expensive?' he asked hesitantly.

'Almost certainly,' replied Jonas with a smile and called up the stairs. 'And a copy of Lang's *Dooms and Legends*, please Frau Gangolffin.'

There was a croak of acknowledgment from the old woman as she climbed slowly down the stairs.

'And about the other matter?' asked Jonas, giving the bookseller a strange smile.

She nodded to Fabian. 'Is he to be trusted?'

'Of course.'

'Very well. Check the street,' she muttered, glaring at Fabian. 'And shut the door.'

Fabian leapt to obey, peering up and down the alleyway. 'No one there,' he said, closing the door behind him with a *clunk*.

The old woman turned to her desk and started to shove it across the floorboards with a horrible scraping sound. Before she had moved it more than a couple of inches however, she was gripped by a coughing fit that was so violent Fabian rushed to her side and began patting her back.

She batted him away with a grunt of irritation and, after wiping the spittle from her chin, gestured to the floor beneath her desk.

Fabian noticed that table's movement had disturbed a rug and revealed the edges of a trapdoor. With the old woman waving him on, he shoved the table a little further until the trapdoor was completely exposed, and then stooped down to lever it open. Hidden beneath the floorboards was a small shelf holding three books. Each one was carefully wrapped in oilskin and fastened with a thick, knotted cord.

Jonas moved Fabian to one side and gazed lovingly at the small, innocent-looking bundles. 'Which one?' he whispered.

Frau Gangolffin backed away from the books; watching them carefully from a few feet away, as though they might leap for her throat at any minute. 'The middle one,' she muttered, with a note of fear in her voice.

Quick as a flash, Jonas snatched the book, secreted it in a pocket and slammed the trapdoor shut.

As he signalled for Fabian to move the table back into place, the boy noticed that his uncle was flushed with excitement.

Jonas took a deep, relieved breath, and smiled at Fabian. 'Don't mention what you've seen, my boy. Frau Gangolffin has some particularly disreputable competitors, and they'd all dearly love to know about that trapdoor.'

Fabian nodded in reply.

'I believe that's everything,' said Jonas, giving the old woman a stiff bow. She was already climbing slowly back up the stairs though, and if she heard him she gave no sign of it.

'Well, Fabian, we're almost done,' Jonas said as they stepped out onto the street. 'I just have one last call to make, and then we can head home.'

Fabian suddenly realised how exhausted he was. He nodded sleepily and stumbled after his uncle, making no pretence of supporting the elderly gentleman as he tottered back towards the quayside. Before they reached the river, Jonas veered off down another narrow winding street and after a few lefts and rights, Fabian gave up trying to work out which direction they were heading in. The routes criss-crossed and doubled back on themselves in a mind-boggling confusion of pitch dark side streets and crooked, sombrous alleyways. Tiredness added to Fabian's bewilderment and he began to feel as though everything that had happened to him since his father left him in the coach had been nothing more than a strange dream.

A predawn glow was just beginning to lift the gloom a little when Jonas led them onto a street full of narrow tenements, huddled together against the wall of a large park. Cheerful lights flickered in many of the small, square windows, and figures flitted hurriedly in and out of the open doorways.

Fabian pointed out an iron bench, just outside the entrance to the park. 'Wait there for a while, lad,' he said. 'I have one last bit of business to attend to.'

Fabian eyed the tall, crooked building with concern. 'Will you need my help climbing the stairs?' he asked.

Jonas grinned and ruffled his hair. 'Bless you, son, no. I have friends in there who will be more than happy to take my hand.'

Fabian blushed, as he realised what kind of house it was. 'Oh, of course,' he muttered

Jonas began to walk away and then hesitated, pursing his lips as he looked up and down the street. He came back to Fabian and placed a hand on his shoulder, stooping so that their eyes were level. 'Best keep yourself out of view,' he said, frowning. 'Altdorf at night is, well…' He stumbled over his words, looking a little anxious. Then he shrugged and his mouth split into a broad grin. 'You'll be fine,' he said patting Fabian's shoulder. 'Anyway, I won't be long.' With that he hobbled off into the darkness.

Fabian rushed over to the bench and did his best to become invisible. As he sat there, trying desperately to stay awake, Fabian saw a stream of people rushing by: ne'er-do-wells of every class and creed, from rowdy, drunken dockhands to sinister, hooded nobles, none of whom seemed to notice him as he crouched sleepily by the park gate.

After a few minutes had passed, Fabian began to get the unnerving feeling he was being watched. He studied the faces of the passers-by, but everyone he saw was intent on either getting in or out of one the houses as quickly as possible. None of them were paying him any attention at all. So why was his skin crawling so unpleasantly? A movement caught his eye in an alleyway directly opposite. He peered into the shadows, but it was still too dark to see very clearly. Was that a barrel, or a crouched figure, he wondered? Despite his best instincts, he rose from the bench and started walking across the street towards the alleyway. As he neared the hunched shape, it suddenly leapt from the ground and dashed silently back up the alley, quickly disappearing from view. Fabian's fear grew, as he realised his suspicions had been correct: someone *had* been watching him. The idea horrified him and he looked anxiously up at the house Jonas had entered, praying he would not be left alone for much longer.

Fabian passed another awful fifteen minutes on the bench, crippled by fear and flinching at every shape that rushed past. Finally, he saw a tired Jonas step back out onto the street and head towards him, leaning heavily on his cane and finally looking as old as Fabian knew he must be.

'Is everything alright?' asked Jonas with a yawn, as he saw the fear in Fabian's eyes.

'Yes, of course,' he replied. 'I'm a little tired, that's all.'

'Of course you are, my boy. We should get you home. Isolde will be expecting us.' He nodded to the wide, moonlit lawns of the park. 'We can cut back through here.'

A flagged path dissected the park, lined by tall, noble oaks, and low, serpentine yews. In the grey calm just before the dawn, it was one of the few places in the city that Fabian hadn't felt claustrophobic. The path was broad, straight and silent and it seemed that for the briefest of moments that Altdorf was asleep.

They had just spied the gates on the far side of the park when Jonas paused and frowned at Fabian. 'Did you hear that?' he asked.

Fabian shook his head, but something in his uncle's tone reminded of him of the figure he saw fleeing up the alleyway.

Jonas stayed stock still, listening carefully. After a few minutes he curled his lip in disdain. 'It seems that the evening's entertainment isn't over.' He reached beneath the black velvet of his doublet and withdrew a long knife. He flipped it in his hand and held it out to Fabian, handle first. 'Just in case,' he said, with a wry smile.

The sound of running feet came from behind them and Jonas and Fabian turned to see five slender figures sprinting towards them out of the darkness. Fabian recognised the gypsy bandanas that covered their faces from the men in the Recalcitrant Club. A cold fury replaced his fear, as he pictured the treacherous Calderino murdering his frail old uncle. He finally felt as though he had a relative who understood him and these dogs were going to butcher him.

With a howl of rage, Fabian dropped his book and charged at the masked figures, brandishing his knife as though it were a lance. Every heroic tale he had ever read flooded through his mind as he leapt at the first runner, planting a well-placed boot in the man's face and sending them both tumbling backwards onto the grass. Without a pause for breath, he climbed to his feet and threw the knife with all his strength at the second runner. It spun through the air, flashing in the moonlight before embedding itself deep in the man's thigh.

He screamed in pain and tumbled to his knees, clutching at the blade and spitting out a stream of insults in a language Fabian did not recognise.

Fabian flew at the man and pounded his fist into the side of his head, sending him sprawling across the flagstones. 'The books were forgeries!' he cried, his voice cracking with emotion. 'Keep your hands off my uncle!' Then he gasped in pain as his face suddenly slammed against a flagstone. He realised vaguely that someone had just punched him, but as the stars whirled over his head, he could not quite work out how to operate his legs.

A furious, swarthy face snarled down at him. 'Stay out of this, you ridiculous child,' cried Calderino, ripping the bandana from his face and spitting on the path. 'I'd be quite happy to slit your throat too.'

Fabian tried to climb to his feet, but his legs collapsed beneath him and his stomach emptied its contents noisily across the path. He could do nothing but watch in helpless, mute despair as the men drew their knives and stepped towards his defenceless uncle.

CHAPTER FOURTEEN
Kindred Spirits

Fabian writhed across the ground, still retching as the men circled Jonas. All his strength had vanished and a terrible nausea twisted his guts as he realised his uncle was about to die.

Calderino and his men tossed their slender blades from hand to hand as they closed in on the old man, hurling mocking insults as they prepared to strike. Even the man Fabian had injured managed a grin as he limped towards his prey.

Jonas, however, seemed quite calm. He placed his books carefully on the ground and raised his slender cane, as though intending to use it as a weapon. Then he shook his head sadly. 'You've wasted a lot of my time today, Calderino. Thanks to you I was unable to greet a very important guest, and the lies you told about those books will set my studies back months. But as a club member, I was prepared to forgive your lack of professionalism. Despite my better judgement, I was willing to write the whole thing off to experience.'

Calderino's wiry body shuddered with fury. 'You owe me my money, Wolff!' he screamed. He looked around at his men and pointed his knife at Jonas's head. 'Kill the bastard, quickly. I can't bear to listen to his stupid, pompous voice.'

The man nearest to Jonas sprang, cat-like, bringing his stiletto down towards his face with lightning speed.

Jonas rocked back on his heels with the practiced ease of a dancer. His agility shocked the knifeman and he stumbled past him in confusion. Jonas drew a long, slender sword from within his cane and slid it neatly through the man's ear so that it emerged on the other side of his head in a bright fountain of blood.

The man twitched and lurched for a few seconds, dangling puppet-like from Jonas's sword, then the old man withdrew the blade and the attacker slumped lifelessly to the floor.

Fabian stopped trying to climb to his feet and lay down again in shock. His uncle's movements had been faster and more graceful than any swordsman he had ever seen. He noticed something else, too: as Jonas fought, his lips had moved as fast as his limbs, mouthing strange, silent words and phrases.

Calderino's three remaining men took one look at each other and leapt at Jonas with their blades flashing.

The old man rolled to the ground in a fluid, elegant movement, so fast that the first man to reach him tripped awkwardly over his hunched frame and toppled heavily onto the path. Jonas then rose smoothly to his feet and skewered him through the back of his neck with a quick thrust of his rapier, leaving him gasping horribly for breath and clutching at his severed windpipe.

The second man to reach Jonas jabbed his stiletto at the small of the old man's back, but Jonas simply rolled forward out of harm's way and the knifeman's own momentum sent him crashing to his knees. He had barely cried out in pain before Jonas spun around in a delicate pirouette with his sword held at just the right angle to sever the man's head from his shoulders and send it bouncing away down the path.

At the sight of such formidable skill, the third man tried to halt in his tracks, abandoning his attack and turning it into an attempt to flee, but his leg still had Fabian's knife embedded in it, and as he turned it collapsed beneath him. He slipped on his heels and fell backwards with a cry of fear. Jonas had no need of any more acrobatics. The man was so petrified, Jonas simply took one step forward and, with an artistic flourish, jabbed his sword quickly in and out of the man's left eye, puncturing his brain and leaving him to thrash around for a few seconds like a landed fish, before finally lying still.

Jonas raised his hand to stifle a yawn as he turned to face Calderino. 'That's even more effort I've wasted on you,' he said, taking a languid step towards him. 'You're running up quite a debt.'

Calderino shook his head in horror and backed away into the shadows. 'You're a witch,' he hissed, before turning to sprint away across the silvery lawns.

Fabian looked up at his uncle in awe as he loomed over him. 'I can't believe what you just did,' he groaned, struggling not to vomit again. 'You moved so fast. It was incredible. Even men half your age aren't so agile.'

Jonas looked down at him with a sad smile. 'It's true,' he said, placing the tip of his sword against Fabian's throat.

'What're you doing?' asked Fabian, trying to twist his neck away from the blade.

The smile slipped from Jonas's face, to be replaced by humourless frown that Fabian had not seen before. 'I could never have learned such techniques from any normal swordsman,' he continued. 'And unfortunately, on the rare occasions I'm forced to use them, I must ensure there are no witnesses. It's nothing personal, you understand. It's just crucial that nobody can tell the world of my special talents. Calderino may have eluded me for the moment, but his days are numbered. I'll see to him shortly. You, however, are a different matter.'

'I don't understand,' croaked Fabian, hoarse with panic. 'You're going to kill me?'

Jonas sighed heavily and nodded. 'It *is* most unfortunate,' he said. 'I've already grown quite fond of you. I particularly liked the way you attacked a gang of vicious hired killers without the remotest chance of surviving.'

'Uncle, I beg you,' cried Fabian, grabbing his uncle's leg. 'Don't do this!'

Jonas narrowed his eyes. 'I wonder,' he muttered, pressing the tip of his sword a little harder into the soft flesh under Fabian's chin. The boy whimpered as he felt a thin trickle of blood run around his trembling neck and begin to pool on the ground beneath his head. 'Tell, me Fabian,' said Jonas, lowering his voice to a whisper. 'What do you crave most of all in the world? What do you dream of?'

A host of possible answers filled Fabian's mind. He saw that his life depended on choosing the right one, but which was it? What did his uncle wish to hear? That he wanted to be an honest, law-abiding man, or an infamous villain? Or that he wished to be a great scholar and author, or an artist even? What could it be? He sighed and let his head fall back to the ground, realising that it was hopeless. What ever he said would be wrong. 'If I weren't about to die in this filthy, fish-stinking, cesspit of a city,' he said finally, 'my dream would have been to reinstate my family's honour. And to see a Wolff at the head of the Empire's armies once more; leading us to glorious victories, as my ancestors did, instead of poring over prayer books and building even more temples.' He glared up at Jonas. 'And who knows, maybe if I hadn't been betrayed by such a lying, ungrateful maggot of an uncle, I could have reminded my father that Jakob isn't his only son.'

Jonas continued to frown at him for a few seconds, then a smile spread slowly across his face. He tilted his head back and began to chuckle. Then his chuckles became great, heaving guffaws and he dropped his rapier to the ground with clatter. 'Lying, ungrateful maggot,' he gasped through his laughter. 'Oh, I like that.' He fell to the ground, next to Fabian, still shaking with laughter. 'We truly are kin, you and I,' he said, blinking away a stream of tears.

An overwhelming feeling of relief washed over Fabian as he realised he'd somehow stumbled across the right answer. As a grey dawn crept nervously over the convoluted spires of Altdorf, it found the two Wolffs laughing and rolling hysterically across the park, surrounded by blood and the spread-eagled corpses of their foes.

As they arrived back at the door of the Unknown House, blackbirds were trilling from its eaves and sleepy-eyed merchants were already hurrying past on the way to market.

Isolde was waiting for them: leaning against the doorframe with her arms folded and a despairing look on her face. 'I see you've already introduced our guest to the dubious pleasures of Altdorf's nightlife,' she said with a wry smile.

As his uncle placed a kiss on her outstretched hand, Fabian could hardly believe it was the same woman. Her hair was tied back in a neat, intricate plait, and her eyes were bright and alert. She was no less beautiful, but all trace of her earlier feyness had vanished. She shook her head in reply to Jonas's wry smile and held out her hand to Fabian.

'I doubt Jonas has found time to mention me. I'm Isolde, his wife. It's a pleasure to meet you, Fabian.'

Fabian frowned in confusion, but Jonas's raised eyebrows and fixed smile implied that Fabian should say nothing about their previous encounter, so he simply kissed her hand and gave a low bow. 'The pleasure's all mine, Frau Wolff. Uncle told me you were beautiful, but you surpass even his most enraptured descriptions.'

Isolde pursed her lips in disbelief. 'Hmm. I see he's been giving you lessons in flattery, too.' She gave a good-natured chuckle as she waved them inside. 'Come in. Come in. I doubt he remembered to offer you anything as mundane as food. I thought you'd come scurrying back at first light, so I've rustled you up some breakfast.'

The house was just as gloomy and labyrinthine as the day before, but with Isolde waltzing through its maze of halls and antechambers, humming a merry tune as she went, the atmosphere seemed far less oppressive. She led them to a dining room crammed with suits of rusting armour and dusty, stuffed animals, bears mainly, who crowded around the long table like hungry dinner guests. Fabian shoved a mangy badger from the seat he was offered and began to eat. Isolde had prepared a platter of cold meats, sour bread and scrambled eggs and as soon as Fabian took his first bite he realised how hungry the night's adventures had left him. For a few minutes he forgot everything else in his eagerness to wolf down the food.

After a while he sat back in his chair and found that Isolde had left them. He could still hear her nearby, whistling and bustling around the house, and the sound comforted him for some reason.

'So,' said Jonas, pouring him a cup of tea. 'Where does this leave us, you and I?'

Fabian leant across the table and looked imploringly at his uncle. 'I would never talk of what I saw. You must believe me.'

Jonas nodded and twirled his waxed moustaches thoughtfully. 'And just what exactly *did* you see?'

Fabian shrugged. 'I saw a man too old to walk properly, suddenly become the most agile, deadly swordsman I've ever seen. I saw him slay four trained assassins with no more effort than if he were combing his hair.' He paused, recalling the incident. 'And I saw him utter strange, whispered sentences that seemed to aid him in some way – almost as though the strength and speed of the attack were linked to the force of the words.'

Jonas nodded. 'You've a sharp mind, and you've already guessed at far more than I would usually be comfortable with. However, as I said earlier, I feel we share more than just a bond of blood. Your ambitions remind me very much of my own adolescent dreams.' He took a sip of tea and sat back in his chair, eyeing Fabian carefully.

'I'm a collector of curiosities, Fabian,' he explained. 'Curiosities and antiques of all kinds, and I'm not just talking about physical relics. I'm a kind of archaeologist of ideas, as much as anything. I've spent my whole life digging beneath the oppressive, facile foundations of our universities and colleges, looking for older, broader forms of knowledge. However,' he said, waving at his lined face, 'I'm even more ancient than I look, believe it or not, and I sometimes wonder what will happen to all this accumulated wisdom when I finally grow tired of life. I've no children, you understand.'

He looked around at the rows of glassy eyes that surrounded them. 'I inherited the Unknown House from my great grandfather, Johannes Wolff. I know very little about him, but I believe he may have shared the same desire for strength and glory that burns in the two of us. I'm not sure of his profession, but his house was full of oddities even before I took possession of it, and I also inherited many of its odd guests. They continued to arrive, unannounced, long after Johannes had died, still expecting an unquestioning welcome at the house of a Wolff.' He shrugged. 'So, in exchange for various gifts and pieces of information, I let them keep coming. This house has countless rooms and half of the time I couldn't tell you who's staying in them. But my guests have proved to be an invaluable source of knowledge. Many of them have travelled from the furthest corners of the Old World and are prepared to provide me with the most incredible artefacts in exchange for nothing more than hospitality and discretion. My one condition is that only the most interesting people are admitted. If there's one thing I can't bear, it's a dullard.'

Fabian leant across the table towards Jonas, his eyes wide with excitement. 'Share your learning with me, uncle, I beg you. I've already spent long hours in the library at Berlau, reading of the days before Sigmar. I know much about the Old Faith that preceded our current church.'

'There are things I could show you,' conceded Jonas. 'There are certain techniques and methods that might help you realise your ambitions.' He took a silver chain from around his neck and placed it in Fabian's hand. Fabian recognised it as being identical to the one he saw around Isolde's neck. In the hazy light of the dining room, however, he could now discern the small figurine that hung on the end of it: it was the head of a wolf, carved intricately from a piece of bone. Jonas closed the boy's hand over the pendant and squeezed, until the icon pressed painfully into the flesh of his palm. 'You must swear an oath of secrecy, though, Fabian,' said Jonas, gripping even more tightly. 'And if you ever break this oath, a curse of the most violent, terrible magnitude will come down on you and your family.'

Fabian did not hesitate for a second. 'I swear,' he said. 'I swear I would never tell a soul. Even if it meant my life or the life of my parents.'

Jonas gripped Fabian's hand for a few seconds longer, peering into his eyes as though looking for something. Then he nodded, withdrew the pendant and hung it back around his neck. 'Do not take that oath lightly, my boy,' he said, with a deep sigh. Then, after finishing his tea, he rose to his feet. 'You should probably bathe and get a little sleep,' he said, in stern, serious tones. 'We may only have a few days before you leave and there is much to learn before then.'

Fabian did as he was instructed. Isolde made him a hot bath and showed him to a small attic room that looked out over a noisy, wooden dovecote and a sunlit yard at the back of the house. He was exhausted from the night's exertions, but he still only managed to sleep for a couple of hours. His dreams were filled with visions of his uncle's brutal acrobatics; but it was his own face that was muttering the strange words as he plunged a glinting rapier into the bodies of countless, reeling foes.

He awoke well before midday and leapt from his bed, tingling with excitement at the thought of what awaited him. Jonas was in his study, reading a letter. He didn't look up at Fabian's approach, but acknowledged him by beginning to read out loud. 'The Arch Lector would like to consult a few of his brethren before making a firm commitment, but as you can imagine, we are all very proud that Jakob would even be considered for ordination at such a young age. It is a great honour for our family. As a result of this good news, the Arch Lector has graciously invited us to stay in the cathedral for another week or so. I hope Fabian is not making too much of a nuisance of himself, and look forward to seeing you and making the acquaintance of your wife. Yours, etc, etc, Hieronymus Wolff.'

As he reached the end of the letter, Jonas looked up from his cluttered desk. 'Good. We have a little longer than I expected then. There's something I'd like us to discuss with Puchelperger this evening at the Recalcitrant Club, but before then I think I should introduce you to a few basic martial concepts.' He shook his head. 'It was undoubtedly brave of you to defend me from those Tileans last night, but I've no idea what you thought you could achieve by throwing yourself at them like that.'

Jonas looked around at the crowded shelves that lined the room. Skulls, books, leering painted masks and jars of pale, cloudy liquid filled every available inch of space. 'There's a lifetime of study in this room, Fabian,' he said, rummaging in the drawers of the desk, 'which can make it a little hard to track things down. Ah!' he exclaimed, spotting a small wooden box sat on the desk in front of him. 'Just the thing.' He handed the box to Fabian and turned to look inside a large trunk next to his chair. 'Put it on,' he said, with his head buried in the chest.

Fabian sat next to the fireplace in the same chair he'd used the night before and carefully opened the box. He sighed with pleasure as he saw a silver chain just like his aunt and uncle's, complete with the same wolf's head pendant. He placed it over his neck and relished the feel of the cold metal on his skin.

Jonas's head popped up again and when he saw the chain in place he peered anxiously at Fabian, as though waiting for some kind of adverse reaction. Then he nodded. 'Good, good,' he said and rose from behind the desk with a long needle and a bottle of ink in his hand. 'Now, take off your right shoe.'

'My shoe?'

'Yes, your shoe child – as quick as you like.'

Fabian could not help but feel a little nervous as his uncle crouched before him and took his foot in his hand.

Jonas dipped the needle in the ink and held it a few inches from the sole of Fabian's foot. 'This may hurt a little,' he said before piercing the tough skin of his heel. The old man muttered something under his breath as he worked the ink into Fabian's flesh. It sounded like some kind of tune, but as Fabian winced in discomfort, he could not quite make out the words. 'There,' said Jonas after a few minutes, rising to his feet with a wheeze and a creak of protesting joints. 'All done.' He stepped up to a terrible portrait of Isolde, which hung behind his desk and moved it to one side, revealing a small safe embedded in the wall. He unlocked it and withdrew a sheaf of papers. Then, after closing the safe and sliding the painting back in front of it, he sat down at the desk again.

'Let me see,' he muttered, leafing through the crumbling old parchments. He gave a grunt of satisfaction as he found the one he wanted. 'Right,' he said, taking a stick of chalk from his desk and stepping into the middle of the room. He kicked aside a rug to reveal the dusty floorboards beneath. Fabian noticed that a palimpsest of faded chalk marks covered the wood, where dozens of geometrical symbols has been drawn, erased and redrawn. Jonas crouched down with the chalk in one hand and the paper in the other, and began to transcribe an intricate series of shapes from the parchment to the floor. The symbols and numbers were mind-boggling in their complexity, and Fabian felt the first stirrings of doubt.

'Uncle,' he said, frowning at the shapes.

'Yes?' replied Jonas, with a hint of irritation in his voice as he concentrated on the drawing.

'Is all this, well…' Fabian stumbled over his words as his uncle looked up at him. 'Well, there's nothing heretical about what we're doing, is there?'

'Pah!' snapped Jonas, returning to his work. 'Such words are open to interpretation. Your parents would no doubt think so – and your brother too by the sounds of him. But such prejudice only reveals the paucity of their education – and its blinkered, narrow focus.' He climbed to his feet and gestured to the grotesque scrawl he had created. 'This is science, lad, nothing more, nothing less. But it's a wisdom that stems from an older, more holistic world view than the simple, crude tenets of the Sigmarites.' He pointed to a circle in the centre of the drawing. 'Place your right foot there, and don't move it until I say you can.'

Fabian did as his uncle ordered and noticed that a mixture of blood and ink began to mingle with the chalk marks. After just a few seconds a peculiar warmth began to spread across the sole of his foot. He looked at his uncle in surprise, but the old man simply gave him a brusque nod, before turning to rifle through his books. The heat spread quickly up his legs, though his groin and into his stomach, where it grew in strength and rushed through his chest and into his arms and head. The heat was not unpleasant, and something about Jonas's calm, matter-of-fact demeanour infected Fabian so that he remained unconcerned, even as the chalk marks began to smoke slightly. Fabian beamed as he felt a fierce vitality rush through him. He flexed his muscles and sighed with pleasure as he felt a new strength blossoming in them. He suddenly felt as though he could tear the whole house down with his bare hands if he wanted to.

Jonas heard his sigh and turned away from the bookshelves. He raised his eyebrows at the sight of Fabian's broad grin and the smoke trailing up around his legs. 'That's enough,' he snapped. 'Step back, Fabian.'

Fabian reluctantly lifted his foot out of the circle, but to his delight a vestigial glow of the heat and strength remained in his muscles as he stepped back. He had to stifle the urge to punch something.

'Stand by the door,' said Jonas, seeming slightly annoyed, 'and we'll get down to work.' He grabbed a pair of foils from the wall and stood next to Fabian with a large book in his hand. 'If you're ever going to make something of yourself, you must learn to master the Circle of Defence and the geometrical principles propounded by the Old World's greatest swordsman, Agilwardus.'

'I've never heard of him,' said Fabian, frowning at the intricate diagrams his uncle was holding up to him.

'Of course you haven't. He was burned as a heretic three hundred years ago, simply for being a little ahead of his time. There are only three copies of this wonderful treatise still in existence and they're all in this room.' Jonas placed the book on a lectern, gave Fabian one of the swords and raised his own into an en garde position. 'Remember,' he said with a lupine grin, 'this will hurt me a lot more than it will hurt you.'

As they set out towards the Street of a Hundred Taverns, Fabian was moving even slower than his elderly uncle. He carried bruises on almost every part of his body and the fire in his muscles had been replaced by the dull, throbbing ache of exhaustion. They had trained until well after nightfall, without even a break for food or water, and all he wanted to do now was to collapse onto a bed.

The streets were just as crowded as on the previous night, but Fabian was blind to the figures that swarmed around them. His mind was spinning with a wealth of new information. As his uncle had lunged and parried, he had yelled out a stream of commands. Some of them in languages Fabian never heard before: musical, lilting phrases, or harsh, guttural barks, but he had understood the meanings behind them quite clearly. The energy from the chalk marks had not just filled him with strength, but also a strange intuition. As his blade flashed back and forth in a desperate attempt to fend off Jonas's attacks he had felt his skill growing with each word his uncle hurled at him. When they finally stopped sparring, both of them had collapsed to the floor, gasping for breath and covered in sweat. Fabian had crawled up into a chair, feeling like his head was some kind of strange pupa, bulging and writhing as it struggled to contain an entirely new Fabian, who was straining to burst free from behind his eyes.

Now, as he stumbled after his uncle, Fabian still felt the mass of information twisting somewhere in his head, but it seemed to be biding its time, waiting patiently at the back of his thoughts until it was called upon. He felt its presence as clearly as he felt the weight of the rapier his uncle had tucked in his belt as they left the house.

Jonas left the boy to his thoughts as they made their way to the club, but every now and then he would cast a discreet sidelong glance at him, as though watching for something.

'It's good to see you again, Captain Wolff,' said the flame-haired butler as he welcomed them in out of the heaving throng.

'Thank you, Vogel,' said Jonas, handing him his hat and cloak. 'Has Puchelperger arrived yet?'

Vogel shook his head with a cheerful grin. 'I'm sure he'll be here soon though. I passed on your note myself, and he seemed delighted at the prospect of spending another evening in your company.'

'Very good,' said Jonas, stepping into the lounge and taking the same table as on the previous night. 'Strange,' he said, taking a sip of the drink that appeared before him. 'Puchelperger is usually here well before midnight.'

Fabian gave no reply, still struggling with his thoughts as he took a deep, grateful swig of his own drink.

They waited in a tense silence for nearly an hour, with Jonas drumming his fingers angrily on the table and sighing every few minutes.

'Terrible business with those Tileans last night,' said a ruddy cheeked, whiskery old general, pausing at their table.

'How do you mean?' asked Jonas, a little nervously.

The general shrugged. 'Shouting like that, in the club. It's really not what one expects in an establishment of this quality.'

'Oh,' said Jonas, visibly relieved. 'Quite.'

'If I had my way, anyone as ill-mannered as Calderino would be barred.' He sniffed disdainfully. 'I saw the villain this morning, actually. Practically knocked me over he was in such a hurry.'

'Really?' asked Jonas, taking another sip of his drink and trying to look uninterested.

'Yes. I was leaving Puchelperger's house and the blackguard barged past me on the way to the gate.' He shook his head in disapproval. 'What a scoundrel. He didn't even acknowledge me.'

Jonas lowered his glass carefully to the table. 'Are you sure it was Calderino?' he asked.

The general frowned. 'I may be retired, Wolff, but I've not lost control of my faculties just yet. It was Calderino, I tell you. Whoever recommended that man for membership must be a bloody fool.'

'Well, General Rauch, it's always a pleasure, but I've just remembered I promised Isolde I'd get the boy home a little earlier tonight.' Jonas drained his glass and stood. 'Come, Fabian,' he said striding towards the door.

Fabian smiled apologetically at the general as he rushed after his uncle.

As soon as they were out in the street, Fabian let out a groan of despair. 'This is bad,' he muttered, hobbling away as fast as his old legs would carry him. 'Very, very bad.'

'Do you think Calderino meant to harm Puchelperger?' asked Fabian, taking his uncle's arm and trying to support him a little.

Jonas looked at Fabian in disbelief. 'I think you could probably answer that yourself, don't you? General Rauch is exactly right – the man's a scoundrel. He's too afraid to approach me after what happened last night, so he's turned on my friends.'

Jonas led the way through a baffling sequence of lefts and rights until yet again Fabian had absolutely no idea where they were. They eventually emerged on a wide moonlit avenue, lined with tall plane trees and large, handsome townhouses. Most of the windows were filled with light and the elegant silhouettes of Altdorf's great and good, but there was a house near the end of the avenue that was utterly dark and lifeless. It was this house that Jonas rushed towards. As they approached the spiked iron gate, they saw that it was swinging on its hinges, and as they rushed up to the front door, Jonas pushed it inwards with a gentle shove. 'Unlocked,' he muttered. As the door swung open, the moonlight washed across the polished floorboards and picked out a large crumpled shape lying at the foot of a grand, sweeping staircase.

They rushed towards the prone figure, but before they had got within a few feet of it, they could see the ink black lake that had pooled beneath it.

'Ah, old friend,' groaned Jonas, lifting the corpse's head and revealing an ear-to-ear gash beneath Puchelperger's rolls of fat. 'Whatever you may have done, you did not deserve to die like this – at the hands of a petty criminal.'

Fabian looked nervously up the gloomy stairs. 'Do you think he might still be here?'

Jonas shook his head as he climbed slowly to his feet. 'No, there's no need to be afraid, boy. He's long gone. Probably on his way to butcher someone else dear to me.' Jonas's eyes widened and he staggered backwards, as though someone had slapped him. 'Oh, by the gods,' he muttered. 'Isolde.' He clutched his face in his hands and let out a terrible wail of anguish. 'I'm probably already too late. He knows what time I leave for the club.' He grabbed Fabian's shoulders and looked desperately into his eyes. 'You might make it though boy,' he hissed. 'Run as fast as your young legs will carry you.' He saw the doubt in Fabian's eyes as he pictured himself fighting the Tilean swordsman. 'It will all come back to you,' hissed Jonas. 'Everything I showed you today – even the strength from the sigils, it will all come back when you need it most. But you must be quick,' he cried, pushing him back towards the door.

'But which way do I go?' yelled Fabian in reply. 'I'll never find my way back alone.'

Jonas's face twisted into a mask of fury and for a second Fabian thought he would strike him. Then he took a deep breath to calm himself and looked around the house. His eyes came to rest on the pool of blood that surrounded them. 'Hold out your hand,' he said, stooping to the floor and dipping his finger in the cold, thick liquid.

'Left at the top of this avenue,' said Jonas, drawing a crimson line across Fabian's palm. 'Then a right, then two lefts, two rights and another left.' He stepped back and looked at Fabian with desperation in his eyes. 'Go, I beg you.'

Fabian looked at the crude, sticky map on his hand, and nodded once, before turning and dashing from the house. Fleet with fear, he pounded across the flagstones: barging past drunks and leaping over walls and hedges. As he ran, the map trailed across his skin, gradually losing all its definition and finally, with one turn still remaining, the lines of Puchelperger's blood blurred into a shapeless smear.

'Where now?' gasped Fabian in horror, as he reached a wide junction at the end of a row of tenements. He had no idea which way to turn. His heart was pounding in his chest as he looked up and down the two roads that lay before him, straining to remember the last direction. He groaned in despair. Then, something familiar caught his eye: the large dovecote that sat beneath his bedroom window. He gave a howl of delight and sprinted towards it. After a few seconds he saw the narrow street that led to the Unknown House and dashed up it.

As he ran towards the gate, he saw that just like Puchelperger's it was swinging on its hinges and to his horror, he saw that the front door was ajar too. 'I'm too late,' he panted, stumbling down the path.

He froze as he saw Calderino's face looming out of the darkness towards him. He drew the rapier his uncle had given him, but then he paused. There was something odd about Calderino: he was much taller than Fabian remembered him and his tanned, gaunt face was knotted in fear.

Fabian squinted into the darkness of the hall and slowly made out a second, much larger figure, stooped behind Calderino. The colossal shadow stepped forward into the moonlight and Fabian gave a laugh of relief. Calderino was dangling helplessly in the grip of one of Kobach Ivanov's massive hands. Fabian stepped aside as Kobach hurled the cursing Tilean out of the door. Kobach gave Fabian a brief nod of recognition before turning and closing the door firmly behind him.

Calderino leapt to his feet, spitting insults in his own language and pulling a stiletto from beneath his cape as he stepped towards Fabian. 'If I can't have his whore, you'll do instead,' he hissed, before lashing out with the needle-thin blade.

A stream of droning words fell from Fabian's mouth and the world seemed to slow. He watched the Tilean's blade moving towards his face with a feeling of cool dispassion and stepped easily out of the way. As Calderino tumbled into the space where Fabian had just been standing, the boy casually extended his leg and sent the Tilean sprawling across the path. The man crashed to the flagstones with a grunt and his knife clattered away into the darkness.

The world resumed its usual pace and Calderino clambered to his feet, turning to face Fabian with a look of horror on his face. 'You're just like him,' he gasped, backing away towards the gate. 'You're sorcerers, the pair of you.'

Fabian raised his slender sword, and levelled it at the man's head. 'You should leave,' he said calmly.

Calderino cursed as the gate flew open and Jonas staggered, gasping, onto the path.

'I think not,' said Jonas, grabbing the Tilean's shoulder and ramming his sword up through his chest.

Calderino stiffened with pain as the weapon emerged between his shoulder blades, then he slumped lifelessly in Jonas's arms. The old man laid his body down onto the path and looked back down the street to see if they were being watched. Once he was sure they were alone, he sheathed his sword and stepped towards Fabian, grasping his hand and nodding enthusiastically. 'You see? You've begun a great journey, my boy.' He looked down at Fabian's clean, unused blade and shook his head. 'You've still much to learn though.'

CHAPTER FIFTEEN

Secrets and Lies

'He's become unbearable,' said Fabian, steering his horse through the powdery snow.

Winter had come early to Ostland and the Berlau estate was a kingdom of ivory, frozen ponds and heavy, glittering boughs. 'He was never the most rational soul,' continued Fabian, as his charger picked its way carefully through the waist-high drifts, 'but since we returned from Altdorf, he seems determined to prove his holiness at every turn. Mainly by labelling everyone around him as morally suspect.' He pulled the collar of his fur-lined coat a little tighter, as a fresh flurry of snow rolled across the hills towards them. 'Sigmar knows why they ordained him at such a young age, but it's made him even more in love with his own myth. I dread to think what he wants to talk to me about. I imagine he intends to announce his impending godhood.'

The young man riding beside Fabian threw back his hood to reveal a face that looked like it had been carved from granite; his features had a crude, brutal quality to them and his eyes were as flat and lifeless as a corpse's. He grunted in disgust. 'So why are we running back to the house with our tails between our legs?' He patted the bleeding mass of fur and teeth hanging from his saddle. 'The hunting is good at this time of year.'

Fabian shrugged. 'I hear you, Ludwig, but Jakob's been ensconced in the temple with Brother Braun since the summer, so I suppose even I'm a little interested to know what his news is. But, more than that, for the first time in my life, my father is actually allowing me some leeway.' He clutched the waxed, fur-clad sheath that held his sword. 'My new-found military prowess has achieved the impossible and actually impressed the old man, so I'm determined not to do anything to upset him.' He looked over at his friend. 'Finally, I'm able to remind people that the Wolffs are a family with a proud history – a family not to be trifled with.' He gestured at the grizzled head that was fastened to his saddle. 'Father would never have let me roam the estates like this, marshalling the watch, and cleansing the woods of filth, if I hadn't proved to him that I have skills as impressive as Jakob's. How wonderful it is to finally be able to reinstate some order.'

'And dispatch transgressors,' said Ludwig, leaning forward with a hungry grin on his face.

Fabian looked over at his friend a little nervously. 'Yes, that too I suppose. Although it might be best to keep that under our hats for now.'

Ludwig's head snapped to one side a couple of times in an involuntary twitch. 'They deserve everything they got. The idiot peasantry only understand brute strength, Fabian. We were absolutely right to kill them. It will be a long time before anyone dares to poach from the Berlau estate again.'

Fabian continued to watch Ludwig from the corner of his eye. He was his oldest childhood friend and had been very useful during the months since he had returned from Altdorf, but he was beginning to wonder if he had been a little too open with him. 'Remember, Ludwig,' he said, placing a hand on the reins of the man's horse and bringing it to a stop, 'we should not mention any of my uncle's training techniques either. Father knows my new-found skill is due to Jonas's teachings, but he has no idea of the methods involved. And I don't think he would understand. Such ancient, unorthodox practices could easily be misconstrued by people less cultured than ourselves.'

Ludwig nodded eagerly, continuing to grin. He stretched out his arms, tensing and relaxing the muscles with obvious delight. 'We wouldn't want everyone to have such skills anyway – we'd lose the advantage.' He laughed. 'I imagine that's why your uncle made you swear that ridiculous oath of secrecy – to limit the number of people who might be able to face him in single combat.'

Fabian flinched at the mention of the oath. With so many miles between him and Altdorf, it had seemed no great crime to share what he had learned with his closest friend; but every now and then, he felt a chill of doubt. 'You're probably right,' he muttered, steering his horse onwards down the hill. 'But nevertheless, I'd rather no one else knew.'

He smiled to himself as he remembered the other reason he was happy to visit Berlau: there was a parcel waiting there for him. Since their training sessions in Altdorf, Jonas had sent several packages containing fencing manuals, military textbooks and other, more unusual items. In his most recent letter he had mentioned some dolls, acquired through one of his guests at the Unknown House. They were things of incredible antiquity, believed by Jonas to have originated in far Cathay. The letter explained that despite their grotesque appearance, the dolls contained great power. Jonas claimed that if Fabian placed a single strand of a man's hair beneath the wax skin of one of the dolls, he would be granted unnatural power over the flesh of that man. Fabian had thought immediately of how easy it would be to pluck a hair from his brother's pillow.

They crested the brow of the next hill and saw the white folds of the valley spread out before them. 'Someone's burning the welcome feast,' said Ludwig, nodding to a thin column of black that was snaking up towards the bright, pregnant clouds.

'Odd,' muttered Fabian. The smoke was coming from near the house and it gave him an unpleasant sense of foreboding. He kicked his horse into a canter and cut through the deep snow with as much speed as he could manage.

As they approached the sprawling mass of the house, the source of the smoke became clearer: a pyre had been constructed not far from the gatehouse. Fabian peered through the eddying banks of snow and made out a group of figures, silhouetted against the whiteness. 'What's this?' he muttered, with growing impatience at his horse's slow progress.

His agitation grew as he neared the figures. A loose circle of servants, soldiers and officials was scattered around the smouldering pyre and at the head of them was Brother Braun with his head bowed in silent prayer. Next to the priest was a small, stocky figure, swaddled in a mountain of furs and bright, ceremonial robes. Fabian recognised him immediately as Tischer, the local magistrate, but there was another man by his side he could not place: a wiry, fanatical-looking priest of some kind. Fabian's gaze passed quickly over the stranger and came to rest on a shape near to the pile of charred wood. Jakob was lying a few feet from the pyre, curled up on the snow in a foetal position and shuddering violently.

Fabian reined in his horse as a row of ashen faces turned towards him. At a nudge from the magistrate, Braun looked up from his prayers and saw Fabian riding towards them.

'Fabian,' called Braun, with a look of panic on his face. He began clambering up the hill towards him, but Fabian had now looked beyond Jakob and fixed his eyes on the pyre. His head felt oddly light as he focussed on two corpses fastened to the top of the wreckage. They were burned beyond recognition, but from Jakob's shuddering sobs, he had no doubt who they were. The brightness of the snow seemed to grow suddenly, lancing painfully into his eyes and the whole scene began to spin around him as though he were drunk. He gripped the neck of his horse in an effort to stop himself falling.

'What have you done?' he whispered under his breath, steering his horse down the hill towards his brother. 'What have you done?' he repeated a little louder as he neared Braun who was still clambering up the hill. 'What have you done?' he howled, as he kicked his horse into a gallop, leaving a cloud of snow behind him as he charged down the hill.

'Wait, Fabian,' gasped Braun, reaching out in desperation as the horse thundered past.

'What have you done?' screamed Fabian, leaping from his horse and planting a ferocious kick into Jakob's side.

Jakob spun across the snow and clambered to his feet. His eyes were red raw from crying and he looked across at his brother in confusion.

Fabian strode forward and punched Jakob with such force that his head snapped back with an audible click of bone, sending a spray of red across the crisp, white snow.

Jakob reeled backwards but managed to stay on his feet. The blow seemed to clear his head slightly and he looked at Fabian with a spark of recognition in his eyes. 'Occultists,' he slurred through bloody teeth, trying to explain.

Fabian's face flushed a dark purple and he howled with inarticulate rage, before drawing a long hunting knife from his belt and rushing at his brother.

'Wait,' cried a piercing voice.

Fabian paused to see the wiry priest striding towards him, closely followed by the magistrate and a group of militiamen. The priest had odd, pale eyes that bulged out of his thin face as he approached. 'Jakob only did what he had to,' he said. 'Your parents were engaged in the most depraved, heretical activity. Who knows what havoc they would have wrought if your brother hadn't reported them to me. You should thank him.'

Fabian shook his head in disbelief. 'Who are you?' he gasped, noticing that the guards lined up behind the man were drawing their weapons.

'My name's Otto Sürman,' he replied, 'and I'm a Templar of Sigmar.' He nodded to the guards and officials that surrounded him. 'You should think very carefully about what you say.'

'Sürman's telling the truth, Fabian,' said the magistrate, anxiously rubbing his hands together and cowering behind the priest. 'You know how fond I was of your parents, but there was very convincing evidence. I'd never have sanctioned this if there had been any doubt.'

'Wait a minute,' growled Fabian, ignoring the magistrate and pointing his knife at the witch hunter. 'I recognise your name. You're the man my father banished from his estate, just a few months ago. You locked a village idiot in a cage because he spoke to his birds.' His whole body was trembling with fury as he strode towards Otto. 'I see what this is,' he said, his voice sounding strained and unnatural. 'My father made a fool of you, and this is your vengeance.'

The witch hunter was about to reply when Jakob cried out. 'No, brother, that's not how it is. I found the evidence. They were involved in something terrible.' His voice cracked with emotion as he turned to face the pyre. 'But I didn't realise the punishment would be so...' he placed his head in his hands.

Fabian shook his head in disbelief. 'How could you betray our parents to this charlatan?' As his eyes filled with tears, he let out another keening wail of despair. 'They were starting to notice me. Finally. After all those years in your shadow.'

Sürman cautiously stepped closer to the weeping Fabian and the magistrate signalled for the guards to ready their weapons.

'Your brother's not to blame,' said Sürman as he emptied a small bag onto the snow at Fabian's feet.

'What's that?' snapped Fabian with a dismissive sneer. 'Something you planted on them, no doubt.' As he stooped to examine the objects, the colour drained from his face. They were small, wax dolls; ugly, deformed little things, but there was no disguising their heretical nature. Fabian recognised them immediately from the description in his uncle's letter.

Sürman was just a few feet away and as he saw Fabian's look of recognition, he frowned in confusion. 'Do you–?' he began. But as the magistrate stepped to his side, the witch hunter clamped his mouth tightly shut and said no more.

Fabian's legs folded beneath him and he crumpled silently into the deep snow.

Jakob stepped to his side and looked down at him. 'There's nothing we could have done, brother. They brought this on themselves.'

'No, they didn't,' spat Fabian, 'you did. You and your obsession with holiness.' He climbed back to his feet and leant towards Jakob until their noses were almost touching. 'If you weren't so wrapped up in your own twisted idea of virtue, our parents would still be alive. You've murdered them as surely as if you lit the fire.'

Jakob shook his head in desperate denial, but could think of no words to defend himself.

Fabian's rage returned to him and he drew back the hunting knife.

Before he could strike, the soldiers rushed forward and grabbed his arms, knocking the knife from his grip and dragging him away from his brother.

Fabian slipped, eel-like from their grasp, leaving them stumbling through the snow in confusion. He reached down to retrieve the knife, but then, noticing the dolls at his feet he paused and glanced nervously at the witch hunter. He left the knife where it was and turned to face his brother. 'Just go,' he said, trying to control his breathing. 'You've destroyed everything. The Wolffs are ruined. Don't make me a murderer too.'

Jakob shook his head in a pitiful, mute plea.

Fabian pointed at the bodies. 'Look at what you've done,' he cried.

'You must leave Berlau. If I avenge them, I'll be ruined too.' He nodded at the surrounding whiteness. 'Take your wretched prayers away, Jakob. Be anywhere but here.'

Jakob looked from his brother to the charred corpses of his parents and his face twisted with anguish. Then his shoulders slumped in defeat and he gave a slight nod. 'If it's what you wish,' he muttered, giving his brother one last pleading glance.

Fabian was still trembling with anger and refused to meet his eye. 'If I ever see you again, I won't be responsible for my actions,' he hissed, sounding close to tears. 'But if you swear never return to Berlau, I won't hunt you down.'

Jakob swayed, as though slapped, but gave another weak nod as he turned away. He stumbled off through the valley like a dying man and after just a few minutes his stooped, lonely figure disappeared behind the whirling banks of snowflakes.

CHAPTER SIXTEEN

Massacre at Hagen's Claw

The Iron Duke, Kriegsmarshall Fabian Wolff, surveyed his vast army with a long sigh of satisfaction. 'Have you ever seen anything so beautiful?' he asked the grey-haired captain riding beside him.

The old knight's head jerked sideways in a series of involuntary twitches, then he looked back at the men behind them. 'Never,' he replied as he studied the sea of rippling banners.

Fabian had begun the campaign with a force of considerable size, but over the months, it had grown even larger, becoming an unwieldy host of epic proportions. As the seriousness of the incursion became known, von Raukov had sent reinforcements from every corner of Ostland in support of his beloved protégé. It would be impossible to say exactly how many men were now marching behind him. They numbered in the tens of thousands though, certainly: knights, engineers, spearmen, pistoliers and greatswords, all eager to serve under such a revered general. Fabian's exploits had already become the stuff of legend. After three decades of combat, his mind was as fast as his sword arm; in fact, he was almost as deadly in real life as he was in the tales his agents had spread across the province. The officers under the Iron Duke's command followed him with a fanatical devotion and the elector count had placed complete trust in him. He had achieved almost everything he had ever desired.

'The scouts have returned from Mercy's End, kriegsmarshall,' said the captain. 'Felhamer's run of luck has finally ended. Mormius didn't even stop to pursue the survivors. They just torched the ruins and continued marching south.'

Fabian nodded. 'His only interest seems to be reaching Wolfenberg as quickly as possible. Was there any news of Felhamer himself?'

'None, although I doubt he would have fled with the survivors.'

'No, I imagine you're right, Ludwig – from what I hear, the captain was as honourable as he was stupid. He'll have held out until the very last minute.' As they rode up out of the valley, he raised a hand to shield his eyes from the late afternoon sun and looked down across the rain-drenched hills and forests of Ostland. 'We should meet them very soon,' he said, with a slight tremor in his voice. 'The moment I've waited for, all these years, has finally arrived.' He lifted a pendant from beneath his polished cuirass and studied it closely. It was the ivory wolf's head his uncle had given him all those years ago in the Unknown House. 'After this battle, the name Wolff will never be forgotten,' he said, turning the pendant slowly in his fingers. He lowered his voice and smiled at Ludwig. 'And once my master has accepted the wonderful gift I'm bringing to him, I'll become the mightiest warrior the Old World has ever seen.'

Ludwig shook his head. 'I can understand why the Ruinous Powers would wish you to bring them such a great sacrifice – to lead so many soldiers into their grasp is truly a wondrous gift, but there's something I can't understand.'

Fabian looked around to see if any of the other officers were near enough to overhear. Then he leant closer to Ludwig and nodded for him to continue.

'If you're taking this great army to your master as a sacrifice, will Mormius know not to strike you down, as he has done so many others. Does he understand the bargain you've struck?'

Fabian leant back in his saddle and stroked his moustache. 'I imagine he knows nothing of me, or my true purpose. My master won't care which of us triumphs – either result will amuse him. If I can defeat Mormius and his rabble, and make my great sacrifice, he'll reward me in ways I'm only just beginning to comprehend. But, if I fail, and Mormius lays waste to Wolfenberg, the power I sought will be bestowed on him. We're playthings, nothing more – just an amusing diversion for the Great Deceiver. Mormius will only see me as an obstacle on the road to glory.' Fabian clutched the hilt of his sword and smiled. 'He should make a worthy opponent.'

Ludwig nodded, and rubbed his cold, lifeless eyes. 'Well, whatever the outcome, it will be good to finally reach him. We seem to have been marching for decades.'

Almost half a mile behind Fabian and his officers, rode Baron Maximilian von Düring, at the head of his squadron of Knights Griffon. Beside him rode Jakob, Ratboy and Anna.

'Can you be sure we're talking about the same man?' asked Ratboy, looking at the group of banners at the head of the army. 'Do you really think that's your brother up there?'

Wolff nodded. 'There's no other explanation. I was filled with dread at the thought of my brother marching with this army and now I find he's the man leading it.' His brow was creased in a thunderous scowl. 'It's much worse than I anticipated. Fabian's not the hero these men think he is. His master isn't von Raukov, but some unspeakable, unholy force. I can't imagine what he has planned for this army, but it's certainly not victory.'

'But it makes no sense,' said Maximilian. 'I've been hearing tales of the Iron Duke's victories ever since I first arrived in Ostland. He's driven back countless invasions. Why would he have done that if he's some kind of pawn of the Dark Powers?'

Wolff looked over at his old friend. 'He's playing for higher stakes. All he's ever dreamed of is to be a great hero – the *greatest* hero in fact. As a child, he pictured himself as a valiant knight, torn straight from the old lays and ballads. He always wanted to march at the head of a great Empire army such as this one. He's been carefully biding his time and gradually winning the trust of the elector count, and now he's leading the largest force in the province.'

'Then we should confront him,' cried Ratboy, brandishing his graceful sword. 'We should reveal him as the heretic he is.'

Maximilian shook his head. 'You'd never get within thirty feet of him, boy – unless he wanted you to. His personal honour guard watch him constantly. He calls them the Oberhau and their swordsmanship is legendary. They wield greatswords as easily as if they were rapiers.' He frowned. 'They wear fearsome helmets, fashioned in the shape of a snarling wolf and are famed for their ruthlessness. Rumour has it that the Iron Duke trains each of them personally; but, if your suspicions are correct, maybe there's more to the training than meets the eye.'

Wolff nodded. 'To reveal myself now would be a mistake. Fabian has an entire army fawning at his feet. He'd simply have me arrested. I imagine these Oberhau would have no qualms about executing me, if Fabian ordered them to.'

'Then what will you do?' asked Anna, looking around anxiously at the ranks of marching soldiers that surrounded them.

'Bide my time,' replied Wolff. 'Ostland's on the edge of ruin. Even if I could convince these men that their general is a traitor, I'm not sure I should. It's only Fabian that's holding them together.'

'But if he's a cultist of some kind, he's probably leading them all to their deaths,' she gasped, anxiously stroking the velvety stubble that covered her scalp.

Wolff nodded. 'All I can do is watch and wait.' He turned to Maximilian. 'We should move a little closer to the command group.'

Maximilian nodded and urged his horse into a canter, signalling for the other knights to pick up their pace too.

After a few hours, Maximilian nodded at a large hill that sat at the end of a long, narrow defile. It was topped with five odd, slender towers of stone. 'There's Fabian's destination,' he said, 'Hagen's Claw.'

Wolff peered at the distant hill. 'Have you spoken to my brother then?'

'Not personally, no, but two nights ago, I met with his closest advisor, the captain of the Oberhau.' Maximilian pursed his lips, as though tasting something bitter. 'His name's Ludwig von Groos and apparently he's Fabian's oldest friend, but there's something about the man that made my skin crawl.'

'Von Groos?' muttered Wolff, frowning. 'The name *does* sound familiar, but I spent most of my childhood in a temple. I never really knew my brother's friends. Why did you find this von Groos so unpleasant?'

Maximilian shrugged. 'Hard to say, really. I knew him by reputation anyway. He's considered unusually brutal, even by the standards of the Oberhau, but it wasn't that – there was something in his manner that made me feel on my guard. His words were quite deferential and his tone was perfectly reasonable, but I still felt as though he was mocking me somehow.'

'I see. But he explained Fabian's strategy to you?'

'Yes, although not in any detail. He simply told me the same as he told the other senior officers. The Iron Duke wants to reach an old burial site named Hagen's Claw and have time to dig in before the marauders arrive. His judgement has been sound on every previous occasion, so I simply thanked von Groos for the information and ushered him out of my tent as quickly as I could.' He shuddered at the memory. 'He started leafing through one of my tactical manuals with a ridiculous grin on his face – poking fun at the techniques and asking if I really used them. If I'd not found an excuse to shove him out of the door, I think we might have come to blows. Fabian's plan seems quite logical though. The hill's steep and topped with ancient monoliths, so there'll be plenty of cover and places to position the guns. There's also an unusually narrow valley behind it, so if things go badly, we'd be able to inflict *very* heavy losses on Mormius's men as we withdrew.'

Ratboy watched the smouldering, red sun as it sank behind the hill, silhouetting the towering obelisks that guarded the valley. There were four intact stones and a fifth that was broken and leaning to one side like a thumb. 'Whose tombs are they?' he asked. 'They're like nothing I've ever seen before.'

Maximilian shook his head. 'I've no idea, friend. I know they're old beyond reckoning, but other than that I've only heard rumours and legends. Maybe one of the Ostlanders would know,' he said, waving at the ranks of black and white troops that surrounded them. 'I think even they might struggle though.'

As the sun sank lower, bathing the landscape in scarlet light, the army reached the summit of the hill and began planting their standards between the strange columns. Half of the fifth stone had fallen, to be eagerly embraced by the shrubs and long grass beneath, but those that still stood reached even higher than Ratboy had expected. As he rode between them they seemed to bow over his head, so great was their height. 'Who was Hagen?' he asked in hushed tones, eyeing the obelisks with suspicion.

'I believe he was some kind of tribal warlord – a contemporary of Sigmar's – who met his end here,' answered Maximilian. The polished steel of his visor flashed red as he raised it to get a better view of the stones. 'The Ostlanders tell all sorts of gruesome tales about him. Allegedly, when he suspected one of his men of coveting his wife, he accused him of being no better than a wild scavenger, tied him to one of these stones and pierced his side with a knife. Then he left him to the mercy of the wolves that roam hereabouts.'

Ratboy looked up at the sombre columns with even more suspicion, wondering if it were shadows or dark stains he could see on the lichen-covered stone.

'How did Hagen die?' asked Ratboy.

'Well, if the legends are true, his power corrupted him and eventually he became a disciple of the Dark Gods. Sigmar heard stories of his strange behaviour and travelled out here to confront him. He found Hagen attempting to use the stones as part of some unspeakable rite, so they fought,' Maximilian gave Ratboy a wry smile, 'and Hagen died.'

Wolff saw the concern on Ratboy's face and gave Maximilian a disapproving shake of his head.

The old knight chuckled through his thick, silver beard. 'Very well,' he said. 'I suppose I shouldn't fill your head with legends and ghosts. You'll soon have plenty of mortal foes to keep you busy.' He shrugged. 'Anyway, odd as it is, the Iron Duke had this site in mind right from the start of the campaign. He sent scouts up here weeks ago to prepare for this battle. We're going to engage the enemy *exactly* where he planned to. Whatever your master thinks of him, Fabian is no fool. He must have had good reason to drive us so hard, and ensure that we fought here rather than any other spot.' He waved his men over to one of the few areas of hillside not already swarming with soldiers. 'That seems as good a place as any. Let's prepare ourselves.'

Once they'd reached the spot, Ratboy dropped from his horse and helped his master down from his. Then he perched on one of the pieces of fallen stone and, following the example of the Knights Griffon, began to polish his weapon in preparation for the battle. As he did so, he noticed Wolff looking anxiously through the bustling crowds that covered the hillside. Ratboy followed his gaze and saw the Iron Duke's standard, snapping proudly at the summit: a wolf and a bull, rearing side by side on a black background. He tried to imagine how Wolff must feel, to be so close to his brother, after all these decades.

'I wonder what he'll do, when the time comes to act,' said a voice at his ear.

Ratboy turned to see Anna, watching Wolff too. He dusted down a patch of moss and she sat next to him on the stone.

'A brother is a brother,' she said, sitting next to him. 'Whatever's happened in the past.'

Ratboy shrugged. 'He's been so concerned with tracking Fabian down, but I don't think he ever actually worked out what to do when he found him. I've never seen him so subdued. I suppose he imagined he would be dealing with a soldier, not the head of an army.'

Anna shrugged. 'How's your hand?' she asked, peeling back the bandages. The wound was beginning to heal up, but his fingers had set in a crooked, useless fist. She shook her head and frowned. 'It looks like I managed to stave off any infection, but I doubt you'll ever be much of a musician.'

Ratboy smiled. 'I don't think I was ever destined for artistic greatness.' The pain had been growing worse and he grimaced as he flexed his scarred, bent fingers. 'Some of the movement has returned already,' he said, trying to hide the extent of his discomfort. 'I may even be able to use this fancy sword properly, one day.' He raised the blade in his left hand, so that the metal caught the sun's dying rays. 'I've almost got the hang of using my other hand now anyway.' He looked over at Anna. In all the excitement of the last few days, he had almost forgotten her loss. 'How are you feeling?' he asked.

She continued studying his hand for a few seconds, frowning with worry. Then she placed it back in his lap and studied a ring on her finger. It was the one Wolff had brought from the temple: the one that had belonged to the abbess. As she spoke, she traced her finger over the dove that decorated it. 'The sisters were my only family,' she said. 'I only pray that some of them managed to flee before...' She paused and closed her eyes. When she opened them again, they were bright with tears. 'I doubt a single one of them would have abandoned the people in their care.'

Ratboy took her hand. 'There were soldiers in there with them. They may have evacuated some of the sisters before the fighting started.'

Anna nodded. 'It's possible,' she said, with little conviction. She squeezed Ratboy's hand and took a deep breath. 'I don't feel completely alone now though. You've shown me great kindness.' She met Ratboy's anxious gaze with a smile, then looked out across the gloomy landscape. 'I may not have to wait long before I meet my sisters again, anyway. It seems that nothing can stop this Mormius, or his hideous creatures.'

Ratboy recalled the battle of Mercy's End with a shudder. 'I wonder if Gryphius, or Captain Felhamer escaped,' he said.

She shrugged. 'Felhamer knew those tunnels as well as anyone. Gryphius was carrying a terrible wound though. I don't think we'll see him again.'

Ratboy nodded and looked deep into her eyes. 'And what about you, Anna? You're not seeking a glorious end. What is there here for you? Mormius's hordes will arrive any time now. Who can say what will happen, but I doubt many of us will survive. Shouldn't you head back towards Wolfenberg? You could find other members of your order. I imagine there's much healing to be done in the capital. You should leave while you still can.'

'And would you come with me, Ratboy? This is no place for a young, inexperienced acolyte. A desperate battle won't help to complete your training. You could leave with me, head south and present yourself at the first chapterhouse you find. In a year or so, you'd be a fully trained warrior priest, just like your master. Think how much more use your life could be, if you didn't end it here, as a novice.'

Ratboy shook his head fiercely. 'I would *never* abandon Brother Wolff.' His face flushed with colour and he turned away from the priestess, embarrassed by the passion in his voice. 'He'll need me tonight, more than ever before and if it means my life, then I'll be proud to die by his side.'

Anna nodded and loosed his hand. She gave him a sad smile and climbed to her feet. 'I know,' she said quietly. 'I owe you my life, and if there's anything I can do to aid you, I'll be here to do it.' She looked around at the rows of pale, nervous faces rushing past them. 'And I imagine you won't be the only one who'll need my help.'

Ratboy stood and pulled her towards him. His eyes were wide with emotion, but before he could speak, a chorus of shouts erupted from the surrounding soldiers. The troops' preparations suddenly became much more urgent. Valets and equerries sprinted past and sergeants began barking commands at their men. 'What's happened?' said Ratboy turning from Anna and looking out into the darkness of the surrounding meadows.

'Listen,' said Wolff, stepping past them both and climbing up onto the stone. He looked out across the rippling pools of grass and shadow.

Ratboy held his breath and heard an odd sound on the breeze. He climbed up beside his master and followed his gaze. He could see nothing, but as the wind shifted slightly to the east, the noise suddenly swelled. He heard a horn of some kind, but it was playing no melody he could recognise. The thin, plaintive sound simply undulated slowly up and down, like the baleful song of a wading bird.

There was a clatter of armour as the surrounding men formed themselves into orderly ranks. The dark, feral helmets of the Oberhau could be seen all over the hill, dashing back and forth as they directed regiments into the formations Fabian had requested. The squadrons of knights and pistoliers took up positions near the bottom of the incline, while every man with a bow was ordered up to the summit, to stand alongside the engineers and their bizarre assortment of blackpowder weapons. As the eerie, surging sound grew louder, the archers arrayed themselves in a long line across the top of Hagen's Claw and began to ready their weapons.

'We should take our positions,' said Wolff, placing a hand on Ratboy's shoulder.

They climbed down from the stone and, with Anna in tow, rushed back over to where Maximilian was inspecting his men.

The knights had already mounted their chargers, and as Maximilian looked them up and down he nodded with satisfaction. Despite the panic and noise erupting all around them, the Knights Griffon sat calmly in their saddles, with straight backs and raised chins. To Ratboy, they looked as immovable as the monoliths that towered above them.

'We don't have long,' said Maximilian, turning from his men and facing Wolff. 'Would you do us the honour of giving us your blessing, old friend?'

Wolff paused, dragging himself from his reverie with visible effort. Then he nodded slowly and stepped before the rows of gleaming knights. He unclasped a book from his cuirass, signalled for the men to lower their heads and muttered a quick prayer. To Ratboy, though, his words sounded oddly flat. The passion that usually filled his voice was gone, and he recited the words with a vague, distracted air.

> *Where there is weakness give us strength,*
> *Where there is lowliness, give us majesty,*
> *Where there is death, give us eternity.*

Then he moved along the ranks of men and placed his hand on each of their swords in turn, muttering a blessing as he went:

> *Fill this heart with faith undying,*
> *Gilt this sword, with strength unceasing.*

Once he'd reached the final knight, Wolff climbed up onto his own horse and positioned himself at the front of the squadron, next to Maximilian. There was a look of bleak despondency on his face.

The old knight gave Wolff a concerned glance. 'This isn't the first time we've faced such a foe,' he said, nodding to the row of flickering lights that had begun to appear on the horizon.

Wolff shook his head, but did not look up from where his hands were resting on the pommel of his saddle. 'It's not what's out there that worries me, Maximilian,' he muttered.

Maximilian lowered his voice and leant closer to his old friend. 'I have faith in you, Jakob, even if you do not. Whoever and whatever you face tonight, I know you will emerge victorious.'

Wolff lifted his eyes, and Ratboy saw agony and doubt burning there.

The priest opened his mouth to answer Maximilian, but the words were lost, as Hagen's Claw exploded into an inferno of sound and flame.

All along the hillside, rows of cannon and mortar boomed into life. Ratboy flinched and gripped his horse's reins in terror, taken by surprise as the guns unleashed hell on the vague shapes massing below. With the sound of the guns still ringing in his ears, he looked around and saw to his shame that Wolff, Maximilian and Anna were all sat quite calmly, peering through the growing darkness to see the effect of the volley.

'The range of these things is amazing,' said Maximilian as some of the lights below them flickered and died.

The enemy was still far from the foot of the hill and it was hard to see anything very clearly, but the droning horn faltered for a few seconds and several of Fabian's regiments burst into spontaneous cheers.

'It's a little early to begin victory celebrations,' said Anna, giving Ratboy a wry grin. 'I'm going to move back up the hill, there's nothing I can do in the thick of the fighting. I'll see if I can find the surgeons and wait for the wounded to arrive.' She placed a hand on Ratboy's arm and opened her mouth to say something. Then she changed her mind and simply nodded at him.

He gave her a mute nod in reply and watched her ride away between the ranks of stern-faced soldiers. As she disappeared from view, he felt an almost overwhelming urge to rush after her, but a look at his master's troubled face give him new resolve and he drew his sword instead.

'Here they come,' said Maximilian, snapping his visor down.

Ratboy saw that the tides of light below were now rushing towards the hill at great speed. The drone of the horn shifted up a key, becoming a shrill scream and he began to make out individual figures at the head of Mormius's army. He frowned. There was something odd about the men sprinting towards them. They were clad in crude, brutal armour, tatty shreds of hide and helmets crowned with vicious tusks, but it was not their dress that made him frown. There was something about their proportions that confused him. He turned to Wolff with a question on his lips, but his master was engrossed in his own thoughts and barely seemed to register the army hurtling towards them.

As the men moved closer, other marauders emerged behind them and it was then that Ratboy realised what was so strange about the warriors in the vanguard: they were colossal. The marauders behind them were obviously well built, but they barely reached the waists of the warriors in the front line. As the giants pounded across the field towards them, Ratboy noticed that their faces were as grey as month-old corpses and their canines were grotesquely enlarged – jutting from their drooling mouths like boar tusks. 'What are they?' he gasped.

'Ogres of some kind,' replied Maximilian, his voice ringing oddly through his helmet. 'They're a fearsome breed, from what I've heard. Fond of human flesh.' He raised his sword in silent command and there was a scraping of steel behind him as the ranks of knights all drew their own weapons in perfect unison.

Maximilian gestured to Ratboy's sword. 'That should serve you well, son.'

Ratboy nodded and lifted the ornate weapon higher, but as he saw the haunted expression on Wolff's face, doubt filled him. Just then another, even louder explosion of artillery erupted behind them and Ratboy's horse flinched violently, almost throwing him from the saddle.

'Steady,' said Maximilian, as the first rows of marauders started to dash up the hill towards them, led by the huge, lumbering ogres. As the creatures grew closer, Ratboy realised he could hear their hoarse, grunting breath beneath the wailing of the horn. He looked at Maximilian, wondering what he was waiting for. In a few more minutes the monsters would be all over them. The baron was faceless behind the polished steel of his helmet and did not acknowledge him.

Just as Ratboy was about to speak, a dark shape passed overhead. The archers at the top of the hill had finally loosed their arrows and the dusk grew even deeper as the lethal cloud filled the sky. The marauders were so close by this point that even the fading light could not obscure their outlines. Thousands of black and white-flecked arrows thudded into their thick hides.

Countless ranks of marauders fell screaming back down the hill, clutching at their throats and chests as they went, but the ogres barely stumbled. They hardly seemed to notice the arrows that sank into them. With a chorus of derisive grunts and snarls they simply snapped the shafts and continued rushing up the hill.

'They're unstoppable,' muttered Ratboy, looking around to see if the other soldiers would hold their ground in the face of such a horrendous foe.

'Watch,' said the baron, gently turning Ratboy's face back towards the front line.

The grunting, stomping mass of corruption was only a few feet from the vanguard of Fabian's army when, at the bark of a captain, the soldiers in the frontline raised an impressive array of pistols, muskets and crossbows. The men did not fire however, watching for the captain's signal as the ogres lurched towards them. Soon, they were so close that Ratboy could smell the thick, meaty stink of their flesh.

At the very last minute, the captain stepped out to meet them. It was one of the wolf-helmed Oberhau, and as the first ogre approached him, the captain calmly fired his flintlock pistol into the monster's head, tearing the skin from its skull with a fierce blast of gunpowder. As the report of the pistol echoed across the hillside the creature finally paused. It raised its hands to the pulpy mess where its face had been and gave a grunt of confusion. Then it toppled lifelessly back down the hill.

The captain dropped to one knee, lowered his head and pointed his sword at the enemy. At this silent signal, the entire frontline fired their weapons. The noise of so many guns blasting in concert was incredible and the hillside lit up in a brief, sulphurous flash. It was so bright that for a second the ogres' faces resembled those of grotesque actors, leering out into the footlights of an infernal theatre. Then the lead shot ripped the flesh from their bones and left gaping, blackened holes in their chests. Even in death, though, many of them seemed incapable of halting; stumbling forwards even as viscera spilled through their hands and their legs collapsed beneath them.

As a second thunderous volley tore into them, most of the ogres finally ground to a bloody halt: only one actually managed to blunder, half-blind, into Fabian's army. It was even larger than the others and its misshapen head was crowned with a thick, white mohican. The left side of its face was hanging down around its neck like a glistening scarf, revealing its long teeth in a fierce rictus grin as it stumbled, bellowing, up the hill. Black and white ranks of soldiers crowded around the towering figure, trying to block its way, but the thing's rage and momentum powered it through them. Its only weapon was a rough-hewn piece of sharpened iron, but the crude blade was taller than any of the men who pressed around the ogre and the monster cut them down as easily as grass, pausing only to tear at their faces with its gleaming, exposed teeth.

The ogre wove a spiralling, confused path through the soldiers and Ratboy realised with a rush of dismay that it was heading towards the Knights Griffon. Dozens of blades rose and fell against it, but to no avail. Then, with a crash like waves against rocks the full force of the marauder army ploughed into the Ostlanders. The battle began in earnest and the ogre was forgotten.

A cacophony of screamed commands engulfed Ratboy as the surrounding regiments began charging down the hill, howling with fear and bloodlust as they rushed towards the enemy. Meanwhile, clouds of arrows were still swarming overhead and the *phut phut* of mortar fire had begun, sending whistling, iron balls down into the approaching hordes, where they exploded into fragments of white-hot metal.

Ratboy looked at Maximilian and saw to his surprise that he was still sat utterly still. Watching with calm disdain as Hagen's Claw descended into a riot of fear and pandemonium. Behind the baron, his knights waited, equally patient and at the baron's side, Wolff seemed unaware of the fighting. His huge, armour-clad shape remained motionless, as he studied his hands with a perplexed frown on his face.

The injured ogre was now only a few feet away, hammering its brutal weapon through ranks of men, utterly oblivious to the countless wounds that networked its calloused flesh. With a roar of frustration the thing slammed its huge shard of metal into a row of spearmen attempting to block its way, sending them reeling backwards in a shower of splintered wood and bone. The men screamed in horror and pain as the ogre trampled maniacally over their bodies, crushing ribs, lungs and hearts as it continued up the hill. Then, with a confused snort, the beast found itself facing a dazzling sight: Maximilian and his knights.

Wolff finally looked up from the back of his hands to see a bleeding colossus staring directly at him. The ogre seemed enraged by the priest's air of devotion. Ignoring the knights it made straight for Wolff, raising the huge piece of metal above its head with a belching roar.

Wolff and the surrounding knights scattered their horses just in time as the hunk of iron sliced deep into the soft turf. Anger flashed in Wolff's eyes and as his horse circled the beast, he drew the warhammer from his back, testing its weight as though he'd never held the weapon before.

Ratboy saw the muscles tighten in his master's powerful jaw and wondered if the priest's anger was at the sight of the monster or at the thought of his own inaction.

'Sigmar,' bellowed Wolff, with such fury that everyone within earshot paused and looked in his direction. Even the ogre hesitated, lowering its guard for a second and turning to face the priest with a slack-jawed grunt. 'Absolves you,' continued Wolff, slamming his hammer into the thing's knee. The *crack* of breaking bone rang out, audible even above the gunshots further down the hill.

The ogre's leg folded backwards, sending it crashing to the ground and the last traces of doubt vanished from Wolff's eyes. Dismounting, he grasped the hammer in both hands, strode towards the dazed creature and slammed the weapon into its face. As he did so, the rekindled flames of his devotion rushed from his flesh and into the metal, so that as it connected with the monster's jaw, the head of the hammer was throbbing with white, holy radiance.

The ogre's skull detonated in an explosion of blood and light and it sprawled backwards across the scorched grass.

Wolff looked around at the soldiers charging down the hill with surprise on his face. Then he clambered back onto his horse and turned to face Maximilian, Ratboy and the knights. His ornate, iron cuirass was drenched in the ogre's blood and his face was flushed with exertion but, as he wiped the gore from his shaven head, he smiled at his friends. 'We've work to do,' he said, nodding at the carnage below.

The initial wave of ogres had been replaced by a crush of human marauders so great that the Ostlanders were already being forced to concede ground. A chorus of grunts and screams had replaced the sound of gunfire as the two armies locked together in a heaving, flailing forest of limbs and spears.

Maximilian nodded in reply and signalled for his standard bearer to raise their colours. As the cloth unfurled in the breeze, the baron snapped his reins and began riding down the hill at a slow trot. Behind him, the ranks of knights followed suit, maintaining their neat, orderly lines as they made their way through the battle.

As they neared the bottom of the hill, Ratboy realised that despite the size of Fabian's army, the tide had already turned against them. Marauders were flooding out of the darkness like a plague. The horizon had vanished behind a sea of pale, muscled flesh and scaled, mutated limbs. Ratboy saw horsemen, with long, drooping moustaches and others with helmets fashioned from the skulls of great beasts. Behind them marched blue-eyed tribesmen wearing human pelts and bearded, screaming goliaths with chains woven through their tattooed flesh. Despite their initial display of firepower, the sheer volume of the enemy was now overwhelming the Ostlanders. Guns were useless in close combat and the bare-chested marauders hacked and clawed their way through them in an orgy of bloodletting.

Ratboy swallowed hard as he neared the frontline. The din of clanging swords and screaming wounded was horrendous and as the last traces of sun vanished the slaughter became a strange, gruesome, tableau. The rows of grim faces looked suddenly flat and unreal as silver moonlight threw them into sharp relief.

The crush of bodies was so great that before Ratboy and the others could reach the marauders, their horses ground to a halt, hemmed in by clanking, serried ranks of Empire soldiers, several feet away from the fighting. The heaving mass of shields and spears was rocked by tides of movement, lurching and stumbling from left to right and Ratboy's horse strained beneath him, struggling to keep its balance in the tumult. Despite his fear of the marauders, Ratboy found it worse to be stranded like this, so close, but unable to act.

'What do we do now?' he called to Wolff. The priest was right next to him, but he had to yell to be heard over the clamour.

Wolff was looking back up the hill at the banners that surrounded the command group. There was no sign that Fabian and his officers were going to join the fighting. At the sound of his acolyte's voice, Wolff turned to face him with a frown of confusion. 'What?' he yelled back, leaning forward and cupping his ear.

'What do we do?' repeated Ratboy, raising his voice to a hoarse yell.

Wolff pointed his hammer at the advancing ranks of marauders. Their numbers were quickly overwhelming the Empire soldiers. 'Wait,' he replied, making the sign of the hammer over his chest. 'And pray.'

They did not have to wait long.

Far down in the valley, there was a flash of silver, as a winged figure lifted up over the heads of the marauders. From this distance it was barely more than a glittering speck, but Ratboy thought he could make out multiple pairs of wings, shimmering in the moonlight as it flew towards them. 'It's Mormius,' he gasped, leaning forward in his saddle to try and see more clearly. The din of battle drowned out his words, but he assumed he was right. As Mormius approached, Ratboy saw him raise a long, tapered horn to his lips and the awful, undulating sound echoed around Hagen's Claw again.

At the sound of Mormius's horn, his army surged forward with renewed vigour. They seemed utterly consumed by passion, howling furiously and throwing themselves against the Ostlanders with complete abandon.

The captain of the Oberhau tried to rally his men, swinging his greatsword with such phenomenal speed that a circle of headless corpses quickly built up around him. As the marauders pushed the other Empire troops slowly back up the hill, the captain found himself alone in an island of calm at the heart of the enemy vanguard. As the rows of muscled, mutated barbarians crowded around him the captain's strikes grew so fast his movements were hard to follow. Only the wolf mask of his helmet was visible, seeming to snarl with delight at the constant supply of fresh blood. Finally, inevitably, the circle closed in on him as the marauders used the sheer mass of their bodies to stifle his blows. Ratboy saw the lupine snout of his helmet one last time before it vanished under a tsunami of swords, axes and spears.

As Mormius's horn pealed out across the battlefield, driving his men onwards, Ratboy's concerns about reaching the frontline evaporated. The Ostlanders were now falling in droves and the fight was moving towards him with alarming speed. A nearby group of halberdiers dropped their weapons in panic and tried to scramble back up the hill, but they were blocked by the dignified, immovable presence of the Knights Griffon. The marauders made short work of the stranded men: hacking at their backs with broad, iron axes and ripping out their throats with crab-like claws.

As the last of the halberdiers fell to the ground, Maximilian's knights finally had room to manoeuvre and he waved them on with a twirl of his sword. As their chargers leapt forwards, Ratboy's horse followed suit and he found himself flying towards the screaming, blood-drenched marauders, with Wolff's broad, armoured back just ahead of him.

The knights fought with vicious, carefully drilled efficiency. Their swords rose and fell in graceful arcs, quickly cutting a path through the enemy and leaving a trail of broken claws and splintered shields. Wolff seemed to forget his brother for a moment and let the heat of battle consume him, swinging his hammer with brutal effectiveness and screaming out blessings as he pummelled and crunched his way through the marauders.

Ratboy tried to imitate the knights' unruffled precision, but as the sneering marauders crowded around him, his horse reared in panic and Ratboy lashed out in a desperate frenzy. The strange sword felt light and swift in his hands and his frantic blows were surprisingly effective. Few marauders made it past Wolff's pounding hammer, but those that did met a blur of flashing steel.

Across the hillside, other knightly orders were entering the fray and for a while the enemy's advance slowed. The winged figure of Mormius was still gliding towards Hagen's Claw and as he approached, his horn rang out once more. The wavering note was now so loud that several of the Ostlanders had to clamp their hands over their ears to block out the trilling sound. The marauders exploded into action – driven onwards by the close proximity of their general's rallying cry. Even Maximilian's knights struggled to defend themselves against such unhinged aggression. The bare-chested barbarians threw themselves at the polished armour of the knights with no thought for their own safety. For every one that fell, gutted, to the bloody ground, a dozen others clambered up onto the horses, their eyes rolling wildly as they wrenched and hacked at the men's armour.

The crush of bodies slowly halted the knights' advance. In fact, as the horn drove them to even greater fury, the marauders began to push them back up the hill. As the marauders swarmed over them, Ratboy saw one of the knights dragged from his charger. A crowd of enemy soldiers had grappled and shoved at his horse with such fury that it eventually toppled onto its side, thrashing and kicking in fear as the marauders plunged knives beneath its scalloped armour. The knight rolled clear of the horse and continued to fight with calm dispassion, but down on the ground he stood little chance against the seething mob. The other knights showed no sign of recognition as he vanished beneath a flurry of blows; they simply closed ranks and continued to fight with a quiet dignity as they were forced slowly back towards the monoliths.

A furious roar echoed across the hillside as the marauders greeted the arrival of Mormius. He dropped gracefully down amongst them and folded his flashing wings behind his back. Ratboy found it hard to look directly at him. It seemed almost as though a fragment of the bright, gibbous moon had broken away and fallen to earth. He could see quite clearly how tall the man was though; he was almost as big as the ogres that had led the attack. But as he strode towards the Empire troops, he showed none of the ogres' animal simplicity. He sauntered casually through the carnage, as though promenading into a ballroom, flicking his red hair back from his face as he drew a long, two-handed sword.

The first Ostlanders to face him were so paralysed with fear that Mormius simply ignored them, strolling past the rows of shocked faces and leaving the marauders that followed in his wake to hack them to the ground.

Two of Fabian's honour guard attempted to rally the Ostlanders, charging at Mormius with their two-handed swords above their heads and calling furiously for the ashen-faced onlookers to follow. As they neared the winged colossus, a detachment of swordsmen grudgingly shuffled after them, wide-eyed and trembling in the face of such an unholy vision. As the wolf-helmed Oberhau reached Mormius, they dropped into a low crouch and edged slowly towards him.

At the sight of the two officers, Mormius revealed his perfect teeth in a broad smile. His regal gait became a lurching, twitching stagger, as a fit of laughter gripped him; but then his pretty face twisted with anguish. 'Be calm,' he hissed, in a desperate voice, shaking his head furiously as the soldiers approached. 'It's not funny.' He took a deep, calming breath and his crystal wings spread out behind him, creating a flash of moonlight so powerful that it temporarily blinded the Oberhau. They faltered, raising their hands to try to block the glare and, with a casual flick of his wrist, Mormius lopped their heads from their shoulders.

The swordsmen baulked in the face of such incredible speed and as the giggling, cursing champion stepped towards them they backed away, raising their shields defensively against the glare of his glimmering breastplate.

Mormius continued up the hill. As the terrified Empire soldiers shuffled back, they created a broad path ahead of him, leading straight towards the distant banners of the command group. The only possible danger to the champion seemed to come from himself; as his expression alternated from a leering grin to an agonised scowl, he began slapping his armour-clad fists against the side of his head, punching himself with such force that blood began to flow from his ears.

'We must stop him,' cried Wolff, leaping back up into his saddle. 'If he reaches Fabian something terrible will happen, I can feel it.'

Maximilian nodded and with a wave of his sword, ordered his men to abandon their futile attempt to advance. He led them sideways across the hill, through the moonlit jumble of corpses and broken guns. The crush of bodies was just as great in that direction though, and they soon found themselves mired once more in the mass of struggling soldiers. The knights hacked and shoved with all their strength, but the marauders seemed endless. Ratboy's face and hair were slick with blood and his voice was hoarse from screaming. He paused, mid strike, as a familiar face looked out at him from the heaving throng. He could see no more than a pair of pale eyes, glaring at him from behind the flailing mass of swords and limbs, but something about the face chilled him. He had no time to dwell on it though, as another lumbering brute lashed out at him, swinging a battered sword straight at his head. He parried the blow and kicked the marauder to the floor and when he looked again, the face in the crowd was gone.

Wolff suddenly gave a howl of frustration and Ratboy looked over in alarm, surprised by the desperation in the priest's voice. Wolff's face was purple with rage and his scarlet robes were drenched with sweat and blood. His inability to reach the champion seemed to have driven him to distraction. There was a feral look in his eyes that Ratboy had never seen before.

Wolff leapt from his horse, diving face first into the enemy. His heavy frame hit the northmen with such force that a whole row of them toppled backwards under his weight. Before they could clamber to their feet, Wolff grabbed the nearest one by his greasy hair and slammed his warhammer into his face. 'Bow down before Sigmar!' he screamed, pounding the weapon repeatedly into the man's shattered head and shaking him violently back and forth, even though he was obviously already dead. 'Receive His judgement!'

Ratboy watched in horror as his master ripped and pounded his way through the struggling men. He seemed unhinged; inhuman even. As he bludgeoned his way towards Mormius, the priest was no longer taking heed of who crumpled beneath his bone-crunching hammer blows. Ratboy saw several Empire soldiers, smashed to the ground by his blind, uncontrollable rage. The sight of such untrammelled fervour reminded him of someone and with a sickening rush of fear, Ratboy realised who he had seen in the crowd. It was the witch hunter, Sürman: alive and here with them on Hagen's Claw. He must have trailed them right across the province, but for what purpose? He looked around but could see no sign of the frail old man amongst the crowds of struggling warriors.

Ducking beneath a spear thrust, he dropped from his horse and ran to his master's side. On approaching him, he paused. As Wolff screamed a tirade of furious blessings into the pulped faces of his victims, he suddenly seemed indistinguishable from Sürman. Is that what I will become, wondered Ratboy, lowering his sword in horror. A vision of Raphael's corpse filled his head, surrounded by his adoring crowds of penitent followers, tearing their flesh for the glory of Sigmar. Where were they now? Broken and forgotten on a muddy field. Sacrificed on a whim of his master. Anna's intense, grey eyes suddenly filled Ratboy's thoughts and he looked back up the hill, wondering if he had made a terrible mistake. I can't do this, he suddenly realised, blanching at the sight of so much bloodshed. He turned away from his master and began to climb back up the hill.

Rough hands grabbed him beneath the shoulders and hoisted him up onto a horse. He found himself sat behind Maximilian. The knight's helmet was gone and his steel grey beard was splattered with blood, but he had a fierce grin on his face. 'We'd best keep up with your master, eh lad?' he said, giving Ratboy a suspicious look. 'A wolf needs his pack around him at a time like this.'

Ratboy flushed with embarrassment and nodded, gripping his sword a little tighter.

Wolff's frenzied attack had cleared a path across the hillside, and as Maximilian rode after him, Ratboy got his first clear glimpse of Mormius. The champion was only about two-dozen yards away, and he noticed again that some of his crystal armour was stained and dark. The black shadow had now spread from his left hand all the way down to his waist, and, from the awkward, one-handed way Mormius held his sword, Ratboy guessed he was in a lot of pain.

'He's wounded,' he yelled into Maximilian's ear, pointing at the champion's arm.

The knight nodded as he steered his horse around the struggling figures, closing quickly on Wolff. 'Doubtless his corruption is eating him up from the inside. Should make our job a little easier.'

As they reached Wolff's side, there was no sign of his wrath diminishing. He was fighting towards the gleaming champion with jerking, spasmodic movements that reminded Ratboy of a marionette or an automaton. As he shouldered and punched his way into the clearing around Mormius, the priest's robes were hanging in tatters from beneath his dented armour, but he still had his warhammer grasped firmly in both hands, and it was glowing with a light almost as dazzling as Mormius's armour. 'Blasphemer,' he gasped, slamming his hammer against one of the stone columns with a dull *clang*.

Mormius paused at the sound and looked back. He met Wolff's bloody scowl with a wild grin. 'A priest, a priest, a warrior priest,' he sang, strolling back down the hill towards him. 'Have you come to pray for me?' He gave out a thin shriek of laughter and looked around at the rows of terrified faces that lined his path. 'I think you may be a little late.' His laughter grew so hard that tears welled in his eyes and as he neared Wolff, his face was flushed with colour. 'Your congregation seems to have already written me off.'

'Speak carefully,' yelled Maximilian, as his horse crashed through the rows of cowering soldiers, a little further up the hill. As they rode down towards the champion, Ratboy's pulse began to throb painfully in his temples. Mormius's towering shape was essentially human, but corruption seemed to pour out of him. Ratboy found it impossible to meet the giant's eyes as he turned towards them.

'What's this?' asked Mormius, leaning heavily on his sword as the battle raged around them. He wiped the tears from his eyes and shook his head. 'A welcoming committee? Finally. I was beginning to feel quite snubbed. Anyone would think you people had forgotten your manners.'

Maximilian's horse tossed its mane nervously as the knight rode towards Mormius and Wolff. As they approached him, Ratboy realised that his master, well built as he was, barely reached the flashing plates of Mormius's chest armour.

'You abomination,' muttered Wolff, wiping the gore from his shaven head and striding forwards. He pounded his gauntleted fist against the hammer device on his chest armour. 'Sigmar denounces you, with every muscle, heart and sinew of His Holy Empire.'

The champion's laughter faded as he saw the passion burning in Wolff's eyes. 'I see no muscle here,' he replied, waving his sword nonchalantly at the rows of petrified onlookers. 'Maybe Sigmar has tired of His snivelling, bastard offspring. Maybe He's forsaken you, little priest.'

Wolff gave no reply, but broke into a sprint, raising his hammer to strike as he raced towards Mormius.

Mormius turned slightly so that the crystals of his armour flashed in the moonlight and presented Wolff with an image of his own, livid face.

The priest stumbled in confusion and lowered his hammer.

Mormius stepped to one side and sliced his greatsword at Wolff's neck.

The blade hit Maximilian's sword with a ringing sound. With Mormius distracted by Wolff, the knight had managed to approach the champion and was now just a few feet away. He had extended his sword just in time to parry the blow and save Wolff's life, but Mormius's strength was such that the knight's weapon flew from his hand, spinning across the battlefield towards the crowds of onlookers. The old soldier cried out, clutching his arm.

Mormius rounded on Maximilian and Ratboy with a sardonic smile on his plump lips. He strode towards them, but then stumbled and winced. Ratboy noticed again that the crystals on his left arm were dark and lifeless. In fact, now that he saw it a little closer, he realised that his whole side was atrophied and twisted.

There was a rending metallic crunch as Wolff's hammer slammed into the small of Mormius's back. The champion's eyes widened in shock and he stumbled towards Maximilian's horse. As he fell past them, Ratboy lashed out with his sword and a flash of red erupted from the champion's face. Mormius slammed to the ground like a felled tree.

Wolff strode forwards and struck again, but Mormius rolled to one side and the blow pounded harmlessly against the ground.

The champion lurched to his feet and turned to face his three attackers, batting his long eyelashes in shock and pouting as he clutched his bleeding cheek. Then his mouth set in a determined line as he saw several other Knights Griffon fighting their way through the carnage and lining up behind Maximilian with their swords raised. He lowered his hand from his face, allowing the blood to flow freely down his pale neck and grinned. Then, he rocked back on his heels, rolling his eyes at the moon and letting out another burst of hysterical laughter. 'Little friends,' he gasped, waving his sword at the scene behind them. 'Your determination is commendable, but can't you see? It's already over.'

Wolff and the others turned to see that marauders were now flooding the hillside in such numbers that the Empire troops had no option but to retreat. Huge crowds of the black and white clad figures were rushing back towards the banners at the top of the hill. Trumpets were blaring in several places as the sergeants ordered their men to retreat.

Mormius spread his wings to the breeze that was buffeting the hillside and lifted himself up over the heads of his opponents. 'I've no time to entertain you,' he called, apologetically, as he flew up the hill towards the command group. As he glided over the soldiers, he lifted his long horn from his back and the mournful, undulating sound washed across the hillside once more, driving the marauders to new levels of ferocity as they rushed after him.

Wolff vaulted up onto his horse and without even pausing to acknowledge his friends he raced up the hill.

Maximilian and the other knights charged after him, led by the flashing shape of Mormius. The retreat was quickly becoming a rout. A second wave of ogres had swelled the ranks of marauders and as they grunted and stomped their way into the fray, the Empire soldiers fled for their lives.

As they thundered back up the hill, Ratboy saw that the enemy had even overrun the command tents, trampling the striped canvas to the ground as they chased their prey. 'Where's Fabian?' he called.

Maximilian shook his head and gave no reply as they raced towards the tents.

As they reached the summit, Ratboy saw no sign of the Iron Duke, or his officers. The tents were empty and as the Ostlanders saw they had been abandoned to their fate, they screamed in fear and confusion, before fleeing down into the narrow valley behind Hagen's Claw. Thousands of them were already scrambling and tumbling into the ravine, leaving a trail of broken weapons and banners as they went.

Mormius was flitting back and forth like a carrion bird, searching desperately for Fabian and lashing out at the fleeing shapes in frustration. His great wings were silhouetted against the moon as he landed on top of one of the stone columns and looked down over the battlefield. Even from such a high vantage point, his enemy eluded him and the champion howled and gibbered at the stars, as though the heavens themselves were responsible for Fabian's escape.

Without their general to lead them, the Empire army lost all sense of order and its neat ranks collapsed into an unruly jumble of beleaguered knights and panic-stricken foot soldiers. Ratboy scoured the confusing scene for any sign of his master, but it was impossible to make out individual figures in the riot of plumed helms and tattered banners. This is it, he decided. This is the moment my master feared. Fabian has abandoned his army to its doom. He's led them here to die.

The ringing of swords filled his ears and he turned to see that Maximilian's knights were now a lone island of purity, surrounded by a host of screaming, grotesque brutes. The marauders were clambering over each other in their desperation to attack the knights and Ratboy saw immediately that they were about to be overwhelmed. 'We must flee with the others,' he cried. 'Into the valley.'

Maximilian shook his head and hissed with frustration, lashing out at the clutching fingers trying to drag him from his horse, unwilling to show weakness in the face of such a barbarian rabble. Within seconds of Ratboy's cry, however, the whole front rank of knights collapsed with a scream of twisting metal and injured steeds.

'Retreat,' cried the baron in a despairing voice, as several of his men were dragged to the floor and butchered right before his eyes. 'Pull back into the valley.' He turned his horse up the hill and led his men in a desperate charge away from the advancing hordes.

Even then, on the very edge of defeat, the knights carried themselves with a quiet dignity that belied the hopelessness of their situation. As they reached the summit of the hill, they slowed to a canter and formed themselves back into neat, ordered ranks.

Maximilian and Ratboy looked back to see a myriad of grotesque shapes teeming over the hillside: towering, slack-jawed ogres, sinewy, broad-shouldered barbarians and lumbering, unnatural shapes, all heeding the call of the winged monster perched on top of the obelisk.

'My master's probably down there,' cried Ratboy, straining to be heard over the din and pointing down into the crowded valley on the other side of the hill. 'He'll be trying to find his brother.'

Maximilian had regained his composure and nodded calmly at the acolyte. 'We'd not last a minute up here on our own anyway. And down there we can at least defend our countrymen as they retreat.' He signalled to his men with a flourish of his sword and led them down the hill after the fleeing Ostlanders. 'Whatever Fabian's motives,' he cried as they rode down the hill, 'he was right about this ravine. The pass is so narrow, the marauders will find themselves in a bottleneck as they try to attack. Their numbers will work against them in such a confined space. Mormius will pay dearly for every foot he advances.'

Ratboy nodded vaguely, but he was only half listening to the baron. As they raced down the hill, with the enemy hordes at their backs, he scoured the crowds of fleeing soldiers for any sign of a white-robed girl or an old man with pale, staring eyes.

If there were any officers left alive, Ratboy saw no sign of them as the reached the valley floor. The Ostlanders were less an army than a terrified, demoralised mob. For months, Fabian had been the cornerstone of their faith: the incredible luck and charisma of the Iron Duke had made the impossible seem possible, but now he was gone the full horror of their situation had hit home. Handgunners, swordsmen and halberdiers all piled together in a desperate, headlong stampede through the narrow valley. The Knights Griffon brought up the rear of the fractured army, but all they could do was flee with the others as Mormius swooped down into the ravine at the head of his daemonic host.

'They must stand and fight,' snarled Maximilian, as they raced after the receding army. 'Where's that wretched traitor, Fabian? If no one turns this army around, they'll just spill out onto the plains and be butchered. At least in here we've *some* a chance of seeing the dawn.'

Ratboy nodded weakly, but could think of nothing to say in reply. He had scoured the terrified faces that surrounded them, but had seen no sign of Wolff or Anna. His oath to protect Wolff, whatever the cost, had been proven worthless and he had failed the priestess too. He looked down at his beautiful sword with disgust. What use had it been, in the end? As they fled from Hagen's Claw, all his earlier doubts returned to him. The Empire had raised an army of incredible size, thousands of good men had abandoned their lives in the name of Sigmar and what had it achieved? What began as a noble crusade was about to end as a pitiful farce. He realised his dreams of following in Wolff's footsteps were nothing more than a romantic fantasy. As the army neared the end of the valley, he shook his head in despair and let the sword slip from his hand.

A rolling boom, like the sound of thunder filled the ravine. The horrified Ostlanders looked back over their shoulders to see what fresh horror had been summoned to assault them. The whole army stumbled to a halt and gawped in shock. The far end of the canyon was collapsing in on itself. The walls were engulfed in smoke and dust as a curtain of crumbling rock hurtled down onto Mormius's men. The champion flew clear of the explosion, beating his wings in a desperate attempt to escape the avalanche, but the great host beneath him vanished, as the walls of the valley slid downwards in a lethal, deafening storm of granite.

As the dust and stones settled, the Ostlanders stared in bewildered silence at the huge, silvery cloud rippling towards them. Then a movement far above it caught their eye. All along the sides of the ravine, rows of soldiers began to appear, led by a proud, slender figure clad in dark plate armour and wearing a helmet styled to resemble a wolf's head. Behind him fluttered a black and white banner, showing a wolf and a bull.

A chorus of shocked voices erupted from the men around Ratboy. 'It's the Iron Duke,' they cried. 'He hasn't abandoned us.'

Maximilian tugged at his stiff, silver beard and gave out a bark of laughter. 'The old devil must have planned this. He intended for us to retreat into this ravine.'

Ratboy peered through the thinning smoke and saw the surviving marauders climbing from the rubble. They made a pitiful sight as they dragged themselves clear on twisted, broken limbs while howling up at their champion to save them. Grey dust covered their bodies, giving them the appearance of ghosts, or revenants, crawling from a rocky grave. 'But how could Fabian have predicted the avalanche?'

'He didn't predict it, he created it,' replied Maximilian with a nod of grudging respect. 'I thought it was scouts he sent out here all those weeks back, but they must have been engineers.' He waved along the top of the canyon, where the ranks of soldiers had appeared. 'This whole area must have been lined with blackpowder, primed and waiting for us to lead the marauders to their doom. And meanwhile Fabian kept back a reserve of soldiers, waiting here to strike.'

He shook his head at the pitiful state of the Ostlanders that surrounded them. 'He really must be made of iron though. Rather than let his men know the plan and risk it being discovered by spies, he let them fight on, oblivious to his intentions, until so many had died they were forced to pull back in a genuine retreat.'

Ratboy gasped at the brutal logic: to sacrifice so many men on a gamble made his head spin. What if they hadn't retreated? What if the explosives hadn't detonated? Then he remembered: Fabian would have no qualms about sacrificing Empire soldiers if he was worshiping at the altar of some dark, ancient power.

As Mormius flitted back and forth above his screaming, broken wreck of an army, Fabian led ranks of fresh men down into the valley. With a pounding of drums and hooves they charged into the crowds of wounded marauders.

The soldiers around Ratboy lifted their tired heads and cheered. Then, forgetting their fear and exhaustion, they rushed back down the gully, eager to join the slaughter. Maximilian led his men after them in a slow, stately trot.

At the sight of Fabian, Mormius let out a strangled wail and dived towards him. His wings blurred and he drew his greatsword from his back as he fell. He smashed into the ranks of the Oberhau with the force of a comet, sending a plume of dust from the side of the ravine. For a few minutes, Ratboy struggled to make out what was happening. Then, as the haze cleared, he made out the two men, locked in a fierce duel on an outcrop of rock. The colossal, winged champion dwarfed Fabian, but as he swung his greatsword at him in a flurry of wild, furious blows, the Iron Duke danced easily out of the way, wielding his own sword with calm, controlled skill.

As the lines of fresh, eager-faced soldiers charged down towards them, the surviving marauders turned and fled, limping and clambering back up towards Hagen's Claw. Many of them were too crippled to run and the vengeful Ostlanders fell on them with undisguised glee.

As the clouds of dust folded and banked through the moonlit canyon, Ratboy caught brief glimpses of the carnage. Most of the Empire soldiers had thought themselves as good as dead, and their relief now manifested itself in an orgy of bloodletting. Swords and knives plunged into the struggling marauders as they reached up pathetically towards their embattled champion.

As the Knights Griffon approached the bloody scene, Ratboy saw a familiar face and cried out with delight. The broad-chested shape of his master was striding purposefully though the clouds of dust, still screaming his litany and pounding his two-handed warhammer into the crumpled bodies of his foes.

'Master Wolff,' cried Ratboy, leaping from his horse and sprinting towards him.

At the sound of his acolyte, Wolff looked up from his work with a fierce expression on his face. The ornate scrollwork of his cuirass was glistening with blood and his dark eyes were burning with rage. As he saw Ratboy his eyes cleared a little and his expression softened. He looked down at his gore-splattered chest and limbs in confusion. Then he lowered his hammer to the ground with a *thud* and took in the shocking brutality that surrounded him. In their fury the Ostlanders had become as bestial as the marauders, tearing through the wounded northmen like rabid dogs. As Wolff's fury waned, so did his strength. He had only taken one step towards Ratboy when his legs collapsed beneath him. He dropped to his knees with a grunt of exhaustion.

Ratboy rushed to his side and, taking his arm, helped him to his feet. 'We've won,' he gasped, trying to sound cheerful despite the horrific sights that surrounded them. He gestured to the crowds of figures scrambling back up towards the obelisks. 'The marauders are retreating.'

Wolff's face remained fixed in a grim scowl. 'Where's my brother?' he croaked, through bloody teeth.

Ratboy pointed up to the duelling figures, lunging and slashing at each other on the rocky outcrop. It was an incredible sight. They seemed to Ratboy like gods, locked in a contest to decide the fate of all humanity. Even at this distance though, it was obvious that Mormius was struggling. The whole of his blackened left side looked twisted and deformed and his leg kept buckling beneath him as Fabian forced him closer to the edge of the precipice.

Wolff's amour rattled as he fought through the bloodthirsty mob, trying to get a better view. He and Ratboy both gasped as they saw Fabian plant his boot into the champion's deformed leg and send him stumbling back towards the chasm. Mormius's wings thrashed one last time as he crumpled to the floor, but before he could lift himself, Fabian turned on his heel and sliced his sword cleanly through his neck.

The soldiers ceased their butchery for a moment and an eerie silence descended over the canyon; then, there was an explosion of cheers as Fabian strode calmly into view, with Mormius's severed head dangling from his upraised fist.

CHAPTER SEVENTEEN

Shadows and Ghosts

Anna awoke with cool liquid trickling into her throat. She swallowed it thirstily but immediately gagged. It was thick and tasted of iron and she realised her mouth was filling with someone else's blood. She groaned and struggled to rise, but a heavy weight held her firmly in place. Upon opening her eyes she found that the weight was a dead marauder. The full mass of his stinking flesh was pushing her down onto a wooden floor that was jolting and bouncing painfully against her back. She gasped in disgust. The man's pale, clammy face was pressed right against hers and she could see his eyes rolling in their sockets. His limbs were cold and already stiffening and she guessed she had been trapped under him for some time.

As Anna wrestled with the dead man, a low, guttural voice rang out nearby and she froze. The words meant nothing to her, but she immediately recognised the fierce language of the northern wastes. A second voice replied in the same language, but this one whined in a higher register than the first, speaking in a babbling torrent of bleats and snorts.

The first voice replied with an angry, dismissive grunt and they both fell silent.

Fear crippled Anna. The voices had sounded very close: just a couple of feet away at most. She lay still for a second and tried to calm her breathing. She was surrounded by broken limbs and weapons but through a gap in the corpses she saw a tiny square of sky and realised she was moving. Low, moonlit clouds were rushing overhead and she guessed from the lurching movement beneath her that she was on some kind of cart.

As she listened more carefully, she heard the sound of creaking wheels and horses' hooves and the loud, heavy breathing of the two marauders.

The wheels bounced up over a ridge and as the vehicle slammed back down onto the ground, the corpse's head knocked against Anna's, spilling a fresh load of semi-congealed blood over her face. She groaned and rolled quietly to one side, finally freeing herself from the weight of the corpse. Other bodies lay over her, but she managed to carefully disentangle the mass of torsos and limbs and brought her face up to the surface, gasping for air like a tired swimmer. Luckily for her, the moonlight was too weak to illuminate most of her fellow passengers, but from what little she could make out, the scene resembled an immense butcher's slab. Ostlanders and marauders lay where they had fallen in a confused jumble of broken bones and severed arteries.

Other shapes were travelling beside the cart, slipping through the darkness like ghosts. With a thrill of horror she saw that she was surrounded by marauders: some riding ferocious-looking steeds and others sprinting on foot, but all racing with grim determination from the distant silhouette of Hagen's Claw.

We must have won, thought Anna with a shock. This is no victory parade – they're running away. She nestled back down into the pile of damp bodies, relieved to be unnoticed for the moment. As the cart bounced wildly over the uneven turf of the valley, she saw that huge crowds of northmen were fleeing from the stone towers with no pretence of order. It was a complete rout and Anna's head reeled. The last thing she could remember was fleeing for her life as the hordes of enemy soldiers overran the command tents. She had tried to escape down into the canyon with the others, but as she dashed between the struggling soldiers something had cracked against the back of her head. She must have dropped into the back of this cart and then been gradually covered by the dead and dying.

The hopelessness of her situation suddenly hit her. If she stayed where she was, the marauders would carry her to whatever ungodly destination they were racing for, but if she tried to escape, she would be seen immediately. She shuddered, wondering why the marauders had not detached the cart. What foul purpose did they have in mind for the bodies?

The higher, whining voice cried out again and she felt hands pressing down near her head. She realised one of the drivers must be looking back over her, towards the hill. She froze, doing her best to look like a corpse. The marauder whined again, pointing to something as he leant over her. His face was so close to Anna's that she could smell his rancid breath. Then the other marauder bellowed furiously and wrenched him back onto the driver's seat.

Anna looked cautiously where he had pointed and saw that several of the marauders were dropping to the ground. As she strained to see more clearly, she saw flashes of black and white moving amongst them:

Ostlanders, pursuing the defeated army and hacking them down as they fled.

She dropped back with a sigh of relief. It looked like it would only be a matter of time before all of the marauders were overtaken and slaughtered. As long as she remained hidden beneath the bodies until then, she should be safe.

As she shrugged herself back down beneath the corpses, she felt a movement that didn't seem to come from the wheels below. She looked around and saw a large rat, perched on the face of one of the bodies and watching her intently. There was a spark of intelligence in its eyes that she found a little unnerving, but she decided it was too small to have been the cause of the movement.

She turned the other way and saw that one of the marauders was also staring at her. His plaited hair was slick with blood and she could tell by the black, clotted line around his neck that his throat had been cut. As she watched the man, trying to discern whether it was he who had moved, he suddenly spread his teeth in a wide leering grin and pulled himself towards her.

Anna stifled a scream and squirmed away from him, but she quickly felt her back press against the side of the cart and realised she was trapped.

As the marauder crawled slowly towards her, he opened his mouth wider in an attempt to cry out, but all that emerged from his ruined vocal chords was a faint, liquid croak that was lost beneath the sound of the rattling cart. He freed his legs and lunged across the cart.

Anna tried to worm herself away from the man, but his eyes were fixed on hers with a fierce hunger and as he moved across the mounds of damp, ruptured flesh, he wrapped his hand around the hilt of a broken sword. The blade gleamed with the same cold fire as the marauder's eyes and he jabbed it at her face with a gurgle of amusement.

The two embraced in a silent struggle. Anna gripped his shoulders and shoved with all her strength, but he would not give up. Gradually his grinning face bore down on hers as he forced the shard of metal towards her throat.

Anna fought the urge to scream and reached around for something to use as a lever. Her hand came to rest on a piece of metal and she realised it was the hilt of another sword. Confusion and terror mingled in her head. She had sworn countless oaths to cherish life in all its forms, but as the marauder's broken sword pressed up against her throat, she could not believe it right to simply submit. Everything in her rebelled at the idea of hurting another being, but the psychotic glee in the man's eyes disgusted her. She screamed in despair as a warm fountain of blood washed over her neck.

It was only as the marauder began thrashing about in pain that she realised what she had done. Her trembling hand was still clutching the long sword she had buried in his neck. She had murdered him. Anna closed her eyes and groaned in revulsion as he jerked and twitched violently back and forth. In her horror, she seemed unable to loose the sword, and as the man's struggles grew weaker, she felt every last one of his pitiful, gurgling breaths. Finally, he grew still and, forgetting the danger, she screamed in despair. In that one second everything she knew about herself collapsed. She felt as though she were suddenly trapped inside the mind of a stranger.

Anna did not have long to wallow in her guilt. Her scream had alerted the cart's drivers to her presence and as she shoved the marauder's body to one side, she saw a sinewy, fur-clad youth grinning down at her. His knotted flesh was networked with serpentine, self-inflicted scars and his greasy topknot was dyed a deep, henna red. As he stood up in the driver's seat, he drew a long, curved knife and let out a whooping howl of pleasure.

Anna tried to pull the sword from the corpse, but her terror had jammed it so deep into the flesh that it would not move. She raised her hands in front of her face as the marauder lifted his sword to strike.

There was a staccato thudding sound as four arrows sank deep into his chest, leaving a row of black and white flights buried in his thick furs. He spun his arms for a few seconds, trying to maintain his balance, then he toppled beneath the wheels of the cart. His lifeless body jammed in the axle and the cart lurched out of control. The remaining driver roared in pain as the wheel shattered and the reins sliced through his fingers.

The cart tipped and Anna flew through the air in a shower of weapons and body parts. The air was knocked from her lungs as she slammed down into a clump of long grass. Screams and howls surrounded her as the marauders nearby fought for their survival. Everywhere she looked, Ostlanders were charging out of the shadows, riding down the enemy with swords, lances and spears and howling victoriously as they trampled the northmen underfoot.

Anna looked away from the slaughter and studied the blood on her hands. As struggling figures tumbled past her, she tried to clean her fingers, rubbing them desperately against her white robes, but the more she rubbed, the more blood-stained she became and after a few minutes she let out a low murmur of despair. 'Murderer,' she whispered under her breath.

'Sister,' cried a young, wide-eyed soldier, spotting her sat amidst the carnage. 'Watch yourself,' he yelled as he steered his horse to her side and dismounted.

She flinched at his touch and looked him up and down in terror, taking in his bloody sword and battered breastplate. Then, seeing the concern in his eyes, she relaxed a little and accepted his helping hand. 'Murderer,' she muttered as he pulled her to her feet.

He shook his head in confusion, shaking the tall white plumes on his helmet. 'Who's a murderer?' he asked, looking round at the violence that surrounded them.

'I killed him,' she answered, staring at the young soldier with an intensity he found unnerving.

'Aren't you the priestess who was travelling with the Knights Griffon?' he asked, struggling to meet her eye.

Anna nodded vaguely and continued trying to wipe the blood from her hands.

The young soldier nodded back, relieved at the thought she might be someone else's problem. 'They're still making their way down from Hagen's Claw,' he said lifting her up onto his horse. 'Let's get you back to them.'

As they rode back towards the monuments on the hill, fighting against a tide of victorious soldiers, Anna saw the Iron Duke leading a pack of wolf-helmed Oberhau. They thundered through the heart of the other soldiers, bellowing commands at them as they charged past. Fabian himself had flung back his visor and she caught a brief glimpse of his gaunt face and glittering eye patch. 'They're heading for the forest,' she heard him scream as he rode past her.

As he made his way up the hill, the soldier spotted the unmistakable squadron of Knights Griffon. Despite everything that had occurred that evening, they were still riding with their shoulders thrown back and their chins raised to the heavens. Even the blood of their foes seemed ashamed to stain the knights' armour and it still gleamed and sparkled in the moonlight.

'It's Anna,' cried Ratboy, as he saw the soldier's horse trotting up the hill towards them. Wolff was riding next to him and nodded in reply, but did not slow the speed of his horse as he charged down the hill. Ratboy reined in his own steed and allowed Wolff and the Knights Griffon to race on ahead, so that he could greet the young soldier and his passenger. 'She's alive,' he gasped as the soldier approached.

Recognition flared in the priestess's eyes at the sight of Ratboy and she held her stained hands up to him like a guilty child.

'What's happened?' he cried, grabbing her arms and noticing that her gaze seemed even more passionate than usual.

Anna gave no reply and simply hung her head in shame, but she grasped Ratboy's arms as tightly as he held hers.

Ratboy gave the soldier a questioning look.

'I found her next to a wrecked cart,' he said. 'It looks like some of the marauders had been trying to use it to escape in.' He shook his head. 'It's a bloodbath down there. I thought she would be safer up here with her friends.' He looked at the blood that covered her hands and robes. 'I'm not sure how she got mixed up with the enemy retreat.'

Ratboy frowned in confusion, but nodded all the same. 'Thank you for finding her,' he said, dismounting. He helped Anna down onto the ground, steadying her as the ranks of Ostlanders charged past, screaming for bloody vengeance.

'Anna,' he said, taking her head in his hands in an attempt to make her focus on his words. 'You must stay here. My master and Maximilian are in pursuit of the duke and I must follow, but it's not safe down there. The marauders won't die without a fight.'

Anna's eyes opened even wider as she realised Ratboy meant to abandon her. She shook her head fiercely and threw her arms around him.

The soldier chuckled. 'Looks like she has other ideas.' He looked around at the brooding stones that covered the hillside. 'She's probably no safer up here anyway. Not all of the marauders will have fled.'

Ratboy looked down at the massacre below and grimaced. 'How many are still alive?'

The soldier shook his head and followed Ratboy's gaze. 'Impossible to say. It's even darker down there in the shadow of the forest. Hundreds of them have already fled beneath the trees. The ogres are all dead and the riders from the steppe vanished as quickly as they came. They seem to have lost their fighting spirit,' he laughed. 'The Iron Duke is determined that none should survive to reach their own borders though. He's ordered the whole army to pursue them into the forest.' He laughed again, obviously a little light-headed after their unexpected victory. 'I've a feeling some of our more experienced veterans may have taken the opportunity to slope off. The battle is obviously won, so who can blame them, really. We'd all be making for the nearest town to start the celebrations if it was up to me.'

'So, *is* the battle over?'

The soldier shook his head. 'No, not really, I suppose. I'm only talking about a few people who were a little too eager to return home. The bulk of our men are following the duke into the forest.' He raised his battered sword and grinned enthusiastically. 'After all – there's more than one way to celebrate a victory.' The grin dropped from his face as he remembered something Ratboy had said. 'Did you say that your master is in *pursuit* of the duke?'

Ratboy sneered. 'Yes!' he snapped. 'My master must stop–' he paused as he noticed the frown on the soldier's face. 'Well, yes, of course' he continued, in a softer voice. 'He wishes to assist the duke in any way he can.'

The soldier's eyes narrowed with suspicion, then he gave a curt nod. 'Good luck, friend,' he muttered, snapping the reins of his horse and disappearing down the hill.

Ratboy shook his head at his own stupidity and hoped that no harm would come of his indiscretion. Then he helped Anna up onto his horse and climbed up after her. 'Well, sister,' he said, taking the reins. 'Let's see if we can keep ourselves out of any more trouble.' With that, he rode after the distant, sparkling helms of the Knights Griffon.

'I've killed a man,' whispered Anna into his ear.

Ratboy reined in his horse and looked back at her in confusion.

'Earlier on.' she said, holding up her bloody fingers and shaking her head at him. 'I put a sword through his neck and watched him die.' She groaned in horror at the memory. 'What right had I to take another's life? He would have had parents and children. How could I do such a thing? I was a Sister of Shallya, but what am I now?'

Ratboy lowered her hands. 'Alive.'

Anna simply stared at him.

'We must move fast, if I'm going to catch up with my master,' he said, afraid of the despair in her eyes. He steered his horse down the hill and tried desperately to think of something more useful to say.

Beneath the eaves of the forest, the darkness was almost total. As Fabian's men left behind the open, moonlit fields, they slowed their horses to a walk and peered nervously into the shifting gloom. The Iron Duke's army still numbered in the thousands, but as the ancient trees engulfed it, the host fragmented. Something of the forest's wildness seemed to infect them and as they hunted down the fleeing marauders, the Ostlanders ignored the commands of their officers and blundered wildly through the undergrowth, even abandoning their horses as the slender pines gave way to low, twisted yews and ugly, knotted oaks.

It was only by the flashing armour of Maximilian's knights that Ratboy was able to find his master in the shadows. 'Lord,' he gasped as he climbed down from his horse and rushed after him with Anna following close behind. 'How will you find Fabian in this darkness?'

Wolff looked back and Ratboy saw that his face was still twisted in an animal snarl. Ratboy blanched at his master's fierce glare, feeling that he was looking into the eyes of a stranger. 'I'll find him,' growled the priest.

After a few minutes, as they entered a small hollow, one of the knights grunted in pain and stumbled backwards with a spear jammed under his breastplate.

The rest of the party paused and raised their weapons, scouring the small clearing for any sign of the attackers as the injured knight dropped, wheezing, to his knees.

'There,' cried Maximilian, pointing his sword at a group of figures emerging from the trees.

Ratboy gasped in disgust as the vague shapes entered the pool of moonlight at the centre of the clearing. Most were the same bare-chested northmen they had faced on the hillside, but there were other, stranger things with them. He realised that they were the creatures he had seen before: men with deformed, bestial heads, cloven hooves and thick, greasy hides.

At a signal from Maximilian, the knights fell on the creatures with a flurry of sword strikes.

Wolff launched himself at the marauders with a terrifying combination of hammer blows and scripture. As the knights pushed the other warriors back towards the trees, the priest grabbed one of the beastmen by the scruff of its neck and slammed its head into a tree trunk. The creature collapsed, with a bellow of pain and Wolff placed a foot on its chest and crunched his hammer down into its face. The priest's fury only seemed to grow as the creature stopped breathing and as its dark blood rushed over the roots of the tree, he kept swinging the hammer: pounding the metal into the broken body with spasmodic, jerking blows.

Ratboy saw the look of horror on Anna's face as she watched the priest and he rushed to Wolff's side. The other attackers were already fleeing or dead and as the knights resumed their positions they were also eying Wolff with unease. 'Master,' said Ratboy, placing a hand on the priest's shoulder. 'He's dead.'

Wolff spun around. His face was white with passion as he glared at the acolyte. 'Yes,' he muttered, looking down at the corpse with a slightly confused expression. He staggered back from the dead beastman and raised his dripping hammer towards the heart of the forest. 'We must keep moving,' he gasped, breathlessly.

Maximilian looked at Wolff's pale, blood-splattered face with concern. He stepped after him and placed a hand on his arm. 'Brother Wolff, rest yourself for a moment, I beg you. Your zeal does you credit, but the battle is won.' He looked with distaste at the crumpled mess Wolff had made of the marauder. 'Do we really need to hunt down every last one? My hatred of these beasts is as great as yours, I assure you, but this forest is fey, and unpredictable. I have a feeling that the deeper we go, the stranger it will become. Why not let the stragglers crawl back to their own lands? It would be no bad thing if a few of them lived to spread the word of our decisive victory.' He waved at the calm faces of his knights. 'I've no desire to sacrifice my men in a pointless game of cat and mouse.'

Wolff's black eyes flashed. 'Do as you wish,' he growled, 'but I must continue. Listen,' he said. The surrounding trees echoed with the noise of the victorious army, clattering and hacking their way after their general. 'Fabian's leading these men into the forest for a reason. I don't know exactly what it is, but I know it's going to end in more bloodshed. As you say, the battle's won, but my brother was never interested in victory – he's brought these men here for some dark purpose of his own.' He gripped Maximilian's shoulders. 'I think he means to use them as some kind of sacrifice. I'm not sure how, but I think he's going to use their blood to buy the favour of his dark masters.' He shook his head. 'It's not the marauders I'm pursuing, it's my brother.'

Maximilian turned away with a sigh. 'Tell me, Jakob – how can you be sure Fabian is so evil? He's just led this army to another glorious victory. You saw how he dealt with Mormius.' The baron looked back at Wolff. 'Maybe he's just a brilliant tactician who's eager to protect his homeland?'

Wolff gripped the baron's shoulders even more tightly and glowered at him. 'I know my own brother, Maximilian. I think that deep down I've had my suspicions for decades, but guilt clouded my judgement. As soon as I heard the truth from the witch hunter, Sürman, I knew it had to be right.'

Maximilian shrugged. 'Could this Sürman not have been mistaken?'

Ratboy suddenly gasped and rushed to Wolff's side. 'He's here,' he gasped. 'I saw Sürman's face in the battle. He's followed us.'

Anna let out a groan of dismay, wrapping her arms around herself and looking around at the mass of ancient, winding boughs.

Wolff shook his head at Ratboy. 'I doubt it very much, boy. I hammered a stake into his chest.'

Ratboy gripped his master's arm with an urgent expression on his face. 'I'm sure it was him – I'd never forget those peculiar eyes of his.'

Maximilian took a deep breath and freed himself from the priest's grip. 'Old friend,' he said, still watching Wolff with concern. 'When this witch hunter denounced your brother as a heretic, was it before or after you attacked him with a piece of tree?'

Wolff strode after the knight with a furious expression on his face. 'I *know* Fabian's guilty, Maximilian. He spent his whole childhood dreaming of military glory, but he was useless with a sword and could barely ride a horse. The closest he ever came to battles was reading about them in old folk tales. Then, around the same time as I discovered occult objects in our family home, he suddenly became a deadly warrior.' He shook his head in disgust. 'I was so wrapped up in my own guilt over summoning the witch hunter, it never occurred to me that there might really be a cultist in our family, but now I have no doubt about it at all. I don't know exactly how this will end, but I think this whole campaign is just a way for Fabian to somehow gain even greater strength.' He leant closer to the knight. 'Come with me Maximilian. I *must* find him.'

Maximilian gave a long sigh. He looked around the clearing at the rows of expectant faces. 'Well,' he said finally, 'I'm not sure I really follow your logic, but I don't like the idea of leaving you to go on alone. Your brother's still surrounded by those swordsmen of his, the Oberhau.' He nodded at Wolff's dripping hammer. 'And whether you're right or not, I'm sure they'll defend their lord fiercely. I doubt even you could take them *all* on.' There was a metallic *clang* as he patted Wolff's shoulder and turned to his knights. 'Looks like we still have a little work to do.'

The priest gave a barely perceptible nod of thanks, before turning on his heel and heading off into the trees.

As Maximilian predicted, the deeper they moved into the forest, the stranger it became. Ratboy struggled to keep up with his master's brisk pace as the moonlight began to play tricks on him. Dawn was still several hours away but, as they rushed after the rest of Fabian's army, pale lights flickered at the corner of his vision, only to vanish when he tried to focus on them. He shivered and tried to keep his eyes on the bear-like silhouette of the priest as he shouldered his way through the trees. It was tough going. The forest floor was sloping slowly upwards, and after the exertion of the battle, Ratboy soon grew short of breath.

'Are you sure it was him?' whispered Anna, looming out of the darkness and gripping his arm.

'What?'

'Are you sure it was Sürman you saw on the hill?'

'Oh, yes,' he replied, without slowing his pace or taking his eyes off Wolff. 'I couldn't forget a face like that. He was watching me, I'm sure of it.' He let his eyes flick briefly in Anna's direction. 'I think he must have followed us here.'

Her eyes widened and she clenched her bloodstained hands together. 'How could he have survived such an injury?' she muttered.

Ratboy shook his head as he vaulted a low branch. 'Who knows? I imagine old mendicants like that are hardened by all those years of travel. Maybe he's not as frail as he looks.'

'I knew he'd come for me,' whispered Anna, tightening her grip on Ratboy's arm. 'The day you rescued me I knew it. As soon as I saw he had escaped from your master, I knew he would hunt me down.'

Ratboy frowned. 'He might not be here for you, Anna. He could be after any of us. Wolff's the one who injured him. I can't imagine he'll forget that in a hurry.' He shrugged. 'Anyway, I might be wrong. Maybe he didn't follow us. He might have just seen me in the crowd and wondered where he knew my face from.'

Anna shook her head. 'He's come for me, I can feel it.'

They ran on in silence for a few minutes and then noticed that the trees were thinning slightly and the soldiers ahead of them were slowing their pace.

Up ahead, Wolff reached the top of the wooded slope and paused at the edge of a large clearing. As Ratboy and the others huffed and clattered to his side, Wolff turned and raised his hand, signalling for them to stop at the edge of the trees. 'They're making camp,' he announced, with an incredulous expression on his face.

Ratboy looked past him and saw that it was true. Hundreds of the Ostlanders had gathered on the plateau at the top of the slope, and none of them looked happy to be there. The fervour that had driven them into the forest was fading quickly. There was a tangible feeling of menace about the place that made them wonder if they had been acting entirely under their own volition. They had huddled together for protection and there was a hum of nervous conversation as they eyed the surrounding trees. The wolf-helmed officers of Fabian's honour guard were moving amongst them, and as the nearest one caught sight of Wolff and the Knights Griffon, he strode over and gave Maximilian a stiff bow. 'The kriegsmarshall has granted you all a few hours rest,' he said, waving to the treetops spread out below them. 'The marauders have already hidden themselves throughout the forest. You'll need some sleep before we start the long job of hunting them all down.'

Maximilian looked around at the dismal clearing. 'He wants us to rest here?'

The officer's only reply was a nod and his helmet made it impossible to see his expression.

'Very well,' said Wolff stepping to the baron's side. 'If the Iron Duke wishes it.'

The officer studied Wolff in silence for a few seconds; then he gave another brisk nod and moved on.

'We're completely exposed up here,' said Maximilian, turning to Wolff with a frown. 'Why on earth would we sit out the night in a strange place like this?' He waved at the crowds of tired soldiers flooding into the clearing. They were watching the trees fearfully as they spread out on the long grass. 'If these men are meant to be hunting the marauders, why wait until the morning? They can obviously sense there's something odd about this place and anyway, if they don't move soon, the enemy will be long gone.'

'I expect most of the marauders have already made their escape,' replied Wolff, drumming his fingers on the haft of his weapon. 'My brother didn't bring these men up here to fight. He brought them up here to die.'

'Is he even here though?' asked Ratboy, scouring the hilltop. 'I can see his banner over there with the Oberhau, but I can't actually see the general anywhere.'

They looked over at the tattered black and white standard and the soldiers milling around beneath it. Ratboy was right: there were dozens of Oberhau, cleaning their long, two-handed greatswords and snapping orders at the other Ostlanders, but there was no sign of the general himself. As they watched, a young soldier crossed the clearing and approached Fabian's honour guard. Ratboy felt a chill of fear. He recognised the man immediately as the soldier who had discovered Anna. The young officer spoke urgently to one of the guards and then, after a few minutes he gestured over towards Ratboy and the others. Several of the Oberhau crowded round, quizzing him intently and turning to look at Maximilian and Wolff.

'This looks interesting,' said the baron, tugging at his short silver beard as he watched the exchange. He turned to Wolff with an ironic grin. 'I'm not sure we'll be getting that much rest after all.'

Ratboy gave a nervous cough and looked up at the pair of hoary old veterans. 'I think I might have spoken to that man earlier,' he muttered with a shame-faced expression. 'And accidentally mentioned that we were pursuing the general.'

Wolff's nostrils flared with anger, but when he spoke it was in clipped, controlled tones. 'Was it him, or not?'

Ratboy looked again and nodded. 'It was him – I'm sure of it.'

Wolff grimaced with frustration and closed his eyes for a few seconds to think. Then he turned to the baron. 'Whatever happens,' he said, 'I need to find my brother. I can't die here; not without confronting him.'

'I understand,' replied Maximilian with a stern nod. He looked at his men. It was hard to believe they had just survived a fierce battle. During the whole engagement, only six of their number had fallen and those that remained looked as calm and lethal as if they had just emerged from their chapterhouse. They stood in neat, gleaming rows at the edge of the trees and each of them had their hands folded in exactly the same way across the hilt of their swords. 'We can hold off Fabian's swordsmen for as long as you need us to,' said Maximilian. He waved at the crowds of Ostlanders still shuffling fearfully into the clearing. 'I can't guarantee what everyone else here will do though and even we couldn't hold off an entire army.'

'Leave that to me,' replied Wolff.

The Oberhau finished talking to the young officer and dismissed him. Then, the most senior amongst them huddled together, looking repeatedly towards the Knights Griffon as they talked. Finally, they came to some kind of accord and drew themselves into ordered ranks, before marching over towards Maximilian and his men. All across the clearing, the groups of resting soldiers watched the scene with interest and several of them rose to their feet to get a better view.

The knight at the head of the Oberhau was slightly larger than the others and looked to be their captain. He wore the same dark, burnished armour, but his wolf-shaped helmet and two-handed greatsword were a little more ornate, and a pair of huge, black and white feathers topped his sculpted helmet. Upon reaching Maximilian and Wolff he threw back his visor with a *clunk*. His eyes looked out from the dark metal with a dispassion that Ratboy found utterly chilling. There wasn't a trace of humanity in them. 'Good evening, baron,' he said, nodding at Maximilian. 'I must congratulate you and your men on their work this evening.' He spoke in flat, neutral tones and stood with the casual poise of a relaxed athlete. 'I noticed you were amongst the very last to retreat into the valley.'

'Thank you, Captain von Groos,' replied Maximilian with a deep bow. 'It's a pleasure to–'

A flash of movement interrupted Maximilian's reply. It was so fast that for a few seconds Ratboy struggled to work out what had happened. It was only when Maximilian staggered backwards that the acolyte saw there was a greatsword, buried deep in his chest. Von Groos had shoved it through the baron's cuirass with such force that the blade had sliced through the metal and emerged between his shoulder blades. As he dropped to his knees, Maximilian tried to speak, but all that emerged from his mouth was a thick torrent of dark blood. As he collapsed into his men's arms, with a confused expression on his face, he was already dead.

Von Groos wrenched the blade free with a screech of grinding steel and stepped back.

For once, the Knights Griffon forgot their training. With a chorus of despair and rage, they launched themselves at the Oberhau. Ratboy just managed to drag Anna aside as they slammed into the swordsmen.

There was an explosion of limbs and swords as the Oberhau defended themselves against the vengeful knights. Captain von Groos was already on the floor. Wolff had him by the throat and as Ratboy looked over, he saw the priest slam his forehead into the captain's face, shattering his nose with an audible *crunch*.

The captain muttered a stream of indecipherable words and writhed snake-like from Wolff's grip. As he leapt to his feet, he turned lightly on his heel and brought his two-handed sword down towards the priest's head.

Wolff was nowhere near as fast as his opponent and before he could dodge the blow, the blade slammed into his neck. His ornate gorget took most of the impact, but the edge of the blade scraped across the side of his face, sending up a thin arc of blood and causing him to bark in pain. He rolled forward and rammed his head into the captain's stomach.

Von Groos's breath exploded from his lungs and Wolff lifted him up over his shoulders. The priest draped one arm over the captain's neck and the other over his legs and before von Groos could raise his sword for a second strike, Wolff jerked his elbows downwards and snapped the captain over his broad back, cracking his spine in two. As the priest let him slide down his back onto the floor, von Groos whispered pitifully, then, after a final, rasping breath he fell silent. Wolff glared at the corpse for a few seconds, disappointed he could only kill the man once.

The rest of the Oberhau were faring a little better. Despite their expensive armour and years of training, the Knights Griffon could not seem to lay a single blow on their opponents. As they fought, the Oberhau whispered strange, arcane words and danced easily out of reach with lightning-fast movements.

Wolff backed away from von Groos's corpse and raised a hand to his scarred face to gauge the damage. With a nod of satisfaction he turned his attention to the fight. The combatants were well matched. The Oberhau whirled and slashed with incredible speed, but so far they had been unable to break the proud fury of Maximilian's knights.

Other soldiers had begun swarming around the fight, speechless with shock and unsure what to do. None of them were willing to enter the fray without being sure whose side to take.

Wolff wiped the blood from his cheek and rose up to his full height. He looked out at the gathering crowds and raised his warhammer. 'Men of Ostland,' he cried, loud enough to be heard over the sound of the fighting. 'I'm Jakob Wolff: Templar of Sigmar and brother of Fabian Wolff, your kriegsmarshall.'

A crowd immediately formed around him.

Blood flew from Wolff's face as his booming voice filled the clearing. 'Is that natural?' he cried, waving at the Oberhau. 'Who can fight with such speed?' His voice rose even louder. 'Other than the damned?'

At the sound of Wolff's words, several of the Oberhau tried to break free and rush towards him, but Maximilian's stern-faced men blocked their way.

The soldiers surrounding Wolff looked at each other with confused expressions. A young pistolier stepped forwards. His armour was dented and torn and there was a bloodstained bandage over one side of his face, but he pointed defiantly at the Oberhau. 'They're the Iron Duke's own men,' he cried. 'He's taught them to fight as well as he does.'

'And where do you think your Iron Duke learned such incredible skill?' snapped Wolff, glaring at the pistolier. 'He's my brother, but I won't defend him. Only the Ruinous Powers give such unnatural strength.'

'He's an Ostlander,' the pistolier cried back, looking around at his comrades for support. 'One thing we've all learned to do well is fight.'

A ragged cheer met his words and several of the soldiers raised their weapons in agreement.

Wolff grabbed the man by his jerkin, pulled him close and roared into his face. 'Fight for what?' he cried. He waved at the surrounding trees. 'What are you doing here? The battle is won. Why has the Iron Duke led you to the black heart of this forest? To a place where the enemy has all the advantage? I know Fabian Wolff. He's led you here as a sacrifice. You're a gift. An offering to the very enemy he claims to be hunting.'

There was a chorus of jeers and boos. 'Never,' cried the pistolier, freeing himself from Wolff's grip with a shocked expression on his face. 'How could you accuse him of such a thing?'

'Tell me,' replied Wolff, looking out over the crowd. 'Where's your general now?'

The soldiers looked nervously around the clearing, but the pistolier was undaunted. 'He's most likely scouting the surrounding area, looking for the enemy.'

Wolff shook his head. 'Mormius is dead. His army is already defeated. Those that survived have already fled. Fabian has abandoned you.' He waved at the sinister, twisted trees that surrounded them. 'Here, in this wretched forest.'

A fierce debate broke out amongst the crowd. Some of the soldiers already felt unnerved by their frenzied journey through the trees. It almost felt as though an external force had been driving them onwards. Many of them had been eager to head home even before they reached the clearing and its ominous atmosphere. Wolff's accusations had only made them more anxious to leave. The quarrel quickly grew louder. The men were tired and scared and Wolff's speech had put a name to their fear. There was rattle of swords being drawn and the crowd fragmented into a morass of snarling faces and furious insults.

As the arguments became fights, Ratboy noticed that his master had turned away from the troops. He was peering at something just outside the clearing and Ratboy stepped to his side to see what it was. It was too dark beneath the trees to see very clearly, but Ratboy thought he could make out a face, watching them. 'What is it?' he asked, looking up at the priest. 'Is that Sürman?'

Wolff frowned. 'No, I don't think so. I'm not sure it's even…' his words were lost beneath the din of the battle as he strode off towards the edge of the clearing. He paused briefly at the edge of the trees and looked back at the confusion he had created. The soldiers' frenzy had returned, but now it was directed at each other. It would be several minutes before they remembered the priest who had caused their disagreement. Wolff gave a nod of satisfaction and vanished from view.

Ratboy rushed after him, with Anna close behind. As they plunged into the damp, arboreal gloom they had to reach out and feel their way through the network of roots and shrubs, but Wolff rushed ahead, oblivious to the twigs and branches that lacerated his flesh. Ratboy saw his prey: it was a small deer of some kind, skipping easily through the trees.

'What's he doing?' asked Anna. 'His friend has just been butchered and he decides to go hunting.'

Ratboy shook his head in confusion and cried out. 'Master, where are you going? What about Maximilian's men?'

Wolff ignored his acolyte and blundered on through the trees, chasing the terrified animal. They reached the banks of stagnant pool and the deer paused, knee deep in the moonlit water, looking back at them expectantly. 'Look at it,' gasped Wolff, stopping to catch his breath.

Ratboy peered at the motionless creature. Now that he could see it more clearly, he noticed that there was something very strange about it. Its limbs were crooked and its hide bulged in places where it should have been smooth. It reminded Ratboy of some of the stuffed animals he had seen in Castle Lüneberg. Its eyes were not those of a dumb animal and they gazed back at him with a cool, human intelligence.

'What's that along its back,' whispered Anna, trying not to scare the animal.

Ratboy followed her gaze and saw that all along the deer's hunched, undulating spine there was a flash of iridescent blue, bursting up from under its skin. 'Are they feathers?' he asked.

At the sound of Ratboy's question, the deer bolted. It moved with lightning speed but Wolff was almost as quick, splashing through the water and disappearing back into the trees.

As Ratboy raced after him, he quickly realised that the growth beyond the pool was even more gnarled and closely packed. He and Anna did their best to clamber after the priest, but they felt as though the branches were deliberately lashing out and pressing their ancient weight down on top of them. The strange lights also began to reappear in the corner of Ratboy's vision: flickering sprites that vanished as soon as he tried to pinpoint them. As they struggled deeper and deeper into the brooding heart of the forest, his eyes began to play other tricks on him too. Branches slipped out of reach as he reached for support and leering faces appeared in the knotted trunks, only to vanish when he looked a second time.

'What's that sound?' asked Anna, panting and grunting as she fought through the undergrowth.

Ratboy paused for a second and noticed that beneath the sound of his own laboured breathing, there was a low throbbing noise. It was barely perceptible, but it seemed to emanating from all around them, as though the forest itself were groaning with fear. He shook his head and stumbled onwards after Wolff, terrified at the thought of being left alone in such a place.

After a few minutes, he noticed there was a pale green light pulsating through the trees ahead. He turned to Anna and guessed from her frown that she had seen it too. As they neared the light, the throbbing sound grew louder and Ratboy's nervousness increased. He could no longer see his master, but as they scrambled through the undergrowth he began to make out the source of the strange radiance. There was a grove up ahead that seemed quite distinct from the rest of the forest. An arcade of tall silver birches led proudly towards it, before forming themselves into a perfect circle around the small, raised clearing. The light was bleeding between the gaps in the sentry-like birches, so Ratboy stumbled onto the avenue and raced up towards the clearing. The light was so bright in the grove that he had to shield his eyes as he ran into the dazzling circle of trees.

CHAPTER EIGHTEEN

The Sacred Grove

The grove was filled with blinding light. The glare was so intense Ratboy struggled to see for a few seconds. When his vision cleared, he saw that Wolff was stood just ahead of him, silhouetted against the brightness and watching the deer as it trotted across a carpet of mossy turf. Ratboy saw that the animal's movements had become even more erratic. It lurched into the centre of the grove and dropped to its knees before the hollowed-out bole of an old oak tree. As it fell, its internal organs slipped from beneath its skin in a steaming mess, spilling onto the grass like stew from a pot, to reveal a small, humanoid shape crouched within the hide.

'Sigmar,' whispered Ratboy, as the figure discarded the animal's remains and climbed, gasping, to its feet. 'What's that?'

The creature stretched its slender arms above its head and let out a sigh of satisfaction. As the rest of the deer's innards slid down its back, they revealed a coat of blue feathers that shimmered in the throbbing light. 'Kriegsmarshall,' it said, bowing towards the tree stump, 'the other two are close behind.'

'They're already here, Helwyg,' replied a low voice from somewhere within the inferno of light.

The feathered creature turned to look back at Ratboy and Anna in surprise. His eyes were bright yellow and widened in fear at the sight of them. He dashed away from the sodden remains and vanished into the light.

'Master,' cried Ratboy, rushing towards Wolff but, before he had gone more than a few feet, he froze. The light that washed over his skin felt thick and tangible and it rooted his feet firmly to the spot. He moaned in fear as he felt it entwining his limbs and snaking through his clothes. Within seconds, his entire body was paralysed. The most he could do was roll his eyes from side to side in terror. As he did so, he saw that Anna was frozen too, just a few feet to his left. Tendrils of light snaked between the two of them and Wolff, making a crackling, glimmering triangle. He tried to scream, but even his vocal chords refused to obey. His horror mounted as he realised that he had not seen Wolff move an inch since he and Anna entered the grove. They were all paralysed.

'It's been a long time, Jakob,' said Fabian in an imperious voice, stepping out of the light. His regal features were flushed with pride as he surveyed his handiwork. In his left hand he held an old, battered book, bound in white leather, with a gold knife foiled on the front. Several of its pages were missing and scraps of mismatched parchment had been sewn clumsily into the jacket, but its power was unmistakable. Waves of emerald light were leaking from the paper, rippling through the grass and glittering in the stones on Fabian's eye-patch. 'But I'm sure you remember the promise I made you,' he continued. 'I swore not to hunt you down, but you've brought yourself to me. And I warned you that if we ever met again, I'd have no choice but to kill you.'

The priest tried to answer, but he was completely shrouded in light, and as he strained to escape, the only sound he could make was a strangled groan of frustration.

Fabian strolled slowly towards his brother, still holding the book before him. In his other hand, he held a small black object. As the old general stepped closer, Ratboy realised he was holding the beak of a carrion bird, long and gleaming as he rolled it between his thumb and forefinger.

'You're so old,' muttered Fabian as he reached his paralysed brother. He looked with fascination at Jakob's weather-worn features and ran a finger slowly across his face. 'You've lived a whole lifetime that you didn't deserve.' Fabian's one good eye was the only hint of their shared heritage. Where Jakob was broad and heavy-set, Fabian was slender and graceful; they were as opposite as two men could be, but his eye was as black and dangerous as his brother's. 'Your destiny has finally caught up with you,' he said, pressing the beak into the side of the priest's neck.

Wolff tried to pull away, but the dancing light held him firmly in place and as the curved, filthy beak slipped beneath his skin it sent a dark stream of blood rushing down his thick neck. Fabian gave a low chuckle. 'Bless you, brother. I had my doubts that this would work. My lord had complete confidence in your naïveté, but I thought after all these decades you might have developed a little more insight.'

He stepped back to watch as Wolff's blood pooled on the ground. As soon as the liquid touched the grass, it fanned out into a series of thin, viscous strands, each one twisting and spiralling as though alive. The lines of blood traced around the priest's feet in a complex set of circles, framing him within an elaborate, glistening design.

Fabian shook his head at his brother's confused expression. 'It must be wonderful to see the world in such simple terms – to divide everything along crude fault lines of good and evil, but it does leave one a little blinkered.'

He sighed as he watched his brother struggling. Then he waved at the slender, blue creature watching nervously from the edge of the clearing. 'My eyes have been on you for a long time, Jakob. I've waited and waited for you to realise the truth, but you never did. Your head's still so full of righteousness. Even after all these years, it robs you of sense. You knew I was coming here to make a sacrifice.' He leant forward, so that his face was just inches away from his brother's. 'But not for a minute did you consider that the sacrifice might be you.' He savoured the mute agony in Wolff's eyes. 'Yes, you see it now. Now that you've sent so many innocents to their deaths, believing I was interested in a horde of meat-headed soldiers. I've led you a merry dance, brother, but you embraced the role with enthusiasm. I think you can take credit for all the bystanders you've dragged down with you.' He shrugged. 'To be fair, the idea wasn't mine. I *did* originally intend to buy immortality with the blood of my men. But my master's taste is far more particular. Only a very choice morsel is good enough for such an imaginative appetite.' He raised his hands to the star-speckled heavens and cried out in a dramatic voice. 'Not just the blood of a powerful Sigmarite, but the blood of my own brother! How delectable!' He shook his head. 'I never dreamt you would be so stupid as to bring yourself to me – trotting meekly into my master's own house, but he had faith; he had the vision I lacked.'

The veins in Wolff's neck looked ready to burst as he pulled against the light that enveloped him. Finally, with an incredible effort, he managed to let out a feeble word. 'No,' he croaked.

'Yes,' replied Fabian with a broad smile. 'Yes, yes, yes! You're my gift, Jakob. The whole campaign was nothing but a joke, with you as its moronic punchline. Two entire armies sacrificed, just to make a fool out of you – just to see if you'd take the bait. Everything was leading to this moment. Do you really think it's so easy to stroll from behind the lines of such an army as Mormius's? I thought you would see through the ruse though, I really did. I thought you would spot the handiwork of the Architect of Fate. How could you not recognise the artifices of the Great Beguiler.' He shook his head and his smile became a laugh. 'I could maybe understand your cynical abuse of the flagellants' faith, but what happened at Mercy's End, Jakob? I felt sure you would see sense then. How could you think it was right to abandon all those men? You let Mormius rip the heart out of this province, just so you could pursue a personal vendetta. Don't you see? With you by their side, they would have won. Was there ever such a proud display of Ostland grit as Fel-hamer and his garrison? How could you just leave them all to die? How could you think that was right? You abandoned every article of your faith when you left those men to be butchered.'

Wolff's struggles grew weaker with each word. His shoulders slumped and his chin dropped, until it seemed as though the light was all that was keeping him on his feet. He looked utterly destroyed.

Fabian stepped over towards Anna. 'And what strange company you keep, brother. What a wretched collection of apostates.' He looked down at Anna's bloodstained robes with obvious amusement. 'A murderous Shallyan – who ever heard of such a thing? How quickly we abandon our beliefs in the face of pain.' As Fabian leant closer to the priestess, her body bucked away from him, lurching violently within the prison of light. 'Did you enjoy it, Anna,' he whispered, as he pressed the beak into the side of her neck, 'when you felt him struggling for life?' Anna moaned in horror as blood rushed from her throat, mingling with that of her victim. 'Did you relish the power, as you stopped his heart?' Fabian stepped back to watch as the blood danced around Anna's feet, before writhing across the ground and linking with the pool at Wolff's. 'Did you really think you were left alive in that cart by mere chance?'

He nodded with satisfaction and then moved over to Ratboy. 'And this one, brother' he chuckled. 'Did you know he tried to forsake you?' He sneered with disgust. 'While you were fighting to preserve his homeland, this wretched turncoat was planning his escape. Can you believe that? After everything you've done for him, he tried to abandon you to save his own worthless skin. He wouldn't even be here if the Knights Griffon hadn't caught him trying to worm his way to safety. He lacks your faith, brother. He lacks the faith to kill.'

Ratboy's eyes filled with tears. The truth of Fabian's words cut through him. Fabian was right. The battle had terrified him, but not as much as the sight of Wolff's animal frenzy. That was what he had been fleeing – the fear of such inhumanity. His chest shook with great, heaving sobs. He had pictured many endings to his life as a novice, but never this one: to die by the side of his master after such awful betrayal. Ratboy's desolation was complete. He barely noticed as Fabian slid the beak into his throat and sent a spray of blood down his filthy hauberk. The liquid quickly merged with the morass of crimson symbols on grass.

Fabian turned away from him and flicked through the pages of the book. He muttered a few incoherent lines under his breath and the light grew in brilliance. The tears in Ratboy's eyes fragmented the brilliant display, so that he saw dozens of Fabians stride back up to the ancient tree stump and remove their eye-patches.

As the light grew, so did the throbbing sound. The birches surrounding the grove began to bow and creak with the force of it. At the same time, the strands of blood formed ever more complex shapes around the three captives: eyes merged into fish and flames formed into skulls and all with such frenetic purpose that the liquid seemed to possess an awful, animal sentience.

Ratboy's mind reeled in the face of such an onslaught and he felt his reason slipping away. The trees at the edge of the clearing were now undulating and throbbing in time to the pulses of light, twisting themselves into strange, serpentine shapes. Ratboy gave Wolff a final despairing look, but the priest was hanging like a limp doll, tossed back and forth by the currents of his brother's magic. Ratboy closed his eyes but the awful visions simply burned through his eyelids and flooded his broken heart.

CHAPTER NINETEEN
The Blood of a Wolff

Envy never dies, thought Anna as Fabian's sorcery pawed and scratched at her flesh. Where had she heard those words? For the life of her she could not remember, but as she watched the old general, muttering feverishly over his book, she realised why she had thought of them. In an instant, her mind stripped away the decades and she saw a small boy stood behind the shattered oak; a child consumed by jealousy for his older brother. Her despair began to be replaced by anger. Had so many men really been sacrificed to assuage the petty hatred of a child? Was she really going to die here for such a pathetic reason? Whatever she had done, whatever mistakes she had made, she could not bear to be sacrificed on the altar of some paltry sibling rivalry. She strained her muscles one last time, testing the strength of her bonds, but the column of light that surrounded her was now a furious hurricane of glyphs and visions and there was no way she could break through. As Fabian's incantation droned on in the background she began to seethe with fury. The lattice of energy had lifted the three of them several feet off the ground, coursing through their bodies with such force that they jolted back and forth like branches, battered by a storm.

A movement caught her eye and she twisted her head back over her shoulder. There was a pair of men crouched in the avenue of trees that led up to the grove. They were stood in the darkness beyond the luminous display and she couldn't quite make out their faces, but as the smaller of the two edged forwards, she saw his pale, staring eyes and felt a shock of recognition.

Sürman had finally found her.

Thoughts tumbled through her head. Death, or something worse, was only seconds away. Would the witch hunter do anything? She peered into his strange eyes and flinched at the hatred she found there. She could see that, even now, as unholy energy arced and flashed around the clearing, he was desperate to come to her. If there was ever an ounce of sanity in him it had long gone. She saw a profound madness in his thin, jaundiced features. The only thing keeping his ruined body alive was his hunger for her blood.

She looked around the grove. Fabian was completely lost in rapture. His working eye had rolled back in its socket and his flesh was incandescent with power. The strands of blood and magic that linked her to Wolff and Ratboy were coruscating wildly in time to the rhythm of his words. The throbbing was now so loud she could barely hear him, but the imploring tone was unmistakable: he was using their vitality to summon something. At the heart of the circle of light a nimbus was forming in the bole of the old oak tree. It was too bright to look upon directly, but Anna thought she could see movement stirring deep within it: a foetal shape, twitching and straining for life. Whatever it was, the links between her and the others were feeding it, she was sure of it.

An idea began to form in her mind.

With all her remaining strength, Anna raised her hands above her head and twisted her face into a victorious grin. As she turned towards Sürman, she felt the light playing around her fingertips and laughed with pleasure.

Sürman's eyes bulged at the sight of Anna's ecstatic movements. It was more than he could bear to see her relishing the power that surrounded her. His worst suspicions were confirmed. She was obviously a witch of unbelievable power. He clutched his head in dismay and stumbled into the light, lurching towards her as though dragged by invisible hands.

His companion grabbed him by the shoulder, trying to pull him back to safety, but the witch hunter shrugged him away with a cry that was lost beneath the throbbing hum of Fabian's magic.

Anna twisted her hands into a series of vaguely mystical shapes, trying to ignore the pain that was eating into her limbs and assuming the role of an unrepentant sorceress.

Finally, with a storm of invectives Sürman broke into a run and launched himself at Anna. He grabbed hold of her legs and they both slammed down onto the muddy grass.

The triangle of light collapsed and arcs of power thrashed wildly around the grove, like the flailing limbs of a dying animal. The throbbing ceased immediately and Wolf and Ratboy dropped heavily to the ground.

A hiccupping scream echoed around the clearing.

Anna looked up to see that all of the light had turned back in on its source, pummelling into Fabian's body with such force that it had pinned him to the ground. The book fell from his hand and smoke began to rise from his clothes as the power rippled over his prone body. 'Gods, what have you done?' he screamed at Sürman, as the witch hunter struggled with Anna, attempting to drag her from the clearing.

'Help me Adelman, you oaf,' hissed Sürman, looking back at the hulking figure stood beneath the trees. The man looked at the wild directionless power lashing across the grass and shook his head, white with fear. 'Quick,' said Sürman, wrapping his wiry arms around Anna's legs as she tried to drag herself away.

Anna had almost pulled herself free of the old man's grip when his servant finally plucked up the courage to come after her. He lumbered across the grove and levelled a crossbow at her. Two bolts were loaded in its breach and Anna yelped in pain as the first sank deep into her thigh. As she clutched at the wound, gasping in agony, Adelman lifted her easily over his shoulder and began to carry her back towards the trees, with the grinning witch hunter following closely behind. Anna's screams echoed around the grove, but both Wolff and Ratboy were still spread-eagled on the grass and gave no sign of hearing.

They had almost left the clearing when Adelman stumbled to a halt. He looked down at his chest with an expression of dog-like stupidity. There was a smouldering hole where his chest should have been.

'What are you doing?' snarled Sürman. 'Why've you stopped?' Then he noticed the wound and his eyes widened in fear. As Adelman toppled to the ground, vomiting thick blood across the grass, Sürman and Anna saw the source of his injury. Fabian had struggled to his feet, still enveloped in the green light and was lurching drunkenly towards them. His right hand was extended and crackling with power.

'Leave her,' he said, with light sparking off his teeth.

'She's mine!' screamed Sürman, pinning Anna to the floor and glaring back at him. 'She escaped my justice once but not–'

Fabian silenced the witch hunter with a single flick of his wrist. Light poured from his veins and slammed into the frail old man.

The witch hunter barely had time to cry out in pain before the flesh melted and shrivelled from his face. As he collapsed on top of Anna, his head was little more than a mass of charred bone and smouldering hair.

'Actually, she's mine,' said Fabian, pulling Sürman's smoking remains off Anna and grabbing her arm. The power in his fingers scorched her skin and she cried out in pain. 'I won't be stopped,' he growled, pulling her face towards his.

For the first time, Anna saw Fabian's left eye and she gasped in disgust. The scab had opened and the huge black orb was rolling excitedly in its moist, pus-lined socket. She felt a malign intelligence studying her through the bloated lens and turned away in fear. There was a smell of cooking meat coming from Fabian and she noticed that where the light was leaking through his pores, his skin was blistering and cracking. His determination seemed to blind him to his pain though and, despite Anna's screams and kicks, she found herself being dragged slowly back towards the shattered oak.

Anna gasped as she saw that the foetal shape had already doubled in size. Birdlike talons had erupted from its skin and were scrabbling at the wood in an attempt to climb free. Its flesh was rippling and twitching as it tried to settle on a fixed shape and as they approached it Anna heard the wet, laboured sound of the thing's first breath.

As she struggled to escape, Anna noticed that Wolff had climbed to his knees and was praying to his warhammer. His head was bowed and he was muttering furiously under his breath. The ornate tracery that decorated the head of the weapon was glimmering slightly with a light of its own: not as dramatic as the green fire that was devouring Fabian, but enough to give Anna a fierce rush of hope.

Fabian followed the direction of her gaze and hissed with frustration. He threw her to the ground and stretched out his hand towards Wolff. 'This is my destiny, Jakob,' he shrieked, as light exploded from his arm and hurtled across the clearing towards the priest's head.

Wolff calmly raised his hammer to meet the blast and a deafening explosion filled the grove.

The flash was so bright that for a second Anna was blinded. When her vision cleared, she saw that all traces of magic had vanished. The forest had been plunged back into darkness and Fabian was sprawled, gasping on his back. The bole of the tree was empty once more and there was no sign of the grotesque foetus that had been forming within its bark. Anna's ears rang with the sudden silence as she climbed to her feet. She had forgotten the bolt lodged in her thigh and she cried out in pain, dropping heavily to her knees again.

At the sound of her voice, Fabian lifted his head and gave a weak groan of despair. With the light gone, he saw how scorched and ruined his flesh was. 'What have you done?' he croaked, peering though the darkness at the tree trunk, then turning to look at his brother.

Wolff was still knelt in prayer.

'You can't stop me,' howled Fabian, managing to stand 'Not now, after all my work.' He stumbled across the grove, with burnt clothes and skin trailing behind him like a bridal train. 'You. Can. Not. Stop. Me,' he said, punctuating each word with a punch to Wolff's head.

Jakob took the blows with unflinching stoicism, before rising to his feet and glaring down at his smaller brother. 'This is wrong, Fabian,' he said calmly. 'Whatever has passed between us, you must know I *can't* let you do this.' He adopted a fighting stance and gripped his warhammer firmly in both hands. 'I have to stop you.'

Fabian let out a long, bitter laugh. 'I'm not a child anymore, Jakob,' he said, drawing his sword and mirroring the priest's pose. 'And father isn't here to save you this time.' As he spoke the word 'time' he lunged forward with surprising speed, jamming his blade through a gap at the top of Wolff's vambrace.

Wolff staggered backwards, clutching his arm in shock and trying to stem the flow of blood that rushed down his forearm. He quickly recovered and swung his hammer towards Fabian's head, but the Iron Duke was already gone. Wolff's weapon connected with nothing but air and the priest's momentum sent him crashing to his knees.

Fabian laughed again as he planted a boot into his brother's back and sent him sprawling across the grass. 'So slow,' he chuckled. 'So old.'

Wolff leapt to his feet, gasping for breath. 'You're a Wolff,' he cried. 'Think what that means. Think of your heritage.'

The smile dropped from Fabian's gaunt face and his mouth twisted with rage. 'What would you know of being a Wolff?' he screamed, sending trails of spit from his scorched lips. 'How can you dare to speak of our heritage?' His anger overwhelmed him and he threw back his head, pulling at his own hair and screaming at the stars. 'You ruined everything! I was going to place our family back at the heart of history, where we belong.' His voice cracked and squeaked as he glared at Wolff. 'And you destroyed us. You and your church and your pathetic devotion. You killed our parents, Jakob.' He lurched across the grass with tears of rage flooding down his cheeks. 'How can you dare to even speak to me?' he cried, placing a fierce kick into the side of Wolff's head.

Wolff climbed to his feet and pounded the haft of his hammer into Fabian's breastplate, so that he reeled backwards towards the tree stump. '*I* killed them?' cried Jakob in a voice that sounded as strangled as his brother's. 'What are you talking about? I simply discovered your guilt.' He levelled a finger at Fabian. '*You* brought shame on our family, brother, not me. You diluted our bloodline with heresy and lies.'

Fabian was trembling with fury and his elegant fighting stance was completely forgotten as he ran wildly back towards Wolff. 'You're nothing but a puppet, Jakob,' he cried. 'A puppet of a dying creed.' He lashed out wildly with his sword.

Wolff was faster. His hammer smashed the sword aside and connected with Fabian's head.

The general's neck snapped backwards and he let out a gurgled moan, before toppling backwards into the bole of the tree.

Wolff placed one foot on the tree trunk and raised his hammer for the killing blow.

He paused.

Beneath him, Fabian was trying to speak. His head was horribly misshapen where his skull had cracked and his hair was dark with gore, but he still had the strength to reach out: pawing at his brother's robes in a final, desperate plea: trying to form words with his slack, blood-filled mouth.

Wolff scowled and raised his hammer a little higher, but still he couldn't strike. 'What?' he muttered finally, stooping so that he could place his ear next to his brother's mouth.

Fabian's eye was full of fear, but as he repeated the words, a faint smile played around his mouth. 'The blood of a Wolff runs true,' he whispered, gripping Jakob's shoulder.

The priest flinched. To hear their childhood joke, after all this time, filled him with horror. The years fell away and he saw that the bloody wreck before him was still Fabian. This awful fiend was still his brother. 'I can't do it,' he groaned, amazed by his weakness. He freed himself from Fabian's grip and dropped his warhammer to the grass. Then he stumbled backwards and sat heavily on the ground, with his head in his hands.

Fabian lay there for a few moments, watching his brother with an odd, pained expression on his face. Then, with a gurgling cough, he pulled himself out of the tree trunk and began to limp towards the far side of the grove.

He had only taken a few steps, when a crossbow bolt thudded into his back. He stumbled on for a few more feet, reaching out towards the gloomy boughs, then collapsed onto the grass with a final, ragged breath.

Ratboy approached with the crossbow still in his hand. He stooped and whispered into the corpse's ear. 'I've regained my faith, general,' he said.

CHAPTER TWENTY

Penitents

Jakob lay on his back watching the endless Ostland rain. It billowed and swept across the forest in great columns, falling with such force that dozens of rivulets had begun rushing down the hillside, washing over the priest's battered armour and heading down towards the valley below. A couple of miles away, the ragged fingers of Hagen's Claw pierced the downpour, reaching up towards the dark belly of the clouds like a drowning man. Jakob narrowed his eyes. Even from this distance he could see figures moving beneath the granite columns. Without their general to drive them onwards, the army was dispersing. The soldiers were making their way back to their families and homes, keen to forget the strangeness of the forest. In a few months the crows and other scavengers would have removed any trace of the dead that were left behind. In time, even the broken weapons would disappear beneath the grass and there would be no sign that the battle had ever taken place.

Wolff saw faces in the clouds rushing overhead. His brother's mainly, filled with anguish as he begged for mercy, but there were others too, a whole army of dead souls, all gazing down at him with hatred in their eyes. 'Sigmar forgive me,' he muttered.

'He's waking up,' came a voice from somewhere nearby.

Wolff lifted his head and wiped the rain from his eyes. Ratboy and Anna were sat watching him. They both looked awful. Their rain-lashed faces were white with exhaustion and pain. As Anna climbed to her feet and hobbled towards him, Wolff saw that the crossbow bolt was still embedded in her thigh and the lower part of her robe was black with blood. Ratboy was sat just a few feet away and Wolff guessed it was his voice he had heard. He was rocking back and forth, cradling his damaged hand, but there was a look of fierce determination in his eyes that the priest had never seen before. Wolff could hardly recognise him. He seemed to have aged a lifetime in an evening.

Wolff looked at them both in silence for a few seconds, unsure what to say. He felt somehow naked, ashamed of what they had witnessed during the night. Ashamed that they now knew so much about him. They had not only heard every word of his disgraceful confrontation with Fabian, but they had also seen his weakness and stupidity. It appalled him to think that without Ratboy's courage, Fabian would have escaped. His brother had made him a fool. 'How can I have been so blind?' he said, lowering his head in shame.

'He fooled us all, Jakob,' said Anna, reaching his side and placing a hand on his shoulder.

Wolff winced at the pity in her voice. She had never had any love for him, or his beliefs, so her sudden kindness made his skin crawl. What a pathetic figure he must have become if even Anna felt sorry for him.

'None of us could ever have dreamt that he would engineer a whole campaign – a whole war – just to ensnare his own brother,' she continued. 'That's the thinking of a lunatic. How could we have guessed he was working to such an insane plan? To sacrifice so many innocents,' she stumbled over her words and closed her eyes for a second, 'beggars belief.'

'I should have seen it,' said Wolff, recoiling from her touch. 'I knew him. I should have known.' He threw himself back on the grass. 'And everything he said about me was true. I was blinded by rage. I left all those men to die. I've betrayed everyone: you, the flagellants, Felhamer, Maximilian, Lüneberg, Gryphius – the entire army. Everyone.'

'Nothing he said was true,' replied Ratboy, shaking his head fiercely. 'His whole existence was a lie.' He climbed to his feet and looked down over the sodden trees. 'I *did* lose my nerve for a minute,' he said, with a note of shame in his voice. 'I couldn't recognise you for a while, as we fought through the marauders. I saw something in your face that terrified me.' He rushed to Wolff's side and looked at him with panic in his eyes. 'But Fabian lied. I would never have betrayed you. It was a moment of fear, nothing more.' He dropped to his knees and looked imploringly at his master. 'Even if Maximilian hadn't stopped me, I would've come back. As soon as I came to my senses.' He shook his head. 'I know I wouldn't have abandoned you. That's how I saw that he was nothing more than a cheap trickster. That's how I knew I had the strength to kill him.'

Wolff took Ratboy's hand. 'I never doubted your courage, Anselm. You've nothing to be ashamed of. In fact, you were right to fear me. I could think of nothing but revenge and murder. And even in that one, simple task I failed.' He turned his face to the rain and closed his eyes. 'In the end, I couldn't kill him. If you hadn't been there he would have gone free. It was my faith that failed, not yours.'

For a while the only sound came from the rain, drumming against the hillside. None of them even had the strength to crawl back towards the trees, so they just sat there in a disconsolate silence, letting the water soak through their clothes. Wolff was still staring up at the clouds, and still haunted by his brother's face. In those final seconds, when he saw the fear in Fabian's eye, a kind of awful epiphany had stayed his hand. It was his own religious zeal that had driven his brother down his dark path – he had suddenly seen that quite clearly. What an unbearable child he must have been: always so perfect, always so pious. Who could blame Fabian for rebelling? Who could blame him for attempting to find his own form of devotion?

After a while, Anna looked over at him. 'I think you're wrong, Brother Wolff.'

The priest looked over at her with a frown.

'I don't think it was a lack of faith that stayed your hand,' she continued. 'I think it was your humanity.' She looked at the blood that still covered her hands. 'We're just frail mortals, all of us: nothing more, nothing less. But maybe that's what makes us worth saving?'

'But my brother was a monster! To let him live would have been to loose a great evil on the world. Don't you see? Every decision I've made has led to bloodshed.' He groaned and clutched his head in his hands. 'I'm no better than a dumb animal. I don't even remember half of the battle. In fact, I'm just the same as Fabian. I've been deluding myself all this time that I have to save the Empire from his evil, but in reality, I'm no better than he was.'

Anna shook her head. 'No, Jakob, Fabian was a monster.' She grabbed his hand. 'And the very fact that you let him live proves that you're not. He had become inhuman but, in the end, after everything, you were still just a man. *That's* the difference between the two of you.' There was an intense urgency in her voice and Ratboy suddenly realised why: she was desperate for Wolff to forgive himself, so that she could do the same.

As Wolff looked back at her, a tiny glimmer of hope flashed in his black eyes. They held each other's gaze for a few seconds and then, briefly, the harsh lines of his face relaxed. He gave a barely perceptible nod and squeezed Anna's hand in gratitude. He closed his eyes and muttered a quiet prayer of thanks that was lost beneath the sound of the rain. Then, when he opened his eyes again, he noticed Anna's wounded leg and gave her a brusque nod. 'Let me see if I can I can help,' he said, spreading his hands over the wound.

As a soft, healing light began to leak from the priest's fingertips, Anna looked over at Ratboy with tears in her eyes and a faint smile playing around the corners of her mouth.

CHAPTER TWENTY-ONE

Remembrance

The Great Poppenstein would not be missed. In the few months since his arrival, the villagers of Elghast had quickly grown tired of his tatty costumes and amateurish tricks. Maybe he had been telling the truth when he boasted of his years in the Tsarina's circus, but if so, his age and alcoholism had long since robbed him of any real skill. His hands had trembled as he had performed even the most basic illusions and his juggling had been positively dangerous. When the conjuror's body was discovered, half eaten in the back of his bright red cart, no one was much surprised. The bear, Kusma, seemed destined for better things, and the villagers did not really blame him for wanting to dispose of his less talented partner.

The rain had turned the gardens of remembrance into a treacherous swamp of half-submerged headstones and slippery, flower-strewn paths. A few mourners had turned up, in the vain hope of seeing some of Poppenstein's celebrated circus friends, but they had soon hurried away again when they realised he had misled them about that too. With war continuing to rage across the province, funerals had begun to lose their appeal as a spectator sport. There was hardly a day that passed without some poor wretch being crammed into the packed cemetery.

Erasmus gave a grunt of exertion as he stamped the final mound of sod into place. Mud oozed over his sandals and between his toes and he grimaced in disgust. Then he leant back with his hands on his hips until his back gave a satisfying *crack*. 'Udo,' he called to the raven perched on a nearby headstone. 'Let's get back inside. This weather will be the death of us.'

It was already nine, but there was no sign of sunlight breaking through the low clouds. For weeks now, the village had been smothered in a perpetual gloom. News of the Iron Duke's victory in the north had been greeted with little enthusiasm. Few doubted that it would be long until the next incursion. Even the rumours of his mysterious disappearance held little interest for people so concerned with their own survival. Times were hard and the villagers of Elghast had long since lost their appetite for war. As the priest made his way back through the headstones towards the small temple he pulled his robes a little tighter and gave a long, weary yawn.

The raven remained perched on the stone and let out a peevish croak.

Erasmus paused and looked back over his shoulder. 'Come on, old girl,' he said, peering through the downpour at the huge bird. 'I've not even had my breakfast yet. Let's get inside. If I don't eat some porridge soon, my stomach will digest itself.'

The bird refused to follow Erasmus, but skittered from side-to-side across the top of the stone instead, letting out another harsh cry.

'Udo!' snapped the priest as he stomped back through the ankle-deep mud. 'What on earth's the matter with you?' His robes were now completely soaked and he shuddered as several icy trickles ran down his back. Upon reaching Udo he held out his arm and glared at the bird in an angry silence.

It was only after a few seconds of scowling that he realised they were not alone. There was a figure: a young man, or a boy even, cowering beneath the eaves of a large mausoleum and watching them intently. Erasmus squinted through the rain but could not make out who it was. The mourner was hooded and small, but beyond that he couldn't make out any details. Elghast was barely more than a hamlet and Erasmus knew most of the villagers by name, but this boy did not look familiar. 'Were you a friend of the deceased?' he called to the robed figure.

There was no reply, so he stepped towards him. 'I'm afraid the service is over. Is there anything I can help you with?'

The mourner remained silent.

Erasmus gave an irritated sigh and walked a little closer. 'Are your parents in the village?' he asked, stepping under the roof of the mausoleum.

As he reached the mourner, Erasmus realised his mistake. The stranger was not a boy at all, he was just incredibly hunched and frail.

The man lurched forwards and threw back his hood, revealing a gleaming mask of burnt flesh. 'Heal me,' he whispered. His lips had been burned away, leaving his mouth in a permanent grin and the rest of his face was scorched beyond all recognition. Erasmus had no doubt who the man was though. Despite the awful scarring that covered his skin, his colourless eyes were unmistakable.

'Sigmar help me,' gasped Erasmus, staggering backwards as the witch hunter grabbed hold of his robes. 'Sürman.'

Udo finally launched herself from the headstone, letting out another croak as she headed back towards the temple, leaving the two men struggling desperately in the shadows.

THE JUDGEMENT OF CROWS

Chris Wraight

Johannes Kreisler kept running. He was not good at it. His fat legs laboured under his heaving frame. A thick layer of sweat pooled across his skin, flicking into the night as he swung his heavy arms. Branches whipped across his face. The marshes were no place to be at night at the best of times. And these were most emphatically not the best of times.

He ploughed through a sodden patch of bogweed and briars, staggering as he went. His hose and jerkin were ripped and caked with slime. His old heart thumped furiously.

He risked a backward glance. Nothing. But that didn't mean they weren't there. They were silent, right until the moment they came at you. All he could hear was his own frantic panting; all he could see was his frozen breath against the dark night air. Kreisler felt like a great panicked bull, crashing his way through the soft earth, announcing his presence to every horror skulking in the shadows. There were too many of them, scuttling in the gloom like spiders. All it took was one hand to drag him down, one claw to pull him into the thick folds of the cold earth, and he would be forgotten forever. Just like Bloch. And Ulfika. And all the others. He should have known better. You couldn't go into the marshes. Not since they had come back.

Kreisler plunged across one of many treacherous pools of oily, freezing water. He no longer felt the sharp chill on his breeches. He was fuelled by fear alone, the kind of feral, energising fear which came from being hunted.

Suddenly, he saw lights ahead. Brief, strangled hope rose in his gullet. He'd almost made it. Pulling deep into his last reserves of strength, he pushed on. His flat feet sunk far into the sodden earth. For the first time, he began to believe he might get back, that everything might be all right.

Then they caught him.

The grip on his shoulder was crushing. A spear of cold pierced him, and he screamed, stumbling into the black mud beneath. There was a deathly clatter all around him. Kreisler fell heavily, rolling over in the grime. His hammering heart felt like it would burst. Frantically, hands flailing, he tried to push them off. Their fingers were like beaten iron, not a scrap of warm flesh on them. He felt more of them tug at his clothes. Something was dragging him back into the marshes.

Kreisler let out a second agonised scream. He couldn't see. His eyes were splattered with mud. He could feel them scrabbling all over him, pawing at his portly, warm body. He could hear them too. They were whispering to each other in voices that must once have been human. Even in the midst of his blind panic, he could make out a few words.

'Come with us,' they said, their words resonating like the memory of a nightmare. 'You are full and hot with blood, fat man, just as we were. Come with us…'

Kreisler felt his throat constrict with terror. His screams died. Whimpering, he tried to push himself away from them, to crawl from the whispering horrors clustering over him, to push their knife-sharp fingers from his throat. Then he saw one of their faces thrust over his. There were teeth, human teeth, framed by flaps of leathery skin. A single eye hung precariously in a socket. Old blood streaked the pale skin. Fingers reached for his face; pitiless rods of bone and sinew.

His heart shuddered, his vision went black. So this is death, he thought.

But the final gouging never came. Kreisler felt the flames before he saw them. There were voices, men's voices, and torches. A thin screaming broke out around him. He opened his eyes, and saw bone smashed, flesh ripped. There were heavy footfalls. A brazier was tipped over, and flame surged through the undergrowth beyond. Rough hands pulled him away from the inferno.

'Mother of Sigmar,' grunted a familiar voice close to his ear. 'He's a fat bastard.'

'Just pull,' came another, the note of panic high.

Kreisler felt his senses returning. He was surrounded by men. His own kin, Herrendorfers. In the flickering light, their faces were drawn and terrified. They were all armed. In the middle of the group was the familiar hunched silhouette of Boris.

His vision whirled back to the trees. His pursuers were still there. Some were doused in fire, twitching madly; others hung back from the flames. Their faces were pale in the shadow. Dozens of them. More than ever before. They began to shuffle forward again.

'Back behind the walls!' the old man croaked, his ragged voice breaking in the cold air.

Kreisler was pulled backwards roughly. The noise of burning and screaming rose. He began to regain some strength, and started to stumble along on his own account. The others clustered around him, and they scraped their way back to the gate. They made it, passing under the heavy gatehouse with relief.

Robbed of their prize, the wailing of the dead rose from the marshes. None came after them. They weren't strong enough to take on the axes of the entire village. Not yet.

The gates slammed shut. Kreisler was dropped unceremoniously on the earth inside the walls. He felt nauseous. He couldn't focus, and lay back, pulling air into his lungs in shuddering heaves. Men were running everywhere, lighting fresh fires, calling out instructions. The village was preparing to defend itself, just as it did every night.

Kreisler looked around him. The familiar wattle huts and buildings looked back, as if mocking his failure to escape. They were all filthy, strewn with mud and mottled damp. Pools of oily water lay in the streets, and a low mist curled around the base of the rundown houses. Many of the windows were empty, or covered with rotten wooden planks. Perhaps a little over half of them were still inhabited. The rest belonged to those who had been taken. Or maybe to the few who had got away. Where they were now, none could tell. They had left behind nothing but squalor and despair.

After some time, Boris came back over to Kreisler. The old priest's robes flapped in the icy wind. The torch he carried threw his lined grey face into savage relief. Kreisler felt a surge of emotion.

'Father!' he gasped, tears breaking out across his flabby cheeks.

The priest looked down at him grimly.

'More all the time,' he said, almost to himself.

Boris gazed down wearily at the icon of Sigmar hanging from his neck. He didn't ask why Kreisler had been out in the marshes, or admonish him for putting other lives at risk. He seemed tired and distracted.

'We need help,' he muttered, grudgingly. 'What a wizard starts, a wizard must finish.'

Boris sighed deeply, and looked over towards the gates. Kreisler watched him in confusion, barely understanding his words. Behind him, the doors were sealed with heavy beams, and more braziers were lit. Women came to tend to his wounds. None would sleep in Herrendorf that night. Not until the grey morning came and the horrors shrunk back into the marsh.

Boris limped off, his face creased with concern. Kreisler sagged back against the mud and matted straw of the floor, his vision swimming, ignoring the fussing voices around him. From beyond the village walls, agonised cries of frustration soared into the air and drifted away.

They had been denied their prey this time. But they would be back.

* * *

Katerina Lautermann pulled gently on the reins, and her horse came to a halt. Taking advantage of the rare high ground, she looked around her. In every direction, the bleak marshland stretched towards the horizon. The sky was heavy and low. Rain fell steadily, turning the ground below into a thick soup of filth. Stunted, twisted trees vied with strangling gorse and black grass to cover the landscape. The place looked blighted, ruined, and weary. She felt utterly alone.

She found herself wondering how any people could make a living in such a forsaken place. The squalor and wretchedness of the Ostermark's populace never ceased to amaze her. However pox-ridden, bandit-infested and debauched you thought the last place had been, the Empire was always capable of surprising you. Whispering a minor cleansing spell to keep her nostrils warded from the more noxious of the marsh smells, she pressed on, pushing the horse gently down the long incline towards the village ahead. She'd been told it was cursed. Having seen the country in which it nestled, she could well believe it.

As she went, Katerina stretched her limbs slightly in the saddle. She was cold and stiff after the long ride from Bechafen. The weather was relentlessly chill and damp, the scenery bleak and unremitting. Not for the first time, she found herself cursing Patriarch Klaus, the head of her order. Ever since that business with the orcs in the Grey Mountains, he had become more unpredictable, perhaps vexed by her visible success. So it was that she was given such miserable tasks to perform for him. On her return, things would have to change.

Nevertheless, the message from Herrendorf had piqued her interest for another reason. Radamus Arforl, one of the mightiest wizards of her order. She knew of his lore from when she had been an acolyte. He had done much in the early years of the College to augment its prestige, and then, like so many of their number, had fallen in battle. For three long centuries, no reports of his fate had come to light. Only now, quite without precedent, tidings had come from a forgotten outpost of humanity where his name was remembered with veneration. It piqued her curiosity. Though if she'd known quite how much mud she would have to wade through to get there, she might have been less enthusiastic.

She approached the village. The low trees retreated slightly, creating a wide and mournful clearing. The ground was heavy and waterlogged, and what fields there were looked like they produced a meagre crop. A few thin animals grazed warily at the edge of the forest. In the centre of the open space, the village itself stood. It was walled, and the dark stone rose twice the height of a man on all sides. Though crudely made, the defences looked formidable. Few of the buildings within protruded above the height of the wall. She guessed the houses in such a place would be low, mean affairs. What little wealth Herrendorf had had clearly been placed in its wall. That didn't bode well.

Katerina came up to the gate. There were dark bundles tied to the walls. As she drew closer, she saw what they were. Dead crows, dozens of them, suspended from makeshift gibbets in bundles. She swallowed her distaste, and dismounted. As she landed, filth splattered over her fine leather boots and cloak. She hissed a curse under her breath, and led her horse towards the sturdy gatehouse. Her arrival had been anticipated. There were men clustered under the low arch, waiting. Like frightened children, they looked unwilling to come into the open to meet her. Katerina took a deep breath. Much as she hated peasants, if this business was going to be concluded properly, she'd need to keep civil and bite her tongue.

As she neared the group, one figure limped towards her. He wore the robes of a priest of Sigmar, though they had long since passed their best. He was heavily hunched, and his skin was pale and sickly. Deep rings of grey underscored his eyes, and his thin fingers clutched a staff for balance.

'Welcome, my lady wizard,' he said in a scratchy voice. 'You've found us at last.'

Katerina nodded politely.

'You're Boris, the one who sent the letter?' she asked.

'I am,' said the priest, escorting her towards the crowd. 'Now that the headman has been taken, I'm the last vestige of leadership these people have. Not much for them to rally around, you might think. Maybe so. But I will not leave them.'

He ushered her towards the rest of the villagers.

'This is Albrecht, the gatekeeper,' said Boris, motioning towards a low-browed brute of a man who was holding one of the heavy oak doors open for them.

Katerina surveyed the group of men around her with distaste. They looked back at her with similar animosity, and parted to allow her entry to the village. They seemed extremely protective of the gatehouse, as if it was some kind of enchanted barrier. Dark eyes watched her with that steady, stupid curiosity so common in the mean folk of the Empire. Katerina had to stop herself from turning around, jumping straight back on her horse and riding as fast as she could back to civilisation.

'This is Gerhard, the blacksmith,' continued Boris, apparently oblivious to her discomfort, tediously reeling off the names of the all the men in the welcome party. 'And Weiss, the carpenter.'

The last one looked, if possible, even surlier than the rest. He had a heavy face, marked with days-old stubble. His skin was pale and blotchy, his clothes ragged and poor. He looked at her with open belligerence. This was getting ridiculous. Katerina found her pride getting the better of her. She was an Imperial wizard of the Amethyst Order, capable of razing the whole place to the ground with a single word, and these peasants were being insolent in the extreme.

'Greetings, Herr Weiss,' she said in a voice calculated to belittle him.

'Perhaps you could take my horse. We've been riding long, and she needs water.'

Weiss glowered at her.

'I don't hold with witches,' he said in a thick voice, and turned away, pushing his way through the crowd.

Katerina felt her cheeks flush. There were murmurs of approval from the others. Boris snapped his fingers and a fat man came to his side.

'Kreisler, take the lady's horse and see that it's stabled,' he said sharply, giving his fellow villagers a hard look.

At least that ended the round of introductions. Boris swiftly escorted Katerina to his dwelling place. They passed through the squalid main street, stained with the ever-present pools of filmy marshwater. The villagers seemed to have given up trying to staunch the filth with straw. Piles of refuse had been allowed to gather at the corner of the tired streets, and flies buzzed lazily in the shadows. The buildings, most of which were wooden-framed wattle-and-daub houses with dark thatched roofs, had been allowed to run to near-ruin. Some had even collapsed, and their wooden structures stood open to the chill marsh wind like carcasses.

The priest's chambers were in better order, but still bore the marks of neglect. A stale, damp smell had settled over the whole place, and the windows were dark. It took Katerina a few moments before she ducked under the low lintel and into the gloom of the interior. Once inside, Boris ushered her to a low wooden bench. Clumsy from the ride, she sat down heavily. The priest lit some tallow candles and poured her a flask of beer. She drank greedily, ignoring the sour taste and the acrid smell of the candles. This was as good as it was going to get.

'I apologise for the others, my lady,' he said, sitting opposite her in a battered old wooden chair. 'We get few visitors.'

'Can't imagine why,' said Katerina, dryly, and took another swig.

The priest's chambers were sparse, but relatively clean. Old-looking wooden icons of Sigmar hung from the bare stone walls. On a low table a few leather-bound books rested. They looked well-used. Clearly the man could read, then.

'So,' she said, making herself as comfortable as possible on the bench. 'The place is cursed. That much I can see myself.'

Boris nodded.

'There's no doubt about it, my lady. Each night more come. The unquiet dead. We recognise some of them, folk of Herrendorf we buried years ago. Others we don't. They come from the deep marshes. We can drive them off by fire, but they grow bolder. Something is disturbing them.'

'You've not tried to leave?'

'Some of us did, in the first days. Perhaps a few made it out of the marshes back then. Now none of us do. They wait for the dark, and then they come. I have seen it myself. If we'd delayed sending our tidings much longer, no messenger could have escaped them to tell our tale. The very fact you are here at all is a blessing from Sigmar.'

He looked at her with his rheumy, sombre eyes.

'In any case, this is our home. It is all we have. We have worked here and died here. We cannot leave it to the dead. I will not, at any rate. They are an abomination.'

Katerina looked at him carefully.

'And you think I can help you,' she said. 'Unusual, for a priest to summon a wizard to do his work. If you needed aid, why not ask for it from your own kind?'

Boris shook his head dismissively.

'None could do more than I have,' he said, with a trace of pride. 'I purified the village with the rites of my order, placed wards on the walls, performed rituals of exorcism where the resting places of the corpses were known. None of it works. We are mindful of our history here. A century and more ago, it was a wizard that ended the first of these plagues. An Amethyst mage at that, just like you. It was his spells that laid the dead back in their graves and has kept us warded from evil since. You must work the same spells again, my lady. Nothing else will suffice.'

'You speak of Arforl,' said Katerina, carefully. 'The circumstances of his death have long been unknown to my college. If he indeed died here, my master will be interested.'

Boris nodded eagerly.

'Radamus Arforl. We know the name here, even though so many years have passed. The story is told to our children. We don't forget. He died in the marshes, fighting the living dead. Somewhere out there he still lies, his mausoleum watching over the source of the evil.'

Boris broke into a cough, and for a few moments his ragged body shook. He recovered himself with difficulty. A weary smile flickered on his lips.

'Forgive me,' he said. 'Age, and the burden of care.'

Katerina frowned, ignoring the man's discomfort.

'His mausoleum is in the marshes?' she said. 'I'd like to see it.'

Boris shook his head.

'It has been lost for many years. Now only the legend remains. Some of us have tried to find it, especially now the plague has come again. I tried myself, though I didn't get far. None have done so. It may have been destroyed. Or perhaps it's hidden from ungifted eyes. I hoped there would be secrets there, something to give us a reason for the dead rising again. We don't know why they've come back. If there is an answer, it must surely lie in the past.'

Katerina examined the priest closely as he spoke.

'It was a long time ago,' she said, guardedly. 'The two plagues may be unconnected.'

Boris smiled tolerantly.

'I am an old man,' he said. 'Morr will take me soon. But when I was younger and strong enough to travel, I did all I could to delve into the past. There are scraps of parchment, hidden here and there, fragments of the old chronicles. If you had read them, you would be in no doubt. Arforl was here, my lady, as were the dead. He died here. He saved us. Just as you will do.'

Katerina felt a twinge of disquiet at that. She had no lack of faith in her abilities, but magic was a complicated art, and these villagers couldn't be expected to understand the subtleties involved.

'We'll see about that,' she said. 'You said little in your letter. The dead do not rise by themselves. Did your chronicles name a necromancer?'

'There's a single name in the legends. The Master of Crows. It was he who summoned the dead from the marshes. Arforl defeated him. He destroyed the necromancer's body and cursed his soul. It was in doing so that he was wounded to death. Since then the dead have not returned.'

'Until now.'

'That is so. We don't know why. Some of the stupider members of the village here have even started killing crows. They catch them and hang them from the walls, as if such a thing would ward against the ancient evil. I tell them that the Master of Crows is dead. Even if he'd survived the magic of Arforl, age would have taken him long ago.'

Katerina pursed her lips thoughtfully.

'The necromantic arts are powerful,' she murmured. 'A man may live for as long as the dark magic sustains him. In any case, he may have had a disciple.'

She remembered the surly looks of the villagers, and shook her head.

'Just speculation,' she said. 'I won't know until I begin work. I must see this plague for myself. When will they come again?'

Boris let a shadow of foreboding pass across his face.

'Every night,' he said, his voice lowered. 'You'll see them as soon as darkness falls.'

'Good,' said Katerina, smiling coldly, flexing her fingers slightly. 'I'll look forward to it.'

The night was lit by flame. Braziers had been hauled up on top of the gatehouse and torches mounted high on the walls around the village. In the flickering red light, Herrendorf took on a nightmarish aspect. The flames did little to banish the pervasive cold, and the dim illumination faded quickly towards the eaves of the forest. Low cloud blotted out the stars. The villagers waited for the invasion. Men gripped pitchforks and notched swords, muttering prayers to Morr and Sigmar.

Katerina stood alone in front of the arch of the gate. The doors were open behind her. Only she barred the way. Her dark hair lifted slightly in the chill breeze. She held her staff lightly, letting her thumb rub absently against the smooth wood. Her eyes were closed, her breathing shallow. Though her physical body gave little hint of it, her mind was entirely turned in on itself. She was probing, testing, seeking. The winds of magic were strong, and their unseen currents flowed in long, smooth waves around the entire place. Her magical senses, long used to the lore of death in all its forms, picked out the presence of the Wind of Shyish amongst them. Katerina could almost taste it, almost inhale its pungent smell, even though it had neither savour nor aroma. The sombre notes of the lore of mortality were unmistakeable.

Whereas other magical winds, like that of Aqshy, blazed with force and majesty, the Amethyst force was subtle and elusive. Even some of the great magisters of the colleges had to work hard to detect it. Katerina was one of the few who had never had to try. For some reason, the strange currents of death had always been obvious to her. Now she let her consciousness reach out to caress the fronds of unnatural energy as they coursed through the aethyr.

'What do you see?'

Her concentration broke. Irritated, she snapped her eyes open. Boris had come to stand beside her. He leant heavily against his staff, wheezing slightly. His breathing sounded painful. Like everyone in this wretched place, he was clearly afflicted with some malady or other. In his free hand, he carried a burning torch.

'I sense the power here,' said Katerina, looking back towards the marshes with her normal sight. 'It is old and strong. Something is stirring in the trees beyond, roused by the lore of death. It hangs heavy over the whole place.'

Boris followed her gaze dispassionately, wincing slightly as his laboured breathing slowed to normal.

'So it is every night.'

As he finished speaking, the first of them emerged from the trees. A low murmur rose from the village behind them. There were men high on the walls. Others stood in the open space behind the gates. All looked exhausted. Katerina recognised Gerhard and Kreisler amongst them. All trace of their earlier belligerence had gone, and their faces were drawn.

The unquiet dead approached steadily across the fields, limping and dragging limbs. Katerina surveyed them calmly. She had seen horrors of all kinds in her career, and the figures hauling themselves from the trees were unremarkable. They had once been men, women and children of the Empire, full of life and health. Now their cadavers, entrusted to the earth with the blessings of Morr, had been revived, compelled to rise and stalk the world of the living once more. Some of the undead bore the signs of age; old farmers and their wives who had passed away peacefully in their sleep. But most were young, killed by war, plague or accident, a grim testament to the troubles of the age. Most troublingly of all, amongst them tottered the young, infants who had barely walked in life but who now staggered onwards, their little eyes blank to all but bloodlust. The shambolic host was a mockery of Herrendorf itself, a mirror image of those who drew natural breath.

'So many,' breathed Katerina, grimly.

Boris nodded.

'More all the time. The day will come when there'll be too many.'

'Not while I'm here,' Katerina said firmly, hefting her staff and kindling Amethyst magic along the length of it. She raised the shaft high above her head and called out words of power. The wood blazed with lilac energy.

'By the Wind of Shyish, by the lore of the dead, I command you to return to the realm of departed souls!' she cried, letting the power in her fingers flow through the staff and into the night.

The amethyst wind rushed to her aid, curling around her cloak and arms. The undead paused for a moment. Some of them cocked their ruined heads to one side, as if listening to some far-off, unheard speech. The stragglers at the back stopped, and began to turn back. Katerina allowed herself a smile of satisfaction. This would be easier than she had thought.

But then the Amethyst wind began to drain away, as if extinguished by a gust of chill air. The sickening harmonics of dark magic rolled across the sodden earth, pooling in the hollows and rising up against the smooth stone of the walls. Katerina cast a hasty warding spell around her, and Boris took a step back. The magnitude of the new force was surprising. Where was it coming from?

Heedless of all but the dread commands of their unseen summoner, the undead began their slow march towards the village once more. Where their eyes had been empty before, now they shone with a cold green light. Like a constellation of corrupted stars, the glowing pairs of eyes closed in on the walls.

'What have you done?' hissed Boris, looking at Katerina with consternation. 'This has never happened before.'

Katerina frowned, and fed more power to her staff, soaking up the Amethyst wind where it still lurked.

'The power behind them has responded,' she said. 'It looks like we have a contest.'

The wizard took up the staff and lilac sparks spat from its tip.

'I will not command you again!' she cried, her voice echoing around the clearing. 'Depart while you may, and never return! Your tortured souls may yet find peace. But if you resist, your essence will be shattered for all eternity, never to return either in this world or the next!'

A few of the undead responded as before. One child-figure, once a little girl with pigtails, now a grey-fleshed, eyeless horror in a torn dress, stopped in its tracks, looking up in fear. But the others seemed uncaring. They began to pick up their pace. Parched flesh flapped in the wind as they came, and old bones ground against each other. The silence in their ranks was broken. A weird whispering broke out, the mindless chatter of lost souls. From behind her, Katerina could hear the growing murmurs of unease.

'Close the gates!' came an urgent hiss from somewhere in the crowd of nervous men.

Katerina shook her head with irritation, and planted her staff heavily before her. This would have to be brought to a conclusion. If the undead could not be banished, they would have to be destroyed.

'So be it,' she said in a low voice, and stretched her left arm in front of her.

With a whispered spell, Katerina turned her palm face up. A purple flame burst into life, flickering in the eddying wind. She closed her eyes, and continued to murmur arcane words. Then, with a sudden snap of her wrist, her fist closed over the flame. It extinguished with a sharp snap.

Instantly, the undead nearest her collapsed, clutching at their exposed innards with scrabbling fingers. They clearly had some memory of pain, even if they could no longer truly feel it. Dozens of the limping figures lurched over and crumpled into the mire with streams of lilac energy leaking from their bodies. In place of the green light in their eyes, an Amethyst glow now possessed them. Like a rampant swarm of insects, the purple fire swarmed all over them, stripping the scant strips of skin from them, powdering bones, dissolving cartilage. The whispering was replaced by a frantic high-pitched squealing as the spell did its work. One by one, the walkers were immolated, crushed and blasted apart by the deadly flames of Shyish. Katerina kept her fish clenched, pouring more strength into the casting.

Boris's face lit up, and he dared to hobble back out of Katerina's shadow.

'You're killing them!' he hissed, his eyes alive with relieved glee. Katerina could hear the men behind her inch forward for a better look. But she knew better. The spell was powerful, but it was also draining. For every undead villager who fell, another resisted. The ones most steeped in dark magic were not being destroyed. Slowly, as the weak were swept away, the ranks of stronger attackers came forward. They stalked as slowly as ever, creeping inexorably nearer. They whispered as they came, and now they were close enough for the words to be audible.

'Human creatures, hot with blood,' they chanted in scratchy voices, half-snatched by the wind. 'We were once like you. Soon, you will be like us!'

Katerina felt fresh eddies of dark magic drift towards her, polluting her casting, dousing her power. An icy gust of the unseen wind swept the clearing, and she gasped. Her fist dropped a little, and the Amethyst energy consuming the undead flickered and went out. Boris looked at her in consternation, and crept back under the archway again. Renewed mutters of 'Shut the gate!' rose in volume. The nearest of the skeletal attackers were now within a few yards of Katerina.

With a cry of frustration, Katerina let her consuming spell dissipate. She grabbed her staff in both hands, and it blazed with fresh fire. The flames flared into a scythe shape, crackling and spitting with arcane forces. She swung the blade in a wide arc, and once more the zombies were blasted apart, their loose bones and tendons sent flailing into the dark. Like a harvester, the Amethyst wizard mowed them down as they came.

None came to help her. The villagers, cowed by the ranks of undead closing on them and by the magical forces unleashed, shrunk behind the shelter of the walls. Only Katerina stood between the horde and the entrance, a lone figure wreathed in blistering layers of magic, holding back the growing tide of lurching bodies.

They kept coming. More crept from the cover of the trees. How many? A hundred? Two hundred? It was hard to tell. Katerina began to feel her strength fail. With a fresh cry of anger, she unleashed a fearsome blast of power. The undead near her were flung backwards, clattering into the ranks behind, clearing a wide space. For a moment, the wizard paused, surveying the scene. The undead were in disarray, but even as she watched the fallen were regaining their feet. She couldn't possibly destroy them all. It was as if a lost army had been raised and directed towards her.

With a disgusted shake of her head, she retreated back under the gatehouse.

'Bar the gates!' shouted Boris, and a dozen men ran forward, eager to have the one weak point in the wall sealed off. The thick doors were shut, and heavy oak beams slammed in place. From outside, the whispered chanting began once more. Children's voices were heard wailing in the village as the horrifying voices of the undead permeated the night. With the gates secure, the men went to their positions. Katerina caught unpleasant glances from the villagers as they walked past her. Gerhard and Kreisler averted their eyes. Only the surly Weiss seemed to be missing, which was something of a relief.

Katerina sank back against the interior of the wall, and let the waves of fatigue finally wash over her. Her staff clattered weakly to the floor. With her removal from the clearing, there was nothing to stop the advance of the undead. Soon the sounds of scratching and gouging came from the other side of the stone.

Boris limped up to her. He wasn't obviously angry, but he couldn't hide the disappointment in his face.

'They've never scaled the walls yet,' he said, perhaps by way of consolation. 'We have some success with fire. But there are more tonight than I've ever seen, and even the flames won't stop them forever. It can't be long now.'

Katerina looked up at him, trying to maintain her dignity in the face of defeat. The noises of scrabbling and chanting grew louder.

'This is a setback, nothing more,' she said defiantly. 'Every spell can be countered. You just need to know how to unlock it. Trust me.'

Boris didn't change his expression, but looked worriedly at the gates. Something on the far side had started banging against them rhythmically.

'Of course I trust you,' he said, resignedly. 'What choice do I have?'

The dead failed to breach the walls that night, but they kept coming until dawn. If any looked like scaling the high barrier, they were hurled back again by the tip of a pike. But the gates were battered, and the walls scored with gouges. Only with the coming of the morning sunlight did the assault relent.

They returned the following dusk, and the one after that. No spell was sufficient to break their advance. Though Katerina's magic could blast dozens of them apart as they came, no fire would burn fiercely enough to destroy them all. With every assault they grew bolder, climbing further up the slippery walls on piles of their own fallen, clawing at the gates with growing zeal. Boris was right. They would soon break into the village. Once inside, they would be unstoppable. Time was running out.

After another long night of fruitless spellcasting, Katerina slumped heavily on the bench in Boris's chambers. The cold sheen of dawn had crept across the eastern sky, but it brought little comfort. She had slept little, and the scorn of the villagers had begun to wear on her spirits. It was clear to her that some power had been roused that was beyond her. If a way couldn't be found to counter it, they would all die, far from any possible help.

The thought of leaving entered her mind. If she rode hard, kept to the roads, warded herself carefully at night, she might make it. It wasn't as if she owed the stinking inhabitants of Herrendorf much. And yet, there was still one avenue open. One that offered not only the chance of survival, but of uncovering the secrets of the past as well. Her pride would not allow her to give up on it easily.

As she turned over the various options in her mind, Boris entered the chamber. He had been purifying the gates with holy water. No one thought it would do any good. The old priest sat opposite Katerina. His face looked, if anything, even more sickly than normal. He was at the end of his strength, and clutched on to his staff tightly as he sat down.

'I may have been mistaken,' he said at length, grimacing from some hidden pain. 'Perhaps magic isn't the solution. Or maybe the Amethyst College isn't as powerful as it once was.'

Katerina ignored the dig. The cleric looked bitter.

'Do not lose faith just yet,' she said, quietly. 'There is something else we could try.'

Boris looked at her with little hope in his eyes.

'They were defeated before,' said Katerina. 'The Amethyst wizard Arforl did it. Maybe he knew something that we don't.'

'And what use is that to us?' said Boris. 'Arforl is dead. He can't save us a second time.'

'You forget yourself,' said Katerina, choosing her words carefully. 'I am an initiate of the lore of death. There are many secrets I am privy to. You said he was buried in the marshes. If I could find the place, his spirit may yet dwell there. There are ways of calling it back to the body. It may be our only hope.'

What little blood there was in Boris's face drained away. A look of horror distorted his features.

'You can't mean…'

'Don't be a fool!' snapped Katerina. 'You know well enough what I mean. To summon a shade of Arforl, to interrogate it, to learn the secret of his victory.'

'That is heresy,' whispered Boris, looking as if he had stumbled on a den of Chaos worshippers in his own chapel.

'And if it is?' said Katerina, impatiently. 'In the next week we'll all be dead. The horde of undead continues to grow. Even if we left this place now, all of us, we'd never make it out of the marshes. What you call heresy is our only means of survival. There's no piety in being eaten alive by your former flock.'

Boris looked tortured, and didn't reply at once. Katerina let the idea sink in.

'We've never found the mausoleum,' the priest protested weakly. 'I told you. We tried.'

'You didn't have me with you then,' said Katerina. 'There are hidden signs I can read. Arforl was an Amethyst wizard. Even in death, I'd sense his presence. I just need to get close enough.'

Boris shook his head again.

'It's madness. The marshes are crawling with the dead. If we leave the village we'll never return. Your failure has deranged you.'

Katerina felt her temper rising. There was only one chance, and the fool was incapable of seeing it.

'They're fixed on destroying the village,' she said. 'I have powers of my own. If we stay here, we'll be overwhelmed within the week. Better to risk doing something than die doing nothing at all.'

Boris looked back at her, his face riven with indecision. She could tell he didn't like the idea. But there was something else there, a flicker of something like defiance. Perhaps not all his spirit had been crushed by poverty and sickness. Maybe some spark of ambition remained, buried deeply.

The old priest sighed profoundly, and got up from his seat with difficulty. He walked over to his pile of tomes and parchment, and began to leaf through the pages.

'It's been a while since I looked at these,' he said. 'Perhaps there's some clue I missed. I don't like it, but there's little else on offer. I've pledged to defend this place, after all. And the mausoleum must be out there somewhere.'

Katerina sat back against the hard bench with some satisfaction. He had been convinced. Now the dangerous work would really begin.

The sun was low in the western sky. The stink of marsh gas and rotting vegetation was everywhere. In the grey light, deep green shadows lay like pools of oil. Fronds of mist curled around the wide boles of the trees. Strange, half-recognisable cries of animals echoed deep within the dank hollows. The deep marsh was no place for humans. The hand of man had barely scraped the surface of this country. Herrendorf, like the other scattered settlements in the region, was just a minor pock-mark on the ancient wilds of the Ostermark. If the undead wiped it from the surface of the earth, its passing would be unnoticed, much less mourned.

Katerina found herself reflecting as she trudged through the grime and murk. What was she doing here, far from the bright centre of Altdorf, stuck in a probably hopeless campaign to liberate one stinking settlement from destruction? The reputation of Arforl had intrigued her, it was true. But in future she would have to start being more selective. All of which assumed, of course, that she emerged from the current situation alive.

She turned to see where Boris was. He struggled to keep up with her. After only a few hours of travel out of Herrendorf, he had begun to wheeze thinly. His grey cheeks flapped as he laboured, digging his staff deep into the yielding earth, pulling his feet with effort from the sucking, cloying mud.

He came up to her, his chest heaving, his eyes bloodshot. He looked little better than the undead themselves.

'Are you able to go on?' asked Katerina.

Boris waited a moment for his breathing to settle before replying. When he had recovered, he gave her a wan smile.

'You're despairing of me, aren't you?' he said. 'Perhaps we should have brought men with us.'

Katerina inwardly rolled her eyes. A self-pitying priest was the last thing she needed. If he hadn't claimed to have some insight into where the mausoleum might be, she would have been better off on her own.

'What help would more bodies be, except to draw the dead to us?' she said, scornfully. 'None would come, anyway. We need to make better progress. Night's nearly on us. And we know what that will bring.'

Boris bowed his head at her admonition.

'You needn't pity me, lady wizard,' he said. 'You must have seen what the others have. I'm too old and too sick for this world. I'm dying, whatever the fate of Herrendorf. A year, maybe. No more.'

He raised his face to hers, and there was a determined light in his rheumy eyes.

'So, you see, it doesn't really matter to me what the outcome of this is. I'm dead anyway. I would rather leave this world in the knowledge that my kin have been saved. That's all.'

The priest spoke with conviction, and his voice shook a little. Katerina held his gaze for a few moments. The man meant what he said. This was his task, the one he had studied his whole life to achieve.

'Then we must press on,' she said, curtly. 'We've an hour of light, no more. After that, both our lives will be at risk.'

She turned and walked heavily back into the marsh. The stinking mud clutched at her boots. Slowly and with effort, the old priest limped after her.

Only a few stars glinted through the cloud. The gloom lay heavy. Katerina's staff glowed with a pearlescent light. It wasn't hard to maintain the spell. For some time, she had sensed they were walking into an area thick with the rumour of death. The Wind of Shyish hung thickly on the ground. She could almost reach out and touch it, and her augmented vision could see great eddying swirls of the unnatural force nestling in the gaps between the trees. This reassured her. Wherever the Amethyst wind lurked, her powers were strengthened. It was lucky to have come across such promising signs so soon. Boris may simply have stumbled on the right direction, of course, but it was also possible a more subtle power was at work. Even in death, perhaps the soul of Arforl was dimly aware of their quest. After all, they were both, or had been, wizards of the same colour.

She turned back to see how far behind Boris was. She saw him a few dozen paces off in the gathering darkness, a dark, hunched shape lumbering against the gloom of the half-drowned forest. As her eyes adjusted, a sudden chill passed through her. She stood stock-still, her heart suddenly beating faster.

Boris came up to her laboriously.

'What is it?' he asked through deep breaths.

Katerina pointed her staff back the way he had come. She whispered a brief word, and the glowing tip burst into bright flame. The dark branches around them were thrown into sudden relief.

Boris looked back in the direction the staff pointed. After a moment, he looked back at her.

'Nothing,' he said.

Katerina frowned.

'Really? You see nothing at all?'

She whispered some more arcane words, and the flame changed hue. A thick purple light emanated from it, dousing the trees like liquid. Boris peered into the shadows, screwing his eyes up and squinting grotesquely.

'I don't–' he began, and then suddenly stopped. 'Holy Sigmar…'

Katerina smiled with satisfaction, and released the spell.

'As I suspected,' she said with pleasure. 'You could've walked past this place a thousand times, and seen nothing but trees. This is an illusion of the highest order. I almost missed it myself.'

Where it had appeared that there was nothing more than a close thicket of gnarled and stunted foliage, Katerina's magic had revealed a circular space amidst the wild marshes. The real trees hung back, looking as if every tortured branch was straining to grow away from the clearing. There was a low hill in the centre of the space, perfectly circular and smooth. No grass grew on its bare flanks. In the very middle, a dark tower rose against the night sky. It was unadorned and simple, a single column of ancient stone protruding from the earth. Katerina's illumination glinted coldly off its worn surface. The stench of death was suddenly strong, even to un-gifted senses.

Boris became extremely agitated.

'That is it,' he breathed.

All weariness seemed to have left him, and he began to hobble towards the tower. Katerina accompanied him more watchfully. It was almost certain the place was Arforl's mausoleum. There could be little else in such a desolate place. The slender edifice stank of magic. Thankfully, there was also no sign of the undead. Perhaps they feared the site of their ancient defeat. That alone was reason to be grateful to the long-dead magister.

They approached the base of the tower. There was no device or insignia on the stonework, nor any windows. The walls rose up sheer for maybe forty feet, and were crowned by a simple conical roof. The place was silent. The noises of the forest beyond were strangely muffled. It felt like they had passed into another world.

'There's no door,' said Boris.

He looked at the chill edifice with wonder, the way a child looks at a new wooden toy.

'There's always a door,' said Katerina.

She raised her staff again, and breathed words of uncovering. The tower seemed to sigh, and the stones shimmered in and out of focus. After a few moments, features on the masonry began to reveal themselves. At the summit of the tower, almost lost in shadow against the deepening night sky, a balcony appeared. Narrow windows emerged along the walls, and a low arch was revealed at ground level. The doors were made of banded iron, pitted and worn with age. A heavy stone lintel sat atop the entrance, marked with the rune of Shyish.

Katerina looked at the markings carefully.

'The rune is worn,' she mused. 'It almost looks more like Ulgu than Shyish. They're similar, but still…'

Boris limped over to the door excitedly.

'The legend spoke truly,' he croaked, his grey hands reaching toward the locks on the metal doors, before suddenly hanging back. His nerve seemed to fail him at the last. 'After so long,' he breathed. 'Now that I see it, I wonder if I can face it?'

Katerina ignored him, and approached the doors.

'We'll be safer inside than out here,' she said, calmly breaking the bonds with a gesture. She could sense wards of protection around the place, and powerful magic leaking from between the stones, but the spells were old and nearly exhausted. Clearly, Arforl's entombers had trusted in the power of illusion to keep his resting place hidden.

The doors opened, and a sigh of stale air rushed out. The darkness within was complete. Katerina let her staff give out a little more light, and she went inside, Boris at her heels. The interior of the tower was narrow and claustrophobic. Immediately to her right, spiral stairs coiled upwards. There was nothing else, no adornment, no inscription. They began to climb. The stairs were smooth and without visible blemish. They must have rested here, untrod, since the mausoleum was sealed.

Katerina glanced back. Boris was keeping up as best he could, wheezing and puffing. He seemed to have forgotten his earlier horror at her intentions. Indeed, he was the most animated she could remember him.

They emerged from the stairway into a circular chamber. They were at the top of the tower. Four windows had been set into the otherwise unbroken and unmarked walls. A single open doorway led out to the balcony beyond. There was no moon, but faint starlight limned the ironwork of the railings.

The chamber itself was almost empty. No symbols had been engraved into the stone, and the bare floor was unadorned. Only one item disturbed the room's cold symmetry. In the very centre lay a marble tomb. It was jet black and as smooth as glass. The light from Katerina's staff seemed to soak into it, and there were no reflections. Boris stared at it, fascinated. Maybe he could sense the magic around it. To Katerina, it was bleeding with arcane force. Even in death, Arforl's essence still lingered, buried but not obscured.

'Now we must do what we came to do,' she said, quietly. Her faint words echoed eerily around the circular chamber.

Boris turned to her, his hands shaking slightly.

'Very well,' he said, a nervous expression on his face. 'Waste no time. Even as we linger, Herrendorf must surely be besieged.'

Katerina raised her staff, and the thick Amethyst magic rose to greet it. Great gusts of the deathly wind surged along the length of the shaft, pulsating and resonating powerfully. She closed her eyes, and began to utter the words of power. They were sucked into the stone around her as soon as they were uttered. As she spoke, the chamber began to tremble. Dust drifted down from the ceiling, and Boris took a nervous step back.

Katerina continued, letting her staff channel and refine the raw magic circling the tomb. Her voice rose as the spell picked up momentum. For a few moments, the black casket seemed unaffected. But then, gradually, a soft light kindled above it. The illumination spread slowly, drifted over the glassy surface, bathing it in a dim light. A faint rushing noise could be heard, as if from far away.

Katerina let the magic build up. Despite the travails of the past few days, she felt powerful. It was as if the presence of Arforl augmented her latent strength. The spell was working. The barrier between life and death, never strong in the case of wizards, was being eroded. If anything remained of Arforl, it would not be long in coming. Inwardly, she smiled.

She slammed her staff on the stone. All at once, the light flickered out, and the sound of rushing ceased. The chamber was plunged into darkness. For a heartbeat, nothing stirred. Katerina stayed still and silent. This was the moment. The chamber was drenched in what the ignorant called the magic of death. Only the initiated knew it as it really was, the lore of life unbound. Now it had done its work and the secret of Herrendorf's salvation would be revealed.

'Rise,' she said simply.

There was a mighty crack, and a blaze of light. Boris staggered back, dazzled. Even Katerina had to avert her eyes for a moment. When she looked back up, the casket was just as it had been before. Over it, however, hung a faint shape, insubstantial and vapid. It swayed uneasily, seemingly hovering just on the edge of perception. It looked like the reflection of sunlight on moving water, rippling and transient.

After a few moments, the apparition clarified. It was the shape of a man, tall and forbidding, with a high brow and raven hair. He was dressed in robes of the Amethyst College, and bore a wizard's staff. He looked half-asleep, and his translucent eyes were ill-focused.

'You were Radamus Arforl, wizard of the Amethyst college?' said Katerina, relishing the power flowing through her.

The shade looked at her uncertainly. His eyes still seemed locked somewhere else.

'That was my name,' came a chill voice. It was barely audible, and sounded as if it was coming from far away. 'Who asks?'

Katerina smiled.

'Master wizard Katerina Lautermann, also of the Amethyst College,' she said confidently, allowing her staff to blossom once more with light. Between that and the unearthly radiance of Arforl's shade, the chamber was bathed in a strange mixed light.

'No, you are not the one,' said the shade, looking steadily more alert. His gaze became increasingly fixed. It seemed as if he was solidifying. His piercing eyes swept around the chamber, and alighted on Boris.

'You are the one,' said Arforl, fixing the priest with a pitiless gaze.

'Yes!' cried Boris, rushing forward, letting his staff clatter to the ground. 'It was me! I called you, roused your power! You know what I seek! Grant me it, lord of life and death!'

Katerina whirled around, suddenly consumed by doubt. For the first time, she noticed the crescendo of magic in the room was being fed by another source. Arforl was not merely a passive shade. He was aware, and had been so for some time. Something was wrong.

'Boris?' she said, raising her staff protectively. 'What is this?'

Before the priest could answer, Arforl let slip a sneering laugh.

'The wizard knows nothing!' he said, before turning his baleful gaze on her. 'What did he tell you? That I hold the secret of defeating the unquiet dead? You fool. They're my minions, just as they were a generation ago. Even in my slumber I can rouse them. And yet this place was just enough of a prison to keep my body confined. Only a wizard could break the bonds. You were arrogant, Lautermann. Now there's nothing to contain my power.'

Boris rushed forward.

'So I have served you, my lord!' he cried, a look of ecstasy in his ruined eyes. 'Now heal me! End the pain. I've done as you commanded.'

Katerina was stunned. She felt the waves of dark magic rearing up around her. She began to unravel the unbinding spell, but now nothing would answer her call. Arforl's magic began to blot out all else in the chamber. The shade ignored her. Arforl's image was growing in strength. The waves of malice emanating from him were sickening.

'Heal you?' Arforl said to Boris. 'You're as stupid as she. You'll provide me with a body, and that is all.'

At that, the shade swooped over the horrified priest and locked him in a crushing embrace. Boris screamed, and his limbs flailed jerkily. There was a brief confusion, as the swirling green-tinged vision of Arforl sucked itself on to Boris's jerking body, clawing at his eyes and mouth.

Then the struggle was over. Boris's limbs went limp, then straightened. There was no more hunching or limping. His ravaged form was animated by a new will. Just as the undead had done at Herrendorf, Boris's eyes glowed a sickly green. His lips twisted in a lurid smile. There was a shudder beneath his skin, like cats fighting in a bag, but that too was stamped out. Arforl had consumed him.

Katerina stepped back, placing her staff between her and the possessed Boris.

'These people think you saved them,' she said warily, trying to piece together what was going on.

Arforl laughed using Boris's mouth.

'I know. Ever since this fool dabbled in powers he could not master and began to wake me, the irony has been pleasing. He knew the truth, of course. But the knowledge of death does strange things to a man. I sent him dreams of a cure, an end to his pain. All lies, sadly for him.

There is nothing but pain! Pain and power. You have given him one, and me the other.'

Katerina looked disgusted.

'A traitor, then,' she spat. 'Enough. I may have woken you, but I will not release you.'

She swung her staff around, and waves of amethyst energy screamed across the narrow chamber. Arforl was blasted backwards, hitting the stone wall with a crack. Katerina let her anger flow freely. Her staff sang with energy, hurling bolt after bolt at the unnatural creature before her. She was hurting Arforl, and for a moment he was pinned, writhing, against the edge of the chamber.

'Damn you!' he roared, and a vast well of dark magic burst from his flailing hands.

The shadow tore across Katerina, raking at her eyes and snatching at her staff. She gasped, feeling the icy chill stab at her. She staggered backwards. Her amethyst magic tore away in ribbons. Arforl righted himself, and sent a barrage of seething necromantic essence towards her. She raised her staff for the parry, and the force of the blow nearly broke her arms. His power was unbelievable, as strong as iron and as crushing as stone. She was beaten back, step by grudging step.

Almost before realising it, she had been driven to the far side of the chamber, towards the open doorway to the balcony. She whirled her staff around, trying to combat the waves of dark magic coming from Arforl. Within his torrents of energy she could make out the shapes of jaws snapping and claws rending. There were fleeting, morphing animal shapes in his magic. As quickly as she tore them apart, they re-formed and came at her. She felt cold sweat break out at the nape of her neck. She was being beaten. Arforl came towards her, his eyes glowing eerily, hands outstretched.

'Now you'll pay the price for your curiosity,' he sneered. 'This ruined body repulses me. When your power is spent, yours will make a more fitting vessel.'

Katerina's face distorted in disgust, and she sent a searing stream of amethyst fire directly at him. It halted his advance, but he was equal to it. He replied with spitting bolts of dark force, hurled at her with all the malice he could muster. Katerina desperately parried. Her staff took the brunt of the assault, but one deadly shaft got through, slicing agonisingly into her shoulder. She cried aloud, and staggered backwards. Too late she realised she was out on the balcony. She was dimly aware of high, dark clouds above her, and the whistling of a chill wind. Arforl came towards her, his face still locked in a gloating smile.

Katerina raised her staff wearily, preparing for the final blow. Then she heard the whispering from below. She stole a quick glance over her shoulder. The ground below was crawling with dim shapes.

'Can't tell what they are?' jeered Arforl. 'They're my children, flocking once more to my call. Now, at last, I can join them.'

He clapped his hands together, and a pale green light kindled at the summit of the tower, bathing the scene in a sickly radiance. Katerina could see the hundreds of undead milling at the base of the tower. They were pawing at the stone, though none had yet entered the tower.

Katerina took a deep breath, and gripped her staff tightly. There was no way out. She began to prepare her final defence. She laced the spells with words of destruction and immolation. If Arforl defeated her, there would be nothing left of her body to deface. She wouldn't share Boris's fate.

Arforl raised his arms, and dark magic snaked around him.

'This is the end, Frau Lautermann,' he said.

But then a shudder seemed to pass through the entire tower. Arforl momentarily faltered, and his magic wavered. Katerina looked back over her shoulder warily. A strange presence could be sensed. Below, the horde of undead seemed to turn in on itself. There was a new focus for their mindless bloodlust.

Arforl's face twisted in amazement.

'So he survived,' he murmured, turning his attention from Katerina for a moment.

There was a cry of frustration from the undead below, and a bird-like shape broke from their clutches and into the air. Dark grey wings flapped, and it seemed as if a great carrion crow was heading for the tower. Katerina retreated along the narrow balcony, trying to get away from both Arforl and the newcomer. The traitor wizard followed her out from the chamber, but his attention was focused elsewhere. He hurled a stream of pale green light from his crooked fingers, sparking and crackling as it tore through the night. The wheeling crow evaded the deadly stream of necromantic energy, and landed on the balcony in a flurry of feathers. The shape transmuted with dazzling speed, and soon there was a cloaked figure standing between Katerina and Arforl. He was a Grey wizard, dressed in archaic robes. His staff hummed with power, and his eyes blazed with anger.

Arforl glared at him contemptuously.

'You should be dead,' he said, acidly.

'So should you,' replied the Grey wizard, returning the irony.

He raised a hand, and grey strands of shimmering magic sprung up, clinging to Arforl and pulling him back into the chamber. With a spasm of irritation, the traitor shrugged off the attack. His hands like claws, he summoned a whip of pure dark magic from the aethyr. It curled around his head. He cracked it at the Grey wizard, who leapt with surprising speed to evade the blow.

For a moment, Katerina was stunned. She fell back, trying to work out what was going on. Whoever this interloper was, it was clear he had no love for Arforl, and that at least was reason to be thankful for his intervention.

The best course of action seemed to be to join him. With a deep breath, she raised her staff again and resumed her attack. The flow of amethyst fire rekindled, snapping towards Arforl in flaming barbs. Confronted with two sources of magic, Arforl was beaten back into the chamber. The space was soon swimming in unnatural power. Katerina and the Grey wizard pressed forward, hurling bolts and orbs of sparking energy at the traitor. Arforl responded with equal vigour, blasting gobbets of dark matter at them, slicing at them with his whip. The tower was filled with light and noise. The masonry above them began to shake at the power unleashed, and lines of dust spiralled down from the arched ceiling.

Katerina started to feel her strength ebb. She had been casting magic for days and, despite the ever-present wind of Shyish, she was near her limits. The mysterious Grey wizard beside her was potent, and kept Arforl tied up with a series of unbroken attacks. But Arforl was equal to them. Indeed, the two adversaries seemed strangely well-suited, as if their fighting styles were intimately known to each other. They circled around each other, trading blow after blow. Neither spoke, but their eyes never left the other's. Katerina found herself pushed to the edge of the battle, her contributions increasingly ineffectual.

And then came the sound she had been dreading. The whispering she had come to loathe so much at Herrendorf, the clatter and rustle of dry bone and skin. They had broken through the wards. They were coming up the stairs. The undead had answered their master's call.

She whirled around, just in time to see the first of them clamber into the chamber. Arforl and the Grey wizard remained locked in combat. Katerina swung her staff at the lead skeletal figure, smashing his frame apart and sending the bones skidding across the stone. She was weary to her core, but dredged up the reserves of energy required to ignite her staff with magic once more. Amethyst light blazed from its tip, mixing with the diffuse grey light of the newcomer and the lurid green of the necromancer. She strode forward to meet the shambling host of undead as they emerged into the chamber. Like a blacksmith at his forge, she used her crackling staff to slay them where they stood. She knew that if they managed to enter the chamber in numbers, the fight was over. Just as she had done at Herrendorf, she guarded the doorway alone, the only bulwark against the whispering host of unquiet dead.

Arforl laughed then, a ragged, strangled sound.

'How long can you keep this up, wizards?' he cried, mockingly. 'They'll keep coming forever!'

Katerina knew he was right. She stole a glance at the traitor, desperate for some sign of weakness, some way of turning the tide.

Arforl's face was locked in a rictus of triumph, but there was something manic about his grin. For the first time, it looked forced. There were beads of sweat on his grey brow, and an odd rippling seemed to be taking place under his skin.

'Boris!' hissed Katerina, suddenly aware of what was going on. The old priest was still fighting for his body. This wasn't over yet. There was a chance, but the moment was almost gone.

Ignoring the chattering horrors behind her, Katerina turned and hurled herself towards Arforl in a last, desperate lunge. Summoning all of her remaining strength, she sent a column of raging purple flame coursing towards him. All her residual energy went into the blast, and as it left her she felt stars spin before her eyes. If this failed, then there was nothing left.

The flame smashed into Arforl, dousing him in a raging torrent of amethyst essence. The Grey wizard waded in with spinning balls of cloying matter. The essence of Ulgu splattered into shards on contact with Arforl, digging into his flesh, tearing at his robes. The necromancer was hurled back hard, nearly knocked off his feet by the combined blast. He reeled, staggering against the stone wall, his eyes blurry once more. With a heavy gesture he countered the magic, but then something changed. His skin rippled once more, and his eyes bulged. Arforl let out a choked scream, and started to claw at his own face.

Katerina and the Grey wizard retreated back towards the balcony. Arforl staggered back to his feet, blundering straight into the crowd of undead entering the chamber. Some shrank back in mute reverence. But Boris's body was no longer controlled by a single soul. Others of them sensed the presence of the old priest, and withered hands reached out. Nails clawed against flesh, and blood spurted from Boris's flesh. A mingled scream of two voices rose from the priest's lips. With the scent of blood in the air, the undead went berserk. They rushed forward, biting, scratching, gouging, tearing. With a sickening speed, they tore the body to pieces. Just as the old, ruined head was dragged down into the crowd of scrabbling hands, Katerina thought she glimpsed Boris's rheumy expression in his eyes for a final time. Then he was gone, lost in a hail of dark blood and gore.

For a moment, the undead were locked in their blood frenzy. Katerina and the Grey wizard watched grimly. Over the gorging undead, the insubstantial shade of Arforl appeared once more, ragged and barely visible. His old features were back, though racked with pain. The shade looked around the chamber as if for the first time, a mix of fury and fear marking the once noble face.

Katerina knew she had nothing left, and slumped back against the stone wall. The Grey wizard took command. He raised his staff high, and a vortex of grey energy surged towards it. The Wind of Shyish joined the Wind of Ulgu, and a potent mix of the lore of shadows and death, combined into a maelstrom of shimmering magic. The shade of Arforl, weakened by the death of its host, was sucked into the storm. With a throttled wail, the ghostly form was hurled down once more. A sighing noise escaped from the casket, and Arforl was dragged back within it. The light appeared briefly over the glassy lid, and was extinguished. Bereft of Arforl's necromantic light, the chamber sunk into near darkness.

The undead completed their grisly meal, and pale eyes looked up at the two wizards remaining in the chamber. The green light which had animated them had faded, and they now looked hesitant.

The Grey wizard raised his staff a final time.

'Go now,' he said, in a low, quiet voice. 'Your summoner is defeated. Return to the earth. Sleep. Forget. Trouble the living no more.'

There was magic in his speech, but not much was needed. The animating will behind the living dead had been withdrawn. Slowly, one by one, the vacant, bloodstained faces turned. The skeletal figures withdrew back down the stairs, into the night, and out to their resting places in the wilds. The whispering ceased, and the natural noises of the forest returned.

In the east, a thin line of silver marked the dawn.

Katerina sat wearily on a fallen tree trunk beside the tower. The pale morning chilled her to her soul. Even wrapped tight in her fine cloak, the cold found some way in. She shivered, and looked back up at the slender stone building. The Grey wizard was re-establishing the wards around it. When he was finished, he cleared the lichen from the lintel over the entrance. The rune of Ulgu was revealed more clearly. The tower had never been a place of Amethyst lore. Why hadn't she seen it earlier? Arrogance, perhaps. Or maybe just being too hasty. The error had proved costly.

The wizard came over to her and sat beside her. As he did so, the windows and doors of the tower sunk back into the stone around them. As it had been before, the tower looked impregnable.

Katerina looked up at him.

'The Master of Crows?' she said, letting some bitterness at her conduct stray into her voice.

The Grey wizard nodded, a thin smile on his face. He had ancient-looking features.

'That's what they call me, I believe,' he said.

Katerina sighed, and leant back on her arms. Her body was bone-tired.

'So, the legend was corrupted. You should tell me what's happened here.'

The Master of Crows lost his smile, and sat down opposite her in the mire.

'In the beginning, I didn't know myself,' he said. 'I'd defeated him, all those years ago. I discovered his treachery late, and by the time I found him he had grown strong. I was alone. He raised the dead against me, and I was nearly overcome. But I had more strength then. As the end neared, the dead were destroyed, and we fought a last duel out in the wastes. It must have created quite a show, had there been anyone around to witness it. Four days and nights we fought. The pain was terrible. In the end, he made a mistake. Just one, but it was enough. I defeated him, and believed that I'd killed him. But it proved otherwise.'

He looked wistfully back at the tower.

'Magic's a strange thing,' he said. 'As it turned out, we unleashed something together here. Something in us merged. I don't think he'll ever properly die. And, as it turns out, neither can I. I should have done, years ago. And I should have left this place too, years ago. But I can't do that either.'

Katerina frowned.

'What do you mean? There's nothing stopping you.'

The Grey wizard shook his head.

'For you, that's true. For me, there's no escape. I could follow you along the road to Bechafen for a few miles. And then, sooner or later, you would strangely forget about your companion. I would crest a rise, and be back in Herrendorf. Much as I hate the place, this is home. Forever.'

Katerina looked at him with scepticism.

'But I didn't see you, not when I was there.'

A shudder passed across the Grey wizard's face. For a moment his expression was strangely blurred, and then Weiss's surly features re-established themselves.

'I don't hold with witches,' he growled in his thick, slurred accent.

He grinned.

'Not bad, eh?' he said, retaining Weiss's appearance and demeanour. 'I haven't lost all my skills. And the Wind of Ulgu is strong here, just as Shyish is.'

Katerina shook her head in disbelief. Of all the strange things she had seen, this was amongst the most bizarre.

'So you live amongst them still?' she asked, fascinated despite herself. Weiss nodded.

'Where else can I go? I need to eat. That, at least, hasn't changed. And at first, I was the proper hero. The fact I couldn't leave Herrendorf was strange, but I was confident I could overcome it. Then they noticed I didn't age. For years, I tried to hide it. But you can't, not in a place like this. When I saw children I had known begin to pass into dotage, with me the same as ever, I realised something had to be done. The people here are neither wise nor over-kind. Anything unnatural is culled. So my old self disappeared, and the illusions began. Henrik the cobbler. Johan the farmer. Some others. And now Weiss the carpenter.'

Katerina looked down at the ground, pondering the man's fate.

'And over the years, the story changed,' she murmured. 'Was that Boris's doing?'

'No,' said Weiss. 'The passage of time corrupts all things. Arforl's prison became, in people's minds, Arforl's memorial. You must remember that his reputation in the Empire was then impressive, while we Grey wizards are ever in the shadows. As memory faded and the stories became confused, I must have seemed the more likely villain. And it suited me, after a while. Who cares who defeated whom, as long as the dead lay in their graves? I tended the mausoleum, guarded against Arforl returning, and lived the best life I could. I thought it would last until the End Times. But Boris did stumble across the truth somehow.'

He paused for a moment, looking down at the sodden ground between his feet.

'Don't be too hard on him,' he said. 'He was racked with pain, and death was a terror. When he realised the necromancer was the one in the tomb, not his destroyer, it must have turned his mind. For all his faults, he was a subtle man, Boris. It was he that reached out to the shade and began to rouse it. He was not the first to seek escape from death, nor will he be the last. But he couldn't complete the task. For that he needed a wizard. You.'

Katerina pursed her lips, feeling her mood sink further. She had been duped, and the knowledge of it was bitter.

'I have caused great pain here.'

Weiss shook his head.

'You were not to know. I am the guardian of this place. I was too slow to suspect the priest. I looked for the secret of Arforl's revival in the wrong place. Of all those who could have been responsible, I thought the old man was least likely. It's my dereliction which has brought this on Herrendorf.'

'You've been here on your own too long,' said Katerina. 'You've given up your secret to me. I could bring help. This magic could be unravelled.'

Weiss gave a gruff laugh.

'Unless the witch hunters are now more tender than I remember them, my presence had better remain a secret, I think. I am an abomination, Frau Lautermann. Arforl's necromancy sustains me. It would be the interrogation chamber for me, if they could somehow drag me to it.'

Katerina started to protest, but then saw the look in his face. She let her eyes drop. She knew the ways of the Temple of Sigmar just as well as he did. It would be hard enough explaining Boris's death to them.

She slowly climbed to her feet, and brushed her clothes down. It was hardly worth the bother. They were streaked with dried mud.

'I should go,' she said. 'The plague has been ended.'

Weiss nodded.

'What will you tell them about Arforl?' he asked.

'I don't know yet. No one likes to discover that their hero is a traitor. But perhaps I'll have to tell the truth.'

Weiss looked back at the tower.

'You could say he still watches over Herrendorf,' he said, grimly. 'That's true at least.'

'It's not him, though, is it?' she said. 'You're the guardian of this place.

I'll study Arforl's records when I get back to Altdorf. If I find anything, I'll send tidings. There may be a cure.'

Weiss bowed in thanks.

'I hold little hope. There's neither death nor honour for me here. But such is the way of the world. We were never promised happiness, were we?'

Katerina found herself lost for words. It was time to go. He recognised it too. She bowed, and began to walk away. After going down the path for a few paces, she looked back over her shoulder. Weiss had gone in the opposite direction, back into the marshes. His Grey wizard's robes had returned. As he disappeared into the thin mist of the morning, a solitary crow flew high in the pale sky. It shadowed him for a few moments, before flying west, away from the rising sun. There was a bitter caw, and it was gone.

AS DEAD AS FLESH

Nick Kyme

'Back! Back into the ground!' Mikael cried, driving his sword into the zombie's gut.

Impaled upon the blade, the undead monster hissed and snarled at the templar, reaching out with filthy claws. There was a horrible sucking sound as it dragged itself along the blade, cold steel slipping effortlessly through its rotten innards. It raked a filth-encrusted talon across Mikael's face, tearing a long and bloody gash. Snarling in pain, he ripped the thing in two, wrenching his sword through paper skin. The legs and torso spiralled away as grave dust fell from the corpse like rain.

Strong fingers seized Mikael's shoulder from behind. Hard and sharp, they felt like burning knives as they bit through his armour plate. About to turn, another thing loomed out of the half-dark of the wooden chapel in front of him. Once a butcher, it now had the shambling gait of the undead. It still wore a blood-stained tabard, but the head was caved in and wasted muscle peeked out beneath torn and greying skin. It lunged at him, arms outstretched. Mikael slashed at it, removing an arm, dead blood spattering his neck and face. The creature behind him grabbed at his sword-arm, pushing it down with groping, scraping fingers. The undead butcher pressed forward, reaching out with a claw-like hand, an incoherent moan escaping from its lipless mouth. Mikael grabbed its wrist in a gauntleted fist and broke it. Undeterred, it came at him, snarling teeth - blackened nubs of wasted bone – bared and lunging for his face.

Mikael recoiled. A decaying hand held his ankle. A pox-ridden stable lad, the zombie he had cut in two, dragged its torso along the stone floor. It seized upon the templar's leg, biting at his armoured greaves.

Legs buckling, Mikael tried to resist the burden upon his arms and chest. Sickly morning light seeping through the stained-glass windows was all but eclipsed as a wall of rotten flesh engulfed him. He tried to roar out in defiance, to summon his courage, but a filthy hand filled his mouth. Panic welled within as his armour cracked against the pressure...

Light pierced the dark, as Reiner smashed the one-armed zombie aside with a deft blow from his broadsword. The templar captain drove after it zealously as it floundered in a crumbled heap of bent and twisted limbs, and severed off its head with a brutal swipe.

The fingers clawing at Mikael's back and sword-arm were pulled away as the gnawing claustrophobic dread ebbed, nails, still embedded into his shoulder plates, torn from their fingers. Halbranc was behind him and hefted one of the wretched creatures up above his head, a woman, withered and grey, eyes long since decayed from their sockets. She clawed at the huge knight, a morose wail keening in Mikael's ears as she ripped a long tear in his cloak. Halbranc ignored it and smashed her into the cold stone floor, neck and spine shattering audibly. Mikael held the creature beneath him, stamping hard upon its neck. He crushed its rotten skull with a heavy boot.

Within the dingy chapel, his comrades fought. The place was worn with age, wood cracked and warped. The windows threw murky, dawn light through tarnished glass onto a bloody vista. Valen was bleeding. An ugly ragged wound split his shoulder through his armour padding, the plate-mail long since ripped away. He held his sword waveringly; eyes misted and cold, slumped against a wooden stall. Kalten, and his brother, Vaust who wore a pained expression – left arm tucked tight into his body – protected him. A clutch of undead farm workers armed with rusted scythes and rakes surrounded them.

A cry echoed from the back of the chapel. Mikael recognised the powerful voice of Sigson as he peered through the gloom.

'In the name of Morr, I compel you, return!'

The warrior priest held a gleaming vial aloft. Its contents shimmered as he uttered a prayer to their god and cast it hard at the foul pack harrying the three templars. The vial exploded into the creatures, dousing them with the blessed water within. Long dead flesh burned against the anointed liquid with a shallow hiss, as a foul stench filled the room. Sigson held his breath against the stink and waded in to finish them through clouds of vile smoke.

Another vial shimmered in his hand, but before he could throw it, a creature, nought but a desiccated skeleton, sprang out beneath the stalls and cut a deep wound in Sigson's stomach, piercing his steel breastplate. Sigson cried out, dropping the vial, blessed water eking through stone cracks as the glass shattered. He hacked down at the beast with his sword, but the weapon jarred in its collar bone. The zombie cut a deep slash across his exposed shoulder as he fought to get his sword free.

Sigson fell to his knees. The zombie loomed down upon him, mouth gaping.

Mikael was behind it and rammed his blade through its chest. Congealed blood spat from the wound, black and thick like syrup. Reiner came at it from the front, roaring as he lopped off its head.

The thing slumped into a tangled heap. Mikael yanked out his sword and cleaned the blade on his cloak. The last of the zombies was laid, brutally, to rest.

'Sigson,' Reiner said urgently, helping the priest to his feet. 'The binding. Can you do it?'

Leaning heavily on his captain, Sigson rose grimly with gritted teeth, and nodded.

'Gather them,' he ordered to his comrades.

Mikael, Halbranc, Kalten and Reiner dragged the corpses into a heap before the priest. Vaust watched, bleary-eyed, his brother laid beside him.

Sigson invoked the binding rites of Morr, that which ensured the guardianship of the body and the soul once the two were separated. It was a labour and the veteran priest fought for breath to intone the complicated ritual. The knights knelt beside him, muttering their own prayers to the enigmatic god of death.

Sweat upon his brow, Sigson let out a long and ragged breath.

'It is done.'

Reiner nodded and looked at Mikael.

'Open up the gate,' he ordered.

'Yes, captain.'

Mikael walked over to the chapel gate and hefted the thick wooden bar fixed across, trapping the creatures while they destroyed them.

Light washed into the greyish confines, as if reluctant to enter. A group of worried-looking villagers approached the threshold.

'Is it over? Are we safe?' an elderly man stammered. Several figures cowered behind him. They seemed afraid, perhaps at the abominations within or perhaps at the Templar of Morr stood before them, his armour wrought with skulls and effigies of death.

'It is done,' Mikael told him and turned to Sigson.

The priest, ashen faced, awash with sweat, collapsed. Vaust and Valen were near unconsciousness and the rest of the band was battered and bruised from the battle.

'Bury them face down and sanctify the ground upon the zenith of each Mannslieb,' Reiner told them as he stalked forward, 'Tell me, Alderman,' he added, a full head and shoulders above the man as he regarded him, 'is there a healer in the village?'

'No, I'm sorry,' the Alderman said fearfully. 'The nearest is the Temple of Shallya at Hochsleben, to the west.'

Reiner turned to Mikael, his pale blue eyes like pools of ice.

'Gather the horses,' he ordered. 'We ride to Hochsleben.'

Dawn had turned to greying day by the time they reached the town of Hochsleben. Even as they rode wearily through the gates, Mikael sensed a dark mood, as if the place were laden with some unknown threat.

Treading past the town's threshold, the sentry guards retreated into their gatehouse, nodding a fearful greeting at the dour knights templar. Poor folk walked quickly in groups, hugging rags to their feeble bodies, glancing about at each step. The wealthy rode in closed coaches and with armed escorts, fixed upon their destinations, as if ignorance of their surroundings might protect them.

'There is fear here,' Halbranc remarked beneath his breath as they passed a drunken tramp in the street, a bottle of liquor tinkling in his hand with the last dregs.

Reiner kept his eyes forward, gently urging his steed on.

'It is death.'

Mikael glanced behind him. The tramp shambled off toward an open street. A laden wagon emerged suddenly from his blind side, headed straight for the tramp. The wagoneer drove his beasts heedlessly, intent to get on, to get back, to get away from whatever grim fate had befallen the town. Travelling fast, it would crush the poor wretch!

With a grunt, Mikael spurred his horse, breaking away from his comrades. He rode hard, straight into the path of the wagon, crying out a warning.

'Halt, halt in the name of Morr!'

At the death god's name, the wagoneer pulled at the reins, slewing his cart to hasty stop, just avoiding the fearless templar.

Yelping in fright, the tramp shrank into a ball and cowered in the dirt, dropping his bottle to shatter upon the cobblestones. Realising he wasn't going to die, the tramp sat up and held the broken end of the bottle disconsolately.

The wagoneer shrank before Mikael's stern gaze.

'I didn't see him,' he pleaded, dismounting to check his load.

Something had come loose from beneath the cloth covering the back of the wagon.

It was a human hand. The skin upon it had been removed.

'They're from the mortuary,' the man explained, as if sensing Mikael's question. 'They're to be taken from the town and burned.' He pushed the hand back into the wagon with a stick from his belt and tied the cloth down. 'Victims of the Reaper,' he added, whispering fearfully, and rode off hard down the street without looking back.

Mikael was about to call him back, when a firm hand gripped his shoulder.

'We have found the Temple of Shallya,' Reiner told him. 'Halbranc and

Kalten have taken the others there. They will meet us in the house of Morr.'

Mikael nodded. As he rode away with his captain, he looked back over to where the tramp had been sitting, but he was gone.

Whatever ailed this town they must first pay their respects to Morr before any explanation could be sought. There was darkness here; Mikael felt it as a dull ache in his head, a sensation that grew stronger with each moment. He thought of telling Reiner. His captain was a puritan, cold like steel and as unyielding in matters of faith and heresy. Cold and compassionless, the templar captain might put him to the sword if he thought him bewitched. Mikael stayed quiet.

The Temple of Morr was a huge, gothic structure, stark and imposing in the middle of the poorest quarter in Hochsleben. A mist was forming, the day as bleak as the town's mood. A fine drizzle, exuding from a steel-grey sky, exacerbated the palpable misery felt by the human dregs that cowered in the streets or burrowed into their hovels.

Mikael averted his gaze from them, trying to focus on the monolithic temple. He felt for their suffering, their pain, and pitied them. Perhaps that's why he had gone to the tramp's rescue.

A great wedge of stone steps lay before them, spreading out from the black, oak gates of the temple like the over-extended jaw of some huge skeletal head. Two priests, lowly acolytes, scrubbed feverishly at the steps with buckets of water, their arms and knees sodden, red-faced with effort.

'Morr's blessing,' Reiner said to the priests, dismounting from his steed, a stable lad rushing over to take the reins from him. Another boy came over to Mikael's horse as he dismounted.

'We seek the head of the Temple,' Reiner told them, striding up the steps.

'Morr's blessing,' one of the priests breathed. 'Brother Dolmoth is within the sanctum.'

Reiner nodded his thanks, Mikael close behind him, muttering Morr's blessings with the other priest as he followed, looking down at their endeavours. Faint, but still visible, a stain marred the stone steps. It was dark and thick, like blood.

'I thank Morr for your coming,' Dolmoth told them earnestly. The priest looked ravaged by premature age. There was a shadow beneath his eyes, a worn expression that Mikael believed had come only recently, as if whatever malady seized the town had him in its grip too.

'What is it that ails this place, priest?' Reiner's face was as hard and unmoving as stone.

Dolmoth sagged, as if he could no longer bear an invisible weight upon his shoulders. He sat down upon a wooden stool, bidding the knights to follow.

Harsh grey light seeped through a nearby window, shadows dragging down the priest's features as if they were made of softening clay.

'Last night and on the same night for the past six weeks, a body has been left upon the steps of our temple.'

'It was blood that the acolytes were washing off the steps,' Mikael said.

Reiner looked at him, slightly surprised. He had not noticed it. As they both regarded him, Mikael felt compelled to continue.

'The Reaper,' he said. Dolmoth's expression darkened further, hand trembling as he drank from a silver goblet; a decanter set upon the table filled with communal wine.

'The wagoneer in the street said he carried "victims of the Reaper",' Mikael explained. 'At first I thought he had meant death, but he was referring to a murderer.'

Dolmoth nodded, draining the goblet and reaching to pour another drink.

Reiner grasped his hand.

'You've had enough.'

Brother Dolmoth's eyes, sore and red, held some resistance. But, when he looked at the templar captain, he withdrew.

'Come with me,' he said, his voice little more than a whisper.

Dolmoth led them through the sanctum and across the grounds to a small annex, located in the south wing of the mighty building next to a temple garden. The templars followed him without word or query. A feeling of dread and warning grew in Mikael's gut.

'The body left upon the steps last night,' Dolmoth said. 'Our mortician is examining it. I think you should see it.'

Dolmoth opened a small door to the annex. A corridor stretched before them. Immediately they were struck by the stink of chemicals and unguents.

'Merrick's embalming fluids,' Dolmoth explained and grasping a lantern, hooked at the entrance to the corridor, led them forward.

The corridor was long and dark. Fluttering torches, pitched sporadically in iron sconces, threw little more than a lambent glow onto stark, stone walls that were slick with moisture, black smears visible in the wan light of Dolmoth's swaying lantern.

'Are we heading down?' Mikael asked. He felt the air growing colder and the undeniable sensation of descent.

'The mortuary is located in our temple catacombs. It's an area largely unused by the priests and allows Merrick to work in peace.' Dolmoth had to raise his voice. The corridor was low, the tall, armoured templars forced to hunch beneath the ceiling and Dolmoth ranged ahead of them.

They reached the mortuary. Dolmoth heaved a stout, wooden door open that protested on creaking hinges.

As they entered, the templars stooping further to get through the narrow arch, a man glanced up from a body set upon a metal table. He was thin and wiry, with a silver spike of beard jutting from his jaw and a pepper wash of stubble across the neck and chin. Dressed in a bloody tabard, thick glasses covering his eyes and flecked with blood spatter, this had to be the mortician Dolmoth had spoken of.

'Greetings,' he said, masking his surprise.

'This is Merrick,' Dolmoth told the templars, stood like giants in the tiny chamber. It was filled with all-manner of crude equipment: saws, blades, scalpels, stitch and thread, with wooden racks filled with phials and beakers, a brown, oily liquid within each. Although small, there was a shabby-looking cloth draped over an open archway at the back of the room, which doubtless led to Merrick's private chambers. A bucket rested at the foot of the table. Mikael noticed blood seeping down into it from a funnel attached to the slab above.

'There is little left,' Merrick told him, as if reading his mind.

It wrong-footed the templar and he flashed a glance at Reiner, who stood impassively as he regarded the mortician.

'We wish to see the victim,' he said.

Merrick nodded and gestured to the table. He seemed to wither before Reiner's steely gaze, like most who met the formidable knight.

Dolmoth hung back and covered his mouth. He had seen the victim before, Mikael realised he had been the one who found them.

Merrick flicked a nervous glance at the towering knights, before he concentrated on the corpse.

'As you can see,' he began, 'skin has been removed from the chest, legs, hands and feet and there are marks upon the wrists and ankles.' Merrick turned the left wrist of the victim over. There was a dark, reddish bruise, harsh and violent.

'I have heard of evil men who eat the flesh of the living,' Reiner said, betraying no emotion as he regarded the brutalised body. 'In backward cultures. They are used in rituals to summon daemons and the dead from the grave.'

'And these marks,' Mikael asked, about to touch the bruised skin. before having second thoughts and snapping his hand away. 'The victim was bound.'

'I found them all like that,' Dolmoth muttered from behind his hand. 'Trussed up like meat, backs arched, pain etched upon their faces.'

Reiner stared at the priest cowering in the shadows. Mikael detected the faintest sneer. His captain deplored weakness, almost as much as he deplored the evil creatures that it was his lot to destroy.

'And the lack of blood,' Merrick said, stooping down, a pendant, on a chain around his neck, slipping free of the tabard. 'The victims were all partially exsanguinated.'

'Bled by a daemon,' Reiner muttered darkly, concentrating back on the corpse.

'That pendant,' Mikael said, 'was it given to you by a loved one?' There was a longing in the young templar's voice as a memory sparked of his life before the temple.

Merrick's face darkened, his expression edged with regret.

'It was my wife's,' he said, looking at Mikael. 'She gave it to me before she died. Plague took her long ago. For a time I had my son, but a riot in the town, three months ago, claimed his life. He was crushed to death by Imperial cavalry sent to quell the disorder. He had nothing to do with the rioting. He became embroiled…' Merrick stopped himself, before his emotions bettered him. Sternness crept across his face and he tucked the pendant away, closing his eyes briefly as he a muttered a prayer.

'I'm sorry,' Mikael said and felt his own regret.

'This terror has gone on long enough,' Reiner said, addressing the haggard Dolmoth.

'We will find this Reaper,' he promised, 'And bring Morr's justice down upon his head.' Reiner stalked from the mortuary, full of purpose, passing Dolmoth, who thanked Morr profusely for their deliverance.

Mikael nodded a farewell to Merrick, and gave Morr's blessing to Dolmoth, before hurrying after Reiner.

In the sanctum, Halbranc and Kalten awaited them. 'What news from the Temple of Shallya?' Reiner asked.

'They sleep,' Kalten told him. 'Sigson is badly injured, some of his wounds are infected. Vaust too.'

'And Valen?' said Mikael.

Kalten's face was grim.

'It is feared he will not last the night.'

An uncomfortable silence descended. Reiner quashed it.

'Then it will be Morr's will. We do not mourn our dead, we deliver them to His arms. It is no different for Valen.'

'You are a cold man, Reiner,' Halbranc said. 'I have never known the like, even in an order such as ours.'

Reiner was impassive as he regarded the giant templar, taller even than him and wider still at the shoulders.

'There is little time for compassion, Halbranc. Morr's work is to be done.'

Reiner told them both of what he and Mikael had discovered about the Reaper.

'The Templars of Morr are justly feared,' Reiner said. 'We shall begin by questioning the population about these heinous acts. I doubt there will be any with the stomach to lie, not with Morr's judgement hanging over them.'

'You cannot expect me to work with such shoddy materials,' a sibilant voice said, echoing in the emptiness of the darkened room.

'I'm sorry. I shouldn't have brought the girl, I made a mistake,' another voice pleaded.

'You do want my aid, don't you?'

'Yes, yes of course. I brought you back, didn't I?'

'That you did, and in doing so, your heart became as black as mine,' the voice said sneeringly.

'I am nothing like you.' The second voice tried to sound indignant but lacked conviction.

'Don't delude yourself, you just don't know it. Now, find me another specimen. It has to be perfect, do you understand? Perfect.'

'Yes, I understand. Perfect. I'm sorry. I'll do better next time.'

Even in the fading day, in a town awash with unease, the market continued to do business. In the Empire, it seemed, commerce stopped for nothing.

To better serve their aims, the templars had split up. Reiner and Kalten took the slums ,whilst Mikael and Halbranc surveyed the market.

Across the market square the two of them noticed a butcher selling his wares to a hungry, if skittish, crowd. The man was obese and slovenly, thick fingers holding bloodied joints aloft, his ragged tabard stained with blood and grease. He looked up from his banter, but when he saw the templars, hastily averted his gaze.

'This looks a good place to start,' Halbranc said, immediately suspicious as he stalked forward. 'The bodies trussed up like meat sacks, you said?'

'Yes, but wait Halbranc.'

'Why?'

'Look at him, obese, thick-fingered. His brow is fevered even now from what little exertion it takes to address a crowd. I scarcely believe he could carry a dead body a few feet, let alone up the steps of the Temple of Morr,' Mikael said. 'And the skin cut from the body, it was precise and careful. I doubt this man has the skill.'

'Very well,' said Halbranc. 'Then what do you suggest?'

Mikael thought for a moment. The market stalls were throbbing; people possessed with an urgency to get what they needed quickly, before the onset of night. As he looked around, the shadows seemed to coalesce in the distance.

'There,' he said, pointing towards a worn looking building.

As they approached, Mikael read a sign above the door.

Lothmar's Tannery.

The sign was faded with age, the windows stained by a yellowish grime and covered by thick leather drapes, but the door was open and the darkness within beckoned them.

The room was dark, with the faint stink of musk and spice. A patina of dust rested upon everything inside, tall racks of leather and cured animal hide. The place was crammed and over-burdened, making it feel claustrophobic. The dust-clogged air made Mikael choke.

'May I help you?' a rasping voice came from the back of the room. A man with his back to them stood behind a long, broad, wooden counter. Various cutting and hammering tools hung upon a rack in front of him. He replaced a long, wide knife and pulled something over his head as he turned to face them.

'You have heard of the murderer who blights this town?' Halbranc began, walking forward.

Little light penetrated the tannery. Shadows clawed out from alcoves and dark corners. Mikael felt like the gloom was sticking to him as he followed Halbranc.

Mikael had to mask his shock when he saw the man whom, he gathered was Lothmar.

Half of his face was covered by a leather mask. A blood-shot pupil stared out from an eye-hole, with pink scar-tissue just visible at the fringe of the mask. His hands were covered too, with thick, leather gloves. But despite his obvious afflictions, he was tall and strong. Years of stripping animal carcasses and tearing up toughened hide would do that to a man.

'Would you close that?' he asked, wincing against the feeble light pouring in from the outside.

Mikael nodded, a glance at Halbranc as he eyed the tanner dubiously, and went back to close the door.

Silence descended. A smile cracked the tanner's ravaged face as he saw the templars' discomfort.

'I was burned. Here, in the tannery,' he told them. 'There are vats in the back.' He thumbed behind him to a darkened arch which led further still into the tannery. 'They get hot, to cure the hides and toughen them, so they can be cut and fashioned.'

Halbranc raised an eyebrow.

'I am Lothmar,' he added, offering a hand. 'And yes, I have heard of the Reaper.'

'What have you heard?' Halbranc said, ignoring the hand as he met the man's gaze, despite his unsettling visage.

'That he hasn't been caught, that the town is in fear of him and my business is suffering as a result.' Lothmar was indignant and stood his ground.

'I see your cloak is damaged,' he said. 'I could fashion you a replacement. These are of the highest quality.' He indicated a wooden stand upon which hung an assortment of cloaks and capes. 'I can assure you, they are very supple, like a second skin.'

'I think not,' Halbranc growled.

'Well then, I don't think I can help you further,' Lothmar said.

Mikael rested a hand upon Halbranc's shoulder. His instincts told him the tanner knew nothing.

'We thank you for your time,' Mikael said with respect. This tanner had not balked in the face of interrogation. It seemed the folk of Hochsleben would be more difficult to intimidate than Reiner had predicted.

Even Halbranc relented and nodded. 'Morr's blessing.'

Lothmar nodded back respectfully.

Mikael and Halbranc left the shadows of the tannery, Lothmar watching them leave.

'You're quick to judge, Halbranc,' Mikael said as they made for the market square.

'Men in masks usually have something to hide,' he grumbled.

'He wears his scars on the outside,' Mikael said, 'I trust that over those that harbour theirs within.'

Reiner and Kalten were in the market square. They had learnt nothing from patrolling the slums. Reiner's tactics had only served to make the population less cooperative, either that or a greater fear held their tongues.

'Night approaches,' said Reiner. The sky dimmed like the light around a fading flame and thick clouds billowed overhead, smothering the stars. 'We can learn little more today.'

The other templars were in agreement. They found lodgings at an inn, The Stableman, in short order and retired quickly to bed, battle-weary bones finally demanding rest. Having bid his comrades a good night, only Mikael remained, waiting with the rest of the patrons who were reluctant to leave. He recognised one of them, it was the poor wretch he had saved from the wagon earlier in the day. He was looking forlornly into an empty cup, unaware of the templar's eyes upon him. Mikael turned away and stared into the flickering flames of the dying fire.

He was deeply troubled, a gnawing dread grew within him that he did not understand. With the onset of night, images of his past came back, forming in the hearth like fiery spectres.

The forest rose about him, a cloak of arboreal gloom.

He held a dagger in his hand, stained with his brother's blood.

A deer mewled in the distance, its final dying sounds. Its breath was a cloud of white mist in the cold wintry air. It came in bursts; faster and faster as the deer's heart beat its last.

Mikael looked into its eyes and found his own fear mirrored there. The mewling stopped, the deer was dead.

Mikael cried out, tears flooding from his eyes, cold like daggers of ice as they ran down his cheeks. He looked into the forest void for Stephan, but his brother was gone.

A shallow hiss wrenched Mikael into the present. The innkeeper had doused the burning embers in the hearth.

'Wouldn't want to start a fire, eh?' he said. He was a broad man, thick-jawed with an eye-patch and a scar that ran beneath, all the way down to his neck.

Mikael had stripped out of most of his armour, leaving only a breastplate. He looked like any common sell-sword without his trappings and insignia.

'Chasing monsters, boy?' the innkeeper said with a wry smile.

Shocked at the man's boldness, Mikael was about to protest when the innkeeper stopped him.

'It's written all over your face. I was a captain in the Averheim army. I've my share of them,' he said and leaned in closer.

His voice was little more than a whisper.

'Don't let them consume you, boy. Whatever ill blights your past, there's little you can do about it now.'

'I am a Templar of Morr,' was all Mikael could think of to say, hoping to discourage the innkeeper.

'Then you walk with death, but does he walk with you?'

'I…' Mikael began then rose from his seat, pushing past the innkeeper, and fled out into the night.

As he stood in the darkness, his heart pounded and cooling sweat chilled him. He sucked up a great gulp of air, waiting for his racing heart to subside.

'Can't beat the night air, eh?' Halbranc leant against the wooden beam of the inn's veranda. He held a dark bottle in his hand and drank deeply, then offered it across.

Mikael shook his head.

'Couldn't sleep?' the giant templar asked. Even without his amour, he was huge and imposing. Utterly bald, it was as if he was made from chiselled stone.

Mikael sighed, searching the darkness for an answer that wasn't there.

'Ever since we came to this place, I have had a dark and forbidding feeling, as if–'

Screams suddenly tore into the night.

Mikael and Halbranc drew their swords. His confession would have to wait.

The sound came from further up the street, towards the market. They raced towards it, the bottle shattering as Halbranc cast it aside.

'For the love of Sigmar,' a figure wailed, a distant silhouette gradually coming into focus. 'I've seen it, I've seen it.' It was a woman. Wearing a gaudy dress, thick make-up smeared over her face to hide her age, she was one of Hochsleben's veteran streetwalkers.

At first she ran into Halbranc's arms, but recoiled when she saw the symbols of Morr etched upon his armour.

'What have you seen, woman?' Halbranc demanded, holding her wrist before she fled.

'The Reaper,' she gasped, struggling against Halbranc's iron grip. 'Over there.' Her eyes widened in terror as she tried to pull away.

A short distance away, in the market square, a figure hunched over a heavy burden and dragged it through the street. Shrouded by the darkness, it was impossible to discern the figure's identity.

Halbranc let the streetwalker go and she raced away into the dark.

'Halt,' he bellowed suddenly. 'Halt in the name of Morr.'

Halbranc and Mikael started running forward. The figure looked up at them from whatever it was doing, and ran. The templars sheathed their swords and gave chase.

The figure had left a body in the street. It was a man. A dagger wound through the heart had killed him, but he was otherwise unmolested, although both his hands and feet were bound.

Mikael and Halbranc ran on.

He was fast, a long cloak flapped in his wake as the figure fled from the knights. But Mikael was gaining on him. He darted down an alley and the templar followed, abruptly swallowed by the darkness within.

'Mikael, wait,' Halbranc cried from the mouth of the alleyway.

Mikael glanced back. Halbranc leant against the wall, breathing hard and sweating.

'This is one monster I will not let slip,' Mikael muttered to himself and left Halbranc behind him, driving after the Reaper to become lost in the gloomy alleyway.

Upon racing around a corner, the man vanished. Mikael stopped and drew his sword, listening. The rising breeze whispered in his ear, sibilant and eerie, a bawdy drunk sang raucously, his voice faint, streets away in the distance.

He edged forward, willing his eyes to adjust to the darkness. Formless dark became silhouette before him. He was gripped by a sudden sense of danger behind him. Pain like white heat flared in Mikael's back as he tried to turn. He'd been stabbed. His leggings felt warm and wet, as blood ran down his leg. He glimpsed a flash in the corner of his eye and felt a heavy object smash against his head. Reeling from the attack, Mikael was vaguely aware of glass fragments in his hair.

Vision fogging, he fell. Reaching out into the growing blackness, he clawed at his attacker, pulling something free. He struck the ground hard and a lance of fire pierced his shoulder. He fought it for a moment, then blacked out.

'Idiot!' the voice was hard and angry in the darkened room.

'I'm sorry. Please our pact,' the second voice pleaded.

'Ezekaer is no pawn, dictated to by the likes of you. Corpsemaster they called me. Fellshadow I was known as. I will honour the pact at my choosing. Only I have the skill to grant your desire.'

'Yes, yes, of course. Please, I'm sorry, I'm sorry,' said the second voice, grovelling profusely. 'I had the perfect specimen, but for those templars,' he whined.

The first voice paused, his interest piqued. The atmosphere in the darkness changed. 'Templars you say?' the voice said, anger receding.

'Yes,' answered the second voice, breathless and confused.

'How interesting. Tell me more of these templars…'

A hot spike of pain shot through him as Mikael came too. He thought he could smell pine and the faint musky odour of the forest, but realised he was in the alleyway. Rain was falling. Through the watery haze, three figures stood over him, the black hair of two of them tinged with droplets.

'Mikael,' a voice urged. 'Mikael, are you wounded?' Halbranc stooped down and held his head in a massive hand.

'I think I was stabbed,' he groaned, spitting rain water from his mouth.

Halbranc eased him over and Kalten, who crouched nearby, nodded.

'We must get him to the Temple of Shallya,' Kalten said, rain weighing down his long hair and flecking his beard. 'A piece of the blade is lodged in his armour. And what is that stench?' he said, sniffing Mikael's clothes.

'It's all over him,' Halbranc said. 'I know not.'

'What is this?' Reiner's voice cut through like a cold blade, as he stooped to retrieve something Mikael clutched in his hand.

Halbranc's voice grew dark.

'I have seen that before.'

Reiner held it up. Mikael's head throbbed painfully inside his skull, like a perpetual cannonade, but he focused long enough to recognise what his captain held aloft.

A half-mask with one eye hole cut into it.

'It's the tanner, we spoke to him this afternoon. His lodgings are upon the market square,' Halbranc explained, anger in his voice. He told them quickly of his and Mikael's encounter, of the darkened store, the tanner's shunning of the light and his reference to a cloak that felt like a 'second skin'.

'This wretch is most likely trading with human flesh,' Reiner spat. 'Victims drained of blood, aversion to the light: I can think of no other creature with such despicable traits.'

'A vampire,' said Kalten, crouching at Mikael's side.

Reiner crushed the mask in his hand.

'We head for the tannery. Kalten, you will come with me. Halbranc, take Mikael to the Temple of Shallya and meet us when you can.'

'It lies to the west quarter,' Helbranc told him.

'I remember it,' Reiner said. 'This ends tonight.'

As Halbranc heaved Mikael onto his back with a grunt, and Reiner and Kalten stalked off to confront the Reaper, no one noticed a small figure watching from the shadows. His teeth gleamed white in the darkness as a grin split his features, and he scurried off to report to his master.

He was lost, alone in the darkness. Cold stone pricked his fingers. The air was damp and stale.

Mikael wandered as if blind.

A door opened ahead of him. He drew his sword and felt compelled toward it.

A rising dread filled his stomach. Something was wrong.

He ran, ran with fear at his heels.

Bursting into the light, he entered another room. There were seven bodies chained to the walls, hung up, feet dangling limply above the ground.

A spasm of fear hit Mikael like a physical blow and he recoiled. They wore the armour of Templars of Morr, except that each had his face covered by black shrouds.

Heart thumping Mikael reached out, suddenly within touching distance of one of the bodies and pulled the shroud away.

A pale death mask regarded him beneath. It was Kalten. The templar opened his eyes.

'Mikael,' he moaned with a voice from beyond the grave...

Mikael screamed. Pain burned in him anew and he realised he was awake.

A strong hand held him still as he shook with the night terror, a fevered sweat drenching his clothes.

'Rest easy,' Sigson's voice was calm and soothing as he crouched beside him, 'You are safe.'

'Sigson,' Mikael rasped, breathing hard, 'I had a dream.'

Sigson was abruptly concerned. As the god of dreams, as well as the guardian of the dead, Morr bestowing a vision upon one of his templars was oft portentous and should not be ignored.

'What did you see, Mikael?'

'Where are the others?'

'Valen and Vaust are still recuperating, the fever has passed but they are still bed-ridden,' Sigson explained, nonplussed.

Mikael grabbed Sigson by his jerkin. His hands trembled, his voice infected with urgency. 'No Kalten, Reiner, Halbranc – where are they?'

'Halbranc headed into town a few moments ago, he was leaving by the time I entered your chambers.'

Mikael released the warrior priest and got up from his bed, biting back the pain as he strapped on his armour waiting nearby.

Sigson rose and held Mikael's shoulder.

'What did you see, Mikael?' he urged, gripping tightly so Mikael would listen.

The young templar looked directly into the warrior priest's eyes and spoke as intently as he could.

'I saw death, Sigson. The death of our entire company.'

Sigson's face grew dark as the resonance of what Mikael said struck him. 'I'm coming with you.'

Mikael and Sigson ran through cobbled streets, rain battering against their armour with such fury it was as if nature itself had come to oppose them. They drove on through the downpour, with not a soul in sight until they reached the market square.

Two figures, one huge, the other small and slight by comparison, conversed beyond a wall of driving rain. As they got closer, Mikael recognised the immense form of Halbranc and the wiry mortician, Merrick, in front of him.

Halbranc turned to them both when he saw them.

'What are you doing out here?' he bellowed against the raucous downpour. Overhead, thunder boiled and lightning cracked the sky.

'The others,' Mikael cried back. 'Where are they?' They were forced close, so they could hear each other.

'At the tanners. Lothmar attacked you in the street, you tore off his mask,' Halbranc said, spitting away the water washing over his mouth as he spoke. 'I was headed to them, when I was stopped.' He looked over at Merrick.

The mortician looked half-drowned. His face blue and pale with cold, he clutched a thick but sodden cloak around his body, and shivered. 'Another victim has been found,' he explained, leaning in to speak, voice shaking. 'He is alive and has been taken to the mortuary. The watchmen thought he was dead,' he cried.

'They found him in the street?' Mikael asked, confused.

Merrick nodded, water trickling rapidly down his face.

Raging wind filled the silence. They all breathed hard in the dire conditions. Mikael regarded Merrick closely, before he turned to Halbranc.

'Go with him,' Mikael said. 'We'll meet you there, once we've found the others.'

Halbranc nodded, grateful to be on his way and getting out of the terrible weather.

The party broke up, Halbranc and Merrick heading toward the house of Morr, Mikael and Sigson to the tanners. None were aware of a fifth person on the streets, braving the rain. He watched the entire scene and sticking to the shadows, followed the two templars.

The door to Lothmar's tannery swung open on creaking hinges. Buffeted by the wind and rain, it slammed hard against the frame before being sucked open again.

Mikael forged inside, ahead of Sigson, sword drawn.

Darkness surrounded him but Mikael could tell the shop was empty. He remembered the archway towards the rear.

'There is another chamber beyond that arch,' he whispered to Sigson, who crept behind him.

'I see it.'

The two men moved carefully in the gloom toward the archway. As they reached it, a cold draft wafted up at them, stone steps descending into a cellar below.

The swinging door slammed hard against the frame behind them, rupturing the silence. They turned as one, weapons raised, but there was no one there.

Mikael blew out his nerves, and, with a glance at Sigson, headed down the steps. A crack in the roof above threw a shaft of moonlight within.

A body slumped in the stairwell was illuminated, a sword in its hand. It was Reiner.

Mikael felt dizzy and for a moment thought he would fall, but gathered himself and raced to the bottom.

He lifted his captain's chin. Reiner's eyes opened a crack. There was an ugly bruise upon his forehead and a bloody gash where he'd been struck.

'He was already dead,' he mumbled, semi-conscious.

A door was ahead. It was open, and dark within.

'Where is Kalten?' Mikael asked, his sense of dread growing.

'I don't know, we were ambushed.'

Mikael looked back, Sigson was behind him.

The two of them entered the room. A lantern was hooked up just inside. Oil hissed as Mikael ignited it and yellow light washed over the room.

Just beyond the lambent glow of the lantern, Lothmar lay dead, his throat slit, mask ripped callously from his face, exposing his scars. Mikael crouched over his body. The wan light revealed the pallor of Lothmar's skin, white like alabaster. His right eye, unblemished from the accident was pink.

'He was no vampire,' Mikael said, voice tinged with regret.

'An albino,' Sigson said, crouched next to him. 'But if not this poor soul, then why cut them?'

'A ritual perhaps, or maybe the murders were meant to look like Lothmar's work, or that of a butcher, with wrists and ankles tied.'

'There might be a way to know for certain,' Sigson said. 'Move aside.' Sigson leant over Lothmar's body and muttered a prayer beneath his breath. The air tingled as he invoked the power of his god. The hairs rose on the back of Mikael's neck. Morr had answered.

'Push down upon his chest,' Sigson ordered, intent on the tanner and leaned down, putting his ear to Lothmar's mouth. 'Morr will do the rest.'

'Who attacked you?' he whispered, and nodded to Mikael, who pushed down as instructed.

The last breath in Lothmar's lungs eked out.

'A man… a stranger,' he wheezed, the words drawn out and laboured. 'He wore… a mask. Terrible… odour…' Then there was silence, the air within him finally expired.

'There is no more,' Sigson said, getting to his feet. Mikael did the same and turned to the door. A figure stood there.

They drew their swords.

'Identify yourself!' Mikael demanded.

'Do not be alarmed,' a deep and confident voice told them. A figure stepped into the lantern light.

It was a man, perhaps close to his forties with greying hair and a thinning beard, but strong and powerfully built beneath simple brown robes. A breastplate covered his chest, etched into it the symbol of a fiery comet. Hanging down from his neck was a silver talisman that bore the sigil of a hammer.

'I am Rathorne,' he said. 'Warrior priest of Sigmar.' A short figure shuffled out of the darkness to hunch beside him, a pitiable wretch dressed in nought but rags. Mikael recognised, once again, the tramp he had rescued.

'You,' he said, accusingly.

'What business have you here?' Sigson asked, sword raised.

'Please,' Rathorne said. 'Put down your weapons. We are here for the same purpose.'

'What might that be?' Mikael asked, unwilling to relent.

'To catch the Reaper and end his murderous rampage.'

They lowered their swords.

'Your expressions demand explanations,' Rathorne began. 'But since your comrade is wounded and our prey loose, I'll keep them short. I have been tracking this devil since I heard of the dire happenings in this town more than four weeks ago. His movements have been a mystery to me but I did not want to reveal myself lest I alert him. When your company arrived I thought you might provoke a mistake, so I had Vislen follow you.' The impish tramp bowed and grinned, revealing a set of perfect, white teeth.

'It seems we are allies then,' Mikael said, noting the distaste in Rathorne's eyes, and sheathed his sword. Sigson did the same.

'But we have reached a dead end,' Mikael explained. 'Although one of our comrades is questioning a survivor of the attacks as we speak. Aside from that, all we know is he drains his victim's blood and bears an unpleasant odour.'

'Much like the stench that clings to you,' Rathorne said, breathing in the stink of Mikael's clothes. 'It is consistent with vampirism.' He glanced down at Vislen, who shuffled over to the templar and began sniffing at him.

'What is he doing?' Mikael asked, raising his arms and looking down suspiciously at the runtish tramp.

Vislen shuffled back to his master, and, as Rathorne leaned down, whispered into his ear.

'Embalming fluid,' Rathorne announced, 'and something else.'

The warrior priest moved over to Mikael and examined the wound in his back, now a dark red mark in his jerkin, just below the back-plate.

Rathorne dug into the wound with his fingers and as Mikael was about to recoil said,

'Hold, there is something left in the wound.'

The young templar winced in pain, neck arched around so he could see what the Sigmarite was doing. Rathorne pulled a tiny sliver of metal out of the wound, letting it fall into his open palm.

He looked up at the two templars.

'A scalpel blade.'

'Merrick,' Mikael spat with anger. Realisation dawned soon after. 'Halbranc,' he gasped and raced to the door. 'Sigson,' he said, turning, 'stay with Reiner. I must get to the mortuary.'

He felt a hand on his arm. Looking back he was met by Rathorne's intense gaze. 'You mean we.'

Mikael was defiant at the priest's interference but had no time to argue.

'Then, come on,' he said, and he and Rathorne sped out of the tannery into the night.

Bolting through the Temple of Morr, acolytes and priests scattering in their wake, Mikael and Rathorne were quickly at the door to the mortuary.

A muffled voice emanated from beyond. It was Merrick, he was talking to someone.

'...but what of our pact, your promise to me,' Merrick urged desperately. 'I have fulfilled my part of the bargain. I have your amulet, you are bound to it and my bidding. I didn't mean to tarnish this one, but he struggled so, and I have brought you a new body to replace it.'

A muted cry, as if through a gag, echoed in the chamber, faint but discernable. Mikael recognised Halbranc's voice and heaved at the door.

It was locked tight.

'Stand aside,' Rathorne ordered, taking an icon of Sigmar from his robes as he pushed in front of the templar.

'By the order of Sigmar,' he bellowed with conviction, loosing a warhammer from a leather loop at his waist, swivelling it in his hand as he tested the grip. 'Get back,' he said to Mikael.

'Open this door!' Rathorne struck, and the door was smashed open, splinters flying as it slammed into the adjacent wall with a heavy *thunk*. The warrior priest waded in immediately, Mikael was right behind him.

He gasped when he saw Kalten's body on the mortuary table, as the dream came back. His throat was slit but had been done so with a struggle; numerous deep cuts lacerating his neck, face and chest, his features now horribly mutilated. In the far corner, Halbranc struggled. His head was bruised and he was gagged, hands and feet both bound with thick rope. And before them stood Merrick, the pitiable mortician who had lost his family, the pendant his wife had given him hanging around his neck. The man Mikael had felt the deepest sympathy for. But now there was a darkness about his eyes and face, the shadow of a driven man, one who was willing to do absolutely anything to achieve his goal.

'Where did you get that amulet?' Mikael demanded, a raised hand compelling Rathorne to wait.

Merrick looked down at it, toying with it in his fingers, as it glowed with an evil light. 'A forgotten chamber in the catacombs,' Merrick confessed, with a glance at the veiled off room at the back of the mortuary. He struggled within himself now, at the final moment, he realised the consequences of his deeds, the innocents he had killed. 'I stole it, watched the priests for months. I knew I could bind him to it, that he would do my will.'

'Merrick, you fool,' Mikael spat, wrenching the mortician back into the present.

'I... It's for my son,' he said, weeping, the old Merrick returned for but a moment. 'I didn't want to kill them,' he said forlornly, eyes pleading forgiveness. 'But I couldn't use the mortuary, they would find out, I would lose him.'

'Speak no further,' an evil voice echoed in the chamber. Not Merrick, someone else, beyond the curtain at the back of the room and with it came an ancient menace, one that spoke across the ages. 'Perform the binding rites.'

'What have you done?' Mikael said, edging forward.

'You'll not stop me!' Merrick cried.

Rathorne surged toward him, icon outstretched.

The evil voice spoke again and chanting filled the room. A dark nimbus of power played about the pendant around Merrick's neck as he mimicked it.

At last, Mikael realised it was no gift from his dead wife.

'Rathorne, wait!' he cried.

But the warrior priest was upon him, 'Down hell-kite!' he bellowed, thrusting the icon toward him.

A man possessed, Merrick launched himself at Rathorne, grabbing the priest's wrists as he completed the ritual.

'Night stalker,' Rathorne raged through clenched teeth as he struggled, 'feel the burning truth of Sigmar's wrath,' he spat, pushing the icon against Merrick's cheek, but nothing happened.

Upon the slab, Mikael watched in horror as the dead eyes of Kalten flicked open.

'Fool,' he said, in a reedy, rasping voice that was not his own. 'He is no vampire, he is my pawn,' he added, rising up from the slab and grasping his fallen sword.

Rathorne wrenched himself free from Merrick's grasp and faced off against Kalten's reanimated corpse.

'But my son, you promised to bring him back. What of our pact?'

Merrick wailed, rushing toward the undead monster, sobbing.

The thing that used to be Kalten turned to him. 'The body is mine. It was always mine.' He smashed Merrick aside with a swipe of a mighty arm. The mortician clattered into the wooden racking, shattering the vials and bottles, chemicals spreading across the floor. Amidst the foul unguents and oils he lay still.

'By Sigmar's hand...' Rathorne cried, charging forward.

'Silence!' Kalten bellowed, blasting the warrior priest back into the wall with black fire from his eyes. Rathorne slumped unconscious, faint smoke rising from his hair and robes.

As Kalten turned, Mikael raked his blade across the undead templar's eyes.

Kalten reeled from the blow, blinded, but recovered quickly, blocking a swipe aimed at his neck.

'Clever,' he rasped, lashing out with his blade.

Mikael parried, and edged around to the creature's left.

'But I don't need these eyes to see,' the monster told him, matching his movements.

'Release him,' Mikael spat as he drove a powerful thrust into Kalten's chest, right through his heart. He pushed hard into the wound, using the blade like a spear and smashed Kalten into the wall. Kalten's flailing sword clattered against a lantern, knocking it and the blade to the ground. Oil and flame ran inexorably to the spilled chemicals pooling near Merrick, who had shaken himself to.

'I won't die so easily,' it said mockingly, locking its hands around Mikael's throat.

Fire flared at the back of the chamber, Merrick dragging himself clear just in time.

'Rathorne,' Mikael urged through strangled gasps.

The warrior priest stirred and looked up through blood-shot eyes.

'Get Halbranc out, warn the priests.'

Dazedly, Rathorne obeyed and dragged a semi-conscious Halbranc to his feet as Mikael and Kalten struggled.

The young templar released his sword and smashed his fists down hard against Kalten's wrists. Rigor setting in, the fingers slipped away, losing their grip.

In the corner of his eye, Mikael saw Rathorne and Halbranc escape down the corridor as he backed away.

Kalten ambled toward him, Mikael's blade still stuck in his chest.

Smoke billowed as fire swathed the room, angry and intense as it roared amongst the stored chemicals. Bottles shattered with the heat.

A shadow leapt through the smoke and flame from the back of the chamber. It was Merrick. He dove upon Kalten's back and dragged him down. His clothes were on fire and they spread to the undead creature.

'You promised me, you bastard!' he cried, pulling the monster into the fire, using its body to shield him.

The flames ravaged Kalten's skin, cracking his armour, burning hair and cloth alike.

'No, the undead thing cried. 'I was to be reborn!'

Mikael tried to go to Merrick's aid, but couldn't reach him through the wall of fire and smoke.

'Merrick!' he cried, against the roaring inferno, hand before his face to ward off the heat.

Clutched in a fiery embrace, a dark miasma exuded from Kalten's mouth and seeped into Merrick as he wailed in anger and anguish. Kalten's corpse fell to the ground and burned. Merrick backed away, ripping off his burning shirt and clutched his face, screaming, the fire burning it red raw.

'Merrick!' Mikael cried again, coughing as smoke filled his lungs.

Strong hands grasped Mikael's shoulders and dragged him away from the conflagration. Rathorne had come back for him and heaved him out of the room just before the roof collapsed, and Merrick was lost to his sight.

Reaching the outside, flames danced before Mikael's eyes. His lungs were choking with smoke and his skin burned. As he collapsed, the last thing he saw was Merrick screaming, surrounded by fire, the image forever seared onto his memory.

Mikael awoke in the Temple of Shallya. It was night and the rain had abated to a fine drizzle. He sat up in bed and allowed the moon, coming through a high window, to bathe him in its beam.

'Show yourself,' he said, looking out into the gloom.

A shadow moved at the far end of the room and stepped into the moonlight.

'I see the encounter has not dulled your instincts.' It was Sigson. 'I was trying not to wake you.'

'Where are the others?'

'Resting, as you should be.'

'There should be no rest for me,' Mikael said, broodingly. 'I left that poor man to die.'

'You make it sound like he was innocent,' Sigson said. 'Resurrecting the dead and killing those people, he was no better than the necromancer he foolishly consorted with.'

'You sound like Reiner.'

'I sound like a Templar of Morr,' Sigson corrected him, agitation in his voice.

'Grief had driven him mad, Sigson. Mad to the point where he was capable of bloody and brutal murder.'

'Then his love for his son was his undoing. The dead should not be interfered with. That way lies heresy and damnation.'

Mikael fell silent. He knew Sigson was right and yet he thought he might have saved him, redeemed his soul some how.

'The dream I had,' Mikael began. 'I saw Kalten's face. He was dead.'

'There was nothing you could have done to prevent that, Mikael. Halbranc and Reiner are both alive, mainly thanks to you. You cannot save everyone.'

'At least we can leave this place, now that it's over,' he muttered. 'Perhaps Merrick will find some peace at last, as well.'

Sigson's expression changed.

'You don't know?' he said.

'Know what?'

'When the fires were doused, I scoured the ruins of the mortuary. Kalten's body was burned, almost to ash, within his armour. But there was no sign of Merrick.'

'He survived? How?'

'I don't know, but I doubt he is in Hochsleben now and pursuit would be pointless, we have no idea of his direction.'

'When I saw him at the last Sigson, he was burned and I saw something enter his body, like a black mist. At the time I thought it a trick of the smoke and flames, but now...'

'So then,' Sigson said severely, 'it seems that Merrick was not the only one to escape the fire.'

'Then he is a renegade, and a dangerous one at that. It is our duty to hunt him down.'

'Yes, and we will,' he said rising, and walked over to the door to Mikael's chamber. When he turned, his face was grim. 'Rest, Mikael. Morning is not far off, and you'll need your strength for what is to come, I fear.'

The door shut, and, as a cloud smothered the moon, Mikael was left alone in the darkness.

DEAD MAN'S HAND

Nick Kyme

The guard was dead. He fell to the ground at Krieger's feet, his broken neck a pulpy, twisted mass.

Krieger clenched a fist, felt the knuckles crack. It was good to kill again. He regarded the corpse impassively from above, rubbing the angry red rings around his wrists left by the manacles.

A sound beyond the dungeon gate alerted him. He ducked down and slowly dragged the guard's body away from the viewing slit, then waited, listening intently in the gloom. He heard only his own breath and the mind-numbing retort of dripping water from the sewer beneath.

Rising slowly, Krieger felt anew the bruises from the beatings they had given him. He'd sobbed as they'd done it. They'd become complacent and negligent, removing his manacles and leg irons to make beating him easier. The mistake had cost one guard his life, but Krieger's retribution was just beginning.

Krieger heaved the guard's corpse along a stone floor, thick with grime, shushing him mockingly, touching his finger to his lips. He was alone in an interrogation cell. There were no windows and it smelled of vomit and blood. At the back of the chamber was a cot. The rest of the room, dank and filth-smeared, was empty save for a single wooden chair, bolted to the floor. Short chains were fixed to it. Spatters of Krieger's blood showed up, dark and thick, around it.

The witch hunter would be here soon, the guard had boasted of it. Working quickly, Krieger concealed the guard's body beneath a stinking, lice-ridden blanket. The man had the sloping forehead and common features of a low-born; the blanket seemed oddly fitting as a mortuary veil. Donning the guard's helmet, he quickly carved a symbol into the dead man's flesh with his dagger.

After he was finished, Krieger fixed his attention back on the vision slit.

Three sharp raps came from the other side of the door. Volper sprang to his feet. He fumbled with the iron keys, slipping one into the lock. Bolts scraping, he opened the vision slit.

'I 'ope you spat in that gruel,' he said, peering through it as he eased the door open a crack. A shadowy figure wearing a helmet looked back at him. As it drew close Volper saw bloodshot eyes, filled with murderous intent.

Instinctively, stupidly, the guard reached for his sword with shaking fingers. Looking back through the vision slit, he saw a flash of steel.

Krieger rammed the dagger through the vision slit, driving it into the guard's eye. Wedging his foot into the door, he reached around and pushed him thrashing onto the blade. Krieger held him there a moment, waiting patiently for the spasms to subside. Then, opening the door inwards, he allowed Volper's body to fall inside.

Krieger stepped over the guard's body and into the sickly light of the corridor. There was a sewer grate a few feet away. Krieger padded up to it and saw it was embedded with rust and slime. Age and wear had weakened it though. With effort, cold gnawing at him as he perspired, he carved away the filth at the edges of the sewer grate with the guard's dagger, stopping occasionally to listen for signs of intrusion.

Using the fallen guard's sword he levered the grate open, sliding and scraping it to one side. A foul stench assailed him. Krieger ignored it, pushing the grate wide open. He went back to the dead guard, took the man's boots and put them on before pushing the body into the sewer. There was a dull splash as the guard hit the turgid water below. Krieger followed, standing on a slim ledge inside the sewer tunnel and pulling the grate back. With a final glance up into the dungeon, he plunged into the mire beneath.

Effluent came up to his waist and he held his breath against the horrible stink, wading through it quickly. A half-devoured animal carcass bobbed in the filthy water like a macabre buoy. The guard's body was gone; weighed down by his armour the sea of waste had swallowed him.

After several long minutes, the sewage began to ebb and Krieger saw a circle of faint and dingy light ahead. He waded towards it – the hope of his freedom his incentive – and emerged from the edge of the tunnel into the day.

Blinking back the harsh light, Krieger looked down into a rocky gorge. Beyond that, the surrounding land was thick with pine. But from his vantage point he could see a stream. It ran all the way out of the forest and to a settlement, about a mile from the edge of the treeline. Krieger saw chimney smoke spiralling into the turbulent sky. He knew this place.

Climbing carefully but urgently, Krieger made his way down the rocky embankment, negotiating a mass of boulders and slipping occasionally on scattered scree. Gratefully, he descended into the thick forest and kept running until he came upon a clearing. Krieger took a moment to appreciate his freedom, filling his lungs with the smell of it and gazing into the heavens. Clouds crept across the sky, filled with the threat of rain, as the wind steadily picked up.

Without time to linger, Krieger moved on and found the stream he had seen from the edge of the tunnel. He ran into it and eagerly washed away the sewer stench. Following the stream, he soon reached the fringe of the forest. The town was ahead. It was waiting for him. Dark clouds gathered above it, echoing Krieger's mood.

Clenching his fists, he said, 'There will be a reckoning.'

The town square of Galstadt was alive with people. Thronging crowds clapped and danced and laughed as jugglers, fire-eaters and all manner of street entertainers dazzled them with their skill and pantomime. Huge garlands hung from windows and archways; acrobats leapt and whirled amongst the crowds and flower petals filled the air with dazzling colour. Even the darkening sky overhead could not dampen the carnival mood.

A massive cheer erupted from the townsfolk and assembled soldiery as a vast and ornate casket was brought into view. Held aloft by six proud men-at-arms, it shimmered with an unearthly lustre. Behind it rode a retinue of knights mounted on snorting steeds, austere and powerful in full armour. The crowds gathered in their hundreds to welcome the return of their count and his brave knights.

As he rode through the town, Count Gunther Halstein regarded the crowds impassively. His steed stumbled on a loose cobblestone and moved its flank awkwardly. A sudden sharp pain seared Count Gunther's chest, just below his heart, and he grimaced.

'My lord?' Bastion, Gunther's knight captain, was at his side immediately. 'Is it your wound?'

Irritably, the count waved away Bastion's concern. 'These people,' he whispered, resuming his smiling façade, 'they know nothing of the sacrifice, Bastion, the danger beyond these walls.'

'No, they do not,' Bastion replied. His voice held a tinge of knightly arrogance. 'But we survived the Lands of the Dead, with the prize,' he added. 'Let them bask.'

Bastion flashed a confident smile, but the count's gaze travelled upward, to the banner of their order fluttering in the growing breeze; a heart wreathed in flames. Framed against a steel sky, it reminded him of an animal struggling for breath.

For Count Gunther, the endless desert was never far from his thoughts. Despite the cold, he still felt the sun on his back, the sand in his throat and the maddening silence of windless days.

Thunder rumbled overhead, rousing the count from his dark reverie. Ahead of the returning crusaders, the great wooden gates of his keep opened. Rain was falling as the knights filed in, filling the great courtyard beyond. Count Gunther was the last of them. He lingered in the gateway and failed to notice the dispersing crowds as he watched the darkening horizon.

'A storm is coming,' he muttered.

The doors closed, throwing their shadow upon him, shutting the outside world from his sight.

Lenchard the witch hunter stalked from the cell, his hard footfalls resonant against the dungeon floor. He was followed by two templars, wearing the black steel armour of Morr.

The three of them walked quickly down the long corridor from the cell and approached a shallow set of stone steps that led up to the barracks of Thorne Keep. A nigh-on impregnable bastion, the keep rested on a broad spike of rock, surrounded by pine forest. It was a garrison for the Elector Count of Stirland's soldiery, with thick and high walls, so it was also used as a place to hold and interrogate prisoners. Never had one of the detainees escaped – until now.

A guard, a thin, fraught-looking man, wearing a studded leather hauberk and kettle helmet, was waiting for Lenchard and the two templars. The witch hunter emerged menacingly from the gloom. 'The prisoner is gone,' he muttered darkly.

Dieter Lenchard was thick-set, even beneath his leather armour, his facial features bony and well-defined. He wore a severe expression, framed by a tight-fitting skull cap stretched over his head, and the guardsman balked at his formidable presence.

'Where is your sergeant?' Lenchard asked.

The guard tried to muster his voice but could only point towards the steps.

'Captain Reiner,' the witch hunter said, without looking back as he addressed one of the templars, the older of the two, a stern looking man with short black hair and cold eyes. Lenchard marched up the steps, black cloak lashing in his wake, 'with me.'

Reiner turned to the other templar beside him, a bald giant that looked as if he were made of stone, 'Halbranc, wait here until Sigson has finished his work.'

Halbranc nodded and faced the quailing guard.

Like the Black Knights of Morr, the templars' breastplates and greaves were etched with symbols of death and mortality. For many they were a bad omen of impending doom and misfortune.

Confronted with Halbranc, the guard swallowed hard and made the sign of Sigmar.

The massive templar folded his arms and leaned forward. Close up, the guard could see a patchwork of old scars as the shadows pooled into the chiselled depths of the templar's face. Halbranc snarled at him.

The guard shrank away, finding the solid, unyielding wall at his back. 'That's enough,' said Reiner in a cold voice that came from above.

'Yes, Captain Reiner,' Halbranc said dutifully. He looked into the guard's fearful eyes and smiled.

'Just you and me now, my friend,' he whispered.

Mikael, a young Templar of Morr, waited in the courtyard of Thorne Keep, just outside the stables. His comrades, the twins Valen and Vaust, were with him, standing silently. The three of them had been left with the knights' horses, while Reiner, Halbranc and their warrior priest, Sigson, conducted their investigations. It was to be a short stay it seemed – the portcullis was raised and the drawbridge lowered for their departure.

Reiner emerged from the entrance to the barracks, as impassive and unemotional as ever.

'Make our steeds ready,' he said to them as he approached, 'we are leaving soon.'

The twins moved quickly to the stables and began immediately untying the horses' reins, testing stirrups and checking saddles.

'What happened?' Mikael asked.

Reiner fixed the young templar with an icy glare.

'The prisoner has escaped.'

'How is that possible?'

Reiner kept his gaze on Mikael for a moment. The penetrating silence held an unspoken question. It was one Mikael was familiar with, the threat Reiner saw in all inquiring minds.

'By killing at least one of the guards,' he explained coldly.

A pistol shot echoed around the stone courtyard from the barracks.

All in the courtyard started at the sound. The horses whinnied in fear, Valen and Vaust gripping their reins tightly, patting the beasts' flanks to soothe them. Only Reiner betrayed no emotion, as hollow and deadly as the shot reverberating around the keep. It had come from the direction of the cells.

After a moment, Lenchard appeared, tucking a smoking pistol into his belt. Valen held the reins to the witch hunter's steed, which he'd walked from the stables. Without a word, Lenchard took them, securing his pistols and sabre before mounting up. The young templar bowed his head respectfully.

'Inform your priest,' the witch hunter said to Reiner, 'the guard sergeant is in need of Morr's blessing.'

Reiner gathered the reins of his own horse, utterly unmoved. 'How long do we have?' he asked the witch hunter curtly.

Lenchard steadied his steed. His eyes were dark rings of shadow, his face a pepper-wash of stubble.

'The heretic may have an hour, possibly two hours' head start.'

Reiner turned to Valen and Vaust and said, 'Ride on ahead, find his trail.'

The twins nodded as one. Sometimes their seemingly empathic synchronicity was unnerving, Mikael thought, as he watched them mount up and ride swiftly through the gates.

'Once Sigson is done speaking to the dead guard we will join them,' Reiner said, noting the look of veiled disgust on the witch hunter's face. He ignored it and switched his attention to Mikael.

Ever since that night at Hochsleben, when Kalten had died at the hands of the crazed mortician Merrick, the captain of Morr had watched Mikael closely. The young templar had foreseen his comrade's death in a vision, but spoke nothing of it to Reiner. But he suspected something, Mikael was certain of it. Only Sigson knew for sure.

'He yielded nothing.' The warrior priest Sigson came out of the darkness, face drawn and laboured. Communication with the dead was a gift from their god Morr, protector of the deceased, but it was taxing and often left the priest weak. 'He had a violent death, but that is all I could tell.'

Halbranc followed Sigson. The terrified guard came after, scurrying quickly past the giant templar and into the courtyard.

Reiner was about to mount up when Sigson's voice stopped him. 'However, his face bore some interesting wounds.'

The captain's expression was questioning.

'A mark; carved after death, I believe.'

'A ritual mark?' Mikael asked, abruptly aware of Reiner's gaze upon him, his silence penetrating, searching.

'Perhaps. There was little time for examination. I suspect the other guard was dumped in the sewer. I have performed the binding rites on the body we do have though,' said Sigson, 'and our dead watch sergeant,' he added for Lenchard's benefit.

Reiner addressed the guard who had followed Halbranc out.

'Have your men go down there and find him, it might provide some clue to the fugitive's whereabouts.'

'No,' Lenchard stated curtly, 'I know where Krieger is going. There is but one thing occupying his mind.'

This time it was the witch hunter who received Reiner's questioning gaze.

'The thing that dominates the mind of any killer regarding his captors,' Lenchard said, pausing to steer his horse toward the gate, 'revenge.'

Krieger watched the road from his shelter in the trees. The chilling rain ran off the leafy canopy above and down his face and neck. He crouched, betraying no sign of discomfort. A figure loomed through the downpour, coming towards him. It was a farmer, driving his cart hard, cloak wrapped tight around his body, his hood drawn against the lashing rain. The cart drew nearer, and all other sounds faded. Krieger heard only his own breath. He drew the stolen dagger from his belt and waited until the cart came so close he could see into the man's eyes. The rain smothered Krieger's approach. Lightning cracked. The flash from the blade was the last thing the driver ever saw.

Count Gunther was alone in the dark, empty hall. He sat upon an ornate throne set in the centre of the room. A large window threw grey light into the darkness, illuminating a huge tapestry which dominated the wall before him. The man depicted in it looked just like the count.

Gunther raised a silver goblet to the portrait as he regarded his likeness. A twisted, haggard man bedecked in finery and the coldness of wealth, stared back at him. At the edge of the tapestry were the names of all his forefathers. Soon his would be added to them.

'To you, father.' His voice was edged with bitterness. 'You would be proud.'

Gunther slumped in the seat, exhausted. As the room grew darker he closed his eyes, remembering the desert.

Krieger knelt before him in the stillness of the tent, head bent low. The night was chill and Count Gunther repressed a shudder as he regarded the traitor. Krieger was stripped to the waist; arms and armour removed. Bastion and Rogan waited either side, watching the prisoner. Despite the cold, he did not shiver, nor make any sound or motion.

'You are accused of heresy,' Gunther told him. 'You stole these dark manuscripts from the tomb, why?' He brandished the scrolls before him in a gauntleted hand.

Krieger said nothing.

'Answer me!' Gunther struck his captive hard across the face. Krieger fell to the ground hard but, with effort, dragged himself up.

'What was your purpose here?' Gunther hissed, seizing Krieger's chin to face him.

The traitor's eyes were cold and penetrating. 'To kill you.'

Krieger head butted the count hard in the face. Springing forward he ripped a dagger from Gunther's belt, ramming it into the count's chest.

Bastion and Rogan dove upon Krieger. Rogan punched the traitor in the neck, bringing him down as Bastion disarmed him.

With a grimace, Gunther withdrew the dagger. Blood seeped from the wound onto his tunic. Cries for the surgeon filled his senses as madness and panic took hold.

Thunder resonated around the chamber. Count Gunther awoke,

startled. White heat burned in his chest, as fresh pain sprang from the wound. He looked up, suddenly aware of someone else in the room.

Captain Bastion waited in the shadows. He had taken off his armour and now wore a simple grey tunic and leather breeches, though he still carried a sword at his belt.

'Bastion.' The statement held an unspoken question.

'A matter has arisen that requires your attention, my liege,' Bastion said, bowing respectfully. 'This incessant rain threatens the banks of the Averlecht; there is a danger they may burst.'

The count saw the rain thrashing hard against the window. It was the first time he'd noticed it.

'I have workers buoying up the bank with earth and sandbags,' Bastion told his master. 'There is little else to be done.'

'Good. Keep me informed and I will visit the site in the morning.'

'As you wish, sire.' Bastion bowed, and walked away. He was almost at the door when Gunther spoke. 'What of the other matter?' he asked.

'It has been secured as instructed,' Bastion said, without looking back, and left the room.

Gunther nodded, looking far away into the gloom. 'Good. That is good.'

About an hour after the templars left Thorne Keep, Valen and Vaust found the body of a farmer. He lay in a growing quagmire of earth, face-down and sprawled in the middle of a back road. A cart, presumably once owned by the dead man, lay half embedded in a nearby ditch. The horse was gone; its traces had been slashed.

Mikael crouched next to the farmer in the pouring rain. He'd removed his gauntlet, and rested a hand on the man's neck.

'Still warm,' he said, looking up at Reiner.

The captain had dismounted and was standing with Sigson. Valen and Vaust held the reins of their horses between them, also on foot. The four knights formed a circle around Mikael as they regarded the body. Halbranc was mounted, waiting further up the road, maintaining a silent watch as night crept over the horizon. Lenchard stayed near the other knights, but remained on his steed, preferring not to soil his leather boots with the mud of the road to ascertain facts he already knew.

'This is how you found him?' Reiner asked the brothers.

'Yes, captain,' they answered together.

The farmer's body sank further into the mire. Sigson crouched down next to Mikael and carefully tilted the dead man's head to one side, brushing away the earth clinging to his face.

'We can learn nothing more here,' Reiner said and was about to signal for them to get back on their horses when Sigson spoke.

'There is another mark. Like the one upon the guard.'

Mikael leaned in for a closer look, pulling on his gauntlet.

'Is it a scarab beetle?' Lenchard asked the warrior priest.

'Yes,' Sigson said suspiciously, looking up at the witch hunter. 'How did you know that?'

'It matters not,' Lenchard replied, dismissively, facing the road ahead. 'Krieger has a horse now. We must press on and hope we are not too late.'

'Too late for what?' Sigson asked but Lenchard was already riding away into the darkness.

'To your steeds!' Reiner bellowed, stirring his templars into action.

Sigson seized Reiner's arm, before he could mount his horse. 'What is this? This witch hunter knows more than he's telling us.'

'That is possible.' Reiner's voice was cold and hollow. 'But we are in Herr Lenchard's charge by the order of our temple. It is our duty to deliver him to the heretic.' Reiner looked down at his arm. 'Unhand me.'

Sigson took his hand away and stood back.

Mikael had stood up during the exchange, taking the reins of his and Sigson's horse from Valen, and watched as the two men parted. The tension between the captain and priest was written upon Sigson's face as he turned away from Reiner.

'Do you trust him, Mikael?' Sigson asked quietly as he took the reins of his horse from the young templar.

'I don't know,' Mikael told him, 'but he is certainly hiding something.'

'I agree,' said the warrior priest, then asked, 'Any more dreams since Hochsleben?'

Mikael shook his head.

The old priest held Mikael's gaze a moment, as if determining whether the young knight had told him the truth or not. The rain trickled down his face, tiny rivulets forming in the age lines, coursing to his chin and dripping off the grey spike of beard that jutted out. In his eyes there was a warning. 'Don't ever speak of them to Reiner.'

'I still feel his death on my conscience, Sigson,' Mikael said, watching the others as they mounted their horses.

'As do we all, my son,' said the priest, grunting as he swung himself into his saddle.

Mikael mounted up, trying to crush the memories and push away the dark omens gnawing at his mind.

Overhead, the storm wracked the sky with forks of lightning and tremulous thunder, as the silhouette of a man hurried to the outer wall of Galstadt. Unseen by the workers, toiling hard in the downpour, he moved along the wall quickly like a creeping shadow, before plunging into the deepening tributary that fed the town's wells and sewers.

Limbs aching, his muscles fuelled by vengeful desire, Krieger swam through the shallow drain in the town's wall, diving deep to crawl through the murky water, beneath the rusting bars that went only halfway to the ground. He emerged into a wide tunnel which was illuminated by a narrow shaft in the wall to his left. Krieger crept into it and climbed up a shallow incline, the water gushing below him. Reaching the top of the shaft, he heaved opened an iron grate blocking his ascent and levered himself out.

He had emerged in a long chamber, probably the lowest level of the keep. Barrels and sacks were strewn about the room. Krieger waited for a moment in the silence, getting his bearings. He was in the east wing storeroom. Across a corridor and up a flight of stairs he would be in the great hall. Padding quietly down the low room, the rain thrumming distantly beyond the walls, Krieger saw a knight ahead with his back to him.

Drawing his dagger, he crept silently towards his prey.

Count Gunther and Captain Bastion stood upon a grassy ridge at the outskirts of Galstadt. They wore heavy cloaks, with hoods drawn, to ward off the unrelenting rain.

'If that river is breached, Bastion, it will flood the town, the lower levels of the keep and we'll lose many lives,' the count told him.

'We are doing all in our power to prevent that,' Bastion replied, looking at the workers below as they strived frantically to reinforce the bank.

Men toiled with great heaps of earth as others brought fresh mounds on wooden barrows. Some drove carts through the worsening mire with rocks gathered from the edge of the mountains, some three miles away, and sand-filled sacking. They fought in the constant rain, stripped down to the waist, digging trenches to lessen the river's strength.

Bastion looked back to the horizon, hoping for a sign that the storm might abate. Instead, he saw a rider coming towards them from the town.

'Knight Garrant,' Count Gunther addressed the rider as he approached. He reined in his steed, dismounted and trod steadily up to the ridge. Garrant was a broad man, half armoured with breastplate and vambraces, and wearing a heavy, cowled cloak. When he got to the top of the ridge, he pulled back his hood revealing a noble face, framed by thick reddish hair.

'My liege,' the knight's voice was severe. 'I have bad news.'

The count grew suddenly pale, his eyes questioning.

'It is Rogan, my lord. He's dead.'

Gunther regarded Rogan's corpse, slumped against the interior wall of the keep's east tower. He was joined by Bastion and Garrant, the redhaired knight carrying a lantern. Inside, the tower was dark and fairly bare; just a bench and an empty rack for stowing weapons. It was commonly used as a watch station. A stout trapdoor was in the centre of the circular chamber, which led down to the lower levels. Two wooden doors, opposite each other, allowed egress to the walls of the keep

– this was where the count and his knights had entered. Wind whipped through a thin window that looked out over Galdstadt, making the lantern flame flicker. It cast ghoulish shadows over Rogan's body.

'In the name of Sigmar, how could this happen?' Count Gunther asked sombrely.

Garrant crouched down next to the body, setting the lantern down and examining the dead man's head. It hung limply at an unnatural angle.

'His neck is broken,' he uttered flatly.

'He was with us in the Lands of the Dead,' Captain Bastion hissed anxiously into his lord's ear.

'I know that,' snapped the count.

Bastion stalked away, clearly disturbed. He went to the window for some air: Rogan was already beginning to stink. He looked through the thin opening and saw something to take his mind off his dead comrade. 'We have visitors,' he said.

Count Gunther and Garrant looked over to him.

Bastion's expression was severe as he peered outwards. 'They are knights of Morr.' It was a bad omen.

'Remove the body and gather the knights,' ordered the count, a grim feeling clutching at him. 'We'll meet them in the town square.'

The templars of Morr rode wearily towards the gates of Galstadt; they had travelled through the night in horrendous conditions and were at the end of their endurance. They passed numerous workers as they went. Mikael noticed the looks of fear, mistrust and even hatred as the men paused in their labours to regard the Black Knights.

'It is man's nature to fear mortality,' Sigson, who was riding alongside the young templar, told him. 'They fear us and so they hate and distrust us.'

'It is our greatest weapon,' Reiner's voice was like chilling sleet, from the head of the group. 'Never forget that.'

Mikael eyed him carefully and was silent. There was little that escaped the captain's attention. It frightened the young knight.

'A warning, templars,' intoned Lenchard who led the party, his voice powerful even through the downpour. 'The people of Galstadt are devout Sigmarites, their knights are of the Order of the Fiery Heart; they are their protectors and are not well known for their tolerance of other faiths, particularly Morr worshippers.'

'We come to them as allies, though,' said Valen, nonplussed. He tightened his grip on the company standard, partly from the slickness caused by the rain and partly to reassert the grip on his faith, of which the banner was a symbol.

'They will not see it that way. Tread carefully, that is all.'

The templars reached the outer gates of Galstadt, a small party of guards watching them intently, through the driving rain, from atop a high wall.

'Who are you and what is your business?' one of the guards asked, shouting to be heard. He wore a simple grey tunic, leather armour and pot-helmet, and carried a hooked halberd.

'I am Dieter Lenchard, an emissary of Sigmar's holy church,' the witch hunter said, brandishing a talisman etched with the twin-tailed comet. 'Open the gate,' he demanded.

The guard called below and the gate swung open slowly.

The Black Knights filed through into a small walled courtyard, which was little more than a staging area. There were stables on either side, each protected by a short wooden roof. A second gate at the far end of the courtyard, a stout-looking gatehouse appended to it, led into the town proper. As they entered, the guards waiting for them retreated fearfully and made the sign of Sigmar.

Reiner could barely hide his contempt as the templars of Morr and the witch hunter dismounted, allowing their horses to be led to the stables by grooms.

'Follow me,' Lenchard told the knights, bidding a guard to open the second gate and walking out of the courtyard and into the town itself.

Mere feet into Galstadt, the streets thronging with dour looking people, a beggar stumbled into Reiner, dropping a gnarled stick. The captain reached out and grabbed the wretch's arm.

'My apologies noble lord,' the beggar said, from beneath a thick black hood. The poor creature was obviously blind and pawed at the knight to get his bearings.

Reiner released his grip, disgust on his face, and watched coldly as the beggar slumped to his knees and clawed around in the dirt, searching for his walking stick. Mercifully, he found it quickly and shuffled off into the rain-soaked crowds.

Mikael bit back his anger. Reiner despised the weak and the poor. To him they were little better than the foul creatures they hunted. 'A weak body leads to a weak mind,' was Reiner's creed. 'That way there is only darkness.'

The remembered words of the doctrine in his thoughts, Mikael followed the rest of the knights as they made their way further into Galstadt. When they reached the town square, they stopped. Before them were six mounted knights. They wore half-armour, with the symbol of a heart wreathed in flames over their breast and left shoulder. Their swords were drawn.

'What have you embroiled us in witch hunter?' Sigson hissed accusingly.

Lenchard ignored him, instead addressing the mounted knights. 'I seek an audience with Count Gunther Halstein,' he began, 'on a matter of some import.'

'I am he,' one of the knights, his armour slightly more ornate and arrayed with decorative gold filigree, said from the middle of the group. It was the count. The man had a regal bearing and wore a closely cropped beard that showed signs of premature grey. His eyes were haunted by dark shadows and betrayed the austere façade, as he regarded the strangers suspiciously.

'What is this matter of which you speak?' Count Gunther asked.

Lenchard held the count's gaze. 'A man called Karl Krieger,' he said.

Count Halstein's face darkened briefly, then a mask of indifference slipped over it. 'He was executed this very morning for crimes of heresy, after interrogation by witch hunters. Why should I be concerned about a dead man?'

'Because he has escaped and I was to be his interrogator.'

The count was unable to keep the shock and fear from his face, this time. He instantly thought of Rogan, dead in the tower.

'Holy Sigmar,' he breathed, realising what had happened at once. 'He's already here.'

Rogan's body lay on a stout wooden table in one of the keep's halls. It was a sparse chamber with a lofty ceiling, crossed with thick wooden beams. Faded portraits and tarnished militaria clung to the walls. A dust clogged arras hung down one side of the room, on sharp hooks. The dead knight had been stripped of his apparel. A blanket covered the lower half of his body.

Count Gunther and Captain Bastion presided over the body on one side of the table, while on the other Sigson examined the dead knight, the witch hunter having convinced the count that the priest of Morr might be able to learn something useful. Gunther had refused communication with the corpse though.

Reiner, Mikael and the other knights of Morr waited patiently behind Sigson. The warrior priest conducted his work in silence. Mikael caught the dark glances of the Sigmarites – Garrant and two others waiting in the shadows at the edge of the hall – and saw they were still armed. The tension was almost palpable. He didn't need the prescience of Morr to tell him there was danger here. And there was a stench about the place too. Perhaps this was a sign from his god, for it reeked of death.

'Strangulation,' Sigson asserted, pointing out the lividity around the neck. He too had stripped out of his breastplate and arm greaves. He moved the head to one side, inspecting the cheek. 'No mark,' he muttered.

'What do you mean?' Count Gunther asked.

'Krieger has killed two already, that we know of,' Sigson told him, 'and each had a mark carved into the cheek.'

'Perhaps he was interrupted,' Bastion suggested.

'Whatever the cause, Bastion, I want Krieger found and brought before me,' Gunther ordered, before returning his attention to the priest. 'My men and I are tired and their forbearance is stretched to the limit. This is over,' he said, pulling the blanket back over Rogan's body, much to Sigson's chagrin.

'Garrant, conduct a full search of the keep. I want double watches come nightfall.'

Garrant uttered his compliance and left the room.

'And what would you have us do, count?' Reiner said. It was the first time he'd spoken since entering the keep.

'I will make a barrack house available, other than that keep out of our way.'

Reiner nodded, but his cold eyes never left Count Gunther's face.

'I have some questions,' Lenchard said from the shadows then added, addressing Reiner, 'Your men look weary. I suggest you get them to the barracks.'

'Halbranc,' the captain of Morr said, without averting his icy gaze from the witch hunter, 'you heard Herr Lenchard.'

Halbranc nodded and looked over to Sigson.

'I'll follow shortly,' said the priest, washing his hands in a clay bowl. Reiner showed no signs of movement. Clearly, he wanted to hear what the witch hunter had to say.

With that, Halbranc and the other knights left the chamber.

The barrack house was at the end of a long corridor, past the keep's training ground. Mikael watched as knights paired off and sparred with each other using wooden swords. He felt a sudden pain in his skull – it had happened before, in Hochsleben, just before he'd been attacked by Merrick. Wincing, Mikael saw four Sigmarite knights approaching.

Halbranc tensed beside him, but they continued towards the barrack house.

As they passed, the Sigmarites regarded Mikael and his comrades darkly, and one leant out, jarring Vaust's shoulder deliberately.

'Little better than necromancers,' the Sigmarite muttered.

'What did you say?' Vaust demanded, whirling on his heel to confront him.

Mikael went to lightly restrain him, but Vaust shook the young templar off. 'No, speak up!'

The Sigmarite, a thin-faced, white-haired youth flashed a contemptible smile. 'Those who consort with the dead are not to be trusted,' he spat.

Vaust drew his sword, Valen likewise behind him. Mikael tried to stand between them, but the Sigmarites had drawn their blades too.

'Knights of Morr, sheath your swords,' Halbranc warned, placing his massive form between them. Even the belligerent Sigmarites backed down before the giant templar. But the white-haired Sigmarite felt the presence of his fellows behind him and found his courage. Eyes filled with violent intent, he was about to act when a command stopped him.

'Put down your sword!' Garrant bellowed, stalking towards them. 'What is going on here?' he demanded angrily.

'Nothing, just a misunderstanding,' Halbranc said. 'We'll be on our way,' he added, holding Vaust hard by the back of his neck and turning him around. Mikael followed suite, and as the knights were walking away he heard Garrant mutter. 'The sooner, the better.'

Halbranc stopped. An uneasy silence filled the corridor. Mikael heard the leather of the giant's gauntlets crack into a fist. He could feel the gaze of Garrant and his fellows boring into him. Halbranc released his grip. They walked away. Mikael breathed again.

It was night. The scrape of Halbranc's whetstone against his sword blade penetrated the frustrated silence. He sat on the end of a small cot and worked hard at the weapon – a mighty zweihander and one of several blades he carried – until its edge was razor-keen. He seemed lost in the routine of it as if scraping out past sins that tarnished his blade. Mikael knew little about the giant templar, save that he was a mercenary once and had fought in many armies, across many continents. Halbranc never spoke of it. Perhaps he didn't care to.

The two brothers, Valen and Vaust, were sitting on stools at a low wooden table in the middle of the room. They had found a deck of cards and were playing out a game of skulls. Like Halbranc, they were restless, preferring action instead of prolonged bouts of inactivity.

Reiner and Sigson were still absent, doubtless conversing with the witch hunter, Lenchard. None of them had slept.

Mikael sat on the opposite cot to Halbranc, his attention on the window next to him. Outside, in the flickering light of several lanterns, the shadows of workers still toiled. As he stared up into the blackened sky, Mikael felt his eyelids grow heavy as a dream engulfed him...

A great sun burned down upon the barren desert.

Mikael was alone in a mighty desert that seemed like it was on fire. Yet he felt no heat or wind.

Cresting a mighty rise he looked across a deep valley. An old man dressed in black robes was standing upon a high dune. With a gnarled finger he beckoned Mikael across the valley towards him.

Mikael took a tentative step forward. His foot plunged into a mire of sand and suddenly the entire side of the dune was shifting, collapsing beneath him!

He fell, tumbling down the side of the valley. Spitting sand from his mouth, he looked up into the sunlight. The man had gone.

A sudden trembling began beneath him. Mikael scrambled back, clawing handfuls of sand as he did so. A great spike pierced the valley floor before him, reaching ever higher into the burning sky. A tower of obsidian followed, surging upwards, pushing out great waves of sand. Slowly, a huge black skull emerged like some terrible, mythic beast. Rivulets of sand flowed from the gargantuan eye and nose sockets and as the mouth broke through the churning dunes created by its emergence, a huge black door was revealed. It opened and there stood a towering figure.

Its mummified flesh bore the taint of ages and it wore the armour of a knight of Sigmar. It reached out towards Mikael with a filthy talon-like hand. The creature's mouth opened and uttered, 'Setti-Ra...'

Mikael woke with a sudden start. There was a commotion outside. Halbranc was on his feet, a short sword in his hand, going for the door. Valen had fallen asleep at the card table but sprang up, alert at the sound. Vaust was nowhere to be seen.

Grabbing his own blade, Mikael went to join Halbranc. He pulled the door open and saw three Sigmarite knights running away down the corridor. Another knight was running towards the barracks. It was Vaust.

When Vaust reached the door, he was panting heavily for breath. 'They've found another body,' he gasped.

Twenty knights had gathered in the hall of the east wing when Mikael and the others arrived, Count Gunther and his retinue amongst them. They encircled the body of a slain knight and the Morr worshippers had to force their way through.

'Back away,' ordered the count, fighting to get past the throng of knights. 'Holy Sigmar,' he breathed. The knight lay slumped within an alcove, his face covered in shadows.

Reiner and Sigson appeared amidst the crowd. The warrior priest went instantly to the dead knight, crouching down to examine it.

The knights fell abruptly into silence. Mikael heard mutterings of discontent. Valen and Vaust closed in around him, Halbranc at their back. Reiner kept his cold gaze on Sigson but held his sword hilt ready.

'He has been strangled,' Sigson told the count. 'With some force – his neck is broken.' Sigson carefully tilted the dead knight's head, searching for another mark. Light spilled onto the corpse, illuminating the face.

'By the hand of Morr,' Vaust gasped. It was the knight he had confronted in the corridor.

'You argued with this man,' said Garrant, accusingly. 'Where were you tonight?'

'I was restless,' Vaust admitted, 'So I toured the east wing.' He cast a sideways glance at Reiner. There would be repercussions from this. The captain took disobedience very seriously.

'And you met up with this knight,' Garrant continued, 'to settle your differences.'

There were angry murmurings from the Sigmarites. Mikael felt the same tension he had back in the corridor with Halbranc.

'No. I saw no one,' Vaust protested through gritted teeth.

'You drew swords first,' Garrant said. 'I saw it with my own eyes.'

Some of the Sigmarites nodded in agreement. Mikael noticed that the count had moved to the back of the group, Bastion alongside him.

'Is the chamber intact?' he heard Count Gunther mutter above the increasingly belligerent Sigmarites.

The captain nodded.

'You killed him,' one of the knights from the crowd spat suddenly, stepping towards Vaust. Valen put him down with one punch.

The hall exploded into chaos. Three Sigmarite knights waded forward to take on Valen, but Halbranc and Reiner intervened. Halbranc smashed the first two into the crowd, while Reiner brought the other to his knees with a powerful uppercut. Several of the knights of Sigmar bellowed battle oaths and charged in, weapons drawn.

Mikael drew his sword. Valen and Vaust followed his lead.

A pistol shot rang out, reverberating around the mighty hall. Lenchard stood upon a table, smoke rising from the barrel of the weapon.

'Cease!' he commanded. 'Listen.'

From outside there was a sound like thunder.

'The river,' Count Gunther realised suddenly. He turned to Garrant. 'Gather up all the men,' he said. 'If the bank breaks the flood waters will take this keep and us with it.'

Garrant nodded, gave a last dark glance at the knights of Morr, and started bellowing orders.

Reiner approached the count. 'This is what Krieger has been waiting for,' he said. 'To slip away and kill again in the confusion.'

Gunther looked him in the eye. 'I need every man on that river bank.'

'Then let us help.'

The count hesitated at first then nodded. 'Very well.'

Reiner turned to his knights and gestured for them to follow.

As they were leaving Mikael saw Gunther conversing with Bastion once more. 'Take two men,' he said, 'and guard the vault – lock it.'

Mikael had no time to linger and left the hall to join his comrades. Again the strange stench of death assailed him.

'This place reeks of the dead,' Mikael whispered to Halbranc.

'Careful lad,' said the giant, 'they'll be blaming us for that too,' he added, smiling.

Thunder raged in the heavens and lightning split the blackness.

Mikael carried two heavy sacks of sand towards the breach in the bank. At the river there was chaos.

A cart lay on its side, sinking into the earth. Men heaved at it, trying to free the thrashing horse trapped beneath. Others held ropes onto workers wading into the river itself with sacks and rocks. Workers and knights battled together, heaving great clods of earth into the raging river flow. A great train of them moved from the keep to the riverbank, bringing earth in barrows, pails and tools in an effort to save the keep and the town. The rain battered men down as they struggled to lift the sodden earth, digging the crude trenches ever deeper to divert the water.

Mikael slung down a second sack. Straightening his back and wiping the moisture from his brow, he looked up at the keep. A flash of lightning cast it in stark silhouette. It was a dark and forbidding image. Another bolt lit up the night and through the lashing rain, Mikael thought he saw a figure, away from the river, creeping up a shallow embankment towards the keep. Blinking back the rain and buffeting wind he looked back again, but the figure was gone. He trod back up the shallow rise to the keep.

Halbranc was in the courtyard.

'Works up a sweat eh, lad?'

Mikael nodded. His muscles burned, they'd been fighting the flood waters for over an hour.

They headed towards the cellars, through a trapdoor in the courtyard and down shallow steps, where supplies of sand bags and barrows were kept.

Mikael stopped part way down the stairs. 'Something is wrong,' he said.

'What is it, Mikael?' Halbranc drew his short sword, searching in the half darkness.

Mikael advanced slowly. The torches set in the cellar walls spluttered and cast flickering shadows. The floor shimmered and moved.

'It's flooded,' Mikael said, taking the last of the steps and plunging, waist deep, into the water.

'Can you smell that?' he whispered. The storm outside was dulled down here, resonant and foreboding. Suddenly the rest of the knights seemed very far away.

'Smells like death.' Halbranc watched the darkness ahead.

An ill-feeling grew in the pit of Mikael's stomach as they waded through the flooded cellar.

'Wait,' he hissed. Something was floating down towards them on a light current. Mikael drew his sword.

The thing drifted into the corona of light cast by one of the torches. It was a man's body, partially decomposed.

'Another knight?' Halbranc asked, covering his mouth at the stench.

'I don't know,' Mikael said, leaning in close. 'His neck is broken,' he added, looking back towards Halbranc, 'and I've smelled this stench since we arrived. This man has been long dead.'

A shadow passed over the entrance to the cellar above.

'Down here!' Halbranc bellowed.

Four men entered the trapdoor into the cellar; Lenchard followed by Count Gunther and two of his knights.

'We may have another victim,' Halbranc told them, picking a torch off the wall to illuminate the man's rotting features.

Gunther's eyes grew wide and fearful. 'That's Karl Krieger,' he rasped.

'Then we are looking for the wrong man,' Mikael told them.

Realisation dawned upon the count's face. He plunged into the water, pushing past the templars of Morr and the floating corpse. 'The vault,' he muttered, wading down the flooded corridor, fuelled by anxious desperation.

Mikael sheathed his sword and followed. After a few minutes they reached a corner, around it a shallow slope led up to a massive iron door. Count Gunther stopped. The rain outside throbbed against the walls as the door swung open on creaking hinges.

At Mikael's urging, they moved towards the door. Halbranc gripped it and heaved it open.

Inside was a simple stone room. At the centre rested an ornate throne, encrusted with jewels and worn gold filigree. At the foot of the throne lay three dead knights. Mikael recognised one of them as Bastion. They had all been strangled.

'Just what did you bring back with you from the desert?' Mikael asked Count Gunther, drawing his sword.

The count turned on him, initially shocked the templar even knew of it then said, 'My father... Falken Halstein...'

In the thick shadows at the back of the room, something stirred. Stepping out of the gloom was a creature that resembled Gunther. Its tarnished armour bore the emblem of the fiery heart. Its flesh was desiccated, worn to shrivelled leather by the hostile conditions of the desert. As it lumbered towards them, its eyes flared with remembered hate.

It came at Gunther. The Sigmarite knights rushed forward to protect him. Swinging its mighty arm, the creature smashed one of the knights into the wall with a sickening crunch of bone. From a rotting scabbard it drew a rusted sword and ran the second through, lifting him screaming into the air. As the beast withdrew its sword, the knight slipping off like discarded meat, Halbranc charged at it, hacking down two-handed upon its arm but his blade rebounded.

'Its skin is like iron,' he cried, fending off a blow that almost knocked him down. Mikael went to his side.

The creature held up a withered hand. Mikael couldn't move, halted by the malevolent will of the undead knight. It spoke with a voice that held the weight of ages. 'I am Setti-Ra. A reign of terror shall sweep your lands and beyond at my rebirth. Slumbering legions will rise once more and bathe the deserts in blood. Kneel now before me.'

Mikael felt a terrible weight pressing down upon him. His legs were buckling against it. He tried to mutter a prayer to Morr, but was unable. Halbranc was on his knees; sweat coursing down his reddened face.

'Only fire and the will of Sigmar can purge the creature from this body.'

The voice of Lenchard was like crystal water as it broke the power of Setti-Ra. With the burden lifted, Mikael arose. Halbranc struggled to his feet beside him.

The Black Knights backed away.

Around the chamber, the torches spluttered and died as the water lapped languidly at their feet.

'We must get to higher ground,' Mikael said, 'draw the creature out.'

'No.' It was Count Gunther. Sword drawn, he blocked the doorway. Mikael noticed the creature's gaze was fixed upon the count.

Lenchard saw it too. 'He is under the creature's thrall,' he growled.

Mikael pushed the witch hunter aside, parrying a blow from Gunther's sword. Behind him, Setti-Ra advanced.

'Keep it back!' Mikael cried, hearing the clash of steel as Halbranc and Lenchard fought the creature.

Count Gunther's eyes were covered by a milky white sheen. When he spoke, it was as if he were the creature's mouthpiece.

'The will of Setti-Ra be done, the living shall perish before his–'

The count collapsed to the ground before he could finish. Reiner stood behind him. The other knights of Morr were with him. They had heard the commotion below and gone down to investigate. The captain's eyes grew suddenly wide and a strange keening sensation resonated in Mikael's skull. The young templar dove to the side as, dragging Count Gunther clear, Reiner bellowed, 'Down!'

Lenchard was smashed through the doorway and tumbled down the slope.

'Out. Now!' Reiner cried.

Halbranc backed out of the room, heaving Mikael with him as the beast lumbered after them.

'Seal the doors,' Reiner ordered.

Valen and Vaust pushed the doors shut as Sigson slid down a heavy, metal brace. From within, the distant thudding retort of the creature's blows could be heard almost instantly.

Outside the vault, Mikael nodded his thanks to his captain who responded coldly.

'That door will not hold it long, make ready.'

'Our swords won't kill it,' Mikael said, 'we must get to higher ground and burn it.'

A sudden powerful blow echoed against the iron door as part of it bent outwards.

'The barrel ramp...' Count Gunther muttered, sluggishly. He was slowly coming round and rubbed his head where Reiner had struck him to break the creature's hold. 'It leads to the hall above...' He pointed down the slope where a corridor branched off.

Reiner looked over at it, then back at the count.

'It wants me dead,' Count Gunther said. 'My father killed this creature long ago; in me it sees him and desires vengeance. I can lure it.'

Sigson went over to the count, and helped him to his feet. 'Can you stand?'

The count nodded.

Another blow from within the vault caused a hefty split in the iron.

'We must leave, now,' Reiner told them. 'Vaust, lead them,' he ordered.

The young templar ran to the head of the group and back down the slope towards the corridor Gunther had shown them, his brother following closely behind.

Halbranc hefted Lenchard onto his shoulder as Mikael and Reiner went last with the count. They were backing down the slope, a few feet from the vault, when the iron door finally fell with a screech of twisting metal. Bolts came free from the wall with a shower of dust and debris, and Setti-Ra stepped out onto the slope, driven by primal instincts.

The knights of Morr goaded the creature on. They retreated up the barrel ramp, making sure the creature saw where they were going. Ahead, Vaust smashed through a trapdoor that led to the hall.

Crouched in the room above, the two brothers heaved an unconscious Lenchard out of the cellars from Halbranc's shoulder. The giant followed, then Sigson, then Reiner, Mikael and the count.

'The creature is close,' the weakened count gasped. 'There,' he said, pointing to another archway.

Heaving the ailing count between them, Reiner and Mikael were right behind the others who stood in the great hall. The tapestry of Falken Halstein loomed large, about to witness his horrifying undead self.

Putting the witch hunter down, Halbranc hefted a massive torch from an iron sconce. Mikael and Reiner did the same.

'Protect the count,' Reiner said to Valen and Vaust. The brothers took Gunther between them to an alcove at the back of the room.

With a bellow of rage, Setti-Ra emerged from the trapdoor opening.

Halbranc lunged forward, thrusting the burning torch into the creature's body. It hurled the templar aside. The torch clattered to the ground, and was smothered. Flames licked over the aging corpse but died quickly.

Sigson stepped forward, the holy book of Morr in his hand.

'In the name of Morr, I compel you,' he uttered, his voice loud and powerful.

The creature stopped as if suddenly held by an invisible bond.

'I compel you,' Sigson repeated, stepping towards it, arm outstretched, his open palm facing towards it. Mikael and Reiner thrust their torches at the beast. Sigson screamed and fell to the ground as Setti-Ra broke his hold.

Though the undead thing burned, the flames were dying out quickly.

'Force it into the tapestry,' Mikael cried, launching himself at the creature. At the same time, Halbranc rammed into it with his shoulder and Reiner tackled the beast's legs. It toppled, slowly like a felled tree, tearing at the huge portrait that caught alight with the remaining flames licking its body. The tapestry pulled free and smothered the foul creature, fire spreading eagerly now over the corpse, as it thrashed and flailed for terrible unlife.

Flames mirrored in his eyes, Gunther looked at the burning form of his father, at the tapestry destroyed and his family history with it.

With the knights of Morr encircling it, the creature gradually stopped struggling and slumped down amidst a pall of foul smoke as it was burned to ash, the spirit of Setti-Ra banished along with it.

'Please,' Gunther rasped, tears in his eyes, 'put him out.'

It was dark in the infirmary. Mikael stared from one of the windows onto the town below. The rain had abated at last and the waters were dispersing. Workers shored up the earthen banks, to make certain they would hold. Across the darkened sky, there was a light to the south as the sun began to rise. Looking back into the room, he saw Lenchard was awake. Reiner and the others waited silently in the shadows. Sigson was by the witch hunter's side.

'You owe us some answers,' he said.

Lenchard's head bore a thick bandage and his face was covered in small cuts and bruises. He winced as he smiled back at the warrior priest.

'There is a cult called the Scarabs,' he relented. 'Fanatical men, they worship the Tomb King Setti-Ra, believing the heart of he who defeated their king would bring about his resurrection.'

'Gunther's father,' Sigson asserted.

'Yes, but they need the living heart and since Falken Halstein was dead, they came for his son,' Lenchard said, getting up out of bed.

'Krieger could not have known that Setti-Ra had inhabited the body of Falken Halstein; such a body could not sustain an undead lord. I was wrong; Krieger came here with a mission, not for revenge but to kill Count Gunther and take his heart. He stumbled upon the creature and it killed him, and so we are still no closer to finding the cult,' he continued, strapping on his weapons.

'*We*,' said Reiner coldly.

From a pouch by his bedside Lenchard produced a scroll of parchment, which he gave to the captain.

'This is a missive from your temple,' he explained as Reiner read it, 'stating that you and your knights are seconded into my service until the cult is found or it is deemed fit to release you.'

Sigson laughed mirthlessly and walked out of the room.

Reiner sealed the scroll up and handed it back to Lenchard. 'So be it,' he said without emotion and left after Sigson. Slowly the rest of the knights followed. Mikael was the last. As he was about to leave, Lenchard said, 'It's Mikael, isn't it?'

Mikael nodded.

'Tell me, Mikael,' the witch hunter said, his expression curious, 'how did you know about the desert? I heard you speak of it to the count.'

A pang of anxiety rose suddenly in Mikael's chest. He thought only the count had heard him.

'I overheard it,' he countered, backing away.

'Of course,' Lenchard said, watching the young templar as he followed after his comrades. 'Of course you did.'

In the hall, the knights of Morr were making ready to leave, checking weapons and armour before heading out the keep and Galstadt for good. The Black Knights had clearly worn out their welcome, and as they fixed blades and tightened belts, a small group of Knights of the Fiery Heart had gathered. The Morr worshippers were standing opposite them, clustered close together, Halbranc putting himself deliberately between Vaust and the glowering Sigmarites. Mikael stood next to the giant, alongside him was Valen. Sigson was sat down, reading his prayer book, while Reiner and Lenchard, who conversed quietly in a nearby corner of the room, waited for Count Gunther so they could observe the proper etiquette for their departure.

As far as Mikael was concerned, it couldn't happen soon enough, his eyes on Garrant, as he and the other knights exchanged dark glances.

'Doubtless, they are making sure we leave,' Halbranc chuckled.

Mikael was about to answer when a door, thudding insistently at the far end of the hall from a strong draught running through the keep, distracted him. Something about it was odd, slightly incongruous.

'Something doesn't feel right,' he said. 'This is taking too long.' Mikael walked quickly over to Garrant, trying to ignore the glare of Reiner, who had been listening to the witch hunter. Sigson saw the young templar too, and put down his prayer book.

'Your lord,' Mikael asked the Sigmarite. 'Where is he?'

Garrant was slightly perturbed by what he perceived as insolence, but something about the young templar's tone got his attention.

'He's in the chapel,' Garrant said, pointing to the door at the end of the room. 'A priest offered to bless his father's ashes.'

'What priest?' Sigson asked, suddenly appearing next to Mikael.

'From the town,' the Sigmarite explained. 'An old blind man.'

The templar and warrior priest looked at each other, with grave faces.

'Show us this chapel,' Mikael said urgently.

The chapel was a small room, little more than an antechamber from the great hall. Inside, there was a stone altar on top of which was an urn containing Falken Halstein's ashes. Count Gunther lay next to the altar. He was dead, his heart removed from his chest. A scarab beetle had been carved into the flesh of his left cheek.

'The blind man,' Mikael said to Sigson, abruptly aware that Reiner and the others had followed them.

'What?'

'The one that stumbled into Reiner at the gates,' he said, pointing at his captain. 'He addressed him as "noble lord". How could he have known he was a knight if he were blind? I saw him on the ridge during the flood, but thought it was my imagination.'

'You're right.' Lenchard spoke with a hint of resignation, standing in the doorway. 'We have been fools; a second Scarab cultist.'

Sigson bent over near the body.

'The blood is still warm,' he said, looking up at Reiner.

A look of disgusted anger passed briefly over the captain's face. 'Get to the gates,' he ordered.

By the time they reached the gatehouse, it was too late. The guard was already dead, his body propped up on a wooden stool. Protruding from his neck was a curved bladed dagger that bore a gold scarab hilt.

Lenchard examined it.

'They are taunting us,' he said bitterly to the knights of Morr standing around him. 'Get the horses,' he told them, rushing out of the gatehouse, heading for the stable yard. 'They have the heart and the means with which to resurrect Setti-Ra. We must find the cultist's trail. We ride, now!'

The knights followed after him, mounting up quickly and racing through the gates. Driving his steed hard, Mikael looked to the lightening horizon and felt time suddenly ebbing away as if an hourglass were turned and they were all slipping through it.

SANCTITY

Nick Kyme

Dawn light crept over the horizon as the wagon emerged from the gathering mist, heading for Hochenheim. The driver urged on the beast pulling the huge wagon, and the creature's heaving flanks were lathered in feverish sweat. Behind it, the forest was a dense black line. Drakwald they called it: a place of shadows, fraught with dark imaginings. Yarik knew it well.

From his position in the watchtower, he watched the wagon intently as it got closer to the village gates. Years ago, Yarik had worked as a road warden for Baron Krugedorf. During his tenure guarding the highways of the land Yarik had seen it all. Never, though, had he witnessed a wagon travelling alone in this part of the forest. On the edge of the Drakwald forest, even the villages required defences. Hochenheim itself was surrounded by a solid wooden stockade, with two watchtowers and a stout gate, bolted shut at night. Yet this wagon appeared to be without protection; he couldn't see a single outrider.

Grimacing, Yarik got to his feet.

'Wait here,' he growled to Falker. The young Middenlander, cradling a loaded crossbow, nodded obediently.

A speck of flame flared in the half-light as Yarik drew deeply on his pipe. Below him, Hochenheim was waking. Fires were being stoked to ward off a chill morning, a frail old woman was wringing out clothes before attaching them to a line, and the resonant din of a smithy at his anvil emanated from an unseen forge.

Trudging down the wooden steps of the tower, Yarik saw the gates were opening, as they did every day at dawn. As he reached the village entrance, he tried to rub the arthritis out of his hands, remembering wistfully the lost strength of former days, and went to greet the wagon.

'Ho there,' Yarik called, showing his palm in a gesture for the driver to stop at the open gateway.

The wagon looked even more massive up close. Six stout, iron-shod wheels accommodated its weight, and leather flaps covered both sides. The horse pulling it wore a sacking hood over its head, coarse slits in it serving as eyeholes. It was incredible that one beast could bear such a burden.

Yarik gripped the pommel of his sheathed sword as he went to speak to the driver. He moved to pat the beast's flank, but recoiled when it turned sharply with a muted snarl. The wagonner laid a hand on the horse's rump, soothing the creature's belligerence. He held the reins nonchalantly as he leant back, a bizarre, patchwork coat flapping down over his body. Long, black hair shrouded most of his face, and he wore a thin, curled moustache with a tightly cropped spike of beard. Yarik judged men by their eyes, but this fellow's were difficult to discern, obscured by a tall, wide-brimmed hat.

'State your business,' Yarik barked, his breath misting the cold morning air.

'Greetings noble lord,' uttered the driver silkily. 'I am Zanikoff,' he declared, 'and my business, put simply…' he said, leaping from his seat and landing with a flourish, as a bunch of paper flowers appeared in his hand, '…is entertainment,' Zanikoff concluded, with a devilish smile. A flick of the wrist and the flowers vanished.

Yarik was taken aback by the sudden display and half-drew his sword. 'We don't harbour sorcerers here,' he told the stranger.

Behind him, a crowd had gathered.

'I do not intend to bewitch you,' said Zanikoff plaintively, 'merely beguile you with trickery and show.' He moved beyond the gates and towards the crowd. The flowers reappeared in his other hand. 'It's just sleight of hand,' he explained, with a wink, and put his finger to his lips.

Zanikoff turned his attention to the mystified onlookers. He produced a long cane from one of his coat sleeves and walked over to them, singling out a village maiden. He bowed, and gave her the tattered paper flowers. Blushing, the maiden took them.

'Milady,' Zanikoff purred, before twirling to face a young boy, watching the impromptu pantomime open-mouthed. The boy's eyes sparkled at three silver coins that had appeared in Zanikoff's splayed fingers. Juggling them effortlessly, he threw the coins high into the air. The boy tried to follow, but lost them in the light.

'I know what you're thinking,' Zanikoff said, leaning in towards the boy. 'Where are they?' he whispered. Reaching behind the boy's ear, his hand emerged holding a silver coin. 'Here, all the time,' he said, flicking the coin to the boy, who snatched it eagerly.

'Ladies and gentlemen,' Zanikoff continued, walking back to the wagon, which had made its way through the gates and into the square, Yarik starting at its sudden appearance. 'I am Zanikoff,' he said, doffing his hat with a mock courtly bow, 'and may I present for your edification, your delectation and delight, your sheer, pure and unadulterated gratification...' Zanikoff took a deep breath, observing the befuddled faces with veiled amusement, '...the Carnival of Mystery!' He smacked the side of the wagon with his cane and the leather flap covering it rolled away to reveal a garish banner beneath. Two theatrical masks – one happy, the other sad – were described upon it, surrounded by a myriad of colourful images. Amazing beasts, jugglers, sword swallowers, fire-eaters, clowns and acrobats all vied for the crowd's attention. 'Carnival of Mystery' was etched above and below in faded archaic script, and read by the few literate onlookers. The banner was well worn and cracked in places, but still it drew excited gasps.

'What do you want here?' asked Yarik.

Zanikoff swaggered towards the old soldier theatrically.

'Why, that is simple,' he said, eyes widening with glee, 'to perform.' He rapped three more times on the wagon and the back fell open. A menagerie of gaudy characters issued forth. Fire-eaters painted in bizarre tattoos were joined by brutish strongmen, jesters and jugglers, while musicians played out merry tunes on drums and pipes, wearing fantastical costumes, their faces concealed by decadent masks.

'Plays and pantomime is what we offer,' Zanikoff informed the awe-struck Hochenheimers, 'great tales of valour,' he said deeply, puffing up his chest. 'Tragedy,' he added with a sorrowful frown, 'and comedy!' he concluded raucously, a jester slipping onto his arse to the collective laughter of the entire village.

'Meagre tribute is all we ask,' Zanikoff said, growing serious, shifting his attention back to Yarik. 'To bestow such gifts of mirth and merriment, we crave a simple indulgence.'

Yarik looked back at him nonplussed.

'A stage,' said Zanikoff, a wide grin spreading across his handsome features.

A raised wooden platform in the village square, usually used for storing sacks of grain, was cleared quickly and turned into a makeshift stage. A vast array of backdrops and pantomime furnishings dressed it. The fixtures looked old and slightly tarnished, but the bedazzled villagers of Hochenheim paid these details no heed. A great apple tree overshadowed the stage. It was the biggest in all of Hochenheim and a symbol of the village, its abundant blossoms full of the promise of spring.

Yarik sat on a barrel, away from the thronging crowd that cooed and called, and laughed at the antics of the Carnival of Mystery. Smoking his pipe, he noticed Alderman Greims, and even Mayor Hansat, entranced by the troupe of masked players. Yarik was secretly impressed by their realistic costumes, turning them into maidens, monsters and mythic heroes.

Other entertainments were going on around the main stage, too: a jester performed tumbling tricks and a ventriloquist with a hand puppet regaled a group of children with his talents. It appeared as if they were moving away from the main crowd. The puppet was a bedraggled looking thing, a mangy dog with one eye, but the engrossed youngsters seemed oblivious.

There was no sign of Zanikoff. After introducing the various festivities, he had vanished. Yarik didn't trust him and wanted to know where he was. He swept his gaze across the crowd and thought he saw something in the shadow of the village tavern, the Black Bear. The wagon Zanikoff and his troupe had arrived in was stationed there, along with the hooded steed. As Yarik got up, he didn't relish reacquainting himself with that beast.

Negotiating the crowd, he headed for the wagon. The noise was almost deafening, such were the raucous cheers and thunderous laughter. But Yarik kept his eyes on the tight alley next to the Black Bear and the thing in the shadows that had caught his attention. For a moment, out of the corner of his eye, he thought he saw a lone young girl following the puppeteer further away from the stage, but he soon lost sight of her, more intent on his investigations.

As he got closer, Yarik saw Zanikoff. He was hefting something heavy into the wagon and after a moment inside, emerged unburdened. Yarik's suspicions grew and for a moment he thought about seeking out Falker; he hadn't seen the young Middenlander for hours.

Yarik pressed on, unperturbed, but by the time he reached the Black Bear, Zanikoff had gone. The wagon door was open, so, giving the horse a wide berth, he worked his way around the wagon. Darkness persisted within. He drew his dagger and took a tentative step up inside.

The wagon's interior was vast; it seemed far larger inside than outside. Yarik willed his eyes to adjust quicker to the dark and his beating heart not to thump so loudly. Taking another step, Yarik realised there was something at the back of the wagon, something big. He swore he could hear it breathing, and a horrible stink assailed his nostrils. Another horse? It would explain how the animal he had seen could carry such a burden if it were shared. As Yarik got closer, he discerned a misshapen silhouette, too large and grotesque to be a horse. His days as a road warden, and all the things he had seen dwelling in the deepest bowels of the Drakwald, returned to him and suddenly he knew what this thing was.

'By the gods,' he breathed, reaching slowly for his sword and backing away.

'My noble lord Yarik,' said Zanikoff from behind him.

Yarik turned quickly to find the carnival master blocking his path, his long, sleek silhouette described by the light at the wagon door as he stood just outside.

Yarik's mind and body screamed at him to flee, but somehow, through sheer force of will, he compelled himself to stay. To flee now would mean death, he was certain of that.

Behind him, there was the faint rattling of chains as the creature shifted. Yarik started to slide out his sword.

'Would you like to peek?' Zanikoff intoned playfully.

Yarik shook his head weakly, mouthing the words he was desperate to articulate. The drone of the crowd was distant now, as if heard from underwater. 'No?' Zanikoff answered for him. 'Tell me,' he said, 'do you know what curiosity did to the cat?'

Yarik couldn't speak, his mouth sketching words noiselessly. He couldn't even shake his head. Hot breath lapped at his neck; the nause-ating stench of decay came with it, making him retch and it took all of his resolve not to vomit. Warm piss trickled down his leg and tears filled his eyes, as all those years of hunting and fighting in the dark, all that fortitude and bravery, were stripped away.

'I thought not,' Zanikoff said, stepping back from the wagon's entrance. 'Let me educate you.' The door slammed shut and Yarik was trapped.

Outside, Zanikoff watched with some satisfaction as the wagon rocked violently back and forth, the cries of the ex-road warden quickly muted, much like his fellow soldier's had been. Molmoth was ever ravenous, his appetite seldom sated for long.

In the distance, a mother cried out for her child, but the roaring crowd, oblivious in adulation, smothered her desperate call.

Zanikoff smiled, watching as the players sprang through the village, spreading their gifts. The seeds had been sown and soon, very soon, the harvest would begin.

The beating of drums was like thunder across the open plain. Atop a craggy rise a force of knights knelt in prayer, their silver armour gleaming, framed against a blackening horizon. They surrounded a great stone temple with two doves flying above it, despite the approaching storm. A priestess stood at the centre of the penitent warriors, a sword at her side, a book in her hand. She looked down at the foot of the great rise where their enemies gathered, eager for slaughter.

To the west, there massed a mighty horde, thousands strong, black banners fluttering. Armoured warriors, faces obscured by metal, stood side-by-side with loping daemons. Whelp masters held snarling hounds as they strained at the leash, while above the sound of drums was joined by the beating of wings. A champion of the Dark Gods waited amongst them, riding a huge and fearsome steed. His armour was the colour of night and the slits in his helm flared with flame-red malevolence.

From the east came rotting warriors encased in husks of rusted armour, their tarnished blades held aloft in tribute. Daemons: horned, cyclopean creatures riddled with decay, capered with them. Their silent lord sat upon an emaciated steed. A ragged hood concealed his face, and pustule ravaged, bone-thin hands clutched a pitted scythe.

At some unseen command, the armies of darkness charged, zealous fury lending them vigour. The knights rose as one to meet them. The priestess raised her sword, tears streaming down her face.

Fury charged the air and the smell of steel filled it. The sound of the charging legions resonated throughout the hillside and then, at last, as the three armies met, a great peal of thunder roiled across the heavens and lightning tore down with all the anger of the gods.

'Wake up.'

Steel crashed.

'Mikael…'

Blood ran like rain.

'Wake up.'

Lightning flashed.

'Mikael!'

Mikael awoke, gasping for breath, as strong hands shook him. Cold pricked at his sweat soaked face. His heart beat with the sound of remembered thunder. Instinctively, he reached for his sword. He found the templar blade readily, felt the skull-shaped pommel.

'Easy son,' said a giant man clad in thick, black armour, wrought with sigils of death and mortality. They were the symbols of their god, Morr. It was Halbranc, his brother-at-arms.

'You slept like the dead,' he said, voice deep and resonant. He crouched over the young knight, a broad smile cracking his battle-scarred face.

Mikael looked around, trying to get his bearings. He was surrounded by trees. A light snow, drifting in a fitful winter breeze, laid a white veneer over their camp. The others were already up it seemed; the previous night's fire a blackened scar on the forest floor. Mikael hugged his black cloak around him. He'd stripped off his black armour. It lay cradled in a blanket. Recall rushed back.

They'd been in the Drakwald for three days, hunting in the shadows and the dark. They'd left their horses at the Road Warden's Rest, a fortified coaching inn several miles back, as the forest was too thick and too dangerous for steeds to venture into. They'd been searching blindly for a renegade, with no guarantee of success, a warlock of the Cult of the Burning Hand.

Halbranc stood up. His formidable presence cast a long shadow; he was every inch the avenging knight of Morr. The hilt of his zweihander protruded from beneath his cloak and was strapped to his back. Snow fell upon his bald pate, but his chiselled features betrayed no discomfort.

'Strap on your armour,' he said, passing Mikael a breastplate with a gauntleted hand. 'Valen has found the renegade's trail.'

'You are certain it is Kleiten?' asked Reiner, without emotion. He stood over the young templar scout, one hand resting on the pommel of his blade.

'I cannot be sure,' Valen answered his captain, 'but something has come this way recently and the earth is scorched, yet there are no signs of burnt kindling.'

Reiner turned to Sigson; his cold blue eyes held a question.

'The cult has been known to use the Wind of Aqshy in its magics,' said the warrior priest, drawing his cloak tight to his body as he suppressed a shiver.

Reiner held Sigson's gaze, unmoving.

'Kleiten is a fire wizard,' Sigson elaborated, wiping an encrusted veneer of frost from his grey spike of beard.

'Your knowledge of the arcane is… unsettling,' said Reiner with some consideration. He turned back to Valen, who was already on his feet. His twin brother, Vaust was alongside him.

'Find what's keeping Halbranc,' said Reiner. 'We follow the trail.'

Vaust nodded, hurrying back to the nearby campsite to find Reiner's second in command. The fact they were so close only made it all the more galling that they'd missed the renegade's trail earlier. Vaust had only just set off when Halbranc and Mikael emerged into the clearing where their comrades congregated.

'Where is Köller?' Reiner asked. He was the only knight still not present.

'Here,' a low voice answered. Köller emerged from the shadows, regarding his fellow knights with hooded eyes.

Death was no stranger to any of those who came into the service of Morr. Every man in that clearing had a story of loss. Most kept such tragedies to themselves and Köller was no exception, but he bore a particularly terrible burden, and one that never seemed to lift.

Reiner's look was reproachful.

'I'm sorry,' Köller said. 'I was searching for further signs.'

'This is the Drakwald,' Reiner reminded him. 'We stay together.' The captain turned to Valen. 'Lead the way,' he ordered icily, with a final piercing look at Mikael.

The youthful knight couldn't hold his gaze and was glad when Reiner stalked off after the scout.

'I doubt he feels it,' Halbranc whispered to Mikael as they trudged after the others.

'Feels what?'

'The cold,' Halbranc said, a broad smile splitting his craggy features. 'I wonder if he "feels" at all.'

Halbranc laughed, slapping Mikael on the back, sending shudders through his armour.

'Come on,' he urged.

It happened quickly. One moment they were following Valen as he stalked the renegade's trail, the next Köller had started off alone, running as if all the hellish daemons of Chaos were after him.

Reiner had immediately signalled the rest of the knights to pursue.

Mikael was close behind the fleeing knight, hot breath misting in the air as he exerted himself.

'Köller!' a voice echoed from the gloom. 'Köller, where are you going?' It was Vaust, at Mikael's heels.

Köller paused to wave them on and then continued.

'Köll–' Vaust's shout was arrested by a giant hand covering his mouth.

'Quiet, you fool,' Halbranc hissed in his ear. 'You'll have every denizen of the Drakwald upon us.'

Mikael saw his captain, several feet across from him; slashes of black between the stout trunks of trees as he followed silently and stealthily after Köller. Mikael wasn't sure whether his captain wanted to catch him to prevent mishap or to put him to the sword for his erratic behaviour. Reiner's stony demeanour made it impossible to tell.

They were gaining. Ahead, the forest had thickened and Köller was finding it hard going. Valen headed the chasing pack. He made good headway, despite the weight of his armour and the snow underfoot.

Halbranc was not so adept. He slipped, barging through the clawing bracken, and was lost from sight. Sigson was nowhere to be seen.

Mikael managed to stick close to Valen. He was an Ostermarker by birth. A childhood spent in the deep forests of that province had taught him much about traversing them. His was a childhood tainted by tragedy. Thoughts sprang unbidden into Mikael's mind: the flash of the dagger, a cry in the dark, the creaking of the rope.

Searing pain brought Mikael back, a sharp branch slashing open his cheek as he ran past it. None of them were wearing their helmets: they dulled awareness. To be so disadvantaged in a forest, the Drakwald of all places, was unwise. Mikael's blood felt hot as it ran down his face. He wiped it away, instead focusing on getting to Köller. The Drakwald was no place for a mindless chase into shadows.

Köller stopped abruptly as if whatever had been compelling him had gone.

Valen reached him first, followed by Mikael a few moments later.

'Köller, what happened?' Valen asked.

The rest of the company caught up, Vaust then Reiner. A battered Halbranc brought up the rear with Sigson, the old priest bent over and gasping for breath.

Köller turned to face Valen.

'A woman,' he gasped, 'she wanted me… to follow.'

Mikael had seen nothing. There were no tracks in the snow and no broken branches. He noticed a dark glance pass between Reiner and Sigson. Both men knew of the unseen dangers of the Drakwald, of the phantoms of those long dead, calling others to join them in damnation, of strange magics that possessed men and enslaved them.

'What is that?' Valen asked suddenly, pointing through a gap in the trees.

Mikael followed his gaze.

Beyond the tree line, a light invaded the forest shadow, and a few hundred feet beyond stood a walled settlement. A simple road led up to it, emerging from another part of the Drakwald.

'It's a village,' said Mikael.

Two dilapidated watchtowers stood at the village's entrance, an iron-bound gate hanging limply on a rusted hinge between them. A wooden stockade wall surrounded the village and, getting closer, the knights saw that the wall was cracked, age-worn timber yielding to the ravages of time.

Passing through the yawning gateway they saw a line of frost-caked clothes, eroded by decay, swinging in the breeze. Chimneys were dormant, emaciated animals wandered aimlessly, and a great tree stood withered and forlorn, wasted apples clinging to skeletal branches. Silence reigned; the village was empty, ghost-like.

'What happened here?' asked Mikael. It reminded him of home, back in Ostermark. He found the thought saddening.

'I see no signs of a battle,' growled Halbranc.

'Let us find out,' said Reiner. 'Knights, draw swords,' he ordered and they drew as one, a chorus of scraping steel.

The captain signalled the knights to split into groups. Reiner moved up the village square with Valen and Vaust, and Halbranc accompanied Köller who ranged right, while Mikael and Sigson went left.

After searching several hovels without success, Mikael came to a blacksmith's forge. Peering tentatively inside, he saw that tools were left out. A horseshoe sat upon the anvil, pinched between a pair of rusted metal tongs. A lantern swung noisily on a chain set into the roof.

'It's as if this place has been abandoned for years,' he muttered to himself.

'You're bleeding, Mikael,' said Sigson, noticing the cut on Mikael's cheek.

'It's nothing,' he said absently, wiping away the blood and crouching down, as he noticed something in the frosty earth at his feet.

'What is it?' asked Sigson, joining him.

'I'm not sure.' Mikael brushed the snow away carefully with his hand, revealing something large and flat. 'Looks like a sign,' he said.

'Dropped by the smithy, perhaps,' Sigson wondered. 'What does it say?'

Mikael swept away the grime and filth, using his dagger to chip away at the rusted metal.

'Hochenheim.'

There was a distant cry, Köller's voice preventing further exploration. The knight and the priest got up and dashed outside.

Halbranc was running after Köller with the other knights in tow.

'I saw her,' cried Köller, 'the woman, she is here,' he said, disappearing from view behind a dishevelled tavern.

They found Köller standing before a tombstone, a mass of other graves arrayed around him in a garden of Morr.

Mikael saw Reiner mutter a prayer to the deathgod, before entering.

'She was here,' said Köller.

Mikael looked down at the grave which was marked by a nondescript and unadorned headstone.

Reiner stalked away with a meaningful glance at Sigson who nodded, and went to Köller. Mikael couldn't hear what the priest was saying, but his tone was soothing.

'What is happening?' Köller cried out. 'I swear I saw…' The young knight paused, looking out beyond the cemetery.

Mikael followed his gaze to a steep hillside.

At first he saw the shadows at the crest of the hill; then he heard cries and the clash of steel.

With the winter sun almost faded behind them, the templars of Morr reached the top of the hillside, where they saw a large stone temple. Outside it, a battle raged.

Mikael made out a horde of misshapen creatures in the twilight. They surrounded a band of knights, who were backing off towards the temple. One knight was torn down by a claw-handed freak, his torso severed in two, turning the snow crimson.

'Mutants,' Halbranc hissed.

'Sigson, who are these men?' asked Reiner, his eyes never leaving the brutal combat.

'They bear the livery of the Baron of Krugedorf, it's a town in this province,' Sigson replied, discerning the design on the knights' tabards. The warrior priest was learned not just in matters of his faith, his knowledge extended far beyond that purview, a valuable asset the knights often called upon.

Mikael went over to the warrior priest, slipping on the snow. He crashed into the ground, reopening the cut in his cheek. Blood dripped down onto the snow, blossoming readily. He saw a piece of cloth sticking out of the snow, and, picking it up, used it to stem the bleeding.

At the temple, another knight was dragged, screaming, to his death.

'We must aid them!' Vaust hissed urgently.

Reiner had seen enough.

'Such abominations must not be allowed to endure,' he growled, donning his helmet and sliding the skull faceplate down as he got to his feet.

The other knights followed suit, each drawing down the death masks that were part of their helmets, a symbol of their intent to do battle. Mikael quickly tucked the cloth beneath his armoured greave before pulling down his own faceplate.

'Knights! To arms!' Reiner bellowed, drawing his sword.

Charging over the rise, the knights struck the mutant horde with righteous fury.

Valen and Vaust waded in silently. Vaust hacked the leg off one creature, its features obliterated by boils. Valen impaled another, his blade sinking into the distended maw of a half man, half beast.

Halbranc carved a red ruin in the diseased throng, opening up a massively bloated monster with his zweihander, maggot-ridden entrails sloughing from the ragged tear in its belly.

Sigson cut down a horned mutant before reaching into his robes and pulling out a glass vial of shimmering liquid.

'I cast thee back into the void,' he intoned, hurling the holy water at the bloated creature's disgorged intestines. The stink of burning viscera tainted the breeze.

A goat-headed man brayed its defiance at Mikael. The templar roared, cutting the beast's head from its shoulders, black blood fountaining.

Reiner was deadly.

'I am Morr's instrument, through me is His will enacted,' he uttered, tearing into the abominations with ruthless efficiency.

Köller though, was unstoppable.

Misshapen limbs and grotesque heads fell like macabre rain upon the ground as he carved through the horde like a butcher.

Recognising allies when they saw them, the Krugedorf knights rallied and redoubled their efforts.

'Knights of Morr, to me!' Reiner cried, seeking to break through the back of the encircling creatures.

The templars of Morr followed dutifully, smashing a hole in the mutants' death pincer.

'Look,' cried one of the Krugedorf knights.

A veritable sea of boil ridden, plague ravaged wretches erupted over the rise.

Hacking down a cloven-hoofed monstrosity, Mikael noticed another group watching them, far behind the onrushing horde. At the centre was a thin figure, his long coat flapping in the breeze. It might have been his imagination, but Mikael swore he saw it bow towards the knights.

'We cannot overcome such odds,' said Sigson, gutting a beast on his blade.

'Your priest is right,' said a Krugedorf knight. Mikael assumed it was their leader. His face, hidden behind his blood spattered helmet, was unreadable. 'I have men in the temple,' he added, cutting down another mutant, 'we can regroup there.'

'Agreed,' said Reiner, felling another as he backed away from the reinforcements.

The knights of Krugedorf and Morr raced the short distance to the temple and hurled themselves through the entrance, slamming shut the door immediately after them.

Mikael looked back to see two armour-clad warriors, with swords drawn.

'They are allies,' the Krugedorf leader told them, 'knights of Morr. Quickly,' he added urgently, his voice dull and resonant inside his helmet, 'we must barricade the entrances.'

Halbranc needed little encouragement. Hefting a massive wooden bench up over his head, he slammed it down against the door. Reiner dragged over another, ramming it against a window, a Krugedorf knight bracing it with a massive wrought iron candlestick. Mikael and another Krugedorfer heaved a statue of some long-forgotten saint across the final window.

The tide of mutants crashed against the temple. The door shuddered as the debased creatures hammered on it with unholy vigour, massing like diseased surf. Claws and pockmarked talons reached in through gaps in the barricades, only to be cut off. Others were impaled as the knights thrust their blades through the openings in desperation, rewarded with disembodied mutant screams. At last, amidst shouting and crashing steel, the barrage stopped. Dust motes drifted silently from the ceiling. After a few moments, Valen peered through an opening in one of the barricades.

'They have gone,' he said quietly.

'For now,' said the Krugedorf leader, removing his helmet. Long blond hair fell down onto his shoulders as a handsome face was revealed in the light of a flickering torch ensconced on one of the walls.

The knights stood in a small entrance chamber at the back of which was a gateless arch that led into a long chapel, full of overturned pews. Strangely, this place, although dusty and ancient, bore no signs of the blight that had afflicted the rest of Hochenheim.

'You think they will return?' asked Mikael of the blond-haired noble.

'They will return,' a deep voice said from the shadows. Another knight stepped forward, his ornate helmet covering the upper half of his face. He wore a black beard, and a mace hung at his hip, slick with blood.

'I am Heinrich of Krugedorf,' the blond-haired knight interjected, extending a gauntleted hand towards Reiner.

'Reiner,' the captain growled warily, shaking Heinrich's hand as he lifted the death mask and removed his helmet, 'servant of Morr,' he added. The others followed his example and introduced themselves to the strangers.

Heinrich gestured to his warriors.

'Goiter,' he said. The dark-bearded knight remained unmoved. 'Kurn,' he continued. Kurn, sticking to the shadows, was broad, and taller even than Halbranc. He wore a full-faced helmet, a mighty zweihander at his side, and gave a mute greeting. 'Mordan.' A youthful, wiry-looking knight, with a number of small daggers up his right arm nodded. His left arm was harnessed in a sling. 'And Veiter,' Heinrich concluded.

The last knight smiled and bowed slightly, twin short swords sheathed at his hips. His hair was the colour of sackcloth, his eyes suspicious and alert.

The Krugedorfers were unshaven and drawn. Clearly they too had been on the road, and they each bore the crest of what Mikael assumed must be the Baron of Krugedorf: a red shield with a bearded stag at opposite diagonals, doubtless some reference to the hunting heritage of their lord.

'What is your purpose here?' asked Reiner.

'We come on an errand from our liege-lord, the baron,' said Heinrich. 'We are to salvage the relics of this temple and take them to a place of safety,' he explained.

'Then let us help you. We can reclaim them together,' said Reiner matter-of-factly, 'and leave this damned place.' He turned to Halbranc. 'Fortify the entrance,' he ordered, 'Mikael and Sigson with me, the rest, assist Halbranc.'

'I'm afraid it isn't quite that simple,' warned Heinrich.

Reiner turned to face him. His expression demanded explanations.

'Beyond this door lies the relic chamber,' Heinrich informed them.

Reiner, Sigson and Mikael, together with Heinrich and Kurn, stood in a long, narrow corridor at the foot of a set of stone steps. The stairway had led them to these catacombs from a trapdoor in the chapel and now they faced a single, stone door.

'I warn you,' Heinrich intoned darkly, 'there is peril beyond it. Steel yourselves.'

'Knights of Morr fear not the darkness,' Reiner told him with the utmost certainty.

Mikael felt his heart beating.

Heinrich motioned to Kurn, and the silent giant gripped the great iron manacle of the door and heaved with all his considerable might. As the door ground open, noisily kicking up grit and dust, Mikael gripped his sword. There was a long, wide room beyond it, flickering torches illuminating the threshold. Further in, there was only darkness.

'I see little peril here,' Sigson remarked, driven by curiosity as he stepped beyond the shallow cordon of light.

'Wait!' Heinrich warned.

'There is noth–' he said, and then cried out as a long cut appeared on his arm.

Heinrich hauled him back into the light.

Mikael muttered a prayer to Morr as a shimmering, ethereal blade materialised in the darkness. A hand coalesced around it, then an arm, and then a torso, until the spectre was revealed. Hollow, sunken eyes, ragged robes and skeletal limbs marked this thing as a wight, one of the unquiet dead.

More phantoms appeared alongside, their faces pitiless and cold. In their unearthly lustre they revealed the ancient bones of priests and other relics. But it was the woman, kneeling in silent vigil, dressed in dishevelled robes, who got the knights' attention. She was flesh and blood. Her hair was lank, her face wizened and encrusted with filth. She chanted wordlessly. Behind her was a second, much smaller, chamber, delineated by a wide arch. Set in the back wall was a large circular window coated in dust so thick it blocked out the light.

Looking at her, Mikael felt an overwhelming sense of sadness.

'There,' Heinrich intoned quietly, interrupting Mikael's thoughts, 'you see the witch?'

Reiner nodded sternly.

'We found her hiding in this place, doubtless seeking refuge from those who might put her to the torch,' he spat.

Reiner's jaw locked.

'Before we could slay her, she summoned these... spirits,' Heinrich continued. 'We have been unable to approach her since. As those who follow the Lord of Death and Dreams, do you think you can lay these ghosts to rest?'

Reiner looked to Sigson, who held onto his arm, his expression pained.

'It will take time,' the warrior priest told them.

Night, it seemed, came all too swiftly, but there had been no more attacks on the temple. The knights worked quickly, bolstering the barricades and lighting the remaining torches in the chapel. The mutants knew they were there, no sense in trying to hide their presence and the heat was welcome respite against the cold.

Mikael stared into the flames, hugging his arms around his body as he sat on one of the wooden pews, the wrathful wind providing a moaning chorus to his thoughts.

'Sigson has yet to return,' Halbranc said. Mikael wasn't even aware he was next to him and started at the big man's sudden presence.

'Easy,' he said, 'it's just me, lad.' He handed Mikael a slice of salted pork, but the young knight refused it.

'This silence unnerves me,' Mikael admitted. 'I have no care for it,' he added, looking around the room.

Valen and Vaust talked quietly amongst themselves as they ate, making the most of the opportunity before the fighting started again. Köller lay on the floor, his cloak wrapped tight around him, shivering in his sleep. Reiner had stayed with Sigson.

Mikael knew the captain didn't trust the Krugedorf knights. His gaze fell to them next, regarding the knights of Morr beneath the glow of torchlight, the faint hubbub of whispers barely audible. But then Reiner trusted no one, not even his own men.

'Don't dwell on it,' Halbranc advised. 'Here,' he said, producing a small silver flask from beneath his cloak, 'take a swig of this; it'll warm your blood.'

Mikael shook his head.

'If Reiner saw that…' he began.

'I dare say he would not approve,' Halbranc agreed, 'but then our fearless captain approves of very little,' he said, taking a belt of liquor from the flask, grimacing as it scorched his throat.

'You don't know what you're missing,' he said afterwards.

Mikael smiled; the ephemeral expression fading as he looked into Halbranc's eyes. He knew very little of the man's history, save that he was once a mercenary and had fought across much of the Empire and beyond. There was a sadness in him, one that he could not shake, only dull with alcohol. He'd heard him at night, crying in his sleep at dark dreams that Mikael could only guess at. Halbranc would never admit to the hidden pain in his soul, but he knew that Mikael was aware of it.

'How are there so many of them?' Mikael asked, finding the abrupt silence uncomfortable.

'Them?' Halbranc asked, concealing the flask beneath his cloak.

'The mutants.'

'What do you think happened to all the villagers?' asked Halbranc grimly, getting to his feet. 'We fought them today.'

'By the breath of Morr,' Mikael said, at last understanding.

'Do not think on it,' Halbranc told him sternly. 'Get some sleep,' he added, his face softening. 'We don't know when we might get another opportunity.'

'Don't worry,' he said, 'I'll keep a watch. Don't feel much like sleeping, anyway.'

Mikael watched Halbranc go to stand at the barricade, peering out into the night. He sank back against the pew. It was hard and unyielding, but he was exhausted, the cold and his dark thoughts sapping his endurance. Reluctantly, he fell into a fitful sleep.

The forest rose up around him, thick branches tugging at his clothes, briars scraping exposed flesh. There was a dagger in his hand. It was stained with blood. He was running; a shadow figure a few paces ahead. He almost reached it when he saw a mighty bearded stag looking at him from a sun dappled clearing. A second, identical beast emerged from the forest beside it.

The two creatures charged each other, locking antlers fiercely. He watched, horrified as the antlers started to merge together in a terrible union, the stags becoming one hideous, mutated beast.

Four baleful eyes stared back at him from a single head as the abomination burst into bright red flame.

Mikael awoke to desperate cries and rushing feet. He saw Vaust, struggling to hold back the wooden bench at the window. Valen lay on the floor beneath him, clutching his shoulder. Halbranc was running to him, Heinrich not far behind.

Goiter dragged Köller up, muttering a curse.

Kurn's armoured bulk was pressed against the door, while Mordan and Veiter hefted another bench between them to seal the second window, which gaped open, the statue in rubble beneath.

Mikael caught a glimpse of Reiner in the corner of his eye, appearing from the trapdoor. There was no sign of Sigson. He must still be in the relic room. Getting to his feet, Mikael ran towards Vaust. Then the temple door exploded.

Halbranc and Heinrich were thrown to the ground. Kurn bore the brunt of the blast, engulfed in a splinter storm of broken wood and iron. Incredibly, he stayed upright.

Flames lapped at the edges of the shattered door, the twisted iron jutting out like broken limbs. Smoke issued through the huge gap, shifting figures visible through it. The stench was unmistakeable: blackpowder.

The mutants howled as they emerged through the haze and into the temple. Kurn swept his blade in a punishing arc, but missed as a creature dressed like a macabre jester thwarted his aim. It rode around on a skeletal hobbyhorse with a cadaverous head. It smashed the massive Krugedorf knight to the ground with a huge, unwieldy mace.

Mikael charged at the grotesque jester, but his path was blocked by two girls holding hands. He wavered for a moment, his blade stayed by their apparent innocence. Then he saw their hands, fused together in a gelatinous mass of flesh and knew they were not children. Snarling viciously, revealing deadly fangs, they sprang on top of Mikael. The templar dropped his sword, desperately trying to fend off the weird sisters as they clawed and bit.

He felt their weight lifting and vaguely saw the hideous twins flailing off into the dark. Halbranc stood before him.

'Pick up your swor–' he began, but was smashed aside, a hugely obese woman crushing him into the wall with her bulk.

Reiner raced to Halbranc's aid, blade in hand, but was confronted by a diminutive, sallow-skinned freak, mouth sewn shut crudely with thick, black thread. In one hand it clutched a rusted dagger; on the other was the puppet of a mangy dog. The mute shook the puppet free, revealing a small, daemon-like creature, instead of a hand.

'Die!' the daemon-hand hissed, its voice bubbling like melting flesh.

Reiner roared, cutting the daemon thing off at the wrist and sending it flying. The mute scampered after it, ducking and weaving under the blades of the other knights as it went.

At the wall, Halbranc was slowly being smothered. Mikael and Reiner plunged their swords into the hideous woman crushing him. The creature laughed, black ooze running down the knights' blades, corroding the metal. They dropped their weapons as the caustic blood devoured them.

Mikael was reaching for another blade, when a long shadow fell across him. He turned quickly, short sword in hand and found himself gazing up at an incredibly tall, thin man, a strange, almost infantile head on his shoulders. It swung a massive glaive at the templar, who leapt to avoid it, chunks of flagstone debris erupting in his wake. He sprang up to face it, abhorred as the creature's head detached from its body and with a horrifying screech launched itself at the temple roof, thin, spidery legs punching from the cranium and gaining purchase in solid stone. The spider-thing chittered as it came towards him, the headless freak still swinging the glaive. There was the flash of silver and the spider-thing fell, a dagger protruding from its forehead. Both the stickman and the spider-thing retreated.

Mikael turned to see Mordan, another dagger in his hand, about to throw it when he was split in two, a grotesquely muscled freak with a tiny hooded head, cutting him down with an axe.

Mikael lost the creature amidst the chaos, his attention arrested by Halbranc's muffled cries as he was still pinned by the obese woman.

Reiner had shaken off another mutant and was moving in, when Heinrich appeared beside them, hefting a torch from the wall and ramming the fiery brand into the obese freak's wound. Its jaw distended horribly to reveal the half-digested corpse of a Krugedorf knight, slain in the first battle, as it recoiled from the fire, shuffling away into the shadows.

Gasping for breath, Halbranc slumped to his knees, his zweihander clattering to the ground.

Around them, the smoke was clearing, the freaks defeated, but Mordan was dead and Valen badly wounded.

Mikael regarded the carnage, the corpses of slain villagers, afflicted by the plague, were everywhere, but of the macabre circus freaks, there was no sign.

'I brought down at least one,' growled Goiter, apparently reading Mikael's mind as he wiped the gore from his mace.

'I too felled one of them that could not have lived,' offered Vaust.

'Daemons,' Reiner spat, under his breath.

'Whatever those things were, we cannot remain here,' said Heinrich, gesturing to the charred ruin of the door. 'When they return, and return they will, we will be defenceless.'

'Is there another way out?' Reiner asked, looking out impassively into the darkness.

'A secret passage leads to the surface from the relic room,' said Heinrich.

Reiner turned, an inquisitive look flashing briefly over his face.

'If your priest is successful and banishes the spirits…' Heinrich let the thought hang in the air for them to finish.

Then we live, Mikael thought.

'The passageway before the relic room is narrow,' Reiner said. 'It will be easier to defend. We fight in pairs, rotating as each pair gets tired. We'll make our stand there.'

Without further preamble, Reiner stalked over to the trapdoor, the others following him.

They had waited for over an hour in the creeping dark of the catacombs, Sigson's muffled prayers emanating through the door of the relic room.

Mikael was listening to it when he noticed Veiter looking at him. The Krugedorf knight evoked an uneasy feeling in the young templar, and he quickly averted his gaze, shifting it to the other knights.

Vaust was ever watchful over his brother who grimaced in pain next to him. Halbranc and Reiner stood quietly, the former lost in thought, the latter an emotionless statue. Köller sat opposite Mikael and looked sullen, the dark mask upon his face as always.

Of the Krugedorf knights, Goiter and Kurn stood sentinel at the entrance to the passageway. They seemed oddly restless. Even Heinrich, alongside Veiter, appeared on edge.

'What troubles you?' Mikael asked.

Heinrich opened his mouth to answer when the trapdoor caved in and stone fell like rain.

The torches in the passageway guttered and died, engulfing the knights in blackness. Amidst a deluge of broken stone slabs and ruined wood, something large and terrible filled the end of the passageway. The charnel house stink of its breath infected the air.

Goiter turned to shout to Heinrich as something thick and wet lashed out of the dark, and suddenly Goiter was no more, the sickening crunch of bone a macabre echo of his existence.

Overcoming the mind-numbing terror threatening to unman him, Mikael drew his sword.

'We cannot prevail here,' Heinrich breathed, fear in his voice.

Reiner, backing away from the beast, looked over his shoulder at the solid stone door behind him.

'Into the relic room!' he bellowed.

Acting quickly, Halbranc got to the door first. 'Watch my back,' the giant snarled, and heaved on the iron door manacle.

It wouldn't yield.

The massive Krugedorfer, Kurn, appeared alongside him. Together, with the stone grinding in their ears, the knights opened the door.

Inside, Sigson was kneeling on the floor. He'd stepped beyond the cordon of light and was encircled by grave dust, facing off against the witch. In front of him was a black candle, its flame casting a bright aura. The warrior priest was bathed in sweat, his features creased with exertion. Around him, the spirits wailed silently, trying to tear at him with unearthly claws, only repelled by the priest's wards.

The knights paused at the portal when they saw the spirits. The thing in the corridor was a worse terror though and the knights piled inside. Sigson was unaware of their presence, entranced as he invoked the banishment ritual. Kurn heaved the door shut behind them.

Heart racing, Mikael leant heavily against the wall. Something fell from his arm greave, dislodged in the panic. He stooped and picked up a section of cloth. It was the same piece he'd used to staunch his bleeding face outside the temple. He hadn't paid much attention to it. Now that it lay open in his hands, Mikael saw it bore the crest of the Krugedorf knights: a red shield, two bearded stags at opposite diagonals. He suddenly recalled his dream of the stags coming together in a blaze of flame, and wondered what it meant. He half heard Sigson chant the banishment rites and felt the same sadness as he had before. Only it wasn't sadness, it was something else. It felt like… pleading.

Two stags coming together.

Mikael looked again at the cloth. He held a corner in each hand and folded them in on each other, then turned them up, forcing the image of the two stags together.

His heart quickened as the realisation of what was before him struck like a hammer blow. In his hand, the cloth folded over to reveal an entirely different image: a burning hand.

'Sigson, no!' he cried.

He was too late. Sigson had finished the ritual.

The candle flared impossibly bright, and white light flooded the chamber. The witch screamed, flung back with the force of her broken summoning, the spirits crying out in unison as they were expelled in a blinding coruscation.

The knights were thrown down with the sheer power of the invocation, ears ringing with the screams of the damned.

Blinking back the stark after-image, virtually seared upon his retinas, Mikael saw that Heinrich was on his feet and running towards the arch at the back of the room.

'Slay them!' he cried.

Kurn's zweihander was drawn, and he smashed Vaust aside with the flat of the blade. The knight struck the wall hard and fell into a crumpled heap, next to his semi-conscious brother.

Veiter, eyes aglow with balefire, leapt at Reiner, but the captain of Morr was ready and parried his double-handed assault. The Chaos knight snarled, revealing fangs.

'Knights, to arms, the servants of Chaos are among us!' Reiner bellowed.

Sigson staggered to his feet, drawing his blade with shaking hands.

Kurn's armoured boot put him down as he advanced on Halbranc.

The two giants clashed, zweihander on zweihander, the scrape of churning metal and flashing sparks filling the air around them.

'By the hand of Morr,' Halbranc breathed. Face-to-face with the beast, he saw that Kurn's helmet was fused to his neck, the eyeholes empty voids of hate.

The stone door thundered as whatever was outside tried to get in. Mikael gave it little heed, as he ran past the battling knights. He was intent on Heinrich, who was through the archway at the back of the room and into the antechamber.

'Heinrich!' he cried, flinging his short sword at the traitor captain.

The Krugedorfer turned and parried the blade out of the air with unnatural quickness.

'Unwise to relinquish your only weapon,' he said, licking his lips with a serpentine tongue, and stepping backwards into the centre of the antechamber.

'You want the relics for yourself,' Mikael said accusingly.

'Fool,' Heinrich spat. 'Whatever feeble trinkets reside in this place are of no interest to me. It is the temple that I covet,' he said.

'Ignis!' he then cried and a tongue of flame spread furiously around him, describing a rune-etched symbol on the ground, an unholy icon of Chaos.

Exultant, Heinrich threw his head back and the flames rose to the ceiling.

Mikael backed away from the conflagration. Through the blaze, a hazy silhouette was visible.

'Dormamu, I supplicate myself before you. Make me your host,' Heinrich uttered with a voice like prophecy.

His treachery was clear. He meant to summon a daemon.

The inferno intensified as Heinrich's shadow form was lifted off the ground, the deep and unholy resonance of another voice coming from the fire as Heinrich reasserted his pledge.

'He seeks to re-consecrate the circle,' the witch cried desperately from behind Mikael, vying against the raging din of the fire.

Shading his eyes, heat searing his face, Mikael turned to her.

She staggered to her feet.

'Help me,' she begged.

Suddenly, Kurn loomed behind her, zweihander raised, Halbranc lying prone and defeated, his breastplate smashed.

'No!' Mikael cried as the blade fell. She would be cut in twain.

The blade failed to strike; an aura of blue light surrounding her repulsed it.

Witness to a miracle, Mikael had a sudden epiphany as if the light had opened his eyes for the first time. She was no witch. She was a priestess, the guardian of this place, and he must protect her at all costs.

Mikael took up his thrown short sword and rushed at Kurn, knowing he was no match for the Krugedorfer.

The giant turned his attention to the young knight, exuding menace.

Mikael raised his weapon, awaiting the deathblow that would shatter it and his body. It never came.

Kurn recoiled wordlessly, like an automaton, as Köller's blade smashed down onto his pauldron.

Seeing his opportunity, Mikael came at the Chaos warrior from the front, plunging his sword into Kurn's breastplate. He withdrew it savagely, then watched horrified as black sand spilled from the wound. The knight reached out to crush him with a mailed fist.

Köller cleaved it off with a two-handed blow. Still Kurn lived, and whirling around, smashed Köller into the wall.

Mikael gripped his blade, incredulous that the thing before him still endured.

This was his last chance. 'Morr, guide my hand,' he breathed and thrust his sword deep into the eye slit of Kurn's helmet. The giant staggered, trying to clutch at the weapon embedded in his skull with a hand that no longer existed. At last, he fell, like a hewn oak, thunderously to the ground and was still. But it wasn't over yet. The door to the relic room shuddered, cracks appearing in the stone. Mikael turned to the priestess.

She closed her eyes as she muttered words of power. The knight's defence in her honour had granted her the time she needed to perform some ritual.

The cracks in the stone door widened and finally it split and crumbled. The terrible shadow filling it retreated and a horde of bloodshot, plague-infected eyes regarded them.

Mikael was about to run to intercept the creatures, when he felt the light touch of the priestess on his arm. He looked back.

Her eyes opened, burning with a deep blue lustre. The heat from the conflagration surrounding Heinrich visibly ebbed. Even the mutants paused at the doorway, as if sensing something.

'Stop her!' Heinrich cried from within the inferno, his voice deep and ageless.

Only Veiter remained.

Reiner advanced on the last Krugedorfer, the mutant horde faltering at the doorway.

Flinging his blade at Reiner to distract him, Veiter ran. He fled through the arch at the back of the chamber, lost suddenly behind the inferno.

Reiner was about to give chase. A plague creature grabbed his arm, its rusting cleaver about to strike, when the priestess spoke.

'No.'

The cleaver was blasted aside by some unseen force as her voice echoed through the chamber. It was followed by a terrible wail as the dread spirits returned.

Ghostly faces and ethereal bodies became as one as they coalesced into a swirling, spectral maelstrom.

'Purge this place,' she said.

The spirit host swept through the temple like a cleansing wave, accompanied by a wrathful wind, searing plague-ridden flesh and shredding bone. Holy light blazed furiously as the dust and grime clogging the window was destroyed. A lance of power came through it and engulfed the Chaos circle, extinguishing the flames surrounding Heinrich.

Mikael shielded his eyes against its glory.

Then the light was gone, as quickly as it had manifested, and the vengeful spirits with it.

His vision returning, Mikael saw Sigson crouching down next to the priestess.

Mikael went over to him.

He held her in his arms. She was beautiful, the dirt and grime on her face washed away, her hair golden and pure, her robes no longer torn. A radiant blue aura surrounded her.

'My time here is ended,' she told them. 'The sanctity of this place has been preserved.'

'What do you mean?' Mikael asked, his mind reeling from what he had witnessed.

She pressed something into the young knight's hands.

It looked like a book, old and unadorned, but with a small silver clasp in the centre. Mikael unhooked it and opened it out, revealing that it was no book, but a triptych. Three wooden plates within described a battle. In the middle a temple, two doves flying above in a stormy sky; below them, a force of knights surrounded by holy light, a priestess at their heart; to the left, an army of black-armoured warriors and daemons, led by a mighty dark knight on a fell steed; to the right, a plague ridden horde, their skeletal master holding a scythe aloft…

It was the battle from Mikael's dream.

'This place of power has existed for centuries,' said the priestess. 'The prosperity of the village, the relic in your hands,' she said, looking at Mikael, 'ensures its purity. Every one hundred years it is contested. Every one hundred years a guardian is selected to watch over it, to remain here for another century until it is contested again and the next guardian called.'

'A hundred years,' breathed Sigson, 'but that would mean…'

'Yes, I will die,' she said, smiling faintly. 'When the plague came I was weakened. I could not prevail without help. Now the malady that ravaged this place has been lifted and the new guardian is here to take my place.'

Mikael took a deep breath and exhaled his resignation. The dream had been a sign, he could see that now. It was his calling.

'I am the guardian,' he said solemnly.

The priestess turned, a trace of amusement upon her face, 'No, it is not you of whom I speak,' she said, looking beyond the two knights.

Mikael and Sigson turned as one, following her gaze.

Köller staggered to his feet, the light from the window bathing him was a startling affirmation. He looked shocked at first; then, as if suddenly enlightened, he knelt down, bowing his head and laying his sword before him.

Sigson gasped, as the priestess shimmered and faded, the blue aura surrounding her flaring bright in Köller's eyes as he looked up, bathing the room in azure. Then it was gone, and Köller returned to normal.

The remaining knights of Morr stood around him, their wounds miraculously healed.

'What happened here?' Reiner asked darkly.

Mikael looked back to the corridor. Of the creature and the plague horde, there was no sign; even those mutants who had entered the chamber were gone.

'A miracle,' the young knight breathed.

Reiner walked to the back of the room, apparently unmoved.

He regarded Heinrich's charred remains in a circle of ash. He scattered them into nothing with his boot.

'Our work here is done,' he said, his voice like ice. He turned on his heel, and with a glance at Köller, stalked out of the room.

'What will you do?' Mikael asked Köller.

He looked different, lifted.

'I will remain here,' he said, 'and protect this place in the name of Morr.'

Silence persisted, the gravity of the moment and Köller's undertaking sinking in.

'It is a noble deed, Köller,' said Sigson. 'A great evil has been averted this night.' He bowed solemnly and left the chamber after Reiner.

Valen and Vaust followed, a nod at Köller before they went.

'Fare thee well, lad,' Halbranc said, joining the others.

Mikael handed Köller the triptych. 'This belongs here, I think.'

Köller accepted it gratefully. 'Yours is a great destiny, Mikael. Do not fear it.'

Mikael opened his mouth to speak, but couldn't find any words. Instead, he turned and walked away into the darkness.

Outside the temple, the knights made ready.

'Your orders, Captain Reiner?' Halbranc asked, securing his zweihander.

'We head back to the Road Warden's Rest, get the horses and make for the nearest temple of Morr,' he said. 'There is much to report.'

He stalked off, back the way they had come when first happening upon Hochenheim.

Mikael thought of Köller and found his heart heavy as he walked through the ramshackle village gates and back into the Drakwald. As he did, he looked back at Hochenheim one last time. There, in the village square, he noticed the great tree and upon its branches the smallest of blossoms.

THE MIRACLE AT BERLAU

Darius Hinks

Ratboy awoke to a world of silence and pain.

Charred rafters were tumbling from a temple roof to reveal a heavy, pewter sky. Stone lintels were smashing across flagstones, pulling down walls and windows as they went. Fragments of skin, teeth and bone were bouncing across the floor, while overhead, flaming pages of the *Deus Sigmar* drifted beneath what remained of the vaulted ceiling. But none of it made a sound.

Other senses quickly returned to him. He felt the hard stone of the temple floor pressing into his blistered back, and he could clearly smell the meaty aroma of embers, smouldering on his upturned face; but nothing reached his ears.

He lurched up from the blood-slick floor and noticed something moving through the chaos. A figure was dragging itself through the tumbling masonry. It kept to the shadows and was hard to see clearly, but its awkward, jerking movements unnerved him. He shuddered and closed his eyes. When he looked again it was almost gone. A single, glistening thread was briefly visible, as it slid out through the temple door, then it disappeared into the growing morning light.

A whistling began in Ratboy's head as he stumbled through the smoke and confusion. He pounded his skull, pummelling the side of his face with his bloodied fist and, to his surprise, this seemed to help. He felt something shift in his left ear and finally, with a fizzing, popping screech, sound returned to him.

As the agony in his head eased, he began to notice other pains: his left side was badly scorched and the leather of his coat had merged with his arm like new skin. Blisters were erupting all over his scrawny neck. He lifted a hand to his face and winced at the smell of burnt flesh, but as he flexed his fingers he smiled. Still works, he thought. He picked the glowing embers from his face, ran a nervous hand over his aching skull and laughed with relief. 'I'm alive,' he muttered.

Memory came back to him with a rush of adrenaline. Brother Wolff, he thought, scanning the room. He quickly spotted the old priest, slumped awkwardly beneath a pile of rubble and he limped to his master's side. 'Jakob,' he whispered, taking his hand, 'My lord.' The priest's chest armour was scorched and dented and the grey stubble that covered his head was dark with blood, but he still lived. 'It's a miracle,' said Ratboy, helping him to his feet.

Wolff looked down at his torso and shook his head in despair. 'I've failed,' he muttered. Then, his bloodshot eyes focused on Ratboy. 'What are you doing here?' he snapped, grabbing the boy's arm.

Ratboy was about to reply when a large section of the roof erupted with fresh flames and they were forced to flee, stumbling punch-drunk from the building.

They fell out into the grey Ostland dawn and clambered slowly up to the edge of the forest. From there, the temple looked a little more stable: one of the walls had given way and the tower was slumped at a slightly odd angle, but it looked mostly intact. The flames were already subsiding. Wolff examined his torso again and began to gingerly remove a row of pouches that was strapped to his chest.

'They didn't all explode,' said Ratboy. 'That's why you survived.'

Wolff nodded, then scowled at his servant. 'Did you follow me from the camp last night?' Then he took his servant's head in his hands and peered intently at him. 'Your ears – are you hurt?'

Ratboy noticed a gentle warmth flowing down his neck and realised he was bleeding from the side of his head. The priest ignored his murmurs of complaint and clasped the boy's head even tighter. Eventually, a different kind of heat blossomed behind Ratboy's eyes and he slipped into unconsciousness.

When Ratboy came to, the midday sun was already warming the grounds of the temple. He lay there for a while, looking down across the little clearing and listening to the harsh cawing of ravens perched on the temple roof. He ran a hand over his battered, skinny limbs, struggling to believe they were still intact. The pain in his side had eased a little and he smiled with the simple joy of being alive. Something about the birdsong seemed odd though. He listened to the sounds of the forest; sounds he had thought lost to him. Beneath the birdsong and the creaking of branches, he thought he heard words: soft, singsong voices, calling to him. 'Firefirefire,' they whispered. Then an odd smell reached him – an acrid, offal stink that had no place in such an idyllic scene.

He climbed to his feet, suddenly afraid, and limped quickly back down to the temple. 'Brother Wolff?' he called, peering cautiously into the gloom. There was no reply. A faint haze of smoke still lingered in the air, but the roof was no longer falling and he decided it was safe to enter. In a far corner, he saw the priest's shadow, thrown across the wall by a flickering oil lamp. The old man was clearing dust off a headstone and peering closely at an inscription.

'Brother Wolff,' he said, crossing the temple, 'did you kill him? I thought I saw something earlier. I think it was a man, but it didn't look, well…'

The priest gave no reply and continued staring at the headstone.

'Lord?'

Wolff looked up at Ratboy with despair on his face. 'What? What did you say?'

'The Reaver – did he die?'

The priest frowned for a few seconds, then raised his eyebrows in recognition. 'Oh, the Norscan, no, I found parts of him over there,' he gestured to a crumpled mound near the altar, 'but he survived the blast. Not for long though, I think. Nearly half the powder detonated. He must be burned beyond recognition.' He looked around at the ruined building and frowned. 'I seem to have lost my warhammer though. I think it may have been destroyed by the explosion.'

Ratboy knew what such a loss would mean to the priest. The hammer was more than just a weapon – it was a powerful icon of his faith. Wolff would feel lost without it. He could not help smiling at the sight of his master's familiar scowl however. 'I didn't expect to see you again,' he said.

'You spied on me?' replied Wolff.

Ratboy nodded, with a rueful smile. 'I wondered what had dragged you from your tent so early. Even you don't usually rise until dawn, so I crept through the moonlight to see what you were up to. I don't know what you said to those poor engineers, but it seemed to wake them up pretty sharpish.'

Wolff gave a short bark of laughter. 'What a bunch of rogues. I think they'd only stopped drinking a couple of hours earlier.' He shook his head. 'And on the eve of such an important battle.'

'Well – you seemed to sober them up pretty quickly. I saw them give you those blackpowder weapons, but I couldn't understand why you hid them beneath your cloak. Or why you crept out of the camp like that. Why would you head off into the forest on your own, with the enemy camped so close by?'

Wolff sighed. 'You've seen the way the marauders rally at the site of their champion – the Reaver as you called him.'

'Of course – and I've seen the way he watches your every move.'

Wolff nodded and smiled. 'You have your wits about you boy. Yes, you're right – he knows me. Even in that pit of corruption he calls a brain he knows what I represent to the regiment: hope. Ever since I rallied Maximillian's pistoliers at the Battle for Hogel Bridge, he's had me in his sights. Even then, as I led the charge across to the west bank, I realised he was desperately trying to separate me from the others, but our firepower was too great.'

'I remember,' said Ratboy with a grimace. 'He lashed the marauders half to death trying to get to you, but they just fell in their dozens, their bellies full of shot. The river ran red before he finally gave up.'

'Yes – and so it's been in every battle of the campaign, leaving us at this bloody impasse. And he knows this deadlock will continue until one of us dies, but so far he's been unable to corner me.' Wolff looked away, as though he were suddenly embarrassed. 'So, I thought I'd give him the chance he's been looking for. He knew as well as I did that there was a Sigmarite temple in the heart of this wood; the kind of temple a priest might be foolish enough to visit.' He paused and took a long breath. 'I knew I couldn't survive an encounter with such a creature, but that fitted in with my own plans.'

Ratboy laughed, trying to hide his shock. 'You wanted to die?' He noticed that Wolff was not listening, but staring at the headstone again. 'Brother Wolff?'

'What kind of a miracle,' muttered the priest, 'could happen here?'

Ratboy edged closer to the headstone to get a better look. Most of the engraving was scorched beyond recognition, but the names were still just about legible: Hieronymus and Margarethe Wolff.

'Wolff?' asked Ratboy. 'Are these your relatives?'

The priest looked up at him. 'My parents.' He sat down heavily next to the stone and massaged his bloody, shaven scalp. 'As soon as I led the Reaver into this clearing, I knew I had the right place. He was on me so fast though, I hardly had the chance to look around. I had no intention of surviving, as you guessed, but I was determined not to die alone.' He paused, and looked up at Ratboy with a feverish look in his eye. 'My faith has always been a means to an end. Its usefulness was always going to be finite.'

Ratboy's thin, beak-nosed face flushed a deep red. 'I'm not sure I know what you mean.'

'Of course you don't.' A dull *clang* rang out as Wolff kicked the headstone with his ironclad boot. 'This is a mark of my inescapable sin. A sin beyond reckoning. A sin against my own parents. My faith has never been anything more than atonement and today was to be my final penance.' He snapped the silver hammer that hung around his neck and threw it to the floor in disgust. 'But now I see that there is no penance. Nothing can atone for what I've done. I've failed. I can't even die.' He looked up at the ruined ceiling. 'I think my *willingness* to die gave me an edge though. The Reaver thought me easy prey, out here in the woods, away from our guns and cavalry. His gods have bestowed many gifts on him,' he grimaced, '*many* gifts.' He tapped the scorch marks on his breast-plate and gave a grim smile. 'If it wasn't for my final trick, he would've finished me.'

Ratboy's mind was cast back to the odd figure he saw crawling from the temple, and he shuddered, relieved he had seen no more of the creature. He looked back at the stone. 'But if these are your parents then this must be–'

'My home, yes. A place so banished from my thoughts I flinched when I saw it on the general's campaign map. So great is my shame.'

'Why should you be ashamed, Brother Wolff? You're an inspiration to the entire regiment. Your faith *shines* out of you. How can you dismiss it so easily?'

'My faith? Oh yes, my faith has always inspired, but to what end? And anyway, what's the use?' His voice cracked. 'What use is a religion so powerless it can't even erase my own crimes? How could it lift this darkness that hangs over us?' He sighed and clenched his broad, power-ful hands, until the old scars that networked them throbbed a deep red. Then he began to speak in a loud voice, as though addressing a crowd. 'At the age of ten my parents sent me to a local priest, Aldus Braun, boasting of my piety and learning. Even at that tender age I possessed an unusual, infectious fervour. The priest taught me to read, and I quickly surpassed him. Within a year I had devoured every text in his library. At the age of eleven, I could quote the *Deus Sigmar* in its entirety, and with such conviction it would make you weep to hear it. It could have ended there, the happy tale of a devout childhood, but my parents wanted more.

'My older brother, Fabian was a useless wastrel, as is most of our aris-tocracy. He did no real harm: gambling, duelling, womanising and the like; nothing unusual for a young duke, but he was an embarrassment to my parents, so they focused all their energies on me: their perfect, pious, prodigal son. Soon, I was the sneak of the village. Every suspicious look or deed reported back to Brother Braun, until there wasn't a crone within fifteen miles who would dare pluck a herb.'

'So, you were an eager apprentice. I see no shame in that. You were being trained for a lifetime of holy servitude.'

Wolff shook his head and smiled. 'But they trained me too well, you see. Unbridled faith is a dangerous dog to unleash, unless you know how to call it off. Brother Braun was summoned to Altdorf for a while and I returned to the old house.' He gestured out through a broken window. 'If you climbed that hill you could probably still see it, sitting smugly at the north end of the valley. Fabian was too busy chasing peas-ant girls to entertain his little brother, and as the summer passed I grew progressively more bored. Finally, with my parents away hunting, and the house empty, I found myself rummaging in the attics.' He paused, and took a long breath. 'With hindsight, the things I found were so pitifully innocent: just some wooden idols; nature gods, nothing more than that. Relics of a more innocent age, I suppose. But of course, my shining faith, as you so elegantly described it, drove me on.

'With Braun away in Altdorf, I didn't know where to turn. My righteous young mind was convinced their souls were in peril. I was mindless with fear, desperate to tell someone before they returned. Otto Sürman was the name of my saviour.' He looked up at Ratboy. 'I threw myself on his mercy, much as you did mine. They told me he was a priest of Sigmar, but witch hunter would have been a more accurate description. Or maybe rabid, mindless zealot might have done better. Utterly unhinged. The worst kind of backwater tyrant. Thriving on fear like a vampire.' He spat bitterly on the floor. 'I betrayed my family to a monster.'

Wolff gripped the headstone and screwed his eyes tightly shut. 'As my parents burned, the militia had to hold my brother back, or he would have torn me to pieces. He swore that if I ever stepped foot in the province again, he would rip out my heart with his bare hands.' He looked at Ratboy with an awful, despairing grin. 'I can still hear their cries. They begged for mercy as the flames took hold.'

Ratboy lowered his head, afraid of Wolff's terrible gaze.

'So you see, you've chosen a very poor prophet for your inspiration. I can lead no one to salvation. For these last years my faith has been no more than a useless burden. Nothing I have done in Sigmar's name has ever eased my guilt. My pain just grew, year on year, until eventually I merely hoped to die in the most effective way possible. I thought that to sacrifice myself here might save the regiment and maybe redeem me at the same time. As soon as I saw the name of Berlau on the map, way back at the start of the campaign, I realised what a perfect symmetry it would make, to die here. I still hoped I could repay the old debt somehow.' He gave a hollow laugh. 'What a fool. Who could repay such a thing? Do you see? There was no occultist in my parents' house. Just a couple of old dolls; dolls my parents had probably never laid eyes on. They burned for nothing.' He cradled his head in his hands. 'I saw guilt where there was only love.'

To see the priest in such despair shocked Ratboy deeply and he could think of no words of comfort. After a while he backed away, leaving Jakob to his grief. He decided to head back to the encampment and fetch help. The priest seemed utterly bereft and Ratboy feared for his sanity.

As he passed the base of the crumbling tower, however, he spotted something glittering in the dust and stopped. A metal block of some kind was sticking out of the rubble. He stooped to investigate, only to be distracted by something even more interesting. The explosion had shifted the tower's lower stones to reveal a small staircase, leading down into the foundations of the temple. He stepped closer and realised it must have once been some kind of priest hole, now revealed for all the world to see. Intrigued, he lit a lamp and climbed down into the darkness. It was a library of sorts. Most of the abandoned temple had obviously been looted years ago, but this tiny chamber was still intact. Ratboy placed the lamp on the table and opened a book.

Months before, as a starving refugee, he had thrown himself on the mercy of the army as it marched through Ostland but the soldiers had caught him stealing food and punished him cruelly. They were men on the edge of defeat and their fear made animals of them. They spat on his tattered clothes, kicked his filthy, skinny body and christened him 'Ratboy'. Finally, they chased him from the camp with a leather 'tail' nailed to his back. When Wolff found him snivelling and bleeding on the outskirts of the camp he was in a truly wretched state. The old man took pity on him and employed the boy as a servant. The priest was taciturn and ill-tempered, but as the army marched on, he kept his new acolyte from harm. More than this, to Ratboy's delight, as Wolff healed the young boy, he also taught him to read. Ratboy had surprised himself with his own aptitude and, peering now at the graceful script in front of him, he felt a familiar rush of pleasure as he began to read. It was the journal of Aldus Braun, the priest who mentored Wolff all those decades ago. Ratboy poured over the text, reliving the childhood exploits of his grizzled old master. He lost himself in Braun's tales of his young protégé, forgetting for a while the sorry state Jakob had come to.

Dates were carefully foiled on the books' leather spines and, before leaving, Ratboy plucked a volume from a shelf to read the priest's last words. The final entry was written in a more hurried hand than the others. It made for interesting reading:

I can live with this burden no longer. To think that the boy should spend his entire life with such guilt is unthinkable. The fault was never his and he must be told. I am riding tonight to confront the witch hunter, Sürman, and demand he reveal the truth. I fully expect him to comply. It will doubtless be the end of his 'career' but I consider that a small price to pay for correcting such a mistake. To have burned the Wolffs on the flimsy evidence of a child was a travesty of justice in the first place, but to then discover the real occultist, and attempt to hide the truth, is beyond the pale. If Sürman will not admit his mistake and reveal the true guilty party, then I will accuse him openly. I am not afraid. I have absolute faith that Sigmar himself will protect me from Sürman's hungry pyre.

I will ride out this very night to see him.

As Ratboy read and re-read the words his eyes grew wide. He snatched up the book and dashed back upstairs. 'Jakob,' he cried, 'look at this.'

The priest was still crouched by the headstone, gazing into his open hands. 'What is it?' he muttered, taking the book. At first he flicked through the pages with a dismissive sneer on his face. 'Braun. What a yokel he was. How little he knew of the world. Hiding out here in the comfort of his–' As he turned to the last entry, the priest fell silent. He stood upright and held the lamp over the pages. 'What's this?' he whispered, shaking his head. The colour drained from his leathery skin. 'What's this?' He grabbed Ratboy by the shoulders and lifted him from his feet so that their faces were level. 'Where did you find–'

The movement that silenced the priest was so fast Ratboy struggled to follow it.

Something flashed in the corner of his eye and he found himself on the far side of the temple, crushed against the altar, fresh blood in his eyes. He wiped his face and tried to draw a breath, but all the air had left his lungs. As he lay there, gasping, he saw Wolff stagger across the flagstones, wrapped in a vision of hell. It was the same creature Ratboy had seen earlier, but this time he could not take his eyes off it. From the furs and skulls, he guessed it must once have been the Reaver. He had witnessed the bloody champion many times, leading the enemy into battle, but he was now transformed beyond all recognition; every trace of humanity gone from him. What was once a man was now a heaving mass of charred skin, pulsating flesh and snarling, hissing jaws. As Ratboy struggled for breath, the already weakened priest struggled in vain to throw off the monster, cursing it bitterly as he staggered backwards towards the exit.

He has no weapon, thought Ratboy with horror. He forced himself to his feet and began to claw desperately around in the rubble, trying to find anything the priest could use to defend himself.

A scream came from outside. The monster had thrown the priest to the ground, thrashing him with countless limbs and attempting to attach one of its gaping maws to his face. Wolff was holding its deformed head at arm's length, but he was already trembling with exhaustion.

Ratboy dashed to the priest hole, thinking he might find some kind of icon or staff.

Wolff howled in pain and Ratboy turned to see that the creature's head was now fixed onto his neck.

He ducked down into the priest hole, but to his dismay there was nothing: just books and a desk, not so much as a quill. He groaned with despair and leapt back up the steps, deciding to fight the creature with his bare hands. As he reached the top step, he stubbed his foot on something and stopped to curse. Only then did he realise it was the same shiny object he had noticed earlier. 'Metal!' he gasped, and began to clear away the stones, thinking he might have found a candleholder. 'Sigmar,' he muttered when he realised what a treasure he had unearthed: the priest's warhammer.

He struggled outside with it to see that the creature had climbed off the priest and was standing over him, taunting its victim. Its words were lisping and confused as they chorused through a dozen inhuman mouths: 'Nownownow, littlelittlelittle, manman,' it slurred as it writhed and danced gleefully over him. 'Wherewherewhere isis youryour firefirenownownow?'

Ratboy had intended to hand the hammer over to his master, but Wolff was barely conscious. Blood was rushing from his neck and his eyes were tightly closed in pain.

Ratboy hesitated. The monster was oblivious to him, intent on its prey as it leant closer and drew a long, sharpened bone from within its folds of flesh, all the while singing its gleeful song. 'Wherewherewhere isis youryour firefirenownownow?'

Ratboy tested the weight of the warhammer in his hands, unsure whether he could even swing it. I should flee, he decided. I would barely even mark the creature. It would just kill me too. He backed quietly towards the temple.

A memory halted him in his steps: a vision of kindness in the priest's face as he nursed him back to health all those months earlier. Suddenly the weapon felt lighter. He lunged forward with all his strength, bringing the hammer down in a great sweeping arc towards the beast's head.

The hammer connected with the misshapen skull and it collapsed inwards with a muffled crunch, as easily as a piece of damp wood. The thing's writhing ceased and it reached up in a spasm of pain, then sank silently to the floor, dropping its bone knife at Ratboy's feet.

Ratboy staggered backwards, shocked by his success. The warhammer suddenly regained its weight, and he let it clatter to the floor. 'I killed it,' he gasped, looking at his bloodied hands in disbelief. He began to giggle.

A moist popping sound silenced him and he looked down at the beast's body in horror. In the area where he had destroyed its head, dozens of snarling mouths were quickly bursting from the bloody flesh. Ratboy reeled with shock as the mouths swelled and multiplied, each one hissing and belching merrily at him. 'Littlelittlelittlemanmanan,' they sang. 'Eateateateateateateat.'

It launched itself from the floor and sent him staggering back into the temple, desperately trying to fend off its snapping jaws and flailing limbs.

Ratboy screamed for help, knowing that no one would hear him. In his panic, he barely registered the various wounds appearing all over his face and chest as the monster quickly overwhelmed him. Finally, he found himself pinned against the altar, with no place left to go. The thing pressed him firmly against the stone and placed a blackened tentacle over his mouth to silence him. A terrible stench of rotting innards filled Ratboy's nostrils and he recognised it as the same smell that had so disturbed him earlier, outside the temple. The beast's claws and teeth grew still as the largest of its heads stretched forward, until it was only an inch from Ratboy's face. He could see his own silent scream reflected in the unblinking blackness of its eyes.

'Eateateateateateat,' it whispered to him. 'Eateateateatthethelittlelittle manman.'

Ratboy closed his eyes and waited for the end.

He felt the thing's limbs tighten around his body, then its whole body grew stiff and its voices rose in pitch, turning into a furious chorus of snarls and howls. After a few seconds Ratboy opened his eyes in confusion and saw the monster's bone knife protruding from its own glistening chest.

The creature's limbs loosed their grip and it slid to the floor with a wheezing sound, a knife through its heart, finally dead.

Ratboy found himself face-to-face with Wolff. The old man managed to stand for a few more seconds, smiling through his pain, then he too dropped to the floor.

As the two men made their slow ascent back up through the forest, sounds of battle began to greet them: the thunder of horses crossing the plain, the lurid drone of enemy horns and the dull thud of steel against leather. Even from here though, they could tell the tide was turning. Without the Reaver to lead them, the marauders were being driven slowly back out of the valley. The long deadlock was finally broken.

Wolff paused to catch his breath, leaning heavily against a tree. Ratboy had bandaged his master's neck as well as he could, but the cloth was already black with blood. The old priest's face was grey and drawn with pain. The despair had faded from his eyes though; replaced with a new look of defiance. He looked down at his blistered young servant and smiled. 'I think there was a miracle in there after all.' He lifted his warhammer so that the metal glinted in the dappled sunlight. 'I thought I was saving you that day, when I rescued you from the soldiers, but I think, in the end, you saved me. Thanks to you, my friend, I know my despair was needless.' He placed a hand on Ratboy's shoulder. 'Come,' he said, staggering back towards the battle.

As the priest left the trees and entered the heaving carnage of the fight, he held his hammer aloft and stood motionless for a moment, smiling up at the roiling sky as bloody figures crashed all around him, like waves breaking on a rock.

As Ratboy ran to his side, he thought he saw a light, bleeding from the old man's skin, shining out as a beacon to those who would falter and doubt.

THE MARCH OF DOOM

by Chris Wraight

Mathilde screamed.

Her flabby body shook and her lips rippled. Spittle flailed into the air, glistening like pearls.

The men and women around her screamed too. Ragged arms punched up, clad in scraps of filth-soaked wool and leather. Fists clenched knuckle-white and veins stood out on necks like rigging ropes pulled tight.

They weren't afraid. They had forgotten how to feel fear. They only remembered hate, glory and life. Their whole existence had become a scream: a long, never-ending scream of affirmation and violence.

They charged. They ran up the mud-slick slope, churning through the grime and falling over one another to get to the enemy.

Mathilde was in the front rank, screaming all the while, hearing her voice go hoarse. She lumbered up the incline, scrabbling at the earth with her free hand, slipping on the trodden-down turf.

The rain hammered, turning the furrowed dirt into a mire of grey slurry. The sky, low and dark, scowled at them. Far in the east, the Drakwald treeline rippled, black and matted like hair.

At the top of the slope were the beastmen.

They bellowed and stamped their hooves. Blunt-edged blades swung and tattered hide standards swayed.

There were hundreds of them. They stank of old blood and musk and wet hides. They roared out a deafening challenge of hoarse bellows.

'Death to the unclean!' screamed Mathilde, reaching the crest of the slope and hurling herself into the press of warped flesh beyond.

Like the meeting of two dirty seas of bilge, the armies crunched together. Less than a thousand strong on either side, there were no glittering flashes of plate armour or bright pennants waving in the sunlight. Every exposed piece of skin was caked in mud and crusted with scabs and sores and weeping wounds. The humans smelled almost as bad as the beasts, and some were hairier.

It was a scrum of hacking, punching, gouging, raking, stabbing and throttling. No strategy, no tactics, just a collision of two sets of frost-raw hatred.

Mathilde ducked as a horse-faced gor swung clumsily at her. Before she could respond, its head was ripped from its neck by a bald-headed man with the image of the comet branded across his face.

A scrawny ungor leapt up into her path, all scraggly limbs and stretched grey flesh. It swiped at her with a dirty gouge, keeping it high, expecting her to respond with her cleaver.

Mathilde laughed as she punched out with her fist, and laughed again as the ungor's skull bounced away. She laughed as she lashed out towards its face, and giggled as her fingers plunged into eye-sockets to gouge out the balls of jelly within. When she tore up its throat, snapping the sinews with savage pulls and wrenching the gristly sockets of the spine out, she was chortling like a young girl.

The beasts were all a head taller than their human opponents. They were stronger, better-armed and possessed of the ingrained and wily battle lust of all their kind, but the crazed army of screaming fanatics came at them like a river in spring-flood, pouring over defences and rushing into contact.

Dozens of human zealots died on the mad run up the slope. Many more were cut down by the beastmen as they crashed into blade-reach. They were bludgeoned into a stupor, gutted with metal or eviscerated by grinding sets of teeth.

It didn't matter. It didn't slow them. They pushed on, wiping the blood from their staring eyes and screaming praise to Sigmar in unison. They were one body, one form, one vengeance.

Mathilde swung round, seeing a big wargor rush at her with red eyes and slavering jaws. She slammed her cleaver up, jamming into the oncoming dirk and feeling the impact judder down her arm. Then she rushed in close, hauling her blade back across and tearing with her fingers, going for those red eyes again as if they were rubies.

The gor blunted the blade attack, then smashed her down to her knees with a single blow from its head-sized fist. It loomed over her, preparing for the kill.

Mathilde reeled and her vision went blurry. She had a vague sense that she was about to die and it gave her a sudden rush of ecstatic fury.

'Sigmar!' she screamed, lurching back to her feet and blundering around for her assailant.

But the gor had gone.

In its place was a single massive figure. He towered above the humans around him, resplendent in heavy, rain-dulled plate armour. A mournful face loomed up through the storm-lashed murk, slab-featured and hard as pig-iron. At his forehead was a fragment of scripture, bound tight with strips of stained leather. Huge arms, each clad in rings of tarnished steel, hefted a gigantic warhammer. Blood – the blood of the dead gor – ran down the shaft in muddy rivulets.

Mathilde felt a fresh surge of joy. She'd never stopped screaming, but now her cries were redoubled.

'Father!' she roared, feeling the scar of her comet-brand pucker on her forehead. All around her, more zealots took up the cry. 'Blessed Father!'

If he heard her, Luthor Huss of the Church of Sigmar, the man who had given her everything and who had demanded everything, made no sign. He strode onwards, swinging the massive hammer one-handed, his face set like beaten metal and his mouth clamped into a rigid line of determination. Those thin lips parted only once, and then only for a single word.

Mathilde wasn't close enough to hear what he said. By then she was fighting again, striking out with the cleaver for the honour and glory of Sigmar, and words ceased to have meaning in the haze and crash of righteous combat.

But Huss had spoken. He had spoken softly amid the rush and slaughter; just the one word, before the hammer swung again.

'Kohlsdorf,' he had said, and his voice was bitter.

'You know, I think, that you're asking the impossible,' said the Margrave Bors von Aachen.

His voice was calm. Kind, even. As he spoke, his thick lips, glossy with recently drunk wine, twitched into a beneficent smile.

Huss looked back at him. The priest's face was a study in disdain.

'I never ask the impossible,' Huss said. His deep voice was quiet. 'In Sigmar, all things are possible. I ask you to enact the will of Sigmar. Thus, I ask only what is possible.'

Von Aachen looked around the room, and his eyes twinkled with amusement.

'Very nice,' he said. 'A priest with an education.'

He sat back in his chair, and his fat chin wobbled.

The margrave was dressed in robes of silk and ermine, and they stretched smoothly over his round stomach. The town's burghers, eight of them, sat in a semi-circle on either side of him on low wooden chairs. Though it was not yet midday, rows of torches burned against the walls of the audience chamber.

Huss stood before them all, shoulders back, feet apart, hands clasped on the heel of his upturned warhammer. His thick armour plate reflected the light of the torches, as did his shaved head. He was a foot taller than the largest of the other men and his shoulders were as broad as von Aachen's gut.

The sky outside was dark with the coming storm. The straw on the floor was stale, and the stone of the walls was grimy and crumbling.

Kohlsdorf was not a rich place.

Huss looked around him steadily. As his eyes ran over the faces of the burghers before him, they looked down, one by one.

'The beastmen are out of the Drakwald,' Huss said. 'They can be defeated, but must be cowed by strength. Now, before the herd-rage draws more from the trees. Wait for them to get here, drunk on killing, and they will slay you all.'

Von Aachen gestured lazily at the walls around him.

'These walls are five feet thick, priest. I have men-at-arms here, and supplies, and protection. They would not get in here, not if there were a thousand of them.'

Huss narrowed his eyes.

'Your people are unprotected. Villages are already burning.'

Von Aachen raised an eyebrow.

'My *people*?' He looked faintly disgusted. 'If those who clamour for succour are too slow or witless to seek refuge here, then they will learn their folly soon enough.'

Von Aachen shook his head.

'Orders have been given. No man will join you. Leave these walls, and you will be on your own.'

Huss listened patiently. His face remained static, though his eyes, set deep in a bleak visage, glowed darkly.

'I will not be on my own,' he said softly.

Von Aachen looked at him with some sympathy then, as if remonstrating with a village simpleton.

'Listen to me. There are no proper troops garrisoned between here and the forest's edge. The beasts may ransack our villages, but that will only wear out their fury and they'll kill only serfs. Stay here. Weather the storm until it blows over.'

Only then did anger flash from Huss's eyes. Only then, at the mention of *serfs*, did his voice rise.

'They are the sons and daughters of the Heldenhammer.'

Huss still spoke quietly, but the tone had changed.

'They are his beloved, for whom he bled and wept. They are the soul of his Empire. They are the heirs to his glory.'

As his speech echoed around the audience chamber, the burghers shifted uneasily in their seats. The flames in the torches suddenly seemed to burn more strongly.

'If you will not fight for them, I will. I will show them what they can become. I will fill their hearts with holy fire and their limbs with the strength of their fathers. They will forget their sorrow and remember their fury.'

He took up the warhammer and hefted it into a two-handed grip.

'I will take the fight to the beast. I will go east and I will purge their filth from the realms of men.'

Von Aachen swallowed, struggling to hold Huss's pitiless gaze.

'And when I have done these things, I will return.' Raw contempt rang from Huss's voice. 'Pray, margrave, that I do so before the beasts tear your throat from your body and feast on your fat, stupid flesh.'

The stink of the pyres rose up into the sodden air. Columns of dirty black smoke rolled across the ridged earth, heavy and acrid. The wind whipped them up, dragging them in tatters across the scene of carnage.

The zealots knelt in prayer, heedless of the blood on their rags and the bite of the rain-studded breeze. The bodies of the beastmen had been piled into a jumbled heap and set alight. Each one had been ritually mutilated before the oils had been poured over them – an eye torn out, or a clawed finger pulled off. It was a small statement, but one that meant much to the zealots. Only the bodies of the glorious dead, the human defenders of the Drakwald, went to their long rest as they had fallen.

Huss stood on the crest of the rise, arms crossed, watching the grey light of the sun fall away into the west. The rain ran down his armour, washing the blood from the steel.

For fourteen days he'd been in the wilds, gathering the scattered survivors of the beastman incursion to him and moulding them into something like a fighting force. Fourteen days since leaving that fat man in his grimy, depressing provincial town with its crumbling walls and complacent dreams of safety.

Only now was he turning back, following the gathering gangs of beastmen as they trekked west toward the prize that they really wanted.

Even as he watched, a column of figures emerged from out of the growing gloom. They came slowly, limping and dragging heavy bundles. Some bore horrific wounds. Their eyes were hollow with fatigue.

Huss waited for them to arrive. He said nothing, but his eyes, those dark and taciturn eyes, softened a fraction.

'Rise,' he said at last, just as the first newcomers shuffled towards the light of the pyres.

All around him, his army of zealots hauled themselves from their knees and opened their eyes. They turned to watch the newcomers. There was no hostility in their ravaged faces. Out in the wilderness, all were as desperate as the other.

The foremost traveller came up to Huss, halting a few paces before the huge warrior priest. He was a skinny man with a dirty beard and red-rimmed eyes. His stark ribcage was visible under claw-rents in his clothing.

'Are you Huss?' he asked, his dry voice rasping.

Huss nodded. 'What are you seeking?' he asked.

The man's shoulders slumped. He looked on the verge of desperate tears. All of those behind him did too. They had been destroyed. It had long been said in the hostile marches of the northern Empire that the only thing worse than being killed in a beastman attack was surviving one.

'I do not know,' he said, his voice cracking from grief and exhaustion, his head hanging in bitter, angry shame. 'Mercy of Sigmar, I *do not know*.'

Huss walked over to him and placed his gauntlet on the man's shoulder. He had to stoop to do so, though the movement was tender. Those huge hands, the ones that had ripped through the beastmen with the fury of the gods, went gently now.

'I will show you, son of Sigmar,' said Huss. His voice was commanding, though he did not raise it.

The man looked up at him, and his tear-reddened eyes gave away his yearning. All of his fellow travellers, each clad in rags and shivering against the wind, did likewise.

'I will give you weapons, and the spirit to use them. I will make you strong again. I will make you the instruments of the Lord of Men.'

Huss gestured towards the pyres of burning beast-flesh.

'This is what we have done to them. This is what we will do to every one of them. Give yourselves to me, let me mould you into disciples, and you will do this too.'

Huss leaned closer, his eyes locked on the man's ravaged face.

'Will you do that, son of Sigmar? Will you give yourself?'

The refugee looked up at him and a desperate, keening hope flared up in his rheumy eyes.

'I will,' he said, his voice grasping. 'Show me, lord, how to serve. Show me how to kill for you.'

Already, hymns of praise were breaking out from the zealots, keen to have new blood among their ranks. Though no signal had been given, several of them approached Huss. They had long metal brands in their hands, glowing angrily red from the pyres. The heads had been fashioned into the shape of the twin-tailed comet.

Huss took one up. He held the hot metal before the refugee, and the heat of it made the air shimmer. The man's eyes widened nervously, but he held his ground.

'This is the mark of service,' said Huss, lowering the brand over the man's trembling forehead. 'This is the mark of the march of doom.'

He moved the brand into position.

'Try not to fear. Pain is fleeting. Salvation, I tell you, is eternal.'

From the fringes of the forest, they travelled out across the broken plains, west towards the curve of the river that lay like a band of grey steel across the charred earth.

The zealots went at a punishing pace, chanting as they went. They strode through the seas of black mud, going tirelessly even as the wind hurled sleet and rain in their faces and their old wounds refused to heal.

At the head of the column, four hulking men in stiff leather jerkins carried braziers aloft. The fires never went out. Flames raged in the iron cages, red as hearts, trailing long lines of peat-dark smoke behind them.

They passed villages, all destroyed. Walls were ground down, thatch burned, wells despoiled. Filth was everywhere, the stinking spoor of the beastmen. Hoof-prints studded the clay, deep and waterlogged.

The zealots only paused to tear down the beasts' standards, ragged poles surmounted with skulls and feathers and daubed with blood. The poles were shattered with ritual denunciations, and Huss cast out the spirits of ruin that dwelt within.

Then the march would start again, the fearsome, grinding journey, ever moving steadily west, accompanied by the holler of hymns and rolling cries of fervour.

More joined them all the time. They came from all directions, attracted by the clamour, or stumbling across them at random, or perhaps guided by some other subtle force. Huss's forces swelled to over a thousand. He made the sign of the comet to each and every one of them as they staggered up to him, blessing them and making sure they had a weapon to wield. At the end of each day, fires would be lit and the brands heated.

On occasion, he would ask new disciples if they had seen bands of beastmen. The answer was always the same.

'Heading west, lord.'

And Huss would nod and give the order to march once again.

The tenth day after the battle on the ridge, the zealots reached their destination. They crested the summit of a low, bleak hill. Below them, the land stretched away in a maze of dreary marshes, broken by thickets of wiry grasses and glistening like tallow in the diffuse light.

A walled town burned on the horizon. The smoke of many fires rose up in columns, looking like the outstretched fingers of a vengeful god reaching down from the darkening heavens.

Huss looked at the vista coolly. For a long time, he said nothing. His dark eyes narrowed, peering out through the murk.

His zealots waited for the order. They struggled to restrain themselves, but waited for the word. Always, they would wait for the word.

Huss kept them waiting a little longer.

It was not clear to him that Kohlsdorf merited saving. The margrave's refusal to meet the beastmen before their blood-frenzy reached its peak had doomed dozens of outlying settlements to ruin. Now the horde had gorged deep on manflesh, and the stench of blood on the wind had drawn more gors from the deep forest. The fact that von Aachen's faith in his walls had proved misguided was no consolation.

It could have been different. So much could have been avoided.

So Huss weighed up the issue, knowing guidance would be shown to him, seeking the truth as he always did in reverent, disciplined silence.

Once the decision had been made, he moved swiftly, taking up his warhammer and hefting it in both hands.

'Sons and daughters,' he announced, his voice ringing out over the assembled ranks. 'For the sake of He who gathers the righteous to His side in glory.'

His thin lips broke into a cold smile.

'Kill them all.'

Mathilde was near the back, stuck with the old, sick ones who ran in a shambling, stumbling mess of limbs. Weeks of near-starvation on the march had made her skin loose and flabby, but she still had most of a lifetime's worth of fat to burn through.

The front rank of zealots had already broken through the walls and she came in their wake, tumbling over collapsed brickwork and pushing aside teetering planks of rotten wood. Once in, they all rampaged down the narrow streets, baying like hounds. The musk of the beast was every-where, and they went after it, their eyes blazing with frenzy.

Kohlsdorf was a ruin. Fires raged out of control and other screams, screams of pain and terror, broke out from the centre of the town. Bodies lay across the mud, their necks twisted and their bones broken. Slicks of dung and viscera hung from every exposed surface, already swarming with clouds of bulbous flies.

Mathilde couldn't run faster. Her wobbling bulk held her back and her short legs slipped in the grime. She could only watch as the skinnier zealots sprinted into battle ahead of her, their scrawny limbs pumping and their skull-like faces distorted into masks of animal loathing.

But she did her bit. She screamed with the rest of them and lurched along as fast as she could, sniffing out the stench of the beastmen and hefting her cleaver two-handed.

The hunt consumed her. She had already forgotten her other self, the blacksmith's chattel, raising nine bawling children and scrabbling around for a living in the hard earth of Middenland. She had forgotten the grind of water-carrying, the backbreaking labour in the fields and the rare snatches of laughter when the sun broke out and made the dank soil bloom with flowers.

They were all dead now, those children. Her husband too, gutted open with a rusty blade and torn apart by that red-eyed beast that had come out of the trees. Mathilde had run away then, screaming and weeping, out into the wilds, lost in a world of terror, just like all the others who had got free of the cull.

But then she'd found Huss and the burning pain of the comet brand had purged her fear from her. Now she feared nothing. Now she never ran from anything. Now she was a daughter of Sigmar, a blazing light in the darkness of a fallen world.

'Kill them all!' she screamed, echoing Huss's final order, hunting through the ruins. 'Find them, and kill them all!'

She lurched around the shell of an old tavern and got her wish. A courtyard opened up in front of her, fenced with shabby, leaning buildings and covered in a patchy layer of foetid straw. In the distance, the heavy stone walls of a Sigmarite chapel loomed through curtains of smoke. The townsfolk had made their last stand in there, and the beastmen milled around it, hurling rocks at the lead-lined windows and hammering on the doors with iron axes. The foremost zealots were already plunging into the horde, lashing out in fury.

'Death!' screeched Mathilde, running straight at the beasts. 'Death! Death!'

She whirled the cleaver over her head, and flakes of old blood showered over her. Still screaming, her mouth stretched wide and her yellow teeth bared, Mathilde ran at the horde, her eyes lit up with joy.

Huss swung the warhammer in a vicious backhanded curve, and its blunt head connected with a wet crack. A goat-faced gor careered back from the impact, chest caved in. It bleated briefly in choking, gasping agony before being dragged down by a dozen scrabbling hands. Zealots clambered all over it, gouging at its eyes, tearing the skin from its face, ripping tufts of hair from its bloodied hide.

By then Huss was already moving, striding out into the thick of the fighting, hauling his weapon in wide, bone-breaking arcs. He was immense, a towering bulwark of stability in the midst of the confused press of bodies.

All around him, zealots threw themselves at the beastmen. The courtyard was packed with bodies, human and abhuman. Neither side gave any quarter. The beasts, disturbed from the prospect of fresh slaughter, raged at the incoming ranks of zealots, keeping their horned heads low and using them to gore and maim. The zealots rushed back at them, heedless of the death on every side, clambering over the bodies of the slain just to get close enough to stab or punch or bite.

They died in droves. They didn't care. They had ceased to be individual souls, fretting about their own lives or ambitions, and had become part of just one mass, a driven expression of incoherent defiance. They just kept coming, blind to the slaughter around them, possessed by the only thought that remained in their minds.

Kill. Kill. Kill.

At the forefront, driving them on, was Huss. His armour flashed red from the fires. As he plunged deeper into the ranks of the beasts, blood flew around him like a halo. Lumbering wargors pushed their way towards him, bellowing their challenge. One by one, he cut them down, crunching through gnarled skulls and breaking apart warped limbs. The warhammer rose and fell like the tolling of a mighty bell and the blood-halo flared out further.

Huss issued no battle-cry. His lips only moved in silent prayer. His face remained locked in a rigid mask of concentration. Unlike his raving disciples, he was implacable. He fought methodically, intensely, moving stride by stride across the courtyard until he was standing under the eaves of the chapel's porch.

The doors had been broken. Huss slammed aside a bellowing gor, breaking its back against the stone doorway, and kicked the remaining slivers of wood apart. Messy noises of killing echoed out from the nave.

Huss went inside, swinging his warhammer around him in wide loops. Two gors reared up out of the shadows, poised to leap at his throat. Huss, still striding, let the hammer come back round. The golden hammerhead flashed across, crunching into the skull of the first beastman and sweeping it into the path of the other one. Stunned, the gors skittered across the floor, losing their footing. By then, Huss's zealots had poured through the doorway. They leapt on the prone beasts, fingers outstretched, jaws wide, blades poised to rip.

Huss strode down the nave, mouthing his endless cycle of prayer, face set. Men were alive inside the chapel. Up ahead, around the high altar with its stained cotton cloth and tarnished candles, a dozen or so humans fought on. They were surrounded by a gang of beastmen, all hacking away at the diminishing band of defenders.

One beast stood out from the others. It was massive, far bigger than the gors around it. As Huss approached, it turned to face him, perhaps warned by some animal sense.

It had the long face of a bull, broken by curved tusks and flared-wide nostrils. Its skin was the black of old scabs and sigils of destruction had been painted across the exposed flesh in virulent strokes. Huge shoulders wielded a mighty double-headed axe. A long ragged cloak hung down its back, roughly stitched with what looked like human sinew. Its tiny eyes raged, and it pawed the ground with knife-sharp hooves.

It laid eyes on the warrior priest and instantly issued a throaty, hoarse bellow of challenge. The axe blade flashed as it swung round and the creature charged.

Huss braced himself, bringing his warhammer up. The beast's axe whistled in, aimed at his chest. Huss parried and the two weapons locked together with a jarring, echoing clang.

Huss grunted, and the impact forced him on to the back foot. The beast snarled in anticipation of a quick kill and thrust down with all its strength. Huss felt his arms blaze with the pain of resistance, and released the pressure.

The beastman lurched forwards, snapping with its huge jaws. Huss spun back, letting the beast's momentum carry it off-balance. He checked himself and swung the hammerhead back, going for the moving flank. The beast, adjusting quickly, veered away from the hammer and pulled the axe back for another swing.

The blade scythed round, heading for the priest's neck. Huss pulled away again, evading the cutting edge by a finger's width, before powering back in close. He lunged forward, letting the hammer fall away, and launched into a savage head-butt.

The skulls connected with a heavy snap. Caught by surprise, the creature staggered backwards. Huss punched out with his free left gauntlet, sending the beast reeling further, before swinging across with the warhammer.

The hammerhead hit just below the beastman's jaw, smashing clean through the bone and ripping it out. The creature yowled in gurgling agony, spraying gouts of hot, black blood from the gaping wound. Grabbing the shaft of the warhammer two-handed, Huss hauled it back across, swivelling on his heel to generate extra force.

The beast's skull shattered, cracking open like an earthenware jar. The monster tottered back, somehow still on its feet despite the blood leaking from its open neck-stump and sluicing down its chest, before crashing to the ground. Its heavy body twitched for a few moments before shuddering into stillness.

Breathing heavily, Huss looked up. All across the chapel, his vengeful zealots were tearing after the remaining beastmen. There was still fighting in the aisles, but the master of the warband had been defeated.

There was no cry of victory. No smile broke across that severe face. Huss looked up at the altar for a moment, his eyes locked on the sacred stone, and raised the gore-streaked warhammer in salute.

'By your grace,' he whispered, still breathing heavily.

And then he was moving again, the warhammer swinging, looking for more prey.

She had never been pretty. Even in life, her face had been heavy and blotched, ravaged by a poor existence in the harsh northern Empire and made worse by weeks of privation.

In death, her face was hideous. The left cheek had been ripped away, exposing the teeth of her jaw. An eye had gone, leaving a deep well, slowly filling with blood. Her belly, a sagging bag of wobbly flesh, hung out from her ripped clothes, studded with puncture wounds.

Huss looked down at her. His expression was gentle.

He didn't know her name. He rarely knew the names of those who entered his service. Names, in truth, meant very little to him.

Actions, on the other hand, mattered a great deal. The fat woman had died with the corpses of beasts all around her. There was still the echo of a grin on what remained of her features.

She was glorious.

'Daughter of Sigmar,' Huss breathed, smoothing the remaining eyelid over the remaining eye.

He knelt by her still-warm body for some time, and his own eyes closed. He would pray long for her.

'Lord Huss!'

The hard, querulous voice of Margrave von Aachen broke his concentration. Huss gritted his teeth, irritated by the sacrilege. Slowly, letting his movements convey exactly how he felt about the margrave, he rose from the body of the fallen zealot.

The interior of the chapel was stuffed with corpses. Beastmen and humans lay on top of one another, locked in twisted, cold embraces. The stench was already powerful. The pyres would be assembled soon, and flames would come; one set for the righteous, another for the damned. The sound of sobbing came from the courtyard outside – tears of relief, grief and release. The fighting was over, but the rebuilding had yet to begin.

Huss looked at von Aachen. The fat man had lost his robes of silk. He wore a jerkin that didn't fit and his white hair was disarranged and dirty. He'd been one of those sheltering behind the altar and no doubt others had perished to keep him alive there.

'Lord priest,' gasped the margrave, and fell down at Huss's knees. He was trembling. 'I am sorry. You were right. We tried to resist them. By the gods, we tried, but there were–'

He looked up, his eyes filled with a pathetic mix of remorse and fear.

'You were *right*, priest,' he said. 'What can I do? Gold? Titles? I have them. Tell me, what can I do?'

Huss gazed down coldly. The margrave's knee rested on the body of the fat woman. He hadn't even noticed.

He contemplated killing him. He contemplated kicking him heavily in the face, again and again, mashing his fat features into a sponge of muscle and blood.

That would make him feel better. It would be suitable sanction for the ruin of the lands he had been given to guard.

It would be indulgent, though. It would be... bestial.

'You can make amends, margrave,' said Huss, reaching for the leather belt at his waist. He drew out a long metal shaft. 'That is what you can do.'

Von Aachen's eyes widened as he saw the twin-tailed comet device at the end of the shaft. The iron was cool, as black as old ashes.

But he knew what it was. He knew how quickly it would heat up, growing warmer under flame until it was throbbing red like the dying sun.

'What do you–'

'All the penitent carry this mark,' said Huss, his voice soft. 'Are you penitent, margrave? Do you strive for purity of soul?'

Von Aachen shook his head vigorously. That wasn't what he'd had in mind. A new terror spread across his pale face, and he began to clamber to his feet.

Huss leaned forward, clamping an iron gauntlet on the margrave's shoulder and keeping him on his knees. As he did so, the shadow of the brand fell across the man's forehead, picking out where the scar would be.

'Build a fire, my children,' Huss said out loud, knowing it would take only moments for the kindling to catch. 'We have a new disciple for the march.'

He gave the margrave a savage smile as he spoke, remembering the devotion of those who had liberated Kohlsdorf. From the corner of his eye, he saw zealots rushing to fulfill his order. Von Aachen struggled, but he was pitifully weak.

'Try not to fear,' said Huss, turning the brand over and watching the different shadows it cast across the fat man's face. 'Pain is fleeting.'

Then his smile truly broke out, a beatific glow that briefly transformed Huss's melancholy face like sunlight lancing through old stained glass.

'Salvation, I tell you, is eternal.'

ABOUT THE AUTHORS

Chris Wraight is the author of the Horus Heresy novel *Scars* and the Space Wolves novels *Battle of the Fang* and *Blood of Asaheim*. He has also written the Space Marine Battles novel *Wrath of Iron*, along with *Schwarzhelm & Helborg: Swords of the Emperor* and *Luthor Huss* in the Warhammer universe. He's based in a leafy bit of south-west England, and when not struggling to meet deadlines enjoys running through scenic parts of it.

Nick Kyme is the author of the Tome of Fire trilogy featuring the Salamanders. He has also written for the Horus Heresy, Space Marine Battles and Time of Legends series with the novels *Vulkan Lives*, *Damnos* and *The Great Betrayal*. In addition, he has penned a host of short stories and several novellas, including *Feat of Iron* which was a *New York Times* bestseller in the Horus Heresy collection *The Primarchs*. He lives and works in Nottingham.

Darius Hinks's first novel, *Warrior Priest*, won the *David Gemmell Morningstar* award for best newcomer. Since then he has carved a bloody swathe through the Warhammer World in works such as *Island of Blood*, *Sigvald* and *Razumov's Tomb*. Recently, he has ventured into the Warhammer 40,000 universe with the Space Marine Battles novella *Sanctus*. He plans to return to the grim darkness of the far future after he has finished telling the tale of the forest god Orion.